Politics, sex, corruption, blackmail, lies . . . and that's just the first three pages!"

As teenagers, Alison and Derek were lovers—but chose opposite directions which tore them apart.

Now adults, the pursuit of their incompatible dreams turns them into enemies who must deny their love for each other. But the real-world consequences of their actions bring them together in an alliance of mutual self-preservation—and cause them both to question their every belief.

TRUST YOUR ENEMIES IS A NOVEL IDEAS that's packed with action and adventure. It's a political thriller—but one like no other you've ever read.

Alison McGuire is the indispensable "right-hand" to Australia's next Prime Minister. She's one step away from achieving the goal of a lifetime . . . when she's suddenly ensnared in a web of power and intrigue by Frank McKurn, a devious, Machiavellian politician.

In her frantic race for survival, Alison must deliver a knockout blow to demolish McKurn . . .

To win, they must risk everything

In desperation, Alison turns for help to the key people in her life: An acerbic-tongued newspaper columnist—who ends up in a coma. A secretive computer hacker who discovers incriminating evidence—and then is forced into hiding. A police officer who's abruptly removed from a crucial investigation. A politician supposedly on her side—who shows his true, spineless colors at the worst possible moment.

With her every resource exhausted, she faces a life-or-death question: Can she trust Derek Olsson—the man she once loved? The man she mistakenly thinks deceived and betrayed her, who she now regards as an enemy?

Meanwhile, Olsson is nowhere to be found. He's on the run, wanted by the police for a murder he claims he didn't commit. A drug-dealing Triad king has offered a reward for his head. And a powerful politician must shut Olsson's mouth—or risk spending the rest of his life in prison.

**A battle of liberty
against power**

Only by joining forces can Alison and Olsson both survive. The irony is that they don't yet know it. Alison must first overcome her anger and bury the hatchet—and time is running out.

A shadowy contract hit man is pursuing them both. Known only as "The Assassin," he has never failed.

But *Trust Your Enemies* is far more than a page-turning action novel. You'll be plunged into the seamy underbelly of partisan politics, a world where no one is a friend and—paradoxically—the only people you can really trust may be your enemies. Woven through the novel are challenging and controversial themes, ranging from the psychological motives behind power and corruption to the eternal human desire for freedom and individualism. The key characters learn, dramatically, that when you make the wrong choices, you get the opposite of what you set out to achieve—and then take you on an inspiring journey of moral redemption and personal liberation that will have you cheering when you reach THE END.

By the same author

FICTION:
Give Me Liberty (co-edited with Martin H. Greenberg)
Visions of Liberty (co-edited with Martin H. Greenberg)
Freedom! (co-edited with Martin H. Greenberg)

NON-FICTION:
Understanding Inflation
How To Get A Second Passport
The Nature of Market Cycles
*The Winning Investment Habits of Warren Buffett & George Soros:
    Harness the Genius of the World's Richest Investors*
*When God Speaks for Himself: The Words of God You'll <u>Never</u>
    Hear in Church or Sunday School* (with George Forrai)
*Ayn Rand's 5 Surprisingly Simple Rules for Judging Political
    Candidates: Never be fooled by a politician again!*
*Free eBook: How to Make Money By Sitting On Your Butt
    (http://marktier.com/sitting)*

Trust Your Enemies

MARK TIER

inversebooks HONG KONG

My enormous thanks and gratitude go to
Jo Ann, who saved it, and
Raquel, who helped make it

Contents

PART ONE: *"Trust Your Enemies . . ."*   **7**

"Those whom the Gods would destroy they
first make mad with power."
— Greek proverb

CHAPTER

1	A Truckload of Monkeys	9
2	Between Heaven and Hell	17
3	"Vengeance Shall Be Mine . . ."	25
4	"For A While . . ."	39
5	The Long Arm of Paradise	47
6	A Woman from Mars	56
7	Shark Bait	64
8	Fallout	70
9	"Wish Me Luck . . ."	80
10	"Value Added"	86
11	Murphy's Law	91
12	The Siren's Song	102
13	Night Vision	114
14	The Frosty Lady	123
15	Tinkle, Tinkle, Little Star	140
16	Fairy Tales?	148
17	"Mum's the Word"	155
18	Pillow Talk	171
19	Pendulum of Fear	181
20	Virginity Hill	189
21	Without Notice	200
22	Sly Grog	208
23	A Man of Influence	221
24	Hobson's Choice	229
25	Rolling the Dice	238
26	The Ice Queen	248
27	Fingers of Fate	257
28	The Lion's Den	267
29	Sixth Uncle	279
30	The Girls from Issan	287
31	Merchants of Death	298
32	Hollow Idol	313
33	Chains of Love	326
34	Hacker for Hire	336
35	Collision Course	345

PART TWO: "But Not Your Friends . . ."   *359*

"Take what you want," said God, "and
pay for it." — Spanish proverb

36	Masquerade	361
37	The Sound of Thunder	372
38	My Enemy's Enemy	382
39	True Son	396
40	Mexican Standoff	407
41	Virtuoso	422
42	The Smile of God	431
43	A Matter of Trust	450
44	"Get a Dog"	456
45	Down Payment	470
46	Gone Fishing	489
47	Election Fever	505
48	Hanging Judge	515
49	"As Ye Sow . . ."	523
50	Run Like Hell	539
51	"Fair Go!"	555
52	Blank Cheque	566
53	Lost and Found	580
54	Off the Record	584
55	Citizen's Arrest	596
56	What Goes Around . . .	604
57	Invasive Procedures	621
58	Rue the Day	631
59	Blowback	639
60	No Sanctuary	648
61	Unintended Consequences	662
62	Judgement Day	670
63	Disappearing Act	684
64	Mission Accomplished?	690
65	". . . for I Have Sinned . . ."	699
66	End of the Line	706
67	Inversion	712
68	Pay the Piper!	719
69	Black Holes	724
70	"Chicago Rules"	733
71	Fireworks	744
72	Mandate of Heaven	754
73	Fun & Games	763
74	"Et Tu, Mate?"	770
75	"Why Not?"	780
	Acknowledgements	785
	Cast of Characters and Glossary of Terms	786
	About the Author	788

PART ONE

"Trust Your Enemies . . ."

"Those whom the Gods
would destroy they
first make mad
with power."
— Greek proverb

1   **A Truckload of Monkeys**

SENATOR FRANK MCKURN'S EYES roved over Alison McGuire's body as if it were a *Playboy* centerfold in 3-D.

"I have a proposition for you, Alison."

"I can't imagine how any proposition from you, Senator," Alison replied, her sapphire eyes cold and hard, "could possibly interest me."

McKurn grinned, his thick, stubby fingers snapping the corner of the only item on his desk, a fat manila envelope.

"Oh, I do believe I'll be able to change your mind."

Alison was startled by McKurn's tone of absolute certainty; she tucked a curl of her jet-black hair back into place to cover the slight trembling of her hand.

In her fourteen years in Parliament House, Alison had dealt with McKurn many times—but carefully avoided being alone with him.

Until now.

McKurn had insisted on this meeting and she couldn't find a way to refuse.

A lanky, imperious six foot five, Senator Frank McKurn towered over every other Senator and Member of the House. In his mid-seventies, he wore his age well. But thanks to his crooked nose, bushy, unkempt eyebrows, leathery skin, and the pinkish cast to the whites of his eyes, even wearing an impeccably tailored suit and a $200 tie he looked like a laborer, talked like one, and was built, people whispered, like a brick shithouse: solid, tough, smelly, and slimy.

"It's really very simple," McKurn said with a smile—a smile that did nothing to improve the look of his face. "When Kydd stands down as Prime Minister, everyone expects Anthony Royn to step into his shoes—but I intend to make sure Cracken knocks Royn out of the ring."

"And I, Senator, will do everything I can to make sure your little weasel loses."

McKurn's eyes danced with merriment, as if Alison's response had been an especially funny joke. He grinned wryly; a crooked grin that sent cold, tingling fingers of fear shooting up and down Alison's spine.

"I think not, Alison," McKurn said, his grin broadening, his fingers idly tapping the envelope. "I think not."

McKurn picked up the envelope, leant back in his chair, pulled several sheets of paper half out, gazing at each one with obvious satisfaction for a long moment. His eyes flicked to Alison as if he was gauging her reaction . . . or making some kind of comparison. Alison couldn't tell. But she could feel his eyes lingering for brief moments on her full lips, on the shape of her breasts, and following the outline of her body as it curved into her waist and then flared to her hips.

Alison found her gaze glued to the back of papers, frantic to know what was on the other side.

"You know, Alison," McKurn said with a broad smile that made Alison's stomach quake, "I've admired you from the moment I first saw you."

"Do you expect me to take that as a compliment, Senator?"

"And I've always thought you had a great body," McKurn continued, as if Alison hadn't spoken. "Until recently, I didn't know how stunning it really is."

Alison's long fingers stiffened, her fingertips turning white as stone, gripping the edge of the desk for support. She struggled to speak, but felt as though the muscles of her throat and neck were no longer connected to the rest of her body. "Wh-what do you mean?"

"Very simple." McKurn tossed a single sheet from the envelope onto the desk in front of Alison.

Not a document but a full-color printout. Of her. Naked.

A scream welled up from deep inside her, but she found she could hardly breathe. She was looking at her own face, consumed with ecstasy, framed by her black hair spilling in all directions over a downy pillow. Her pale skin, which the sun reddened but never tanned, was flushed, her deep blue eyes glowed, her nipples were taut, a man's hand on one full breast. A hand she recognized.

Her face turned to ice as she glared at McKurn, half-rising from the chair as words struggled with each other to spill out. After a moment, her mouth opened in the beginning of a yell, but instead she growled: "You—you *bastard.*"

"Sit *down.* And shut *up.*" McKurn's face was hard, his lips tight. He leant forward, his eyes narrowed into pinpoints. He was breathing heavily; Alison flinched as the faint but sour taste of his breath floated towards her. Against her will, she felt herself transfixed as she sank back into the chair, avoiding his eyes by focusing on the broken lines of the bulbous, crooked nose jutting from his craggy face.

Alison shuddered. Long ago, McKurn's nose was broken in a street brawl and hadn't been set properly afterwards. When people remarked on it McKurn would comment, with a malicious laugh, "You shoulda seen the other guy."

The "other guy" had died in hospital.

"No one talks to me like that." McKurn didn't raised his voice, but he spat his words through narrowed lips. "*No one,* you understand?"

Alison clamped her mouth tightly shut. *I won't give him the satisfaction of a reply,* she thought.

McKurn shrugged faintly and threw another picture on the table, then another.

"They leave nothing to the imagination, do they?"

She held her lips tight, but couldn't prevent her eyes from widening as each picture showed a different part of her naked body.

"I must apologize for the quality," McKurn said matter-of-factly. "They were printed off a video."

"A what?"

"A video. Complete, I might add, with sound effects."

Alison's eyes flew wildly around the room. Was she really in *Parliament House?* Was she listening to the president of the Senate—in his *own office?* To the most powerful politician in Australia after the prime minister? For a moment, she felt as though she were looking down on herself from somewhere near the ceiling, observing but coldly ignoring the undisguised terror and disgust surging through her body. And she could hear a voice, an ageless voice, responding to her questions: *Yes, Alison. And you're seeing how he became so powerful.*

Holy Mother of God, I'm having hallucinations. As that thought came, the strange vision disappeared.

McKurn tossed the last one on the desk. Alison saw a grainy blow-up of herself passionately kissing Derek Olsson.

"Convinced yet?" McKurn asked, now watching her with satisfaction and undisguised lust.

Alison became aware of how she was hunched down in the chair like a frightened rabbit. She began to straighten up—but recalled a lesson from Machiavelli. *Keep your enemies continually off guard: Make sure they always underestimate you.*

So she didn't move. Let him think I'm beaten, she decided, and just making futile protests.

"Convinced," she said slowly, straining with the effort to effect a normal tone of voice, "of precisely what?"

"Alison," McKurn said with a sigh, "I've always thought your intelligence matched, if not exceeded, your beauty. Don't disappoint me now."

"Why should I give a damn whether I disappoint you or not?" Alison replied, her teeth clenched.

McKurn shook his head like a teacher whose favorite student had just let him down. His fingers tapped loudly on the pictures strewn across his desk as he watched Alison, waiting.

Alison tried to move her gaze away from the pictures, to look anywhere else, even at McKurn. But she felt as though she no longer had any control over all the little muscles around her eyes.

"Just think," said McKurn. "I can make you famous. All I have to do is post this video on the internet, and you'll be a worldwide sensation. The latest sex bomb, the newest *femme fatale.* The world's paparazzi will follow your every move. There'll be pictures of you everywhere—and double-page spreads of the juiciest ones in the sleazier tabloids."

Leering at her, McKurn picked up the phone. "One phone call, Alison. That's all it will take."

Alison's skin crawled at the thought of people everywhere drooling at the most private parts of her body—at the most private parts of her *self.* Just walking down the street . . . *I'd feel violated again . . . and again . . . knowing that every man would have seen me. I'd have to move to the middle of the Sahara. Or join a nunnery. I'll never be able to show myself in Parliament House again.*

And her mother. Just knowing that her only daughter's naked body was cavorting in pornographic Technicolor for anyone and everyone to see would give Mum a heart attack.

"NO!" Alison said angrily, glaring at McKurn. "You can't."

"Really?" McKurn laughed. Not a laugh that invited her to join him. "Why on earth not?"

Somewhere in the background she heard that strange yet familiar voice: *Take note, Alison. This is how he operates. This is a lesson in power you'll never get from Royn—or even Kydd.*

Though her heart seemed to be hammering in her ears, and her stomach churned with rising panic, she forced herself to speak.

"So?" she said, still unable to look up. "I had a romantic weekend with Derek Olsson. So what? Who gives a damn?"

"You didn't go to bed with just anybody, Alison. You had a dirty weekend with *Derek Olsson,* who's now in jail and about to be convicted of a brutal drug murder."

"Derek is no murderer." *He just can't be.*

"Really?" McKurn chuckled, a thick eyebrow rising in a question mark. "You must be the only person in the whole country who thinks that."

"I know," Alison said under her breath, her eyes dropping to focus on the edge of the desk.

McKurn shrugged, and waved a picture of Olsson's face under her eyes. "And he's obviously up to his eyeballs in the rackets."

"That's completely ridiculous."

"Get real, Alison. Whether he's a racketeer or not doesn't matter. It doesn't even matter if he's innocent of the murder he's charged with. This is *politics,* Alison. What has truth, or right and wrong, got to do with it? Absolutely *nothing.* Most people will believe whatever the media tells them to believe. As far as the press is concerned, the famous Derek Olsson, the business sensation they once drooled over, is nothing but a gangster and a hoodlum."

When Alison said nothing, McKurn added in a quiet, hissing voice, "And you, Alison, will be nothing but a gangster's moll."

He's turned the tables on me, she realized.

Three months ago when her boss, Anthony Royn, asked her to "Get the goods on McKurn," she'd leapt at the assignment. *Now he's "got the goods" on me instead.*

She lifted her head stiffly against the strain of the locked muscles of her neck, forcing herself to look McKurn straight in the eye. But the room was spinning. The vision that had driven her since she was sixteen flashed into her mind: Alison McGuire striding through the corridors of power, dispensing justice and righting wrongs—a crusading Joan of Arc. As McKurn's face came into focus, her vision seemed to shatter in front of her eyes, like a fragile crystal being smashed into a thousand pieces.

"No!" she cried, involuntarily.

"*Yes,* Alison."

McKurn's face morphed into the image of the Devil Incarnate Father Ryan painted in one Sunday morning sermon when she was a mere six years old. An image which gave her nightmares for weeks afterward.

With an effort, she forced herself to look deep into the pinkish pinpoints that were McKurn's eyes . . . and decided that Father Ryan had never experienced and knew *nothing* of the depth of evil he'd been trying to portray.

"So this is how a slimeball like you," she hissed, "gets people to do your bidding."

"Wake up, Alison," McKurn's voice boomed across the room. He stood halfway out of his chair, leaning across his desk, his face looming over her. "From now on, when I tell you to jump through hoops, you ask 'how many?'"

Alison tensed her muscles against McKurn's onslaught—but felt herself cringing back in her chair. *I should walk out of here,* she thought to herself. But her shaking legs refused to move.

"That's better," McKurn said as he lowered himself back into his chair, his eyes glinting with satisfaction.

"I see," Alison sighed thoughtfully, as if to herself. Straightening her body, she forced herself to look directly into McKurn's eyes. "So," she shrugged, "you can run me out of politics. What good does that do you?"

McKurn seemed amused. "Really, Alison. If that's all I achieved. . . . What do they call you in the Press Gallery? Oh yes, *The Power Behind the Throne.* Knocking you out would kick away Royn's main prop. He'd be easy game."

Alison shook her head. "I'm not indispensable. Royn's still Kydd's favorite. You can't get around it."

"You're not thinking clearly. As former 'Drug Czar,' Anthony Royn has built his political career around a take-no-hostages anti-drug program." McKurn picked up the picture of her and Olsson kissing passionately and waved it under her nose. "But it turns out that all along his chief political adviser, the much-vaunted Alison McGuire, was really a gangster's deceitful moll who gave Olsson the inside dope on every move the great 'Anti-Drug Crusader' was about to make." McKurn chuckled. "Royn will be seen as the witless dupe he really is, whose every move was orchestrated by the gangster's strumpet. Who's going to believe Royn has the balls to occupy the highest office in the land then? He'll be laughed out of politics. Not even Kydd would stand up for him."

"You make it sound very plausible." Alison spoke with a coolness she did not feel. "But Royn could easily surprise you."

"I don't want any surprises," McKurn said. "That's why *you're* going to help me make Cracken, not Royn, the next prime minister."

"What? You mean. . . . You want me to be your *spy* in Royn's office? Is that what you're proposing? You must be out of your mind, Senator."

"Am I?" McKurn laughed, fingering the pictures.

"So, let me get this clear," she said slowly. "You want me to give up everything I've worked for, betray my principles, deceive everyone who trusts me and pimp on them just so you can put that little weasel Paul Cracken into power?"

"It seems we understand each other."

"And what am I supposed to get out of this?"

"Why, Alison, you'll be on the winning team of course."

"That's hardly something to look forward to—if it's *your* team."

"And, of course, I won't post that video."

"You think that's enough incentive for me to do what you want me to do?"

McKurn grinned, his bushy eyebrows peaking into two inverted Vs. *Like horns,* Alison thought.

"It's your choice, Alison. But do you really want everyone in the world to watch you and your boyfriend fucking like rabbits?"

"He's not my boyfriend."

"I suppose not—since he took up with that pesky Karla Preston who writes for his newspapers." McKurn shrugged. "More grist for the mill: Olsson's just a heartless womanizer who dips into the company store, and Alison McGuire, so-called 'power behind the throne,' was mere putty in his hands."

Oh, Derek, she thought, feeling tears in her eyes, *how could all this be happening?* But Olsson was now doubly out of reach: he *was* in jail, though she didn't believe for a moment that he was a murderer. And she hadn't seen him since—since that weekend.

She shook her head. *I can't think about that right now.* Dabbing the corner of her eyes with a fingertip, she took a deep breath and looked as steadily as she could at McKurn.

"I've got a better idea," Alison said heatedly. "Why don't you just go ahead and post the damn video. If you're right, that will get you what you want."

"What would be the fun in that?" McKurn exclaimed. Idly picking up a picture he murmured, "I wouldn't get everything I want." Picking up another he added, "Not *quite* everything."

Breathing heavily, McKurn placed the pictures he was admiring in front of Alison. Gently stroking one of them with his finger he said, "Did anyone ever tell you, Alison," McKurn asked, "that you have a great arse?"

Somewhere deep down, Alison felt that some part of herself knew and understood the real meaning of McKurn's words—but she clamped down tight, refusing to let that awareness rise into her consciousness.

He moved his finger to the erect nipple on the other picture, covering Olsson's hand as he did. "And your breasts, Alison. One rarely sees such perfection."

McKurn looked up from the picture to focus on her breasts. Alison shivered as though she was being caressed by his ice-cold hands rather than his eyes.

Her throat dry, Alison had to swallow a couple of times before she could speak. "I thought young girls were more your style," she spat, her voice tinged with contempt. "Preferably under the age of consent."

"For beauty such as yours, Alison, I've made an exception."

"Dream on." Alison tried to push herself up, to leap across the table to physically shatter McKurn's leering grin. But her legs were trembling; she had to thrust with her hands on the desk to find the leverage to heave herself into a standing position.

Now looking down on McKurn she felt momentarily in command. *One day,* she silently swore to him, *we'll meet in a dark alley and only I will come out.* She heard her own voice repeating her *Sensei's* words: "The purpose of the martial arts is self-defence." *Well, it would be,* she thought in reply—and smiled at the image of McKurn's arms, legs, and neck twisted in impossible angles.

"I'm glad you find this amusing," McKurn said with surprise.

"I'd rather walk under a bus."

"That," said McKurn coldly, "can be arranged."

He means it, Alison thought. *I should be shocked.* But she felt a strange, if hollow, sense of triumph as the pieces of the jigsaw puzzle that was McKurn fell into place: *Everything I've thought about you, McKurn, is true—but can I prove it?* "You mean like the guy you put in hospital?"

"That was self-defence."

"Oh, come on, Senator. You expect me to believe that now? That was Sydney in the nineteen-fifties. Just about every cop in town was for sale back then. And witnesses can always be intimidated, can't they?"

"You'd better be careful what you say, and who you say it to, Alison."

"Or what? You'll sue me for slander? That would be fun."

"You obviously need some time to mull over everything I've said. I'll give you a week. If you haven't accepted my offer by this time next Friday, that video goes up—and we can all say 'Goodbye' to Alison McGuire."

Glaring fiercely at McKurn she shook her head. *"Never."*

Gathering the shreds of her dignity around her she walked out of his office without looking back.

McKurn laughed, calling after her, "One week, remember."

In the corridor, she slammed the door behind her. Heart racing, head spinning, she grabbed at the wall for support and leant breathlessly against it. *One week,* she thought between gulps of air. *What can I do in one week?*

It was late Friday afternoon. Parliament was already half-empty; in offices all over the country people were getting ready for their weekends—if they hadn't taken off for the beach already.

McKurn chose this time on purpose.

The week wouldn't start till Monday—and what could she do over the weekend?

"Are you all right, Miss? You look terrible."

She lifted her head to see people looking at her strangely as they hurried past. A security guard was standing in front of her looking concerned—and, no doubt, checking the ID hanging around her neck at the same time.

"I'll be fine. Thanks. It must be something I ate."

She pushed off from the wall and walked slowly in the direction of Royn's office. Remembering the guard's comment she turned into the first bathroom she passed.

"You do look terrible," she said to her image in the mirror. Somehow, the ritual of washing her face and re-applying her makeup made her feel a little better.

"Well, Alison," she said to her reflection, "what are we going to do?" As if in answer, the thought came to her: *Never lay all your cards on the table.* "He's overconfident," she muttered. "He's told more than he should have. He was boasting."

He's made a mistake . . . but how can I use it against him?

"I need some help, don't I?" she said to the mirror. Her thoughts turned to Olsson—but she shook her head. What could he do, even if he wasn't stuck in jail?

She sighed, stretched to her full height, and looked herself in the eye until she saw the fire and determination come back.

No, she vowed to her mother. *Never,* she pledged to her younger self, and to the vision that fuelled her since she was sixteen. "No, McKurn," she swore, "I *won't* do anything you want," she said to herself. *But how,* the voice in her head responded, *can you refuse?* "There's a way—and even if it's the dark alley, I'll find it."

But her stomach chose that moment to rebel. She stumbled into the nearest cubicle where she threw up.

*****

WHEN ALISON REACHED HER office, she went straight to the safe and pulled out her file on McKurn. But everything in those pages was etched in her memory. *No facts. Sydney,* she thought. *He grew up in Sydney. I could visit Mum and Dad. I could visit Derek. In jail?* Alison shuddered. *I could talk to his partner, Ross Traynor.*

"Stop kidding yourself, Alison," she said sternly. "You could phone Ross and ask him how Derek's doing."

Still, there might be something I can do in Sydney. She quickly tidied up, closed the safe, folded up her laptop . . . and stopped.

"My enemy's enemy. . . ." she muttered to herself with a glint in her eye. *Of course. Randolph Kydd—McKurn's most powerful enemy.* "Yes," she said out loud. "That's who I should talk to."

She'd always looked forward to her meetings with Kydd. He treated her as if she were a favorite granddaughter; she always felt a tinge of awe, as if she were sitting at the feet of the Master. But those meetings, when they weren't with Royn as well, were always arranged by or for him.

I should call Royn first, she thought. And shook her head. *Then I'd have to tell him why.* She looked at the phone. *This is an emergency. He'll understand.*

She picked up the handset—and put it down again. *The phone. If I could tap McKurn's phone.*

But a court order would be needed. She knew several Federal Police officers—but none of them owed her enough favors to risk his job doing something as patently illegal as that. "Pity," she said as she dialled Kydd's office.

"Larry, it's Alison," she said as she got through to Kydd's personal assistant. "Is the Prime Minister still here?"

"Yes, but he's about to walk out the door for the airport."

"Oh. Any chance of a quick word before he goes? I've got something to ask him that really can't wait till Monday."

"Hang on, I'll check."

A moment later she jerked the handset away from her ear as Kydd's voice boomed at the only volume setting he knew: extra loud. "Yes, my dear, what's so urgent?"

Alison stopped her hand from leaping to her mouth.

"Well, Prime Minister." She paused. *What am I going to say?* she asked herself. *I can't tell him the truth—I'm going to have to lie to the Prime Minister.* "I need some advice . . . about Senator McKurn, Prime Minister."

"Pah—McKurn." Kydd spat his words. "Always trouble. What now?"

"I've been digging into his past—"

"And how's it going?"

"Not too well. I've collected lots of rumors. But no facts, no *evidence.*"

"He's a clever bastard—trickier than a truckload of monkeys. Covers his tracks too well, damn him."

"Now, he . . . he's. . . ." Alison felt herself freezing up, as if something was stopping her from uttering the words she was about to say.

"I can tell that something is bothering you," Kydd said kindly. "But please get to the point, Alison. I've got a plane to catch."

"Sorry, Prime Minister," Alison said with a silent moan. "The problem is—" she took a deep breath, and her words tumbled out "—I've just discovered he's got wind of what I've been doing, and I need to come up with something concrete fast to head him off. I thought you might have some idea, some suggestion, someone I could talk to. . . ."

"This is a distressing development, Alison. One I don't like at all."

"No, Prime Minister." Alison made no attempt to hide the shakiness in her voice.

"Talk to Sidney Royn, Anthony's father. Back when he was attorney-general, he started an investigation into corruption, mainly targeting the New South Wales state government—McKurn's home territory." Kydd's voice turned thoughtful. "You know, I've never completely understood why Sid quit politics. He was at the top of his game. Maybe, just maybe—"

"Maybe McKurn had something to do with it?"

"That's what I'm wondering." Kydd looked at his watch. "I'd better get moving. Call Sid. If I come up with something else you'll be the first to know. And remember, my door is always open to you, Alison."

"Thank you, Prime Minister."

SHE GRIPPED HER HANDS to still them and felt the calluses from years of Aikido and Karate. She chopped the edge of one hand into the palm of the other, imagining she was smashing McKurn's neck.

Yes, I've got enough time before the flight, she thought, looking at the clock. *I'll call Sidney Royn on the way.*

Right now, I'm going to go and break some bricks.

2 Between Heaven and Hell

"**H**EY, TOFF. WHYDJA DO it?"

"Forty-six, forty-seven, forty-eight. . . ." In one corner of the exercise yard at Long Bay Penitentiary, Derek Olsson counted push-ups.

"Hey! Toff! We're talking to ya."

From the corners of his eyes, Olsson noticed five pairs of feet in a rough semicircle around him.

"Do what," he said, without breaking the rhythm of his pushups.

Everyone doing time here seemed to have a nickname: Olsson's was the "Toff" because of his wealth. These five were known as the "Rollers," partly because anyone who got in their way got rolled. Their leader was "King Kong": to the other prisoners, he was unquestionably the king, and he was bigger, meaner, and had more murders to his credit than the other four members of his gang. Wherever the Rollers moved they were surrounded by a meter or two of empty space as the other prisoners kept a respectful distance.

"Whydja kill that guy?" said the King. "You were livin' rich, ya got all the money in the world, hot and cold running girls, I'll bet. Whydja do it?"

"I didn't."

"Come on. You're gonna get life, same as us. *We* ain't gonna tell anyone anyways, so ya might as well be straight with us—and come clean."

"I am being straight with you."

The King rolled his eyes.

"Anyways, we gotta message we have to give ya."

"I'm listening," said Olsson.

"From someone called Luck Suck," said one of the other men.

"Lock Sook, you dummy," said the King.

"Whatever," said the other man with a laugh.

Olsson stopped at full stretch and looked up. "Perhaps you'd better make sure you know who the message is from before you deliver it," he said. He'd chosen this spot because it was shaded from the heat of the afternoon sun. But he became aware the five men stood to block his view of the prison guards—and their view of him.

"I don't think he gives a shit about our pronunciation." The five Rollers all thought this comment was extremely funny.

While they laughed, Olsson continued his push-ups. But his rhythm was slower, his motions shallower; he inched his feet forward a little; though he still appeared to be looking at the ground, his eyes were turned so he could study the men in his peripheral vision.

They stood with their hands in their pockets and expectation on their hard, unforgiving faces. The King grunted, and in unison the five men pulled out their hands. Olsson saw a piece of wood sharpened to a point in one man's hand, a nail protruding from a small block of wood in another's, a jury-rigged knuckleduster on a third. At the same moment the King lunged with his foot, aiming to kick Olsson in the gut. *Ah,* thought Olsson without surprise, *it's that kind of message.*

Olsson pushed up with his arms and legs, turning his body at the same time. His awareness seemed to shrink to the tips of his fingers and toes. The five men became five shifting shapes in space, connected with him and to each other by faint lines of movement, like a three-dimensional geometric puzzle.

When the King's foot arrived, Olsson's stomach was no longer there.

As Olsson's body left the ground he saw his hands slice sharply upwards, connecting *one two three four* with the back of the King's ankle, transferring the inertia of his body to the King's leg at the same time. The foot flew up in the air, forcing the King off balance. He fell backwards, groaning as the back of his head cracked onto the hard pavement. The other four Rollers looked stunned as they watched the King's foot come to rest on the ground at an impossible angle.

Olsson landed gracefully on the balls of his feet, his knees slightly bent, his hands held like straight knives in front of him. In the background he was aware of faint yells of "Fight! Fight!"

"Well, gentlemen," he said amiably. "Why don't we just agree you've delivered your message—and now you can all fuck off."

The faces on the four remaining shapes crystallized in Olsson's vision. They hesitated, flashing glances at each other. But his words, Olsson noted, had made them angrier. Sure enough, as one of the shapes moved onto the attack, the other three followed and they rushed Olsson—but as a straggle, not a team.

The faint connecting lines in Olsson's mind turned into arrows of motion so when the nearest shape arrived, its fist in full swing, Olsson was already gliding out of its way. In one fluid, twirling motion one of his hands arced out, touching the shape's shoulder, nudging the man in the direction he'd been moving so his head slammed into the wall where Olsson had been doing his pushups just moments ago.

The man's head hit the concrete wall with a sharp crack and he collapsed in a heap, but he'd already disappeared from Olsson's awareness. His twirl turned into a ballet-like pirouette as one foot sailed out in mid-air and connected to a kneecap with a crunch. The third shape fell into the path of the fourth.

Olsson seemed to swirl faster into a second pirouette as his other foot floated up and into the fourth shape's crotch, his knee then continuing the upward arc to meet the man's head as he doubled over, groaning loudly.

"Jesus H. Christ," a voice nearby said breathlessly, and Olsson suddenly realized he'd lost track of the last shape, only to feel an arm go around his neck and something sharp resting none too gently on the right side of his throat just under his jaw. His eyes did a fast scan of the other four men. Must be the wooden knife, he concluded.

"Looks like you got me," Olsson said. He let his body relax as though he was admitting defeat, and felt the man's grip around his neck slacken just a touch.

"Yeah, looks like I do."

"Oh well," said Olsson despondently, "what—"

Olsson never finished his sentence.

As he spoke, his feet lifted from the ground, his left elbow jabbed deep into the man's stomach while his other hand pushed up on the wrist of the hand holding the makeshift knife. The last Roller staggered against the unexpected weight of Olsson's whole body now hanging from his arm, grunted with surprise as Olsson's elbow dug deep into his stomach, and collapsed on Olsson's back.

Olsson's body seemed to rise as if his legs were springs. The man's struggling body rolled off Olsson's back and to one side as Olsson used the wrist he still held as a lever to roll him onto his stomach. Then Olsson dropped, leaning his weight on one knee just above the man's hips, twisting the man's arm behind his back, pushing his hand towards the back of his neck.

"Youch. My arm, my arm," the man yelled.

"Oh, I'm hurting you, am I?" Olsson said. "Isn't that a shame. Now, you were saying you had a message for me?"

"Seems like we're the ones who got the message."

"Quite," said Olsson, only now breathing hard and fast.

"Jesus H. Christ," said the same voice again.

Olsson looked up to see a weedy man—the "Rat"—gaping at him in awe, and staring at the five bodies lying on the ground, two of them unconscious, the other three groaning in pain. "How the hell did you do *that?*"

With a crooked grin, Olsson shrugged. "Practice."

The Rat shook his head in disbelief. "You're bleeding," he said.

Olsson put his free hand to his ear. It felt warm and sticky; and now he was aware of it, it hurt. "Thanks," said Olsson with a smile. He pulled out his handkerchief and held it to the side of his head.

Olsson now saw the other prisoners crowded around, looking at Olsson with a new respect: in the prison hierarchy, he'd just taken the place of the alpha male.

But quite a few of the prisoners seemed disappointed. *They missed out on the show,* Olsson chuckled to himself. *By the time they got here, it was all over.*

"Out of the way. Move out of the way."

A prison guard, swinging his truncheon in the direction of anyone who didn't move fast enough, squeezed his way through the crowd, followed by three more.

"You," he shouted at Olsson. "Stand up and let that prisoner go."

Olsson rose slowly and carefully to his feet.

"Well, well, well," the guard said, beating one hand with his truncheon in time to his words. "What happened here?"

"He—" the Rat started to say.

Olsson looked at the weedy man quizzically.

"Self-defence, swear to God," the Rat said to the guard. "It was like something out of one of those Kung Fu movies. Unbelievable."

Bob. That was the guard's name, Olsson remembered. Bob the Swagman—because he swaggered rather than walked.

"Sheesh." Shaking his head, the Swagman looked down at the five toughest men in the prison yard. He took a step back, as if to keep himself as far away from Olsson as he could. "You and you," he said to two of the guards, "handcuff him and lock him up tight. And you," he said to the third one, "call an ambulance—and tell them to bring five stretchers."

"What about the Toff?" said a prisoner. "He's bleeding."

"Nothing less than he deserves, I'm sure," the Swagman grinned.

A rumbling sound came from behind the Swagman; the prisoners didn't approve.

The Swagman realized where he was standing. "And they'll need a first aid kit," he said. But he glared at Olsson. *I'll get you later,* he seemed to be saying.

As the "Toff," as something of a celebrity, Derek Olsson was known to everyone in the prison, including the guards. A broad-shouldered man of average height and a ready grin, Olsson's hazel-green eyes always sparkled with amusement as they did now, as if everything he looked at were some kind of a joke. Women felt he was just a warm and friendly, grown-up teddy bear waiting to be cuddled; men, while aware of a restrained power, that he was someone they could unreservedly trust.

The two guards hesitated, eyeing Olsson as though he was not the tame puppy he had seemed, but a wild, deadly, even feral wolf.

Olsson stood relaxed, as though he was lounging in his living room rather than standing in a prison yard with blood oozing from the gash on his ear, the only sign, other than the five bodies at his feet, that he had been in a fight.

Truncheons at the ready, the guards met no resistance as they each grabbed a muscled arm and roughly handcuffed his wrists behind his back. As they led him away, the prisoners cheered.

OLSSON COLLAPSED ONTO the hard bed as the door swung shut and the locks clicked into place. *And you figured having the police convinced you're a murderer was as bad as it could get,* he thought, staring at the ceiling. *How wrong you were. Now Luk Suk believes you killed that man—and it's not his style to waste time with a trial before executing his judgement.*

*****

HER TAXI FROM SYDNEY airport was driven by a dour Russian or Ukrainian of very few words, which suited Alison just fine. But her mood lifted the moment it turned into the familiar streets of Balmain where she'd grown up. Where, much to her mother's distress, she'd zoomed around the roads on her bike even before the training wheels had come off.

Everything was so much simpler then, Alison sighed as the taxi pulled up in front of her parents' home.

The McGuire home was an old, nondescript, three-bedroom brick house that looked just like all the other houses on the street. But as Alison stepped through the gate, she felt like she was going back to heaven. The front door opened and her parents crowded in the entrance, smiling broadly.

Alison dropped her bags and ran into their arms. For a long moment, enfolded by them both, her head nestling against her father's broad chest, she felt five years old again without a care in the world.

As a child, Alison McGuire was loved as no other child had ever been loved. When she was born, her sparkling sapphire eyes wide open, her father, Joe McGuire, had collapsed to his knees with relief. For nine long months he'd lived in the shadow of constant fear: at forty, with Maggie McGuire's history of miscarriages, pregnancy could be a sentence of death for the woman he loved.

Even though Alison was now thirty-four, Joe and Maggie McGuire still treated their only child as if she was a gift from God.

"You look tired, Alison," Maggie said after a while. "Go freshen up. Dinner's almost ready—your favorites."

"Of course," said Joe, beaming.

As SHE DID WHENEVER she came home, Alison stood in the middle of her bedroom and breathed the air of her childhood. It was the smallest room in the house—cramped to her friends, but to Alison it was warm and cozy. And *safe,* with bars on the windows and a bolt on the door.

The room was just as she'd left it when she'd moved to Canberra a few weeks after graduating from Sydney University. Her English, history and political science textbooks were still on the shelves, along with the tennis cup she'd won in the inter-school competition; and pictures . . . her smiling, impish face at around three, clutching a stray kitten she'd brought home from one of her expeditions around the neighborhood . . . with her parents, who were making no attempt to hide their pride in their daughter, standing by the organ in the church where she played on Sundays . . . her body caught in mid-leap above the Aikido mat, her black hair streaming like wings buoying her in space as she flew through the air with unstoppable motion, arms and legs outstretched.

She turned to look at the picture dominating the opposite wall. She stepped closer to study herself, aged sixteen, standing radiant—and all too innocent—on the steps leading up to the main entrance of Parliament House, a constant reminder of her dream and her goal: to be working *there,* at the center of power, where it was possible to change the world.

Shrugging away the tears that came into her eyes, she sat down at her desk and opened a drawer. At the bottom, underneath papers and odds and ends, was a large picture, face down. She gingerly pulled it out of the drawer and stared into the soft hazel-green eyes of Derek Olsson. She smiled back at his wide grin, his tousled brown hair that grew, it seemed, in all directions at once and was the despair of barbers everywhere. She reached out a finger to touch the deep dimple that appeared on his cheek whenever he smiled. To look at him at seventeen was to see the face of a Greek god fallen to earth, of joyous possibilities untouched by pain or suffering. But his face was turned slightly to one side; she knew that hidden from the camera's lens was the faint shadow of a bruise. He'd got it playing rugby, he told anyone who asked. But Alison was one of the few people who knew where it really came from.

Her mother's voice calling from the dining room interrupted her thoughts. "Dinner's on the table, Alison."

"Coming, Mum."

She roughly pushed the picture back into the drawer, face down as she'd found it. As she headed to the bathroom to wash her hands and face, she passed the closed door of the spare bedroom without seeing it.

"TELL ME, ALISON," HER mother asked as they took their places at the table. "Do you think Derek Olsson is really a murderer?"

Alison shook her head. "I just don't understand what's going on, Mum. It's got to be a mistake. Derek couldn't have done anything like that. I'm sure of it."

"He was such a nice boy. But maybe he's changed. It happens, you know."

"He has, but not in that way."

"Oh, so you're still seeing him?"

"From time to time."

"He was the one I liked best of all your boys. And he's been very successful, hasn't he?"

"Oh, Mother. You're not going to start trying to marry me off again, are you?"

"Well, Alison, your clock is ticking. And we're not getting any younger you know."

"I know," she sighed.

"Given he's in jail," her father said gruffly, "it's just as well you didn't marry him."

Alison looked at her father with a wry grin. "You're probably right, Dad," she said. *But for other reasons,* she added to herself.

Her father, Alison knew, would be scandalized by her association with anyone accused of a crime, even if he was proven innocent later. Unless, of course, that person was a striker or a union organizer. Such were her father's loyalties that he'd always stand by a union man, regardless of the crime, if his actions could be viewed as furthering the workers' cause. Though not, of course, a union man who'd done something like run off with the members' money. "Capitalist turncoat," he'd say of such a person. "A traitor to the working class."

Silence reigned for a few minutes as they polished off the roast lamb, onions and potatoes. Without having to ask, Alison knew her mother had dashed to the supermarket the moment after Alison had called to say she was coming and had spent the rest of the afternoon in the kitchen, preparing this feast.

"You didn't say how long you're staying this time," Maggie said as she and Alison cleared the dishes.

"Till Sunday morning."

"So you won't be coming to church with us?"

Alison smiled and shook her head. "I have an early flight to Melbourne."

"Melbourne?" Joe said. "Going to see that primped up popinjay you work for?"

"No, Dad. His father, Sidney Royn."

"Why him?"

"He has some information I need. At least, I hope he does."

Alison and Maggie disappeared into the kitchen and returned a moment later with dessert.

Eyeing her husband, Maggie said, "So what would you like to do tomorrow, Alison? We could all have lunch at the Fish Market. You always loved that place."

"That would be fun," Alison said as she sat back down. Looking at the large bowl of white, fluffy semolina snow, the red raspberries beside it, and the huge jug of fresh cream, she added, "And I'd better go to the *dojo* sometime tomorrow, to work off this dessert."

Maggie laughed; Joe just downed the rest of his whisky and said,

"Every day when I think of you working for those capitalist lackeys, I feel I've failed as your father."

"Oh, Daddy," Alison said, her face melting. "You're the bestest Daddy in the world." She smiled as she spoke as she had when she was five years old.

Joe's face softened. "Well—" he started to say, momentarily lost for words.

"And yes," Alison continued quietly, "we have our differences. But not on what's right and what's wrong—just on the best way to make things better."

"Electing a Labor Party government—a *workers'* government," Joe replied, "is the best way to make things better."

"You could be right," Alison said softly, "and I'll be the first to admit it. But after all, the Labor government started the whole process of deregulation and freeing up the markets that you so detest."

"Thatcherites," Joe snorted. "Every damn one of them. But at least they had the support of the unions. Your Conservatives are out to destroy the working man."

"I know," Alison sighed. "Unions have certainly declined since the Conservatives came to power."

"Declined?" Joe glared. "The union movement has been *gutted.*"

Alison nodded. "But, just the same, you—and lots of working men just like you—are millionaires today."

"Only if we sold our home," Joe grunted. "Which we'll never do."

As a young couple—Joe loading and unloading ships at the nearby docks, Maggie working in a supermarket—they had scrimped and saved to buy their proudest asset: their home. Today, the docks were slated for redevelopment. The Dockworkers' Union, of which Joe was a lifelong member, was a shadow of its former self, hit by the Conservative government's workplace legislation—which Joe, unsurprisingly, loathed as "anti-union."

Balmain, once a sleepy semi-industrial area, had been "gentrified" along with the neighboring inner western suburbs a short bus ride from the city. As property prices soared, many members of the McGuire family and their friends had cashed in their unexpected wealth, sold their homes and retired to cheaper properties strung along beaches from the Central Coast north of Sydney as far as the Sunshine Coast past Brisbane. Every winter, Joe and Maggie packed up their car and visited them, but always returned home after a month or so with a sigh of relief. Alison chuckled—very quietly— to herself. Her father would never change his ways: he was, without doubt, the most conservative person she knew.

"And only," Joe added, "because the Conservatives have ridden on the back of what Labor achieved."

Alison knew her father's words were true, and that if she said anything she would have to agree with him. So, staring at him without blinking, she kept her mouth tightly shut.

"So," Joe McGuire said, scenting victory, "what are you going to do about the Sandeman Islands?"

"Daddy! That's hardly fair."

"Is it? Or do you think more Australian boys should die just so your lah-de-dah boss and that pompous ass Randolph Kydd can continue sucking up to the Americans?"

"Joe," Maggie cried.

"Well," said Joe, turning on his wife, "it's true, isn't it?"

"Daddy . . . " Alison breathed. But she found she could no longer look her father in the eye.

Fifteen months before, a routine meeting of the Pacific Islands Forum agreed to send troops, police and aid to help the government of the sleepy, tropical Sandeman Islands bring various separatist movements under control.

Not long after soldiers from Australia and New Zealand, along with token contingents from Fiji, Papua New Guinea and other Forum members had begun operations, an Australian wildcatter struck oil off Jazeerat el-Bihar—Arabic for "Spice Island," the westernmost island of the Sandemans. It was the first time the Sandemans had been world news since the battles of the Coral Sea and Guadalcanal in 1942 and '43.

Oil was something really worth fighting about.

Papua New Guinea to the west and the Solomon Islands to the north both claimed part of the presumed under-sea oil lake was theirs. While Toribaya, the capital, prospered, grumblings of discontent in the outlying islands at their neglect and poverty was turning into a full-scale guerrilla war to grab control of the oil windfall.

To the public, Australian forces in the Sandemans had been a non-issue—"the sort of 'Good Thing' we should do," those few people who ever thought about it said, "to help a poor country get its act together." That all changed earlier in the week, when three

Australian soldiers were killed in an ambush—in a country Australians knew only as an idyllic, tropical holiday resort. Alison had known for days that at its next meeting Cabinet was going to authorize the sending of more troops to the Sandemans.

"So tell me, Alison," Joe demanded, "that Jeremy's regiment *isn't* going to be sent up there."

Alison's cousin, newly minted army lieutenant Jeremy McGuire, was part of the regiment next in line to go. As her father spoke, Alison couldn't help but see Jeremy's smiling face, shattered by a bullet. With a jerk she remembered: *I was involved in making the decisions that led to our troops' being in the Sandemans. When someone dies I'm partly responsible.*

"I don't want *anyone* to die," Alison said, her eyes downcast.

Seeing her expression, Joe shook his head and sighed.

"So when something really *important* has to be decided, a matter of life and death, where's the power and influence you were after? Looks to me like your strategy isn't working."

You might be right, Daddy, Alison thought weakly. *More right than you'd ever want to imagine.*

"Sometimes. . . ." Alison looked helplessly at her father, reluctant to concede anything to him at all. "Sometimes. . . . It's just . . . it never pays to step in front of a speeding train."

Joe leaned back, relaxing in acknowledgement of his daughter's concession. "Better to live and fight another day than be a martyr to a lost cause."

"True," Alison nodded in agreement, her eyes brimming. "After all, I'm still *your* daughter, Daddy."

"That's right," said Maggie. "Stubborn as a mule."

Even Joe joined in their laughter.

"Joe," said Maggie quickly, pointing to the clock on the wall, "you go and watch your favorite show while Alison and I clean up."

"I'll read for a bit," Alison said a while later when her parents went to bed. But in the warmth and comfort of the living room, she quickly started nodding off until she imagined—or was she dreaming?—her mother's voice cooing, "Bedtime, Alison."

She laughed, and ambled slowly towards her room. About to enter, she stopped, looking at the closed door of the spare bedroom. *Should I?* she asked herself. She reached for the doorknob. . . .

Dare I?

Trembling from the memories, Alison yanked her hand away from the doorknob as if it was a hot stove. Using the wall for support, she stumbled into her bedroom and shot the bolt on the door, something she hadn't done for a long, long time.

3 "Vengeance Shall Be Mine . . ."

A LISON WOKE, BATHED IN sweat.
Have I even been asleep?
Her body trembling, she threw back the sheets to feel the coolness of the morning air, and opened her eyes to try and shake the imprint of the nightmare that terrorized her as a teenager . . . except, now, the faces in her dream were no longer indistinct: every one of them had the pink eyes and bulbous nose of Senator Frank McKurn.

The room was bathed in a soft, rosy pink glow as the light of the sun filtered through the curtains. It was a warm, comfortable feeling to wake up to. But even with her eyes wide open, on this morning she hardly noticed it: the afterimage of her nightmare seemed fixed in her field of vision.

She sat on the edge of the bed, imagining a long, hot shower. But that would only make her feel clean on the outside. She dug into the cupboard for an old T-shirt and a worn tracksuit and pulled on her running shoes. She stopped to wash the aftermath of the dream from her face, and tied her long black hair back into a ponytail before striding into the corridor.

Halfway to the front door, Alison stopped and looked back over her shoulder to see her parents sitting at the dining table. "Morning Mum, Dad," she said. "I'm going for a long bike ride. I'll be back in an hour or two." And she was gone.

AT AN INTERSECTION SHE waited for the light to change, the bike shuddering slightly as she rested her weight on the front pedal while gripping the brake levers to rein it back. As the light turned green she relaxed her fingers and the bike sprang forward at the release of coiled energy. She grinned when she crossed the intersection ahead of the car accelerating beside her. She leaned the bike hard into a turn, skidding around the corner without slowing, like a Grand Prix racer. As a car in front blinked a turn, she spun the bike to the center of the road and slid at speed along the double yellow line through the small gap between the turning car and an oncoming truck. She caught a glimpse of the truckie's wide eyes glaring at her, his mouth an "O," as she flew past.

Nearing a hill she stood on the pedals and pumped faster; at the crest without the slightest pause to catch her breath she leant into the wind and accelerated downhill, knowing without seeing when she flew past her old primary school, the corner store where she had counted out her pennies for a candy, the familiar houses of school friends where she'd spent many happy afternoons, at this moment not even aware of their names or faces. Her mind was filled with the rhythm of the whirling balls of her feet on the pedals, of the strain in her leg muscles and the tension between her shoulder blades as her fingers clenched the handlebars to the sound of her breath coming hard and deep. Every crack and pothole in the road ahead jumped out at her in sharp relief, and here and there a slight unevenness in the road appeared to her as two different shades of black. The dashed lines painted on the road, with the little cats-eyes that twinkled when the sun was at the right angle, formed a boundary on her right; the wheels of parked cars on her left; the red and yellow blinking lights of a car ahead were just an obstacle to be surpassed without any letup in effort.

As she reached the crest of another hill she was momentarily surprised by the glare of the sun's light bouncing from Sydney Harbor below her. She drank in the sudden sight of sea and sky, skidding her bike to a halt. Her breathing, hard and fast, slowed as she stopped, the pounding ache in the muscles of her legs now energizing her body and permeating it with warmth.

Her eyes were attracted by a mass of color packed into a tiny garden nearby. She saw roses, rhododendrons, bougainvillea, primroses, blooms she didn't recognize. The branch of a eucalyptus tree rustled at the edge of her vision. *I never noticed that before,* she thought as she saw that leaves along the same branch could be subtly different shades of the same green. Her eyes swivelled slowly from tree to tree as she searched for the birds twittering in the background. And somewhere far away was the raucous laughter of a kookaburra.

With a faint smile, she became aware that the sense of her nightmare and the feelings that had haunted her since awakening had now faded into the distance.

Good morning to you, Mr. Kookaburra, she thought to herself. *I wish I had something to laugh about, like you.*

As she let herself coast down the hill towards the bay she caught a glimpse of her deep blue eyes in the bike's tiny mirror. Dull when she woke, they now gleamed again like sapphires.

She pulled to a stop at a tiny coffee shop towards the end of the main shopping street which ended, at the bottom of the hill, at the water. From one of the small tables crammed onto the narrow footpath outside, she could see the bay below. The sun shimmered across the deep blue expanse of water; the soft breeze cooled her as it stirred the leaves of a nearby tree with a soothing rhythm. She ordered a cappuccino and croissant, and took a jug of water and a glass to the outside table. She sat, gulping the water, looking at glittering yachts and cruisers crawling towards the sea. When her order came, she sat back contented at last, the sun warming her face, the muscles of her body luxuriantly tired, sipped her cappuccino—and nearly dropped it in her lap as a new thought flashed into her mind: *McKurn. That's how he got the video.*

Carefully putting the cup back down, she thought back to when she and Derek had arrived at the Sandview Hideaway Hotel. There was some mistake in their booking, they were told. As compensation, they'd been upgraded to the Honeymoon Suite.

The Honeymoon Suite. . . . It must have been wired. By who? McKurn? Some independent operator who sold it to McKurn? And just how many copies of that video are there?

"McKurn could even own the hotel," Alison muttered to herself. He'd been living on the fringes of society since he was fourteen—some sixty years. In his late twenties, he'd weaseled his way into politics. It was impossible to tell how much money he'd skimmed in that time, *so he must have money stashed all over the place.*

A hotel like that . . . a perfect investment for a bastard like him.

Innocent newlyweds could end up in McKurn's private library of porn. Not-so-innocent businessmen or politicians on a weekend fling away from their wives would be vulnerable to McKurn's grisly methods of persuasion.

Ownership, she realized, is something that can be traced.

My God, she thought, jerking to attention. *Did McKurn just get lucky? Or did he know we were going to be there?* She looked at the other people sipping coffee and at the passers-by, trying not to be obvious. *Am I being followed?* she wondered. She shook her head. *It could be anybody . . . or nobody.*

She'd been toying with the idea of visiting Olsson in jail, but now firmly rejected it, just in case. "I'll call Ross instead."

She pulled her cellphone halfway out of her pocket—and stopped. She knew, from the Federal Police briefings she'd attended, that just about anyone with some technical knowledge could build gadgets to monitor mobile phone calls. *I must be going paranoid,* she thought. Nevertheless, she checked there was nobody within hearing distance before she made the call.

After a few rings an answering machine kicked in. Alison hung up, thought for a moment, called again and left a message asking Ross Traynor to call her.

She eyed the weekend sailors scattered across the bay, all looking forward to a pleasant and uneventful day of sailing around the harbor or fishing out to sea. *Damn you, McKurn,* she thought, clenching her fists. *I should be doing something like that, not worrying about what could happen in one week. No . . . only six days left. . . .*

She stood up angrily, almost knocking over the table as she did. She glared at the couple nearby who were now looking at her strangely, and jumped onto her bike. Pumping the pedals hard up the hill, she suddenly slowed as a police car cruised by.

Of course, she thought. *The police. Time to see how many favors I can call in.*

*****

"I can have Olsson's solicitor here in thirty minutes."

Ross Traynor glared at the overweight, uniformed clerk at the visitor's entrance to Long Bay jail, waving his cellphone under the man's nose at the same time.

"As I told you, sir," the clerk said, now speaking defensively, "the prisoner has been in some trouble and is temporarily off-limits to visitors."

"Really? I've been through all your red tape and I have a pre-arranged appointment to see Derek Olsson now," Traynor said firmly.

"We have our procedures, sir."

"And will they stand up to legal scrutiny? Let's find out," Traynor said, opening his phone to dial a number.

"If you just wait a minute, sir," he said, glowering at Traynor, "I'll ask my superior to talk to you."

"Go right ahead—but I'm going to talk to Olsson's solicitor, just the same."

A few minutes later another man, with pips on his shoulders, came to the desk. Before the officer could speak Traynor said, "Olsson's solicitor is ready to jump in his car—and you know what that means. He also wants to know *what* kind of trouble Olsson was in, *why* he hasn't been informed, *whether* the police were called to investigate and, if so, was *Olsson* at fault?"

"Ah, well I've only just come on duty," the officer said hesitantly, reluctantly adding, "sir. But I will ensure that the prisoner's solicitor is informed. If there's anything to inform him of."

Traynor repeated the officer's words into his cellphone, and after listening, nodded. Turning back to the officer, he asked, "So, do I get to keep my appointment? Or will we need to disturb a magistrate's peaceful Saturday morning for a ruling? It's your call."

The officer scowled at Traynor. "Okay, you can come in," he said gracelessly. And then he smiled as he said, "Keep in mind that we'll be seeing a lot more of you in the years to come."

"I wouldn't count on it," Traynor said with a conviction he didn't feel.

"Are you hurt?" Traynor asked, as he saw the plaster on Olsson's ear.

"Nothing serious," Olsson smiled. "Just a scratch."

They sat on opposite sides of a long, wide table that made touching, although permitted, difficult. Prison guards stood around the room, supposedly out of hearing distance. At another table, a woman was crying as a prisoner tried to comfort her; further along, a child was showing her father some pictures she'd drawn. Like Olsson, all the prisoners wore white overalls with no pockets.

"What happened? They said you were in some trouble," Traynor asked anxiously.

"Nothing significant," Olsson said, waving a hand dismissively. "More importantly, how's everyone holding up?"

"Well, we're losing a few people, but InterFreight hasn't lost any customers. Lynette's job running your newspapers is a lot tougher than mine. Circulations have dropped a bit; and morale, especially among the journalists, is a problem. But Karla, apparently, has been doing a great job of convincing people you've been framed. Anyway, Lynette will tell you more herself. She said she'd come to see you sometime next week, before the trial."

"Ah yes," Olsson leaned back. "The trial. What have the lawyers and private eyes come up with?"

Traynor shrugged. "Lots of maybe useful background information. But nothing we can wave in court come Friday."

"Tell me in a nutshell."

"A lot of people, it turns out, could have a motive to kill the guy you've been charged with murdering. Vincent Leung's gang was encroaching on just about every other gang's turf, so we've got a long list of possible suspects. But that's all we've got at the moment— suspects."

Olsson nodded. "Well, I'd hoped for more—but I can't say I'm surprised."

"They're working on developing contacts and so on in those gangs—but God knows how long it will take to dig up anything we can actually use." Traynor emphasized his words by slapping his hand on the table. The noise drew the prison guards' attention and Traynor's skin crawled. He hated these visits; he couldn't stand seeing his best friend and business partner locked up like some kind of animal in a zoo. He felt claustrophobic the moment he came anywhere near the jail; once he was inside he was desperate to get out again. Yet Olsson, who couldn't just get up and walk away, sat comfortably relaxed, projecting an unearthly calm. Perversely, Traynor found that made him feel even more nervous.

"Maybe I just got unlucky," Olsson said.

"Or maybe not."

"Yeah, that's a possibility too." Olsson leant forward, his face suddenly turning serious. "Well, I've got some news. Bad news."

"What's that?"

"I found out yesterday that, like the police, *Luk Suk* is convinced I did it."

"Holy cow," Traynor breathed. "That *really* sucks."

"So it's time for Plan B."

Traynor nodded. "Okay," he sighed. "I guess I figured it would come to that anyway, one way or the other."

*****

THE SHRILLING OF THE phone in her pocket startled her.

Alison had been growing edgier all morning. She'd gone through the contacts she'd made in her fourteen years in politics, noting who might have information or be able to find it, trying to figure out how she could get it from them without tipping her hand, without telling anyone what she was after or, especially, who she was trying to nail.

When Royn was Minister for Justice and Customs—his portfolio prior to becoming Deputy Prime Minister and Minister for Foreign Affairs—Alison had made hundreds of contacts in the Australian Customs Service and the Federal Police, both at that time areas of Royn's responsibility.

But midway through making her list, the memory of the many investigations she'd been associated with made her stop.

Police and Customs could throw hundreds of people into an urgent investigation. Even then, they wouldn't expect to find the culprit by the end of next week. And the average criminal actually helped the police in some way, by leaving something at the scene of the crime—a fingerprint, a hair, a witness—that would eventually lead the police to his door, or by making some dumb mistake.

McKurn had to be in a completely different league—how else could he have survived for so long without ever being caught?

How am I, acting entirely on my own, going to be able to nail this bastard by Friday?

NOW, SHE WAS ONCE again sitting in the sun, having lunch with her parents at the Fish Market on the waterfront. The fresh calamari, scallops, and fish and chips were delicious, but she had to force herself to just nibble a bit here and a morsel there.

"Are you all right, Alison?" her mother had asked. "You look like you didn't get enough sleep."

"I'm fine, Mum," she'd said. "I've just got a problem at work that's really bothering me."

Joe began to say something but Maggie, putting her hand on his, said, "Not now, love."

When her phone rang, she pulled it quickly from her pocket to turn off its disturbing sound. But when she saw it was Ross Traynor calling she stood up. "Excuse me a moment," she said, "I need to take this call."

She walked along the promenade packed with families having a Saturday afternoon out, heading towards the parking lot where there were hardly any people. Sleek, well-fed seagulls scattered out of her path. An adventurous ibis grabbed a stray piece of fish from a table with its long beak. A couple of pelicans perched nearby, their cavernous lower beaks hanging open, waiting for one of the many children to throw something their way.

"Alison," Traynor said, a smile in his voice. "How are you doing?"

"I've been better. And you?"

"I've been much better." Ross Traynor laughed sourly.

"How's Derek?"

"Holding up amazingly well. I saw him this morning, and his aura of calm is unnerving, like he didn't have a worry in the world."

"That sounds like Derek. Meditation and martial arts. You should try them some time."

"Yeah, maybe," Traynor said doubtfully.

"Anyway, Ross, can you tell me what's going on? I don't for one minute believe Derek is a murderer."

"It's a frame-up, Alison. We're both sure of it. But why? Who can tell."

"But the evidence?"

"That's the problem. It's a very good frame-up. The police have no doubt Derek did it. No doubt at all."

"So when it comes to the trial?"

"We'll find the real culprit . . . eventually. But by Friday, when the trial is scheduled to begin? I don't know."

Friday, Alison thought. "I surely hope so," she said.

"Do you want me to tell him anything?"

"Yes," she breathed. "Tell him I'm thinking of him."

"I will."

"And Ross," she said, hesitating, "this may sound like a silly question, but do you know of any private investigators, someone who's good at digging up information—who can maybe even tap phones."

"Haven't you got access to a whole bureaucracy devoted to that sort of thing?" Ross asked in surprise.

"Well, yes. But this is . . . how shall I put it . . . unofficial."

Traynor was silent for so long that Alison thought she must have lost the connection. "Are you still there?" she asked.

"Yes. Just thinking. Look, I don't know any private detectives I can recommend. But there's one option. Very expensive, though."

"That's okay," Alison sighed, "so long I get results."

"Oh yes," Traynor replied. "You'll get results all right."

"How do I get in touch with him?"

"Are you really sure you want to do this, Alison?"

"Absolutely." *Right now,* she thought desperately, *I'd even consider selling my soul to the devil.*

"Okay. Meet me in one hour at the place where . . . where the four of us used to go after school. Do you remember?"

"Of course. I'll see you there."

JOE AND MAGGIE'S ADOPTION of modern technology was limited to a mobile phone they carried for emergencies—but almost never turned on. So after seeing Ross Traynor, Alison set up her laptop on the dining table and connected through her mobile phone.

What did Ross say? Ah yes. . . . She logged into a free, web-based email program and set up an account.

I need a handle—a codename, she thought when she was asked for her name. She smiled wryly as she remembered a Bible quotation: *Vengeance shall be mine, saith the Lord.*

"Saith" it shall be. "Saith Lord."

Typing in the email address Traynor had given her, she wrote:

Hi. I'm Saith. The Jackal sent me.

She started wondering how long she'd have to wait when an email appeared in the inbox.

whats the color of the jackals shoes

I know the answer to that.

Blue and white with purple polka dots—but he doesn't wear shoes, they're thongs.

ok. do you have pgp

No. What's that?

google it. when youve installed it send me your public key. u home office internet cafe where? own computer someone elses?

Home. Own laptop.

ok c u l8er

It took her about an hour to install the encryption program on her computer and figure out how to use it. Then she encrypted a short message and uploaded it to the "Saith Lord" email address. Five minutes later she had a reply: a long, encrypted, laundry list of instructions using terms like "anonymizers" and "tunnels" that she didn't understand, along with three new email addresses.

Whenever she logged onto the internet, she learnt, she left a trail pointing back to her. The purpose of the complicated instructions was to eliminate that trail. A "tunnel," she discovered, was a program that established an encrypted link between her computer and an internet site. Once the "tunnel" was in place, not even her own internet service provider could tell where on the internet she was going.

All internet traffic is sent in small "packets" of information, and reassembled at the other end. Between computer A and website B, her data could be retransmitted from up to a dozen different web servers as it travelled around the world. Each of these web servers might keep a copy, making it easy for a snoop to read. By going through the encrypted "tunnel," those data packets were rendered meaningless to outsiders.

The "anonymizer" was the final layer of protection. Websites automatically keep a log of information about every visitor: how long they stayed, which pages they looked at— and the IP address of the gateway where they connected to the internet. Every IP address is unique. Just by knowing it you can tell what city and country a person is connecting from, and which company—often, the person's email provider—owns the gateway. The anonymizer would disguise her real location.

Police and security agencies—and talented hackers—could, if they so wished, piece all this information together and find out who was looking at what pages on which websites at any particular time of day—and even read their emails and know who they'd sent them to or received them from. But these techniques—which, it turned out, were used in places where all internet traffic was monitored and censored, like China and Iran, so people could keep their activities hidden from the authorities—made such snooping impossible.

But . . . why do Ross—and, presumably, Derek—know a guy like this? What are they up to?

IT WAS WELL AFTER dinner when she'd thought she had it all worked out. To be sure, she read through the instructions again. They concluded:

this is how we communicate in future. every message u send MUST be encrypted.

u save it as a DRAFT at email address A. u send me an innocuous message "molly

was wondering if youd be free for dinner friday nite" whatever FROM email address
B TO email address C

whenever i have something 4 u process reversed. i save message encrypted as
DRAFT at address A and send vague message TO address B FROM address C.
content of message irrelevant. the message is the signal you need to check the draft
folder in email address A

so u must check address B regularly DO NOT FORWARD ANY MESSAGES wud
leave tracks no tracks understood?

whenever u access above email addresses go via tunnel site and anonymizer

finally whenever you send or receive messages must WIPE messages off disk when
done DON'T SAVE ANYTHING NO TRACKS NO TRACKS NO TRACKS

Here goes, she thought. She typed:

All done. I'm ready. What next?

After encrypting it, she went through the tunnel and anonymizer and logged into
email address A. And stopped, frozen, her finger above the key that would save it to the
Draft folder.

So I have no idea who I'm dealing with, she thought. And if all this works, he—
whoever it was had to be a computer geek so 99-to-1 it was a "he"—he won't know who
he's dealing with either.

"Can I trust this guy?" she had asked Traynor. "As far as we know, yes," he had replied.
As far as we know . . . what kind of guarantee is that?

The ageless voice inside her head chose that moment to ask: *What choice do you
have, Alison?*

None, she thought in answer.

And hit the key.

Then she remembered she had to send some meaningless email from address B to
address C. She typed:

I'm ready to talk—Saith.

How long will I need to wait for an answer? she wondered.

She sat staring blankly at the computer screen, suddenly aware of her aching shoulders
and sore back. When she saw a reply in the inbox, she had no idea how much time had
slipped by. She looked at the clock. *Eleven o'clock on Saturday night. Definitely a geek,
married to his computer.*

so what do u want she read.

Can you tap phones?

sure but depends

On what?

who where etc

What a cumbersome way of communicating. Better to give him the works.

Senator Frank McKurn. And any of his associates, like Paul Cracken. But what I'm
really after is to nobble the bastard, preferably something that will put him in jail for
a very long time. So I need hard evidence that will stand up in court. Short of that,
something that will emasculate him.

sounds like fun. u buying exclusive?

Exclusive? Please explain

means for your eyes only or can i sell info over and over exclusive costs more

Tell you what: the more you can spread it around, the more I'll pay you mckurn eh? yum yum lots of dirt but wont be cheap

Like how much?

to put mckurn away? well into six figures if i can find the info

My God, thought Alison, *where will I get that kind of money?* . . . *I'll worry about that later.*

I need FACTS. Stories I have; stand-up-in-court facts I don't—and they're worth paying for. But if we're talking that sort of money I'm only willing to pay on results.

fair enough no honey no money but you have to cover basic costs and i start only when i have a retainer in hand

How much is that? And how do I get it to you?

$10,000 to start with in a swiss bank account your problem to get it there

Okay. Send me the account information and so on.

in a mo. u send me names addresses phone numbers home office girlfriends whatever plus anything else that would save me time and u money. and remember banks must tell mr plod about every t/t of 10 grand or more so send in 2 lumps pref from 2 different banks and best not yours

"Mr. Plod?"

police cops feds fuzz

Okay, understood

check draft folder in a mo for a/c info wl b in touch after $$$$s in hand bi 4 now

Keeping only the bank account information and passwords, Alison carefully closed everything down. *I have an early flight to Melbourne,* she reminded herself. But she felt exhausted, unable to move. When she eventually fell gratefully into bed, even though she was dog-tired, it was some time before she finally drifted off into a troubled sleep.

THE SUN HAD BARELY risen when Alison slipped quietly from her parents' home to catch a taxi to the airport for her early morning flight to Melbourne.

Three hours later she swung her rental car onto the kilometer-long driveway of Sidney Royn's Mount Macedon estate to the thought: *Mum and Dad are probably going to church about now.*

The two-storey, ivy-covered Tudor-style house, surrounded by manicured lawns, sculptured flowerbeds, smartly clipped hedges, mature oak and poplar trees looked, as it was meant to look, like an ancient manor house that had been transported, stone by stone, from a British aristocrat's country retreat. In reality, the oldest part of the house dated from barely a hundred years ago.

Opening the solid oak front door as Alison stepped out of the car, Sidney Royn exemplified the patrician image the Royn family had so successfully fostered since Max Royn had become accepted into the Melbourne establishment in the 1880s.

The Royn family's wealth was a consequence of the Victorian gold rush. Not from anything as messy as sweatily grubbing for gold nuggets in the dust and dirt of the goldfields, but from their ancestors' being in the right place at the right time.

Though they did their best not to remember it, the seeds of that wealth were planted by an ex-convict, Malcolm Royn, known as "Blackie" for his jet-black hair, the black eyes he sported from his many brawls, and because he was widely despised as a blackguard.

He'd left Sydney in 1837, barely one step ahead of his creditors, for the newly established village of Melbourne, then merely a handful of wattle and daub huts and a few dozen tents housing, at most, a few hundred people. He arrived in time to participate in Melbourne's first land sale. For £15—using money, it was later said, that rightfully belonged to a number of Sydney establishments—Malcolm Royn bought two of the hundred half-acre lots on offer.

Malcolm Royn tried his hand at a number of businesses, all of which failed. Finally, he opened a pub, which was, at last, successful. But as he drank most of the profits he was forced, from time to time, to sell off a small chunk of his land to stay afloat.

Then, in 1851, gold was discovered at Castlemaine, 120 kilometers away, quickly followed by even bigger finds in Ballarat and Bendigo. The Victorian gold rush was on. In just three years Melbourne's population skyrocketed from 29,000 to 123,000. Land once sold for £15 an acre could only be had for £35,000 or more. Malcolm Royn's no-questions-asked pub became a favorite watering hole for gold miners who'd struck it rich and wanted to celebrate with whisky, champagne, and high-class whores.

The land Malcolm Royn had purchased for £15 was, today, prime downtown property in the City of Melbourne, now developed with hotels, shops, and offices worth hundreds of millions of dollars. Most of it still belonged to the Royn family.

The family fortune was consolidated by Malcolm Royn's son Max, who speculated wildly in the land boom of 1880s, but wisely paid down his debts before prices peaked. After the crash, he turned around and picked up swathes of prime property in the city and suburbs for a song—including a large parcel of land fronting the Yarra River which, as the suburb of Toorak, would become the favored home of Melbourne's rich and famous. Max Royn became a member of the Melbourne Cricket Club, an honor brusquely denied to his father; his children went to the exclusive Melbourne Grammar School. In the boom-time atmosphere, where few people wanted their past to be scrutinized too closely, his ancestry was quietly forgotten.

Before he died, Max Royn tied up his legacy in a maze of trusts, companies, and charitable foundations to protect his wealth from the two deadly enemies of all such fortunes: taxation, and profligate great-grandchildren. As a result, the Royn family remained one of the city's biggest landlords to this day.

At the dawn of the twentieth century, it was inevitable that the Royns—now paragons of virtue in Melbourne society—turned their attention to politics and charitable works. Some, of course, became gentlemen farmers, playboys, or wastrels living off their allowance. One was even forced into bankruptcy by the steely-eyed trustees' refusal to come to his rescue—just as Max Royn had intended. But a Royn was involved in the movement to unite the Australian colonies into a federation; Royns were active in state and local politics; and when Sidney Royn was elected to the federal parliament, it was the third time a Royn had been sent to Canberra from the safe, blue-ribbon Conservative Party seat of Higgins—which included the wealthy suburb of Toorak.

"I trust you had a comfortable flight, Alison," Sidney Royn said as, with a graceful flourish of his arm, he ushered her into the wide corridor.

"Passable thank you, Mr. Royn," Alison smiled. In fact, she'd dozed fitfully most of the way from Sydney, unable to get comfortable no matter which way she squirmed, feeling sad she'd been too preoccupied to spend much time with her parents. And the drive from the airport, though only forty minutes long, hadn't made her feel any better.

Even though he was at home on a Sunday morning, Sidney Royn wore grey slacks, a crisp white shirt and a blue blazer. His only concessions to informality were his tie less shirt, and a pair of well-worn leather slippers on his feet. He was tall; his height emphasized by a thinness bordering on the gaunt that was typical of some people in their eighties, as he was. "Let's sit on the verandah out the back," he said. "It's my favorite spot at this time of day."

When Alison was seated comfortably in a soft armchair, Royn asked, "And could I offer you something—tea, or coffee?"

"Coffee, please. Strong. And how is Mrs. Royn?"

"Nancy? She's fine. She's gone to church but she'll be back before lunch. I hope you can join us."

"I would be delighted," Alison said.

As she waited she felt herself sinking deeper into the soft cushions, idly admiring the gardens, the tennis court, and the nearby swimming pool.

When Sidney Royn returned with the coffee, he noticed how Alison was gazing at the pool. "If you'd like to go for a swim first," he said, "I'm sure you'll find a bathing suit that will fit in the changing room over there."

"Thank you Mr. Royn. But I really don't want to impose on your hospitality."

"Alison, it's no imposition at all," he said, smiling warmly. "At my age, as you'll one day discover for yourself, time is something I have too much of, and charming visitors are far too rare."

"Well, thank you again," she said. "Very enticing. But that would mean I'd have to get out of this comfortable chair, and leave you alone. And that wouldn't feel right."

"You youngsters," Sidney Royn said, grinning, as he sat down opposite her. "All work and no play. So tell me more about what brought you here today."

Alison took a deep breath and tried to speak in a normal tone. "McKurn."

"Ah yes," said Sidney Royn, leaning back in his chair. "Dear old Frank—speaking for myself, I can't say I'm sorry to have seen the last of that bastard." Then he looked at Alison sharply. "So what's he done now?"

"A few months ago, the minister—Tony—asked me to see what I could dig up on McKurn's activities. *Get the goods on McKurn,*' was the phrase he used. I think the idea came from the Prime Minister."

"Ah yes—Randolph Kydd." To Alison's surprise, a look of distaste flashed across Royn's face. "So what did you come up with?"

"Stories. Rumors. Whispers," Alison said. "Lots of them—but nothing concrete. No *evidence.*"

"You did this all on your own?"

Alison nodded. "Yes, we kept it confidential, just between me and the minister."

"Then I'm not surprised. Did you know that while I was Attorney-General we started an investigation into corruption? It wasn't stated openly, of course, but McKurn was the main target."

"Yes. The Prime Minister told me, and suggested I talk to you."

Royn's eyes narrowed. "So when you called me you'd just spoken to Randolph?"

Alison nodded.

"So, my dear, what's the urgency?"

Alison's head jerked back slightly and her eyes blinked rapidly. *How did he guess?* she asked herself. She took a deep breath before replying, "McKurn seems to have found out I've been digging into his past, so I need something to hang over his head, and quickly too."

Sidney Royn nodded thoughtfully. "I'll be right back," he said.

A few minutes later he returned carrying two thick ring binders, stuffed with paper.

"I kept a copy of the investigation—strictly off the record, you understand."

Alison nodded, her eyes fixed on the files, a flicker of hope stirring in her breast.

Royn opened one of the binders, and began turning the pages rapidly. "Ah, yes, here it is," he said, stopping to scan one of the pages.

Alison leant forward, assuming he was about to show it to her. But instead, he looked at her in a sad, compassionate way. "This," he said intently, indicating the files, "resulted in several arrests—but as far as McKurn is concerned . . . ? Almost nothing but rumors, the same sort of thing you have. And we had dozens of investigators all over the country working on it night and day. Do you see what I'm getting at, Alison?"

Alison nodded mutely.

"And here," he said, stabbing the document with his fingers, "is a statement from a man, a Sydney gang leader, who swore he'd made payoffs to McKurn. A couple of weeks later, he simply disappeared, and no one's ever seen or heard from him since."

Royn flicked through the file, looking for another document. "This is the transcript of an interview with a well-known member of the New South Wales state government. He admitted to all kinds of minor graft—fixing parking tickets, building permits and the like. He had no choice: we had him cold. But when the subject came to McKurn. . . . This is the interviewer's comment: 'When we asked him about McKurn, he just clammed up. He was obviously terrified—and couldn't even bring himself to say he knew nothing.'"

Royn closed the file and sat back in his chair. "McKurn's tracks are all over this file. But they're like the Abominable Snowman: lots of people claim they've witnessed its passage—strange footprints and the like—but no one's ever actually seen it."

Alison nodded again, her heart sinking. "But maybe there's something there. . . ."

"There could be," Royn conceded. "Perhaps something you could correlate with more recent information. But this is twenty years old, so maybe it's completely useless. But if you want to take it, you're welcome to it."

"Thank you. Yes."

"It's probably best if I keep the original. I have a photocopier in the study, though, and you're free to copy anything you want."

I'll take a later flight, Alison thought. "I'm sure I'll find something I can use," she said, looking at the thick files hopefully.

"One thing I do recall," said Royn. "After I resigned from Parliament, the task force on corruption I'd set up was wound down. Right at the end, a senior Sydney police officer agreed to be interviewed. But he never was. His name's in here somewhere. If you can track him down—he must be retired by now—he might talk to you."

"Do you know why he was never questioned?"

Sidney Royn shrugged. "McKurn has long fingers is all one can presume."

"And did he—" Alison hesitated "—did McKurn have anything to do with your resignation?"

Royn shook his head half-heartedly. "That's not why I left politics. Well—not the main reason. . . . But I'd certainly prefer you didn't mention to anyone that you got this file from me."

"I understand." *I understand too well,* she thought, her eyes shrouding as she unwillingly remembered the look on McKurn's face as he'd leered at her.

Royn cleared his throat, a sound that interrupted Alison's thoughts. She looked up to see that he was gazing at her sadly again. "I see," he sighed. "There's something else, isn't there."

"Something else?" Alison stared at him, a lance of fear stabbing in her stomach.

"Something you haven't told me."

Alison looked into his kind, concerned but resolute eyes—and felt her composure beginning to desert her.

"Isn't there, Alison," he said firmly; a statement, not a question.

Alison tried to speak, but her mouth wouldn't move. She had trouble breathing, and her stomach froze. She gave the briefest of nods as she turned her head away so Royn wouldn't see the tears streaming down her face.

Sidney Royn disappeared and returned with a box of tissues that he placed at Alison's side.

"With McKurn," he said understandingly, "there's *always* something else."

Alison tried to stop the sobs welling up inside her. But they overcame her every effort. "Where's a bathroom I can use?" she asked.

When Alison returned her face was dry but her skin was clearly wan and pale beneath her makeup. She smiled weakly at Sidney Royn as she sat down.

After a few moments of silence, he said softly, "This is not a burden you can carry alone, you know, Alison. I trust I've already made that clear."

Alison said nothing.

"You need to talk to someone," Royn said, "and I'd be honored if it was me."

Alison shook her head violently. "I—I can't—"

"And it affects Tony, too, doesn't it?"

She nodded wordlessly, her eyes pleading with him to stop asking her questions.

"And you told him the same story you told me? About McKurn finding out what you were doing?"

Alison nodded again. "And the Prime Minister," she muttered, so softly that Royn had to ask her to repeat it.

Alison felt a rising nervousness at the warm and understanding look on Sidney Royn's face. Her deep need to confide in someone battled with her fear, with the *shame* she would feel if anybody else *knew.* After long moments of agonizing, almost stuttering, she began to speak.

"McKurn has a video—"

"Of?"

Alison shook her head again. ". . . he threatened to release it if I didn't. . . ."

"Didn't . . . ?"

". . . didn't spy for him . . . if I didn't alert him to everything we're doing and thinking so he could ensure Cracken becomes Prime Minister when Kydd goes."

"And the video is so bad that—"

"—it would destroy me, and probably Tony as well."

"What could be that deadly?"

"I can't say—I won't say. I'm sorry Mr. Royn, I just don't want anyone to know."

"I see," said Royn, nodding thoughtfully. "So tell me, instead, who else is in the video."

Alison looked at him fearfully. "Derek Olsson," she whispered.

Sidney Royn was leaning forward, listening carefully, so this time he heard her. "Ah, the drug murder."

"He's innocent," Alison said fiercely. "He's . . . the whole thing is a frame-up."

Royn held up his hand. "All I know is what's in the papers. And, of course, at the moment he's only the alleged murderer—though that's not what the press would have you believe. So even if what you say is true, John Q. Public won't buy your story for a second."

"I know," Alison groaned.

"That bastard," Royn said suddenly. "The doctor should have strangled him at birth."

"I agree," Alison said fiercely. "I could even do it myself."

"I hope you're not serious," Royn said with concern.

"Sometimes, I just feel that way."

Royn nodded. "Putting that thought aside, pleasant though it is, you *must* tell Tony."

"I—I don't know how I could."

"You need his help. You can't fight McKurn alone. And it's Tony's fight too. He needs to know."

Alison's mouth was open but she made no sound.

"Promise me, Alison, that you'll tell him."

She looked at him appealingly, but it was clear he was determined. *And he's right,* she thought to herself. *And I can certainly use the help.*

She nodded.

"Tomorrow," Royn said, a hint of steel in his voice.

Alison sighed deeply. "Okay," she said reluctantly. "I will."

She bowed her head as she spoke, studying the patterns the tiles formed on the floor. *How am I going to face Anthony Royn tomorrow morning?* Alison asked herself.

The only answer was the gnawing knot of apprehension in her stomach.

4 "For A While . . ."

Towering over the Sandeman Airlines flight attendant, Karla Preston stepped out the door of the 737 into a furnace. Mingled with the heat were the smell of smoke and the stench of rotting garbage coming from the shantytown beyond.

WELLCOME TO TORIBAYA
CAPITAL OF THE SANDEMAN ISLANDS
TROPICAL PAR DISE

"Some paradise," she muttered, grimacing at the faded sign hanging crookedly above the terminal building.

Yet as the plane had descended the Sandeman Islands were strung out below her, glistening, white-haloed emeralds in a cobalt sea. The white rims of the islands grew into wide, pristine, inviting beaches, sparkling rolls of surf lapping onto the shore. The emerald-green resolved into trees dotted with what looked like the thatched roofs of small villages, and tracks and narrow roads making random, crisscross patterns through the greenness. It was easy to feel herself floating on one of those beaches, the grains of sand on her back, bathing in the sun as the waves lapped over her feet. . . . Ah, she thought to herself, what bliss that would be. . . .

It was almost impossible to grasp the reality: that perhaps in those trees right *there*, she thought as the plane flew lazily over one shimmering island, right *now*, Australian soldiers and rebels were shooting at each other.

Then they were flying over dense jungle, which seemed to be rising up to meet them. Suddenly, the ground dropped away sharply and the jungle and the dazzling beaches disappeared from view. Karla jerked upright, her hands gripping the armrests tightly as she stared, wide-eyed, down on densely packed buildings that seemed to have been jammed, higgledy-piggledy, into every available square millimeter . . . wrapped in a low blanket of grey, smoky haze . . . hardly a trace of greenery to be seen.

As the ground came closer Karla shuddered as she saw that the buildings were shacks and lean-tos made, it seemed, from corrugated iron and cardboard . . . and one, more solidly built building, the only one looking as if it would not blow away in the next storm: a small church. She caught glimpses of barefooted children playing in the dirt, of an old woman bent low under a huge bundle, of tiny shops with crude signs, of a narrow, twisting street clogged with bicycles.

Towards the sea, a few tall, glassy buildings jutted out from the haze rolling out over the water. And on the other side of a muddy-grey stream, protected from the shanties by fences, walls, and wide, grassy strips that made her think of moats, was an area that could have been a transplanted Sydney suburb, complete with manicured lawns, swimming pools and several cars in every driveway.

And then they were over the runway, a tall fence at the edge of the airfield now hiding the shanties from view. As the plane touched down with a mild bump, and eventually came to a halt a short walk from the terminal building, Karla played the images back in her mind. *It's a different world,* she thought, *like I'm on another planet.*

Over the intercom, a flight attendant announced, "Welcome to the sunny Sandeman Islands. If you want to set your watches, it's still Sunday afternoon, but the time is now 5:23 PM, one hour ahead of Sydney time. Thank you for flying Sandeman Airlines, and we hope you enjoy your stay."

"So do I," Karla said to herself. "So do I."

HALFWAY DOWN THE STEPS, she was already feeling sticky from the heat. As Derek Olsson had promised, there was someone here to meet her, a man carrying a sign with her name on it standing at the bottom of the steps. Quite unnecessary, she thought. But Olsson had insisted. "It's a dangerous place, Karla." She agreed, reluctantly. Perfectly capable of looking after herself, to her own surprise she rather enjoyed Olsson's protectiveness.

At the thought of Olsson, she shook her head. When police armed with a search warrant had woken them up at some ungodly hour in the morning a couple of weeks ago, Olsson had treated it as some kind of joke. "It's not April Fools' Day today, is it?" he'd asked the humorless detective-inspector.

But the police proceeded to turn Olsson's penthouse apartment upside down—and then found the knife, wrapped in one of his shirts, wedged underneath the spare tire in the boot of Olsson's car. For an instant she found herself believing he was a murderer . . . a thought which disappeared at Olsson's look of total surprise, of frozen shock, his inability to utter a sound.

But there was a hidden, secretive side to Derek Olsson, so now and then she wondered. . . .

"Miss Karla Preston?"

Karla stood five feet nine inches in her bare feet, nearly a head taller than the short, dark, elegantly dressed man waiting for her at the bottom of the steps. His black trousers and crisp, white shirt seemed oddly out of place amongst the handful of casually dressed Australian tourists, a couple of them wearing just shorts, T-shirts and thongs, and airport workers in well-worn, greasy overalls. With a touch of jealousy she noticed that although he was also standing bareheaded in the hot, tropical sun, there was not a bead of sweat on his face.

"That's me," she said, wiping her brow, feeling a little strange that she had to look down to make eye contact. "And you are . . . ?"

"My name is Uqumagani," the man said, speaking English with an Australian accent. And switching to a broad Australian accent, he added, "But me mates call me Uqu."

Karla laughed. "Mr. Uqumagani," she smiled warmly, reacting to her usually reliable first impression that this man would become a good friend. "I'm pleased to meet you," she said as she stretched out her hand, ". . . and I hope I pronounced your name correctly."

Uqumagani grinned broadly. "Indeed you have," he nodded, "and as you've probably guessed, I'm to be your guide while you're here."

"I'm looking forward to it already, but I'm roasting. Could we get out of this heat?"

"Of course. Please follow me."

Karla didn't walk daintily but strode like a man, and while her hips swung as she walked, so did her arms in a rather unfeminine way. With just a few steps she caught up with Uqu, and slowed her pace to walk beside him.

"I'm wondering, Miss Preston," Uqu asked, "if you speak like you write."

"Pretty much," Karla replied.

Uqu stopped, and turned to face her. "In that case," he said, "while you're here, and especially in there—" he indicated the terminal building "—when an official has a question or something, please let *me* do all the talking."

"That bad, eh?" Karla laughed.

"It can be," Uqu said. "Especially for a Westerner who is too . . . direct."

"Like me, you mean."

"Exactly."

"Okay," said Karla. "I'll try to keep my mouth shut. So how do you know how I write? Are my columns published here?"

"Oh no." Uqu shook his head, laughing. "I read them on the internet. A local newspaper that published one of your articles would probably be shut down the same day."

"Really?" said Karla with surprise.

"Oh yes," said Uqu.

Shaking her head, Karla followed Uqu into the terminal. The Sandeman Islands, she recalled, were peopled by Melanesians, who'd spread from the Philippines to Malaysia, Indonesia, and across the Pacific as far as Hawaii in just the past thousand or so years; and Papuans, who'd arrived tens of thousands of years earlier in Papua New Guinea, the Sandemans' closest neighbor to the west. Uqu, she thought, with his chocolate-brown skin, must have ancestors in both camps.

RELIEVED TO BE IN the air-conditioned coolness of the terminal, Karla nervously eyed the submachine gun-toting soldiers who seemed to outnumber the passengers as she followed Uqu to the lane marked DIPLOMATS ONLY.

The uniformed lady behind the immigration counter flicked through her passport idly—and stopped. Karla noticed it was open at the page with the visa which journalists, though not tourists, required.

The other passengers, to her annoyance, were moving through quickly; and she saw that Uqu was fidgeting nervously. She was about to ask him why when the lady immigration officer abruptly said, "For a while," and walked off with Karla's passport to a glassed-in office to the side of the immigration hall. The woman handed the passport to the portly man behind the desk. He was carrying on an animated conversation on the phone and seemed in no hurry to acknowledge the woman's presence.

"For a while?" Karla asked Uqu.

"Ah," said Uqu, "that's local parlance for 'wait'."

"And what's happening?" Karla asked.

"I'm not sure," he answered with a forced smile. "Yesterday, the government announced new restrictions on journalists. Maybe it's something to do with that."

"You don't like it, do you?"

"No, I don't. Captain Irgi's ego," he said, indicating the official in the office, "is bigger than his stomach. He's the chief today, and he can be difficult to deal with. Be better if someone else was on duty."

Captain Irgi smiled broadly, almost licking his lips in anticipation as he waddled towards her, his belly straining at his jacket and flopping over his belt in time with his steps.

Karla was used to men reacting to her in that way, though she didn't quite appreciate why every male eye turned to look at her whenever she walked into a room. She was muscular, not unattractively so—and nowhere near enough to get her picture in a bodybuilding magazine. Just muscular enough to disqualify her from ever thinking of being a model, a movie star, a pinup girl. She knew she was no beauty—and that she wasn't ugly either. She was neither: but looking at her own face in the mirror she knew it was the kind of face you could easily forget the moment you looked away, framed by straight, nondescript, mousy brown hair. She considered herself so plain she wondered why her parents hadn't called her "Jane."

Yet the name "Karla"—meaning "strong and womanly"—fitted her like a glove. And, coming from somewhere completely outside her own awareness, she radiated a sexuality that triggered some dormant sixth sense in even the most insensitive of men, drawing their eyes like moths to a flame.

Seeing Irgi's slight swagger and his self-satisfied smirk, Karla saw an officious little man who too obviously enjoyed the power he exercised, and took an instant dislike to him. And although she'd pledged to Uqu to keep her acerbic, razor-sharp tongue sheathed, she made no attempt to otherwise disguise how she felt.

Too late, she realized that Irgi had seen her reaction. His smile turned into a frown, and he loudly slapped her passport on the counter as he reached it, the female official following a few paces behind him.

"Oh dear," said Uqu, "this doesn't look so good."

Karla saw Uqu surreptitiously pull out a wad of bills, keeping them carefully out of Irgi's sight, peel some off and fold them into his hand. Seeing Karla's puzzled look he said an almost silent "Shhh" as a scowling captain Irgi glared at them both.

"Good afternoon, captain," said Uqu, with a slight bow.

Irgi nodded at him brusquely, and turning his attention back to Karla. "Miss . . . ah . . . Preston is it? Visa issued week ago, yes?" he said.

"Yes, last week. That's right."

"Well, new regulations yesterday, as maybe you don't know already. So visa not valid today."

"Really?" she said, pulling herself up to her full height so she towered over Irgi. "That's totally ridiculous."

Irgi bristled and opened his mouth to speak when Uqu broke in, nudging Karla quiet.

"Indeed, captain," Uqu said with another slight bow, speaking in a calming, almost obsequious tone. "I heard about those new rules. So I'd appreciate, with your permission, sir, if I may have a look at that visa?"

Irgi eyed him with a touch of disdain, and then shrugged. "Here."

Uqu seemed to study the passport intently, and then snapped it shut with a flourish. If Karla hadn't been watching closely, she would have missed the moment when Uqu, moving his hands like a magician, slipped the banknotes inside. Then he handed it back to Irgi with the comment, "You know, captain, I thought those new rules came into effect tomorrow, so I'm not so sure. Perhaps you'd like to take another look at the visa."

Irgi raised an eyebrow, but opened the passport and made a pretence of studying the visa again. After a while he nodded at Uqu saying, "Yes, I see what you mean. Okay—this time. But," he added, glaring at Karla as he handed the passport back to her, "you better register with police tomorrow."

"It shall be done," said Uqu.

As they headed for the baggage carousel Karla looked inside her passport. The money had, of course, gone—but Irgi was a better magician than Uqu: she hadn't seen a thing.

"THAT IMMIGRATION LADY WILL be upset," Uqu said as he wheeled the baggage trolley out of the terminal.

"Oh? Why is that?" Karla asked.

"I put in enough money for both of them. But I doubt she'll ever see even one *tingi* of it."

"And when you said Irgi was 'difficult,' you meant 'expensive,' right?"

Uqu laughed. "You catch on quick."

As they walked out of the terminal back into the sweltering heat, they were surrounded by men, pushing against each other to be the closest, shouting "Taxi?" "Hotel?" "Taxi?" "Cheap," "Best ride, mum."

"*No go no go*," Uqu told them in a lilting voice, waving them away. Smiling at Karla and admiring her at the same time, the drivers quietly stepped back to let them through, and slowly drifted back towards the taxis parked by the kerb.

"Most of those taxis should be in a junkyard," Karla said to Uqu.

Uqu glanced at them and shrugged. "This way," he said.

Karla was stopped by a soft tug at her skirt. She turned to see a little girl looking up at her with big, pleading eyes, her arms and legs looking like sticks. "How old are you?" Karla said; not more than five, she thought. "And what are you doing *here?*"

Without making a sound, the little girl held out a cupped hand, and then brought it to her mouth. "You're hungry . . . ?"

"No, she's not," said Uqu, turning back from the kerb; but if Karla heard him, she took no notice.

Tagging behind the little girl was an even smaller, barefoot boy, whose only piece of clothing was pair of tattered shorts way too big for him. A dirty piece of string tied tightly around his waist kept them from falling down. His nose was runny and flies darted around his face.

Pulling a tissue from her handbag, Karla knelt down and wiped his nose. "Boy, you could do with a bath." He seemed as indifferent to her touch as he had been to the flies'. The girl had grabbed the boy's hand, as if to protect him, but when Karla looked at her she smiled tentatively. "Here," Karla said, handing the small pack of tissues to the girl, "take these." The girl took the packet and felt the soft texture of a tissue like child with a new toy.

Karla was about to reach into her handbag when she realized she only had Australian currency. "Uqu," she said, standing up, "could you lend me some *tingi* please?" As Karla stood she saw half-a-dozen other children, all in a similar condition, eyeing her inquisitively from a safe distance. They broke into smiles as she looked in their direction.

Uqu was frowning impatiently. "I don't think that's a good idea, mum," he said. At the sound of Uqu's voice, the children scattered, stopping a few meters further away, watching him warily.

"And why is that?"

"Because it doesn't go to them."

"What do you mean?"

"They're trained to be beggars. They have a quota—ten or twenty *tingi* a day—they have to hand over to their minder."

"And if they don't?"

"They're beaten." Karla noticed a bruise, partly covered by his shirt, on the shoulder of one of the boys.

"Why don't they run away?"

Uqu shook his head sadly. "Where to? There's nowhere for them to go."

"Why not back to their parents?"

"The ones who aren't orphans were probably sold to the minder by their parents."

"You can't sell people—that's slavery."

Uqu shrugged. "We're not in Australia, mum."

"Jesus," she said. "This is straight out of Charles Dickens. . . . So what can I do?"

"Nothing."

She looked sharply at Uqu, a fiery look in her eyes. "This is normal to you, isn't it?" she said.

Uqu held his expression blank, but nodded, almost imperceptibly.

"Well, it's not normal to *me*."

Towards the end of the terminal building were some carts selling drinks and snacks. "Let's go, Uqu," she commanded, motioning towards them. "At least I can give these kids a decent meal. Tell them all to come down there with us—and they can eat and drink as much as they can."

"All of them?"

"Right. And any others who turn up."

"You'll be late," Uqu protested.

"For what?" Karla retorted. "Tonight, as I recall, all I'm going to do is hang out with a bunch of other Aussie journalists staying at the hotel. They'll still be in the bar . . . even if we don't get there till midnight."

Uqu shrugged. "As you say, mum."

"And one other thing," Karla said. "Give each of them twenty *tingi*. What's that . . . about one Australian dollar?"—Uqu nodded—"At least tonight they won't get a beating."

An hour or so later, when Uqu finally persuaded Karla to get into the waiting car, sitting beside her in the back seat, they were fare-welled by a delegation of nearly a dozen kids who'd all clearly eaten too much. As the car pulled out of the parking lot, Uqu said, chuckling, "Those kids will probably all be sick."

Karla looked at him sharply. "You disapprove?"

Uqu turned his head away, gazing into the distance. "Not exactly," he said slowly. "You . . . make me feel . . . ashamed that such things should be happening here."

"You see that sort of thing so often don't even notice it any more, right?" Karla said, looking into his eyes.

Uqu nodded. "I guess so."

Karla slumped back into the seat. "Do other people here feel the same way?"

Uqu nodded again. "Inshallah. That's what we say."

"Inshallah? Are you a Muslim, then?"

"No. Catholic. But before the Westerners came and brought Christianity, the islands were mostly Muslim."

"I see. 'As Allah—or God—wills.' Yes, I guess it works for anybody."

"There's no word like it in our language—or yours."

"Nothing can be done," Karla mused, "but it's much stronger than that. Nothing *can* be done . . . so nothing *will* be done."

"That's right," said Uqu. "So nothing *is* done."

The car swerved to avoid a pothole, and crawled to a stop as it passed through the airport gate. Beyond the high wall that shielded the airfield from the rest of the town was a narrow road jammed with cars, motorbikes, trucks, buses, bicycles—and people. The sidewalks were crammed with stalls selling snacks, clothes, brightly colored fabrics, pots and pans and every imaginable kind of bric-a-brac; and the stalls were crammed with people—mostly, Karla thought, looking, chatting, and generally having a good time, but not buying much of anything. Pedestrians spilled out onto the street, ignoring the honking cars and beeping bikes.

"Very traffic," the driver commented. Seeing a small gap he accelerated sharply, gaining a couple of meters, and seconds later hit the brakes, throwing Karla and Uqu forward.

Uqu leaned forward and exchanged a few harsh words in Pidgin English with the driver, which ended with the driver shrugging.

"What was that about?" asked Karla.

"I asked him to drive more gently, and he said, 'Sure . . . if you want to be here till morning.'"

Karla laughed. "It looks like they're having a party," she said, pointing to the crowded footpath.

"It's the Sunday market."

Behind the stalls were shanties like those Karla had seen from the air. Before the car jerked forward again, she could see down a dim, narrow, muddy laneway, hardly wide enough for two people to pass.

A cloud of dark, oily-looking smoke engulfed the car as the battered pickup truck in front of them moved forward another meter.

"So that's where the smog comes from," Karla said.

"Yes, and from cooking fires in the shanties. Normally, the winds blow the smoke away. Right now, though, it's still."

"They don't have electricity?"

"Some do. Most don't."

Karla shook her head. "And that truck in front of us . . . don't they have any regulations here?"

"Oh yes," said Uqu, and chuckled at Karla's puzzlement. "All those vehicles are certificated emission-free."

"Then how come all these buses and trucks are belching smoke?" Karla asked.

"That's simple. It's cheaper to pay a hundred *tingi* for the certificate than fix the exhaust system."

"You mean, to the officials? Like Captain Irgi?"

"Right."

"So how many Captain Irgis are there in the government of the Sandeman Islands?" Karla asked.

"Oh," shrugged Uqu, "about all of them."

"Even the top officials? Like the prime minister?"

"Of course," said Uqu. "He's the worst of the lot."

Sirens suddenly cut through the air above the babble, music, and noise of the crowd. Helmeted police on motorcycles, blue lights flashing, edged along the road, waving cars, motorcycles and bicycles alike towards the sides of the road; people started melting away. In moments, the street was clear of pedestrians and bicycles as they squeezed onto the already-crowded sidewalks, leaving just enough room for the police to clear a narrow lane down the center of the street.

Creeping down the road behind the police was an army jeep, loaded with soldiers carrying submachine guns, leading two stretched limousines with darkened windows, and finally another army jeep bringing up the rear. They all had flashing lights and sirens blaring.

"What's going on?" Karla asked.

"Some big wheel is coming. I think it's the foreign minister who's leaving tonight for Canberra."

"Why all the soldiers and police?" Karla asked. "These people seem so friendly."

"The police escort is normal. The army jeeps are new," said Uqu.

"So why—?"

"Since those Australian soldiers died last week, the guerrillas have been making all sorts of threats. So I guess they're taking extra precautions."

The driver hunched down, creeping slowly forward. Not far down the road, Karla could see a bridge where the crowded market came to an end. The tall buildings she'd seen from the plane, one of them no doubt being her hotel, began just a few hundred meters past the bridge.

Something flew in the air, an arc of flame—a spinning bottle alight at one end—and shattered on the leading jeep. There was a small explosion and flames spread over it, engulfing the soldiers.

"My God," said Karla, leaning forward in her seat and pulling her camera out of her bag. "That smells like petrol burning . . . *it's a Molotov cocktail.*"

Seconds later, another one hit the roof of the first limousine, and in moments it, too, was covered in flames.

"Get down," Uqu screamed, squeezing himself as best he could on the floor behind the driver's seat. *"Get down!"*

Soldiers, some with tails of fire, jumped off the jeep and began shooting in all directions. Guns from the rear jeep joined in.

Karla opened the window and leant out, taking pictures as fast as she could.

"No, no!" shouted Uqu, yanking her back inside the car.

There was a loud *crack* and a small hole suddenly appeared in the windscreen. The driver slumped over the wheel and the car's wheels spun, squealing, as his weight pushed down on the accelerator. The car gathered speed and weaved across the road, scraped against the burning jeep and slammed into the burning limousine, throwing Karla forward.

Her head hit the back of the seat in front of her, and that was the last thing she remembered.

5 The Long Arm of Paradise

A FEW MINUTES BEFORE eight on Monday morning Anthony Royn, Minister for Foreign Affairs, Deputy Prime Minister, and Deputy Leader of the governing Conservative Party, stormed into his Parliament House office in Canberra.

His staff looked up with fond anticipation, expecting to see the boyish grin, the soft, twinkling, hazel eyes framed by the halo of golden hair that had won untold thousands of votes—and not a few hearts—for the Conservative Party nationwide.

But their smiles died at the sour scowl on Royn's face, and their cheery greetings of "Good morning, Minister," trailed off to nothing.

Instead of ambling through the outer office, smiling, chatting, and cracking a joke or two as he normally did, Royn ignored his staff completely. He headed straight for his private office walking so fast he was almost running, and slammed the door behind him.

A moment later, his door swung open.

"Alison—*now!*" Royn shouted.

And he slammed the door shut again.

WHEN ALISON MCGUIRE HEARD Royn call her name, she buried her head in her hands. "It's the damn headlines," she muttered to herself. "No wonder he's in such a foul mood."

Dominating the morning headlines were Sunday's terrorist bombing in Toribaya, an Australian journalist's brush with death at the hands of government troops, and Karla Preston's eye-witness story in Sydney's *Mercury* which threatened the government's—and Royn's—credibility.

Next to a dramatic, front-page picture of flaming soldiers jumping from a burning jeep, Karla Preston flatly contradicted the Sandeman government's official statement that some twenty terrorists had been killed, and many more wounded, in a vicious (but fruitless) attack on their foreign minister as he headed for the airport. Alison didn't need to read Karla's commentary again to recall her accusations. . . .

The Sandeman government's claim they killed twenty terrorists is a flat-out lie.

I was there. I saw their troops—supposedly trained by Australians—fire their guns in panic, shooting randomly into a crowded street market. The so-called "terrorists" who died or were wounded were all innocent bystanders, who wanted nothing more than to enjoy themselves on a sunny Sunday afternoon.

What's more, the driver of my car was knocked unconscious by a random bullet. The car ran out of control and rammed into the foreign minister's limousine. If I hadn't been rescued by Australian soldiers—a ready reaction unit that was helicoptered in—

I'd now be languishing a Sandeman Islands' jail, along with my driver and guide, as one of the so-called "terrorists."

From what I've seen and experienced so far I can only conclude that Australian policy here is a shambles, and that the three Australian soldiers who died here six days ago died for absolutely nothing.

I have to tell him about McKurn today, she thought. And now this has happened.

The phone on her desk rang. "Yes, Minister . . . sorry Minister," she said. "Just getting my files together. I'll be right there."

Slamming the phone down, she wearily pushed herself to her feet. The previous evening, she'd taken the last flight from Melbourne back to Canberra; and then stayed up till three in the morning reading through the two thick files Sidney Royn had given her . . . the third night in a row she hadn't had enough sleep.

Grabbing the pile of papers she had ready for her regular morning meeting with Royn, she hurried out of her office.

As Alison came into Royn's private office, a phone on his desk rang: his direct line.

"What is it?" Royn snapped as he answered it. "Oh, sorry Prime Minister." He was silent for a moment. "Yes Prime Minister . . . yes Prime Minister."

He slammed the phone down. "Darn it. I haven't been here five minutes. . . . The man must be telepathic."

"What did he want?" asked Alison as she sat down opposite Royn.

"When I got off the plane in Canberra I was ambushed by the press," said Royn, as if he hadn't heard her.

"About . . . ?"

"That journalist who was almost killed yesterday in the Sandeman Islands by government troops. 'Minister, what can you say about our training program in the Sandemans when Australian-trained troops are shooting randomly into crowds?'" Royn mimicked a reporter's voice so well Alison knew who'd asked the question. Changing his tone completely, "'Minister, how do you react to the comment that Australian policy in the Sandemans is in a shambles.' I tell you, if that Karla Preston woman had been there I might have strangled her on the spot."

"And how did you handle them?" Alison asked.

"Not very well." Royn scowled as he spoke. "Basically, I said something like: 'This is certainly a very worrying report—if it is true. When we've been able to establish the facts, I'll have something more to tell you.'"

"And did that keep them quiet?"

Royn shook his head. "Not really—but it was better than 'No comment.'"

Alison nodded. "So tell me Minister," she asked, pointing towards the phone on his desk, "what did the Prime Minister want?"

Royn's face darkened. "After making an unprintable comment about journalists and how we shouldn't let them out of the country, he said that as well as deciding about troop levels in committee this morning, we had to come up with a unified stance that will kill these 'scabrous and irresponsible reports,' as he put it. And he's depending on me to get us out of this mess."

"What if the reports are true?" Alison asked.

"We'll smother it."

"It might be too big to smother."

"What do you mean?"

"I talked to Captain Peter McMurray this morning. He led the team that rescued Karla Preston. He confirmed everything she said."

"I see," said Royn thoughtfully. "Including the bit about Australian policy being a shambles?"

"In a way, yes. The Sandeman troops escorting the convoy were elite forces."

"You're joking."

Alison shook her head. "The prime minister up there grabs the soldiers who top our training courses, and adds them to his own personal guard unit. So those soldiers who shot into the crowd yesterday. . . ."

". . . were the pick of the bunch. If that gets out it will be a disaster."

"Too right. The first time they see any action they go to pieces. That could make a total mockery of our entire operation there. Anyway, McMurray said it was total chaos, bodies everywhere. As McMurray tried to restore some order, the foreign minister—who, he said, was 'scared shitless'—ordered his soldiers to arrest the occupants of the journalist's car. Then he demanded that McMurray use his helicopter to take him the rest of the way to the airport."

"What did McMurray do then?"

"He radioed the helicopter pilot and told him to rush back to base and come back with every medic and spare soldier he could find."

"I bet that made the minister happy."

Alison grinned. "McMurray, unfortunately, is no diplomat. You know you're meeting Sandemans' foreign minister today at eleven, after Cabinet committee."

Royn groaned. "I forgot."

"It was just a courtesy call. But now, instead of spending five minutes exchanging meaningless pleasantries, you're going to have to smooth some feathers.

"What do you mean?"

Alison chuckled. "McMurray said after he'd radioed the helicopter crew the minister cursed him and tried to order him about as if he were some lackey. So McMurray told him: 'You've only got a few hundred meters to go to get to the airport. If you're in such a hurry you can bloody well walk.'"

Royn burst out laughing. "He said that? To the minister?"

"Yes," said Alison, chuckling. "And then, when McMurray saw there was an Australian woman in the car, he said he'd take them into custody—and medivaced them out right under the foreign minister's nose."

Royn groaned. "It's not going to be a pleasant meeting. How come none of this was in that woman's story?"

"She was knocked unconscious when her car rammed into the foreign minister's limousine."

"Thank God for small mercies." Then his face turned serious and he sighed deeply. "I see we've got a big mess to clean up."

"Right," said Alison, looking at her watch. "And we've got an hour and a bit to get you ready for the National Security Committee at nine-thirty."

"Okay, why don't you huddle with Doug and whoever else you need for about thirty minutes. And then we'll all get together for a council of war."

"We're already on it," said Alison. "And we've come up with one possibility: this could be an opportunity to bring the Sandemans into line. Instead of trying to smooth the Foreign Minister's feathers, you could read him the riot act instead."

Royn looked at her in surprise. "So I could," he said, brightening up. "And Defence has been pushing for more command and control up there. Give me some options, and I'll bring them up in the Cabinet committee." Royn looked at the pile of newspapers on the corner of his desk. With a sudden thrust of his arm he swept them onto the floor. "I certainly won't be reading *them* this morning."

"One other thing," said Alison, handing him a report from the Ministry of Justice and Customs. "I've highlighted the relevant paragraphs."

Since becoming Minister for Foreign Affairs, Royn made sure he was kept informed of anything of interest in his previous portfolio. He quickly scanned the paragraphs Alison had marked. . . .

At the same time as a turf war is brewing between local drug dealers and gangs connected to the Chinese Triads, the street price of heroin has plummeted some 20-25% compared to a year ago as a new supplier has come into the market with a much higher quality product.

Little is known about this new entrant in the drug market, beyond the underworld nickname for him (or her): "The Candyman."

"The Candyman, eh?" Royn said looking up. "Curious." He threw the report on his desk. With a nod towards Alison he turned to read a file, but looked up as he realized Alison was still standing there.

"Yes, Alison?"

"Minister," she said, breathing deeply. "There's something I need to tell you."

"To do with the Sandemans?" he asked.

Alison mutely shook her head.

Royn looked at her with annoyance. "Not now, Alison. I've too much on my plate as it is."

Alison seemed to deflate. "Later, then," she said softly.

But Royn was once again absorbed in the open file, and didn't hear her.

*****

"Look!" shouted a deep male voice. "It's Karla Preston."

Karla turned towards the sound and saw a group of men sitting at a table on the far side of the hotel coffee shop. Recognizing two of them, she knew they were the Australian correspondents stationed in Toribaya. One of the journalists was standing, beckoning to her. As she headed in their direction, one by one they stood, calling out: "Well done, Karla." "Congratulations." "Good on yer luv."—and applauded.

Alan Massey, a pudgy, balding man wearing horn-rimmed glasses, shook Karla's hand vigorously.

"Hi Alan." Karla leaned over and gave him a peck on the cheek. "Good morning, gentlemen—" she said to the three journalists she hadn't met before "—and Robin. I see you're all up at the crack of dawn, in hot pursuit of tomorrow's news," she grinned. "Or are you waiting for it to fall in your laps?"

"At least we're not making it," one chuckled.

Robin Cartwright, a grey-haired, red-faced man, growled, "Yeah, you've really set the cat among the pigeons."

"Well, Robin, I see you're full of good cheer as usual."

"Scotch, actually. Like to join me?"

"At this time in the morning?"

"You haven't been outside yet?" Cartwright asked. Karla shook her head. "The hotel's been cordoned off by government troops. 'For your own safety, sir.' We can't go out and no one's taking our calls. An enforced day off, so we might as well all get pissed. Why wait till lunchtime?"

"Hmm," said Karla. "I have a stack of interviews scheduled for today, including one with the Prime Minister."

"That wily old fart," said Cartwright. "Never talks to the press, so that's something of a coup. Waste of time, though. He speaks in clichés and answers questions in circles. So you're not going to miss anything."

Karla knew he was right. *But I'd miss is my impression of him. That would be a shame.*

"We'll see," she said.

"The bastards are restricting our movements 'for our own safety' eh?" said a beefy man. "Balls. They're tightening the screws. They've heard of freedom of the press—and they don't like it one bit."

"Seen the *Toribaya Pravda?*" asked another, waving a copy of *The Sandeman Times.* "'Vicious terrorist attack foiled by brave soldiers.' I liked your story better."

"Miss Preston," a somewhat nervous young man asked. "I'm Will Sanders from News24/7. Could I interview you?"

"Will," Karla beamed at him, reaching across the table to shake his hand. "Call me 'Karla.' Sure. Any time."

"It must have been terrible, being shot at and all that," said Sanders.

"It all happened so fast the idea of danger didn't really occur to me."

"What happened after that?" Alan Massey asked.

"I was knocked out. The next thing I remember I woke up with a headache and one of the handsomest men I've ever seen looking over me. I thought I must have died and gone to heaven."

"Heaven?" said Cartwright. "Last time I heard you were an atheist."

"I was speaking metaphorically, Robin. If I had gone to heaven I probably would have died—of a heart attack."

"That's another metaphor, is it?

"Yes, Robin," she said patiently. "It's in the dictionary, under 'M.'"

"So who was this guy?" Massey asked, scowling at Cartwright.

"Captain Peter McMurray, who led the team that cleaned up the mess. After the doctors looked me over, they drove me over here to the hotel. Thankfully, they'd rescued all my luggage along with us."

"You were lucky," said Will Sanders.

"Yes," said Karla gravely, "we all were."

After a moment of uncomfortable silence, Massey said, "Karla, my apologies. Let me introduce these other reprobates. Robin you already know—and the less said the better."

"Up yours," said Robin Cartwright, lifting his glass in a fake salute.

"This is Gary Hunt from the *Melbourne Gazette*, and Dick Erin, ABC."

"Please to meet you all, gentlemen," said Karla as she gazed deeply into the eyes of each one in turn. Gary Hunt was the round, beefy fellow with a deep voice. "I like your articles—especially the think pieces," Karla said to him. Dick Erin was a thin, lanky man who seemed to flop everywhere. "I've seen you on TV," she said. "You have a great presence."

"Thanks," he grinned. "Can I interview you too—a more sober, thoughtful discussion," he said, taking a dig at Will Sanders, who winced slightly.

"Which hardly anyone will listen to, being on the ABC," cut in Cartwright.

"Just the elite—the people who count," Dick Erin shot back. And turning to Sanders he said, "Why don't you interview Karla now, live?"

"That's a good idea, Dick. Thank you."

"My pleasure," said Erin.

"Would that be all right, Miss Preston—I mean, Karla?" Will Sanders asked.

"Sure," she said. "After I've had my breakfast."

"Great. Thank you," he gushed, and moved away to make a call.

"What's going on with Derek Olsson?" Alan Massey asked.

Karla turned somber. "It's a frame-up," she said. "That's the only explanation that makes any sense."

"But the evidence seems solid." said Cartwright.

"That's the problem," Karla said. "It's too damn good."

"Couldn't make head or tail of it myself," Massey said. "But then, I don't know him as well as you do."

"Ah," said Cartwright, "the age-old story—the boss getting into the pants of the hired help."

"At least he's got something worth putting there—unlike you," Karla grinned.

"I tell you, my fearsome reputation precedes me wherever I go. When the ladies of the night see me coming, they all run and hide."

"It's your face, mate, not your equipment that scares them."

"It's pickled anyway," said Erin.

"What, his face or his equipment?"

"Both," said Erin.

"I think I'll go and talk to the bartender. At least I'll be able to have an intellectually stimulating conversation," said Cartwright; but he made no move to leave. "Babes in the woods," he confided to Karla, smiling. "They'd be lost without me."

"You're incorrigible, Robin—but I love you nevertheless," she said.

"So what are you doing tonight? Or, considering our choices for the rest of the day, what are you doing right now?"

"Right now," she said, laughing, "I'm going to have breakfast."

"Later, then," he said, waving his empty glass at a passing waitress.

"Don't get your knickers in a twist waiting up for me, Robin."

"Miss Preston?" said a voice behind them.

Karla turned to see a uniformed hotel concierge with some envelopes in his hand. "That's me," she said.

"I have some mail and messages for you." He handed her the envelopes. Three were computer-printed hotel messages—phone messages, presumably. The other two were letters, both in heavy, parchment envelopes with impressive insignia. One, she saw, was labelled Ofis Prime Minister. She tore it open. Inside was a brief letter:

Dear Miss Preston:

We regret that due to unforeseen circumstances, the Prime Minister will not able to interviewed with you this morning, as previously scheduled.

It was signed by the Prime Minister's personal assistant.

Quickly, she ripped open the others. "Look at these," she said, throwing them onto the table. "Every government official I was scheduled to interview has expressed their 'regrets.'"

"They all say the same thing," said Dick Erin as he scanned them. "Even the ungrammatical wording is almost identical."

"Payback time, perhaps?" said Massey.

"No great loss," said Cartwright. "What would they have told you anyway? Just more lies."

"Most likely," she sighed. "But I've still got a couple of businessmen to interview."

Cartwright leaned forward with a serious look on his face. "Betcha ten bucks there'll be two more messages for you within the hour."

Karla had a witty comeback on the tip of her tongue when she saw Cartwright lay a ten dollar bill on the table in front of her.

"Well, Robin," she said eventually. "You might be a lecherous old bastard, but you're a *perceptive* lecherous old bastard. So if it's all the same to you, I think I'll go and sample the breakfast buffet instead."

FORTY MINUTES LATER KARLA sat with Will Sanders at a quiet table on the far side of the coffee shop. Sanders gave her a headphone and mike which, like the one Sanders wore, was plugged into his cellphone.

As she put her headphone on she heard the announcer back in Sydney, ". . . and here's Will Sanders up in the Sandeman Islands. Over to you, Will."

"Thanks, Dave. And good morning Australia."

As he went on air, Sanders seemed to grow a couple of centimeters taller, his voice deepened, commanding authority, and all traces of his previous nervousness disappeared.

"I'm with Karla Preston who writes a column in the Sydney *Mercury* and other papers. Karla witnessed the terrorist attack on the Sandemans' foreign minister last night. Karla, were you injured in the attack?"

"Not seriously. Just a bump on my head. The car I was in plowed into the foreign minister's limousine and I was knocked out cold."

"In your column this morning, you accused the Sandeman Islands government of lying. That's a serious charge."

"Damn right it's serious—and it's true. I saw the attack. Two Molotov cocktails were thrown at the convoy. I couldn't tell exactly where they came from, and I certainly didn't see—couldn't see—who threw them. The footpaths were too crowded with people and street stalls."

"Didn't the soldiers go after the bombers?"

"No," said Karla. "They just stood in the middle of the street and fired in all directions. Not even targeting the area the bombs most likely came from."

"But the government claimed that twenty terrorists were killed—"

"Dead bodies can't talk back. Twenty people, *blameless* people died. So the government calls them terrorists and claims a victory. If I hadn't witnessed it, no one would have questioned their blatant—"

"Wait, wait," said Sanders urgently. "We've been cut off . . . I think. Hullo. Dave. Are you there? . . . *Anyone* there . . . ?" He picked up his cellphone. "No signal," he said. "That's strange."

"Indeed it is," said Karla. "Let's see. . . ." Karla sped at a fast walk across to the other journalists; Sanders gathered up his equipment and trailed after her. "Have any of you got a signal on your cellphone?" she asked.

Almost in unison, the four other journalists pulled out their cellphones and shook their heads. "Just the phone company," said Cartwright. "Totally unreliable."

"Has this happened to you before?" Karla asked. They all nodded.

"I'm not so sure," she said. Karla went to the coffee shop reception counter and asked to use their phone. When the hotel operator answered she asked for an outside line. "I'm sorry ma'am, the lines have just gone down. It happens now and then."

When Karla came back to the table Dick Erin had his laptop open. "No internet access," he said, looking up at her. "I can get on the hotel wireless network okay, but no further."

"So three different networks—mobile, landline and internet—go out at the same time," Karla said. "What are the chances of that being a phone company 'glitch'?"

"Not very high," said Erin.

"We've been cut off," said Karla.

"So, Karla," Cartwright asked, "what were you saying on radio that the authorities here didn't want anyone back in Oz to know?"

"They listen in . . . ?" Karla said with muted surprise.

Cartwright shrugged. "Who knows? I wouldn't put it past them—but it assumes a level of efficiency I've yet to see in this place."

"Whatever the reason is, I don't like it one little bit," said Karla.

They were interrupted by the same concierge as before, who handed Karla two envelopes.

Cartwright looked at her and smiled. Raising his glass he said, "Pity. About the only thing I like about this godforsaken country is that the booze is cheap. Ten bucks would have refilled my glass quite a few times."

Karla slowly opened the messages and, shrugging, threw them on the table. "So much for that."

"Cheer up, Karla," said Cartwright. "Look at it this way: you've got a free day in paradise with good company and cheap booze. What more could you ask for?"

"How about . . . freedom? Thanks, Robin. Another time, perhaps. Right now, I think I'll go up to my room."

"To do what—write an article you can't file?"

Karla grinned. "Maybe. See you guys later."

As she neared the elevators a businessman stepped out and strode across the lobby towards the hotel entrance. A hotel security guard stopped him, pointing at the soldiers outside. Karla could hear the angry tone of the businessman's voice. Then the guard said something and after a moment the businessman sat down in a nearby armchair and pulled out his cellphone.

Karla began walking towards the entrance. As she neared the security guard the businessman jumped up and cut in front of her.

"There's no signal," he said angrily to the guard. "How can I arrange a pass if I can't phone out?"

The guard just shrugged. "Inshallah," he said, his face blank.

The businessman growled and turned on his heel, nearly bumping into Karla.

"Scurvy little country," he said as he saw her. "They couldn't organize a piss-up in a brewery," he added as he stormed back towards the lifts.

"Do you have a pass, mum?" the guard asked Karla.

"No," she said. "Why would I need a pass?"

"If you don't have a pass, you can't go outside."

"Are you going to stop me?"

The guard shrugged. "They will," he said, indicating the soldiers.

As Karla opened the door and stepped into the heat three soldiers turned and blocked her way. She took another step and one of them moved directly in front of her, vaguely waving his submachine gun in her direction.

"Where's your pass?"

An officer, looking like he'd just come off a parade ground, strutted towards her. The three pips on his shoulders indicated he was a captain, and Karla smiled at the "fruit salad" of ribbons adorning his chest. To look her in the eye, the captain had to tilt his head up, which seemed to make him angrier.

"Why would I need a pass just to go for a walk?" Karla asked.

"You need a pass just to step outside that door."

"Why? What sort of a place *is* this?"

The captain barked an order and the three soldiers stiffened, brought their submachine guns to the ready, and pointed them at Karla.

Karla shivered as she eyed the wrong end of three gun barrels, nervously aware that each soldier had his finger on the trigger. "You're making a big mistake," she said, hoping the captain didn't notice her shaking knees.

"I don't think so," the officer said. "This hotel, and the area around it, is under martial law, so either you get back inside now, or. . . ." He negligently waved one hand in the direction of the guns.

Karla nodded slowly. "That," she said, looking at the gun barrels, "is an argument I understand."

She backed slowly inside, and walked as calmly as she could towards the lifts without a glance back.

"Where the hell is Uqu?" she growled as the lift doors slid shut in front of her.

6 A Woman from Mars

RANDOLPH KYDD LOOMED LARGE, both in Australian politics and in person. One opposition wit claimed Kydd's circumference, according to his tailor, equalled his height. "The tailor is a solid Labor Party man—one of the workers."

"That's right," Kydd replied. "He's a worker and *I* provide the work. Lots of it."

True or not, no one doubted that—excluding the four letter and other unprintable words most commonly attached to his name—Randolph Kydd was best described by the word *round*. His appearance was a study in circles and ovals. His torso looked like a water-filled balloon held from above: much wider at the bottom than at the top. His head, which began with not a double but a triple chin, seemed to sit on that torso without the intervention of a neck. His face was a smaller replica of his torso, his massive jowls folding over his chins, topped by a shiny, round and completely bald head. His fleshy lips jutted out slightly from his face, a pair of semi-circles when viewed from the side. And as his dark, penetrating eyes, two small circles turned into bright pinpoints by yet more folds of flesh, darted from face to face along the table and came to rest on an empty seat, his expression turned into a glowering frown.

As his bulk lumbered into the Cabinet room, the second hand on the wall clock a few ticks short of nine-thirty, the chatter of the four men and the one woman assembled at the long oval table for the meeting of the Cabinet's National Security Committee was replaced with a chorus of "Good morning, Prime Minister."

"Good morning, ladies and gentlemen," Kydd boomed sourly at the one empty seat. "I see we're not ready to begin."

Kydd's voice began in the pit of his stomach, rumbled through his throat like gravel in a cement mixer, and erupted from the slash of his mouth with the force and latent energy of lava spouting from a volcano. When his words were directed at an opponent, they could demolish him with the accuracy and explosiveness of a laser-guided missile. In his conversational mode, his words would merely bounce around the walls, as they did now, even in the plushly furnished, thickly carpeted, sound-deadened Cabinet room.

As Kydd levered his weight into his chair, set at the center of one side of the long table, Anthony Royn stepped through the door. "That damn Preston woman was being interviewed—" he said as he entered, and stopped in mid-sentence and mid-motion as realized Kydd's censorious gaze was fixed on him.

"Morning Prime Minister, everyone," he muttered as he scurried to his seat, Kydd's glowering eyes following him the whole way. As Deputy Prime Minister, second in the chain of command, his position at the table was facing Kydd. In the long moment it took him to reach his place, sit down, and arrange his papers in front of him the only noise in the room was the sound of his movements.

To Kydd's left Treasurer Paul Cracken, a wiry man of average height, sat slightly hunched over like a vulture ready to pounce at the slightest weakness, his deep-set eyes smirking at Royn. Though just two years older than Royn, Cracken's dark brown hair was already receding noticeably. Out of Kydd's sight, Cracken waggled a claw-like, tobacco-stained finger at Royn and mouthed the words, "Naughty boy." Royn felt his hackles rise, but with a conscious effort calmed himself and gave Cracken a quick, mocking smile.

Kydd's voice broke the silence. "I don't think we have much to smile about this morning." He spoke to the room but everyone who'd seen Royn's grin knew who the comment was for. "So, *if* we may now begin," he continued, frowning at the wall clock, "originally this meeting had just one item on the agenda: whether we should send more troops and police to the Sandeman Islands. Now, thanks to 'that damn Preston woman,' as Tony so aptly described her, we have a few other items as well." Looking quickly from face to face he said, "Now, you've all read Victor's *Sandeman Islands Situation Report*"—and from the tone of his voice it was clear Kydd meant "you'd all *better* have read it"—"so Victor, perhaps you could give us a quick summary, to make sure we've all grasped the implications."

Victor Bergstrom, Minister for Defence, was a gentlemanly, soft-spoken, grey-haired man in his early sixties. To everyone's surprise, including his own, he'd risen slowly through the ranks in the Conservative Party to his current position of fourth, after the Treasurer, in Kydd's hierarchy. With his courtly, old-world manners, even he agreed he didn't have the *chutzpah* to succeed in the rough and tumble of today's politics. But by being everybody's friend and a threat to none, he'd assumed the role of peacemaker within the Parliamentary Conservative Party. Often, when there was a fiercely contested fight for a position and neither of the front-runners could gain a majority, Bergstrom was drafted as a compromise candidate, one who guaranteed the restoration of consensus. The warring parties could retire, gracefully, without either side feeling they had lost the battle. And without resentment: nobody resented Bergstrom's success, in significant part because they knew that because of his age, he'd retire from the scene in a couple of years at most.

As Bergstrom cleared his throat everyone leaned forward slightly to be sure they'd catch his words.

"Since the three Australian . . . ah . . . casualties last week, we think the situation in the Sandemans has deteriorated markedly. The various guerrilla groups have been crowing at their success and issuing threats left, right and center. As yesterday's . . . ah . . . incident demonstrates, they're stepping up their terror tactics."

"How many . . . ah . . . *incidents* as you call them," Cracken cut in sarcastically, "like this have there been in the capital?"

"A few," Bergstrom admitted. "A bombing in a shopping mall a few months ago. And a couple of low level officials, like town councillors, have been assassinated or kidnapped in the past year. But this is the first time they've attacked a high official, and one surrounded by police and soldiers."

"Soldiers?" Cracken spat. "More like a gaggle of trained monkeys."

"Yes . . . ah . . . well," said Bergstrom stumbling. "Unfortunately, we've investigated yesterday's incident, and the soldiers who were guarding the foreign minister were the elite of the Sandemans' forces."

"The elite?" Cracken said. "Sounds like we'll have to—"

"Paul!" Kydd spoke sharply at his usual volume—directly into Cracken's ear; Cracken's head jerked. "Let Victor finish before you bring out your knives."

"Yes, Prime Minister," Cracken mumbled, glowering when he saw Royn flash him a victorious smile.

"Well," Bergstrom continued, seemingly unruffled, "as you know our forces are there in a peace-keeping, advisory and training capacity. We don't have command authority over Sandeman troops. It turns out the prime minister has used the troops who did best in our training programs to form his own, personal guard. The other troops, who are actually out in the field, are doing okay when Australian advisors accompany them."

"And when they don't?" asked Kydd, gently.

"Well, they do as little as possible. Stay in a village guarding it, but never run patrols in the surrounding area to flush out guerrillas, that sort of thing. And the desertion rate of these troops is quite high. Unlike our soldiers, they lack commitment."

"This is indeed distressing news, Victor," said Kydd. "Pray continue."

"It's not quite so bad as it seems. As I said, Sandeman troops are fair to medium when supervised in the field, and get better as they gain experience. The prime minister's guard unit, however, has basically been parading around the palace in formation, practicing their spit and polish—but no exercises, not even firing practice. Hardly a surprise they fell to pieces when push came to shove."

Bergstrom paused, but when Kydd said nothing he continued, "The best solution, we believe, is to significantly increase the presence of Australian troops, carry out more Australian-only and Australian-commanded combined operations, and seek some sort of joint command over the Sandeman army—a face-saving formula that actually puts us in the driver's seat."

"So," said Cracken cautiously, eyeing Kydd to see if he'd react, "it seems the Sandeman troops have no interest in dying for their prime minister. So why should we send our young men up there to die in their place?"

"Your concern for our young men's lives is extremely moving," Royn sneered. "I'm touched."

"Well, that too," Cracken mumbled sheepishly. "Of course no one wants anyone to die. But with the. . . . I'm talking about body bags—which may not be an issue today. But it's an issue that could kick us in the balls sooner or later—most likely at the next election."

"Well, Paul," said Victor Bergstrom, trying to inject a tone of calm into the discussion, "what are our other options?"

"Well, we could send the Papuans in. They'd make mince-meat of the terrorists in no time."

"Hardly an election-winning alternative, Paul," Helen Arkness, the Immigration Minister, said softly in a chiding tone of voice. Her gentle, motherly bearing was deceptive: in the male-dominated arena of politics, Helen Arkness usually gave better than she got.

"Or perhaps you'd rather we brought our boys home," Royn snapped, "and have a hostile, government of separatists and terrorists sitting on an oil lake up there instead."

"Of course not," Cracken barked in reply. "Don't be ridiculous."

"Enough!" Kydd roared, glowering at Royn and Cracken alternately. "Let's keep to the *point.*"

"Yes, Prime Minister," said Royn. "We do have another option—at least, another string to our bow." At Royn's words, six heads turned to look at him in anticipation.

"Do go on, Tony," said Kydd.

"I'm meeting Sandemans' foreign minister at eleven. He'll be in a very bad mood. Aside from surviving a Molotov cocktail yesterday, when he demanded he be helicoptered the rest of the way to the airport, the Australian captain in charge apparently told him, 'If you're in such a hurry you can bloody well walk.'"

The Cabinet room echoed with laughter. "So either I could work to smooth his ruffled feathers. Or I could read him the riot act. What do you think?"

Kydd nodded thoughtfully. "Victor, what's your reaction?"

"Well," said Bergstrom turning towards Royn, "if you can get him to agree to Australian command of all forces in the Sandemans—under some sort of face saving measure of course—Defence would be eternally grateful."

"At least for the next ten minutes," said Cracken scornfully.

Bergstrom looked at Cracken sourly, and shrugged.

"I guess I could make the point that the only alternative, due to the delicate political situation here in Australia—"

"You mean body bags," Cracken interjected.

"Quite," said Royn, nodding. "Anyway, due to the. . . . I could say instead of adding to our troop commitment there we'd invite the Papuans to increase their peace-keeping forces instead."

"He'll never agree," said Bergstrom.

"Indeed," said Royn.

"But he wants to save his little brown arse—" said Cracken.

"Paul," said Helen Arkness, shaking her head. "Sometime I wonder how you ever got to be a minister, let alone Treasurer."

"Elbows," Cracken said with a smirk.

"He certainly will want to save his. . . ." Kydd scowled at Cracken as he spoke. "So, Tony, if you and Victor can set up the options so he has to agree to what we want, I say give him hell."

Kydd looked around to see everyone nodding. "So are we agreed?" he asked.

There was a chorus of, "Yes, Prime Minister."

"Good," said Kydd. "Now, we have question time at twelve-thirty, and no doubt all the questions will be on the Sandeman Islands and that damned Preston woman—"

"Dead bodies can't talk back," Royn muttered to himself.

"What was that, Tony?" Kydd asked.

"Dead bodies can't talk back," Royn repeated. "That's what she—the Preston woman—said on the radio this morning."

"Ah," said Cracken. "So how many of the other 'terrorists' the Sandeman government claims to have killed were actually bystanders who got in the way of a bullet by mistake?"

"Exactly," said Royn.

"And how long before the press ask the same question?" Cracken said.

"Not long enough," Kydd growled. "And—"

He stopped at a loud knock on the door. After a moment, the door opened and one of Bergstrom's assistants stood there.

"Excuse me, Prime Minister, Ministers," he said. "I'm sorry to interrupt, but I have an urgent message for my minister."

"Deliver it, then," said Kydd, "and be quick about it."

"Yes, Prime Minister." The assistant scurried into the room and handed the message to Bergstrom.

"Thank you," he said, waving his assistant away. As the door closed again, Bergstrom said, "It seems the . . . ah . . . Sandeman government has cut all the phone lines and so on with the outside world. The hotel where the Australian journalists—including Miss Preston—are all staying, has been placed under martial law. It's surrounded by troops who aren't letting any Australians, or Caucasians, out."

"Just what we need," said Cracken. "*Another . . . ah . . .* incident."

"We're still in satellite communication with our troops there?" Kydd asked.

"Of course, Prime Minister," Bergstrom nodded.

"Better get a detachment of our soldiers down to that hotel, then. Personally, I'd rather let those damn journalists sink or swim on their own. Politically, though. . . ."

"We'll protect them," said Bergstrom.

"Good," said Kydd. "Anything else?"

"Three different guerrilla groups," said Cracken quickly, "have claimed responsibility for yesterday's attack. Presumably, at least two of them are lying."

"This better be relevant," said Kydd sternly.

"It's very relevant," Cracken replied forcefully. "What do we actually *know* about all the guerrilla groups up there? Is it some coordinated conspiracy? Or are they just disparate groups of dissatisfied citizens who, like the Sandeman Islands soldiers who desert, simply have no respect for their government and want something better?"

"The Muslims are the biggest group—" said Bergstrom.

"Perhaps that's just because they're the biggest minority."

"—and they're the only ones who seem flush with money."

"And where does that money come from?" Cracken asked.

"Well, we say it's al Qaeda—" said Royn.

"I know that, Tony. I wasn't born yesterday, for Christ's sake. Look, al Qaeda is the convenient, catch-all, Big Bad Wolf of international terrorism. Saying al Qaeda is behind everything keeps the gullible John and Jane Q. Citizens quaking in their boots. There's no need to repeat the *spin* we put on this in *here,* for heaven's sake. What I want you to tell me is: what the fuck do we actually, unequivocally *know?* Are *you*—" Cracken stabbed his finger at Royn "—or *you*—" he pointed at Bergstrom "—willing to stand up in Parliament and swear the Muslim terrorists are part of the international jihadist conspiracy, who just take orders from some international puppet master running everything from behind the scenes?"

"Well," said Bergstrom, "when you put it that way. . . ."

"Victor," Cracken said, slapping his palm on the table, "this is the kind of thing Defence should know. Do they?"

"Well . . . ah. . . ."

"So our soldiers are going in blind, and we don't really have any idea what the fuck is *really* going on up there. Is that the case, Victor?"

"Sometimes, Paul," Helen Arkness cut in, "you almost carry your weight—even though you talk like an illiterate hoodlum."

"Thank you, Helen," Cracken smiled.

"Victor," said Kydd, "it seems that whatever else we do we'd better beef up our intelligence-gathering up there. Throw everything into it—military intelligence, the Federal Police, ASIO's spooks, the lot. Anyone objects or proves obstructive, tell the bastard to expect a call from *me.*"

"Yes, Prime Minister," Bergstrom said.

"Anything else?" Kydd asked. When no one spoke he slapped the table and said, "Twelve-fifteen, then."

*****

Karla answered the knock on her door to see a somewhat bedraggled Uqu standing in the hotel corridor, a bandage on his head and a backpack hanging on one shoulder.

"What on earth has happened to you?" she asked.

"I wasn't hurt. So after the doctor looked me over, they sent me home. When I got out the gate of the Australian base, I was picked up for a little 'questioning.'"

"I see," Karla said slowly. "Come on in."

Uqu wore a rumpled shirt and baggy pants that looked like they needed a laundry. *He doesn't look like the same person today,* she suddenly thought.

"Were you hurt much? That bandage looks pretty bad."

"A few sore muscles, that's all." Uqu broke into a big, toothy smile at Karla's puzzled look, and pulled the bandage off his head. Underneath were just a couple of Band-Aids.

"What?" she said.

"You're going to be deported. The police will be here soon to put you on the next flight back to Sydney."

"They will? Why? A silly question. They don't like me, right?"

"The other journalists have pretty much abided by the restrictions. I guess you didn't even know there were any. As far as they're concerned, you're a troublemaker."

Karla grinned. "That's not the first time I've been called a 'troublemaker.'" She sat down and then stood up again. "Damn it," she said angrily, "I only just got here. I'm not ready to leave yet."

"There is another option," said Uqu.

"There is? You mean . . . get out here somehow? . . . But the hotel's surrounded by troops, right? How do we escape—through the kitchen or something?"

"No," said Uqu, still smiling. "We walk out the front door." Pulling something out of his backpack he said, "Excuse me a moment." He turned his back and pulled off his shirt. Karla had time to notice a small bruise on his muscly back as he pulled another garment over his head. He turned around to face her, putting on a Muslim-style cap as he did.

Karla gasped. "You're completely different. Unrecognizable."

The shirt he was now wearing, collarless, made from thin cotton with a couple of faint, embroidered gold stripes was, she realized, the kind of native-style dress she'd seen in some of the tourist brochures.

"Good, it will work then. They won't connect me with the man with a bandaged head who came into the hotel. And this hat," he said, tapping his head, "is worn by Muslims who've made the pilgrimage to Mecca—the *hajj*. So I'll get respect, even from the Christians."

"I see."

"And you," said Uqu, pulling a black, shapeless garment from his backpack, "wear this."

"What is it?"

"A burqa."

"A burqa? Like Muslim women wear?" Karla held it to her shoulders and it nearly reached the floor.

"That's right. It's the biggest one I could find."

"I'll die of heat stroke wearing that."

Uqu shrugged. "It's your choice—but this is the only way I can think of to get you out of the hotel. Dressed like this, we can walk out the front door and nobody will question us."

"I see. Yes . . . it should work. So it's that—"

"—or let them put you on the plane back to Sydney. After, no doubt, a little 'questioning.'"

Karla shuddered. "I see."

"And where will we go?"

"To the one place where you'll be safe. But there's a condition: you say nothing about this place to anyone."

"I can't agree to that."

"If you don't agree, I can't take you there," Uqu said. "Anywhere else we go—" Uqu shrugged helplessly "—people will talk and the police will find us in a week or less."

"You're not giving me a choice, Uqu. But never? That's a hell of long time."

Uqu grinned. "Not never. When the time comes, you'll have a great story. An exclusive."

"That sounds a lot better than a 'little questioning.'"

"I need to go to ground for a while, too. Right now, the authorities think I'm under Australian protection. But in a few days they'll figure the Aussies will have forgotten about me, and I don't want to be here then."

"No—I wouldn't want you to be here either."

Uqu looked at Karla with surprise at her expression of concern, and then his look hardened. "Something else you should think about is that you'd be a fugitive, having evaded a deportation order."

"And I haven't registered with the police, either."

"No. Two offences they can throw at you. So there's no telling what might happen to you if they catch up with us."

"I see," she said. "And how would I get back to Australia? I won't be able to turn up at the airport and get on a plane."

"Where we're going, that can be arranged."

Karla thought for a moment—and felt a boiling anger rising up inside her. "Damn them," she spat. "I'm not going to be shoved around by some tinpot little tyrant."

"That's what I thought you'd decide."

"Getting to know me, huh? . . . Okay, what about my luggage?"

"I'm afraid you can only bring what will fit in this backpack," Uqu said.

"How about a small carry bag as well?"

"That's okay too."

Karla stood. "All right," she breathed. "Should I bring my laptop? Will I be able to recharge it . . . ?"

"Sometimes," said Uqu.

"—I'll bring it anyway. Do I have time for a shower?

Uqu shook his head. "I don't really know, but let's not take the chance."

"Fair enough."

Karla emptied her suitcase onto the bed, threw some clothes into the backpack, and added a few items from the bathroom, her laptop, and a few other valuables.

"Okay, that should do it. What about the rest?" she said, pointing at the remaining clothes on the bed.

"I'll throw them back in the suitcase." Noticing Karla's cellphone on the bed, Uqu said, "Turn off your cellphone so they can't trace us."

"Okay" she nodded. Studying the clothes strewn across the bed she added, "I guess I'll miss a couple of those dresses, but I'll live. Uqu, I'd appreciate if you went into the bathroom while I change."

She stripped off her clothes and, eyeing the burqa with disdain, pulled on a T-shirt and shorts, and finally her sturdy walking boots. Knocking on the bathroom door, she said, "Okay, Uqu, you can come out now."

Karla held the burqa at arm's length while Uqu repacked the suitcase. "Okay," she sighed, "let's see if I can get into this." In a few minutes a tall figure in black stood before her in the mirror, with just a thin slit through which she could make out her eyes.

"It works, Uqu," she said in a muffled voice. "You can hardly tell what color my eyes or skin are." Noticing her hands, she hid them behind the long arm-folds of black cloth. "How's that?" she asked, turning towards Uqu.

"Great. No one would think you're a Westerner," Uqu said, "but you're tall—too tall. It's the only thing we can't disguise. So can you sort of hunch down or something— anything to make you seem shorter than you are."

"You mean, like this?" Watching herself in the mirror she bent forward slightly, dropping her shoulders and looking down towards the ground. She was still tall compared to Uqu, but somehow she gave the impression of meekness and submission and no longer seemed to tower over him like some giantess.

"Will that do it?" she asked; and straightened up, flexing her shoulders and throwing back the veil. "I'll get a backache. And I'm already suffocating in this outfit and we're still in air-conditioned comfort. How do those Saudi women stand it? It gets really hot there. Forty-five degrees or more."

"A lifetime of submission and obedience," said Uqu seriously. "And one thing to keep in mind: until we get to safety I'm your lord and master. When I tell you to do something, you say 'Yes, Massa.' And you never speak unless spoken to."

"That's two things, Uqu—no, three."

Uqu grinned. "We Muslim males don't have to be consistent or logical—certainly not to women."

"Got it, your lordship . . . though that's not an attitude restricted to Muslim males."

"Whatever," he said picking up the carry bag. "*You* wear the backpack and follow me—always a pace or two behind."

"I don't seem to have any other choice, do I?" Karla mumbled to herself.

KARLA SQUEEZED HERSELF INTO the back of the lift, nervously eyeing the alien figures reflected into the infinite distance in the lift's mirrored walls. *God,* she thought, *I look like—I feel like a woman from Mars.*

The lift stopped at an intermediate floor and a Caucasian man stepped in. He gave her a strange, searching look and he frowned as his eyes fell on Uqu. He seemed uncomfortable, Karla thought. But then he just stared into the distance trying to ignore them both.

When the lift arrived at the ground floor the man stepped out first. Karla shuffled behind Uqu, feeling like she was trying to disappear. The lobby's width to the hotel entrance seemed to stretch forever; through the doors she could see the same soldiers standing guard outside. An Australian—the man's voice seemed to echo across the lobby into her ears—was having a heated discussion with one of the soldiers. Eventually, a couple of the soldiers simply herded him back inside the hotel.

She'd hardly walked more than three steps from the lift when she heard raucous, off-key singing coming from the direction of the coffee shop. She turned to see a clearly drunken Robin Cartwright staggering in her direction, supported by an almost equally drunken Alan Massey, both completely oblivious to the sour looks of the other guests, annoyed at the racket they were making.

Under her veil Karla smiled, thinking how really outraged the other guests would be if they were able to understand the pornographic ditty the inebriated pair were butchering.

Suddenly, their off-key singing was drowned out by the sound of sirens. Karla looked up cautiously to see two trucks screech to a halt outside the hotel. Soldiers and police piled out and ran through the entrance, fanning out to encircle the lobby. She heard a commanding voice demanding, *"Kanda b'long Karla Preston ka? Wikwik."*

Karla stopped in her tracks, and felt herself quaking uncontrollably. *My God,* she thought, eyeing the two drunks as they stumbled closer. *This burqa won't hide me from them. And they're so drunk, God knows what they'd do. . . .*

A few paces ahead Uqu turned and barked something at her in Pidgin English. All she could make out was *"nogood wimmen"*—but she understood his tone of voice. "At least he hasn't lost his cool," she mumbled under her breath. She started shuffling after him, trying to shrink, hoping to make herself invisible, as the sound of hobnailed boots thumping on the parquet floor came closer and closer . . . and stopped in front of her. She froze as she saw the snouts of two submachine gun barrels swinging in her direction.

7 Shark Bait

DIGNIFIED AS IT WAS, the imposing main entrance of Parliament House was mainly used by the public. Side and rear entrances were used by staff, journalists, Members, Senators, and Ministers.

The Prime Minister had his own, personal entrance, and was the only person who could enter Parliament House without going through a metal detector.

Randolph Kydd, Anthony Royn and Victor Bergstrom formed a greeting line as a stretched Cadillac flying the Sandeman flag pulled up in the Prime Minister's courtyard.

"At least he's not running on Sandeman time," Royn said with a smile, knowing Kydd would be furious if he was kept waiting for even a couple of minutes.

"Just as bloody well," Kydd growled.

Abdullah Nimabi, the Sandeman Islands Foreign Minister, slowly emerged from the limousine, followed by the High Commissioner, as ambassadors between members of the British Commonwealth were called. A second car, a nondescript Toyota, stopped behind the limo and half-a-dozen aides, all men, loaded with files and briefcases piled out. Two of them were dressed like Nimabi, in long, white, flowing robes with fez-like hats, while the others wore suits and ties.

"Foreign Minister," Kydd boomed, his face assuming a warm expression as he waddled up to Nimabi to vigorously shake his hand. "Welcome, and I'm so glad you're safe. High Commissioner," he added with a nod.

"Thank you, Prime Minister," Nimabi said with a slight bow. "It is indeed a pleasure to be here."

Royn judged that Nimabi's expression didn't match his words, and he gained the impression their meeting was not, after all, going to be a pleasant experience. But he hadn't buried himself in drama at school and university for nothing. Summoning his winning smile, and injecting his well-known charm into his voice, he took Nimabi's hand in one of his and clasped his shoulder with the other. "Abdullah. What a pleasure to see you. . . . It must have been a terrible ordeal."

Nimabi's face brightened. "Tony," he said. "Indeed, it was. But as you can see, I'm all in one piece."

"Inshallah," said Royn, "as I believe you would say."

"Indeed," Nimabi nodded, his smile widening.

Suppressing a shudder, Royn had the sense that, to Nimabi, "Inshallah" also applied to the dead and wounded bystanders and the Sandeman soldiers now in hospital with third degree burns.

Turning to Bergstrom, Royn said, "Victor, of course, you know. And Victor, I'm sure you've met the High Commissioner before."

"Indeed," said Bergstrom. "Welcome."

"Good to see you again," said Nimabi, shaking Bergstrom's hand.

"I've invited Victor to join us," said Royn as he gently shepherded Nimabi inside. Nimabi just nodded.

"I'll look forward to talking to you later, then," said Kydd as Royn and Nimabi moved past him.

"An honor, as always, Prime Minister," Nimabi said, inclining his head.

As they walked through the corridor to the conference room, Royn chatted gaily to Nimabi as if he were a long-lost brother, slowing his pace to keep time with the shorter man, and hanging back slightly so Nimabi would feel that he was in the lead. Behind them were Bergstrom and the High Commissioner, followed by Nimabi's aides, who were, in turn, discreetly trailed by a couple of plain-clothed guards aware that none of the visitors had passed through security before entering Parliament House.

*****

ROBIN CARTWRIGHT, SUPPORTED BY Alan Massey, continued to reel through the hotel's lobby, too absorbed in their duet and in staying upright to notice the soldiers and police storming in

Cartwright lurched and Massey stumbled under his weight, almost bowling over one of the soldiers standing in front of Karla.

A great sense of relief flooded over her as the soldiers' submachine guns turned to point at the two drunks. She began to straighten herself up—stopping herself in mid-motion. Furtively, she looked around through the eye-slit, having to turn her head as her field of vision was restricted. *Like every other part of me,* she thought. But nobody seemed to have noticed anything. She bit back on a comment she would have made at any other time. *Nearly blew it,* she thought. *But they didn't recognize me. It's working.*

"Shorry," Cartwright muttered, vaguely in the direction of the soldier. Massey grunted something unintelligible, and they moved to continue their stagger in the direction of the bathroom.

But the two soldiers stood in front of them, blocking their way.

"Shcuzhe ush," said Cartwright, starting to push between the soldiers. But he stopped short, surprise on his face, as one of the soldiers poked his submachine gun in Cartwright's belly.

"Careful where you poke that thing, mate," said Massey. "He'll throw up over your shiny new boots if you keep doing that."

Frozen in place, Karla wondered if the soldiers had understood a word Massey had said—and nervously expected them to turn back to her at any moment. Uqu barked something and she shifted her gaze back to his feet. He was beckoning at her impatiently. She took one tentative step, and then another; Uqu strode ahead confidently, even a bit cockily, but she couldn't really tell. Not without dropping her meek, submissive pose. *That's more of a straitjacket than the damned burqa.*

Behind her, Cartwright's and Massey's voices rose in complaint, but she resisted the impulse to look back to see what was happening. She kept her eyes on the hotel entrance which, thankfully, was slowly coming closer, along with shiny boots arrayed to her right and left. She continued to shuffle along, her back aching from the uncharacteristic pose when suddenly Uqu stopped. She came to a halt a step behind him. He and a man she couldn't see were exchanging words in Pidgin, but she recognized the voice . . . *the captain.*

Karla's knees started shaking again and with an iron will she steadied herself without having to reach out for support.

Uqu laughed and so did the other man. *Uqu, goddammit, move. That captain will recognize me.* She tensed her body, waiting for the hail of bullets she was convinced would come at any second.

Uqu spoke for what must have been just a few minutes but felt like hours, and then both he and the captain laughed again, long and loudly. *At last,* she saw Uqu's feet move and she almost tripped over her own feet as she tried to follow in step and work out the kinks in her leg muscles at the same time. The wheels of a car pulled up in front of her, and she almost groaned when she saw flakes of rust peeling off the bottom of the car's body: it was another heap that shouldn't be on the road, like the jalopies she'd seen at the airport. She looked up cautiously and saw Uqu motioning impatiently at her. *Of course he's not going to open the door for me, or anything civilized like that,* she thought.

As she scrambled slowly into the car, trying not to expose any skin, Uqu held a finger to his lips. She nodded mutely and sank back into the seat with a sigh of relief. But she remembered to keep her eyes fixed to the floor.

The upholstery was torn and tattered; the taxi shook and rattled as it moved. They seemed to spend most of the journey sitting, waiting for the traffic to move; when the car was stationary Karla could hear a nasty clunk-clunk-clunk sound coming from the engine.

Uqu sat in the front seat next to the driver, engaging him in animated conversation. Karla felt they must have had enough time to tell each other their life stories when the taxi finally stopped and Uqu opened his door.

She levered herself out of the taxi with a feeling of relief, and wonderment that they'd arrived in one piece. To her surprise, Uqu was standing in front of an alley leading inside a shanty town, saying something to a couple of boys standing idly on the chipped footpath. *What are we doing here?*

She saw the two urchins nod and scamper away; she followed Uqu as he picked his way along the alley, the mud squelching on her boots, people pushing against her as they passed each other on the narrow path. *I wanted to see this—but I can't even look.*

Uqu stepped through a doorway and she looked up to see where he'd gone. He was inside a dark room beckoning her to follow. "We made it," he said as he closed the door behind her, turning on a light, a naked bulb hanging from the ceiling. He took off his *hajj* cap and Karla noticed it was slightly discolored by beads of sweat.

"Can I relax now?" she asked. "And put down this backpack?"

"Of course, but keep the burqa on," he said in a soft voice. "We won't be here for very long. And speak quietly. There's no real privacy here at all."

Karla became aware of some neighbors chattering, the noise of people walking along the path, and a couple of radio stations and somebody's boom box competing with each other to be heard, and nodded. *And no peace, either.* "Can I at least take this damn veil off for a while?"

"Sure."

She put down the backpack and yanked off the headgear, breathed deeply, and shook her hair out gratefully. But as she stood up to stretch, she bumped her head against the roof.

The floor was packed dirt; the walls were bare corrugated iron. Instead of a window there was a narrow opening between the roof and the top of the outside wall that barely brightened the room. Whether it was there for light or ventilation, or simply as a result of poor construction, Karla couldn't say.

Spying a stool in a corner of the room she set herself down and stretched. Uqu was busy packing things into a large, shabby backpack. "What are you doing, Uqu?" she asked.

"Just getting together stuff we need," he said.

"What's that?" as she saw him put a rather large box into the bag; it looked new, unlike everything else she could see.

"A satellite dish," he said, holding up the box.

"A what?"

"So you can stay in touch while we're out in the middle of nowhere."

"You've thought of everything."

"Well, it wasn't me, exactly," he replied.

"Derek Olsson, then?"

"One of his assistants."

"Have you ever met him?"

Uqu shook his head.

"So what do you actually do for a living—and what do you do for him?" she asked.

"I offer liaison services."

"Meaning?"

"I smooth the way between Westerners and the local people they want to do business with. Another term for my job is fixer."

"Ah, I see. Taking care of bribes and that sort of thing."

"That sort of thing. Right. Or, as my sociology professor might have put it," he said with a smile, "'negotiating the sliding interface between two incompatible and mutually incomprehensible cultures.'"

"I had a professor like that once," Karla laughed. "So tell me Uqu, do you work for Olsson?"

"Mostly, but not exclusively."

"And what business does Olsson have here?"

"Freight. They only have a small office, a couple of people. But every year, there are licences to renew, permits, and so on. There's always some customs problem to be sorted out. And then there's the occasional visiting fireman, like you."

"I think I get the picture," Karla said measuredly.

"Okay," said Uqu zipping the backpack shut. "We're nearly ready to go."

"And where are we going?"

"We're going to take a boat trip."

"So I need to put this back on?" said Karla, holding up the veil.

"Yes," said Uqu, pulling off his shirt, "and I need to change." He put on an ordinary T-shirt, kicked off his shoes and put on sneakers instead, and replaced the *hajj* cap with a black, fez-like hat of the kind Muslims in Malaysia and Indonesia wore.

"So you're still posing as a Muslim, I see," said Karla.

"Right, but not the one who left the hotel. While you, of course—" he giggled uncomfortably "—are still one of my, uh, four wives."

Karla laughed. "I'd make your life such hell you'll be dying to say 'I divorce thee' three times."

Uqu smiled. "Well, I might as well enjoy being Muslim while I can. After all, I can look forward to those seventy-two virgins waiting for me in heaven."

"I wonder what the virgins think of that arrangement."

"I doubt anyone ever bothered to ask them their opinion."

"You'd be right about that," Karla said sourly. As she put the veil back on she asked him, "How long will I have to wear this?"

"I'm afraid you'll need to keep it on till we get where we'll be spending the night."

"And how long will that be?"

"Probably till sunset."

"Great," Karla groaned.

At that moment there was a knock on the door and one of the urchins poked his head into the room. "P'lis come wik-wik," he said. "Look b'long you."

"Police?" said Karla. "Is that what he said?"

The urchin looked at her strangely, and a hand flew to her mouth: she knew he'd recognized that, under her disguise, was some foreigner.

Uqu glared at her briefly; and spoke quickly to the urchin. The boy seemed to like whatever Uqu had said to him: he grinned broadly and stood straighter. When Uqu pushed a wad of notes into his hand, he looked like he would burst, and disappeared out the door.

"Come on," said Uqu. "And *keep quiet,*" he hissed.

"What did you ask him to do?"

"Create a diversion. Which won't be hard: no one here likes the police. Now, shush."

Karla followed close behind Uqu as he wound through the narrow, twisted alleyways. Behind her, she could hear shouts of "P'lis-p'lis, p'lis-p'lis," which were taken up around the shanties. People poured into the alleys clogging them, slowing their progress to a snail's pace.

*****

"WE DON'T HAVE MUCH time," Randolph Kydd said as he entered the committee room, smiling when he saw that everyone was present. "So, Tony, tell us what happened with Nimabi."

"Unfortunately," Royn said, shivering as he recalled the coldness that had fallen over his meeting with the Sandeman's foreign minister, a chill not caused by the air conditioning, "the short answer is nothing—yet. I raised all our concerns—"

"Conditions, you mean," said Cracken.

"Precisely," Royn nodded, "and he claimed they were all new to him."

"Which I doubt," said Bergstrom. "Our commanders have made our concerns about Sandeman troops' incompetence very clear to their counterparts up there."

"The only thing which was really new," said Royn, "was the lousy performance of their elite troops."

"Which he blamed on our training," Bergstrom said in disgust.

"Anyway," said Royn looking at the clock. "He promised to 'convey your concerns to his colleagues,' as he put it, and we'll meet again at five. But in my estimate, he doesn't want to agree to anything we want."

"I think you're right," said Cracken.

He's agreeing with me? Royn wasn't the only person in the room who looked at Cracken in surprise.

"Treasury has been investigating the Sandemans' finances," Cracken continued. "It's a total shambles. What's relevant here is that we've traced some of the millions of dollars people like Nimabi have been raking off the top and salting away in Swiss bank accounts and the like. My sense is the only thing Nimabi and his so-called 'colleagues' really give a damn about is preparing for their retirement in some luxurious bolt-hole, and if their country collapses around them, so be it."

"Their value-system . . . " said Royn, thinking of his sense of Nimabi when they met in the courtyard, "it's very different from ours."

"You're saying," Kydd rumbled, "that we've been mistaken in assuming their priorities and ours are the same: to stabilize the islands."

"That's what I'm coming to believe, Prime Minister," said Cracken.

"I want to see that report. Now."

"I can have a preliminary summary ready this afternoon."

Kydd nodded. "Good."

"So where does that leave us?" said Helen Arkness. "The real question is: are we going to send in more troops if we don't get concessions from the Sandemans? And if we don't send more troops, is our whole mission up there going to fall apart?"

"I couldn't have put it better, Helen," said Cracken.

"I have the feeling," Kydd rumbled, "that if we're not careful this could blow up in our faces. So cancel everything else you have for the rest of the day. After question time, we'll continue until we have very clear answers to Helen's well-put questions."

"And if the opposition tries to maul us in question time," asked Helen, "how will we respond, given that we have no ammunition to blast them with?"

"We'll fudge it, like we always do," Kydd growled.

*****

As Anthony Royn left for the Cabinet committee meeting, Alison McGuire checked her email. There, in a message from one of her Federal Police contacts, was the phone number of the senior Sydney policeman who was now in retirement. She recognized the area code: somewhere on the coast north of Sydney.

"Here goes," she said, picking up the phone.

And put the phone down again. *No tracks,* she remembered with a smile. *And I have to go to the bank.*

"I'll be back in an hour or so," she told Mary as she left the office.

Ten minutes away from Parliament House she found a payphone, and dialled the number.

"Am I speaking to Mr. Roger Kelly?" she asked when a man's voice answered.

"That's me. And who are you?"

"I'm—" Alison hesitated. *I guess I have no choice,* she thought. "I'm Alison McGuire, and I'm calling from Parliament House, in Canberra."

"Parliament House? What on earth for?"

"Well, Mr. Kelly, you'll recall that some twenty years ago, you agreed to talk to an Attorney-General's inquiry, but the inquiry wound down before you could be interviewed. I'm wondering if—"

"—if I'd answer some questions now? Is that what you're about to say?"

"Yes."

"Look lady, I don't know you from Eve—"

"You can easily check," Alison said.

"—but even if I did, I went fishing this morning. I want to go fishing tomorrow morning—and the morning after, and the morning after that. I *don't* want to go out to sea one day and end up as shark bait, you understand? So goodbye, and don't ever call back."

Alison held the phone's handset, staring at it in disbelief as it went dead. She thought of the hours she'd spent going through the files Sidney Royn had given her. *Just one lead, one decent lead in all those piles of paper—and he's slammed the door in my face.*

8 Fallout

IT TOOK FOREVER—OR so it felt to Karla—to make their way through the crowded alleys to the edge of the shanty-town. Her nervousness grew whenever she lost sight of Uqu, which happened frequently, and she wondered what she should do if she ever saw a soldier or a policeman heading towards her.

After a while she noticed that while the narrow paths were full of people, they were mostly children and teenagers. *Why aren't they in school?* she wondered. Most of the adults she could see were standing in doorways, peeking out nervously. She was dying to ask Uqu what was going on, but could see that, for whatever reason, no one here seemed to have any affection for the police.

They emerged into a narrow street bustling with vehicles belching black smoke, honking incessantly at the pedestrians and tricycles that never seemed in any hurry to get out of anyone's way. Uqu flagged down one of the tricycles and Karla gratefully squeezed into the narrow seat. As the driver pushed down on his pedals he grunted in surprise——*presumably,* Karla thought, *at my extra weight.* They crawled interminably through the slow traffic; despite the heat, Karla was thankful for the first time for the veil covering her face, which filtered out some of the ever-present exhaust fumes.

Eventually they arrived at a jetty, set midway between the airport and a power station with a tall chimney spewing fumes and coal dust into the air. Karla spent an uncomfortable ten or twenty minutes sitting on a bench, sweating in the full glare of the afternoon sun, while Uqu wandered up and down the jetty, negotiating with the dozens of boatmen who all tried to get his attention at once. "Hurry up," she murmured, nervously twitching every time she saw someone who looked like a policemen; anxiously listening for the sound of police sirens which she was sure would come at any moment.

At long last, Uqu waved her over to one of the boats. Unfortunately, it was one with no awning to shade the passengers. *I guess it's cheaper,* she thought. *No—if Olsson's paying, money's not a problem. This must be the kind of boat the locals use.* As if to confirm her guess, she saw a couple of tourists getting out of a covered boat.

Uqu indicated that Karla should sit in the front, which was thankfully at the other end of the boat from the noisy, belching engine. Uqu sat behind with the boatman, a respectable distance separating this supposedly devout Muslim woman from the strange man in the rear.

The boat, known locally as a *banca,* had a knife-like bow turned upwards from the long, narrow and open hull. On each side hung bamboo outriggers which acted as stabilizers, making the boat look like a trimaran. Depending on the wind or the direction they were travelling in, one of the outriggers dug into the water while the other lifted into the air.

The seat was nothing but a hard, narrow plank with nowhere to rest her back. Still, once they were out on the water, the steady sea breeze took the edge of the heat, and she welcomed the times when the bow smashed into a wave and cool seawater splashed over her. Occasionally, she could hear voices over the *chug-chug-chug* of the motor, but she didn't turn around to see what Uqu was doing.

THE SUN HAD SUNK nearly to the horizon by the time their *banca* pulled up on a deserted beach.

While Uqu paid off the boatman, Karla stood on the beach with her backpack and carry bag. As the boatman pushed off, Uqu began walking towards one end of the beach. Karla looked at him angrily; then, realizing the boatman could still see them, picked up her bags, resumed her hunched persona, and trudged slowly after him. When she reached the trees she saw Uqu sitting on a fallen log watching the boat chugging away.

"We can relax now," he said. "And you don't need to wear that any more."

Karla pulled off the black robes as fast as she could. As the sea breeze brushed her skin she stood tall, breathed deeply, and spread her arms wide. "Aah, that feels so good."

Uqu, she saw, was no longer wearing the fez. "What shall I do with this?" she asked, holding the bundle of black cloth at arm's length.

"Better keep it," said Uqu. "It might come in handy."

"Okay . . . but I hope I never have to wear it again."

Karla looked longingly at the surf lapping up on the beach. "I'd love to go for a swim."

"Tomorrow," said Uqu, looking at the angle of the sun. "It will be dark soon."

"Okay. . . . So tell me," she demanded, "what happened back there? Those yells of 'P'lis-p'lis, p'lis-p'lis'?"

Uqu laughed. "Simple," he said. "The police aren't welcome in the shanties, will only ever go in during the day—and only in pairs. Probably half of the people in the shanties are breaking the law if only in petty ways. Stalls that don't have a licence—all of them, I'd guess. Illegal stills; moonshine parlors—that sort of thing. So people love to crowd the alleys and make life difficult for the cops . . . and give whoever they're looking for a chance to get away."

"I see," she said. "Neat. But it sure slowed us down too." Karla shuddered at the memory. And her shoulders still ached from trying to keep her head down to the same level as the locals. "Never again, I hope."

She sat down on a thick tree root growing horizontally from the trunk. "Now where to?"

"There's a village a couple of kilometers that way," he said, pointing inland in the direction they'd walked. "But we're not going there. Five kilometers or so the other way—" he pointed towards the other end of the beach "—is another village. That's where we're going."

"You, Mr. Uqumagani," she said with a strange glitter in her eyes, "have a very devious mind."

"I do?" Uqu said, puzzled.

"Yes," said Karla, catching his eyes with hers, "you do. First, you walk into the hotel with a prominent bandage on your head. You walk out as a well-dressed Muslim who's been on the *hajj* with a Muslim lady in tow. When we leave the shanties you're yet again different—and we take a different path out. We ride a tricycle, not a more expensive taxi, just as a poor man from the shanties might. At the jetty, you spend time negotiating the best price, right?—" Uqu nodded "—and if anyone asks our boatman he tells them a Muslim couple went in that direction; but in fact two different people are going the other way. How am I doing so far?"

"It seems I am an open book to you," he smiled.

Karla shook her head. "I'm not so sure. I have the feeling I'm just beginning to sense the labyrinth of your mind."

"Labyrinth? Oh—maze." Uqu smiled happily. "That's a good description."

"Of the incomprehensible culture?"

Uqu nodded. "That sort of thing."

"So what kind of people are we from now on?"

"You're some kind of Australian tourist, and I'm your guide."

"Ah, good: we get to switch roles." Uqu's face went blank and Karla nodded understandingly. "Up to a point," she said.

"Right," Uqu smiled. "You have your camera, right? Can you hang it round your neck?"

"Okay. But if I'm a tourist, why am I trekking around in the boondocks instead of lazing on some pristine beach eyeing cute young guys like you?"

Uqu grinned and shrugged. "You're a crazy Aussie. To people here, that will go without saying."

"Okay," Karla said skeptically. "You're the expert."

"There's one thing we should do."

"What's that?" said Karla skeptically, noting the gleam in Uqu's eyes.

"Disguise you somehow."

"I'm still going to stand out."

Uqu nodded. "All I can think of is give you a haircut."

"What?" she said, her hands going to her head. "No you don't."

Uqu laughed. "Okay, but think about it," his voice taking a serious tone as he added, "and there's your name."

"What's wrong with my name?"

"Nothing. Except that every official and half the population are going to be looking for one Karla Preston. So it might be a good idea if you used a different name."

"Makes sense," said Karla. "How about . . . 'Katya'? I've always liked that name."

"Fine, but Katya who?"

"Hmm. Peters . . . Paddington . . . Pelham . . . "

"How about trying some other letter of the alphabet," Uqu suggested.

Karla nodded. "Good idea. . . . Okay, Horton. And if I'm asked to show an ID, what do I do then?"

"Nothing . . . provided you let *me* do all the talking."

"Okay," Karla nodded. "I've learnt my lesson."

"Good," said Uqu. Standing up he added, with a slight bow, "So, Miss Katya Horton, we'd better get going."

"Why did you choose this village?" Karla asked as they walked along the edge of beach, careful not to leave any footprints in the sand. "Do you know people here?"

"No," Uqu replied. "It's about as far as we could get today without arriving after dark. And the people here will be delighted to have visitors. I have some small gifts in this bag to repay their hospitality." Uqu stopped at the end of the beach. "Okay," he said, "I'm pretty sure that track leads to the village."

"And if it doesn't?"

"The village is right on a beach, so all we have to do is follow the coastline."

"Okay," Karla nodded.

"Follow me then," said Uqu. "And no more talking—just in case."

"Just in case of what?"

"Actually, wild pigs and snakes are the worst dangers here. But who knows? Maybe there are some guerrillas—or police—around."

"Now you tell me," said Karla.

With a last look at the pure white sandy beach and the sinking sun, she followed Uqu along the rough, narrow track into the gloomy, deepening shadows of the jungle ahead.

*****

"WHAT I'M TRYING TO impress on you, Abdullah," Royn said, clamping down on his rising anger and irritability, "is that the situation in the Sandemans has changed dramatically since we first came to your government's assistance."

"I'm afraid, Tony," Nimabi said coolly, "that I don't see how any of the fundamentals are any different."

Royn suppressed a sigh. *Seven o'clock already,* he noticed. The two hours they'd been meeting felt more like two days. To his right, along the long conference table, were ranged Victor Bergstrom and his staff who were all clearly irritated that nothing had yet been achieved. Aside from himself, he thought—and, perhaps, the Foreign Affairs department head, Kieran Fairchild—only Alison on his immediate left was doing a better job of keeping command of whatever she was feeling.

Or is she? he thought. On the other side of the table the Sandemans High Commissioner and Nimabi's staff seemed to spend most of their time casting side-long glances at Alison, the only woman at the meeting, as a way to relieve their boredom. Alison's aura of icy calm and her mechanical movements as she passed a paper to him might be more in reaction to the male looks than an expression of control.

"We have to consider the fallout from yesterday's attack on you," Royn said, a little more sharply than he'd intended. "You know what happened in question time." He wondered how much longer he could hold onto his diplomatic tone of voice. *King Lear was easier than this,* he thought.

"Yes," Nimabi said, with a faint smile. "You got mauled."

"Indeed. But more to the point, *why?* Because we've been supporting a government whose troops randomly kill innocent people and call them 'terrorists.'"

"That damn journalist—" Nimabi said angrily.

"She certainly blatantly contradicted your official press release, didn't she?" said Royn, knowing that what Nimabi was complaining about was that the truth had gotten out. "And do you know what we're asking ourselves now?"

Nimabi shook his head.

"How many of the other dead bodies your government claims were terrorists were actually innocent bystanders."

"I imagine there may have been the occasional one," Nimabi allowed.

"And how long do you think it will be before other people—like Australian journalists—start asking the same question?"

"We've managed to restrict their movements quite effectively," said Nimabi, "so they might ask—but they won't get any answers."

"Except for one, who seems to be roaming around freely at the moment."

"She'll eventually be found and deported," Nimabi said with an air of assurance that, somehow, made Royn feel even more uncomfortable.

"She happens to be a real and persistent pain in the neck, who is extraordinarily popular here. So it might be a . . . politic idea, Abdullah, if you remind your people they can't point to *her* body and claim she was a terrorist."

"The very idea," Nimabi protested. "You can't imagine we—"

"Of course not," said Royn with a conviction he didn't feel. "But I'm sure lots of other people would assume exactly that."

"I'll keep that in mind," Nimabi said icily.

"And then, there's the fallout from the discovery of oil off el-Bihar."

"The problems all lie at the Papuan's and Solomon Islands' doors, as you very well know, Tony. They're just trying to grab the riches that are rightfully *ours.*"

Tiny as it was compared to world oil production, the recently discovered oil field would in one fell swoop increase the Sandeman's GNP by fifty percent; royalties would *triple* the government's annual revenue and would (so the islanders believed) eliminate the country's unemployment problem almost overnight by providing thousands of high-paying jobs.

Suddenly courted by the world's oil majors, the Sandeman's government had auctioned dozens of exploration licences, and promised a "New Era" for the islands—and a "New Deal" for the islanders.

"Well," Royn said carefully, "the Papuans and Solomons have certainly put a spanner in the works—"

"Is that how you'd describe it?" Nimabi demanded, his underlying anger showing on his face for just a moment. "They're threatening our entire economy."

Two months ago, the government of neighboring Papua New Guinea claimed the oil fields extended into its territory, demanded a percentage of oil royalties, and sent one of its coastguard vessels to patrol what they claimed was the dividing line in the ocean between Papua New Guinea and the Sandeman Islands—a line several kilometers east of the one drawn on Sandeman maps. The next day, the Solomon Islands followed suit—even though the oil field was so far away from its territory the Solomon's claim was dubious at best. All exploration stopped, as did the construction of oil rigs and pipelines on the original field, as the oil companies waited to see how the dispute would be resolved.

"We don't believe," said Royn, "that either the Papuan or Solomons governments can be blamed for the fact that your government borrowed millions of dollars from the world's banks—at outrageous interest rates, I might add—on the promise of future oil revenues to fund massive new infrastructure projects."

"Ours is a very poor country, as you very well know. Our people deserve to benefit from our windfall as quickly as possible."

"I quite agree with you, Abdullah. And it's now a much poorer country, loaded with new debts it may not be able to repay—and you're asking us to come to your rescue."

"Mere temporary bridging finance, that's all we're asking for."

"As I've already pointed out, the view of our Treasury is that the best thing for the Sandemans to do is get the oil money flowing again by wrapping up negotiations with Papua New Guinea and the Solomons as quickly as possible."

"Well, you know our position on that," Nimabi said emphatically—Royn stifled a groan—"but I will certainly ask our Treasurer to study your proposal in detail."

"As you say, Abdullah," Royn shrugged. "But it does leave everything rather up in the air while your people—not to mention our soldiers—are the ones who are suffering."

"I realize that. Unfortunately, my hands are tied."

"Which brings me to the next issue: the el-Bihar Islanders are saying it's their oil—and demanding their 'fair share' of the monies."

"It's a national asset," Nimabi said gruffly.

"What I'm getting at, Abdullah, is different: namely, that oil is fuelling their separatist tendencies, and leading other outlying islands to follow suit."

"This is severely increasing the terrorist problem," Bergstrom interjected.

"Which is why we're asking for increased assistance."

"As we've made clear," said Bergstrom heatedly, "we're willing to provide that assistance, but only with the assurance of joint operational command of all forces in the Sandemans—"

"As a cover for Australian command," Nimabi protested. "We are an independent, sovereign government—"

"—a government that's bankrupt," said Bergstrom, glaring at Nimabi, "and depends on the Australian *voter* for its survival."

"Gentlemen, gentlemen." Royn said, trying to inject a note of calm he didn't really feel. "It's getting late, and I'm sure we're all rather tired. But Victor does have a point, Abdullah. It's really the Australian voter and taxpayer you and your colleagues have to consider. Right now, they're not in the mood to send more soldiers or more money to the Sandemans without some assurance they'll be used wisely."

"I hear you, Tony—but as I trust I've pointed out, there are some things we feel are too onerous for us to bear."

Royn nodded. "Yes, I can see that, Abdullah. But—" he smiled wryly "—our hands are also tied. We all live in the awareness that every three years we have to face the voters, and at this juncture there are certain courses of action which, we feel, would be electoral suicide."

"We all have those concerns to worry about," Nimabi said woodenly.

"I'd really appreciate if you could convey the intensity of our feelings on these concerns to your colleagues so that, one would trust, we can finalize these discussions as quickly as we can."

"I'll see what I can do, Tony. But I must say that at this juncture I'm really not in a position to make any promises."

"I understand."

"NIMABI DIDN'T GIVE AN inch," Royn muttered to Alison as they slowly walked back to their office.

"I wonder what or who they expect will bail them out?" she asked.

"You've read the Treasury report?"

Alison nodded. "Pretty gruesome reading."

"So it may be they're simply prepared to desert a sinking ship."

"Well, if Treasury's right, they certainly all have nice little nest eggs hidden away."

Royn opened the office door and ushered Alison through first. "Indeed they do," he said.

"Minister," Alison said quietly as they stepped into the outer office, "I need to talk to you."

"SO LET ME SEE if I've got this right."

Anthony Royn stood looming over Alison McGuire, glaring at her, clenching and unclenching his fists. "McKurn wants you to be his 'mole' so I *lose* the contest for party leadership to *Cracken* when Kydd retires. And if you don't agree, he'll destroy us both with that video he's got."

"Minister," Alison said softly, straightening up in her chair, "it's not *me* you should be angry with."

Royn looked down at his hands, noticed how close to her he was standing, and sheepishly took a step backwards. "Yes," he mumbled guiltily. "I suppose you're right."

He turned and walked unsteadily around his desk and collapsed in his chair. "Sorry," he groaned, his head in his hands. "As if it wasn't bad enough already—this must be the worst day of my life."

He looked up to see Alison nodding understandingly. "Pretty much," she agreed. "And yes, that's what McKurn told me."

"I didn't even know you knew Derek Olsson."

Alison smiled wistfully. "We met in high school, Minister."

"And you've been . . . lovers ever since?" Royn asked, feeling disoriented—and strangely disappointed. "I can't understand why you've never told me before—especially after he was arrested."

"I had no reason to mention it—and I haven't seen him for over a year."

"Oh, well—any more bad news I should know?"

"Only that I have to give McKurn my answer by Friday."

"Blimey. That's no time at all. And to think," Royn said angrily, "just one more step. . . . If I lost to Cracken in a fair fight, that would be bad enough. But to lose—no, to be *pushed out of the race*. . . . No," Royn said, shaking his fist. "No," he said more quietly, "we have to get McKurn before he gets us. That's what it boils down to."

"Yes," Alison agreed, "but how? So far, I seem to have hit a brick wall. There are still a few possibilities in your father's file—but I don't know how to follow them up. And I don't really have the skills or resources. We need an investigator of some kind—a private eye, perhaps."

"That sounds like a good idea," Royn said thoughtfully. "But the time—" He shook his head. "Wouldn't produce any results by Friday. But there's the legal angle." Royn leaned forward excitedly. "After all, it's blackmail. We could probably get an injunction, something like that. I'm pretty rusty on this aspect of the law. . . ."

"I don't know if that would work, Minister," Alison said with a shake of her head. "He could just put up the video anyway and claim someone else did it. God knows how many copies there are."

"Maybe," Royn conceded. "But I'll check. You never know what might be possible."

"I'd offer to resign, Minister . . . " Alison said in a rush, "if I thought it would be of any help."

"Resign?" Royn seemed astonished at the idea. "That would be admitting defeat. We haven't begun to fight yet, Alison. . . ."

"No, Minister, I'm not offering," said Alison, visibly relaxing at Royn's use of the word *we*. "If I quit, everyone would believe the drug connection was true."

"I thought you were serious for a moment," said Royn, visibly calming. "It's bad enough around here when you're on vacation."

Alison smiled, inclining her head at his implied compliment.

"How has McKurn survived all these years," Royn said, his voice barely louder than a whisper, "without being caught out?"

"If I knew that, Minister, we'd have the bastard."

Royn nodded, surprised at the sound of steel in Alison's voice, and at the violent way she slapped the edge of one hand into the palm of the other. "We'll find a way, Minister," she said, a hard edge to her voice. "You can't do whatever McKurn's been doing for fifty-odd years without leaving tracks somewhere."

"I suppose so." Royn's eyes narrowed as he studied her. "You've got something up your sleeve, I think."

Alison laughed hollowly. "Only breaking his neck. And right now," she added coldly, her voice menacing and her eyes hard, "I'd do just that—if I could get away with it."

"I think I'd join you—" Royn stopped in mid-sentence, feeling appalled as he relished the thought at the same time.

ROYN SAT BACK IN his chair, staring into space, thinking of the ruthlessness he'd never seen Alison exhibit before. *It was as if—for just a moment—she had turned into someone else,* he thought, *someone I don't know.*

He had to fight back. *How?* His mind wandered at the impossible question as he sank further back into the leather cushioning. His phone rang a couple of times. He ignored it. There was a knock on his door. He ignored that too.

Suddenly the division bell rang, signalling there was about to be a vote in the House and he had four minutes to get there.

"Blast," he said, pushing himself awkwardly to his feet. He walked quickly into his bathroom to see a ghostly reflection looking back at him in the mirror. Splashing water on his face he muttered, "That'll have to do."

"Your wife phoned Minister. Twice," Mary called out to him as he ran through the outer office and into the corridor towards the House. Mary couldn't tell whether Royn had even heard her.

Royn had no idea what the vote was about, and at that moment he didn't care. He joined the line of Members entering the House and simply followed the Party Whip's directions, returning to his office as quickly as he could. The other Members who said "Hi, Tony," or directed some comment at him were puzzled when Royn ignored them or merely vaguely nodded his head in their direction.

BACK BEHIND HIS DESK, Royn looked at the phone for a long moment before picking it up and dialling.

"Hi Mel," he said when the phone was answered.

"Tony," Melanie Royn's voice was edged with anger and suspicion. "I called and called. Mary said you were in your office—but you didn't answer. What on earth were you *doing?*"

"Digesting . . . trying to digest some awful news. Ghastly news."

"Uh-huh." Melanie's grunted comment was larded with skepticism.

"I really need to talk to you about it."

"Okay. I'm listening."

"Oh, Mel," Royn said despairingly, leaning into the phone as if that would bring them closer. "I—it's something—I wish you were here."

"Well I'm not! It will have to wait till Friday, then, won't it. That's when you're back home next, isn't it?"

"It can't wait. Mel . . . I was hoping you could fly up tomorrow—"

"You know I don't like Canberra."

"Please, Mel. I really need you."

"And I don't need you? All this time I'm here looking after the kids by myself. It's like they don't have a father any more."

Royn winced guiltily, as he always did whenever she reminded him of how much of his time he'd had to spend away from the family. At the same time, he felt an angry response rising within him: *"For heaven's sake Melanie, they're not kids any more—"*

But he stopped himself from speaking those words: the last thing he needed right now was another shouting match. "Oh, Mel," he said contritely, "I'm sorry—"

"You've said you're sorry. I don't know how many times you've said you're sorry. But you never *do* anything about it."

"Mel, that's hardly fair. . . ."

"Really? Anyway, tomorrow night is Zoë's parent and teacher night—another one you're going to miss. So there's no way I could go to Canberra, anyway."

Royn jerked back from the phone at the cool indifference in her voice. "Okay," he sighed, knowing he had to appease her, "you remember Senator McKurn?"

"How could I forget that bastard."

Royn thought of the time Melanie had first met McKurn, how she'd wrinkled her cute, turned-up nose in disgust and pulled her hand away from his a little more quickly than was polite.

"And you know that bastard, as you so aptly describe him, is backing Cracken against me—"

"Little Dick," Melanie interjected, using the nickname she'd given him in high school.

"—indeed," Royn smiled. "Well, he's blackmailing Alison in a way—"

"Fire her, then. I've always said she was trouble."

Really? Royn remembered the time, quite a few years ago now, when Melanie and Alison had been the best of friends.

"I wish it were that simple."

"And why isn't it?" Melanie demanded.

"Because McKurn is just using Alison as a way to get to me. And if he succeeds . . . I'll be booted out of politics. Laughed out. And Cracken will be the next Prime Minister."

"Surely not," she said. "Won't Kydd stop McKurn?"

"Kydd's loyalty runs only skin deep—"

"That's true," Melanie sighed.

"—and this is so devastating he'd freeze me out in a second."

"You'd better tell me all about it, then."

As Royn spoke he became more relaxed, feeling like they'd gone back in time, to the days when they'd been inseparable. As teenagers, they'd gone door-knocking, hand-in-hand, to help in his father's election campaigns. The first time he and Paul Cracken had battled, for the presidency of the Young Conservative Club at Melbourne Grammar School, Cracken, a "scholarship boy" literally from the other side of the tracks, had exaggerated his impoverished background and mocked Royn as a "Silver Spoon." When Melanie heard about it, she had breathlessly confided—to a bunch of Grammar School boys—that she had it on good authority from one of her girlfriends that Cracken was "woefully under-equipped in the . . . ah . . . nether regions."

Much to Cracken's annoyance, the nickname "Little Dick" spread around the school like wildfire. In the changing room, a few weeks after his crushing defeat, Royn saw that Melanie's information was dead wrong—and he'd realized she must have made it up on the spot.

He smiled at the memory; they'd been allies in *everything.*

When his father resigned from Parliament, it was she who'd masterminded his victory over Cracken for preselection. While Royn knocked on doors, spoke at meetings, phoned party members, and generally charmed as many people as he could, Melanie worked long hours to counter Cracken's unashamed branch-stacking, uncovered the dummy names he'd added to the party's rolls, and persuaded some key party functionaries to switch their support from Cracken to Royn.

Royn recalled fondly that being eight months pregnant—and so much sexier than usual—hadn't slowed her down one bit.

But then. . . . Their second son, Richard, decided to come into the world on polling day. So instead of being at her side, as he had been for the birth of their first son, Max, Royn was out on the hustings and didn't get to the hospital until thirty minutes after Richard was born.

"I see . . . " said Melanie when Royn had finished. "This is worse than any stunt Cracken ever pulled."

"Far worse," Royn agreed.

"I guess if you quit, the problem would go away—"

"But I'm so close . . . "

"I know," she sighed. The change in her tone of voice made Royn wonder whether, if he became Prime Minister, he'd end up living in the Prime Minister's Lodge alone.

"If you did," Melanie continued, uncertainty in her voice, "maybe we could have a life again. But to give into a scum like McKurn? No way. Quitting would be the coward's way out."

"Exactly my feeling."

"So, what are you going to do?" she asked.

"I'm going to fight."

"But—hang on. *Zoë!*" Melanie shouted, *"where on earth have you been? I'll have to go, Tony. Your daughter has no sense of time whatsoever. And God knows what she's been up to."*

"She's eighteen," Royn mused, "so she's probably up to the same things we were up to at her age." Royn smiled at the memory.

"That's what I'm worried about. Call me later."

"Melanie, I love you—" he said.

But the phone was dead.

*****

ALISON SAT HUNCHED ON her sofa, a near-empty glass of wine in her hand, idly watching TV. *It's still a dumb show,* she thought, *even with the sound turned off.*

She emptied the glass and looked at the bottle of wine sitting on the coffee table in front of her. *This isn't going to solve anything,* she chided herself. Shrugging, she poured the rest of the wine into her glass and took another sip.

Friday, she thought, eyeing the thick files of Sidney Royn's investigation stacked next to the wine bottle. *Nothing there . . . not now the cop turned me down. Three days to Friday—and what can I do? Just wait for the computer geek—"Mystery Man."*

She'd sent him a message when she got home—The money's gone—along with McKurn's and Cracken's phone numbers, and the other related information she could find. Shortly afterwards, she had a reply: got it i'm on it

Her laptop sat open on the dining table. She thought of checking again to see if there was another message. "What's the point?" she mumbled. "He's not going to solve my problem in a couple of hours. Probably not even in three days."

There must be something else I could be doing. But her mind felt like a blank slate.

She drained the wine from the glass in one long gulp. *Well,* she thought, *maybe I'll get a good night's sleep for a change.*

She let herself fall back into the soft cushions, feeling her exhaustion and tiredness, willing herself to give in to it. But it seemed the more she tried to relax, the tighter the knot of tension in her stomach became.

On the TV screen, a man looked lustfully at a girl. Alison sat upright. *Sometimes, men think with their penises. . . .*

She stood up and walked quickly, almost running, into her bedroom. It took her but a moment to find the sheer silk blouse she'd had in mind. *Perfect,* she thought.

She put it on and observed herself in the mirror, studying the blouse's effect. "You don't fight your opponent," she remembered her Aikido *Sensei* saying. "You don't resist. Instead, you help your opponent go wherever he wants to go, so *you* control where he ultimately ends up."

She gathered some of the silk fabric beneath her breasts, noticing how that emphasized their shape and prominence. *A little invisible mending will do it,* she thought with satisfaction.

"Okay, McKurn. . . ."

She straightened her posture, pulled her shoulders back, and smiled at her reflection in the mirror.

9 "Wish Me Luck..."

On the Run...
"For A While"
By Karla Preston
OlssonPress Syndicate Exclusive
Monday: **Somewhere in the Sandeman Islands**

I'm on the run.

This afternoon I slipped out of my hotel minutes ahead of soldiers and police who were about to drag me off to the airport and put me on the next plane back to Australia.

It seems the prime minister of this country and his cronies didn't like my story yesterday exposing his government's lies. So they decided to eliminate the source of their discomfort: me.

But no primped up, would-be dictator who believes freedom of the press might be okay so long as it doesn't happen on his watch—which is how this prime minister increasingly looks to me—is going to push me around.

I'll be okay, at least for a while—but I am worried about what might have happened to the other journalists here. This morning, we woke up to find our hotel surrounded by government troops. "For your own safety," we were told, no Australians were allowed out of the building.

Later, in the middle of being interviewed on News24/7, the phone connection suddenly went dead. We thought it must have been the phone company dropping the line. After all, this is the country where somebody once said that ninety percent of the people are waiting for a telephone, while the other ten percent are waiting for a dial tone.

It wasn't the local phone company this time. Nobody in the hotel could get a cellphone signal, the hotel's landlines didn't work, and no internet either. Maybe someone in authority here had been listening in and didn't like what I was telling you guys back in Oz—or maybe they were planning to do something else they didn't want any Australian journalists to know about.

Whatever the reason, I scarpered out of there PDQ (pretty-damn-quick), so I've no idea what happened to my colleagues. Maybe they're all still having a wild party in the hotel bar—or maybe the Australian government will have to send in our troops to rescue them from God knows what.

I can't say. All I can say is that if you haven't heard from anyone in the Sandemans in the last 24 hours, now you know why.

I was lucky to find a working internet connection—a rickety one that keeps cutting out—so I've no idea when (or, for that matter, how) I'll be filing my next report.

Till then I'll be out of touch "for a while" as they say in this country. Which basically means you'll have to wait anything from a minute or two till God knows when.

Meanwhile, wish me luck (I may need it)—and may your God go with you.

Alison gasped, imagining Karla Preston somewhere alone in a strange place where armed terrorists could be lurking anywhere in the shadows. *That woman has guts,* she thought admiringly.

At the same time, she was computing the story's likely political fallout, grimacing as she imagined how the press would leap on the news of one of their own being persecuted by a supposedly "friendly" government—as Australian soldiers were dying in its defence.

With a sigh she closed the newspaper, and immediately turned it over to hide the headlines. "I've had better days," she muttered, "and it's only eight o'clock."

She heard Royn's "Good morning, Mary," and looked up to see him coming towards her office with a big smile on his face. *Wait till he sees the papers,* she thought.

"Alison!" Royn strode into her office, bouncing with energy, pausing only to carefully close the door behind him.

"Remember that J&C report you gave me yesterday," Royn said as he sat down opposite her, leaning forward eagerly, "about this mysterious 'Candyman'? How about we persuade Bruce—" naming Bruce Spring who'd succeeded Royn as Minister for Justice and Customs "—to set up a task force to find out just who he is. We could use it as a cover to dig up stuff about McKurn. And wouldn't it be something to put that Candyman bastard out of business?"

"A wonderful idea. Shall I set up a meeting?"

"Please do," said Royn. "As soon as possible."

"I will. Now, sorry to spoil your mood," she said, turning the newspaper over to show him the front page, "but you'd better take a look at today's headlines."

**KYDD WAFFLES ON
SANDEMANS CRISIS
"We're having discussions"
INSIDE: Opposition wipes floor in Question Time**
One of the papers had a front-page editorial headlined:

**Democracy and Freedom?
Sandemans say "No thanks, not for us"**
"Holy cow. That's worse than I imagined it would be."

"It doesn't get better." Alison opened the paper to Karla's column. "You'd better read this. And today's editorials uniformly describe our stance as 'rudderless' and 'gutless,' and demand to know why we're letting the Sandemans get away with pillorying our journalists for telling the truth."

Royn groaned as he read Karla's column. "If anything happens to that Preston woman, we'll be crucified." A moment later he looked up and asked Alison, "Are the phone lines to the Sandemans still cut, do you know?"

"Yes," she answered. "I tried making a call this morning."

Royn leaned back in his chair, drumming his fingers on Alison's desk. "Okay," he sighed after a moment. "When we meet with Nimabi later this afternoon, I'm going to have to throw the book at him."

"But first, remember, you're chairing the foreign ministers' meeting this morning on the Sandemans' oil deadlock."

"I know," Royn groaned, "and I thought yesterday was a bad day."

"It's about to get even worse," Alison said as she handed him a thin file.

"How?" Royn gasped, his fingers gingerly taking the document as if it could turn out to be explosive.

"This is an early warning from the Attorney-General's department. One of the companies which paid for an exploration licence in the Sandemans will file a case this morning before an adjudicator in Singapore, to seek a refund of the money it paid the Sandemans, plus damages."

"Oh no." Royn flicked the folder open and began reading. "On what grounds?"

"The right term is 'fraudulent conveyance,' I think—the company is claiming the Sandemans sold them something they had no right to sell."

Royn nodded and moaned at the same time. "If the Sandemans loses that case," he said, looking up, "their position on the oil negotiations gets pretty much blown out of the water."

"And if the Treasury's right about their finances," Alison said, "where would they find the money if they have to pay the company back?"

*****

"A PRIVATE WORD, ABDULLAH, if you will, before we begin," Royn said, his arm gesturing behind his back to indicate that Alison and Doug Selkirk should go ahead into the conference room.

Royn had met Nimabi and his assistants at the entrance to Parliament House, and beyond Royn's cheery "Good afternoon, Abdullah," and the curt nod of Nimabi's head in reply, they walked along the corridors towards the conference room in stony silence.

Nimabi looked up slowly in reaction to Royn's words, his eyes narrowing in suspicion, his face a glowering stone mask. It was the same expression he'd worn when he'd walked out of the morning's negotiations: in what appeared to be a coordinated move, the Papuan and Solomon Islands foreign ministers had leapt on the Singapore case to harden their own demands, and deadlock turned into gridlock.

"A *private* word, if you would be so kind," Royn repeated softly, his face friendly but intense, when he noticed Nimabi's assistants standing behind them, waiting for instructions. Nimabi stared doubtfully at Royn, and then nodded his head. At an impatient wave of his hand, his assistants filed dutifully into the conference room.

"This Singapore business is very worrying, Abdullah," Royn said quietly, after he'd made sure the door was firmly shut. "Very worrying indeed . . . for us all."

"They'd have to get an order from a Sandemans' court to collect anything—if they win," Nimabi growled.

"Quite probably, I'm sure," said Royn, almost failing to keep his smile in place. "But the ramifications. . . . What I'd like to suggest you and your colleagues think about, Abdullah, is how crucially important it is for you to either win this case, or find some other way to bring it to an agreeable settlement."

"Settle? Never—"

Royn raised his hand. "Please hear me out, Abdullah. I'm not speaking as Minister for Foreign Affairs, but as a friend—a friend who is also a qualified lawyer. Much as I would like to, I really can't give you legal advice of any kind. But I do strongly urge you to get the very best legal counsel you can find, and carefully consider all the possible outcomes and implications . . . not just the legal ones, if you know what I mean. I wish I could say more, but. . . ."

"You've said—" Nimabi began, anger in his voice. And stopped as though it had taken him a moment to listen between Royn's words to appreciate their subtext. His face softened slightly as he nodded. "Thank you, Tony. I do understand."

"And one other thought, Abdullah."

Nimabi looked at Royn with a mixture of curiosity . . . and suspicion.

"Only when, or indeed, if you're ready, it might be a very . . . ah . . . diplomatic idea if your office were to suggest a resumption of this morning's negotiations in some neutral place like . . . oh, say . . . Singapore. That way you could, potentially, kill two birds with one stone."

After a moment Nimabi replied, "As you say, Tony . . . if. . . ."

"Quite," Royn nodded. "And we never had this discussion," Royn added with a grin.

Nimabi nodded but did not return the grin. "Mutual deniability."

"Quite." Royn opened the door of the conference room, standing back to allow Nimabi to enter first. "Shall we . . . ?"

NIMABI'S HEAD DIPPED A millimeter or two as his eyes stopped on Bergstrom's face; but he came to a halt and frowned when he saw Paul Cracken at the table. He turned towards Royn, his glowering mask back in place.

"I invited Paul along at the last minute," Royn said quickly, "since finance is one of the topics for discussion."

When Nimabi looked at Royn skeptically he turned to Alison and said sharply, "Alison! I'd asked you to talk to the Foreign Minister's assistant about this—" As Royn spoke, he turned his head towards Alison and, with the eye hidden from Nimabi and his associates, slowly winked.

"Oh yes, Minister," Alison burbled as she caught Royn's hint. "I called and couldn't get through, and then—" she bowed her head in mock shame "—I forgot."

Royn felt like applauding her performance—and laughing at the same time at the thought that Alison, who had a memory like an elephant, had forgotten a thing.

"My apologies, Abdullah," Royn said to Nimabi as they both took their seats. Nimabi just nodded, seeming mollified.

Royn had been nervous when he asked Cracken to join the meeting. "Paul, just remember to be diplomatic—if you can," he'd said. "You think you're the *only* one who can put on an act?" Cracken had snapped in reply.

To Royn's surprise, Cracken followed his lead, keeping his mouth shut while, for almost an hour, Royn and Nimabi, with an occasional comment from Bergstrom, did little more than calmly restate their positions of the day before. The only difference, Royn thought, was that with Cracken and a couple of members of his staff also at the table, the room felt rather crowded.

Royn could feel Cracken's growing impatience as it became increasingly clear—although not stated it in so many words—that neither side was willing to concede an inch to the other.

When Alison passed him a note, Time to break the log-jam?, Royn realized he'd been repeating himself. He paused to gather his thoughts. He felt like saying to Nimabi: *Wake up, for heaven's sake. The worst thing that could happen to us is that we lose the next election. But you and your precious prime minister could be strung up on lampposts.*

Instead, Royn said, "Here's something I think you should take a look at, Abdullah," and pushed a sheet of paper across the conference table. "These are figures taken from our Treasury's analysis of the Sandemans' finances."

Nimabi studied it carefully, and then looked up. "I don't see the significance of these numbers," he said coldly, "or how they relate to our discussions today."

But, Royn noticed, a look of concern crossed the Sandeman high ommissioner's face as he Nimabi's other associates craned their eyes to look at the paper. Nimabi scowled at them and flipped the sheet over.

"If I may, Tony," said Paul Cracken.

"Of course," said Royn, leaning back in his chair.

"As you can see, Minister," Cracken was saying, "the numbers show the oil companies paid over a million dollars *more* in licence fees, according to their accounts, than your government *received,* according to your Treasury's records. Quite a discrepancy."

To Royn's ear, Cracken's tone was hardly soothing, sounding brittle like a schoolteacher instructing an errant student. But perhaps, he reflected as he watched Nimabi for signs of a reaction, that was just his own, almost Pavlovian response to his rival's voice.

"What's the point of all this?" Nimabi demanded. "You can't hold *us* responsible for an oil company's accounting mistakes."

"I'm sure you're aware, Minister," said Cracken, "of the severe penalties Western governments like ours have enacted for company officers who file inaccurate information. So we're quite satisfied the company figures are correct. It's not as though these numbers are estimates: they wrote you cheques, after all."

Nimabi shrugged. "No doubt our Treasury figures are preliminary, or something."

"That's what we thought at first," said Cracken, now with a smile on his face. "But it seems the monies actually received in the Sandeman government's bank accounts match the oil companies' figures. . . ."

"There you are," said Nimabi with obvious relief. "Quite obviously a mistake."

"I'm afraid, Minister," said Cracken—who, Royn thought, seemed to be clearly enjoying himself—"this is hardly the first time this kind of discrepancy has appeared when your Treasury is accounting for international receipts."

"What do you mean?" said Nimabi, now showing signs of anxiety. "And how could you know?" He suddenly rose to his feet. "You've been sending spies into our country?" he said angrily. "That's *unconscionable.*"

Royn braced himself for Cracken to leap to his feet and respond to Nimabi in kind— or for Nimabi to simply walk out, as he had done this morning. But Royn noticed that Nimabi's fingers were nervously clutching the list of figures as if it were a chain holding him in place. Cracken merely tilted his head back to look Nimabi calmly in the eye, saying, "Not at all, Minister. The very thought." Cracken shook his head in disbelief— and Royn chuckled quietly to himself: *So I'm not the only one who can put on an act.*

"It's simple. The world's anti-money laundering laws," Cracken continued, "make just about everybody's bank account an open book—if you receive cooperation from the American, British and other authorities, as we usually do. So we can see the actual amounts wired into your accounts, and where they came from."

"Well," said Nimabi uncomfortably, slowly settling back into his seat, "I suggest you should take up this is a matter with our Treasurer rather than with me."

"Perhaps," said Cracken. "We'd certainly appreciate if you'd pass this information on to him. But," he added, taking another sheet of paper from the file, "your Treasury has also been making payments which don't seem to be reflected in the government accounts."

"We don't have the resources," said Nimabi frostily, "you have available within your Treasury department. Such errors are quite understandable."

"Except this list of . . . ah . . . errors is rather unusual," said Cracken, "Significant payments to bank accounts in places like Switzerland, the Cayman Islands, Bermuda, and similar places. Payments that have been going on for many years."

"I have no doubt our Treasurer will be happy to explain what these were all for," said Nimabi shrugging nonchalantly, an effect, Royn noticed, that was undercut by the way he briefly glared at Cracken before he could bring his expression under control. And where Nimabi's self-control was almost iron-clad, Royn could see that the junior members of his staff, ranged to Nimabi's right and left, looked puzzled, worried, and were whispering to each other.

"Though I hardly see," Nimabi said, giving his associates such a fierce glare that they did their best to turn into wooden statues, "what business it is of yours."

"Abdullah," said Royn gently, a look of compassion on his face directed towards Nimabi, "I've been through this report. There's more, and it's very worrying. One aspect, however, you may not appreciate."

Nimabi looked at Royn suspiciously. "What could that be?" he demanded.

"The danger is that someone in our Treasury department, or someone else who's seen the report, might believe—erroneously of course—that this information deserves a wider public."

"Are you threatening me?" Nimabi asked angrily.

"Threatening you, Abdullah?" Royn projected an air of being misunderstood. "Most certainly not. This hazard, unfortunate and illegal as it is, is one of the problems we face in a democracy such as ours. If that were to happen. . . ." Royn shook his head sadly, and paused.

"Yes," said Nimabi, "it would be very . . . unfortunate."

"Very," Royn agreed. "For all of us."

Bergstrom, who'd kept his counsel for the most of the meeting, broke the short silence. "If I may make a suggestion."

"Please do, Victor," said Royn.

"Paul, you could classify this report at the highest level. Numbered copies, that sort of thing. Then, if any of this report were leaked, it would be easy to find out who did it. And under the Crimes Act, the penalties for divulging classified information are far more severe."

"Yes," said Cracken, "I suppose we could. . . ."

"That," said Nimabi, "sounds like a very good idea."

"I agree," said Royn.

"It would, however," Cracken said doubtfully, "be very unusual to classify such a routine document."

"But it could be done," Nimabi said anxiously.

"I'm sure it could be done," said Cracken. "But I'll have to check with my head of department first."

Nimabi looked at Cracken skeptically and nodded slowly.

"I see it's time for dinner," said Royn. So, with your agreement Abdullah, could we adjourn at this point, and reconvene tomorrow? Hopefully, then, we could wrap everything up."

Nimabi's eyes flicked from Royn, to Cracken, to Bergstrom, and back. After a moment he nodded. "Okay," he said sourly.

"I'D COUNTED ABDULLAH AS a friend," said Royn sadly as he, Alison and his department head, Kieran Fairchild, left the meeting. "As much of a friend as you can have in this line of work."

"Yes," said Alison in a neutral voice, "but something had to be done."

"I know," Royn sighed. "I just wish it could have been done by someone else. Quite likely, we—I've now turned Nimabi and maybe the whole Sandemans cabinet into enemies."

"Were they really our friends to begin with?" Alison asked. "Or just fair-weather friends?"

Royn sighed again. "Probably the latter."

Alison nodded. "And Minister, tomorrow I bet he'll agree to everything. But when it comes to implementation . . . the people up in the Sandemans will prove highly uncooperative, managing to find countless obstacles that just can't be easily overcome."

"And if you're right," said Royn uncomfortably, "we'll be left holding the ball—with more Australian boys' lives at stake."

10   "Value Added"

"CAN WE STOP HERE?" Karla asked. "That's the most beautiful beach I've ever seen—but what happened to it?" The beach was a gentle, extended crescent-shaped arc of pure, white sand, nearly a kilometer wide. It was protected, at the two tips of the crescent, by rocky promontories jutting into to sea.

Uqu spoke to the boatman and the *banca* chugged towards the shore, rising and falling with the swell. Karla saw waves racing to shore to crash with a loud roar and an eruption of spray at the far end of the beach, while nearby the waves lapped gently on the shimmering sand. The *banca* turned its nose towards the calmer end of the beach, sheltered by one of the peninsulas from the raging seas, Karla could imagine little children playing happily in the gentle swell while exhilarated surfers slalomed to shore towards the other point of the sandy arc.

"This is amazing," Karla shouted into the whistle of the wind.

Gripping the *banca*'s bow for support she rose to her feet and leaned into the wind. Her hair, now bleached blond at Uqu's insistence, with a few strands of grey to make her look older, blew around her face; her body swayed in time to the *banca*'s rocking motion.

Her gaze roved in delighted wonder from the spray-kissed rocks at one end, across nearly a kilometer of unbroken sand to a ring of low jungle-covered hills, and along the white crescent to its center, where her eyes came to an abrupt halt.

In the dead center of the beach stood a derelict construction site: ugly concrete pillars, some blackened and broken, poked from the ground, bent and rusted metal rods protruding from their ends.

As she slowly fell back to the bench, she turned to ask Uqu, "Who would desecrate such a wonderful place with an ugly building like that?"

"An Australian resort company, as it happens," Uqu said, "in partnership with some local interests—all fronts for politicians. It was going to be a multi-storey hotel."

"But . . . will it be finished? Not that I'm complaining."

"El-Bihar Islanders are nearly all Muslims. They protested at having an establishment serving alcohol with semi-naked Western women cavorting in bikinis on their territory. They boycotted the site, and wouldn't let any local people work on it."

"But surely, the people here need jobs, don't they?" Karla asked as the *banca* came to rest on the sand of Jazeerat el-Bihar with a soft thump.

Uqu smiled. "Actually, not so many Bihar islanders," Uqu said as he helped Karla down from the boat.

Karla pulled off her boots and flopped down on the sand. "This is wonderful," she said, stretching her arms and legs and wriggling to imprint the shape of her body in the sand, relaxing with a loud "Aaaah," as she felt supported at every point. "But surely—"

she lazily waved her hand to indicate the lush greenery behind her "—there's no industry here. And surely they don't grow spices any more."

"You'll see soon enough," Uqu said with a knowing smile.

Karla's eyes narrowed, and then she laughed. Lying back spread-eagled on the soft sand she chuckled, "Have it your way, then, Mr. Mysterious. Okay . . . but there must be plenty of people from the other islands who'd be happy to work here."

"Indeed," said Uqu, squatting down beside her. "So the Muslims organized, drove them away, sabotaged equipment, and raised a stink in Parliament. One of the project's sponsors was Abdullah Nimabi, whose constituency is right here. I think the decisive factor in stopping the project was that Nimabi would have lost his seat at the next election if he hadn't withdrawn his support."

"So are those ugly concrete blocks just going to sit there till they fall apart?"

"Inshallah," Uqu said with a smile. "The Australians sold out to a company from Dubai, which pledged to turn it into an alcohol- and bikini-free Muslim resort, and a Dubai airline even promised to fly into Toribaya. That got everyone excited . . . until the majority, mostly Catholics, realized the islands would be crawling with Arabs and women in black. So its ultimate fate is still up in the air."

"Don't Muslim women wear burqas here?"

"Only a few. Most just wear a scarf covering their hair—a gaily colored one at that. And some don't even go that far. Islam here is nothing like it is in Saudi Arabia. Though," Uqu added sourly, "that's beginning to change."

"I see," she said thoughtfully.

Karla wiped the sweat from her forehead. She was all too aware of the almost intense heat of the afternoon sun, and the way every bone and muscle in her body seemed to ache from their long journey.

For three days and three nights, Karla had played tourist, island-hopping by *banca* and ferry along the coral atolls of the Sandeman Reef stretching the full length of the southern side of the islands. They'd avoided the resorts dotting the atolls, stopping at tiny villages where they were welcomed and fêted with banquets of blackened or roasted freshly caught fish, cooked on the sand. Tiny villages where, it seemed, *tingi* were met with shrugs of incomprehension, while the villagers eagerly accepted the gifts Uqu had brought: candies, chocolates, mirrors, needles, thread, and the like.

In the mornings they'd waken, like the villagers, with the sunrise. At dawn, it was blessedly cool, but the sun appeared all too quickly over the horizon and, even at that early hour it felt like a ball of fire focused on *her*. In just an hour or two, she'd be sweating even while standing in shade—and she was all too aware that every item of the few clothes she'd been able to carry were now sodden with sweat, salt-spray, or both. She'd washed herself, awkwardly, standing by a barrel and splashing herself with scoops of cool water; each night she'd fallen into an exhausted sleep on a thin reed mat on a hard dirt floor. She was a spoiled Westerner, she thought, taking for granted luxuries the happy, smiling villagers had never even heard of—smiling people who didn't even seem to know they were poor. Despite the warm, carefree hospitality she'd never experienced before, there were moments when she longed for a piping hot shower, a thick, juicy steak, clean, crisp clothes—and a very soft bed.

As there was no awning on the *banca* they'd hired for the last stage of their journey, after five hours sitting on a hard bench in the hot sun she felt bleached, patches of her skin were bright red, and her hair had become so dry she imagined strands would just break off. She sat up and looked longingly at the waves lapping onto the sand. "I've got to go for a swim," she said.

"Um . . ." Uqu stood up and looked around. "Well," he said doubtfully, "there's no one in sight. . . ."

"Oh—no bikinis?"

"Right."

"That's all I've got," she shrugged, standing to get her backpack from the *banca*.

"I think," said Uqu carefully, "it would be a good idea to respect the islanders' sensibilities—for your own safety."

"But there's no one around."

"Not now. But that could change at any time.

Karla nodded, and smiled. "I hate being told what to do . . . but you make your point. I'll wear a T-shirt then, okay?"

"That would do it. And tomorrow," said Uqu looking at his watch, "will be Friday. . . ."

"Friday? I've completely lost track of time. . . . Tomorrow?"—Karla squinted at Uqu, a question in her eyes—"What do you mean by that?"

"It will be the Muslim day of prayer—their Sabbath. We should lie low so we don't unwittingly offend anyone."

"I see. I could spend the whole day here."

"A good idea." Uqu nodded, and rose to his feet to pay off the *banca* still sitting on the beach. "And Inkaya, the village where we're heading, is just over the ridge," he said, pointing to where a track cut through the tangled jungle. "We could walk there in half-an-hour if you like."

"Sure. I could use the exercise."

From the top of the rise they could look down the small village of Inkaya nestling by the ocean—a scattering of thatched or tin roofs and quite a few larger buildings, one shining whitely through the trees. Beyond it was a long pier, crowded with *bancas*, a couple of larger vessels, fishing boats Karla thought, were tied up at the end. A sea of green carpeted the hillside down to the water's edge.

As they walked down the gentle slope Karla saw women working in the forest of shrubs covering the slope right and left. They wore scarves, long skirts, and loose blouses which covered their arms to their wrists, and were pulling leaves from the shrubs, piling them into wide wicker baskets. As the baskets filled, men brought empty ones and dragged the full ones down towards the village. The women looked at her with interest, as did the men they passed on the path—except their looks were tinged with suspicion.

"Those shrubs look familiar," Karla said, going up to one taller than she was, and smelling it. "I've seen it before—or maybe a picture—but I can't remember what it's called."

She turned to see Uqu smiling at her.

"*Ganja,*" he said.

"Marijuana?"

"Right. That's why so few of the islanders were interested in working on a construction site. And that's what makes el-Bihar Island the richest place in the Sandemans."

"I see. And they sell it—"

"—in Australia—"

"—of course. I bet I've had some of it myself."

She looked around again with renewed interest, noticing the shrubs were planted in between much taller trees. "I see," she said. "It would be hard to spot from the air, but it's not hidden from close scrutiny. So I bet this is the real reason the locals didn't want that hotel on their island."

Uqu just smiled.

"But surely, all this," she said, waving at the marijuana plants stretching as far as the eye could see, "can't be a secret from the locals."

"Of course not," said Uqu. "Everybody knows—and everybody benefits."

"Everybody? On the island?"

"And everybody in power."

"*Everybody . . . ?*" Karla held up her hand before Uqu could speak. "I'm beginning to believe the picture you're painting."

As they came nearer to the village the wide track made a dog-leg. Beyond it was a clearing with two large structures, partially shaded by large, drooping trees. The roofs of both were made of tin and covered with camouflage-style netting. One had no walls, like a large gazebo, and the space under the shelter was filled with leaves all the way to the ceiling, hanging out to dry. Men and women were busy adding the newly harvested leaves from the baskets. The other building was enclosed, with air-conditioners poking through the walls, the sound of a diesel engine fracturing the natural sounds of the jungle. The smell of marijuana hung heavily in the air. "What's in there?" she asked. "The smoking room?"

Uqu laughed. "That's the hash factory, and where they press the marijuana into blocks and wrap it for shipment. This is the main industry on el-Bihar, and making hashish and hash oil is 'value added,' as economists would say. Many more dollars per kilo shipped."

"I presume all this is highly illegal."

"Not exactly. It's a grey area of the law," said Uqu. "But, anyway, in the Sandemans, laws are made to be broken."

"What do you mean by that?"

"*No one* would work for the government just for the salaries they get."

Karla's mouth fell open. "I'm being a bit slow on the uptake . . . I shouldn't really be surprised by now, should I?"

Uqu smiled.

"I'd love to look in there," Karla said, pointing at the hashish factory.

"They might let you—if they trust you to keep your word."

"Of course I will," Karla protested. "I don't see anything wrong with what they're doing. But the moment the Australian government got wind of this they'd have crop-dusters up here spraying weed-killer everywhere. They'd destroy el-Bihar's economy completely."

"Which is why they want to keep it quiet for as long as they can."

A hundred or so meters further along the path they came to the outskirts of the village. Men and women alike looked at Karla curiously as she passed; and as they walked on towards the village square, she felt like the Pied Piper as a growing number of small children followed her excitedly.

Inkaya looked more affluent than the villages where they'd spent the last three nights, but otherwise not too different. The houses, even those with walls of logs and roofs of thatch, were better built, and here and there were some made of concrete. Unlike the other villages, nearly all had a TV aerial bolted to the roof. The main path—hardly a street—was wide, but just grass and dirt that would surely turn into mud when it rained.

They stopped at the edge of the village square, a wide-open expanse of trimmed grass dotted with a few large trees and benches, with one corner given over to colorful playground equipment which looked brand new. On one side was a shining, domed building made of white stone. "That's the mosque," said Uqu. "Partially financed with Saudi money. And over opposite us is the school." Uqu pointed to several wooden buildings, some large, some small, and Karla became aware of the sound of children's voices drifting across the square.

"A vast improvement," Karla said. "Schools" in some of the other villages were little more than a teacher standing under a thatched roof with no walls.

"It's the best-equipped school in the country, outside of Toribaya," Uqu said.

He led the way to the other side of the square, to a large, open roofed-over area with lots of tables and chairs and several small stalls along the sides offering different foods and drinks. In the center, a group of older men sat around a table chatting, drinking tea, and smoking, and Karla breathed in an aroma that was a mixture of cigarette smoke and *ganja*—and a fainter smell of fish wafting from the pier.

"Well, there are certainly some things I like about this place," Karla smiled. "Not Amsterdam, perhaps—but way cheaper, I'm sure."

As they walked towards the open area Uqu said, "In a moment, I'll introduce you to Inkaya's headman. His name is Tungi. He speaks some English. And you should address him as Tungi-*ga*."

"'Ga'?"

"It's is like 'sir' in English. The feminine is *'gaat'.*"

Uqu signalled Karla to wait and went up to the men and said a few words. One of the oldest stood up, and when he smiled at Karla she could see he had only three front teeth, all black. She smiled back sensing that, despite the way he shambled slightly as he walked towards her, he was a man of authority used to receiving respect.

"Ah, 'Orton-*gaat*," he said, dipping his head in a slight bow, "our village welcome you."

"Tungi-*ga*," she said, inclining her head in return at Uqu's silent urging. "Thank you. I'm pleased to be here."

A loud, angry voice came from the other side of the village square. A slight young man wearing white robes strode out of the mosque. Karla realized he was glaring at her bare arms and legs, her uncovered hair, and her prominent breasts. Behind him, she could see two heads covered in black peering out from behind the door.

The chatter of the old men ceased, the smiles disappearing from their faces. The village headman turned and said something sternly to the young man.

"Who is he?" Karla asked Uqu.

"If he's who I think he is, his name is Gurundi—and he's probably the most dangerous man in the country."

"Him?" Karla asked in surprise. *He's hardly more than a boy . . . with two chips on each shoulder.* The young man waved his hands in emphasis; his stick-like arms, so thin as though tendons without muscles held his bones together, were briefly outlined in the long sleeves of his robe. "But he looks so—so frail. So weak."

Uqu nodded. "Too many people underestimate his potential, just as you have."

Karla shook her head. "And what's the headman saying to him?" she asked.

"That we—and you in particular—are honored guests, protected by Allah in the Muslim tradition. And he'd better watch his step. But I wouldn't trust him one inch."

11   Murphy's Law

"WHAT'S REALLY GOING ON in Sandemans?"
Alison, who'd been thinking what a good job the seamstress had done as she fastened the last button of her silk blouse, turned up the TV's volume. She recognized Robin Cartwright, from the *Melbourne Examiner*, next to the familiar face of Rowena Watson, host of the morning talk show *Good Morning Australia*.

He's in the studio, she realized. *I thought he was in Toribaya.*

"The fact is, we don't really know," Cartwright was saying.

"But you were on the spot—"

"Yes and no. We've been pretty much confined to the hotel and treated like mushrooms: kept in the dark and fed manure."

"Meaning . . . ?"

"—we get official press releases, which are about as informative as toilet paper and half as useful. The government up there is trying to freeze us out, to impose a news blackout. The people I used to be able to squeeze a little information out of just won't talk to me any more. The Aussie soldiers would give us some of the lowdown on the side—unofficially, of course. But since Sunday's attack they've clammed up tighter than a gnat's arsehole."

"Mr. *Cartwright*," said Rowena. "This is a family program."

"Sorry," Cartwright grinned, winking at the camera.

"But there is one journalist on the loose up there somewhere, right? Karla Preston."

"Right," Cartwright nodded, his face turning serious. "Yesterday I learned the Sandeman government has ordered its soldiers to find her and bring her in. I figured it was safer for me to be here when I broke the news."

"Why is that?"

"Simple. Our hotel was placed under martial law and surrounded by trigger-happy soldiers with submachine guns. This news will drive them crazy, so I didn't want to file the story from up there."

"What do you think will happen to Karla Preston now?"

"I'm not sure," Cartwright said gravely. "But you know what happened last Sunday so I, for one, wouldn't want to be in Karla's shoes when the Sandeman soldiers catch up with her."

"Nor would I," said Rowena, shuddering as she turned to face the camera. "We'll be right back in a moment. . . ."

Half-dressed, Alison sat shakily on the bed and hit the mute button as the program went to a commercial break.

"My God," she breathed, wondering if anyone in the Sandeman government cared whether Karla Preston was captured dead or alive. *It looks like our deal with Nimabi is already unravelling,* she thought, *and it's only two days old.*

She thought furiously, and picked up her cellphone. "Doug?" she said, when Royn's press secretary answered. "Have you got your TV on?"

"You mean Cartwright?"

"Exactly. There's going to be hell to pay."

"I'll be on my way in about ten minutes."

"See you there. I'll call Justin."

She punched another number. When Victor Bergstrom's PA, Justin McWinter, answered grumpily, she said curtly, "You'd better turn on *Good Morning Australia* right now."

"Alison?" he said sleepily. "Why?"

"Just do it, Justin. Sandeman soldiers have been sent to find Karla Preston and bring her in. What should we do, if anything? We have to come up with some options for our ministers pretty damn quick."

"We're getting situation reports from TV now?"

"It seems your sources up there leave a lot to be desired."

"Our sources . . . ?"

"Justin, I suggest you get to your office in about ten minutes. I imagine your minister will be pretty pissed off with you if you don't have your head around this issue by the time he arrives."

"I suppose you have a point—if this journalist can be trusted."

"Justin!" said Alison, finally losing her patience. "That's something you'd better be in a position to tell him." She irritably punched END CALL and, seeing that Cartwright was talking again, turned up the TV.

". . . hard for Westerners to really understand what countries like the Sandemans are like. So, Rowena, let me ask you a question."

"I'm supposed to be the interviewer," she said with a smile.

Cartwright grinned. "Where were you born?" he asked.

"Here in Sydney."

"So, do you think of yourself as a Sydney-sider first, or an Australian first?"

"Australian, of course," Rowena said.

"Of course," said Cartwright, nodding. "In the Sandemans, it's the other way around. And you know the old joke, first prize is a week in Melbourne, second prize is two weeks . . . ?"

Rowena Watson laughed as she nodded.

"In the Sandemans they mean it. It's like . . . " Cartwright groped for words. "If we were Sandeman Islanders we'd hate, or at least despise each other just because you're from Sydney and I'm from Melbourne."

Rowena shook her head. "You're pulling my leg! That makes no sense."

"No to us. But it does to them. The Sandemans isn't really a country at all but a bunch of warring clans and tribes. Another question: if somebody wanted to get rich, what would you recommend they do?"

"Oh, become a doctor or a lawyer, or start a business."

"How about a career in government?"

"Don't be ridiculous," Rowena said.

"I assure you, Rowena, I'm deadly serious. The Sandemans is one of the most corrupt countries on earth. That means bribery. You get pulled over by a cop, you give him about a dollar and he forgets to write the ticket. The cops come to arrest you—pay them enough and they go away. You want to build a house, start a business, even register your car or get a passport . . . *every* permit or licence needs a payment under the table. Government contracts don't go to the lowest bidder but to the contractor who kicks back the most money. A courtroom isn't a place where justice is done, or even seen to be done, but a bidding war between the contestants which is won by the person who pays more to the judge. And getting elected is like winning the lottery. Since they auctioned off all those oil exploration licences, the traffic there has slowed to almost a halt with all the new BMWs, Audis, Jaguars and the like clogging the roads—driven by politicians and senior bureaucrats."

"Even the prime minister?"

"Ah yes," Cartwright smiled broadly. "Aruma Bagambi. That old devil has a garage full of them: BMWs, Cadillacs—even a Ferrari. There's nowhere in the whole godforsaken country where you can drive a Ferrari fast enough to get out of third gear. How on earth can you afford a Ferrari on a salary of about twenty thousand dollars a year?"

"You just can't."

"Of course not, if that's your only source of cash. We Westerners naïvely go into places like the Sandemans—or Vietnam or Iraq—and think that because they have a parliament, police, and law courts, their society is pretty much like ours." Cartwright shook his head. "They're not. They might be wearing clothes that look like ours, but they're not even made of the same fabric. So we always end up making a pig's breakfast of things."

"It's hard to imagine. . . ." said Rowena.

"That's right—which is why we keep on screwing up."

Rowena Watson seemed at a loss for words, but recovered almost instantly. "Thank you Robin." As she spoke, the camera moved into a close-up. "Derek Olsson's murder trial starts today. Is he guilty, as everyone seems to think? And if he is, what's his motive? More after the break. . . ."

Derek, Alison thought, *if only I could be there. . . .* She shook her head. *I'll send him a message through Ross,* she decided, and after a moment's hesitation flicked the TV off. *Got to get moving. . . .*

*****

ANTHONY ROYN UNLOCKED THE main door to his office, unable to recall the last time he'd arrived before anyone else.

He was up early not because he was full of energy and raring to go, but for the exact opposite reason: he'd tossed and turned all night long and gave up trying to get to sleep before the sun rose.

He made himself an extra-strong cup of coffee and sat at his desk waiting for the caffeine to hit. He gazed blankly at his diary to remind himself of what he had to do today, but his thoughts kept returning to McKurn . . . and Melanie. *The only good thing about today,* he thought, *is that it's Friday, and I'll be flying back home to Melbourne tonight . . . and Melanie.*

His eyes locked longingly on a picture of Melanie set prominently on his desk, her face lit with a brilliant smile, directed at him as he'd taken the shot . . . some twenty years ago.

But his thoughts returned to the question, *How is Alison going to answer McKurn's so-called proposition?* He groaned. That had been their incessant topic of conversation for the whole week, and they still had no lever to fight back with.

Perhaps the Candyman inquiry might produce something on McKurn in a few weeks. Months, more likely. Too late. What was left? The legal option—charging McKurn with blackmail—which would probably result in everything coming out anyway. *That* would mean he could look forward to the satisfaction of seeing McKurn sent to jail—from the torment and shame of dishonorable retirement.

Looking again at Melanie's photo, he asked himself: *Would you stand by me then?*

Vaguely aware of a sound on the edge of his consciousness, he looked up to see Alison McGuire walking across the silent carpet to his desk.

He began to say "Good morning, Alison," when he saw that she was smiling. And then he stared, open-mouthed. She wasn't dressed in the usual way that downplayed her femininity. She wore clothes that, while perfectly proper office wear, emphasized and even amplified her raw animal magnetism. His eyes were drawn by the sheer fabric of her blouse to slide over the outline of her breasts, and admire the curves of her waist and hips, her shapely legs, and the way her skirt swayed with the rhythm of her motion.

"Have you got a hot date tonight, or what?" he asked.

Alison's only reaction was to smile even more broadly; and as she moved to sit down opposite him she seemed to grow a couple of centimeters taller, projecting an air of confidence and control that made no sense to him whatsoever.

"A hot date?" Alison said, her sapphire eyes sparkling with amusement. "No, only McKurn." She placed her laptop on his desk as she spoke.

"McKurn? You've dressed up for *McKurn?*" He felt embarrassed at the hint of envy in his voice.

Alison's eyes narrowed, and she laughed. "Of course. Don't you think his reaction will be the same as yours?"

"Oh, I guess." Bewildered by her inexplicable confidence, impatiently he said, "Alison! I don't get it. What's to smile about?"

"You'll see. Listen to this," Alison said, pushing a button on the laptop.

"Gladys?"

"Yes . . . ah, John. Your usual?"

Royn leant forward. "That's McKurn!"

Alison nodded.

"Of course," said McKurn.

"It's your lucky day. We have a new one, almost virginal. Inexperienced but *hot.*"

The woman's voice sounded like she was cooing in McKurn's ear.

"You've tapped his phone?"

Alison smiled happily.

"That's illegal!"

"Very," Alison agreed.

"Okay." McKurn's voice was enthusiastic. "I can hardly wait."

"You realize, of course, that she's. . . ."

"It's worth the risk. Send her over."

"And who's the woman?"

"That would be easy enough to find out," Alison said as she closed the lid of her laptop. "He was calling a call girl agency—Aphrodite's, it's called—here in Canberra."

"Heaven's above. So the rumors are true."

"So it seems."

"How did you get that?" Royn asked.

"Through a friend—" *no need to mention it was Olsson's partner,* she thought "—who recommended someone who seems to know what he's doing."

"So now I understand what you're smiling about. With this, we could nail him."

"Unfortunately, this can't be used as evidence."

"No," said Royn emphatically. "Of course not. But imagine, to catch him *in flagrante delicto.* . . . Wouldn't that be something."

"Yes it would," Alison agreed. "And at his age, he wouldn't last very long in jail, either," she added happily.

"But if the . . . tapping can be traced to you . . . ?" Royn asked worriedly.

Alison shook her head firmly. "There's no link. No tracks."

"You're sure?"

"As sure as I can be."

She'd found this file—along with half-a-dozen others, mostly mundane calls like ordering pizza, all headed by the phone number called—when she'd checked her encrypted email account the previous evening. Along with another email:

it begins. you'll get these files automatically. voice activated so you get everything up to you to find the gems. happy listening!

"So who is this guy, this tapper?"

"I actually don't know. All contact is through cutouts. He—and I'm only assuming it's a he—doesn't know who I am and I don't know who he is. There is one other thing, though."

"Which is?"

"His services are not cheap. He said information to nail McKurn to the wall would probably run well into six figures. I've sent him a ten thousand dollar deposit, but I certainly don't have hundreds of thousands of dollars to spare."

"If he keeps producing material like this," Royn said cheerfully, "no problem." As he spoke, he felt a warning at the edge of his mind: he could be implicated as an accomplice to illegal activities. With a frown, he resisted the urge to push the thought aside and said, "This puts me in a difficult position, you realize?"

"In what way?"

"As a member of the bar, I'm required to report any evidence of a crime to the police. And as a former Minister for Justice and Customs—effectively, Assistant Attorney-General—if this ever came out I'd have to resign. I might be disbarred as well."

"I see," said Alison, studying Royn intently for a sign of where he was heading. "Which is the same as your future if McKurn wins."

Royn nodded, his face taut with strain.

"What McKurn's doing is illegal," Alison said. "Unfortunately, the only way we can fight him is with the same means."

"I know," said Royn. "And I also know it's not as though we have any real choice. But—" Royn leaned forward to emphasize his words, his face solemn "—no one must ever know."

"No one else will," Alison said.

"Aside from you and I, there's only one other person we can trust: Melanie. She has to know. Okay?"

"Certainly, Minister."

Royn leaned back, the strain disappearing from his face as he nodded. "Good."

"Thank you, Minister." She dipped her head in apparent appreciation—to hide any reaction she might show as the memory of a familiar voice flashed into her mind saying, "Does it, Alison? *Does* the end justify the means?"

"We can feed ideas to the Candyman Inquiry," said Royn.

"And to the police," said Alison. "I've also asked him if he can trace the ownership of the hotel where the . . . ah . . . video was taken."

"Good. But it doesn't solve the problem of what you're going to say to McKurn when you meet him today. You can't walk in and play that recording to him as you just did to me."

"That would be premature," Alison said. "Here's what I've got in mind. . . ."

*****

FELIKS ILYICH NAZAROV LIKED to say he was named after Lenin and the founder of Lenin's *Cheka,* predecessor to the MVD, NKVD, and KGB (his first employer), Feliks Dzerzhinsky. In reality, the patronymic he shared with Vladimir Ilyich Lenin came from his father, as Lenin's had from his, and his grandfather was named Feliks. Trained as a *Spetsnaz* assassin, the KGB sent him to Afghanistan where he rose to captain and spent the five happiest years of his life.

The collapse of the Soviet Union left Nazarov at a loose end. After a couple of boring, low-paying, dead-end jobs and a short stint with the Russian mafia, he'd hired himself out as a mercenary, fighting in a variety of African brushfire wars. That's where he'd teamed up with Mats de Brouw, a young South African Boer who regretted the end of apartheid, and Nick Shultz, an older American, a tough sergeant who'd been cashiered from the U.S. Marine Corps.

The three former mercenaries had moved to Australia where they were hired, five years ago, by a man they'd never met. All contact, including all instructions, was through encrypted email or via mobile phone—never the same number twice. Aside from a few soft "no casualty" standover tactics, usually to get information, they had spent most of their time shadowing, taking pictures or making recordings of people making drug sales, cops and other minor officials accepting bribes, and members of various underworld gangs plying their trade.

Today's mission was different: to liberate Derek Olsson from the prison van taking him to court. To complicate matters, their instructions came with the usual caveat from their unknown employer: *no casualties.* So Nazarov armed his team with tranquilizer guns of the kind usually used to capture wild animals.

De Brouw trailed the van along Anzac Parade from Long Bay Jail on a motorbike, giving a running commentary via walkie-talkie. Nazarov, dressed as a policeman sitting on what looked like a police motorcycle, was parked on the median strip at the intersection where they planned the ambush. Also on the median strip, Shultz waited in the "wrecker"—a tractor with a jack-hammer on its long front arm that could pound its way through the prison van's weak point: the bullet-proof glass. Four "young punks" (as Shultz described them), also on motorbikes, carried chocks to immobilize the van when it stopped at the red light. They were also armed with tranquilizer guns.

Nazarov, Shultz, and de Brouw all carried pistols as well—despite the "no casualties" instructions. Assuming a tranquilizer gun scored a hit, it could take took fifteen minutes for the sedative to take effect.

"Roadwork ahead," de Brouw's South African-accented voice crackled over the radio. "The van's slowed to a crawl."

"Okay," Nazarov replied.

"Holy shit!" De Brouw was now shouting. "The road workers are fakes. It's a setup. They're after the van. Surrounded it. They're wearing masks and carrying guns—not popguns! A truck is blocking the intersection."

"Where are you?" Nazarov said. "Exactly."

"Anzac Parade. Middle of a block, three, maybe four lights from you. There's a railing along the center strip blocking the van from getting to the other side."

"Not far. Everyone. Get there as fast as you can. Two, dump the wrecker and take the getaway van down there."

"Two, on the way," said Shultz.

"Everyone else, count off so I know you've heard me."

A straggle of "Seven," "Five," "Six," crackled over the air.

"Four!" Nazarov screamed. "Wake up."

"I've had a problem—"

"Who gives a damn? Just get your arse moving."

"Where do we have to go?"

Jesus, Nazarov groaned to himself. *This sure isn't a crack Spetsnaz team.* "Just head south till you see a truck blocking the other side of the road."

"Okay, got it."

Nazarov revved up his motorbike and switched on his siren. Blue lights flashing, he weaved across the traffic heading to the center of Sydney and when he got to the other side of the road he twisted the accelerator hard.

"Just remember, you guys," Nazarov said as he expertly skidded the bike around a car moving out of his way too slowly, "I'm the cop on the BMW motorcycle with the sunglasses. The real cops are probably on the way. Shoot me by mistake, you don't get paid. *Got it?*"

This time, they counted off almost in unison.

"Three," Nazarov said to de Brouw. "How many are there?"

"Eight or nine."

"Weapons?"

"Shotguns. And a couple of AK-47s."

"Oh, shit."

"They're standing guard around the van. Two of them are doing something under the back door."

"Can you get under cover and start picking them off?"

"No problem. Plenty of stalled cars."

"Okay. But wait till at least two more of our guys are there. Otherwise they'll all come after you."

"They've shot a cop," de Brouw yelled. "A cop came up on a motorbike and they just gunned him down."

"So now you know who we're dealing with," Nazarov said.

"What do you mean?" someone asked.

"They shoot to kill—so keep your heads down."

"They've got the back door open," De Brouw said, his tone now measured. "They've thrown something in and are leaning on the door."

"Gas, I bet," said Nazarov. "Aside from Three, who's in position?"

"I am—Five."

"Seven, almost there."

"Five and Three, line up on a target. Seven, as soon as you're in position—and make it quick—give the order to fire. Report."

"Three, ready."

"Five, ready."

The radio crackled again. "Seven, *fire.*"

Unlike rifles and pistols, the single-shot tranquilizer guns, powered with compressed carbon-dioxide gas, were noiseless. If the men got their heads down fast, their targets would have no idea what hit them, or where the shots came from.

"Two hits, I think," said de Brouw. "One guy's having trouble standing up. They're all looking around, puzzled, as though they can't figure out what hit them."

"Good," said Nazarov. "Reload—fast. Two, Four, Six, report when you're in position."

"Here," said someone.

"Identify yourself, goddammit."

"Four."

Of course.

"They're opening the back door of the van. They're pulling someone out."

"Six, ready."

Nazarov could see a truck slant-ways across the opposite lane, just past the intersection ahead—and heard sirens in the distance coming, it seemed, from every direction. He switched off his siren and braked sharply to a crawl, coming to a halt just across the intersection, about fifty meters from the truck. A wide, grassy median strip divided the three lanes in each direction. He jumped the bike across the kerb onto the median strip where a handful of trees gave him some shelter. The other side of the strip was blocked by a chest-high railing, which began just past a pedestrian crossing. He could see one broken headlight of the van, which looked as though it had smashed into the side of the truck; three figures wearing road workers' orange tunics were clearly visible. He fixed their positions firmly in his mind and began to reach for the tranquilizer gun strapped to his back.

I don't think the "no casualties" order applies to these thugs, he thought.

He pulled his 17-shot Glock semi-automatic from its holster.

"Two," Shultz's American-accented voice drawled, "I'm in position right across the road from the van."

Nazarov looked up and could see the getaway van parked near the pedestrian crossing opposite the truck.

"Two, stay put and wait for my signal to move. Everybody else, select a target and wait for my instruction. Three, what's happening now?"

"They've got someone unconscious and look like they're ready to carry him somewhere."

"Which direction?"

"Across the median strip, I think."

"Okay." He crouched forward to lie on top of the bike, his pistol at the ready. "Ready . . ." he ordered, ". . . aim . . ." With his other hand he gunned the throttle. ". . . fire *now.*" The BMW surged forward through the trees and as it accelerated he guided it towards the beginning of the railing, squeezing off shots which went wild but forced the thugs to keep their heads down.

"Some cop has just shot at them," de Brouw said in his ear. "One of them's down."

"That's me," Nazarov said.

"We hit one more . . . no, two more."

Nazarov was too busy to reply. As he closed in on the prison van he planted one foot hard on the brake and pushed upwards with both feet, letting go of the bike as it smashed into the railing. He cleared the railing to see that he was flying straight towards one of the gunmen, who was swinging his shotgun in his direction. Nazarov squeezed off a couple of shots and smashed into the man, using the man's body to cushion his landing. He continued his forward movement into a roll, which ended with him squatting on the ground, his pistol aimed at the thug. One more shot finished him off.

"Anyone behind me? Three, can you tell?"

Inside the van, two uniformed prison officers lay, unmoving, on the floor.

"They've seen you," said de Brouw. "They're turning back to fire at you."

Without looking back, Nazarov dived into the back of the prison van, pulling the door half-closed behind him. As he moved he could hear the *thunk* of bullets and the peppering of buckshot around him, followed by a rattle of impacts on the door. He kept his head down as a stray bullet ricocheted around the inside of the van.

"Three. What's happening now?"

The airwaves were silent, but he could hear the faint sound of sirens in the distance.

"Three. Three. Come in."

He realized the thick metal of the van's body was blocking radio contact. He carefully peeked out the back of the van. ". . . come in, come in . . . " De Brouw's voice cracked with static.

"I can hear you now. What's happening?"

"Four of them are carrying the prisoner across the other side of the road."

"Two, can you see what kind of car they're taking, and the number plate?"

"Two, will do."

"Watch out," said Three. "There's one coming to the back door. And he's got an AK-47."

"Everyone, pick him off if you can. Two, use your pistol."

He transferred the Glock to his left hand and as he saw the end of an AK-47 poke into the van he fired a few shots low, underneath the door.

"He's down. I got another," said de Brouw.

"Any others still up and about?" the Russian asked.

"Not that I can see."

"Take a closer look."

After a moment, de Brouw said, "All clear."

"Okay." Nazarov stepped carefully out of the van. "The cops are on the way. We gotta get out of here fast. Three, get on your bike and follow their car. Stay back."

"No problem," said de Brouw.

"And dump the dart gun."

"Okay."

"Four, Five, Six, Seven, pick up two of the unconscious bodies—not the dead ones. And carry them to the median strip. And *run.*"

"Two here," Shultz said. "They're in a blue panel van. AY-something—number plate's dirty. They've just taken off."

"Three, I see it."

The other four members of his team picked up two orange-clad "road workers" and carried them the to the median strip. "Two, get moving."

The getaway van's engine screamed as it accelerated across the road with a squeal of tyres, braking to a halt in the middle of the pedestrian crossing. Nazarov ran across the grass and opened the back door. "Throw those scum in the back," he ordered. "And get in too."

He jumped into the front seat beside Shultz. The others piled in after him, and the van accelerated down the street as a policeman on a motorbike came roaring towards them, more police cars a few hundred meters further along the road.

"Slow down," Nazarov ordered. He leant out the window and fired three shots in quick succession as the policeman turned his bike towards the van, aiming for the motorcycle's tyres. One bullet grazed the rear tyre; the policemen skidded out of control, smashed into the kerb where he was thrown to a reasonably soft landing on the grass of the median strip.

"Go."

"We'll be followed," said Shultz as he accelerated down a side street with a screech of tyres skidding on the tarmac.

Nazarov nodded, and turned to look at the four men behind him. "Leave the dart guns and strip off to your shirts and we'll drop you off up the road so you can disappear."

"When do we get paid?" asked one of them.

Nazarov took four envelopes from the glove box and handed them to the four "young punks." "That's part payment. The rest in a day or two, at the usual place. I'll call you."

"This is only about a quarter of what we agreed," said one of the men as he riffled through the bills in the envelope. "Why should we trust you for the rest?"

Nazarov shrugged. "Look, nothing went according to plan, including the final payment. Sorry, but I've got some other business I have to take care of first." He jerked his thumb towards the back of the van where the two bodies lay.

The van turned another corner and jerked to a stop in the middle of the road, a car coming up behind them honking as it, too, pulled to a halt. Nazarov turned his head to glare at the four men, who were muttering to each other, eyeing their employer with suspicion. "If you like, we could sit here all day and argue about it . . . and let the police catch us. So I suggest you get moving now."

Grumbling, the men got out. Now dressed indistinguishably from people wandering along the sidewalk, they melded into the crowd and disappeared from view.

"Wait," said Nazarov. Still in his full policeman's uniform and helmet, he pulled the visor down, stepped out of the van and walked slowly towards the car behind. The driver's angry expression disappeared, to be replaced with a worried, fawning look. Nazarov calmly pulled out his Glock, shot out the car's front tyres, and jumped into van's back seat.

"Go! That will stall the cops for a few minutes."

Shultz nodded.

"And can you remember this number?" He reeled off the number plate of the car he'd just turned into a roadblock. "The boss will, no doubt, want to compensate the driver for the damage."

"Strange man," the driver drawled.

"Indeed," Nazarov agreed as he leant over the back of the seat. "Let's see what we've got here."

He tore the masks off the two unconscious men.

"Ah," he said as he took off his helmet. "Asians, both of them—Chinese maybe? . . . Let me know if Mats calls in."

Shultz nodded.

Nazarov turned the two men face down and tied their hands behind their back. "No ID, no nothing," he said as he ran his hands over their bodies and checked all their pockets. Then he threw a blanket over the two bodies to hide them from prying eyes and pulled out his cellphone to dial a number. A muffled voice answered after one ring.

"Somebody else snatched him," said Nazarov. "We're following them."

"Any idea who?" The voice was hard to understand, mainly from the distorter the man at the other end was using to make sure his voice couldn't be identified. Nazarov knew the number he had just called was a pre-paid SIM card which would be thrown away after this operation, just as his would be.

"We grabbed two of them. Chinese most likely."

There was a long pause at the other end. "I see," said the man slowly. *"Find him."*

"We will. And when these bodies talk I'll let you know what they say." Turning to Schultz, he asked, "How much further till we get to the garage?"

"About a click and a half. These damn Sydney streets though—nothing in a straight line. We have to go back on the main road for about two blocks, which will put us right in the middle of the traffic heading for the city."

"No other way?"

"Nyet, tovarisch," Schultz grinned.

Nazarov knew from long experience that when Schultz said there's no other way, there was no other way. "We'll just have to chance it, then."

"We'll pay them guys off, just like we promised?" asked Schultz.

"Of course," said Nazarov, "but not in the way they expect."

"That'll be fun," Schultz laughed. "We'll be doing a public service. We should get a medal."

Nazarov joined in his laughter. "Well," he said, "that little exercise sure beat taking pictures."

"Damn right. Almost like being back in Africa—for ten minutes."

"Not as young as I used to be though." Nazarov rubbed his shoulder as he spoke. A thick, heavy-set man in his mid-forties with hardly a gram of fat on his body, he been leading a sedentary life compared to his time as a soldier. "Bumped my shoulder when I landed."

"I'm glad I got the soft, air-conditioned job," Schultz, ten years older than his captain, said with a smile. "You did damn well, considering."

"Yes, it went well . . . considering we were beaten to the punch."

12 The Siren's Song

BREATHING DEEPLY, ALISON MCGUIRE stretched out her hands and examined them carefully in the mirror.

They weren't shaking. . . . *Well,* she thought, *not noticeably.*

She finished retouching her makeup, added a whiff of perfume behind her ears, and straightened her skirt for the third time. She again practiced a few movements—a minute, almost imperceptible flutter of the eyelids; a slight wettening of her lips that made them glisten; a sway of the hips that made her skirt swing and lift just above her knees. She admired the way her black, high-heeled shoes emphasized her shapely legs and ankles; at the same time she evaluated her reflection in the way she imagined a man would look at a woman.

I'm as ready as I'll ever be, she thought.

With another deep breath she walked slowly out of the bathroom and into the corridor; although she'd just washed and carefully dried her hands, her palms were already damp with perspiration.

As she walked through the palatial suite of the President of the Senate into McKurn's office she replayed in her mind the words of her tennis coach: "Anyone can hit a ball, Alison. Good players control the ball. But *great* players use the ball *to control how their opponent moves.*"

"ALISON," MCKURN SAID WITH a smile, his eyes widening as he looked at her with undisguised appreciation.

With a nod of her head, Alison walked towards the visitor's chair, while McKurn came out from behind his desk. "Let's sit over there," he said, indicating the armchairs in one corner, "where it's more comfortable."

"Thank you, Senator," Alison said with the warm smile she'd practiced in the mirror, continuing to move towards the same chair she'd sat in the week before, "but for the moment I'd feel more comfortable here . . . if that's okay with you."

"As you wish," McKurn said, his tone of voice indicating disappointment. As McKurn turned back to his desk he said, "Well, you've had a week to consider my proposition. Do you have your answer?"

"Indeed I do, Senator."

"And it is . . . ?"

"Yes . . . but."

"But?" said McKurn, his voice rising in surprise. "You're in no position to make any conditions, Alison."

"On the contrary, Senator," Alison said with as much conviction as she could muster, "you're in no position to refuse them."

"Really?" McKurn said with a laugh.

"If you really want what you say you want." As she spoke, she sat slightly straighter, pulling her shoulders back as she moved; at the same time she slowly crossed her legs. As one leg moved over the other, her skirt slipped up to expose her knees.

Captured by the flash of her skin, McKurn's eyes caressed Alison's legs at the same time as his face reddened with anger at her words.

But Alison smiled invitingly as she moved her body—showing no response to his festering rage—and McKurn's anger faded as his eyes followed Alison's movements. He shrugged. "It will, at least, be amusing to hear whatever you have in mind."

"First of all," said Alison, surprised the nervous flutter in her stomach didn't color her tone of voice, "I've reserved one of the smaller conference rooms. I'd really prefer to continue our discussion there."

"I certainly don't think so," said McKurn firmly.

Alison shrugged. "It's your choice."

McKurn laughed. "Why on earth should I move from here?"

Alison leant forward slightly, pleased to note how McKurn's eyes followed the movement of her breasts. "A short walk along the corridor is all I'm asking, Senator," she said in an inviting voice, her eyes looking at him warmly. "Such a small matter, Senator, to indulge me in. Hardly worth losing everything over, is it?"

"Alison," McKurn said, chuckling. "You don't trust me. I should be offended." He spread his arms wide. "I assure you, there is no recording equipment of any kind in this office."

Alison smiled. "You see right through me, Senator," she said as she slowly, languidly, uncrossed her legs and rose to her feet. "Allow me to lead the way, Senator."

She could feel McKurn's eyes on her back as she walked towards the door, her skirt swaying with a slightly exaggerated movement of her hips. With a hand on the doorknob she half-turned so McKurn could see her body in profile, and tempted him with her gaze. "Come," she said, softly.

"And if I don't?"

"You should remember that the moment you post that video," she said calmly, "I've got nothing to lose."

"And what is that supposed to mean?"

Alison smiled modestly. "I assure you, Senator," she said matter-of-factly, as if she were talking about the weather, "that you really don't want to find out."

McKurn settled deeper into his chair. But as Alison opened the door and took a slow but determined step through, she could see that his gaze was transfixed. After a moment of indecisiveness, his eyes won his internal debate and he said, sourly, "Okay, have it your way. But we'll use a different conference room."

"I'm listening," McKurn said irritably, as he shifted his body this way and that, trying to find a comfortable position in the creaky conference room chair . . . and failing.

Alison sat calmly on the other side of the glass-topped conference table, her legs crossed to expose her knees, the chair set back a little from the table to ensure they would be in McKurn's field of vision.

"Certainly Senator," she said meekly. "First of all, there's a serious obstacle relating to the video. . . ."

"You mean," said McKurn chuckling, "that I have it?"

"Aside from that, Senator," Alison smiled. "Just how many copies are there? Who, aside from you, has one? Who else has seen it? And how can I be certain there aren't any other copies floating around?"

"I have absolute trust in the people working for me," said McKurn coldly.

"Unfortunately, Senator, that is not a good enough reason for *me* to also trust them. I can't agree to anything if there's the slightest danger someone else might release that video just for kicks."

"I'm afraid, Alison, you'll just have to accept my word."

"I'm sorry, Senator, but you're asking far more than I can give. But if that's your final decision. . . ." Alison shrugged indifferently.

McKurn leaned forward, his eyes focusing on her face rather than her body, searching her expression, trying to gauge her intent.

Alison sat calmly, waiting.

"You know what will happen if you leave now," McKurn exploded.

Observing him distantly, Alison smiled at him coldly. "Indeed I do, Senator. And I've had a whole week to think about it."

Then she leaned forward, gazing girlishly into McKurn's eyes. "Is what I'm asking so unreasonable, Senator? And in fact," she said, slowly straightening her body while holding his gaze, "what I'm asking is as much for your own safety as it is for mine."

"Really?" McKurn laughed. "It's hard for me to believe you'd have the slightest concern for my safety."

"This happens to be a matter where our interests coincide. For example, if I were to accuse you of blackmail now, who'd believe me?"

McKurn grunted. "No one, of course."

"Right," said Alison. "But if the video is released after I've been acting as your . . . spy, it would be a very different story. Then you could be implicated in far more than just blackmail . . . and everything you've spent your whole life building would come tumbling down."

McKurn was listening intently, Alison noted with a feeling of quiet satisfaction, as if she'd come up with an angle that hadn't occurred to him.

"And I'm sure," Alison continued, "that jail is not where you plan to while away the last years of your life."

"Most certainly not," said McKurn forcefully. "Okay," he snapped. "I'll think about it. Anything else you want?"

"Thank you, Senator," Alison said with a demure nod of her head. She took a moment to collect her thoughts. "Yes, just one other thing: if you want me to be instrumental in making your side the winning team—which is, after all, what you're asking—I want to be rewarded commensurately. I'm not interested in being treated like . . . say, a secretary, who merely follows instructions."

"And what kind of reward do you have in mind?" McKurn asked, a hint of eagerness in his voice.

"You're in your seventies, Senator, so when you retire I'll still be in my prime." Alison leaned towards McKurn, her eyes intense, one hand outstretched as though she were grasping for something. "So I'm asking you to make me the number two in your organization."

The tone of her voice hardened as she added, making a statement of fact rather than request, "When you retire, I will take over."

McKurn jerked back in surprise and laughed, a long and deep jovial belly laugh that invited Alison to join in. As his laugh died into a wide smile he wiped a tear away from one eye. "So I was right," he murmured so softly that Alison had to strain to catch his words. "We are cut from the same cloth."

Alison felt herself beginning to relax, and quickly stopped herself. But she nodded her head in a small, almost imperceptible movement, as though she was indicating her agreement.

McKurn leant one elbow on the table and rested his chin on his hand, gazing at Alison as if he was seeing something in her he had not expected to find. "There's just one problem with that, my dear." He now appeared relaxed and at ease. "Once you become familiar with my operations, how can I be sure you won't turn on me?"

"You'll just have to *trust* me, Senator," Alison said with a wide grin, leaning forward slightly and straightening her shoulders as she spoke.

McKurn laughed. "I didn't get *here*," he said seriously, but with no menace in his voice, "by trusting *anybody*. And I'm certainly not going to start now."

"Of course not," Alison agreed.

"If I agree—*if*, mind you—how can you be sure I won't get what I want, but freeze you out at the same time?"

"That's a chance I'm willing to take," Alison smiled, watching the way McKurn's eyes followed her as she leant deeper into her chair. "After all, who else in your organization, aside from you, is any match for me? Cracken? Don't make me laugh."

"You certainly have the potential," McKurn said admiringly. "Yes, Alison, I have to grant you that." He nodded as he spoke. "That's certainly an interesting idea, one I'll give some thought to."

"So if my two requests are agreeable, Senator, then I will become your . . . informant, and your willing assistant."

McKurn nodded, as if he were indicating his asset. "But, Alison," he said, "aren't you forgetting something?"

"I think not," Alison said, suddenly turning cold.

"Oh yes, my dear," said McKurn. "There's one crucial part of my proposal you've omitted to mention."

Alison shook her head. "That's not something I can . . . bring myself to do."

McKurn spread his arms on the table. "At my age do you really think I care deeply whether or not Cracken becomes prime minister? Or what happens to Royn—or you, for that matter? Or that I really give a damn who steps into my shoes when I'm gone?" McKurn shook his head sadly. "It's just a game, Alison. It didn't start that way, of course, but when you've been playing the same game as long as I have, it loses most of its excitement." He leaned forward as if to emphasize his words, a smile on his face as his eyes seemed to catch fire. "Do you understand what I'm saying? What really keeps me going?"

Alison nodded, recalling the sound of McKurn's voice on the recording she'd played for Royn earlier that morning. *Yes, you bastard,* she thought, *I understand all too well.*

"So you see, Alison, my offer to you is a seamless whole. It's all or it's nothing, *capisce?*"

Alison had prepared herself for this moment . . . so she'd thought. But her muscles refused to respond to her commands and she cringed away from him fearfully. As she desperately tried to regain her self-control, she was aware that McKurn had begun to breathe heavily, his eyes glittering, his expression face a study in intensity as it seemed that, for a brief moment, the primary focus of his attention had become her emotional reaction.

Though she already knew how she was going to respond, she felt the words choking in her throat.

She forced herself to speak. *"Okay,* Senator," she said, her eyes downcast, *"if* you agree to my two conditions."

For the first time, McKurn's six-foot-five frame seemed comfortable in the too-small chair. His face lit into a self-satisfied smile as he gazed at her approvingly.

"But *once* is all you get."

McKurn raised an eyebrow, but nodded slowly.

"Then I believe we have what lawyers would call 'Heads of Agreement.'" Alison said, her self-control slowly returning. "Would you like me to type them up so we can both sign off?"

McKurn roared with laughter. "I hardly think that will be necessary."

"Since we are agreed, in principle," Alison said, her mouth in a wry smile as her eyes studied McKurn coolly, "let me know when I can inspect your security procedures. A week from today, perhaps?"

McKurn chuckled. "If not sooner," he said rising to his feet and stretching his long arm across the table, "and it will be a very pleasant change to be working with someone as quick and as charming as you."

"Thank you, Senator," Alison said with a tiny flutter of her eyelids. As she also stood, she covertly wiped the palm of her hand on the back of her chair and, willing the muscles in her arm to stay rock-steady, she reached across the table to shake his proffered hand.

*****

Not far from the intersection where Nazarov had planned to ambush the prison van, Shultz had rented a double garage. The SUV, which Shultz and de Brouw had stolen that very morning, was now parked there next to a Volvo station wagon.

"Where will we take them?" Shultz asked as the two men transferred the still-sleeping bodies of the two Asian men into the back of the Volvo.

"Good question," said Nazarov. "What's the latest from Mats?"

"Still heading south."

"Why?" Nazarov asked himself. "They have a hideout, or they're going to move him somewhere. Boat or plane. I can't think of anything else—can you?"

"Nope."

"And these guys?"

"Pump them for information and get rid of them as fast as we can."

Shultz nodded, and seeing Nazarov suddenly deep in thought, he began vacuuming the inside of the SUV; then carefully wiped all the vehicle's surfaces to remove any trace of their presence. As Shultz was replacing the fake number plates on the SUV with the originals, Nazarov announced, "We'll leave them here, along with the dart guns—if we can wake them up now."

Shultz was looking in the back of the Volvo. "One of them's stirring."

They levered the younger Asian man out of the Volvo and propped him up on a rickety stool. Using water from a dirty basin at the back of the garage, Shultz poured it over the man's face, and his eyes slowly opened.

Still dressed as a policeman, Nazarov lounged on the side of the Volvo as Shultz stood near the man. "I thought we should have a little, private chat before taking you down to the station."

Breathing heavily, the man's head twisted left and right to take in his surroundings; his eyes flicked warily at Shultz and came to rest on Nazarov. He opened his mouth and mumbled something incomprehensible as though he had trouble controlling his voice.

"Sorry," said Nazarov. "What did you say?"

With a deep breath, the man tried again. "Lawyer," he spluttered. "Wanna lawyer."

"There's plenty of time for that," Nazarov said with a smile. "A policeman has been murdered. When that happens, we use everything we can to find the culprit."

"I had nothing to do with it."

Nazarov nodded kindly, noting the Chinese man's Australian accent.

"We think it was one of the others," he said gently. "Ballistics, of course, will tell the story, won't they? But, you see—" he leant forward and spoke more softly "—you were a member of the gang, no question of that. So you could still be charged with aiding and abetting murder. What's the penalty?" he asked, looking to Shultz. "Seven to ten years?"

"Something like that," Shultz drawled. As Shultz spoke, a puzzled look crossed the man's face.

"On the other hand, you could turn state's evidence, and we could arrange a deal where you get off with a light sentence—perhaps just probation."

The man shook his head violently, his eyes fearful. "No!" he said emphatically.

Nazarov shrugged. "How old are you? Mid-twenties?"

The young man nodded. "Twenty-six."

"All those years ahead of you. Pity to spend the next ten of them in jail, wouldn't you say?"

The man just shrugged blankly, appearing indifferent to the choice.

"So," Nazarov continued conversationally, "which triad gang do you belong to?"

Again, the man shook his head violently. "I want a lawyer," he demanded. "I know my rights."

"Of course," said Nazarov. "When we get to the station. Right now, the only right you have is the right to answer my questions."

"You're not really policemen."

"What makes you think so?" Nazarov asked, a pained expression on his face.

"You've got rules you're supposed to follow, and this ain't in the rules."

"Quite so," Nazarov agreed. "But there are times when we, ah—bend the rules a little. And hunting for a cop-killer is one of those times. Don't worry. When we get down to the station, no one will believe you if you tell them about our little diversion. There'll be no evidence—no bruises, if you know what I mean—to support it. So . . . which triad?"

The man's mouth tightened and he shook his head.

Nazarov nodded to Shultz.

With a quick, sudden movement, Shultz stuffed an oily rag into the Asian man's mouth as the fist of his other hand swung down hard on the man's crotch. Muffled as he was, the man's scream still echoed through the garage. Panting hard through the gag, tears came into his eyes as he struggled to pull his hands free. Failing to loosen his bonds, he shifted his position and crossed his legs to protect himself.

"As I was saying," said Nazarov, appearing not to have taken any notice of Shultz's punch, "which triad do you belong to?"

Shultz pulled the rag away from the man's mouth and held a fist near the man's face. Gulping for air, he cringed away from Shultz, and turned to look at Nazarov with a silent appeal for help. As he saw the faint smile on Nazarov's face his shoulders slumped.

"The Golden Dragon," he sighed

"And where were you going to take the prisoner?"

"I don't know. No! Don't hurt me," he sobbed as Shultz brought his fist to within an inch of his eyes. "I'm just a foot soldier. Nobody tells me anything except to give orders— and I follow them. That's all. I don't know anything else, honest."

"Would your friend know?" Nazarov asked, motioning with his head to the back of the Volvo.

"He might." The man was babbling now. "But he doesn't speak much English. He came here from Hong Kong just a week ago."

"Any others from Hong Kong?"

"Yes. Four. Real tough guys, every one of them." He shivered as he spoke. "They were in charge of the operation. Like I said, I just did what I was told."

Nazarov nodded but said nothing. The prisoner looked alternately at Shultz grinning at him and Nazarov deep in thought, their silence more unnerving than Shultz's sudden violence. "Ask me anything else you like," he said to fill the vacuum with sound. "Anything you want to know I'll tell you—if I can."

"Who's your boss?"

"Ultimately, some guy in Hong Kong. I've no idea who. The Sydney boss was Vincent Leung."

"Was?"

The man nodded. "He was killed a couple of weeks ago. Murdered. By that Olsson character. You know, the one in the van."

"We'd need an interpreter to talk to the other guy?"

"That's right," the man nodded vigorously.

"Chinese?"

"Yes. Cantonese."

"Well, thank you," said Nazarov with a smile as he stood upright. "I guess we'll have to wait until we get to the station where we'll have a translator available."

Nazarov looked at his former sergeant and nodded his head slightly. Alerted by the movement, the man lifted his head to look at Shultz. At the same time, Shultz grabbed the man's hair and jerked his head back. Shultz's other hand reached into his boot and came out with a thin knife lovingly and painstakingly sharpened to a needle-point, both edges sharper than razors. A look of realization flashed on the man's face but his scream turned into a gurgle as Shultz rammed his knife upwards into the man's throat, penetrating the brain.

"Where shall we put them?" Shultz asked as he wiped his knife clean on the man's clothes.

"In the van. Keep the smell down so no one will notice it for a few weeks."

"Of course, *tovarisch*."

*****

Detective-inspector Rudi Durant closed his cellphone with a sharp *crack* that rang out like a rifle shot in the silent corridor outside the courtroom. At the sound his assistant, Detective-Sergeant Simon Lee, sitting on the bench beside him, looked up with surprise but kept his face blank, saying nothing, when he saw Durant's expression. Durant stood and, as Lee began to follow suit, Durant indicated "wait" with a vague wave of his hand.

A solidly built, barrel-chested man in his mid-fifties, Durant moved with surprising speed into the courtroom where he leant down to exchange a few whispered words with the crown prosecutor. A few moments later he charged out at the same speed with the quick, long steps of a long-distance marathon runner.

"Let's go," he said as he passed Lee.

"Where?" Lee asked as he jumped up to follow, running, despite his longer legs, to catch up to his boss. Durant didn't answer, but dialled a number on his cellphone as he sped through the corridors which connected to the police station behind the court building and into the parking lot on the other side, Lee always a couple of steps behind.

Durant's steely-grey hair was cropped short like a new army recruit's, and the suit he wore had clearly seen better days. But one look from his cold, hard eyes was enough to make even a hardened criminal flinch. His bearing was one of a man of authority, used to command; senior police officers found themselves automatically moving out of his way as he tore through the corridors as if he was the only person in the building.

"Anzac Parade," he grunted to Lee as they got into their car. "And pull out all the stops." Lee grinned as he switched on the siren and gunned the engine.

"Super," Durant said into the phone. "Durant. Olsson's been grabbed, out of the prison van on the way to court. . . . Right. And a constable has been murdered. . . . Yes, that's exactly what I was going to ask you. Thanks. I'm on my way."

"Olsson's been what?" Lee asked in surprise as Durant closed his phone.

"Snatched," said Durant angrily. "Right out from under our noses."

"And a policeman's been murdered, you said?"

"Right. There was some kind of gun battle and now you know everything I know. The Super's agreed to put our names down for the task force that will be set up to get Olsson back where he belongs."

Lee nodded as he punched a long blast from his horn at a car ahead, which was too slow to get out of his way.

"Bastards," Durant said irritably, smashing his fist on the car's door as he spoke. "But we'll find them."

Lee knew why Durant was boiling: they'd been waiting in the court to give evidence in Derek Olsson's trial and now, when it looked certain Olsson was about to be put away for a long, long time, Durant's most high-profile arrest in a lengthy and distinguished career had slipped through his fingers at the last moment.

Anzac Parade was a long four- to six-lane divided thoroughfare starting at Centennial Park near the outskirts of the city which ran past Long Bay Jail to the south. The pile-up of traffic ahead was the first sign they were nearing the crime scene: despite the siren—and theirs was not the only one, as all officers who could be spared converged from all over the city—it took them some fifteen minutes to cover the last few kilometers. They walked the last couple of blocks—past so many cars, vans, motorcycles, and other police vehicles it looked like a parking lot for a police convention.

The whole block along the carriageway where the stationary, and now empty, prison van still stood had been cordoned off. Cars trapped behind the van were still stuck there as untangling the traffic was not at the top of the list of police priorities.

Four ambulances had been called. A paramedic from the first one to arrive was directed to the policeman whose motorcycle had been shot out from under him. His bike had skidded into the median strip as a bullet shredded the rear tyre. But apart from feeling slightly dazed and suffering from a few minor bruises and a severely damaged pride, he was unhurt.

The other paramedics surrounded an Asian man in black who lay on the asphalt behind the prison van. He was semi-conscious and breathing with difficulty. Blood was oozing from his chest and the bicep of his left arm. After a police photographer took pictures for the record, the medics quickly established that his blood pressure was low and cut away his clothing, exposing bullet wounds in his chest and arm. Covering his nose and mouth with an oxygen mask, they taped sterile gauze bandages over the wounds and gently lifted him into a stretcher. In moments the ambulance was speeding, its sirens blaring, in the direction of the nearest hospital.

The second ambulance slowly carried away the dead policeman, its lights flashing silently as though in tribute, while the third one carried a man who seemed to be coming out of some drug-induced coma to hospital, and the fourth took three dead hijackers to the morgue with no ceremony whatsoever.

Meanwhile, senior police officers interviewed the prison guards—including the two from the back of the van who, though groggy, insisted they were all right—while others fanned out to collect any evidence they could find and interview bystanders and drivers and record contact information in case they were needed for further questioning or, at some time in the future, as witnesses in court. One driver described the gun battle— admitting he hadn't seen everything as he'd ducked down under the steering wheel of his car when the bullets started to fly. When another bystander confirmed the story of a motorcycle policeman shooting two of the men attacking the prison van, police radios across the city called for the policeman in question to come forward.

None ever did.

Simon Lee was directed to join the team of officers interviewing witnesses while Durant's eyes roved over the scene, examining every detail as he walked slowly towards the police van where Superintendent Norman Bates, the local area commander—LAC for short—had set up a temporary headquarters.

"Ah, Rudi," Bates said as he saw Durant. "Your man, I believe."

"He was. And he will be again."

"You'll be on the task force then?"

Durant nodded. "The Super said he'd get me on. So mind if I look around?"

"No worries."

"I've never seen a gun like this," Durant said, pointing to the tranquilizer gun that, along with a couple of shotguns, an AK-47, shell casings, and the baker's dozen of darts gathered from around the van, were laid out on the roadway encased in plastic evidence bags. "What is it?"

When a constable who'd been born on a farm explained Durant simply shook his head in disbelief. "Inaccurate, unreliable—and silent, you say?" The constable nodded. "What's the point?"

Shrugging, and shaking his head, the constable indicated the darts. "That's far too many darts for one of these guns to fire in a short time, so there must have been more than one shooter."

"Thanks," Durant nodded. Turning to Bates he asked, "Any idea yet how they got him out of the van?"

"Too early to say," Bates replied, "but it looks like an inside job."

"And no sign of this mysterious policeman?"

Bates shook his head. "He must have been a fake—no real cop would have left the scene. At least, not without calling in."

"Right," said Durant, and turned to survey the whole area. After a moment, he walked slowly back and forth through the parked cars trying to reconstruct the sequence of events in his mind based solely on what he could see: he'd get the interview reports later. Drivers whose progress to the city and their jobs had been blocked for more than an hour glared at him as he walked by; Durant ignored them as he committed the position of the van and the ROADWORK AHEAD signs to memory, and studied the remains of a BMW motorcycle wrapped around the now-bent railing.

Half an hour later, alternately nodding and shaking his head, he returned to the police van where the evidence was being packed up for transport to the labs. "Any chance of a preliminary report tomorrow?" he asked one of the ballistics team.

"We'll rush it, sir," said a sergeant who recognized Durant, "but it will still take a week or more, especially considering how much there is to analyze."

Durant nodded, imperfectly masking his impatience. The sergeant smiled. "I know, sir, you want instant results; we want to make sure we have everything a hundred percent right first."

"That's the way it is," Durant agreed.

"I doubt we'll have time to write anything up by tomorrow. Give us a call and we'll tell you whatever we can."

"Thanks, I'll do just that," Durant said.

*****

THE PRESSES IN THE basement rumbled to a stop. On the fifteenth floor, Sir Philip French felt the faint vibration cease. His eyes flicked to the clock on the wall. On cue, his door flew open and a messenger sprinted in and dropped the afternoon edition of Friday's *Sydney Today* on his desk. The messenger was grinning like he'd just broken the four-minute mile, and French returned the grin.

French liked to think his was the last copy off the press. He insisted his staff saw the last-printed, not the first, of each edition. "If you can't get it right in the type," he would say, "you can't get it right and you won't be working for me." French's were the best-proofed newspapers in Australia. He knew it only saved a moment, but when those moments were added together. . . .

Sir Philip French made every moment count.

But as he turned to focus on the paper's headline his smile turned into a scowl:

DEREK OLSSON SNATCHED
Prison Van Hijacked on Way to Trial
COP KILLED IN GANGLAND SHOOTOUT

When his afternoon paper, the *News*, was the number one-selling Sydney daily that headline would boost circulation by 30,000 or more. But the *News* had died along with most of its afternoon counterparts around the world some two decades ago. He'd started *Sydney Today*—one of those thin, free papers handed out at bus stops and railways stations—in a fit of nostalgia to recapture the "good old days." A vain attempt: printing tens of thousands of extra copies of a *free* paper and rushing to get them on the streets held no thrill for him at all.

"The bastard's on the loose again, damn it," French grumbled. A few years ago Derek Olsson, self-made road transport millionaire, had unexpectedly branched into country newspapers, put French's Wagga Wagga *Morning Mail* at the bottom of a deep red hole and almost wiped out the profits of several others. The streams of cash his regional papers kicked off was drying up—just when he needed it for the on-going circulation battle between his morning *Express* and Henry Sykes' *Mercury,* and to finance other parts of his publishing empire, including the expense—and extravagance—of the new French building.

Not that the French publishing group was in dire straits. French's son Nicholas ran the magazine, radio and TV divisions, and they were all healthy. But French had kept his son away from his newspapers, his first love. Probably a mistake: he was better suited to the old days of newspapering, when the press was king of all media and competition was ruthless, no holds barred. He'd been slow to adapt, especially to the internet which was taking away newspapers' readers, advertisers, profits—and French's major source of excitement.

Maybe it's time to hand everything over to Nicky, he mused. *And do what—play golf?*

With a last look at *Sydney Today,* he threw it in the bin and turned back to the numbers he'd been going through: columns of red ink—mainly caused by Olsson.

Olsson had started his papers with the newest four-color presses and non-union labor. French's regional papers, overstaffed at union rates, immediately looked like dowdy and old-fashioned dinosaurs compared to Olsson's bright, breezy and crusading publications.

French groaned at the bottom line: the millions of dollars—tens of millions—he'd have to invest just to match his competitor's products. And he'd still be stuck with the cranky, obstinate, and high-priced unions, so Olsson would still have the low cost operation. Closing his losing papers down—the only real alternative—was something he just couldn't face.

Well, not today anyway.

And Olsson, with his Sydney and Melbourne *Weekend*s, and his financial weekly *MoneyWeek,* had started nibbling at the advertising revenues of French's mainstay city publications.

Worst of all, though the circulations of Olsson's papers had dropped a bit since Olsson's arrest, people hadn't returned to reading French's papers. And as Olsson had built a superb team—including a slew of his own best journalists and executives hired away at salaries French just couldn't afford to match—the OlssonPress juggernaut hadn't slowed one bit.

Where would it all end?

As was his habit, at six o'clock French headed for his small apartment on the penthouse floor for a pre-dinner nap. Like the boardroom next to it, the apartment had walls of glass and was surrounded by rooftop gardens. When it was first built, French could see the whole sweep of the city of Sydney, from the Heads at the mouth of Sydney harbor all the way to the Sydney Harbor Bridge and beyond.

His view had been built out over the years, and now the gardens wilted at the bottom of a man-made canyon. The latest addition to the city skyline—which would be Sydney's tallest building—was growing next door, casting the gardens into daylong shadow. In a few months, new gardens would be planted atop that building, seventy-nine storeys in the air, just above the neon signs at the four points of the compass which would spell one word: FRENCH.

He smiled at the thought that the sight of his name would dominate the Sydney skyline for years, if not decades to come.

"Sit down, Phil."

"What?" French looked in surprise at the figure lounging in an armchair, set in a dark corner of the apartment's living room. He flicked on the light.

"What are *you* doing here?"

"You haven't kept your part of the deal," the man said. His voice was deep, and although he spoke calmly, almost nonchalantly, French couldn't help but be aware of the threat behind his words.

"And how did you get in?"

"Really, Phil, don't be so naïve. An amateur could pick those locks. I'd be happy to recommend a locking system that would stop even me. For an extra fee, of course."

"You haven't delivered in full," French replied, sitting down shakily.

"You got what you wanted. I framed Olsson for you, fair and square. So he escaped? So what. Not my problem. You owe me, and I want the rest of my money. Now."

"He hasn't gone to trial—and that's the real test of whether your frame stands up. He's on the loose again. God knows what's going to happen. I've paid you half already—and the job's only half-done. That seems fair to me."

"Olsson's on the run, Phil," the man said in a tone appropriate for a wayward child. "Cops all over the country will be after him—he'll be Australia's Most Wanted till he's caught. His escape will merely prove to everyone he's guilty. I don't see any difference between that and twenty-five years to life."

"There's a big difference," said French. "In jail, he's locked up, effectively dead to the world. On the loose, anything could happen."

"It won't."

"Maybe not," French allowed. "But Olsson on the run wasn't part of the deal. He's a smart, devious bastard, so I sure don't trust him to lie down and play dead."

"You're saying you want me to wait for the other fifty grand? No way."

"You're being paid on results. You get paid when you deliver those results, not before."

"I don't think so Phil." The man stood and loomed over French, clenching and unclenching his right fist under French's nose. French could see his muscles rippling under his shirt as he moved.

"I'm a frail old man, as you can see," French smiled, leaning back in the armchair with an air of serenity he didn't really feel, "so you'll have no trouble beating me up any time you like. Go ahead—if you'd like the cops to arrest you for the murder they now think Olsson committed."

"Ha. They're not going to take any notice of a tip-off from you—especially one from the grave."

"Do you think I'm stupid?" French snorted. And leaning forward slightly he said, "If anything happens to me they'll receive a recording of our conversation—the one where we set up this deal. They'd believe *that,* don't you think?"

The man's thick hand closed tightly around French's throat. French tried gasping for breath—but couldn't. He struggled futilely until the gangster relaxed his hand without letting go of French's neck.

"Just a little sample of what's to come—if you don't pay me and give me that recording."

French breathed hard and pulled a tiny MP3 player from his pocket. The man grabbed it out of his hand. "Is this the only copy?" he asked with a glare.

"There's something else you should think about," French said as he slowly shook his head, "now Olsson's out and about."

"What," the man said scornfully. His hand tightened again.

"Something that could mean life or death for you," French said quickly. "Sit down and I'll tell you."

Suspiciously, the man released his stranglehold and pulled a chair over from by the small dining table to sit less than an arm's length from French.

"I'm listening."

"What's Olsson going to do now?"

"Try and get the hell out of the country as fast as he can, I guess. So what's the problem?"

French smiled. "Maybe," he said, looking the man hard in the eyes. "But if you asked me, I'd say it's more his style to find out who *really* murdered Vincent Leung."

  Night Vision

THE LAST FLIGHT FROM Canberra was nearly an hour late, so it was nearer ten PM than nine when Anthony Royn arrived at the family's Melbourne home—a stately, three-storey, seven-bedroom mansion nestling by the Yarra river at the end of a cul de sac in the most exclusive section of Toorak. He'd called Melanie to let her know; when she didn't meet him at the front door, he was convinced he was in for a frosty reception.

He called her name but the house was silent. He padded across the thick carpet of the reception area, went past the staircase and into the large living room, and stopped when he saw her curled up on the big armchair by the fire, sound asleep.

He smiled. She was still as breathtakingly beautiful at fifty as she had been when they had first fallen in love: love at first sight, according to family legend, when they gazed at each other across the playground in primary school. She was nine and he was ten when she made up her mind *he* was the man she was going to marry. His memory of that moment was a little fuzzy (not that he ever admitted it)—but Melanie's, so she said, was crystal clear.

It was quite a few years since she'd retold that particular story.

She was tiny then and tiny now, like an imp or a pixie, who could stand five feet tall only wearing high heels. She was so short that once, after they'd had an argument while on vacation, she'd disappeared from their hotel room. He searched high and low but couldn't find her . . . only to see her, when the sun peeked through the curtains, peacefully asleep, curled up in their suitcase.

She stirred, as though she'd felt his gaze. "Tony," she said with half a smile, her enormous brown eyes studying him distantly, stretching her body in a way Royn found enticing. "Hi, sleepy-head," Royn smiled warmly, his eyes twinkling, as he knelt down by the chair and gathered her into his arms. He kissed her ear and whispered, "How would you like to go to Singapore. You and me?"

Melanie smiled at him, and Royn felt his temperature rising. "Sure," she said. "When?"

"Monday."

"Monday?" A puzzled look replaced the smile as if a light had been suddenly switched off, and then her lips pouted in understanding. "Oh, you mean for work . . . you, me, and Alison, right?"

"Well . . . that's the excuse."

"What's the occasion?" she asked, her voice dull, almost without interest in the answer.

"Nimabi offered to resume negotiations on the oil deadlock . . . on Tuesday in Singapore."

"I see. So I suppose you'd want me to join you in all those boring ceremonial dinners and stuff."

Royn nodded glumly.

"Well . . . " she said thoughtfully, a spark on interest in her eyes, "I suppose I could work on the wives for you."

"What do you mean?"

"If everything I've heard about the Sandemans and those other places is true, they'll all want to keep going on shopping trips to Singapore and the like. And they can only do so if the money keeps flowing. Nothing like a bit of pressure from your wife to get you pointed in the right direction, is there?"

"Ah," said Royn with a grin, "that would probably do it . . . the woman's touch, especially your touch."

Melanie wasn't sure whether to smile or frown. "Okay then," she said flatly, without committing herself one way or the other.

"Great."

"And let's take Zoë—and the boys if they want to come. A real Royn family outing with Dad so busy we'll hardly ever see him."

"What? Take them out of school?"

"They're on holiday next week, mid-term break . . . or have you've forgotten already?"

"I—well, it's been a tough week."

"It certainly has." Melanie yawned. "I was asleep . . . I was so tired. Oh, and your dinner's in the oven."

Royn nuzzled closer, tightening his loose embrace. "I'm hungry for something else right now."

"Tony," she giggled. Melanie wriggled her body in a way that excited him even more—but somehow ended up with her sliding out of his embrace. With a peck on his cheek she slowly stood up. "I'm too tired," she said. "And the reason I'm tired is Zoë." Her voice rose as she continued. "She's completely out of control. She went out somewhere tonight with some friends dressed like a call girl—and she wouldn't tell me where she was going or who she was going with. She's supposed to be home by midnight, but I'll bet she'll be late. Again. It really is time her *father* had a serious word to her."

"I see," said Royn, making no attempt to hide his disappointment.

Melanie shrugged helplessly. "I just don't know what to do with her. So I'd really appreciate if you could stay up and wait for her this time, and read her the riot act when she gets home . . . and let me get a good night's sleep for a change."

Royn frowned, his eyes downcast.

Melanie stepped closer to him, resting her hand gently on his arm. "Please, do this for me, Tony," she said, appealing mutely with her eyes, her body sliding ever closer to him. "And for Zoë."

Royn nodded. "Okay," he said half-heartedly.

"Thank you." Melanie smiled. Her movement toward him ended with another quick peck on his cheek.

She yawned. "I'm sorry, Tony, but I must go to sleep."

Royn nodded again. "Okay," he sighed. "I'll be up—later, I guess."

He watched her wistfully until she had disappeared up the stairs and then stomped into the kitchen where he pecked at his dinner. Eventually, he sank into the deep armchair by the fire—still warm from Melanie's body—with a novel he'd been meaning to read for some time. But his thoughts were racing and he could hardly focus on the words in front of him. Slowly, almost against his will, the warmth of the fire and the comfort of the cushions slowly relaxed him until he began to doze fitfully.

He woke with a start, and shivered, suddenly feeling the cold: the fire had gone out and the thermostat for the central heating had automatically ratcheted down before midnight.

A glance at his watch told him it was after two. *I must have missed her,* he thought. But then he heard another *creak* on the stairs—*that* must have been the sound that woke him—and the scampering of feet.

"Zoë!" he called, letting the book slide onto the floor as he pushed himself up. Peering around the side of the high-winged armchair he saw his daughter standing sheepishly three-quarters of the way up the stairs.

"Hi, Daddy." Zoë smiled coyly at him. "Goodnight. See you in the morning." With a little wave of one hand she turned to run the rest of the way upstairs.

"Zoë," he said a little more sharply than he'd intended.

"It's late, Daddy," she said with an impish smile making her look so like Melanie when she was younger that his heart melted. Though she had the same turned-up nose, she was taller than her mother. And her dark brown hair, in some weird, spiky hairdo, was dyed bright red, something Melanie had never done. She was wearing a tight pair of jeans that hugged her hips, strapless evening shoes and a skimpy tank top that left a wide gap of skin around her waist and her shoulders bare. Her lipstick—what was left of it—was smeared around her mouth. He had thought Melanie's remark about her being dressed like a hooker was a bit over the top—but it wasn't far off the mark after all.

"Yes, it is late, isn't it?" Royn said. "In fact, it's after two."

"Right, so I'd better be getting to bed—hadn't you?"

Royn shook his head. "I think that you and I, just the two of us, should have a little chat. And right now, while your mother is still asleep, is the perfect time, don't you think?"

Zoë shrugged and moved to continue up the stairs, one eye watching for her father's reaction.

"Your mother said you'd promised to be back home by midnight," Royn said sternly, "and you're over two hours late."

Zoë stood still. "We got held up."

"Really? It wasn't the traffic, was it?" Royn said sarcastically. "Look. Zoë, if you had a good reason for being late you should have called to let us know. Or asked if you could stay out later. But you did neither of those things. And it seems this is far from the first time you haven't kept your word."

"Gawd," Zoë said nervously. "Living in this house is like living in a convent."

"Really? I didn't know nuns dressed up like that and hung out with boys till way past midnight."

"Daddy."

"Come and sit down please, Zoë."

"Daddy, *please*—can this wait till morning?" she pleaded. "I'm *so* tired."

"No," Royn said, frowning while Zoë reluctantly—and very slowly—came down the stairs.

As she sat down, she looked up at Royn defiantly and asked, "Why is there one rule for me and a different one for *you?*"

"What do you mean by that?"

"I've heard the stories about you and Mummy. Very romantic and all that—but you were way younger then than I am now. That's hardly fair."

Royn coughed, covering his mouth and turning his face as he did. But when he turned back Zoë was smiling at him, knowing she'd scored a point: he hadn't been able to disguise the deep flush that covered his cheeks.

"Things were very different then," he said.

"Really," Zoë laughed scornfully. "Do tell."

"Really. First, there was no AIDS to worry about. And no drug-resistant strains of STDs either. And then—" He recalled the rare occasions he'd met Zoë's current boyfriend, always a different boy "—your mother and I were inseparable from the very beginning. So there were no chances of either of us catching anything." *Well, almost none,* he thought guiltily. "And third, we kept to our parents' rules—and we certainly didn't break them outrageously as you seem to be doing."

"So you lied to your parents, did you?"

Royn shook his head. "No. We never lied to them. They just never suspected a thing . . . so they never asked."

"So you'd prefer that I—that I deceive you? Is that what you're saying?"

"Why—is there something you feel you need to deceive us about?" Royn asked with a smile.

Zoë glared at her father, but didn't answer.

"And did you know," Royn continued, "that you can get an infection from oral sex too?"

Zoë's jaw dropped.

"So tomorrow we'd better take you down to a VD clinic for a check-up—and a pregnancy test."

"No, Daddy. You can't. I *won't.*"

"Why ever not?

"It would be so—so embarrassing. So *humiliating*"

"Better to be embarrassed than infected, don't you think?"

"You're punishing me when I haven't done anything wrong."

"It's not a punishment, Zoë. It's a precaution."

"And do you think Mummy will agree to this?" she demanded.

"Of course. Indeed, she told me to read you the riot act—which I guess I've just done."

Zoë sighed. "Mummy's so unreasonable. She just doesn't understand."

"I think she understands all too well. That's why we both worry about you so much."

Zoë slumped in the chair, her eyes glistening. "There's nothing to worry about," she muttered—but Royn felt sure he heard a hint of doubt in her tone of voice.

"Well, we'll know tomorrow, my dear."

Zoë glared at him. "I can hardly wait."

As he watched Zoë trudge dejectedly up to her room, Royn stood and stretched. *I did exactly what Melanie asked me,* he thought, feeling very pleased with himself. After a few moments he, too, went up the stairs, but with a new spring in his step. When he climbed into bed he cuddled up close to Melanie, one hand gently holding her breast. She wriggled a bit closer to him without waking up—and in just a moment Royn was sound asleep as well, dreaming happy dreams.

*****

"There's a light flashing out to sea."

Nazarov woke like a cat, fully alert, when he heard de Brouw's voice. "What's the time?" he asked.

"Two am."

"Let's see what's happening," Nazarov whispered as he pulled himself out of his sleeping bag.

They'd set up camp on a rise half a kilometer from the house where the Chinese gang had taken Olsson. They overlooked a small, isolated weekender set on top of a rocky promontory jutting out to sea on the coast about a hundred and fifty kilometers south of Sydney. A verandah hung out over the cliff giving the occupants an uninterrupted view of the sweep of the ocean, and the coastline for kilometers in each direction.

There was no moon. A few stars glittered through scattered, wispy clouds floating high above. Land, sea, sky, rocks, and trees were a kaleidoscope of blacks and dark greys. Light splashing from the house on the promontory was the sole patch of brightness, the only visible sign of other people nearby. Nazarov peered out into the darkness, but could see nothing.

De Brouw passed him the night-vision binoculars and indicated where to focus them. In the middle of the blackness the infrared goggles turned the heat of a ship's engine into a patch of faint brightness; small, moving stick-figures were people walking around on the deck.

Putting down the binoculars, Nazarov could now make out the outline of the ship as a slightly different shade of black.

Then a brilliant point flashed twice from where the ship lay in the shadowy pool of the ocean.

"There it is again."

De Brouw and Nazarov quickly moved their focus back to their faintly lit surroundings: they knew from bitter experience that keeping their night vision intact would give them a decided advantage over men coming from bright light into the darkness of night.

"I thought ships were supposed to show lights at night," said de Brouw.

"Right," said Nazarov. "So that ship must be here for Olsson. Wake Shultz. Time to move."

"There were four of them," de Brouw reported when Nazarov and Shultz arrived late the previous afternoon. "The three who carried the man across the divider, plus the driver. About half an hour ago, four more came."

"All armed?"

"Yes, with the same weapons as far as I can tell. I saw them unloading shotguns. I saw one man with a pistol on his belt, and there could be others."

They'd spent the rest of the afternoon and evening surveying the ground. To the right of the house, a track with steps cut into the hillside led down to a wide beach, a scattered handful of weekenders on the slopes behind it.

To the left of the promontory the coastline formed a small, V-shaped bay. As the surf rolled into the bay from somewhere across the Pacific Ocean, the waves surged, accelerating as the V narrowed, so even when the ocean was quiet the waves reached the tip of the V so fast they smashed into the rocks with a spectacular explosion of sound and spray.

"You could climb that slope," Nazarov reported after he'd scouted it, "but no boat could get in there, except in daylight when the sea was absolutely still."

Every hour or so after the sun went down, a man loosely carrying a shotgun came out the side door of the house, walked around it peering into the bush as he did, and then went back inside. Otherwise, all was quiet except for the pounding of the sea, the rustle of the wind in the trees, and the chirps of birds and crickets. In the brief silences between waves, they could hear occasional voices, and, now and then, a faint but perturbing *click-click-clat* sound. De Brouw volunteered to see if he could find out what was causing it.

He moved so silently that in the muted starlight Nazarov and Shultz could only follow his progress through the infrared binoculars. He appeared like a shadow in the light spilling from the verandah, crawling down the left-hand side of the house, carefully peeking into windows as he passed.

"They're drinking tea and playing that Chinese game, Mah-jong," de Brouw told them on his return, grinning widely. "Don't worry," he said. "I wasn't seen. They have lookouts on the verandah. Otherwise, they're all busy gambling."

"Any idea where our man is?"

"I didn't see him. The back rooms are dark, so most likely in there."

"We'll take them as they come out."

They settled down to wait, two of them sleeping with their weapons at hand while the other stood watch.

Nazarov and Shultz had brought a small arsenal with them, selected from the cache of weapons they'd had smuggled into Australia over the years. Each man had an AK-47, and in holsters on their belts were Glock-17s. In addition, Nazarov and de Brouw each had U.S. Army issue M24 sniper rifles, along with the latest American telescopic and laser sights, equipped with night vision, bought brand-new on the black market in Baghdad. A box of grenades had come from the same source.

THROUGH THE NIGHT-VISION binoculars, Nazarov could see human figures moving slowly from the ship towards the shore. "A boat's coming in. Time to go."

They began crawling towards the house. De Brouw made for the two vehicles parked behind the back of the house. He plunged his knife into the sidewalls of the tyres, the *whoosh* of escaping air drowned by the pounding of the surf. When both vehicles were disabled, he crawled back to stand behind a large tree about fifteen meters behind the house from where he had a clear view of the side door and the top of the path down to the beach.

Carrying a couple of grenades, Shultz crept through the bush until he was hidden beside the path leading down to the beach, where he, too, had a clear view of the side door.

Nazarov lay behind some shrubbery about ten meters further back from de Brouw, his sniper rifle at the ready. Each man had a clear view of the target area and of each other; and they were positioned so it made no difference whether the Chinese planned to take Olsson down the path or to a car.

About ten minutes later, the side door of the house opened and figures came out in silence, clearly illuminated by the shaft of light splashing from the open door. The first man walked out carrying a torch, a shotgun slung across his back. The second man, holding an AK-47, was followed by two men holding a Caucasian man in a prison uniform; his feet were hobbled and hands tied behind his back. Nazarov and de Brouw tracked the two men holding the prisoner with their laser sights; as the fifth Chinese man stepped out into the light they opened fire almost simultaneously. The two men holding the prisoner both dropped followed a moment later by the man in front and the man behind. As he heard the *crack* of the M24s, Shultz threw a grenade through the open door, followed a moment later by the rattle of his AK-47 as he fired a burst into the open doorway.

The man who'd been leading the file dropped his torch and grabbed for his shotgun. As he began to swing it towards the sound of the AK-47, three bullets tore into his body almost simultaneously.

Olsson stood on the path looking dazed. "Get down," Nazarov shouted at him as he de Brouw began running, alternately, in short spurts toward the doorway. They'd dropped the M24s and now carried their AK-47s. Shultz fired another burst from his AK-47 into the doorway as Nazarov and de Brouw approached.

Without looking at Olsson, de Brouw sprayed bullets through the doorway while Nazarov stood behind him. After listening for an instant and hearing nothing he peeked through the door. "All quiet," he said. A moment later he added, "One missing."

He sprinted in a crouch towards the verandah while Nazarov moved to the back of the house. "Get out of the light," he hissed to Olsson as he moved.

From behind the house came the sound of a motor starting. One of the vehicles lurched forward on its flat tyres and Nazarov sprinted around and emptied his magazine through the car's rear window as it bumped away. It slowed to a halt, stalling with a couple of jerks. Changing magazines, Nazarov crept forward, and seeing the driver slumped over the wheel, opened the driver's door. The man wasn't moving, but Nazarov fired one bullet into his brain just in case.

"All clear," de Brouw said as he came walking out the side door. The three converged on Olsson. Shultz pulled out his knife and cut through Olsson's bonds.

"That's better," Olsson said as he rubbed his wrists and stamped his feet. As he looked at the Chinese men sprawled across the path, he clearly felt sick.

"Are you okay?" Nazarov asked.

"Just hungry, thirsty, and tired," Olsson said with half a smile. "I should thank you gentlemen, I presume," he added, his face losing even more color as his eyes scanned the bodies.

"They won't bother you again," Shultz grinned.

"No," Olsson agreed, shivering as he spoke. *"They* won't."

A light flashed in the surf near the beach below. "They'll be disappointed," Shultz grinned.

"Somebody's heard us," Nazarov said, peering towards the far of the beach where light from a window suddenly streamed through the trees. "Follow me," he said to Olsson. As he jogged towards the car, Olsson trudged slowly behind.

"Where are we?" asked Olsson as he caught up with Nazarov who'd stopped to scoop up his M24.

"About one-fifty clicks south of Sydney."

Olsson nodded. Looking strangely at the M24 he said, "Overkill?"

"No such thing."

Nazarov could tell that Olsson's gaze was fixed on his, but Olsson's face was shrouded in shadow so Nazarov couldn't make out his expression. It occurred to him, though, that Olsson had probably never seen a dead body before, let alone eight.

The four men were silent as Shultz drove the Volvo slowly, without lights, along the dirt track to the main road. He let the car coast the last few meters, the engine no more than a quiet purr, using the handbrake to bring the car to a stop. The Volvo was half-hidden by the tall trees lining the road, but he had a clear view of the road in both directions. They waited while a car whizzed by, followed by a semi-trailer. When the road was clear, and there was no sign of headlights in the distance, he planted his foot on the accelerator. The wheels spun in the dirt and the car slid onto the highway and he flicked on the headlights. In moments they were speeding along the highway, just another car travelling through the night. Shultz set the cruise control for 98 KPH—no point in getting a speeding ticket, especially with that armory in the back.

They all breathed a sigh of relief as they topped the next rise. Nazarov pulled out his phone and made a call. "We've got him," he said. He listened for a few moments and then passed the phone to Olsson. "He wants to talk to you—but don't say anything, okay?"

Olsson nodded, listened, and passed the phone back to Nazarov. "He wants to know if you got everything," he said.

"Yes."

"Any questions?"

"No."

"No questions," said Nazarov into the phone. After a moment he said, "We'll be an hour and a half or so," and put the phone back in his pocket.

"Here," he said to Olsson, pulling a bag from the back of the wagon. "You'd better get out of that prison uniform. Not the sort of thing to be wearing wandering around Sydney, even in the dead of night."

IT WAS NEAR FOUR AM when the Volvo stopped at a deserted corner in a mostly industrial area not far from Sydney airport.

Olsson waited until the car disappeared from view and then walked quickly down a side street. Though he only had to walk one block, his step was light as he revelled in the unfamiliar freedom to breathe the night air and move where he wanted, when he wanted.

At the corner he saw Ross Traynor standing nervously half in shadow. "Thank God," he said as Olsson reached him.

"Never been happier to see you," Olsson said with a smile.

"IT WAS LUK SUK'S men, you know, who grabbed me," Olsson said. Traynor nodded his head as he drove. "They're all dead." Olsson paled at the memory. "Bodies everywhere. Sickening!"

Traynor shrugged. "It was you or them, Derek—"

"But they didn't deserve to die," Olsson said angrily.

"They would have happily killed you, right?"

"Yes. But—"

"But what? They live by the law of the jungle. Kill or be killed."

"Yes—but I don't have to live by their rules."

Traynor looked at Olsson quizzically. "You expect them to live by *yours?*"

Olsson shook his head. "I . . . suppose not. But there must have been a better way."

"Derek! Why do you have to make what's simple so complicated?"

Olsson sighed. "Maybe," he said doubtfully. "Anyway, Luk Suk is sure going to be madder than hell now."

Traynor nodded.

"Half of them were from Hong Kong. The other half locals."

"How do you know?"

"By their accents, the way they spoke Cantonese. A couple of the younger Australian guys could hardly speak the language at all."

"So we should assume that Luk Suk has lost some of his best men."

"Exactly. If Luk Suk can't find me, he might come after you—or Judy and your kids. So take them on a long holiday somewhere far away."

"So," Traynor said with a grin, "we *both* need to live by the law of the jungle for a while."

"I suppose so," Olsson admitted reluctantly.

"What about the businesses?"

"They'll be all right—or they won't. What's more important: your business or your life?"

Traynor looked at Olsson and nodded. It was question that didn't need an answer. "And what are you going to do?"

"Look after some . . . things."

"Okay," Traynor laughed. "Be secretive then."

Traynor slowed the car as they drove past a motel. Then he went around the block and swung into the motel's parking lot. "Just making sure there's no one around," he commented.

He unlocked the door of a room and handed the key to Olsson.

The only imprint of Traynor's presence on the motel room was a battered suitcase and a large backpack sitting by the bed. Olsson grabbed the backpack, carefully took out a laptop and then upended the bag so the rest of its contents fell onto the bed. He fiddled with the fabric on the bottom and opened a hidden compartment. Inside, there were five envelopes. He sat on the bed while he slowly examined their contents.

The first four contained passports—two Australian, one British, and one from New Zealand—together with matching driver's licences, credit cards, and other IDs in four different names, none of them "Derek Olsson."

The fifth envelope, much thicker, held a dozen SIM cards, several more credit cards in yet different names, all issued on foreign banks and each accompanied by a driver's licence, half Australian and half from other countries, and a large stack of $100 bills.

Olsson's eyes flicked to the suitcase.

Traynor grinned. "I already checked. It's all there."

"And some clothes I presume."

"Of course. They've been there a while though, so I hope they still fit."

"The least of my troubles."

Traynor handed Olsson a key chain. "It's the old, burgundy Toyota we parked next to."

"Who owns it?"

"Registered in a company name," Traynor said. "A dummy of course."

"Okay," Olsson nodded, and picked up one of the envelopes at random, checking the name on a credit card. "Okay. So I'm Joe Schuster for the moment." He closed his eyes and stretched. "Boy, do I need a shower. And sleep."

"Not here, I hope."

Olsson shook his head. "I'll drive for an hour or so and then crash. Thanks, Ross," he said, standing up to embrace his friend. "You need to get back home to look after Judy and the kids."

AFTER LEAVING THE MOTEL, "Joe Schuster" stopped at the first fast-food place he found open where he ate two hamburgers washed down with coffee and Coke. He then drove for two more hours and checked into a nondescript roadside motel.

He was so tired that his head had hardly hit the pillow when he collapsed into the first deep, untroubled sleep he'd had in several weeks.

14　The Frosty Lady

WHEN A MAJOR CRIME was committed the State Crime Command established a task force, headed by a detective-superintendent, which could draw specialists as needed from different police units in the city and, if need be, from anywhere in the state or even further afield. TASKFORCE OVERFLOW had two major crimes to investigate: the kidnapping and recapture of Derek Olsson and the murder of Constable O'Reilly.

As requested, Rudi Durant and Simon Lee were members. While the team was assembled they'd spent the previous afternoon, evening, and early hours of Saturday morning preparing a report to present to the first gathering of the task force, which was scheduled to begin at noon. Lee collated the faxed and emailed transcripts of interviews and other reports gathered at the crime scene by police officers who had now—mostly—returned to their original stations around the city. Durant worked the phone, cajoling information from the overworked ballistics, lab, medical and other teams.

Durant's desk, like every other available surface in his cramped office in the Surry Hills police station, gave the impression of creaking beneath the weight of neatly stacked piles of files, folders, reports, and papers. On one side of the desk, Durant made notes in handwriting which reflected his personality: precise, to the point, and well-organized; on the other side Lee read through the transcripts of interviews, police reports, and his and Durant's hastily scribbled records of phone conversations, reorganizing them as he did.

The dead motorcycle policeman was riddled with AK-47 bullets, fired from two different guns; Ballistics didn't think the bullets came from the abandoned AK-47.

The two dead Chinese gang members, however, had been shot with a different caliber altogether, both bullets having been fired from the same gun . . . the gun which had shot out the back tyre of the police motorcycle, and the front tyres of a car found later in a side street blocking traffic. A 9mm, probably fired from a Glock or similar weapon, the lab scientists thought.

The BMW they found at the scene was not a missing police bike, but one painted and modified, complete with false number plates, to look like one. When the engine numbers were matched to the registration records, it appeared the BMW belonged to a seventy-year-old pensioner in a wheelchair with no criminal record who protested he'd never ever ridden, let alone owned a motorcycle. Four other motorcycles, all stolen, were also found abandoned.

The darts contained the same anaesthetic vets used to bring down wild animals. As far as the lab could estimate at this stage, the dosage was set for an animal with the same body weight as a man.

The prison van was an armored truck similar to the ones banks used to move money and valuables around the city. The tiny windows were all bullet-proof, the exterior was armor-plated, the doors double-locked and bolted from the inside. It was like a bank vault on wheels, supposedly impossible to open . . . unless you had the key.

According to the prison guards with Olsson, a whiff of some irritant gas had been pumped—somehow—into the back of the van. They were then warned that if they didn't open the door, a different gas would be pumped in—and they'd all die. "So we opened it. Then the bastards gassed us."

The team that had gone over the van had found a hole drilled in an inconspicuous place through the armor plate; since the guards had not reported the sound of drilling, the assumption was it had been done beforehand by, presumably, someone on the inside. When they inspected the other vans, they found tiny holes drilled in the same place in each one. A week earlier, one of the mechanics—a new hire—hadn't turned up to work and hadn't been heard of again. The prison authorities were embarrassed to discover his identity was fake.

The previous afternoon, Lee and Durant had interviewed one of the prisoners in his hospital bed whose only words had been "I want a lawyer"—in Cantonese at that. His solicitor, one they both knew well from previous cases involving triad members, advised his client to refuse to answer any and every question he was asked—and scowled silently when Lee, who had emigrated to Australia from Hong Kong as a child, questioned him in Cantonese. The second prisoner was still in intensive care. They'd be able to interview him soon—but he'd have the same solicitor so they knew they'd get the same result.

However, it turned out that both the Chinese men in custody had arrived from Hong Kong less than a week ago. The Hong Kong police were very efficient, and less than three hours after he'd send his request for information via Interpol, Durant had an email detailing everything they knew about these two men, which turned out to be a lot.

Both were, according to the Hong Kong police, known members of the Golden Dragon gang, the same triad whose Sydney boss had been Vincent Leung. Both had prison records for violent crimes; and both were suspected to have been responsible for several murders.

The two dead Asian men had not been identified, but one of them matched the description of a known member of the Sydney branch of the Golden Dragon.

It was after ten AM when Durant finished going through his notes—which, Lee knew, could now be typed up for filing without further editing—and he fixed his eyes on Lee and asked him:

"What do you think, Simon?"

In the two years Simon Lee had been Durant's assistant, he'd become used to Durant's style of grilling him about a case. For the first few months Lee had felt extremely nervous, especially when Durant mercilessly chewed him out for overlooking some essential part of the available evidence. But he quickly realized that Durant's Socratic practice of initially concealing his own conclusions and forcing Lee to voice his first was the best training in police methodology and logical thinking he'd ever had. Perhaps that was why so many of Durant's previous assistants had gone on to spectacular careers of their own.

But before Lee could answer, the door opened and a constable walked in waving a couple of sheets of paper. "Excuse me, sir, you'd better look at this."

Being closer, Lee grabbed first for the papers the constable was carrying, but with a smile, Durant held out his hand and Lee passed them over. "A bloody graveyard," Durant said as he finished the first page and handed it to Lee. Looking up at the constable still standing by the door Durant said, "Thanks. I presume the LAC has called the experts in?"

"Yes, sir," replied the constable. "Officers from Ballistics and Homicide have already hot-footed it down to the south coast. Nice day for it, eh?"

Durant grinned. "I don't suppose they'll have much time to enjoy it."

"I guess not, sir. Anything else?"

"Not right now." As the constable left he turned to Lee, "Well, Simon, do you think this is connected in any way?"

"Well," said Lee thoughtfully, "it looks like two gangs were after Olsson. One we now know about: the Golden Dragon Triad. The second one—with someone masquerading as a policeman—tried to snatch Olsson from the Golden Dragon gang. It appears they're the ones who killed two triad members—and immobilized the others with tranquilizer guns." Lee shook his head. "That I just don't understand."

"So what's the connection?"

"I'm hypothesizing of course," Lee said carefully, "but the triad had to take Olsson somewhere. Why the south coast? Beats me," he shrugged, hastily adding, "at the moment. But this report says they found eight Asian bodies, all dead, all riddled with bullets. Shotguns and AK-47s were found there too, the same kind of weapons as at the ambush. It seems a logical assumption they were also Golden Dragon members."

"But remember," said Durant, "what seems obvious is often dead wrong."

Lee smiled. "I realize that, but I haven't had time to think up any other possibilities yet."

"So the next—obvious—question: why are they dead and who killed them?"

"Again," said Lee, "the logical culprit is the second gang. Perhaps they were tailed from Anzac Parade."

"Or maybe Olsson escaped on his own . . . you've seen that report about the fight in the prison yard?"

Lee nodded, and studied the fax. "Possible, I suppose. I guess we'll have to ask the medical examiner if there are any wounds or bruises on the bodies other than bullet wounds. Added to which there's a big difference between a one-against-five fight in the prison yard, and one man against eight armed men."

Durant nodded. "There's another possibility: aside from some third outfit spiriting Olsson away, some of the triad members took him somewhere else and killed the rest to eliminate any evidence."

Lee shook his head. "No boss, I can't buy it."

"Remote, but—"

Lee leant forward to emphasize his words. "A triad member will be executed for, say, betrayal. But wanton killing like that? No way—there's too much loyalty in the triad, up and down, for that to happen. Anyway, you see how *all* the guys in hospital simply clammed up. Their boss wouldn't fear exposure that way."

"You're probably right," Durant conceded.

"Anyway," Lee said, "at the moment I'm willing to bet that some of those bodies down there will be identified as members of the Golden Dragon, and we'll find the gun that killed Constable O'Reilly."

"I only bet on sure things—is this one of them?"

"Aaah . . . virtually a sure thing."

"Not good enough. Though I agree, it's certainly the leading hypothesis. Anything else, Simon?"

Durant grinned as Lee searched through the piles of paper.

"I'll put you out of your misery. Is there anything strange about this second gang?"

"Well . . . we don't know who they are, so. . . ." Lee shrugged helplessly.

"Assume it's the same gang—at both Anzac Parade and the south coast—and read that fax again."

"The number of bodies . . . " Lee murmured as he read, ". . . some kind of explosion, possibly a grenade . . . the man who called the police from the beach house at three AM said he thought he was having a dream, reliving his time in Vietnam . . . but it turned out to be a real gun battle. The *scale* of the violence, of the killing. . . ."

"Damn right—gun battles on Sydney streets followed by a St. Valentine's Day-style massacre. You'd think we were in Chicago, not Sydney," Durant said angrily, shaking his head. "And shotguns I can understand. There must be hundreds, possibly thousands of them that were never registered or turned in when guns were banned a few years ago. AK-47s, unfortunately, are too easily available on the black market. But a Glock—and grenades? Where did they get them?"

"Stolen from the army, perhaps? Or even . . . the police. Except for the grenades, of course."

"If it was police issue, we'd know about it. Unless some quartermaster is sitting on his thumbs. Be a good idea to check—and with the army too, to see if they're missing any munitions. But that's not the really strange thing."

"It's not?" said Lee. "Then what is?"

"Why haven't we heard about this gang before? There's no shortage of murderous bastards in the underworld. But these guys take the cake for violence. So where have they been all this time? And why haven't we ever heard of them—until *now?*"

"I see . . . " said Lee. "But then, if they're such a violent gang, why the tranquilizer guns? That makes no sense whatsoever."

Durant nodded, sighing. "I can't figure that out either. Too many damn puzzles."

"But the Hong Kong angle is looking more solid," said Lee.

While they were searching Olsson's penthouse apartment in the Rocks area of Sydney, just before they arrested him for murder, Olsson's answering machine picked up a call and a man left a message in a menacing tone of voice in a language—Cantonese—only Sergeant Lee understood. Translated, it went:

> *Ah-son.* I sure as hell don't like the line your newspapers are taking—what's gotten into you? And I've just heard you seem to be branching out on your own. That's not the deal and it's not on. You'd better explain yourself and it better be good . . . if you know what's good for you. I expect to see you Thursday in Bangkok at the usual place.

Olsson had merely shrugged when Durant asked him about the message; and his solicitor had advised him he was under no obligation to answer any of Durant's questions, so he didn't.

Durant nodded. "Right. But does that mean Olsson was connected to the Golden Dragon Triad—or some other outfit . . . or what?"

Lee shrugged. "Or, maybe, Olsson was involved with the Golden Dragon and 'branched out' on his own—if we can believe that message."

"And why meet in Bangkok?"

Lee shrugged. "Could be dozens of reasons—including, of course, that the guy calling was from Thailand. But there's something else I've dug up which points more firmly to Hong Kong. Olsson dropped out of Sydney University when he was nineteen, near the end of his very first semester. He bought a round-the-world-ticket, and his first stop was Hong Kong."

"What was his second stop?" Durant asked skeptically.

"I don't know. Airlines don't keep records that long. I talked to his mother and his sister. His mother seems to be a bit gaga, and his sister refused to talk to me when she found out I was a policeman. Said we were persecuting him."

"That merely moves the pointer one degree closer to Hong Kong. Not enough."

"I agree. But there's something else. Now, I don't know where this is all leading—if it goes anywhere. But it makes me suspicious."

"Okay," said Durant. "What have you got?"

"Seven years after he flew out of Sydney for Hong Kong, he came back and partnered with Ross Traynor who had a struggling freight operation that basically ran a few trucks between Sydney and Brisbane—and that's when InterFreight started to take off."

"And in between?"

Lee shrugged and spread his hands. "At the moment, I have no idea what he was up to."

"Continue—but make it quick."

"I spoke to an executive at one of InterFreight's competitors, who said they must have been exceptionally well-financed to expand as quickly as they did: all the trucks, warehouses, and other equipment they purchased would have cost tens of millions of dollars. But InterFreight is only capitalized at one hundred thousand dollars."

"So where did all those millions come from?"

"Exactly my question. Presumably, it was loaned to InterFreight but no bank would lend that much money to a hundred-thousand-dollar company—and certainly not on a personal guarantee from two guys with not much more than their shares in InterFreight between them. Twenty-five and a half percent of the shares each, by the way. The other forty-nine percent is owned by a Swiss lawyer in Zurich, presumably as a nominee for somebody else."

"I don't really see how that explains anything."

"No—but it raises an interesting question: how could a nineteen-year-old university dropout gain access to or accumulate tens of millions of dollars in seven years? It's not impossible, I know—just very unlikely."

"Could his family have staked him?" Durant asked.

Lee shook his head. "He grew up in Balmain. His father, Sven Olsson, was a car mechanic who turned into a drunken bum. Sven's been picked up for vagrancy and disorderly conduct quite a few times over the last fifteen years."

"Could Olsson have inherited some money?"

"Unlikely. His father came to Australia from Denmark in his early twenties—assisted immigration."

"One of those ten quid, one-way ticket jobs?"

"Right. Olsson's maternal grandfather, Jack Dent, is still alive. Quite an upright citizen by all accounts. He has some money—he sold his garage when he retired—and his own house in Annandale, fully paid off. But one of the local policemen remembers there was some kind of bad blood between grandfather and grandson, so it seems unlikely Olsson would get anything from granddad."

"I see," said Durant. "All very interesting . . . but where does it take us?"

"At the moment, nowhere. But I would like to go to Hong Kong myself and see what I could dig up."

Durant chuckled. "It'd be pretty tough to squeeze the money out of the super for what he'd suspect was an all-expenses-paid holiday for you."

"You know, it's been a long time since I've been to Hong Kong anyway—and quite a while since I've taken any leave. . . ."

"You think there's something there, do you?"

Lee nodded. "Just a gut feeling—but a strong one."

"Sometimes they pan out. Do you know anyone in the Hong Kong police?" Lee shook his head. "Well, worth emailing them a few questions, see what they can tell us."

"I will."

"Anything else—?" Durant paused for a second but Lee shook his head. "So, since it's a sunny Saturday afternoon, what do you say to a drive down to the south coast?"

"To Ulladulla, I presume," Lee said, his smile disappearing.

"Exactly."

"You didn't have something planned this evening, I trust?"

"Nothing that can't be put off," Lee grumbled.

"Okay . . . so let's get this task force meeting over and done with. I'll have a quiet word with the Super and then we can take a leisurely drive."

"Great," said Lee.

*****

IN THE ENORMOUS, FOUR-POSTER bed in the master bedroom on the top floor, Anthony Royn slowly stirred from a deep but restless sleep. Without opening his eyes he moved his hand slowly towards the other side of the bed, rolling over as he did. When his hand reached the other edge of the mattress he realized he was alone.

With a soft sigh he half-opened his eyes to check the time: after ten. Hardly surprising then, considering Melanie had gone to bed several hours before him . . . but he felt let down nonetheless.

On the other hand . . . , he thought, brightening as he remembered just why he'd stayed up last night. . . . He grinned. Bouncing out of bed he dived into the shower.

"GOOD MORNING," HE SAID cheerfully as, fifteen minutes later, he walked through the kitchen door. And stopped: Zoë was sobbing breathlessly, her head nestled to Melanie's chest; Melanie's arms hugged her tightly, protectively.

And Melanie was glaring at him.

"How could you do such a thing?" she growled. "And to your own daughter."

"You said—"

"I certainly did not," she said, cutting him off. "Anyway, I called Dr. Bristow and Zoë has none of the symptoms. But since you're so suspicious—though there's clearly no reason to be—I'll get one of those pregnancy test kits down at the chemist, just to make you happy."

Royn stood with his mouth hanging open, fighting the burst of anger surging inside of him. He glared back at Melanie and strode towards the coffee pot, his mouth now tight. The coffee was lukewarm, but he poured himself a cup anyway.

He turned, intending to walk straight back out the door—and paused. "Well," he muttered, "I'm glad to hear there's nothing to worry about after all."

As he left the kitchen he glanced back to see Zoë looking at him, a triumphant smile on her face.

Women, he thought as he slowed his pace, wondering what he was going to do with himself now. *Doesn't matter what you do; you just can't win.*

His thoughts were interrupted by the sound of a dog yapping from the street outside. *Sheesh,* he sighed, *if we had a dog it'd be a bitch.*

He started to amble towards the stairs and slowed almost to a halt; then he began to run up the stairs, slowing when he realized he was spilling coffee all over the carpet. *Too bad,* he thought.

He made a phone call from the bedroom and then, smiling, went to his dressing room and changed into a patched pair of jeans, a T-shirt, a worn pair of running shoes, adding his tatty old gardening hat for effect. He dumped the rest of the now-cold coffee in the washbasin and ran down the stairs, two or three steps at a time. "I'm going to see a man about a dog," he said to Melanie with a smile as he dumped the coffee cup in the kitchen sink.

"Will you be back for lunch?" she asked in surprise.

He shrugged in answer and disappeared through the side door leading from the kitchen into the garage. He passed the Bentley, the Porsche, the Mercedes, the BMW—and opened the door of the old VW which, when new, had been his first car. *It needs a spin anyway,* he thought. *I hope it starts.*

The engine *whirred* a couple of time before roaring to life. He drove out of the garage, driving off without a backward glance.

"GIMME A PINT, MATE."

Anthony Royn stood drumming his fingers on the bar, his eyes searching for Collin Renfrew. Renfrew stood six-and-a-half-feet in his socks, his legs like two rakes supporting a torso not that much thicker. He stood out, as another student in their law class had put it, "like a thin streak of Pelican shit." So when Royn didn't see him, he didn't need to look twice.

"Here you are, mate."

"Thanks," Royn said. He took a long swallow and carried his beer outside into the pub's beer garden, but Renfrew was still nowhere to be seen.

Shrugging, Royn sat down at an empty table, half-shaded from the warm autumn sun by an old oak tree casting its leafy arms like a giant umbrella across a baker's dozen of tables. He stared blankly into his glass, his mind bubbling like the foam with memories of Melanie . . . the way she'd looked at him once, summoning him with her eyes, and how he'd walked helplessly across an empty street . . . the day they went horseback riding to a distant, isolated hill where, with the rising excitement of slowly exploring each other's bodies, discarding one piece of clothing at a time, and fumbling with mutual intent, they both lost their virginity on the soft, sun-kissed grass . . . of her wondrous smile, shrouded in white when—twenty-seven years ago—she had replied, "I do" . . . and the wonder he still felt that she would say it . . . and the way he'd looked at Melanie last night, curled up asleep, knowing those memories, those feelings, were still real today. . . .

Yet now, there were also arguments, anger, and the harsh words that had driven him away that morning . . . where had they come from? When did it all begin? Images floated through his head . . . of how children made their simple life complicated . . . of how their lives had changed when he gave up law for politics . . . of how, as Minister for Foreign Affairs, he spent even more time on a plane. . . .

At each memory he shook his head, until he remembered the day they'd proudly accompanied their first-born son, Max, to his first day at school; and the night the Conservative Party swept into government. . . .

BY SEVEN-FORTY THAT SATURDAY night, less than two hours after counting began, it was clear the Conservatives had an unassailable lead. On Sunday morning, Kydd called to make him Special Minister for State; he and Melanie—pregnant for the third time, though it hardly showed yet—bundled Max and Ricky into the car to celebrate with Royn's parents.

Anthony Royn had been in federal parliament for six years, an opposition shadow minister for five of those years. Easy years. He was in Canberra only when Parliament was sitting, and Melanie and the children usually travelled there with him.

He became a minister with the never-ending responsibilities of running a department in Canberra, a month before Max started school . . . in Melbourne. As he progressed up the political ladder he spent more and more time in Canberra or on a plane while Melanie, he thought, became more mother than wife—and revelled in her social standing in Melbourne society as Mrs. Royn.

But it had all happened so slowly neither of them had noticed it, like two pulsing rivers joining into one . . . becoming divided by larger and longer islands as it grew wider and shallower, until it was no longer clear whether there was one river, or two.

He took another gulp of his beer, looking around vaguely—but still no sign of Renfrew. He let his thoughts drift back to the Monday, the second day after the election.

He'd been sitting in his electoral office grappling to understand the issues he would face as a minister of state. Running through his head was his father's advice— "The important thing, Tony, is to take charge immediately from Day One. Or those public servants will run rings around you"—well-meaning advice that somehow made everything more difficult: he'd now be in charge of thousands of career public servants, experienced administrators and managers who knew all the ropes while he, the new kid on the block, had only ever "commanded" secretaries and a handful of assistants.

Feeling overwhelmed, he welcomed the interruption when he heard a strange voice saying:

"Mr. Royn?"

He looked up in surprise to see a very attractive young woman—or a teenager?— standing on the other side of his desk.

"And you are . . . ?" he'd asked while his eyes admired the curves of her waist and breasts.

"Alison McGuire."

He felt a brief moment of desire—as he still did when he saw her unexpectedly, along with the thought, *Yes, I would like to sleep with her*. That thought was nowadays replaced with a feeling that gave him even greater satisfaction: the knowledge that every other male in the Parliament had the same desire, while he was widely believed to be the only one who'd ever achieved success. "I don't recall having any appointments this morning."

"I just . . . walked in, Minister."

His keen ears picked up the slight quaver in her voice, and he noticed there was no sign of that hint of nervousness in her confident stance, in the way she held her body loosely erect.

"Not 'Minister' for a week or so yet," he smiled, wondering whether he should throw her out . . . but she looked vaguely familiar. If she was a constituent with a problem, sending her away would be a bad idea. At the same time he was astonished she had gotten past his formidable assistant, Mrs. Willow.

"Miss McGuire," he said in a slightly deeper tone, a touch of severity in his voice. "How can I help you?"

She sat down, taking his words as permission—or maybe, the feeling came to him, as if it were she who was handing out the favors. "I wish to apply for a job—" she paused, as though permitting his thoughts to catch up with hers "—as your personal assistant."

He hesitated, resisting the urge to shout "But I have one . . . and how the hell did you get past her?" followed by the urge to run into the next room to see if she was still there.

"Mr. Royn," she continued, taking his silence to be permission to speak, "with your new responsibilities, you'll need someone extra to help you in Canberra . . . and you won't be able to spend so much time in the electorate. . . ."

Exactly some of the issues he'd been thinking about this morning, Royn thought. Momentarily lost in the cadence of her voice and the brilliant sapphires that were her eyes, Miss McGuire—that is, he hastily corrected himself, someone *like* Miss McGuire— would be the perfect complement to his new position.

"So, Miss McGuire," he had said, determined to reassert control in his own office, "why should I hire you?"

Alison smiled demurely. "Aside from the fact that I can type and answer the phone and do all the other things a personal assistant needs do, I can get into places where I'm not expected."

"So it would seem."

"And places you would never be allowed."

"What kind of places could they be?"

"The ladies' room, for example. Amazing the useful gossip you can pick up there. More importantly," she added, holding his eyes with hers and subtly shifting her body, "while I know I have a lot to learn about politics—though I've spent the last four summers as an intern in Parliament House, so I do know my way around—most politicians and officials in Canberra are men. I can guarantee they'll tell me things they'll never tell you. Things you'll need to know."

"Interesting points. So tell me, Miss McGuire, if I were to hire you, what would be the first thing you'd advise me to do?"

Alison McGuire studied him before saying, "Get a new wardrobe."

"What? Why?"

"To control the impression you make, and because your tie doesn't go with that shirt, which doesn't go with your suit, which is clearly very expensive—"

"Of course. It's from Savile Row."

"That's the problem. Not many people in this country are as wealthy as the Royn family. Australians like to think they live in a classless society. It's a bad idea to remind them they don't."

"I see, I never thought of it that way—although my wife has said something similar, about stuff not matching."

Alison nodded. "It's the sort of thing women are more likely to see than men—and women are more than fifty-one percent of the voters. . . ."

"True," Royn nodded. He'd gained the impression she had set her mind on working for him—and he was impressed by the matter of fact way she all but disguised it. "I should be doing other things right now. So why don't you leave me your resume and I'll—"

"Certainly." She pulled a thick file from her shoulder bag and handed it across the desk.

Royn opened the file and riffled through the pages. "What's this?" he asked with a puzzled look. "It's fifty-something pages long."

"It's a case study of a new development in the States on using polling to fine-tune political messages. I tested it in the New South Wales state election back in March and wrote up the results."

"And you think it's something I can use?"

"I think it's something you should use. In fact, I've had a very lucrative offer from a major polling company to help create this very service for them to market . . . to any politician who wants to use it."

"I see. How old are you, Miss McGuire?"

"Twenty."

"Rather young for such a position, don't you think?"

"I believe my youth will prove to be an asset for you, rather than an obstacle. But for that reason I'm certainly willing to work as an intern for you . . . until the end of this summer."

"Why not take the offer you already have?"

"I'd prefer to work in Canberra . . . Minister . . . and in Parliament House."

"Hmm. So, were I to ask you to be an intern, when could you start? Tomorrow?"

"Wednesday, Mr. Royn. I have my last exam tomorrow morning."

"Exam? In what?"

"Political Science," Alison smiled. "The last exam of my last year at university."

"I see." He looked at the file. "Your contact information is here—Balmain, I see. Sydney University, I presume?"

Alison nodded.

"So let me give it some thought and I'll get back to you. But while you're here, I'd like you to have a talk to my wife . . . I'm sure she's still at home. Since you both seem to think I have no dress sense, I'll be intrigued at her reaction to your ideas."

When Royn returned home later that afternoon, he discovered Melanie and Alison deep in conversation, with Max and Ricky both demanding Alison play with them again. Melanie had arranged—"If it's agreeable with you, of course, my dear"—that she and Alison would go and study clothes, fabrics, styles, tailors and accessories on Wednesday. As a result, he now had pasted on the inside of his wardrobe—and suitcases—a chart telling him what ties, shirts, suits, socks and even shoes went with each other, and what he should wear depending on the impression—somber, light, authoritative, and so on— he wanted to give that day. He was now regularly listed in the women's magazines among the best-dressed men in Australia. Looking back, he was now unsure whether it was he or Melanie who had made the final decision to make Alison McGuire his personal assistant.

Melanie and Alison had been the best of friends, always conspiring together until . . . what? Nothing had happened between them that he could remember. Yet Melanie's attitude to Alison had cooled, seemingly in lockstep with the growing problems in their marriage, reaching the point where . . . what had Melanie said about Alison on the phone the other day? "Fire her, then. I've always said she was trouble." Royn shook his head.

That's a course that should be in all universities, he thought: *How To Understand Women.* But, perhaps, no one was qualified to teach it.

"Tony. *Tony? Is that you?*"

Royn raised his eyes see the smiling face of Collin Renfrew towering over him. "I nearly didn't recognize you—what's with the hat, for heaven's sake. Want another?"

Royn looked at his glass, surprised to see it was nearly empty. "Sure," he said, tipping the glass back and chugging down the remainder of his pint in a couple of short gulps.

"Another pint?" Renfrew raised one eyebrow as he asked.

"Sure," Royn said again.

Renfrew shrugged and came back a few minutes later, a foaming pint in one hand and a smaller middy in the other for himself.

"Cheers," Royn said, clinking Renfrew's glass.

"So tell me, Tony," Renfrew said as he sat down opposite Royn, "when will you send out the invites for the booze-up at the PM's Lodge?"

"Booze-up?" Royn frowned as he looked at Renfrew through puzzled eyes. "The Lodge? What on earth are you talking about?"

"The Great Conman, of course. All your old mates are waiting for you to give him a nudge—though some of them think you're just going to cool your heels until he keels over."

"Conman?"

"Christ, Tony." Renfrew shook his head in mock sadness. "You're a bit bloody slow this morning. I'm talking about *Kydd*—Kydd, Kydding, Conman."

"Is that what you call him?"

"Fits doesn't it?" Renfrew smiled. "The randy old goat could sell ice cubes to an Eskimo, you gotta admit."

Royn smiled. "I suppose he could."

"So when are you going to make your move? Or has the old bastard got you conned too?"

Royn shrugged. "I don't know," he groaned. "I don't even want to think about it right now."

"I see," said Renfrew. "Well . . . you'd better tell me about your problem, then."

"Women. Tell me, Collin, what you know about women."

"Mate, you're asking me?"

"Sure, you always seem to have some pretty bird in tow."

Renfrew shrugged. "But never the same one. Anyway, you know I tried marriage twice, so whatever you want to know about marital and divorce law, I'm your man. But relationships? With women? You should know better than to ask. 'Slam, bang, thank you, ma'am' is more my style."

"No complications, either."

"Only getting them into bed. That's complication enough."

"What an easy life you have," Royn shook his head, and took another swig from his beer. "Sheesh. And now my daughter's ganging up on me as well."

"That's a problem I don't have. . . . Well, not so far as I know, anyway."

Royn laughed.

"So what was it you wanted to see me about that you didn't want to talk about on the phone—or in the office?"

Royn took a deep breath. "I need a recommendation," he began slowly, "a . . . private eye."

Renfrew looked at him sharply. "What for?"

"I'd . . . rather not say."

"That much trouble, eh?"

Royn nodded gravely and handed him a folded sheet of paper. Renfrew's eyebrows wrinkled quizzically as he scanned it. "This is weird—let me get it straight. You want me to find a good private detective and tell him to send an email to this address. That's it?"

Royn nodded, and—remembering Alison's careful instructions—craned over the table to look at the list again. "But he has to send it from a dummy email address, not his real one. That's crucial."

Shaking his head, Renfrew said, "And then he'll be asked a question, and he has to give this answer."

Royn nodded. "Right. And do NOT email or fax these instructions. You must hand them over in person—and then forget about it."

"This is so bizarre, Tony, how could I forget it? But I can certainly keep my mouth shut." Renfrew smiled. "That, after all, is one of the things lawyers get paid for."

"Good." said Royn. "Because one other requirement is my name is never mentioned—to anybody, ever. Okay?"

Renfrew nodded. "Okay. Legal privilege and all that. But," said Renfrew, his face clouding over, "a judge can set that aside in certain circumstances, as you very well know. In which case—"

"I can live with that."

"You'll have to."

Royn nodded resignedly. "I guess so. . . ."

"And what about payment?" asked Renfrew. "They're certain to ask me about it."

"I suppose . . . could that go through you? Keep me out of it?"

Renfrew nodded.

"Discretion," Royn said. "That's imperative. And an outfit with national coverage would be best."

"Okay. I can think of two possibilities. . . . It would help if you could give me a little more—hell, some detail about what you're after."

"I'd . . . rather not."

"Okay," Renfrew grinned broadly, "so when she's been caught in the act, so to speak, do I get the case?"

"Huh?" Royn said, masking his surprise with a smile. "Maybe . . . but no promises."

"Fair enough. . . . How about a game of darts then—bet you ten bucks I can still beat you."

"Sure," said Royn. Picking up the two empty beer glasses, he added, "My shout, I believe."

*****

The Frosty Lady. A neon mermaid with pendulous, dripping breasts rose from a frothy glass of beer above the wide door.

Alison McGuire stared at the sign in disgust. Why, of all the bars in Canberra, had he chosen this one? Overriding the powerful impulse to turn and walk away, she opened the door, wondering if she was doing the right thing.

Half in and half out of the doorway of the gloomy bar, her nose assaulted by the odor of stale beer and sweaty bodies, she peered through her sunglasses, toying with them nervously, seeing only a darkness of grey shadows made even bleaker by the contrast of bright sunlight streaming from behind her. A drunken male voice shouted over the tinny sound of an old jukebox turned up too loud for its ancient speakers, "Hey, luv, shut the bloody door, would ya," followed by another, "Yeah, make up your bleeding mind."

Alison let the door swing shut, leaving the sunglasses in place.

She made her way slowly along the long bar to her left. As her eyes adjusted she could make out the white splotches of singlets on broad, muscled, sun-bronzed shoulders, of tables weighed down by jugs, pints and schooners of beer, of men's eyes lingering on her as she passed. She returned glance for glance . . . but saw no one looking even vaguely like Derek Olsson.

Her worn T-shirt and faded jeans fit the bar's tone perfectly, but her dark red leather handbag and the silver and jade bracelet on her thin wrist—a long-ago present from Olsson she'd added on a last-minute impulse—made her look completely out of place. As one of the few women in the bar, she realized that how she'd dressed would have made no difference whatsoever.

Sliding into an empty booth in the far corner, she glanced at her watch: five after five. "He said he'd be here at five. I'll give him five more minutes," she muttered, her discomfort and annoyance rising with every male look passing her way. She drummed her fingers on the table as she waited, asking herself why he wanted to see her—and whether she really wanted to see him again. *And if he shows up, should I tell him about the video?* Two minutes, then three, then four ticked by as she stared into space, arguing with herself. *It concerns him, too. . . . Maybe he can help. . . . I wouldn't ask* him. *And what could* he *do? . . . Are you trying to protect* him, *Alison? Don't be ridiculous!*—and still no sign of him.

A rather pudgy, unshaven man, who looked like he'd been holding up the long bar for quite some time, shuffled towards her, a glass in each hand. He shambled closer; he seemed vaguely familiar. But his clothes were shabby and she smelt a faint odor of something rotten, like someone who hadn't had a shower for a while, except worse.

His eyes were obscured by tinted spectacles.

"Vodka and tonic, right?" the man said, his speech slurred, as he placed a drink in front of her and sat down opposite.

"You've got the wrong person, bud," Alison snapped.

"I don't think so," the man said quietly with a wide grin, the slur gone from his words.

Alison gasped. Pushing up her sunglasses she peered closely at his face. His hair was the same shade as her own: jet black, as was the stubble of his beard. His face seemed chubby from a distance, but close-up she saw it was actually lean, except for his bulging cheeks. He wore a jacket and pants not even the Salvation Army would want, she thought; so baggy she couldn't make out the shape of his body.

But there, in the middle of his cheek, was that very familiar dimple.

"It can't be you." Her eyes went from the dimple to his hair: tamed—lying flat against his head, nothing like Olsson's unruly brown locks—and back to the dimple. Her hand began to reach out to touch his cheek. "It just can't."

"Why not, Alison?"

"Derek!"

Olsson nodded. He took off his glasses to clean them with a napkin; Alison found herself smiling at the warmth and memories of his soft eyes.

"Are you all right?" she asked urgently, one hand tightly clutching his. "I couldn't stand thinking of you locked up like an animal in a cage. How could you take it?"

"I survived." Olsson returned her grip, caressing her wrist gently with his fingertips.

"Is it safe for you to be here?"

"Possibly not. So I shouldn't stay too long."

"And what's that awful smell?"

Olsson patted the side pocket of his jacket. "A small piece of a rotting fish," he grinned. "Very effective, eh? But I don't think I'll be wanting to wear this jacket again."

Alison laughed. Then her shoulders dropped, her hand on Olsson's relaxed its grip, the muscles in her arms loosened, as though a tension that hadn't been apparent was draining from her body. A single tear rolled down one cheek; her laughter stopped as suddenly as it had begun.

She jerked upright and pulled her hand from his. "But if you're going to ask whether I've forgiven you, the answer is no."

Olsson dropped his eyes; the spectacles slipped from his fingers with a faint rattle that could barely be heard above the background chatter and slurps of beer.

Olsson shook his head.

"So why did you want to see me? And here of all places."

"Why did you come?" Olsson asked softly.

"Just answer my question, Derek."

"I was worried about you."

"Do you really expect me to believe that?"

Olsson leaned forward, his forearms digging into the table's edge, his hands clasped in front of him. He gazed silently into her eyes, his face serious, and then as he spoke he was weighing his words carefully, "You're in danger, Alison?"

Not hearing his question mark, Alison flinched at his words, covering her reaction with a forced laugh and a puzzled expression. "Me?"

Olsson sighed, leaning slowly back into the cushions of the booth. But his eyes would not let hers go.

"Yes, you," he said. "Ross told me he gave you a referral."

"He shouldn't have."

"I disagree."

"It's none of his business—or yours."

"I'm making it my business."

"I haven't asked you to."

"You have the entire federal bureaucracy at your disposal—thousands of cops and spooks you can call on. So just tell me, Alison, why you need to do something . . . 'unofficially'?"

Alison's lips twisted into a smile. "To gather 'unofficial' information."

"On who?"

"On . . . potential troublemakers."

"Who'd make trouble for whom?"

"Royn," Alison said firmly, adding in a slightly softer tone, "mainly."

Olsson breathed long and deep, nodding his head slowly. "I see," he said. "So you're not going to tell me."

"What's to tell? Anyway, as you pointed out I have a whole government bureaucracy to protect me from danger—should I ever need it."

"Alison—your answers only leave more questions."

"Do they?" She laughed at her own words. "Anyway," she said, a flash of anger behind her eyes, "what can one man—on the run from the law—do that thousands of professionals can't?"

"Nothing—if he doesn't know what the problem is."

"Well," Alison said, standing up and reaching for her handbag, "it's very sweet of you to offer, Derek, but I don't see why you're trying to make me believe you care."

"I've always cared, Alison," Olsson said softly.

"You have a strange way of showing it."

"By offering to help you?"

"You know that's not what I mean."

Olsson bowed his head. Slowly looking up, speaking hoarsely in a whisper Alison had to strain to hear, he said, "I know I've given you enough reason—"

"Enough reason? A thousand times enough."

Olsson squirmed uncomfortably, as if her words were waves of raging surf shattering him on a rocky shore.

"I should never have come here." Her eyes flashed as she spun on her heel, and took a quick step towards the entry door.

"Wait."

Alison turned at the insistence in Olsson's voice; she hesitated at the mute appeal in his eyes; her hand went to the silver and jade bracelet on her wrist.

"Take this," he said, offering her a slip of paper, his eyes going to the bracelet, wondering if she was thinking about throwing it back at him.

"What's that?" Her nose wrinkled at the paper as if it had been wrapped around the rotten fish; she made no move to accept it.

"An email address. If you ever need me."

Alison's body swayed back, away from him, but her feet wouldn't follow. Her eyes gleamed with fury—and glinted in the faint light as if beads of condensation were forming on an ice-cold glass. She said nothing, her lips tight.

In one swift movement Olsson stood and stuffed the paper in a side pocket of her handbag.

Alison stepped back, letting her hands drop. "Another promise you'll break, I suppose," she said. With a shrug she turned away towards the door.

Olsson stood watching her as she stormed out of the bar, hoping she'd look back. Alison, her glass untouched, nonetheless reeled slightly, like someone who'd had one drink too many.

ANOTHER PAIR OF EYES, belonging to a nondescript man who'd been nursing a beer at a darkened, corner table, followed Alison's progress with veiled interest. As she passed him he dialled a number on his cellphone, listened, and then dialled another. "She met a guy I don't recognize. He looks like a bum—not her type. But somehow . . . I got the impression of a lovers' quarrel. Very strange. Too dark here to get a decent picture. She's leaving now. Do you want me to follow her—or him?"

As he closed the phone he watched admiringly as the harsh sun highlighted the shape of Alison's body before the door swung shut behind her. He then turned back to his beer, waiting patiently, as he did most of the time, to see how long the bum would stay—and where he would go after that.

*****

MELANIE LOOKED AT THE clock when she heard the buzz of the doorbell. Six thirty . . . *and he's still not home.*

With a sigh, she stood up and walked out of the living room into the foyer. The doorbell buzzed again and again, repeatedly. Who could it be?

She saw Zoë coming down the stairs in a dressing gown. "I'll get it," Melanie called. "Are you expecting anyone?" Zoë shook her head and turned back up the stairs.

"I'm coming, I'm coming," Melanie yelled. The buzzing didn't stop, even when she opened the door to see Anthony Royn leaning, slumped against the door jamb, his eyes and face red, his finger stuck to the door bell button.

"Hi, beautiful," he said with a big smile.

"You're drunk," Melanie glared, wrinkling her nose at the strong, sour smell of his breath. She slapped his hand away from the buzzer.

"You too?" Royn laughed. He leaned forward, grabbing for the doorway as he half-stumbled, and said in a low, conspiratorial voice, "They wouldn't let me drive anywhere. Made me get into a taxi—shaid I'd had too much to drink. Foolsh."

"Just as well, " she said contemptuously. "Deputy Prime Minister Anthony Royn picked up for drunken driving would make a great spread in the Sunday papers."

Royn smiled. "Made some new friends," he giggled. "Somebody said I looked like Anthony Royn and I said, 'Curse of my life, being compared to that bastard.' They all thought I was a good Labor man, then. Fooled 'em, didn't I?" His giggles came almost hysterically—until they turned into a fit of hiccupping.

"Did I ever tell you, Mel," he said, his eyes roving slowly over Melanie's body, "how mush I love you?"

Holding onto the doorway with one hand, Royn reached out with the other towards Melanie's shoulder. Melanie's nose curled up and her mouth wrinkled into a frown as she took a step backward; Royn's arm hit empty air and continued to swing around, his fingers slipping off the door jamb and, stumbling, he fell in a heap. "Whatcha do that for?" he asked looking up in surprise. "I'm your husband."

Royn, slowly and awkwardly, picked himself up, moving a little closer to Melanie in the process. "I have rights . . . " he mumbled to himself. ". . . I think . . . shomewhere in marital law. . . ." His eyes were screwed up as he tried to remember. "Shomewhere. . . ."

"Not in that state, you don't." Melanie took another step back, and raised her voice as she spoke with rising contempt. "You're nothing but a liquid lunch."

"Lunch? I—I think I ate shomething . . . I can't remember." From his position halfway off the floor, Royn angled his head up, looking hurt and puzzled. Melanie glared at him, making no attempt to hide her obvious distaste.

Grunting, Royn finally managed to get himself up, wobbled slightly and, breathing hard, edged his way backwards to lean on the wall behind him.

"You've been gone over eight hours without a word. You wouldn't answer your phone. You've been drinking yourself to death by the looks of it. With who?—" her eyes narrowed in suspicion "—so what do you want me think?"

"And with damn good reason."

"Good reason—?"

"Damn right. You asked me to do shomething and I did 'zactly what you wanted. Next day you bawl me out—and not in private, either. And Zoë got 'zactly what *she* wanted . . . how can we expect to have *any* control over her now? Every day I'm away I miss you terribly. Whenever I phone you always find shomething to bitch about. When I come back home, dying to see you, you make me feel it would be better if I hadn't. So I went and had a beer or two, jusht what I needed."

"*I'm* always bitching—?"

"Damn right."

"—when you leave me all alone in this enormous house—"

"Thash your choice—"

"And who'd look after the kids then?"

"They're not kids any more."

"—while you're up in Canberra—"

"Jush an hour away." Royn raised his voice, his eyes glaring redder. "Yet shomehow going with me to New York, London and Paris is never a problem for you."

"That's different."

"Really."

"And God knows what you're up to up there . . . especially when you don't even take my calls."

"What are you accusing me of now? Working my guts out, thash what I'm doing in Canberra. . . . Hell! I don't even need to work. No Royn needs to work."

"What would you do then—sit around here all day?"

"Why—would that be a problem for you?"

"It wo—" Melanie's voice stopped in the middle of the word, her face frozen as if in fright about what she might have been about to say.

"Jush tell me one thing, Melanie." Royn made to take a step towards her and as he began to lurch, changed his mind. "Jush when did you stop loving me?"

Melanie's big eyes grew even larger. "I—I—" she stuttered, her hand flying to her chest. With an effort she stilled her lips, as if to arrest any other sound in mid motion, although no sound was stirring in her breast other than the thumping of her heart.

"Stop it. Stop it. *Stop it.*"

Royn and Melanie turned as one to see Zoë standing halfway down the staircase, her fists trembling by her thighs, blinking back tears. "You're never here, Dad—"

"Yesh I am and . . . " Royn protested mildly, his voice trailing off when he remembered where he'd spent the day.

"—and you pushed him into politics—" Zoë turned to face her mother "—you and Grandpa. And you're always clucking around me like an old mother hen—it drives me up the wall."

"Me?—it's all my fault?" Melanie said, turning her glare to her daughter.

"And the way you're always bickering and arguing and shouting at each other," Zoë continued as if no one had spoken, "why don't you get a divorce? You might as well—at least life would be peaceful around here for a change."

Royn and Melanie stared at their daughter open-mouthed. Zoë's cellphone rang. "Tom! Yes. Come and pick me up now. . . . Yes, right away . . . I've got to get *out* of here."

She glared at her parents. "I'm going out—now. I can't stand it any more."

"Tom? Who's Tom?" Royn mumbled.

"Zoë. . . ." Melanie started to say plaintively.

"And I'll be back when I'm good and ready and not before." Zoë's tears smeared her makeup into black lines under her eyes; she stormed out the still-open front door, slamming it loudly behind her.

Melanie stared at the closed door, her body shaking with uncontrollable sobs, wet rivers racing from her eyes to her chin. She slowly turned to look at Royn.

"Why are we doing this to each other, Tony?" she asked, her voice trembling between gasps for air. "Why?"

Royn took a half-stumbling step towards her, hugging her tightly, partly leaning on her for support, awkwardly dabbing her eyes and cheeks with the end of his sleeve. He swayed slightly, losing his balance and they both sank awkwardly to the floor, hugging each other for support as they slowly collapsed. They sat looking into each other's tear-streaked eyes.

"I jush don't know, Mel. But I wish to God it would stop."

15 Tinkle, Tinkle, Little Star

A WHOLE SUNDAY MORNING *with nothing to do . . . but worry,* Alison thought as she opened her eyes to stare blankly at the ceiling. She burrowed back under the blankets . . . but it didn't make any difference: even with her eyes closed, even though she still felt sleepy she was, nonetheless, wide-awake. Reluctantly, she threw back the covers and sat on the side of the bed as though considering the blank expanse of the day before her. After a while she came to a decision: *Go for a run.*

An hour and a half later, she jogged towards her favorite coffee shop in Manuka, a small complex of trendy boutiques, restaurants, and cafés little more than one city block in size. To Alison, it was one of the few places in Canberra with any real personality of its own. The main street was lined with tables along the footpath. It was the sort of place where, if she closed her eyes, the smell of coffee and croissants, the bustle of people and the soft sound of music in the background, could make her think she was sitting at a sidewalk café in Paris, not Canberra . . . for just a moment.

As she ran by the tables, a couple of young men, barely out of their teens, seemed to be undressing her with their eyes. She glared at them so severely that they both turned away, embarrassed.

But when she reached her destination she stopped, cold, as she saw her reflection in the plate glass door. Her thick black hair was plastered to her head; the T-shirt she'd grabbed in haste was old and tattered; and the loose tracksuit pants made her look shapeless from the waist down. *Maybe I should feel complimented,* she thought. *After all, how often do kids like them give any 34-year-old woman, let alone a dishevelled one, "The Look"?*

"Morning. Louie," she said to the swarthy, elderly man behind the counter as she stepped inside.

"Morning, Miss McGuire," Louie replied. "The usual?"

"Thanks," she nodded, putting a twenty-dollar bill on the counter. "I think I'll sit out in the sun."

"Okay, I'll bring it out to you. And you look like you could use this," Louie said, handing her a large bottle of water.

"Most definitely," said Alison. After a long gulp she asked, "And what have your customers been talking about this week?"

"Aside from the weather, and who's divorcing whom?" Louie's eyes twinkled. Alison said nothing. They played this game every Sunday morning. "The Sandemans, of course. They all want to nuke the terrorists who killed those soldiers. And most of them wonder why the hell we're involved in this no-account little country, don't think we should be sending more troops up there—and reckon our forces oughta all come home so there are no more deaths."

"Ah, I see. A perfectly balanced sample. And what do you think?"

Louie looked at Alison intently before he spoke. "I saw enough death and destruction in the second world war to last me several lifetimes. First Mussolini's *fascisti*—" he spat the word "—and then the Germans and the Americans. I was lucky." He rolled up the sleeve of his left arm. "See that," he said, pointing to a ring of faint scars on his upper arm. "Over sixty years ago. American bullets—which saved my life. They shattered my arm— but I spent what was left of the war in hospital. And I never saw any of my comrades again. I'm sure they all died. You know, we would have all melted into the hills except for one thing: the Germans were behind us and we knew they'd shoot us if we tried to run away. So we shot at the Americans instead. But not too well . . . the war was over for us by then, but we were still stuck in it.

"So if you really want to know what I think I'll tell you."

"Yes, Louie, I really do."

"I think if people like your puffed up peacock of a boss want to send young kids out to die, they should at least have the decency to lead them into battle themselves."

Alison burst out laughing.

"I'm not being funny," said Louie, irritably.

"I know," said Alison, speaking between giggles. "But you've got to admit, the picture of Anthony Royn and the rest of the wheezing, overweight Cabinet stalking through the jungle or jumping out of foxholes and trying to duck bullets is pretty hilarious."

Louie chuckled. "Make the bastards think three times, though."

"That it would," she agreed.

Alison gathered up the five Sunday papers from the newspaper rack—two from Melbourne, two from Sydney, and the local Canberra *Sunday Guardian*—and took them out to a sidewalk table. With a sigh, starting with the newspaper on top of the pile, she flicked through the pages rapidly, scanning the headlines, occasionally reading a couple of paragraphs, looking for any mention of Royn, or any comment or article relevant to him in some way, before moving on. By the time Louie brought her order, she'd already dropped the first paper in the nearby garbage can.

"Do you ever actually read the papers?" Louie asked as he wedged a small tray with her cappuccino, croissant, and change onto the small table.

Alison laughed. "Hardly ever."

"I can tell you there's no need to read the local one. Your boss didn't rate a mention today."

"Ah," she replied. "Well, I want to see what's on at the movies."

"Nothing worth watching." Louie said. "Unless of course you've got a hot date. Then any movie will do."

"Louie," she laughed, reaching for her coffee, "you're probably right."

BACK IN HER KINGSTON apartment, she threw the two unread Sunday papers, with a few pages torn from the others, on the table and saw the message light flashing on the phone. It was from Royn, who answered when she called back.

"I'll be taking the morning flight to Singapore tomorrow, along with Melanie and the kids. We're all going," he said.

"Anything you need me to do?"

"Just let the Australian High Commission up there know—and arrange a courtesy call on the Singapore Foreign Minister late that afternoon, if possible."

"Certainly, Minister. What about hotels and so on?"

"All taken care of."

"Okay. I'll get a midnight flight tomorrow so I'll be there Tuesday morning."

"See you there."

Putting down the phone, she opened her laptop—and grimaced. Screening the growing volume of the geek's phone taps was taking more and more of her time. Aside from some interesting gossip between McKurn and Cracken, only one, so far, had been of any direct use. It was the sort of work that should be delegated—but she couldn't think of anyone she could entrust it to. Except, maybe, the computer geek . . . but then, he'd probably miss some connection only she could make. Shrugging, she set up the connections and went to have a shower while the emails downloaded.

Her hair still wrapped in a towel, she saw a message from the geek thanking her for the information—her summary of Sidney Royn's report—she'd sent him the previous day. And then she scrolled through one phone call after another, discarding most of them, until, half an hour later, she came to a man's voice she hadn't heard before:

"She met a guy I don't recognize. He looks like a bum—not her type. But somehow . . . I got the impression of a lovers' quarrel. Very strange. Too dark here to get a decent picture. She's leaving now. Do you want me to follow her—or him?"

After a pause, McKurn's voice replied, "Very odd . . . so follow the guy. Find out who he is. We can pick up the girl any time. And use the other number in future, dammit."

"I did. But you haven't switched the bloody thing on—and I can't wait."

"He looks like a bum," the man had said. *Could he be talking about Derek?* she asked herself in surprise. She looked at the time on the message—*We were in the bar*—and played it again.

"Is McKurn having me followed?" she muttered, looking unseeingly at the screen. "I wouldn't put it past him. . . . Or is the timing just a coincidence? And what's "the other number"? I should warn him anyway. . . ."

She picked up her cellphone and scrolled through the incoming calls, but Olsson's call yesterday morning to arrange their meeting yesterday was marked UNKNOWN.

She went to her wardrobe to get his email address, still stuffed in the side pocket of her red handbag. Holding the scrap of paper in her hand, she stopped in the doorway of her bedroom, feeling a rising anger and frustration. *Why should I?* she asked herself. *He could be in danger,* came another voice. "As if he's not!" Uncertain steps carried her back to the laptop. Hesitating, her fingers resting on the keys, until she muttered "Whatever," quickly typed You may have been followed out of the bar yesterday . . . and clicked the SEND button.

"Damn it all, Derek," she said to the silent computer, "if you hadn't. . . . Well, maybe we could have had a life."

*****

"TINKLE TINKLE LITTLE STAR," the children sang, "how I wonder wot you are."

Karla stood next to the teacher, grinning broadly at the thirty-odd children, aged nine and ten, who smiled hesitantly back at her. At Uqu's insistence, she wore an ankle-length skirt, a shirt with long sleeves, a flowery scarf partly covering her hair. The only way to find something that would fit was to have them tailor-made, a process which took all of two-and-a-half hours. Made of thin cotton, the clothes—even with sleeves that covered her wrists—were surprisingly cool. And so cheap—a mere 125 *tingi,* six dollars something—she'd ordered two more sets.

"Stop, stop," she said, raising her hands.

"Very good. But it's not 'tinkle, tinkle, little star.' It's '*tw*inkle *tw*inkle. . . .' Everybody, say '*winkle.*'"

"Winkle," the children chorused.

"Good," Karla smiled. So it's the 'tw' sound that's the problem, she thought.

Karla had been apprehensive when Arang'anat, one of the school's teachers had invited her—implored her—to help teach the children English. Karla had protested, "I've never stood in front of a class of children before."

"But your English speak, 'Orton-*gaat*." Arang'anat said. "Have no problem teach."

"And I'm not a teacher either—what would I do?" When she realized Arang'anat *was* an English teacher, she agreed.

Karla had met Arang'anat in the women's dormitory complex at one edge of the village where she had been billeted for the past three nights. Arang'anat was one of the many unmarried women—almost all young—who lived there. For the most part, they had come from other parts of el-Bihar to work in the fish-processing plant, *ganja* fields or hashish factory. The dormitory was presided over by elderly, unsmiling ladies and was surrounded by a high bamboo fence, with a gate that was locked a couple of hours after sundown. The old ladies griped when 'Orton-*gaat* refused to abide by those rules and sat smoking *ganja* and drinking mint tea with the men till late evening, grumbled when Karla returned and they had to unlock the gate, and even after they were reminded in no uncertain terms that Karla was an honored guest of the village, continued to nag the village elders incessantly at every opportunity.

But to the fifty-odd young women in the dorm, Karla was the object of endless fascination. She slept, as they all did, on a mat on the hard, packed-dirt floor. The first night she was hardly spoken to, but there were sporadic giggles and some "oohs" and "aahs" when Karla took off all her clothes in the dim light to change into her pajamas. As she bent, naked, to dig her pajamas out of her backpack she became aware of a dozen pairs of enormous eyes staring at her in surprise. Karla thought nothing of it until, waking the next morning, she realized the other women had all slept in their ordinary clothes. And the next morning, in the showers, they were fascinated by Karla's pale skin, her light pink nipples, and the strange light reddish color of her pubic hair—and shocked, as Karla showered naked. To Karla's surprise all the women showered in a long, shapeless, shift-like dress which covered them from under their arms to their ankles.

Few words were spoken that morning as the women sang their way to the mosque in answer to the call for dawn prayers. Karla spent the daylight hours at the beach with Uqu—which, the next day, raised many giggled questions. An unchaperoned, unmarried woman alone all day with a man, Karla discovered, was the stuff of scandal.

Meals were served at long tables sheltered by a thatched roof but otherwise open to the elements. At breakfast on the second morning one woman—who introduced herself as Arang'anat—boldly brought her tray over and sat down opposite Karla. Shyly, haltingly she began to ask seemingly innocuous questions like "Where you from?" "How old?" "Married?" and, gesturing politely towards Karla's shorts and T-shirt, "All women in Australia your clothes wear?"

Slowly, as they talked, the women at the other end of the table edged closer and a few more drifted over. Karla became the center of a circle of breathless eyes and questioning mouths as each young woman competed with the others to persuade Arang'anat to translate their question next, giggling or oohing as Arang'anat translated Karla's answer until the elderly woman who'd supervised the meal barked something and they all, except for Arang'anat, leapt up guiltily, picked up plates and trays and carted them off to the kitchen.

"We now tables must clean, dishes must wash," Arang'anat explained as she stood.

Karla noticed that apart from the women who'd been sitting with her, the canteen was empty.

"Where is everyone else?"

"To work. Our day off."

"I see," said Karla, "a woman's day off."

Arang'anat said nothing but looked puzzled.

"Is there a men's dorm?" Karla asked.

"Dorm?"

"A place like this where men workers sleep."

Arang'anat nodded.

"So do the men clean up the dishes on their day off?"

"Oh no," said Arang'anat, looking as if Karla had just pronounced a heresy.

Karla gathered some plates and stood. "I can help."

"No no, Arang'anat protested. "You guest."

Karla smiled. "I'm a woman, too, right?"

Afterwards, they gathered again and, shyly, Arang'anat produced a scrap of newspaper and a pouch of *ganja* and began to roll the leaves into a thin tube. "You like?" she asked Karla, a worried look on her face.

"Sure," said Karla with a smile, resisting her automatic reaction to turn up her nose at the use of newspaper. She searched in her pockets and found the packet of cigarette papers she'd bought in a village store. "A bit early, I would have thought," she said as she passed the small packet across the table.

Arang'anat smiled broadly. "Here okay. Outside no can."

For the next couple of hours, Karla was grilled—very politely, guardedly, and circuitously but with single-minded determination, despite continuous giggling interrupted only by shocked silences—about the mating and marriage habits of the Australian female; about the clothes she wore; whether it was true that a Western woman could choose any job she liked and go anywhere she liked . . . by herself; if it was really true that Australian women all went to the beach and lay in the sun with no clothes on—and how were the women punished after they'd inevitably been raped by any and every passing male.

"Te'winkle, te'winkle, little star," the children sang, "how I wonder wot you are."

"Very good," Karla clapped, surprised at how much she was enjoying herself. "Now—"

The classroom door was pushed open forcefully, swinging all the way to the wall with a loud *thunk,* and Gurundi, stepped into the classroom. He strode up to Karla, demanding angrily, "You 'ere wot do?"

"I'm helping teach these children English," said Karla, taking a step towards him. "More to the point, what are you doing here?"

Gurundi's eyes widened as Karla moved; his mouth hung open, for a moment speechless. Karla noticed that the children, who a moment before had been smiling and happy and were full of energy had now shrunk into their seats. A few were even shaking.

She saw that Uqu, who had positioned himself discreetly just outside the classroom, had silently followed Gurundi inside, a worried look on his face.

"Well?" Karla demanded, her hands on her hips, her gravelly voice sounding like a monarch questioning an errant courtier. "Explain yourself."

The boys' eyes were riveted, waiting apprehensively on Gurundi, who took half a step backwards, his pale China face turning rapidly into deeper and deeper shades of red. The girls, sitting on the other side of the room, watched Karla nervously . . . and with guarded awe. Karla felt a light tap on her elbow and looked back to see Arang'anat's fingers barely touching her, her shoulders drooping, her body meek, her eyes flicking fearfully towards Gurundi as she softly pleaded, "Please, 'Orton-*gaat,* no more—"

"You!" Gurundi shouted, his voice strangely high-pitched. "You now stop. . . ." His halting English failed him and he turned on Arang'anat and unleashed a stream of invective in the local dialect. Arang'anat cowered away from him, hiding herself behind Karla's body.

Uqu was gesturing wildly to attract Karla's attention—but Karla didn't see him, or chose not to. She took one stride closer to Gurundi so she towered over him. "You are an ill-mannered, miserable excuse for a man," she growled. "You have no business here. And you should be ashamed of yourself—no honorable person treats any human being, male or female, like that. Now, get out of here before I throw you out."

Gurundi, his head awkwardly tilted back to look up at Karla, seemed frozen in place, his only movement a slight quivering in his shoulders.

Behind her, Karla heard Arang'anat whisper, in a fragile voice, "'Orton-*gaat,* please, no more trouble."

But Karla herself was beyond listening. After a long moment glaring at Gurundi who refused to move—or was incapable of doing so—she grabbed his arm in a tight, painful hold. Fuming, Gurundi struggled to release her grip, but Karla held tight and marched him out of the door, half-lifting him to help him on his way. In the hallway she released her grip, and pointing imperiously towards the exit, commanded him, "Now, go."

Gurundi's eyes blazed at her—but, slowly, he turned and slunk way.

Karla was unaware that Uqu had stepped out behind her and quietly closed the classroom door until, when she saw Gurundi reach the outdoors, she spun around to continue her English lesson.

"You have just made an enemy," said Uqu quietly.

"Someone had to bring him down a peg or two—and I was happy it could be me."

"But you'll soon be gone from here while, unfortunately, that nice young lady teacher will not. And it's *she* who will bear the brunt of his anger."

"Oh my God . . . you're right." Karla tried to push past Uqu, but he held his ground, blocking her way.

"Do you know what he was saying to her?"

Karla shook her head. "Only that it was awful, whatever it was."

"He told her she was corrupting the village's children by bringing an infidel into the classroom, and she'd probably end up in hell or worse. There was more, much more, I'm sure, if you hadn't cut him short."

"I should—"

"Another time would be better. Let's hope Gurundi is licking his wounds so we can talk to the village elders first."

"We need to do that?" Karla asked.

"Do you understand what actually happened in there?" Uqu asked as he nudged her along the corridor.

"I chewed out a despicable runt of a man who—" Karla stopped when she noticed Uqu was shaking his head, smiling sadly. "So, tell me, what actually happened in there?"

"The village's current spiritual leader, the most influential young Muslim in the country, was just humbled, even disgraced in public—"

"Nothing more or less than he deserved."

"Perhaps," said Uqu. "Tungi, the village headman, has the authority to chew him out—but even he would do it politely. Now, though, Gurundi has just been manhandled by a *woman*—which, given his position, is a sacrilege—in a culture—"

"—where women are seen and not heard."

"Right," said Uqu. "And when they are seen, they do exactly what a man orders them to do."

As they walked across the square Karla noticed gratefully that Gurundi was nowhere to be seen. In the restaurant, Tungi-*ga* listened without comment, and with several quizzical, sidelong glances at Karla, as Uqu related what had happened. *"Matalam,"* was all he said when Uqu finished.

Karla took a table while Uqu went to order tea. The school bell rang. Tungi stood and walked slowly in the direction of the school.

"What do you know about Gurundi, anyway?" Karla asked as Uqu sat down, passing her a cup of tea. "You seem to think he's important and influential—why?"

"A few years ago, he came first in a Saudi-sponsored competition. The winner was the one who best-memorized and recited chapters from the Koran in Arabic."

"So he speaks Arabic, then?"

Uqu shook his head. "He memorized passages without understanding their meaning. The prize was a scholarship: two years at an Islamic school in Indonesia. He came back as a celebrity—and one of the few Sandeman Muslims who has had any formal schooling in Islam. So when the local imam became ill and died, he was offered the position of Khatib—who delivers the sermon at Friday prayers, a sort of assistant-imam if you like—until a trained imam could be found. Young men from all over the islands come to listen to him, to learn from him. Unfortunately, most of them are now out in the hills somewhere, toting guns."

"I see. So he's preaching . . . ?"

"Fire and brimstone. Death to America. Expel the infidels . . . and so on."

"So that's what he learnt in Indonesia then?"

"So it seems."

"But if he doesn't speak Arabic," Karla said slowly, "and his English isn't much good. . . ." She stopped. "Is there a translation of the Koran in the local language?"

Uqu shook his head. "Not as far as I know. The Bible, yes, but the Koran . . . I don't think so. But in his two years in Indonesia he's been taught what it all means—by Saudi-trained Wahhabists."

"I see," said Karla thoughtfully. "So he's hardly had a balanced education."

"Quite the opposite," Uqu said sourly.

*****

It had been an uneventful flight, except for the bitching when, about an hour out of Sydney, the chief steward had regretfully announced that the plane had completely run out of alcoholic drinks. Someone in the back started singing *The Pub With No Beer,* to be joined by over a hundred voices.

But Lieutenant Jeremy McGuire—sitting with the other officers and the senior sergeants in the business class section of the Qantas 767—noticed there was no similar shortage of soft drinks and snacks, so he wondered if the supply of booze had been limited intentionally.

As the most junior officer, Jeremy had the job of checking that all other 253 soldiers had safely disembarked from the plane before it was his turn. As he stepped outside, his nose wrinkled at the smell—and he stifled a grin as he saw that the other officers and the men, even in summer uniform, were already sweating in the glare of the tropical sun.

At the bottom of the steps he smartly returned the straggled salutes of the dozen soldiers waiting to board the plane. Unlike the soldiers who'd just arrived who, though standing easy, stood in neat, orderly rows on the tarmac, these veterans were lounging and chatting. Their uniforms were clean but wrinkled, their boots needed spit and polish, their floppy hats were stained with sweat and dirt. They came to a sloppy sort of attention as they saluted him—but then he noted one man with an enormous bandage on his head and another with his arm in a sling, and decided to make no comment.

"Good luck, sir," said one of the men as he made his way up the steps.

"Thank you. I hope we won't need it."

The soldier smiled knowingly but said nothing.

Looking up at the crooked sign, Wellcome to Toribaya, he wondered what sort of welcome he and his men would be receiving.

16 Fairy Tales?

DEREK OLSSON STARED AT his laptop, yawning as he read: You may have been followed out of the bar yesterday. "What a nuisance," he muttered.

Thanks, he replied; and on an impulse attached his public key to the message so Alison could send him encrypted messages.

"If I was followed, I guess 'Joe Schuster' is going to have to go into retirement for a while."

He padded over to the suitcase and rummaged inside it until he found a floppy beach hat. "Good." Pulling it down over his hair as far it would go, he checked the result in the mirror, and nodded. He pulled out two envelopes from the bottom of the small suitcase, took the passports from each envelope, studied the pictures, and then put one of the envelopes back. Taking out what looked like a tube of toothpaste he went into the bathroom and sat down in front of the mirror, wet his hair, squeezed the tube over the hairbrush and proceeded to brush the ointment into his hair.

"Half an hour to dry," he said, reading the instructions. Looking in the mirror, he decided to leave the stubble of beard till later.

Padding back to the laptop, he finished drafting the email he'd been working on, checked for other messages, packed everything up, and when the thirty minutes were up, got into the shower. As he dried himself, a face with reddish hair stared back at him from the mirror.

Shortly afterwards Derek Olsson, still masquerading as "Joe Schuster," walked out of the motel room wearing a loud pink shirt and jeans, tinted glasses, and a hat to conceal the changed color of his hair. He threw his luggage into the back seat of the Toyota and wandered over to the reception office to check out.

He spent the night in a nondescript motel in Goulburn, a little over an hour's drive from Canberra, where he'd gratefully crashed for twelve solid hours of sleep. As he slowly drove out of the parking lot he heard an engine come to life; as he turned the next corner, in the mirror he saw a grey Holden Commodore nosing out onto the street and, grinning, wondered whether the driver had had any sleep.

He drove carefully through the unfamiliar streets of Goulburn until he turned onto the highway towards Sydney, where he slowly accelerated until the speedometer reached 135 KPH, as if he was in a hurry to get somewhere . . . but stuck to that speed as if he had no idea someone might be on his tail. *Too bad if "Joe" gets a speeding ticket,* he thought.

Sure enough, he could see the grey Commodore sticking a kilometer or so behind him, the driver trying to pretend he wasn't really there by staying in the outside lane except when he had to pass another car. "Joe Schuster" relaxed back in the driver's seat, doing his best to look like a speeding driver who wanted to avoid getting a speeding ticket—slowing down at the tops of hills, for example, as one place the police liked to hide in waiting was at the bottom of a steep descent.

Okay, so I'm definitely being followed. How to throw him off the scent?

*****

"HAS THIS SCURRILOUS WEBSITE got anything to do with you?" Through the earpiece of the phone, McKurn's angry voice burned in Alison's ear.

"Senator?" Alison asked, as calmly as she could. "What on earth are you talking about?"

"McKurnWatch.com. Some bastard—" he spat his words "—has put up a website filled with scandalous rubbish libelling me. Better for you if you own up right now—if it's something you have done."

"McKurnWatch.com, did you say? Just wait a moment, please, Senator. . . ." As she spoke, her fingers danced over her keyboard and in a moment the web page flashed up, the sole illustration a famous cartoon of McKurn, his eyebrows devil's peaks and his bulbous nose bigger, and much uglier, than Pinocchio's:

McKurnWatch.com

Hi there Boys & Girls!

In the mood for a not-so-fairy tale? Poor boy makes good—with a twist?

This is the saga of how a poor boy from a rich and exclusive neighborhood rose against all odds to become one of the nation's most honored and powerful people through skullduggery, corruption, drugs, prostitution, intimidation and murder . . . and no one really knows anything about how he did it. (Mainly because most of those who did know something are now wearing concrete boots.)

So sit back, put up your feet, and "listen up."

Once upon a time, not so long ago and certainly not so far away, a young kid named Frank (who never lived up to his name . . . but I'm getting ahead of myself) grew up in a rich family in one of Sydney's more exclusive eastern suburbs. Daddy was a businessman who'd made some really good investments so the family lived high on the hog, in a big mansion in Bellvue Hill with a wonderful view of the harbour, maids, gardeners, cars, drivers, the lot . . . the whole box and dice.

Every day the family driver took the young Frank to kindergarten—at Cranbrook, no less. Nothing but the best for young Frankie you see. It was a good life.

But Daddy had been hit hard by the Great Depression, though he managed to hang onto his money for a while. However, just before World War II—which bailed everyone else out—Daddy (not to mention Frank) was broke, bankrupt, *kaput.*

Not quite totally: he did manage to save a small shop in Rose Bay with an apartment above (mainly because it was in his wife's name).

Still, Daddy scrimped to keep his son (the apple of his eye—though God knows why) at Cranbrook (but what a comedown—poor little Frankie had to give up the mansion with the swimming pool for a pokey little flat, and had to take the tram to school . . . while the rich kids who were still rich kids still arrived in limos . . . a formative experience, perhaps, especially at such a young age?) and in pocket money which, once he entered high school, he mostly spent on gambling and girls.

It wasn't long before the school authorities became aware that young Frankie had got a couple of girls pregnant—but of course he denied he was at fault. He'd also become rowdy, rebellious, and uncontrollable—the exact opposite of the "goodie-

goodie" Cranbrook boy they were trying to mould. (Wrong material with young Frankie.)

Anyway, at the tender age of 14 (that's right, he was a quick learner) Frank decided to quit school, mainly to deny the school the pleasure of expelling him.

In any case, aside from arithmetic (to count his money) what else did the school have to teach him that would be useful in his life to come of blackmail, standover tactics, and schmoozing with "ethically challenged" cops, bureaucrats and politicians?

Much to his father's disappointment, Frank then disappeared, presumably into the underworld. While we don't know for sure, it's a good guess since when Frank surfaced a few years later it was thanks to a gang fight that resulted in Frank almost being charged with manslaughter.

News to you? I'll betcha—but he wriggled out of that one, you see. His *real* education was going gangbusters.

More about that (and lots of other good—well, better—stuff) to come. So hang onto your seats for our next installment.

—The McKurn Watcher

With great difficulty, Alison stopped herself from bursting into laughter.

"Yes, Senator," she said with a straight face, "I see what you mean."

"Filth." McKurn spat through the phone. "So . . . answer my question."

"You think I . . . ?" Unable to continue restraining herself, her laughter echoed through the outer office.

"Goddammit, Alison," McKurn growled. "This is not funny."

"Quite so, Senator," she replied, still chuckling and dabbing her eyes with a tissue. "But what is hilarious is why you think I'd do something as stupid as that."

"I suppose you wouldn't . . . maybe."

"No maybe about it. . . . Why don't you take some legal action to close it down?" Alison asked.

"The damn site is set up in the U.S., where the libel laws are a lot weaker than they are here."

"Presumably, though, whoever set it up is an Australian—so you could take legal action here."

"If we could find out whose it was—but the ownership is cloaked."

"Oh dear," Alison replied, hoping her smile was not reflected in her voice. "Well, I'm afraid I don't have any more suggestions. And, uh, Senator, unfortunately I won't be able to meet you until Friday at the earliest—maybe not even till next Monday."

"Whyever not?"

"I have to go to Singapore tonight with the minister—the Sandeman oil negotiations. I won't be back until Thursday or Friday night."

"I suppose that will have to do then," McKurn said gracelessly. "Till Monday." And the phone went dead.

Alison turned back to her computer where the McKurnWatch page was still showing. Noticing an option to sign up "for further thrilling installments of Frankie's life story," she entered an email address and clicked SUBSCRIBE NOW.

*****

HALFWAY TO SYDNEY, OLSSON pulled into a diner set in the center of the freeway. Out of the corner of his eye, he noticed the Commodore pull into a parking space on the other side of the parking lot.

He rummaged around in the backpack until he found what he was looking for, and then pulled a dull grey T-shirt from the suitcase.

At a leisurely pace, making sure he could be seen, the T-shirt bunched up in his hand out of sight, he strolled into the diner and went into the bathroom. In a cubicle, he took off his shirt, put on the grey T-shirt, and put the pink shirt back on over it. He was washing his hands, whistling, when another man strolled in and went to the urinals. Their eyes met for just a moment; Olsson smiled pleasantly but the other man quickly looked away.

He stood in line for a while, bought a coffee, and sat drinking it for a few minutes. The other man had come out of the bathroom a moment after he did, and spent a while looking sideways at the menus pinned to the wall behind the counter as if he were deciding what to order, yet positioned so he could also see Olsson without having to turn his head. When Olsson sat down with his coffee, the man stood in line. But when Olsson stood up, carrying his coffee out of the diner, he saw the man tense up, and as Olsson walked outside, the man sprinted for another exit.

Back on the highway towards Sydney, Olsson took out his cellphone and made a call. He had to wait a minute or so for an operator, but soon closed the cellphone with a satisfied smile, and accelerated until he was, once again, speeding along at a steady 135.

*****

ONLY TWICE, ON THE long boat ride from Toribaya, had Karla been able to hook up her laptop to the satellite dish Uqu carried. Inkaya, Karla was pleased to discover, had a small internet café where she could check her email and talk to the office—at any time of day.

"Have they lifted the communications blackout, do you know?" she asked Uqu.

He shrugged in reply. "I don't know. But we're a long way from Toribaya. Maybe el-Bihar connects direct into the Papua New Guinea network, just a few kilometers across the water."

Karla remembered standing on the pier, looking at the island just a stone's throw away, it seemed, across the narrow strait. Now and then, a *banca* made the short crossing without any apparent hindrance—at least, not from the uniformed official sitting or, more likely, sleeping at the end of the pier.

Seeing the internet café was empty, except for the cashier at the front, Karla whispered to Uqu, "The people back in Sydney told me Australian troops are trying to find me as well."

"I'm more worried about Sandeman soldiers showing up here," Uqu murmured softly in reply. "But even if they don't, any day now a picture of you will get to the local police station—I doubt your blonde hair will do you much good then."

"Meaning . . . ?"

"It's not going to be safe for you to stay here much longer."

Karla nodded. "Then—"

"Not now," said Uqu. "Let's talk about it later."

"Okay," said Karla, looking at her laptop blankly She closed it, put it in her backpack, and said, "Let's go for a walk."

They walked slowly past the school where children were playing—too quietly, it seemed to Karla. Or was it just her imagination? She shook her head as she thought again of Arang'anat, and how everybody's attitude towards her had changed since she'd marched Gurundi from the school. She was still welcomed at the elder's table but more coldly, out of politeness now, she thought. And the grouchy old ladies who ran the dormitory had made it clear that she, too, must now abide by the curfew—and Karla saw that, for the first time, they were really happy.

There were no more giggling, *ganja*-smoking chats. Many of the other women in the dorm avoided her, some even eyeing her disdainfully. Others looked at her longingly, and a few even came up to her when no one else was around, whispering *"Matalam, matalam"*—"Thank you, thank you"—with a quick smile before nervously scurrying away.

But what really hurt was how Arang'anat trudged around lethargically, the red, frightened wetness of her eyes now seeming a permanent feature of her expression, and the way Arang'anat avoided her.

Late the previous evening, Karla couldn't stand it any more and walked up to her saying, "I'm sorry." Karla was relieved as Arang'anat allowed herself to be folded into a tight embrace. "I had no idea. . . ."

"How much I wish like you I could be," Arang'anat said, shaking in Karla's arms. Looking up at Karla she said tearfully, "But, I no can; I no can." A few minutes later she shuffled away muttering, "Inshallah."

"Inshallah," Karla thought angrily. *Damn that attitude.* She wondered if there was some way she could spirit Arang'anat off to Australia. At that idea, depressing thoughts came into her mind: *Would she want to go?* And: *If she were in Australia, would she change? And if so, how much and how quickly?*

"Yes," said Karla as they reached the beach, "I think I've worn out my welcome, sad to say."

"Time to go?" Uqu asked.

"Right," said Karla. "But where—and how?"

"Back to Australia? Or—"

"Or where?"

"Well, you wanted to meet some separatists. We could go for a trek up in the hills."

"And then?"

"Australia."

"How? Just take a *banca* over there?" Karla asked, pointing towards the nearby tip of Papua New Guinea.

"Not a good idea. The Papuans might send you back here, intern you, or let you go. We're not sure how they'd react."

"What then?"

"The fishing boat at the end of the pier."

"Take that? To where?"

"North Queensland."

"How long would that take?"

"It's fast, but it would still be quite a while."

Karla looked at the boat, her eyes narrowing. "That's how the *ganja* and hash get to Australia, isn't it?"

Uqu nodded. "It's all been arranged. You can take the next boat whenever you want."

"The next boat?"

"One goes every day or two."

"Makes sense."

"The village elders agreed long before you got here—and they're men of their word, no matter what might have happened."

"You mean Gurundi?"

"Exactly. And I can tell you, few of the elders disapprove of what you did, only that you, a woman, did it."

"I see. So we could go for a trek, as you put it, and then I can take the boat . . . ?"

"Right. But, perhaps we should leave in the morning?"

"Okay," Karla nodded with a feeling of relief. "Now that's decided, let's go back to the internet café. I still have some things to do."

*****

WHEN HE REACHED THE outskirts of Sydney, Olsson turned off the Sydney-Melbourne highway onto the M5 toll way, which went past Sydney Airport to the eastern suburbs.

The traffic was now heavier, so the Commodore stayed closer to him than it had on the open highway. And Olsson now stuck to the speed limit, as most other cars did on this road. He took the exit to Sydney Airport and a few minutes later drove up the ramp to the departures level of the international terminal, the Commodore still on his tail, just half-a-dozen cars behind.

He drove all the way to the end and swung into an empty parking space. He leapt out of the car, grabbing his suitcases from the back seat, and walked through the glass doors. As they closed behind him, he heard a voice calling, "Hey, mister. You can't leave your car here."

"Be just a moment," Olsson shouted back.

As he turned right, as if heading for a check-in counter, he could see the Commodore stop beside his Toyota, the driver hesitating before stepping out, only to be accosted by an airport parking policeman. Olsson grinned: drivers were supposed to stay with their cars and a car without a driver would be quickly towed away.

Once out of sight of the door he ran towards the escalators, wheeling the larger suitcase behind him, and went down towards arrivals. As he stood on the escalator, to the surprise of the people nearby he ripped off his shirt, grimacing slightly as a few of the buttons flew off, and stuffed the pink shirt, beach hat, and tinted glasses into the side of the suitcase.

On the arrivals level, fluffing up his now-reddish hair, Olsson stopped at the rental car counter. Waving his gold card and driver's licence, he was handed a set of keys with the words, "All ready for you, Mr. Brewster. Have a nice day."

A few minutes later, he pulled out of the parking lot and headed back towards the highway. He grinned when he noticed the man run out of the arrivals door near the rental car counters, looking around frantically for a black-haired man in a pink shirt . . . who was nowhere to be seen.

*****

ON MONDAY AFTERNOON, THE NSW Police announced a reward of $200,000 for information leading to Olsson's arrest.

Durant was disturbed and puzzled to learn the underworld's grapevine had been abuzz since the previous Saturday with the news that someone else was also offering a reward for Derek Olsson: $100,000 dead; $500,000 alive.

Who? Durant wondered. And why?

*****

ALISON LEFT THE OFFICE earlier than usual that afternoon, to have time to pack before her connecting flight to Melbourne. When she got home she sent a message:

You have anything to do with McKurnWatch.com?

An answer arrived a little while later:

like it?

Never thought of you as a writer.

nor did i. no extra charge by the way

Thanks. Keep it up.

When she checked the email address she'd given Royn she found a message from the private investigators Royn had arranged to hire: You have some kind of work you need done?—and she sent the question she'd already prepared.

COMFORTABLY ENSCONCED IN THE Singapore Airlines first class lounge at Melbourne airport, with several hours to wait for her onward flight, she went through her email address book and prepared a list of the email addresses of all the federal parliamentarians, press gallery reporters, and any other similar contacts she could think of, after making sure each one she added was publicly available—like those from a parliamentarian's home page on the web. Then she trawled through websites of state parliaments, newspapers, TV and radio stations, and other likely looking websites for email addresses to add to her list, collecting close to three hundred she'd send to the geek, suggesting he add them to the email list for "Frankie's saga."

Just as her flight was called, she spied the private eye's answer in her inbox, and quickly sent the same message she'd received from the geek:

Next step: install the encryption program, and send me your public key.

17   "Mum's the Word"

Arang'anat hugged Karla tearfully. "I know you to go have to . . . but I wish you stay."

Karla was dressed for a trek: T-shirt, shorts, and walking boots, covered by a long skirt over her shorts, and a headscarf she'd take off when she was out of the village. "I'd like to stay too, if I could," Karla replied. "But we can stay in touch."

"How?"

"Do you have an email address?"

Arang'anat shook her head. "About them I've heard. . . ."

"I'm sure if you just go to the internet café, they'll show you how to set one up."

"Maybe. But . . . wot then *ka?*"

"You send me an email." Karla said, handing her a slip of paper, "and we can write to each other."

Arang'anat nodded uncertainly.

"And I want you to have this," said Karla giving her another piece of paper . . . a $100 bill.

Arang'anat looked at it and shook her head, looking offended. "No can, no can. Not from you," she protested, trying to push the bill back into Karla's hand.

"I want you to keep it," said Karla gently. "Save it, put it away for a rainy day."

"Rainy day?"

"In case something happens, some emergency . . . just in case."

"Too much. Too much."

"If you never need it," Karla said, folding her hands over Arang'anat's, "you can give it back to me."

"You one day come back?" Arang'anat asked, her eyes hopeful.

"One day, I promise. And if we stay in touch by email then I'll be able to tell you when I'm coming—and you can tell me where to find you."

"Thank you."

With a last embrace, Karla slung her backpack over one shoulder and walked towards the gate, Arang'anat walking beside her.

Shyly—and to the obvious disapproval of most of the other women waiting to see Karla leave—two younger girls came up to Karla to shake her hand. *"Matalam. matalam."*

"May Allah be with you," Karla replied.

As Karla went through the gate to where Uqu was waiting for her, Arang'anat stood watching her walking down the path, waving as Karla waved back before she disappeared from view around a corner . . . and stood looking down the empty path for a long while afterwards.

At the village square, Karla stopped to say "Goodbye" and *"Matalam"* to the elders, while Uqu packed several large bottles of water and packets of food.

"Do we have far to go?" Karla asked, eyeing the water bottles.

In the center of Jazeerat el-Bihar was a hill, called K'mah, some three hundred meters high, shaped like a cone. *Probably—hopefully,* Karla thought, *an* extinct *volcano.* Uqu pointed to the peak. "Up there somewhere. It will probably take most of the day."

"A long way," Karla said, in the tone of someone more used to walking to the corner store than climbing a mountain.

A couple of kilometers from Inkaya, Karla stopped in surprise as a man dressed like a soldier but in worn clothes that didn't match, a pistol at his belt, sprang out of the jungle into the center of the narrow path in front of them. She grabbed Uqu's arm. "What are we going to do now?" she asked.

Uqu smiled. "He's our guide."

He was a small, wiry man, his dark brown face leathery from years of exposure to the sun. Karla had discovered that people here were often a lot younger than the age they looked. This man could have been around forty, so she figured he was really in his early thirties.

He certainly had the energy of a much younger man. The way he moved, in short spurts, always alert, sometimes skipping from one rock to another, reminded her of the motion of a mountain goat. As she hadn't been introduced, and didn't even know if Uqu knew his name, she decided to call him Mountain Man.

He led the way, followed by Karla, with Uqu bringing up the rear. As the sun rose in the sky the path kept getting steeper, and the track narrowed as the jungle thickened. After a couple of hours of walking, with just one very short break for water, Karla found herself losing her breath as she tried to keep up with Mountain Man's pace, his quicker, surer steps outpacing her longer legs. He stopped and when she caught up with him, he silently offered with a couple of gestures to carry her backpack. After a moment, she gratefully took it off and passed it to him. Relieved of the weight, she found the going a lot easier, but her backpack could have been a feather for all the difference it made to Mountain Man's nimble steps.

Whenever she could see the peak of K'mah through the jungle—so thick that in places it grew tangled over the track, turning the sun's light into a dim shade of green— their destination didn't seem to be getting any closer. A while back, she had hoped they had passed the halfway mark; now, she was sure, night would fall before they arrived at wherever they were going.

The track made a dogleg and for a moment she lost sight of their guide. When she reached the bend he was nowhere to be seen—but she gasped when she saw, instead, half a dozen soldiers, real ones she realized, blocking the path. They all carried submachine guns. The men stood relaxed, smiling; they held their guns loosely, their fingers not on but near the triggers. But there was no mistaking where they all pointed: at her. To Karla, they looked very different from the soldiers in the hotel lobby. It wasn't that their uniforms were dirty and well-worn, some torn in places, or that they all needed a shower and a shave. It was something about the way they stood that made the soldiers in the hotel's lobby, with their shiny boots, sparkling buttons, and fresh, starched clothes ironed to a knife-edge seem like toy soldiers, as though they were big kids playing at war; these men looked as if they'd seen death and meted it out themselves.

Karla stifled a scream and spun about, looking for Uqu. A voice behind her yelled, *"Stop!"* as she saw what must have been Uqu's shoes and ankles disappearing through a small opening in the undergrowth. "Damn you, Uqu," she shouted.

Two men came up behind her and grabbed her arms. One of them saw the movement of Uqu's disappearance and raised his submachine gun. As he pressed the trigger Karla leant her weight into him, pushing his arms up at the same time. The burst of fire sprayed the sky. As the soldier recovered, he pushed her angrily out of the way and said something to the group behind him.

Karla noticed that the soldiers were all dressed and armed the same way, and none wore any insignia of rank. But one of them stood out when he barked something to one of the soldiers who'd spoken. From the way this man spoke and held his body Karla concluded he was an officer, or, at least, the group's commander. Her supposition was confirmed with the imperious gesture that followed his words, and the immediate actions of the two soldiers who let go of her and disappeared into the jungle after Uqu.

The officer stood studying her; Karla cringed away as his eyes took an inventory of her body. "Fancy that," he said. "I do believe we have found Miss Karla Bloody Preston."

The Australian-accented voice—another product, Karla figured, of the Australian effort to upgrade the quality of the Sandeman army—wasn't the same voice as the captain's at the hotel; but from the self-satisfied, smirking way he was looking at her, it was clear they'd both come from the same mould. "Your lucky day," he laughed. "Tomorrow, you'll be back in Toribaya."

Two other soldiers came up to her, roughly grabbed her arms and tied her wrists together tightly behind her back. "In a moment—as soon as my two men come back with your cowardly friend—we'll be going for a little walk," the officer said with a broad smile.

But five minutes passed, then ten with no sign of the two men. The officer sent another man to investigate; he went fearfully, but returned a few moments later. "They b'long sleep, suh," he said, "head knockknock."

The two unconscious men, who'd been stripped of their guns, ammunition, belts, and boots, were dragged unceremoniously onto the track. The officer poured water from his canteen in their faces and they both opened their eyes, groaning, their hands going to their heads. The officer kicked them and they scrambled slowly to their feet. "Fools," he spat. "Go—you lead."

He pointed along the track in the direction Karla had been going. The two men got to their feet and took position at the head of the group, one turning to say to the officer, "No guns. We no guns."

"Move," the officer replied, swinging his submachine gun vaguely in their direction. As the two men started gingerly picking their way along the track with their bare feet, he shouted, "Wikwik, wikwik," and roughly pushed Karla to get her moving.

*****

THREE TIME ZONES WEST, Alison McGuire flung herself onto the wide, comfortable bed in the Four Seasons Hotel in Singapore. She lay there, looking blankly at the ceiling, thinking that the day's packed schedule would hardly give her a break until late evening, knowing she should be getting ready for work, but wondering where she'd find the energy to move.

There was no question: first class was wonderful. And she'd thoroughly enjoyed it—except, despite several stiff drinks and a real bed, she felt as though she'd had no sleep until just before the plane landed. *I've had better flights sitting up all night in the back of a packed, cramped 747.*

Standing, she slowly did a series of exercises to stretch the kinks out of her muscles. She plugged in her laptop, sent Royn a text message telling him she'd arrived, and went and stood in the shower, luxuriating as the hot, pulsing jets of water massaged her body . . . until, sooner than she'd hoped, the phone rang.

Sighing as she turned off the shower, she picked up the bathroom extension. "Good morning Minister. . . . Okay . . . how about in thirty or forty minutes?"

Wrapped in a towel, knowing she didn't have much time, she scanned her emails, deciding to leave them all for later—except the one from the Melbourne private eye. She quickly rewrote the geek's instructions about tunnels, anonymizers, and communicating, set up three email addresses, encrypted her message and sent it. Checking the clock again, she decided it was more important to get the investigator moving than to be on time for breakfast with her boss. She wrote a second message to tell the investigator that the assignment was Senator Frank McKurn.

A THICK FILE UNDER her arm, Alison walked through the ornate, plushly furnished living room of the Presidential suite at the top of the Four Seasons Hotel and into the separate dining room where a sumptuous buffet-style breakfast lined one wall. Two waiters stood unobtrusively at attention, and a chef was poised to meet any special order on the spot. Alison filled her plate more out of duty than hunger, and as she and Royn talked about the day's agenda she forced herself to eat, papers strewn across the long table, hardly tasting the food, just so she'd have the fuel to last to the end of the day.

"So," said Royn as he stood to indicate their meeting had come to its end, "we're going to meet Nimabi and the rest in . . . ninety minutes."

Alison nodded, but did not follow Royn's hint. "Minister," she said sharply, "I'm not sure how much longer I can take it, this . . . pressure."

"Pressure?" Royn asked, slowly sitting back down. "Perhaps you'd better explain."

"McKurn," she said with quiet anger, her eyes flicking to the hotel staff standing nearby.

Royn stepped across to the buffet and after a few words the hotel staff filed out of the room. Royn shut the door behind them. Taking his seat again he said, "Okay. Tell me what's on your mind."

"McKurn will give me his answer on Monday. I've been in touch with the private eye and if he accepts, then maybe he can start this week . . . but how long before he gets results?" She shrugged despondently. "Who knows? And no new incriminating phone conversations—not a thing. I think McKurn has a phone number we don't know about—and, as you know, the geek hasn't been able to tap into his Parliament House phones. If he did then—God help me—I wouldn't have time to do anything except listen to phone messages. As it is, there's probably two, maybe three hours of messages piled up I haven't had time to get to." She lifted the day's agenda and waved it in front of Royn. "And with all this, when will I be able to start? Midnight?"

Royn nodded sagely. "It's definitely too much. If only we could get you an assistant."

"Yes—but who could we trust?" Alison shook her head, her eyes glistening. "And the geek hasn't come up with anything new . . . says he's still working on it. The Candyman Inquiry is progressing with the speed of a leisurely government bureaucracy. They're still arguing about the terms of the inquiry, for heaven's sake. I feel like we've run out of options." Alison's words tumbled out faster and faster, slurring together, her voice level and pitch both rising the longer she spoke. "I'm worried I'll have no choice but to accept

McKurn's answer on Monday, that we're not going to get him, that we're never going to get him. I can't sleep. I can't focus. I'm . . . afraid."

"We will get the bastard," Royn said forcefully. "But . . . playing double agent for a while will certainly be tough to pull off."

"Yes," she muttered. *And more.* As a tear rolled down one cheek, Royn leaned forward and laid a comforting hand on top of Alison's.

"But we can—"

"We can *what?*" a woman's angry voice cut in. "You'd better explain what's going on here?"

Royn and Alison turned their heads to see Melanie standing in the doorway, her face a red mask of anger, her shoulders tight as though she was restraining herself. Royn sheepishly withdrew his hand.

Alison glowered at Melanie. "Senator Frank McKurn," she said, spitting the words like bullets, "that's what's 'going on.'"

"Really," Melanie said sarcastically, taking a few steps closer towards Alison.

"Yes, Mel," Royn said with a sigh. "Really."

"Too much for you, is it?" Melanie said, her eyes focused on Alison, speaking as if her husband wasn't present. "Or is it just that time of the month?"

"You have no idea what you're talking about," Alison said coldly, and gathering up her papers stomped out of the room, pushing rudely past Melanie as she opened the door.

"Alison. Find Kieran," Royn said loudly, naming Kieran Fairchild, Secretary of the Department of Foreign Affairs. "Fill him in and tell him to meet me here in one hour—or less. Call the office and get them to put Doug—or whoever you like—on the next plane. And then take the rest of the day off. I can call you if I need anything."

"Thank you, Minister." Nodding at Royn and glaring at Melanie, Alison closed the door with a little more force than necessary.

MAX AND RICKY ROYN were battling each other on the PlayStation in the living room, the game projected onto an enormous screen. As Alison strode through, they called, "Hi, Allie," in unison, using the name Ricky had given her when he was five years old.

Alison turned and stopped, surprised she had failed to see them—or Zoë, who sat curled up in an armchair deep in conversation, her laptop on her knees and headphones covering her ears.

"You sick?" Ricky asked.

Alison shook her head. "No, but I've been better." Max and Ricky were so alike they were often mistaken for twins—especially now when, at nineteen and twenty, they were about the same height. They enjoyed adding to the confusion by dyeing their hair— Max's black, Ricky's blond—the same color. Alison studied the two young versions of their blond father sitting together on the sofa. "Sorry, Max," she grinned, "your hair's not the right shade of blond."

"Ah, well," said Max with a smile, "guess I can't fool you, eh?"

Hearing raised voices leaking out of the dining room, Ricky said, "At it again, are they?"

"Yeah," said Max sadly. "Hey, *Zo,*" he shouted across to his sister. Holding one of the headphone's earpieces away from her head, Zoë looked up. "What?" she said impatiently.

"Wanna have breakfast by the pool?" Max asked.

"Yeah," said Ricky, "before it gets too hot."

"But there's that buffet in the. . . ." Her voice trailed off as she heard her mother's angry voice through the thick door. "Good idea," she said. And with a conspiratorial smile that invited her brothers to join in, added, "And let's turn off our cellphones and not tell them where we're going." Then she noticed Alison still standing by the main door.

Before she could speak, Alison smiled and said, "Don't worry Zo. Mum's the word."

"Thanks, Allie," Zoë said, grinning back.

*****

THE ROYAL ARMS HOTEL.

Derek Olsson stood looking up at the sign before walking in.

In Sydney's Rocks area, the "ye olde British-style" pub was a regular hangout for journalists and staff who worked in the OlssonPress offices just a few hundred meters away along George Street. This was where he'd come to know Karla, on those evenings when he joined his staff members for a drink on the way to his penthouse apartment, just around the corner. As he walked up to the bar he—as expected—recognized several OlssonPress employees sitting around a table. He took his beer to a small table near them, one of the few empty tables in the crowded pub. But over the loud babble of conversation he couldn't make out what they were talking about.

He smiled as one of them—someone he'd often shared a beer with—gazed his way . . . and his eyes kept moving without a pause. Good confirmation that his glasses, beard, and slicked-back reddish hair were doing their job.

He looked at the beer glass, turning it through 360 degrees. *There's no question. It's the same. . . . But does that mean anything?*

BEFORE COMING TO THE hotel, Olsson had made a list. He shredded it when he'd finished, but he remembered it all too clearly. At the top he'd written:

WHO framed me?

WHY?

HOW?

I'm playing amateur detective, so what should I look for? he asked himself. . . . Motive. And Opportunity.

MOTIVE:

Revenge

Revenge? Who could have a grudge against me only murder would satisfy? Try as he could, he could think of only one name:

Luk Suk

But why would Luk Suk kill Vincent Leung, his own man? If his purpose was to set me up, he would have chosen someone else for me to "murder."

He thought about that for a moment and then shook his head. *Not his style,* he decided. Luk Suk could be devious, but he preferred the simple and the straightforward. In Sydney, it would be so easy to walk up to someone in the street, especially at night, put a bullet in his head or a knife in his gut and slip silently away. *If Luk Suk wanted to get rid of me, that's HIS way of doing it.*

He crossed off Luk Suk's name.

To divert suspicion

Somebody had a reason to kill Vincent Leung—and wanted to get away with it. Hence . . . make the police think someone else did it. Me.

So, who might want to kill Vincent Leung, and why? He wrote:

Me

Luk Suk

One of Leung's henchmen who was after a quick promotion

A competing gang

Somebody else

What was his motive for killing Vincent Leung? That was the big, gaping hole in Durant's case which could be overlooked because the evidence was so solid. Break the evidence, and the case would collapse.

He looked at the other four categories; while none could be ruled out, a competing gang seemed the logical suspect.

Olsson sat back and pondered what he knew about Sydney's underworld. The Golden Dragon Triad was heavily involved in the drug business. Knocking Leung out of the picture might slow them down—if only for a while—to another gang's advantage. If it was obviously the work of another gang, the Triad would, presumably, go on the warpath. Every reason to divert suspicion.

The complexity of the frame-up argued against one man acting alone, though it couldn't be eliminated completely, so he put a large red "X" with a question mark next to "henchman." Luk Suk? He shook his head. *Too many people would be involved; too easy for Leung to get wind of it.* Again, Luk Suk's style would be to send a hit man from Hong Kong. He repeated his "X?" notation.

Somebody else? Olsson shrugged. *Too many possibilities.* Only an investigation ruling out a gang would produce evidence or hints leading in some other direction.

Next question: Was I chosen *intentionally* or *randomly?*

INTENTIONALLY: someone wanted to get Vincent Leung AND me out of the way.

What possible connection could anyone make between him and Vincent Leung? He recalled the series his papers ran on how the drug trade corrupted police, politics, and the law, and Karla's articles advocating drug legalization. Politicians, especially Royn, condemned the idea. Letters to the editor ran three to one against legalization. The campaign gained no traction and posed no danger to the underworld's most lucrative business.

His papers' exposés of petty corruption . . . policeman on the beat taking bribes to waive a speeding ticket, town councillors implicated in fixing building permits, and the like. All petty, local stuff—and nothing to do with drugs or the Golden Dragon Triad.

So that couldn't be the connection, he thought. But my papers. They're a weapon I could use.

RANDOMLY: Why choose ME? Surely there are easier targets. . . .

He asked himself who he'd select if he were planning a frame-up. The intricacies of the frame-up argued in favor of going after someone easier . . . yet that very complexity made the evidence against him more compelling, especially in the absence of a motive.

He shrugged. He couldn't strike either possibility out. All that was left was his gut feel, which leaned towards INTENTIONALLY, so against it he wrote: Seems more likely. / And next to RANDOMLY: Can't be ruled out.

He turned to his laptop and found his lawyer's summary of the crime scene and the evidence:

Vincent Leung was found dead in his apartment by the cleaning lady about 11AM.

He'd been knifed. Estimated time of death: between midnight and 3AM.

Later, the traces of blood on the knife discovered in the boot of Derek Olsson's car
turned out to be the same type as the victim's; DNA analysis confirmed it was the
victim's.

The doorman on Leung's building swears he saw Olsson enter the building, with
Leung, around 11 PM the night before.

One strand of hair and two flakes of skin were found caught in the victim's
fingernails. The DNA test matched them to Olsson.

A nearly empty bottle of beer and two glasses were found on the coffee table in
Leung's apartment. Olsson's fingerprints were on one of them.

The only other fingerprints found in the apartment were Leung's and the cleaning
lady's. Several doorknobs had been wiped clean. The only fingerprints found on the
front door knobs were the cleaning lady's, indicating they must have been wiped
clean before she arrived.

The frame-up was well-organized, and cleverly done. Someone had gone to a lot of
trouble to collect bits of Olsson's hair and skin and a beer glass with his fingerprints
on it. They'd also had to find someone who looked like Olsson, someone who Vincent
Leung would willingly take to his apartment—and at eleven o'clock at night, hardly the
time a casual acquaintance drops by. *Was Leung gay?* Olsson wondered, *or did Leung
think they needed somewhere private to discuss something . . . ?*

Or . . . Vincent Leung had come home by himself, and the doorman had been paid
to identify Olsson.

Too dangerous, Olsson thought, shaking his head. What if the doorman turns out to
be an unreliable witness or breaks down in the witness box under pressure . . . ?

Or . . . he was someone recommended to Leung by Luk Suk or a trusted sidekick.

Too many logical possibilities, he thought. But the glass with my fingerprints. . . .

Was that the key?

He'd secured a picture of the beer glass by asking Ross Traynor to request their lawyer
to get one from the police. With the picture had come a note:

There were over a dozen beer glasses of different shapes and sizes in his
apartment. It looks like he collected them from different pubs.

Or they were planted to give that impression?

It was the kind of glass brewers supplied to thousands of pubs and bars all over the
country, a standard size with a brewery's logo—but nothing to identify which bar it
came from.

Exactly like the glass he was now holding in the Royal Arms Hotel.

Olsson preferred wine, and rarely drank beer, one glass at this pub being the main
exception.

He drank his beer slowly, watching the waiters move from table to table and the
barmen pour drinks. They were all too busy to notice what the customers were doing.

The OlssonPress group began drifting out the door and in a moment their table was
deserted, except for the empty glasses. He could reach out, pocket one now, and no one
would ever know.

As his eyes followed a waitress's progress towards the bar they stopped, fixed on the
back of a man's shoulder. A few white flakes of dandruff littered the dark fabric of his
suit . . . and a hair. *Hair falls out all the time,* he thought, one hand touching his head.
He tried to grab a single hair with his fingers . . . it was easy to grab a clump of hair but
difficult to take hold of just one strand. He tried jerking out several strands of hair at
once. He stopped when it hurt, *without* pulling anything out.

And the flakes of skin? He dragged the fingernails of one hand over his cheek. If Vincent Leung had tried to defend himself from his murderer, why just two flakes of skin? Wouldn't there be more?

And then . . . there was putting the knife in my car. Whoever had done that had been able to get into his high-security apartment in a high-security building without setting off any alarms, open the boot of a locked Mercedes and then get out again without leaving any trace. *Which,* he thought as he drained the rest of his beer, *puts every underworld gang on the list of suspects.*

DEEP IN THOUGHT, OLSSON left the bar and trudged along George Street without any particular destination in mind.

"Hey, mister," a voice wheedled, "can you spare the price of a hamburger?"

Olsson would have taken no notice, except the voice seemed vaguely familiar. He turned to see a balding, grey-haired bum sitting in a doorway. The bum's red-lined eyes looked vaguely in his direction without hope; several days' stubble sprouted from his face like dark fungus; both he and his clothes needed a long, hot bath; a paper bag in the shape of a bottle poked out of the bum's jacket pocket.

But the shape of the bum's jaw, and the bushy eyebrows. . . .

"Dad," he stopped himself from saying and cringed away shaking, his stomach threatening to revolt. It had been—how long?—some eighteen years since he'd last seen his father, and at least seventeen since he'd given him more than a passing thought. He took two long fast paces, intending to get himself past the stomach-churning sight and long-buried memories as fast as possible.

You, Olsson thought, *who pride yourself on being unable to hurt a fly. . . .*

He turned back. "Here," he said, pulling a wad of notes from his wallet and dropping them towards his father's outstretched hand. The bum's eyes lit up like a Christmas tree as fifty and twenty-dollar notes floated down in front of him. The breeze scattered a few along the footpath; he scrabbled for them.

"Don't drink it all at once," Olsson added as he thrust his wallet back in his pocket.

Sven Olsson was leaning forward, reaching for one of the notes; when Olsson spoke he stopped in mid stretch and his bleary eyes looked at his benefactor strangely. Had he recognized Derek's voice? But an instant later Sven Olsson's eyes. glinting. turned to the scattered bills. "Thank you, sir. Thank you, thank you," the bum babbled as he scrambled to pick them all up. As Olsson walked away, his father was unsteadily pulling himself to his feet, turning in the direction of the nearest pub.

Instead of hailing a taxi, he decided to walk. He wasn't surprised his father had turned into a drunken bum, but to actually see the reality was like opening a memory vault he'd thought was securely locked.

He stopped in mid pace, halfway across a side street, frozen in place until the angry *honk-honk* of a car made him realize where he was. His father must have known of his son's success, he was thinking. It was not the sort of story anyone could avoid. Yet, he'd never come asking for money or help. Because he knew what the answer would be? Pride? Or . . . perhaps . . . fear. . . .

DEREK OLSSON WAS BORN with a question in his mouth.

Whenever his mother snapped "You mustn't go out on the street alone," he'd reply "Why not?" Told "You're not old enough to do that," he'd answer, "Why not?" When his father growled, "That's not allowed," he'd say, "Why not?" A question he kept repeating until he'd accumulated sufficient cuffs and bruises to learn to avoid his father's presence as much as possible.

Sven Olsson had come to Australia from Denmark in his early twenties. Instead of finding the new life and prosperity he'd dreamed of, he ended up in a dead-end job and felt he'd been pressured into a shotgun marriage with a woman he didn't love who was pregnant with a baby he didn't want. His bouts of heavy drinking became more frequent and his unpredictable temper more violent, targeted at the focal points of his resentment: his wife, and the children he referred to indiscriminately as "your brats" or "the goddamn bastards."

Derek was born two years after his brother, Lars; his sister Jessica arrived fourteen months later. A year after that, Sven unintentionally made sure there were no more: bowing to her husband's drunken and far from gentle demands, Molly Olsson wheedled $500 from her mother for an abortion. But Sven found the money, drank most of it and with the rest paid some back street quack who botched the job. Molly Olsson spent a week in hospital and no longer had any need to take the pill.

Derek Olsson couldn't remember a week going by without his suffering a bruise, a welt, or worse. If not from his father, then from Lars who, whenever beaten by his father, turned around and got his revenge by beating up his younger brother. Whenever his father threatened his sister, Derek would attempt to protect her. When he was young, Sven would just laugh and push him out of the way. As Jessica graduated from being a tomboy trying to keep up with her brothers to a curvaceous adolescent, his father threatened her more often and his threat seemed more malicious; Derek became more determined to protect his sister . . . which just made Sven Olsson madder and more dangerous.

Molly Olsson retreated from her husband by walking around the house like a ghost pretending to be invisible and bowing wordlessly to her husband's every demand. Derek Olsson stayed at school late, played with friends afterwards or retreated into his room where he dreamed of being the knight in shining armor, the rags-to-riches slum boy who became a mover and shaker on Wall Street or the heroes of the other myths and fables he devoured.

When he was seventeen he discovered Aikido. When Lars went to hit him some ten weeks after his first lesson he found himself unconsciously following an Aikido routine. Much to his surprise, Lars ended up falling flat on his face. "You tripped me up," Lars complained as he pulled himself to his feet. "Fight fair, you goddamn bastard," he yelled, and launched himself at Derek again, his fists pumping.

"You're the bastard," Derek replied as he consciously stepped out of Lars' way and, in textbook fashion, took one of his wrists as it flew by and twisted it painfully so Lars ended up kneeling with his head touching the floor.

"Want me to break it?" Derek asked.

"You wouldn't dare!"

"Why not?" Derek laughed. "I've been wanting to do this for seventeen years."

When Lars was silent, Derek said, "I tell you what, I won't break your arm if you promise you'll never touch me again."

After a moment Lars said, "Okay."

"Promise?"

"Promise."

As Derek released him Lars sprung up and around and tried to pummel him. A moment later he was, again, kneeling awkwardly on the ground. This time Derek kept twisting until there was an audible snap.

When their father came home, he gave Derek a black eye, but Lars spent the next six weeks with his arm in a cast. Now and then Lars would wave his cast in Derek's direction, threatening to "smash your head in." Derek simply smiled and calmly replied, "Want me to break your other arm too?"

When the cast came off, Lars' arm never regained its full strength and Lars never hit his brother again.

A few months later Derek came home late to be greeted by his father's angry voice: "It's after eleven—where the hell have you been?"

Damn, Derek Olsson thought to himself as his father's bleary eyes glared at him, a shot glass and a nearly empty bottle of Aquavit on the table. *He's still awake—and drunk as usual.* Derek, who'd been tiptoeing towards the kitchen in his bare feet, froze and let his shoes and his Aikido bag drop to the floor.

It's now or never. He allowed his pent-up resentment and anger to surge through his muscles. Taking a deep breath to steady himself, he said, "Since when have you given a shit where I am or what I'm doing—except when you want someone to beat up on."

Sven Olsson's face turned a brighter shade of red as he pushed himself off the sofa. "You little bastard," he snarled, shaking his head in disbelief. "Seems I'll have to teach you a little respect—speaking to your own father like that."

"Respect?" Derek spat back. "You don't deserve respect—from me or anybody else."

As his father lurched towards him Derek tensed to counter the ingrained reaction of cringing away from his father's hand as it came swinging towards his face—a reaction instilled from the untold hundreds of times his father had slapped him in the seventeen years since he'd been born.

Derek Olsson had dreamt of this moment for almost as long as he could remember. No longer a defenceless child, he now stood a shade taller than his father; but Sven Olsson was almost twice his weight. Most of that extra weight, however, was in his belly, while Derek, though lighter, was all hard muscle. And sober.

Since discovering Aikido, he'd practiced this movement in his mind and on the mat countless times. On the mat with a friendly "opponent" he smoothly blocked the blow and glided out of the way. Every time.

But now, facing his father, reflexive fear in his stomach slowed him down. Instead of blocking his father's blow, aimed at his cheek, he deflected it so the fist connected with the tip of his nose.

Nevertheless, for the first time in his life he'd stood up to his father, and Sven Olsson faltered in shock. With a roar, Sven bunched his hands into fists and lunged at Derek's belly. But Derek had time to recover and whirl out of the way, nudging his father as he turned to send the older man crashing into the wall.

Dazed, Sven Olsson pushed himself off the wall and lunged again. But Derek's life-long fear of his father retreated in the face of his overpowering determination to win, and in a moment Sven Olsson was on the floor pinned by Derek's body in a painful arm lock.

"Let me go, goddamn you."

Derek slightly increased the pressure of the arm lock, and his father screamed in pain. "Shut the fuck up, or I'll do to your arm what I did to Lars."

"What's all the noise about—?"

Derek glanced behind him to see his mother standing in the doorway of the living room, shivering as she rubbed the sleep from her eyes, staring at her son in disbelief. "Derek. Wh-what are you doing?" she shrieked.

"I'm teaching Dad a much-needed lesson—in respect." Derek squeezed his father's arm as he spoke.

"Bullshit," his father yelped, struggling for release. "When I get up I'm going to beat the living daylights out of you."

Derek leant closer to his father's ear, pressing down with his weight on his father's back. "If you get up."

"Derek," said his mother, "you wouldn't."

"Why not?" asked Derek, in his trademark reply. When his mother said nothing he asked, "Give me one good reason why I shouldn't."

"You might go to jail," she gulped.

"Yes—and that's about the only thing stopping me from breaking his bloody neck right this minute."

"You don't have the guts," his father snapped.

Derek squeezed the arm again. "You're hardly in a position to argue right now, Dad."

"You—" his father spluttered between yelps of pain. "You can go to hell, and good riddance."

"*No,*" Molly Olsson screamed in a voice that sent shivers through the spines of both father and son. "Never. You'll not take my son away from me. If anybody leaves this house it will be *you,* not Derek."

Distracted by his mother's scream, Derek slightly loosened his grip and Sven Olsson lunged for Molly's ankle, knocking her off balance. Derek smashed his fist into the side of his father's head, saying, "There's ten thousand of those punches still to come before we're even"—and pinned his father to the floor again.

Dazed, Sven Olsson's eyes flicked uncomprehendingly between his wife and his son.

"Now it's your turn to listen to me," said Derek. "Promise you'll never touch me or Lars or Ma or Jessica again."

Sven Olsson shrank limply from his son's glare.

"I'm not going to let you up till you promise me that," Derek demanded. "And if you break that promise, I will break your neck."

His father opened his mouth to speak—and froze at the menace in his son's face, and the fist clenched in easy swinging distance from his nose.

"No," said Molly Olsson, as she picked herself up. "Even if he gives his word, he'll never keep it. You, of all people, should know that. He's got to go."

The tiny, mousy woman who crept around the house like a shadow burned with a fury Derek had never seen before: her hands tensed into fists, her blazing eyes and rigid mouth transforming her normally sallow, hollow-cheeked face. As she stepped forward into the dim light to stand looming over her husband, Olsson saw a red welt on the side of her face that hadn't been there in the morning, just above a faint bruise his father had planted there the week before.

Derek looked at his father's face and knew his mother was right. Sven Olsson was not a man to be trusted.

"You're right, Ma," said Derek, nodding. "Why don't you go and pack a few things for him and we'll throw him out right now."

But his mother was shaking, her face drawn and pale as if she'd seen a ghost. Her eyes slowly turned towards her son, but at first she didn't seem to recognize him. *She's overwhelmed, scared of what she's done,* Derek thought. "Ma," he ordered, "move."

"You can't," his father sputtered.

"Why not?" said Derek. "It will be like heaven to come home and know you're not here."

"Yes," his mother muttered at last, shuffling out the door, "it will."

"How will you pay the rent?—you'll get nothing from me."

"We get bugger all from you anyway—you spend all your money on booze."

"I'll get even with you—all of you—if it's the last thing I do."

Derek picked up the small bag Molly had placed on the floor, threw it at his father and slammed the front door. He felt his rush of energy drain away, leaving him with a hollow emptiness tinged with unaccustomed guilt. "He's gone, Ma. And I've got his keys," he said, waving them, "so he can't get back in."

Molly now seemed deflated, uncertain, and pleading with Derek as if he was now in command asked, "Oh, Derek, what are we going to do now? What's going to happen to us all?"

What's going to happen . . . ? Derek asked himself. The absence of his father, something he'd dreamed of for as long as he could remember, suddenly took on several new aspects he'd never considered before. He was about to respond, "I don't know, Ma," but stopped himself just in time, telling his mother, instead:

"In the morning we'll call Grandpa. He'll know what to do."

As a child, Derek Olsson had always looked forward to visiting his grandparents. His grandmother, Jennifer Dent, was a warm, loving person who doted on him, and always prepared his favorites dishes. And his grandfather, he felt, was the exact opposite of his parents. For one thing, whenever Derek said "Why?" or "Why not?" Jack Dent would answer patiently and at length. If he didn't know the answer he'd simply say, "I don't know . . . let's see if we can find out." So they'd go to the local library and consult the encyclopedia, or ask one of the many people Jack Dent seemed to know.

One day Dent returned home to see his grandson on the floor attempting to put back together a clock he'd taken apart, the pieces spread all over the carpet. Derek looked at his grandfather with a flash of fear—but Dent crouched down on the floor and said, "If you need some help, just let me know."

Several hours later, when neither of them could get the clock working, Dent took Derek and the clock down to the local watchmaker who quickly showed them where they'd gone wrong. And he'd take Derek with him to his service station, where Derek was allowed to pump petrol, serve behind the counter, and "help" the mechanics fix the cars.

"Maybe I could make a car one day," seven-year-old Derek said.

"Why not?" his grandfather laughed.

It was a dark day for young Derek when Jack Dent had a mild stroke and was forced to sell the business he'd built from a tiny garage on a back street into a thriving service station on Sydney's busiest thoroughfare, Parramatta Road. The first thing the new owner did was fire Sven Olsson, who Dent had kept on mainly as disguised charity for his daughter. Still, from time to time, his grandfather would take him there, but the new owner looked at Derek Olsson skeptically. Eventually, Jack Dent persuaded him to give Derek a part-time job on a trial basis—and he had worked part-time at the service station ever since.

Jack Dent did know what to do; the following morning Molly and her three children moved to live with the Dents.

Derek soon discovered that living with his grandparents was a very different proposition from occasional morning or afternoon visits. For all his seventeen years, he'd pretty much come and gone as he'd pleased. Now, he had to be sitting at the dinner table at one minute to six every evening. Breakfast and lunch were similarly scheduled. At ten o'clock every morning, rain or shine, Jack Dent would go for his daily walk. At five PM he'd have one careful measure of whisky; and at seven he'd watch the news. Everything had its place in his grandfather's house, which was so clean and tidy he came to feel he was living in a museum, and he got into trouble every time he left something lying around.

His grandmother almost never protested the way her husband ruled with an inflexible iron fist. But once in a while, when Jack Dent started to chew his grandson out for some transgression she'd interject, "Now, now, Jack. Derek's had a terrible time. Let him adjust."

Dent would glare at her—but relent.

His mother, however, glowed in a way he'd never seen before, looking more and more like the photographs of the pretty young girl scattered around the house. But she refused to leave the house after dark and would never go out during the day alone. And when Derek vaguely wondered when they'd move back home, she replied, "Oh, Derek, I'm sorry but I really can't think about that sort of thing just yet."

His sister Jessica felt right at home, grateful that Jack Dent's rules and regulations brought a much-needed order to her life. Lars, like Derek, chafed under those rules. But he'd been working since he'd dropped out of school a couple of years ago and quickly decided the time had come for him to move out on his own.

To regain his lost freedom, Derek quickly found tasks to keep him out late—duties Jack Dent found he couldn't argue with. "We're studying at the library tonight—exams are coming up, you know." "I'm going to work more shifts at the service station, starting Sunday morning. Now we have nothing at all from Dad, I have to help Mum out." "We have extra rugby practice—I'm the team captain, so I have to be there."

In this way, he achieved a balance between the freedom he'd always cherished and the order he'd never had. And though he would never admit it, with his father gone, his mother peaceful, his sister happy, and his elder brother no longer beating on him, this was the happiest period of his life. For when Derek did follow Dent's rules, his grandfather treated him with the same respect, love and attention he always had. Derek found he lived for those moments: Jack Dent was the only person he had ever loved and idolized.

HIS FATHER'S EYES, DEREK Olsson thought as he walked the streets of Sydney, hadn't changed in eighteen years. The fat had gone from his body; he now looked gaunt, underfed. His eyes were redder, blearier . . . but the look, the mind behind them, he sensed, was unchanged. The memory of his youthful guilt faded and all that remained was the revulsion he'd felt when he'd recognized what his father had become.

When he reached the guest house he staved off sleep long enough to send Traynor an email: Ask the lawyer to see if he can find out whether the Royal Arms Hotel—that pub in the Rocks—has any gangland connections. Also, I'd like to know exactly where the hair and flakes of skin were found—which fingers of which hand. And whether just TWO flakes of skin seem unusual or suspicious in any way.

He threw himself on the bed and collapsed, drained, feeling sleep welcoming him . . . only to jerk upright, his arms pushing him into a sitting position on the bed.

Lars, he thought, now wide awake. *It couldn't be . . . or could it?*

As teenagers, he and Lars were occasionally confused. He recalled a shopkeeper once saying "Hi Lars" as he'd walked through the door. As he reached the counter, the man said, "Oh, you're not Lars, you must be his brother." That had happened from time to time, though never from someone who knew them well.

In the line-up at the police station, the doorman studied him for nearly a minute before stating "That's him." His long look made sense if he'd seen *Lars* with Leung.

Would Lars bear a grudge for eighteen years? Yes . . . every time he used his weaker arm, he'd remember.

There were probably hundreds of people who looked enough like Derek Olsson to fool the doorman . . . but only one you could trust to keep his trap completely shut.

He had no idea where Lars was. His mother treasured the Christmas card Lars sent her every year, his only contact with his family. Molly Olsson would study the postmark on the envelope and rush to the atlas to see where her oldest son was: almost never the same place twice, as if Lars had turned into a tramp.

"I'll just have to find him," Olsson mumbled. He drifted off to sleep shuddering at the uncomfortable thought: *And when I find him, will he confess . . . or will I have to break his other arm after all?*

*****

BEYOND THE FACT THAT she was lying on hard ground inside a small tent, out of sight of lustful male eyes, guarded by two soldiers standing outside, Karla had no idea where she was.

The sun was on the way down by the time the two stumbling men, their feet bleeding and sore, led them into a small camp, set on a rise somewhere in the middle of the jungle. It had been slow going, not just because of bare feet, but because the other soldiers moved nervously, their guns at the ready, jumping at the sound of every bird whistle, every movement of some unknown animal in the jungle, and even—until they were chewed out by the officer—letting loose a few bursts of fire at nothing Karla could see.

Her hair was plastered to her head from the long, hot walk, every exposed patch of skin had been burnt a painful red by the sun, her now dirt-streaked, sweat-stained clothes were glued to her skin, and she itched everywhere she couldn't reach. She shuddered helplessly at the way the soldiers all looked at her . . . but she was simply pushed into the tent and left there.

She found that thoughts of what would inevitably come were pushed away by small irritants that grew larger and larger. An itch on her nose she could do nothing about with her hands tied behind her back. Continual sniffles as if she was getting a cold, caused by something she'd always taken for granted: she couldn't blow her nose. The urge to do so began to overshadow her desire to go to the bathroom. Unable to do more than roll over, and to awkwardly move her legs and neck, it felt as though her body had turned into a network of aching, screaming muscles. She was equally aware of every drop of dried sweat on each square inch of skin, of the scratches on her legs and knees, of the twinges that felt like incipient cramps rippling through her feet and toes, still imprisoned in her walking boots—and of the many blisters on her soles.

Eventually, the tent flap opened and a man stepped through. She braced herself, but the soldier merely put a bowl on the floor, along with a plastic spoon. Karla waved her arms behind her, saying, "Can you untie me, please? Otherwise, how can I eat?"

The man looked at her and disappeared. She groaned, thinking she would have to assuage her hunger was lapping at the bowl like a dog. But a moment later, two soldiers came in, untied her, and re-tied her wrists in front of her. Now, at least, she was able to flex her aching arms. "Water, please," she rasped through her dry throat, and water was brought a moment later.

She drank deeply, and greedily, and, with her wrists bound together awkwardly, spooned the thin rice gruel into her mouth. Some vegetables and a few unidentifiable pieces of meat floated in the soup; the vegetables she ate, the meat she left behind. She was still hungry, though no longer starving, and still a little thirsty although all the water was gone. Now, however, she had only one thought: a bathroom. She poked her head through the tent flap, saying "bathroom" to the soldier outside. He looked at her uncomprehendingly, and said something to another soldier passing by. A few minutes later the officer came back.

"I need to go to the bathroom," she said to him, "rather desperately, in fact."

"Is that so?" the officer said condescendingly. "Well, I suppose we can't have you messing up our lovely tent, then, can we?" and laughed at his own joke. The two guards joined in half-heartedly, although they clearly hadn't understood what he'd said.

Karla was led to a shallow, smelly hole in the ground near one edge of the camp. She wrinkled her nose and looked around, aware the makeshift toilet was in full view of the camp.

"Can you please untie me?" Karla asked. "Otherwise—" she looked at the hole in the ground "—I don't see how I can."

The officer said something to the soldiers who removed the rope.

"And would you kindly turn your backs while I. . . ."

The officer shook his head. "We will have to look. We can't have you running off somewhere, now can we?" He laughed again. "But we promise, we won't enjoy looking."

Karla glared at him briefly. Turning her back on the officer gave her small satisfaction as she pulled down her shorts. At least afterwards, as she was tied up again and bundled back into the tent, she felt a whole lot better.

Lying down again she reflected on what she'd been able to see. A few soldiers, their guns in their laps, sat around on the edge of the camp looking out. But most of the soldiers had parked themselves around a small fire in the center, talking and chatting as if they didn't have a care in the world—until she emerged from the tent. She still shivered at the vivid image of two dozen men eyeing her shamelessly in the sudden silence.

The officer strutted around as if he'd just won the lottery—which, in capturing her, Karla thought, perhaps he had. And though she couldn't be sure, it seemed, from brief glints reflected from the light of the fire and the way a man here or there would hold his head back, an arm up, that they were passing a bottle around.

What she knew of military procedure came from reading a couple of novels and seeing a few B–grade movies which—if movies on subjects she knew something about were anything to go by—had little to do with reality. Still, she felt certain that lighting a fire at night and advertising your position was not the best strategy, and letting your soldiers sit around it having a party in potentially hostile territory was hardly a good idea.

She was tired and dying to go to sleep. No matter which way she turned she could not get comfortable on the hard dirt; every time her mind began to drift, it focused on her anger at Uqu and Mountain Man for abandoning her to this uncertain fate. As the night deepened, the soldiers' noise grew in volume as they drank more and more, and she was sure she'd have stayed wide awake even if she'd been lying on a soft mattress rather than a mat covering the unforgiving ground. Although she couldn't understand a word they were saying, she was convinced the songs they sang were lewd and their raucous laughter had more to do with dirty jokes and *ganja* cigarettes than any sense of happiness. And all the while she imagined against her will what was going to happen when those soldiers had finally had enough to drink. . . .

18 Pillow Talk

KARLA WASN'T AWARE SHE had drifted off into a fitful sleep until she felt a hand go over her mouth and a voice whispering, "Quiet," in her ear. She struggled and tried to bite the hand until she heard, "*Orton-gaat,* it's Uqu. Thanks for saving my life back there, by the way."

Another man appeared—holding a long knife. Karla began to struggle again.

"It's our friendly guide," Uqu said. "He's going to cut those ropes."

Mountain Man, she thought, and relaxed as the bonds were finally gone.

Soft, indistinct sounds drifted through the wall of the tent. Suddenly, there was a burst of gunfire; a moment later it seemed guns were being fired from every direction. Uqu and Mountain Man threw themselves on top of Karla, covering her. The firing stopped as quickly as it had begun, and a few moments later she could hear voices. Uqu and Mountain Man slowly sat up, and somebody poked his head through the tent flap, his thumb flashing up, grinning "Okayokay. . . ." followed by a few words Karla couldn't understand.

"We can go out now," said Uqu. Haltingly, Karla followed the two men into the outside air. The embers of the fire still glowed a dull red, and the moon, three-quarters full, cast its eerie light from halfway into the starry heavens. She could see dozens of men moving around the camp—while others were laying still on the ground.

Karla gasped. "Are they all dead?"

"Just sleeping—I think," said Uqu. "I'll ask our guide to find out, shall I?" After a couple of words, Mountain Man disappeared into the gloom.

"What's the time, anyway?" she asked.

"Getting on for two in the morning."

As Karla walked slowly around the camp, flexing and stretching her stiff, sore muscles, it was easy to tell the soldiers from the rebels—separatists? Terrorists? What were they, exactly?—from their motley uniforms. None, as far as she could tell, wore anything that matched in the way the Sandeman soldiers' uniforms did.

They were pulling boots from unconscious men, tending wounded from both sides— seemingly indiscriminately—collecting weapons and all the other equipment they could find. She saw the officer sitting, cringing away from three men looming over him menacingly, all trace of his imperiousness gone. Being questioned, perhaps?

She turned away. Maybe he deserves it, she thought. But she didn't have to watch someone being humiliated.

"Just one dead," Uqu said, breaking into her thoughts. She saw Mountain Man standing next to Uqu, grinning, his teeth a moonlit flash in his dark, shadowy face. She stretched out her hand to shake his; after a moment he understood the gesture and eagerly grasped her hand in his. *"Matalam,"* she said. "Very much." He said nothing, but grinned even more broadly, dipping his head slightly.

"We crept into the camp. Most soldiers were asleep," Uqu told her. "The other we simply knocked on the head. Until someone—maybe the officer over there—started firing. But by then it was all over—only a couple of the Sandeman soldiers were still up and about."

"I'm glad to be free—very glad," she said. "But I'm sorry someone had to die. It seems such a waste."

"This whole thing is a waste," said Uqu.

Karla just nodded tiredly and sat down on a fallen log. Uqu squatted nearby.

"So where did you go," she asked, "when the soldiers appeared?"

"I made a split-second decision. I figured there was nothing I could do to help you by staying, but maybe something I could do by getting away. Plus, I didn't think they'd too careful about my safety. I had a feeling I'd probably end up being reported as shot, trying to escape."

Karla remembered the way the officer had treated his soldiers. "Quite possibly."

"Had you been anyone else, I'm sure you'd have been in great danger. But I was also pretty certain they had orders you had to be delivered in one, unbroken piece."

"I think you're probably right," Karla said, remembering that none of her deepest fears had been realized. "But you stopped them from delivering their 'package'—me."

"I didn't," Uqu laughed. "We were being shadowed by a few of the separatists all the way from Inkaya. It was they—and our guide—who took care of the two soldiers sent after me. Then our guide and I trekked back to their base for reinforcements, while the others trailed you to the camp."

"I see."

All of a sudden, Mountain Man stood in front of them, seemingly appearing from nowhere. "Now go. All go. B'long house." he said.

"B'long house?" Karla asked.

"Home," Uqu said. "Including you."

"Me? Oh, you mean—?"

"Right. We're going to put you on a boat. Now. It's waiting just a few kilometers from here."

"How can you . . . ?" She stopped as she saw a man outlined in the embers speaking into a cellphone. "Of course. Modern technology. Okay then, let's go . . . who should I thank?"

"Their leader . . . but you just thanked him."

"Mountain Man?" she said.

Uqu looked at her in surprise. "Yes, I suppose that's a good name for him."

"So what are they going to do to the soldiers—kill them all?" she shuddered.

"Oh no. Look." Uqu turned and pointed towards the fire, which was now burning more brightly: someone had thrown some more logs onto the coals and they were catching alight.

Karla saw the Sandeman soldiers sitting in a circle around the fire. Taking a few steps closer she could see they were roped together.

"Won't they raise the alarm?" she asked.

"Eventually, yes. But I don't imagine they'll be in much of a hurry. Anyway, it will take them a while to get free, and by the time they do we'll be long gone. They're not going to chase us. All their weapons and supplies—and boots—have been confiscated." Uqu chuckled. "That's how Mountain Man resupplies his men."

As they all began to leave the camp Karla estimated there were thirty to forty men altogether. Then she thought she recognized the two men who'd been forced to walk all the way back to camp in bare feet. She stepped closer to be sure.

"Are they prisoners?" she asked Uqu.

Mountain Man overheard her. "No, no," he grinned. "Join up."

"What?" Karla asked.

"They've switched sides," Uqu explained. "It happens all the time, though there's not much traffic in the other direction."

Karla noticed some of the soldiers tied up by the fire were wearing bandages. "Ah . . ." she said. "They treat the soldiers well, do they?"

"The enlisted men, yes. They get a lot of converts that way . . . and a lot of soldiers who are reluctant to shoot at them."

"Makes sense."

"Not all the separatist groups behave this way, unfortunately."

The bulk of the men, all carrying something extra—a second weapon, a radio, a backpack full of supplies—turned towards the inland peak. Uqu, Mountain Man, and a few others guided Karla in the opposite direction. It was slow going with just the light of the moon to guide them, and while Karla stumbled from time to time, the separatists moved as though they could find their way even in complete darkness. Although it might have been only a few kilometers, it was something like an hour and a half before the jungle gave way to a small beach. An inflatable rubber dinghy was pulled up on the sand, a couple of men standing by it, smoking. In the distance, out to sea, Karla could see the shape of the fishing boat, like the one moored at the village pier, outlined in shadow against the horizon.

Taking Uqu by surprise, Karla took hold of his face in both her hands and kissed him on the cheeks. "Thanks for everything. You've been wonderful."

Karla felt sure Uqu was blushing—though she guessed she wouldn't have been able to tell, even in broad daylight.

"It was my pleasure . . . Karla."

Mountain Man touched her shoulder, pointing at the dinghy waiting on the small beach.

"Time to go," Uqu said.

"*Matalam, matalam,* for everything." She planted a kiss on Mountain Man's cheek, much to his astonishment, and they walked down the beach towards the boat. As she stepped in, Uqu said, "They'll look after you. Just keep your head down so to speak— they're a bit nervous about having you on board and keeping you safe if they're ever stopped by the Australians."

Karla nodded. "Thanks again, Uqu." And turning to the sailors said, "*Matalam,*" with a smile.

The boatmen smiled back as they pushed the dinghy into gentle waves and jumped in behind her. A powerful outboard motor revved up, sounding strangely muffled, and the little boat flew across the tips of the waves towards the fishing boat half a kilometer offshore. Karla looked back at the two dim figures on the beach, waving until they were out of sight.

Uqu and Mountain Man stood watching the boat head out to sea until Karla was a dim stick figure in the distance. The men who'd accompanied them turned inland; Uqu and Mountain Man walked silently along the coast towards Inkaya.

*****

As much as he wanted to do nothing more than just lie there until he could fall back to sleep, Derek Olsson forced himself awake. *I have to find Lars,* he thought. *He could be the key.*

Splashing water on his face, he spent several hours going through the online phone directory, calling every "Olsson" he could find anywhere in the country—without result. He tried all the variations he could think of—Olssen, Ollson, Olsen, Olson—with only aching ears to show for all efforts. Finally, he emailed his partner, Ross, asking him to get the lawyers and private investigators to dig up his brother's whereabouts. Pull out all the stops, he wrote. He may be the key we're looking for.

*****

As "neutral territory," the Four Seasons was the venue for the Foreign Ministers' meeting. The other Foreign Ministers and their staff were staying in other hotels scattered the length of Orchard Road, Singapore's main shopping street. Alison stood outside the conference room waiting for Royn. She nodded and smiled as the Papua New Guinea and Solomon Islands delegations filed in, idly chatting with Kieran Fairchild and other members of the Australian contingent. She stifled a grin at the number of Australians present, considering that Royn was merely to be the neutral chairman. When Royn had challenged the numbers Fairchild proposed, the Secretary of the Department of Foreign Affairs had answered, "But Minister, you never know when some last-minute drafting or certain expertise will be urgently required." Alison had considered asking whether Fairchild had ever heard of the internet—or the telephone. But she'd held her peace.

"Good morning, Alison," Royn said woodenly as he reached the door. Alison hadn't seen Royn since Melanie had interrupted their discussion the previous morning.

"Good morning, Minister," Alison replied. "Everyone's here except for Nimabi and company. They're running quite late."

"Shall we . . . ?" Royn asked, gesturing towards the door.

"A quick word first," Alison said quietly, continuing before Royn could comment, her voice dropping to a whisper. "They've accepted, but they want a deposit of a hundred thousand first, before they'll start."

"Good work . . . but a steep price. How do we . . . ?" Royn stopped as he saw Nimabi leading the Sandemans' delegation along the corridor. "Good morning, Abdullah," he said, grinning broadly.

"Good morning," Nimabi said softly with a wry smile as Royn held the door open for him.

"My God," Royn breathed, surprised to see Nimabi's face wasn't the same stony, unyielding mask he'd worn the previous day. "He looks . . . different," he mumbled. "Strange . . . I wonder why."

"What happened yesterday?" Alison asked.

"Absolutely nothing," Royn said quietly, gesturing for Alison to precede him. "Everybody stonewalled. I figured we're in for another day of the same."

Royn and Alison took their places at the round table, rather like the tables Chinese restaurants use for large parties, set in the center of the room. One foreign minister sat at each point of the compass, each flanked by two of his aides, one on either side. Other staff members sat behind.

When Royn declared the meeting open he was surprised when Nimabi, who'd hardly said a word other than "No" the previous day, spoke first. "I was wondering, gentlemen, if, just perhaps," Nimabi said tentatively, "we could agree, in principle at any rate, to let the geologists decide the extent of the oil deposits."

Royn's eyes widened at Nimabi's words. But to hide his astonishment he had to quickly appear as if he was going through some of the papers in front of him when the Papuan Foreign Minister chimed in, "You know, Abdullah—" addressing Nimabi by his given name for the first time in the past few weeks "—that makes eminent sense to me."

"A very good idea," added the Solomons minister.

The logjam had broken, and Royn had no idea how, why, or what had happened for all three ministers to turn, overnight, from irreconcilable combatants into the best of friends; after weeks of fruitless negotiations, they reached a Heads of Agreement covering all areas of their dispute in less than two hours.

"Well, gentlemen," said Royn when everything seemed decided. "May I suggest we adjourn while our appropriate staff members remain to draw up the necessary papers?" The three foreign ministers nodded in agreement. "And," Royn added, "since yesterday's meeting was so . . . arduous . . . may I suggest we resume at the same time tomorrow morning?"

Royn's proposal was accepted unanimously and such camaraderie pervaded the room that the four ministers decided to have a private lunch together.

Royn lost count of the number of bottles of vintage wine they'd imbibed—a pleasure which Nimabi enjoyed just as much as the others. By dessert, the stiff formality of foreign policy had disappeared, replaced with uproarious laughter at bawdy stories and dirty jokes, often mangled by slurred tongues.

After a pause while waiters cleared the table and served coffee and liqueurs, the Papuan minister turned to Nimabi and said, "I'm curious about something, Abdullah. My wife said a number of things last night that have been bothering me, to say the least."

"Really?" asked Nimabi with obvious interest. "What?"

"Well, to start with, she said she had a headache." All four men laughed. "But then she added she'd made some kind of pact—though she didn't say who with—and that her headache probably wouldn't go away—"

Royn watched in surprise as the other two Foreign Ministers both tried to speak at once—and then argued as they each tried to give way to the other.

After a moment of laughter, Nimabi was given the floor. "Very strange," he said, "because my wife and I had a blazing row last night. Very unusual for her."

"What about?" the Papuan minister asked.

"About . . . how it would be my fault if we simply couldn't afford make any shopping trips like this one for a long time to come, among other things," Nimabi replied. "And she was certain she could convince all the other Sandeman minister's wives—even the prime minister's wife—to take the same stand as her."

". . . and my wife got all upset," the Solomons foreign minister added, "saying 'You stupid men. What are you all fighting about when there's obviously so much money to go around?'"

The three ministers turned on Royn as one. "Our wives had lunch together with yours yesterday," Nimabi said accusingly. "So, Tony, did you get your wife to plant this little stratagem?"

"Me?" said Royn with unfeigned innocence. "I can assure you, gentlemen, that only a woman's mind could be so devious as to come up with something like this. When it comes to scheming, I'm just not in the same league."

*****

Mountain Man disappeared into the jungle as they neared Inkaya, leaving Uqu, hot, sweaty, and tired, to trudge alone into the village square.

The elders were, as usual for that time of day, smoking, drinking tea, and talking around a table in the restaurant. They looked up in surprise as Uqu came in and sat down, unasked, at the table. Drinking endless cups of cool water, he spoke for a long time. He answered questions, and when he finished he went and sat alone at another table while the elders talked and argued with each other. After about fifteen minutes, Uqu heard Tungi speak sharply in a raised voice and the others fell silent. One by one, they all nodded. Tungi stood up and led the other elders towards Uqu, who stood as he saw them coming.

Without a word, Tungi nodded gravely. With Uqu in the lead, the entire village council walked out of the village the way Uqu had come. Uqu stopped where Mountain Man had disappeared and heard a voice calling him. The elders followed Uqu into a small clearing in the overgrowth where Mountain Man was standing.

Apparently, no introduction was needed as they all smiled at each other and Tungi just said, "Please, speak."

As Uqu had done, the Mountain Man spoke for a long time and answered many questions. When the elders were satisfied, Tungi said, *"Matalam,"* and Mountain Man disappeared.

Tungi led the elders, Uqu in tow, back to the village. When they reached the canteen, Tungi ordered a young man, "Tell Gurundi the village council wants to see him. Now."

Tungi was about to send one of the elders across the square when Gurundi finally emerged from the mosque and ambled nonchalantly across the square. "Tungi-*ga*, gentlemen, you asked to see me?" he said as he walked towards the table where the elders were sitting, waiting, stopping a couple of meters away.

The elders sat on one side of a long table, Tungi at the center, and Uqu at one end. Nobody stood behind the counter, and there was nobody else in the seating area. Gurundi stood, facing Tungi, behind the sole chair on the other side of the table. His eyes moved from one elder's stony face to the next until his gaze reached Uqu.

"What is the meaning of this?" he asked in the local dialect, his gaze fixing on Tungi.

"Sit," said Tungi, gesturing impatiently at the sole chair facing him.

"I demand to know—"

Tungi cut him off angrily. "You will demand nothing. You will speak only when spoken to. And only when you have taken your seat will we begin."

"Begin what—?" Gurundi stopped, his mouth frozen open in mid-sentence, as he saw Tungi's brilliant eyes fixed on his face. In slow motion, he stepped over to the chair and sat down.

Tungi leaned forward. "Tell me, are you aware of the tradition of *diyafah* handed down to us from the very lips of the Prophet Mohammed, peace be upon him?"

"Yes," Gurundi said hoarsely.

"Then perhaps you'd care to remind us of the details, Gurundi-*ga*."

Gurundi licked his lips. "The Prophet, peace be upon him, enjoins us to welcome strangers into our midst."

"And when such a stranger is welcomed, how are we enjoined to treat him?"

"With respect."

"Quite. But isn't there more?

"Yes," said Gurundi quietly.

"Which is . . . ?"

"The stranger—" Gurundi now spoke as if he were giving a lecture "—is to be protected from harm."

"Exactly," said Tungi with a nod. "And is it not true that the *hadith* says, 'If you believe in Allah and his Prophet, be hospitable to your guest'?"

"That is my understanding," Gurundi said guardedly.

"And being part of the *hadith*," Tungi continued, "it is part of the Islamic law, is it not?" Gurundi nodded silently.

"And what is the penalty for a member of the community who transgresses those rules?"

"In the Prophet's days, peace be upon him, humiliation, even banishment."

"And who decided?"

"The punishment?" Gurundi asked. When Tungi nodded he said, "The tribal chieftain."

"And in our community, who is the equivalent of the tribal chieftain?"

"You are, Tungi-*ga*."

"Thank you, Gurundi-*ga*. Also my understanding. So, we would appreciate—" he spread his arms to include the other elders "—if you would be so kind as to explain to us what happened in the school the other day."

"I stopped the infidel woman from corrupting our children."

"A laudable aim indeed," Tungi said; Gurundi relaxed. "So in the process," Tungi continued, "would you say you treated 'Orton-*gaat* with respect?"

"The infidel woman?" Gurundi's body stiffened.

"The stranger to whom we offered *diyafah*," Tungi said. When Gurundi made no reply, Tungi asked, "Did you, for example, understand the English words the children were singing?"

Gurundi shook his head.

"Did you ascertain exactly what our guest was doing in the classroom?"

Gurundi shook his head again.

"Did you ask the teacher, Arang'anat-*gaat*, for an explanation?"

"You would consider a woman's word the equal of mine?" Gurundi asked with an air of surprise.

"We are not asking for her word," Tungi said, his voice hard, "but for yours. . . . And we are waiting to hear them."

Gurundi glared at Tungi. "I did what needed to be done, in the name of Allah and the Prophet—peace be upon him—for the good of our community and our children."

"There were also thirty young children present," Tungi said with hardly a pause. "Do you think your behavior set a good example for those impressionable young children to follow?"

"Yes," Gurundi said fervently.

"Including the words you said to the teacher herself?"

Gurundi looked for support towards the elder who had first championed his appointment as stand-in for the village imam, but the elder turned his face away. "I—I admit," he said softly, looking back towards Tungi, but at his hands rather than his face, "that I may, perhaps, have overreacted."

"You may be interested to learn that the song in question was a harmless children's nursery rhyme. 'Orton-*gaat* was using it to help our children improve their pronunciation, vocabulary, and understanding of English—and doing it very well, apparently. Indeed, until yesterday I was not aware our English teachers' command of English is less than perfect. With that knowledge, would you say that in your treatment of 'Orton-*gaat* you also overreacted?"

After a pause, Gurundi replied in small voice, "Perhaps."

"And would you say you treated 'Orton-*gaat* with respect?"

Gurundi's eyes flicked from one elder's face to another, looking for some sign of support. Finding none, he turned back to Tungi in stony silence.

After waiting another moment for Gurundi to reply, Tungi said, "Well, it is quite clear to all of us that you did not. Furthermore, we do not agree you have set a good example to our young children—quite the opposite. And even worse: the reaction your actions provoked are an example of behavior none of us want our children following."

"What the infidel woman did—"

"We're not here to discuss what she did, only what you did."

"What I did," Gurundi said slowly, "I did as a representative of Allah in this community."

"Breaking the rules handed down to us by the Prophet from Allah in the process?" Tungi asked, a skeptical expression on his face.

A long silence settled over the table as Tungi and Gurundi glared at each other.

With a sigh of resignation, Tungi turned towards the end of the long table, where Uqu was sitting. "Uqu-*ga*," he said, "would you be so kind as to tell us what you know."

"Certainly, Tungi-*ga*," Uqu said with a bow of his head. "Yesterday, about noon—" as he spoke, he turned to face Gurundi "—'Orton-*gaat* was captured by Sandeman soldiers. Last night, separatist forces raided the soldiers' camp and freed her. Under interrogation, the officer in charge swore they had been tipped off as to 'Orton-*gaat*'s whereabouts by someone in this village."

"Would you have any idea," Tungi asked Gurundi, "who the person in our village might be?"

"Someone doing his Islamic duty," Gurundi said with a smile.

"And who might that be?"

Gurundi shrugged.

Turning to Uqu, Tungi asked, "Did the officer identify the person who tipped them off?"

"Yes," said Uqu. "The village's religious leader."

Tungi turned to Gurundi. "Is this true?"

"No," Gurundi said, an involuntary quaver in his voice.

"You're lying," Tungi said; the other village elders all nodded at Tungi's words.

"You prefer the word of an infidel to *mine*?" Gurundi said angrily.

Tungi glared at Gurundi, and tersely announced, "Uqu-*ga*'s account has been verified by an honest and devout Muslim we all know and trust. Some thirty others stand ready to come forth and tell us the same story."

"I demand these men be brought forward—if they exist."

"Are you doubting my word?" Tungi asked angrily.

"This is not a court of infidel law," another elder interjected.

"Quite so," said Tungi. "It is not necessary to bring others here to merely repeat what we have all heard from their mouths—and what you have been told they said. . . . To repeat the question: was it you who told the infidel soldiers where they could find 'Orton-*gaat*, thereby causing harm to the guest I welcomed into our midst in Allah's name—and who you were duty-bound to protect, as it is spoken in the *hadith*?"

Gurundi stood up, standing tall to look down on the village elders. "Yes," he declaimed. "And I'd do it again."

"Sit down," Tungi said coldly.

Gurundi's nerve deserted him as he slowly sank back in the chair.

Tungi's head lifted higher as he let his body lean into the back of his chair. "It is the unanimous decision of this village council that you be banished evermore from our community and Jazeerat el-Bihar, with immediate effect."

"What?" Gurundi cried, his shoulders shaking, his eyes shifting nervously without pause. "You can't—"

"It is done," Tungi said coldly. He stood, and an instant later the other elders also stood as one. "Come. Get whatever you can carry. There is a *banca* waiting to take you away."

THE NEWS SPREAD THROUGH the village at the electronic speed of text messaging, and a small crowd gathered near the playground chatting and speculating with each other about what was going on and why. Led by Arang'anat, the teachers and staff of the school left their duties and drifted out, one by one, to join the crowd.

As Gurundi stepped out of the mosque, his head held high, his face angry, his eyes fierce, a hush fell over the square. The two black-shrouded women followed behind, each loaded with luggage. A couple of the village elders then emerged to join Tungi and the remainder of the council who were waiting outside. With Tungi leading the way, the other elders surrounding Gurundi and the two women like an escort, the group moved in the direction of the pier.

As Gurundi passed near where Arang'anat was standing, she heard him say, "You'll regret this," to Tungi, a pace in front of him. Tungi ignored him.

The procession filed down to the pier, the crowd ambling silently behind, Arang'anat among the first to move. As they reached the pier, one of the elders looked back and made a gesture like a stop sign; a few children ducked through and scuttled along the pier, hiding behind whatever cover they could find, but the other villagers stood still.

Except Arang'anat, who gingerly took three steps onto the pier, from where she could have a better view.

She saw Gurundi climbing into the *banca,* and stood watching as it headed out to sea, a tentative smile on her face. Her heart leapt as Tungi neared her, inclined his head briefly in her direction, and said respectfully, "Arang'anat-*gaat*."

"May Allah be praised," she breathed softly, smiling, to herself.

Only when the *banca* disappeared from view did she turn for the short walk back to the school—and her waiting class. No longer trudging, she walked with an uncharacteristic, almost masculine air.

*****

WITH HER AFTERNOON NOW free, Alison cleared her backlog of emails, sent the geek some more names to add to the ones for the McKurnWatch list she'd sent the previous day. Then she informed the private eye that payment would be handled through their original contact in the normal way—with complete, detailed invoices, and so on. She also sent them a copy of her summary of Sidney Royn's report, asking them to advise her how they planned to proceed.

Finally, though not with relief, she turned to the stack of waiting phone messages. As she played each message her hopes drooped further until she seriously thought of just deleting the remaining ones without even checking them. She thought of going to the gym, or for a walk or a swim. "Afterwards, Alison," she told herself. "Not many left." Five minutes later, only half-listening, she straightened up in her chair in disbelief, replayed the message—and called Royn's suite.

"There's something you should hear, Minister."

"Fine," Royn said. "Why don't you bring it up?"

"Okay . . . is Melanie there?"

"She's gone shopping—celebrating with the other ministers' wives, I believe."

"I'll be right up, then."

Placing her laptop on the dining table in Royn's suite, she clicked play. When the phone was picked up, McKurn's voice spoke ominously:

"Your payment's late."

"Frankie—"

"No names, you imbecile."

"Mate, it will just be a couple more days. I promise."

"It had better be . . . or you know what's going happen."

"Don't worry F—mate. Two days, that's all."

"I'll be waiting."

"That voice sounds familiar," said Royn.

"Does the number mean anything?" Alison asked, pointing to the phone number at the head of the email.

"That's a parliamentary number," Royn said. "New South Wales Parliament. Play it again."

Royn listened carefully as Alison replayed the message. "It's a state politician. A Conservative member of the New South Wales state Parliament . . . I've met him . . . I'll think of his name in a minute." He grinned at Alison. "Maybe we've hit the jackpot."

"Maybe," said Alison, a touch of reservation evident in her voice. "A second string to our bow in any event.

"At least," said Royn excitedly. "I know—how about getting your geek guy to tap his phone too?"

Alison shook her head vigorously. "No, no, Minister. I've already got too much to handle. Better if we get the private eye to tail him. This is more up his alley . . . find out what rackets this member is involved in, and what, if anything, is his relationship to McKurn." She looked questioningly at Royn.

Royn nodded hesitantly. "Okay."

"Thank you. So when you remember his name—no, wait a minute." Alison's fingers flew across the laptop's keyboard and in a moment she was looking at a list of all NSW state parliamentarians. She turned the laptop so Royn could see the screen, and scrolled down the list slowly until Royn said, "Harry Weinbaum . . . ?" His voice was unsteady, and as he turned slowly to look at Alison his face was frozen, his mouth half-open, his eyes unfocused. Shaking his head he added, "But it can't be him. Surely not."

Alison clicked on a link that went to Weinbaum's page on the New South Wales parliamentary site. A picture of a ruddy-faced man with a shock of grey hair stared at Royn.

"I can't believe. . . . Play his voice again, please."

Royn listened to the conversation for the third time. Halfway through he said, "That's him all right. Harry Weinbaum of all people. Who'd have thought it? He's one of the last people I'd have ever suspected of having anything to do with McKurn."

"A dark secret."

"Indeed."

"I wonder how many other people like him are in McKurn's pocket."

"Sheesh," said Royn. "It could be anybody."

"It certainly seems so," said Alison. "Is it okay with you, then, for me to go ahead and tell the private eye to check him out?"

"You bet," Royn said.

19 Pendulum of Fear

AT THE END OF her last lap, Alison let her muscles relax and her body glided slowly to the edge of the hotel pool. She floated before letting her feet sink to the bottom; her eyes scanned the mass of pink bougainvillea and oleanders surrounding the third-floor pool. Eventually, almost against her will, she realized she'd lost track of time, and there was probably only a couple of hours left before she had to leave for the airport.

Royn had persuaded the foreign ministers to wait till Thursday afternoon to issue a statement to the press to make it seem it took three tough, tortuous days of negotiation to reach an agreement. Alison was grateful: the extra day in Singapore made it impossible for her to meet with McKurn until Monday at the earliest. *Still too soon,* she thought, wondering how she could postpone it again while knowing she couldn't. As she pushed herself up out of the pool, her mind wandered in the early morning heat to imagine what his answers could be—and how she might respond.

She forced McKurn from her mind as she strode to the table where she'd left her towel, oblivious to the admiring male glances following her bikini-clad movements. Wrapped in the hotel's soft dressing gown she ordered breakfast and, with a sigh, opened her laptop and began scanning the accumulated emails, more appearing in an apparently endless stream as the wireless connection cut in. She decided to begin with the poll results from Conservative Party headquarters.

On the surface, they seemed confusing: seventy-three percent of voters answered YES to the question, "Should Australia withdraw its troops from the Sandeman Islands immediately?" while sixty-four percent answered NO when asked, "Should Australia abandon an ally in the middle of a fight?" To Alison the meaning of these and the responses to the other questions were very clear but potentially double-edged: the way to sell (or, she shuddered, "spin") the Sandemans to the voters today was as "keeping our word" and "sticking with our friends." But that most voters wanted to pull the troops out now was more worrying: polls taken before the army's casualties in the Sandemans demonstrated that most people hadn't even known Australian troops were there. She didn't have to take a survey to know how voters would answer the question, "Should Australia abandon an ally we know we cannot trust?"

The Sandeman involvement, previously under the voters' radar, was now a hot issue; in war—as in politics for that matter—if today's promise didn't produce the expected results, it could easily turn into tomorrow's boomerang.

The results of a poll Royn's office took every month or two was more encouraging: "if an election were held tomorrow" the Conservative Party would actually increase its vote with Royn as leader—but lose seats if Cracken were, though still beating Labor.

But Cracken was seen as the leader who would be "most decisive" in a crisis. Royn trailed a poor second as he had every time this topic was polled. *Royn needs to appear more decisive,* Alison thought—*although, too often, "decisive" decisions turn out to be unpopular ones.*

A few minutes before she had to get ready for her flight, she received an email from a friend: have you seen this? She clicked the link and was directed to the Sydney *Mercury's* widely read gossip column:

> **"Lies! All Lies!" says Senator McKurn.** A new website claims to be telling the "real" life story of the Conservative Party's senior Senator, Frank McKurn. Fascinating reading. But McKurn's lawyers made it very clear it was "All lies, defamatory lies"; and that if we repeated a single word from this website—or even mentioned its name—we'd be sued for libel and slander.
>
> "So why haven't you sued them?" we asked. "We're working on it," was the only answer we were given.
>
> Who put up this site? Despite the best efforts of our techie friends here at the *Mercury,* we have no idea—and we get the impression McKurn's lawyers don't either.
>
> We have been told—off the record, of course—that similar rumors about McKurn's past have been circulating for years; now there are now some [very quiet] rumblings from some Conservative party higher-ups to the effect that McKurn better get his act together, and quick.
>
> We can say no more except . . . Happy Googling.

At last, she smiled happily, *some good news.* Clearly, the list she'd sent to the geek had already begun to pay off. And McKurn would be under a lot of pressure on Monday, which could only be to her advantage.

Her arm, stretched out to fold down the laptop's screen, froze in mid-motion as she became aware that the small knot of tension in her stomach had dissipated, replaced by a warm, if faint, glow. Her eyes were caught again by the mass of colorful flowers, her attention drawn to the oleanders . . . *poison,* she thought, *wrapped in beauty. . . .*

"It is better," Niccoló Machiavelli had once said, "to be feared than to be loved." Her fight with McKurn, she realized, hinged on a balance of *fear. Perhaps,* she thought, *the pendulum of fear is beginning to swing the other way.*

*****

THREE TIME ZONES EAST, a helicopter flew over the south-eastern peninsula of Jazeerat el-Bihar. Jeremy McGuire, thankful for the cooling wind from the chopper's blades that blew away some of the heat rising from the ground just twenty meters below, sat by the open door, studying the island where he and his platoon would be spending the next few weeks . . . or months. This part of the island looked like a great spot for a vacation: just a couple of small villages along the coast on an otherwise uninhabited peninsula; from time to time, he was sure, they'd be able to dive into the thundering surf racing up the empty white beaches. But most of the time, he thought, we'll be there . . . tearing his eyes away from the pristine sand to the thick, green jungle covering much of the island, thinning only towards the peak of the volcanic cone of K'mah in the center.

But just the same, he felt lucky. . . .

From a briefing he and other officers attended, he learnt that every one of the Sandeman Islands had its own, seemingly home-grown, separatist group. Some were little more than local bandit gangs, using a political umbrella to claim some legitimacy. On some islands there were more than one . . . like el-Bihar's eastern neighbor, St. Christopher's Island. That island's population was evenly split between Muslims, who mainly lived on the el-Bihar side, and Christians to the east. The two groups hated both each other and the government in Toribaya. They even disagreed about the island's name: the Muslims resented the official name, St. Christopher's Island, demanding it should be called by its original Arabic name, Jazeerat el-Misk—Fragrant Island—a demand which the Catholic population unsurprisingly denounced. With not two but three separatists groups, all fighting each other as well as government troops, St. Christopher's was the most violent of the Sandeman Islands. Jeremy felt sorry for his fellow officers who were to be sent there.

On Jazeerat el-Bihar, by comparison, the sole separatist group known as Islamic Purity—which had mobilized the islanders to stop the construction of the beach resort near Inkaya—seemed to follow a peaceful, Gandhi-style strategy in preference to violence.

Maybe that was about to change. According to Captain McMurray, one Sandeman soldier was shot two days ago—the very first casualty on el-Bihar. Why, though, were their Sandeman counterparts keeping their mouths clammed tightly shut about what, "if anything," they'd been doing on the island?

The Australian army was setting up a small base on what promised to be a very pleasant location at the end of the peninsula, with beaches on three sides and jungle on the other. The base was intended to support, resupply, and reinforce operations on St. Christopher's Island. Jeremy's platoon's job would be, initially, to defend the camp's perimeter. As the helicopter flew towards the base low over the shore, giving Jeremy a final bird's eye view of the surrounding terrain—and the pier the army engineers were constructing at one end of a wide, enticing beach—he thought it wouldn't be long before his platoon would be sent scouting inland. Or, worse, rotated onto St. Christopher's to give the troops there a break at what, from the air, looked more like a holiday resort than an army outpost.

*****

IN SYDNEY'S UNDERWORLD, THE Greek's headquarters was no secret: a raunchy Kings Cross nightclub colloquially known as the "Bare Bottoms Club." It was in the center of the Greek's home turf: a long strip of such nightclubs lining both sides of Darlinghurst Road, a third of them also owned by the Greek.

Nazarov, Shultz, and de Brouw stood before the ornate double entrance doors in the first stop of their latest assignment: find out which underworld gang was behind the murder of Vincent Leung.

Some five minutes after Nazarov knocked, one of the doors opened slightly, a chain holding it in place, an eye looking out from the darkness behind. "Yeah?" a voice said skeptically. "Whadya want?"

"We're here to see ze Greek," said Nazarov, exaggerating his Russian accent.

"He sure won't see you if you don't learn a little respect first." The man moved to push the door closed, but Nazarov's foot prevented the door from moving.

"We're full of rezpect for ze Greek," said Nazarov with a smile. "His name is known far and wide, which is why we've come halfway around ze world to see him."

"Is he expecting you?"

"No. But he will want to see us."

"I doubt it. Have a nice flight home." But Nazarov's foot still prevented the man from closing the door.

Nazarov took a small packet from his pocket. "Just give him zis. A small sample of what we can offer. And tell him we can match ze 'Candyman' on price and quality." Nazarov poked it through the small gap and the man took it gingerly and slammed the door.

A few minutes later the door partially opened and the same man, pointing at Nazarov, said, "You can come in." He pulled the door fully open to reveal a wide staircase that would be glittering when the lights were turned on, but now just seemed dull and grimy.

As Nazarov stepped through, the man walked a few rungs up the stairs—and the door was closed behind him. Nazarov turned to see two other men, both with bulges under their jackets, grinning by the door. "Up against the wall," said one of them, "and spread your legs." Nazarov complied and was efficiently, and none too gently, searched.

"He's clean," the same voice said. "You can go up. We'll be right behind."

The nightclub above was littered with glasses, some half-empty; ashtrays spilled onto the tables. The air smelt of stale beer, stale smoke—and the aroma of an expensive cigar.

The Greek—Demas Chrysanthopoulos—sat puffing a thick cigar at a dimly lit, circular table near the bar with three other equally beefy looking thugs. Nazarov's packet lay in the center of the table. Chrysanthopoulos was a broad-shouldered, heavily muscled man in his mid to late forties, a few streaks of grey in his otherwise black hair. His thick fingers drummed the table as his dark black eyes, set wide above a long, prominent nose, studied Nazarov skeptically. "And who the hell are you?" he demanded in a deep, rumbling voice.

"Anatoli Sergeyevich Borzovsky," Nazarov said with a slight bow of his head, "at your service, Mr. Chrysanzopoulos."

Chrysanthopoulos shook his head. "Never heard of you."

Nazarov moved to take a seat opposite Chrysanthopoulos but one of the bodyguards grabbed his shoulder. "You've been invited in," said the voice behind him. "I didn't hear any invitation to sit down. Did you? Mr. whoever-you-are?"

"Borzovsky," said Nazarov, shrugging, letting go of the back of the chair.

Chrysanthopoulos motioned and one of three men at the table passed the packet back to Nazarov. "I don't know what this is," Chrysanthopoulos said, "and I don't want to know. I don't take gifts—or samples—from strangers."

Nazarov shrugged as he dropped the packet into the side pocket of his jacket. He couldn't tell whether it had been opened, but he felt certain it was now a bit lighter.

"You may not know me, Mr. Chrysanzopoulos, but I'm not a total stranger."

"Really?" said Chrysanthopoulos.

"And I have somezing for you zat will prove it."

"I can't imagine what that would be."

"If I may," Nazarov said, patting his jacket pocket.

Chrysanthopoulos nodded. "Okay. Just take it out slowly."

Nazarov reached into his pocket and—aware of the two men standing watchfully behind him—carefully withdrew a crinkled scrap of paper, unfolded it and leant forward to drop it on the table in front of the Greek.

Chrysanthopoulos looked at the piece of paper without touching it. Handwritten, in both Russian and English, it read:

TO WHOM IT MAY CONCERN

Anatoli Sergeyevich Borzovsky is a trusted friend.

It was signed—also in Russian and English—Andrei Mikhailovich Kuznetsov.

Nazarov, Shultz and de Brouw had decided to try the frontal approach first, posing as drug suppliers offering a good deal as a way to, they hoped, meet the heads of the various Sydney gangs. Late the previous evening de Brouw had purchased a packet of heroin, which was carefully repackaged to remove any traces identifying its origin, while Nazarov, with Shultz's assistance, had forged the letter and spent several hours "aging" it.

Looking at the letter's signature, Chrysanthopoulos said, "I haven't seen you before."

"No," Nazarov laughed. "I was on . . . holiday in Siberia, all expenses paid courtesy of ze government, ze last time Andrei visited Sydney."

"And how is Andrei these days?"

"Not too good. But, hopefully, he'll be feeling a whole lot better in a few weeks."

"How's that?"

"We're working on springing him from jail," said Nazarov. "Ze operation should go off shortly after we get back to Moscow. And I don't zink we'll need to be quite as imaginative as whoever it was who grabbed zat Olzon guy from ze prison van ze ozer day."

As he spoke, Nazarov kept his eyes fixed to Chrysanthopoulos' face. At the mention of Olsson's name, Nazarov was positive he saw the Greek's eyes narrow fractionally, and his mouth begin to twist into a sour look . . . which became a sour smile.

"Good luck then," said Chrysanthopoulos. "And when Andrei's out, perhaps you can ask him to give me a call so he can vouch for you in person."

"Sure," said Nazarov. "Just give me a number where he can reach you."

"Give him the number," Chrysanthopoulos said to his men at the table. One of them man went behind the bar and came back with a sheet of paper; he passed it to Nazarov.

"Zank you," said Nazarov. "And would you like my contact number so you could—"

"Sure," said Chrysanthopoulos grinning. "Why don't you ask Andrei to give it to me when he calls."

"Fine," said Nazarov. And he reached out for the letter.

Chrysanthopoulos slid it away from him. "I'll hang onto this so I can remember what Andrei wrote . . . for when he calls."

"Fine," said Nazarov.

"So have a nice trip home," Chrysanthopoulos said, waving his thick fingers in a gesture of dismissal.

"Suspicious bastard," said Nazarov, as he sketched his meeting with the Greek. "But I get the feeling he's mixed up with this Olsson business somehow."

"So what next?" asked Shultz.

"Let's try the same trick on a couple of other gang leaders before we start interrogating their minions," Nazarov replied.

"Have to be quick, though," said de Brouw. "We could walk into trouble if the word gets around these Russians are showing up with multiple copies of the same letter."

"Indeed," said Nazarov. "So the South Americans . . . or the Lebanese?"

*****

Derek Olsson read the solicitor's reply to his questions and went for a walk around the block to think through his next step. Returning to his room, he began to write. . . .

Hi Ross:

Please send this email to our solicitor (delete any reference to me so that, as far as he's concerned, it comes from you); ask him to rewrite it in his own words and send it to Inspector Durant.

He may object to giving the prosecution key elements of our case, but at this stage in the game that doesn't matter. I want Durant to question his own evidence and think about other suspects. It's a long shot, I admit—but we've got to try every angle.

Here it is:

There are serious problems with your case against Derek Olsson:

What's his MOTIVE for killing Vincent Leung? Where's the evidence or history that might support any motive you care to come up with? This is a big hole in your case. Some of the evidence against him is questionable.

If my client was framed, all the evidence you have against him was planted. This would mean someone entered Olsson's apartment and planted the murder weapon wrapped in one of his shirts—without setting off any alarms or otherwise leaving any trace. Given the security systems in place this would obviously be a difficult task, but not totally impossible.

By your office's own admission the placement of the hair and TWO flakes of skin, found under three different fingernails of the victim's left hand, are highly unusual, to say the least. This lends weight to the thesis that my client was framed.

Can you think of a scenario that would produce just this result, and no other? My associates and I cannot.

The beer glass with my client's fingerprints may have come from the Royal Arms Hotel in the Rocks, the only place he drinks beer from a glass. One of the owners of this hotel, via nominees, is Demas Chrysanthopoulos, otherwise known as "The Greek." If this is a fact you don't already know, I'd be happy to provide you with the evidence.

Chrysanthopoulos has a very powerful motive for getting Vincent Leung out of the way—and an even more powerful motive for getting someone else to hang for it.

My client would appreciate, in the interests of justice, that you carefully consider these questions.

Secondly, of course, if Olsson was framed, it means the real murderer—whether Chrysanthopoulos, one of his gang, or someone else—is right now walking around like a free man.

After encrypting it, Olsson saved it in the "draft" folder of a web-based email address, and sent a dummy message to a different, also dummy, email address.

*****

THE FISHING BOAT'S CAPTAIN had graciously offered Karla his tiny cabin which, like the rest of the boat, smelled overpoweringly of fish. Between the smell and the never-ending rising and falling and rolling and yawing and bobbing of the small boat on the Pacific Ocean waves and the itching aftermath of her sunburn, Karla spent the first two and a half days of the voyage lying miserably on the narrow bed, with only occasional forays onto the deck. She still had some of the marijuana and hashish she'd bought in the village, and she tried smoking a joint as a way to calm her stomach. But it only gave her the munchies, which made her feel even worse.

When she finally, unsteadily, emerged, she stood on the deck for a long time breathing the fresh, salty air, revelling in the sight of the open sky. Seeing only endless ocean in every direction without land or even another vessel in sight, she hoped the captain knew where he was and where he was going. She was surprised to see the waves were nowhere near as big as her stomach had insisted they had to be.

After she finally ate something that actually stayed down, the captain led her to the wheelhouse, the highest structure on the boat, and spread out a large chart.

"We here. Now," he said, a gold front tooth glittering in the middle of his smile. Karla wondered how he could smile as widely as he did with his apparently continual cigarette still hanging from one corner of his mouth, his stubby, tobacco-stained finger in the middle of the Coral Sea.

"And here," he said, pointing near Cairns on the north Queensland coast, "we you take."

"*Matalam,* captain," Karla said. "How long—how many days?"

"Days?" He stubbed out the cigarette stub and immediately lit another one. The aroma of cloves from the Indonesian-style cigarette overwhelmed the ever-present smell of fish. "Four, five, six," he said, shrugging. "We first stop, then go."

Stop? Where? Why? And for what? Karla wondered, noticing that this time the captain—Captain Gold, she decided to call him—had not pointed to the map.

Most of the time, the crew who weren't busy in the engine room seemed to have little to do but sluice down the deck and polish (or re-polish) the fittings. Whenever a plane was sighted or another vessel came near, the boat slowed and the sailors busied themselves castings lines and nets into the water. Alone again on the high seas, the sailors brought in the nets and cleaned and gutted the fish. Sometimes, though, they simply emptied them back into the sea.

"Way home, fish. Lots," the captain grinned when Karla asked him. *So they're just keeping up appearances,* she thought.

She often walked around the deck—but carefully and not too often, keeping Uqu's admonition in mind. She talked to the sailors and smiled with them but either their English was limited or they'd been warned not to speak to her, or both. With nothing to read—and no English-language books or magazines on board—she typed an article until her laptop's battery ran out, and then switched to pen and paper. But mostly she lay on the narrow bed or stood on deck watching the sun, the clouds, the rolling sea, pondering what she'd learnt in the Sandemans—and what she hadn't learnt.

To begin with: Uqu. Despite his obvious friendliness and apparent openness, he really was a Mystery Man, she decided . . . his mind indeed a labyrinth. Urbane and educated, he finished high school in Australia, and graduated from the University of Queensland. He came home to a country where most kids went to schools (if they went to school) nowhere near as well-equipped as the one in Inkaya with teachers, presumably, who weren't even up to Arang'anat's standard. A man who spoke English like a native in a society where most people spoke broken English at best. A Catholic—who was welcomed as a friend by Muslims on el-Bihar, from Tungi to Mountain Man. A man who worked just part-time for InterFreight—who, nevertheless, seemed to be readily available whenever Olsson's people called . . . she'd had no sense that his role as her guide had any time limit. A man from a family wealthy enough to educate their son abroad—who knew the intricate details of the marijuana trade on the Sandeman backwater of el-Bihar, a place producing nothing that could be exported by his employer. A place, she guessed, few people in Toribaya knew anything about and even fewer ever visited.

The more she reflected on Uqu's seeming contradictions, the more obvious the gaps in her knowledge of the Sandemans became. She regretted her exposure to the country had been so—albeit necessarily—brief. She'd seen some of the poorer and more isolated areas, places that tourists, foreign diplomats, businessmen, and even foreigners working on the oil field on el-Bihar's northern shore probably never went to except on the way to somewhere else. She'd spent the bulk of her time in a Muslim village, one hardly typical of the rest of the country—and probably totally different from other Muslim villages.

Why, she asked herself, had someone with Uqu's obvious talents decided to stay in a backwater like the Sandemans when he could have worked in Australia—or even have gone to the States or anywhere else in the world he wanted? His work, as he'd described it, didn't seem like a full-time occupation.

She was convinced there was something, probably many things, he hadn't told her. For example, she wondered: what did he *really* do for Derek Olsson?

*****

"Sergeant Lee has come up with something interesting," Durant said as he and Lee were ushered into the office of Superintendent Zimmerman, commander of task force overflow.

"Go ahead," said Zimmerman.

Lee explained his suspicions about Derek Olsson's possible connection to the Golden Dragon Triad, his questions about how he'd amassed the money to start InterFreight—and what had he been up to for seven years in Hong Kong.

"All very intriguing," Zimmerman said dismissively, "but I don't see how answering any of those questions will help us recapture Derek Olsson."

"Right now, I don't know, sir," said Lee. "But the Hong Kong police report stated Olsson's passport, wallet, ticket, and money were all stolen. The date indicates it happened within a week of his leaving Sydney. What's more, he gave his address as Chung King Mansions."

"I assume that address is significant in some way," said Zimmerman.

"Yes, sir. It's a real flophouse, the place you stay in Hong Kong if you're strapped for cash."

"You realize, Sergeant, that if Rudi hadn't brought you here I'd have stopped listening a long time ago. So if you have a point, you'd better get to it now."

"Yes, sir. Now we know that Olsson was completely penniless in Hong Kong—yet seven years later he returns to Australia with oodles of money at his disposal. I want to go up there and find out how he did it."

"And you're about to ask for expenses—?"

"No, boss," Durant cut in. "Sergeant Lee wants to take some of his leave, and intends to buy his own ticket."

"When?"

"Tonight, sir, if I'm allowed."

Zimmerman glared at Durant. "You asked to be put on the task force," he said, "and I got you both on. Now you're proposing that Lee goes off on a wild goose chase in the middle of one of the biggest operations the New South Wales police has ever put on? With all due respect, Rudi, you must be out of your mind."

"Perhaps," said Durant nodding. "But Sergeant Lee has a hunch his trip will pay off—and I'm willing to back it."

As Lee came under Zimmerman's gaze he shifted uncomfortably in his chair. "And how long do you think you'll be away?" Zimmerman asked.

"If all goes well, sir, I could be back Tuesday or Wednesday night."

"'If all goes well . . .'" Zimmerman said sarcastically. "As far as I'm concerned, if it doesn't go well, it means there's nothing to find. Can you spare him for a couple of days, Rudi?"

Durant nodded. "I'll work twenty-six hours a day if I have to."

"I see," said Zimmerman doubtfully. "Okay, Sergeant. But I expect to see you back here, on the job, bright and early on Wednesday morning."

"Thank you sir. I will be."

"But it seems to me," said Zimmerman with a sigh, "you're going fishing without a rod, let alone any bait."

"Quite possibly, sir," said Lee.

As Durant and Lee stood up to go Zimmerman smiled for the first time. "But if you do come back with something, Sergeant Lee, I want to be the first to know."

20 Virginity Hill

MONDAY IN CANBERRA DAWNED clear and bathed in sunlight as if to reflect Anthony Royn's sunny mood. From his window seat, he gazed across the uninterrupted cityscape—no trace of cloud, no sign of the mist that often shrouded the city on winter mornings impeded his view—to the white mass of Parliament House. Behind it, a near-full moon was sinking to the horizon. Before the plane banked towards the runway, Royn felt McKurn's face leering down at him from a perch far above.

But not even that discomforting thought could impact on the Cheshire Cat grin he'd worn since a giggling Melanie, naked under her dressing gown, had hugged him "Goodbye" on the steps of their Melbourne home.

It had been a long time since she'd done that. . . .

"I'M NOT GOING TO that dinner tonight," Melanie announced in a loud voice as she opened the door to their suite at the Four Seasons. Behind her, a bellhop dutifully wheeled a trolley loaded with packages, the fruits of her afternoon shopping expedition. "Tell them I'm sick or something."

As she tipped the bellhop she glowered towards the darkened corridor leading to the bedrooms and in an impatient voice yelled even louder, "Tony? Are you here? Did you hear what I said?"

Royn shuffled along the corridor, touching the wall for support as he moved. "Hi, Mel," he croaked.

"You look awful."

Royn coughed violently. "It works," he whispered, gasping for breath as he spoke, "doesn't it?"

"What works? You should be in bed."

Royn suddenly straightened up and grinned widely. "I used your makeup," he said, his voice now normal.

"This is no time for theatrics," Melanie glared.

"On the contrary, my dear," Royn said. Still grinning, he carefully wiped away a dark ring under one eye with a tissue. "I just had a drink with the Singaporean Foreign Minister."

"Don't you have an official dinner with him and a whole bunch of other boring officials?"

"Did," Royn chuckled. "But I pleaded illness." He finished wiping the reddish pallor from his nose. "He took one look at me and it was a very quick drink, I can tell you. He didn't want to catch whatever I had."

"Why?" Melanie demanded.

"Because I don't want to be bored either," he said, stepping closer, "and I've got a better idea."

"You do?" Melanie whispered. As she felt Royn's arms go around her she let herself be pulled gently to his chest.

"Yes. A quiet dinner, just you and me."

"What about the kids?"

"Oh, they've gone nightclubbing or something."

"Have they now. And whose idea was that?"

Royn shrugged. "I really can't say."

Melanie sighed. "Okay, then," she said guardedly.

"There's just one catch. I shouldn't go gallivanting around town, seeing as how sick I'm supposed to be. So dinner here?"

Melanie laughed. "You've missed the other eye."

The weight of their argument over Alison felt like a third, increasingly unwelcome presence at the dining table. Those concerns soon melted away from the candlelight, the champagne, and the way Melanie allowed Royn to lead their conversation into the happiest times of the past.

Afterwards, they snuggled on the couch and idly watched a movie. When they heard a scrabble at the door and Ricky's, "You've put the key in the wrong way, you schmuck," it was Melanie who placed a finger to her lips and, tugging Royn off the couch, led the way to their bedroom.

On their last day in Singapore the Royns took a boat ride, toured the island—stopping at a park where Zoë shrieked as a cheeky monkey dropped from a branch and yanked a bag of peanuts from her hand—and crossed the causeway to look at the markets in Johor Bahru, Malaysia. "Shopping," Ricky moaned. "Who wants to go shopping?" But he ended up spending the most money—on pirated computer games and DVDs. At the end of an indolent day filled with laughter—the most contentious issues being "what's for lunch?" and "where will we go next?"—Melanie was half-dozing as they sipped champagne from the limousine's bar, her head resting on Royn's shoulder.

That night, about halfway to Melbourne, Royn tugged Melanie awake and dragged her, hushing her questions, from the flat, first-class seat, past the mostly sleeping passengers all the way to a bathroom at the back of economy. She quickly grasped his intent and giggled; he had to clamp his hand over her mouth as they joined the Mile High Club. As they walked off the plane they smiled and touched each other constantly.

"Why can't you two be like this all the time?" Zoë demanded sourly.

"Yeah," Max and Ricky chorused.

Melanie shrugged; Royn, squeezing her hand, said, "That's a good question, Zoë. Could you give us a little time to work on the answer?"

"Okay," Zoë said skeptically. "But don't take too long about it."

The boys returned to their university dorms, Zoë went to stay with a friend, so Royn and Melanie were alone when they sat down to lunch. The vastness of their empty Toorak mansion suddenly weighed on Melanie's shoulders. "Back to reality," she grumbled.

"Meaning?" Royn prompted.

"Yesterday and last night," she giggled, "were a wonderful but brief fantasy, Tony. But now—" her shoulders slumped "—we're in the real world."

"Do you want it to always be like that?"

"No."

"Let's go horse-riding," Royn said, a sudden glint in his eye.

"What?"

"Mum and Dad are away for the weekend. We can have Mount Macedon to ourselves."

"I don't understand."

"You will, Mel. You will. Scout's honor."

Anthony Royn spurred his mare to a gallop. Pointing to a gnarled oak halfway up a hill about two kilometers from the Mount Macedon stables, he shouted back to Melanie, "I'll race you to that tree."

"Hey, no fair," Melanie shrieked.

Royn laughed. "What do you expect, my love?" he shouted over the thrumming beat of the horse's hooves. "You married a politician."

Melanie's head kissed her stallion's neck as she pushed her horse for every ounce of speed, and her larger horse with the lighter load swiftly shrank the gap. As Royn neared the oak, he slowed to a canter so they reached the tree at the same time.

"Beat you," Melanie said.

"How do you figure that?" Royn asked.

"You stole a head start—and I caught up. Anyway," she grinned mischievously, "I always win."

Royn laughed. "Let's keep going."

"Where to?"

Royn just smiled. "You'll see."

They rode up a narrow trail off the dirt track, over one hill and up another, going deeper into the bush. The ground grew rockier and the vegetation sparser until they reached the bottom of a small, steep hill where Royn dismounted.

Melanie sat rock-steady in the saddle, her nose wrinkling as she eyed the bare, stony ground. "Hardly the spot for a picnic."

Royn's eyes twinkled with suppressed laughter. "Don't you recognize this place?" he asked, a crooked, cheeky grin on his face.

Melanie's face suddenly turned bright red. "Oh my God—how could I forget? It's been so long."

"Too long."

Melanie leapt off her horse and threw her arms around Royn's neck. She pulled his face down to hers. "What a brilliant idea, Tony," she said through her kiss.

"It hasn't changed," Melanie exclaimed as they reached the small, grassy plateau at the top of the rocky trail.

"It has—a bit." Royn was looking over the edge of the plateau, the boundary of the Royn's Mount Macedon estate. Melanie stepped beside him. Here, the crown of the hill ended abruptly; a craggy cliff-face plunging almost vertically to what had once been open country, inhabited only by sheep, cows, and kangaroos.

Melanie wrinkled her nose at the once pristine bush, now a transplanted suburb. She pulled him back to the center of the knoll. "It looks the same from here," she grinned, pulling him down on the blanket she had spread on the ground.

"It's a bit colder today," Royn grinned.

"We can take care of that."

The first time they'd climbed to this spot it was mid-summer, a merciless sun smoldering in a cloudless sky. Melanie was fourteen, he fifteen. It was a day of fumbling exploration, of mounting excitement, of pain and ecstasy—and the temperature rose with each piece of discarded clothing despite the cool and welcome breeze.

They called it Virginity Hill in honor of what they'd left on its peak. They came again and again—until marriage, children and Canberra overwhelmed their private moments.

"We should build something here," Royn said afterwards as they snuggled against each other under the blankets. "A little hut. Or a gazebo. For our old age."

Melanie laughed. "And how would we get here—when we're too creaky to ride a horse . . . or do anything else for that matter?"

Royn shrugged. "We'll manage, somehow. But that's what I want, Mel—to grow old with you."

"That's what you said when we were here, like this, when you asked me to marry you."

"It's still true."

"Is it? Monday, tomorrow—"

"I don't have to go."

"What do you mean?"

"I can quit."

Melanie's body tensed in surprise. "And let McKurn win? No way."

"The hell with McKurn, and Canberra, and everything else—if that's what it takes."

"But you can't," she said, a hint of desperation in her voice.

"Why not?" Royn said, clasping her naked breast, her nipple responding immediately to his touch.

"Tony." Melanie pushed herself up to glare down on him. "I'm being serious."

"So am I."

Melanie sighed, kissed him lightly on the lips and rested her head again on his shoulder. But at the same time, she gently pushed his hand away from her breast. "Don't you want to be Prime Minister?" she asked. "You're so close."

"Sure," Royn said. "It would be nice. But if it means going to back to the way we've been, you and I, the price is too high. I'd rather stay right here."

"I love you, Tony," Melanie said. "I've never stopped loving you—though there were times when I forgot. But I don't want you to give up."

"I won't—if we're back together as a team. It's not worth it any other way."

"I'm sorry, Tony. I feel like I abandoned you."

"No, Mel. We just forgot what's really important. We took us for granted—and look how we ended up."

"We did, didn't we?"

"Do you want to live in the Prime Minister's Lodge . . . ?"

"The fun part is getting there." Her eyes sparkled.

"Then let's get there. When we get bored with it, we quit."

"But if Kydd won't go—?"

"Well . . . " Royn shrugged.

"We'll have to push him out."

"I guess so."

"One more election. If he doesn't go and won't be pushed—"

Royn grinned. "We build that hut."

Melanie laughed. "Deal."

"Done."

"Let's seal it, then," Melanie said, holding out her hand.

"I've got a better way," Royn chuckled, his mouth closing over her breast.

"Tony, you're not fifteen any more."

"I am today," he said. "Give me an hour and I'll prove it."

"When you were fifteen, you didn't need an hour."

THE AUSTRALIAN CAPITAL SITS 300 kilometers southwest of Sydney—a three-and-a-half hour drive if you stick to the speed limit. The city arose on land where the main inhabitants, since 1825, had been sheep. Even further away, about 650 kilometers to the south, lies Australia's second most populous city: Melbourne.

The capital's odd location in the middle of nowhere was the result of a deal between the six British colonies covering the Australian continent when they united into a federation. Politicians from New South Wales wanted their state capital, Sydney, to also be the national capital. Victoria's representatives felt the same way about Melbourne. The other four colonies, already feeling overshadowed by Sydney and Melbourne, preferred the new capital to be almost anywhere else. So it was agreed that the capital would be within New South Wales, but at least a hundred miles from Sydney. In exchange, until the new city was built, the interim capital of Australia would be Melbourne.

The Chicago architect Walter Burley Griffin won a worldwide competition held in 1911 to design Canberra, as the new capital would be known. He predicted it would be "unlike any other city in the world."

As indeed it is.

In cities that grew helter-skelter, like London, streets go every which way, or follow the ups and downs and skirt the obstacles of the land. Cities laid out in advance often follow a grid pattern, like New York north of 14th Street. Even Brasilia, another capital city built miles from anywhere, is designed on a grid pattern, though its grid curves like a boomerang.

Canberra is a study in circles. The plan is dominated by a large circle south of the lake with Parliament House in the center, and a second to the north which encloses nothing but a park of grass and trees that hardly anyone ever uses. Suburban streets curve away from the main avenues, with connecting streets often—and, for drivers, annoyingly—shaped like an S to preserve the theme. The only exceptions are the major thoroughfares between different parts of the city, though a few are semi-circular, making them about the only roads in the city where it's possible to drive more than a few blocks in a straight line. Burley Griffin's subconscious aim, some wit once claimed, must have been to make Canberra the ideal environment for politicians and bureaucrats.

Parliament House hugs a low hill in the center of the largest of Canberra's circles, State Circle. The building's main entrance looks across the artificial lake, named after the city's architect, towards Anzac Parade, a wide avenue leading to the War Memorial beyond. It's built in the shape of two boomerangs joined at the center, capped by an enormous spire flying an oversized Australian flag. The arms of each boomerang slope upwards from the ground, covered in grass. It was possible to walk from one side of the building to another over its roof—until access was blocked off for fear of a terrorist attack. Much of the building, which has 4,500 rooms, is buried under the hill. But the chambers of the House of Representatives and the Senate, together with parliamentarians' offices and meeting rooms, are free-standing buildings, the House within the arc of one boomerang, the Senate within the other.

As Parliament meets sixteen or seventeen weeks a year, most MPs and Senators fly into what the Duke of Edinburgh once called "a city without a soul," and leave as soon as possible after Parliament rises. So at Canberra airport that morning the parking lot overflowed with white government limousines and their uniformed drivers, waiting patiently for their arriving passengers.

Elsewhere in Canberra, nobody took much notice of the budding hive of political activity that sunny Monday morning. The main exceptions were political staffers in Parliament House and journalists in the parliamentary press gallery, who were all sharpening their pencils at the prospect of the jousts and fireworks they knew would come—and the city's call girls, who were anticipating a very profitable week.

ROYN'S LIMOUSINE SWUNG AROUND the circles and disappeared into the mouth of the ministerial wing's underground parking lot. Absorbed in the memory of Melanie's warmth he hardly noticed the car had come to a stop until the driver prompted him.

His smile drooped as he stepped through the metal detector into the inner sanctum of the Parliament. *But I'm no longer alone,* he reminded himself, and strode along the corridors with the sense Melanie was beside him, grinning broadly at everyone he passed.

"Morning all!" he said as he walked in his office a few minutes after eight. Alison, as always, was in her office, but only a couple of other members of his staff were also there this early. "Good morning, Minister," they chorused in reply.

When Royn's door swung shut, Alison glanced at her reflection in a small mirror and grimaced. The dark rings under her eyes seemed to be peeping through the thick makeup she'd applied this morning. The faint flush of pink in her cheeks she'd achieved from her early morning run had long gone and now her skin tone was more grey than pale. With half an eye on the clock, she touched up her face. *I hate heavy makeup days,* she thought distastefully.

With an effort she turned to her laptop to reread the geek's latest email:
hotel you asked about managed by a Hong Kong-based boutique management company very up market resorts seems legit. is owned by a swiss company address c/o swiss lawyer Zurich. . . .
Interesting. Suggestive. But useful . . . ? She still couldn't decide.
wired mckurn's canberra apartment sydney home too risky voice activated
"Voice activated" turned out to mean "noise activated." The recorder switched on every time McKurn walked across the room; an extra-large file turned out to be a neighbor practicing the piano.

Only one of the recordings from the new tap held any interest: a phone shrilled—the kind of ring tone suggesting a mobile—and she heard McKurn saying ". . . we'll have a mole in Royn's office soon, probably from tomorrow. . . . You'll find out who in good time. . . . That's right, make life a lot easier. . . ."

With a last—reluctant—glance in the mirror she picked up her files and walked into Royn's office. As she took a chair she was aware that Royn's eyes were on her face, almost as if he was a doctor performing an examination. "Looks like you haven't slept too well," he said after a moment.

"Is it that obvious?" she asked, her voice tight.

Royn laughed. "I doubt anyone else will notice. I can see you're wearing some kind of cosmetic mask. Covering up lack of sleep, given what's on the agenda today, is my guess."

Alison nodded, her shoulders relaxing.

"So . . . anything in the papers this morning?"

"Not much. Just a couple of reports that several backbenchers—on both sides of the house—will have some nasty questions for Senator McKurn today."

"So . . . " Royn said with a smile, "question time should be fun for a change."

"Indeed," Alison grinned, but the expression in her eyes did not match the one on her lips.

"Have our . . . snoops . . . come up with anything new?" Royn asked.

"The geek says the hotel where . . . where that video was made is owned by a Swiss company. The 'snoops' have a twenty-four hour watch on McKurn, they're looking into Weinbaum, and investigating APHRODITE's call girl agency here in Canberra. I've also got the geek to tap the agency phone . . . but the recordings go to them, not me. I've also passed them as much information on McKurn as I have, and they'll see what they can confirm. The only real news from them is that expenses will mount up really quickly."

Royn nodded. "I can handle it for a couple of months without a problem—let's hope that's enough."

"Thank you, Minister."

"Alison," Royn said, his body leaning forward to emphasize his somber tone, "we're in this fight together—aren't we?"

"Of course, Minister," Alison replied. *Up to a point.* "It's just that. . . ."

"I know," Royn said, raising his hands and shaking his head, "you couldn't do this alone. Nor could I, Alison."

If it wasn't for me, the words formed in her mind, *you wouldn't be in this trouble.* But she stopped herself from uttering them. Alison couldn't look Royn in the eye; she bowed her head, dropping her gaze to the desk.

"You've seen the polls, I presume?" Royn asked. Alison looked up to see Royn now relaxed back in his chair, smiling again as if nothing had happened. "Pretty good, eh?"

"The polls?" Alison said. "Oh, yes. They do look good—if you don't read between the lines."

Royn frowned. "What do you mean?"

"The public's mood will shift the moment there are more casualties—or other bad news. And then, the Sandemans could blow up on us . . . politically."

Royn nodded. "I see what you mean."

"And what do you think could happen when Karla Preston finally resurfaces?"

"Still no news?"

Alison shook her head.

"That woman is trouble," Royn said. "When she turns up, the chances are all hell will break loose."

"That's my guess, too."

"And if she doesn't turn up . . . ?"

"That could be worse," said Alison.

"Especially if they find her body."

"God forbid."

Royn leant back in his chair, idly tapping the desk with one finger. "So you're convinced," he said slowly, "the Sandemans will cause us more problems, sooner or later, one way or another."

"That's right, probably sooner. The word from Defence is they still haven't ironed out an agreement for 'joint command'—the Sandeman officials are still stalling."

Royn sighed. "I'd better have a word with Nimabi."

"And you know what he'll say. . . ."

"*Well, I'm sorry, Tony, but I've done everything I can,*" said Royn, mimicking the lilt of Nimabi's voice, "and so on and so forth. . . . I know," his eyes brightening at his thought,

"I'll tell him we've come across some 'possibly insuperable obstacles' to classifying the Treasury report."

"That should help."

"When we're finished here, please get him on the phone for me."

Alison nodded.

"But the other poll results . . . me versus Cracken. . . ."

"Yes, they're much better."

"Right," said Royn with a smile, and taking a deep breath he added, "I think we should set up a meeting of the Push." Named after the gangs that controlled the Sydney Rocks area before the First World War, the "Push" was an informal committee of Royn's closest, most loyal supporters within the party room.

"Really?" said Alison, her eyes widening. "To what end?"

"To spread the word," Royn replied, "and to get a sense of the party room—how they'd feel about a leadership spill."

"Are you seriously thinking of challenging Kydd?"

"I don't know," said Royn. "But I would like to know whether it's an option—or whether the party room would be dead set against it."

"And if Kydd gets wind of it, what then?"

Royn shrugged. "I can say . . . it was over-enthusiasm on the part of my supporters."

"And do you think Kydd will believe that?"

"Probably not," Royn grinned.

"I don't understand, Minister," Alison said with a puzzled look. "In the past, you've simply been willing to wait for Kydd to retire. What's changed your mind?"

Royn shifted his weight uncomfortably. "Melanie."

"Melanie?"

"Yes. She seems to think that Kydd won't go by himself, and will have to be pushed."

"She's probably right."

"So Melanie and I agreed. . . ."

"Sorry, Minister," Alison said, "but you've lost me. Last I heard you two were arguing . . . viciously, it seemed."

"True," Royn grinned. "But this weekend . . . since Friday in Singapore. . . ."

Royn gazed into the distance, his face flushed; Alison eyes widened at the sudden glow on his face. For an instant the light behind him turned his hair into a golden halo.

"Anyway," Royn continued, "we came to an agreement."

"Which, I presume, has something to do with Kydd."

"Yes, well . . . in part . . . " Royn fidgeted with a pen as his voice trailed off. "Well," he repeated, "it concerns, you, too I suppose. . . . In a nutshell, I get to be PM soon after the next election . . . or I quit politics and Melanie and I go and sit on the beach. Or something like that. And on that basis—" Royn let go of the pen, his hands now resting on his desk, and his eyes began to twinkle again "—Melanie will pitch in again. It will be like the old days. Frankly, I'm looking forward to it."

"And if Kydd keeps hanging on . . . ?"

"He's sixty-nine now. Surely he can't hang on for much longer."

Alison shrugged. "Who can say? Look at your father . . . eighty-something and still going strong. And if you do push him out, who do you think he'll throw his weight behind in the election for the next leader? It won't be you, Minister."

"I guess not—but surely he wouldn't support Cracken."

Alison shook her head. "I doubt it. But he has so much influence in the party room, if he backed some dark horse he would probably throw the leadership succession wide open. You'd no longer walk it in."

"I see what you mean."

"Don't get me wrong, Minister. If you want to go for it, I'm right behind you. But we should think all the angles through, first."

"We should."

"Do you still want me to set up a meeting of the Push?"

"No . . . just make sure they all see the poll results."

Alison nodded. "I'll take care of it. One other thing, Minister: we shouldn't make any moves while McKurn's threat is hanging over us."

Royn nodded glumly.

"And speaking of McKurn," Alison said, her fingers tightening and her gaze falling as she spoke, "I have to meet him this afternoon. Based on one of the phone taps, I think he's confident of reaching an agreement today."

"So he must be ready to meet your conditions, then."

"Presumably," Alison said softly, her throat tight.

"That's good," Royn said; as he noticed Alison's eyes dropping as her head turned away he added, "I suppose. . . ."

Alison looked up suddenly. "I'm not looking forward to the role of . . . double agent."

"No . . . but it shouldn't be for too long."

"We can't know that. I feel I'll be entering a race—without any idea of where the finishing line is."

"We've got so many irons in the fire something will pay off, sooner or later."

"It's the later I'm worried about."

"It will be a strain . . . but what's the alternative? Lie down and give in?"

Lie down? Give in? Alison shuddered at the thought. "Never!" she said fiercely, her eyes glaring, thinking, *I wish you hadn't used those words.* With a sigh, she continued, "The problem is, the longer it takes to come up with something, the more information I'll have to give McKurn. And it will have to be real: he'd quickly know if I was giving him disinformation. Initially, I'm sure I'll be able to string him along. But if we don't 'get the goods' on him sooner, then I'll have to feed him information that could seriously damage us."

"What else can we do?"

"I don't know," said Alison helplessly. "Except: put a bomb under the Candyman Inquiry, otherwise it won't produce anything useful in time to do us any good. They're in motion, but they've decided they'll begin by collating and cross-referencing information on the drug trade. They're not treating investigation as a priority."

"That's not a bad idea, I guess," said Royn, "but—

"—it's not what we want."

"That's for sure," Royn agreed. "I'll have a quiet word with Bruce today."

"But please do me a favor and make sure it's a firm word."

"I certainly will. Bruce needs a bit more spine—so I'll have to give it to him."

"Good idea," Alison said, with a quick smile. "And . . . I think I should have some little nugget of information to give McKurn, if need be."

"Why?"

"To prove my supposedly 'good intentions.'" Alison laughed sourly as she spoke.

"Makes sense," Royn said. "But what?"

"Why don't I tell him about the Candyman Inquiry? It will be common knowledge. Whenever it gets moving. There's no reason to hide that the impetus to set it up came from you, is there?"

"Quite the contrary, I'd have thought."

*****

"Do you have the sense we're being watched?"

"Can't say I have, Sarge," Jeremy McGuire whispered back as he glanced around the small jungle clearing where his platoon had stopped for a short break. "What have you seen or heard?"

"Nothing. That's the problem. I just have this prickly sensation that someone's watching me—us. I wouldn't even mention it, but it's what saved my life in Afghanistan."

Like everyone else, Jeremy had heard the story of how Sergeant "Paddy" Byrne had yelled "Get down!" to his platoon and ducked behind a rocky outcrop just seconds before machine gun fire raked their position. Everyone had attributed his yell to pure dumb luck—and Byrne had never said anything to correct them. Jeremy imagined it was probably the first time Byrne had mentioned the real cause to anyone.

"So it wasn't the 'luck of the Irish,' eh?" Jeremy smiled.

"No, sir," said Byrne.

As a second lieutenant, Jeremy outranked Byrne. But Jeremy was fresh from Duntroon—the Australian equivalent of West Point and Sandhurst—while Byrne was a veteran of campaigns in Afghanistan and East Timor. Jeremy quickly gained the respect of his Sergeant and the platoon by asking for and listening carefully to his Sergeant's advice. "Who do you think it might be?"

"Well, if somebody is shadowing us," Byrne replied, "I don't think it's Sandeman troops. From what I've seen of them, they'd have given themselves away by now. So my guess is it's the guerrillas."

"Makes sense," Jeremy nodded. "After all, this is supposed to be where they hide out." They had reached the bottom of K'mah, the conical peak in the center of el-Bihar. They both looked up towards the top.

"Jungle all the way," said Byrne.

"Solid, too."

Two days before, just when his men had settled into their newly constructed barracks (with a crudely drawn sign reading BEACH VILLAS hanging over the entrance, while someone else had put up a sign next to the helicopter pad reading: WELCOME TO SURFERS' PARADISE NORTH), Captain McMurray sent Jeremy's platoon to sweep the island for any sign of Karla Preston. "We've traced her path and it looks like she went to either St. Christopher's or el-Bihar," he'd told Jeremy. "And there are rumors floating around Toribaya that she's with the guerrillas, she's being held by Sandeman troops somewhere, *and* she's been spirited off to Papua New Guinea. So God knows where she is."

"It's a big island, sir."

"More troops are on the way."

"Sir, will this be joint operation with the Sandeman forces?"

"No," McMurray replied. "They're busy doing something on el-Bihar but won't tell us what. Report anything you learn about their activities."

"Yes, sir. But—we won't have a translator with us."

"I'm afraid not."

"So what do you think of going up there, Sergeant?"

"The guerrillas know this ground and we don't," said Byrne. "We don't even have any idea how many there are, what weapons they have—or anything else about them. We could end up walking straight into a trap."

"I'd say you're right," Jeremy nodded. "No point in going for the Victoria Cross," he added, referring to a medal rarely awarded to anyone who hadn't died heroically in action. "Let's have a look at the map."

Byrne unfolded his map of the island. "We're here," he said. "I suggest we skirt around the bottom of K'mah, taking note of any paths or trails, and head for here instead." Byrne pointed at the village of Inkaya.

Jeremy nodded. "Makes sense," he said. "In any case, that's another of our objectives. No doubt we'll be shadowed there too."

*****

"Not a trace," Durant said with disgust. "It's as though the bastard's disappeared off the face of the earth."

"And the sightings?" Superintendent Zimmerman asked.

"Dozens of them. Olsson's been 'seen' all over the county. Even in New Zealand. False—every damn one of them. What's more, his business partner, Ross Traynor has scarpered too. He pulled his kids out of school and the whole family took off to the U.S. a couple of days after Olsson was snatched. He hasn't been heard from since. No one in the company knows where he is—or they aren't talking."

"Presumably," Zimmerman said, "Traynor's involved too, somehow."

Durant nodded.

"And the butchers?" Although taskforce overflow had yet to establish any connection between Olsson and the mystery gang of murderers, their nickname for the mysterious gang was "Olsson's Butchers."

"Nothing there either. Except the bodies. Our informants tell us no one in the underworld has ever heard of them either. A complete blank. It's incredible."

"So, Inspector, what do you make of it all?"

Durant shook his head. "I've never come across anything like this before. Normally, there are enough hints, rumors, and evidence, however flimsy, so we have *some* suspects. But nothing? Either we've been incredibly unlucky, or there's someone behind this outfit who's very smart."

Zimmerman nodded. "Let's hope it's just bad luck . . . so far."

When Durant returned to his office he found the email from Olsson's solicitor. He read it dismissively and was about to delete it when something in the back of his mind made him read it again, slowly and more carefully.

He turned back to the files he'd been working on, but the irreverent thought kept entering his mind like an itch that needed to be scratched: *There just MIGHT be something unusual about the placement of the hair and flakes of skin. . . .*

"I'll have a chat to the pathologist," he muttered, "next time I see him. If I remember. . . ."

21 Without Notice

"A QUESTION WITHOUT NOTICE for the Prime Minister."

Alison sat glued to the screen of her desktop computer, watching as the camera focused on Ian Nash, the gruff, stocky Leader of the Opposition, whose unruly shock of red hair added a lively splash of color to the rows of dark grey and blue suits filling the benches of the House of Representatives.

She could have walked down to the House and watched from the gallery. But by tuning in over the internet she could monitor the Senate on her laptop at the same time—and no one would become aware of her interest.

"Serious allegations have been made," Nash was saying, "that a senior member of the other place—and your colleague for countless decades—" from the angle of Nash's gaze, Alison knew he was glaring at Randolph Kydd "—has been engaged in corrupt and illegal practices for some fifty years. This may be the first time such allegations have been made in print, but it's not first time such allegations have been heard. Some twenty years ago, the Attorney-General set up an inquiry ostensibly to investigate corruption in government. The unstated focus of that inquiry was the very same person who stands, once again, accused of corruption and other practices dishonoring the sacred trust he has so lightly assumed. This previous inquiry, I might add, was wound down under mysterious circumstances and never issued a report.

"So I ask the Prime Minister if he will *immediately* establish a Royal Commission to look into these allegations—unless, of course, he is willing to stand up in this place and state, unequivocally and for the record, that these accusations are baseless, and that the honor and reputation of the target of these accusations is, in fact, beyond question."

Question time—like the dominant green of the House (as in Britain's lower house, the House of Commons) and the Senate's red (as in the House of Lords)—is just one of many British inheritances incorporated in Australian parliamentary procedure. It's a time when members of the opposition get to ask questions which, they hope, will surprise a minister, catch him off guard and cause enough embarrassment or controversy to make headlines in the next day's papers. It's also a time when government backbenchers can plant "Dorothy Dixers," leading questions that allow a minister to push some government achievement or savage the opposition. Aside from divisions, when members vote on bills, it's the only time when the House or Senate is full. At other times, there are usually just enough members present to ensure a quorum.

Alison waited as the picture switched to another camera showing Kydd lumbering to his feet, his mouth an enormous semi-circle of a smile. His eyes glinted mockingly in Nash's direction as he stepped to the lectern set on the long table running down the center of the House floor, dividing the government from the opposition. He coughed as if he was clearing his throat.

"I'm surprised that the honorable member and Leader of Her Majesty's Loyal Opposition is so gullible," Kydd's familiar voice rumbled, "that he would believe what he sees on the internet . . . even if his assistant has printed out a copy for him to read. Does he still believe in the Tooth Fairy and the Easter Bunny as well? And has the honorable member forgotten the timeless principle of English law—and of basic Aussie fairness— that the accused be confronted by his accuser? So why, may I ask, is the honorable member repeating, in this place, unsubstantiated rumors from person or persons not only unknown but who have gone to great lengths to hide their identities from public scrutiny?

"Someone is accusing Australia's most senior Senator of corrupt and illegal behavior. Someone who hasn't got the guts to stand up and be counted. So I say him, whoever he or she is, and to *you*, sir, when you have some facts, some *evidence* to lay upon the table, present them to the Attorney-General for action. And if the honorable member can't put up, then the best thing for him to do is shut up."

A chorus of "Hear! Hear!" was heard from the Conservative Party members on the government side of the House. To Alison's ears it was muted, even perfunctory, with none of the yelling and thumping that often accompanied Kydd's demolition of an opponent.

"As I recall," Kydd continued, "the inquiry referred to by the honorable member did not issue a report because there was nothing to report. It seems to me there's nothing mysterious about it. And if there was an 'unstated focus' to that inquiry—another unsubstantiated rumor the honorable member chooses to repeat in this place—there can't have been anything in it either."

McKurn's angry face appeared on Alison's laptop, which was tuned to the Senate proceedings. Alison turned up the volume to hear him saying, ". . . nothing but lies— and I challenge Senator Tyndall to repeat his question and his allegations outside this building. But I know he hasn't got the guts to do so."

Seeing a vein almost popping on McKurn's forehead—*That's the word . . . livid,* she thought—she knew Senator Tyndall certainly would not repeat his question outside Parliament. Whatever was said in the House or Senate was protected by parliamentary privilege; if the Senator was foolish enough to repeat his question anywhere else, McKurn's lawyers would paper him with writs for libel and slander from here to Thursday.

On her desktop. Kydd was speaking again, answering another question—presumably a planted "Dorothy Dixer."

". . . our Great Traditions of Freedom of Conscience and Freedom of Speech," Kydd was saying, looking up slightly as he spoke, sounding as if he was reciting a litany, "enable anyone to say anything they like, no matter how stupid. And if something be libelous or scandalous, remedies already exist through the courts so no further government action is required. In any event, surely anyone so credulous to take any notice of such uncorroborated and—until some evidence is produced to the contrary—baseless rumors is, I submit, at least three sandwiches short of a picnic."

Leaping to his feet, Nash's *"A point of order, Mr. Speaker"* thundered over the shouts of "Hear! Hear!" from the government side and "Shame!" from the opposition members.

"Order! Order!" The Speaker's gavel rapped sharply until quiet returned to the House. "The Leader of the Opposition has the floor."

"I demand the Prime Minister apologize for his last remark and withdraw it."

Alison smiled as Kydd's voice boomed, "I see no need to withdraw my previous remark. But I will certainly apologize to the honorable member if he—clearly, mistakenly—was under the impression that it referred to him."

The government benches erupted into gales of laughter, overwhelming the cries of "Shame!" from the opposition side. Nash stood glowering at Kydd for a long moment, his face the same shade of red as his hair. He looked towards the Speaker and then back to Kydd—and slowly resumed his seat.

*****

Attack, Alison thought as she entered McKurn's office, *is the best form of defence.*

Without waiting for McKurn to offer, she took the seat on the other side of his desk, saying, "So in question time you flatly denied everything."

McKurn watched Alison with approval as she moved across the room. At her words, his eyes narrowed and focused on her face. "But of course."

Alison snuggled comfortably into the office chair, letting her arms relax on its wooden arms, as she replied, "And you had the Prime Minister's support in the House."

"Do you think so?" McKurn asked. "Did you hear him?"

Alison nodded, matching McKurn's gaze, breathing slowly to maintain her appearance of calm—and to hold down the rising tension within her.

"But did you listen carefully to what he said?"

"I thought I did."

McKurn waved a couple of sheets of paper. "A transcript." He placed the two sheets in front of him, scanning them as he spoke. "Kydd attacked whoever who put up that damn website, casting very effective aspersions on whoever-it-is's character. The randy old goat is good at that sort of thing. But the bastard uttered not one word of actual support for me."

"I suppose he didn't, now you mention it."

"He even broadcast an invitation for people to come forward with evidence. As though he was mocking me . . . *challenging* me."

"Do you think anyone will?"

"Come forward?" McKurn's asked, his lips slowly curling into a cruel grin that made Alison spine tingle. "I doubt that very much."

"I see . . . but do you think anyone really believed your denial?" she asked, keeping an eye on the vein on McKurn's forehead.

"Of course."

"A majority? Most people would say that when there's a stink there must be something rotten behind it."

The vein on McKurn's forehead pulsed. "Let the bastards—who the hell give a rat's arse what the *hoi polloi* thinks?"

Alison controlled her response to McKurn's outburst, merely raising one eyebrow and letting her mouth show the beginnings of a smile. "Really, Senator? That's the opposite of what you were telling me last time we met."

"It is?" McKurn leant forward slightly, squinting at Alison's expression. "Whose side are you on anyway?" he growled.

"The same side as you, Senator," Alison said with a demure smile. "My side."

McKurn's eyes widened, his lips twisted into a grin—and then he laughed, a deep belly laugh that shook his whole body. "Fair enough," he said, pulling out a handkerchief to wipe his eyes. "But in your case, Alison," he added, still chuckling, "instead of whispered rumors there'll be incontrovertible visual evidence for people to focus on. And they will focus on it . . . in the millions."

"No doubt," said Alison, her lips compressed as she spoke, "if they ever get the opportunity." Looking McKurn hard in the eyes, she continued, "I'm looking forward to you telling me how you can guarantee that can't happen."

"Without my say-so."

"Indeed," Alison murmured without moving.

"Since you insist . . . down to business. There are four copies of the video. A DVD and a hard drive in a safety deposit box. The others are on a DVD and a hard drive in secure storage in our . . . computer center."

"From where they can be easily copied."

"Only by people with access to the storeroom . . . and the right passwords."

"Passwords? Plural?"

"Right. One to gain access to the drive, a second to decrypt the file."

"And how many people have the passwords?"

"Only two: me and one other."

"And how many people have seen the video—or parts of it?"

"The same two people."

"And who can access the safety deposit box?"

"Only me."

"That all sounds very secure . . . and you've personally checked all these arrangements?"

"Of course not. I have other people for that."

"So this is what they've told you."

McKurn nodded. "I've no reason to doubt they're telling me the truth—and every reason to believe they are."

"How can you be so sure?"

"Because I know the loyalty of my people; they're handsomely paid for it—and they know what would happen if ever they betray me."

"But unfortunately," Alison replied, leaning forward a little to give McKurn a better view of her cleavage, "I don't know that."

"You don't believe me?" McKurn said, a pained expression on his face, which was undercut by the way he grinned at her.

"Oh, I imagine you're telling me what you believe. But even if you'd checked all those arrangements personally, I still wouldn't be satisfied."

"You don't trust me?"

"I think we've already covered that question, haven't we, Senator?"

"I suppose we have," McKurn chuckled.

"For me to be convinced, I need to see the entire setup—from recording to safety deposit box—and talk to all the people involved."

"I'm willing to indulge you up to a point, Alison. But no further."

"That may not be enough for you to . . . get what you want. And if I'm to be your successor, what difference does it make anyway?"

McKurn shrugged. "As I said, I don't really care who takes over after I'm gone. But you seem to be expecting access to crucial parts of my operation as a condition." McKurn shook his head. "That kind of access is something you'll have to earn."

"So, Senator, we seem to be at some kind of impasse."

"Not really," McKurn smiled, placing one hand on the phone. "One phone call, remember—that's all it takes."

"Go ahead, Senator. Make it."

"You're daring me?" McKurn asked. His hand rested on the phone as his eyes searched Alison's expression. When Alison just held his gaze in silence he said, "Is that what you're doing?"

"Go ahead. Make your choice." Alison looked steadily at McKurn, and then turned her head and pointing at the phone, she added, "Who would you rather have? Me—or Cracken?"

McKurn laughed again, looking at Alison with appreciation. He nodded slightly and, his eyes twinkling at her, picked up the phone and dialled.

Alison tensed. Letting her hands fall below the edge of the desk, out of McKurn's line of sight, she stiffened her right hand, turning it into a blade, the muscles in her right arm hardening. At the same time, she shifted her weight so she was poised to leap to her feet. Even though he was leaning towards her as he reached for his phone so she could see dandruff and glimpses of his scalp where his white hair was thinning, his neck was slightly out of reach. So her eyes watched McKurn's hand as he pushed the buttons on the phone. Loose skin hung from his flabby wrist and the veins stood out on the back of his hand . . . the wrist of an old man with weak, frail bones . . . *it would take me less than a second. . . .*

"Ivan. . . . I'm going to send someone to see you—" Alison suppressed a shudder at the risk she'd taken, holding herself rigid so McKurn would not notice her state "—You'll recognize her. . . . That's right, Alison McGuire. . . . So, Saturday morning . . . ?" Turning to Alison he said, "He can't this weekend—anytime during the week is okay though."

Alison slowly shook her head. "How about the following Saturday morning instead?"

McKurn covered the phone's mouthpiece with his hand, his eyes turning to scowl at Alison. "This week, Alison," he growled.

"Parliament's sitting. I have to be here."

"But it's not sitting on Friday, is it?"

"No," Alison said. "But that doesn't mean I won't need to be here."

"Friday evening then."

Alison appeared to consider the option, and then slowly nodded her head.

"Friday evening or late afternoon," McKurn said into the phone. "I'll confirm the details later."

As he finished the call, McKurn turned to Alison who now appeared to be lounging, relaxed like a cat, as if she were taking it easy by a pool rather than sitting in an office. "One good turn deserves another," he said, all signs of his earlier humor gone. "So you'll start working for me today. I expect daily reports. And secondly, you'll be taking a risk commensurate with mine: should anything you learn from Ivan leak out, then releasing the video will just be the first step in your demise. . . . Do I make myself clear?"

"Crystal clear, Senator."

"And assuming your meeting on Friday with Ivan is satisfactory," McKurn smirked, eyeing Alison's breasts as they slowly rose and fell in time with her breathing, "then the next step will be to consummate our agreement."

*****

Is McKurn still having me followed?

That question had been plaguing Alison since she got back from Singapore. Every time she drove home, as she was now, she varied her route slightly and kept checking the rear view mirrors to see if she could tell. Even on her pre-dawn run, she'd cautiously eyed the occasional jogger or passing car, and felt a jolt of fear when she thought she saw the same one twice.

When she reached her apartment, she leant against the closed and bolted door, taking a few deep breaths until she felt more relaxed. Safe. As she cleared a space on the table for her laptop by pushing a couple of piles of paper out of the way, her eye stopped on the phone. "My God," she gasped, and quickly covering her mouth with one hand she thought: *If I can arrange to tap McKurn's phones, he can surely tap mine.*

She shook her head—*I'm being paranoid. Nevertheless*, she decided as she poured herself a vodka and tonic, *I'll have it checked for bugs.* About to throw herself onto the sofa, she grabbed the bottle and brought it with her. The vodka calmed her but a few moments later her stomach started growling. She'd had no lunch—she hadn't wanted to eat before seeing McKurn—and afterwards she'd forgotten about food altogether. Without looking, she pulled a packaged dinner out of the freezer and put it in the microwave. She picked at it while checking her emails.

McKurn had given her a cellphone number she hadn't known about for her "daily reports." She was typing a message to the geek to add that new number to the list of taps, when she was interrupted by the buzz of the doorbell.

"What are *you* doing here?" Alison asked, when she saw who it was.

"I thought it's time we had a chat, just you and me," Melanie Royn said. She stood in the hallway, a small, wheeled suitcase behind her.

"Why?" Alison scowled, taking half a step into the doorway to block it completely.

"I—" Melanie faltered at Alison's movement; resisting the urge to step backwards, she lowered her head. "I . . . I'm sorry I lost my temper in Singapore," she said softly. "And I'm hoping," she continued, raising her eyes to look at Alison again, "that even if we can't be friends again, at least we can be allies. We are on the same side, after all."

"If we are," Alison said skeptically, "where have you been lately?"

"You're not making this easy, are you?"

"Why should I? Whatever's been going on between you and the minister has nothing to do with me. So tell me," Alison said, stretching her body so she seemed to tower over Melanie, "do you *still* think I'm sleeping with the minister?" When Melanie didn't answer, she added, "That's what you thought, isn't it?"

Melanie trembled. "You know how he is with women—and how they flock to him as if—"

"To the best of my knowledge," Alison snapped, "the minister has remained totally faithful to you, even on those trips where visiting dignitaries are offered geishas and the like to keep them warm at night. Though I can't imagine why."

Teardrops formed in the corners of Melanie's eyes, hanging there before rolling down her cheeks. "Alison . . . " Melanie spoke softly, and then threw back her head saying, "I wish I could believe that."

"It's true!"

Melanie sighed. "Don't tell me you have never been in a situation where your mind has raced with all kinds of suspicions?"

Alison nodded slowly. "Yes," she breathed, her face softening, "I have." The two women stared into each other's eyes, and Alison stepped back from the door. "I think we could both use a stiff drink."

"Thank you, yes."

Leaving her suitcase by the door, Melanie let herself sink into one of the armchairs. With a sigh of pleasure, she closed her eyes and rested her head on the soft cushion.

"What would you like?" Alison asked.

"Rum and Coke—if you have it," Melanie smiled, her eyelids fluttering open. "A strong one, please." Her gaze moved from watching Alison and rested on the half-empty vodka bottle on the coffee table. Her lips tightened, and she quickly turned her head to look around the room.

"Cozy," she said as Alison put a glass in front of her. "I've always liked what you've done to this room." But she safw files and papers heaped on the dining table in unstable stacks surrounding an open laptop—next to what must have been the half-eaten remains of Alison's dinner. Her now-critical eye decided the room was long overdue for vacuuming, and the coffee table hadn't been wiped down in a while either. Her gaze returned to Alison's face and she saw what she hadn't noticed before: the pale skin, the dark rings under Alison's eyes which were unusually dull and slightly bloodshot.

"Thank you," Alison said warmly as she sat down on the sofa, splashed some vodka into her own glass and topped it off with tonic water. Melanie sipped at her drink as she watched Alison take a long gulp from hers; when she put her glass back on the table, it was half-empty.

Alison kicked off her shoes and sat cross-legged on the sofa. "You know the minister's at an official dinner tonight."

"Yes," Melanie said, "for some visiting bigwig. I'll see him afterwards at the townhouse."

"He didn't mention you were coming up tonight."

Melanie smiled. "He doesn't know. Yet. I came here straight from the airport. You won't tell him—I hope."

Alison paused and, smiling, shook her head. "I hope he doesn't die of shock as I almost did."

Melanie giggled. "Of excitement, more likely."

Alison's smile faded, to be replaced by what Melanie felt as a deep melancholy. Speaking softly, Alison said, "I hope you and the minister get back to where you used to be. Did I ever tell you," she added wistfully, "that *yours* is the kind of relationship I wanted to have with somebody?"

"Wanted?" Melanie shook her head, and leant forward. "Why use the past tense?"

Alison spread her hands as she shrugged. Her eyes dropped. "Did I?" she said, leaning back, her hands now gripping her knees.

"Yes, Alison, you did."

Alison sighed. "I guess . . . it just doesn't seem possible . . . right now. . . ."

"But surely, you've come close. You must have. . . ."

"Once. Briefly. A long time ago."

"With . . . Derek Olsson?"

Alison stared at Melanie, her mouth an "O." She inclined her head slightly: half a nod. "Anyway," she said, leaning back again, trying to get comfortable, "that's over."

"Is it?" Melanie said without thinking.

Alison looked at her blankly for an instant. "But you didn't come here to talk about me," she said, ". . . did you?"

"No." Becoming aware she'd been intensely studying Alison's reactions and of the tension in her arms and shoulders from leaning forward for so long, Melanie let herself sink back into the softness of the armchair. "McKurn."

"McKurn?" Alison repeated, emptying the rest of her glass.

"That's why I'm here. To help."

"Good." Alison's eyes turned to her laptop. "Let me fill you in," she said.

"I'D BETTER CALL A taxi," Melanie said a while later.

"No need. I'll drop you off." As they both stood up Alison noticed Melanie's glance at her empty glass. "Don't worry," she said. "I haven't had that much to drink. But maybe . . . if you hadn't come . . . I might have finished off the whole bottle."

"If I were in your shoes," Melanie said with a shudder, "I probably would have."

"I just hope this business with McKurn is over soon."

"So do I," said Melanie, "long before the next election."

*****

IT WAS LATE WHEN Royn returned to his Yarralumla townhouse. He whistled as he unlocked the door and automatically reached for the light switches—and froze when he saw the glare of the living room lights.

Burglars?

Gently placing his briefcase on the floor, he hesitated, wondering if it would be better it he backed off, went outside and called the police. *Don't be silly,* he thought. But he was positive that when he'd left that morning the lights had been off—that he hadn't even turned them on. *I must have.* Just the same, he grabbed for the only possible weapon at hand: a long, furled umbrella from the stand by the entrance.

Holding his breath, he tiptoed soundlessly into the living room. It was empty. He looked around and noticed a wine glass—one he certainly hadn't used—on the counter separating the kitchen from the main room, that the cushions on the sofa had been rearranged, and that the little red light on the TV set was on. From the small bathroom under the stairs he heard the sound of a toilet flushing. He crept silently towards the bathroom door, his umbrella raised, when the door opened and Melanie stepped out—wearing a translucent nightie.

"Melanie!"

"Is it raining?" Melanie asked, her laughter shaking her body.

"B-burglars," he stuttered, feeling silly all of a sudden; the umbrella fell to the floor. "I thought maybe there were burglars in the house."

"Just me."

Melanie stepped towards him at the same moment he moved towards her. She threw her arms around his neck, lifting her lips towards his. Royn enfolded her, lifting her off the ground as his hands caressed her at the same time. She tightened her embrace around his neck and pressing her body to his kissed him hard and long.

"What's that smell?" she asked when they came up for air.

"What smell?"

"Perfume."

"Really?" Royn shrugged. "I was sitting between two old women at dinner—one of them an insufferably dreary British dowager."

"Poor Tony. All those boring functions you have to attend."

"Indeed," he said as he lifted Melanie to carry her up the stairs.

"Don't you think you should shut the front door first?"

22 Sly Grog

Good morning Boys & Girls!

Ready for the next thrilling installment of the "Frankie McKurn Saga"?

Light a fag, roll a joint, take a snort, inject some caffeine . . . whatever turns you on . . . and listen up.

Frankie McKurn has had several run-ins with the cops—and has even spent some time in jail (though never for very long. Just as well for *old* Frankie: a convicted felon with a year or more's "porridge" [jail time] can't be a member of parliament).

His first appearance on the police blotter was at the tender age of 17. One evening, the police raided a "sly grog shop" in Balmain, arrested staff and patrons alike, and carted them—and the liquor—off to the cop shop.

What, you may wonder, is (or was) a "sly grog shop"? A little history.

Back in the First World War (1914-18 for the history-challenged reader), to reduce drunkenness and increase productivity, the government ordered all pubs to close at 6PM. This was a "temporary wartime measure" . . . which lasted until 1955 in New South Wales and longer in some other states.

But just because the pubs were shut didn't mean there was any slump in demand for late night drinking. The underworld was quick to fill the gap and pretty soon there were "sly grog shops" scattered all over the country.

Why didn't the cops shut them down? There was no great public outcry and no political mileage in doing so. The reverse, if anything: the average Aussie certainly saw (and still sees) nothing wrong with having a drink pretty much anytime he or she likes. And in New South Wales, in particular, the Labor Party opposed the occasional tentative move against the sly groggers as an infringement on "the working man's rights" . . . and to the benefit of party funds (no doubt the more important consideration).

Every now and then, of course, the cops had to make a show of enforcing the law . . . which is how young Frankie got caught in the net.

Had he stopped by for a quick beer after work? No. He was *at* work. Illegal businesses need enforcers, big, strong men who are quick with their fists. Just like young Frankie.

At the cop shop, the police went through the ritual of recording everyone's name and then let them all go. The press announced the police raid the next morning and the cops could bask in the glow, the "proof" that they *weren't* corrupt and that they *had* enforced the law by closing down an illegal bar.

Which they had . . . for one night.

(What happened to the liquor, you may well wonder? Simple: what the cops didn't drink themselves they sold back to the underworld.)

Since this was the first time young Frankie had been through this charade, he made a mistake: he gave his real name, unlike the "regulars" who all treated the experience like the joke it really was.

Of course, no one was actually charged. That hardly ever happened.

The "sly grog" spawned by 6PM closing was the underworld's first big cash cow, followed soon thereafter by off-course betting shops. By the time young Frankie came onto the scene in the late 1940s, these underworld businesses were well-established and proved fertile ground for our young "hero."

As we shall see in future installments.

— The McKurn Watcher

PS. Memo to Kydd: ask and ye shall receive.

"That's the geek's work?" Melanie asked when she finished reading the issue of McKurnWatch which had just arrived.

"That's right," Alison replied.

They were sitting together behind Alison's desk, the office door closed, speaking in hushed whispers.

"So he's been in jail, eh? McKurn will be furious," Melanie giggled.

"Maybe he'll have a heart attack," Alison chuckled.

"We should be so lucky."

We can but hope, Alison thought.

"So," Melanie said, turning to look at Alison. "How do we divide up the work?"

"I really appreciate your help," Alison said as she switched the screen to the list of audio files.

"You've already said that," Melanie said with a smile, touching Alison's arm.

Alison smiled back. "I guess I have. It's just such a relief."

"I don't know how you've managed."

"Nor do I." Pointing at the screen, Alison continued, "I guess we just take half each. I'll set up a new email address, get the geek to send some of the files there, and show you how it all works."

"I tried to follow what you were doing last night—you're using programs I've never even heard of."

Alison nodded. "Some I'd never heard of before."

"Well, I don't know," Melanie said. "I'm no computer whiz. In fact, I've never even installed a program. Any time I need something more complicated than spell check, I ask Zoë or one of the boys to do it."

"I see. . . . Do you have a laptop?"

"No. I just use the family computer at home."

"In that case, the best thing would be to buy one today so I can set it up for you and show you how to use it. It wouldn't be a good idea to use the family computer in any case."

"Why not?"

"If you use the same computer as your kids do, they could easily get into your files."

"Why would they?"

"Because they're computer-literate and insatiably curious."

"But if they know something—"

"They might let something slip to someone else. Not intentionally. At the moment, only three people know about this: you, the minister, and me. And it must stay that way."

"You don't trust my children—is that the issue here?"

"No, it's not," Alison said. "I trust them to be fully behind us. But if one of them finds something, the others will know in no time flat."

Melanie nodded.

"They'll feel part of something important, some sort of spy game, right? One of them is bound to let something slip to one of their friends—quite innocently. Then, who knows who else will find out?"

"Maybe," Melanie said, unconvinced.

"And, Melanie, would you really want them to know what this is all about?"

"No," Melanie said with a start. "Definitely not."

"Okay, then," Alison sighed. "Laptop . . . ?"

As Melanie nodded Anthony Royn opened the door. "I'm off to see Kydd," he said.

"You are?" said Alison. "I didn't know you had a meeting with him."

Royn smiled. "Well, you two have been closeted together all morning."

"Good luck, dear," said Melanie. "I'm going shopping . . . to buy a laptop."

"A what?"

"Alison's instructions."

"Oh. Got to go—you know Kydd doesn't like to be kept waiting."

As Royn left her office, Alison turned to Melanie. "*Why* is he going to see Kydd?"

Melanie shrugged. "He's going to raise the succession issue—"

"Oh my God," Alison gasped. "He mustn't."

"Whyever not?" Melanie asked. "Anyway, he's going to do it very obliquely."

Alison shook her head. "Kydd's paranoid. Remember his first rule of politics?"

Melanie looked up at Alison and slowly nodded, her eyes and mouth wide.

"So how do you think he's going to react?" Alison ran to the door—and stopped. "I'll never catch up with him now."

She turned back to the desk and dialled a number.

"Larry? It's Alison. . . . Yes. Is the minister, Tony Royn, there? . . . Oh. . . . Okay, thanks."

She sank into the chair, opposite Melanie, her head in her hands. "He's just gone in."

*****

THE FOUR WALLS OF Randolph Kydd's office recorded his fifty years in politics through the luminaries he'd met: pictures of Kydd with the Queens, Kings, Princes, Emperors, Presidents and Prime Ministers of thirty-nine different countries (at last count). Not forgotten were famous people like Nobel Prize-winning economists and best-selling authors, and the not-so-famous people who were politically important, like the Mayors of Sydney and Melbourne and other major cities, and all the current state Premiers. Those pictures were centrally displayed whenever one of them visited Canberra but otherwise—as now—were tucked in corners and other out-of-the-way places as befitted their lesser prominence.

The prime minister had a large office with walls to match—and every square inch was covered with pictures of Kydd with somebody. Hundreds of them.

Kydd settled his bulk into the wide chair behind a desk which was incongruously small, given the spaciousness of the room. It was a frail, feminine table, with flecks of gilt peeling from the ancient woodwork, far too small to be a desk for a prime minister . . . or anybody else. A gift from the Queen—to the government, not Kydd, even though he treated it as his prize possession—it had once belonged to Queen Victoria, making it so valuable it really belonged in a museum.

In front of Kydd was what he thought of as The Phone, which he felt gave him direct, puppeteer-like control over a hundred thousand bodies at the other end . . . layers of secretaries, bureaucrats, and functionaries whose only purpose was to serve *him*.

With a smile he picked up The Phone and dialled a number.

"Frankie," he chuckled when McKurn answered, his jowls wobbling. "I see you've got a problem or two."

"Nothing for you to get excited about, you randy old bastard."

"Oh, I don't know, *Frankie* . . . " Kydd wheezed as he spoke. "Did your Dad really call you that?"

"None of your fucking business."

"I wouldn't be so sure. Feels to me like it might be a good time for you to be thinking seriously about enjoying that stash I'm sure you've got tucked away for your retirement . . . before it's too late."

"Over your dead body."

"I'd say, me old mate, it's more likely to be your body than mine."

"Mate?" McKurn laughed. "That'll be the day. Anyway, you worry about your problems and I'll worry about mine."

"Unfortunately, it looks like you are turning into a problem for me—not to mention for the party."

"Are you suggesting I retire for the good of the party?"

Kydd laughed. "I know better than to appeal to your better nature."

"I'm surprised you're appealing to me at all."

"Appealing? To you?" Kydd chortled. "You must be joking. I'm just giving you a friendly warning that you'd better kill these rumors permanently or my guess is little Frankie will get his just deserts . . . at last."

"I'm working on it."

"The problem is, Frankie, mud sticks."

"You should know. You're the expert at throwing it." As McKurn slammed down the phone Kydd heard him mutter, "Arsehole."

Kydd laughed.

As ANTHONY ROYN ENTERED his office, Randolph Kydd's dark eyes, two small circles turned into bright pinpoints by overlapping folds of flesh, flashed a glance at his watch and darted back to Royn with a slight look of censure. "I realize," he boomed, "you no doubt have immaculate reasons for your slight delay. . . ."

Royn's step faltered, his sense that this office would inevitably, one day, be his disappearing under the glare of Kydd's censorious eyes. "Ah . . . yes . . . I—"

Kydd dismissed his excuses with a wave of his fingers. Though he gestured a great deal as he spoke, his gestures began and ended at the wrist. And rather than shaking his head, he would wobble his jowls—as he did now. "Time, my boy. *Time.* I never keep people waiting, mainly because people expect to wait around here."

As a politician, Royn recognized when another one massaged the truth. Wisely, he kept those thoughts to himself.

Wrinkling his nose at the stale smell of cigar smoke permeating the room, Royn strode towards the chair in front of Kydd's desk, but Kydd's fingers waved him in the direction of the sofa. "Over there, Tony, over there. Let's be comfortable."

A Churchillian cigar clenched between his teeth, Kydd levered his massive body upright by gripping the arms of his chair and heaving with all four limbs at once. As Royn sank gratefully into a soft armchair he watched breathlessly—as he did every time he saw Kydd do this—waiting for him to make some slip that would send his massive weight crashing on the weak, fragile Victorian desk and shattering it to smithereens. Royn felt a touch of disappointment when Kydd's manouver was successful. He waddled across the room to plonk himself down the sofa in the place where he always sat: in a large concave depression where the springs had almost given out.

"So, Tony," Kydd rumbled, coughing as he placed his cigar in the nearby ashtray. "What was it you wanted to talk to me about?"

"Well . . . Prime Minister . . . ah . . . it's these damn press stories that keep popping up from time to time. . . ."

Royn passed a newspaper clipping to Kydd, who scowled at the headline, "Tired Old Party" Needs New Blood.

"I saw that," he spat. Then, scowling at Royn, he added, "You're not about to suggest it's time for me to pack it in, are you Tony?"

"No, no, Prime Minister. But I think it is time we killed these stories somehow."

"Who cares what these so-called 'opinion leaders' chatter on about?"

"In the electorate at large? Almost nobody. But here in Canberra? Everyone."

"So what?" Kydd shrugged, his sour expression making it clear this was not a topic he wanted to think about.

"These stories sow uncertainty within the party. And they could give Nash the idea to make an issue of our leadership—and the uncertainty about the succession. That's what I'm getting at."

"Hmmm. Maybe. . . . But . . . this is not like you, Tony. Who put you up to this—Alison?"

"No, no, Prime Minister. Actually, it was my wife, Melanie, who mentioned it."

"Ah, women," said Kydd. He paused to relight the cigar; Royn held his breath as a cloud of smoke floated in his direction: smoking was actually *verboten* in Parliament House, but who was going to stop the Prime Minister? *Not me,* Royn thought.

"A woman in politics is like a snake in the grass," Kydd was saying. "You never know when it's going to jump out and bite you." Kydd's laugh boomed at Royn's expression of disbelief. "Look, Tony," he continued, taking a sip from a glass of water on the side table, "this is just between you and me. I'd never repeat this in public—those damn feminist bitches would be jumping all over me. But if I've learnt anything in my sixty-nine years it's this: no man will ever understand a woman completely. Men. They're simple. Sex, money, power, or all three. That's about it. Easy to figure out. Easy to manipulate. Predictable. It's women—" he seemed to spit out the word "—who always do the thing you least expect when it's going to hurt you most.

"And no question, Melanie is a superb backroom operator and numbers man . . . ah, woman. And Alison—your right hand, so to speak, very capable and damn sexy too . . . a dangerous combination, I might add. She's the best man who wears skirts I've ever come across. But they're still both women. Remember that, too."

Melanie? . . . Alison? thought Royn. *Not to be trusted?* But he knew better than to disagree with Kydd whenever he had a fixed opinion . . . or at any other time. So he just nodded his head and said, "Very good point."

Royn felt his stomach clench as, frowning, Kydd squinted at Royn for a long moment.

"I suppose . . . " Kydd wheezed eventually, his gaze unmoving, ". . . it's something to think about."

"Anyway," Royn said, forcing his voice into a light tone as his stomach tightened, "with ten months to go before we have to call an election, there's no rush."

"True," Kydd muttered, his mouth an upside down semi-circle. Royn felt as though Kydd's eyes were slicing into him as Kydd added, "Have you . . . or Melanie . . . come up with any ideas for handling this?"

"Well . . . to kill these stories we need to remove any doubt."

"And how could we do that?" Kydd took another puff on his cigar, which was followed by a deep, liquid cough.

"Well . . . I haven't really given it a lot of thought, Prime Minister."

"But," said Kydd, doubt written all over his face, "something must have come to mind . . . ?"

Royn sighed. "Ah," he said, trying and failing to look Kydd in the eye as he spoke, "only the two obvious things, Prime Minister."

"Which are?"

"Announce a timetable of some kind, or something to make it clear to all and sundry that you have plenty of years to go—" Royn's voice trailed off as he concluded "—like a medical. . . ."

"Damn doctors," Kydd coughed, "always fussing around." Kydd leaned forward slightly, his body still as his eyes seemed to burn into Royn's flesh. "Or a leadership spill . . . was that on your list?"

"Prime Minister. How could you think such a thing," Royn protested. "I've looked up to you since I was a kid—when you and Dad used to sit around and discuss politics. *Nothing* will change that."

"Hmm." Kydd slowly sank back in the sofa, looking unconvinced. "You've got to remember, Tony, that in this position, ultimately you can't fully trust anyone. Loyalty in this business is always conditional. But I've always thought of you as the exception that proves the rule. I'd be very disappointed if it were to turn out I'd made a mistake."

"Prime Minister!" Royn lifted his head so he was sitting tall, his back straight. His face solemn, he spoke with all the persuasion he could muster. "I swear that will never happen." But at the sound of his own words, he wondered if, by raising the issue at all, the mistake had already been made.

*****

FOR A GANGSTER, THE Colombian, Jorge Gonzalez, seemed to be a man of reasonably regular habits. For example, no matter how late he got home, he left his apartment a little after noon to pump iron at the gym. At least, he had for each of the three days Nazarov, Shultz, and de Brouw had been shadowing him.

Which is why, just before noon, the three men trudged up the stairs of the apartment building until they reached a fuse box on the wall outside the Colombian's front door.

After visiting the Greek, Nazarov and his associates had paid similar calls on the South American and Lebanese gang leaders—with similar, inconclusive results. So they switched strategy to "squeezing" second-level gang members for information. Gonzalez was their first target.

When Gonzalez opened his door, wearing gym shorts and a singlet that displayed his well-muscled arms, shoulders, and legs, he saw three men from the electric company: one was doing something to the electrical box while the other two, caps low over their foreheads, stood around smoking cigarettes.

"Hey," said Gonzalez said angrily. "Smoking's not allowed."

"Really?" said Nazarov, blowing a mouthful of smoke in Gonzalez' direction, "I didn't know that." Turning to Shultz, he asked, "Did you?"

"Nah," Shultz replied, blowing a smoke ring.

Gonzalez stepped closer to Nazarov and flexed his muscles. "I've got a good mind to complain to the electric company." The tendons in his neck stood out as he spoke, his black eyes glaring coldly at the two smokers.

"You do that," said Nazarov.

"I think I will," said Gonzalez, turning to go back inside.

As he stepped through his door Nazarov and Shultz dropped their cigarettes and rushed him, knocking him face down onto the carpeted floor. They both held him down as he kicked and tried to punch them with one hand and push himself up with the other while Shultz covered his nose and mouth with a pad soaked in chloroform. After a few moments, his struggles weakened.

"That should do it," said Nazarov.

De Brouw came in carrying the toolboxes they'd brought as part of their disguise, closing the door behind him. Instead of a cap, he now wore a stocking over his head. Nazarov and Shultz let Gonzalez go and quickly pulled stockings over their heads as well.

Gonzalez groaned, and tried to get up.

"We'll help you," said Nazarov. He and Shultz picked him up and threw him on the sofa. As Gonzalez fell, a wild swing from one of his powerful arms caught Shultz in the stomach.

Shultz grunted and pulled out his knife, waving its sharp tip a hair's breadth from Gonzalez' nose. "I wouldn't do that again," he said. Gonzalez tried to escape the knife by pushing himself deeper into the sofa. "Agreed?"

Gonzalez nodded his head drunkenly as Nazarov and de Brouw clipped a pair of handcuffs over his wrists.

"Ssso," Gonzalez said, slurring his words, "you're not here to fix the lights."

"Smart man. For a muscle man," said Shultz.

Gonzalez glared at him and lashed out with one foot.

"Not so smart after all," Shultz smiled as he dug his knife into Gonzalez' bicep.

"No," Gonzalez shrieked.

"I thought we had a deal," said Shultz, showing Gonzalez the bloodstained tip.

"*Bueno.* A deal. That's right."

"Good," said Shultz, placing the blade of his knife just above Gonzalez' elbow. "Now you already know how sharp this knife is, right?"

Gonzalez' head bobbed up and down quickly, his eyes unable to move from the glittering blade.

"Do you know what happens when a tendon is cut?" Shultz asked.

Gonzalez shook his head, his eyes trying to look at Shultz and the knife at the same time.

"Would you like to find out?" Shultz asked, pressing the knife a little harder.

"No," Gonzalez shrieked again in deep gasps, his head swinging violently from side to side. "No. Please, no!"

De Brouw sat on the other side of Gonzalez, while Nazarov pulled up a chair and sat in front of him. "Now," he said, "there's no need to be difficult. We're just here to ask you a few friendly questions—"

"You're not being very friendly, then," Gonzalez said, lifting his bound wrists and eyeing the knife.

"—and show you a few pictures."

"Of what—your holiday snapshots?"

Nazarov just grinned as de Brouw passed him a thick envelope from one of the toolboxes. Nazarov pulled out a picture and admired it before holding it in front of Gonzalez. "This one came out rather well, don't you think?"

"What's this?"

"You mean, you don't recognize yourself?" Nazarov asked.

Gonzalez looked at the picture as thought he was studying it carefully before answering. "I suppose it looks like someone who looks a bit like me," he said. "Big deal."

Nazarov took out a few more pictures, glancing at them briefly until he found the one he was looking for. "You're quite photogenic actually, didn't you know?"

"Fuck you," Gonzalez said, spitting at the picture.

Nazarov flipped the picture around. "Good shot," he said, grinning at Gonzalez. "You hit yourself right in the eye." He leant over and wiped the spittle off the print on Gonzalez' singlet, and studied the result. "Oh dear. These prints cost about a dollar each. We'll have to ask you to pay for a new one."

"Go fuck yourself," said Gonzalez. Shultz applied a tiny pressure to the knife. "Okay, okay, who gives a shit about a lousy dollar."

"Now, José—"

"My name is Jorge," Gonzalez protested, pronouncing it *Hor-hay*, the Spanish way.

"He sounds like a horse," Shultz laughed.

"Listen, spic," Nazarov said, his hard, dark eyes glittering, "you're in no position to argue."

Gonzalez turned his head towards Shultz, the knife, and back to Nazarov. He shrugged . . . carefully.

"That's better," said Nazarov. "As I was saying, José, if we were to give these pictures to the cops, what do you think would happen?"

Gonzalez pursed his lips but said nothing.

"Not sure? Well, you see this guy here," Nazarov said, pointing to the other man in the pictures, "the one you're selling the dope to—"

"Dope?" said Gonzalez. "Could be talcum powder for all we know."

Nazarov grinned. "From what we know about you spic arseholes, it probably was. Most of it anyway. But if you keep interrupting we're going to be here all day. And I'm sure you don't want to disappoint your boss by showing up late for work. He has a pretty short temper, I hear." Nazarov paused, but Gonzalez just kept his mouth shut. "Now, this other guy, he's well-known to the police as a minor pusher. Been arrested a few times but somehow managed to get off. Connections, I suppose. I don't think his connections would help against this kind of evidence. My guess is, the cops will do a deal with him: he dobs you in and in return he gets a reduced sentence. Fair guess?"

"I'm just a businessman—"

"Save your spiel for the cops," Nazarov snapped.

Narrowing his lips, Gonzalez stared back at Nazarov, his twitching facial muscles betraying his attempt to keep his face expressionless. And as hard as he tried, he couldn't prevent his gaze from now and then flicking to the blade pressed against his skin.

Nazarov sighed, and waved the envelope at Gonzalez. "We've got lots more . . . ah . . . holiday snapshots." He selected another picture and shoved it close to Gonzalez' face. "Caught in the act," he said. "Good camera work if I say so myself." The light in the picture was poor, but it clearly showed Gonzalez crouched over another man, his fist embedded in the side of the man's head. "You know what happened to this guy, don't you?" Nazarov asked.

Gonzalez shrugged, as if the question held no interest for him.

"He spent a day in a coma and then died."

"Is that so?" Gonzalez asked. "If I'd known, I'd have sent flowers."

"Very funny," said Nazarov without smiling. "Did you know that when you punch someone like that you leave lots of little flakes of skin behind? . . . No? . . . No doubt the police found those little bits of your skin and analyzed them. Then they'd have tried to match them with the DNA samples they have in storage. But you're still walking around like a free man, so I presume you don't have a record. Not in this country, anyway. The cops will keep those skin samples till Judgement Day. So if we give them this picture, along with your name, address, and phone number, they'll come calling. And you, my friend, will be looking at a long, all-expenses-paid vacation as a guest of the government."

Gonzalez sighed, his shoulders drooping and his body deflating as if all the air inside him was whistling out through the hole of his mouth. "Okay," he said at last, "what do you want?"

"Information."

"What kind of information?"

"Like . . . when—and of course where—you're expecting drug shipments, where you store it, who you sell it to, how you move it around. To start with."

"Not asking much, are you?"

"Well, we're not asking for anything you don't know."

"And what do you do with this information?"

"We're traders. We sell it to the highest bidder."

"The cops?"

"Nah," Nazarov shook his head. "They don't pay enough."

Gonzalez looked puzzled. "Who else would be interested?"

"Let me give you an example. Say the Greek or the Lebanese or someone else was expecting a large shipment of high quality smack. Say we knew when and where they were going to pick it up and make the trade. Do you think your boss would be interested in picking up a couple of kilos—and the money for it—for free?"

Gonzalez nodded. "Damn right he would."

"How much would he be willing to pay to know the time, place, and how many of the opposition would be there?"

"No idea," Gonzalez shrugged. "Ten or twenty grand, maybe."

Simultaneously, Nazarov, Shultz and de Brouw burst out laughing.

"You really are a funny fellow," said Shultz, still chuckling.

"We think a fairer split," Nazarov smiled, "would be you keep the smack, we get the money."

"I don't know if my boss would go for it."

Nazarov shrugged. "If your boss won't, some other gang boss will."

"So . . . if I tell you something, you're going to auction it off to some other outfit? Is that it?"

"You've got it." Gonzalez was about to protest when Nazarov went on. "But it's a two-way street. You will be our exclusive contact in your mob—so you'll be able to get the credit for bringing lucrative opportunities to your boss's attention."

"I don't know. . . ." Gonzalez shook his head slowly. "They'd cut my throat the moment they suspected anything. I don't think so."

Shrugging, Nazarov held up one of the pictures. "You always have a choice."

"And you're such a pretty boy," de Brouw said, softly stroking Gonzalez' arm. "I'm sure you'll be in great demand behind bars."

Gonzalez shrank away from de Brouw and stared at him wide-eyed; he didn't even flinch as the point of Shultz' knife dug into his side. His face contorted, and he made strangled sounds as if he was choking. Then he bent over the way he was facing and brought his bound hands up to his face.

"He's going to throw up," de Brouw said, quickly standing up to get out of Gonzalez's way.

Gonzalez' body shuddered, he coughed and gasped for air and then sat up, slowly beginning to breathe again normally.

"So," said Nazarov as if nothing had happened, "what's it to be?"

"Whatever you like," Gonzalez yelled. "Just so long as. . . ." De Brouw sat back down. "Keep away from me, you—you goddamn *poofter.*" With a shudder, his eyes flicked between de Brouw and Shultz. They both sat unmoving, and Gonzalez slowly turned his head back to Nazarov.

"What can I tell you, then?" As he spoke, his shoulders slumped, his head dropped, and he buried his face in his hands.

"You spics sell a lot of coke as well as heroin. First question, then: where's your factory?"

Gonzalez raised his head, his mouth open, but no words came out. Nazarov fanned a few of the pictures.

"Okay," he sighed. "It's over in Redfern." Groaning, he gave Nazarov the address. "There are lookouts all over the place, though," he added with a smile. "And they have a whole arsenal in there: sawn-off shotguns, AK-47s, pistols, the lot. Good luck."

"Good boy," said de Brouw. Gonzalez glared at him and began to pull away until he remembered the knife still pressing against his elbow.

"What about drug shipments?" Nazarov asked. "Anything planned?"

"Something's coming in a couple of weeks. The details aren't set yet, though."

Nazarov took out a pen. "Give me your arm," he said.

"Why?" Gonzalez asked, looking frightened.

"I need something to write on."

Tentatively, Gonzalez extended his arm; Nazarov leaned over and wrote a phone number on his skin. "There," he said. "When you know the details, send me a text at this number. Okay?"

Gonzalez slowly nodded, swallowing hard against the bile threatening to rise in his throat.

"Good," said Nazarov. "That'll be enough to keep us busy for a while." As he stood, de Brouw and Shultz also began to rise.

"What about these?" Gonzalez asked, lifting the handcuffs.

Nazarov stood unmoving.

"You're not going to leave me like this, are you?"

With a grin, Nazarov pulled a key from his pocket. Gonzalez eagerly lifted his hands. But with a frown, Nazarov sat back down. "Oh yeah," he said, "one other thing. We're curious about this Vincent Leung guy."

"Who?"

"You're trying to tell me you don't know who he was?"

"Was?"

"The triad chief who was killed recently."

"The Dragon man?"

"Yeah."

"Why didn't you say so? He's dead. What else so do you want to know?"

"Who killed him?"

"They arrested the guy who killed him, didn't they?"

"That's what they say. He a member of your gang?"

"I don't even know the man's name."

"Derek Olsson, I believe."

Gonzalez shrugged.

Shultz ran the tip of his knife over Gonzalez' bicep, the slight pressure leaving a scratch that slowly oozed blood.

"What are you doing?" Gonzalez shrieked, a hand, its range of movement constrained by the handcuffs, making the sign of the cross. "I swear on my immortal soul I know nothing about it."

"Your gang had nothing to do with it?"

Gonzalez' head bobbed left and right vigorously, his eyes looking in horror at the red lines on his arm. "No. *Dios mio,* you've got to believe me!"

"I believe you," said Nazarov as he bent to unlock the handcuffs. But he grabbed Gonzalez' wrists instead, leaning with his weight to pin them on Gonzalez' knees. Simultaneously Shultz pushed Gonzalez' shoulder into the sofa while de Brouw jerked Gonzalez' head back by the hair with one hand and slapped another chloroform pad over his nose and mouth. He held it there until Gonzalez' body went limp.

*****

"McKurn," Alison muttered, as she saw the number on her cellphone. *What does he want?*

Taking a deep breath, she answered. "Yes, Senator?"

"Alison. A little birdie told me Royn met with Kydd this morning. Tell me what they discussed."

"He ... ah ... went to show Kydd those poll results I told you about yesterday, Senator."

"Is that all?"

"He's been in meetings or in the House ever since, so he hasn't had a chance to tell me anything about their discussion."

"I see. . . ." McKurn paused. "And the moment you know what they talked about, you'll tell me, right?"

"Of course, Senator."

Aware she was visible through the glass wall of her office, she forced her hand to put the cellphone down slowly and naturally on the desk. She pulled a tissue from the box, wiped her sweaty palms, and let them lie in her lap until they stopped shaking.

*****

The sun was low on the horizon as Jeremy's men—two of the three sections of his platoon—reached the outskirts of Inkaya. They'd stopped for a quick but welcome swim on the beach near the unfinished hotel. They passed what looked like two more derelict buildings as they neared the village: one was just a roof without walls, the other was enclosed with holes in the wall where once, presumably, had been air conditioners.

"Seems like a strange place for buildings like that," Jeremy observed.

"Something to do with the hotel construction, perhaps?" Sergeant Byrne replied.

Jeremy shrugged. "Maybe. We'll take a look in the morning."

For the past two days they'd moved slowly and carefully through the jungle and seen . . . next to nothing. Two more trails led up to the conical peak which they marked on the map, a clearing which had, probably, once been a campsite.

And they'd seen nobody.

"It's eerie," Byrne had commented, "as though people had been warned to keep out of our way."

As the platoon filed into the village, the soldiers attracted a growing number of smiling, skipping children. The soldiers smiled back, some letting their weapons drop from the ready position. "Keep your guard up," Byrne snapped. "We've no idea what to expect."

As they reached the village square they saw a group of elderly men standing in front of a cabana-like building—a roof with no walls—with a dozen or so long tables scattered around the dirt floor.

"Looks like we have a welcoming committee," Jeremy said.

"Seems they knew we were coming," Byrne replied.

"The kids could have warned them, I suppose."

"Maybe," Byrne replied, his tone laced with skepticism. "And see that playground—new equipment. This place looks a bit more prosperous than other villages I've seen here."

"Fishing, perhaps?" Jeremy said, indicating the fishing boat being unloaded at the end of the pier and wrinkling his nose at the strong fishy smell that drifted towards them, brought by the soft, cooling breeze from the water.

"Could be," Byrne grunted.

A gnarled old man took a step towards them. He spread his arms and smiled; Jeremy stifled a gasp as he saw that he had only three, black, front teeth. "Welcome," the man said. "Aussie soldiers, first time see." As he spoke, his smile stretched even further towards his ears.

"Thank you," said Jeremy.

The man started to reply, then turned his head to one side saying, "Arang'anat-*gaat*."

A young woman wearing a headscarf stepped forward from where she'd been waiting, unnoticed, behind the men.

"To Inkaya, welcome," she said, smiling briefly at Jeremy before lowering her eyes. "My name Arang'anat. I for you translate." With a slight bow, she turned towards Tungi. "Tungi-*ga*," she said, "village leader." Indicating the other men she added, "Elders council."

"We are honored," Jeremy replied. "I am Lieutenant McGuire. This is Sergeant Byrne."

"M'gire-*ga*," Arang'anat replied, inclining her head again. "Byrne-*ga*. Tungi-*ga* you invite to talk. And drinks for your men—tea, water, juice, all can offer."

Jeremy looked at Byrne whose eyes had been scanning the growing group of villagers standing at a respectful distance in a wide circle, smiling as they watched. Byrne nodded briefly. "Suggest by sections, sir," he said softly.

"A good idea, Sergeant," Jeremy nodded. Turning to Tungi, he said, "Your offer is most welcome."

Arang'anat spoke a few words to the elders who all smiled at Jeremy and Byrne and began walking towards a large table set near the counter.

"Please, come," Arang'anat said.

"After you, ma'am," Jeremy said with a flourish of his arm.

Arang'anat looked at him in bewilderment until his words sank in.

"Here," Byrne whispered, "women follow behind."

"I see."

Arang'anat took a tentative step—but then waited for Jeremy to go ahead.

At Byrne's order, the men dropped their knapsacks in a pile and half of them took seats while the other half, standing at ease, formed a loose cordon around the building. A moment later, several young girls brought out trays laden with cups of tea, glasses of water, and juice. The men gaped at them, and as soon as they had placed the trays on the table the girls disappeared as quickly as they could.

"Mind your manners," Byrne growled as he took a seat next to Jeremy. The elders sat along the opposite side, Tungi in the middle, with Arang'anat at one end. As Byrne sat down they, too, were served with refreshments.

They all sat in silence, studying each other as they sipped their drinks. Then Tungi said something to Arang'anat.

"Tungi-*ga* asks if we can some way help you," she said. "If you anything want to know."

"Thank you." Jeremy inclined his head towards Tungi as he spoke. "Indeed there is," he said, taking a photo of Karla Preston from his shirt pocket and placing on the table opposite Tungi. "We're looking for this woman. Have you ever seen her before?"

As Arang'anat strained to see the picture she gasped—and looked guiltily at Tungi.

Tungi's expression remained stoic as he slowly nodded his head. "Preston-*gaat*," he said.

At Tungi's signal, Arang'anat said, "She here, two, three days."

"How long ago?" Jeremy asked.

"Seven days. One week."

"Do you know where she went?"

Arang'anat turned to Tungi, translating Jeremy's question. Tungi looked searchingly at Jeremy, frowning, as if he were carefully considering his answer.

After he'd spoken, Arang'anat turned to Jeremy, her words catching in her throat. "She to K'mah went."

Jeremy frowned. "Do you have any idea why?"

Arang'anat smiled. "She a writer, yes?"

"Yes," Jeremy nodded. "A journalist."

"She talk to—" Arang'anat paused, searching for a word "—dissidents want."

"But . . . seven days ago? That's a long time. And you've heard nothing about her since?"

Arang'anat shook her head, tears appearing in the corners of her eyes. "I pray to Allah every day she safe."

23 A Man of Influence

Karla woke, half-opening her eyes. It was pitch black and the boat was rocking from side to side. Was that what had woken her? The *slap-slap-slap* of the waves against the hull was unusually loud; gone were the engine's steady *throb* and its comforting vibration which lulled her to sleep each night. Straining her ears she could just make out the faint tone of the engine as it idled.

The boat must have stopped. Why?

Now wide-awake she knelt on the narrow bed and peered through the tiny porthole. All she could see were the endless, rolling waves, the night sky filled with stars as the boat rocked one way and dark water as it rolled the other. Then there was a *thump* and a jar that rattled everything in the room, followed by the sound of feet scrabbling above her.

Had they hit something? Were they going to sink?

She went to open the door. It was locked.

She pounded on the door and yelled—but nobody came.

She peeked back through the porthole. The boat was now just rocking gently; no longer was the glass momentarily covered by the waves, and no longer was the small circle of the porthole alternately filled just with stars. She studied the waves for a long moment and decided everything seemed stable. *We're not sinking. If we were, surely they wouldn't leave me here.* Holding her watch close to the porthole she could make out the time in the faint starlight: around three in the morning.

She beat on the door again. Again, there was no response. She wondered if anyone had heard her. From the bumps and thumps coming from above, she doubted it.

When she'd looked at their position on the chart they were still days away from land. What's more, if they stayed on the same course for much longer, they'd pass by Cairns several hundred kilometers out to sea. Was the captain just being cautious? Or was there another reason? For the next half-an-hour, she sat in silent thought contemplating the possibilities.

In the fishing boat's hold, the sailors had been working fast. First, they hauled the iced plastic buckets of fish on the deck. From underneath, they pulled out big boxes heavily encased in a thick plastic wrap, and levered them up onto the deck where they were stacked by a second group of sailors.

A sleek, clearly expensive yacht was coming closer, gliding silently alongside until the two boats touched, beam-to-beam, with a *thump*. Without a word from either crew ropes were passed between the two boats to join them together. Then the boxes were passed across to the yacht where they quickly disappeared below decks. After about thirty minutes of hard, sweaty work, the ropes were released and the two vessels pulled apart. The fishing boat headed south, staying well in international waters; the yacht turned northwest towards the Australian coast.

As the engine sounds returned to normal and the boat got under way, Karla lay back down, soothed by the vibrations—but stayed alert. Sure enough, about fifteen minutes later there was a *click* from the direction of the door.

They've unlocked it, she thought, slowly, silently, sitting up on the bed. So they were doing something they didn't want me to see—and they don't know I woke up.

Why, she wondered, had they had stopped?

The fishing boats at the village pier . . . the marijuana plantation and hashish factory—"And they sell it . . . ?" *In Australia,* Uqu had told her.

A rendezvous? In the middle of the night, in the middle of nowhere, had another boat come to take the cargo on the last leg of its journey?

What other reason could there be?

*****

"Sir," asked Sergeant Byrne, "how long ago do you think that construction site on the beach was abandoned?"

"A year," Jeremy said. "Maybe longer."

"This padlock is new."

Jeremy leaned down to look at the lock on the door of the abandoned building. "So it is. What do you think that means, Sarge?"

"Well," said Byrne, scratching his head, "if these buildings had something to do with the construction site—storage, say—then the padlock should be old too."

"It's not exactly convenient to the beach, though, is it?"

Byrne shook his head. "Or to the village, either."

Jeremy looked up at the hole in the wall above, just the right size and shape for an air conditioner. "If this building was air conditioned," he said, "there must be power. But there are no power lines."

"A generator, then."

Jeremy nodded. He walked around the building, trying to find a chink in the wall he could look through. "Can't see inside anywhere," he said.

"Well-built—better than just about anything we saw in the village," said Byrne. "But maybe we can get a look-in through there." He pointed at the hole above.

Jeremy nodded, and a few minutes later one of the soldiers was standing on the shoulders of two others. "It's blocked, Sarge," he reported. "A sheet of plywood by the looks of it."

"Can you push it aside?" Byrne asked.

"—without breaking anything," Jeremy added.

The soldier managed to push one corner of the plywood out of the way. "It's too dark inside, sir."

"Mac," Byrne ordered. "Could you send someone back to the beach to get a torch."

"Sure, Sarge," Corporal MacDougal replied.

They'd spent the night camped on the beach. Half the platoon was packing up the camp while Jeremy, Byrne, and the other men had come to look at the abandoned buildings. Jeremy had politely turned down Tungi's suggestion they spend the night in the village, but could not refuse Tungi's hospitality completely. After protracted negotiations—which revolved around Tungi's refusal to accept payment ("It's against our traditions") and Jeremy's insistence that he was unable to accept Tungi's invitation without payment ("It's against our customs")—Jeremy made a donation to the school's funds, and the village put on a feast which the men all agreed was "the best feed we've had since we left home."

A torch was soon brought from the beach and the same soldier clambered back onto the shoulders of his fellows. "Looks like some sort of machinery, Sarge."

"What kind of condition is it in?" Byrne asked.

"Like new, Sarge. At least, well maintained. But no idea what it's for."

"Lemme have a look," said Byrne.

"It'll take four of us to hold you up, Sarge," one private groaned.

"It's all muscle," Byrne said with a grin.

"That's the problem," said another.

It only took two, but they pretended to be about to collapse under Byrne's weight until he ordered, "Hold still, damn you." After a moment, he jumped down and shrugged. "Can't tell what it's for either. " Turning to Jeremy he asked, "Do you think it's worth going back to the village and asking Tungi-*ga* what these buildings are for?"

Jeremy shook his head. "If they are hiding something, he wouldn't tell us the truth, would he? And by going back and asking, we'd only be showing our interest in them."

"I think they already know."

"Being watched again?"

"I think so, sir."

"I wouldn't be surprised," Jeremy said. "We're finished here, then."

Byrne nodded. "Let's go," he ordered.

"Sarge, wait a moment," Corporal MacDougal said. He was standing a few meters up the path to the beach staring into the jungle.

"What is it, MacDougal?"

"You see all these plants." MacDougal pointed at the meter-high shrubs covering most of the ground under the trees.

"Weeds?" said Byrne.

"Maybe," MacDougal said. "But they're all around the same height, and it seems to me they've been planted in rows. Not straight, but rows just the same."

Byrne and Jeremy went to stand near MacDougal. "Could be rows," Jeremy said.

"In Toribaya," MacDougal said, "you can buy marijuana just about anywhere—"

"Is that so, Mac?" said Byrne sharply.

"So I've been told, Sarge."

Byrne smiled. "You think that's what these plants are?"

MacDougal shrugged. "I've no idea, Sarge." He pointed to the trees. "You couldn't see these from the air, so if it's something they want to hide . . . could be."

Jeremy took a few pictures with his cellphone, and pulled off a branch from one of the shrubs. "Good work, Mac."

"Thank you, sir."

"Someone will know what they are," Jeremy said.

"Okay men," Byrne said. "Let's get moving. Back to home cooking."

*****

"Sorry," Alison said as she walked towards her office after her morning meeting with Royn. "My mind must have been somewhere else."

"I just asked you," said Mary, "if you know whether Melanie will be coming in today."

"Not as far as I know, Mary," Alison replied as she entered her office.

As she dumped her files on her desk, she heard Mary's voice saying to someone else in the front office, "Seems like Alison has been in some other world this past week or so."

How true, she thought, her gaze freezing as it reached the cellphone lying on her desk. *Can't put it off any longer.*

She went to the bathroom and, as she came back into her office, she closed the door behind her. She took a moment longer than necessary to get comfortable before reaching for her cellphone to dial what she thought of as McKurn's "unlisted" cellphone number . . . and stopped when she saw that her fingers were shaking. *It's just a phone call—what's happening to me?*

She'd felt on top of the world all morning . . . until she left Royn's office knowing she had to call McKurn. Though Royn knew what she was doing and what she was going to tell McKurn, she still felt a gnawing sense of betrayal.

Her optimism came from the private eye's summary of everything they knew—whether true or rumored—about McKurn, and how they planned to proceed.

They'd done their legwork, coming up with information that would embarrass McKurn: at sixteen, he'd spend nine months in reform school, the result of a knife fight with another gang member, and three different stretches in Long Bay Jail of up to four months. Grainy photos photocopied from old Sydney newspapers of the nineteen-sixties and -seventies showed McKurn with known underworld figures like Perce Galea, Abe "Mr. Sin" Saffron and "Stan-the-Man" Smith.

And then there was the story that McKurn was part-owner of an office supply outfit, Paper Supplies Pty. Ltd., that had become the exclusive supplier to the New South Wales government for mundane items like pens, pencils and paper in the early seventies—a contract the company still held. More recently—a year after Paul Cracken became Treasurer—the same company had gotten a nice chunk of the federal government's stationery business.

What really lifted Alison's hopes was the news that Leon Price—the Sydney politician mentioned in Sidney Royn's report—was willing to make a deathbed confession. Dying from pleurisy, kidney failure, and an assortment of other ailments of old age, he agreed to "tell all"—*provided* his life would be protected until he died from natural causes.

Royn had agreed to the expense, saying excitedly, "McKurn's goose is going to be well and truly cooked."

Perhaps I'm not going to have to play double-agent for much longer after all, she thought as the highlights of the private eye's report flashed through her mind; her fingers no longer shook as she dialled McKurn's "unlisted" number.

"Senator?"

"Good morning, Alison," said McKurn. "You have some information for me, I trust?"

"Indeed, Senator. As I thought, the minister discussed the poll results with the Prime Minister yesterday. You know, the ones that show he'd be streets ahead of Cracken."

"I know what you're talking about, Alison," McKurn said irritably. "Tell me something I don't know."

"Kydd was not very happy with the minister," Alison said, "especially since the poll showed Royn would top Kydd's record at the last election." McKurn chuckled in her ear. "He immediately became suspicious that Royn might be considering a spill. Royn came back from that meeting with his tail between his legs."

McKurn laughed. "That's nice to know. Maybe we can help sow a little more discord there."

"There certainly seem to be possibilities in that direction, Senator," Alison said as she thought: *Blast. I didn't mean to give him any ideas.*

"Royn's basic strategy at the moment is to do whatever's necessary to keep Kydd's support while making sure the MPs—especially those in marginal constituencies—all know they should hitch themselves to him, not Cracken, if they want to keep their seats."

"Alison—that's been quite obvious all along," McKurn growled.

"Indeed, Senator. But I'm confirming it for you—isn't that the sort of thing you want?"

"Quite so, Alison. Quite so. And that's all?"

"That's it. Since Kydd's retirement doesn't seem imminent, we haven't given it serious thought. So there's no real plan, as such."

"I see. Good. Anything else?"

"Only that the Candyman Inquiry will finally get under way today."

"That should be fun to watch," said McKurn.

Let's hope so, Alison thought.

She slumped back when the call ended, massaging the tension from her shoulders on the back of the chair. *How much longer can I take this?* she asked herself, not knowing the answer.

*****

Rudi Durant opened his office door to see Simon Lee grinning at him, his luggage piled up in a corner.

"How was the flight?" Durant asked, his voice deadpan.

"Tiring," said Lee.

"Find out anything?"

Lee nodded, his grin looking like a permanent addition to his face.

"So tell me!" said Durant as he took his seat.

"The Super said he wanted to be the first to know. I could be run out of the force if I disobeyed a superior officer's direct order, couldn't I?"

Durant chuckled. "Or—if he thinks what you've come up with is a complete waste of his and your time—sent back to being a local Detective. How embarrassing would that be?"

"True enough," Lee laughed, pulling out his notebook. "But I couldn't resist. Remember the seven-year gap in Olsson's history, his seven-year absence from Australia? He spent most of that time in Hong Kong, ending up as an assistant manager at an investment bank—one of those boutique things. The Hong Kong police believe the bank in question is a front for the Golden Dragon Triad—money-laundering and the like."

"I see," said Durant. "But 'believe' doesn't sound bankable . . . ?"

"We knew Vincent Leung was head of the Golden Dragon Triad here—but couldn't take it to court. That's what they mean when they say 'believe.'"

Durant nodded. "Fair enough. So there could be an Olsson connection with the Golden Dragon lot. What else?"

"You're overlooking something . . . sir," Lee said, grinning as he shook his head. "Banks don't hire people for management positions without at least a university degree; better yet an MBA. And it's very unusual for small, Chinese-owned and run outfits in Hong Kong to hire an unqualified *gweilo*—a foreigner—for such a position."

Durant looked at Lee in surprise. "You're right, Simon," he said slowly. "Very suspicious."

"About a year after Olsson's arrival in Hong Kong, he was making so many entries and exits at the airport—almost once a week—that his name appeared on an Immigration Department watch list."

"Did they ever pin anything on him?"

"Unfortunately, not." Lee shook his head. "He was often searched. A couple of times his suitcase was full of cash—"

"And he wasn't arrested?"

"That wasn't illegal in Hong Kong then, or even reportable. So the immigration officer I met said he was a courier of some kind. And he gave me this." Lee pulled a computer printout from his briefcase and passed it over to Durant.

"What's this?" Durant asked as he scanned it.

"That's a printout of Olsson's entries and exits since Hong Kong Immigration computerized their arrival and departure records. It seems he's been going to Hong Kong about twice a year."

"Well . . . he could afford it, couldn't he?"

"True . . . but why?"

"Visit old friends?"

Lee shrugged. "Maybe. But InterFreight doesn't have an office there, and you don't go to Hong Kong to buy equipment for a freight company. But it is a place full of rich people with money to invest. Perhaps that forty-nine percent investor in InterFreight is the Golden Triad gang, or someone related to them."

"So," said Durant, "we still come back to the same question: where did he get the money?"

"And if it was Triad money," said Lee, *"why?"*

"What's in it for them?" Durant mused.

"Exactly."

"A good question, but I see what you're getting at. And I'll have a quiet word to my mates in the Drug Squad and ask them to keep their eyes and ears open for any connection, including rumors, between drugs and InterFreight." Durant grinned. "You know, we'll make an investigator out of you yet."

Lee smiled broadly: from Durant, faint praise was a major compliment.

"I'd say there's no question the Super will be interested in what you've dug up," Durant said as he picked up the phone. He let the phone ring until he was transferred to the voice-messaging prompt. "Durant here, Super. Sergeant Lee is back and says he has some interesting information."

As Durant hung up Lee asked, "Anything come up while I've been away, sir?"

"No breakthroughs. No sign of Olsson. But there are some disturbing developments. Remember that the place near Ulladulla was sprayed with bullets? They were identified as coming from three different AK-47s. But two of the Chinese gang died from a single shot between the eyes: *those* bullets were not fired from AK-47s."

Lee's mouth hung open. "Single shots . . . a sharpshooter?"

"That's what they think," Durant nodded. "Maybe a military sniper rifle."

"Where the hell would that come from?"

"God knows," Durant sighed. "The Army says none of their weapons are missing. No missing grenades, either. But that's not the worst of it—"

"It's not?"

"Nope. Just yesterday we found two more dead Chinese, both killed with a knife. Throats cut. They were in the back of a SUV in a garage a couple of kilometers from where Olsson was snatched. The stink—" Durant's nose wrinkled at the memory "—somebody complained about it, which is how the bodies were discovered. The SUV fits the description of the vehicle seen fleeing from the ambush with members of the second gang—the one that shot out the tyres on the police motor bike." Seeing Lee was about to say something, Durant held up his hand. "It gets worse. Over the weekend four more bodies were found—"

"That's eighteen bodies altogether?"

"Right. They'd been dumped in the bottom of a hole in the ground at an abandoned building site. Like the two bodies found in the SUV, these four had also been knifed. But they'd been tortured first—genitals, fingers cut off, chests and arms slashed, that sort of thing." Durant shuddered. "It was like they'd been played with—gruesome."

"Do we know who they were?"

"Young punks. Aussies, not Chinese, with records of petty theft and the like."

"Any leads?"

Durant shook his head. "None! But my gut tells me the same thugs sliced them, killed the two Chinese in the SUV, *and* are responsible for the massacre in Ulladulla."

"Jesus Christ," Lee breathed. "Do we have any leads to these murderous bastards, any idea who they are?"

"Not a thing," Durant said sourly, "except this."

He passed Lee a printout of the email from Olsson's lawyer. "What do you think?" he asked when Lee finished reading.

"Eighteen bodies aren't evidence?"

"In the absence of a connection with Olsson, I'm afraid they're not. After all, Maybe Olsson was rescued by a gang of Good Samaritans."

"Do you believe that?"

"Of course not. Olsson is up to his eyeballs in . . . something."

"But what?"

"That's the problem. And there's another problem: there were no signs that Leung struggled with his murderer before he was killed."

"That doesn't mean he didn't."

"It doesn't," Durant said sourly. "But that damned ambulance-chaser has a point about the hair and—"

Durant's words were cut off the shrill of his phone. "Super? . . . Right, we're on our way."

*****

"Zulu, this is Charlie Alpha, over."

"Zulu" was the call sign of the base, and "Charlie Alpha" was Jeremy's call sign as commander of the "Charlie" platoon. Had Sergeant Byrne been speaking, it would have been "Charlie Bravo." And—much to his regret—Corporal MacDougal had the honor of being "Charlie Charlie."

"This is Zulu. Go ahead Charlie Alpha, over."

"Charlie Alpha. Can you patch me through to Hotel and scramble, over."

"Zulu. Wait one, over."

A couple of minutes later another voice came through the radio's headphones. "Charlie Alpha, this is Hotel, over." Jeremy recognized Captain McMurray's voice.

"Charlie Alpha. We've just visited Anakaya, a village halfway between Zulu and Inkaya, and have some news, over."

"Hotel. Go ahead, over."

"Charlie Alpha. A week ago a group of Sandeman soldiers arrived from inland, carrying the body of one of their men. The villagers were told he'd been shot by guerrillas. They also learnt that these soldiers had captured a white woman, and that the guerrillas had attacked them and spirited the woman away, over."

"Hotel. I see. Anything else? Over."

"Charlie Alpha. The soldiers were taken off by boat and about two days later a larger force of Sandeman soldiers landed, over a hundred of them according to the villagers, and went inland, over."

"Hotel. Did you see any sign of those soldiers while you were scouting around? Over."

"Charlie Alpha. Negative, over."

"Hotel. Good work, Charlie Alpha. Over and out."

*****

Alison yawned as she followed Royn through the entrance of his townhouse.

Melanie sat at the dining table, hunched over her new laptop, headphones covering her ears. Royn glanced at Alison with a smile and a finger to his mouth, and tiptoed until he was standing behind Melanie. He placed his hands on her shoulders and ran them down towards her breasts.

Melanie yelped. "You gave me a fright," she said as she turned to smile at Royn, her lips held up to him for a long kiss.

As she usually did when she saw her boss and his wife acting like aging lovebirds, the picture of Derek Olsson at seventeen flashed into Alison's mind, and she grieved for what-might-have-been.

When Royn stood again, his hands still caressing her shoulders, he asked, "How are you, Mel?"

"Better now," she smiled. "But my ears are sore—" she let the headphones drop on the table "—and my head hurts from listening to McKurn's voice all day."

"Time for a drink," Royn said, heading towards the bar. "How about you, Mel? Alison? Vodka and tonic?"

"Thanks," Alison said as she joined Melanie at the table.

"Wait," Melanie said with a grin. "Listen to this first and tell me what you make of it." She unplugged the headphones and turned up the laptop's volume.

Voice: Senator. These approvals are taking far too long. And I had it on good authority that you were a man of influence.

McKurn: I *told* you there are no guarantees.

Voice: These damn blackfellas—someone should line the bastards up and shoot 'em. They've held us up for so long we're close to running out of cash.

McKurn, laughing: I feel your pain.

Voice: You will if you've put any money in our stock. You can kiss it goodbye.

Royn whistled as he slowly sat down next to Melanie.

"I see why you didn't want me to do this in the office," Melanie said.

"Indeed," Alison nodded. "Any idea who he's talking to?"

Melanie shook her head. "I was hoping one of you might know."

"No idea," said Royn with a shrug.

"So what do you make of it?" Melanie asked.

"A company needs a permit of some kind—and will go bankrupt without it," Alison said. "McKurn promised to help get the permit—and would make a killing when the company's shares hit the roof. That's my guess."

"The . . . ah . . . Aborigines are holding up their project," said Royn. "A mining company, perhaps?"

"Could be a mining concession," Alison said. "Or timber—even a factory. Pretty wide choice."

"That's what I was afraid of." Melanie's shoulders slumped. "If only we knew who he was talking to—"

"There is a way to find out," Alison said, her sapphire eyes sparkling once again. "All we have to do is ask people."

"How can we do that," said Royn, "without blowing our cover?"

Alison smiled. "Ask the geek to put it on McKurnWatch with the question: 'Who is McKurn talking to?' If the press picks it up, the voice is sure to be identified."

"But then McKurn would know someone's listening to his phone conversations," Melanie objected.

"That call was on his cellphone. Anyone could have picked it up out of the air."

"Is that true?" Royn asked.

"According to a Federal Police briefing I attended, yes," said Alison.

Royn nodded approvingly. "Seems worth the risk. . . . What do you think, Mel?"

"I'd like to be there to see McKurn's face," Melanie grinned mischievously, "when the geek's email hits."

24 Hobson's Choice

"They lied to us, Prime Minister," Victor Bergstrom was saying. "Brigadier Thierry—our commanding officer up there—agrees. In fact, those were his very words."

Anthony Royn sighed. "I'm neither surprised nor shocked."

"They had this Karla Preston woman," Cracken said, "lost her—and told us they knew nothing about her whereabouts."

"Exactly," said Bergstrom.

"General," Kydd said, "can we send some of our troops to get her back from the guerrillas?"

"We could, Prime Minister," said General Arthur Riddell, Chief of the Defence Force and the only additional face at this hastily called meeting of the Cabinet's National Security Committee.

"Better do it, then," said Kydd. "Now, let's get back to the main business at hand."

Each committee member had a copy of the CONFIDENTIAL, TOP SECRET report. In his summary, General Riddell concluded, "The separatists' strength appears to be growing. The situation on St. Christopher's Island, in particular, is deteriorating. In our judgement, the forces are there to deal with the situation—but only with a unified command. Only then can we follow a unified strategy and concentrate forces where they'll do the most good. Without that, or a dramatic increase in the number of Australian troops, the outlook for getting the separatists under control is bleak."

"To put it another way," Randolph Kydd rumbled, "two weeks ago we had a deal—and they've reneged."

"They insist they're fully committed to our agreement," said Bergstrom. "They just haven't delivered."

"What's the difference?" Cracken snapped.

"In effect," said Bergstrom, "none."

"So, Victor," Kydd asked, "what are our options?"

Before Bergstrom could speak, Cracken cut in: "Sending more troops so Sandeman forces can go back and lounge around in their barracks isn't one of them. The public wouldn't stand for it."

"Quite so," someone said, and several heads around the table nodded.

"With soldiers in Afghanistan and East Timor, as well as the Sandemans," General Riddell said, "we don't have much room for manouver."

Nodding towards Riddell, Kydd said, "Victor?" His slightly impatient tone commanded silence from everyone else.

"If the Sandeman authorities aren't coming to the party," said Bergstrom, "our military options are basically three: do nothing, and hope we can muddle through; increase our strength there; or withdraw."

"Hobson's choice," said Cracken.

"Indeed," said Bergstrom. "And with your kind permission, Paul, I'll conclude my remarks."

"Of course, Victor," Cracken mumbled, his cheeks flushing.

"If we do nothing now, we'll only have to make one of the other two choices later. Sending in more troops, aside from being unpopular, has no guarantee of success. We need the Sandeman troops at our side and the Sandeman authorities behind us to be most effective."

"Could you explain that a little more, please Victor?" Kydd asked.

"Certainly, Prime Minister. If large numbers of Australian troops go in, we could be seen as an occupying army, which would only fuel the resistance. Secondly, whatever their failings, the ordinary Sandeman soldiers are reasonably effective in joint operations They're very cooperative at the platoon and company level—none of this obstructionism we're experiencing at the top. They respect and tend to look to our soldiers for leadership. More importantly, we gain the cooperation of the local villagers, and so our intelligence—and I emphasize at the local level—is much better. Without Sandeman assistance, we could be flying blind, and be resented rather than welcomed."

"Each separatist group is local," said Riddell. "There are few signs of unity. If we don't nip them in the bud, that will change. They'll be much harder to dislodge if they present a united front. They get minimal support from the islanders—at the moment. Strategically, now is the best time to go after them. Yesterday would have been better."

"And tomorrow will be worse," said Helen Arkness.

"Exactly so, madam."

"So your preferred option, General," Kydd's voice boomed before anyone else could speak, "is to have all forces under your—or should I say Brigadier Thierry's command."

"Precisely, Prime Minister. End this interference from their 'fruit salad' generals." Riddell's voice dripped with sarcasm.

"Are you referring to the Sandeman Prime Minister's brother, by any chance, General?" Royn asked.

Riddell nodded. "The man has no military knowledge or experience—couldn't tell one end of a howitzer from another. That doesn't stop him from thinking he's a general and issuing orders left, right, and center. The only thing he's any good for is strutting around in his uniform, with every medal the Sandemans can offer hanging off his chest and a bunch of others he probably picked up at a flea market."

"I take it you're not very impressed," Kydd chuckled, his jowls wobbling.

Riddell made no comment; he didn't seem to find the subject in any way amusing.

"Do you have the joint command structure already worked out, General?" Kydd asked.

"We do," said Riddell. "We can put it into action tomorrow—there are no operational difficulties. Only political ones."

"Give me an example, Victor," said Kydd.

"It keeps coming back to the . . . ah . . . 'fruit salad' general," Bergstrom said. "As a general he supposedly outranks Brigadier Thierry, and under the 'joint' operational command structure we envisage, he'd have nothing to do. But if we overcame that objection, they'd find something else."

"I see. It looks like we need a battering ram to break the logjam," said Kydd.

"That seems to be the only solution, Prime Minister," said Bergstrom.

"The problem is, now that *you*—" Cracken looked at Royn as he spoke "—have got the oil money flowing again up there, they're going to feel less beholden to us. That reduces our leverage over the bastards."

"And what," demanded Kydd, "is our leverage?"

Cracken replied immediately: "Cut off the money, pull out our troops—and leak the Treasury report. And there is a fourth possibility—though I'm hesitant to mention it."

"You?" asked Royn, pointedly raising one eyebrow. "Hesitant?"

"Which is?" asked Bergstrom with interest.

"A more cooperative government up there might certainly make a difference."

"What are you suggesting," Royn said sarcastically, "a coup?"

"I suggested nothing. But maybe that's not a bad idea."

"And where, Paul," Royn said slowly, "would you find a Sandeman politician you could trust?"

"I'd say," said Cracken, smiling mischievously, "that's your department, not mine."

"And *I'd* say," said Kydd, "we drop this topic right now. And if anybody asks, it was never discussed at this table—is that clear?" Kydd's eyes moved from one face to another, finally coming to rest on Cracken with an expression of unmistakable disapproval. He waited until everyone said, "Yes, Prime Minister."

HALF AN HOUR LATER Anthony Royn, his face drawn, strode straight into Alison's office. "Alison, get me Nimabi on the phone immediately . . . please."

"Bad meeting?" Alison asked.

Royn nodded. "And I'm the hatchet man."

"We're considering our options, Abdullah," Royn said fifteen minutes later. "We've yet to make a decision, but I thought I should let you know that withdrawal is at the top of the list."

"You *can't*. I mean—"

"I know exactly what you mean: how long do you think the Sandeman army will last without us to give them spine? Especially on St. Christopher's Island? We estimate three to four weeks."

"And if the Papuans were to make a lighting raid on el-Bihar—which is effectively defenceless—to grab all the oil, what then?"

"You should have thought about that before."

"This—it's just blackmail."

"Really, Abdullah. Two weeks ago we made a deal. We've already kept our side of the bargain and sent reinforcements. We've been waiting and waiting for you to keep your word—and we can't wait any longer. Is that clear?"

"But, as I understand it, there are all kinds of issues still to be resolved. For example, Thierry is only a brigadier. He can't be in overall command—our generals outrank him."

"That's exactly the kind of foot-dragging tactic we're totally fed up with," Royn said impatiently. "We'll send someone of higher rank, set up a separate task force under Thierry—or promote him to Field Marshal. Use your imagination. The simplest thing would be for your so-called commander-in-chief to retire."

"This is outrageous—"

"No, Abdullah, failing to keep your word when people are being killed is outrageous. Anyway, check your watch. Exactly twenty-four hours from now, if you haven't agreed to our proposed joint command structure and put everything in place for its implementation, that Treasury report will be, sadly, leaked to the press."

"This . . . this is pure extortion."

"Call it whatever you like. We've all had enough. We're giving you a straightforward, either-or, black-and-white, yes-or-no choice—and you've got twenty-four hours to make it, Abdullah."

*****

"HEY, NAZIR. . . . IT'S PASHA you dummy—wake up. . . . Yeah, well take an aspirin. . . . I blew my cash last night, so why don't we pick up some pocket money at a corner store first? . . . . Then? Well, what about a bit of snatch—a nice, young, firm schoolgirl, say. . . . Yeah, a lunchtime snatch, ha, ha, . . . Okay, I'll pick you up in about half an hour."

When Pasha Kuri walked out his front door, he saw an electric company van parked by a telegraph pole. A ladder was propped up against the pole and three workmen stood around the bottom, looking up. As he reached his car, parked behind the van, one of the men began to climb the ladder.

He shrugged and turned the key. The starter motor whined but the engine didn't catch. "Damn." He tried again with the same result. On his third try the starter motor turned over sluggishly. "Damn battery's giving out," he muttered.

He opened the bonnet and went to see if he could figure out what was wrong.

"Won't start, mate?" one of the workmen asked.

"No," Kuri said, shaking his head.

"Maybe I can help," the workman offered.

"Please do." Kuri frowned as he looked at his watch. "I'd appreciate it."

The workman leant over the engine, poked here and there, and within a couple of minutes stood up saying, "See that connection? It's come loose."

As Kuri bent his head over the engine, the workman slammed the bonnet down hard on the back of his head. "Oops, sorry about that, mate."

KURI CAME TO LYING on an unfamiliar bed, a gag in his mouth. His hands automatically tried to hold his throbbing head—but they were chained to the bed.

He strained hard against the bonds but all he achieved were sore wrists. The room suddenly brightened and he heard a voice with an accent he couldn't identify saying, "At last. Our Lebanese sleeping beauty is awake."

Three men came into the room through the now-open door, their faces hooded.

"And who the fuck are you?" he growled.

"I'll do the asking and you'll do the answering," said de Brouw.

"You bastard," he spat, recognizing de Brouw's voice. "Like hell I will."

De Brouw's fist smacked onto the side of his chin. Kuri yelped at the pain.

"If you hit him that hard, you schmuck," said Shultz, "he won't be able to talk. Hit him somewhere else. And you—" Shultz poked Kuri's forehead "—he *likes* hitting people, so it would be a good idea to answer his questions."

"Fuck you, too."

De Brouw punched him hard in the stomach.

De Brouw stepped to one side as Nazarov pulled up a chair by the bed. "Sorry about that," he said. "My associates tend to get overzealous from time to time."

Kuri's eyes flicked warily between the three hoods.

"We're just after a little information, and then we'll drop you back home—or anywhere else you like."

Kuri said nothing.

Nazarov made the same proposition to Kuri he'd made to Gonzalez. Kuri just listened in sullen silence until Nazarov finished.

"That's it?" he asked.

Nazarov nodded.

Kuri spat at Nazarov's face.

Nazarov stood, wiping away the spittle trickling down his hood, shaking his head sadly. "You shouldn't have done that."

Kuri rolled over to face the wall.

Shultz came forward and roughly forced him back. De Brouw stood by him, holding a needle.

"What's that?" the Lebanese asked, fear showing in his eyes for the first time.

"Heroin," said Nazarov. "Poetic justice, don't you think?"

"No. Please. No!" Kuri tried to shrink away from de Brouw, but Shultz held him firmly in place.

"Rather talk?" said Nazarov.

Kuri looked at him, shuddering for a long moment, and shook his head.

"As you like it," Nazarov said, nodding to de Brouw.

De Brouw grabbed Kuri's arm roughly, thrust the needle into a vein and squeezed the plunger home.

"No no no no no!"

*****

Senator Frank McKurn, the most senior figure in the governing Conservative Party in both age and length of service, could, in theory, have had any ministry of Cabinet rank he desired. One insuperable obstacle stood in his way: Prime Minister Randolph Kydd. After a brief stint as Minister for Mining and Energy in the first Kydd government, Kydd kicked McKurn "upstairs" as soon possible, where he became President of the Senate.

McKurn objected bitterly to Kydd's decision—in public. Privately, he was perfectly happy with the arrangement. He avoided the burdens and pressures all ministers faced—and the prominence which could have led to undue scrutiny of his activities. Much better, he knew, to work through proxies like Cracken.

As Senate President, McKurn had a plushly appointed office with its own dining room and garden, duties that were light, often ceremonial, and occasionally tedious. He had the responsibility, shared with the Vice-President of the Senate from the opposition party, of running the affairs of the Senate, presiding over its meetings, and meeting heads of state and other prominent visitors as the Senate's representative. And in his hands were certain jealously guarded powers, such as control over the Senate's agenda.

A few minutes after noon McKurn, sitting in the President's chair, acceded to Labor Party Senator Felix Haughtry's request for permission to introduce a private member's bill.

McKurn's ruling was met with considerable surprise. The senators expected the next item on the agenda would be the last: a motion to adjourn.

Haughtry proposed an extension of the libel and slander laws to expand the definition of "publish" to include the conduits for libellous information, including internet service providers and even the owners of the wires and cables that browsers used to access websites around the world.

"It should be clear," Haughtry was saying, "from the recent slanderous and anonymous attacks on one of our most senior members—the kind of cowardly and vicious attack that could happen to any one of you, to any person of any station in life, prominent or not—that the libel laws were written for another age, and need to be updated to meet the realities of today's world of instantaneous, electronic communication. . . ."

Haughtry's words were greeted with gasps that onlookers took be ones of amazement. They were, but from three different impulses: *appreciation,* for the sneaky and audacious way in which McKurn was clearly demonstrating his power; *disapproval* from the freedom-of-speech champions present, at the outrageous extension of the libel and slander laws into areas they were never meant to go; and *fear,* as Senators, journalists and visitors in the galleries who understood what was going on looked at Haughtry with the question in their minds: *What has McKurn got on him?*

*****

WHILE SENATOR HAUGHTRY WAS presenting his private member's bill in the Senate, a McKurnWatch email landed in subscribers' inboxes:

McKurnWatch.com
"The website that must not be named"

We must interrupt the fascinating "Frankie McKurn Saga"—even though we're still in the "prologue" stage of this riveting historical drama—for the very latest (though not, sad to say, concluding) installment.

But . . .

Roll out the champagne, Boy & Girls. Not-so-young-any-more Frankie has been caught in the act!

There can be no doubt that Frankie's still up to his old tricks, and that he's risen up the rungs of corruption from sly grog bouncer to the rarefied level of corporate crime.

A loyal reader—one of those techie people (I presume) who builds gadgets to listen into other people's cellphone conversations (naughty, naughty) was kind enough to send in a recording of Frankie on the phone. Just click on Frankie's nose in the cartoon (you can't miss it) to hear Frankie's liquid tones for yourself, talking to . . . WHO?

That's the question . . . though everything else is clear (as you'll find out for yourself when you "listen in"): Frankie's up to his eyeballs in a scam with some shady stock promoter to fix permits and permissions so they can both make a killing in the stock market.

But, as I mentioned, there's still the question: WHO is Frankie talking to? If you think you can identify Frankie's partner-in-crime, just nominate your candidate in the comment box below.

The first person to correctly identify this mystery voice will be the first person honoured in "The McKurnWatch Hall of Fame."

Naturally, you may prefer NOT to use your real name—no problem: no names, no pack drill (and when dealing with a sleaze like Senator Frank McKurn, that's a good policy to follow).

Of course, if you use a pseudonym you won't be able to bask in the glory of blowing the whistle on young Frankie. Beats wearing concrete boots, though, don't you think?

Happy guessing.

— The McKurn Watcher

PS. My apologies if you've had any problems reaching McKurnWatch.com recently. Somebody (it's not hard to guess who) has been attacking the website, flaming it, trying to overburden the servers and shut us down. They did succeed—but not for long. Now, with mirror sites all over the place and other defensive measures, future access won't be a problem (tough luck, Frankie).

Within two hours, 179 people had nominated seventeen different candidates as "The Voice"—some of them clearly frivolous. Shortly afterwards, a reporter from *The Western Miner* phoned Lester Edleton, a Perth-based stock promoter with a shady reputation, and asked whether he had ever spoken to Senator Frank McKurn.

"Yeah, I have. So what?" Edleton said—and, as the reporter recorded the conversation, his words were broadcast nationwide ten minutes later on News24/7.

"And you talked to him about the problems you've had getting permits for your Metal Mountain Exploration company?"

"I did—and what's wrong with that?

"Depends what you talked about. For example, did you offer him stock to 'fix' the problems for you?"

"Don't be ridiculous. I just assumed he's a smart bastard and knows a quick buck when it's staring him in the face."

"So Senator McKurn is not one of your shareholders . . . ?

"Look, mate, the share register's an open book. McKurn's name isn't on it—you can check for yourself."

"Do you stand by your statement that Aborigines should be lined up and shot?"

"I was angry—I am angry," said Edleton. "This native title business has tied the mining industry hand and foot. It's totally unreasonable—did you know that over fourteen *thousand* applications to mine are held up because of it—just in Western Australia? Every Australian is poorer because hundreds of millions, maybe billions of dollars of minerals under the ground can't be exported—not to mention the thousands of jobs that haven't been created."

When the News24/7 announcer came back on the air, he tersely added that "Senator McKurn was unavailable for comment."

The implication was: "Senator McKurn doesn't *wish* to comment." But McKurn was at that moment discharging his duties as President of the Senate. It wasn't till an hour later, when the Senate had adjourned, that a reporter managed to get through to McKurn.

"What if some people think this Edleton guy is a sharp operator?" McKurn said, his anger muted but still evident. "So what? He's a voter too and last time I looked he's still entitled to talk to his representatives in Parliament. And if he thinks everyone else is like him, that's his problem, not mine. My finances are an open book. I own no shares, only investment trusts—which are all invested in blue chips."

"And do you agree with him that Aboriginals should be lined up and shot?"

"Don't be ridiculous," McKurn snapped. "But there's no question some of these native title restrictions go too far."

"The implications of that phone call—"

"You realize it's illegal to tap a phone conversation without a court order. I'm going to insist the police find out who this hacker is and that he suffers the full consequences of his illegal—and unconscionable—action."

Good luck, Alison McGuire chuckled: she was lounging comfortably in her office, the grin on her face larger than the Cheshire Cat's.

"What promises did you make to Lester Edleton, Senator?"

"Promises?" McKurn laughed. "All I said I'd do is look into it, and if I thought he had a case I'd submit my opinion to the appropriate regulators."

"So what did you tell the 'appropriate regulators'?"

"As it turned out, the area he wanted to explore is mainly on Aboriginal land, so it was up to the leaders of that Aboriginal community to say 'yea' or 'nay,' not the state or federal government. So there was nothing for me to do."

Alison McGuire switched the radio off as the announcer's voice replaced McKurn's.

He's rattled, she thought with a smile, but she couldn't help but admire the way McKurn had persuasively protested his innocence—and subtly brushed off every question. *Polished . . . but will it convince anyone? Where there's smoke. . . .*

With Melanie's help reducing her burden, Alison felt much lighter. With pressure mounting on McKurn from more and more fronts, maybe he'd make a fatal mistake. And the taps of McKurn's "unlisted" cellphone held out the promise of a breakthrough.

She heard McKurn's all but abusive anger as he ordered someone to find whoever was behind McKurnWatch.com.

And when we find him, what do we do?

I don't give a shit, so long as he's stopped.

There were a few conversations with Cracken and other of his supporters in the party room, discussing the numbers. "We've got to be prepared," McKurn had said. "Royn hasn't got a post-Kydd plan; we have, so we have one advantage. And who knows what Kydd's health is really like? What if he drops dead tomorrow? It pays to be prepared."

And an unknown voice asked, "How much longer are you going to be able to protect me, Frankie?"

*****

"Your apartment's clean, Alison." Federal Police Sergeant Jason Kowalski grinned suggestively as he packed up his debugging equipment.

"Thanks, Jason," she said, smiling wanly in return. "I appreciate it."

"No problem," he said. "I still don't understand why you think someone might be bugging you."

"Put it down to paranoia," Alison replied. "But—there are ways of bugging besides putting a listening device on a phone, aren't there?"

"Oh yes. If you have authorized access to the phone company's computers. That's how we do it."

"I see. . . ."

"Time for a nightcap?" Jason asked, looking puzzled.

"Sorry, Jason. Not tonight. I'm too tired."

"You know, Alison, it seems like you've been very antisocial this past few weeks."

"I've just been so busy," she said, giving him a peck on the cheek. "You're still as sweet as ever, Jason. But it's time for me to go to my bed—" Jason looked at her hopefully as she pushed him gently on his chest in the direction of the door "—and for you to go to yours."

It was true; she had been busy. Every Wednesday night, staffers from Parliament House gathered at restaurants and bars in Kingston, a short walk from her apartment. On weekends were barbecues and parties. For the past two weeks she'd turned down every invitation. She frequently saw Jason at such get-togethers and, occasionally, they'd meet for a quiet dinner or a drink. Jason always, not so subtly, attempted to revive the brief relationship they'd once had.

When she'd first come to Canberra, journalists, other staffers, even politicians—not all of them single—had invited her on dates. She'd found that simply fluttering her eyelids was an easy way to loosen a man's tongue. There was a journalist in the press gallery—witty, urbane—who, she later realized, reminded her of Derek Olsson. Their shared idealism had initially drawn them together; as he became jaded and cynical, they drifted apart until their interest in politics was all they had left in common.

At the next election a tall, blond, handsome man entered Parliament as its youngest member. Just a few years older than she, Bruce Spring had won his seat as a "new breed of Conservative." In his maiden speech he elegantly declared that "government *per se* is not the problem; too much government is. Nor, as the members of Her Majesty's Loyal Opposition would have it, is government the solution. Government has its proper role: to provide the basic legal, security, and infrastructure framework which enables society to flourish. And to always stand ready to help. Not to interfere, not to command or deny, but to assist people to lift themselves up by their own bootstraps—especially those among us who are disadvantaged in some way. Ultimately, happiness comes from self-actualization and the fulfillment of one's own dreams. That, of course, is something no one—and certainly not *government*—can give another person. What government can and definitely should do is limit itself to building, as it were, the scaffolding that makes possible and fosters individual and community achievement."

With Bruce Spring, she found a unity of purpose she'd never experienced before. She brought him into Royn's circle and they enthusiastically championed each other's policy ideas; Spring, within the party, Alison, to Royn and sometimes Kydd. Her memories of Derek faded into the background, as if that part of her life was over, done and dealt with.

But as Spring jockeyed for position within the party hierarchy, Alison began to get the uncomfortable feeling that Spring's commitment to any cause other than the cause of Bruce Spring was little more than skin-deep. That feeling flourished into an open break come the next election, three years later. With the polls favoring Labor, Kydd announced a slew of what he called "give-backs"—little more than using the government's budget surplus to buy himself the election. Tax cuts were promised; welfare was handed out to groups thought to favor Labor; hospitals, schools, roads, bridges, and police forces—mostly in marginal electorates tipping towards the opposition—suddenly received new largesse. Spring enthusiastically championed Kydd's proposals, and merely shrugged when Alison pointed out that most of them went against his declared political philosophy. "To achieve anything, Alison, we have to *win*."

"No matter what?" she replied. From his answer she concluded he was just another political opportunist.

That was all before Derek Olsson suddenly came back to complicate her life after a seven-year absence . . . that he still hadn't fully explained. She shook her head. *Never mind that now.*

25   Rolling the Dice

A HELICOPTER SWUNG AROUND K'mah, the cone-shaped hill at the center of Jazeerat el-Bihar. At a leisurely pace, it made a full circuit twice before landing on the peak. A single Australian soldier stepped out. As the helicopter lifted back into the air and turned towards the Australian base the soldier unfurled a white flag, sat down . . . and waited.

For some forty minutes the soldier sat unmoving, hearing and seeing nothing, until three men stepped silently out of the brush like ghosts, guns at the ready and trained on him. He eyed them carefully, part of his brain admiring their clear military discipline which contradicted their motley dress, a mixture of cast-off uniforms, jeans, T-shirts, military boots, sandshoes, and flip-flops. But their AK-47s, if not new, all looked clean and well oiled, and the men held them as if they knew exactly how to use them. Moving very slowly, the soldier raised his hands above his head and rose to his feet.

More men appeared, making not the slightest sound, surrounding the soldier. The first three moved forward until one stood in front of him, the barrel of his gun a mere meter from his chest. The second man opened the flap of his holster. It was empty. The third emptied his knapsack, kept the radio and cellphone and put everything else back.

The soldier studied the man in front of him in mutual silence. At least a head shorter, he was a small, wiry man, with a leathery dark-brown face and a huge white grin. His intelligent eyes exuded a sense of authority the soldier could almost touch.

"*Matalam,*" he said when the third man finished repacking the knapsack, slung his AK-47 over his shoulder, and indicated with a gesture that the soldier should sit.

"*Mata—?*" the soldier repeated. "Oh. . . ." He nodded. "Thank you."

They both sat, the small, wiry man sitting comfortably balanced on his heels.

The others relaxed too, but the soldier noticed their eyes were fixed on him.

Another guerrilla, looking as if he should still have been in school, asked, "Who you?"

"Lieutenant Jeremy McGuire."

"What want?"

"I came here to ask you if you could tell me anything about a woman by the name of Karla Preston."

The man Karla had named Mountain Man smiled. "Ah, Presdon-*gaat.*"

THE DAY BEFORE, JEREMY had told Captain McMurray: "I'd like to go in alone, sir. Unarmed."

"Why alone? Why not in force?"

"They know the ground and we don't. There'll be casualties, most of them *ours.* If we go in shooting they won't be any mood to give us any information later on. If I go in alone, they might talk to me."

"And they might just shoot you."

"That's a possibility," Jeremy said. "But I don't think they will."

"Why not? They shot a Sandeman soldier not so long ago."

"That was the first, and only casualty ever on this island. Sandeman troops went all the way across without a challenge. As you know from Lieutenant Sanders' report, they found the guerrillas' hideout in the mountain, but they never saw one of them. My guess is the guerrillas simply melted away and came back in behind them. If it had been any of those groups on St. Christopher's it would have been a different story. Everything indicates this group favors Gandhi-like tactics."

"Can you prove that, *lieutenant?*"

"No, sir." Jeremy spoke stiffly, reacting to McMurray's "lieutenant." "But that's my considered opinion from circumstantial evidence."

"You could be right, Jeremy. If you're wrong, what then?"

"You can send in a force to retrieve my body."

"Okay," said McMurray after a long pause. "Put it in writing."

When McMurray approved his plan, he added, "You've got twenty-four hours. If you haven't come out by then, we'll come in and get you."

*****

THE INTENSE OPPOSITION TO Senator Haughtry's proposed extension of the libel and slander laws was a major story on that morning's TV and radio news: the media, the phone and cable companies, even supermarket chains, all fearing they'd be caught in Haughtry's wider net, were forming a united front to shoot it down.

The media hadn't picked up that McKurn was the real motive force behind Haughtry's bill. Alison sent the geek a message: Haughtry is in McKurn's pocket. Can't prove it at the moment—but am positive.

But it was the page one headline on *Business Day,* the national financial daily, that grabbed Alison's attention: Lester Edleton's Chequered History: *Metal Mountain, His Latest Questionable Venture.*

She snatched it up and started reading the article before sitting down.

Yesterday's revelation that Lester Edleton had talked to Senator Frank McKurn about securing mining permits for his company, Metal Mountain Exploration NL [No Liability], is not the first time the Perth stock promoter has been a center of controversy.

He first came to the mining industry's attention ten years ago as "Manager, Investor Relations" for high-flying Kalgoorlie Nickel Ventures, whose stock went from a few cents to more than $100 a share in a matter of months, and then collapsed back under a dollar. Edleton's explanation at the time: "We drilled here and found nickel, and the price went up. We drilled half-a-mile away and found nickel and the price skyrocketed. We drilled in between and found nothing, and the price collapsed."

In the subsequent ASIC investigation, several of the company's officers, who'd dumped their shares just before the last drilling report was released, were convicted of insider trading. Edleton was under suspicion, but was never charged: although he sold most of his shares between $90 and $100, his selling took place before the third drill hole was completed.

After being involved in several speculative mining ventures which never got off the ground, he aggressively promoted Grubstake Mining NL: its stock price rose from 45 cents to a high of $5 based on several promising drilling reports. Accounting irregularities led to an ASIC investigation which revealed that, among other things, Edleton had used Grubstake Mining NL as his personal bank account. Trading in Grubstake Mining NL's shares was suspended. Under pressure from ASIC, Edleton resigned as managing director and the company was placed in voluntary administration. When the administrator demanded Edleton repay the money he'd "borrowed," Edleton, whose main asset was his now-unsalable shares in the company, filed for bankruptcy. ASIC then banned him from being a director of an Australian company for life.

He reappeared a year ago as CEO of Metal Mountain Exploration NL; Edleton's wife is the major shareholder and managing director. Metal Mountain's share price zoomed when it announced the discovery of a rich gold deposit 250 kilometres north of Coolgardie, WA. The indications were the main deposit lay outside the boundaries of his tenement.

"We applied for permits next door," Edleton told *Business Day,* "but when news leaked out about the expected size of the deposit, eight different Aboriginal groups claimed the area was sacred ground. Negotiations have proved fruitless."

Edleton believes the gold deposit is "enormous," and freely admits he talked "to anybody and everybody who might be able to help us get all the necessary permits."

His first call to Senator McKurn was made about a month ago, when Metal Mountain was close to running out of cash and its share price had sunk from a high of $3.20 to 17 cents. Three weeks ago, two Zurich-based companies filed notices that they each owned more thanf 5% of Metal Mountain. As the share price continued to fall, these investors' holdings have risen to 10% and 8.2% respectively. A third company, whose address is given "care of" a lawyer's office in Vaduz, Liechtenstein, has accumulated 6.5%. As Edleton's wife owns 53.5% of Metal Mountain, the remaining free float is now just 21.8% of the total shares.

The identity of the beneficial owners of these shares is veiled behind Switzerland's and Liechtenstein's tight secrecy laws. Of course, these new investors may be entirely legitimate. But it would not be the first time Australian investors have hidden behind a Swiss front to profit from inside information.

Holding the newspaper, Alison ran through the outer office towards Royn's closed door. "He said he wasn't to be disturbed," Mary called, but Alison didn't hear her—or ignored her cry—and rushed in breathlessly to stand in front of Royn's desk.

Royn was talking on the phone; he glared as the door swung open; his face softened when he saw who it was. Nevertheless, he waved Alison irritably towards a chair, but she remained standing.

After a moment he said, "Can I call you back in ten or fifteen minutes? Something's come up. . . . Thanks, bye." Turning to Alison he said, "I instructed Mary I wasn't to be interrupted," Royn said.

"Sorry, Minister. I didn't realize."

"Okay," he sighed, "what's so important?"

"Did you see this morning's *Business Day?*" she asked, waving the paper in his direction.

When Royn shook his head, she retold Edleton's chequered history, concluding, ". . . and you'll recall that while the Sandview HideAway Villas is managed by a Hong Kong-based boutique hotel operator, the property is owned by a Swiss company."

"You're thinking it could be the same owner as a shareholder in this gold company?" Alison nodded. "But I don't know how to find out."

"I'll call my broker," said Royn. "He'll know." A moment later Royn turned to Alison, "He's going to look it up now on the internet." Royn repeated an address; Alison shook her head. "What's the other address, Fred?" he asked. When Royn repeated it, Alison shrieked, "It's the same. It must be—" She stopped when she saw Royn raise a finger to his lips.

"Thanks, Fred," he said, putting down the phone. "So it's the same address, huh?" he said to Alison. "But that doesn't prove it's the same ultimate owner."

"No," said Alison, suddenly looking deflated. "But a couple of weeks ago one of the Aboriginal leaders negotiating with Metal Mountain complained to the police he'd been threatened with violence if he didn't come to an agreement."

"Really?"

"Yes! And then all the Aborigines went walkabout leaving Metal Mountain with no one to negotiate with." Alison laughed. "This has McKurn's fingerprints written all over it—and it's nice to know he's not invincible."

"It's highly suggestive. But what can we do with this information?"

"I don't know."

"It looks like McKurn's behind the scenes—but I can't take it to court."

"No, we need more information—but from Switzerland of all places?"

"Why don't you ask the geek? You never know. . . ."

"I will," said Alison. "Thank you, Minister."

"I'd better get back to my phone call," Royn said.

But Alison was already halfway out of his office.

*****

THE SHADOWS WERE LENGTHENING when Jeremy McGuire walked into the clearing at the bottom of K'mah where Sergeant Byrne and his platoon were waiting for him.

Mountain Man and his men had guided Jeremy down the hill, returned his radio and cellphone . . . and disappeared. Jeremy shook his head, wondering how they could do that—and how he and his men could learn to do the same.

"They claim they rescued Karla Preston from the Sandeman troops and put her on a boat, indicating the direction of Papua New Guinea," he told McMurray later. "They were very courteous, very polite and friendly, and told me and showed me nothing. They're *excellent* soldiers. Totally disciplined, extremely well-trained. On their home ground, definitely much better than we are. I think they know every rock and tree on that whole hill. You want their troops fighting with you, not against you. I saw about twenty in all, but I'd say there were more. And somewhere on that hill they have an excellent cook."

"Did you get any sense of what they were after?"

"All they said was that everyone on the island wanted to be left alone to mind their own business, and if everybody else did the same it would be a much better world."

"Hard to argue with. What did you say?"

"I said I could understand, but unfortunately I'm only a lieutenant, not a general."

*****

IT WAS SEVEN THIRTY in the evening. Alison McGuire walked past a pub in central Sydney overflowing with the noise of happy drinkers. She passed a café, also busy, on the corner where she turned into Bridge Street where the traffic was light and she felt she was the only pedestrian on the street—though for a moment she had the impression someone ducked into a doorway behind her.

Halfway along the block, she stopped in front of an office building. Except for the reflections of streetlights and the few neon signs still flashing, the building's sleek glass wall rising into the sky was completely dark. In the lobby, a doorman sat, bored, behind his small counter.

She pulled her overcoat tighter as a defence against the sudden gust of cold wind. The doorman looked at her quizzically, and she forced her feet to carry her up the wide marble steps into the lobby. She hesitated when she was asked to sign in, scribbled *Andie Merton—not very imaginative*—almost illegibly in the column headed NAME and took the lift to the seventh floor.

The offices of Andrews, Zolisky & Smythe, Solicitors, occupied the entire seventh floor. Behind glass doors at one end of the lift lobby was a lavish but dimly lit reception area. Alison pressed the buzzer next to the keypad and waited, shifting her weight from one foot to the other, her eyes glued to the second hand on the clock on the wall behind the counter. It seemed to stick for so long at each mark before jerking to the next that, she thought, its battery must be running down.

But only twenty-four seconds passed when a flabby, pasty-faced, balding middle-aged-looking man scurried into the lobby, eyed her sideways, leant over the counter—a movement which was followed by a *click* from the lock in front of her—and continued his scurry across the lobby to pull the door open.

Alison realized her initial impression of him was mistaken. He was not middle-aged but probably a bit younger than she was. No grey or white was visible amongst the thinning, nondescript brown of his hair, which was brushed carefully over the bald spot on top of his head. She decided he must be one of those men who go prematurely bald, a conclusion confirmed when she noticed the clumps of hair, like rows in a plantation, across the front of his receding hairline. He was also taller than she'd thought at first glance—or would be if he didn't walk with a permanent stoop: his shoulders hunched and his head looking in the direction of the floor rather than straight ahead.

"You must be Ivan," she said.

The man nodded. "And you are . . . ?" he asked.

"Alison McGuire."

"Oh yes," Ivan said sheepishly, turning his eyes away. "Of course."

She suppressed a grin at the realization that Ivan had been looking at the outline of her breasts under the coat and not her face, as if it were *them* he recognized.

"Follow me, please."

Through another door protected with a keypad lock, Ivan led her into a large space crowded with a maze of empty legal cubicles inhabited only by eyeless computer screens, past a conference room and wood-panelled partner's office to what appeared to be a blank wall at the end of the kitchen area. As Ivan ran a card through another keypad and then punched a code, Alison saw the door: it was embedded into the wall, a thin line that could easily be mistaken for decoration.

Ivan pushed the door open saying, "Welcome to the inner sanctum." Alison walked through and felt a shiver as the door swung noiselessly shut behind her.

She stood in a long narrow room. Cupboards and shelves untidily stacked with books, papers, printers and computer supplies lined the wall behind her. As if by way of contrast, the counter under the windows was scrupulously neat, except for one dirty coffee cup. The windows were heavily barred, frosted glass, letting in light but not sight. Three desktop computers sat on the counter, one with two enormous screens.

"Now," said Ivan. His voice squeaked as though it needed oiling; he gazed at her ankles, with occasional sideways glances at her body. "The Senator said to show you anything you wanted to see. Not that there's much to see."

Alison grasped that in this effectively windowless, locked room, Ivan was at home. He can deal with computers—but not people. And women? Has he ever had a girlfriend . . . one who cared for him, not his money?

"Well," Alison said, the hint of a purr in her voice, "it may not look like much, but appearances can be deceptive, can't they?" She took a slow step towards the counter, letting her handbag fall on the countertop.

Ivan's gaze move upwards from her ankles to her knees. "I suppose so. But, what do you mean?"

"Only that—" She stopped. "It's nice and warm in here. Is it okay if I hang my coat on this chair?" Her hand reached out to touch the fabric on the back of one of the chairs, almost a caress.

Ivan nodded without a word.

"From what little I understand—" as she spoke, she slowly removed her overcoat, one arm at a time, with exaggerated movements "—it all sounds so complicated."

Ivan seemed to stand a little straighter; Alison smiled, and draped the coat carefully over the back of the chair. "That's better." She unbuttoned her cardigan so it hung around her loosely.

Ivan's eyes were now fixated on the plunging neckline of Alison's blouse. "I suppose it is fairly complex," Ivan said, a touch of pride in his voice.

"Oh yes," Alison purred admiringly, *especially to "poor little me,"* she thought to herself, stifling her desire to laugh. "So, Ivan," she asked, "where do you keep the videos?"

Ivan looked at another door, set at the right-hand end of the narrow office.

"The Senator did say to show me everything, after all."

Ivan nodded, turning reluctantly to unlock the door which required a key on top of a card swipe and a code. Alison followed Ivan into a small windowless room, goose bumps covering her arms and legs at the gust of cold air coming from the open door.

"It's cold in here," Alison said, pulling the cardigan around her. Her eyes were held by the DVD boxes and hard drives, stacked three or four deep, on the shelves lining most of the four walls of the small room. *There must be hundreds and hundreds, and on one of them. . . .*

"Yes. These servers," said Ivan, pointing to what looked like two ordinary computers that were a bit larger than desktops, "have to be kept cool all the time." He paused while Alison's gaze slowly reacted to his voice. "One of them's a backup—a fail-safe. They're continuously recording, twenty-four hours a day." Between the two servers was a rack of hard drives, their lights flashing.

"You keep everything?"

"Oh no," Ivan said. "They automatically overwrite the oldest file until I instruct otherwise. We're linked to the hotel's reservation systems, so I know who has a booking, and I'm notified whenever someone checks into the honeymoon suite, and who they are."

"Do the hotel people know that?"

"Oh no," Ivan smiled, looking pleased with himself. "It all happens automatically, and they have absolutely no idea."

"I see," said Alison. "So how do you decide which ones to keep?"

"Well, I might recognize the name. But you'd be surprised how many times 'Mr. and Mrs. Smith' and 'Mr. and Mrs. Jones' check into that suite." His cheeks went pink, his voice level dropping so Alison had to strain to hear his words. "So quite often I have to look to decide whether to keep it or not."

"And some names are flagged for an upgrade to the honeymoon suite, is that right?"

"Ah . . . quite so," Ivan said as he studied the interlinked strands of different-colored fabric in carpet.

"What happens next?" Alison asked.

Ivan pointed to a regular desktop computer next to the servers. "The videos files are compressed and transferred to DVDs and external hard drives through this computer. The originals, of course, are being overwritten all the time by the next recording."

"What happens to the copies?" Alison asked.

"One set of DVDs is kept here, along with an external hard drive." Ivan waved at the crowded shelves. "The Senator takes the other DVD, and the second hard drive. When I've made the copies, I play one on the two-screen computer outside."

"That could take hours—days."

"It could, but I don't really watch them. I just run them through at high speed until I see what looks like one of—"

"—the juiciest bits."

Ivan blushed again and nodded. "Right," he mumbled. "And when I've made about a dozen prints, I stop, and put everything back in here."

"So no one really watches the whole video?"

"Oh no. Even though the cameras are set so they don't transmit anything when the room is dark—there'd be no picture," he explained, "most of what's recorded is just an empty room."

"So if the couple turns off the lights when they go to bed . . . ?"

Ivan shrugged. "There may not be anything worth seeing. One se—" Embarrassed, Ivan stopped and started again. "One guy did that, but there were plenty of torrid scenes on the sofa in the other room his wife would find highly persuasive. The only time I might go through the whole recording is when I have to make an edited version. But the prints nearly always do the trick—at least, that's what I assume."

Alison gritted her teeth to stop herself from nodding in agreement. "But when you're editing, or making prints," she asked, "someone else could see what you're working on it."

"Oh no." Ivan shook his head vigorously. "I only do it at night or weekends, when no one else is here."

"So the only copies are the ones in this room and the ones the Senator has."

"Right," Ivan nodded.

"There's just one thing, Ivan," she said, edging slightly nearer to him. "You're here all alone, so you could make as many copies of these—" her arm swept the room "—as you care to."

"Oh no," Ivan protested. "I could never do that. I—I wouldn't, I . . . *couldn't* betray the Senator."

For the first time, Ivan lifted his face to look directly at Alison, except his eyes kept flicking every which way, rolling around like those of a snared rabbit. He shook his head in sharp, short, violent movements. "Never."

Ivan's the weak link in McKurn's security, she thought, wondering what kind of leverage would be needed to change his mind. She could feel the waves of helpless fear emanating from his shaking body, and it came to her that he was completely defenceless, that she could immobilize him in one swift movement—and remove the copies of her with Olsson from the shelf. *If I can find them,* she added mentally as she noticed the boxes were identified only by number.

What good would it do me? McKurn still has a backup.

Alison reached out and placed her hand gently on his arm, just above the elbow; he flinched, as though her fingers carried an electric shock. "I understand, Ivan," she said softly, gripping his arm a little harder in emphasis.

Then she stepped back and asked, "How does the signal come from the cameras to here? Over the internet?"

"Oh no," he said, relieved to be talking about bits and bytes again, "over a dedicated high-speed line. These servers are not connected to the internet."

"Who set up the cameras in the honeymoon suite? You?"

Ivan nodded.

"And all the wiring?"

Ivan nodded again.

"Didn't the hotel staff suspect something?"

"No. It was done while renovations were in progress. Nobody noticed a few extra workmen."

"But, to get here," Alison said, gesturing towards the servers, "the signal travels from the cameras through a phone company's wires, right?"

Ivan smiled serenely as if he knew what she would say next.

"So someone could tap into that line anywhere along its route?"

"Of course. Quite easily done." Then Ivan grinned broadly, reminding Alison of a little boy who just put something over on you. "But the signal's encrypted—you know, scrambled—so it wouldn't do them any good."

"It seems you've thought of everything," Alison said admiringly.

Ivan beamed at her compliment. "I believe I have."

"I suppose, then, I've seen everything there is to see in here."

"That's right."

Stepping into the other room she asked, "What goes on in here, then?"

"Oh—other stuff," Ivan said noncommittally as he closed the door behind him. He pointed at the two large screens. "That's where I do the editing."

Alison nodded. "But that computer's on the internet, isn't it?"

"Yes, but I always take it offline first."

Except when you forget, Alison thought as she spied a faint flush on Ivan's pale cheeks. "So why have all this here, tucked away in the back of a solicitor's office?"

Ivan shrugged. "That's where it is. That's all I know."

Or all you'll tell me. The words "legal privilege" flashed into her mind. An extra layer of protection against prying eyes—and camouflage.

As Alison retrieved her jacket and her handbag, she saw a label with a printed number affixed to a phone. She leant closer to read it, repeated it to herself silently several times while tracing the numbers on her palm as an aid to memory.

"That's it for now then, I guess," she said, taking one last look at the room.

Ivan shepherded her back to the lift lobby. Waiting for the lift, she saw him take out his cellphone as he disappeared into the interior offices of ANDREWS, ZOLISKY & SMYTHE.

SHE WAS BUTTONING HER coat against the cold when her cellphone rang.

"What's the verdict?" McKurn asked.

"Ah, Senator," she said. *He didn't waste any time.* "Well . . . your security looks pretty good—but not quite good enough, I'm afraid."

"Naturally, I'd welcome any suggestions for improvements—but I've done as much as I'm able and willing to do to reassure you. So it's time for your final answer. Yes, or no."

"You mean—right now?"

"That's exactly what I mean."

She felt her whole body protesting—and heard the cold, unfeeling words of the ageless voice inside her mind, *What choice do you have, Alison?*

"I—I'll call you back in an hour." She closed her phone without giving McKurn the opportunity to respond.

She stopped in the first pub she came to and ordered a double brandy at the bar. *For medicinal purposes,* she thought. She swirled the brandy in the snifter and brought it to her lips. She spluttered slightly at her too-large a gulp, but she could feel the warmth sliding down her throat and beginning to spread through her body. *Slow down, Alison,* she thought to herself.

As she made herself sip the rest of the brandy at a leisurely pace she forced herself to focus on the whirlwind of thoughts, options and possibilities competing for her attention. But in the foreground of her mind was an image she couldn't push away, no matter how hard she tried: the flabby folds of flesh on McKurn's grotesque, naked body.

She drained the last drop of brandy and stared at the empty glass. "Same again, Miss?" the bartender asked.

Alison began to hand the glass across the bar but said, "No," in a tone more suitable for McKurn than the bartender. She didn't notice his strange look as she stood and walked outside in the refreshingly freezing air.

I've got to think, she told herself. She began walking aimlessly along the mostly deserted streets of central Sydney's office district, telling, *willing* herself to *Think, Alison. Think, think, think.*

Time, I need more time. It's as though nothing has really changed—except time is running out.

The geek . . . McKurnWatch . . . the Candyman Inquiry . . . Royn's private eye . . . she thought of everything she'd put in motion, of all the possibilities they held out . . . provided there was enough time for those possibilities to become real.

If she could just put McKurn off somehow . . . but how long did she need? A week? Two? A month? *There's no way of knowing.* She had to agree—and then delay, delay, delay.

The shock of her cellphone interrupted her thoughts. *It can't be an hour.* She looked at her watch: over an hour had passed.

There's never enough time.

"Time's up, Alison."

"It is? I suppose it is," she said.

"What's your answer?"

"Tell me, Senator, what have you got on Ivan?"

McKurn chuckled. "I said no more questions, Alison. But maybe I'll give you an answer tomorrow night."

"Tomorrow night? You must be joking, Senator."

"No, Alison, I'm not. Either we have a deal or we don't. And if we do, you're in Sydney, I'm in Sydney, so why wait to consummate it?"

A thousand and one reasons, she thought. "If my answer is 'Yes,'" she said.

"And what is your answer?"

What choice do I have? Delay . . . delay. "I can make tomorrow night—but I doubt you'd enjoy yourself, Senator."

"Oh—why?"

"It's that time of the month."

"Hmm," McKurn grunted doubtfully. "Next Saturday, then."

I can't do this, she thought, again imagining McKurn's grotesque, naked body.

"Are you still there?"

"I guess you leave me no choice."

"Is that a 'Yes'?"

I can't say "yes," and I can't say "no."

"Alison?"

"Yes," she said weakly, fumbling as she put her cellphone back into her handbag.

Before she could take a step, Alison's vision blurred, everything turned black, the world began to spin. A funeral march beat upon her ears, to the sound of cackling laughter. She felt herself beginning to fall and reached out to a wall. Leaning against it, she squeezed her eyes shut; slowly, the dizziness started to fade. When she felt able to let her eyes flutter open, she saw the music and laughter was coming from a bar two doors away.

As soon as she felt able to move, she flagged down the first passing taxi and collapsed into the back seat.

THE DARK WINDOWS AND the light over the front door were signals her parents had long ago gone to sleep. *Just as well,* Alison thought when she saw her reddened eyes, pale cheeks, the tortured reflection of a ghost in the bathroom mirror. She felt tired—wrung out but unable to sleep. Tiptoeing back to the living room, she poured herself a large helping of her father's Scotch and sat sipping and brooding on the sofa until she felt herself nodding off.

Her feet dragged behind her like ingots of lead as she turned towards her bedroom. Halfway she stumbled and stood, gazing blankly into the dullness of the corridor ahead, unable to remember which way to go. As she was standing in front of a door, she opened it. *But I'm sure I left the light on,* she thought groggily. About to step into a musty lightless room, she knew she'd opened the long-closed door of her old bedroom by mistake.

Without her conscious volition, with the feeling but not the words of the thought *it's now or never,* the muscles in her arm impelled her hand to reach out and flick on the light.

Her old bedroom had become a storeroom, filled with memories . . . her memories. . . . Books, mostly dog-eared, having first passed through her many cousins' hands; dolls and cuddly toys missing arms or legs, or covered in patches; half a Meccano set; a box of Lego made from the remains of an unknown number of hand-me-downs; a dollhouse her father had painstakingly and lovingly rebuilt from the remains of three others.

A raggedy one-armed teddy bear her mother had sewn together from two others sat atop the dollhouse. "Ted!" she exclaimed with delight as she stepped inside to pick him up and clasp him to her chest. "So this is where you've been all this time."

Hugging Ted, she slowly turned full circle, remembering her life as a galaxy of flashing sparks stretching into the far distance. . . .

But no longer. . . .

Now, bent under the weight of her present, she stood on the edge of the universe beyond where there was—not the black darkness that comes from an absence of light but a blank nothingness.

Assailed by the smell of mothballs and dust, she let her eyes stray slowly from her old desk to the bed. *I guess hardly anyone comes in here.* And with a sharp, indrawn breath she remembered: *I haven't been in here since . . . since. . . .*

Alison screamed.

Squeezing Ted hard she ran out of the room slamming the door behind her.

She leant trembling against the wall, her breath coming in deep sobs.

"Alison." Maggie McGuire stepped into the corridor, tying her dressing gown around her with Joe, rubbing his eyes, his face twisted with fear and concern, close behind her.

"Alison," Maggie cried. "You didn't go in there, did you . . . ?"

Alison collapsed into her mother's arms. "Oh, Mama, Mama," she cried.

26 The Ice Queen

"IT'S OUR LUCKY DAY."

Three youths stood in the doorway to her bedroom, their eyes glinting and roving over her body with delight. Their look was not the shy longing and poorly disguised desire of the boys at school but shameless, naked lust.

The sound of the door being smashed open still rang in her ears, drowning out the loud music she'd been playing . . . the music, she now realized, which masked every other sound.

Alison leapt up from her desk where she'd been buried in her books. Glaring at them she snapped, "Get out of here," and sprung at them, her fists aiming at the nearest face.

They laughed.

They caught her arms as she moved to punch them, threw her on her bed and ripped off her clothes. She struggled, she kicked, she scratched—wishing for the first time her nails were long and sharp so they'd leave bloody tracks on their faces and arms while at the same time trying to use her hands to hold her bra in place. She twisted her legs into a knot to protect herself and they roughly pulled them apart. When a hand came close to her face she bit deeply, smiling for a brief moment at the bitter taste of blood. Then sharp daggers of pain covered her scalp as a hand yanked her hair hard, snapping her head down. Her face was slapped once, twice, three times, leaving deep red and blue welts on her pale cheeks. She screamed, she yelled, she swore, she prayed for God's help. They turned the music up even louder; nobody heard her screams.

They held her down on her bed, her arms and legs locked in bruising grips, while they took turns raping her. She screamed even louder as she felt herself being penetrated, torn, shredded; again and again. Unstoppable tears streamed down her face, her body wracked until she was overcome by a terrifying numbness as though her body had disappeared. She cursed them until her throat was so hoarse her words became the meaningless, unintelligible sounds of a tortured animal. Only God could help her now; she pleaded to Him desperately to send them all to hell, unable to understand why He was taking so long to rescue her. . . .

A DAZED, LIMP BAG of skin, the act of gasping for air, like a corpse coming back from the dead, brought back the pain in waves of razor-like slashes. *I'm being punished for the crime of . . . what?* The pain went so deep she could feel it pounding in her very soul. Her favorite CD—she *hated* it now—still played at full volume. But she had no energy to move. . . .

But no hands gripped her arms; no weight held her down. *They're gone—and the pain hasn't stopped!* She touched herself and pulled her hand away, her fingertips wet. *Blood.*

I've been raped. *I've been raped.* I'm dirty, filthy, *fallen* . . . I want to die. . . . Like a sound from a distant horizon she heard Father Ryan's voice, a fragment of a Sunday sermon . . . ". . . and God puts us here on earth to suffer so that through our suffering we will come to know His infinite love and the love of his Holy Son Jesus Christ and the Holy Ghost. . . ."

I have suffered, she thought. I am suffering . . . with my whole being . . . can this be what I deserve?—part of God's Plan for *me?* With a last shudder she lapsed into merciful darkness, unable to grasp how this could be God's way of showing His Infinite Love. . . .

MUSIC WAS BLARING THROUGH the shattered glass of a front window when Joe and Maggie returned from the movies: Alison's music. While Joe fumbled for the front door key in seeming slow motion Maggie, shouting "Alison! Alison!" as if her voice even at its highest pitch could penetrate beyond the wall of throbbing sound, struggled to lever herself between the shards of glass in the open window. When Joe finally got the door open she shot under his arm as if she'd been blasted from a cannon.

She screamed: a long, hard piercing scream of woe that could be heard across the street as she found Alison naked on her bed, covered with dark bruises and stains of half-dried blood, curled up in a fetal ball, seemingly dead to the world.

"My baby, my baby!" she sobbed, trembling with the fear they'd come home far too late, the blood pounding through her veins with guilt at their laughter in the movie theater and the time they'd lingered on afterwards over a slow coffee. As she gathered Alison tightly in her arms, the flood of relief enveloped her as she felt the warmth of Alison's body and saw the faint flutter of breath on her lips; relief which turned into a flood of tears at the wide, grisly wounds smeared across her once-pristine cheeks. At the same time, Maggie tried to cover her daughter with the bedspread as if she had four hands not just two.

Joe stood in the doorway, stunned into motionlessness. "My God! What the f— . . . what happened?" As if waking from a nightmare, he ran to help Maggie cover their daughter. His hand dragged the bedspread and brushed against Alison's shoulder; her eyes fluttered briefly open; she cringed away from her father's touch—her face a sculpture of terror.

Joe remained standing, mutely frozen in place but shrinking—as if his bones had turned to rubber. He started to shake, tears rolling one after another down his face.

Suddenly feeling like the only tower of strength, in a drill sergeant's voice Maggie ordered, "Joe, make yourself useful. Turn that music off. Call Dr. McTavish. Get some blankets. And hot water—and towels. Now. Move!"

As Joe made the supreme effort to drag himself out the door he looked back to see Alison's body shivering as if gripped by a nightmare, a picture that would never fade from his memory for as long as he would live.

Warmed by blankets and Maggie's embrace, Alison's breathing was coming more strongly by the time Dr. McTavish arrived, though in sudden pants, as if she were holding her muscles in chains against the pain of any movement until she had no choice but to hungrily gasp for air. Maggie talked to her softly, not knowing what to say and not sure of what she'd said, her mind in a whirl, cursing her impulse to go to a movie tonight of all nights, praying to God that Alison's bruises would heal without leaving any scars as she wiped them as gently as she could with a warm towel while Alison whimpered quietly at the slightest touch.

Alison had yet to speak a word, but Maggie didn't need to ask: the broken window, the smashed door of Alison's room, her torn and mangled clothes strewn across the floor and the tracks of Alison's blood spoke with heartbreaking silence. "I don't understand," she heard Joe say as Dr. McTavish stepped into the room. "This sort of thing just doesn't happen around here. I've always thought it was such a safe street." Maggie wondered if she'd ever feel safe in this house again.

From time to time, Alison's eyes would open and look at her mother's face through red waves of mist. Alison's wide eyes held hers as they had when she was a baby but they were now dull, more black than blue, her sparkling life nowhere to be found; on her face was the expression of a hurt kitten and an unanswerable question, "Why me?"

As McTavish's large body and craggy face loomed over her, Alison gave out a dry sob and burrowed her head deeply into Maggie's breast. Maggie looked at him with a mute plea for help. McTavish took everything in with a glance, nodded his head and stepped backwards out of her room, grabbing Joe by the shoulder as he moved, pushing him towards the living room.

"This will pass—eventually," McTavish said, with as much conviction as he could muster.

"God, I hope so."

"Joe, get yourself a whisky or something. And one for me too. And sit down while I make a couple of calls."

The clock on the mantelpiece said 11:30. "I hope she's still awake," he muttered to himself as he dialled a number. A sleepy voice answered. "Dori, Mac here. There's been a rape—can you come over right away? Please. She needs you."

Then he called the police. "This is Dr. Graham McTavish. There's been a rape and a break-in—certainly looks like that, anyway. Could you send someone over—but for Christ's sake, whatever you do don't send any men. . . . Please, get a policewoman out of bed if you have to. . . . No, this can't wait till morning—and if you send a guy it will just make everything worse. Much worse. And one other thing: if you can, for God's sake send a woman who's really simpatico, if you know what I mean. . . . Yes, it's that bad."

A moment later Maggie came into the room. "She's sleeping, thank God. If you can call it sleep," she said, and as she collapsed next to Joe all her strength and apparent coolness deserted her.

"Quiet, Maggie," McTavish said gently as she started to wail. "You'll only wake her." He handed her his Scotch. "Here, drink this."

"Wha . . . wha . . . what are we going to do?"

"It's going to be tough. You know that. For a while—maybe quite a while. But let's think about it tomorrow. You know Dori—I mean, Dr. Doreen Hart? She's on the way. Alison has to be examined. She's been hurt. She bled, and she may have been damaged. The police are coming. Policewomen I hope. There'll have to be samples taken, tests made—you know, things like that."

"My God," Maggie screamed, inconsolable. "She's only fifteen. Oh, Heavenly Father," she moaned, casting her eyes to the ceiling as if she could see beyond, "why did this have to happen? Why did this have to happen to *her?*"

Almost hidden under the pile of blankets, Alison half-listened to Doreen Hart's comforting voice as it droned steadily, hypnotically, the fingers glued to her mother's hand slowly loosening their grip—only to tighten violently at words like "hospital," "test," and "examination." *No,* she screamed in silence. *No one will touch me again. Ever.*

Dr. Hart's gentle but unrelenting pressure ultimately swayed Alison to sigh in resignation, and nod her head. Ice cold air bit into her skin and soft fingers delicately touched her body; Alison, her teeth clenched, willed her body into acceptance—but her body seemed to have a mind of its own and every touch came with a different, stabbing memory.

Covered again, tucked in by her mother's hands, she drifted into a restless sleep only to awaken at a strange new voice. Through heavy eyelids she saw a young woman's pale face, framed by tousled hair, her expression a study in concern, while her fingers fidgeted with nervousness—or irritation. "Miss McGuire," the woman said hesitantly, "I'm constable Annabelle Myers."

As a novice constable and the lowest-ranking person at the local police station, it was Annabelle who had received the midnight call. Described by one of her instructors as "too emotional for the job," she was unable to completely disguise the annoyance she'd felt at being brusquely ordered from her comfortable bed.

"I—I'm—I wish I didn't have to disturb you right now, but I would like to ask you a few questions, if I may."

Alison burrowed deeper under the blankets, saying nothing.

Alison was the first rape victim Annabelle had ever met; the first she'd had to question; and as her male partner, at Dr. McTavish's insistence, scoured the house for evidence, it was the first time she'd had to handle anything entirely on her own. As she took in Alison's reaction, she desperately tried to remember how she was supposed to behave in situations like these. But her coolness evaporated as her words erupted like a stream of lava boiling from a volcano's peak, "I want to catch the animals who did this to you and put them where they belong—behind bars." She dug her fingers into the edge of the mattress to stop her unconscious reaching out to Alison. And with an effort to control her voice added, "But I can only do that with your help."

Maggie and Dr. Hart both gasped in surprise, but Alison's eyes seemed to reflect the constable's fire for a long moment as if they were the only two people in the room until, slowly and deliberately, she nodded her agreement. But as Annabelle asked her questions, Alison's mouth would open but no answers would come—until Annabelle turned her interview into a grisly game of twenty questions. "How many? One?" Shake. "Two?" Shake. Her eyes widened, *Three?* Nod. "Oh, my God."

As the wordless answers continued, the gaps between her questions lengthened as she seemed to match Alison's terror with an inner terror of her own. After a longer pause, she said, "I—I—think I can make a preliminary report. But maybe I could talk to you again tomorrow?"

Alison mouthed a silent "Yes," and her free hand inched across the bedspread to clutch Annabelle's fingers in a surprisingly powerful grip.

Alison awoke to the blinding glare of hot, harsh, unforgiving lights, to something piercing the skin somewhere between her legs. Her piercing wail shattered the unfamiliar voices chattering indifferently in the background into a hushed silence. She looked down to see herself covered in something blue; her eyes stopped on Doreen Hart who was leaning over her lower body; Alison glared at her accusingly.

"No, Alison," Dr. Hart said, looking up with a sad smile, "it's just a local anesthetic to take away any pain."

A memory of a violent shudder drifted into Alison's mind, her answer to the doctor's distant voice when she had made the offer. Alison could feel a warm numbness spreading over her loins and a jumble of half-formed images . . . of being carried . . . of a siren that wailed without end . . . of phrases like "permanent damage" and the soft sound of her mother's cry . . . tumbled through her mind.

"Can you feel anything?"

Dr. Hart's soft voice jolted her back into the glaring light. She tried to make sense of what she was being asked, aware of *something*—as though her nerves were transmitting messages to her brain, messages that were empty of meaning or sensation. She continued to be aware that things were being done to her, but the more meaningful feeling was the warmth of her mother's hand; with a brief look into her mother's concerned eyes she let herself drift, only recalling, later, a fragment of sound she could not believe:

". . . some bruising, some tearing that need a few stitches . . . nothing really serious. . . ."

When Maggie brought her home the following afternoon, she reached the door of her bedroom and stopped. She sat in the living room, wrapped in a blanket, while Maggie made up the empty room, half the size, and Joe moved as many of her possessions there as he could fit in. Later, at Alison's insistence, he added bars to the windows and a bolt to the door. She insisted the sheets from her bed be burned. She lit the bonfire herself, throwing the hateful CD on the roaring flames, watching it twist and curl in the flaming heat.

She would wake at ten o'clock, eleven o'clock, even noon, after ten or twelve hours of sleep—without any rest—afraid, every night, to let her eyes close and take her to where the nightmare was waiting for her . . . not that the morning sun would drive it completely away.

She wouldn't go outside the house for weeks, not even to go to church. Especially not to church, though she said nothing to her parents about that. Father Ryan called, often, to bring comfort to Alison if he could . . . but he only managed to comfort her mother: he and Maggie would often pray together. Point blank, Alison refused to see him or, except for Annabelle and Doreen Hart, anyone else.

Her friends would knock, phone, send flowers, chocolates, or cards Alison wouldn't read. Once, as Maggie accepted delivery of yet another bouquet, she heard Alison mutter, "You'd think there'd been a funeral."

She glanced at Alison's listless body and lifeless eyes, her hand leaping to her mouth at the horrifying realization that something *had* died; in her prayers she pleaded with God to bring her daughter back to life.

At night, they wordlessly watched TV until Maggie led her husband off to bed. She'd return a few minutes later to sit with Alison a while, after throwing out the empty bottle of Scotch.

In time, Alison was persuaded to talk to one of her friends. First Lorraine Adams, her oldest friend from just two blocks away, then others, one by one. The day came when Alison announced she was going out with them—and Maggie breathed a great sigh of relief.

Alison started running, running hard and long so that by the time she got home she was dripping with sweat and so limp from exhaustion she felt a great sense of relief. One day she declared she was ready to go back to school.

She found it really hard to concentrate in class. But the break times were the worst. Everybody knew what had happened to her. Nobody knew how to act towards her. Everyone was nervous and looked at her strangely. And in some circles was the belief that if a girl was raped, she must have encouraged it somehow.

On the third or fourth day back at school, three boys sniggered as she walked past. One of them made a lewd comment.

Her face froze. She turned back and walked towards them, looking so fierce that the boys physically shrank back from her. Her eyes had narrowed and were cold and piercing. She walked straight up to the boy who'd spoken and slapped his face with all the energy and resentment stored up within her. She dimly noticed an ugly red handprint on the boy's face. "In your dreams, arsehole," she spat. "And all *you* could look forward to is a sore hand."

Fanning out like a ripple cascading across the surface of a pond, a stunned silence descended over the playground, one student whispering to another until all the chatter stopped and heads turned to Alison with disbelief. Sure, everybody had heard things like that on TV or at movies you were supposed to be eighteen to see. But who'd have believed someone like *Alison* would know them—let alone use them. And in school, too.

Nobody bothered her again.

One Saturday morning, in the park near the local shopping center, curiosity pulled her towards a crowd of people watching something on a makeshift stage. It was a martial arts demonstration. Something called Aikido. She watched with vague interest as an old man who seemed to hobble rather than walk demonstrated various holds and throws with other people dressed in the same strange garb as his.

The stage cleared and a skinny girl about Alison's age stepped into the center. The old man picked up a loudspeaker.

"Ladies and gentlemen," he said. "This is Larissa. She's fifteen years old and she weighs just forty-five kilos. As you can see," he smiled, "there's not much of her." A few giggles came from audience. "She'd like to invite anyone to come up and hit her. To try and hit her. You, sir—" he pointed at a big beefy, man "—how about you?"

"Oh, come on," the man in the audience said. "That wouldn't be fair."

"You're quite right, sir. But I promise she'll be gentle with you." Laughter rippled through the crowd. Sheepishly, the man took a step forward. "Come on, you can do it," someone in the crowd shouted.

"Give it a go, mate."

"Afraid or something?"

"Who, me?" the man said. "Course not."

"Great. Just take your shoes off before you get on the mat. Now, run at her as hard as you can, hit her, do whatever you like."

"You're joking."

"No, I'm serious."

The girl bowed towards him.

"You do the same, please. It's part of the Aikido ritual."

The man returned the bow and walked slowly up to the tiny girl and made an ineffectual jab towards her, more pat than a hit. All of a sudden, he was face down on the mat, the girl sitting on top of him, his arm twisted in an odd-looking way. Alison had no idea how he'd gotten into that position—or how the girl had done it.

Alison found herself walking up to the stage without volition, as if some unknown force had taken command of her body. "Me. I want to be next," she told the old man.

He gave her a puzzled look, thinking she'd said, "Me. *I* will be next."

"Yes, ma'am," he answered.

She took off her shoes at the edge of the mat on the stage and she and the girl bowed to each other. They looked at each other for a long moment. "I can't do this," she said. "I mean, I can't do this to *you*. Why would I hit you or whatever? Is it okay if I pretend you're someone else?"

The girl looked at her for a minute and then nodded her head. But Alison noticed she tensed her body slightly and seemed to become a little more alert.

Alison closed her eyes, imagining her tormentors . . . and the memory of her pain suddenly sharpened in her loins. She leapt at the girl with a blood-curdling scream that sent shivers down the bystanders' spines.

The next thing Alison knew she was flying through the air. She thought the girl had touched her, but she wasn't sure. She landed on her back and the *thump* forced all the air from her lungs.

"Ouch," she said, "that hurt."

"Sorry," said the girl, "but you were serious. Wild."

Alison turned her head. The girl was behind her now, looking towards her. But other than turning about, she hadn't seemed to have moved at all.

"*You* did that to me?" Alison looked around, but the old man and the other people in the funny robes were exactly where they'd been before.

The girl nodded.

"Wow." Alison picked herself up and started to walk towards the old man. She stopped, turned and bowed to the girl. "What's your name again?" she asked.

"Larissa. But you can call me Ris."

"Thank you . . . Ris. I'm Alison. Thank you."

To the old man she said, "Can you teach me something—now?"

She felt his searching gaze—but the wild animal he'd seen the moment before she'd leapt had gone back to wherever it had come from. Standing before him now was just a young girl who was obviously troubled about . . . something.

"My name is Edward Tozen. But when you're on the mat, Alison, you address me as *Sensei*. That's Japanese for teacher."

"Yes . . . *Sensei*."

"I tell you what. We'll demonstrate something for you—" as he said "you" he swept his arm around the audience to include them all, though he kept his eyes fixed on Alison's "—and then maybe Ris or one of the others will teach it to you. So long as you agree not to scream at them."

Alison smiled and her face seemed to light up. She bowed to Tozen. "Thank you . . . *Sensei*."

Tozen waved her to the side of the stage and waddled over and said a few words to the group of what must have been his students. Two of them walked onto the mat as Larissa retired. One of them, a girl, stood in the center of the mat. The second, a man, stood at the edge.

"Fiona, here in the center of the mat," said Tozen through the loudspeaker, "is in a bar with a few friends. Jack has had a few beers too many, making him God's gift to womankind. He notices Fiona and takes a fancy to her." Jack walked across the mat to stand in front of Fiona. "We're not interested in listening to Jack trying to convince Fiona he's God's answer to all her prayers. We'll just fast-forward to the point when Jack tries to give her a kiss."

Alison waited for Fiona to throw Jack across the stage—exactly what he deserved. But as Jack moved closer Fiona acted as if she wanted him to kiss her. She reached up and put her left hand behind his head, inviting him in. The other hand grasped his chin as if to pull him down. But then she pushed his chin *up* quickly with her right hand. Jack's head flipped back; she gave him a nudge, and Jack lost his balance, falling to the floor flat on his back.

"Whew," said Alison. "I want to learn how to do that."

EDWARD TOZEN WASN'T SURPRISED at the passion and intensity Alison brought to Aikido. If he'd given classes every day instead of three times a week, she'd have been at every one. When somebody told him her story he finally understood—and knew where the wild animal had come from. From then on he was careful to say and do nothing she could misinterpret.

Aikido became Alison's release, and she revelled in the growing control she had over her body. But there was one difference: Aikido was not a game to win, like tennis; or a sport, like running; or a pastime, like playing volleyball on the beach with her friends. For Alison Aikido was life—and *survival.* Aikido became her protection, her armor, and she quickly mastered enough to sense she need never feel frightened and helpless ever again. As she found herself walking boldly towards someone who reminded her of her rapists instead of crossing to the other side of the road, she slowly relaxed and let people get just that little bit closer.

Even so, she still lived with the knowledge that the pain was still with her, somewhere inside. Dr. Hart had gently suggested—once—that it might help if she saw a therapist. But she wasn't crazy—was she?

Now and then, the pain would come back, usually when some boy tried to touch her. Even when she wanted the boy to touch her. But the wild animal, thankfully, seemed to have gone at last.

One day a new student joined the Aikido class. She'd seen him around the school. He was a year ahead of her. His name was Derek Olsson.

She'd heard a lot about him. He was one of the guys all the girls talked about: a straight-A student—and captain of the football team. He seemed to swagger a little when he walked. "Sure fancies himself," Alison remarked one day to her friends.

They stared back at her blankly. "What do you mean?" one asked.

"He's so handsome," sighed another.

Alison just shook her head.

Tozen's students worked mostly in pairs. One would practice a movement with a partner, and then they'd reverse roles. So Alison often practiced with the male students. She found it didn't bother her . . . while they were on the mat.

So now and then she was paired up with Olsson. She felt he was the kind of guy who'd never had a girl turn him down. So whenever he tried to be friendly, she cut him dead.

But she had to admit he was good. He picked up Aikido almost as fast as she had. But he wasn't as good as he thought he was.

Some three months after he joined the class, they were working together on a movement ending with the "attacker" being held flat on the floor with the body weight of the "victim." Olsson was a bit clumsy and landed on top of her a bit too hard. Suddenly, she felt suffocated and trapped. Without conscious thought, she lashed out with her foot, kicking him hard in the crotch. "God," he screamed—and let go. She whirled from under him and a moment later their positions were reversed: she pushed his face into the floor with an arm lock that, she knew, hurt.

"Enough," he cried, slapping the mat with his free hand. She obeyed the signal to release, and let him go.

"What was that?" he asked as he rolled on his back, rubbing his arm. "Christ, you're like a wildcat who needs to be tamed."

It was his grin that prompted her to spit, "If that were true, it won't be done by a mere boy."

Tozen was about to scold Alison. But then he asked himself, was it Olsson who should really be chewed out? So he began talking about control, how Aikido meant not just controlling your opponent by using his movement to turn him the way you wanted him to go. It also meant control and restraint of your own movements.

He was talking to the class, but Alison knew he was talking just to her. Her ears burning, she bit back on the temptation to say "Sorry" to Olsson. No . . . she didn't regret what she'd done. Not one bit.

THE STORY OF OLSSON'S fate at Alison's hand spread through the high school with the speed of a bushfire at the end of a dry, scorching summer. A second story was being was whispered breathlessly, in hidden moments, from ear to eager ear: "Have you heard that someone said to Olsson: 'Alison McGuire. Now there's a chick I bet you'll never get into bed.' And you know what Olsson said? . . . 'Melt the Ice Queen? Why not?'"

When finally . . . nervously . . . whispered to Alison, she spied Olsson sitting on the end of a bench, alone, on the opposite edge of the playground; she marched in a straight line towards him, a group of boys in her path melting out of her way, eyeing her with a new respect.

"So that's how you think of me?" Alison demanded as she came to a halt in front of Olsson, breathing hard. "As a challenge to your questionable manhood?"

Olsson was sitting hunched down, his back to the playground, his head bowed, an elbow on his knee cradling his chin, his eyes on the ground as if they were studiously counting blades of grass or crumbs of soil. As Alison's angry voice shattered his thoughts, he looked up in surprise. "Huh?" he asked, his head shaking in puzzlement. "What on earth are you talking about?"

"Deny it then—deny that you accepted a challenge to get me into bed."

"Ah," he said, finally understanding.

"Well?" she demanded, when Olsson said nothing more.

Olsson's face softened. "So tell me, Alison," he said quietly, "why do you care what I think of you?"

"What?" Alison almost shouted. "What makes you think I care about *you* in the slightest?"

She spun on her heel and stalked away. Over her shoulder she threw back the words, "You're so arrogant, so . . . presumptuous."

27 Fingers of Fate

AROUND MIDNIGHT, CAPTAIN GOLD came scurrying down from the bridge, the ever-present cigarette still in his mouth. "Time," he grinned, pointing in the direction of the Australian coast. "You now home, eh?"

Karla nodded, looking longingly towards a dim, dark line in the distance—across a wide, black expanse of water.

After ten days at sea, the motion of the fishing boat had come to feel quite normal; but one look at the small, inflatable dinghy bobbing up and down at the bottom of the ladder and Karla felt seasick again. The coast was some ninety kilometers away. That rubber dinghy had to get her there—*and* through the Great Barrier Reef. She tightened the straps of her life-jacket and hugged her orange oilskin closer, shivering as if Neptune's cold, wet fingers were already climbing up her back in welcome.

Captain Gold's eyes sparkled as he held up a small PDA-like device that was nearly all screen. "GPS," he said, waving one arm towards the distance coast. "No worries, mate." His gold front tooth flashed in the light from the GPS.

Karla couldn't even fake a smile in return. From el-Bihar they'd stayed well outside Australia's two hundred kilometer "exclusive economic zone." Now, they had to drop her off *and* clear Australian waters . . . between sunset and sunrise. The tiny dinghy was fast but not fast enough to spare her four, even five hours of splashing across the ocean in almost total darkness—and then the reef. She wasn't convinced a GPS would guarantee they'd ever reach the deserted beach, some thirty kilometers north of Cairns, where they planned to take her. If they reached land . . . in the right place . . . she would be able to walk a few kilometers inland to a road where she could thumb a ride from a passing car. Passing through the islands and sunken reefs had seemed straightforward enough back then, when the sun had been shining. But now? With not even the moon to light their way? She shook her head.

Captain Gold handed the GPS to a sailor who was wearing knee-high rubber boots and, as she was, a bright orange oilskin. The sailor scuttled down the rope ladder into the dinghy, indicating she should follow.

Captain Gold slapped her on the shoulder again. "Happy trip," he grinned.

With an effort, Karla managed to partially match his smile. "*Matalam,*" she said, shaking the captain's hand.

"No worries."

"No worries indeed," Karla muttered as she began to gingerly back down the swaying rope ladder. Captain Gold leant on the rail watching her, smiling and waving. As she reached the dinghy, her last glimpse of the captain was of him shielding his lighter from the wind in an unsuccessful attempt to fire up yet another cigarette.

Karla sat in the middle of the dinghy, opposite the oilskin-wrapped bundle containing her few possessions. The sailor with the GPS, who seemed to be in charge, sat in the back along with a second sailor who held the rudder. A third was in the bow.

The sailors pulled the hoods of their oilskins over their heads; she did the same. She was handed a plastic scoop with a short handle. The sailor made baling motions at the small puddle of water sloshing around the bottom. *We haven't even started yet.*

Karla slid backwards as the dinghy surged forward. She grabbed for the rope running down the side to steady herself. The dinghy's bow had risen up in the air as the helmsman twisted the throttle, and with a muffled roar, two fountains of spray spread behind them like wings. The dinghy seemed to spend half the time in the air before slapping down on the water with a thump, jarring her spine. Beyond the white bubbling wake were the fishing boat's dim lights. Karla watched them getting further away, far too quickly for comfort. It wasn't long before the lights bobbed below a wave and never reappeared.

Now the only light came from the screen of the GPS, faintly illuminating the sailor's face, and from a torch held by the sailor in the bow. He pointed it forward to help light the way, Karla figured—but the light was so weak the torch's batteries must be almost dead. She peered ahead but beyond a few meters was total blackness. The perfect night for not being seen, and the perfect night for crashing into something equally unseen . . . what kind of debris would be floating around the ocean? Soft drink cans, bottles, bits of wood, all kinds of junk dropped overboard . . . what would happen if they hit a sodden, half-sunken log at this speed? Even if the lookout spotted it, it would be too late.

Water slopped around the bottom of the boat no matter how hard she scooped it over the side. Her boots were soaked; the wetness crept up her jeans; her face and hair were damp from the continual fine spray. Her arm ached from baling; her bottom ached from sitting in one, cramped position; her back ached from the endless *thumping* of the boat.

How accurately would the GPS pinpoint their position? Within ten meters? Ten feet? How good was its map of the Barrier Reef? Its sharp fingers of coral could rip out the dinghy's cushion of air in seconds. Her life-jacket would keep her afloat, but what was left of the boat would be stuck on the coral or dragged into the depths by the weight of the outboard along with her laptop and everything else.

Karla felt helpless—like a prisoner of Fate whose life is determined by unseeable, unknowable, invisible and angry beings in the sky. Ahead was the blackness: the unseeable, the unknowable. Fate, personified.

She now looked at the GPS with a wave of relief . . . technology making the unknowable known. She watched how the sailor holding it seemed to take no notice of the boat or its progress but kept his eyes fixed to the screen. Every now and then he'd touch the helmsman, gesture, and the dinghy's course would alter ever so slightly. The helmsman was intent on the sea, the waves, and the lookout in front who leaned forward and never looked back.

They were skilled men; they knew what they were doing. For the first time she felt her destiny was in their competent hands rather than Neptune's unpredictable fingers of fate.

The question of how and why they'd gained their expertise was pushed from her mind when, without warning, the boat slowed, coming almost to a halt as the motor quieted to a dull purr. Karla had no idea how much time had passed, and no way of telling. But from the sound of waves crashing nearby . . . from both sides . . . she knew where they must be. *The Reef . . . we must be nearly there.*

Ahead was still the familiar blackness, but it seemed to loom higher. The lookout swung his light slowly left and right . . . it seemed so much brighter now that when she looked around she could see so much more. *My eyes have adjusted,* she thought.

The light caught white breakers. *Too close . . . or are they?* It was impossible to gauge the distance.

The dinghy crept forward, surging as it was caught by the swell, accelerating unpredictably as it rode the surf, the helmsman suddenly swinging the boat one way and then the other. The boat's eyes, Karla thought, were those of the sailor holding the GPS, not the lookout in the bow. *Like a plane coming in on an instrument landing in a fogbound airport.*

For the first time, the lookout waved. The dinghy slowed to a crawl, lifted by a wave which crashed down in a spray of surf as the dinghy thumped once more. But this *thump* felt harder and then . . . it didn't rise again.

Land.

The lookout jumped out of the boat and hauled it further up the beach. Grinning, the sailors helped Karla stand and step out onto the sand, a wave lapping over her boots halfway up to her knees. A moment later one of the sailors brought her backpack and shoulder bag, and at his gesture, she pulled off the life-jacket and oilskin.

"*Matalam,*" she said, resisting the urge to kneel and kiss the ground of *home.*

The sailors grinned, the whiteness of their teeth caught by the starlight. They pushed the dinghy back into the water. In a moment, all Karla could see was the faint light of the torch and then . . . nothing.

It was two, maybe three in the morning, she estimated. What time did the sun rise at this latitude? For that matter, what day of the week was it? She'd completely lost track.

Out to sea was an occasional faint brightness. The torch must be intentionally weak . . . anyone who saw it from the shore would write it off as luminescence—or an overactive imagination. The outboard couldn't be heard over the roar of the surf. *The perfect smuggler's boat,* she thought with a smile.

Her boots squelched with every step as she trudged slowly and carefully away from the sea, squinting to make out rocks or other obstacles in the sand. Soaked from the waist down and the neck up, the breeze made her feel like she was inside a refrigerator.

She found the sandbank at the edge of the beach by bumping into it. Tired, her back still aching from the boat ride and her knees creaking as she slowly sat down, she gratefully rested her back against the sandbank and heaped a blanket of sand over herself. As she warmed, she began to feel more comfortable.

She hadn't even known she'd fallen asleep until the light of the sun rising above the water startled her eyes open.

"Coffee, steak and eggs—and a long shower," she said to herself as she stepped into the room of a small motel on the outskirts of Cairns. "And some new clothes." But as she closed the door, the soft bed, its clean sheets, the plumped up pillows all beckoned to her almost irresistibly. Every ache in her body chose that moment to compete for her attention, as if demanding she lie down. She shook her head; there were things she needed to do first.

Plugging in her laptop and cellphone to recharge, she stripped off the clothes that earned her a wrinkled nose from the truck driver who'd given her a ride and stepped into the shower. She felt mildly guilty when, quite some time later, the hot water ran out.

She mentally apologized to any other guest who, at this moment, was about to use the shower.

An hour later, dressed in clean and—with relief—dry clothes, she walked towards a shopping center about two kilometers away, calling Lynette McPherson, the OlssonPress managing director, on the way.

"Karla, you're back! How are you?"

"Worn out but glad to be home," said Karla.

"Where are you now?"

"Cairns."

"When will you be back in Sydney?"

"I desperately need sleep. So I'll get a flight to Sydney tomorrow. And I've never been to Cairns before."

"We'll have one of our legal eagles meet you at the airport."

"Lawyers? What on earth for?"

"Did you show your passport at immigration or go through customs when you landed?"

"Ah—I guess not."

"That, my girl, is an offence under sub-section something-or-other. Strangely enough, as an Australian citizen you haven't done anything illegal—so long as you present yourself to Immigration within two working days."

"I see. Why don't I do it here in Cairns and get it over and done with?"

"It's not that simple. While you haven't broken the law—provided, of course, you didn't bring in anything you shouldn't have—" *Oops,* Karla thought, remembering the little stash of marijuana and hashish in her backpack "—whoever brought you in did. Our lawyers are positive the Federal Police—and who knows who else?—will want to question you. The best strategy is to visit them instead of waiting till they come knocking."

"Okay then. Have you heard from Derek? How is he?"

"We know he's all right," said Lynette, "but not where he is. Nor do the police."

"That's something at any rate."

KARLA PRESTON LAUGHED. HER laugh was loud and penetrating; all eyes in the small café turned towards her. Her laugh was also deep and contagious: in a moment half the people the café were laughing or giggling too, though they had no idea why. Perhaps, some thought, spying the open newspaper on her table, she was reading the comics.

It wasn't a cartoon that had prompted her laughter:

Sandeman Government
Lies—Again

By Robin Cartwright
Friday: **Toribaya, Sandeman Islands**

For three weeks Sandeman authorities have denied any knowledge of missing OlssonPress journalist Karla Preston's whereabouts. But Sandeman troops found her ten days ago—and failed to inform the Australian government.

Villagers in Ankaya, a small village on the Sandeman island of Jazeerat el-Bihar, reported that a woman identified as Karla Preston was found by Sandeman soldiers— and then captured by a band of guerrillas in a midnight attack which left one Sandeman soldier dead.

Australian officials refused to answer any questions, other than saying they were doing "everything we can to find her." In private, however, they're fuming. "The

Sandeman's behavior is inexcusable," was one of the few comments I heard that is suitable for publication in a family newspaper. . . .

Karla skimmed the rest of the article, her laughter stopping when she read: Karla Preston hasn't been seen since and more and more people are doubtful she is still alive. *I had no idea. . . . And the whole time I was feeling very safe . . . except last night . . . while hundreds of people are looking for me afraid I might already be dead.*

She felt a stab of anger at Lynette—but what should she have done instead?

Shrugging, she polished off the rest of her steak and eggs. Now more energized, she headed back to the motel, her laptop—and sleep.

*****

"ALISON," EDWARD TOZEN SMILED broadly as Alison entered the *dojo*. "Welcome back."

"*Sensei.*" Alison smiled in return as she bowed.

"Would you like to lead the class, Alison?"

"Thank you, *Sensei*, but I'd rather just work out today."

"You're just in time," Tozen said, waving her towards the mat. "We're about to begin."

She'd woken less than an hour ago, her head throbbing with a violent hangover, as tired as if she hadn't slept at all. A coffee and two aspirins was all she could manage for breakfast—and she was still waiting for the aspirins to have an effect.

"I'm glad I made it," she said as brightly as she could.

Stepping into the *dojo* felt like travelling back in time. Even though he must be eighty-something now, Tozen was still there, looking unchanged, like the *dojo* itself, still teaching, the pillar holding everything together. Even the schedule was the same: an intermediate class at ten on Saturdays.

As she stepped onto the mat, the connections she'd associated with the *dojo* from her very first lesson came flooding back. She felt wrapped in a cocoon of safety, her energy level shot up as if she were standing on a recharger, and her movements quickly returned to the graceful arcs of easy flow. But as she buried herself in the exercises, as the strength surged back into her muscles and her head slowly cleared, she had a vague, hollow sense that something was missing—but what? When she'd given up trying to figure it out, the memory of the teenage Derek Olsson flashed into her mind—that he, like her, had always been at every class—that even though she had, then, despised him, she missed his presence just the same.

Derek? she wondered, shaking her head. *Why should I think of him . . . now?*

She smiled at the memory of the class where—*Let's be honest*—she had kneed him in the groin. He'd waited for her at the door afterwards and had the gall—the impudence— to ask if she'd like to stop for a coffee. "You must be joking," she replied coldly as she strode past him without a pause or a backward glance.

They had both mastered Aikido quickly, though Alison was the first to wear a black belt. After a few more months, Tozen first asked Alison, then Derek, to lead classes from time to time. At one point when the number of beginners had ballooned, Tozen persuaded them to lead the classes together.

Alison was surprised to find she enjoyed the joint teaching and even began to look forward to it. It was rather like Aikido practiced at a higher mental level. They responded smoothly to each other's cues; when one moved in a new direction the other automatically followed, and Derek made no attempt to impress her or overreach his ability. He deferred to her superior skills and was happy to follow, just as she was when he led.

But off the mat, Alison turned back into the "Ice Queen." She continued to make a point of ignoring him; he seemed indifferent to her. There were times when he'd walk past her in a corridor at school as if she simply didn't exist. Yet at other times she'd turn to see him gazing at her across the playground; he made no pretence that he'd actually been looking somewhere else and continued to look at her as though he had every right to—the mere hint of a smile the only reaction to her glare of disapproval. At a school dance Alison couldn't understand why she felt a touch of jealousy when he came in with some other girl, or why she felt annoyed that while he partnered many girls he never asked her for a dance. *I suppose,* she thought afterwards, *to deny me the pleasure of refusing him.*

One day she accepted his invitation to "buy you a cup of coffee."

"For here or takeaway?" the server asked as she took their order.

"Here," Derek said; "Takeaway," Alison said at the same time.

Derek looked at her quizzically.

"I agreed to let you buy me a cup of coffee," she said, her voice cold, her face taking on the unfriendliest expression she could muster. "I didn't say I'd drink it with you."

She waited for the inevitable angry or offended reaction—but Derek just laughed. She glared at him thinking, *He's always so infuriating.*

They waited in silence until the coffees were ready. "Thanks," he said, grinning as he passed Alison her cup. "I never make the same mistake twice."

Now, what did he mean by that? she asked herself as she stalked out of the coffee shop.

He continued the occasional invitations; she continued to reject them. After one particularly smooth joint session, as she stepped out into the dark, wintry evening, pulling her jacket around her to protect her from the wind that felt like it had blown all the way from Antarctica without gaining any warmth along the way, she heard her voice saying "Okay." When he seemed neither surprised nor pleased, she almost told him she'd changed her mind.

Only in the café around the corner did she notice the dark bruise on his cheek. "What happened to you?" Her hand began to reach across the table as if to wipe the bruise away, but she angrily jerked it back to her side. "In a fight, I suppose," she added brusquely.

"Yes. With my father."

"Your father did that? To you? Why?"

"He was drunk. As usual."

"My God," she breathed, her hand going to her mouth. "You hear about that sort of thing—but I never thought—was it bad?"

Derek nodded slowly. "But it's not going to happen again."

"What?"

"That's why I took up Aikido: to protect myself—and my little sister."

"Jessica? Where is she? I didn't see her at school today."

Derek gently touched his bruised cheek. "No. And you won't see her for a few more days."

"You mean—?"

Derek nodded.

"Oh, my God," she said involuntarily, her body trembling as she thought: *Once was bad enough. . . .* Her voice stuttered. "And did he—has he—?"

Derek looked puzzled, and then slowly shook his head. "Not yet."

"To live with that sort of terror every day . . . " Alison said quietly as they carried their coffees to a table. "How can she stand it . . . how can you?"

"I don't know," Derek said softly, his eyes looking into the distance. "You don't even know there's a choice, not to begin with. And then—any option you can think of is even more frightening. . . . You feel so helpless. . . ."

"But now?"

"I'm . . . not sure. . . ."

His eyes suddenly focused on hers, and he leant forward slightly and asked, his voice now solemn, "Alison, do you believe in God?"

"*What?*" Alison stared at him, trying to make sense of his words. "I—I—I don't know any more." And she thought: *I've never said that before, to anyone. Why did I have to say it to* him?

"If there is a God, what sort of being must He be to sit by and watch while you and I are being made to suffer? For what—original sin? For the crime of being born?"

"I—I've never thought about it."

"So if there is a God and you're standing in front of Him one day, what are you going to tell Him?"

"What a question." Alison shivered, watching Derek nervously. "What would you say?"

"I'd tell Him to go to hell."

"You'd say what?"

Derek, his eyes intense, did not respond to her question but asked, "And would I be wrong?"

Alison's eyes widened, her mouth hung open—but she couldn't speak. Her muscles turned rigid with shock at Derek's blasphemy, yet a part of her felt like cheering him on. She tried to make sense of her confusion—but all that happened was her head began to ache. Eventually, she managed to stutter, "I—I—don't want to think about."

"I'm sorry, Alison. I didn't mean to upset you."

"I'll . . . be okay. And it wasn't really you that upset me."

Derek nodded, his soft eyes kind and somehow calming—and understanding. And yet, she suddenly felt, discomforting: eyes that seemed to peer directly into her soul.

"I need some air—I think I'd best go."

She avoided him for the next few days. But she couldn't stop herself from thinking about him—and his infernal questions—and looking at him from time to time from the corner of her eyes.

She saw the muscled frame of the football player—the rugger bugger—but there was no sign of the boyish grin of the strutting ladies' man who fancied himself so much. She slowly became aware that when he looked at her, Derek's eyes weren't roving up and down her body or flicking to her breasts or hips but were firmly focused on her eyes and face. Eyes, she noticed, that were green—or were they hazel?—with no trace of the pity that so many others showed her. Soft eyes projecting such a well of compassion and understanding that, without thinking, she reached out hungrily. No words were needed for her to sense that even deeper within him was a recognition of her inner strength, a connection that, at fleeting moments, made her feel ten feet tall. Could this really be the same person she'd humiliated on the mat?

*****

"COME BACK SOON, ALISON. Any time. And don't leave it so long," Tozen said as she left the *dojo.*

"Thank you, *Sensei.*"

Her eyes sparkled, her muscles flowed with energy, her headache was gone—but her stomach was still a hollow knot, and something in the back of her mind was nagging at her, something she needed to do—but it wouldn't rise to consciousness. And just as Olsson's ghostly presence had seemed to haunt her on the mat, wherever she looked was a memory . . . *we walked there . . . we argued there—I was so mad at him . . . and around that corner. . . .*

She tried to push the memories of Derek out of her mind—but began to think of McKurn instead. *Simple choice* . . . and, almost without her conscious intention, she let her steps carry her around the corner to the café where, so often, she and Olsson sat and talked.

For a week afterwards, Derek didn't repeat his invitation for coffee, so Alison asked him if he could help her with her maths.

"What I like about maths," he said as he effortlessly untangled her problems, explaining everything so clearly she felt, for the first time, that she finally understood, "is that the rules are all clear and logical. Either two plus two equals four—or it doesn't. If it doesn't, the whole of mathematics just falls apart. So two plus two must equal four. It's a self-contained reality where everything makes perfect sense."

"Even weird things that make no sense—like imaginary numbers?" Alison asked. "The square root of minus one?"

"Sure. They follow the rules. What's really weird is that imaginary numbers have applications in the real world—which makes you wonder about the real world, doesn't it?"

"I don't know," Alison shrugged, feeling that now he wasn't making any more sense than imaginary numbers. "I'm having enough trouble with real numbers as it is."

She began to look forward to her talks with him as much as she looked forward to their teaching Aikido together. Eventually, they spent so much time in each other's company that Alison felt sure she and Derek were the only people at school who didn't think they were a couple, an "item." As they talked, Alison learnt that Derek was a voracious reader, had a part-time job in a petrol station and was the proud owner of a Mini he'd bought for peanuts from a junkyard and rebuilt himself—and that his grandfather was the only person he truly admired and revered. And no matter how lightly they chattered about books and movies or what had happened at school, inevitably Derek would come up with one of his questions.

"What's your purpose in life?" he asked her one day.

"Revenge." The word came out of Alison's mouth instantly. She had no need to think, to reflect. But now the word was out there, in front of her, it felt so right. Yes, she'd thought of it before. Many times. But until now she'd never uttered it—and somehow saying it made it feel far more real. *Damn it,* she thought, *that's the second time I've told him something I've never admitted to anyone else.*

Almost unwillingly, her eyes moved back to Derek's face. She saw him nodding with a smile of understanding. Suddenly, she felt her very soul had been stripped bare, that he could see into her deepest, innermost secrets and desires, and even those parts of her self she was barely aware of. She felt giddy, being pulled towards him like iron filings to a magnet, while recoiling backwards to escape the sense of his X-ray eyes even as she was glued to the chair, unable to move. She took a deep breath and gripped the table's edge to steady herself.

"Doesn't it say in the Bible," Derek asked quietly, "'Vengeance shall be mine, saith the Lord'?"

"The Lord had His chance—and He didn't show up. So it's up to me." Alison's gaze dropped to his hand: his fingers were long, like a piano player's, but there were traces of grease under his fingernails. *If I don't look at his eyes, she thought, he won't be able to see me . . . and I'll be safe.*

"Ah. . . . I see. And when you have your revenge, *then* what?"

Derek had a frustrating way of leaving her speechless.

One day she felt so angry with him that she missed cues and stumbled in front of the Aikido class. Derek smoothly stepped in to make it look as if nothing had happened—which didn't improve her mood one whit. Afterwards, she stalked outside and waited, accosting him when he emerged. "So what's this I hear about you going to movies and hanging out with that slut, Marian? She's an airhead."

"True," Derek grinned. "but she's fun to be with—in small doses."

"And I'm not?"

"I didn't say that, Alison."

"Keeps you warm at night, does she?"

Derek blushed.

"You take her out but you've never invited me to go to a movie."

"So . . . would you like to go the movies with me?"

"With you? Never!"

Derek shrugged. "Why do you think I never asked you?"

A week or so later her mother said to her when she got home, "Some nice-looking boy brought some flowers for you, Alison."

"You keep them, Mum."

"There's a card."

Alison shrugged—but opened it. There was just the one word: TRUCE? *He can stew for a while,* she thought.

Maggie put the flowers on the dining room table. But that night, as Alison went to bed, she took them to her room. Maggie smiled knowingly in the morning; Alison lifted a warning finger and said, "Don't say it, Mother. Not a word."

"LIKE ANOTHER COFFEE, LUV?"

Alison looked up to see the motherly face of the café's owner smiling at her. She looked at her cup: it was empty, and she had no memory of drinking it. She turned her wrist to check the time . . . but she never wore her watch when she worked out.

"Do you know what time it is?" Alison asked.

"It's just gone noon."

"Heavens above," Alison said, leaping to her feet. "I've been sitting here daydreaming for nearly an hour."

STEPPING THROUGH THE FRONT door of her parents' house was like entering a cocoon; the feeling wrapped around her warmly, and she felt protected from the world outside. Alison leant again the door, breathing in the familiarity, the sense of . . . *I've been in Canberra all these years,* she thought, *but this still feels like home.*

"Mum. Dad. I'm back," she called.

Maggie came out of the kitchen and they hugged. "Are you okay, Alison?" Maggie asked.

"I'm fine, thanks, Mum," she said, *except for the tension in my stomach. . . .*

"Dad's in the garden." Maggie looked at her daughter as if she knew something wasn't right, but she said no more.

"I'd better have a shower."

As she was soaking in the steamy water, the thought that had been nagging in the back of her mind all morning came to her fully formed. Excited, she dressed quickly, went online and sent a message to the geek:

Have located where McKurn keeps sensitive computer records. Security seems

pretty tight, and I'm wondering if you might be able to break it.

In response to his describe all relevant details, she sent him a long email, outlining all the security and other arrangements in as much detail as she could recall. A while later she received the geek's reply: doesn't sound promising but wl check it out and let you know. wl cost extra

Understood. Thanks.

Her mother's voice interrupted her thoughts. "What do you feel like for lunch, Alison?"

"Oh—anything, thanks, Mum," she said without looking up and turned to the mountain of waiting emails.

She stopped. Glancing at her mother in the kitchen, the rattle of plates and cutlery signalling she was already busy, Alison snapped the lid of her laptop shut and followed her mother into the kitchen.

"It's a bit chilly outside today, Mum—but sunny. Shall we have lunch at the Fish Market again, instead? No phone calls, I promise."

And at least I never went there with Derek.

28 The Lion's Den

THE OlssonPress's FIRST SHOT had been fired the previous Friday afternoon: its Sydney and Melbourne *Weekend*s—chatty entertainment guides to the respective city's bars, clubs, bands, theaters, and movies—both published a Guide to Buying Drugs. Each Guide came complete with a "location map" of the drug dealers' "supermarkets," and was illustrated with pictures of packets of heroin and marijuana (they claimed) and cash (quite obviously) exchanging hands.

The buyers' faces were blacked out. The dealers' faces weren't.

That Friday evening, the parks and street corners where drug dealers usually gathered swarmed with disappointed sightseers: having also seen the Guide, the dealers decided to stay home.

At the same time a national, wall-to-wall TV and radio campaign advertised that, starting Sunday, the Sykes' and OlssonPress papers would reveal how the underworld reached out its tentacles to corrupt police, bureaucrats, and politicians with gobs of cash. "Names will be named," the ads promised. "In Sunday's first installment: a well-known politician caught red-handed taking money from known gangsters."

The OlssonPress was a chain of small-town dailies, mainly scattered across the countryside of New South Wales and Victoria, plus some suburban giveaways in Sydney and Melbourne. Its exclusives—like Karla Preston's articles—were syndicated to Henry Sykes' chain of city papers, which included Sydney's *Mercury* and the *Melbourne Examiner*. At first, although impressed with the supporting evidence, Sykes was concerned about libel and slander suits, and so refused to carry the drug exposé. Only when OlssonPress executives signed an agreement to assume liability for all and any damages Sykes and his papers might suffer did he order the stories to run.

With front-page headlines like **BRIBED!** (**BRIBED?** in the Sykes' press), every OlssonPress and Sykes' Sunday newspaper hit all-time sales records (while, much to his disgust, Sir Philip French's Sunday sales fell to an all-time low).

Underneath the headline was a slightly fuzzy picture, taken in dim light, of Harry Weinbaum, a member of the NSW state parliament, sitting with a well-known member of Sydney's Lebanese gang, counting a pile of cash. The picture was captioned: Caught in the act! A streamer across the bottom of the page promised: TOMORROW: Melbourne's Bent Copper.

The OlssonPress' only national publication *MoneyWeek,* also published on Sundays, carried a lengthy investigative analysis of the connection between drugs, cash, and corruption.

Late on Saturday night, a package was delivered to the Surry Hills police station in Sydney. It contained enough evidence there to convict Harry Weinbaum several times over. But, somehow, Weinbaum had gotten wind of the scoop and had fled the city. Acting on an anonymous tip, the police in Dunedoo—a small country town three hundred and sixty kilometers northwest of Sydney—arrested Weinbaum at a petrol station where he'd stopped to fill up. It was pure coincidence—so the OlssonPress spokesperson later claimed—that an OlssonPress reporter and photographer happened to be at the same petrol station in the middle of nowhere at the right time to record the arrest in living color.

In the furor these stories created, the return of Karla Preston's column was almost buried:

**Abducted by Soldiers;
Rescued by "Terrorists"**

By Karla Preston
OlssonPress Syndicate Exclusive
Saturday: **Cairns, Queensland**

I'm back in Oz—and glad to be back. Though I had a wonderful if, on occasion, terrifying time in the Sandemans.

Having spent the last week literally at sea, I have been unavoidably out of touch. So first, I want to say a big "Thank you" to my friends and associates in the media, government, and elsewhere who were concerned for my safety—and even to those readers who just wanted to see my articles back so they could shake their heads about how wrong-headed I am. (You're mistaken, naturally—but keep reading: maybe, one day, I'll get you to change your mind.)

I deeply appreciate your concern. And there is, in fact, a lot to be concerned about—though not so much about me.

I was surprised, for example, that my disappearance had become something of a *cause célèbre*. But I'm even more surprised the Sandeman authorities seem to have been unable to tell the Australian government anything about what had happened to me.

You see, they knew exactly where I was. At least, until I was rescued by "terrorists"— from the Sandeman troops who had captured me and imprisoned me, tied up, under guard. (I spent an evening in a state which, had I been somewhat younger, I'd describe as "being terrified of losing my virginity." The "terrorists" were gentlemen compared to the soldiers . . . but more about that tomorrow.)

So, once again, the Sandeman government reveals itself as devious, deceptive, dishonest, and completely untrustworthy.

Is this the kind of government the old farts in Canberra, thousands of kilometers from the front lines—who've never faced a danger greater than being chauffeured across a busy intersection—want to support? Is this what they consider an objective worthy of the expenditure of other people's lives—*your* sons', *your* nephews', and *your* brothers'? Is this the kind of policy *you,* as a voter, support and approve of . . . and, through your taxes, want to prop up?

What do you think? Why not let your member and senator know.

After all, they're supposed to be your representatives. Which means they're supposed to push our demands in parliament, not meekly follow the instructions of some party apparatchik.

About time—don't you think?—that *we* remind *them* that *we* pay their salaries and lush pensions, that *we* fund their lavish expense accounts including free (to them) first-class air tickets and all the rest, that *they* work for *us.*

*****

KARLA'S BACK.

Derek Olsson chuckled as he read her words.

His first impulse, when he'd seen her column in the *Sunday Mercury,* was to rush out of the coffee shop to her apartment a few kilometers further along Glebe Point Road. He immediately restrained himself. *In fact,* he thought as he looked along the street, *I've been here too long. It's time to move on.*

This was the street where Karla shopped. Her bus to the city and the OlssonPress office stopped some ten meters away; he found himself watching each one that stopped in case Karla was a passenger.

Karla was back—but he couldn't see her. Although constantly by himself since his arrest, he now felt *alone.* He missed her sparkling wit, their deep, philosophical conversations, the way their minds moved in lockstep: when one changed the subject one hundred and eighty degrees in mid-phrase the other would effortlessly follow along . . . all beyond reach.

He sat looking vaguely at the headline, **BRIBED?** They'd done a good job. That story and those to follow would stir up a hornet's nest. Something would give. . . .

So would he if he didn't do something.

He took one last look along the street that had become so familiar. Time to find some place else to stay, he decided, where no one has even heard of Derek Olsson; change your look, hair color and identity.

HE HAD FILLED HIS days by reading the newspapers, going through his businesses' daily financial and sales reports, making the occasional phone call and sending the occasional email—their paths over the internet suitably disguised—to various managers. His businesses ticked over without needing much of his or even Ross's attention. They'd built a good team.

He kept pestering Ross for information from the lawyers and private eyes about Lars; nevertheless a week passed before it finally arrived:

> Sorry it's taken so long, but Lars Olsson seems to have spent most of his time with no fixed address, leaving very few traces.
>
> But we found him.
>
> He's living at 3 Avoca Street, Noosa Heads in a house he bought two weeks ago. He put down a deposit of 10% of the house's value of $350,000. He currently works as a waiter in a Noosa fast-food restaurant.
>
> As far as we can tell, over the past eighteen years he has worked at a wide variety of unskilled jobs all over the country—roustabout, waiter, builder's laborer, dishwasher and the like.
>
> While we have not compiled a complete record—just let me know if you want more—it would appear he has rarely held the same job for more than six months.
>
> There is no record of his ever being married.

Noosa Heads, an expensive resort town a few hours north of Brisbane. *Where,* Olsson wondered, *did Lars get the money?* He typed an email:

> A man called Lars Olsson lives at 3 Avoca Street, Noosa Heads. He bought a house there just two weeks ago. Could you get a look inside his bank accounts? No idea what bank or banks. I want to know what has come in and gone out over the past few months—amounts and sources if possible.

He encrypted and sent the email; a while later receiving an answer:
probably can do wl take time tho cant say how long wl make priority but v busy right now ok?

He was now certain Lars was involved. He was torn between jumping on a plane to twist a confession from him and waiting until he had evidence which would make it easier to get him to talk. Fighting his impatience, he decided to wait: *After all,* he told himself, *if he's just bought a house he won't be going anywhere.*

Having learnt "The Greek" was a part owner of the Royal Arms Hotel, Olsson spent some time shadowing him and his operation. One evening he'd gone to the Bare Bottoms Club as a customer, watching the Greek, noting who he was with and who he talked to, assuming automatically the thuggish-looking ones were thugs while the average-looking people were customers . . . until he recognized a prominent state politician who obviously knew the Greek well, by the way the Greek was plying him with girls and champagne. The politician looked more like an archetypical thug than the Greek himself.

He chatted to the bar girls who lined up to have their palms read. It was a trick he'd learnt from a friend who believed in palm reading, astrology, auras, past lives, fortune-tellers—and just about every other superstition. By watching his friend's routine for a while, Olsson found he could easily replicate the patter: just make a few vague statements and follow the cues of the credulous who immediately believed he had some kind of "psychic" power.

Palm reading was the perfect icebreaker: it took but a moment for each bar girl to start spilling out her life story. Even the most hard-bitten whore—who should have known better—was delighted to be told that when she turned thirty-one, or whatever age in the near but sufficiently distant future, some rich and handsome guy would fall desperately in love with her and she'd live happily ever after.

Like many a gangster, Demas Chrysanthopoulos—"the Greek"—was superstitious; but when he sat down opposite Olsson asking for his palm to be read, Olsson's heart nearly stopped. The Greek was all smiles, but Olsson froze as their eyes met. *Cold, jet-black eyes. The eyes of a killer.*
Just like Luk Suk's.

Physically, there was no comparison. Chrysanthopoulos was a tall, broad-shouldered man, with a gold chain resting on a hairy chest exposed by a silk shirt unbuttoned halfway to his waist, his muscles rippling under the fabric as he moved, broadcasting his power. Luk Suk was slightly built, shorter tconhan Olsson, and favored carefully tailored suits with padded shoulders and elevated shoes to disguise the weakness of his physique. But Luk Suk stood and moved in a way that oozed confidence and authority, an impression reinforced by the two musclemen who trailed him everywhere: a pair of Rottweilers ready to spring into action at his slightest command.

As if to confirm he'd noticed Olsson's reaction and approved of it, Chrysanthopoulos nodded his head slightly. *Fear,* Olsson thought. *He's used to invoking fear in others—like Luk Suk.*

Olsson took the Greek's hand to hide his momentary confusion and studied it in serious silence for a while: broad, beefy, and strong, it was a hand powerful enough to snap a neck with one quick movement. *And probably has. More than once.*

Olsson turned the Greek's hand this way and that, looking at the lines and folds on the side of his hand as well as the palm. Through the corners of his eyes he studied his options. He was hemmed into the booth by the girls surrounding the table, now fascinated to see what he'd tell the Greek. A couple of thugs stood lazily behind Chrysanthopoulos.

There was, presumably, an exit behind the bar but he didn't know where it led. The club was now fairly busy, leaving no clear path to the front door. And, of course, there were a couple of doormen at the bottom of the stairs leading to the street. *One slip,* he thought, *and I'd be done for. Only one way out, then. . . .*

Noticing the Greek's growing impatience, Olsson launched into his well-honed routine, breathing deeply to control the tension in his neck and shoulders. "Here," he said pointing at a line on the Greek's palm. "You see, your heart line is broken. So you've had several troubled relationships and probably left a trail of broken hearts." *And who hasn't?*

The Greek nodded, clearly pleased.

"But now. . . ." Olsson paused as if to study the heart line more closely. "You're in a stable relationship—" the Greek nodded, totally unaware that Olsson only needed to look at the chunky wedding ring on his finger to know that "—but you can't help straying from time to time."

The Greek nodded again, delighted to have his masculine prowess confirmed.

"Four children. . . ."

"Three," the Greek corrected.

Olsson shook his head. "There must be one you don't know about, then."

The Greek roared with laughter. "Maybe more than one."

Olsson just nodded, careful not to let his sense of relief affect his heightened awareness. *It's so easy.* He felt not the slightest bit guilty at capitalizing on the way people fell prey to their own superstitions, to their own desire to believe.

"So what does my future hold?" the Greek asked.

He's hooked. "Well, although your Fate is written in your hand," Olsson said, "the future is not fixed in stone, despite what some people say." *Nothing like a little pompous mumbo jumbo to lull the "mark."*

"You always have a choice. I can't see it clearly right now—I'm feeling a bit drained—read too many palms in one go. And your aura is so powerful. . . . " *Flattery will get you everywhere.* "But it involves travel . . . or perhaps, moving. Yes. If you were to live somewhere else, you could look forward to a long and uneventful life. If you stay here, though, I see some kind of danger hovering around you. . . ."

"Excitement or boredom? Is that what you're saying?"

Olsson nodded. "That's one way of looking at it, I suppose."

The Greek smiled broadly. "True enough," he said. "I like to live dangerously."

Olsson let the Greek's hand go and fell back into the cushions of the booth as if he was exhausted. He wiped his forehead with a napkin. "I need a break."

The Greek waved to a waitress. "Champagne!" he yelled. "Champagne for our friend here. And I don't even know your name," he added, looking at Olsson.

"Joe," said Olsson. "Joe Brewster."

"For Joe!"

The Greek stayed long enough to drink one glass of champagne with Olsson before moving to talk to someone else. Olsson took the opportunity to extricate himself from the bar.

As he sucked in the cool midnight air he told himself sternly that he had taken far too many risks to merely "take the measure" of the Greek, and gain the impression that the Greek was perfectly capable of killing Vincent Leung or anyone else without a second thought—something Olsson already knew.

To kill a whole day, he'd ridden his motorbike around Balmain, choosing a weekday when he knew Parliament was in session so there'd be no chance of bumping into Alison by accident. The ghosts of his memory took on flesh as he circled past everywhere he and Alison had spent time together . . . Alison's house . . . the *dojo* . . . the Traynors' place. . . . He slowed as he came to their old high school, grinning as he remembered catching up to her one morning, asking if he could ride with her the rest of the way to school.

"It's a free country," she had shrugged, indifferently, otherwise ignoring him.

"Is it?" Olsson asked.

She'd glared at him. "Do you question absolutely everything?"

"Of course. Don't you?"

Her answer had been to accelerate her bike away from him.

He remembered how alive he'd felt whenever they were together, and how tormented he'd been when she became angry with him, usually as a result of one of his "infuriating" questions. Suspecting—no: certain—his affection was not returned, he tried to stay out of her way . . . and failed. Except on those occasions when she sought him out first, as though there was some invisible force pulling them together.

Without conscious planning, he ended up at the coffee shop around the corner from the *dojo* where they'd so often sat and talked. And just as he had sat here aged eighteen in this very same seat, wondering why he loved Alison—if indeed it was love he felt—so now, thirty-five, he again asked himself the same questions.

Was it love? Or a strange obsession?

What is love, anyway? He couldn't answer that question then—or now. *Why do I turn everything into a philosophical question?* he asked himself—chuckling when he realized that, in itself, was a philosophical question.

It was her fiery nature that had first attracted him; her unyielding determination; her fixity of purpose. That, and being bested—humiliated—on the mat, turned her into a challenge as well. His "Melt the Ice Queen?" remark—something Alison threw back in his face every now and then—was a "macho" response made at an age when all boys exaggerated their masculinity to each other. "Macho Man," he smiled grimly: his mask, hiding the reality underneath. It had been automatic, not a matter of conscious choice: a sensitive, caring, touchy-feely teenage boy wouldn't survive the locker room mentality of the strutting male teenager.

He'd regretted his remark almost as soon as he'd made it. But it added to the challenge, made him persistent, and when that persistence, all so slowly, paid off, his feelings changed dramatically.

He found he could talk to her about anything, even his deepest, most private thoughts and fears. He had baited her with his "infernal questions" even while speaking from the heart. But she responded—yes, with anger. But she took him seriously. In time it seemed as if he were stretching her mind, that she enjoyed it—and stretched his in turn. He knew that she also felt safe enough with him to tell him inner thoughts she'd confided to no one else.

That she'd been hurt appealed to his male protectiveness. What other boys saw as her overwhelming strength provoked his admiration; the sense that, even so, she was fragile, made him cautious. They hardly ever touched, he never made a pass at her, never responded overtly to her sexual appeal until one day she complained, exasperated, "What do you think I am? A mind without a body?"

The door to the coffee shop swung open; he saw Alison coming towards him and was gripped with the same excitement, anticipation, and flood of desire he always felt when he saw her. And the unconscious sense of harmony which developed from their teaching Aikido together, which persisted off the mat even while being denied. Even now, just one look was enough to know the other's mood, and sometimes the other's thoughts as well.

But it was just someone who looked like Alison; he felt overcome with disappointment. Never mind that seeing her here, now, was a very bad idea . . . if she walked through the door, nothing else would matter.

He shook his head sadly. A gulf still loomed between them. She still remembered the way he'd scorned her aim of being "in the center of power"; she knew that in the years since he hadn't changed his mind. But—there were things he hadn't told her . . . couldn't tell her. And somehow she knew, as if she could now see inside him a place that was locked, bolted, and shuttered to her, with no clue as to what was hidden inside.

If only I'd never taken that plane—

He looked glumly into his empty coffee cup: too many what-might-have-beens. *All water under the bridge now.*

He wandered idly past the *dojo,* feeling as though he sensed her presence; as if, should he walk inside, there she'd be. . . .

Love? Obsession? Seventeen years later he was no closer to an answer except . . . when they were together, even when they argued, the world seemed brighter, crisper; he felt more himself than at any other time. And he missed her.

But Alison, he thought, was like a surging, unpredictable river: oases of calm pools turning into spinning whirlpools, unexpected waterfalls and rapids forming treacherous undertows and pounding into glistening, rocky walls. While Karla was self-sufficient, like a wide lake, its calm waters stirring in a wind barely touching the deep stillness beneath.

Yet . . . while he was remembering Alison all thoughts of Karla disappeared from his mind. *What does that tell you?* He smiled to himself at the question which answered itself.

*****

"It's called *The Three Little Wolves and the Big Bad Pig.*"

"No, no, no," the children cried. "That's not right, Alison," a serious little girl said sternly. "You've got the story backwards."

Alison smiled. "Look," she said. She held up the book. The children craned to see the cover picturing three cute wolves taking a break from building a house. "See? This is a different story."

Alison sat on the floor of the playroom, three-year-old Billy sitting on her knee, sucking his thumb and resting comfortably against her; half-a-dozen other young children crowded the space in front of her.

"Want to hear it anyway?" Alison asked.

"Yes, Alison," the children chorused happily.

"Once upon a time," she read, "there were three cuddly little wolves with soft fur and fluffy tails. . . ."

For over ten years, when she was in Canberra and had a free Sunday afternoon, she'd come to this Children's Shelter to play with, read to and just be with the children—all orphans. The orphanage was originally located in an old house needing renovation. The children slept two, three, even four to a room; the furniture, books, toys, and most of the clothes the children wore looked like the cast-offs donated to charity that they were.

Now, thanks to Alison, the orphanage was in a brand-new building. Except when there was a sudden influx of new children, each kid had a room to him- or herself. Hundreds of children's books lined one wall of the playroom with which now had about every kind of toy and gadget a kid could desire.

WHEN SHE'D FIRST PRESENTED the idea to Royn he'd protested, "A good idea, but . . . orphans? I don't mean to seem insensitive," he added hastily, "but how can we sell it to people. . . ?" He looked embarrassed as his voice trailed off awkwardly.

"You mean," said Alison, "how can we make it a vote-winner?"

When Royn nodded she said, "Simple. Call it . . . 'Humane Conservatism.' Be the 'Caring Conservative.' We're not out to regulate everybody's life, create more dependents, or set up more self-perpetuating government programs. We want to help people pull themselves up by their own bootstraps. We want to make it easier for people who are already helping others, not replace them.

"We'll do it economically by recognizing the magnificent work of charities like St. Vincent de Paul, and offer them additional support. No government orphanages: there's no way a government department can hope to replicate the caring and compassion of the wonderful people who dedicate their lives to looking after the unfortunate children who have lost their parents. What the government can do is remove some of the disadvantages these children suffer. Provide the books and toys that parents buy for their kids, for example. Computers. Funds for schoolbooks and after-school activities—ballet classes, piano lessons, and so on. Even some pocket money for the kids. Grants to improve facilities so every orphan could have his or her own room. That sort of thing. Sit down first with the charities and find out what they need and where we can—and can't—help.

"Then, we can use the same approach with rape victims, battered womn, abused children and other disadvantaged groups . . . and steal the 'social conscience' vote away from Labor. And after all," she added with a broad smile, "what politician is going to oppose giving books to orphans?"

"That's brilliant, Alison!" Royn said with admiration. "There are times when I think you should be sitting in this chair, instead of me."

"God forbid. Then I'd have to kiss babies and shake hands and make speeches and fend off all those pesky reporters trying to find out who I was sleeping with. And be nice to people I can't stand to be anywhere near. I'm much happier where I am."

"If you ever change your mind," Royn grinned, "I'm sure we can find you a nice, safe electorate—just so long as it's not mine you want."

Helping orphans became the first Conservative Party initiative that could have come straight from the opposition Labor Party's playbook.

But there were times when Alison thought the result of her idea had turned into a mixed blessing. It had spawned a new government department—or, rather, a small agency to administer the program . . . which seemed to grow larger with every passing year as the bureaucrats came up with new schemes for grants, assistance and so on that increased their staff and budget. And worse, while the program's original purpose had been to supplement the charities' work, as the program's budget rose the agency slowly increased its interference in orphanages' operations, pointing out they now provided the bulk of the orphanages' funding.

And to Alison, the children didn't seem to be any happier. Indeed, they now seemed to spend much of their time fighting over which TV channel to watch, or whose turn it was to play on the computer, while most of the books stood unread on the shelves and the toys gathered dust in their storage boxes unplayed-with—a few still in their original, shrink-wrapped packaging. The occasional child—usually an older one—actually resisted being adopted if it meant going to a home whose facilities didn't compare with the orphanages'.

But she didn't keep coming back to see the results—especially the imperfect ones—of a government program she'd initiated. What drew her to the orphanage initially were the children and the sense she could pass on just a little of what she'd been lucky enough to receive from her parents. What kept her returning—especially after her thirtieth birthday when she began casting long, wistful looks at mothers walking along the street with their toddlers—was that here she could gain some sense of what it meant to be a mother.

From time to time, Alison wondered if she'd ever succumb to "baby hunger," some kind of primeval instinct that afflicted some women in their late thirties and early forties—not all of them childless. Two career women she knew had simply stopped taking the pill and one of them didn't even know who the father of her child was. But both were delighted to be mothers regardless of the cost—and it wasn't difficult for Alison to imagine herself following their example.

SHE HUGGED ALL THE children "goodbye," wiped away Billy's tears, and shook her head sorrowfully when the children asked hopefully, "See you next Sunday, Alison?"

"They all love your visits, Alison," said one of the nuns as she left, "and really look forward to them—it's a real pity you can't come every Sunday."

"I wish I could, Sister," said Alison.

"Especially little Billy. He clings to you, and gets really upset when you don't come back. It's as if you remind of him of his mother."

The nun's subtext, she realized, was: "If you can't come every Sunday, it might be better if you didn't come at all."

She's an expert in creating guilt, Alison thought. *But . . . she could be right.* And when she thought about her real reasons for coming, she wondered if she was really doing the children—or herself—any favors.

And she drove home . . . slowly, tears blurring her vision . . . trying to make sense of a world where you set out to help others and end up being rewarded with induced guilt . . . and wondering whether someone like McKurn was the true product of the establishment you'd committed your life to.

*****

THREE MEN IN SUITS descended on Karla Preston as she strode out of the gate at Sydney airport. Two, who seemed to be together, were wearing sturdy shoes, nondescript grey suits and white shirts, looking as if they'd both come out of the same mould, even though one of them looked Eurasian. The word *Police* popped into Karla's mind of its own accord. The third man looked like he'd just stepped out of an Armani advertisement.

"Are you Karla Preston?" the Eurasian man asked officiously.

"Perhaps you would be so kind to identify yourself," the man in Armani asked the grey suit.

"Just hold your horses," Karla said, raising her voice and one commanding hand, stretching herself to her full height so she stood eye to eye with the Eurasian man. Her deep, authoritative tone caused the three men to look at her in surprise as the heads of other deplaning passengers turned to see what was going on. "Perhaps you'd all be kind enough to tell me just who the hell you are—" she turned to look at the Armani man who was now smiling at her wryly "—starting with *you.*"

"Miss Preston," he said with obvious appreciation, handing her his card. "I'm Mike Rubin from the law firm of Butler & Taylor. Lynette, I believe, said you'd be expecting me."

"She did," Karla said. "But I didn't expect two welcoming committees."

"Me neither," Rubin grinned as he handed his business cards to the two men in grey. "And you two gentlemen are . . . ?"

"Sergeant Ramon Clarke, Federal Police," said the Eurasian man who'd spoken first.

"Fallow, ASIO," the second man grunted.

"Could I see your ID please gentlemen?" Rubin asked.

"Miss Preston," said Clarke, "are we to assume that Mr.—ah—" he looked at Rubin's card "—Rubin acts for you?"

"That's correct," she said.

"We were hoping we could ask you some questions," Clarke said.

"Did you receive my message," Rubin asked, "suggesting we make an appointment tomorrow or Tuesday?"

Clarke nodded. "But when we saw Miss Preston's column this morning, we decided we couldn't wait. Especially Mr. Fallow, here."

"And what possible questions can ASIO want to ask me?" Karla asked

"Perhaps we could move somewhere a little more private first," Fallow said quietly, eyeing the departure lounge now crowded with passengers waiting for their flight.

"Sure," said Karla. "I, for one, could use a decent cup of coffee."

"We have an interview room available," said Clarke, "and coffee we can certainly do."

"Let me just clarify something first," said Rubin. "Do you have a warrant to arrest or detain my client? Is she a suspect of some kind?"

Clarke and Fallow shook their heads. "As I already said, all we want to do is see if Miss Preston can help with our investigations," said Clarke.

"Excuse me a moment then, gentlemen, and I'll confer with my client."

Rubin and Karla moved away and talked quietly for a few minutes while Clarke and Fallow eyed them uneasily. When they came back Rubin said, "My client is perfectly happy to cooperate with both of you, although another time and place would be far more convenient. But since you've come all this way let's see what we can cover in thirty minutes."

Declining Clarke's suggested interview room, Rubin led a search for a quiet table in the terminal which, on a busy Sunday afternoon, was not easy to find. The two grey suits eventually agreed to a booth which, though surrounded by customers at other tables, was relatively private. Rubin placed his recorder in the center of the table and switched it on. "First of all, gentlemen," Rubin said, "we admit that my client has entered the country without passing through Immigration, but that is not a criminal offence."

"Provided," Clarke said, "she fronts up to Immigration within two working days."

"Which she will do tomorrow," said Rubin.

"The crew of this boat," Clarke said, "have almost certainly committed an offence by entering Australian waters without permission. And there's always the possibility, of course, that they're smugglers." He began questioning Karla about the boat and the crew—"What kind of boat?" "Do you know its name?" "The names of any of the crew?" But Karla, grateful for the risks they'd taken to bring her back, immediately felt protective of them, and while she answered the rest of Clarke's questions truthfully, he ended up frustrated at how little information he'd obtained—and clearly doubtful she'd told him everything she knew.

"And is this all the baggage you brought with you into Australia?" Clarke asked her, pointing at her backpack and carry bag.

"Except for the things I bought in Cairns, which I'm mostly wearing, yes."

"May I take a look?"

"Any objection?" asked Rubin.

Karla shook her head—relieved that Lynette had remarked, "provided, of course, you didn't bring in anything you shouldn't have," which had prompted her to mail the marijuana to her apartment instead of carrying it on the plane.

Clarke reached for her bags but Rubin stopped him. "I'd appreciate if you would sign a statement afterwards that you have searched her bags. She can take it with her to Immigration tomorrow."

"And if I find something?" Clarke growled.

"Then I imagine you'll arrest her, so it won't matter."

Clarke nodded sourly, and began to go thoroughly through every pocket and corner of Karla's bags.

"And you, Mr. Fallow," Rubin said, "have been very quiet. What brings you here?"

"My interest, Miss Preston," he said in a voice so soft it barely carried above the background chatter, "is in the terrorists. I'd appreciate whatever information you can give me about them."

"There's not much I can tell you," Karla said. "But you could have saved yourself the trip—it will all be in my column tomorrow. In fact," she said pulling out her laptop, "why don't you read it now? Save time—and I don't know that I can tell you much more than what I've already written."

Fallow scowled briefly, but scrolled quickly through her words. "What about the casualty—one Sandeman soldier died."

"I didn't see anything—I kept my head down until the shooting stopped. But just between you and me, it wouldn't surprise me if the Sandeman captain shot the soldier himself—for not shooting back or something like that."

"You expect me to believe that?"

"I'm not saying that's what happened. But from what I saw of the captain and the way he treated his troops, that would be perfectly in character."

"How many terrorists were there? Where was their base of operations? What weapons did they carry?"

"Look, Mr. Fallow, I was with them for just a few hours. It was the middle of the night. They took me to a beach where this boat picked me up. They were simply much nicer people than the Sandeman soldiers—well, certainly nicer than the captain, who was a real arsehole. I was overjoyed to be rescued. I felt safe, something I didn't feel the whole time I was with the Sandeman soldiers. What else can I tell you? It's all in the article— including the fact that their weapons seemed to all come from the Sandeman Army's arsenal."

"Well, gentlemen," said Rubin, "thank you for coming. If there's nothing else, I'm sure we've all got things we'd rather be doing for what's left of our weekend."

*****

IT TOOK THREE DAYS to break the Lebanese.

Every three or four hours, for two days, he was injected with heroin laced, unknown to him, with a trace of crack. On the third day of his confinement he was left alone, shaking for hours with withdrawal symptoms and screaming endlessly for relief. Eventually the three hooded men came in. His eyes were fixed on the needle in de Brouw's hand.

"So," said Nazarov pulling up a chair, "are you ready to talk?"

Kuri nodded desperately, and began to talk. He'd say one thing and then plead for the injection. Nazarov would shake his head. "Tell me more first."

Finally, when Nazarov seemed satisfied, he nodded to de Brouw who took his arm. Kuri's expression of gratitude as he looked at de Brouw almost masked his pain.

"Wait," Nazarov said sharply, pushing de Brouw's hand, and the needle, away. "One other thing."

Kuri's eyes pleaded with Nazarov. "Anything," he croaked.

"What do you know about the Vincent Leung murder?"

"Nothing," he sobbed. "Nothing at all."

"It wasn't your gang who killed him, then?"

"No." His head shook back and forth violently, but his wild, blood-red eyes never left the needle. "We had nothing to do with it."

Nazarov nodded and de Brouw administered the injection. Kuri relaxed as the drug hit him.

As he calmed down Nazarov handed him a copy of that morning's *Mercury*. "Looks like you've just become famous," he said.

Kuri gasped as he saw his face on the front page next to Weinbaum, his face a mask of terror.

"We were planning to take you back home—" said Nazarov.

"No," Kuri shrieked. "The cops will be waiting for me."

Nazarov shrugged. "So where would you prefer?"

"Anywhere else. I don't care. Just not home!"

"Okay."

Kuri continued to grow calmer until he fell into a peaceful, drugged sleep.

Later, in the middle of the night, they gave him another injection and dumped his unconscious body in an alleyway. Some twenty minutes later, the police found him there. "Jesus, what a stink," said one policeman, holding his nose. "Too right," said another. "We'll have to hose this poor bastard down as soon as we get him back to the station."

29 Sixth Uncle

AT NINE AM ON Monday morning, claiming libel by McKurnWatch.com on behalf of their client, Senator Frank McKurn, the firm of ANDREWS, ZOLISKY & SMYTHE, SOLICITORS, sought and were granted a temporary *ex parte* injunction which ordered all internet service providers in Australia to block access to the website McKurnWatch.com.

The suit named as defendants the unknown owners and writers of McKurnWatch.com, the American company that hosted the website and every internet provider in the country, from the major phone and cable companies to the smallest "mom and pop" outfit.

The judge gave them two weeks to serve a libel suit against the website's actual owners, or his order would expire.

*****

"MELBOURNE'S BENT COPPER"—FEATURED on the front pages of Monday's Sykes' and OlssonPress papers—turned out to be a senior Superintendent who was a favored candidate to become Victoria's next Police Commissioner.

When the Melbourne police received a packet of information from the OlssonPress on Sunday afternoon, they went to arrest him. But by then he'd flown the coop: after seeing the Sunday papers, he'd rushed to the airport to grab a flight to Los Angeles where he was detained before he could take an onward flight to Brazil.

Tomorrow, the papers promised, Australia's most corrupt Mayor.

"It seems they've learnt their lesson," said Royn.

"What do you mean by that?" Alison asked.

"They're giving no indication of which city or even which state has the dubious honor of hosting the country's most corrupt mayor."

"I see," chuckled Alison. "So I wonder how many mayors are making hasty travel plans as we speak."

"Indeed," Royn laughed. "I guess we'll find out tomorrow." His laughter came to an abrupt halt as his eyes turned to the copy of the *Mercury* sitting on his desk. "Depending on who it exposes, this corruption series could be very damaging," he said, slamming his fist on top of the newspaper. "But we can capitalize on it."

"The Candyman Inquiry?"

"Exactly," said Royn. "Set up a meeting with Bruce this morning. We can use these exposés to create a sense of urgency. And beef up the enquiry, broaden it, and even go public. We'll show we're already on top of it, and if Bruce goes on TV promising action, those damn foot-draggers will have to fall in line."

"Don't be too optimistic," Alison grinned. "They should also interview Weinbaum, and see if they can get advance copies of the OlssonPress' evidence at the same time as the police. Okay, now . . . have you spoken to Mary yet this morning?"

Royn nodded. "Briefly. She gave me this," he said, the smile disappearing from his face as he picked up a sheet of paper from his desk. "Nine hundred and thirty-seven emails, thanks to that damned Preston woman. And only ten percent of them support our presence in the Sandemans."

"They're still coming in," Alison said.

"Gawd," Royn groaned. "And she really savaged the Sandeman troops this morning. She's making us look so bad I sometimes wish she'd been lost at sea."

"So . . . " Alison said hesitantly, "why don't you invite her in for a chat?"

"Now, why would you suggest that?" Royn asked, looking puzzled. "Isn't she Olsson's current girlfriend?"

"So it seems," Alison said sourly. "But she does have a completely different perspective on the Sandemans—one we're not getting anywhere else. And since she's so hostile, you might be able to do what you've done with other opponents: disarm them with your charm."

"Maybe," Royn said doubtfully. "Though I have the sense it won't work with her."

"You're probably right," Alison said. "From what I hear around the press gallery, her bite is worse than her bark." She passed Royn a sheet of paper from her file. "Take a look at this. It just came in from the geek."

paper supplies received its first new south wales government contract in 1972. just a few months afterwards there was a change of ownership: mckurn's wife had a 45% interest, now owned by the same swiss company that owns the hideaway hotel.

of particular interest: as you can see from the enclosed accounts of the company (which, of course, you should not have access to without a court order) the company has just two customers: the federal and nsw state governments. and its profits are surprisingly low considering that everything they sell is much cheaper down at the supermarket or the big office supply stores.

the most likely reason: a lot of what they sell (pens and pencils for example) is imported from cheap-labor countries like china. by "re-invoicing"—that is, the goods are first sold to a tax haven company, which then on-sells them to the australian company at a significant markup—the REAL profits are banked tax-free in the cayman islands or somewhere like that. if the fuzz were sent in to look at their books, i'm sure that's what they'd find.

"Now, that's very interesting," Royn said as Alison took the sheet from him and fed it into the shredder by his desk. "Looks like a boondoggle to me. But we don't have any proof that McKurn's behind this Swiss company. We can't just go and ask that Swiss lawyer."

"Not much point," said Alison. "But closer to home there's the Cracken connection."

"Ah yes," said Royn, with a broad smile. "If Paul had something to do with that company getting the federal government contract—"

"That would be the end of him." Alison's eyes glittered as she spoke. "And I'm working on two, maybe three avenues of attack."

"The Auditor-General would be one," Royn said.

"Quite so," said Alison. "But we can't just send him a copy of the geek's email—I have to figure out the best approach. Hopefully, I'll have it all worked tomorrow."

"Good," said Royn. "But there's no question in my mind, now, that McKurn's involved in all kinds of shady deals and questionable practices."

"All we need is some bankable evidence," Alison said.

"It will come," said Royn. "After all, just one of our leads needs to pay off."

"We're getting closer," Alison agreed. *But quickly enough?* "The private investigators will begin interviewing Leon Price today, but it'll be a slow process. He's weak, and pleurisy affects the linings of the lungs so he has great trouble breathing, even with oxygen. And even more trouble talking."

"Confession, they say, is good for the soul," Royn chuckled. "so let's just hope he names some names."

*****

"Derek. *Derek!* Make them stop. Oh *please,* make them *stop!*"

Derek Olsson stared open-mouthed at his sister's tear-streaked face on the screen of his laptop. She screamed, the tip of a knife nicking her throat, drawing a single drop of blood.

"Ah-son," a voice he knew all too well chuckled in Cantonese, "if you'd like to see your little sister again in one piece, you'd better give me a call immediately. You know my number. And you know I don't like to wait."

The video clip ended, Jessica's head thrown back, away from the knife-point, her mouth wide open in mid-scream, frozen tears glittering in the harsh light.

Olsson stood, his eyes watering and his stomach heaving as he turned away from the screen; he could feel bile creeping up his throat. "Damn you, Luk Suk," he swore, smashing his fist at the wall . . . but he forced himself to stop in mid-motion, the skin of his knuckles just brushing the target, for fear his fist would go straight through to the other side, and the noise would attract unwanted attention from the other residents of the guest house. He glared at the locked muscles of his arm, feeling the accompanying lines of stress across his shoulders. He willed his arm to relax; slowly, it fell back to his side. But his shoulders didn't follow suit. Aware of a headache beginning at the bottom of his neck, he forced himself to return to the laptop.

Turning off the sound he ran the video again, stopping it frequently to study the picture carefully. Shaking his head he ran through it a third time: there was simply nothing in the background giving any clue of where in the world Jessica might be. Information from the email's header showed that the message had been sent from Bangkok. But the video itself could have been taken anywhere.

He stood again, and paced the room, four steps each way, back and forth, again and again, until he came to a decision. Opening another program on the computer, he donned a set of headphones and dialled a phone number.

"Hullo?"

Damn, he thought, remembering the day he'd stormed out of his grandfather's house in anger at the man he'd once idolized, never to return, *it's him.* Slurring his voice, he asked, "Is Jessica there, please?"

"Ah . . . no."

"Could I speak to Molly, then."

"Wait a moment."

Olsson slumped back in the chair, his body limp. Speaking to his grandfather had sent his tension level notching several rungs higher than his reaction to Jessica's torture.

"Hullo." His mother's voice was faint, hesitant.

"Hi, Mum," he said. "It's Derek."

"Derek? Are you all right? What's going on?—I don't understand any of it."

"I'm fine, Mum. Where's Jessica?"

"Jessica? I don't know."

"When did you see her last?"

"I'm not sure, Derek. A while . . . I think."

"And nobody's gone looking for her?"

"Derek, you're not angry with me are you?"

"Of course not, Mum. But I am worried. About Jessica."

"Worried? Yes, I suppose so. Dad," she said, her voice level in Olsson's ear falling as she turned away from the phone, "where is Jessica, do you know? . . . He doesn't know either Derek."

"Ask him when he last saw her." Olsson could hear a touch of anxiety in his mother's voice as she spoke to her father, though he couldn't make out the words.

"Two days ago, he says," she told him when she turned back to the phone.

"Two days? Has he tried to find her? Has anyone?"

"Well . . . I don't know . . . really Derek, why are you so angry?"

"Jessica's missing, Mum. She's in trouble. I'm sure of it. I want you to do something for me—and for her."

"If I can. . . ." Molly Olsson's voice faltered as she spoke.

"I want you to tell the police that Jessica is missing. Then the police will go looking for her and bring her home."

"That would be nice. I miss her you know. Where could she be?"

"That's why I'd like you to go and tell the police, so they'll find her," Olsson said patiently.

"Well, I don't know if I can do that, Derek. I don't go out very much you know," she said doubtfully. "I don't really like going out any more. . . ."

"Okay, Mum. You can call them. Do you have a pen or pencil handy?"

"Let me see. . . ."

While he waited, Olsson scrabbled through the phone directory until he found the number he was looking for.

"Yes, Derek," his mother said, "I have a pencil."

"Write down this number then. . . ."

"Oh. Wait. I'll have to find something to write on."

Olsson felt his eyes dampen and grabbed at a tissue. Has she been taking her medicine? he wondered. Without Jessica to make sure, maybe not. One thing at a time, that's all she can handle . . . I'll call back later to check. . . . I guess I should be glad that Mum doesn't—can't—really understand what's going on. Small comfort.

"Okay, Derek. Now what do you want me to do with this?"

"Write down this phone number." He repeated the number, slowly, twice, and then made his mother read it back to him. "That's the phone number of the Annandale police station. I want you to call them and tell them about Jessica, okay? They'll know what do to."

"All right, Derek. . . . And when are you going to come and visit me again?'

"In a while, Mum. I can't right now, I'm afraid."

"I know . . . you're always so busy. . . ."

"I'm sorry, Mum. I'll come as soon as I can. Now, could you tell Grandpa I need to talk to him, please?"

"Do you think that's such a good idea, Derek?"

"It's important, Mum. About Jessica."

"Wait a moment, then."

Olsson breathed deeply while he waited for his grandfather, Jack Dent, to come on the line. He felt just a slight tremor when he heard the familiar, grating voice. "Your mother insisted I talk to you. I can't imagine why."

"Jessica's been missing for two days. . . ."

"It's happened before," Dent said disapprovingly.

"For two days?"

"Well . . . no . . . now that you mention it."

"And did she tell you she'd be away?"

"Ah . . . not this time, no."

"Jessica's missing. I want you to take Mum down to the police station *now*, this minute, and file a missing persons report on Jessica."

"And if I don't, what then?"

"Jesus. Just what sort of a grandfather—or father—are you?"

There was a wheezing silence on the other end of the phone.

"Well, just remember," Olsson said angrily, "when you get to the Pearly Gates—" *and the sooner the better,* he thought "—your sins of omission will be weighed just as heavily as your other sins." He cut the line and yanked off the headphones.

I'm sorry, Jess, he thought as he looked at her image still dominating the screen. *This has nothing to do with you.*

Feeling his mind drifting he did a few pushups and stretches to get himself focused again. "Okay," he muttered to himself with a sigh, "I know what I need to do next—so do it."

Putting the headphones back on, he made another call.

"Inspector Durant?" Olsson asked when his call was put through.

"That's right. Who is this?"

"Derek Olsson."

"Olsson? I find that hard to believe." He covered the mouthpiece of the phone. "Trace this call," he said urgently to Simon Lee.

"Today is not April Fools' Day, either, Inspector," said Olsson.

"Okay." Durant drew his words out into a drawl. "So it is you. I must say, though, you've got a nerve."

"I'm calling to report a kidnapping."

"Really," Durant said sarcastically.

"That's right, really. And oh, by the way, go ahead and trace the call by all means. It won't do you any good."

"We'll see. . . . So tell me," Durant asked skeptically, "who's been kidnapped—and what's the evidence?" Durant asked.

"My sister. The evidence is a video I have just received. She's being held by the Golden Dragon Triad. But I've no idea where she's being held. She may not even be in Australia any more."

"Is that the outfit that has put a half-a-million dollar reward on your head?"

"That's right."

"Why?"

"Because they, like you, mistakenly believe I killed Vincent Leung."

"If that's the case, why didn't they simply kill you on Anzac Parade?"

"When you see the video of my sister, I think you'll have an idea of what they had in mind for me."

"What do you plan to do—drop it off at my office?"

"Hardly, Inspector. Give me your email address and I'll send it to you."

"I really don't have time for this sort of thing."

"Call the Annandale police station. Within the hour, you'll find that she's been reported missing."

"I'm rather busy right now, so if I remember, I might give them a call in the morning."

"There's no need to string me along. You'll have plenty of time to trace the call without resorting to tactics like that."

Durant grunted. "Well . . . I'm willing to play along. For a minute or two anyway. So, do you know who's holding her?"

"Yes. His name is Wong Sui-hung, but everyone calls him 'Luk Suk.'"

"Look Sook?" Durant repeated. "What sort of name is that?"

"It's a title, like Godfather. It means sixth uncle—he's the sixth leader of the Golden Dragon Triad. *El Supremo*—of the Hong Kong gang, which makes him leader of the triad world-wide."

"Does he identify himself on the video?"

"No. But I recognize his voice. The Hong Kong police, I'm sure, will be able to confirm that."

"Really, Olsson, I have enough on my plate without going off on another wild-goose chase."

"I've called you, Inspector, because I know you're a straight-shooter. Jessica's been missing for two days and no one knows where she is."

"So why hasn't she been reported missing before now?"

"Because I only just learnt about it. She lives with my mother and grandfather. My mother has Alzheimer's and hardly knows what day of the week it is and my grandfather is an arsehole. I just put a bomb under him . . . metaphorically speaking, I hasten to add. Call him. One phone call will confirm what I've been saying."

"Hmm," said Durant doubtfully. "Well, give me the number . . . maybe there's something in what you're saying."

"There's no 'maybe' about it, Inspector." After dictating the phone number, Olsson continued, "Jessica's life is in danger. Luk Suk is using her as bait to get me. If he gets wind that the police are looking for her, he may simply have her killed."

"Why don't you just make the trade—if that's what he wants? Solve everybody's problems."

"I don't trust him to release her, for one thing—would you?"

"I'm in no position to judge . . . I don't know him as well as you obviously do."

Lee pushed a note into Durant's hand. It's a Sydney number used by one of those voice-over-the-internet phone services, he read.

"So where in the world are you?" As Durant spoke he wrote: See how far you can trace it.

They're working on it, Lee wrote. Durant nodded and indicated that Lee should pick up an extension.

Olsson laughed. "I told you it would be a waste of time. By the time you find out, if you ever do, I'll be long gone."

"Don't count on it," Durant growled.

"So will you give me your email address?"

"Okay," Durant said, a shrug in his voice.

"Check your email shortly."

"I'll find you sooner or later, you know."

"I doubt it, Inspector. I'd say the next time you'll see me will be when I bring you the real murderer of Vincent Leung."

"I already know."

"You've been very cleverly misled, Inspector . . . as my solicitor's email pointed out. You've read it by now, I presume."

"Of course. Speculative questions, not evidence."

"But, as I'm sure you very well know, such evidence can be validly interpreted in more than one way."

"Not, I think, in this case."

"One day, Inspector, you'll have to eat your words."

TEN MINUTES LATER, DURANT'S eyes widened as Jessica Olsson screamed and Lee's expression froze at the Cantonese words. At Durant's impatient glance, Lee hastily translated them.

"Seems like Olsson was telling the truth," Durant growled.

Lee nodded and pointing at the email, "I'll go look for someone who's computer savvy. He may be able to tell, by looking at Olsson's email, where in the world it was sent from."

In another ten minutes Durant had a transcript of Luk Suk's words, learnt that Olsson's call couldn't be traced beyond the Sydney number, and that Olsson's email had been sent from what looked like a web-based email service in Colombia. But it didn't follow that Olsson was in South America. "He could be anywhere in the world, sir. We'd have to get a look at the email service's records to find out where."

"Colombia," Durant groaned as he picked up the phone. "Super, can I see you immediately? It's urgent."

*****

AFTER TWO DAYS, JESSICA could be anywhere.

Olsson checked the date on Luk Suk's email: it had been sent late the previous evening. *I'll have to call him soon,* Olsson thought. *In a day or two . . . ?* He recalled Luk Suk's words, *"And you know I don't like to wait,"* and shook his head; the muscles on his back tightened uncomfortably as he imagined what Luk Suk could do to Jessica. *No . . . tomorrow . . . or would that be too late?*

He paced the room again, in long, impatient steps, spinning on his heels as he reached the wall, back and forth, back and forth, clenching and unclenching his fists as he strode. After a few minutes he stopped, grabbed his helmet and ran down the stairs. Outside, he leapt on his motorcycle and wove through the traffic along Glebe Point Road, heading in the direction of Annandale. "Slow down," he muttered to himself as he noticed the angry glare of a driver he'd cut in front of. "The last thing you want right now is too much attention."

When he neared his grandfather's house in Annandale he slowed the bike to a crawl. *Good,* he thought with a smile at the police car parked in front. As he passed it the bike was almost wobbling from the lack of momentum. He turned at the next corner, looped around the side streets and, a few minutes later, headed towards the house again from the other direction. He could picture his mother inside, probably spooked by the arrival of the police, panicking as she fully realized for the first time that something terrible must have happened to her daughter. He noticed that the bike was slowing, as if of its own accord, so that it would come to a stop behind the police car. *What am I thinking?* he asked himself. He pushed away his urge to go in to comfort his mother and gunned the motorcycle's engine so that it roared along the street with a sharp burst of acceleration.

As he heard the squeal of the back tyre and the throbbing growl of the engine, he let the accelerator grip go and looked quickly right, left, and behind . . . but no one had taken any notice of the sudden noise.

Back in his room, he donned the headphones to make another phone call, which was answered by the surprised voice of Lew Campbell, head of InterFreight and OlssonPress security. "Is that really you, boss?"

Olsson smiled. "That's right, Lew."

"You're taking too many chances, aren't you? And are you sure this call can't be traced?" Campbell asked.

"No. At least, not in time."

"Okay," Campbell said, stretching out his words, "I sure hope you're right. . . . I suppose there's something you want me to do."

"Right. My sister Jessica has been kidnapped by the Golden Dragon Triad. I want you to see if you can trace her—pull out all the stops."

"Okay . . . " Campbell drawled, as if lengthening his words would give him time to think. "Isn't this more a matter for the police?"

"They've already been informed—I called Durant—"

"Jesus, boss, you shouldn't be let out without a minder."

Olsson laughed—but his laugh left a bitter taste in his own mouth. "Just see what you can do, okay Lew?"

"Okay, boss, but. . . ."

"Yes, Lew. What?"

"I used to be a cop, as you know. I'm obliged to tell them about your call."

"I see. . . ." Olsson paused. "Well, go ahead. Let's keep on the right side of the law."

"Very funny, boss," Campbell sighed. "All right, then. I'll do whatever we can to find your sister, though we're not really set up for this sort of thing. First, you'd better tell me everything you know. . . ."

Afterwards, Olsson stared blankly at the computer screen, unaware of the incessant drum roll of the fingernails of his right hand as they *click-click-click*ed on the tabletop. *Lew's probably right,* he thought. "So if he draws a blank, what then?"

His eyes turned to his backpack, sitting on a chair by the table. "Just one thing left, then." He rummaged through the backpack until his hand closed around an external hard drive. He plugged in into the computer, typed the password for access and began going through the files.

"Time to cash in some chips."

30 The Girls from Issan

"CHANGE OF PLANS, GUYS," Nazarov announced.

"What now?" asked de Brouw.

The next target on their list was one of the Greek's henchmen, and they were ready to make the snatch later that day.

Nazarov shook his head. "I don't get it. We'll have to grab the Greek's guy later. We have to pick someone from the Golden Dragon Triad. Here." Nazarov handed Shultz and de Brouw a printout of the email he'd received that morning. "He's even given us a list of their names and addresses—and their pictures." He paused while Shultz and de Brouw read their new instructions.

> It will be tough to make these bastards talk—"omerta" and all that—so you'll probably need to lean on several just to get one to answer. And I'm after this info desperately—preferably yesterday—so please pull out all the stops.

"If they're going to be tougher than the Lebanese—" de Brouw began.

"—we'd better pick up two or three of them at once." Shultz finished.

"Right," said Nazarov. "But at the moment we're only set up to accommodate one at a time."

"It won't be hard to make some alterations," said Shultz.

"True," Nazarov agreed. "But it will take time."

"Which he's not giving us," said Shultz. "I don't like it. We've always been able to plan everything carefully before. That's what's kept us out of trouble."

"And if we stretch ourselves too thin," de Brouw added, "the greater the risk we'll be running that something will go wrong."

"We can take advantage of the 'opt out' clause in his instructions," said de Brouw, looking more cheerful.

"What's that?" the other two asked simultaneously.

De Brouw spread his hands, smiling. "If these Dragon guys are hard to break, they're hard to break. Can't get around that. He's already admitted that up front. So I suggest we hurry—slowly. If he gets impatient we just tell him—'like you said, Boss, it sure is hard to make these bastards talk.'"

*****

"IS THIS KARLA PRESTON?"

"Yes. Who am I talking to?" Karla asked.

"I'm Alison McGuire, from Anthony—"

"Well . . . hullo. This *is* a surprise."

"Yes," said Alison, "for both of us, I imagine."

"And for some reason," said Karla, "unlike some politicians I could name, I don't think you're calling to complain about something I've written."

"No, I'm not," Alison chuckled, "but I could if you like."

"It's hardly a good investment of your time—or anyone else's."

"Miss Preston, I had already figured that out."

"Good. And call me Karla . . . Alison."

"Okay . . . Karla. I'm calling because my boss—"

"Anthony Royn."

"Right. . . . And he'd like to talk to you—"

"Talk to me?" said Karla. "What on earth for?"

"To get more background on the Sandeman Islands. A different perspective."

"Okay. Let me suggest you also invite Robin Cartwright."

Alison laughed. "That's a good idea—though I'm not sure how the minister will take to meeting both of you at the same time. Anyway, he might still be in Toribaya. I'll check. When would work best for you?"

"Later in the week would be fine."

"So where should I send your ticket?" Alison asked.

"Ticket?" Karla replied.

"Airline ticket. Since we've invited you, you're entitled to expenses at least, plus an honorarium for your time."

"If you make the meeting in the afternoon I'll drive down in the morning."

"Those kind of expenses are covered too."

"I guess I'm not making myself clear," said Karla irritably, "so let me put it this way: I'm not a receiver of stolen goods."

"What do you mean by that?"

"I mean that all the government's money is extorted from the people by force, without their consent—"

"'Without their consent'? Alison said heatedly. "This is a democracy, after all."

"So it is," Karla sighed. "But if taxation were truly voluntary, do you think enough money would be collected to pay your salary? We can talk about it some other time if you want to. In any case, I won't be coming to Canberra just to talk to your boss. So I'll pay my own way, okay?"

Strange woman, Alison thought as she put down the phone and turned back to skimming the newspapers. She chuckled at an item in the *Mercury's* gossip column:

> **Conservatives to Dump McKurn?** We hear mutterings from Conservative Party members and bigwigs that Senate President Frank McKurn may be turning into a liability the Conservative Party can't afford. As yet, no one is willing to speak for the record, but a small group of CP senators are sharpening their knives and counting heads to see if a motion to eject McKurn from his comfortable sinecure of President would succeed. If it did, the next move could be to drop him from the CP Senate ticket altogether.
>
> But with his hard core of supporters and his take-no-prisoners style, any move to oust McKurn will end up as a venomous battle royale on the Senate floor.
>
> Watch this space!

Turning to another article, she grinned as she read that the same coalition that had formed to fight Senator Haughtry's bill to extend the libel laws was debating whether to attack McKurn's *ex parte* injunction. The smaller companies were taking the lead, but it looked as if they'd be outvoted by the bigger ones, one spokesman being quoted as saying "it's no skin off our nose."

In another article, a lawyer described McKurn's injunction as being "against every known principle of law, justice and plain common sense," and warned it was the "thin end of the wedge" that could lead to the unrestricted censorship of the internet.

McKurn, she decided, had made a strategic error. Civil libertarians would be up in arms; as "McKurnWatch.com" had been now been named in McKurn's application, "McKurnWatch.com" was now freely mentioned in both the press and on radio and TV, some of the more daring talkback radio hosts even quoting a few juicy paragraphs from the website's emails. The net result, Alison felt sure, was that tens of thousands more people would flock to the website before access was cut off to see what the fuss was all about.

But. . . .

The smile disappeared from her face as she faced *her* reality: *none of this will be of any help to me.*

Just five days left before. . . . She didn't want to think about it. *But I must.*

Dragging her feet, she gathered her files together for her regular morning meeting with Royn.

*****

"Ah-son. What a pleasure to hear from you."

"I got your message," Olsson replied in Cantonese.

"Just in time, too," said Luk Suk.

"Just in time for what?"

Luk Suk laughed. "I was getting ready to send you another message. Since nobody knows your current address, I was thinking of sending it to your mother instead."

"What kind of message?"

"Good question. We hadn't actually decided. Some of my boys were in favor of sending a finger or two. Personally, my preference was an ear."

"Jessica's ear—?"

"Not mine, that's for sure." Luk Suk laughed uproariously at his own comment.

"You'd give my mother a heart attack, you bastard."

"Ah-son, such language," he chuckled. "If you want to see your sister again, alive and in one piece," Luk Suk growled, his voice sounding as though it was dripping with ice, "you've got till Thursday to meet me in Bangkok."

"That's impossible," said Olsson. "But there's something else we need to settle before I even think about meeting you in Bangkok—or anywhere else."

"And what, *Ah-Son,* could that possibly be?" Luk Suk's tone was that of a parent patiently humoring a small child.

"I'm willing to trade places with Jessica. But I will *not* simply walk into your arms while she's still in your possession."

"Naturally, I'll release your sister—when you give yourself up to me," Luk Suk said smoothly. "I'm simply not going to discuss anything else with you."

"And why should I trust you?"

"Maybe you can't," Luk Suk chuckled. "And after all, what's one little sister compared to all the fine men you have cost me. But I'm not giving you any other choice, *Ah-Son.* Is that clear? So Thursday—"

"I can't just wander down to the airport and jump on a plane—I'd be arrested."

"You've got a fistful of false passports, so what's the problem?"

"Sure I do—and I can't get at them right now without alerting the cops. It will take me time to make other arrangements."

"I can get one to you tomorrow."

"Sure you can—if I give you my address. Don't make me laugh. Today is Tuesday. This is not Bangkok or Hong Kong. It will take me a few days to get a false passport that's quality work. So Sunday or Monday is the earliest I could be in Bangkok."

"Thursday, I said, and Thursday I meant," Luk Suk growled. "We can make all the travel arrangements . . . even pay your airfare." Luk Suk laughed.

"That's not very funny. And the answer is no."

"In that case, maybe your mother will have a heart attack."

"No," said Olsson, raising his voice. "You listen to me. You touch one hair on my sister's head—"

"Threatening me is hazardous to your health."

"If you can find me—and if you could we wouldn't be having this conversation. On the other hand, I can find you easily, any time I like. You'll never see me coming. I can wait years, if necessary. You'll spend the rest of your life looking over your shoulder, wondering when the axe will fall."

"Assuming you live long enough."

"My death will make no difference. That's already taken care of. Think of it this way: whatever happens to Jessica will happen to you—with interest. Don't make the mistake of underestimating me: if you keep losing your goons at the rate they've been disappearing, there'll be nobody left to stand in my way."

Luk Suk was silent for a moment. "You've got till Sunday. If you're not here on Sunday, the first package goes to your mother."

Before Olsson could reply, the line went dead.

*****

"WILL YOU LOCK UP?"

Alison looked up to see Mary standing in the doorway. "Am I the last one then?"

"That's right," Mary smiled. "See you tomorrow."

"Bye."

Alison watched Mary all but skipping out the door . . . to go back home to a husband and her little boy. It made her aware that all she had to go home to was an empty apartment, so she decided to stay where she was for a while longer. *Not,* she thought as she gazed through the glass wall at the vacant desks, *that an empty office is much of an improvement.*

Now she was alone, however, she could at least get the day's backlog of phone taps out of the way. But she turned to her laptop a new email caught her eye:

McKurnWatch.com

"The website that ~~must not~~ can now be named" [Thanks, Frankie!]

Good evening Boys & Girls!

Excuse me for taking a moment to blow my own trumpet, but have I hit a nerve or what?

Poor Frankie! He must be losing his marbles. Since he sent his tame legal eagles into court yesterday to try and block access to this website, visits have gone off the scale. They're up so much that McKurnWatch.com could even hit the top one hundred in the next website rankings.

Thanks, Frankie. I owe you one ☺.

Unfortunately (for him) Frankie has completely lost the plot.

Sure, McKurnWatch.com will be "off the air" for a couple of weeks, once the internet service providers get around to blocking it. But I've already set up three alternative websites (listed below) and can just keep setting up more if necessary.

Worse—for Frankie—there's simply no way he or anyone else can stop me sending you continuing installments of his life story. Just to be on the safe side, though, why don't you forward this email to every friend you think would enjoy it, so they can sign up for future installments *now,* avoiding any possible obstacles they might face later on.

Finally, the judge gave Frankie his injunction on the basis that I'm libelling him.

Am I? Granted, I've made the occasional snide remark that might not get past the editor of your family newspaper, but libel assumes I'm telling fibs.

As Frankie well knows, every fact I've published is true—and I can *and will* prove it.

Meanwhile, perhaps we should all spare a thought for poor Frankie: instead of lighting that next joint or popping that next pill, why not drop it in the mail to *him?* (Senator Frankie McKurn, Parliament House, Canberra ACT 2600 will get his attention). After all, he needs it more than you do right now, don't you think?

— The McKurn Watcher

PS. If you do decide to make a small contribution to relieving poor Frankie's angst, remember this: it would be MOST unwise to put your return address on the envelope.

Alison laughed, long and loud, as much with relief as from the imagined sight of a large pile of envelopes addressed to Senator *Frankie* McKurn. *I wonder how many will come in. That will be an interesting statistic.*

McKurn's phone calls were, as usual, mostly routine, salted with the occasional intriguing hint or implication that, if it could be untangled, might lead to something solid—as Melanie, hoping to come across another "nugget," sometimes complained when she and Alison compared notes each day.

And then, Alison reached a call McKurn had made to someone called "Phil":

"Phil, this anti-corruption campaign in the press is damaging—"

"You're not kidding. My circulations have gone through the floor."

"I'm not talking about your fucking newspapers, Phil. I want those goddamn presses stopped."

"You're not the only one."

"Why do you think I called you?"

"Your main problem is Sykes—his papers are the heavy hitters."

"Sykes I can take care of—he knows when to play ball. It's this Olsson bastard I can't touch."

"He's immune to . . . ah . . . pressure, eh?"

"At the moment, yes. So—got any ideas?"

For a long moment, all Alison could hear was the breathing of the two men.

"Maybe. I'll get back to you."

"Make it snappy . . . okay?"

Who was "Phil" . . . and at a Sydney number? Alison wondered. *Newspapers . . . circulations . . . gone through the floor.* "Not Sir Philip French, surely?" she said in surprise.

But no one else named "Phil" owned any Australian newspapers . . . well, maybe in some country town, but none that would lose circulation to the Sykes' dailies. She had met French a few times—but wasn't sure if that's who McKurn was talking to. *If it is French, Royn or Melanie will recognize his voice.*

On a second phone call, made a couple of hours later, Alison heard the same two voices:

"Frank, it'll cost you two hundred grand, half up front."

"Worth it—if it happens. But where's the guarantee? Twenty-five percent down, no more."

"Sorry, Frank, he says it's a take it or leave it offer."

"What the hell. And what, exactly, do I get?"

"You wanted the presses stopped. They'll be stopped."

"And when will this happen?"

"Saturday at the latest, maybe Friday."

"Okay, Phil. That'll have to do."

I should tell Derek. But anger toward him, rising from within, held her back. *All that really matters,* she finally decided, *is that if I can stop McKurn from getting something he wants, I MUST do it.*

Derek: I have wind that McKurn and French (I think it's French) are going to somehow "stop your presses" by Saturday or maybe Friday night. I have no idea how, but the "why" is simple enough: your papers' corruption exposés—Alison.

She encrypted her text with Olsson's public key, and sent it to him. Just as she finished with her emails, she saw a reply in her inbox:

Hi Alison: Thanks for the "heads up"—but what exactly are you involved in to be getting such information? Listening to their phone conversations? Or what? My offer to help is still open—and always will be. But from Thursday I'll be out of touch for a week or so—so if there's ANYTHING you think I might be able to do, please let me know right away—Love, Derek.

Love, Derek.

She felt tears forming in the corners of her eyes, losing herself in the remembered feeling of being enfolded in his powerful arms, everything bottled up in her heart spilling out. *He'd listen. He'd understand . . . in a way no one else ever does. . . .*

No memory of the disputes and sometimes-bitter arguments that often followed their previous separations entered her mind. Only the thought, *He does care about me,* as she looked at his email, and she fondly savored the memories of those moments when she'd been overjoyed to see him. . . .

Derek Olsson had skipped school and Aikido for three or four days. To her own annoyance, Alison missed seeing him around. As she stepped out of the *dojo* that evening so many years ago, she was surprised at the stab of pleasure she felt when she saw Derek Olsson lounging by the door.

Derek seemed to snap to attention as he saw her. "Alison," he said, his voice urgent. "Can I ask you something?"

"So long as it's not another one of your infernal questions," she grinned, making no attempt to disguise her pleasure.

"No. It's about my mother. A favor. I wonder if you could talk to her."

"Why? And why me?"

"Remember I told you I signed up for Aikido to defend myself from my father?"

Alison nodded, her eyes focusing on his cheek as if to see whether his bruise was still there.

"I threw him out of the house."

"You did what?" she said.

"I threw him out. Tuesday night. And we haven't seen him since."

"My God—you're full of surprises."

"We moved to my grandparents' house—but Mum's in a fragile state."

"But—what could I do?"

"A lot. I hope. If you have time, can I tell you about it now?"

It seemed so natural to go with him to the coffee shop around the corner, to enjoy the sudden warmth of his closeness and to listen as much to the cadence of his voice as to his actual words as he explained, leaning forward, earnestly, ". . . so you see, Ma's happier than I've ever seen her. And she feels safe—but it's like she's gone back to being a child again. I get the feeling she doesn't ever want to leave her parents' home again. What's worse, though, is that she never does anything, never initiates anything. She's so passive it's like. . . ." Derek waved his hand, groping for a word. "It's like she not all there."

"You really love your mother, don't you."

"I—I . . . don't know." Derek's eyes gazed unfocused into the distance. "When I was little—" his voice was almost whispering as if he were talking to himself rather than her, and Alison had to lean closer to hear him "—Ma would sometimes try and protect me when Dad got angry. But all that meant was that she got beaten up too. And more and more . . . well, she just wasn't there. Most of the time I wished I was an orphan."

Alison jerked back in her chair. "I. . . . I just can't imagine feeling like that." Slowly, her hand reached out to gently touch the shadow of the bruise on his cheek. "But you do care for her—I can see that."

"Yes," said Derek softly, clasping her hand tightly, "I do."

Breathing heavily, he slowly straightened up, lowering her hand to rest on the table as he moved. "Your skin is so soft."

Alison gently loosened his grip, but her warm expression didn't change as she asked, "I'd be happy to talk to your mother. But—why me?"

"Well . . . it's because . . . Aikido. It's the only thing I can think of. Ma's so afraid. She's afraid that Dad will come around one day when everyone else is out. She won't go outside by herself—even to the shops nearby—because she'd afraid Dad might be lurking around a corner. So I was thinking, if she picked up just a few defensive moves, she might stop feeling so frightened. Grandpa and I suggested it, but she wouldn't hear of it. So I thought you—I mean, with your strength. . . ." He shrugged helplessly. "I can't persuade her, but you could. . . ."

"I know what you're getting at," she said, an edge to her voice. "But—maybe I can."

"Thank you," he said with a sigh of relief. "So any time you like, just let me know."

Alison stood up. "Let's do it now."

"Now?" Derek looked up at her in surprise. "Sure," he smiled. "My grandparents' home is over on the other side of Annandale. I can drive you."

ALISON AND DEREK'S MOTHER disappeared into Molly's room, so Derek randomly grabbed a few books from his desk. As he carried them back to the living room, he put his ear to his mother's door, but all he could hear was a faint murmur of conversation.

He was idly flicking through one book after another, without any of them engaging his interest, when he heard a grunt. He looked up to see his grandfather glaring at him.

"Oops," he said, and quickly moved to the sofa: without thinking, he'd sat in Jack Dent's favorite chair.

Dent glanced at Derek's books as he sat down. "What are these—Kant . . . Wittgenstein . . . *Karl Marx?* What on earth are they teaching at your school—communism?"

"Hardly, Grandpa. They're philosophy books, not schoolbooks—I'm trying to make sense of it all."

"Philosophy," Dent snorted. "A waste of time. You know, I left school when I was fourteen and never regretted it—and never looked back. Guts, that's what you need. All this highfalutin' nonsense they teach kids these days. . . ."

Dent stopped in mid-flow, his face lighting up with a smile. Derek turned to see Alison standing in the doorway, tears in her eyes. "I'm sorry, Derek." She shook her head. "In time . . . maybe. . . ." she shrugged. And then noticing Dent, she smiled, "Oh, you must be Derek's grandfather."

"That's right," he said, standing up. "I'm Jack Dent." He held out his hand with a slight bow, eyeing Alison appreciatively as he moved.

"This is Alison McGuire, Grandpa," said Derek. "She came to talk to Ma."

Derek noticed the warmth draining from Alison's face at Dent's look; she took his hand and shook it coldly.

"Welcome to our modest home. Could I offer something—tea, or coffee, or a soft drink?"

"Thank you, Mr. Dent," Alison said thoughtfully, looking at him with a new interest. Then, she smiled sweetly at him. "I'm afraid I have to get back home now, so perhaps another time, okay?"

"Certainly," Dent said, his smile broadening. "And call me Jack."

"I'll drive you back, of course," said Derek.

"A good idea, Derek," Dent said. "You can never be too sure these days, young lady."

Alison smiled at Dent demurely with a slight flutter of her eyelashes. "Goodbye, then . . . Jack," she said.

"Bye, Alison."

"That's a relief," Derek sighed as they stepped outside. "I had to get out of there—sometimes Grandpa just drives me up the wall," he growled.

"Oh, I don't know, he seems rather like a puppy," she said distastefully.

"So that's what you were doing."

"What?" she asked innocently.

"Charming Grandpa—and turning him into a puppy."

"It was so easy," she laughed.

Derek shook his head. "What were you going to say about Ma?—he didn't even ask!"

Alison's face turned serious and the tears came back to her eyes. "She's so frightened . . . I don't think it would matter what she had—a black belt, a shotgun . . . she's so scared of your Dad she'd just freeze up and let him do whatever he wanted."

"I see," said Derek thoughtfully. "She's always been afraid of Dad, for as long as I can remember."

Alison found a support group for battered women. "But it's in the evenings," Molly protested. She agreed to go only if Alison and Derek escorted her there and back. After a few meetings Alison told Derek, "She just sits there, hardly saying a word. I think the only reason she goes is that she likes to see you and me together."

"She likes you, Alison. A lot. She's always talking about you."

"And hinting . . . ?"

Derek blushed. "Yes, I must admit, she does that."

*****

"YES, THAT'S RIGHT. YOUNG—and Asian. Thai if you can. . . . Okay, I'll be here."

Hanson McLeod stretched out on the bed of his room at Canberra's Lakeside Hotel and waited. He hadn't known what to think of this particular assignment to begin with. Everything was so mysterious, so hush-hush. Except in an emergency, all communication was by encrypted email; instructions came the same way. They had no idea who their client was; they'd been hired by a lawyer who'd refused to tell them. "As far as you're concerned," he'd said, "I'm your client."

The target of the investigation was the powerful federal senator, Frank McKurn, making him wonder if they were unwittingly involved in some complex political back-stabbing operation; the extent of the investigation, tying up over half their investigators nation-wide, combined with the client's "money no object" mentality, made him think that their real client might be a government department . . . in which case it was possible everything they were doing could be illegal. The high-quality phone taps they were being sent reinforced that hypothesis.

But as they learnt more about McKurn, McLeod ceased wondering about the client's identity and became keen to put McKurn away for bonking underage girls. Even if all they could prove was that he frequented prostitutes, the resulting scandal would force him to resign.

About half an hour later, his reverie was interrupted by the doorbell. A young Thai girl stood timidly in the corridor, entering the room reluctantly with a fearful glance behind her.

McLeod just nodded without saying anything and went to open the connecting door to the next room. To the girl's surprise, a middle-aged Asian woman came through. The girl looked confused and a little frightened, as though she assumed she was going to be required to participate in some kinky group sex.

Smiling warmly, the Asian woman said in Thai, "Please come in. Take a seat."

The girl froze and gasped; only after a long moment did she partially regain her composure and clasp her hands together, bow her head, and diffidently utter the respectful Thai greeting, *"Sawadee-ka."*

The older woman returned the traditional Thai *wai* with the same bow. "My name is Orawan," she said, and began talking quietly in Thai.

The girl listened, perched on the edge of a chair, a bird ready to fly away at the slightest hint of danger. Now and then she nervously eyed McLeod, sitting quietly on the other side of the room practicing invisibility, following the conversation as best he could in his broken Thai.

It took fifteen to twenty minutes for Orawan to gain the young girl's trust. The girl began to relax, responding in short, curt sentences—and forgot about McLeod. When Orawan promised her, "You'll *never* have to go back, and *I'll* keep you safe," the young girl burst into tears, became demonstrative, and talked non-stop for quite a while.

At one point, McLeod saw Orawan gesture towards him and he understood she was telling the girl, "he's my husband."

"Hanson," Orawan said, "this is Lawan."

Lawan turned towards him with a broad smile and bowed, saying, *"Sawadee-ka."*

"Sawadee-krap, Lawan," McLeod replied, returning Lawan's *wai*.

Then the two women continued talking as if he'd ceased to exist.

Orawan came from Issan region of Thailand, bordering Laos and Cambodia. In addition to Thai, she spoke Issan, a Laotian dialect, and passable Khmer. Almost half the girls in the bars in Bangkok came from Issan, but Orawan was not one of them. Her father was a shopkeeper who was prosperous by Issan standards; she had won a scholarship to Mahidol University in Bangkok; on graduation she had joined the police force. She'd been among the Thai police who'd attended a criminology course in Melbourne, which is where McLeod, then a member of the Victorian police, had met her.

After their marriage, Orawan made a name for herself in Melbourne by becoming the first Thai policewoman in the Victorian police. She and McLeod had broken up several prostitution rackets built on sex slavery. From the nature of Orawan's occasional glances, McLeod knew they were on the verge of breaking up another.

Orawan showed a picture of McKurn to Lawan, who immediately giggled uncontrollably. When she'd calmed down she spoke to Orawan so rapidly that McLeod could hardly make out a single word. But whatever she said caused Orawan to laugh raucously. McLeod continued to wait, knowing he'd share in the joke later on. When nearly an hour had gone by since the girl had come into the room, McLeod pointedly looked at his watch several times until Orawan caught his hint and turned to face him.

"Lawan is from Issan," Orawan told McLeod. "She is eighteen and has been here for about three months. Same old story—lured by stories of riches, passport and all ID's taken and effectively imprisoned when she arrived. She was repeatedly raped and beaten into submission—and turned into a heroin addict to keep her on the leash. And beyond a few dollars, she's yet to see any of her earnings—all sorts of bills and fees she has to pay back first. So she was told."

"Any other girls like her?"

Orawan nodded. "Two more from Issan; a Cambodian and a Vietnamese. But she doesn't know where they're housed. She can describe the house, but it could be just about anywhere in Canberra. A minder takes the girls to the client and brings them back."

McLeod nodded. "Let's think this through. Do we have enough to nail this so-called agency?"

"I'd say we have enough for the police to get a warrant to raid it," Orawan said.

"Quite likely," McLeod agreed. "But in terms of the evidence we have, it will be her word against everybody else's. So—"

"I know what you're going to say next and the answer is 'No,'" Orawan said sharply, her eyes suddenly on fire. "She *can't* go back. I've already promised her that she won't have to. And if she did, could she keep a secret like this?" Orawan shook her head. "If the word gets out, the girls will all be in Perth or Adelaide or somewhere before we can move in."

"Agreed," said McLeod, knowing there was no point in debating with Orawan when she'd made up her mind. "Lawan will be okay. In the worst case she'll be deported back to Thailand—"

"Penniless. We have to make them pay."

"We've done that before," McLeod smiled. "But we need one more witness."

"I almost forgot," Orawan said. Scrabbling inside her handbag, she found the picture she was looking for and showed it to Lawan.

"Phuong!" Lawan shrieked, throwing a series of questions at Orawan.

"It's the Vietnamese girl," Orawan told McLeod, placing a quieting hand on Lawan's arm. It was a dim picture they'd taken late last week of a girl entering McKurn's apartment building.

"Good," said McLeod. "Unfortunately, it doesn't prove that she was going to visit McKurn."

"I know," said Orawan, her voice downbeat. "But we basically have no choice. It's a condition of your investigator's licence that you inform the police the moment you have any evidence of a crime."

"What about the minder?" McLeod asked. "Does she know where he is?"

"He'll be downstairs, waiting for Lawan," Orawan said. "Prostitution is legal, but forcing girls into prostitution isn't. Maybe he'll squeal to save his own skin."

"Can she describe him?"

"She already did. Big, muscled, light hair, and a tiny scar on the side of his forehead." Orawan traced a short line on her own forehead, near the hairline, and Lawan nodded eagerly.

"Okay then. It's up to me to persuade the police to act immediately. But first, what was so funny about McKurn?"

Orawan smiled. "The girls apparently liked him—at least, as much as you can like a john. He was a big tipper, but the best part was that it was all over in five minutes."

McLeod chuckled. "If that gets out, McKurn will never live it down."

The day he arrived in Canberra, McLeod paid a courtesy call on an old friend, Inspector Zack Latham of the ACT (Australian Capital Territory) Police. "Let's hope Zack will come to the party," he said as he picked up the phone.

"If you can persuade my father to agree to our marriage," Orawan beamed, "you can persuade anyone."

Thirty minutes later, the ACT police took Lawan's minder into custody. "We know him quite well," a police sergeant said to McLeod as the minder was taken into an interview room after they'd heard Lawan's testimony with Orawan translating. "I think he'll sing."

An hour later, the police raided the offices of APHRODITE'S, arresting the woman known as "Gladys" and carting all the paperwork away for further investigation.

*****

ALISON LEARNT ABOUT THE raid the next morning, spying the headline splashed across the top of the *Canberra Guardian* while she was out jogging. When she returned home, she found a report from the Melbourne private investigators in her inbox.

Now, all she had to do was wait until McKurn's name was discovered in the agency's records.

31 Merchants of Death

Two days before, Sandeman troops on St. Christopher's Island suffered heavy casualties in a coordinated attack by two Islamic separatist groups which had, previously, spent their energy fighting each other.

Australian and Sandeman troops poured into St. Christopher's Island and Zulu base in the first major operation of the new "joint" operation command. The coastal towns were easily secured; troops were now moving inland to encircle and flush out the guerrillas.

Five helicopters sat on the pad at Zulu base: two Tiger helicopter gunships, known as "Firebirds"; two Sikorsky S-70s transports; a third Sikorsky, large red crosses painted on its sides, waited for a call that had yet to come. A Navy patrol boat was moored at the end of a makeshift jetty, and a frigate patrolled off the shore of St. Christopher's Island as a floating artillery base. Two unmanned Predators circled St. Christopher's 24 hours a day.

Jeremy McGuire sat in the Zulu base command center, one eye on the LCD screens showing the Predators' surveillance, the other on the clock. His shift would end soon and he intended to go body-surfing on the beach before breakfast.

As part of the face-saving compromise that made "joint" operations possible, all Australian officers were bumped up a rank so Sandeman officers with less training and experience didn't outrank them. Brigadier Thierry was now Major-General, Jeremy a captain—the equal of his Sandeman counterpart, Captain Ranga N'gaandi, sitting to his left.

Jeremy's reverie was rudely interrupted by the radio. "Zulu, this is Alpha One. We're under fire. Request a Firebird ASAP, over."

Jeremy looked at the map of St. Christopher's Island. Alpha Platoon's position was marked about a third of the way to the center of the island.

In moments "Firebird One" was lifting off; a series of flashing red dots on the LCD screen indicated targets where "Marauder"—the Navy's floating artillery base—would lay a barrage around Alpha platoon's position.

Colonel Lucas Cantrell came striding into the room. Except for his slightly puffy eyes, dark stubble of beard, and the fact that he was still doing up the top button of his shirt, Cantrell looked as though he'd just walked off the parade ground. "Jeremy, Ranga," he nodded. "Please bring me up to date."

Cantrell briefly studied the map as he listened to the situation report and then asked, "Has Major . . . uh, Colonel Raymond asked for anything?"

"Not yet, sir," said Jeremy.

"Okay, I'll have a word to him."

Cantrell sat behind and talked to Raymond—the officer commanding the forces on St. Christopher's Island. "He says he has everything under control—at the moment,"

Cantrell called out. "But get two platoons ready to go and warm those choppers up so they can take off at the drop of a hat."

"Yes, sir," Jeremy and N'gaandi said in unison.

The radio crackled again: "Zulu, this is Alpha One. Got one of those toy birdies on standby?" A flashing red cross appeared on one of the screens near Alpha platoon's position, as the coordinates were flashed across from the platoon leader's laptop. "That's a machine gun nest. Appreciate if you could get rid of it for us, over."

On a second screen, infrared imaging from a Predator showed the outlines of four human figures as red blobs. Streaks of bright flashes streamed from a bright red outline—the heat of a machine gun barrel—from a point in front of one of the figures.

On his laptop out in the field, Jeremy knew, the platoon leader was seeing the same picture. Jeremy looked at Cantrell, who nodded. "Pass him over to Sarge," Jeremy said, indicating Sergeant Bowman at the console behind him. "He's itching to try out his new toy."

The red cross moved to just behind the infrared shapes and the camera zoomed out so that Alpha Platoon's position was visible. A line appeared overlaid on the picture indicated the distance was 193 meters.

"Alpha One," said Bowman, "this is ToyBird One. Howzat? Over."

"Perfect. Over."

Jeremy turned his head and nodded to Bowman. "Alpha One, you'd better duck now. Over."

"We're already ducking. . . . Shit a fucking brick. You got the bastards. . . . Uh, over."

"You're most welcome. ToyBird One, over and out."

"That," said N'gaandi, "is abso-bloody-lutely amazing," as everybody in the control room applauded and Sergeant Bowman took a bow.

"Captain," Colonel Cantrell's voice boomed from behind them, "you are abso-bloody-lutely right." Turning to the two Predator operators he said, "Let's see what else your babies can do."

"Sir?" asked Bowman, slightly puzzled.

"Those bastards are going to be running away now. That's my guess. See if you can find them—and give those Firebirds some target practice."

"You bet, sir."

As a figure was caught by a Predator's camera, the operator spoke into his microphone. A moment later the figure stopped moving. "Eerie," Bowman said, "like watching a movie with the sound off."

Cantrell had moved to stand behind the two sergeants operating the Predators. One of the screens now showed a file of three figures moving rapidly up a hill. The operator was about to pass the location to a Firebird when Cantrell said, "Wait. Let's see where those bastards are going."

The screen followed the three figures until, one after the other in rapid succession, they disappeared. "Can you zoom in on that spot, Sarge?" Cantrell asked.

"Sure can," said Bowman.

The screen showed nothing. Then Bowman switched the resolution to regular light and the screen turned grey-green in the early morning sun with a black patch in the center.

"What do you make of that?" Cantrell asked.

"I'd say," said Bowman, "it's a cave—or a tunnel entrance."

"That's what I figured. So why don't you two flyboys each put one of your zingers right down that hole."

"Yes, sir," both sergeants said enthusiastically.

The LCD screens on both sides of the map now showed the same picture. Red crosses appeared over the tunnel mouth and a minute later there was a tiny, momentary streak of red followed by some flashes of light. Thirty seconds later was another flash of light, and the grey-green above the tunnel mouth seemed to slide downwards. "You've caused a landslide by the looks of it," said Cantrell.

"I don't think there'll be anyone coming out of that hole again," Bowman grinned.

"Good work. Some toys, eh?"

"Sir. Colonel." Jeremy's weak voice floated under the loud yells of agreement of the Predators' operators.

Cantrell had been aware that the radios had been going nonstop while he'd been watching the Predators. He turned in response to Jeremy's unusually weak voice to see both captains looking at him. Jeremy's face was pale.

"What's up, son?" Cantrell asked softly.

When Jeremy, appearing frozen with shock, didn't speak, N'gaandi said, his voice and his body shaking, "They took some prisoners, and one of them blew himself up, taking three of our guys with him."

"A fucking *kamikaze*," Colonel Cantrell growled. "Right. We're going to go in and wipe those bastards out."

*****

"Just answer one question," said Nazarov, "and you can go back to your buddies in one piece."

The Chinese man was handcuffed and tied to a bed in a second room of the "safe house" that Nazarov, Shultz, and de Brouw had hastily converted into a prison. He looked at Nazarov incuriously, without any reaction.

"All we want to know," said Nazarov, "is what you did with Jessica Olsson."

The man's name was Kung Chee-wah. Now that Vincent Leung was dead, he was third in the hierarchy of Sydney's Golden Dragon Triad. They'd grabbed him earlier that morning in the parking lot of his Rushcutters Bay apartment building, leaving his bodyguard unconscious on the concrete floor.

"Of course, we do give you a choice," said Nazarov, pointing to de Brouw who held up a hypodermic needle. Kung's eyes moved to the needle and then back to Nazarov. He didn't appear to be the slightest bit interested in either the question or the needle.

"Do you know what's in that syringe?" Nazarov asked. Kung's face stayed a study in blankness. "Heroin. A couple of days of that and you'll be hooked for life, you understand. Of course, if you just tell me where Jessica Olsson is, then we'll drop you back where we found you."

Kung didn't move.

Nazarov nodded; de Brouw grabbed an arm and emptied the syringe.

"I'll go and check on our other guest," said Shultz.

Nazarov and de Brouw heard Shultz' scream and ran into the room where they'd imprisoned Alvin Chong, the first member of the Golden Dragon Triad they'd picked up just the previous day. He was a short, stocky Chinese man built like a Mr. Universe contestant. Shultz was pinioned on top of him, one of Chong's arms squeezing Shultz' throat. Blood poured from a wound on the side of Shultz' head. Shultz was breathing hoarsely, his eyelids fluttering, almost unconscious.

Chong was still chained to the bed: chains bound his ankles together and tightly to each side of the bed. His wrists were chained separately to allow him a little freedom of movement. Nazarov and de Brouw could see that the chain on the arm pinning Shultz was still firmly fixed to the railing of the bed. But as de Brouw, who was ahead of Nazarov, neared Chong his second arm lashed out and the chain swung unerringly toward de Brouw's head. De Brouw ducked just in time for the swinging end of the chain to miss his ear, but he staggered as it grazed the top of his head. Chong yanked the chain back, wrapping it around de Brouw's neck, pulling de Brouw so he fell on top of Shultz. The bed creaked under the sudden weight, De Brouw struggled, but Chong managed to pin one of de Brouw's legs with his knees, and his other hand gripped de Brouw's head, turning it hard.

"Want me to break your buddy's neck?" he asked Nazarov.

Nazarov shook his head.

"You'd better undo these chains then."

Nazarov hesitated. Chong's cold black eyes just looked distantly at Nazarov, but there was a faint smile on Chong's lips as he slowly twisted de Brouw's head a little further towards breaking point.

"Okay, okay. You win," said Nazarov. He pulled a bunch of keys from his pocket and leant down by the Dragon man's ankles. "Feet first, okay?" he said.

Nazarov's body obscured the Dragon man's view of his hands. With one hand Nazarov jangled the keys near Chong's ankles while his other hand reached into Shultz' boot and pulled out the thin, sharp blade Shultz always carried there—and jammed it up to the hilt into Chong's scrotum.

Chong screamed, his fingers loosening their grip on de Brouw's head for just a second. That was long enough for Nazarov to slap de Brouw's head out of the way, bring up the knife and plunge it into the side of Chong's neck, upwards, into the brain. Chong spluttered, his eyes looking at Nazarov in defeat, and then his body went limp.

Nazarov unwound the chain from around de Brouw's neck. De Brouw slumped to the floor beside the bed, rubbing his neck with one hand and the top of his head with the other. "Boy, that was close." he grunted. "Too damn close."

Nazarov nodded. "Shultz looks in a bad way," he said.

While de Brouw recovered, Nazarov went for the first aid kit. "It's only a surface wound," he said as he bandaged it while Shultz still lay on Chong's still and now smelly body. "But he's going to have a sore head for a while."

"Just as well he has a thick head," de Brouw said.

"I heard that," Shultz moaned.

"Mats is right," Nazarov grinned.

"Fuck you, too," said Shultz, groaning as he tried to lift his head.

"As I came in he just whipped up that damn chain," Shultz said later, woozy from the pain-killers he'd taken, "and almost throttled me. If you'd come in a minute or two later, I'd have probably been dead. Jesus, he was strong."

"He sure was," said de Brouw pointing at the broken wooden leg in the middle of the bed against the wall to which his wrist had been chained. "That's how he got free. He must have yanked on it till it gave."

"Amazing," said Shultz. "And pumped full of drugs too."

After a moment of silence, when they marvelled at Chong's strength, resistance, and their lucky escape, Shultz said, "So we're down to one."

"I don't think he'll talk either," said Nazarov.

"Doesn't look like it," said de Brouw. "We'd better get ready to pick up a third Dragon guy." Pointing at Chong's body. "And what do we do with him?"

"Make him disappear," said Nazarov.

****

Karla Preston strode into Anthony Royn's office suite displaying none of the diffidence or hesitancy of the first-time visitor—nor was there the slightest touch of the awe that even successful businessmen and popular celebrities usually exhibited in the inner sanctums of power. Rather, Alison thought, she moved as if she were the owner and had every right to be there, or with the indifference of someone walking along the aisles of a supermarket. Alison couldn't quite make up her mind which impression was the more accurate.

Unusually, as Alison came out of her office to greet the visitor, it was she who felt slightly hesitant—and strangely apprehensive. Was it the knowledge that she was about to meet Olsson's current girlfriend? Or was she nervous about confronting the person whose writing was so unforgiving, so scornful and belligerent, so . . . opinionated? Alison searched for some sign of the acid tongue, the sardonic wit and the mocking tone of her columns—and failed to find it.

Karla Preston was smiling, stopping to chat gaily with each person she passed. Alison overheard Mary talking about her little boy as though Karla were a long-lost friend. Nor did she bear the slightest resemblance to a harridan or a harpy. On the contrary, she looked surprisingly plain, ordinary and unmemorable, except for her uneven suntan— bronzed arms and face but pale white shoulders—and her outrageous dress: a flowery, multi-hued shock of bright colors that, if more subdued, was the sort of design you'd expect a grandmother, not a young woman, to be wearing. It was a simple shift, gathered with a chain at the waist, more suitable for wearing to the beach than to an office of any kind, topped off by an equally outrageous wide-brimmed straw hat. Although her clothes seemed impertinently out of place, the overall effect was, Alison had to admit, surprisingly elegant, spoiled only by the battered, nondescript carry-all slung over one shoulder.

Karla Preston's only physical attribute that was in any way unusual was her height, but unlike many tall women she made no apology for being tall. Rather, she emphasized this by wearing sandals with high heels.

And then, there were her eyes. . . .

It was an unusual sensation, Alison thought, to have to tilt her head up to look at another woman's face. As she did, she felt Karla's eyes searching hers as if they were X-rays, and she had the cold sensation that Karla was looking directly into her, inside her, without asking permission, with the sense she wasn't going to take "No" for an answer. The last time Alison remembered feeling as exposed as she did now was with Derek Olsson. His look was warm and understanding; Karla's was razor-edged and invasive.

"Who twisted your soul?" Karla said to her softly, in a voice that no one else could hear.

"Wh-what?" Alison found she couldn't move, as though Karla's eyes held her pinned, until Robin Cartwright's voice broke the spell. With relief, she turned away with the feeling that, at some level, she knew exactly what Karla meant.

"Very nice," said Cartwright as he ambled into the office. "Plush. So . . . this is what you get for our money, eh?" Spying Karla, he planted a kiss on her cheek, all the while looking appreciatively at Alison. "Karla, I insist you introduce me to this gorgeous creature."

"Alison McGuire, this is Robin Cartwright," Karla said.

"Miss McGuire," Cartwright said, taking Alison's hand with both of his, "this is such a pleasure. And as I'm a stranger to Canberra—"

"You're such a liar, Robin," Karla laughed. Turning to Alison, she said, "He's been coming to Canberra since before you were born—probably since before your father was born. So just ignore him, Alison. Unfortunately, he's so thick-skinned that doesn't make him go away."

"You're such a spoilsport, Karla," Cartwright protested.

"I don't think I'm telling Alison anything she hadn't already figured out the moment she saw you."

"If I can interrupt this love fest," Alison said with a wooden smile as she gently took her hand back from Cartwright's grip, "perhaps we can get down to business."

As if on cue, Anthony Royn stepped out of his office. "Minister," said Alison, "this is Karla Preston . . . Robin Cartwright."

"Thank you for coming." Anthony Royn's smile encompassed both his visitors, but his eyes focused on Karla. "Miss Preston," he said. As he held out his hand and Karla shook it, some sort of electricity seemed to pass between them. Royn looked at her appreciatively—a little longer than was polite—and Alison had the fleeting impression that if they'd been rabbits, they'd already be over in the corner.

Then Alison noticed the way Doug Selkirk's eyes, and those of the other men in office, followed Karla wherever she went—when there was nothing in her plain looks, her almost-masculine, dominating demeanor, and her gravelly, unfeminine voice that should attract a male's attention. Karla, she realized, had an effect on men similar to Royn's effect on women: when Royn looked at a woman whom men would dismissively describe as "an old bag" her eyes would light up as though she just been given the honor of being recognized as the sexiest creature on earth.

"Mr. Cartwright," said Royn. "I've heard a lot about you. . . ."

"None of it good, I'm sure," Karla smiled.

Alison stifled a grin at Royn's expression: he was clearly unsettled at the direct, almost contemptuous way these two journalists were treating him. She toyed with the impulse to sit back and let this meeting take its natural course but decided she really should come to Royn's rescue. "Would you like some tea or coffee?" she asked Karla and Cartwright as she took a step towards Royn's office. "And shall I hang up your hat, Karla?"

"Yes, come on in," said Royn as he took the hint.

"Tea, please," said Karla.

Alison's eyes narrowed slightly in surprise as Karla took off her hat and she saw that the reporter's faded blonde hair was mousy brown at the roots. *Is she really a fake after all?* she asked herself.

Karla caught her reaction, her free hand automatically touching her head, and chuckled. "Disguise," she said. "In the Sandemans."

"I see," Alison nodded, feeling as though Karla had read her thoughts.

"I'll have a Scotch, thanks," said Cartwright.

"At this time in the morning?" Alison asked in surprise.

"You want me to talk?" Cartwright grinned. "Talk requires lubrication."

"I'll see what we can do."

As Karla and Cartwright settled into the sofa, Royn opened a cabinet containing an array of bottles and glasses. Spying a bottle of Black Label, Cartwright said. "Black Label, thanks. And make it a triple while you're at it." At Royn's raised eyebrow, Cartwright added, "Think of it as a tax refund."

Royn shrugged, splashed a large measure of Scotch into a glass and, after a moment's hesitation, brought both the glass and the bottle of Black Label over and placed them on the coffee table in front of Cartwright. At the same time, Alison and Mary came in with the other drink requests.

"Ah," said Cartwright, saluting Royn with his glass, "a man after my own heart."

"Not exactly," Royn smiled. "Cirrhosis of the liver will remove one small annoyance from the daily mountain of newsprint."

"We'd miss you, Robin," Karla said, placing a hand on his knee. "But not that much."

Cartwright groaned, Royn chuckled, and Alison grimaced as she took a seat at one end of the coffee table, Royn on her right and Karla to her left.

"Miss Preston—" Royn began.

"Karla. And I don't know if you're aware of this, we've actually met once before."

"We have?" Royn said with surprise. "If we had, I'm sure I'd remember you."

"Just after you became Minister for Justice and Customs, you gave a talk at Sydney University. And afterwards a young girl asked you a very pointed question—"

"And you—?"

"—asked the question."

SYDNEY UNIVERSITY'S GREAT HALL was packed when Anthony Royn walked up to the podium, throwing his jacket on a chair and loosening his tie as he began to speak. "To put it in a nutshell, as Minister for Justice and Customs it's my job to protect Australia's borders and to protect you from criminals. . . ."

Unlike too many politicians, who gave a dry-as-dust talk from a perspective of self-righteousness, Royn tailored his message to the audience and didn't take himself too seriously. Or, at least, he didn't appear to. After talking about how his duties affected the people on the room for all of thirty-five seconds, he turned to the drug trade, his voice becoming stronger, his movements passionate, with a fire in his eyes that hadn't been there before.

". . . and as you may be aware," he concluded, "I have a very personal interest in coming down as hard as I can on drug smugglers. Just a few weeks ago, my older brother Sam died from an overdose of heroin." Royn's eyes were glistening, his breathing rough. "Sam and I were very close. . . ."

Royn stopped to dab his eyes with his handkerchief. "I'm sorry," he said after a moment, "but it's still hard for me to talk about his death."

After a deep breath, he continued, "In one sense it wasn't a surprise. Sam had been an addict for a long time. It was terrible to see him fall apart. He became thinner, lost energy, lost his interest in life. He'd been an artist. Modestly successful. He had a few exhibitions and many people in the business thought he had a great deal of promise. But as the addiction took hold, his paintings became weirder and projected stronger and stronger feelings of depression until no one really wanted to look at them. They were the last thing you'd want to wake up to in the morning.

"Our family did everything we could. He dried out several times. But, every time, he went back to it. And you know, it was strangely a relief when he did. His addiction had such a strong hold over him that in those brief times when he was clean, he was even more unbearable than when he was injecting poison into his veins.

"Heroin changed him from someone who was living his life at full tilt from the moment he woke up in the morning to someone who was dying before our very eyes. He told me the drugs gave him artistic visions. And there's no question that—at first—some of his paintings were stunning. And he was sure he could stop any time he wanted to.

"But he was wrong."

Royn paused, looking searchingly at the audience, using the pause to take several gulps of air.

"Sam thought he was immortal, invulnerable. When I was twenty, I felt the same. But he wasn't. He was human. And for the last ten years I've been watching him die.

"It's not something I want to see happen to any of you. It's not something you want to see happen to anyone you love—or even to someone you know.

"While I can't bring Sam back to life, I can promise you that I will do everything within my power to stamp out this poisonous trade once and for all. Make no mistake about it: the people who will sell you drugs are callous thugs. They have no respect for human life; they're selling powdered death. They know it—and they don't care. They *intentionally* turn impressionable people into heroin, cocaine and crack addicts who must then turn to crime or prostitution to support their addiction. Most Australians want them locked up. So do I.

"I pledge to you to put these merchants of death behind bars where they belong so that every one of you here today, and everyone you know, can lead a long, healthy, and drug-free life."

As an eerie hush blanketed the room, a younger Karla Preston wiped her eyes, and tears streamed down the face of a girl sitting near her. After a long instant, when the silence seemed to stretch uncomfortably, someone began to clap and almost instantly applause rolled like thunder across the hall.

Anthony Royn stood firmly in the center of the stage, his arms slightly akimbo, his golden hair radiant—perhaps a trick of the light, Karla thought—his eyes warm and glowing as they moved slowly to scan the room; there were instants when it seemed he was holding her eyes, as if they were alone. She imagined he was soaking in the applause, drinking the energy that was flowing towards him in waves.

As the volume of the applause began to fall, he slowly raised his arms. "Thank you," he said, as the applause died and chairs scraped as people took their seats again.

"It's hard for me to express how deeply I appreciate your response." Royn paused, looked at his watch and said, "But I'm afraid I'll have to leave in about fifteen minutes. Until then, though, I'd love to hear any questions or comments you have."

After Royn had taken a couple of questions, Karla's hand shot up and she raised her body slightly to lift her head above the level of the audience. She fixed Royn with a warm gaze that looked adoring and sorrowful at the same time. As she had hoped, Royn turned to her—gratefully she thought. Indicating his watch said, "Madam, yours will have to be the last question."

"Mr. Royn," she said, standing to her full height. "I'm sure I am not alone in saying how deeply moved I have been by your talk today. How I wish there was something more I could do than just say how sad I feel about the tragedy of your brother's death, and extend my condolences to you and your family in your time of grief." Her gravelly voice carried easily and clearly across the room. A number of voices shouted, "Here, here," accompanied by a ripple of applause.

"Thank you," Royn said. "I appreciate that."

"Yet, I have a question. People have certainly died from an overdose of sleeping pills or other regulated drugs—by choice. But not from impurities or unpredictable variations in a prescription drug's strength. So surely, if heroin had been legal and regulated and of constant quality in the same way as prescription medicines, wouldn't your brother still be alive today?"

Royn seemed to rock backward on the stage, as if from the force of Karla's words, his face frozen, his eyes glistening, clearly overcome by a deep sadness while flashing anger towards her. His answer was stumbling, and he left the podium with no sign of his normal panache.

"That question was cruel," Alison said.

"So I was told at the time."

"And there's something you wouldn't know," Alison continued. "According to the police, Sam Royn had been given heroin of a purity normally never available—almost a hundred percent heroin instead of the usual fifty percent, plus or minus. The police concluded that Sam had been given it intentionally, so that when he took what he thought was a normal amount, he would in fact overdose. The underworld, in other words, sent the minister a gruesome message."

"That's terrible." said Karla, clearly shocked. "Awful. But it simply makes my question even more compelling—a question that the minister still hasn't answered." Karla spoke evenly, now looking openly at Royn.

Anthony Royn was glowering at Karla with the same mixture of sadness and anger he'd displayed all those years ago. "My answer," he growled, his face reddening, "is the same today as it was then: lock the murdering bastards up."

"A great idea," said Cartwright as he splashed more Black Label into his glass. "Bring on Prohibition, I say."

"That's different," Royn snapped.

"Really?" said Cartwright. "You were talking about cirrhosis of the liver a moment ago."

"And alcohol kills brain cells," said Karla with a smile, "which explains a lot about your state of mind, Robin."

"The minister's views on this issue are exceptionally clear," Alison said severely before Cartwright could frame a riposte, "and this topic is not on our agenda today."

"Ah . . . quite so," Royn said, slowly regaining his composure, turning in Karla's direction but avoiding her eyes. "It would seem you have quite an influence," the tone of his voice making it perfectly clear that he totally disapproved of Karla's influence. "The mail system in Parliament House has been a bit strained since your column on Sunday— quite an achievement."

"And what have they been saying?"

"Overwhelmingly agreeing with you." Royn shook his head. "Some of them actually ordering us to get our act together. Kydd read a few of the ones from his constituents, addressed to him, and became apoplectic."

"I'm glad to hear it," Karla grinned. "Reminding you of your proper place in society just once every three years is not nearly often enough."

Seeing Royn's anger beginning to rise once again, Alison distracted his attention with a gesture and, raising her voice slightly, said to Karla, "We've read what you've written about the Sandemans, so what we'd appreciate is what else you can tell us. Even your impressions would be valuable."

"I'll do what I can," Karla said, "but I didn't see nearly enough. In retrospect, far too little. What I can tell you is that the Sandemans is a very class-conscious society, where everyone seems to know his station and no one is expected to rise above it."

"Do you mean that nobody can?" asked Alison.

"Oh, no. Just that such an idea wouldn't even occur to most of the people there. By the same token, the people in the upper strata feel they have the divine right to rule. I don't know if you're aware that almost all the politicians and top bureaucrats come from the same twenty-odd families, and that seats in parliament are passed on like private property from father to son or nephew."

"Surely not," said Royn, now sitting back in his armchair, glancing at his watch from time to time.

"Karla's right," said Cartwright. "Each island has one or two dominant, land-owning families who run the place like feudal fiefdoms. By and large, when the so-called separatist groups aren't outright bandits, they see themselves rather like Robin Hood, taking from the local rich and giving back to the poor—minus a huge cut, of course. And they get a lot of popular support when they call for the break-up of the large estates."

"They're socialists?" asked Royn.

"Labels like that are meaningless in the Sandemans," Cartwright chuckled. "A few people have the land and the wealth. The rest don't. Even if the dominant families had gotten their land fair and square in the first place—which they didn't—both the landed and the landless agree that the only rule of ownership is who can grab what and then stop anyone else from grabbing it back. Property rights, to the extent that they exist at all, just enable the landowners to use the police power of the state to stop anyone else stealing what their ancestors stole in the first place."

"And would you agree with that, Karla?" Alison asked.

"Much of what Robin is saying is new to me. But then, I spent most of my time on the Muslim island of Jazeerat el-Bihar—and most of that time in the village of Inkaya. Ownership there seemed mostly communal. The fishery and the plantations seemed to belong to the village and the money was ploughed back into the community—the school in Inkaya, for example, was much better equipped than others I'd seen. And there was no conspicuous wealth, no hacienda on the hill, so to speak. In a sense, the way it was organized seemed more like an Israeli *kibbutz* than anything else. These are my impressions, I hasten to add. But I'm sure they'd be easy enough to confirm."

Remembering his conversations with Nimabi, Royn responded, "So it's a very different culture, then."

"Exactly," said Cartwright, "with rules and customs that are totally alien to ours."

Karla nodded. "That's true. I got to know the villagers reasonably well, especially the women. They were all subservient, and all fully accepted and fully believed that they were, compared to men, second-class beings. I also talked extensively with the Elders, a kind of village council made up of the eldest males, though I don't know if age was the only qualification. They didn't quite know how to take me, and I was treated as a kind of honorary man. Up to a point, anyway. Their main problems were trying to stop the politicians and bureaucrats in Toribaya meddling in their affairs. They said they were quite capable of taking care of themselves without any outside help . . . or interference. They were also very concerned about the influence of militant Islam, which, apparently, had caused a few young hotheads to head off to the hills to join the separatists.

"They joined that terrorist group in the hills there?"

"The ASIO man who talked to me on Sunday made the same mistake: not all the separatist groups in the Sandemans are terrorists. The group on el-Bihar is a case in point. They're terrorists in the same way Mahatma Gandhi was a terrorist. In other words, they're not. But if you label them terrorists and send the army in shooting . . . well, of course, they'll shoot back. Then you'd be able to say, 'See what I told you?' Except, of course, they'd just be defending themselves."

"How can you be sure of that?"

"First of all, the village Elders seemed to have no beef with the separatists—not that they said so in so many words. Quite the opposite, in fact, and I gained the impression that they knew them well and wanted to shield them from any outside scrutiny. But second, and more telling: most of those young hotheads who went to join them were rejected. So they ended up on St. Christopher's Island, where you do have a real terrorist group—two or three of them, in fact."

"Rejected? Why?"

"Because the hotheads saw their main purpose as converting or killing infidels, while the Mountain Men, as I called them, have the same objective as the village elders: to be left alone."

"With the discovery of oil off that island," said Alison, "they'll be fighting a losing battle."

Karla nodded. "With just the internet, and contact with the outside world, they're fighting a losing battle. For example, I think I gave a few of the women there some very *un*-Islamic ideas about what a woman could and should be."

"I can imagine," said Alison with a smile.

"And one other thing: the Sandeman captain who captured me treated his soldiers as if they were cattle, not people. I only met one other Sandeman officer, but he was from the same mould. As Robin said, they see themselves as superior and made no bones about it—and their men, by and large, seemed to accept it as normal. But the Mountain Men interacted with much greater camaraderie, almost democratically—and they follow their leader from respect, not fear."

"What you're saying, in effect, is that our information is incomplete—"

"—or just plain wrong. I've met just one of the groups ASIO labels as 'terrorists.' How many such groups do their agents have first-hand experience of?"

Royn nodded. "That's a good question. Possibly . . . none at all."

"Quite likely," said Cartwright. "As far as I can tell, your spooks sit in Toribaya and compile other people's reports—not to mention rumors—with little if any fieldwork for direct corroboration."

"Perhaps," said Royn doubtfully. "But I'm beginning to think, Mr. Cartwright, that you're a bit too cynical to be taken completely seriously."

"Is that so," said Cartwright. "Well, I take it you know Nimabi is visiting Saudi Arabia?"

Royn nodded.

"Do you know why?"

"Some sort of routine visit, I imagine. And after all, he is a Muslim."

Cartwright shook his head. "The 'courtesy call' story is just a cover. The real reason, from the scuttlebutt I've managed to pick up, is money."

"Money?" said Royn. "I don't get it."

"At the moment—at least until the oil starts gushing, assuming it ever does—they're almost entirely dependent on us. Our troops are propping them up; our money is paying their government's bills . . . what little of it is left after all the sticky fingers it passes through. They feel as though they need our permission to go to the bathroom. They're under our thumb—and they don't like it one bit. They see another source of financing as freedom from our imperialism."

"Imperialism? We're just trying to help them—"

"I know that. You know that. But they bitch that we're always telling them what to do, and all that tired old 'white colonial' rhetoric is being muttered—very quietly—in some circles. If they can get money from somewhere else—"

"But the Saudis—" said Royn.

"Exactly," Cartwright agreed. "Money never comes without strings attached, and Saudi money is worse than most."

"How can that be?" Royn said, shaking his head. "They have so many charities, do so many good works—"

Cartwright chortled. "Really, Mr. Royn. I suppose that's the sort of thing your department tells you, is it?"

"Now that you mention it. . . ." Royn said quietly, with a slow nod.

"Do they tell you that many of the Saudi ruling class are alcoholics?"

"What?" said Royn, dropping his eyes as he remember Nimabi's considerable consumption of wine at the lunch in Singapore.

"Are you sure?" Alison asked.

"I have it on good authority. But all you have to do is get on a British Airways flight out of Jeddah, and if you're in first class you'll see all the bigwigs scoffing down the Scotch and champagne faster than even I can manage. And the ladies take turns in the bathroom to junk the *burqa* and come out looking like Parisian fashion plates."

"I can't say I blame them," said Karla, shuddering.

"What do you mean?" Alison asked, noticing Karla's reaction.

"I escaped from the hotel in Toribaya dressed in a *burqa*. Walked straight through the lobby and out the door just as Sandeman soldiers and police showed up to arrest me. I had to wear the damned thing nearly the whole day. It was so constricting and so hot—even in the air-conditioned hotel. I'll never understand why those Muslim women who are free to give it up choose to keep wearing it."

"Brainwashed," said Cartwright.

"They'd have to be," said Karla.

Like Derek's mother, Alison thought to herself.

Looking at his watch, Royn interjected, "So what if the Saudi leaders are alc—I mean, drink—"

"—aside from being hypocrites?" Cartwright shot back. "Drunkards and dodderers at the top aren't the only similarity between Saudi Arabia and the old Soviet Union. They're both totalitarian societies, closed to outsiders. But the Saudis have two great advantages the Soviets never had."

"You can't be serious," said Royn.

"I'm deadly serious," said Cartwright. "And before you ask, yes, I've been to Saudi Arabia, but no, I haven't seen inside Saudi society. No outsider can—except a male, Arabic-speaking Arab who's accepted as an equal."

"Okay. So what are these two advantages you're talking about?" said Royn irritably. "But I have another meeting in about ten minutes, so make it quick."

"Sure," Cartwright shrugged. "No one ever had qualms or second thoughts about criticizing communism, right? It was only politics or economics, after all. But Islam is a *religion*. That shields it from criticism. Christ. It's even protected by anti-hate-speech laws in many places, including some of our own states. The Saudi's second advantage is money. All that lovely oil that gushes out of the ground at a cost of just a dollar or two a barrel. They use it to spread their own brand of Islam, Wahhabism, throughout the Muslim world. Just as every Soviet embassy had a commissar under the cover of diplomatic immunity whose job it was to support local communist parties and front organizations, so every Saudi embassy has a religious commissar whose job is to spread Wahhabism. They fund mosques, support all kinds of Islamist groups, offer scholarships, run conferences, and train imams. And when those imams come back to, say, the Sandemans, they spruik the same Wahhabist vitriol that Saudi kids learn in school: kill the Jews, death to the Americans, *jihad* against all infidels."

"I know about all that sort of thing," said Royn impatiently. "But it's mostly funded by various Saudi charitable organizations."

"Ha," said Cartwright. "You can't set up a charity, let alone raise money without the Saudi government's permission. And where do you think all those rich Saudis get their money in the first place? From government contracts, of course. They're just pulling the wool over your eyes—there's no difference between Saudi government money and money from a charity. But the important point is this: Wahhabism is not Islam. It was once a tiny, militant, isolated, desert, anti-almost-everybody sect that today, thanks to Saudi oil money, is spreading like the Black Death. At its current rate of expansion, in ten or twenty years it will become the primary form of Islam. And if you think we're having problems with Islamic terrorism now, just you wait."

"But the Saudis are our friends," Royn said.

"Really?" said Cartwright. "They'd as soon stab us in the back. But why should they, when they've got you conned into thinking like that. But don't take my word for anything I've said. Check it all out independently. Because the important thing is this: if I'm right, once the Saudis get their hooks into the Sandemans, in no time at all we'll have a bunch of militant suicide bombers on our very doorstep."

Royn and Alison looked at each other uncomfortably. "Better tell them," Alison said. "It'll be announced shortly anyway."

Royn turned to the two journalists. "This morning, our soldiers took some prisoners on St. Christopher's Island. One of the prisoners blew himself up, taking three of our boys with him."

"So it's already too late," said Cartwright. "You know those two Islamist groups on St. Christopher's who were at each other's throats have joined forces? Some self-described mullah appeared from the next island, Jazeerat el-Bihar—he was banished by the elders of the village, Inkaya—"

"Was his name Gurundi?" Karla asked.

"Sounds about right, I think," said Cartwright.

"He was banished? Any idea why?"

"Something to do with violating the Muslim rules of hospitality—"

"That was me," Karla squealed. "Oh my God. If I hadn't offended him, then—I feel as though *I'm* responsible for the deaths of those soldiers."

"What makes you say that?" Alison asked.

"I was the honored guest. Gurundi—an odious little man, a stand-in for the village imam. I manhandled him. Apparently, that's a serious offence . . . for a woman to lay a hand on a Muslim holy man. And if I hadn't, he'd still be there, and those two Islamist groups would never have gotten together."

"But Karla," Alison protested. "You can't blame yourself for someone else's actions."

"Maybe not. But if you give a murderer a gun, don't you have some responsibility?"

"I—don't know," Alison replied, thinking: *That could have been one of Derek's "infernal" questions.*

"The two terrorist groups probably would have gotten together sometime," said Royn. "If not now, then later."

"Maybe," said Karla. "But Gurundi had spent two years studying in Indonesia . . . at Saudi expense."

"Unintended consequences," said Cartwright, almost as though he was speaking to himself.

"What do you mean by that, Robin?" Karla asked.

"All our actions have consequences—but how often are the results of our actions the ones we intended or expected? Hardly ever. Your little run-in with Gurundi is the perfect metaphor for our presence up there. To be reasonable, how could you have expected that by manhandling the so-called holy man, he'd end up uniting two factions, which led to this morning's attack? So don't blame yourself, my dear." Cartwright put a hand on Karla's knee as he spoke. "The history of the world is the history of unintended consequences. Especially when you're making judgements on the fly, in situations where you don't know all the rules or have all the information. Which is just about all the time."

"You're quite the philosopher," said Alison.

"What you've been saying about the Saudi influence would make a good article," said Karla.

"So it would. Thanks, Karla. I wonder if it will get past the lawyers, though."

"Lawyers?" Royn asked. "What would they have to do with an article in a newspaper?"

"Victoria is one of those places with pretty restrictive anti-hate-speech laws."

"So it is." said Royn. "There was a case—" he searched his memory "—'speaking the truth is no longer an acceptable defence' I think the judge ruled."

"More unintended consequences," said Karla. "And bizarre ones, too."

"Possibly," Royn said as he stood up. "Now, our time is past up. I appreciate your coming—"

"My pleasure," said Cartwright, hoisting the nearly empty bottle of Black Label.

"—maybe I'll ask the department to see if there's anything in what you've been saying."

"They'll just tell you the Saudis are our friends and allies and we can't afford to offend them because they have all that oil," Cartwright said, his voice scornful. "And then they'll drag their heels until, if you haven't forgotten about it altogether, they'll produce a whitewash. If you really want to get at the truth, do it independently."

"An . . . interesting perspective," Royn said.

As Alison ushered the two journalists out of Royn's office, she turned to Karla and said, "Inviting Cartwright was a good idea. Thank you, Karla."

"My pleasure," Karla replied. "Next time you're in Sydney, give me a call. We have a lot to talk about, don't you think?"

"Maybe," Alison said doubtfully.

"So, ALISON, DO YOU think Cartwright has a point?" Royn said. "About the Saudis?"

"And the department?" Alison grinned.

Royn nodded.

"I don't know," Alison replied. "But I think we should find out."

"Let's do this: draft a memo to Fairchild directing him to prepare a report on the relationship between Wahhabism and Saudi society and Saudi foreign policy. Also ask him to identify the, ah, 'religious commissars' in the Saudi embassy here in Canberra, and the extent of Saudi funding of activities of any kind in Australia—and, of course, in the Sandemans. Naturally, this report will be highly confidential."

"And if Fairchild 'drags his heels'?"

"We'll keep reminding him," Royn chuckled. "Which won't make him at all happy."

Alison laughed. "And what about Cartwright's other point—about doing some digging independent of the department?"

Royn was thoughtful, and then nodded. "Could be an interesting test. Why don't we look into putting some researchers together?—academics and the like. But under the umbrella of some think tank." Royn grinned. "For deniability."

"Okay," said Alison, nodding, and passed Royn a document marked CONFIDENTIAL. "This just came in from Defence."

"It seems," said Royn as he skimmed it, "that a certain Lieutenant McGuire—a relation by any chance—?" Alison nodded "—took some samples and pictures of a plant near a village call Inkaya that's been identified as marijuana. They conclude that marijuana is being grown there in commercial quantities."

"I wonder if that's the 'plantation' Karla mentioned."

"If it is, then where are they selling it? And that Preston woman came back from the Sandemans on a fishing boat that simply dropped her off on the coast without being challenged or even noticed." Royn leapt from his chair and leant on his desk, glowering as he spoke. "Our shoreline is wide open—they could smuggle it in anywhere." He began to pace impatiently around the room. "Make sure Bruce sees that report. Get him to find out if there's any evidence of marijuana coming into Australia from the Sandemans."

"And if there is?"

Royn looked at Alison, and smiled bitterly. "What I'd like to do is destroy it," he said, returning slowly to his seat. "So any evidence could give us the pretext, don't you think?"

"It just could," Alison nodded. She had reservations about whether Royn's desired action was wise, given the current state of their relations with the Sandemans. But she would raise them later, when Royn was in a calmer mood. "And Bergstrom wants to see you as soon as possible."

"Do you know what about?"

Alison nodded. "The terrorists on St. Christopher's Island used a machine gun in the attack this morning. They traced the serial number and it was a new one we'd supplied to the Sandeman Army."

"And how did the terrorists get it?"

"According to one of the prisoners, they bought it from a Sandeman quartermaster. The Sandeman Army denies this, saying it was lost in action—"

"And we don't believe them—is that what you're about to say?"

"Right," Alison nodded. "Apparently, items like rifles have been sold to the terrorists—usually by individual soldiers who desert and turn their weapons into cash. But Bergstrom says Thierry is convinced a lot more weapons like machine guns are missing. He suspects organized theft—and wants instructions on how to handle it."

"Sheesh," said Royn, jumping to his feet. "I'll go and see him now."

"One other thing first, Minister."

Seeing Alison's broad smile, Royn sank back into his seat and said, "Better news, I presume."

"I certainly hope so. I got one of my friends in the Federal Police assigned to the Candyman Inquiry, and I've been passing him the names and information the private eye's been getting from Leon Price."

"How that going?" Royn asked.

"Far too slowly," Alison said. "They're lucky if they get five or ten minutes with him before the doctors demand that he rest."

"It sounds like he's on his last legs."

"Possibly. They say he's clearly in no condition to testify in court—though if it ever gets that far he'll probably be long dead and buried."

"If I was McKurn's lawyer," said Royn, leaning back in his chair and pursing lips, "I would challenge any statement Price makes as the blathering drivel of an embittered old man who probably wasn't in his right mind at the time. So whatever he says might only be useful if it can be corroborated, or lead to other lines of investigation."

"I'm afraid so," Alison said. "My Federal Police friend is also pushing the ACT Police's investigation of those agency records to get at McKurn's name as fast as possible."

"Did you mention McKurn specifically?"

"To my contact, yes. But he will only tell the police he's interested because he has information that federal politicians could be implicated."

Royn sat up straightened his shoulders and smiled broadly. "Alison, we're that close—" he closed his finger and thumb so they almost touched "—to nailing him. I can smell it."

32 Hollow Idol

Using the pseudonym "Stuart Wrench," Derek Olsson booked a flight to Bangkok via Singapore in case flights direct from Australia were being watched. He'd had a moment of tension as the immigration officer at Sydney airport compared the face in front of him, with its greying hair and neatly trimmed goatee beard and hairline moustache, to the photo in the British passport which had none of that facial hair. "You should get a new photo, mate," the officer said, his tone disapproving.

"I will most certainly do that, sir," Olsson replied in the British accent he'd been practicing with a voice coach all week. Olsson held his breath as the officer checked the visa and ran the passport through the computer. A moment later he stamped the passport and returned it to Olsson: apparently the computer records were in order, as promised.

As he walked away, Olsson heard the immigration officer say to a companion, "Sometimes these Pommie bastards can be a bit arsty-farsty, eh?"

He smiled, thinking he'd passed the first test—and his tutor should be proud of him. Though she might have a stroke if she knew his real reason for practicing the accent; she'd been under the impression he'd been preparing himself for a role in an amateur performance. *Not entirely untrue.*

He settled back into the wide business class seat that promised a reasonably good night's rest. Instead of drifting into sleep he found himself thinking that his life had moved in an ironic circle: initially, he had come to admire, even look up to Luk Suk as a man who made and lived by his own rules . . . but he'd moved back to Australia to get out from under Luk Suk's thumb—which hadn't worked, because he was now flying to Bangkok to confront him. And now growing in the pit of his stomach was the gnawing sense that the world was too small a place for both of them.

It had begun, he thought as he looked back, the day when Alison, ashen-faced, had come almost stumbling down the stairs from his mother's room in his grandfather's house. She failed to return Jack Dent's greeting, refused to look at him and walked straight outside, a jerk of her head signalling that Derek should follow. When Alison finished telling him what she'd just learnt from his mother, he stormed back into the house.

"So you stood by," Derek snarled at his grandfather, "knowing what was going on, letting Dad beat up my mother—your very own daughter—and me."

"No, it wasn't like that at all," Dent pleaded, his head in his hands.

"Really? Ha! You mean, you saw Ma's bruises, and mine and Lars' and Jessica's—and just closed your eyes? That's even worse."

"No—I wasn't certain."

"But you made damn sure you never found out, one way or the other. *Right?*" Derek demanded, standing over his grandfather, his fists clenched, the tendons on his neck taut.

"That's exactly how it was," said Jennifer Dent. Derek, Dent, Molly, Jessica—and Alison, who was now standing in the background by the front door—turned in unison, all surprised at the hard edge to her voice.

"Jenny—" Dent said in a pleading tone, his eyes glaring at her.

"I've been too quiet for too long," said Jennifer Dent, taking two quick steps to her daughter's side and enfolding her in her arms. "How many times did I plead with you to do something? *You*, who always told me I'd never have to worry about anything, that you'd take care of it. *You*, who knows the mayor, the police commissioner, with your lawyer who you only ever had to ask . . . but never did."

"You knew?" Derek asked her.

"Molly never said anything to me. It was always some accident or another. But, I knew that something was very wrong—but your grandfather here refused to take any action. 'They're married now,' he'd say, 'and let no man tear asunder what God has made.'"

"God?" Derek turned on his grandfather, more furious than ever. "What's God got to do with it? *You're* the one who forced Ma into a marriage she didn't want, not God. How could you do such a thing to your own daughter? A marriage that he didn't want either. You're the one who saddled us with a man you knew was shiftless and couldn't be trusted. . . ."

"But I never knew he was violent. And the . . . shame. . . ."

"Shame? Yours? Or Ma's?"

Dent said nothing.

Derek went over to his mother, taking her hands. "I love you, Ma, but I'm sorry. I can't stay here another minute. I don't want to see Grandpa ever again."

"Derek—no."

"Ma," he said, getting down on his knees so they were eye to eye, "come with me. Let's both get out of here—not back to the old house. Somewhere else. Just you, me, and Jessica. And Lars, if he wants."

"I—I can't, Derek." Tears ran down Molly's face, unconstrained. "Not right now."

He bowed his head. "I understand—and I hope you do, too."

Derek went to live with his friend, Ross Traynor, moving into the room Ross's elder sister vacated when she married. Ross's parents listened quietly as he told the story, his words tumbling out so fast they tripped over each other.

"You're welcome to stay here, Derek, as long as you need to," Ross's mother said. His father nodded his agreement.

"And I'll pay rent."

"There's no need for that," Ross's father protested. "And how can you afford to—you've got your final exams coming up in less than two months. You have to have time to study."

Ross laughed. "That's not true, Dad. Derek never needs to study, damn him."

"Thank you," Derek said. "But I insist on paying my own way. I can do it too—I'll just have to do a bit more tutoring or put in a few more hours at the service station. And I can work there full time over the summer holidays."

"How could he do such a thing?" Derek asked Alison one day, pleading with her to make sense of it for him.

"Look on the bright side, Derek," Alison said, desperately grasping for something positive. "If your parents hadn't married, you wouldn't be here."

"Does that make what he did right?" Derek demanded.

"Of course it doesn't."

"And I should thank him for what he did?"

Alison shook her head. "And your mother—" Alison stopped when she saw Derek frown at her critical tone.

"What about Ma?" Derek gazed at her accusingly.

"You've got to face it Derek. She's responsible, too. She never stood up to her father—or her husband."

"I know," he groaned.

"So tell me, what do you have that she doesn't?

"What do you mean by that?"

"You stood up to your father—and your grandfather. You're still at school but already you're paying your own way. You're independent—not just financially but with all your damn questions too. Molly's not. She's passive; you're active. Maybe Molly had her will beaten out of her as a child—but why did yours survive? Why did you fight back, and she didn't? Why the difference?"

He just shrugged helplessly. "All I know is that I looked up to him, I loved him, Alison. He was my hero—and it turns out he was nothing but a hollow idol. I feel betrayed."

"The problem with Shakespeare," Derek said one day in his English class, "is that every one of his protagonists is flawed and comes to a tragic end. Where can I find someone I can look up to, someone I can admire?"

"Myths and fairy tales," the teacher replied. "That's where. In real life every one of us is flawed—which Shakespeare dramatizes to perfection. That's our fate—there are no heroes."

"Why not?"

The teacher just shook his head wearily. "I guess you're just not old enough to understand."

Derek leaned forward intently on his desk. "Maybe I'm not old enough to have given up." *Or have I?* he asked himself silently.

The teacher glared at him. "What's that supposed to mean . . . ? Never mind. We're wasting time on meaningless frivolity. Turn to page 112. . . ."

But Derek had stopped listening. He opened his book and pretended to follow the teacher's words, but in his mind he was listening to another voice: *Have I given up?*

"That's where I want to be," Alison told Derek excitedly after she returned from a class outing to Canberra. "We saw Parliament in session, and the Prime Minister—"

"In Canberra?" Derek asked skeptically. "You want to be in *politics?*"

"I don't know. I don't think I want to be a politician. But I do want to be in Parliament House, in the center of power, where I can make things happen."

"Really?" he asked. "Why?"

"Why? Because that's where I can make a difference. I'm going to work there over the summer holidays." Noticing that he was looking at her somewhat distantly, she challenged him, "What's wrong with that?"

Olsson shrugged. his eyes seeming to stare through her into the distance as he spoke. "That's just something I'd never do, don't want to do . . . in a place I don't want to be."

"So why are you looking at me that way?" She waited an instant until she could hold his gaze and said, softly, "There's more to it than that, isn't there, Derek?"

He nodded, moving slightly backwards in his seat, which made him look more, not less, uncomfortable.

"So tell me," she demanded.

"Everybody's always telling me what to do. Parents—grandparents—teachers, cops, talking heads on TV and radio," he said heatedly. "But the worst of all are preachers and politicians—and you want to be one of them?"

Alison was clearly hurt and angry at the contempt in his voice. "All I want to do is help people like me, and Molly—and you," she glared. "And that's where I can do it best. Whether you like it or not, I'm going to spend the Christmas holidays in Parliament House as an intern."

"Tell me, then. Can you pass a law to turn my grandfather into what I used to think he was?"

"That's hardly fair!"

"Really?" he challenged her, his cheeks flushing. "What are you going to end up doing in Canberra, Alison? Making laws—more rules telling people like me what do to. Of course no law can change my grandfather—or give spine to my mother either. So you can cross me and her off your list. And there are already laws against rape—do you think more laws would have given you any more protection?"

Slowly, shakily, Alison rose to her feet. "You know that's not what I want to do. You're so unbelievably . . . nauseating."

Fuming, tears streaming down her cheeks, Alison stalked away. For the next couple of weeks, she rebuffed his attempts to talk to her; turned and headed the other away whenever she saw him in school; walked out of the *dojo* after Aikido without a word; and joined Molly at the battered women's group meetings, instead of talking with Derek— while he waited outside, alone.

But Derek didn't seem to care. For the first time, without a word of explanation to *Sensei* Tozen or anyone else, he began missing Aikido classes. His grades at school were slipping, and the MG he and Ross Traynor had been rebuilding sat unfinished and untouched in the garage. One day Ross even cornered Alison at school to tell her, "I don't know if you've noticed, but Derek seems to be going to pieces. Even my parents are worried about him. Do you think there's something you could do?"

"I don't know, Ross," Alison replied. "But I'm not going to talk to him—not till he apologizes."

"For what?" Ross asked.

"He knows."

Ross shook his head. "He just doesn't seem to care, Alison. About anything."

ALISON HAD VOLUNTEERED TO take calls at a Rape Crisis Hotline—and often left in tears. Desperate to talk about it, after an Aikido session when Derek actually showed up, she reluctantly asked him if he'd join her for a coffee.

Ross was right, she thought when Derek merely answered "Sure," with a shrug—as if her invitation made no difference to him one way or the other—and followed her listlessly around the corner.

"They're so afraid, so depressed," she told him, "so ashamed—as if it was their fault. And helpless. Some want to fight back but don't know how. Most are like your mother, Molly, and can't lift a finger in their own defence."

"Teach them Aikido," Derek suggested, a faint glimmer of life behind his eyes.

"Brilliant," said Alison, looking at him warmly in appreciation, her face glowing at the possibilities.

"What would have happened if you'd known Aikido when . . . ?"

"I'd have broken their goddamn arms," she growled happily. "Teach with me. I can tell my story and you can tell yours—and we can show them how easily they can learn to defend themselves. We can really help people like us . . . and your mother."

Alison was leaning forward excitedly, but Derek had just slumped back into his chair, his eyes blank. "I—I'm sorry, Alison, but I just can't."

"Why not?" Alison demanded.

Derek's mouth twisted into a wry grin as Alison turned "his" question around. "That's my question," he chuckled half-heartedly. "Why not? I don't have the energy, for one thing. And this is your crusade, isn't it, Alison? It's not mine. I . . . I don't have a cause. You have the passion to do it; I don't. But I will make one suggestion: our school would be a good place to start."

To everyone's surprise—except Derek's, who watched incuriously from the sidelines—the school hall was packed for Alison's first demonstration, which lasted nearly three hours instead of the allocated ninety minutes. Tozen's Aikido classes overflowed, and despite vociferous opposition from a vocal minority of parents—who either felt personally threatened or thought such topics were better dealt with in private or not at all—once or twice a month she was invited to put on her "road show" at high schools across the city.

As reports trickled in of would-be rapists who'd ended up with broken arms or worse, Alison told Derek excitedly, "You see, you can change the world."

"And you didn't have to be in government to do it."

"But wouldn't it be better if schools were all required to run self-defence programs?"

"Maybe," he replied skeptically.

Derek continued to help her—when she asked for his help. He talked to her—when she initiated a conversation. But he never volunteered anything or asked any more of his infuriating questions. He was, Alison thought, like one of her girlfriends who'd been jilted—except that he didn't snap out of it a week or two later like her friends who quickly fell in "love" with some other boy, but was sinking deeper into a gloomy depression. So the day he asked her, "Like to come with me and see this American evangelist?" she felt a flicker of hope, overwhelmed by surprise—and incredulity bordering on shock.

"You? You want to listen to a *preacher?* I can't believe it."

"He's supposed to be some kind of a saint," Derek shrugged. "I just want to see for myself."

"Derek, I can't believe my ears. After everything you've said about God . . . and preachers?" she shook her head. "Count me out. I've heard more than enough from Father Ryan."

But she didn't speak the words she was thinking: *Are you losing your mind?*

"He had a wonderful presence," Derek told her later. "I guess 'saintly aura' is the only way to describe it. Quite breathtaking. But he preached about Adam and Eve being thrown out of the Garden of Eden. By eating the apple, he said, they rejected morality and were doomed thereafter. Our only hope for salvation is to return to their original state of mindlessly obeying the edicts of God as he, being God's messenger on earth, interprets them. Yes, he says, we have free will—to accept God's word or reject it. Choose between hell—being a rational human being—or heaven—and become an unthinking vegetable. What a choice."

A few weeks later, Derek showed Alison a story he'd ripped out of a newspaper: the evangelist had been charged with having sex with underage girls—and not one, but several. "He convinced me the path to God was through his bed," said one of the girls who'd come forward to testify.

"So much for him," Derek said with a touch of glee that Alison found disturbing.

As though the evangelist had been the first stop on some kind of warped quest, hardly a week went by without Derek telling her a similar story in the same cynical, mocking tone . . . of a businessman said to be a model of honesty—who turned out to have been cooking his company's books . . . a famous philanthropist who'd been caught dipping his fingers into his charity's till . . . a professor held up as an exemplar of moral integrity who was discovered, by his wife, in bed with one of his students . . . a priest who'd abused little boys in his congregation and the archbishop who shielded him—who was now a Cardinal, safely out of reach in the Vatican . . . a champion athlete who'd filed for bankruptcy, the millions of dollars he'd made in prize money and endorsements having disappeared in profligate spending and dumb investments. . . .

"Being good at one thing doesn't mean you have to be good in everything," Alison said. "And failing at something doesn't make you a bad person."

"Doesn't it?" was all he would say in response.

"Who or what are you looking for, Derek?" she asked him softly, her eyes sad and concerned.

"I am looking, aren't I? For what? I guess . . . for someone—anyone—I can look up to."

"Someone to replace your grandfather, you mean?"

"Yes," he replied hoarsely. And projecting a sense of desperation he whispered, ". . . maybe my English teacher was right."

Alison shook her head vigorously. "No. What about the people who don't appear in the papers?"

"You mean, the ones who don't get caught? They probably beat the kids or cheat on their wives."

"No." Alison said angrily. "I mean the ones who have never done anything wrong."

Derek shrugged. "I've just about given up expecting I'll ever find one."

"What about . . . Mother Teresa?"

"Maybe," he said, skeptically.

A little while later he looked more hopeful. "As far as I can tell, everyone says she's wonderful, a living saint." But the following week, he excitedly thrust an article he'd found in an obscure magazine in the library into Alison's hands and demanded, "Read this. Mother Teresa's no saint after all. She takes sick people in, yes. But then she won't even allow their friends and relatives to visit, or give them any medical treatment—just prayer. And she gets millions of dollars in donations every year and nobody knows where it goes."

"That's terrible," Alison said as she read.

"Isn't it. She's a vampire feeding on other people's suffering."

"But that's not what's really terrible."

"What is, then?"

"*You,*" Alison replied. "You've become so cynical it's depressing. Being around you used to be—infuriating, yes, but exciting, challenging. You used to be so alive. Now, you're like a walking black hole of despair. You're not looking for someone to admire—

you're determined to find fault with everyone and everything and prove that no such person exists. That Shakespeare was right. There are lots of people you can admire if you'd just look around you."

"Like who?"

"Like . . . my parents, who battled all their lives to make a home for themselves—and my mother, who risked death to create the one thing they both desperately wanted: a child. Or what about Ross's parents, who happily took you under their roof with love and understanding. They may not be giants, like the people you keep trying to tear down, but they're wonderful people just the same. And what about looking into yourself? What are your admirable qualities? And if you're so concerned about flaws, about imperfections, isn't the most important thing to overcome them, not give into them? So why don't you concentrate on conquering your own defects instead of focusing on people who failed?"

For a change, it was Derek who was speechless.

Derek passed all his finals—but for the first time he did not get straight As.

"What the hell," he said. "I don't want to be a doctor or a lawyer anyway," naming the two courses that needed almost perfect scores for entry, "so what difference does it make?"

"So what do you want to do?" Alison asked.

Derek just shrugged, as listless as ever. "I guess I'll go to university—why not?" He enrolled at Sydney University, taking "maths, physics, and chemistry for fun," he told Alison, "and philosophy for the meaning of life."

"You'd make a great teacher," Alison said, recalling the way he'd explained everything to her so clearly. "Or, with all your damned questions—" she grinned, her voice enthusiastic as though, by projecting it, she could transfer the feeling to him "—a great scientist."

He shook his head wistfully. "I really don't know. In fact, I have no idea what I want to do when I grow up. Be stuck in a lab all day? No thanks. Teaching? Not as a career. I couldn't do the same thing year after year, even if all my students were there because they were desperate to learn. It's like building cars. I've done it, so it's time to do something else."

"What else?"

"I wish I knew, Alison. I wish I knew."

Derek spent the December/January summer vacation pumping petrol, working nights as an assistant waiter, deputy bartender, and all-round gofer in a seedy Balmain bar where, after he'd stopped a few fights, he also became the unofficial bouncer, teaching Aikido and, in what little spare time he had left, reading philosophy. He found himself holding imaginary conversations with Alison, storing up things to tell her when she returned from Canberra.

Alison returned bubbling over with excitement. "It was great," she told Derek. "I met lots of people—politicians, journalists, members of staff, and that's definitely where I want to be. And in the July holidays, I'm going work in a Senator's office." Seeing that Derek was about to speak, she held up her hand. "I know you don't approve, but please don't say anything that would spoil my mood."

Derek smiled. "I was about to say . . . I owe you an apology."

Alison nodded, looking suddenly hopeful. "Have you . . . changed your mind?" she asked softly.

He shook his head with a quiet laugh. "Not exactly. I mean. . . . Canberra. I know I *don't* want to do what you want to do. It still feels wrong to me . . . but now, I'm . . . confused, I guess."

"Confused? About what?"

"What's right and what's wrong. I've been reading different philosophers all summer long—and they all disagree with one another. Some say 'black is white,' while others say 'no, it's red.' Someone else says 'it can be black to you and red to me'—but they all agree that truth is relative. Then another guy says 'since the word "real" doesn't really mean anything, all this talk about "black, white, and red" is completely meaningless.'"

"But surely," Alison protested, "what's right and wrong is just . . . obvious. Isn't it?"

"Apparently not. Except to those philosophers who say morality is handed to us from God. Otherwise," he shrugged, "there's no standard of morality . . . or it's relative, or arbitrary. . . ." His voice trailed off.

"That all makes no sense to me."

"I know," Derek said fervently. "That's why I'm looking forward to uni—hoping this philosophy course will make sense out of it all. So while what you want to do still *feels* wrong to me, I just don't know any more."

"Thank you," Alison said, glowing at him warmly.

Derek dipped his head in acknowledgement. "While I can't prove I'm right, I hate people telling me what to do. I'm *never* going to do to anyone what my father did to me. According to Nietzsche—one of the philosophers I've been reading—the choice is to rule others, or to be ruled." He shrugged again. "I won't let anyone rule me . . . and I don't want to rule anyone else, either."

"Poor Derek. It seems to me you're making something simple really complicated."

"Maybe," he admitted. "I just have to make sense out of everything, that's all. My head spins just thinking about it. Whereas you—" he leant towards her slightly to emphasize his words "—seem to know exactly where you're going. I wish I could feel that way."

"I . . . guess I do," Alison smiled awkwardly, feeling slightly embarrassed. "And I even know . . . well . . . I sort of know who'd I'd like to work for. After uni of course."

"Who?"

"I don't know, exactly. But if I worked for the right politician, I could have a lot of influence."

"What do you mean by the 'right' politician?"

"Well . . . for example . . . Anthony Royn."

"Who's he?"

"You really don't know, do you?"

Derek shook his head. "You know me, Alison. I couldn't give a stuff about politics or politicians. As far as I'm concerned, they're all liars and cheats. Remember that minister who had to resign because he'd padded his travel expenses? And that senator who hadn't fully disclosed his investments and was busted for buying stock on the sly just before government approvals were announced? They're all the same."

"That's not true," she protested.

Derek pointedly raised one eyebrow, but simply said, "Okay. Maybe not all of them. Anyway, tell me about this Royn character."

"He was elected only a couple of years ago, but already he's Randolph Kydd's favorite. . . . You know who he is, don't you?"

"The leader of some party or other."

"He's the leader of the Conservatives, and they're in opposition."

"So Royn's a Conservative?" When Alison nodded, Derek laughed. "You'll give your father a heart attack."

"I know," she said miserably.

"Why not a Labor politician, then?"

"I want to work for someone who's got a good chance of getting to the top—"

"Hitch yourself to a star, you mean?"

Alison scowled at him. "You have such a way with words," she said sarcastically. "But . . . yes."

"Sorry to interrupt," he grinned, not looking at all apologetic.

"As I was saying," she glared, "I learnt—mainly from the journalists, who were all very helpful—"

"You mean, you charmed them, turning them into puppies, like you did with my grandfather?"

"Derek!"

"That was a compliment, Alison."

"Really?" Alison said skeptically. "It didn't sound like one to me."

"Sorry," he shrugged. "Please, go on. . . ."

"Okay. So . . . the Labor Party is rife with factions so you never know who's going to end up where. While Royn stays in Kydd's favor, he'll keep moving up in the Conservative Party hierarchy."

"But Labor's in government."

"They won't always be. The Conservatives' structure is also a lot looser, and their ideology. According to most of the people I talked to," she giggled, "their only ideology is winning votes."

It was Derek's turn to frown. "How's that significant?"

"If I can persuade whoever I'm working for that something I want to get through is a vote-winner, I won't have to also fight an ideological battle." Derek seemed about to say something, but when he hesitated she went on, "Royn's also young; he's going places; he's really popular—I met him, briefly, and he's such a nice guy, not like some of them—and he's got movie star looks—"

"Oh, I see."

"That's got nothing to do with it. I mean, with me." But she averted her eyes as she felt the flush of warmth flood her cheeks. "It means—he wins votes. Anyway, he's happily married too."

"What are his beliefs, his aims?"

"I—don't really know, yet. But he strikes me as a kind of Little Boy Lost."

"I see," he said.

"What do you see?" she demanded. "Out with it."

"If you insist. You're telling me that you'd rather work for a Conservative because the Labor Party is too hidebound by its principles, while the Conservatives don't really have any. And you want to pick someone like this guy Royn because he seems to be on the fast track to the top, a vote-winning hunk of no fixed ideals—a moral vacuum—who's the most malleable shooting star you can find. Alison!"

"I'm not. . . . Well, maybe I am, but that's what you have to do. What I want is to be in a position where I can get more support and protection for people like . . . for victims. And if I have to play by their rules to beat them at their own game, okay, I can do that."

"I thought you wanted to make the rules, not follow them."

"I will. But you have to know the rules first."

"Maybe. I'd rather just make my own rules . . . for myself."

"Which are?"

"Aside from hurt no one, I don't know—yet."

"But you hurt your father. And Lars. Didn't you?"

"True," he said. ". . . in self-defence."

"What about your mother? You hurt her when you walked out on her—was that in self-defence?"

"I don't know, Alison," he cried, his head falling into his hands, his body shaking. He raised his face, twisted in pain, to look at her, tears dripping from his eyes. "I . . . I had to leave. . . ."

She reached out her hand to hold his. "I'm sorry, Derek."

Partly because she was somewhat intrigued herself, Alison decided to accompany Derek to hear a visiting Indian guru for "an evening of meditation and spiritual uplift." *There must be something in it,* Alison thought when she saw the guru, a lady with an aura of peace who looked to be in her late twenties but was actually forty-five.

The sounds—*om, mane, padre, hum*—plus the monotonous beat of the Indian music were strangely soothing. Little books were passed around and they began chanting transliterated Sanskrit words. After a while, Alison vaguely noticed that Derek had stopped chanting. Afterwards he almost shouted, "Look at this. It's right here in black and white." Pointing to the English words under the lines of Sanskrit he read: "'The Guru is wise . . . always look up to the Guru . . . even when the Guru is wrong the Guru is right.' There's more, all like that."

"I was just listening to the sounds—they're so enchanting."

"Let's go," he said.

"You go. I'm enjoying this."

Derek shrugged. "Okay, I'll stay."

After the break the guru gave a talk, and afterwards it was time for something called "darshan," to be blessed by the guru. With an impish grin at Alison, Derek jumped up and joined the line of devotees.

"So what did you ask her?" Alison asked when Derek sat beside her again.

"Remember how she was saying that someone becomes a guru by being appointed by the previous guru? So I asked her: 'Who appointed the first guru?'"

"And what did she say?"

"'In our tradition, the Lord Krishna.' Meaning, of course, that the first guru in the chain appointed himself." He smiled at her—a bitter, twisted, smile that made her shudder. "You see Alison, they're all the same."

Alison kept returning to the meditation center; after a few weeks, Derek joined her despite his reservations. "You're right," he said eventually. "If you ignore the meanings and just listen to the sounds, it works. But I can't ignore the meaning completely, so I made up my own sounds, meaningless ones . . . and they have the same effect."

Over time, Derek became calmer and more centered. But as Alison started her last year of school and Derek began at university, his cynicism, far from subsiding became, if anything, more entrenched.

Almost from the first day, the philosophy lecturer had dashed Derek's hopes. "He says he's a deconstructionist," he told Alison.

"What on earth is that?" she asked.

"As far as I can tell," Derek replied, "someone who tears things apart so they can't be put back together.

"Truth?" the lecturer had said. "Consider science—you'd expect to find absolute truths there, right?" When the class agreed he continued, "You'd be wrong. There are no truths in science—not 'Truths' with a capital 'T'. Just hypotheses that have yet to be falsified. So Newton's so-called 'laws' were superseded by Einstein—and now we have quantum mechanics and something called 'string theory' which merely goes to show that science is 'proving'—and I put that word in quotes intentionally—what many philosophers have been saying for centuries: that the universe is essentially incomprehensible."

When Derek told Alison what he'd been "learning," Alison stared at him in horror. "That . . . can't be true," she said. "How can anyone believe such things?"

Derek shrugged. "Lots of people believe in invisible men in the sky so—why not?"

"I suppose," Alison said, unconvinced.

"But it gets worse. For example, he says the eye has a blind spot where the optic nerve connects the eye to the brain—so how can we be sure that what we think we're seeing is really there?"

"So how does he know the eye has a blind spot?" Alison asked.

"Good question."

Towards the end of his first semester at university, Derek Olsson stood outside his old high school lounging by a bright red, two-seater convertible MG sports car with its roof down, circa 1960s, that looked brand new. As the students in their uniforms streamed out of school they crowded enviously around Derek, who was wearing just torn shorts, a battered T-shirt and thongs—and gaped at his car.

"You've finished it," Alison said as she saw him. "It's . . . beautiful."

Derek nodded. "Can I drive you home, ma'am?" he grinned, opening the passenger door.

"Yes—but my bike . . . ?"

"Let's go for a spin, stop for a coffee, and pick up your bike later."

Alison laughed as Derek accelerated the MG and the wind whipped her hair back in a tail behind her. But her laughter stopped when Derek said, "I've quit."

"You've what?"

"Quit university. Dropped out—"

". . . given up . . . ?" Alison said softly.

Derek glanced at her sharply, and with an indifferent shrug and a bitter smile said, "Maybe."

"But Derek, you can't. Don't you care? About your life and yourself? . . . " In a faint voice Alison added, diffidently, ". . . and about me?"

Alison struggled for breath as Derek suddenly swung the car into a vacant parking space, braking violently as he did, the car behind honking angrily at his unexpected movement. Switching off the engine he turned to study her, saying somberly, "Yes, Alison. I do care—about you. As for the rest . . . ?" He shrugged again.

"But . . . Derek. . . ." Alison stared at him, her face frozen in shock, gasping for words and unable find a single one.

"Let's get a drink," he said, pointing to a nearby café and leaping out of the car without opening the door.

"Tell me, then," Alison said as they took a table, "what made you decide to quit? And why, for heaven's sake?"

Derek grinned impishly. "You know this philosophy course has been driving me crazy—it's such a relief to know I'm never going back to it. Anyway, I really put the boot into the lecturer today. . . ."

"So," said Derek rising from the back of the lecture hall. "What you've been telling us is that you don't exist—or that I'm merely a figment of your imagination."

"Well," said the lecturer with surprise, "rather badly put—but in essence, yes."

"Thank you," said Derek, "I just wanted to be clear."

"Well," said the lecturer doubtfully, "true clarity in these matters is a childish expectation. So-called reality is essentially unintelligible and unfathomable."

"Perhaps," said Derek, pulling a rifle out of his bag. "But I think a little demonstration might prove educational."

"What are you doing?" the lecturer asked with a flash of fear.

"Simple," said Derek. "You just said you don't exist, or that I'm merely a figment of your imagination. So this rifle is just another figment, right?"

Derek aimed the gun at the lecturer.

"This can't be happening," he shouted. "Somebody—HELP!—call the police."

"Now why should anybody do that—assuming they exist—just to bring more illusions into the room . . . which is, itself, another construct of your imagination."

The lecturer was frozen, cowering behind the lectern.

"And if I were to pull this trigger, an imaginary bullet might come out and might blow your brains out, but what earthly difference could it make to you—since you don't really exist?"

"But . . . but. . . ."

"But what?" demanded Derek. "After all, you've told us there are no moral absolutes, so if I do pull the trigger, on what basis would I be doing anything wrong?"

The lecturer stood like a petrified statue, his face a mask of terror, his mouth open, his vocal chords frozen.

"You see, you have no answer," Derek said, and squeezed his finger.

There was a loud explosion and the lecturer dropped out of sight. A couple of people screamed as the entire class turned to look at Derek. After a moment's stunned silence, the room broke up in laughter.

The lecturer peeked over the lectern, ducked down again, and slowly stood up. He looked aghast at Derek: hanging from the rifle's barrel was a large flag with the word BANG! in bright red letters, and the lecturer's face turned deep red as the students' laughter ricocheted around the hall.

When hall became silent again, Derek said, "I think we've just proven that your philosophy is full of shit."

Alison hooted with laughter till tears streamed down her cheeks. "You . . . did . . . that?" she spluttered between laughs.

"It was only a toy gun—but it sure looked real."

"But . . . I don't understand."

"Look, I never wanted a philosophy *degree*—what would I do with that? I just wanted to make sense of the world. That lecturer just made everything worse. Take the MG," he said waving a hand to where it was parked on the kerb, a couple of passers-by admiring it. "I rebuilt it, with my own two hands. Is it an illusion? Was I dreaming the whole time?"

"Of course not," Alison said heatedly, taking his hand. "And I'm not a figment of your imagination either."

"No," Derek smiled wistfully. "If you were. . . ."

"If I was . . . what?"

His cheeks flushing, Derek shook his head.

"Go on. Say it," Alison demanded. When he pressed his lips together, his eyes glistening, she said angrily, "If you won't, I will."

"I . . . can't, Alison."

"Because I'm not a virgin any more, is that what you mean?" As she spoke, she couldn't prevent her gaze from lowering.

"No," Derek protested. "That's not what I . . . was thinking." And then he smiled mischievously. "But you are . . . metaphysically speaking."

"Metaphysically?" Alison spluttered, pulling her hand away. "From the way you treat me, you must think I'm a mind without a body."

"No, Alison," Derek said, his lips trembling and his eyes pleading, "I've never, ever thought that."

They sat in uncomfortable silence until Alison sighed, and asked, "Why quit? There are dozens of other courses you could take."

"True," he answered, "except they don't really interest me."

"So what now?"

"I really don't know." He spoke uncertainly. "The only idea I've come up with is to see the world. Sell the MG and buy a round-the-world ticket. I can work in England and Canada. And I'm sure I can stretch my money by picking up the odd job here and there."

"No, Derek," Alison pleaded. "Please don't go."

"Only be for a few months. Then I'll be back."

"Stay here—with me."

"Oh, Alison . . . I—I would love to. But I'm afraid."

"Afraid of what—" Alison's voice trembled, and she seemed on the verge of tears. Of . . . me?"

"No. Afraid . . . because everything I ever care for always turns into dust."

"No, Derek. It doesn't need to be that way."

"And right now, I feel like I'd be a millstone round your neck. I can't—I can't hold you back."

33 **Chains of Love**

ALISON PARKED HER BIKE on the footpath, chaining it to the Victorian-style, iron lace railings of the fence. In place of the pocket-handkerchief lawns of the other houses on the street was a lovingly tended jungle of color, complementing the burnt orange of the walls and bright yellow of the window frames. A path paved with yellowish bricks led from the gate to the front door.

She had been here before, many times. But this time. . . . She shook out her wind-blown hair and combed it with her fingers. She felt strangely exposed without her handbag with its brush and mirror, with nothing on her shoulder or her arm . . . while a tingle of excitement raced up her spine.

As she opened the gate she hesitated. Her hands fluttered as they reached for the handbag that wasn't there . . . for what? She couldn't be sure. Her teeth trembled against her lips as she brushed invisible creases from her dress.

One thought filled her mind: *In a few days he'll be leaving.* . . . and she felt herself being pulled by a desire she couldn't resist towards the front door.

Just moments after she rang the bell she heard steps and the door opened, yet in those fleeting seconds the tension of anticipation in her heart had swelled to become almost unbearable.

"Alison!"

Derek Olsson wore a ragged T-shirt and a pair of shorts, his feet bare, his hair untamed, his mouth open like a freeze-frame caught in mid-sentence. Yet his hazel-green eyes seemed strangely bright as they locked on hers, smiling in welcome, as if to let her know that she was not unexpected.

Alison took a step towards him. "Aren't you going to invite me in?" she asked, her excitement catching in her throat.

"Do you think it wise? With the Traynors on holiday till next weekend?" Derek said softly, his eyes leaving her face to flash up and down the street.

Noticing his glance Alison laughed, the tension in her throat making her laugh sound more nervous than gay. "I know," she said, taking another step so that mere centimeters separated them. "Since when have you cared what other people think?"

Derek seemed cemented to the doorway. One corner of his mouth twisted into half a smile, while his gaze became solemn. "I don't care what other people think," he said, "about me."

"I don't either."

Alison raised her lips and let herself lean towards him, feeling as if she were falling. But as she kissed him she felt his arms gently enfolding her. She let her lips press closer, parting them as if to relieve the pressure. The tips of her nipples hardened as they thrust into his chest, sending an electric shock through her body. She could feel her heart racing and her body felt weak as Derek turned his head slightly, welcoming her tongue, and her arms went tightly around his neck, as if afraid to let go. Derek began to angle his lower torso away, but Alison clutched the small of his back to keep his excitement close. Unhurriedly, the almost invisible touch of his fingers ran slowly down her back, her body trembling at a tender force she had no desire or ability to resist. She felt herself being cocooned by the power of his hard muscles and pressed herself closer into the warmth of his embrace. The edge of her mind sparkled briefly at the slight hesitation of his fingers as they reached the bra strap that wasn't there, but her consciousness was lost in his closeness, in the oneness of melding lips to lips and flesh to flesh, their breaths coming in a single rhythm.

As if by mutual agreement their lips parted. His eyes glowed with the warmth of fierce passion; as they searched her face she felt herself opening to him, like flower petals unfurling in the early morning sun, no longer afraid of what he might see but, rather, wanting him to see everything. And she saw his eyes glowing with an intense feeling of love that was almost impossible for him to bear, one that mirrored her own.

She smiled, feeling this must be what it meant to be blessed, and gently leant harder on his body, as if to signal to him that it was time they moved inside.

"Hold me tight," Derek whispered. One arm gripped her hard around the waist; the other reached down, and she shrieked with surprise and delight as he swept her off her feet. She clung to his neck, letting her head fall back, laughing at her feeling of weightlessness, of the sense that at this moment she was completely at his mercy . . . and always had been. Derek carried her through the doorway, turned, one foot kicked out to nudge the door closed, as his mouth folded around her breast. Her arms hungrily pulled his head closer while her body arched and shook with pleasure so intense she was sure she was about to explode.

"Don't stop," she murmured inaudibly as Derek lifted his head, brushing his lips against her neck, her ears, her eyes, to stand erect, lifting her body higher as he did. She gripping him tighter, wanting to repeat her words but unable to find either breath or energy. Already feeling drained, exhausted, she let her head rest, nuzzling on his shoulder, breathing in his heady masculine scent. Her eyes were closed, but she was aware of his every step, his every movement, the tiny caress of his fingertips, and she let herself relax into the arms supporting her in the air. Only when she felt herself being laid on something soft, his grip loosening, did she allow her eyes to open.

It was a girl's room; Traynor's elder sister's room before she was married. Frilly curtains lined the windows; the duvet on the wide bed was edged with lace. A computer, piles of books, and scattered male clothes which didn't belong and made no impression on the room were the only signs of a male presence. And over Derek's shoulder she saw one picture. . . .

A large blow-up of a girl in a bikini caught at the beginning of a perfect swan dive dominated the wall opposite the bed. Alison knew the girl had just jumped from the springboard though no board was in sight; her arms spread like wings holding her in space, her body straight, her toes pointed and legs so close together she was a shapely mermaid floating on fluffy white clouds scattered across a sapphire sky.

Alison roughly pushed him away and stepped closer to the picture. As she studied the figure, her fists relaxed, the tension in her shoulders dissipated. She slowly turned around, her face a radiant smile, her cheeks flushed, to gaze warmly at Derek sitting on the edge of the bed, watching her with a knowing grin.

"That's me! All this time you've had this here. . . ."

Derek inclined his head; Alison felt as though it was a salute.

"Did you take it?

Derek nodded.

"When? How? I had no idea. . . ."

"You didn't notice me in the water with my camera," he said, his eyes laughing. "You were too busy . . . making the perfect dive."

She stood, feeling naked and defenceless as Derek sat on the edge of the bed, his eyes openly admiring her. Her eyes drank in his gaze, but the tingles on her skin where his eyes touched her body only made her yearn for his hands. The gap of a few steps suddenly yawned between them, and as she moved towards him he stood and they ran into each other's arms.

"Do you know what a torture you've put me through . . . waiting . . . for you?" Derek asked, his lips on her ear.

"Oh, yes," she said happily, at his open acknowledgment that he was hers to command. "But you didn't have to wait."

"But you felt it too, didn't you." He was not asking a question.

"Of course." She pulled her head back to look at him; laughing. Reaching under his T-shirt, savoring the feeling of his skin on her hands, she demanded, "Am I still a mind without a body?"

Derek shook his head. "No. Now you're a body without a mind." As if to demonstrate, his fingers ran down her spine as he unzipped her dress, and she shivered as her skin lay exposed to the cool air.

"Really?" she whispered. "And where's your mind gone?"

"It's . . . a slave to your touch—" he said; his hands slipped under her dress and she gasped with unendurable pleasure in response "—as yours is to mine."

As if in submission to her desire, she felt the fabric of her dress falling away; she gripped his warmth tighter, closer, kissing him hungrily. A faint fear began to form in the pit of her stomach; she clamped down on it but her skin crawled nevertheless at the cold memory of other hands, of other fingers, touching, invading her body.

She felt as though she was floating, with just the vague memory of being lifted again and laid on the soft mattress, lost in the electric sensations of his fingers and lips and tongue as they touched and kissed her neck, her shoulders, her breasts, even her knees and toes, and the insides of her legs. As his mouth moved between her legs she felt her body arch; shuddering, she pushed his head down harder. *This,* came the fleeting, irreverent thought, *must be what it feels like to be in heaven.*

His lips inched across her skin back to hers. She opened her eyes and smiled into his as their lips and bodies kissed. She opened her legs to welcome him, her hands gripping his thighs, her arms clutching him tighter. But as he moved to enter her, the pressure of his body seemed to turn into a leaden weight expelling the air from her lungs. She felt as though she couldn't breathe, and the small knot in her stomach turned into the panic of terror as her nightmare, now feeling real, filled her mind. Her eyes now unseeing, the knowledge of where she was and who she was with fled from her consciousness as she felt she'd gone back in time; every muscle in her body froze rigid in shock, her vaginal muscles becoming a steel wall. Her body turned into a lever pushing him away, throwing him to one side of the bed.

Her knees curled, her shoulders hunched, her muscles turning into rubber with relief as quickly as they had frozen into ice to insulate and protect her from an invader.

She focused back into the present and for half a heartbeat she looked uncomprehendingly at the person beside her, then burst into tears. "I'm sorry, Derek," her voice frightened, sorrowful. "I can't." She shivered on the bed, her eyes pleading, sobbing mindlessly. "I want to but I can't," she said through a rush of tears.

He moved to cradle her head in his hands, to gently kiss her eyes and cheeks. But with a swift, sudden movement she jerked back from his touch, reached for the duvet and tucked it protectively around herself so that just her head remained exposed. "No," she cried through her tears, burrowing her face into the duvet. "No."

"But . . . I love you, Alison," Derek wailed. "I love you."

Alison shook head slowly. "You . . . can't," she whispered, so softly that he couldn't hear her words. Struggling to make the muscles in her legs obey, she stood, swaying slightly, hugging the duvet around her shaking body, stumbling to pick up her dress from the floor. Holding the dress in one hand, she fumbled until she realized she couldn't put it on while holding the doona protectively in place, and began to walk to the bathroom to change.

"Alison. . . ." Derek's voice entreated her, begged her to stop, to listen.

At the doorway she turned to look towards him, unable to lift her eyes from the floor. "I . . . have to go," she said quietly. Derek began to speak but Alison forced her eyes to look at his, pleading, "No. Don't say a thing. Don't . . . make it any . . . harder."

Wordlessly, he waited until she emerged from the bathroom, her face pale but clear, her eyes still red, and followed her to the front door where he stood, frozen, watching the lengthening shadows through sad eyes long after she had ridden away.

*****

"There's a note for you, Alison."

Maggie stood in the doorway to her bedroom holding a small envelope. Alison was lying listlessly on the bed, and made no move to take it. Maggie had the impression she'd been gazing at the picture of Derek Olsson on the shelf above her desk. "He's waiting outside for your answer," she said softly.

"Just tell him—" she stopped to choke back tears "—just tell him 'no,' please, Mum. Whatever it is. . . ." She shook her head.

Maggie sighed and sat down on the bed beside her daughter. She'd expected to see her daughter return from her tryst with Derek Olsson looking bubbly, radiant, and glowing. But she'd returned timid and fearful, as though she was in a state of shock. For two whole days, there'd been no sign of her sparkling eyes or her relentless energy, and she'd spoken no words more significant than "pass the salt, please." Derek had called—often—and she'd simply refused to speak to him.

"Alison," Maggie asked awkwardly, "did he . . . do something to . . . hurt you the other day?"

"No, Mum."

"Then . . . I don't understand."

"I did something that hurt him," Alison said, her eyes glistening. *And me.*

As Maggie had done when Alison was a child and in pain, she took Alison's hand in hers, only to be surprised at the way Alison clutched it, as if in desperation. She slowly nodded, even though she couldn't make sense of Alison's reply, and asked, "Would he forgive you?"

Alison nodded numbly. "He already has."

"And he's going away . . . ?"

"Tomorrow."

"Then—" Maggie looked at Alison for a long moment, gently stroking her forehead. "Alison, I really can't imagine what's going on between the two of you. But you've been moping around for two days like—even worse than—"

She couldn't bring herself to say the words "after you were raped," but Alison nodded, as if she had heard them. "I know, Mum," she said softly.

"—and I'm not going to ask you to explain a thing. But let me ask you just one question: Do you love him?"

Alison gasped, replying in a low, solemn voice, "Yes, Mum, I do. Very much."

"And he loves you."

"He does?" Alison said. *How* can *he?* she thought. "How do you know?" she asked.

Maggie face lit up as she beamed at her daughter. "My darling daughter," she chuckled, "you must be the only person who can't see it. And no, he hasn't told me—not in so many words."

"What do you mean by that?"

Maggie chuckled again. "You'd better ask him."

Alison turned her head away, murmuring, "I can't . . . face him."

Maggie gave no indication of whether she'd heard Alison's words or not. "If you love him, and he loves you, why aren't you together? The poor boy's beside himself, you know—he looks like he's hardly slept for the past two days. Why don't you at least go and talk to him?"

Alison shook her head. "I—can't, Mum. I just can't."

"He's leaving tomorrow, so don't you at least owe it to yourself to read what he has to say?" Maggie asked, tearing the envelope open and handing it to her.

Alison held the envelope gingerly, as if it was about to explode.

"Go on," Maggie urged. "It won't bite you, will it?"

Slowly, awkwardly, her fingers all feeling like thumbs, Alison pulled Derek's note from its envelope. As she read, she could hear the pleading tone of his words:

Dearest Alison: I MUST see you before I go. Please please please. I love you. I love you. Derek.

Looking away to hide her tears, Alison let the note fall. Maggie couldn't bring herself to pick it up, but by turning her head she could make out Derek's words. Measuring her pace, she said softly, almost as if she was talking to herself, "You know, I expected to see you so unbelievably happy when you came back from seeing him the other day—"

Alison turned her head, her eyes narrowing. "What do you mean by that?" she demanded.

Maggie just smiled. "Do you think I didn't know what you intended to do—"

"But how could you know?"

"I was seventeen once," Maggie said grinning, "and I can remember what it felt to be seventeen and in love. And then . . . there was what you were wearing . . . and not wearing . . . when you left to visit him."

Alison gasped, looking at her mother in amazement. "So why didn't you stop me?"

"Could I have stopped you?"

To Maggie's relief, Alison laughed, shaking her head.

"But I wouldn't have stopped you, even if I could have."

"You mean . . . you approve?"

"Not really," said Maggie. "But your happiness comes first."

"Oh, Mama," Alison said, sitting up on the bed to hug her. Suddenly making up her mind, she said, "Okay, Mum. Would you ask him to wait while I get ready?"

"Of course I will," Maggie said. And with the look of a girlish co-conspirator she added, "And tonight, if you're late getting back, I won't stay up waiting for you."

"But . . . ?" Alison's mouth formed an "O." Her eyes widened, and she looked at her mother as if she couldn't be meaning what she'd just said. "What will Dad say?"

Maggie's look was strangely calculating. "He'll never know."

"How—?"

"Leave it to me, okay? Just promise me one thing: take care."

Alison nodded gravely. "Yes, Mum. I will."

"I'M SORRY, DEREK," ALISON said as she closed the front door behind her.

"It's okay," he said. "You're here now. That's all that matters."

Derek seemed to grow an inch or two taller when he saw her coming towards him, his face lighting up, his eyes and mouth smiling in delight. But he stood awkwardly, restraining his hands and arms from reaching out to her. So Alison stepped close to him and, looking up into his eyes, said, "I love you, Derek. Very much."

His face blazed as if warmed by an inner glow, and his arms wrapped around her, gently but firmly pulling her close against his body. He smiled at her wonderingly, his eyes suddenly glistening, and she sank gratefully into the soothing warmth and strength of his embrace.

"So what is your pleasure, my lady?" he asked, whispering in her ear. "Dinner? Coffee? What would you like?"

Alison tilted her head back to look at him. "Surprise me," she said, laughing as she snuggled closer to him and kissed him hard.

He took her hand and led her onto the footpath, opening the door of the MG for her with a flourish. She had the sense that he couldn't quite believe she was really there, or that he was afraid she might disappear, or break like fine porcelain. "Hungry?" he asked as he jumped into the driver's seat.

"Starving," she replied as her stomach reminded her how little she had eaten over the past two days.

"SOMETHING SMELLS REALLY GOOD," Alison said as they came into the dining room of the Traynors' house. "Nothing too complicated," Derek said, going to the stove in the open kitchen. Alison stood at the other side of the counter, eyeing the two places set opposite each other on the long dining table covered with a crisp white tablecloth. Two unlit candles stood in the center.

"That looks like the Traynors' best silver," Alison said. "Are you sure it's okay to use it?"

"Yes—but only for special occasions."

Alison felt herself glowing at his compliment and turned away to hide her embarrassment at being so openly happy—and her disbelief that such happiness was possible. But as she looked at the table settings again and turned to see Derek stirring a pot on the stove while water heated in another, her smile faded. Frowning at him through narrowed eyes she said, "I feel like I've been set up."

"Huh?" Derek said, looking up in surprise.

"You and Mum—you've been conspiring together. Haven't you?"

"No—well . . . not exactly."

"What do you mean? You'd better explain yourself."

Measuring his movements, Derek turned down the heat on the stove, placed the ladle carefully on its rest, put the lid back on the pot, took two wine glasses from the rack and carried them across the to counter, setting one in front of Alison. She noticed her fingers were drumming on the countertop and she forcibly stilled her hand.

"I hoped," he said, opening a bottle of red wine and half-filling the two glasses. "I called three times this morning, you know." Alison dropped her eyes in acknowledgement. "Maggie suggested I write a note and said she'd see what she could do. 'But I can't promise anything,' she said. That's all."

"So she's on your side, is she?"

"You know better than that, Alison. The one she *most* cares about is you."

"That's true," Alison muttered, taking a long sip of wine, aware of the growing warmth in her cheeks. She'd always taken her parents' affection for granted. But now, remembering the impact of her mother's words, and intensely conscious of the way Derek was looking at her, she wondered why the almost overwhelming sense of being loved should make her feel awkward and embarrassed.

She lifted her eyes slowly, a flicker of excitement and a flutter of nervousness taking hold of her stomach in a bizarre chorus as her gaze reached his face. "Mum said she knew that you loved me," she said, breathing softly. "But how did she know?"

Derek chuckled. "Maggie has known—or suspected—for a long time. From the way we look at each other whenever she sees us together, from the questions she asked me when I came to dinner."

"But . . . Dad was the one always grilling you. I don't remember Mum asking you any questions."

"Ah . . . that's because she'd ask them when you'd gone to the bathroom or something, and Joe was watching TV."

"What did she ask?"

"Oh . . . things like 'What do you think is most admirable about Alison?'"

"And how did you answer?"

"Your powerful spirit—and your perceptive mind. And the way, once you've made your mind up to do something, you become an irresistible force. Getting in your way then is like standing in front of an express train."

"You really think so?"

"Oh, yes," he said, his eyes twinkling, lifting his glass to clink against hers.

As he carried a salad and two bowls of spaghetti, he saw Alison moving the table settings. "Didn't I set it properly?" he asked.

"No," she said with mock disapproval. "You put us too far apart." She had moved one of the place settings to the head of the table, next to the other instead of opposite.

He nodded. "You're right."

She felt giddy as Derek held her chair with a flourish; sitting next to him seemed to make her even more lightheaded, as though she were connected to the world only through the overwhelming brilliance of his two soft eyes, the faint, fluttering light of the two candles, and the aroma and taste of the meal he had prepared so lovingly . . . for her. Now and then she had to reach out to touch him as if to reassure herself she wasn't dreaming.

"This is great," she said through a mouthful of spaghetti. "Let me guess. You ordered from Giovanni's." She named a popular Italian restaurant nearby.

"They don't deliver."

"It was . . . in the freezer."

"Nope."

"You made it?" He nodded. "And I didn't even know you could cook. How can you—?"

He untangled her maths, built cars, beat her at tennis, made her look at the world differently—and cooked like a gourmet chef. Whatever he turned his mind to, it seemed, he did expertly and effortlessly while whatever she'd achieved had taken struggle, practice, endless toil, and buckets of sweat.

"What is it, Alison?" His fingers were locked with hers, his voice was warm with concern—and the way he was looking at her now, the way he always looked at her . . . *how can I doubt him?*

"It's just that . . . everything seems to come to you so naturally, so effortlessly, that now and then I just feel inadequate."

"It's hard for me to imagine that you'd ever feel like that. When it comes to determination, who can hold a candle to you? No one. When you decide to do something, you set out to be the best—and you succeed. When you want something, Alison, you're unstoppable—and I'm in awe of you. And—because I always feel like I'm leaning on you for your strength."

"You do?"

"You see," he said with delight, "you don't even notice it."

She was suddenly aware of their differences with a strange clarity. Despite his protestations, he was smarter and more talented, able, it seemed, to learn and do anything—and do it superbly. But it was she who had a direction, a purpose, while he was aimless. His decision to leave, she realized, was an admission of that, and at the same time the hope that he might find a path, a reason . . . a mission. Without that, all the intelligence and ability in the world was essentially meaningless.

Feeling calmer, more able to accept that tomorrow he would be gone, she reached out to clasp his hand and, keeping her thoughts to herself, simply said, "Have I really been your pillar of strength?"

"Yes," he said, leaning across the table to kiss her. "Just don't try and carry all the burdens of the world," he whispered. "Nobody is that strong. Not even you."

THEY TOOK THEIR WINEGLASSES to the verandah at the back. They snuggled on the soft cushions of the wide wicker lounge, gazing at the buildings of the city of Sydney strung out across the water as the sun's last rays faded. Now, the only illumination came from the windows behind them and from the moon when it peeked through scattered clouds.

The verandah—open to the view beyond, yet cocooned by vine-covered trellises of luxuriant green, the faint, sweet perfume of the last hibiscuses and frangipanis hanging in the air—felt like a private arbor in the sky, as though they were floating unseen over the city beyond, absorbed in the sense of each other's presence.

"I love you, Derek," Alison sighed. "And I want you with me always."

His eyes glistened. "That's what I want, more than anything."

"Then never leave me."

"I'm not leaving you. It's something I need to do—"

"But couldn't you do it here? I'll miss you so much."

"Maybe," he conceded. "I just don't know. But . . . you know where you want to go, and where you want to be—and I just can't follow you there. You know I love you, and I know you love me—but if you bind me with chains of love they'll just end up choking both of us."

"But—"

"—if I insisted you came with me, demanded that you gave up the idea of Canberra and politics and changing the world, would you drop everything and come?"

"Yes."

"And would you be happy?"

Alison was silent for a long time. "No," she said softly, shaking her head, the lights of the city beyond blurred by her curtain of tears.

"I'll be back in a few months—even with odd jobs, I doubt my money will last much longer than that."

"And if it does?"

"Then . . . we could have Christmas together in London. Or New York."

"Yes . . . " she said doubtfully. "London. I want to see the Houses of Parliament. And Washington. Congress."

"You just have a one-track mind."

"I guess . . . sometimes I do," she said, smiling to herself, thinking of express trains . . . and of Derek standing in front of one.

She gently pried his glass from his hand, placing it on the end table beside hers. He raised his lips in the expectation of a kiss, but she threw him roughly across the cushions. Her weight on his thighs pinned him to the wicker lounge, which creaked with the rhythm of her motion.

"What are you doing?" he asked in surprise, though she was all too aware that he had made no move to resist her—that his only movements guided and stabilized hers.

"I'm taking my revenge."

He smiled in understanding, and she leaned down to kiss him roughly on the lips. He struggled weakly to bring up his arms to embrace her; she growled, "Just lie back and think of England."

"I guess I have no choice."

"That's right. None at all," she replied, knowing that was true, while knowing at the same time that with a flick of his body he could turn the tables and pin her helplessly to the floor below.

He made no movement as she yanked his jeans and underpants down to his knees, hobbling him. She stared at his upright penis, mesmerized and fascinated but not without a sense of trepidation. But the knot in her stomach was now just a diffuse edginess. Gingerly, she reached out to touch it and with a deep breath held him tightly, smiling to herself as he shuddered and groaned.

She tore off her jeans and slowly lowered herself onto him, waiting for the reaction . . . daring it to come. But all she felt was the tension of her muscles gripping him as she welcomed him inside her. Almost instantly she was rocked by an explosion and then another as his warmth spread inside her.

She collapsed onto him, releasing his arms which instantly wrapped around her. They both shuddered again and again as if from the aftershocks of a massive earthquake. They looked into each other's eyes, the only sound their gasping breaths. No words were needed for her to know beyond doubt that she was enfolded with his love.

"Have you had enough revenge?" he asked.

Time seemed to stop before she could find the energy to form a reply, and the control over her muscles to utter it. "Never," she said weakly.

"So how long are you going to keep me shackled like this?"

"Always," she whispered.

When he just grinned at her happily, she commanded him, "Kiss me again."

"Where?"

"Everywhere."

Across the water, the city had gone to sleep. Alison let her hand stroke his chest, feeling his goose bumps and suddenly aware of her own . . . and the chill of the cool night breeze. With one hand she reached down to pick up her clothes; with the other she clutched his hand and pulled him to his feet.

"It's late," he said, embracing her, all too aware of her naked body against his. "I'll take you home."

Alison laughed. "I'm not going home tonight—if you'll let me borrow your toothbrush."

"That, and anything else you want. But your parents? What will they think? And won't you be in hot water—"

She stopped his flow of words by pressing her lips to his mouth and clasping him tightly. "It's all taken care of," she said at last. "It won't be a problem."

"Really? Joe will hit the roof."

Alison laughed. "I was right. I have been set up—it was a conspiracy, masterminded by my mother, God bless her."

"What do you mean?"

Alison laughed again. "Never mind . . . you can ask her yourself one day. Come on." She stepped out of his embrace and pulled his hand. "I need some more warmth. . . . And one other thing."

"What's that?"

"You can sleep on the plane."

When they finally stood in the airport's departure lounge, Alison couldn't hold back her tears nor Derek his.

"It won't be so long and I'll be back."

"Derek, I'm afraid. . . ."

"Afraid?"

"Afraid I'll never see you again."

"You will, I promise. We'll write, and I'll call you whenever I can."

"It won't be the same. . . ."

"And remember, Christmas in London—or New York."

"Maybe," she breathed, nodding but not fully believing.

Alison stood watching the doorway to immigration where Derek had disappeared at the last possible minute. After a long time she stumbled, her vision blurred, to get the bus home, hearing planes taking off, wishing desperately she was on one—the one— right now.

 Hacker for Hire

CARNAGE! WAS ONE OF the less-venomous banner headlines, as Friday morning's papers reported that four Australian soldiers had been killed in the Sandemans, three of them by a suicide bomber—or *kamikaze* attack, in Major-General Thierry's words—and seven more wounded.

The headlines were more or less what Alison had expected, and, although she wasn't surprised, she was once again overcome by the anguish she'd felt when she'd first heard the news. As she did whenever she thought of the Sandemans—which, these days was far too often—she worried for Jeremy, wondering how much longer he'd be safely away from danger. Not that she'd know if he was in any danger until it was too late; not that there was anything she could do about it. And she grieved for the dead soldiers—and their wives, girlfriends, parents, friends, and cousins . . . and the poor people whose job it was to tell them the awful news. *Thank God I'm not one of them.*

And how, she asked herself, *am I going to face my father tomorrow? And also tomorrow: McKurn.*

"BE WITH YOU IN a minute," Anthony Royn said as she came into his office, without even looking up, so missing Alison's sour expression.

He was engrossed in something in a newspaper which caused him to alternately, growl, smile, grimace, chuckle, and pause briefly in puzzlement. Alison composed herself as she waited, suppressing a smile as she noticed what he was reading.

**Nice Guys
Finish Last?**

By Karla Preston
OlssonPress Syndicate Exclusive
Thursday: **Canberra**

It's easy to appreciate why Anthony Royn has become so popular. Just to begin with, shaking hands with him is an orgasmic experience. And then there's the way he looks at you and listens as if you're the only important person in the world. Yet, when he's talking to someone else you don't feel excluded.

(I'd love to know how he does it. If he could bottle it, he'd be rich. Or should I say, in his case . . . richer.)

And we don't need to mention his movie-star looks.

Anthony Royn is a really nice guy. That's great for winning votes. But does he have what it takes—the steel, the mettle, the ruthlessness a politician needs to get to the top—and stay there?

In politics, don't nice guys finish last?

It's no secret that Anthony Royn and Paul Cracken are the two main contenders for the post-Kydd Conservative leadership, and they're circling the Conservative party room waiting to butt it out like a pair of randy young goats when the cantankerous old one keels over. Well . . . Cracken is. What's Royn been up to? Aside from securing the support of Conservative Members from marginal constituencies by taking polls which regularly show a whole bunch of them would lose their seats with Cracken as leader, not a whole lot.

It's also no secret that Royn is Kydd's favorite, and no one in Canberra believes Royn would be where he is today if Kydd hadn't pulled him up there. But one reason the wily old Kydd has held onto the prime minister's office for so long is that any potential challenger is offered a plum job like Ambassador to France, sidelined, or finds that his local party branches have mysteriously switched their support to some brash neophyte come preselection time. One can only conclude that the only reason Royn isn't enjoying long lunches at *Maxim's de Paris* is because Kydd sees him more as a lapdog than a bull terrier.

Cracken, by comparison, is a poor-boy-made-good—something he never lets anyone forget—and levered himself up through the ranks with his own elbows (with the odd push from Senator McKurn, not something anyone wants to shout from the rooftops these days). He's certainly "got what it takes" in spades, and would grab Kydd by the throat yesterday—if he had the numbers, which he doesn't. But with the personality of a decomposing rattlesnake and the sex appeal of a decrepit Mafioso chieftain, the wonder of it is that Cracken's even a member of parliament, let alone in the race for the next leader.

So the nice guy may finish first after all. That appears to be the consensus view in the Conservative party room: they'll go for the charming vote-winner, even though he may be all show and no substance, if only so they can turn their backs (carefully) on the guy you'd hate to have as a neighbor who needs a decade or two in charm school to convince his fellow party members he's not going to lead them straight to the opposition benches.

Of course, this speculation is really all academic. I expect to be an old maid long before Randolph Kydd walks away from the leadership of his own free will—and who knows who'll be hanging around in the Conservative Party waiting room by then?

"Decomposing rattlesnake," Royn chuckled as he looked up to face Alison. "And the sex appeal of. . . ."

"Yes," said Alison, "I read it too."

"I'll bet Paul's in a bad mood this morning," Royn smirked, clearly relishing the thought.

"I'm surprised you like backhanded compliments," Alison said.

"Back-handed . . . ? Oh, right, I see what you mean. She sure knows how to twist the knife in exactly the right spot."

"Thankfully, she's not saying anything that's particularly new," Alison said. "To us, anyway: it's simply what our polling has shown."

"You mean . . . decisiveness and so on."

"That's right," Alison nodded. "One of the few metrics where Cracken comes out ahead. But the way she says it—"

"That I 'haven't got what it takes'? Is that what you mean?"

"That—plus her whole tone is so disparaging of you—and of Cracken, for that matter—that I don't think her article will do you any good whatsoever."

"Maybe not," Royn shrugged, his eyes twinkling. "But my kids—when they were kids—had a plastic snake. I think I'll give it to Paul."

"And give him another reason to be angry with you? Wouldn't it be better to commiserate with him?"

"He'd die of shock," Royn laughed. "Worth a try, though."

"Can we turn to business, Minister?"

"Yes, of course," Royn said, becoming serious without quite fully succeeding.

"Defence says they're moving in force into St. Christopher's Island with the aim of clearing out all the rebel groups."

"Which will mean more casualties."

"Inevitably. Let's hope it's worth it," Alison said, wondering if any casualties could be justified, even by success. "There's a meeting of the National Security Committee at eleven thirty where you'll be briefed."

"What else?"

"I've wangled for the Auditor-General's office—both Commonwealth and state— to take a quiet look at the stationery contract. But God knows when they'll get to it. And Leon Price has admitted he and McKurn were 'bagmen' for the Premier and other higher-ups in the in the NSW government back in the seventies. He and Price collected wads of cash each week from policemen, contractors, kickbacks from businesses and so on, and distributed it to various politicians and bureaucrats. He's identified almost two dozen people by name so far."

"That's great," said Royn. "If just one of them talks—"

"But Jason says—"

"Jason? Who's he?" Royn asked.

"My Federal Police contact. He says that the police need something at least semi-official—a signed deposition, for example—before they're likely to act. And that it would be better if Price was interviewed by the police—which would give his evidence a lot more weight."

"So, why don't they?"

"Time, and other priorities. This was all twenty and thirty years ago, so they don't see any urgency. Jason says he'll arrange to interview Price after he's signed something, so all he needs to do is get direct confirmation."

"But the private eye will follow up on the people Price named, I trust."

"Yes. But we've stretched their resources pretty thin."

"Cheer up, Alison. We'll get there."

"I know," Alison said wearily. *But not soon enough.*

*****

Derek Olsson transited Singapore and passed through immigration and customs in Bangkok without a hitch. After freshening up in a modest hotel on Soi 7 off Sukhumvit, Olsson bought a SIM card and, back in his hotel room, dialled a number.

"*Sawadee-krap,*" he said when the phone answered. And continuing in Thai, "General Vanich? Derek Olsson. . . . Yes, thank you. . . . An early lunch would be fine. . . . Noon? I'll see you there."

Later, he decrypted an email which he read with mounting excitement:

lars olsson has two bank accounts that i can trace. four weeks ago $20,000 was deposited in one account and $10,000 in the other. prior to those deposits the balances were $11,273.27 and $36,833.45 respectively. two weeks ago $35,000 was withdrawn from the two accounts by cheques payable to a real estate agent anything else you want to know?

"The bastard," Derek Olsson said to himself as he typed a reply: please trace the source of the two payments if at all possible. Pull out all the stops. "He took a payoff to set me up. Well, Lars, I guess I'll be seeing you again when I get back."

IF I get back.

*****

ALISON HAD DECIDED TO postpone facing her father by staying in Canberra overnight and flying to Sydney on Saturday morning. *Pity I can't put McKurn off the same way.*

When she reached home she fixed herself a salad and trolled through the phone taps until she found one that sounded intriguing.

"Henry."

That, she knew, was McKurn's voice.

"Frankie! What an unpleasant surprise."

"Henry's" voice, though obviously male, was high-pitched and squeaky—and very familiar. After a moment, she realized that McKurn was talking to Henry Sykes.

"My name is Frank, goddamn it."

"More and more people are calling you 'Frankie' these days, you know . . . *Frankie.*"

"Well, bugger them all."

"So tell me, Frankie, to what do I owe this honor?"

"I'm calling to ask you to stop publishing these corruption exposés."

"Now, why on earth would I want to do that? They're great circulation builders."

"I could say that they're having a destabilizing influence, bringing into question the integrity of the government and our political institutions—"

"Don't make me laugh, Frankie. The only reason you're calling me is that you have a personal stake in this."

"Think what the hell you like. And as a matter of interest, who's this prominent federal politician whose mug, your ads are promising, will be splashed across the front pages on Sunday?"

"It's not you, Frankie, I can tell you that much. Though maybe your name will appear later in the series."

"You mean there's more?"

"There's certainly another week's worth after Sunday. For all I know, though, they might have an unlimited supply."

"Make Sunday the last one, then."

"Why the hell should I do that, Frankie?"

"Consider it an investment in your health and longevity."

"Threatening me, are you? Now *that* would make a good headline in tomorrow's *Mercury,* don't you think?"

"You wouldn't dare."

"Wouldn't I just? You realize, Frankie, that you've become a lost cause."

"And what the hell do you mean by that?"

"Simple. From what I hear from my Conservative Party mates, you've got a better chance of getting to heaven than you do of being on the Party's Senate ticket at the next election. Your days are numbered, Frankie my dear."

"So if you're not in the mood right now to consider my very reasonable request? Why don't I give you twenty-four hours to think it over."

"I don't need twenty-four hours, Frankie. I don't even need twenty-four seconds. Let me put it this way: if anything happens to me, whether you're behind it or not, the gist of this phone call will be blasted across the next day's *Mercury*. And, of course, the police will get a copy."

"You recorded this? You fucking arsehole. After all I've done for you. . . ."

Henry laughed. "I can't think of anything you've done for me, Frankie. Only *to* me. It's payback time. How do you like it?"

All Alison heard, by way of McKurn's answer, was a *click* as he ended the call.

So whatever might happen to Derek's papers—had he acted on her warning? And been able to stop whatever McKurn and French planned?—the Sykes' papers would hit the streets on Sunday, and next week, as scheduled.

"Good for him," she mumbled. "More people ought to stand up to McKurn. . . ."

Like me.

Angrily, she thrust McKurn from her thoughts and spent another hour going through the rest of the recordings.

But there was nothing else.

Hoping for a break in the APHRODITE case, she called Jason—but his mobile phone was off. After injecting calm into her voice, she left him a message, and then wondered what she could do next. Her eyes stopped at the liquor cabinet—and moved on. *I need a clear head,* she decided, *and sleep. I need sleep.*

About to close her laptop, she noticed a reminder from the Victims' Self-Defence League. Their annual conference was this coming weekend in Sydney. She was to give the closing address on Sunday afternoon. It had been in her schedule for nearly a year. And it wasn't that she'd forgotten about it; she'd just had too many other things on her mind for the past few weeks to give it any thought.

"How can I do it now?" she moaned—the day after her "date" with McKurn. But she knew she had no choice: Alison was the keynote speaker—as the League's Founder. . . .

A few months after she'd begun giving talks at high schools around Sydney, Alison became a regular on several talkback radio shows, was interviewed on TV and by the press, and was even written up in one of the leading women's magazines. Her example proved to be an inspiration, and it wasn't long before other people were giving similar talks at high schools and universities all over the country.

They all came together in a loose federation which was eventually formalized as the Victims' Self-Defence League with Alison, almost against her will, acclaimed as its founder—and its first president.

By then, Alison's nightmare was coming more often, and with added power: continually talking about her experience kept her memory of her rape fresh. So she stepped slowly into the background, and eventually resigned altogether.

"Founder" was not a title she ever claimed herself: it had been given to her by others. The idea had been hers—or, perhaps, it was really Derek's. Others had pushed for and actually set up the organization but she knew that hers was the inspiration and the passion that led to its creation.

Turning her back on the League was unthinkable. . . . Yet, already feeling drained, she wondered if by Sunday there'd be any shred of her passion left for her to find.

Even before she crawled under the blankets she could feel her nightmare lurking in the darkness of her subconscious . . . but instead of the familiar feeling of terror and helplessness she could sense the dread and foreboding that her nightmare was about to become reality. She resisted sleep until, exhausted, she seemed to crumple into unconscious, so tired that her sleep, while restless, was also, mercifully, dreamless.

*****

THEY'D GIVEN KUNG CHEE-WAH his last injection early in the morning, and then let him dry out. He'd been given neither food nor water since the previous evening. If he'd become addicted in the short time he'd been drugged, he'd now be desperate. If not . . . now they had no choice: they'd been instructed to get that night's flight to Bangkok.

"It's time," said de Brouw, standing up.

Nazarov and Shultz followed him into the room where their prisoner was held. Kung was a slightly built man, but after being assaulted by their previous Dragon gang prisoner, Kung was so securely tied down he could hardly move.

"W-water," Kung said weakly. His face was pale, his cheeks gaunt, and his eyes ignored the needle de Brouw carried to fix on the bottle Nazarov held in his hand.

"Sure," said Nazarov, sitting on the edge of the bed. He made a show of opening the bottle of water, holding Kung's head up so he could drink, and bringing the bottle close to his lips. As Kung's lips reached greedily for the mouth of the bottle, Nazarov let a little water splash on this chin, pulled the bottle away and let Kung's head fall back to the bed.

"Just one thing, my friend," he said. "You still haven't answered my question: What did you do with Jessica Olsson?"

Kung ran his tongue around his lips, reaching for any drops of water within range. Nazarov held the bottle above his head and emptied it over Kung's chest.

"Jessica Olsson . . . ?" he said.

Kung said nothing and Shultz handed Nazarov another bottle of water. Nazarov looked at Kung and drank half the water in the bottle himself.

Kung's mouth hung open, his eyes pleading. He seemed to be trying to speak, and after a couple of grunts he said, "B—. B—."

"What was that?"

Kung shook his head violently, fear now written on his face.

"Talk to me," Nazarov said, waving the open bottle near his face.

When Kung said nothing, Nazarov nodded to de Brouw. "No," Kung screamed, doing his best to struggle away from de Brouw as he brought the needle closer.

"So you can talk . . . just answer my question," said Nazarov, "and you can have all the water you want."

Kung looked from de Brouw to Nazarov and back. With a small shake of his head he seemed to shrink, his body going limp, his eyes turning to stare blankly at the ceiling in resignation.

Nazarov shrugged. Kung was so tightly tied his struggles in no way hindered de Brouw from thrusting the needle into a vein.

"Last chance," said Nazarov.

Kung tiredly turned to look vacantly towards Nazarov, and then turned his gaze back to the ceiling.

"Okay," Nazarov said, and de Brouw pushed the plunger home.

"What do you think he was about to say?" Nazarov asked in the corridor as Shultz closed the door and locked Kung in the room.

"Some place beginning with B," said de Brouw.

"Bangkok being the obvious candidate," said Shultz.

"I agree," said Nazarov, "though it could be Brisbane."

"That wouldn't make any sense," de Brouw said. "But Balmain would."

"Or Boondocks," Shultz chuckled.

They all laughed. "I'll tell the Man," said Nazarov, "and let him worry about it."

They spent the next hour packing everything they'd brought into the SUV, parked in the enclosed garage, carefully wiping every surface to remove any fingerprints or other signs of their presence. By the time they'd finished, Kung was unconscious and de Brouw injected him twice more with a heroin-crack cocktail. He then wrapped Kung's fingers around the syringe and let it fall to the floor. They removed the ropes and chains so it would now look as if Kung had died from a self-inflicted overdose.

Once in the SUV, they removed the surgical gloves they'd been wearing and, as they drove away, de Brouw announced, "Three hours to flight time."

"No worries, mate," Shultz drawled, in a poor imitation of an Australian accent.

*****

GOTTLIEB ALTEN THOUGHT OF himself as a ferret who dug out information thought, by its owners, to be securely protected. Like a ferret, he was thin, so scrawny in fact that you wondered if he had any muscles at all. He looked like a pale, wimpy schoolboy; a wallflower whose proper place was on the shelf—or, where he was happiest, behind a computer. "You can get everything you want on the internet these days, 'cept pizza," he once said. "What about girls?" "Plenty of them on the internet too. But okay, sure, like pizza, sometimes I'll order room service."

On a dare, Alten hacked into CIA, U.S. Department of Defense, and MI5 computer systems; just for fun, he altered the university records to give the Vice-Chancellor's dog a Ph.D. in nuclear medicine. As computer security improved, he skulked around the city's wireless networks with his laptop so he could get into networks that were tough to break—without a password. "It's amazing," he once told a fellow hacker. "Companies spend a fortune on network security—and then hand out passwords to every Tom, Dickhead, and Blondebrain," who, unknowingly, passed them onto Alten. Initially, he did it just for fun, but it didn't take him long to find there was a ready market for such passwords.

His future path was clear.

For a short time, Gottlieb Alten worked as an analyst for a prestigious investment management outfit. By poring through old records, newspapers, documents, and accounts he'd reconstruct information a company thought was lost forever. He could pull apart financial statements to reveal embarrassing facts and long-hidden skeletons the company's management itself couldn't even remember. And, by hacking into their computers, unearth information the company didn't want anyone else to know. In the course of his work he'd be invited to boardrooms and CEO's offices where—unbeknownst to both his employers and his hosts—he'd plant bugs so that, later, he could listen in on what the management was sure were private conversations.

Alten's employers put his seemingly magical insight into companies' next moves to very profitable use. They once loaded up on an obscure mining stock at around fifteen cents a share—just days before it announced the discovery of a major nickel deposit. They sold their stake a few days later at $2.50. Another time, Alten's boardroom bugs gave him early warning that a major industrial company was about to announce a massive increase in profits. The company's stock price jumped after the announcement—and Alten's employers banked profits of twenty percent in just over a week.

The regulators became suspicious and investigated. But they could never pinpoint any connection between Alten's employers and anyone who was in a position to pass on inside information.

Gottlieb Alten was the connection.

And although that connection was never discovered, after only ten months at the firm Alten quit: he realized the information he could unveil was worth far, far more than the handsome salary and bonuses he was being paid.

In just another ten months, Alten was independently wealthy and set himself up as a freelance hacker-for-hire . . . hidden behind every firewall and dummy front he could think of. Given his talents, those protections were formidable.

As was his habit on a Friday evening, Alten had ordered "room service." So he was whistling through his teeth as went to answer the doorbell. But—as he always did—he checked the hidden video monitor showing who was standing in the corridor outside his front door. Instead of two sexy girls—he'd ordered a blonde and a redhead—there were three beefy, mean-looking men. They carried large hammers—and were wearing guns on their belts.

Oh-oh.

"I heard something," a man said. "The bastard's there."

Alten saw one of them beating his fist on the door. "Open up, in the name of the law."

Yeah, right, Alten thought. As he scurried into the large room he thought of as "Information Central," a louder noise came from the door: *They're going to break it down.*

To anyone walking into the living room of his harbor-side apartment it seemed just like any other luxury residence in Sydney's posh suburb of Potts Point, a thirty-minute walk from the city. But the large back room, made by combining two already-large bedrooms, looked completely out of place, as though it had been transported from a computer warehouse in some grotty industrial area.

Alten sat in front of one of the half-a-dozen active computers lining the walls, opened a window and typed a command. *Just more thing.* While he waited to make sure the routine started properly, he called the emergency number to report the break-in. "They're armed with pistols so I suggest you send the SWAT team."

The computer screens shut down, one by one. The program he'd set in motion was doing its job: his hard drives were backed up to a server installed in a locked cupboard; the computers then wiped their hard drives clean and turned themselves off. By the time those thugs broke through, they wouldn't even find an operating system. Meanwhile, the server was copying everything to two remote sites over the internet. Once done, the server would also have empty disks.

Meanwhile, an encrypted email was sent automatically to his clients:

if you're receiving this email, it means ive been put out action temporarily. wl be back
in touch as soon as possible tho have no idea when that wl be. to be on the safe
side, do NOT communicate with me until you hear from me again

Alten looked up as the hammering on the front door was now accompanied by the sound of wood breaking and metal groaning.

"Time for me to get out of here," he muttered.

He picked up what looked like a TV remote control and tapped out a seven-digit code on the number pad. A portion of a bench in the back corner of the room slowly rose along with a slab of the concrete floor. Keeping hold of the remote and grabbing his two laptops, he strode across and carried them down an iron ladder screwed onto the wall beneath. He tapped the code again and waited for the hole in the ceiling to close. When it did, he collapsed on the narrow bed with a deep sigh of relief.

Gottlieb Alten was all too well aware that no protection could ever be one hundred percent unbreakable. So under another name, he'd also purchased the apartment below his and rented it out. But first, he'd carved out this small room with a hidden exit to the back stairs, a bolthole with the only other access from above. The work had been done so skillfully that his tenants never realized that their apartment was a tiny bit smaller than it should have been.

It was not a pretty room. It had no windows, the machinery that lifted the square in the ceiling occupied one corner, and the iron rungs up the wall were another scenic blot. The room was also cramped, just large enough for a narrow bed along one wall, a bench and a wash-basin along the other, and only enough room for a stool in between. There was no toilet: Alten hoped he wouldn't need to stay there long enough to need one. Ventilation came from the building's central air conditioning system—one of the reasons Alten had chosen these apartments over others he had checked out.

On the bench was a computer. Alten turned it on and noted with satisfaction that it immediately began downloading his information backups from the internet—over a different connection from the one in his "Information Central" above. He put on the headphones and opened another program. In a moment he could hear the sounds of the men upstairs, and the computer's screen divided into half-a-dozen windows, each one showing a different view of the apartment he'd just vacated.

"There's no sign of the bastard," one of the intruders said.

Another man was unlocking the apartment's back door. As he opened it a fourth thug came through. "Anyone come out here?" he was asked.

"Whadda you think?"

"That sound you heard," someone said, "must have been your imagination."

"The hell it was."

"Where the fuck is he, then?"

A fifth man was sitting at one of Alten's computers. He'd turned them all on, it seemed, but the six screens remained blank. While the thugs were all muscle, he was all flab; pasty-faced, he looked more like Alten than one of the muscle-men, who called him "Professor." He put a CD into one of the computers and rebooted it. Alten smiled. The man was booting the computer from the CD drive and in a moment he'd be able see that the computer's hard drives were blank.

Another, different, muffled noise came through the headphones. Through the camera in the living room Alten saw four policemen wearing bullet-proof vests and carrying submachine guns run, crouching, into the living room; two stood either side of the corridor that led to the bedrooms, the other two ducked down behind sofas and armchairs for cover.

One of the thugs wandered into the room—to be welcomed by a barrel in his gut. A moment later, two more policemen came in through the back door. The two thugs in the kitchen froze, and raised their hands. A few minutes later, Alten chuckled silently as the intruders were all handcuffed and led away without a shot having been fired.

Putting down the headphones he lay back on the bed, wondering how much time he should let pass before leaving his "priest hole." But he didn't wait aimlessly: he began to figure out how he'd go about finding who had rumbled him and what chink in his armor they had discovered. He'd have to fix that up before he could resume business as usual.

35 Collision Course

ALISON GASPED AS SHE read the geek's email: . . . ive been put out action temporarily. . . . *What has happened to him?* . . . to be on the safe side, do NOT communicate with me until you hear from me again. . . . *When will that be?*

The time-stamp showed it had been sent around ten PM last night—but looking at the inbox she could see the phone taps were still all functioning. *But he can't do anything new until . . . when?* she asked herself.

She sat at the dining table in her apartment, her head in her hands, staring blankly at the laptop screen. She thought of Leon Price's confession . . . McKurn's stationery scam . . . the links to Weinbaum . . . French . . . every possibility she'd uncovered that led to McKurn's demise was still . . . a possibility.

But tonight she had to give McKurn his pound of flesh . . . unless. . . .

She snatched at her cellphone and dialled. "Jason. It's Alison. What news do you have?"

"Hi, Alison. Some . . . but not much I'm afraid."

"You mean," Alison said despondently, "you can't link 'John' to McKurn?"

"No. Well . . . not yet, anyway. APHRODITE'S had a number of clients referred to by a first name only—like 'John.' But there was John One, John Two, and John Three . . . just to start with. They're working on putting names to the nicknames—tracing the agency's payments and receipts through the banks, for example. But that will take time. And for them it's not a high priority: they have an open and shut case of sex slavery, intimidation, and so on. So they're not terribly excited about identifying customers. In any case, hiring a prostitute is not illegal, so even if they can put names to the customers, there's no crime they can be charged with. So their attitude is, Why bother?"

"What about underage girls?"

"There were none on the books—"

"Which doesn't mean there weren't any."

"I know that, Alison. And by the same token, prostitution is mostly a cash business, so there may not be a money trail back to McKurn. I assure you, they will figure out the money trail . . . eventually. But there is one thing—"

"What?" Alison demanded.

"Thanks to that Thai lady—she's a real tiger—the five Asian girls have all identified McKurn as a customer."

"They have? That's enough to hang him with."

"Hold your horses, Alison. McKurn can simply deny it as mistaken identity. And the girls' ID of McKurn may not stand up in court—not that it would ever go to court since—"

"I know. I know. McKurn hasn't done anything illegal, just immoral."

"Exactly."

"I wish you'd told me that before."

"I only just learnt it myself."

"I'm sorry, Jason—I really appreciate your help. It's just that—"

"I know—you want to get him."

"Damn right," said Alison heatedly. *And if not yesterday, then by lunchtime.* "And what did they get out of Weinbaum?" she asked. "Anything?"

"A little, but not what you're after."

"Jason, I *know* he's in league with McKurn."

"But we don't have any evidence," Jason protested.

Yes we do, she thought, remembering the McKurn-Weinbaum conversation. *But it was acquired illegally. . . .* "I guess," she sighed, "you'll just have to put it down to woman's intuition."

"Sorry, Alison. You may be right, but I need more than that."

"I know. . . ."

To calm herself down and clear her head she went for a short, but fast run. It helped, but not enough: she needed something she could hold over McKurn's head—something she could trade, something she could threaten to release if McKurn didn't hold back the video of her and Derek.

One possibility, she decided. She found the recording she had in mind and played it back:

"Gladys?"

"Yes . . . ah, John. Your usual?"

"Of course," said McKurn.

"It's your lucky day. We have a new one, almost virginal. Inexperienced but *hot,"*
The woman's voice sounded like she was cooing in McKurn's ear.

"Okay," McKurn's voice was enthusiastic. "I can hardly wait."

"You realize, of course, that she's. . . ."

"It's worth the risk. Send her over."

Would that do the trick? she asked herself. Undecided, she copied the "John-Gladys" phone conversation to her MP3 player, and then typed an email to Royn's private eye:

I have learnt that the five Asian girls you so wonderfully liberated have all identified Senator Frank McKurn as one of their customers. I wonder if they would be agreeable to being interviewed about McKurn, and if so whether you would be kind enough to make a "home" video, with appropriate translation, and send it to me.

Even if I can't stop him dead, I'll make him pay.

She looked at the list of phone taps. A moment ago, the prospect of going through them all had felt as appealing as pulling herself up a vertical cliff by her fingernails. Now, she attacked them, and less than an hour later she closed the last one. She marked the ones that were suggestive or hinted at possibilities worth following up; none were directly incriminating, but that didn't dent her mood. There was only a slight tremble in her fingers when she phoned for a cab to take her to the airport . . . and her flight to Sydney.

*****

Introducing himself as "Stuart Wrench," Olsson met Nazarov, Shultz, and de Brouw at the airport and took them to breakfast at a rooftop café at a hotel which overlooked Luk Suk's compound.

"That," Olsson said in his best British accent, "is most probably where the Jessica girl is being held."

"Lots of guards," said Shultz. "And nasty-looking dogs, too."

"Right," said Olsson. "Along with uniformed guards are others, not in uniform but obviously armed, patrolling the grounds."

"And plenty of barbed wire and glass on top of the walls too," said de Brouw.

"They're armed," said Nazarov who was looking through pair of binoculars. He passed them first to Shultz and then to de Brouw.

"So what's our assignment?" Nazarov asked as they took a table near the edge where they could keep an eye on the compound below.

"Basically, rescue me, probably from there," Olsson said, indicating Luk Suk's house below, "and then snatch this guy." He passed them three photographs of Luk Suk. "He's the Golden Triad boss."

The three mercenaries studied the photo. "Okay," Shultz drawled after a while, "but I don't get it. You're here—how are you going to get there? Just walk in? And why."

"I'd better lay out the whole situation. What will happen tomorrow," Olsson told them, "is that I'm going to meet Luk Suk at police headquarters. . . ."

"Where?" Nazarov and Shultz chorused.

Olsson smiled. "Neutral territory. We'll both be detained there until Jessica Olsson is released, unharmed, into the hands of Inspector Rudi Durant of the New South Wales police in Sydney."

"How long will that take?" de Brouw asked.

Olsson shrugged. "It all depends on where she is now. If she's in Sydney, just a few hours. If she's here—as we think she is—it might take a day or more. We'll just have to wait and see."

"How will we know when she gets to this Inspector?" Nazarov asked.

Olsson handed them each a SIM card. "Use these. Someone in Sydney will call you to let you know."

"Why should this Luk Suk guy agree to be holed with the Thai police?"

"I'm sure he won't agree," Olsson chuckled. "But he'll have no choice. Don't worry, it's all taken care of."

"Worry is one of the things we're paid to do," said Nazarov. "So please give me all the details."

Olsson nodded. "Fair enough. Tomorrow morning Luk Suk will receive an invitation from a police general to pay him a visit—immediately. He'll agree to that. In fact, one of you could watch from up here to confirm that he does. At headquarters, the general will make him a proposition—me, in exchange for the Jessica girl—and we'll wait there until we know she's safe."

"A police general?" de Brouw asked in surprise. "Now why would someone like that be involved in what's, basically, a gang dispute?"

"Connections," Olsson replied. "That's one of the things I'm paid for. Unfortunately, after the exchange, I'll have used up all my credit, so we'll be well and truly on our own."

"What if Luk Suk doesn't agree to make the exchange?" asked Shultz.

"Then I'll walk out of the police station, and so will he—twenty-four hours later."

"So we'll have twenty-four hours to figure out Plan B," said Nazarov.

"Precisely," Olsson agreed. "I don't think it will come to that—but it could."

"Okay," said Nazarov. "What happens after the girl is delivered to Durant?"

"Then I'll leave police headquarters with Luk Suk as a prisoner. No doubt I'll be handcuffed, shackled, God knows what. Your job is to follow me wherever I'm taken, spring me, and grab Luk Suk—in that order, of course."

"How many exits does this police place have?" de Brouw asked.

"Uh . . . I don't know," Olsson admitted. "I've always gone in through the front door."

"We need to know," said Nazarov. "We'll check it out. Now, where will he take you?"

Olsson shrugged. "There, I imagine," he said, pointing to the house. "But I really can't say."

"I wouldn't take you there," said Nazarov, "because that's where you'd expect to be taken. And if this Luk Suk guy has half a brain, he'll know you'll have back-up of some kind arranged."

"He's nobody's fool," said Olsson, "but is he a battle-hardened strategic thinker?"

"He must be," said Nazarov, "in his own way."

"And in his own field." Olsson pointed to Luk Suk's compound. "That looks pretty well guarded to me—from attack by a bunch of gangsters. But from a former *Spetsnaz* . . . ?"

"Maybe," Nazarov conceded. "But the first thing you learn in our business is never take anything for granted."

"Of course," Shultz drawled, "there's just one minor problem. A lot of those guys down there look like Thais. There are only three of us, and not one of us speaks Thai or knows our way around the back streets."

"That's where Suchart comes in."

"Your driver? What help could he be?"

"You'd be surprised," Olsson chuckled. "But he does rather blend into the background, wouldn't you say?"

"You'd better tell us more, then," said Nazarov.

Olsson leaned over the railing and pointed at the heavy traffic snarled along Sukhumvit. "See all those motorcycles?" he asked. "With a few phone calls, Suchart could put a fleet of two or three hundred of those bikes at your disposal, all of them with cellphones, naturally enough."

"I'm not sure I see how that could help," said de Brouw.

"See how the motorcycles are just zipping between the cars? Luk Suk will take me in a car or van. If you follow him in another car, you'll stand out like a sore thumb. But if a hundred motorcycles follow him, with you on the back of three of them. . . ."

The three mercenaries nodded. "You're talking sense," said Nazarov. "What else could Suchart do?"

Olsson smiled. "Say you'd like a dozen experienced hit men for backup. Give him a couple of hours' notice and you'll have Bangkok's finest."

"Do you mean that literally?"

"Indubitably," Olsson grinned, "some of them will be policemen, but not all. And if you want weapons of any kind, he's your man."

"We'll have to pay for all this, won't we?"

Olsson shook his head. "Suchart will handle that. And before you ask, he effectively has an unlimited line of credit."

Nazarov nodded doubtfully. "We'll sit down with him after this."

"One question," Shultz asked. "Why don't we just grab the Luk Suk guy now?"

Olsson shook his head. "After the Jessica girl is freed, by all means. But not before."

"Why not?" Shultz asked.

"I've been led to believe you've already had some conversations with some of his men. Did they prove fruitful?"

The three men shook their heads. "Not a word," said Nazarov, "unless you count 'B—. B—.' as a word."

"Would the Luk Suk character be any different?"

"He might be," said de Brouw.

"But he probably won't," said Shultz.

"Precisely, dear boy," said Olsson.

"So why," drawled Shultz, "are you willing to trade places with Jessica Olsson?"

"Because," said Nazarov, "he's really *Derek Olsson . . .* aren't you?"

"What makes you think that?" Olsson asked innocently.

"It's the way you move," said Nazarov. "You can change the color of your hair, grow the funny beard, and talk different—but you can't change your physique or your underlying manner."

"And sorry," said de Brouw, "but your Pommie accent, dear boy, is as phony as an old whore's promise."

"And," said Shultz, "we already know that the Chinks want Derek Olsson. Why would they agree to swap Jessica Olsson for anyone but him? And why would you, if you're not Olsson, agree to be traded?"

Olsson shrugged. "Think what you like—what difference does it make?"

"We like to get paid," said Shultz, "so if you're the Man—"

"The Man?"

"Yeah . . . the boss, the big cheese, honcho numero uno—"

"I've got your drift," said Olsson, holding up his hand. "I can only presume, gentlemen, that, like me, you get paid by results. So if you have to get me out to claim your reward, and I am numero uno, as you so quaintly put it, you'd better make bloody sure you succeed, don't you think?"

*****

THE CRYSTAL GLASSES AND silver cutlery glittered in the low candlelight; the dark, highly polished wood of the long dining table glowed with flickering reflection.

"Let's go riding tomorrow—can we Gramps?" Zoë asked.

"Zoë!" Melanie said. "Don't talk with your mouth full."

"Oh, mother," Zoë glared. She turned to Nancy Royn. "Grandma, did you tell Dad to keep his mouth shut and all that stuff all the time too?"

"Yes," Nancy Royn smiled. "But it was a total waste of time."

"Mother," Anthony Royn spluttered, a fork full of food in his mouth.

"Yeah, Dad," said Zoë, glaring again at her mother.

"Of course you can go riding in the morning, Zo," Sidney Royn said gently. "In fact, I'll join you."

"Want to have a race?" Zoë asked.

Sidney Royn shook his head. "A slow canter is all I'm good for these days," he said. "But maybe Max and Ricky will."

"Nah," Ricky said. "Horse-riding's for sissies."

"That's not what you said the weekend my girlfriends came up to Mount Macedon."

"That was different," Ricky growled.

"You just know you'd lose," Zoë shot back.

The phone rang; while sister and brother continued to bicker Sidney Royn went to answer it. "It's for you, Tony," he said.

Anthony Royn wiped his mouth and folded his napkin before walking over to the phone. His words didn't carry above the loud table chatter, and only Melanie noticed that, as he listened, Royn seemed shaken, the color slowly draining from his face.

He stared vacantly into space as he slowly replaced the handset, missing the cradle at his first try. He stumbled back to the table rather like a drunk having trouble standing up straight—even though his first glass of wine sat on the table, more than half full.

"What is it, darling?" Melanie asked as Royn resumed his seat.

"Kydd's had a heart attack."

Six heads turned to look at Royn; all conversation ceased.

Royn raised his head slowly, looking blankly towards Melanie. "A massive one, apparently," he said woodenly, his eyes slowly focusing on Melanie's face. "He's in intensive care. . . . It's touch and go whether he'll make it. . . . Fifty-fifty they say. . . . But the way they spoke, it sounded to me as though they don't really expect him to recover."

"He will," said Sidney Royn, everyone turning in surprise at the venom in his voice.

"I . . . don't know," said Anthony Royn. "He's overweight, he smokes too much—and he's ignored all his doctors' advice."

"We'll see," said Melanie, reaching her hand across the table to take Royn's. "I guess that means we should go to Sydney . . . in the morning. The last flight's already gone."

"Morning will be fine," Royn said. "He's not conscious now anyway."

"Tony," said Sidney Royn. His words were crisp, businesslike. "The first thing you need to do is inform the Governor-General. His protocol officers will know what to do next. But I really don't think they'll need to do anything . . . unless Kydd dies. You're automatically Acting Prime Minister, and while Kydd's incapacitated that means you'll be Prime Minister, both *de facto* and *de jure*."

"Thanks, Dad."

"So here's your opportunity to show everyone what you're really made of—and throw that Preston woman's words back in her face."

Royn nodded, looking at that moment nothing like prime ministerial material.

"Hey, Dad," said Ricky excitedly. "Since you're Acting PM, does that mean we can all go to Sydney with you in the VIP jet?"

"Technically, Ricky, yes," Sidney Royn said severely. "But if your father's first act was to grab for his privileges like a greedy youngster I can think of, how do you think the press and the voters might react?"

"Ah—yes, Gramps," Ricky said sheepishly, his ears turning red. "I suppose you're right."

"Of course he's right, you bonehead," said Max.

"Enough, you two," said Melanie.

"I don't know about the rest of you," said Nancy Royn, "but I've lost my appetite."

Sidney Royn nodded. "I think we could all use a stiff brandy," he said as he rose to his feet.

"Can I finish your steak, then, Gramps?" Ricky asked.

Zoë wrinkled her nose. "Ricky, you're disgusting."

"Ah . . . never mind then."

Grinning, Max dug his elbow into Ricky's side. "We'll clear up, okay, Grandma?" he said.

"Thank you, Max."

Sidney Royn put a tray with a bottle of cognac and seven brandy snifters on the table and began pouring, handing the first—large—one to his son.

"Thanks Dad," Anthony Royn said. Turning on his mobile phone he added, "I'll call Alison and get her to handle all the minutiae." He punched Alison's mobile number but there was no answer and he left a message. "It must be off," he muttered. He called her home phone with the same result. "Damn it, Alison," he growled, "where the hell are you?"

"Do you have her parents' number in Sydney?" Melanie asked.

"Somewhere here. . . ." Royn punched another number, and after a brief, if somewhat tense discussion, he asked ". . . if you would kindly ask Alison to call me urgently. . . . Thank you, Mr. McGuire," he said as he shut his phone. "Alison's father is not one of my fans," he grinned. "He said she's out for dinner."

"Why don't you go into the living room where we can all be more comfortable," said Sidney Royn, "and I'll call the Governor-General on your behalf."

"Thanks, Dad," Anthony Royn smiled.

WARMED BY THE GLOWING fire and mellowed by a second bottle of cognac, the conversation drifted lazily, guided mainly by Sidney Royn's reminiscences of his days in politics.

A while later, when the color had returned to Royn's cheeks and the vitality to his manner, Melanie leant towards him with undisguised anticipation, saying softly, "You know what this means, Tony, don't you?"

Royn looked puzzled. "What?"

"This could be the perfect time for Cracken to make a move—or, at least, to stake out his position. You're going to have to beat him to the punch."

"Which means," Royn said, "we're going to have to put McKurn out of action first."

*****

DEREK OLSSON'S FIRST NEWSPAPER was *The Twin City Times* in Albury-Wodonga, two towns lying astride the Murray River which defines most of the border between the states of New South Wales and Victoria. It met the established *Albury-Wodonga Independent* head on. Founded in the 1890s by Alexander Houghton, a dynamic local businessman, the *Independent* quickly became the region's leading daily. But by the turn of the 21st century, the *Independent* was a tired monopoly fought over by the baker's dozen of Houghton's great- and great-great grandchildren whose main interest was the fat dividend cheques their cash cow threw off.

Olsson's *Twin City Times* was a wake-up call for Alexander Houghton's heirs. His state-of-the art, computerized Goss Uniliner presses could print an all-color *Twin City Times* with twice as many pages three times as fast with a fraction of the labor it took to produce the *Independent.* The only place the *Independent* ran a tighter ship was in the editorial department. Olsson had lured away some of their best journalists, managers, and ad salesmen with salary offers that made the *Independent*'s remaining managers shake their heads in despair. Indeed, even in the opinion of other publishers, Olsson's editorial department looked to be grossly over-staffed.

The regional press, Olsson had discovered, was really a local press. National news, except the most significant, ran a distant second to just about anything local; world news was buried somewhere inside—and in some regional papers hardly appeared at all. An observation from the editor of a tiny country weekly glued itself into Olsson's mind. "The reason people buy my paper," the editor had told him, "is that everyone in town knows their name and picture will be published at least once a year. They just don't know when."

The *Twin City Times'* clean, modern layout made the *Independent* look like an aged dowager. And from its first issue, it published far more local news than the *Independent*, and every local bridge club, dog lovers' society, primary school football team—you name it—had its "day in the *Times*" at least once a year, even if it was only on page 52.

The *Times* was also a crusading paper, and its favorite crusade was against corruption. Some unlucky policeman was photographed taking $50 for not writing a traffic ticket. When it turned out that the driver was a reporter for the paper some people felt that wasn't "fair play."

But the following week, the same policeman was in much hotter water when the *Times* revealed he'd fixed a large number of tickets for a certain local councillor—and the councillor's prominent friends. The policeman, the councillor, and most of his friends spent some time in jail or paid heavy fines.

Every month or two the *Times* uncovered another corrupt official, and questions were even asked in Parliament as politicians tried to jump on the anti-corruption bandwagon. But behind the scenes were questions like "How did these bastards find out?" and "Shit, who's next?"

In just a few months the *Twin City Times* overtook the *Independent* as the circulation leader. A year later, Alexander Houghton's descendants threw in the towel and shut their newspaper's doors.

About six months after he'd launched the *Twin City Times,* the reason for the seemingly bloated editorial staff became clear: Olsson started his second daily, the *Wagga Wagga Bulletin,* a clone of the *Times* in almost every respect. Printed on the same presses, it was shipped in InterFreight trucks from a brand new freight terminal shared with the OlssonPress plant to Wagga, just over an hour away. But for French's deep pockets, his former cash cow the *Wagga Morning News* would have shared the same fate as the *Albury-Wodonga Independent.*

Within two years, Olsson had repeated the same formula on the outskirts of Melbourne and then near Liverpool on the edge of Sydney, publishing two to four dailies from each central plant, each of which shared a modern, computerized InterFreight terminal. Even with *MoneyWeek,* the *Sydney* and *Melbourne Weekends* and some suburban and country weeklies, his three Goss presses still had plenty of spare capacity to print for other publishers all over the country.

At nine PM that Saturday evening, the five gleaming towers of the Goss Uniliners were silent as the printers came back from their dinner break. The magazine sections of the Sunday *Twin-City Times* and the *Wagga Wagga Bulletin* had been printed at the beginning of the shift. They were carefully stacked, ready to be automatically inserted when the news sections were printed later. First, though, they would print the few thousand copies of *MoneyWeek* to be delivered along with the Sundays.

Ever since Lew Campbell, the OlssonPress and InterFreight security chief, had told him about the threat to "stop the presses," printmaster Hugh Matson had spent every waking moment at the plant, watching over the presses as if they were his babies—as, in a very real sense, they were. No visitors had been allowed; extra security guards were present at all times; all employees, especially recent hires, had been vetted again; everything was checked and rechecked; and as a final precaution, Matson had ordered that the presses be run slower than normal.

So far, nothing had happened and nothing suspicious had been discovered, either here at the *Twin Cities'* plant, or at its Sydney and Melbourne counterparts, where similar precautions were taken.

Matson's anxiety was increasing at the approach of the "Friday or Saturday night" deadline specified in the warning. He ordered the presses to roll at a slow 10,000 copies per hour compared to the presses' maximum speed of 75,000 copies per hour which could print the full run of both daily newspapers in under sixty minutes. Even though the presses smoothly turned rolls of paper and tubs of ink into finished copies of *MoneyWeek,* with everything working perfectly, Matson could not relax. He walked around the towers as they rumbled, listening for any out-of-place-sound, watching for any undue spray of ink or unusual wrinkle in the paper. He hovered over the console in the glassed-off control room, his eyes glued to the screen, dials and warning lights that looked nearly as complicated as the cockpit of a jet. So when the alarms sounded and the presses were automatically shut down, he didn't see until afterwards that the paper, fed from an enormous roll at the bottom of one tower, had torn, and the sudden release of tension had jammed the point where the five streams of paper from the five towers came together to be folded and cut into single newspapers.

Paper breaks like this happened occasionally, but the cause of this break was not some weak spot in the paper. The bearings carrying the plate that, when inked, transferred the image of the page to the paper had, literally, ground to a halt. In the moments before the presses shut down automatically, the sudden seizure of one roller had caused a second one to screech to a halt. It was immediately clear that one of the five towers was out of action, but it took much longer to determine why: fine grit had been introduced into the lubricant on the roller's bearings, ruining them completely.

After informing Olsson's security chief, Lew Campbell, Matson called the printmasters at the Melbourne and Sydney presses. They checked all the lubricants of their Goss presses, but after a couple of hours of painstaking scrutiny, found nothing out of order.

Press breakdowns, while infrequent, did happen, and newspapers—even the fiercest competitors—had an informal arrangement to help each other out. So Matson called the printmaster at French's *Wagga Morning News*—and immediately afterwards spoke to Lew Campbell again. "Doesn't have enough paper, he told me—the lying bastard. I told him: 'I can ship you plenty of paper.' He tells me it's the wrong size for his presses. Bullshit. We go way back. I could tell from his tone that he was really embarrassed, as though he'd been ordered not to cooperate with us."

Two hours behind schedule, the presses in the Melbourne and Sydney plants began to roll. The Melbourne Goss had barely started up when the computer control system crashed and everything stopped. Attempts to reboot the system failed. It wasn't until the next day that engineers discovered that a computer worm, which must have been introduced into the system by someone on the premises with authorized access, had wiped the system clean.

Half an hour later the Sydney presses continued to print as normal, the papers coming off neatly folded and stacked—with pages that were half blank. The black ink was contaminated with a thickening agent that blocked the ink jets on most of the towers.

In Melbourne and Sydney, the Sykes' presses came to the rescue—after they'd finished printing their own papers. In the Albury plant, it was nearly three AM when the lubricants had been completely flushed from two of the five towers and replaced, and Matson began to print the Sundays' news sections. With just forty percent of normal capacity, it would take several hours to complete the run. Worse, though, it had to be printed in three sections instead of one, and then those sections put together along with the previously printed magazine sections. To complement the inserting machines, journalists, office staff, their spouses, elder children, and any friends they could round up were drafted to assemble the finished papers by hand. It was eight AM before the last of the 40,000 copies of the Wagga and Albury-Wodonga papers were ready to be trucked out.

The presses had been stopped. But, if late, the Olsson Sundays still reached most of their readers . . . with the face of the latest in their line-up of corruption, Federal Labor Senator Felix Haughtry, grinning in full color on the front page.

*****

ALISON'S HANDS WERE COLD as the door to the hotel suite opened to reveal a smiling Frank McKurn, a scattering of grey and white hairs showing though his open-necked shirt. His eyes glinted in anticipation.

"Ah, my dear," he said, taking Alison's hand and kissing it in emulation of a man of chivalry. "Come in, come in."

Alison stayed the impulse to pull her hand back, hiding the revulsion she felt at his touch by letting her arm hang limply from his fingers. She shivered at the touch of his lips, and as he let her hand go it fell to her side as though her arm were lifeless.

"That's hardly the right attitude, you know," McKurn said

"I'm not one of your good-time girls, Senator," she said icily.

"So I see," McKurn said sourly as his eyes ran up and down her body. Alison wore a loose black sweater that concealed her curves, black slacks that shapelessly covered her legs, low-heeled shoes and no makeup. McKurn shrugged. "Come in."

As she stepped into the room McKurn let the door swing shut and, waving his hand at the sofa, said, "Take a seat. Can I offer you a drink?"

"Vodka and tonic. Light on the tonic," she said tonelessly.

Alison gingerly sat at one end of the couch, sitting as though she was attempting to shrink her body to disappear between the cushions. A part of her self was cringing in the expectation that McKurn was about to sit next to her, screaming for her to *get out of here now.*

But McKurn wasn't watching her, and made no move towards her. He picked up the TV remote from the coffee table, which was tuned into a news program with the sound off, and fingered the volume control saying, "There's something on the news I've been waiting for."

What had sounded like a low background whisper became the announcer's voice. ". . . the government's environmental policy came under attack today from an unexpected source." A freeze-frame of McKurn appeared to one side of the announcer's head and suddenly expanded to fill the screen, McKurn's voice filling the room.

While Alison watched she was aware that McKurn had moved behind her and heard the sounds of cans being popped and of ice tinkling against glass.

"Many of you, no doubt, will accuse me of being very slow to accept the danger of global warming," McKurn was saying. He stood behind a lectern marked SAVING THE PLANET. "But people who know me well know that I am the cautious sort who must first be convinced by facts, by scientific evidence, especially before supporting the kind of sweeping government measures required to counteract global warming—measures that would radically affect the lifestyle of every Australian. Having extensively studied the issue, I have become convinced that today, except for nuclear weapons, we as a species face no greater danger than environmental catastrophe. As a member of the Conservative Party, and as President of the Senate, it is incumbent on me to do everything I can to change our party's and government's insensitive dismissal of this issue. . . ."

McKurn sat down and placed a glass in front of her; Alison hungrily took a long swallow. "You?" she said, her eyes darting to his face and back to the news. "Turning into a greenie?"

McKurn chuckled. He lounged in the middle of the sofa, his long legs spreading under the coffee table, his arms outstretched right and left along the back of the sofa—without touching her. "Don't be ridiculous. The ice-caps on Mars are melting," McKurn said contemptuously, "and I suppose the greenies will claim the Mars Rover did it. Just six thousand years ago Sydney Harbor was almost twice as big as it is now, and half of Brisbane and Melbourne were underwater—caused, no doubt, by all our ancestors' camp fires." McKurn's words were dripping with unconcealed contempt. "But I sure know a bandwagon when I see one."

"For a moment," Alison said, equally contemptuous, "I thought you were taking a stand on principle."

"Ha," he grinned. "And there's nothing I enjoy more than adding to Kydd's discomfort."

McKurn flicked off the TV and Alison drained her glass, continuing to watch the now-blank screen, but against her will focusing on McKurn's every movement in her peripheral vision.

"Well, my dear," McKurn said, shifting his position to face her, "they have a superb Chateaubriand. . . ."

"I'm not hungry." Indicating her glass, she added, "But I could use another drink."

McKurn had hardly touched his own glass. He looked at her reflectively, his lips pursed. "Suit yourself," he shrugged. A few minutes later he returned and placed it in front of her. As Alison reached for it he sat down beside her and put an arm around her shoulders to pull her closer to him. She automatically resisted, moving her body in the opposite direction. But already squeezed next to the arm of the sofa, she could only lean over it. The fingers of her hand had immediately straightened, *en garde,* her arms and shoulders becoming rigid as she fought against her impulse to move onto the attack.

McKurn sighed, shaking his head. "That won't do, Alison."

"If you want willing cooperation," Alison snapped, gulping her drink as she spoke, "or the appearance of it, you'd better call someone else, Senator."

"I had a feeling you might react like that," McKurn said coldly, his eyes glittering at her in a way that sent a shiver of fear crawling up Alison's spine. He leant over to the laptop sitting on the coffee table and pressed the ENTER key. "There's something I thought you'd like to see . . . in full."

Alison's face appeared on the screen, her lips slightly open as they met another pair of lips in a long, slow kiss. Derek's face was turned towards hers but she could easily recognize his jungle of hair. The picture changed to his hand caressing her breast, her nipple lengthening as it hardened.

Her eyes glazed over, unseeing, but she couldn't tune out her voice saying, "Oh, Derek, Derek, more . . . " and she frantically groped into her handbag until her hand closed around the MP3 player.

The argument she'd had with herself in the taxi flashed through her mind. She had listened again to "John" and "Gladys," and knew that its release would certainly embarrass McKurn, and maybe even force him out of politics. But it did not live up to Niccolo Machiavelli's advice, that "if an injury has to be done to a man it should be so severe that his vengeance need not be feared."

McKurn's video was in a different league. It would devastate her and wreck her life. *Be better just to walk away.*

So, why don't you? The cold, ageless voice somewhere inside pulled her up short.
Because I can't throw away everything I've worked for.
And if you go through with it, you're not? the voice asked.
Alison found she had no answer to the question.
"Turn it off, damn you," Alison yelled.
McKurn stopped the video; Alison's face, tipped back—her mouth open in mid-scream, her eyes rolled back, frozen in mid-ecstasy—filled the screen; McKurn turned to look at her admiringly, staring, almost gaping at her breasts half-outlined by her sweater as he had looked at her naked breasts on the screen.
"One phone call, remember, Alison," McKurn growled as he leered at her.
Alison leant over and slammed the laptop's lid closed and sprang to her feet. "Let's get it over with." She pulled a condom from her handbag and thrust it into McKurn's hand. "Wear this."
McKurn looked about to object.
"It's not negotiable!" Alison spun on her heel and turned in the direction of the adjacent bedroom. But as she reached the door her steps slowed; halfway to the king size bed she stopped. "I—can't—do—this," she muttered.
Faced with the reality of the bed, all her previous thoughts, decisions, and resolve flew from her mind. She turned around to see McKurn standing, smiling, in the doorway. *Just once,* she thought. *Only a few minutes . . . that's all.* But if McKurn hadn't been blocking the door she would have run straight through it and out of the hotel. She couldn't bring herself to move in the other direction.
"Well, my dear," McKurn said coldly, "are you going to keep me waiting here all night?"
Not a bad idea, Alison thought. But as she looked at him, delving deep within herself for some other—any other—alternative, knowing she'd run out of options and had no choice.
Sighing, she turned her back on McKurn, kicked off her shoes, yanked the sweater over her head and pulled off her slacks. Now wearing just her bra and panties she dived under the covers of the bed feeling as if she was jumping into an arctic ice pool. She turned her head away from McKurn—like a little child who, by hiding her face behind her mother's skirts, could make herself invisible. She tried to connect with that meditative state she occasionally reached where her mind felt disconnected from her body, as if she could mentally disappear and leave her body behind, limp and lifeless. But a shock of cold air on her skin brought her sharply back to reality as the covers were pulled off the bed. She turned to see McKurn, naked, kneeling on the edge of the bed, his erect penis, encased in its plastic shroud, was an enlarged replica of his bulbous nose. In rising excitement, his eyes freely roamed her body for a long moment, and then he ran his fingers slowly across one breast and along her soft skin to her thighs. Quivering, Alison rolled away from his touch, and his hands moved to fumble with the strap of her bra. She felt a glimmer of a smile as he muttered, "Damn things are like chastity belts." As the catch finally came undone, he roughly pulled her onto her back with one hand as he slipped the shoulder strap along her arm with the other and her breasts stood free.
Alison closed her eyes, breathing deeply as she felt his mouth close over her breast, a hand gripping the other. Her fingers dug into the mattress, clutching so fiercely she felt she must be punching holes in the sheets. She cringed at the feeling of his drool on her nipple—and then felt his hands pulling off her panties. Her body remained limp, unresponsive. She tried to force her mind to drift away, to leave her body an unwelcoming corpse, but she couldn't help but be aware of every touch, every movement.

She half-opened her eyes for an instant, seeing McKurn's face looming over her, his red face contorted in anticipation, his eyes glittering as if he'd turned into the personification of unbridled, ruthless power . . . and at the same time she realized his satisfaction, his game, was not that of lust but of humiliation—that his purpose was to dishonor, degrade, demean, debase—and *control.* Alison felt gripped by overwhelming fear, weakening as she cringed away in horror at the same moment as, leaning his weight on her arms to pin her spread-eagled beneath him, McKurn thrust and entered and she felt his warm, hard skin sliding deep inside her. . . .

She could feel his skin! "You cheating bastard!" She screamed, a long keening wail that made her wonder who could be in such pain—a scream that brought a twisted smile to McKurn's lips.

I'm being raped again. . . .

Alison's scream became the roar of an animal in pain.

McKurn's grip tightened, his fingers imprinting bruises on her arms—and he laughed.

Beyond reason, Alison's body arched as her vaginal muscles froze into a knot.

Through a red haze, Alison was vaguely aware of McKurn's grunt of pleasure—which turned into a whimper of pain as she twisted her body throwing him to one side, a knee slamming between his legs as he fell away from her. McKurn's hand went to his scrotum, his legs crossing automatically in self-protection.

Taking hold of a wrist, Alison rolled over him and, as she came to her feet standing by the bed, the momentum of her body through the lever of his arm flipped McKurn over onto his stomach.

Panting, she became aware of a sticky wetness dribbling between her thighs, prompting the ageless voice inside her mind to comment: *And you thought you could trust this insect? Ha!*

With a snarl of pleasure she dropped, her knee slamming into his back and pushing the air from his lungs. She twisted his arm to his neck—and, in slow motion, higher, beyond any arc it was designed to reach, until she heard a *crack.*

McKurn screamed, a howl that made Alison shudder with a strange, unfamiliar sense of satisfaction. "Stop," he pleaded, gasping for breath. "Stop!"

Alison began to relax her grip, responding unconsciously to the movement of his free hand pounding the bed until she remembered with surprise that she was no longer on the Aikido mat. She let him go and stood up, her face lighting up a slow smile: one of his arms now lay limp and useless on his back. McKurn tried to move it and cried at the pain.

Blubbering, his eyes glaring redly at her through throbbing tears, McKurn reached slowly for the phone beside the bed with his undamaged arm. Before he could touch it, Alison grabbed the handset, yanked it hard, and threw it across the room where it shattered on a mirror, leaving a crack like an explosion in the center of the glass.

She stood looking down on McKurn's frail, twisted body, her breaths coming in gulps, her breasts heaving as she stood frozen in indecision. Her skin crawled wherever McKurn had touched her, itching as though his fingers were leaves of poison ivy. Involuntarily, her gaze fixed on the bathroom door . . . and for how many hours would she have to stand in a steaming hot shower before feeling clean again? But she felt that if she moved at all, if she allowed one foot to take a single step, she'd begin to run like the wind until she could run no more.

"You'll pay for this," McKurn growled.

Alison turned to look at him, studying him like a pale specimen flattened under a microscope. His shoulder was turning red and beginning to swell. His pale white skin sagged; the body that looked so powerful in a suit turned out to be muscle that had turned to fat; his legs were thin, his knees knobby, the end of one toenail a dirty grey. To quell her growing feeling of nausea, her eyes searched for her clothes and she began to pull them on.

"Call a doctor or an ambulance for God's sake," McKurn moaned.

"I should save everyone the trouble," Alison growled as she zipped up her slacks.

"What do you mean?" McKurn asked weakly, apprehension in his voice.

"I mean," she said as she adjusted her sweater, "I should finish what I started."

"You wouldn't dare."

Alison knelt by the side of the bed so she could look McKurn in the eye, and closing one hand around his throat squeezed gently. "It would be so easy. I could just squeeze a little harder—" McKurn spluttered, gasping for air, fear writ large in his eyes "—or with one slash of this hand and I could break your neck." She showed him the hardened edge of her other hand, and slashed it downwards, shattering the clock-radio on the bedside table. "See what I mean? Easy."

McKurn tried to nod his head, his eyes watching her hand.

"You're a liar, a cheat, and a parasite, Frankie," she spat. "You've never done a decent thing in your whole life. Give me one reason you deserve to live for another minute."

As he opened his mouth to speak she relaxed the hand around his throat. "Because," he gulped, "you'd go to jail."

"That," Alison chuckled, "is a reason I shouldn't kill you. Not a reason you should *live*."

"I—I—" McKurn's voice trailed off.

"You'd better think of something better than that before you meet your Maker," Alison said as she stood. McKurn shrank away as if she was now looming over him, like the angel of death. "But I won't break your neck, Frankie. At least . . . not today."

As Alison turned away, McKurn opened his mouth to speak, but changed his mind. He wheezed as he struggled to lever himself with one arm to a sitting position, wincing each time his broken arm flailed behind him. His nipples and stomach, Alison noticed, seemed to form the eyes and mouth of a cartoon sketch, a parody of himself.

Stepping into her shoes, she said, "I'll see you in Canberra, Frankie." She strode out of the room without a backward glance. In the corridor, she slammed the door to McKurn's suite and leant on it to catch her breath.

"One phone call, Alison," McKurn had said. "That's all it will take." Now he had no reason not to make that call, how long would it be before he did?

She smiled at the strange sense that—somehow—it just wasn't so important any more. And thought:

Now, I've got nothing left to lose—and everything to gain.

"... But Not Your Friends"

"Take what you want,"
said God,
"and pay for it."
— Spanish proverb

36 Masquerade

Hong Kong. A city that never sleeps. But sometimes it slows down.
Around five in the morning is one of those times. The city is awakening to another sweltering summer's day while the night dwellers are closing up shop and making their separate ways to home and slumber. The sun has yet to rise but is beginning to streak the clouds; streetlights and neon signs are still shining, their colors washed out by the slowly brightening sky.

Yet there is bustle, even if it is subdued.

Groups of mostly elderly people gather in parks for Tai Chi exercises in the cool of the early morning. A trickle of early risers join the night owls at the 24-hour McDonald's; Chinese restaurants with sausages and meats hanging in their windows are beginning to open their doors, as are the noodle stands on the footpaths. Here and there, people negotiate their way past high piles of newsprint where groups of newspaper vendors, taking up most of the sidewalk, busily collate the morning papers. With practiced speed they stuff the classified and business and feature and other sections inside the main news pages of Hong Kong's two English and seven Chinese dailies. Papers are unloaded and reloaded into cars and vans parked awkwardly nearby, oblivious to the NO PARKING and NO STANDING signs that would earn them a ticket any other time of day. As the lights of the Pink Pussy, Bottoms Up, and other Kowloon bars flick out, groups of girlie-girls in mini-skirts trickle out onto the footpaths, their high heels clacking in time to their chattering. The occasional male passer-by ogles their bobbing breasts, swaying hips, and naked midriffs—only to be ignored by their cold, hard eyes.

Unable to sleep, Derek Olsson wandered aimlessly along these streets that only last night teemed with honking buses, trucks, cars, taxis, and people spilling out from the crowded footpaths—now empty and deserted. He angrily kicked a flattened soda can, part of the previous day's accumulation of cigarette butts, drink cartons, orange peels, and other rubbish no longer hidden by the roaring traffic, and watched it arc and rattle along the asphalt with a momentary flicker of satisfaction.

A mere week ago—seven short days—he'd walked off the plane from Sydney to the feeling that Hong Kong had put out a welcome mat just for him. Oblivious to the heat, he immediately plunged into the floods of people jostling along the narrow footpaths, moving contentedly with the current as it took him from one new sight and sound to another, captivated by everyone's haste to fulfill some urgent purpose—if only to escape the sticky heat by scurrying to the next air-conditioned building. "The energy in this place is amazing," he wrote to Alison, "and the Cantonese seem to shout rather than speak. Maybe that's the only way they can be heard above the background noise—but even friends and lovers sometimes sound like they're arguing."

Like everything else about the city, the sharp alien sounds of the singsong Chinese dialect intrigued him. In just a few days of repeating what he'd heard without understanding he'd mastered a few basic phrases. Sometimes, especially when he asked, *"Gay door jin?"*—"How much?"—he'd be greeted with a broad smile of approval and a rattle of Cantonese. Until he learned *"M sik goong"*—"I don't speak the language"— which just brought another smile.

Wherever he went, he bought a postcard for Alison and, less often, one for his mother or sister. On some, like his description of the heart-stopping ride on the Peak Tram, a seemingly vertical climb from the bowels of the city to Hong Kong's highest point, his words to Alison flowed in circles to every available white corner; on others, like a junk gliding along the harbor past Hong Kong's skyline behind, had just a word or two on the back: "Breathtaking" or "You'd love this!"

At night, alone in a restaurant, his exhilaration turned into words that tumbled onto paper as he wrote to Alison about the sweaty crush of humanity on the buses and ferries; of rushing to get out of a sudden torrential downpour—and how, when the rain stopped, everything steamed dry in minutes; of the strange mélange of Nigerians, Arabs, Indians, and other shoestring travellers he met at the cheap guesthouse—one of dozens leavened with cheap, mostly Indian restaurants all stacked like bricks in Chung King Mansions, a tall building just a few blocks from the Peninsula Hotel, where mirror-black Rolls-Royces decorated the forecourt. He recounted relentlessly bargaining with the persistent hawkers offering "genuine" Rolex watches or "Hong Kong best tailor suit" ("What would *I* do with a suit?") until they realized he was not a buyer of anything. He didn't mention the evening a raunchy, dark-skinned girl, whose oversized breasts strained to leap from her undersized bra, had yanked him by his arm over faint resistance and pulled him off the street into a bar filled with barely-dressed women.

He felt liberated. Free. There were moments when he leapt into the air for no conceivable reason, or sprinted a few blocks oblivious to the sweat dripping past his eyebrows and plastering his T-shirt to his frame. The locals shook their heads wonderingly at the sight, muttering a few insulting words about crazy *gweilos*. Neither past nor future, just the *now* to be filled with new sights, sounds and experiences. And when Hong Kong started to become familiar? He'd simply get on a plane and take off to a new *now*.

He was becoming more determined to put off his journey's end as long as he could. Except Alison, he knew, would pull him back like an arrow in flight which eventually returns to earth. The sense of her absence—which is how it felt, as if it were she, not he, who'd flown away—was an ache that would come at odd moments. *If only she was here with me*, he'd think, *life would be complete*.

But she was on a journey to a different destination—at least she *had* a destination. And, perhaps—there was always the hope—Christmas in London or New York might change her mind. As for the rest? There was all the time in the world.

Except that now he blindly walked the empty streets, numb from lack of sleep and so focused on framing a letter to Alison that he bumped into a kerb, a light pole, and a passer-by, mumbling "Sorry" without even looking up. No matter which way he put his words together, they always sounded like the last thing he wanted to send her: a plea for help. He was relieved when the aroma of rice and noodles bubbling from a passing street stall prompted a growl from his stomach. He stopped in front of the McDonald's, jangling the coins in his pocket. Deciding he'd better conserve his cash, he walked on and ordered the cheapest dish, a bowl of *congee*—rice porridge—from a nearby food stall instead.

When he'd returned to the cheap room in Chung King Mansions, the three other young men he shared it with were gone. The door to his locker was swinging open and all his possessions, including his passport and ticket, missing. *Stupid!* he castigated himself. Even most of his cash was hidden in the lining of his backpack—*as if that would keep it safe.*

Now all he had was the clothes he was wearing plus the few hundred dollars in his wallet—and how long would that last? And what about his ticket? Would it be reissued? Would he have to buy a new one? If so, with what?

The *congee* was filling, but it left him feeling empty. He stared at the bottom of the bowl, scooping up the last flake of rice, vaguely trying to identify if the empty feeling was for want or food, or something else, when a girl's loud screeching, sounding like chalk grating on a blackboard, accompanied by her high-pitched, angry voice, drew his and everyone else's attention.

From the doorway of a bar about ten meters away, a shrieking, skimpily dressed girl was being pulled by her long hair by a squat, powerfully built Chinese man. Olsson couldn't catch a single word of the girl's Cantonese, but from her tone he was positive she was letting loose a stream of invective casting doubt on the Chinese man's paternity, masculinity, ancestry, and, no doubt, everything else about him. The girl tottered on her high heels as the man whacked her, at which the volume and intensity of her curses increased.

The handful of other people at the noodle stand buried their heads back into their bowls; the few people walking along the street crossed over or looked the other way. Their indifference made Olsson angrier.

Dropping his spoon, he jumped up and sprinted towards the man whose arm was raised ready for another swipe at the girl. Shouting, "Lay off, you bastard," Olsson grabbed the man's wrist and twisted his arm behind him.

The Chinese man let go of the girl's hair and turned in astonishment. Growling something incomprehensible, he wrenched his wrist from Olsson's grasp and swung a foot. For a fleeting moment, the rippling muscles of the man's leg stood out in sharp relief, and Olsson wondered if he'd taken on more than he could handle. But the thought fled from his mind as he found himself smoothly stepping into the man's kick. Instead of the foot connecting with the side of his chest to bowl him over or even crush a rib, Olsson took hold of the man's leg with one hand and helped it on its upward way. The man lost his balance, slammed into the thick plate glass of a small jewelry shop and slumped onto the pavement.

Stunned at his own prowess, the thought *Sensei Tozen would be proud* flashed into his mind. Yet as that thought came he imagined Tozen's voice scolding him for being so impetuous.

Now worried how badly the man might be hurt, he bent towards him but the girl shrieked at him and pushed him roughly away. Tears in her eyes, she glared at Olsson and resumed her tirade, now directed at him, and crouched over the groaning, semi-conscious man, gently slapping his face, trying to revive him.

It was a lovers' quarrel? Olsson asked himself, gawking at the girl, slowly shaking his head, open-mouthed.

Shrugging, he turned back towards his seat as if the pressure of girl's words were pushing him away—and stopped as he remembered his bowl was now empty. He had nowhere to go but things to do. Find the consulate, sort out his passport, the airline office for his ticket—which should he do first?—but they wouldn't open for hours yet. . . .

"Hey you!" From behind him, a man's gravelly American voice broke into the whirl of his thoughts.

As he raised his head and began to twirl around, he was surprised to see his way blocked by a tall Chinese man, looking uncomfortable in an ill-fitting suit that had a strange bulge under one arm.

"Yes, *you*," said the American voice.

Olsson turned to face the voice worthy of a John Wayne clone and found himself looking down on a short, slightly built, dapper Chinese man dressed in an obviously expensive and probably tailored dark grey suit, an incongruously bright red silk handkerchief spilling from his jacket pocket. His face was lean, a tiny scar to one side of his hooded eyes giving him a sinister look that went with his loud cowboy accent. But the corners of his mouth were turned up in the beginnings of a smile, and to Olsson the eyes behind the slits of his eyelids seemed to be looking at him with curiosity rather than malice. Standing next to him was another muscle man, wearing the same bulge. "You've caused me a problem," the dapper man said, "and I don't like problems."

Suddenly sensing that the muscle man who'd blocked his path had stepped closer to him Olsson spun away. Two steps took him off the footpath onto the street, putting a comfortable distance between him and the three men. "*I* have?" he said, now standing relaxed, his arms hanging loosely by his sides, eying the dapper man with interest, seemingly ignoring but nevertheless totally aware of the two sidekicks. The dapper man grinned at Olsson, a wave of his hand stopping the two men from rushing Olsson. "Yes, you have." He barked something at the girl and seemed satisfied with her answer. "He's breathing, you'll be pleased to know," he said to Olsson, "but I doubt he'll be able to work for a few days."

"Is that so?" said Olsson. "Perhaps you should hire people with better manners."

"I didn't hire him for his manners."

Olsson shrugged. "That much, at least, is obvious."

"Perhaps you oughta fill his shoes."

"Doing what?"

The man pointed behind him. "Doorman and bouncer in that bar. Hmm—I don't suppose you speak any Cantonese?"

"*M sik goong*," Olsson said.

The man laughed. "No matter. You'd be a novelty—for a few days."

Olsson shrugged. "Why not? I've done that before. What's the pay?"

"Five hundred dollars a night."

"American dollars?"

"Hong Kong dollars," the Chinese man chuckled.

Olsson shook his head and pointed at the unconscious man. "The same as him. Should be more, since I'm obviously better."

"Are you? Maybe you just got lucky."

"You think so?" Olsson said, pursing his lips in a wry smile.

"In that case, how about a demonstration?"

"What do you have in mind?"

The man simply grinned and barked something. While his words were still in the air, the two muscle men rushed Olsson simultaneously. They seemed slightly puzzled as Olsson made no immediate move. Only when they were almost upon him did he step sideways towards one of the men, blocking the upraised fist with one arm and spinning behind him to direct his momentum into the path of the second man. As the two men crashed together Olsson reached the boss and lightly held the small man's wrist. "Why don't you tell your two goons to get lost," he said calmly.

The two men had picked themselves up and were cautiously stepping towards Olsson.

"I'm not convinced that's such a good idea."

"*I'd* say," said Olsson with a brief squeeze of his hand—noticing that the man didn't seem to display any sense of fear, as though he was convinced of his own authority, "it's a better idea than letting them hang around."

After a short exchange in Cantonese, the two men walked slowly around Olsson, keeping their distance, picked up the still-unconscious man, and carried him into the bar. A moment later, one of them came out and stationed himself at the door.

"Okay?"

"Sure," said Olsson, letting go of the short man's wrist, "so long as he stays there."

"Two to one," said the man, grinning. "Impressive."

"Two to one?" Olsson shook his head. "No, just one to one. What's the point in going after the brawn when you can go for the brains."

"A thinking man, I see," he said with a laugh.

Unconsciously reacting to the appreciation in the man's eyes, Olsson held out his hand; the man's grasp was surprisingly strong given his thin fingers and slight build. "A pleasure to meet you Mr.—ah—"

"Everyone calls me 'Luk Suk'."

"Mr. Luk Suk." Olsson rolled the words in his mouth. He noticed that the shoulders of the man's suit were padded. In short men, that could be a way of compensating for a sense of inferiority. But there was no indication of that in his manner or in the way he looked at Olsson. They both knew that Olsson was stronger and quicker, that physically Luk Suk was in his power. But somehow, Olsson was dimly aware, the moment he let go of Luk Suk's wrist the authority began to flow the other way.

"Good intonation," Luk Suk said approvingly. "But just Luk Suk. It's a title. It means something like 'chairman of the board'. And yours?"

"Derek Olsson."

"*Ah-son sinsang.*" His brow furrowed. "Okay," he said, having clearly come to a decision. "A thousand a night."

"*Sinsang?*"

"Mister."

"*M-goi,*" Olsson said. "And a thousand a night sounds okay—cash and no receipt."

"Done," Luk Suk said. "Good accent. Been in Hong Kong for a while . . . ?"

"Nope. Just a week."

"Really? Most *gweilos* who've been here for years don't speak Cantonese as well as you do."

Olsson shrugged. "I just seem to have . . . picked it up, I guess."

"Come, I'll treat you to the best breakfast in Hong Kong." As Olsson turned towards the Peninsula Hotel, just behind them, Luk Suk placed a hand gently on Olsson's elbow and pulled him in the opposite direction. "Not there," Luk Suk laughed at Olsson's puzzled look. "Somewhere much better." Olsson found himself falling in step, following the man towards a noodle stand further along the next street. As they walked away, a hand signal from Luk Suk indicated that his muscle man should stay in place. He watched them disappear around a corner with surprise on his face.

A WEEK LATER, TSANG Kwan-yau, the man Olsson had replaced, came back apparently none the worse from the knock on his head. This was the moment Olsson had been dreading. He had enough money for a new passport and to pay the hefty fee the airline was demanding for the reissue of his ticket—but nowhere near enough to replace the savings that would have financed two or three months' of travel. He could buy a one-way ticket back to Sydney. But that would be to admit defeat. *No way.*

So pleasure competed with surprise on his face when Luk Suk asked him to stay on.

"Sure," he said. "At fifteen hundred a night."

"I don't know," Luk Suk said. "You're working illegally, you know, so—"

"So deport me," Olsson shrugged. "I'm worth it, and you know it."

That was true: Olsson had novelty value. Passers-by—local and *gweilo*—slowed or stopped in surprise when they saw his white face. All the bars had a barker out front to pull in customers. Some were middle-aged crones—mama-sans or former bar-girls long past their sell-by date—who screeched "San Mig beer just thirty dollar," or "Sexy girls. Just one drink." At others, one or two of the girls were on display; their sales technique was to try and pull passing men inside—when they could be bothered. Olsson's neat black slacks, crisp white shirt, and black bow tie suggested this bar was a class above the others. He engaged passers-by in a soft-sell of friendly conversation which was welcoming rather than off-putting. To newcomers who didn't know their way around, he'd freely explain how everything worked; to the doubters he'd say, "Just come in and have a beer—and a good look. You don't *have* to buy the girls a drink." But most of them, once the girls got to work, did.

Luk Suk laughed. Gripping Olsson's shoulder he said, "Okay, *Ah-son.* I like a man who knows his own worth."

When they heard how he'd come to replace Tsang, the bar girls and waitresses called him "Mr. Kung Fu." They flirted with him, more out of habit than ardor; he read their palms; they told him their hopes and their troubles; he picked up enough words of Thai, Russian, Mandarin, Vietnamese and Tagalog to greet each one in her own language when they arrived each afternoon. Because he seemed indifferent to their advances they became more brazen, squeezing up next to him when he took a break, whispering breathlessly in his ear, shamelessly brushing him with their breasts when they passed him. When he showed them the picture of Alison he carried in his wallet they were relieved: they'd decided he must be gay.

"Ah, she's so beautiful," said the leggy blonde Russian girl, who always introduced herself as "Veronika—with a 'k'."

"You leave her behind, all alone?" said one of the Cantonese waitresses. "You one crazy *gweilo.*"

"Yeah. *Why?*" asked another.

"To see the world."

"So what you do *here?*"

Olsson shrugged. "Same as you. Money."

When they learnt his nineteenth birthday was imminent—"My God, you're just a *baby,*" they laughed—they persuaded him to join them for a birthday breakfast. "We'll cook something up for you," they giggled. Eleven bar girls, plus a few of the waitresses, crammed into the tiny apartment four of the girls shared. Olsson refused the offer of tequila, nursed a beer, accepted the joints that were passed around and turned up his nose as the white powder came out.

"You . . . disapprove?" asked one of them.

Olsson shook his head. "That stuff's not for me, and I don't think it's a good idea. But no one has the right to stop you choosing your own life. And," he added more softly, "I understand."

The bar girls were all in Hong Kong on six-month contracts as "entertainers." They told him about the brothers and sisters they were sending to school, the aged or sick parents and elderly aunts and uncles they were supporting, or the little house they would build in their village when they went back. These and their other plans weren't pipe-dreams: between selling ladies' drinks and spending the night with customers they could take home more money than Olsson. But Olsson hoarded his money while they couldn't resist the little and not-so-little luxuries they'd never had . . . next month, they vowed, they'd save something. Olsson persuaded a few of them to open bank accounts but that didn't seem to make much difference in their spending habits: the accounts came with ATM cards. And some of them could only make it through a night of being pawed by strange men in a drugged or drunken daze. The ones who'd turned to drugs would have little to show for their efforts when their contracts ended.

The music was turned high to compete with the rattling air conditioner and the girls' constant chatter and barely won, but the air conditioner lost to the heat of a dozen bodies swaying to the pounding beat. They danced alone, with each other—but for themselves, with none of the flirting, sexy wiggles, and lurid come-ons they gave the male customers, and him, in the bar.

As the temperature rose and the tequila flowed, the air became heavy with the sticky fragrance of perfume, the sweet aroma of marijuana and the acrid swirl of cigarette smoke. Mesmerized by their glistening movements, a girl on one side using him as a pillow as she dozed, another bouncing up and down to the rhythm of the music, he realized his birthday was just an excuse for a party: a reason to escape for a short while into their own world, with no concerns, no distractions, and nothing to worry about. He decided he should wait for an invitation to join in their dance, but none came.

Later, when his stomach was full, his eyes half-closed, dazed from the alcohol and marijuana, but mainly drunk from the heady female scent inhaled with every breath, Veronika giggled as she squeezed herself next to him on the small, already overladen sofa. "You know what your birthday present is?" she whispered in his ear.

Olsson shook his head. "I have no idea."

"All of us." Veronika kissed him softly on the lips. Until that moment, the girls had all been acting as if he were an honorary female. As if her kiss was a signal, other hands began caressing him, unbuttoning his shirt, undoing his belt. Other lips kissed his ears, his nipples, his thighs, and a mouth closed around his penis.

That evening Olsson stumbled into the bar tired and hung over—and feeling contentedly wrung out.

He didn't mention that party to Alison, or that his cash and everything else had been stolen. He did tell her he had a job in a bar—as a waiter. "Since I'm making a bit of money, I'll probably stay in Hong Kong a little longer," he wrote, "but Christmas in London or New York is looking better." He apologized that his letters were shorter and came less often. "Working nights and sleeping days is disorienting. I don't think I could ever get used to it. I feel for those poor bastards who work the night shift: when do they get to have a social life, for one thing?"

He mentioned he couldn't find an Aikido class and had taken up Karate—"You should try it."—and how "the boss seems to have taken a shine to me. He's an intriguing businessman who lives by his own rules." But he couldn't bring himself to tell her what he'd learnt from one of the girls who'd had asked him, in a hushed whisper: "Do you know who Luk Suk *really* is? No? He's head of the Golden Dragon Triad . . . doesn't that bother you?" "Should it?" he'd replied.

Luk Suk came to the bar that night, as he did every day or two. "Happy birthday," he chuckled. "I hear you had quite a party." When Olsson flushed, Luk Suk laughed and slapped him on the shoulder. "Oh, to be young again."

The girls, waitresses, and bartender all smiled when Luk Suk stepped through the doorway. He knew everyone's name and had a quiet word to each person as he made his zigzag progress to the small office tucked behind the mirrored dais where the girls took turns dancing as a dare to customers. He'd listen sympathetically to a problem, sometimes making a suggestion, sometimes offering help. Olsson had also taken to asking Luk Suk's advice—even when he didn't need it.

Once a month everyone in the bar was invited to an afternoon cruise around the harbor on his junk. *Little things,* Olsson thought, *that inspire loyalty—and make us feel indebted.*

Now and then Luk Suk would take one of the girls home for the night—something they looked forward to. "You get a great night's sleep for a change," one of them told Olsson. "On full pay," another giggled.

The next payday, Luk Suk gave him a thousand dollar bonus. "You're good for business," he smiled. His expression becoming serious, he asked, "Your visa's about to run out, right?"

Olsson nodded. When he'd finally received his new passport he'd been granted a three-week extension to the three weeks he'd been given at the airport. He had just one week left.

"So what do you plan to do?" Luk Suk asked.

"I'm not sure."

"How about making some serious money?"

"Doing what?"

"Nothing strenuous. Take some stuff to Bangkok, spend a couple of nights there and bring something else back for me. Two thousand dollars—*American* dollars, not Hong Kong. And when you come back you'll get another stamp in your passport."

"Two *grand?*" Olsson's eyes widened and he was silent, thinking of how much sooner he could resume his travels with that in his pocket. "That's . . . nearly three thousand Australian."

Luk Suk nodded. "Plus expenses."

Olsson frowned. "What's the catch? Why don't you just call FedEx?"

Luk Suk grinned wryly. "Can't do that. Take a break. Let's talk about it."

Luk Suk had taken him a few times for tea or *dim sum* at one or another of his favorite, hole-in-the-wall Chinese restaurants. This time, he made Olsson put on a jacket and guided him towards the Swiss restaurant at the Peninsula Hotel. The *maitre d'* welcomed Luk Suk gravely and, while he didn't bow and scrape, his deferential manner gave the impression that his head was about to touch the floor. They were led to a quiet booth tucked away from prying ears. Three waiters hovered over them to the annoyance of other customers trying to attract their attention.

"Hungry?" Luk Suk asked. When Olsson nodded, he ordered Caesar salads, a beef fondue and a half-bottle of Swiss white wine without referring to the menu. But Olsson did, and he blinked at the prices, especially of the wine.

After the waiters had poured the wine, one of them hovered nearby until Luk Suk waved him away.

"So how do you like it?" Luk Suk asked as Olsson took a sip of the wine.

"Wonderful. I've never had a wine like this before." *In fact,* he thought, studying Luk Suk for some hint as to why he'd brought him to this place, *I've never been in a plush restaurant like this before.*

Even sitting down, Olsson towered over Luk Suk, whose diminutive figure seemed dwarf-like once he'd sunk into the high, wide, and very soft leather seat. "A most excellent year," he said, swirling the wine in the glass and holding it under his nose. "Aah," he sighed. He took a small taste and seemed to hold it in his mouth for a long moment before swallowing. Olsson followed his example, only now appreciating the wine's fruity aroma, and then feeling its cool pungency almost biting into the soft flesh on the inside of his cheeks. *A wine to be savored, not drunk.*

The salads came; they ate and sipped in silence. Olsson had been puzzled the first time Luk Suk invited him to *dim sum;* he was surprised by Luk Suk's wide-ranging interests and found his depth of knowledge, as befitting a man of the world, bewitching. Luk Suk enjoyed their conversations as much as Olsson did. He became sure Luk Suk's pleasure had the same source as his: the cut and thrust of argument and the excitement of stretching your mind.

One day, Luk Suk's eyes lit up when he mentioned Nietzsche and Olsson knew what he was talking about. "I had great fun taking philosophy, at the University of Texas in Austin. Went to high school there too—which," Luk Suk smiled, "explains the accent. You?"

"I devoured dozens, maybe over a hundred philosophy books—and dropped out of philosophy at university halfway through the first semester," and he told how he'd demonstrated the lecturer's philosophy was full of shit.

"*That* would have been worth seeing," Luk Suk laughed, looking at Olsson with a new respect. "So you disagree with Nietzsche?"

"I reject both his choices," Olsson replied. "I refuse to be Nietzsche's *ubermensch*— the 'over' man. And I have no desire to be ruled by one of them, either."

"There's another choice?" Luk Suk said, his tone a challenge.

"There *is,*" Olsson said, reacting to Luk Suk's tone rather than his words. "To neither rule, nor be ruled."

Luk Suk smiled. "That's simply not possible. Not even Nietzsche's *ubermensch* can be overlord *all the time.*"

"Why on earth not?"

"Even Einstein had to go home to his wife."

"I . . . see . . . I think. *Context,* right? Like the businessman who's the tyrannical boss in the office and the meek, hen-pecked husband at home?"

Luk Suk smiled with delight. "Exactly."

"I'll have to think about that."

At other times, Luk Suk slipped easily into the role of teacher. "From the papers," Olsson once asked him, "most people think Hong Kong will be a disaster area when China takes it back in 1997. What do you think?"

"I doubt it," Luk Suk answered. "The Chinese, you see, don't really *care* about Hong Kong."

"You mean—they don't want it back?"

"Of course they do. The same way a little kid wants his toy back. He doesn't want to *play* with it. He just doesn't want the *other kid* to have it."

Olsson was thoughtful for a long moment; Luk Suk waited in patient silence. "So you're implying that all foreign policy can be analyzed as mother-daughter, father-son, brother-sister, friend-enemy and so on."

Luk Suk gazed into the distance. "Sure," he said. "Countries don't act or think. Only people do. Saying 'China did this' or 'the United States did that' is misleading journalistic shorthand. Foreign policy is just people fighting over power."

Luk Suk's manner with Olsson was that of a friend or colleague, not of employer-employee. Somehow, it seemed to enhance rather than diminish his authority. *That,* Olsson realized, *is how he treats everyone.* And Olsson began to feel comfortable with Luk Suk in a way he'd only felt once before: with his grandfather. *Of course,* he chided himself, thinking of Shakespeare, *it won't last forever. It never does.*

Today Olsson waited for Luk Suk to speak first. But he was feeling a little tipsy by the time the fondue was served along with another pricey half-bottle of red wine—Luk Suk barely touched his wine, so Olsson's glass was the one refilled. "It's a long night," Luk Suk explained with a twinkle in his eye. "We shouldn't drink too much."

"The world's full of evil, you know, Derek," Luk Suk said when the waiters had left them. "To survive you can't let it touch you."

"Shouldn't you stand up to it? Oppose it?"

"Avoiding it is better—and safer. So far I've succeeded."

"Have you? Some people would say you're . . . that what *you* do is evil."

Luk Suk leaned back and spread his arms wide. "But Derek, no *thing* can be evil. Only people can—agreed?" When Olsson nodded, Luk Suk asked, "So what *is* evil?"

"Hurting people."

"That's always a bad idea."

"Why is that?"

"Whenever you hurt someone you create an enemy. That's bad for business."

"So you've never hurt anybody?"

"Sometimes it's unavoidable."

Olsson's smile faded. "That's true," he said quietly.

"So does who I am bother you, then?" Luk Suk asked.

Olsson smiled. "It *might*—if I knew all the details."

"But it doesn't now."

"No. I've seen the way you are with people, and I can see you're a good person—whatever else you may be. And from what I *know*—the bar—whether everything about it is legal or not I don't know . . . but everyone is there by their own free choice. If the law gets in the way of voluntary acts between consenting adults, well, the law is an arse."

"And drugs?"

"You mean, *illegal* drugs, like marijuana and cocaine?"

Luk Suk nodded.

Olsson smiled. "So *that's* why you can't call FedEx?"

"You're quick." Luk Suk seemed delighted. "But only half right."

After a moment, Olsson asked, "Which half?"

Luk Suk laughed. "Cash to Bangkok. Drugs back. So what's your reaction?"

"I'm not surprised, if that's what you mean. You're a triad chieftain, so I'd be surprised if you *weren't* in the drug business" Olsson shrugged.

"So what *would* bother you?"

"Violence. Murder."

"In self-defence?"

"That's the only justification."

"I agree," said Luk Suk. "So what do you think about making a little trip to Bangkok?"

"It sounds like it could be fun," Olsson smiled. "But it's hardly free of risk."

Luk Suk nodded. "True. But the risks are much lower than you might think."

"Really?"

"That's right. You're not on anybody's list, so there are only two risks. If you look nervous you could be stopped and searched. The other one is a random search. But you'd take flights that are scheduled to arrive at busy times, reducing that risk considerably."

"And if I *am* stopped?"

"A hundred thousand American dollars sounds like a lot of money, but it's not that hard to hide. It will be packed between the lining and the walls of a suitcase. It will only be found if a customs official decides to cut the lining to look behind it. Otherwise, they could empty the suitcase and not see it. And that will be in Thailand, so you'd have to spend a night, maybe two, in jail. But I have connections there, so you'd be sprung pretty quickly."

"But here? We're talking about drugs, not money. Different story."

"So we take extra precautions. The heroin is packed between the lining and the outside of the suitcase in the same way. But it's carefully sealed—vacuum packed so there's no smell for the sniffer-dogs to detect—in thin sheets so the walls of the suitcase aren't noticeably thicker. If you pat them, it just feels as though the suitcase is cushioned. That's why not one of our couriers has been caught. You won't be the first, I'm certain of that." Luk Suk leant forward to give his next words greater emphasis. "I like you, *Ah-son*. If I thought the risk was too great, I wouldn't ask you. You know that."

Olsson slowly nodded his head. Luk Suk's words and the tone of his voice were reassuring, and Olsson's mind had drifted to think how two thousand American dollars would cut weeks off the time he'd need to work to restore his savings. "I'll have to think it over," he said. "But . . . should you be telling me all this? I mean, if I say 'no'. . . ."

Luk Suk shrugged. "I trust you, *Ah-son*. And in any case—" he waved his arm to indicate the empty tables nearby "—there's no one here to overhear us."

Taking drugs may be stupid, but is not immoral, he told himself. *But—they're illegal. Which is the problem.* Would he be caught? *That* was the issue. For the rest of the evening his mind floated between that question and thoughts of the money—that, if everything went smoothly he could replenish his savings *and* buy a ticket for Alison; of the excitement of outwitting government officials—right under their noses; of the certainty in Luk Suk's voice—and the sense that he trusted Olsson implicitly.

Worn out from the long night of standing on his feet at the door of the bar when he was already exhausted from lack of sleep, still feeling the after-effects of the wine, he fell into a deep sleep the moment his head hit the pillow. He had a confused dream, cruising atop a red London double-decker bus, through Piccadilly Circus and Trafalgar Square, past the Empire State Building and getting off to climb up the Statue of Liberty, Alison at his side her hand clasping his. When he woke, the ache of her absence was a cramp in his stomach. The next day he told Luk Suk, "Why not?"

37 The Sound of Thunder

ORAWAN MCLEOD STOOD, HER feet apart and her hands on her hips, glaring at her husband. *"Why* should they make that video? *That's* what I want to know."

"They'd repay a debt—" Hanson McLeod protested.

"They don't *owe* a debt."

"Wouldn't they like to see McKurn ruined?"

"Why should they care about McKurn? What's in it for *them?"*

Hanson McLeod sighed. As always, Orawan was fiercely protectively of her charges—worse, he thought, than any mother hen. He knew when he was beaten.

"Gratitude?" he said weakly.

Orawan snorted. "And if the video gets on the internet then their family and friends back home will know they worked as—"

"They'll all know anyway," McLeod protested.

"That's what everyone will *assume.* But there'll be no *evidence—"*

"What do you mean, no evidence? *They* will be exhibits one to five in court, testifying they were forced into sex slavery. *Their* pictures will be on TV and all over the internet. They'll be broadcast in Thailand and God knows where else. No evidence? Don't be ridiculous."

"Who are you calling ridiculous?" Orawan demanded, her dusky cheeks turning a dark, dusky red. "Anyway, they don't want to do it, and that's *that."*

"They don't want to do it? Or *you* don't want them to do it?"

"You're impossible. Go and talk to them yourself, see what they say."

He did. In his halting Thai—with Orawan glaring in the background—he confirmed what he already knew: Orawan had taught them to say "No," a word that didn't come easily to most Asians where "Yes" often meant "Maybe" and "Maybe" usually meant "Most likely not." Orawan had been in the West long enough to say "No," without any qualms—at least, when she was speaking English.

McLeod could tell that he, a Western male, could sway them. He knew "repaying a debt" was a powerful motivator in their culture. But he could also tell that they really *didn't* want to publicly identify McKurn, and he was secretly proud of Orawan for stiffening their resolve. Turning to her, he said, "Fair enough. I'll send them that message."

Orawan smiled at him—and he melted as he always did. As he passed she planted a long kiss on his mouth. "You're a wonderful man, Hanson," she said. "Most of the time, anyway."

*****

". . . CONSIDER THE BATTERED WIFE," Alison was saying. "Why doesn't she leave her husband? She has a choice—stay or leave—and she knows it. So why does she stay?"

Alison stood at the podium, her gaze skimming the audience to make brief eye contact with the four hundred-plus members of the Victims' Self-Defence League squeezed into every available seat in the conference hall. Nineteen years ago it was just an informal get-together of like-minded people exchanging notes and ideas. It had grown into a fully-fledged organization offering self-defence courses, counselling, hotlines and other support services, and training programs for its members.

"She has what I call the *Victim Mentality*. It's her self-image, that she's a victim, *and deserves to be one*. We know these women—we've all met them, right?"

Alison paused. There was a ripple of nodding heads, and isolated comments of "Right!" and "Certainly have."

She cupped an ear and raised her voice. "I can't hear you."

"RIGHT!"

Alison smiled. She'd arrived a mere fifteen minutes before her talk. Maureen Hendrickson, the League's president, had welcomed her with the comment, "You look like something the cat wouldn't even *want* to drag in." Despite her heavy makeup, her eyes had been red and puffy, her skin pale. She had moved listlessly, even stumbling as she mounted the steps to the small stage. Most of that wasn't obvious to the people beyond the front few rows; but the lack of energy in her voice and demeanor *was*. The audience shifted in their seats, as if they couldn't get comfortable.

But as Alison warmed to her message, her underlying anger injected passion into her voice and vigor into her manner: her words now commanded attention and the audience obeyed. Though still wan, her cheeks were flushed, her eyes brighter, her movements more graceful and precise.

"These women all know they have a choice. They *dream* about leaving their violent husbands every day. Yet, every *day* they refuse to make that choice.

"*Why?*

"When they come to us, we teach them the skills of self-defence. Which they *all* master—if they stay the course . . . am I *right?*"

"RIGHT!" the audience roared as one.

"But then—?" Alison let her question hang in silence for a couple of heartbeats. Her expression now somber, she dropped her voice barely above a whisper "—what happens when that terrible moment comes . . . when they need to *use* those skills?"

Four hundred pairs of eyes focused on Alison in hushed expectancy until, one after another, a rising cacophony of voices began to shout, "Nothing." "They freeze up." "They're too scared."

Alison nodded, asking for silence with a queenly wave of her hand. "You're right. Too often, nothing happens. They freeze. They *submit*. Why? Because they know, deep down, *they don't deserve to win*. They know, deep down, that they *deserve* their punishment."

Alison stared at a woman seated in the back of the room—Molly Olsson? *She* can't *be here. Surely not.* Then the woman smiled, and Alison realized she was seeing someone with a strong resemblance.

"They *know* they have the skills to defend themselves, to turn the tables on their attackers. They've *proved it* on the mat to their own satisfaction. But, deep down, they believe *they don't have the right to use what they know they know.*

"Because they know they were born to be a victim."

But I wasn't. She stood frozen for a long moment, lost in the implications of that thought, until a cough in the audience reminded her where she was.

"Most of us here today were victims ourselves once, " Alison continued, as if her pause was intended, "so you know *exactly* what I'm talking about. I'm also sure that many of you—once upon a time in another life—felt you, too, were born to be a victim." Now, most heads were nodding sagely. "So you know that mentality can be changed—because you've done it.

"But life continues to give you hard choices. Life continues to put you in situations where, if you fight back, you stand to lose something you value. And *when* that happens, do you have the temptation to give in? To *submit*—as you once did before?" The shudder she felt at the memory of McKurn seemed to underline her words. "Because, sad to say, overcoming the Victim Mentality *once* is no guarantee that it's completely *gone.*"

She paused to breathe, and as she lightened her tone of voice the tension in the room slowly subsided.

"In a sense, I'm not telling you anything you haven't already talked about, one way or another. All of us have inspired others by telling our stories of how we fought back—and lived. But too many victims, even as they're caught up in that story, are telling themselves, 'I could *never* do *that.*'

"How can we reach out to them? How can we help them change their minds? I'm afraid that's one of the questions I'm leaving you with, a question *I* can't answer. But I'm sure that some of you *have* an answer—or will find one.

"Finally, it's crucially important to guard against any reappearance of the Victim Mentality in *ourselves.* When another one of those tough choices comes at us out of nowhere, it's imperative we do *not* procrastinate, do *not* let things snowball until they grow into hard or even impossible decisions.

"*And* . . . that we vow to always—*always*—fight back." Her voice echoed through the hall, and as she paused her eyes seemed to be tracking an invisible movement on the rear wall. A few heads in the audience even turned to see what had caught her attention. But only she could see the image of McKurn cringing at her words, scuttling into the distance to escape them.

Her eyes now sparkled as her smile, slowly widening, encompassed the entire room. "Remember the famous quotation, attributed to Edmund Burke: 'All that is necessary for the triumph of evil is that good men do *nothing.*' That saying should be engraved on our souls.

"Why?

"If *every* victim was *always* willing *and able* to fight back, where would that leave the thugs and bullies of the world?

"Imagine a world where hooligans, standover merchants, sadistic husbands, and brutal tyrants—the Hitlers, Stalins, and Pol Pots—all had *no one to victimize.*"

The only sound in the room was the faint, almost inaudible hiss of air blowing through the air conditioning vents. The audience members were frozen in their seats, their eyes alight with the images and implications of Alison's words. Then, as if the four hundred-plus people were of one mind, the room thundered with long waves of applause, and Alison seemed to rock backwards from its force. As she steadied herself, her somber face lightening into a thin smile leavening her angry passion, the roar intensified as people cheered, swayed, and raised their arms so their hands clapped rhythmically above their heads.

The waves of applause faded into a moment's silence, and the hall slowly filled with the sounds of chairs scraping, papers rustling, and people talking.

Maureen touched her arm and said something. Alison turned, momentarily surprised she was not alone on the podium. "Oh—Maureen. Sorry. I must have been daydreaming."

"That was a speech and a half," Maureen repeated. "What happened to you?—I've never heard you like that before."

"I was . . . inspired," Alison said, turning an automatic grimace into a quick grin.

"You can say that again. I must admit, I was a bit worried when you arrived."

"You weren't the only one," Alison laughed.

The audience began trickling out the now-open rear doors, but the mass of the people crowded around Alison, throwing questions and congratulations to her; a few, it seemed, came just to get near her and even touch her as if she was some pop star. Nearly thirty minutes later some fifty people still congregated around Alison, reluctantly moving away only when Maureen's words, "I'm sorry, ladies and gentlemen, but you'll have to excuse us," finally dispersed them.

"After that, I believe you need something cool and probably alcoholic," she said to Alison.

"You must be reading my mind," Alison smiled.

"We have something in the back room. It's the only place we'll get some peace and quiet."

"A quick one, as I've got to get going—"

"I know," Maureen nodded. "But your boss can wait an extra fifteen minutes or so. Something rather worrying has come up."

"What's that?"

"Sit down first," Maureen said as they stepped from the plushly carpeted conference hall into an undecorated room with stacks of tables, chairs, and other equipment for meetings, conferences, dinners and the like. A trestle table covered with papers served as an office. Alison took a chair as Maureen handed her a drink.

"That's strong," Alison said when she took a sip.

"I think you're going to need it," Maureen replied. "What I want to talk to you about . . . has to do with the martial arts program in schools you and Royn pushed through."

"That's been quite a success."

"Well, yes . . . and no."

"Lots of students sign up for it—"

"That's the 'yes' part."

"—so what's the 'no'?"

"We did a study—" Maureen dug into a pile of paper until she found the file she was looking for and passed it to Alison. "Here. Read it later."

"Tell me the bad news."

"You know the two problems: even when the courses are free, many of the kids who really need it just won't sign up. And teaching them the skills is easy enough, but—as you just said so eloquently—giving them the gumption to actually *use* them is another story. . . ."

"Maureen!" Alison sighed. "It's not like you to beat around the bush. It must be *really* bad news. *Out* with it."

"Okay," Maureen said reluctantly. "According to this study, maybe half the people who *need* it—you know, the victims and potential victims—come along. And there's quite a high dropout rate. But close to a hundred percent of schools' *thugs and bullies* join in—and keep coming back for more. They *love* it, goddamn them—especially the more violent martial arts like Karate."

"Oh my God, that's terrible. Is there anything we can do about it? There's got to be some way to stop the bastards—" Alison stopped when she saw Maureen's helpless look.

"We just got this report. We'd assumed it would be something we could talk about today—but we decided to say nothing about it."

"Oh, *hell* . . . unintended consequences."

"What?" Maureen asked. "Oh, I see. Quite. And you know what? If they'd had to *pay* to attend, not a single one of those bully-boys would have signed up."

*****

LUK SUK SMILED BROADLY at police general Chuasiriporn as he stepped into a well-furnished, though not lavish corner office in the Bangkok headquarters of the Royal Thai Police. His smile encompassed a second police general sitting next to Chuasiriporn behind the desk. The two generals were a contrast in opposites: Chuasiriporn was tall, heavily built and tending towards fat, his hair prematurely grey, his light skin suggesting a Chinese heritage—and seemed uncomfortable. The second general, whom Luk Suk had never met before, was about the same height as Luk Suk, dark, lean, swarthy and his face as calm as a stone Buddha. Chuasiriporn had invited him to "an important meeting": the other general's cold, black look suggested it was not going to be the friendly conversation he'd been expecting.

But his step faltered and his eyes narrowed quizzically at the sight of the well-dressed, vaguely familiar foreigner with a goatee beard lounging to one side of the desk.

Chuasiriporn, always delighted to see him, did not return Luk Suk's smile. Gesturing him to a chair at the opposite end of the desk from the foreigner, Chuasiriporn said, "This is General Vanich, and this *farang* I believe you already know."

"He looks like someone I should know, but I can't place him." Luk Suk frowned at Chuasiriporn. They were drinking, golfing, and whoring buddies who had a long-standing and mutually profitable relationship. But Chuasiriporn's impassive face gave no hint to the inexplicable change in his manner

"Derek Olsson."

"Ah-son!" Luk Suk jumped to his feet

"Please *sit,*" General Chuasiriporn said, his parade-ground tone giving Luk Suk no choice but to obey.

As Luk Suk slowly resumed his seat, his angry expression softened to one of concern as he saw Chuasiriporn watching him indifferently, his face a wooden mask. "What's—?" He paused as the implications of Chuasiriporn's manner sank in. "What's going on, General?" he said respectfully.

"It has been alleged that you are holding this man's sister, Jessica Olsson, against her will," said Chuasiriporn.

"Who made this allegation—*him?*"

"No point in denying it, *Wong sinsang,*" said Olsson, pointedly using his name not his title. "They've seen your video."

"Exactly. And we have reason to believe that the lady in question is here in Bangkok." Chuasiriporn looked at Luk Suk with disapproval. "Kidnapping foreign tourists is . . . bad for business."

"I . . . understand," Luk Suk said meekly.

"So you are to deliver this lady to Inspector Durant of the Sydney police—"

"Where—*here?*" asked Luk Suk.

Chuasiriporn shook his head. "In Sydney. And when the inspector confirms receipt of the lady—undamaged in any way—then you may leave and take Mr. Olsson with you."

"But *he's* another foreigner—"

"True," Chuasiriporn shrugged. "But he's a fugitive from Australian justice who, it seems, has entered Thailand on a false passport. So. . . ."

"I see." Luk Suk nodded. "And if I am unable to . . . ah . . . arrange this exchange?"

"Olsson walks, and you will be our guest here for the next twenty-four hours. If you *can* arrange it, you both will stay here, incommunicado, until Inspector Durant confirms receipt."

Luk Suk nodded. He cast a questioning glance towards General Vanich who had yet to say a word, and glared at Olsson.

Olsson grinned back. "What have you got to complain about?" he chuckled. "Isn't this what you wanted? Or did you want to eat your cake and have it too?"

"Ah-son—"

"Enough!" said Chuasiriporn. "What's your decision?"

General Vanich looked at his watch. "There's a Thai Airlines flight leaving for Sydney later this evening," he said. "I'm sure there'll be no trouble getting a seat. And a little first class treatment might improve the lady's disposition, don't you think?"

Luk Suk turned to Vanich. His eyes flicked to Olsson and back to Vanich as if he'd finally made a connection.

"Okay," he said, his body slightly bowed as if weighed by a sudden burden. "If I may make a phone call. . . ."

*****

Trailed by police—who would follow him everywhere while he was Acting Prime Minister—Anthony Royn and Melanie stepped quietly into Randolph Kydd's hospital room.

Kydd forced a weak smile, twisted by one side of his face which wasn't fully cooperating. He lay on his back, his movement restricted by the maze of wires and tubes connecting him to heart and brain wave monitoring machines and intravenous drips. His face was wan, as if the heart attack had consumed all the blood in his cheeks, and his flesh of his jowls sagged in folds against the pillow, making him look as though he'd lost several kilos overnight.

"Five minutes *only*," the doctor had stressed. "His heart attack was accompanied by a mild stroke so he's *very* weak. Don't say a *single* thing that might upset him."

"I imagine," Royn grinned, "that just *being* here is upsetting him enough."

"You're not wrong about that."

"Ah . . . Tony, Melanie." Kydd's now-hoarse voice, barely above a whisper, had lost its boom. "Sorry I can't get up."

"Don't trouble yourself, Prime Minister," Royn said, automatically stepping into the bedside manner of a sympathetic doctor to hide his shock at Kydd's appearance.

"So what did the doctors tell *you*, Tony? They wouldn't tell me a thing."

Royn and Melanie leaned closer to better catch his words, which hissed as though his tongue stuck to the roof of his mouth on every "S."

"Only that you have to rest up for a while," said Royn.

"Damn them. All they *would* say is that I've got to quit smoking and drinking, exercise and eat fucking *vegetables* for Chrissakes—excuse my French," he added with flick of his eyes towards Melanie, and gasped for breath. "What's the point? That's what I want to know. Anyway, Tony, are you ready to step into my shoes?"

"It's a bit early to be talking about that, Prime Minister."

"Take it easy," Melanie said, putting a hand on his forehead. "You've got to get your strength back."

"I know, I know. That's about all I hear." Nonetheless, Kydd visibly relaxed at Melanie's touch. "Anyway, what are Cracken and McKurn up to, do you know? I can feel the bastards dancing on my grave already."

As Royn hesitated a moment, framing a response, Melanie said, "We hear rumblings, Prime Minister. But that's all so far."

"That'd be right."

"We'll hold the fort till you get back, Prime Minister," Royn said.

"And we're already figuring out how to put Cracken in his place," said Melanie with a smile. "So don't worry—"

"Don't *worry?*" Kydd looked at Melanie quizzically, as if he'd detected an undertone in her voice that he didn't like. "That's about all I *can* do. No politics they say. No TV, no radio, no newspapers or magazines. They're keeping me completely cut off." Seeing Melanie look towards the TV set in the room he added, "Just dumb movies, that's all. Not that I've watched any yet. Haven't been awake long enough."

"I'm sure that will only be for a few days, Prime Minister," Royn said soothingly, "until you're up and about."

"Yeah, right."

"Your five minutes are up," the doctor's voice came through the door. A nurse came in after him. "And time for your medication, Prime Minister."

"And what are you going to pump into me this time?" Kydd growled.

"Something to help you rest and recover."

"You're going to dope me again, are you? Damn you."

"Too much excitement, Prime Minister, is not good for you right now," the doctor said firmly as the nurse turned a small tap on one of the IV tubes attached to Kydd's arm.

"Now that you're in the hot seat, Tony," Kydd whispered as the sedative began to take effect, "remember that if you want a friend in politics, get a dog."

*****

"I broke McKurn's arm, or dislocated his shoulder. Maybe both."

"You did *what?*" Melanie and Royn spoke as one, but Royn's tone was angered while Melanie's was one of admiration.

Royn and Melanie sat on the sofa in Royn's suite at Sydney's Four Seasons Hotel, Alison on the edge of an armchair opposite. The suite overlooked the Sydney Harbour Bridge, which was casting long shadows over the water as the sun neared the horizon to the west. The harbor gleamed faintly pink from streaks of sunset on the darkening grey and black clouds. Royn and Melanie had the grandstand view, but their eyes were glued to Alison.

"*Why?*" Royn asked. "What *happened?*"

"I—" Alison looked down at the floor and whispered, "He wanted . . . I'm sorry, Minister, I can't bring myself to tell you. It doesn't matter now," she said, raising her head and her voice, her eyes now fierce, "but I'm *not* sorry and I *won't* apologize."

"So, Alison," Royn said glaring at her, "what's to stop McKurn releasing that video now, for heaven's sake?"

"*Anthony.*" Melanie's eyes were fierce, her voice cutting. "Calm *down.*"

Royn looked at her sheepishly. "I'm . . . sorry," he mumbled. "It's just . . . a shock."

"It is that. But," Melanie said, looking meaningfully at Alison, "I'm sure he deserved it."

Alison averted her eyes. She had thought she would be able to "tell all" to Melanie later, when it was just the two of them. But then Melanie would tell Royn . . . and Alison realized she wouldn't be able to hold her head up again if *he* knew.

"The way you're talking," Royn said, looking at his wife as if he'd suddenly discovered something new about her, "you sound like you'd like to have done it yourself."

"Damn right I would."

"Luckily for you," Alison said, her lips twisted into half a smile, "you didn't have the opportunity."

"There is that," Melanie agreed. "Ah," she said, "so *that* explains McKurn and Cracken. On the phone taps. McKurn said he'd 'had an accident' and was in hospital, so he'd be out of action for a couple of days."

"*That's* going to be his story, eh?" Alison chuckled. She turned to Royn. "In Parliament next week, everyone's going to ask him why he's walking around with one arm in a cast."

Royn nodded numbly. "But . . . what are we going to *do?*"

"We've got a few days' grace," said Alison. "I called McKurn this afternoon—"

"Not to apologize, I hope," Melanie said.

"Certainly not," Alison laughed. "I told him if he was thinking of releasing that video I had something to show him that might change his mind."

"What do you have?" Royn asked eagerly.

"Remember the sex slave ring our private eye busted? All five of the Asian girls had McKurn as a . . . ah . . . client."

"If that came out—" said Royn.

Alison and Melanie both nodded. "He'd have to resign," Alison said. "Before you get too excited, I don't actually *have* anything to show him—yet. I *hope* to have it in a day or two. But—the girls don't want to do it."

"I don't blame them," said Melanie.

"Me neither," Alison agreed. "But I think I've persuaded them."

"And if they won't?" Royn asked.

"We've got a couple of days to come up with something else to head McKurn off."

"And God knows," said Melanie, "we've got mountains of material."

"But nothing else that delivers a knockout blow," said Alison. "Meantime, Minister, I suggest we assume we're going to *win.*"

Royn nodded glumly.

"Politics is just a stage, right, darling?" Melanie said, gripping his arm. "And for the moment you've got the starring role. All you have to do is play it for all it's worth."

Royn grinned at her. "True, my dear."

"So how *is* the Prime Minister?" Alison asked.

"Not good," said Royn, shaking his head.

"And the doctors' aren't saying anything," said Melanie, "which most likely means—"

"—we'd better plan on the basis he won't make it," Royn said.

"That's what McKurn and Cracken are doing," said Melanie.

"Remember, Kydd is paranoid," Royn said, looking like a schoolboy reminded of a painful lesson. "We have to tread carefully. Have you had any thoughts, Alison?"

"Only that it might be a good idea if you called all the members to tell them what you know," Alison said.

"The *Conservative* members, I hope you mean."

"Plus Nash, of course."

"That's a lot of phone calls," said Royn.

"True," said Alison. "But it's a chance to campaign without campaigning."

"I like it," said Royn.

"Call them alphabetically, darling, so you don't ruffle anyone's feathers."

Royn grinned. "Except the guys in the second half of the alphabet."

Melanie shrugged. *"Someone's* got to be last."

"It's going to be a long night." Royn rolled up his sleeves and reached for his cellphone. "Let's get started."

The first thing Alison saw when she opened her laptop was an email from the private eye. "They won't do it!"

Royn covered the mouthpiece of his phone with one hand. *"Quiet* you two, for heaven's sake," he glared.

"Wind it up," Melanie ordered, the fingers of one hand swivelling to emphasize the urgency. "We need you here, *immediately."*

"What are we going to do now?" Alison groaned.

"Let me have a look," Melanie said.

Sorry, Melanie read, but the girls don't want to do it. We tried—but they just don't want to go public.

"I was talking to Ian Nash. He asked me if I was beating my wife," Royn grinned as he took a seat beside Melanie. "Now, what's all this about?"

"They won't make the video," Alison told him.

"Is there any other way to stop McKurn?" Royn asked.

"Probably not in *time,"* Alison said.

Royn nodded glumly.

"How long have we got?" Melanie asked, looking at Alison. "When does McKurn expect to see you?"

"Tuesday."

"Just a day and a bit to make them change their minds," said Melanie.

"How?" asked Royn.

"If I could just go and talk to them myself," Alison said.

Royn shook his head. "We can't break cover."

"Collin Renfrew!" Melanie said. "Call him *right now."*

"It's Sunday night," Royn protested.

"At his rates, it won't make any difference."

"Yes," Royn breathed heavily. "It's our only chance. So what should I tell him?"

"Those private detectives work for *us,* don't they?" Melanie pointed out. "How much have we paid them so far—"

"Over a hundred thousand."

"—so there you are," Melanie grinned. "They're making a fortune from us. And if it wasn't for us, those girls would still be imprisoned in Canberra forced to bonk all and sundry. They owe you big time."

"True," said Royn.

"All you have to do, darling," Melanie said, stroking his hand, "is get Renfrew to drop everything else he's doing and throw his weight around until they do what we want."

"He doesn't have that much weight," Royn grinned.

"A hundred thousand dollars is a lot of weight," said Alison.

Royn picked up his cellphone. "Collin? Something urgent's come up."

"Tony. It's Sunday night." Royn held his phone slightly away from his ear so Melanie and Alison could hear his tinny, protesting voice. "And you know what you're interrupting right now?"

"I can imagine," said Royn.

"Okay," said Renfrew. "This better be important, Mr. Acting Prime Minister."

"Let me put it this way, mate. There's something I need you to do, and that invitation to the party at the Prime Minister's Lodge you're so keen on hinges on the result *you* get."

"Okay, you've got my attention," Renfrew said slowly. "I suppose this has something to do with Mc—"

"Collin, is that bird you're with *also* covered by attorney privilege?"

"Uh, no. I'll go into the next room."

After he'd explained what he wanted he added, "And Collin, if you need me, just call. Anytime. It's crucially important. Tomorrow's going to be a busy day, but I doubt I'll have anything I can't step out of for a few minutes. Okay?"

"Okay," said Renfrew.

Putting down his phone, Royn reached for his drink. "Ah," he said with a smile. "Those girls will be putty in his hands—Collin can negotiate the pants off any woman walking."

*****

DISCRETION BEING THE BETTER part of valor, Gottlieb Alten decided to take a few days' vacation. So he waited several hours after the police left before slipping out of his "priest hole." He carried just his two laptops and a small backpack with his "escape kit": a spare toothbrush, a change of clothes, and the like, and ten thousand dollars in cash. He took the back stairs down to the underground car park, peeking through the fire-exit door until he was certain no one was around. He took a few steps towards his Lotus Élan, a car that was totally impractical for tooling around a city but which he loved just the same. Shaking his head, he turned towards the nondescript Toyota he used about once a week just to keep the batteries charged. Dropping his bags into the boot, he nosed the car out to the street and drove through the night northwards until he reached Coffs Harbour, a medium-sized town about halfway between Sydney and Brisbane where he could disappear amongst the other weekend tourists.

When he finally connected to the internet he logged into an invitation-only site for hackers to discover that he wasn't the only hacker whose premises had been raided in the past few days.

"I wonder what that means?" he mumbled.

Two other hackers reported the same pattern: a group of masked thugs barging in, holding them prisoner while somebody went through their computers—using not so gentle persuasion to get passwords when required. Nothing had been damaged, nothing stolen and, when the thugs had finished, they simply left.

musta bn looking for something, read one post.

Indeed, thought Alten. *And since they didn't find it they came knocking on my door....*

38 My Enemy's Enemy

*T*ERRORISTS ON THE RUN was a lead story in many Australian newspapers that Monday morning. Sandeman and Australian forces had swept halfway across Saint Christopher's Island, driving the terrorist bands before them. The story was illustrated with a picture of grinning Sandeman and Australian soldiers raising the Sandeman flag on the island's highest peak. "We've taken away the terrorists' safe haven," Colonel Cantrell was reported as saying. "The way it looks, the rest of it is mopping up. And the casualties so far have been overwhelmingly on the other side."

In her column, Karla Preston condemned the weak-kneed major internet providers who had all "gutlessly submitted to court censorship." She listed duplicate McKurnWatch sites "that *aren't* censored," repeated some of the anonymous "McKurn Watcher's" allegations against McKurn, and gave directions on how to use "tunnels" and "anonymizers" to reach *any* blocked website, anywhere in the world.

That same morning, McKurn's lawyers applied to the court to have those duplicate sites blocked as well and filed a writ of libel and slander against the OlssonPress and Sykes newspapers, both of which had published Karla Preston's column.

Another team of lawyers appeared before the same judge at the same time. Representing a small internet service provider owned by the OlssonPress, they sought a reversal of the court's original injunction. "We will prove," they said, "that McKurn has no basis in fact for challenging the allegations made by McKurnWatch as either libellous or slanderous."

When they indicated they'd also contest McKurn's suit against the OlssonPress and Sykes newspapers, the judge set the hearing for both issues for the coming Thursday morning.

*****

ALISON MCGUIRE FINISHED KARLA'S article and leant back in her chair, nursing her third cup of coffee.

It had been a long night. While Royn made his phone calls, Alison and Melanie worked through everything they'd accumulated on McKurn, searching for an alternative "knockout blow." So far without success. It was another night without enough sleep— but, she had to admit, travelling with Royn and Melanie on the VIP jet from Sydney to Canberra that morning, with limousines and a police escort at each end, was a step up in the world.

Sitting on the other side of the desk, Melanie Royn noticed Alison's reaction and asked, "What's that you've just read?"

"More pressure on McKurn," Alison said, passing Karla's article across.

"We've got mountains of stuff we could feed her." Melanie jumped to her feet, her brown eyes flashing. "McKurn wouldn't know what hit him. After all, my enemy's enemy and all that. . . ."

"Maybe," Alison said doubtfully.

"Oh. But isn't she . . . ?" Melanie's voice trailed off.

Alison smiled. "That's right. But as you said. . . . And it's not as though we have that many allies at the moment."

"Sad to say," Melanie said.

Alison sighed and turned to her laptop. "Okay, I'll send her an email." Her fingers flicked across the keyboard. "I should be in Sydney on the weekend, so I could see her then."

"Good luck." Melanie smiled encouragingly at Alison's hesitant tone of voice.

Royn poked his head through the door to her office. "Time to go, Alison."

"Be right with you, Minister."

"Any word from Collin?" Melanie said as she gave Royn a kiss on the cheek.

"Not yet."

"Call me the minute you have, okay?"

"You can count on it," Royn smiled as he turned to leave.

"I'll see you back at your place later," Alison said as she followed Royn out the door.

"I'll be there," Melanie said.

As Acting Prime Minister, Royn had to handle Kydd's duties in addition to his own. Along with Doug Selkirk and other members of his staff, he and Alison were scheduled to be briefed by their counterparts in Kydd's office.

Afterwards, Alison would join Melanie at their Yarralumla townhouse so they could continue analyzing the McKurn material in complete privacy.

*****

"I DON'T SEE THE point of you being here," Orawan McLeod snapped as she ushered Royn's solicitor Collin Renfrew and Ramsay Holloway, owner of the McLeods' employer, Countrywide Investigations, into her living room.

Many times in the past, Orawan had clashed with Holloway—a greying, rotund, energetic bulldog of a man whose British accent had survived his thirty years in Australia intact. And even in high heels and stretching herself to her full height, she felt intimidated by the way Collin Renfrew towered over her—and everyone else. She invited them to sit around the dining table, sitting next to her husband on a chair with a cushion so that she could almost look Renfrew in the eye without tilting her head back.

"It's quite straightforward, Orawan, my dear," Holloway said, unaware of the way Orawan bristled at what she considered his fake cordiality. "Our client has made a request which has been turned down, and I'd like to understand why. Mr. Renfrew represents our ultimate client and has full power of attorney to come to any agreement on his client's behalf."

"As we already told you," Orawan replied, "they simply don't want to make the video."

"But, my dear," Holloway said smoothly, "it seems to me such a simple thing to ask. And think of the client—he's obviously important, and our work is clearly of national significance. Surely *that's* an important consideration . . . ?"

"Important to *you*, not *them*."

"And to *you*, remember," Holloway said with a warning glance. "More to the point, if it wasn't for us—and your superb work, I might add—they'd still be prisoners of that awful agency in Canberra."

"Their release was a *side-effect* of our assignment—just their good luck," Orawan shot back.

"Perhaps," he said, waving a hand dismissively. "But I should remind you, my dear, that we have not achieved our client's primary objective, which was to link McKurn with that call girl agency. Now, in one stroke, they can do that for us. Such a little thing for them to offer in return, don't you think?"

"Perhaps," Orawan replied, matching Holloway's tone and dismissive gesture. "The police also got a nice big case out of it. Are you going to send them a bill as well?"

"Now, don't be silly—"

"The point is," said McLeod, "that they don't want to do it. Are you suggesting we try and force them to change their minds?"

"Of course not," Holloway snapped, beginning to rise. "Obviously, I'd better go and talk to them *myself*."

"Just a moment," Renfrew said, placing a restraining hand on Holloway's arm. "If I may, I'd like to clarify a few points first."

McLeod shrugged. "Fire away."

"Thank you. They understand what's being asked of them?"

"Of course," Orawan snapped. "They're not dumb."

Renfrew smiled at her. "I'm sure they're not. I'm just asking dumb lawyer-type questions, okay?"

Orawan began to smile, but her face quickly returned to a Buddha-like calm.

"Do they understand who McKurn is, and the effect their testimony could have?"

"They know McKurn is a powerful politician," Orawan answered. "But the effect? I don't think so."

"Where they come from things are different," McLeod explained. "People there would be surprised if a rich and powerful man *didn't* have mistresses and the like."

"I see," said Renfrew. "Don't you think they'd like to be instrumental in bringing down a scumbag like McKurn?"

McLeod looked at his wife.

"They probably would," Orawan nodded slowly, "but that's not their problem—or *the* problem."

"What *is* the problem, then, Mrs. McLeod?" Renfrew asked.

"Shame," she said.

"Shame," Renfrew said slowly. "That can be a powerful factor. But—are they too ashamed to *make* the accusation? Or am I missing something?"

"I think they'd be shamed if their friends and neighbors ever saw it," McLeod answered. "Am I right?"

"Yes," said Orawan. "They couldn't hold their heads up in public if everyone had seen them admit to—to—"

Renfrew held up his hand. "I understand. So tell me, Mrs. McLeod—" Renfrew softened his voice and she leaned forward automatically to hear him better "—if we could guarantee that their friends and neighbors would never see it, do you think they'd agree to do it?"

"Maybe," said Orawan doubtfully. "But how can you make that sort of guarantee?"

"We draw up an agreement," Renfrew responded, "which includes a penalty for breach."

"What kind of penalty?"

"Say . . . five thousand dollars each?"

"How about ten thousand?" Orawan countered.

"Well . . . I'd have to clear an amount like that with my client. But I'm sure it's not completely out of the question."

"This agreement you're talking about," said McLeod, "would have to be under Australian law wouldn't it?"

"Victorian actually. But yes."

"What if the agreement is broken when they're all back home and thousands of miles away? How could they collect then?"

"They should have their own legal advice before they sign anything—I, of course, can't represent them. You have a solicitor, I imagine—he or she could be their agent."

"Or someone else," said McLeod, "like Orawan."

"Of course. So could we put this idea to the ladies in question?"

"Good idea," said Holloway, getting to his feet.

At Orawan's grimace, Renfrew said, "You know, Ramsay, perhaps—as the client's representative—I should be the one to accompany Mrs. McLeod, don't you think?"

"If you like," Holloway grumbled.

"This way, Mr. Renfrew," said Orawan.

The five girls were sitting in the McLeod's family room on the other side of the kitchen. Renfrew explained each part of the agreement; Orawan translated his words into Thai, Issan, and Khmer adding, he was sure, her own comments. While he understood nothing of their answers—except for Phuong's halting English—he could tell from their body language that they looked at him in awe when he was introduced as the representative of the client responsible for their freedom and became very excited at the mention of "ten thousand dollars." Apparently, he concluded, that amount would buy them a lot of respect when they returned home. He could also see how they deferred to Orawan, confirming his presumption that she was the key to these negotiations.

When they'd indicated their agreement, Renfrew thanked them solemnly and said to Orawan, "I need to talk to my principal now. So if you'll excuse me. . . .

Renfrew stepped into the back yard, admiring the tropical flowers in a small greenhouse—a touch of Thailand in chilly Melbourne—as he called Royn. "Tony, I think I can break the logjam *if* you okay it. The stumbling block isn't *making* the video, but having it publicly available. In other words, they seem willing to make the accusation that McKurn was their client, so long as it's kept *private*. . . . What's the definition of 'privately'? Good question. Tell me, what exactly do you want to *do* with this video? . . . Okay. So you don't *need* to make it public—so long as McKurn thinks you will. . . . And the money? . . . If you *don't* break the agreement, it doesn't matter what the penalty is. . . . Okay, call me back as soon as you can."

ROYN HAD INTERRUPTED THE briefing to take Renfrew's call, moving outside the Prime Minister's office into the private courtyard. *I could get used to this,* he thought as he admired the garden and the spaciousness of Kydd's offices.

Calling for Alison to join him, he relayed Renfrew's proposal, that the girls would make the video on the condition it was never made public. "So long as McKurn is convinced the girls' accusations will damage him, and so long as he *believes* you'll release them, you'll stop him dead, right?"

"But. . . ." Alison looked at Royn doubtfully.

"He'll be well and truly neutered." Royn grinned. "Castrated. A political eunuch as far as we're concerned. So what would it matter if we agreed—?"

"But then we've got no comeback." Alison swung her head violently from side to side, the tips of her hair slapping her cheeks.

"*He* won't know that."

Alison's eyes locked onto Royn's so fiercely that he felt a flash of fear. "I want *revenge*," she growled.

"So do I," Royn said slowly to emphasize his agreement. "And we can get it *without* the girls' testimony. Just not right away."

"How can you be so certain?" Alison said.

"The 'Dump McKurn' movement is gathering steam; it's looking less likely McKurn will even have a place on the Senate ticket come the next election. That's thanks to rumors with no hard evidence. In cabinet tomorrow I'm going to push for beefing up the Candyman Inquiry. With that and the state *and* federal Auditor-Generals' investigations, we'll have the whole *government* after McKurn. The Sykes and OlssonPress papers have joined the fight too. We *know* we're going to get McKurn."

"In time."

"To *get* that time—not to mention all this," said Royn, sweeping his arm to indicate the courtyard and the Prime Minister's office behind them, "we need a lever to bash McKurn with. And we need it *now*. The girls' testimony is the only one in sight. We really don't have a choice, Alison. Do we?"

"I suppose we don't," Alison conceded reluctantly.

"So we'll agree."

"I guess we have to."

*****

It was late morning when Jessica Olsson walked unsteadily but happily off the Thai Airways flight from Bangkok into the Sydney terminal.

"Jessica Olsson?" a Chinese man asked as she came off the air bridge into the terminal.

Jessica stopped, took a step backwards bumping into the passenger behind her, and said belligerently, "Who are you?"

A second man stepped forward. "This is Detective-Sergeant Simon Lee, Miss Olsson. And I'm Detective-Inspector Rudi Durant."

Jessica turned to look at the stocky, grey-haired speaker as Durant opened his wallet to show Jessica his ID. Lee followed suit.

"What's the meaning of this?" she demanded. "*I* haven't done anything wrong."

"On the contrary, Miss," Durant said. He stepped to one side of the stream of deplaning passengers and nudged Lee in the same direction. "We're here to make sure you're okay, get you through customs and immigration—you don't have a passport with you, right?"

Jessica shook her head.

"Well, we've got all that taken care of. And then we'll take you home. Unless, of course, you'd rather take a taxi."

"I'm . . . ah . . . sorry," Jessica said to the passenger behind her and stepped so she was nearer to Durant than Lee. "Okay . . . I suppose."

"And if you'd like to give a statement once you've rested up, we'd appreciate it. Shall we go?"

Jessica nodded and smiled tentatively at Lee. "I'm sorry, Sergeant," she said. "It's just that you gave me a shock. The people who kidnapped and threatened me were all Chinese, you see."

Lee grinned. "No worries, Miss. I've met some of those bastards myself—and maybe you can help us put them behind bars."

"I . . . hope so."

"Good," said Durant. "Let's go, then." He lagged slightly behind Jessica and Lee to make a quick phone call.

Durant and Lee guided the passport-less Jessica through the paperwork immigration and customs demanded. As they walked into the arrivals area, they didn't notice a man who compared Jessica's face with a picture he was carrying. He snapped a shot with his phone, double-checked Jessica's face against the picture and, satisfied, sent it to a phone number in Thailand. He then dialled a different number, also in Thailand. "She's here in Sydney, with Durant. . . . Okay," he said, and snapped his phone shut, his job done.

*****

"SHE'S ARRIVED," NAZAROV SAID into his walkie-talkie. "All systems go."

From the moment Derek Olsson had walked into the Royal Thai Police headquarters, Nazarov, Shultz and de Brouw kept watch on all the entrances. Dozens of motorcycle riders, arranged by Suchart, each with a passenger carrying a walkie-talkie as well as a cellphone, had been cruising around slowly, lost in the horde of other motorcycles. Spotters sat opposite the gates noting down the number plates of every vehicle that entered or left, and warning Suchart whenever they saw a male *farang*—foreigner—coming or going. A backup team monitored the traffic at Luk Suk's compound on Sukhumvit Soi 12.

De Brouw and Shultz were two of the motorcycle passengers. Their faces hidden by helmets, their skin darkened with makeup and their hair blackened so they seemed no different from the Thai motorcyclists all around them—except both were sweating from the heat.

Nazarov was also uncomfortable, even though he was sitting with Suchart and one of his assistants in an air-conditioned hotel room overlooking the police headquarters complex. After Suchart and the three former mercenaries had surveyed the complex the previous day, he asked Olsson, "Any chance you can meet Luk Suk some other place? It's too big: too many buildings, too many entrances. We might lose you as you come out."

"I wish I'd thought of that," Olsson replied. "But it's too late, I'm afraid. General Vanich suggested it and I agreed. It's where they have their offices."

"Okay," Nazarov nodded reluctantly. "So keep your fingers crossed."

*****

"I TRUST YOU HAD a good night's sleep," General Chuasiriporn grinned as Luk Suk and Derek Olsson were ushered into his office.

"Passable," said Luk Suk tonelessly. Olsson said nothing, but nodded to Chuasiriporn and Vanich, who was also behind the desk.

They'd spent the night in separate cells, isolated from each other and from other prisoners. Small touches like extra blankets and pillows showed that an effort had been made to make them more comfortable. Excellent meals were delivered from a nearby restaurant; if they wanted anything—a snack or a T-bone steak, tea, coffee or even beer or wine—all they had to do was ask.

But a cell was a cell, and Olsson had no illusions about Luk Suk's intentions. *Is this how it feels to be on Death Row?* he asked himself. *Tomorrow morning at dawn. . . .*

He couldn't recall whether he'd slept or not. Each time he lay down his head, thoughts, images and memory fragments tumbled through his mind. He visualized ways he might escape—while certain that Luk Suk wouldn't take any chances, and thinking, *My fate now lies in the hands of Nazarov and his fellow killers.*

He tried to exhaust himself to sleep by doing endless pushups, sit-ups, and working himself into a sweat running on the spot. His muscles craved sleep, but his mind would not cooperate. Supposedly, your life flashes before your eyes in the seconds before you die—*How could anyone know?* he mused. *Like heaven and hell, no one's ever come back to tell us about it.* But his restless mind roved through his past, forcing him to look back at his every decision, his every choice, drawing him to the unavoidable conclusion that every road he had taken had led inevitably and inexorably to this cell, as though his fate had been predetermined. A conclusion he refused to accept, no matter how logical it seemed . . . but could not escape.

"Inspector Durant has called," said Chuasiriporn. "She's with him."

"Good," said Luk Suk, smiling broadly at Olsson. "Let's go."

"Just a moment," said Olsson. "General Vanich, could you turn on my cellphone and check for messages please?"

Vanich nodded. "Nothing yet," he said.

"What are we waiting for?" Luk Suk demanded.

"Independent confirmation," Vanich said.

That came about five minutes later when Vanich turned the phone's screen towards Olsson. He looked at the picture of Jessica with Durant. "Okay," he said. "She's definitely there."

Vanich nodded to Chuasiriporn, ignored Luk Suk, said, "Good luck," to Olsson, and walked out of Chuasiriporn's office.

*****

Two hours later a convoy of three black limousines, all private vehicles, pulled out of the police headquarters and turned left onto Rama I Road. A spotter recognized a number plate and reported it to Suchart at the same time as de Brouw, perched on the back of a motor cycle cruising slowly past, called on his walkie-talkie, "The car Luk Suk came in is coming out now, along with two others."

The three limousines, Luk Suk's car in the lead, came to a halt in the center lane at the stoplights at the intersection with Phaya Thai Road. Motorcycles weaved their way through the idling cars and trucks to mass in front of the vehicles. As his driver edged slowly past the three cars, de Brouw peered inside but could see nothing through their windows darkened against the sun, the heat, and the curious.

The lights changed. Police held up the traffic in the outer lanes to allow the limousines in the center lane to roar forward, tires squealing, their horns warning the motorcyclists to get out of their way. Luk Suk's limousine went straight ahead, the second turned left and the last one turned right where other policemen held up the cross traffic to let it through. "Go straight," de Brouw ordered. "The three limos are going three different ways," he said into the walkie-talkie. "Split the motorcycles into three as well."

"We're on it," said Nazarov's voice in de Brouw's earphone.

After a couple more red lights, Suchart's other motorcycles had caught up with de Brouw. Then, when the lights turned green, the car swung into a freeway entrance—where motorcycles were banned.

"Damn," said de Brouw. "He's taking the freeway." De Brouw's bike swung in the same direction as the car, slowing as it passed the tollbooths. De Brouw watched helplessly as, after paying the toll, the car sped up the on ramp. He saw a hand reach out of the passenger window and place a magnetized blue light on the car's roof. As the car disappeared from view he saw the blue light flashing and heard the siren blaring. "He's making out like he's a fucking police car," de Brouw shouted into the walkie-talkie.

The route from police headquarters to Luk Suk's compound on Sukhumvit Soi 12 was via surface streets. But Nazarov had assumed that Olsson would be taken somewhere else. So when the three-car convoy had turned onto Rama I Road, two cars that had been parked illegally further down the same street roared out into the traffic. Luckily, one of them had followed the limousine that was now on the freeway. But unlike the motorcycles, it was still trapped behind a dozen other cars at the last set of stoplights. So several minutes passed between the time the flashing blue light disappeared and the car arrived at the toll booth.

On the freeway, the limousine accelerated to well over the speed limit, other traffic for the most part getting out of its way. By the time the pursuit car came off the on-ramp its quarry was nowhere in sight.

"We've lost him," Suchart told Nazarov.

"Tell him to keep going, as fast as he can, just in case," Nazarov said. "Is there anything else we can do?"

Suchart barked an order into his walkie-talkie and slowly shook his head. "By the time I could get motorbikes to a freeway exit, that car could be near the airport—or halfway to Pattya."

"Oh, shit," Nazarov growled. "Just keep tailing the other two."

The other two limousines wound their way through different areas of Bangkok, sometimes looping back the way they'd come, but inexorably getting further from the city center. After driving for about an hour, both cars stopped at a roadside stand; two men got out of each car and proceeded to enjoy a leisurely lunch.

At one of the roadside stands, a motorcyclist also stopped and ordered lunch. He took a nearby table and eavesdropped on the two men's conversation.

"Weird job," one of the men commented.

"Easy money, though. I wonder if we *were* followed?"

"Didn't see a thing," the first man said.

After taking their time over lunch the men got back into their limousines and drove back towards the city. The end of their journeys turned out to be a limousine rental company.

About an hour after the three-limousine convoy left police headquarters, a delivery van, scratches and dings suggesting it might be near the end of its useful life, rumbled out onto Rama I Road. Derek Olsson lay on the floor of the van, his wrists handcuffed behind him, his ankles tied together. Luk Suk, sitting uncomfortably on a narrow, makeshift bench, looked down at Olsson and chuckled, "Well, *Ah-son, if* you had anyone lined up to follow you, they're well and truly lost by now."

*****

"Hear something?"

The second Australian soldier cupped his ear. "Dunno," he shrugged. "Maybe."

"Over there," the first soldier whispered, indicating with his submachine gun. "I'm sure of it."

Signalling the platoon behind them to halt, they stood stock still, listening for a while.

"Must have been your imagination."

"Could have been. Let's keep moving."

Perched in the fork of a tree about ten meters from where the Australians stood, Gurundi gritted his teeth against the pain of the cramp in his calf muscle. He'd been wedged in the middle of the "Y" where the tree trunk split in two. He had slipped when his muscle cramped—the noise the soldiers heard. Now, hanging by his fingers and biting his tongue from the pain he could do nothing about, he tried to stop hold his awkward position and stop breathing while the Australian platoon filed almost silently under his tree.

When the last soldier disappeared from view, he began to inch himself down the trunk. Climbing up had been easy; now, those few meters to the ground looked an impossible distance. He slipped the last meter sideways, gashing his leg on a broken branch and landing heavily—and noisily. Stifling a scream at the almost unbearable agony shooting up from the wound, he lay there breathing hard, listing for any sign that the soldiers would turn back.

But all was quiet.

He peered down to see how badly he was hurt, but there was so much blood it was hard to tell. He ripped one sleeve off his shirt and used it to bandage the wound. He needed medical attention, but for the moment he'd have to make out on his own.

The indignity of it all! he fumed.

Lauded as the "Unifier" who'd brought the two squabbling Islamic resistance groups together—an honored, if honorary, member of the ruling councils of both groups—he was now a fugitive, and alone. The guerrilla leaders welcomed his idea for the kamikaze bomber—and then blamed him for the ferocity of their enemies' advance.

The Australian and Sandeman troops had attacked in force, sweeping through St. Christopher's Island from the west, forcing the guerrillas to keep retreating. Each day, their numbers shrank as men were picked off by the enemy, threw down their weapons and surrendered, or simply melted away.

Along with the other guerrillas, Gurundi had hacked his way through impenetrable jungle, collected the morning's dew from leaves in case they couldn't find water, and trudged through mud up to their ankles even as the sun cooked them from above, all the while terrified that one of the invisible rockets that rained down like the devil's judgement from the heavens would land in their path.

They trekked east to try to outrun the soldiers. But whenever they thought they might be getting close to safety, the sound of helicopters reminded them that there was no way they could stay ahead of the infidels. They could only trust to luck—and to Allah.

The previous night, Gurundi fell into an exhausted sleep the moment he lay down, oblivious to the uneven ground and the roots and pebbles that pressed uncomfortably into his body.

He was jerked awake by a deafening explosion, a burst of intense heat and the smell of roasting flesh. He brushed flakes of fire and embers from his body. As he raised his head, he realized the dead tree trunk he'd been sleeping against had protected him from the explosion. But the remnants of leadership of Ansar el-Islam—Defenders of Islam, one of the two Islamic resistance groups on St. Christopher's Island—had just been wiped out.

Luck, it seemed, was on the enemy's side.

Yet—he'd begun to feel that Allah had saved him for some special purpose. At first, as he made his way alone, he cursed his fall from grace. But he'd come to realize that a man by himself had an advantage. As long as he kept his eyes and ears open, he had a good chance of hearing any soldiers before they heard him, giving him time to hide. Twice he had eluded discovery. Three times actually—except that now he was hurt.

But I'm still alive. Allah is still with me.

He bandaged his wound with a sleeve from his shirt. Using a branch as a makeshift crutch, he hobbled slowly downhill he reached a small stream of bubbling water. He stretched his wounded leg into the stream and winced as the cold water poured into the cut.

Now that he could see it, the wound didn't look so bad. The branch had cut a deep furrow into the back of his calf muscle. But he could still wiggle his toes and move his foot up and down, so he assumed the wound would not be disabling—as long as it healed. He scooped mud from the bottom of the stream and packed it into the wound, and used the other sleeve of his shirt as a fresh bandage. He rinsed the bloody sleeve in the running water so he'd have a clean replacement bandage when it dried.

The dank night was closing in, the only light coming from the clouds above that caught the last rays of the setting sun. He knew that sleeping by the stream was probably a bad idea, but his energy had gone. He crawled a few meters until he found a soft patch of grass and mud where he could be somewhat comfortable, and quickly drifted into sleep.

*****

"IF HE WAS IN the car that got on the freeway," Nazarov said, "we've lost him."

"Where else could he have been?" Shultz asked. He and de Brouw sprawled on the sofa in Nazarov's hotel room, revelling in the comfort and the cool after spending the morning perched on the back of motorcycles breathing in exhaust fumes. "The other two limos—even the trunks—were empty. Just the two drivers. Suchart's men checked. I watched them."

Suchart nodded his agreement. He sat at the table where his associates were still working, his chair turned towards them.

Nazarov grinned. "What Luk Suk did was very clever. But if *we'd* had a car that was better positioned for the freeway, we could have kept on his tail."

"Okay," said Shultz "So what?"

"Maybe Olsson wasn't in *any* of the cars," de Brouw said excitedly.

"*That's* what I've been wondering," Nazarov said. "Let's face it. His diversion *worked*. We all assumed that Olsson was in *one* of those three limos. So we threw everything into following *them*."

"While Olsson was still in the cop shop."

Nazarov nodded. "Of course, if he *was* in the limo that took the freeway, he could be anywhere in Thailand by now."

"And if he wasn't?" Shultz asked.

"Maybe he'll be taken back to Soi twelve."

"All you're saying, *tovarisch,* is that Olsson's either in Luk Suk's compound, or he's God knows where in Thailand—or even further afield. That doesn't sound like much progress to me."

"There's another possibility," said de Brouw. "Say Luk Suk set up a bolt hole somewhere else. Then some of his men will go there. If we follow all the vehicles leaving the compound, we *might* strike it lucky."

"Great idea," said Nazarov. He turned to Suchart. "Can you arrange that?"

"Sure," Suchart nodded.

"And find out from the spotters whether there've been any unusual movements in or out of the compound this morning?"

They all waited, their eyes fixed on Suchart, until he finished his call. "Nothing unusual, as far as the lookouts can tell. Maids going shopping, a couple of cars and bikes leaving. They've all returned. A couple of deliveries. Everything looks normal. Same guards patrolling the premises and so on."

"Maybe we should just break in there anyway," Shultz suggested.

"Have we got anything to lose?" de Brouw asked. "After all, what do you think Luk Suk plans to do with Olsson?"

"Kill him," said Shultz.

"And if we *do* break in and he's *not* there," said Nazarov. "then we'll just be telling Luk Suk that there's a rescue team around—"

"And Luk Suk will kill him," said Shultz.

"Right," de Brouw said, and shrugged. "Maybe it's already too late."

*****

AT ONE END OF the Members' Bar in Parliament House, Paul Cracken sat huddled with Jack Quigley, the Conservative Party member for the rural electorate of Riverina. Diagonally opposite, in the otherwise deserted room, were two other Conservatives: Bruce Spring, the Minister for Justice and Customs and one of Royn's most loyal supporters, and Donald Kent who'd won a marginal constituency in the last election by just a couple of hundred votes.

"Now that's funny," said Spring, indicating Cracken and Quigley with a nod of his head. "Those two go together like chalk and cheese."

"Cracken," Kent sneered. "That arsehole would sell his soul to the devil."

"Too late, he already has."

They both laughed.

"Never mind them," Spring said. "These poll results mean only one thing: if Cracken becomes leader, you lose your seat."

"Jeez, Bazza," said Kent, "even Blind Freddy could figure *that* out."

Spring winced at the nickname, but made no protest. He passed a sheet of paper from inside his jacket across to Kent. "These are the members who—like you—would lose their seats if Cracken were leader. I'd appreciate if you could have a quiet word to them as they trickle in."

"Want me to stand at the airport and grab as they come off their flights?" Kent asked.

"If you like," Spring replied sourly.

Kent grinned and waved the list at Spring. "So you don't think Kydd's going to make it, eh?"

"He probably will," Spring shrugged, "but who knows . . . ? Best to be Boy Scouts and—"

"Yeah, yeah. 'Be prepared' and all that. Okay, I will. But you realize that most of these guys would get in line behind Cracken—or even Quigley, for Chris' sake—if *he* were ahead of Royn in the polls."

Spring nodded. *Including you, you bastard,* he thought.

"Some of them might say since these poll results for Royn are better than Kydd's last election, why not go for a spill?"

"That's out of the question," Spring snapped.

"Why? The more I think about it, the more I like it myself."

"If *Royn* caused a spill, he'd lose Kydd's support. He'd be vilified for kicking Kydd while he's down. Either way, it would then be anybody's guess who'd be the next leader. And if it's *not* Royn, you'll be out on your arse come election time."

Kent nodded slowly. "You could be right," he conceded.

"Whether I'm right or not, it's not worth the risk."

"Fair enough," Kent said. "You can count on me to rally the troops. I'd feel a lot better with an increased majority."

". . . SO IF YOU THROW your hat in the ring," Cracken was saying, "you might draw off enough votes from Royn to make the leadership contest go another round."

"Maybe," said Quigley. "But I'd come in third. On the next round it would just be you and Royn. How is that going to help *you?*"

"You'd throw your weight behind me, and that might just do it."

Quigley looked skeptical.

"What have you got to lose, Jack?" Cracken asked. "You know damn well Royn won't nominate you for street sweeper. I'll give you a *ministry*. You bloody well know this is the last chance you'll ever get."

Jack Quigley led a faction within the Conservative Party that had a dozen hard-core members and another five or six "fellow travellers" who usually, though not always, supported him. They bitterly opposed the government's policy to do as little as possible to subsidize farmers—or any other industry. Ironically, it had been the previous Labor government that had actually dismantled the subsidies and tariff protection that earlier Conservative administrations had favored. The country vote had once been exceptionally strong within the Conservative Party and its predecessors—further strengthened by gerrymandering. Today, though, the farmers just didn't have the numbers any more.

That didn't faze Jack Quigley. He was a political throwback to a previous era and, as far as anyone could tell, if he'd noticed that Australia's demographic and economic make-up had changed, it hadn't registered with him. Occasionally, when the rest of the parliamentary party was evenly divided on an issue, he'd sell his faction's votes to the highest bidder. Most of the time, though, the other Conservative Party MPs would unite to oppose whatever-it-was he wanted, just "on principle": they all looked on him as a continual pain in everybody's neck.

"*What* ministry?" Quigley demanded. "Postmaster-General? Chief Arse Wiper?"

"If you like," Cracken smiled.

"I don't have to tell *you* what I'd like."

"If that's what you want, it's yours."

"That's settled, then. *But,*" Quigley growled, jabbing his finger in Cracken's chest, "*you* as glorious God-Almighty-Treasurer are the first to shoot down anything I come up with. I'd rather be a backbencher than minister who never gets anything *through* Cabinet."

Cracken shrugged. "When I'm Prime Minister it will be a different ball game. *I'll* be setting the rules."

"Yeah. You—and McKurn. Everyone knows you're in his pocket. That makes you a hard sell."

"Can't be that hard," Cracken protested. "With McKurn behind me, I got to be Treasurer and gave Royn a run for his money for the Deputy Leadership."

"Last place *I'd* want McKurn is *behind* me."

"Suit yourself," said Cracken.

Quigley eyed Cracken skeptically. "I'd need more than your support to get things past Cabinet. Who else is going to support helping the farmers?"

"It depends on what you want, how it's framed, and the timing. We can easily work all that out so what you want gets through. After all, I know the ins and outs of Treasury—"

"And all their objections."

Cracken grinned. "And how to get around them."

"Okay," said Quigley. "But there's still one other thing. *If*—and that's a big 'if'—I've helped make you PM, how can I be sure you won't renege and leave me high and dry?"

"You'll just have to trust me, won't you?" said Cracken.

"Trust *you?* You're out of your bleeding mind, mate."

"Well, what do you suggest?"

"If you betray me, you turncoat, I'll pull my support and back Royn instead. There'll be a spill quicker than you can say 'Young Frankie.' And that's another problem—maybe 'Young Frankie' is becoming a liability *no one* will want hanging about."

"What do you mean?"

"McKurn's term is nearly up, so at the next half-Senate election he'll have to go to the voters."

"So?" said Cracken with a shrug. "He's number one on the New South Wales Senate ticket."

"He's *been* number one. But I'd say if he doesn't squash all these stories about his shady past pretty damn quick, the 'Dump Young Frankie' movement in the party will put paid to his chances of getting a place on the *bottom* of the ticket."

"That bad, you reckon?" Cracken asked, his eyes still on Quigley's face but no longer focused on him.

"Worse. He can shrug off working as a bouncer in a sly grog shop as a youthful indiscretion. He neatly wriggled out of that mining scandal accusation. But when McKurn smells you can be sure that piles of turds are festering in some closet. Any more revelations, especially *serious* ones, and having McKurn on the ticket will be the kiss of death for the party at the next election—and not just in New South Wales."

"Yes," said Cracken distractedly, "I see what you mean."

"Do you?" Quigley asked, smiling as he watched Cracken's reaction. A loyal McKurn supporter—which, Quigley, thought, was probably a contradiction in terms—should have expressed shock at the idea of McKurn being dumped. But there was a hint of smile in Cracken's expression, which suggested to Quigley that seeing the last of McKurn would not upset Cracken in the least. "Who's going to want to vote for a thug—maybe even a murderer? Who's going to want to vote for a party that puts a gangster *anywhere* on their ticket?"

"A *suspected* thug," Cracken said, his eyes now twinkling.

"Jesus, Paul, you've been in politics long enough to know that a rumor doesn't have to be *proven* to be *deadly.*"

"True . . . and rumors can be hard to fight," Cracken said thoughtfully as he lounged back on the barstool. So, Jack, do we understand each other?"

"I guess we do," said Quigley. "God help me."

*****

"ALISON! COME HERE *QUICK.*"

Alison jumped as Royn's voice exploded from the office intercom. As she strode away from her desk, she searched her memory for some reason Royn might be angry with *her.*

As she walked into his office, before she could say a word Royn exploded again. "Renfrew just called. Everything was agreed, so he thought—but now there's *another* demand."

"Which is?"

"The girls are afraid of McKurn, of concrete boots and heaven knows what else—"

"Not at all unreasonable, Minister," Alison said as she sat down—calm now she knew Royn's anger was directed at somebody else, "when McKurn is involved."

"Yes, I know," Royn moaned, his cellphone still clutched in his hand.

"And what do they want?"

"A twenty-four hour guard—armed. The cost of this is starting to get out of hand."

"Couldn't they go into the witness protection program?"

Royn shook his head. "Renfrew suggested that, but they don't trust the police."

"Understandable."

"So . . . what choice do we have?"

"At this stage—" Alison looked pointedly at her watch "—absolutely none."

"Okay," Royn sighed. "I guess I already knew that and just needed to vent some steam." Grinning half-heartedly, he lifted his cellphone and dialled. "Collin?—Agreed. Provided they sign right now."

Alison cast her glance down. "Thank you, Minister. Without your support—"

"We're in the same boat, Alison."

"But if I hadn't dragged you in—"

"*McKurn* is the only guilty party in this. Remember that."

Alison look at Royn gratefully, her eyes slightly moist. "Maybe there's something we could salvage from all this," she said, with the beginnings of a smile.

"What's that?"

"Hire whichever one of those girls did the negotiating. Whoever she is, she could probably run rings around most of the self-important politicians around here."

"Not a bad idea," Royn laughed.

Alison smiled as she stood to leave—but was stopped by Royn's sharp, "Alison. Wait."

She sank back into her chair, frowning when she saw that the smile had gone from Royn's face, his fingers were nervously fidgeting with a pen and his eyes no longer held hers but strayed around her face without settling in any one place. "Yes, Minister," she asked. "What is it?"

"There's, ah, one other thing."

Alison searched his expression for some clue of what could be so difficult or ominous—and she almost laughed at the stray thought, *He's going to fire me.*

"Melanie thinks. . . ."

"Thinks . . . what?" Alison asked softly.

Royn waited, as if for Alison to rescue him; but Alison's only reaction was to raise an eyebrow. He sighed, his pen waggling even faster in his fingers. "She has this idea that . . . McKurn tried to—ah—*seduce* you."

"Ha," Alison chuckled sourly. "That's hardly the right word, Minister. But—I lost control. I overreacted—"

"You certainly had good cause."

Alison looked up in surprise at the vehemence in Royn's voice. "Well—I didn't mean to make things so much *worse* than they already were."

Royn was now leant back in his chair. He laughed. "Serves him right."

39 True Son

D EREK OLSSON LAY ON his back, his wrists and ankles chained to the four corners of the bed in an upstairs bedroom of Luk Suk's house. He knew it well: it was the room where he'd slept on his previous visits. Coincidence, he wondered, or Luk Suk's twisted sense of humor?

A man with a pistol sat opposite; the bedroom door was left open and a second guard holding a rifle stood in the doorway. Going to the bathroom, his only allowed movement, was a major expedition. Each bond was replaced before the existing one was loosened, and trying to pee with his feet chained together and his wrists handcuffed to two of Luk Suk's men was so awkward he waited till he had no choice. His mind was on constant alert for any possible means of escape, for any edge. But Luk Suk must have heard of the fight in the prison yard and did not intend to allow Olsson another chance to demonstrate his martial arts skills.

Olsson chattered to the guards, addressing each one by name. They spurned his attempts at conversation. Their rough, truculent treatment made their feelings clear: Luk Suk was making a mistake allowing the traitorous *gweilo* to live for a minute longer than necessary. Olsson eventually dozed, awakening at any movement to wonder if this was to be his last moment.

Some time after dark, a guard appeared and said, *"Loban seng kui ha-loy"*—"The boss wants him down below." Handcuffed, the chain between his ankles just long enough for him to shuffle along like an old man, he was led awkwardly down the stairs. One man with a rifle went down ahead of them, backwards; another followed behind; the two men he was bound to gripped his arms and used them as levers to half-carry him down the steps. Olsson exaggerated his difficulty moving, nervously wondering what lay in store for him at the bottom. He continually estimated his chances of making a move. Confident he could disable the two men he was handcuffed to, he could see no way to free his bonds before a dozen bullets had ripped into his body.

A spacious living/dining room dominated the ground floor. The curtains were closed on the floor-to-ceiling glass doors that looked out on the wide verandahs and gardens beyond. As they reached the landing where the stairs along the back and side walls angled at ninety-degrees, Olsson stopped in surprise: a sumptuous buffet was laid out on the heavy rosewood dining table; a bottle of wine sat in a cooler.

The two men grunted and pushed him to keep moving and sat Olsson down on one side of the dining table, ran the chain from his ankles around a table-leg, and took off his handcuffs. One guard muttered, *"Chee-sin"*—crazy—as they stepped beyond his reach. Olsson gratefully stretched his arms while surreptitiously testing the chain. It held.

A few minutes later, a clearly rested Luk Suk strolled down the stairs. "You must be hungry," he grinned.

Olsson nodded guardedly, studying Luk Suk intently for a clue to his mood.

Luk Suk took the seat at the head of the table where, even at full stretch, he was safely out of Olsson's reach. Two of Luk Suk's men stood behind Olsson, similarly beyond reach, their weapons held loosely but nevertheless pointing at his back. The other two now stood blocking the door to the kitchen, presumably to ensure the maids stayed inside and saw nothing.

"Help yourself," Luk Suk said, waving at the dishes and smacking his lips as he heaped food into his bowl. "I thought we should have one last chat. For old time's sake."

Dishes of green beef curry, pepper chicken, a whole steamed fish, vegetables and salad were arrayed between the two men—classic Thai dishes cooked by the chef Luk Suk had lured away from a stylish Thai restaurant in one of Bangkok's five-star hotels. With the sole exception of the rice, every dish was red hot. Even the salad was laced with specks of chilli invisible to the naked eye.

The condemned man has his last supper, Olsson thought, studying each morsel held at the ends of his chopsticks as he conveyed them to his mouth. He wasn't feeling the least bit hungry.

Olsson's face wore the mask of a smile, but it threatened to slip every time he looked at Luk Suk: Jessica's tortured screams flooded his mind, along with the knowledge that he had only hours—or, if he was lucky, days—to live. He forced his fingers to calmly hold his chopsticks, glancing at them now and then to be sure they gave no clue to his inner turmoil.

They ate in uneasy silence, Luk Suk's stony expression giving no hint to his mood until he pushed back his bowl and sighed, "You've disappointed me, *Ah-son.*"

"The feeling's mutual," Olsson replied.

"I treated you like the son I never had," Luk Suk said, shaking his head sadly as he placed the bottle of vintage French white wine where Olsson could reach it, "and look how you've paid me back."

"On the contrary, a true son would want to follow in his father's footsteps. . . ."

"Which you have," Luk Suk pointed out.

Unfortunately, yes, he thought, but said, ". . . and seek his independence. A true father would support him."

"And I haven't?" Luk Suk snapped.

"Of course not. You bound me hand and foot."

"*I* did?" Luk Suk laughed. "In you, I had a willing accomplice."

You did, Olsson thought—not that he was going to admit it. The combination of Luk Suk's approval along with the money, lifestyle, and authority he'd enjoyed, the travel—and, he had to confess to himself, the succession of girls—had been an overpowering combination for the youngster he'd once been. He'd fallen in love with the freewheeling city of Hong Kong where anything was possible, where poor kids would walk past a Rolls-Royce and think: *I could have one of those one day.* In Sydney, the same kid might have felt resentment rather than inspiration—and surreptitiously leave a scratch on the side of the car.

But Hong Kong, before Britain returned it to China, was a city of transients. Most foreigners came for a few years to make money; locals, whether refugees from China or Hong Kong "belongers," were all desperate to get another passport—emigrating, buying, or marrying one—before the Communists took over. The younger Olsson had everything a man could desire—except close friends . . . and love.

"You seduced me," he said accusingly. Olsson controlled the tone of his voice to match and encourage Luk Suk's apparently regretful mood. "I was young, naïve—and lost. How much did you pay Veronika and the other girls for my nineteenth birthday 'present'?" Luk Suk looked down—but not fast enough. Olsson caught the brief widening of his eyes. "I see."

"Veronika," Luk Suk smiled. "Great legs, eh? Did *she* tell you?"

"No. I guessed . . . much later." Olsson smiled, as if at the memory. Maybe Luk Suk was just playing mind games with him, toying with him before executing his final judgement—and Olsson had no illusions that this mood, if real, was merely temporary. But if he could prolong it, he'd buy a little extra time. "They didn't do gang bangs just for fun. Especially not Veronika—what a cold-hearted bitch *she* turned out to be."

Luk Suk shrugged. "You have to admit she put on a great show."

Olsson smiled wistfully. "She sure did," he said. "She took me for a ride—until I realized she was all show."

"Despite all the trouble you've caused me, *Ah-son,* I still like you." Sipping his wine, Luk Suk spoke as if he were thinking aloud. "Even now. Otherwise you wouldn't be sitting *here.*"

"That's hardly the point," Olsson replied. "You liked me—but you *used* me."

"I saw potential in you. I fostered it—and I succeeded. Can you deny that?"

"Potential—for *your* profit."

"And *yours.*" Luk Suk glared at Olsson, challenging him to disagree.

"Until recently, yes. But you set out to use me right from the start. Liking me always came second—and still does."

"No," Luk Suk sadly shook his head—and paused. "Ah . . . I see," he said slowly, and smiled wistfully at Olsson. "Even after all these years, you're still a *gweilo, Ah-son.*"

"Of course," Olsson shrugged, realizing he'd begun to enjoy Luk Suk's company despite himself. "What are you getting at?"

"Independence. *Freedom.* A true *Chinese* son wouldn't even think those words in relation to his father."

"Okay . . . " Olsson said, nodding his understanding. "A cultural difference? Maybe. But it's more than that for me. Since I was a child, freedom and independence is all I've ever wanted." *And someone to look up to, to admire.* "The moment you prevented me from quitting, I vowed to get out from under your thumb, come what may."

"Hence . . . Australia and InterFreight."

"That's right," said Olsson. "It took me a long time to figure out *that* idea."

"Perhaps . . . " Luk Suk said, his voice tinged with regret, ". . . I made a mistake."

"Your mistake was not grooming one of your daughters to take over after you," Olsson said, toying with his chopsticks.

"A *woman?* As Chat Suk—'Seventh Uncle'? Unthinkable."

"Not these days," Olsson replied. "But a *gweilo* as Chat Suk—"

"Out of the question," Luk Suk snapped.

"Too true," Olsson grinned. "But I made a mistake, too. I should have quit after that first trip to Bangkok. I shouldn't have made that trip at all."

"But you enjoyed it," Luk Suk smiled. "I could tell."

"Oh, yes. It was so *exciting.* And there I was, twenty, twenty-one, making piles of money, travelling around the world and meeting all kinds of interesting people while my friends from school were still at university. Heady stuff." Olsson looked intently at Luk Suk, and said, "Remember, you once told me there are no evil things, only evil people?"

"Of course," Luk Suk nodded.

"You're wrong."

"I am?"

"Yes.

"How can that be, *Ah-son?* Good, evil, right, wrong—they don't exist in *things,* only in *people,* as attributes of *consciousness.*"

"But some things, some activities attract evil people—and corrupt others."

"For example?"

"Our business."

"But—we agreed a long time ago that there's nothing evil or morally wrong about the drug trade."

"Quite so. But it's illegal, so—"

"Then where's the *evil* you were talking about? In the laws that make this business so profitable? Or in the people it attracts?"

"In the people it corrupts—the good people who end up doing evil things."

"So in *people,* as I said *Ah-son,*" Luk Suk said triumphantly. "And you're forgetting. . . . Yin and yang. Everyone has the potential for both—for the light and the dark—"

"Are *you* evil?" Olsson demanded.

Luk Suk's head jerked back in surprise. "Of course not."

"But look at us *now,* Luk Suk." Olsson stomped his feet and rattled the chain to emphasize his words. "Is this right—or wrong? Good—or evil?"

"It's . . . necessary."

"You're evading the question. The reality is: we're both forced into a situation where we're *both* committing acts that are evil, by *any* moral code. So if evil exists only in people, not things, then by your own definition you *must* be evil."

"What about self-defence?" Luk Suk countered. "Your *own* exception?"

"But you have *not* acted in self-defence. *I'm* the only one of us who can make that claim."

"Really?" said Luk Suk. "You murdered Vincent Leung—"

"No, I didn't. Somebody else wanted him dead and wanted to get away with the murder. So I was framed, very professionally. What's more, I can prove it."

"So tell me—who's the real murderer?"

"I don't know yet. But I know who impersonated me, and in a week or two he'll lead me to the real killer."

"Is that so?" Luk Suk's voice dripped with sarcasm. "To me, it doesn't look like you'll be going *anywhere* in the near future. Or the *distant* future, for that matter." Luk Suk laughed at his own joke, and shrugged. "So what if you *didn't* kill Vincent? It no longer matters, *Ah-son.* How many of my men have died at your hands? What did you assert you believed—'Do no harm to others,' wasn't it? You can hardly claim to have lived up to *that.*"

"I'd been kidnapped. I was rescued. The kidnappers died in the process." Olsson shrugged. "We're both claiming self-defence—but one of us is wrong. And I know it's not me."

"The fact remains that *you* are responsible for their deaths, *Ah-son.*"

Olsson said nothing, but was thinking of Nazarov: *I unleashed them . . . doesn't that make me answerable for their actions . . . ?*

Luk Suk continued, glaring, "As if that weren't enough, there's this new supplier on the Australian market. The Candyman. No one knows who he is. I know you well, *Ah-*

son. This Candyman's sudden appearance, and the way he seems to operate—that's one reason I think he's *you.* It's as though you've have hidden your identity behind this mythical Candyman—but left your fingerprints all over the place. What's more, I know that some of the Candyman's drugs are coming from markets where you operated for me, through *my* contacts. And some new ones—General Vanich is quite a catch, I must say."

"Suspicions are not evidence."

"Ah." Luk Suk seemed to pounce on Olsson's words. "But you don't *deny* you're the Candyman—which is as good as admitting that you *are.*"

Olsson shrugged. "What's the point? You're obviously going to believe whatever you want to believe."

"And then there are these newspapers of yours. Exposing corruption, pushing drug legalization—you're striking at the heart of our business. What's the idea?"

"Sells newspapers."

"Hardly. The majority of people all over the world support the drug laws—"

"More fool them."

"I'm not complaining. But you build sales by pandering to your readers' prejudices, not by *challenging* them. And the newspaper industry is in decline worldwide. Makes no business sense to me. So what's the point? Penance for guilt? Some sort of hair shirt?"

"You could say that," said Olsson. "But you're acting as if I belong to you. I don't. You seem to think I have to clear my every action with you. I don't. I'm a free agent, and always have been."

Luk Suk laughed. "You should have used the past tense, *Ah-son.* That would have been more appropriate. Right now you *do* belong to me."

His face reddening, Olsson resisted his impulse to jump to his feet and swing futilely at Luk Suk. He clamped his mouth tightly shut, swallowing the words he was about to say: *You threatened my sister, a total innocent. That settles the issue of which of us is guilty as far as I'm concerned.*

Instead, he slumped back in his chair growling, "So it would seem." Taking a deep breath, he leaned forward earnestly. "Just let me find out who *really* killed Vincent Leung. Wouldn't you like to know? Take your revenge on the *real* culprit—who's no doubt taking over your markets as we speak." Aware of the pleading tone that had crept into his voice, Olsson paused, and Luk Suk cut in:

"I don't think so, *Ah-son.* Sure, if you *didn't* kill Vincent Leung, I'd like to know who *did*—"

"What's my motive?" Olsson demanded. "The police can't figure that out. But they don't care—they think the evidence is so solid they don't need to."

Luk Suk laughed. "I know what your motive is, *Ah-son.* To escape. I don't blame you. I'll tell you what, just tell me who impersonated you, and he can lead *us* to your so-called 'real murderer.'"

Olsson chuckled. "I don't think so."

"Anyway," Luk Suk shrugged, "what would I gain? Thanks to the damage *you've* done, *all* the other Sydney gangs are elbowing into our territory." Luk Suk shrugged. "Who *really* killed Vincent Leung no longer matters." Turning to his men, he asked them, "What do you think, boys?"

"Give him to us," one of them said, pointing at Olsson. "*We'll* make him talk." The other three echoed their agreement.

"Not a bad idea," Luk Suk said. "I'll think about it. You know, *Ah-son,* it's a shame that we'll have no more of these philosophical conversations. I shall mourn your passing."

Olsson's mask slipped; for a fraction of a moment his anger and revulsion was obvious. "I'm sure I'll appreciate the flowers."

Luk Suk laughed and rose to his feet. "I'll see you in the morning," he said as he sauntered to the door under the landing leading to his office, "or maybe I won't."

"Who impersonated you, Ah-son? You might as well tell us now." "You tell a good story, *Ah-son,* but it's not good enough," Luk Suk's men laughed as they prodded and kicked him up the stairs.

Chained again to the bed, bruised where Luk Suk's men had treated him roughly, Olsson tried to think of a way out.

But he knew they'd never give him an opening.

The three mercenaries were his only hope.

But thanks to Luk Suk's diversion, Nazarov must have lost the scent.

He strained at his bonds to no avail.

The guards mocked him with their laughter.

His future looked bleak—and short.

He tried to sleep—and failed.

When Olsson came back from his first trip to Bangkok with a suitcase stuffed with heroin, he sailed through Hong Kong customs without a hitch. But the first thing he said to Luk Suk was, "You know it says on the Thai customs form? *Death to drug dealers!* I'm not doing that again. Money, okay. Drugs—no way."

"Fair enough," Luk Suk had smiled and assigned him, as he later joked, to the "department of victimless crimes."

Olsson had come up with ideas to reduce the risks of smuggling. He proposed sealing drugs in waterproof containers and dropping them overboard near one of Hong Kong's many islands where they could later be picked up by a cruising junk. Luk Suk refined it, making a deal with a Chinese official; the drugs were dropped in the grey area on the border between Hong Kong and Chinese waters. Olsson ended up "attached" to a small bank Luk Suk owned through dummies, specializing in money laundering. In the process, he'd made a major contribution to expanding Luk Suk's Golden Dragon Triad into a dominating force in Hong Kong's underworld.

But when, shortly after his twenty-second birthday, Olsson decided it was time to move on, Luk Suk shook his head. "Derek," he said, "I can't let you go. You know too much."

From then on, Olsson quietly schemed to find a way out; it took him years of careful, very secret preparation before he was ready to make his move away from Luk Suk. One last element was needed to complete his complicated jigsaw puzzle: would his old friend Ross Traynor agree to be involved?

After completing his MBA, Traynor had turned down lucrative offers in the city to take charge of his elderly uncle's small road transport business, InterFreight, on the understanding he could buy it out over time. Traynor had cut costs and improved margins, but the company's primary business, on the Sydney to Brisbane route, was slowly but inexorably losing customers to cutthroat competition from the majors, and Traynor didn't have the capital to fight back by entering the far more lucrative Sydney to Melbourne market on any scale. For what Olsson had in mind, Ross Traynor was the perfect partner.

Impulsively, Olsson arranged to meet Traynor at the same time Anthony Royn would be in Sydney; he couldn't resist the opportunity to see Alison again. She'd probably tell him to "Get lost." He shrugged: just *seeing* her, just *once*, would be worth it.

Early one morning he sat, unobtrusively, in the lobby of the Regent hotel. Sure enough, around seven-thirty he saw Alison step from a lift. He would have recognized her anywhere, immediately. His eyes were glued to her trim figure as she walked briskly across the lobby. Her legs and ankles flashed across the carpet in the long strides of someone with a purpose, her knee-length skirt fluttering ahead and behind her with each movement. A laptop bag with papers bulging from its side pockets hung from one shoulder, her handbag on her other arm, which also clutched some newspapers. Her jacket fit snugly—the image of an executive in her prime—and Olsson felt as though he was aware of every line and plane of her body. Without breaking her stride, she looked once in his direction, as if she had felt the caress of his gaze, and for a moment he was looking directly into her familiar, sparkling eyes, framed by long, black curls. Her eyes seemed cold, questioning, searching; he imagined that through them he could feel her inner warmth.

Her glance moved on; all she could see—if she saw anything at all—was an unidentifiable person apparently reading a newspaper, half-obscured by the leaves of a large, leafy pot plant.

His heart pounded as he forced himself to wait. When he could bear it no longer he leapt up, let the newspaper that had lain unnoticed on his lap fall to the floor, and carefully picked up the bouquet of roses lying on the chair at his side.

When he wandered into the coffee shop he was immediately aware of where Alison was sitting—alone: leaning forward, intent on the newspaper spread across her table, a cup poised in mid-air halfway to her lips, held in space by long fingers tipped with dark red nails.

His steps slowed as he neared her table, the petals of the roses dancing slightly from his nervous anticipation. *Why did I stay away so long?* he wondered. *Why did I ever leave her?* He knew there were reasons, good and important ones, but their exact nature escaped him, flung aside as the overwhelming sense of her closeness stirred long-forgotten emotions—heavily tinged with guilt.

He came to a halt beside her table in silent admiration, drinking in the faint, wafting aroma of her perfume.

A long moment passed until Alison became aware of his presence. Her head jerked up in surprise and annoyance. As her glance travelled to the flowers her lips began to smile in welcome to someone she knew . . . until she reached his face. Her lips clamped together, the warmth disappeared from her eyes, replaced by a question and a faint shaking of her head.

"Hullo, Alison," Olsson said, startled himself as he felt drawn into the sapphires of her eyes. "How's Aikido?" he asked, when Alison stared at him blankly. "And did you take up Karate, as I suggested?"

She looked at him as if she were seeing a ghost, puzzled eyes searching his face, until she shrieked. *"Derek!"* Her coffee cup fell from her fingers and the newspaper turned a murky brown as she leapt to her feet and threw her arms around him. "Derek," she repeated. "Where did you come from? Where have you *been?*"

"Hey," he said laughing. "Let me breathe." She loosened her grip, feeling a faint flush come to her cheeks as she studied his face.

Now she saw why she hadn't immediately recognized him. Yes, it was the same Derek Olsson she'd always known. He had the same unruly hair, but he was heavier, musclier, a little chubbier in the cheeks and stomach—and never had she imagined him wearing a suit and tie. But the main difference was his eyes. When they were on her face they were the same compassionate hazel-green eyes she remembered so well. But they kept jerking away from her to dance quickly around the room, as if he wanted to be continually alert to every person, every movement, and every object around him. Eyes, she realized, which would not be taken by surprise.

Eyes which were also very tired. And worried.

Suddenly, in one liquid movement, she took a step away from him, her smile turned into an angry frown, her cheeks darkened from faint pink to deep red and her hand swung in a long arc, exploding with the long-repressed explosion of bitter force on his cheek with a *slap* that resounded is if it had been shot from a gun. As her arm fell back to her side, the impression of her palm and fingers remained as red welts on his skin. From the way he winced, she knew that she had hurt him—and experienced a momentary sensation of guiltless satisfaction.

"I guess I deserve that," he said, bringing his hand to his face.

"Damn right you do. That—and more."

Alison's voice was loud, commanding, and condemning. She was oblivious to the hush that had descended over the coffee shop, to the faces turned in her direction, watching and listening. The tendons in her neck were taut lines contorting her body into a pillar of accusation aimed at Olsson, who had to command his muscles to resist the impulse to flee the all but overwhelming force of her anger.

"It's been seven long years since you disappeared from the face of the earth without so much as a word. And you walk back into my life thinking you can pick up where you left off?"

"I didn't think *that*." Olsson tried to stop bowing his head with shame, and failed. "I'm . . . sorry, Alison. . . ."

"'I'm sorry'? Is *that* all you've got to say? After what you did! 'I'm *sorry*'?"

"I got . . . caught up. . . ."

"Never mind," Alison said weakly, as if her energy had been drained away. Slinging her laptop bag over her shoulder with one hand and picking up her handbag with the other. "I don't want to hear it."

She stalked out of the coffee shop, brushing past Ross Traynor without recognizing him, not even hearing his tentative, "Alison? Is that you?"

Olsson and Traynor watched in silence as Alison disappeared into the lobby.

"She was *livid*. What did you say to her?" Traynor asked.

"I hardly had a chance to say a word," Olsson half-smiled, gesturing to an empty table nearby. But what *she* said. . . ."

Traynor nodded as they sat down. "I heard."

"So did they." Olsson glanced around at the patrons who were now returning their attention to their interrupted meals and conversations. "Better than a soap opera."

"For a moment I thought you and Alison were back together," Traynor said.

"Afraid not." Olsson shook his head sadly. "It's much worse than that. We're enemies now."

"You're *what*?"

"We're—"

Olsson shook his head, stood, and said, "It's a great day to be outside Ross. Let's go for a walk in the park. He began walking out of the coffee shop—without a glance at the roses still lying on a chair.

"No ears," is all Olsson would say to Traynor's bewildered queries as he hurried to keep up with Olsson's long strides. They walked past Circular Quay at the top end of Sydney's business district and around the other side of the terminus for the Manly and other harbor ferries in silence. When they walked through the gates of the Botanic Gardens, Ross exploded, "What the hell's going on, Derek?"

Olsson sighed. "Ross," he said, coming to a sudden halt, "I'm going to have to tell this in my own way, okay? Please, just bear with me."

"Okay," Traynor said, spreading his arms wide. "I guess. It's just that . . . you set up one riddle, only to answer with another."

Olsson sat down heavily on a park bench; Traynor dropped beside him. From their feet the grass sloped downwards to the harbor, the bridge arching to the left, the water sparkling in the sunlight. But other than feeling the warmth of the sun, the way the two men looked at each other they could have been closeted in a dim, windowless room.

"So how's business, Ross?"

"Has that got something to do with you and Alison?"

"You'll see."

Traynor looked at his friend in exasperation. "Okay. I'm keeping my head above water—I guess. . . . To be honest, I'm not sure how much longer I can keep InterFreight going. The competition's just too tough for the little guys."

"I have a Hong Kong investor," Olsson said, "who'd like to build a nationwide transport network. He's prepared to invest whatever it takes—so long as he can see a profit at the end of the day, of course. So naturally, I thought of you."

Traynor's eyes lit up. "You've got my attention, mate."

"The concept is we'd pay off your uncle and operate InterFreight together."

"A partnership, you and me?"

Olsson nodded.

"That'd be great," Traynor grinning. "Like the old days."

"The Hong Kong investor wants forty-nine percent, you and I split the remaining fifty-one percent. The real capital—the millions we'd need to go nationwide—would come in the form of bonds and bank loans guaranteed by the investor."

"So when that's all paid back, we'd control a really big operation."

"That's right," said Olsson somberly. "But there's a catch. And it's a big one."

"What's that?"

"Drugs."

"Drugs? Pharmaceuticals?"

"No. *Illegal* drugs. Heroin, cocaine, marijuana and so on."

"Jesus! You're proposing . . . we go into the *drug* business?"

"No, Ross, I'm not," Olsson replied. "Not exactly. . . ."

"Not exactly? What the hell does *that* mean?" Traynor jumped to his feet and paced back and forth as he spoke. "Your pranks back in high school that got us sent to the headmaster were one thing. And I followed you—I admit it. I looked up to you. Still do. But I'm not a kid any more, and nor are you. For seven years, I've only seen you now and then—that's a helluva long time, Derek. Are you the same Derek Olsson I once knew so well?" Traynor stopped and peered into Olsson's eyes as if he'd find the answer there, and shrugged. "I don't know. . . ."

Olsson looked back evenly. "I haven't changed in any fundamental way, Ross. I assure you."

"You sure look different."

"I haven't been . . . happy."

Traynor sat down again. "You convinced me a long time ago that drugs should all be legalized. But to go *into* that business is something completely different. And you don't have Judy and the kids to worry about."

"I'm proposing we go into the transport business, *not* the drug business, Ross."

Traynor shook his head. "I don't get it?"

Olsson smiled. "A pipeline. InterFreight's business is to carry freight. Packages. If somebody put drugs in a box and ships it through us, well, we can just shrug our shoulders and say, 'Really? Jesus Christ, *we* had *no* idea.'"

Traynor looked at Olsson skeptically. "I don't see how that could work. And even if it does—I don't know that I want any part of it."

"I've gone into the legal angle—*everything.* It works. I can prove it—if you'll give me the chance to take you through it."

Traynor rose to his feet. "I'll think about it. But what's this all got to do with Alison?"

Olsson leaned forward, suddenly intense. "Alison and I are enemies now. But Alison must never know. Promise me that. Don't mention it to anyone. Not even Judy."

"Enemies?—Oh, I get it. Anthony Royn."

"Exactly," said Olsson. "The new drug czar and his War on Drugs—and Alison is his right hand."

*****

WHEN ALISON RETURNED TO the hotel later that evening she found her feet taking her to the front desk. "Could you tell me if Derek Olsson is staying here, please?"

"I'm sorry, ma'am," the concierge said, "but Mr. Olsson checked out this morning."

Alison turned away and stood, unsure of whether the burden she felt she'd worn the whole day had lifted—or now weighed on her more heavily. She silently cursed Derek for coming—and cursed him for disappearing just as suddenly.

Nodding woodenly at the concierge, she dragged one foot after the other until she reached the bank of lifts, thinking: *Probably just as well.*

*****

AROUND ELEVEN PM, A van turned into Luk Suk's compound and backed into the garage. An hour later it pulled out and turned up Soi 12 to Sukhumvit.

"Shit," Shultz cursed. He sat at the window of their hotel corner suite overlooking Luk Suk's compound and Soi 12. "What's going on?" he said to Suchart. "Wake everybody."

Rubbing their eyes, Nazarov and de Brouw reached the window in time to see the van slow as it neared the roadworks blocking the intersection. That afternoon, a team of workmen had dug up half the width of Soi 12 near the corner of Sukhumvit, put up MEN WORKING signs and a makeshift traffic light, and left. The light switched from green to red, but no cars were coming the other way so the van accelerated through the red light and turned onto Sukhumvit. A motorcycle trailed behind; a car parked beyond the roadworks roared into life and accelerated after the motorcycle.

Suchart relayed the report of the spotter on the ground. "Two people were in the front of the vehicle."

"That he could see," said de Brouw.

Suchart nodded.

"So, *now* what the fuck are we gonna do?" Shultz grumbled, looking at Nazarov.

They'd struck it lucky—or so they'd thought. Earlier, Suchart had shown them two lists. "Number plates," he explained. One list was of vehicles leaving police headquarters; a much shorter one showed all the vehicles arriving at Luk Suk's compound. "A supermarket delivery van left police headquarters shortly after noon and showed up twenty minutes later at Luk Suk's compound. It backed up to the garage so no one could see what came out."

"It could have been groceries," de Brouw grinned.

"Yeah, right," said Shultz.

"We'll keep following all the vehicles coming out of Luk Suk's compound," Nazarov said, "just in case. If nothing else comes up, we'll go in tonight, around two or three AM."

"Is Olsson in the vehicle that just left?" de Brouw wondered.

"The only way to know for sure is to get a good look inside it," said Nazarov.

"Set up a roadblock?" de Brouw suggested.

"We'd need a helicopter," Shultz grumbled.

Suchart broke in, "It's taking the freeway. We're still on its tail."

"We'll never catch up with it now," said Shultz.

"At least we'll know where it's going," Nazarov said.

"Fat lot of good that will do," Shultz growled.

"Any other movements on your watch?" de Brouw asked, looking at Shultz.

"No." Shultz shook his head. Nobody came in or out except the guards patrolling inside the wall."

"That light's still on," said de Brouw. Olsson had given them a sketch layout of the house, and de Brouw pointed to the one he'd said he usually slept in.

"The light in Luk Suk's room went out a few minutes ago," Shultz said.

"Before or after the car pulled out of the garage?" Nazarov asked.

"About the same time."

They all studied the house. The kitchen was dark, and light from the office and living room leaked through the curtains.

"Maybe he's still there—" said de Brouw.

"And maybe he isn't," Shultz growled. "As I said, what the fuck are we gonna do *now?* Split up the team?"

"If we do that, what are our chances of breaking in there *successfully?*" de Brouw said, pointing at the house. "And we'd be going in blind at the other end—assuming we catch up with them."

"And if we *don't* split the team and hit the wrong target," said Nazarov, "Olsson's dead."

Shultz and de Brouw nodded glumly.

Nazarov turned to Suchart. "Any ideas?"

Suchart held up his hand while he finished a phone call. "They're heading towards Pattya at high speed. The traffic's so light my men think they've probably been spotted."

"Getting further away every minute," Shultz griped.

"Glad we have such an optimist around to lighten the mood," de Brouw grinned.

"The hell with you," said Shultz. "What's to be optimistic about? Tell me that."

Suchart looked at his watch and turned to Nazarov. "I'll make a couple of calls—but it's late, so. . . ." He shrugged. "We'll see."

"You mean," said Shultz, "don't hold your breath, right?"

Suchart nodded.

"Shit," Shultz grumbled. "That Luk Suk sure is a sneaky bastard."

40 **Mexican Standoff**

ABOUT 1:30 AM, A police car stopped two speedsters on the freeway not too far from Pattya. Five minutes later, Suchart's phone rang.

"Just two men in the car," Suchart told Nazarov. "Both Thai."

As one, Nazarov, Shultz and de Brouw breathed a sigh of relief.

"You're a gem, Suchart," Shultz declared, slapping Suchart on the back hard enough to jerk him forward in his seat. Suchart smiled.

"How long do you need?" Nazarov asked Suchart.

Suchart shrugged. "Any time I make a phone call."

"Is twenty minutes enough time?"

Shultz and de Brouw both nodded.

"Time check: it's one-thirty-nine," Nazarov said, glancing at his watch. "We'll kick off at two."

AT 2:00 AM EVERYTHING was quiet on Sukhumvit Soi 12. A passing observer, had there been one, would have noticed a truck wobble slightly, or heard the springs of its suspension groan. The truck had been parked since about six in the evening next to the wall of Luk Suk's compound, a few meters from its main gate. Nazarov, Shultz, and de Brouw levered themselves through the roof of its cab and slid quietly along the top of its tall van body. De Brouw reached up with a pair of long-handled wire cutters and snipped the phone lines leading into the house.

At 2:01 AM, a succession of *burps* from a fusillade of shots from five rifles, all equipped with silencers, were barely audible against the background murmur of traffic from Sukhumvit. In addition to the three mercenaries on the truck's roof, two sharpshooters hired by Suchart were stationed in a hotel room overlooking the compound. In seconds, the three men and two dogs patrolling inside the compound were all dead, as was the guard in the guardhouse just inside the main gate.

At 2:02 AM a fault in a substation caused a power blackout in the area including Soi 12. The two sharpshooters donned night vision goggles. The three men on the roof of the truck now glowed in the dark: their police-issue Kevlar vests had been sprayed with a paint that was only visible in the night vision goggles. Also wearing gloves, motorcycle helmets, and masks, their exposed skin blackened, they were unrecognizable.

Throwing a blanket over the barbed wire and broken glass layered on top of the thick wall, de Brouw, Shultz, and Nazarov left their rifles on the truck's roof, took out pistols also equipped with silencers, swung over the wall, and dropped, catlike, to the ground. They padded silently around the house, making sure no one was still breathing.

De Brouw and Shultz quietly tried the front and garage doors that were, as expected, locked. In the guardhouse, using his dimmed torch, Nazarov found a large bunch of keys on the guard's body—too many to quickly find the right one. "Plan B," he whispered into the walkie-talkie unit tucked into his helmet.

The three mercenaries gathered near the wall opposite the floor-to-ceiling plate glass doors that led from the terrace into the dining room. "Fire now," Nazarov ordered. The two sharpshooters fired five shots each, leaving a pattern of holes and fine cracks in the glass of the doors.

Alarms rang through the house as the glass broke. With the phone line cut, the alarm system could not send out a signal to the police station or a security service—if that feature were part of its system.

On the fifth shot de Brouw and Shultz ran full tilt at the weakened panes of glass, crashing through them using their Kevlar-covered backs as battering rams, Nazarov dashing in behind. Woken by the alarms, two men who'd been sleeping on sofas in the living/dining room looked around groggily. When they became aware of two shadows smashing through the curtains, they reached for the guns that lay beside them on the floor. Nazarov shot them both with his pistol as their fingers closed around their weapons.

Sounds of movement came from upstairs and from the kitchen area. Shultz felt his way to the office, flicking on his flashlight and crouching down at the same time. "All clear," he whispered and joined Nazarov at the bottom of the stairs. De Brouw ran into the kitchen, catching a maid's shocked face in the sudden glare of his torch. She shrieked. De Brouw followed her as she tried to escape to the maids' quarters, where two other shrieks joined the first. Finding no one else, with his pistol he waved the three women into a windowless storeroom and said the Thai phrase that Suchart had taught him that meant: *Stay put or die.* All three vigorously nodded and shrieked again. De Brouw closed the storeroom door, bolted it, and ran back to join Shultz and Nazarov murmuring, "Maids secured," into his walkie-talkie.

"There's a shooter at the top of the stairs," Nazarov replied.

In the dim light coming through the smashed picture wall, de Brouw could just see that Nazarov and Shultz had taken cover behind the upended dining table. With the alarm still hooting speed was more important than silence. De Brouw crept towards the two bodies lying on the sofas, holstered his pistol, picked up the two rifles and crept back. "Keep the shooter busy," he said. As Shultz and Nazarov fired, de Brouw emptied one rifle into the ceiling, moving it slightly with each shot to leave a pattern of bullet holes where the staircase reached the floor above.

They waited a moment after de Brouw's last shot.

"You got him," said Shultz.

"I'll lead the way," said de Brouw. Dropping the empty rifle, he took the second one and bounded up the stairs three at a time. Nazarov followed him cautiously while Shultz found the alarm box and yanked out wires until the alarm stopped. In the sudden silence they could hear footsteps from above.

De Brouw came to a stop near the top of the stairs and fired a couple of shots randomly. He poked his head into the corridor so that just the top of his helmet showed, and pulled it back immediately. A couple of bullets embedded themselves in the wall to his left. Shifting the rifle into a left-handed grip, he took a deep breath and leaned halfway into the corridor firing as he moved. He saw a muzzle flash from a doorway, and a man's silhouette outlined in the faint light from outside. A bullet whacked into his Kevlar vest and a second one hit his left arm above the elbow. The rifle jerked slightly but he brought it back with his other hand and pulled the trigger twice more. The silhouette fell, the rifle clattering to the floor.

"All clear. I'm hit, but okay," he said. He let the rifle fall, took his pistol with his right hand and ran the few steps to where the man lay and into the bedroom behind. It was empty.

"I'm to the right as you come up the stairs," he said, stationing himself in the doorway. "One bedroom empty. Three more doors. All closed."

Nazarov, followed by Shultz, went to the bedroom door opposite the stairs. "Locked." He padded to the door to de Brouw's left and spun through the doorway into a crouch, de Brouw covering him from behind. Empty.

As he came back to the corridor, the door to de Brouw's right slowly opened. Three pistols took aim. "I'm unarmed," said a voice. Nazarov turned on his flashlight again. A small Chinese man wearing silk pajamas stood in the doorway, his hands in the air.

"Luk Suk," said Nazarov.

"Correct," Luk Suk smiled. "This might be a good time for you to all leave."

"Why?" Nazarov demanded.

"The police are on the way."

"I don't think so," said Nazarov.

Luk Suk laughed. "Not the local police. I called a friend of mine. A general. He wasn't too happy to be woken at two in the morning, I can tell you."

"Just unlock that door," Nazarov pointed at the fourth bedroom.

"Sure," Luk Suk said, taking a step back into his room. "I'll have to get my keys."

"Wait here," Nazarov said, pushing past Luk Suk. He played the flashlight into the room, moving in cautiously. "Clear. Okay, come in slowly and *point* to where your keys are." He motioned to Shultz to go in with Luk Suk.

Nazarov took Shultz' place at the top of the stairs, kicking the body aside so it no longer half-blocked the stairwell. When Luk Suk and Shultz disappeared into the bedroom he spoke softly into the walkie-talkie. "Suchart."

"Here."

"Police may be on the way—not local. Let us know if your spotters see anything."

"Okay."

"We'll need to make a fast getaway. Climb over the fence and unlock the main gate. You'll find the keys in the guardhouse. Then get ready to drive the truck when we come out."

"Will do," said Suchart.

"Better tell the sharpshooters to get the hell out of there."

"Okay."

Luk Suk said something in Cantonese as he unlocked the door.

"What was that?" Nazarov demanded, pressing his pistol to Luk Suk's head.

"Just saying I'm coming in."

"You first." Luk Suk opened the door and Nazarov duck-walked him inside. Shultz followed; de Brouw stood halfway in the doorway.

As Shultz' flashlight lit the room, they could see Olsson chained to the bed. A beefy Chinese man sat next to him, holding a pistol to his head.

"One wrong move," said Luk Suk, "and Olsson dies."

As the flashlight stopped on the man's face, his eyes blinked from the sudden glare. De Brouw's pistol burped and a hole appeared in the man's head just above the top of his nose. The man's body slumped on top of Olsson.

"You were saying?" de Brouw grinned.

Shultz yanked the man's body and let it drop to the floor. "The keys," he said to Luk Suk.

Luk Suk shrugged. "I'm not sure where they are."

Shultz pulled his knife from inside his boot and let the tip trace a faint red line on Luk Suk's cheek. "Perhaps this will jog your memory."

"What are you doing?" Olsson shouted, aghast.

"Shut up, boss," Shultz growled. "This ain't your department."

Luk Suk jerked back from the knife into Nazarov, whose pistol dug into his back. Nazarov's arm pinned Luk Suk against his body. "Okay, okay," Luk Suk shouted, a hand going to his face where it stung; when he drew his hand away he trembled at the sight of his own blood. With an effort, he said, "They're on that key ring."

Shultz grabbed the keys, fumbling for each key until he found the right one, and undid Olsson's chains. "Let's get out of here."

Olsson sat up on the bed rubbing his wrists and flexing his muscles.

"What about him?" Shultz asked, pointing his knife at Luk Suk.

"No point in taking him with us," said de Brouw, levelling his pistol at Luk Suk.

"No!" said Olsson. "Hasn't there been enough killing already?"

"Is that your decision?" Nazarov asked, looking at Olsson, bringing his pistol to Luk Suk's head.

"Yes."

"The *last* thing we need," Shultz said, "is excess baggage."

Suchart's voice came through the walkie-talkies. "Police cars are coming along Sukhumvit. You have five minutes or less."

"We've got to go *now*," said Shultz.

"Get a pair of those handcuffs," Nazarov ordered Shultz, and turned to de Brouw, "Open the gate. Get in the truck and leave the back door open for us."

Shultz grabbed a set of handcuffs from the bed; Nazarov spun Luk Suk around and Shultz locked his wrists behind his back. With his knife, Shultz sliced two strips off a sheet. "We don't want him giving a warning," he said as he stuffed the smaller piece into Luk Suk's mouth, and looped the other tightly around his head to gag him securely. "Let's *go*."

Nazarov and Shultz frog-marched Luk Suk out of the room, half-carrying him as they ran down the stairs. Olsson followed slowly.

"Move!" said Shultz over his shoulder.

At the bottom of the stairs Nazarov and Shultz lifted Luk Suk off the ground, ran out through the broken glass doors and towards the gate.

"Suchart," Nazarov shouted as he came around the corner of the house. "That blanket's still on top of the wire. Can you get it down."

"Okay," Suchart replied. "Three minutes left."

As Nazarov and Shultz threw Luk Suk in the back of the truck Suchart was on top trying to pull the blanket off. It was hooked on the barbed wire. He picked up one of the rifles that still lay there and flipped it over the other side, unsnagging it so that it fell inside the compound.

"Where are the gate keys?" Nazarov asked.

"On the passenger seat," Suchart responded.

Nazarov grabbed the keys and ran back to the gate, pulling it shut. There was one large, old-fashioned key on the chain, which fitted into a keyhole on the outside of the gate. Nazarov pushed the key in the slot but it clearly hadn't been used for a long time. He strained to turn it; the sound of sirens was coming closer. Finally it clicked into place. He threw the keys over the wall, sprinted behind the truck, swung the doors shut, bolted them, and snapped the padlock shut.

Suchart was squeezing himself down from the roof of the cab as Nazarov climbed into the driver's seat. "We're too late," he said as, sirens screaming and lights flashing, police cars swung into Soi 12, their headlights sudden bright arcs in the blacked-out street. "Into the back, Suchart," he said as he passed one rifle after another to Shultz. Suchart disappeared into the van of the truck as the cab was illuminated by the police cars' headlights. Nazarov crouched down, locked both doors, and crawled after Suchart.

"We'll stay here and sit it out," Nazarov said. "Quickly, get into a position where you can't be seen from the front. Then, no sound, no movement, understood?"

A narrow bench ran down each side of the van. Suchart squeezed next to Shultz who'd pinned Luk Suk against the bulkhead behind the driver's seat and held a knife to his throat. "One murmur, one twitch out of you and you're a dead man, you understand?"

Luk Suk nodded carefully, his eyes wide.

Olsson was tying a bandage on de Brouw's arm as if his fingers were all thumbs. Nazarov took over from him, kicking the open first aid kit under the bench. Olsson sat looking worn, tired—and dejected, his head in his hands. Nazarov grabbed his shoulder to push him out of sight.

The police cars stopped outside the gate and around the truck. Their blue and red flashing lights threw menacing shadows through the front window of the cab. The sounds of footsteps and voices surrounded them. The gate rattled, a buzzer sounded; neither brought any response. A light flashed into the truck's cab, followed by the sound of boots scraping on the truck's side. Boots loudly climbed over the bonnet and echoed on the truck's roof; voices shouted from above.

For about five minutes nothing happened. Then someone barked an order and the boots clambered down and jumped off the truck. Engines started, the flashing lights moved, disappearing in the direction of Sukhumvit leaving silence and darkness.

"What's happening?" Olsson asked.

"Shh," said Nazarov. He, Shultz, and de Brouw all looked at Suchart who was speaking quietly into his walkie-talkie.

"They've all left," Suchart whispered. "What now?"

Olsson seemed about to speak and Nazarov raising a warning finger.

"Let's wait five minutes," Nazarov whispered. "Can one of your lookouts come down and check they didn't leave anyone behind?"

Suchart nodded.

A couple of minutes later they heard a motorcycle chug past—and come back.

"All clear," Suchart said.

"Okay, can you drive us out of here and explain just what happened?"

Suchart climbed into the driver's seat, started the engine, and the truck jerked as it took off noisily.

"They saw the bodies over the wall," Suchart told them as he drove. "Someone made a phone call and ordered everyone to leave. He said it was too late for them to do anything, and if anyone was going to get egg on their faces, it might as well be the local police."

"What now?" said Nazarov, looking at Olsson, as the truck turned onto Sukhumvit.

"We should all disappear for a while."

"What about *him*?" Shultz demanded, waving his knife in Luk Suk's face.

"You can't let him live," Nazarov said. "You know that."

Olsson jerked his head up at Nazarov's words. "Why not?"

"Because if you don't kill him today, you'll have to kill him some other time. Unless he kills you first."

Olsson looked at Luk Suk and could see that Nazarov was right.

"I . . . can't do that," Olsson said.

"It's easy enough," said Nazarov, levelling his pistol at Luk Suk. "Just say the word."

Olsson shook his head.

"Here, then, take my pistol."

Olsson looked at the gun Nazarov was holding out to him and shook his head again. "I don't need a pistol."

Muffled sounds came from Luk Suk's throat.

"He's trying to say something," said Olsson. "Take off the gag."

"You know, *Ah-son,*" Luk Suk said after a long, grateful breath, "this man speaks truly."

Olsson looked at him in surprise.

"That's right. It's down to you or me. Only one of us can live. I don't see what your problem is—except that this time you have to do it yourself. Unless, of course, you just give the order. Much simpler." In the dim light Luk Suk's smile looked condescending and ghoulish at the same time.

"What's the big deal?" de Brouw said. "What do you think *he* was planning to do to *you*—invite you to the Sunday school picnic?"

His mouth open, Olsson looked towards de Brouw, but beyond him as if de Brouw was just a pale, unmoving, transparent ghost.

"A gangster with a conscience," Shultz growled. "I don't believe it."

"I'm not—" Olsson coughed, as though to loosen his frozen vocal chords "—a g-gangster."

Luk Suk laughed. "What do you think you've been ever since you started working for me? Office boy?"

Olsson nodded reluctantly. *That's what I've been . . . all along.*

"He's got friends in high places, hasn't he?" Nazarov asked. "Like you."

"Right," said Olsson.

"If you let him go, the Thai cops will be after *you,* won't they?"

"And maybe us, too," Shultz said.

"Could be," Olsson conceded, looking at Luk Suk. *But that's not the issue.*

Then what is? Face it. You'd kill Luk Suk and all his men if necessary . . . you already have, just about. . . .

In self-defence. Not in cold blood.

". . . we're *both* committing acts which are evil, by *any* moral code . . ." he had said to Luk Suk. *Except according to the law of the jungle. . . . Is that the code I've accepted all along?*

"You think this Luk Suk guy's some kind of a saint or something?" de Brouw asked Olsson.

"Ha," Shultz said. "The boss seems to think *he* is."

That's right, Olsson thought, his eyes still fixed on Luk Suk. *And if I kill you now, I'm no different from you after all. . . .*

Luk Suk broke into his thoughts, addressing Nazarov. "Are you sure you gentlemen wouldn't like to move up in the world?" he drawled. "I assure you that with me you can make *much* more money than you ever dreamed of."

"There doesn't seem to be much of your operation left walking around," Nazarov grinned. "I have just one question for you."

Luk Suk raised an eyebrow. "Which is?"

"What would we need *you* for?"

Olsson's gaze turned to Nazarov, his eyes alight with new understanding. *Twice now my life has been saved by these men—who enjoy killing.* He turned back to Luk Suk. *Being surrounded by men like them was inevitable . . . from the moment I followed you, Luk Suk.*

"For Chrissakes, boss," Nazarov said, "are we just going to drive around all fucking day?"

"Make up your bloody mind," Shultz cut in. "It's him or you. Easy choice."

Yes, it is, Olsson thought.

His heart racing, his face drawn and pale, he slowly reached over and gripped Luk Suk's neck with his hand, his thumb moving to the vital point. He felt his stomach churning and felt as though he'd lost control over his fingers, which now refused to move. Luk Suk eyes widened, looking directly into his. Olsson could see the fear and resignation behind them.

"So who's evil now, *Ah-son?*"

"Who corrupted me?" Olsson replied.

"Yin and yang, remember."

We all have the potential. . . .

His eyes still locked on Luk Suk's, the thought *It's you or me . . . the law of the jungle* ran through his head. He flexed his fingers, sensing the soft tissue of Luk Suk's throat. But as he imagined crushing that throat, he felt all his muscles lock in place, his breath coming in forced gasps.

"He's frozen up," said de Brouw. "Battle shock."

Nazarov and Shultz nodded, recalling when a soldier under their command panicked and was unable to fire his rifle, or shot wildly into the air—even when the enemy was spraying bullets directly at *him.*

"Don't trouble yourself, boss," Nazarov said, raising his pistol. "This is *our* job."

Olsson made no reaction, as if he was deaf to Nazarov's words.

Shultz waved his knife. "Better this way," he said. "No holes." He tapped the thin metal wall of the van with his other hand.

"No!" Olsson's hand left Luk Suk's neck to lash Nazarov's wrist, sending his pistol spinning to the back of the van while with his other hand he pushed Shultz' knife away.

Nazarov rubbed his wrist and nodded approvingly at Olsson. "You're *fast.*"

Olsson turned to Nazarov. "If it has to be done, *I* have to do it."

"You haven't got the guts," Luk Suk grinned.

Olsson dropped his hands. "You—you give me your word. Perpetual truce. We simply forget each other and go our separate ways—"

"His word ain't worth shit," Shultz cut in, spitting at Luk Suk's feet for emphasis.

Olsson saw the cunning look he knew so well flash across Luk Suk's face. *Shultz is right.* He thought of letting Nazarov or Shultz do his dirty work. *Then I can pretend I'm not involved. . . .*

He shook his head.

"What the hell are you waiting for?" de Brouw demanded.

Nazarov shrugged. "The first time is always the hardest."

"Not for me," said de Brouw.

Olsson shuddered at de Brouw's nonchalant tone, at the sense of being surrounded by vicious animals. *But that's not fair,* he thought. *Animals never kill just for fun . . . unless they're diseased or insane. I'm in the company of psychopaths. . . .*

In one swift movement his hand was again at Luk Suk's neck. But as he squeezed, his body and even his fingers shook. Unable to watch, Olsson closed his eyes . . . but the rhythm of Luk Suk's pulse seemed to beat through his fingers as it faltered . . . and stopped. Luk Suk's neck tugged at his hand; Olsson opened his eyes in surprise as Luk Suk's body collapsed, accompanied by a gruesome thump as his head slumped against the bulkhead.

Overwhelmed by the revulsion of what he'd just done, Olsson threw up all over Luk Suk's pajamas.

"Boss," Shultz grumbled, "you've left your DNA all over the body. We'll have to burn it or something."

*****

"Good morning, Senator."

"You!"

McKurn sat awkwardly at his desk, his right arm locked in a heavy cast from shoulder to elbow. He glared at Alison McGuire as she walked calmly into his office, slamming the door behind her. McKurn winced as he pushed himself slowly to his feet. "Get the fuck outta here."

"That will be my pleasure, Senator," Alison smiled. "But you seem to have forgotten something."

"What's that?" McKurn growled as he struggled to his feet.

"I have something to show you." Alison said as she put her laptop on the desk. "So," she said, leaning towards him, her face now hard, "sit down. And *shut up.*"

"You can't talk to *me* like that."

"I just did. What are you going to do about it?"

His face reddening, McKurn mumbled, "Nothing—right now," and winced again as he sank back into his chair.

"Good boy," Alison said approvingly, grinning at the tone of her mother's voice coming from her lips. "And how's your shoulder, Senator?" she asked as she opened her laptop.

"Damn you."

Alison laughed. Veins jumped out from McKurn's forehead. "Just take a look at this, Senator." She turned the laptop towards him. Five Asian girls appeared on the screen, sitting in a semi-circle facing the camera.

"Who the hell are they?" McKurn growled.

"Don't tell me you've forgotten *all* of them, Senator."

A woman off-camera said something in another language; subtitles across the bottom of the screen read: Do you recognize this man? A photograph of McKurn replaced the girls.

All five girls giggled and nodded their heads in unison. We called him John, the subtitles read, but I saw his face on TV once. His real name is Frank McKurn.

So you know him?

Yes. One of the girls spoke in the same language as the questioner; the others nodded. He was one of our, ah . . . clients.

For what?

After another short silence, one of the girls, hiding her mouth behind a hand and looking away from the camera spoke softly. The others girls looked down, ashamed, but reluctantly nodded their heads as the single word, Sex, appeared on the bottom of the screen.

All of you?

Giggling again, but without looking up, they all answered: Yes.

And what's so funny?

The five girls all spoke at once and a series of subtitles chased each other across the screen.

He was one of our favorites . . .

. . . yeah . . .

. . . it was all over in five minutes. This time, the translator joined in the laughter.

Alison stopped the video.

"So?" asked McKurn.

"There's more, Senator. Would you like to hear them go into detail about your sexual prowess?"

"What's the point?"

"Do you want me to spell it out for you?"

McKurn shrugged. "Get it over with."

"It's really quite simple. Frequenting prostitutes is enough to get you run out of town. But 'Five-Minute Frankie' would be *laughed* out of Parliament."

"It's a fabrication."

Alison shook her head. "These are the five Asian sex slaves who were forced into prostitution at the Aphrodite's call girl agency—which you patronized."

"That's bullshit," said McKurn.

"Really, Senator?" Alison grinned. "They've all signed affidavits identifying you as a customer."

"I . . . see. I presume you have something in mind?"

"I thought that would be obvious. You've threatened to ruin me with that damn video of yours. Release it now, and we can *also* kiss goodbye to 'Five-Minute Frankie.'"

"So . . . " McKurn nodded slowly. "A Mexican standoff."

"Exactly."

McKurn's eyes narrowed. "And how did you get ahold of this?"

Alison grinned. "An . . . admirer sent it to me."

"You expect me to believe that?"

"Frankly, I don't care what you believe," Alison grinned as she rose to her feet. Her eyes flashing she picked up her laptop and said, "A pleasure doing business with you, Senator—for a change." Spinning on her heel, she strode towards the door.

*****

"THE PRIME MINSTER IS recovering, but very slowly," Royn reported to the assembled Cabinet. "The doctors expect to move him out of intensive care in a day or two."

"Will he have a *full* recovery?" Cracken asked.

"That remains to be seen," said Royn.

"What exactly *is* his condition, then, Tony?" Helen Arkness asked.

Fifteen Cabinet ministers, thirteen junior ministers of the Outer Cabinet, and the cabinet secretary who took the minutes filled every seat at the long cabinet table— except Kydd's chair, left symbolically vacant. Thirteen parliamentary secretaries— junior Members and Senators being groomed for higher things whose job was to assist ministers—were arrayed around the walls of the room.

"When I saw him on Sunday he didn't look good." Royn glanced at his notes. "But I'm told the color is returning to his cheeks and he's giving everyone a hell of a time. His mind was not affected, but he has a mild paralysis of the left side of his body. Whether he regains full use of his body remains to be seen. But he'll be able to get around in a wheelchair or even with crutches. So I imagine he'll be back at the helm in a couple of weeks."

"That's good to know," said Victor Bergstrom.

"It certainly is," said Royn, leading a chorus of agreement. All the ministers chimed in, some less enthusiastically than others.

"Turning to current business," Royn said, "perhaps you could bring us up to date on the Sandeman situation, Victor."

"The news is all good for a change," said Bergstrom.

"If you ignore the body bags," Cracken interjected.

"Ah . . . yes," Bergstrom said. "But the Islamic terrorists have been pretty much swept from St. Christopher's Island; the third, Catholic group has been seriously weakened—and they've lost their rationale for existence now that the Islamic groups have been destroyed."

"But have they?" asked Cracken.

"Paul," Royn snapped, "save your questions until Victor is finished, if you don't mind."

"I *do* mind—"

"And so do I," said Bergstrom. Cracken began another interjection but Bergstrom simply ignored him and raised his voice. "As I was saying, St. Christopher's Island has been pretty much pacified. The terrorist groups folded so quickly that we don't have detailed plans for the next step. But this success has proven the wisdom of operating Australian and Sandeman forces together. Plans are being developed which are, in a nutshell, to repeat the same sweeps on the other islands until the terrorist groups across the country have been broken. Now, Paul, what was your question?"

"Some of the terrorists have been killed—"

"Over a hundred, as far as we can estimate," said Bergstrom.

"—but what about the ones who *haven't?*" Cracken continued.

Bergstrom shrugged. "They've been dispersed."

"To *where?*"

"They're no longer a threat."

"Not *today,* perhaps. But what about *tomorrow? Where* have they gone? Are they regrouping? Have they teamed up with terrorists on other islands? And—if not more important—we know from experience in similar situations in other countries that such a success as we've just had can inspire other hotheads to sign up. It can even attract terrorists from abroad. Can you answer these questions, Victor?"

"We're . . . ah . . . fully aware of these concerns, Paul. And we're closely monitoring the situation."

"Meaning," said Cracken sarcastically, "you haven't got a frigging clue."

"Not today," said Bergstrom, pursing his lips in disapproval. "But our intelligence gathering is on-going so we *will* know, and soon."

"I'm sure you're right, Victor," Royn said before Cracken could speak. "I'd like to suggest that we commend our troops—any objections? . . . Good. I'll draft a suitable message. And Victor, this would be a good moment for you to visit Toribaya ostensibly for a conference with your opposite number there."

"Ostensibly?" Bergstrom asked.

Royn nodded. "While you're up there you could hand out some medals, that sort of thing. Raise morale—"

"—and provide some good photo ops," Cracken interjected.

"Indeed," Royn agreed.

"Good idea," said Bergstrom.

"Good. Shall we move on?" When no one objected, Royn said, "There's just one other item on today's agenda before 'other business.' Corruption."

"You mean all these stories in the Olsson and Sykes' papers?" asked Helen Arkness. "The media's out for blood."

"Indeed they are," said Royn. "With this morning's exposure of a senior bureaucrat in the South Australian state treasury, a total of *ten* high officials at all levels of government have been arrested on corruption charges. There've been two top state public servants, two senior police officers—including one who was slated to be the next Victorian Police Commissioner—a mayor, two councillors, two state parliamentarians and a federal Senator—"

"A *Labor* Senator," Cracken pointed out.

"Unfortunately, Paul," Royn said, "we can't claim the high moral ground. Both state parliamentarians were Conservatives."

"And what about these storm clouds gathering around Senator McKurn, Paul?" Helen Arkness said. "If McKurn is next, I'd say we've got a very big problem."

"Exactly so, Helen," said Royn. "What do *you* think, Paul?"

"Well," Cracken said uncomfortably, "I guess we'll just have to wait and see."

"This is far more serious than you seen to think," Royn continued. "Ten isn't many, compared to everybody in government service. But they're all high officials protecting and facilitating serious crimes, mostly drug-related, not minor cases of some minister padding his travel expenses. The public's perception is that government is *riddled* with corruption. If we do nothing, we'll face a crisis of confidence.

"To stave that off, we need to show that we're *serious* about rooting out corruption. To be serious and to be *seen* to be serious, we need an investigation that's completely independent of all government and political pressures. One that's well-financed and has wide authority. My suggestion is to beef up the Candyman Inquiry into a Royal Commission."

"You've brought this up before and we've agreed to leave the Candyman Inquiry as it is. What's changed?" Cracken demanded. "Other than the fact that *you're* now chairing this meeting—and that this is your pet hobby-horse? Perhaps you need to be reminded that you're only *Acting* Prime Minister."

"Thank you, Paul," Royn snapped. "You have such an irritating fondness for stressing the obvious. It's a pity you don't have all the facts. One thing that's changed is the crisis of confidence I have already mentioned—"

"Oh, bollocks," said Cracken.

"Do you have your head in the sand or what, Paul?" Helen Arkness snapped. "Already, people are asking why the OlssonPress, a *private company,* is coming up with this ironclad evidence when the state and federal police *aren't.* Do you know what they're saying about the police?"

"I imagine you're about to enlighten us," said Cracken.

"They're asking whether the police are failing because they're *incompetent,* or because they're *also corrupt.*"

"So I'm sure even *you,* Paul, can now see how serious this is." Royn glared at Cracken when he looked as though he was about to speak again. "So if you have no objections—and even if you *do*—perhaps you could do us all the favor of keeping your mouth well and truly *shut* while Bruce brings you and everyone else up to date on *other* facts you're not aware of."

Cracken glowered at Royn, but said nothing.

"Nobody knows who this Candyman really is," said Spring. "He appeared as a new supplier of illegal drugs a year or so ago. He or she now supplies over sixty percent of the

Australian market for heroin, and an even higher percentage for marijuana, hashish, Buddha sticks, and the like. He's achieved this dominance by offering higher quality at a lower price."

"A proven formula," Stanley Chow, the Minister for Trade, grinned. "How has this affected the *other* suppliers?"

"Our information is that most gangs are abandoning their traditional suppliers and turning to him."

"Hardly a surprise," said Chow.

"I suppose not," Spring replied. "But just in the past couple of weeks there've been two new, and very worrying, developments. And with your permission, ladies and gentlemen, I'd like to invite Inspector Sean Reynolds of the Federal Police, a senior member of the Candyman Inquiry, to brief us."

"Fine by me," said Royn. "Are we agreed? . . .Bring him in, then, Bruce."

A moment later a uniformed police inspector, his shirt crisply white and the toes of his shoes black mirrors, marched in.

"Inspector," said Royn, "welcome. Perhaps you'd like to take this chair." He indicated Kydd's seat.

"With your permission, Prime Minister," Reynolds said deferentially.

"Acting Prime Minister," Cracken hissed under his breath.

"I think I'd prefer to stand." Reynolds wheeled Kydd's chair back and placed his briefcase on the table.

"I've been asked to brief you on two developments related to this Candyman fella. The first is that having dominated the supply of heroin and marijuana, he's begun to selectively *deny* supplies to certain gangs. We're not clear why. But the result of his action—and we're assuming it's a he," Reynolds said, glancing at Helen Arkness and the handful of other women present, "just for convenience—"

"I'm sure he is a 'he', Inspector," Helen Arkness grinned.

"Most likely you're right, ma'am," said Reynolds, taking a deep breath before continuing. "The result has been an increase in inter-gang violence as gangs denied supplies attempt to steal them from others. These attacks have a strange aspect: several times, the police have been tipped off *beforehand,* resulting in quite a few arrests. Gratifying, but nevertheless curious."

"As though someone was using the police as their enforcers—is that what you're getting at?" asked Spring.

"That, sir, is one theory, and certainly a favored one. But," he shrugged, "there's no evidence as yet, one way *or* the other."

"And your second development, Inspector?" Helen Arkness prompted.

"If I may *show* you . . . ?" Reynolds looked quizzically at Royn as he began to open his briefcase. At Royn's "Go ahead, Inspector," he took out four packets, all in sealed Ziploc bags, and passed them around. "This is evidence, so *please,* ladies and gentlemen, don't break the seal."

"Evidence of what, Inspector?" asked Helen Arkness.

"The white powder you can see through the plastic is heroin, ma'am." One minister dropped the packet he was holding as if his fingers were suddenly on fire. "But note the packaging—*inside* the Ziploc bag, of course. It's vacuum packed and sealed."

Stanley Chow was holding a packet, turning it slightly back and forth to catch the light. "It has a 3-D effect. Expensive packaging is my guess. Hard to duplicate."

"Yes, sir," said Reynolds. "It's a hologram—"

"'Burmese Gold,'" Chow read. "Eighty percent. There's a list of other ingredients, and at the bottom it says: 'For your own safety, burn the outer package after opening.' Intriguing."

"Yes, sir. There are three more varieties: Afghan Number One, Colombian High, and the cheapest one which is called Silver Triangle."

"Branding," said Chow. "Very clever. And I suppose the Silver Triangle is some sort of mixture—like no-name brandy compared to cognac."

"Exactly so, sir," Reynolds nodded. "At eighty percent, this heroin is *much* higher quality than any other drug supplier offers, and it's being retailed at not much above wholesale—"

"Is this coming from the same Candyman guy?" Chow asked.

"We *think* so, sir."

"Branding," Chow said, "low prices, high and presumably *consistent* quality. It looks like he's trying to cut everyone else out of the market. I presume the customers love it."

"Yes, sir. They're flocking to it. Though it appears to be available in only a limited number of places."

"At selected retailers only?" Chow grinned.

"Exactly. And every time the police raid one, they've all disappeared—been tipped off."

"Protection," said Chow.

"Unfortunately, sir, it seems obvious you are right."

"Are you suggesting corruption seems pretty widespread in the police forces, Inspector?" Royn asked.

"I wouldn't say widespread, Prime Minister," Reynolds said gravely. "But it's more of a problem, it seems, than we had assumed."

"Is there any indication that these lower prices have resulted in *more customers* for these drugs?" Chow asked.

"As in more addicts? Not as far as we can tell, sir—though that's to be expected, I imagine. But there *has* been a small, statistically significant *decline* in the number of crimes committed by addicts to support their habit."

"So this 'Candyman fella' is performing a public service."

"That's not how *we* look at it, sir," Reynolds scowled.

"I'm just joking, Inspector," Chow grinned.

Royn looked at Chow skeptically. *Was* he joking? With Chow, it was often hard to tell: he had a tendency to state his opinions at precisely the wrong moment, as with his private comment to several businessmen that unions were "havens for feather-bedding layabouts"—unaware that a reporter was standing just behind him.

Convinced that the racist vote would always stand between him and his ambition to be Prime Minister, Chow didn't seem to care. Popular in his electorate and too powerful within the Conservative Party to be pushed aside, he was something of a loose cannon everyone had to live with.

"Inspector," said Spring, "you didn't mention that marijuana and hashish is also on the market in the same style of packaging."

"Thank you, sir. That's correct. Perhaps I should have brought some samples, but they're bulkier."

"They've got brand names too?" Chow asked.

"Yes, sir. Black Mexican Gold, Maui Wowie High, Silver Sticks, and so on."

"Thank you, Inspector," said Royn. "A very disturbing presentation. I'm sure that many of us have lots of questions. But we need to move on, so could you wait outside and be available for questions later?"

"Certainly, sir." Reynolds gathered the evidence bags and strode into the corridor.

"So, ladies and gentlemen," Royn said, "are you now convinced of the seriousness of the situation?"

"So it would seem," said Cracken. "But a Royal Commission—that's like riding a scorpion. Why not make it a *Senate* enquiry? At least we'll still have *control.*"

"What if there's another Felix Haughtry in the Senate?" Helen Arkness demanded. "And *he's* on the Senate committee of enquiry. What then, Paul?" When Cracken said nothing, she added, "The press will make a mockery of it in short order," said Helen Arkness.

"How, Helen?" Cracken smirked. "Do tell."

"Who's President of the Senate, Paul? Is that a question beyond your capacity to grasp?"

"I'm not *dumb,* Helen."

"Sometimes I wonder, Paul," Helen Arkness replied. "So I'll spell it out for you. Who's in charge of making appointments to such a committee? McKurn. What's the obvious implication that even Blind Freddy could see? That McKurn will stack the committee to ensure *he* isn't a subject of their investigations. It will be seen as a farce—which is exactly what it will be."

"I agree with Paul on this," said Stanley Chow. "Once a Royal Commission takes off, you never know where it's going to end up—and you've got no way of reining it in. But I also agree with Tony. The situation is *definitely* serious. How many more officials are going to be exposed? We don't know and the OlssonPress people won't say. But we're looking at a serious electoral liability if lots of Conservatives end up being indicted. Much better if we shunt them out of sight—quietly bury them, so to speak. Keep the focus on the police and officials—and, of course, Labor Party members. Hopefully, we can find a way to set it up so it's *seen* to be independent, while keeping ultimate control."

"That, Stanley, is the ideal solution," Royn said. "But how can it be done? Maybe there's a way, but I haven't thought of one yet." His gaze swivelled to encompass everyone present as he asked, "At this point, is there a consensus that a high-powered investigation into these corruption and drug problems is needed? If so, we can leave the actual structure till later—say, Thursday?"

"That's not much time," said Cracken.

"We don't *have* much time, Paul," Royn said. "Who will headline in tomorrow's papers? And the next? We can't wait to act. And why should we?"

"Hear, hear," said several Ministers at once.

"The problem with decisions made too quickly," Cracken warned, "is that they can come back later and bite us in the arse."

"Eloquently put, as usual," said Helen Arkness sarcastically.

Cracken grinned.

"Could I have a show of hands?" Royn asked.

"Is there a motion before us?" Cracken said. "I haven't heard one." He looked around. "Has anyone else?"

"Yes, Paul," Royn said patiently. "That we agree a high-powered investigation into corruption and drugs is necessary, and that we'll agree to the specific structure of that investigation on Thursday."

"That's *two* motions, Tony," Cracken said. "And on the second one, I think we should consider our *options* on Thursday."

"I agree," said Chow.

"Fair enough," said Royn. "A show of hands?"

Both motions were passed, the first unanimously, the second with a small number of dissenters.

*****

Alison kicked off her shoes and danced a little jig as stepped through the door of her apartment. She let herself flop onto the sofa. "What bliss."

Since walking out of McKurn's office that morning she felt she was walking on air. The burden she'd been carrying for the past few weeks was lifted. That evening, she and Melanie went out to celebrate, and Royn had joined them for a late dinner after the House rose for the evening. They drank two bottles of wine at dinner and before that— she couldn't remember. But she felt as though the alcohol had had no effect. Or, perhaps, she'd been feeling drunk the whole day.

The flashing of the message light on her phone caught her eye. There was just one message, from Jason Kowalski.

"I forgot." Jason had called while she was with Melanie; she'd promised to call him back later. Now, it was *much* later. He was probably asleep. Alison smiled to herself as she dialled his number. *If it's me calling, he won't mind too much.*

"Hullo." Jason's voice sounded grumpy.

"Jason. I'm sorry. I hope it's not too late. I just got home."

"Oh—Alison." He yawned. "It is a bit, but it's okay."

"You said you might have something interesting for me."

"I do. On Friday night, the Sydney police arrested five men in a Sydney apartment for breaking and entering and carrying illegal weapons. One of the men arrested was at the computers. This was the *third* computer guy's place that was busted into last week. The other two both made a living as hackers, it seems."

"That's certainly intriguing. . . ." *Hang on a minute,* she thought. *Friday night. That's when the geek was put out of action.* "But I don't see a connection."

"None of them said a word. They let their lawyers do the talking. But they must have been looking for *something* kept on computers. Then I remembered McKurn and I thought: McKurnWatch. So I thought of you."

"You know, I think you might be right." *I'm fishing in the dark, but. . . .* "Tell me something then: do you have a name for this computer guy?"

"Hang on a mo. I'll check the report. . . . Yes, Ivan Mettner."

Ivan. She paused to steady her voice. "That's interesting. Could you do me a favor and email me his mug shot?"

"Do you know this Ivan guy?"

"I know *a* computer guy called Ivan. Until I see his picture, I won't know if it's the same person."

"I . . . suppose I could . . . if you tell me what you know about him."

"Sure—if it's the same Ivan."

"Okay then. Check your email in the morning."

"Thanks, Jason. You're a wonder. I owe you one."

"I'll remember that."

He's going to break the rules for me—again, she thought as she put down the phone. *Am I corrupting him, too?*

The following morning a police mug shot of Ivan Mettner stared at her from her laptop's screen. The same Ivan who'd shown her McKurn's security setup.

I promised to tell Jason, she thought. *But. . . .* She felt sorry for him. *He's trapped, as I am. . . . "All that is necessary for the triumph of evil". . . . The words I used . . . "should be engraved on our souls". . . .*

If I do nothing, am I helping McKurn . . . ?

41 Virtuoso

IT WAS LATE AFTERNOON when the taxi from Hat Lek rattled to a stop near the immigration post on the Thai border with Cambodia. The last thirty kilometers of the journey from Bangkok—by bus, minibus, and now taxi—hugged the beaches along a thin, coastal strip between the Gulf of Thailand and the Cambodian border barely more than a kilometer wide.

"Ah, that's a relief." A bleary-eyed Derek Olsson—or the red-headed, clean-shaven "Joe Brewster" he had once again become—stepped out of the taxi, stretched, and looked at the Cambodian border post twenty or so meters further on.

"Nearly there." Suspecting that Luk Suk's friend, General Chuasiriporn, might add his name to the police WANTED list, he planned to lie low in Phnom Penh for a while before making his way back to Sydney.

Suchart climbed out behind him. Toting their luggage they joined the line at immigration which included quite a few *farangs*—one reason they'd selected this exit point. Just a day trip from Bangkok, foreigners living in Thailand on tourist visas could leave Thailand, walk a few meters to get a Cambodian visa and then turn around and be back in Bangkok the same evening with a new stamp in their passports good for thirty more days.

"Joe Brewster" presented his passport, now including a fake Thai arrival stamp, and the official barely looked at it as he stamped him out of Thailand. After haggling with the Cambodian officials, who attempted to overcharge Olsson for his visa, they were assaulted by motorcycle drivers offering rides to Koh Kong. "Let's get a drink first," said Olsson, stifling a yawn. "I need some caffeine."

The restaurants in the small border village of Phumi Chrouy Kaoh, such as they were, seemed much of a muchness—open to the street with Formica tables and stools spilling over the sidewalk—so Olsson simply stopped at one that seemed a bit cleaner than the others.

While Suchart had disposed of Luk Suk's body "where it will never be found"—Olsson never asked for the details—Olsson had gratefully crashed. But he'd slept only fitfully, half-waking several times in a cold sweat with the vague memory of a terrible dream that refused to come into focus. He'd dozed most of the journey from Bangkok, barely aware of inviting vistas of blue-green sea and bright yellow sand that reflected the burning afternoon sun through the vehicles' darkened windows.

Olsson sat listlessly as they sipped their drinks; Suchart picked up a newspaper lying on a nearby table, one of the more sensational Thai-language tabloids. The rustling of the paper as he turned the pages eventually caught Olsson's attention and he gasped as he saw, filling the cover, the picture of a girl, clearly dead. Her expression was one of frozen anguish: the bloody slashes mutilating her once-pretty face had been inflicted while she was still alive.

"What's that about?" Olsson asked.

Suchart passed the paper to Olsson. A sick certainty grew in his stomach as he slowly read it. "Three bar girls . . . tortured to death . . . found this morning," he muttered under his breath. *"Fourth time . . .* in five years . . . other similar cases in. . . . What are these words, Suchart?"

"Phnom Penh and Vientiane."

Throwing the paper down he said to Suchart, "When you get back to Bangkok, would you get me all the details of these cases, especially the dates? Also the ones in Cambodia and Laos."

Suchart nodded, searching Olsson's face as he slowly said, "You're thinking it might—"

"Get me those dates and I'll know."

*****

IN COURT THAT THURSDAY morning, lawyers for the OlssonPress—who also represented Sykes Publications—produced police, school and other records demonstrating that the business of Senator McKurn's father had in fact gone bankrupt, that McKurn's mother had owned a shop and apartment in Rose Bay, that McKurn had quit Cranbrook at the age of fourteen. They submitted an annotation from the then-headmaster's notes that McKurn had become rowdy, uncontrollable, and that the mothers of two girls had accused him of impregnating their daughters, along with police records showing he'd been suspected of manslaughter, had once worked in a sly grog shop, and had spent a short time in jail for assault. In sum, they substantiated every charge Karla Preston had reprinted from McKurnWatch.com.

The judge summarily dismissed McKurn's request for an injunction against the OlssonPress and Sykes Publications. "But," he continued, "given that other allegations made by this McKurnWatch outfit have not been rebutted, the injunction blocking access to McKurnWatch.com stands. However, I remind you that this injunction is *temporary.* Unless you serve a suit against the *owners* of this website, as you promised to do, the injunction will expire two weeks after it was issued. That is: at 10:29 AM next Monday."

"Next case."

*****

GOTTLIEB ALTEN SPENT AN hour or so thinking about the email he'd received from his most recent client, "Saith Lord":

> FYI, last week the homes or offices at least three hackers were broken into, the last one on Friday night in a Potts Point apartment where police "caught them in the act." Along with the thugs was a computer guy who, it turns out, works for McKurn. His place of business is the office in Bligh Street I told you about.
>
> My guess is they were looking for whoever is behind McKurnWatch. By the way, they have not answered any of the police's questions, and the police do not know of the connection to McKurn.

Alten checked the hackers' website, emailed guarded questions to a few of his contacts—and waited for their answers which, when they arrived, all confirmed what he'd already concluded: that "Saith Lord's" message was accurate.

Whoever he (or she?) was, he'd thought, he obviously had high-level sources of information.

Gottlieb Alten was back in business.

He still had one decision to make: return to his Potts Point apartment or set up anew somewhere else? He tended towards the first—if only because he'd had enough of hotel rooms and a new place would take time to establish. But "better safe than sorry" had been his operational creed, and so far it had served him well.

He shrugged. Meanwhile, he had his laptops. What else did you need these days?

His eye kept travelling to the time. He had no idea how long the proceedings would take, but was certain he would be notified of the upshot within minutes of the judge making his decision. While he waited, he reread and changed a word here and there in the document he was working on. When the email finally arrived, he made a few minor alterations—and sent it out:

McKurnWatch.com

"The website that ~~must not~~ can now be named" [Thanks, Frankie!]

G'day Boys & Girls!

And what a good day it is! If you've ever felt like a champagne brunch, here's a great excuse: In Sydney this morning, a clearly incorruptible judge well and truly caned our Frankie's fingers. If the caning hadn't been metaphorical, dear Frankie would have blood on his hands. (Dare I say it? again.)

OlssonPress lawyers produced documents confirming the "allegations" in Karla Preston's column—which were goodly chunks of the first two McKurnWatches (which she reprinted with attribution . . . bless her heart).

Meanwhile, *somebody* sent a group of thugs on uninvited visits to several law-abiding hackers' homes to peek inside their computers. The assumption is they were trying to put McKurnWatch out of business. The cops picked them up instead (tough luck, guys).

Today—in celebration of poor Frankie's sad loss in court—some more highlights from his fascinating life saga.

At the tender age of 21, our young hero married the luscious (by all accounts) Lucy Nolan. It was, as the fairy tales go, a match made in heaven. But a mere twelve months after they'd tied the knot and vowed "till death do us part," Lucy moved back to mama. Apparently, she'd discovered what her husband actually did for a living.

Our Frankie, it seems, was truly upset, and went on a bender that landed him in jail, charged with assault. The object of the assault: the three (that's right, *three)* police officers who were trying to arrest him for drunk and disorderly behavior.

He told his sad tale of being the distraught, abandoned, heart-broken husband in court—and what a real tear-jerker it is! (It's in the court records.) The judge must have thought so too: he gave him just thirty days in the clink—a mere ten days for each clobbered copper.

By the way, I'm inclined to think that young Frankie *was* deeply in love with poor Lucy. [Come on! Give the guy the benefit of the doubt. This may be his only redeeming feature.]

Fast-forward some fifteen years. McKurn was now heavily involved in NSW state politics—not as a politician but as a "gofer" for top, mostly bent, pollies.

Around the same time, he decided to get married again. It's hard to imagine it was for love this second go around. The lady in question had just inherited a nice pile of money from Daddy, and was somewhat older than Frankie.

Only now did Frankie ask Lucy for a divorce. Good Catholic she was, she refused Frankie's request point blank.

Sad to report, poor Lucy died soon thereafter in a hit-and-run car accident. While the dirt was still settling on her grave, Frankie took his second wife.

We know almost nothing about this second marriage. But we can infer that it was one of those separate-bedrooms/separate-lives deals. Frankie had wormed his way into the NSW Conservative Party, to be rewarded "for services rendered" with a place on the NSW Senate ticket—and mislabelled as "a representative of the working class." In his ten years in the Senate before his second wife's death, there is just one record of their joint appearance at *any* function: hubbie's first inauguration in Canberra.

When Mrs. McKurn #2 followed wife #1 (of cancer, says the death certificate) Frankie inherited her pile of money, *and* received a nice payout from her life insurance policy.

While she was alive the second Mrs. McKurn made a number of interesting investments. Her fellow shareholders were all wives of *other* interesting characters: senior state politicians, senior cops (including two NSW police commissioners!), and leading underworld figures. These investments all had two things in common: they were in companies whose only customer was the NSW state government, and in those illegal street-front casinos that proliferated around Sydney in the sixties and seventies. You know, the ones with the flashing neon signs that the cops could never find—except on payoff-day.

Shortly before she died, Mrs. McKurn sold her shareholdings for a song . . . mere pennies on the dollar. The buyers: companies whose ultimate owners—Swiss companies, Liechtenstein Anstalts, and offshore trusts—were veiled behind a Byzantine corporate structure, replete with one-dollar dummy companies, cross-shareholding, nominee directors, non-profit organizations, and the like.

Intriguingly, a couple of these Swiss/Liechtenstein investors recently took a big bath in the shares of a west Australian mining outfit by the handle of Metal Mountain Exploration NL. The manager of that company? One Lester Edleton, the "shady stock promoter" caught on tape chatting to our Frankie a while back.

— The McKurnWatcher

PS. It seems Frankie *hasn't* signed up for McKurnWatch—at least, not in his own name. I think that's a shame: would *you* want to miss out on your own biography?

If you know his email address why don't you do him a favor and forward him a copy? If you prefer, send it to me, and *I'll* send it to him on your behalf.

*****

Royn looked up in surprise at Alison's broad smile as she entered his office. "What's the good news?" he grinned.

"We're on a roll. Leon Price's confession is in the bag."

"Fantastic." Knowing that Melanie was in Alison's office, Royn was uncomfortably aware of how Alison's vitality, the way her eyes sparkled and cheeks glowed, made her even more desirable than usual. "But I thought it was going to take forever."

"Oh, there's more to come. But we've already got enough to hang McKurn—if it's confirmed."

"What *do* we have?" he asked.

Alison passed Royn a single sheet of paper as she sat down opposite him. "That's the private eye's report and summary of what Price has said so far."

"I see . . . he and McKurn collected bundles of cash from major crime figures and senior police officers, including the Commissioner. And parcelled it out to various senior politicians, including the *Premier* for heaven's sake."

"Everyone knows the Premier was Sydney's biggest crook back then. But look at the people Price names."

"Yeah. It looks like a laundry list of Sydney's underworld and everyone at the top of the New South Wales state government at the time. Which is exactly the problem."

"How so?"

"Some of them are already dead," Royn frowned. "But the only way any of the others can corroborate any of Price's statements is by incriminating *himself.*"

"One of them's bound to have a grudge against McKurn he wants to pay back," Alison said, her voice hopeful. "There's more to come, and once the police get onto it, someone's bound to sing."

Royn nodded. "Especially if they offer immunity in exchange. . . ."

"We only need a couple of them," said Alison.

"Fingers crossed," Royn smiled. "What else have you got?"

"Nimabi's back in Toribaya," Alison sighed. "He's announced the Saudis will set up an embassy there, and has promised to sponsor the Sandemans for membership of OPEC."

"Nimabi will be on a high," Royn groaned. "Any other announcements? Loans? That sort of thing?"

Alison shook her head. "No. But if Cartwright can be believed, money will certainly follow."

"Anything from Foreign Affairs?"

"Fairchild hasn't mentioned a thing."

"Let's send him a memo." Royn swung back in his chair to gather his thoughts. "Ask for Foreign Affairs' evaluation of the impact this Saudi embassy might have on Islam in the Sandemans, in the light of Saudi activities here and in other countries, and what—if anything—that could imply for our future relations."

Alison smiled. "That, at least, implies a bit more urgency."

"Let's put a bit more pressure on him," Royn grinned. "Sign it from me as Acting Prime Minister—and address it to both Fairchild *and* ASIO."

"I'd guess we'll have the ASIO report first," Alison said.

"I'm not going to bet against you on *that.* Now, I've got some rather puzzling news. According to Bruce, Stanley Chow is being very evasive on who he'd support for leader if Kydd steps down. Do you have any inside information on that?"

Alison shook her head. "McKurn must have changed the number of his private cellphone: no taps on the old number for two days."

"Does McKurn suspect something?"

Alison shrugged. "Maybe—or it's just paranoia."

"He's certainly got a lot of things to be paranoid about right now," Royn laughed.

"What a nice change *that* is," Alison smiled. "What else did Bruce say about Stanley Chow?"

"Bruce showed him the polls results and so on," Royn said, "but Stanley didn't seem to take much notice."

"His seat is safe, even from a *big* swing to Labor."

"True. . . ." Royn's eyes stared vacantly at Alison. "Could *he* be toying with the idea of running for Party Leader, do you think?"

"*Deputy* Leader is more likely," said Alison. "Maybe Cracken's made him an offer—we know he's done a deal with Quigley."

"Hmmm. How many votes can Stanley swing?"

"Half a dozen, maybe a few more," Alison said. "Influence rather than guarantee. You can ask Stanley yourself in about half an hour."

"Still got no idea *why* he wants this meeting?"

"He hasn't said—except that it's urgent *and* important."

"We'll find out soon enough. But it would be premature for *me* to talk to him about the leadership right now. I'll leave that to Bruce. Now, how's that poll report coming along?"

As Acting Prime Minister, Royn could direct the Party organization to conduct a poll on the corruption issue rather than paying for it himself; and order the Cabinet Policy Unit to prepare an analysis of the options—slanted, of course, to his favored proposal, the Royal Commission. Despite its title, the Cabinet Policy Unit was composed of political staffers, not public servants, and was controlled by and reported to the Prime Minister, not Cabinet. It was one of a number of resources the Prime Minster had at his exclusive disposal which helped him dominate his Ministers, their departments—and the party.

"I've been promised it within the hour, so you'll have it in time for Cabinet," Alison said. "The preliminary result is unequivocal: at least eighty percent of the public are in favor of swift, decisive and *apolitical* action."

"Good," Royn smiled. "But there are some rumblings in Cabinet. Yesterday, I had a clear majority—so I thought. But now I'm not sure."

"I have a feeling that's what Stanley wants to talk about." Alison said.

"You could be right. Anything else? . . . No? I'll grab a coffee at 'Aussies' and be back in time for Stanley."

Royn called it "Politics by Wandering Around."

As one electoral success followed another, Kydd had become more remote and isolated from the party room. For the past couple of years, he'd kept in touch with the members' thoughts and opinions almost solely through his lieutenants. Royn had decided to keep his door open to members, and once or twice a day, he'd take out half an hour or so and wander through the corridors or sit at the "Aussies" coffee shop and buttonhole whoever passed by. Added to which, he'd thought, while he was Acting Prime Minister it was a good way to demonstrate the kind of leader the members would have if they elected him.

It turned out to be a popular move. Even members who, he knew, were committed to Cracken or Quigley were pleased with the ease they could gain the top man's ear; he might even have swayed a few in his favor. But he soon discovered one major disadvantage: every member took the opportunity to pitch his or her own pet project—and Royn had to take care not to alienate anyone by appearing opposed to it, no matter how dumb it was.

"Sounds like a good, even important idea," he'd say noncommittally. "But is the *right thing to do?*—and can you convince your fellow Conservatives that it is, and that *they* should support it too? Can you present it as a vote-winner? That always makes it easier to get the party behind you—though, mind you, I'm *not* saying we should refrain from doing the right thing just because it's unpopular. And finally, can it be done *economically?*"

Although most agreed with the logic, for a few too many members that was quite clearly *not* what they wanted to hear.

"So tell me, Stanley," Royn asked. "What's so important and urgent?"

"It's your Royal Commission idea, Tony. You *can't,* you *mustn't* go ahead with it."

"Why is that?"

"You're proposing it should be set up with no limits—" Royn nodded "—and once it's in operation we'll have no control over it, right?"

"Right," Royn agreed. "That's the only way—"

Chow cut him off. "I know your reasons. And I *agree* with them—"

"You *do?*" Royn said in surprise.

"Yes," said Chow, "except for one thing. McKurn."

"What about McKurn?"

"You haven't thought this through, Tony."

"Of course I have," Royn protested.

Chow shook his head. "If this Royal Commission has its head, McKurn is an obvious target, right?"

"Well . . . yes. I suppose so," Royn said cautiously, not wanting to admit to any specific interest in McKurn.

"McKurn's basically being accused of being a gangster. If this Royal Commission of yours digs up evidence confirming just *one* of these rumors about McKurn, what's going to happen to *us*—you and me and the party—come the next election?"

"Hopefully, we'd get some kudos for cleaning house."

"Tony! It's more likely we'll be tagged as the party of corruption for harboring a gangster at the top."

"An election's not due for ten months—"

"And if you keep plugging this Royal Commission, we could be in Opposition in eleven. Keep it as a departmental or Federal Police inquiry. Beef it up all you like. But at least then, if it turns up evidence incriminating McKurn, we can have a quiet word with him and pressure him to resign—"

"—and let the bastard off Scot-free?"

Chow's eyes narrowed. "There are other ways of handling him. But look, Tony—" Chow spread his arms "—all I'm trying to do is warn you of the dangers I, and a number of others see from a Royal Commission—"

"Including Paul, I suppose."

Chow chuckled. "I'm not so sure. He's certainly opposed to the Royal Commission idea, but—just between you and me—I get the impression that he wouldn't be sorry to see the back of McKurn."

"Who *would* be?" Royn grinned.

Chow laughed. "Hardly anyone, I'd say." Leaning forward, his tone now solemn, he said, "Propose a Royal Commission *after* we've won an election, and you'll have my wholehearted support."

"But now—?"

"I'll have to vote against you in Cabinet. And I think you'd be well advised *not* to bring it to Cabinet—I'm not the only one who can see the writing on the wall."

Royn nodded thoughtfully. "You certainly make a compelling case."

"And does Kydd support you?" Chow asked.

"I—don't know, actually."

"You'd better find out what *he* thinks. How will he react if he finds he's saddled with a Royal Commission he doesn't want?"

"Good point," Royn nodded. "I'll be seeing him again on the weekend."

"Does that mean you'll postpone further discussion in Cabinet until *after* you've talked with him?"

Royn considered his response. "That's . . . probably a good idea."

"Thanks, Tony," Chow said as he rose to his feet. "So I guess Cabinet this morning will be pretty quick today?"

"Yes, Stanley," Royn said sourly, "it will."

"So, what do you think?" Royn asked Alison and Melanie after he'd summarized Chow's objections to a Royal Commission.

"Makes complete sense to me," said Melanie sharply. "Why jeopardize the main prize, Tony? You're nearly *there*. Why take *any* risk? McKurn's been neutered so we don't have to worry about him—and we can deal with him in our own time."

Royn looked at Alison.

"Kydd will agree with Stanley," Alison said noncommittally. "And Melanie."

"But you don't like it," Royn said.

"No, dammit, I *don't,*" Alison said with sudden anger. "I don't want to let the bastard off the hook."

"We're not going to," Melanie said, placing a hand on Alison's arm.

"There's no guarantee the bastard will stay dead, either."

"So we'll keep gathering evidence against him until we can go for the kill."

When will that be? Alison wondered, her gaze suddenly focused intently on Melanie; she could see that for Melanie everything, even McKurn, was a distant second to Royn's ascent to the top.

To her own surprise, Alison realized her own priorities were the opposite. If getting even with McKurn meant abandoning the goal she'd been aiming at since she was sixteen, so be it.

"I'd better wait until I've talked to Kydd," Royn said.

Alison nodded. "I don't want to wait," she said. "I *will*. But I certainly don't *want* to."

Pleading a headache, Alison had declined Royn's invitation to join them for dinner, and went to the gym. The anger she'd felt since Royn decided to suspend the attack on McKurn no longer felt so overwhelming . . . but it still simmered within.

She knew, intellectually, that Royn had made the right move: *go for the gold, and clean up everything else later.* She also knew that's the same advice *she* rather than Melanie, Chow—or Kydd—would have given Royn—if she didn't feel personally involved.

She was angry with McKurn. And with herself. But she'd been afraid she wouldn't be able to hold it back from spilling over to Royn or Melanie.

Thoughts jumbled through her mind as she pounded the mat. *Just one step. If Kydd's too ill, I'll be Chief Political Adviser to the Prime Minster. But letting McKurn get away with it—that's too high a price to pay. . . . Now there's no reason to meet Karla—should I anyway? Of all people, she's an ally?*

Still, the evidence against McKurn was accumulating . . . *I can always act alone . . .* and, she had to admit, the Candyman Inquiry was beginning to produce results—though not, as yet, about McKurn. In a report that arrived just before she'd left for the day was the summary of an interview with someone (not identified) who claimed he'd actually met and worked for the Candyman—although "met" wasn't exactly the right term:

> . . . the "meeting" took place over the internet. The subject sat in front of a webcam, but no equivalent image appeared on his computer screen. The voice he heard through headphones was muffled, presumably disguised. Following that "meeting"— which could be best described as a "job interview"—all further communications were

by encrypted email with the occasional call from a mobile phone number (never the same number twice). In each case, the voice was muffled and unrecognizable.

Even stranger, the man told of the clear instruction *no violence,* except in self-defence—and then, only when absolutely necessary. "Run like hell," he said he was told, "is the first rule of defence."

Run like hell. . . . Alison remembered *Sensei* Tozen saying exactly those same words. "The philosophy of Aikido," he had said, "is that you fight only if you really have no other choice."

Just who is this Candyman?

Back home, she was idly flipping channels when McKurn's face flashed on the screen. "Senator," an off-camera reporter asked, "some experts accuse you of censorship."

That afternoon in the Senate, McKurn stepped down from the President's chair to reintroduce the private member's bill to amend the libel and slander laws originally sponsored by the now-disgraced and jailed Senator Felix Haughtry. The scuttlebutt around Parliament House was that he couldn't persuade another Senator to front for him.

In an impassioned speech, he demanded, ". . . the law *must* be amended to make the scurrilous, unsubstantiated, and *anonymous* rumors of the type I'm being subjected to *impossible. You* could be next."

Another Conservative Senator moved that McKurn's proposal be referred to a Senate committee for further study "due to the possibly warranted, but nevertheless draconian changes the esteemed Senator is proposing." The motion passed. An hour later, one veteran political journalist from the press gallery was writing: "McKurn's fellow Conservatives don't seem to be in too much of a rush to have these 'McKurnWatch.com' allegations stopped. Several Senators from both parties are confident the matter will be slowly strangled to death in committee."

On the screen, McKurn, sitting behind the desk in his office, answered angrily, "Most certainly *not.* I stand firmly for freedom of speech. *Anyone* at any time should be able to stand up and say whatever he or she thinks. But sneakily and dishonestly hiding your identity behind a hi-tech firewall? That's beyond the pale."

"What comment would you make about your wife's alleged investments?"

"What my dear departed wife did with her money was *her* concern, not *mine,*" McKurn answered testily. "But . . . this gutless, anonymous *person. . . .*" He stopped, as if words had failed him. His eyes turned moist, and tear trembled in the corner of one eye for a long moment before rolling down his cheek. "This . . . ugly slander of two wonderful women who can no longer talk back, that's—" McKurn's breath was short, as if his words were choking in his throat "—that's *unconscionable. . . .*"

The camera zoomed into two pictures sitting prominently on his otherwise-empty desk—pictures Alison had never seen before, anywhere in his office. One captured an ecstatically smiling couple: a much younger be-suited Frank McKurn with a beautiful young woman in a wedding dress at his side; the second was of a much older woman, coolly elegant.

"The only women I ever loved. . . ." McKurn was saying. "Look," he said, opening his wallet, and the camera zoomed in on smaller replicas of the same two pictures. "I carry them with me everywhere. Hardly an hour passes when I don't think of them."

He sniffled, and pulled a large white handkerchief from his pocket to wipe his eyes.

"Senator—" one of the reporters began to ask.

McKurn shook his head. "Sorry, no more questions. Not right now."

A virtuoso performance, Alison thought. *The lying bastard.*

42   The Smile of God

A SHANTY TOWN SPRANG UP across the neck of the peninsula occupied by Zulu base on Jazeerat el-Bihar. It supplied the base with services like laundries, fresh meat, and vegetables, and fulfilled the soldiers' recreational requirements for cheap booze, loose women, and illicit drugs. The base commander bowed to the inevitable. A second barbed wire fence was built, twenty meters behind the base's initial perimeter, and the land between the two fences was cleared. During daylight hours, off-duty soldiers hopped from bar to brothel and back under the watchful eyes of a contingent of military police.

Nicknamed "The Strip," it was little more than two rows of makeshift buildings parallelling the fence, separated by a wide "avenue" of packed dirt which just a drizzle of rain turned into mud. The bars and brothels began at the gate of Zulu base. Strategically placed opposite that gate was the Firehouse, the biggest and ritziest bar of them all, with a warren of "rooms"—cheap mattresses separated by curtains—at the back. Like the other bars, it was little more than a tin roof held up by tree trunks sawn from the nearby jungle, some even taking root and sprouting leaves. The only solid construction was the bar itself, with its precious array of alcohol in its dozens of varieties. Blaring music drowned out the racket of the generator behind.

In the slow mornings, girls would sometimes stand and gyrate in front of the Firehouse taunting the MPs at the gate. By mid-afternoon, the rowdiest time of day, the bars were packed and the girls were all busy inside, one way or another. Soldiers from the morning shift gulped their fill, knowing they could stagger across the road by the sundown curfew and sleep off the effects before their next shift began. Here and there, soldiers soon to go on the night shift were easily identified by the coffee or soft drink on the rough table in front of them.

Around three-thirty, a pickup truck rattled up to the gate, a trail of exhaust marking its passage; a Chinese man got out and began chatting to one of the guards. An army truck pulled up on the other side of the gate and the Chinese man's two helpers unloaded the bales of laundry, passing them to the soldiers who randomly inspected the bundles of sheets, towels, and uniforms.

So no one took any notice of the portly man who wandered along the Strip and turned into the Firehouse. Nor was anyone aware that the man was being discreetly trailed by another. As the portly man stepped into the doorway of the bar the man behind suddenly ran up to him, pulled out a pistol and shot him in the back of the head. At approximately the same moment, two waiters who'd been lounging by the door drew pistols and simultaneously shot the man. All three ran out the back of the bar, disappearing before anyone could stop them.

The cacophony of music from the bars blanketed the sounds. One MP at the gate looked up, dismissing what he heard as backfires. The other MPs were busy checking the laundry. It was a couple of minutes before a soldier coming out of the Firehouse nearly tripped over the body and bellowed at the MPs, "Some guy's been shot. You'd better come and take a look."

A gate guard ran across the street, took one look at the body with its bloody head blocking the doorway and yelled a few words into his radio. His call brought MPs at a run from further along the Strip.

They found explosives strapped around the man's waist. They immediately called in the bomb experts and cleared the Firehouse and all the other bars, ordering all the soldiers back to base—including those they found in the back rooms and brothels, some of them still zipping up their pants as they grumbled all the way back.

Only a few of the soldiers in the Firehouse could give a lucid account of what had happened. "Why didn't you grab one of the waiters?" they were asked. "It happened too quickly," "It was too crowded," "I was totally stunned—just long enough," were some of the answers.

The Strip was placed off-limits to all uniformed personnel "until further notice"; within a few days it became a ghost town.

The military police major could only conclude that a would-be suicide bomber had been killed by persons unknown before he could blow himself up—along with as many as sixty-five Australian and Sandeman soldiers, and twenty to thirty of the workers in the bar.

But *who* had fired the shots? And *why?*

They were questions for which no one had an answer.

*****

ALISON IDLY FLIPPED THROUGH a newspaper while she waited. Now calmer after working on the mat with *Sensei* Tozen, she was still unsure about meeting Karla Preston, and felt slightly nervous at the prospect. She chuckled at a small ad listing the websites where you could visit the still-blocked McKurnWatch. The ads had appeared daily since Karla's article the week before. McKurn's lawyers dutifully trooped to court each morning to have the new sites included in the original order; the next day the ads appeared again—with a list of *different* websites. *The mouse must be driving the elephant crazy.* Alison grinned at the thought.

"Did I just pass the *dojo* where you and Derek met?"

Alison looked up to see Karla Preston pulling up the chair opposite. Karla's eyes seemed to drill into her; Alison felt frozen, as if caught in the glare of a spotlight.

"And this, I presume—" Karla quickly scanned the inside of the coffee shop and her eyes, now glinting with humor, rested once again on Alison's face "—is where you two used to sit and talk after your workout."

Alison stared wordlessly at Karla. She'd chosen this coffee shop as familiar, home territory—but now she felt as though Karla had somehow defiled it, putting her at a disadvantage at the same time.

"Right here," Karla continued, "at this very table."

"Did he tell you that, *too?*" Alison demanded.

Karla laughed. "Oh, no. I just guessed. When people come to the same place again and again, they tend to have a favorite table. That's all."

"Do you make a habit of shocking people?"

"Whenever I can. That's my business." Karla laughed again, a booming, infectious laugh that turned people's heads; unconsciously, Alison began to smile—until she became aware of what she was doing. Karla's voice, following her laugh, seemed soft, almost conspiratorial, "I've been told I have an annoying habit of always speaking my mind."

"No matter what the consequences? Even if your words might hurt someone?"

"That's right—no matter what. I have to live with myself. What's more important in life than that? The best way I know is to remain true to myself at all times."

"That's . . . sometimes hard to do," Alison said, unable to prevent the image of McKurn and everything he represented from flashing through her mind. *Her words,* she thought, *as if she knows.*

"True," Karla agreed, now looking at Alison as if she had a fleeting glimpse of the solution to a puzzle, "but worth it."

The hint of a scowl on her face, Alison just nodded.

"You know," Karla said, injecting a lighter tone into her voice, "I wasn't sure till I walked in that you'd actually be here."

Now Alison laughed, with relief as much as humor. "Till *you* walked in, *I* wasn't sure I'd be here either."

"I'm glad you stayed," said Karla.

"Why?" Alison asked suspiciously. "From where I sit, you're media enemy number one."

"Political combatants, perhaps," Karla grinned. "But enemies? I don't think so. After all, didn't you propose we meet so you could leak something to me? Then we'd be allies. At least, temporarily."

"That . . . was part of the reason," Alison conceded.

"*Was?*" Karla grinned. "Let me guess—again. Politics *is* the 'art of compromise'. So there's been some deal done on whatever you wanted to feed me, right?"

"Are you some sort of mind reader?" Alison asked with a flash of anger.

"Not at all," Karla protested. "When I see two plus two, I automatically think four." She shrugged. "That's all there is to it. In politics, I see compromise. Which ain't in *my* vocabulary." Karla chuckled. "I'd make a lousy politician, not that I'd ever be one. Or work for one."

"You know, I detested you," Alison said, not aware she'd used the past tense. "I've read everything you've written and I disagree with just about every one of your opinions. Even the way you use the English language. Like starting sentences and paragraphs with 'and'—that's not grammatically correct, you know."

"At least you've read everything I've written. That means you must enjoy it."

"It makes me angry. I enjoy *that.*" They both laughed, but Karla's laugh was hollow, as if she understood not only what Alison was saying, but *why* she said it.

"So you know," Karla said, "that I hold everything you do, especially your boss and the institution you both work for, in complete contempt."

"I've noticed that," Alison said. "So why are you glad I stayed?"

Karla grinned. "Because I like you, and I think we could be great friends."

"I'm not sure that I'm going to like *you,*" Alison replied.

"That's a step forward from detesting me."

Alison grinned. "True," she conceded, surprised at the thought that Karla was *intriguing.*

"And why did you stay?" Karla asked.

"Curiosity, I guess."

"About me?" Karla asked. "Or, about—"

"—Derek's girlfriend? Both," Alison grinned. "But at least I know now what you see in each other."

"What's that?"

"You both think much the same way."

"Yes," Karla sighed, her eyes fixed on something in the far distance. "True. . . ." she mused. "Alison," Karla said tentatively, "there's something I need to talk to you about."

Alison stared at the sudden change in Karla's expression. Her lower lip trembled slightly, her cheeks had turned a faint pink, and her eyes were now hard; though focused in her direction, Alison knew from her tone of voice that Karla's look had nothing to do with *her*. "About—?" she said softly.

"Derek. A suspicion I have. . . . But somewhere—" she looked around "—more private. Maybe we could just wander around a bit when you've finished your coffee—?"

Do I really want her to tell me anything about Derek? Even as the question came, she knew couldn't refuse this confidence, whatever it turned out to be. "Okay," she said slowly. Looking at the remains of her coffee she shrugged and stood. "It's gone cold anyway," she said.

Meandering in the general direction of her parents' house, Karla told Alison about Uqu, his connection with Olsson, the marijuana plantation, and hash factory in Inkaya— and how she'd been locked in her cabin on the boat that had taken her to Cairns. "So I'm pretty sure Derek is up to his eyeballs in the drug business."

"But—according to you," Alison said, "there's nothing wrong with that."

"No there isn't," said Karla. "But it's illegal—"

"—and that bothers you?"

"No," Karla chuckled. "It's the company you have to keep in an illegal business. *That's* what bothers me. Nine or ten people *died* when Derek was swiped from the prison van."

Alison stopped; Karla turned around to face her. "And you think *Derek* must be responsible for their deaths?"

"And how many others?" Karla said. "Murder and violence come with the territory."

"But—they were all gangsters, weren't they?"

"But did they deserve to *die?*" Karla said angrily. "And even if they did, that's really beside the point. Was Derek in any way responsible for their deaths? I can't see how he *wasn't*. Doesn't that bother you?"

"I . . . hadn't thought it through before," Alison replied. *I was just glad Derek was safe,* she thought.

"It all fits together, you know," said Karla, so absorbed in her own thoughts that she didn't notice Alison's reaction. "He never talks about his time in Hong Kong, let alone what he did there. Where did the money come from to start InterFreight? His friend Ross was struggling to pay the rent until Derek became his partner, and the next thing you know he's Businessman of the Year. Now, they've *both* gone underground—"

"Ross too?" Alison asked, nearly tripping over a tiny crack in the pavement.

"Yes, he's gone as well," Karla said. "It all adds up to a not-very-pretty picture."

"Yes, it does," Alison said in a faint voice as she asked herself: *Could she be right? What was he really up to in Hong Kong? He always held something back, something he didn't want to tell me.*

"Do you think I could be right?"

"I hope not," said Alison, afraid that she was.

"I take that as a 'yes'."

"You—it *could* be," Alison said reluctantly. "What do you plan to do, then?"

"When Derek gets back from wherever he is, he's going to have a lot of explaining to do. And he'd damn well better be *convincing*."

Alison grinned. *"That* will be worth seeing."

*****

GURUNDI REMOVED THE CRUCIFIX, the symbol of the infidel world he hated, and thrust the nailed Jesus Christ into the dirt behind him. Facing west, towards Mecca, he fell to his knees and salaamed. He had no prayer mat but Allah, he was sure, would understand. He prayed for forgiveness of whatever sins he was about to commit or had committed, sure in his own mind that Allah understood they were necessary for him to complete his still unknown mission. When he stood he felt calm again, filled with the sense that Allah looked down approvingly on his plan to deceive the godless infidels. He hung the crucifix around his neck but as it touched his skin it felt like it was burning into his chest.

He'd woken up by the stream, his leg on fire. He washed and bandaged it again, thinking it might be infected. But there was nothing he could do about it. So he limped painfully, following the stream in the hope that it would eventually lead him to a town or village where he could get help. In the middle of the day he collapsed. With no energy, he lay there, shivering in the heat of the midday sun, waiting to die. Sometime later he felt as though he was being carried, stretched out on something soft, his leg throbbing—and then the pain faded as if he was drifting away from it. *I don't want to die,* he heard—or imagined—himself screaming.

At some point he half opened his eyes to see an old woman's kindly face smiling at him. She poured a little water on his lips; he spluttered and greedily gulped more when it was offered. *I'm definitely dreaming,* he thought as he lapsed back into unconsciousness.

He woke the next day, horrified to see the Virgin Mary looking down at him next to a cross.

He'd been found by an old man and his wife who lived alone in a small shack an hour or so's walk from the nearest village. They scraped a living from a vegetable garden, a few pigs, and the fish and animals they could catch. The woman had a reputation as a healer; it was she who'd nursed him back to health. He realized he'd reached the eastern, Catholic part of the island. He feigned unconsciousness until it came to him that these infidels must be doing Allah's will. Then it was easy. He told them he'd been wounded by Muslim guerrillas. While pretending to be asleep he'd heard them praying and so was able to pretend to join them. When he mentioned that he'd lost his crucifix somewhere in the struggle, the old man had carved him a new one.

When his leg healed, he thanked them profusely. But now he walked with a limp— and cursed the foreign infidel invaders with every step. The couple understood that he had to rejoin his unit, and showed him how to reach the nearby village. He passed around it and now stood on a dirt road leading to the small town on the coast. He wasn't sure what he was going to do next, but in the back of his mind was the idea of going to Toribaya where classmates from Indonesia would help him. Where the foreign infidels were based.

He sensed that Allah had saved him for a *reason,* and that he was on a journey to a destination that was yet to be revealed. Even donning the hated crucifix became just another test of his faith.

His fingers closed over the wad of notes in his pocket: he'd seen where the old couple hid their money when they thought he was asleep. With a renewed sense of purpose, he strode through the outskirts of the village—his limp, for the moment, forgotten.

Allah will provide.

*****

"WHAT DID KYDD SAY when you saw him this morning, Tony?" Sidney Royn asked the moment Melanie and Nancy Royn left them alone. They sat in the high-winged armchairs by the fire in the living room of Anthony Royn's Toorak House—which he no longer thought of it as "his" when his parents were there.

"The doctors told him he *must* take it easy for a few months if he wants to fully recover," said Royn.

"As in quit."

"Exactly so. He looks better than he did last Sunday, but he's still very weak. He can hobble around a bit on crutches. He'll need a wheelchair to get around without wearing himself out."

"I bet that annoys him no end," Sidney Royn smiled.

Royn chuckled. "He's stroppier than ever. He's angry—at the world for giving him a raw deal, at the doctors for telling him what he doesn't want to hear, and at his own body most of all, I think, for letting him down."

"I can imagine," Sidney Royn said. From the barely suppressed glee in his voice, Royn gained the impression that his father was relishing the thought of Kydd as an invalid.

"You don't like him much, do you, Dad?"

"Am I that obvious?"

Royn nodded. As he stood up to throw another log on the fire he asked, "Just what happened between you and him?"

"I've never told you, have I?"

"No, Dad, you never have."

Sidney Royn settled back to gaze into the distant past. "He and I were rivals for the leadership of the party. It was about a year after we lost government, where I was Attorney-General. The previous leader decided to quit. It turned into a bitter, drawn-out, no-holds-barred fight—the sort of thing that he was far more suited to than I. Eventually, he and McKurn—"

"Kydd and McKurn were *allies?*"

"Allies is the wrong word when it comes to Kydd, Tony. Or McKurn for that matter. They formed a brief coalition of convenience. McKurn threw his influence behind Kydd's grab for the leadership; Kydd promised to give McKurn what he wanted: Minister of Mining and Energy in the next Conservative government. McKurn never approached *me* for a deal—he knew I'd never give him the time of day."

"But I'd always thought you and Kydd were *friends,*" Royn protested. "I can still remember the times Kydd visited you when I was only so high—"

"Yes, we were—or so I thought. Randy persuaded me to go into politics. We made a good team—until the leadership came up for grabs. Everybody assumed I'd be the next leader—the natural Conservative, the patrician, the *Royn* and all that. Then Kydd stepped into the ring, the street-fighter who used every underhand trick in the book—"

"Like Paul Cracken."

"Quite so. I was fooled by my own self-image. So were lots of others, all *certain* that someone like Randolph Kydd could *never* be leader. Of the *Labor* Party maybe, but of the Conservatives? Not a chance. Ha!" Sidney Royn laughed sourly. "Another political prognostication a little wide of the mark."

"But Dad—" Anthony Royn said, a puzzled look on his face, "Kydd was elected *unopposed.*"

"When it became obvious he had the numbers to win, I withdrew from the race so the party would end up unified. Kydd asked me to be shadow Attorney-General, but—"

"Yes?" Anthony Royn prompted, when his father seemed to be debating whether or not to say whatever had come into his mind. "Come on, Dad. You should finish what you started."

Sidney Royn smiled. "So be it," he said. "Remember that inquiry? Your gal Alison came to have a look at the report."

"McKurn was the hidden focus, right?"

"That was all Kydd's idea—I bet *that's* news," Sidney Royn grinned.

"He suggested much the same thing to me, too," Royn said.

"That's our Randy." There was a hard, bitter edge to Sidney Royn's voice. "Always gets someone else to do his dirty work—and take the fall. The way he won the leadership made that very clear to me. I decided I'd had enough of dirty politics—and Kydd. So I quit."

"Take it easy, Dad. No point in *you* having a heart attack *too.*" Royn said, stunned at the impossible thought that his father, a rock-solid pillar of strength, had been outwitted . . . defeated. *If Dad didn't have what it takes to beat them, how on earth will I?*

Sidney Royn took a deep breath. "You're right," he said, forcing a grin. "Certainly not over Kydd. And sure enough, as soon as the Conservatives were back in government, Kydd got rid of McKurn as soon as he could. Kicked him upstairs to the presidency of the senate—so much for them being *allies.*"

"But—Kydd's always treated me so *well.* . . ."

"Maybe he feels guilty—but I doubt it." Sidney Royn's laugh bordered on a cackle. "You seemed content to wait in the wings, not force succession. I imagine that's part of it. He always liked you." Sidney Royn shrugged. "I've no real inkling of his *underlying* motivation. But you can be sure it's *his* interests he's taking care of, not yours."

Lost in thought, Anthony Royn nodded. "I can see that."

"Keep it in mind at all times," Sidney Royn said. "So tell me, Tony, is Randy in any condition to take back the helm of state?"

"The doctors certainly don't think so. But," Royn shrugged, "maybe he could. Seeing his condition, I hinted that maybe he should retire—very delicately, I thought. But he looked like he was ready to tear out my throat. He said, and I quote. . . ." Royn paused for a minute, shifted his body weight, and when he opened his mouth it was in Kydd's booming voice, "'If Roosevelt could win World War II driving a wheelchair, then I can sure as hell wheel myself through *our* piddling little crises for a few months.'"

"You do that so *well,*" Sidney Royn said appreciatively. "If my eyes were closed, I'd be sure *he* was sitting right where you are."

Anthony Royn forced a weak smile, swallowing the bitter thought that he would have much preferred his father's appreciation of his dramatic talents years ago. "I think the only way he'll go willingly is in a wooden box."

"That'd be right," Sidney Royn said sourly.

"He gave me lots of advice—"

"So you could warm his seat till he gets back, I suppose."

Royn nodded. "But something he said has been sticking in my mind. Just a moment." Once again, it was if Randolph Kydd had entered the room. "Listen, my boy. I know you're the right man to come after me—and *somebody* has to, after all. You've got all the makings of a good, if not excellent Prime Minister. Except for one thing: the killer instinct. That's the only way you can keep all those bastards in the party in line. Cracken's got it—and not much else. You've got to surprise your enemies—and move in *immediately* for the kill. Kick 'em while they're down: that's the only way you can be certain to win. But you've got to get them down *first*. Remember that."

"Stab 'em in the back and put the boot in while they're bleeding," Sidney Royn said sourly. "That's Kydd's *modus operandi*."

Royn nodded. "Yes, but—"

"Tony, he's *challenging* you to throw him out—giving you an engraved invitation he's confident you won't accept. You *are* the right man for the job, Tony—because you're *not* like him. But in one way he's wrong: when it comes to fighting the Crackens of the world, you've got Melanie on your side. What a gal *she* is, made to be a politician's wife." Sidney Royn's eyes lit up, he leaned forward eagerly, and continued before Anthony Royn could say a word. "You've got the numbers so I hear—you should *take* his invitation."

"I couldn't agree more." They both turned as Melanie came into the room, Nancy Royn behind her. "That's *exactly* what I've been telling him, Sid."

"You see," said Sidney Royn. "I was right. What more confirmation could you want, Tony?"

Anthony Royn opened his mouth to protest as Nancy Royn said, "Dinner is now ready. Would you like to open the wine, my dear?"

"Certainly," said Sidney Royn. He stood up and putting a gracious hand on Melanie's elbow, escorted her to the dining room. "So you think he should go for it?" he said to Melanie. "But what if. . . ."

Lost in conversation, Melanie and Sidney Royn stepped past Nancy Royn, who stood in the doorway smiling at her son. "I think that's what keeps him going you know, Tony," she said. "To see you complete his ambitions. But remember, at the end of the day it's always *your* decision."

"Thanks, Mum," Anthony Royn said. But he thought: *If only you'd said that to me thirty years ago. . . .*

*****

"Is Karla *right*, Derek? What do you have to say for yourself?"

The dimpled photograph of the seventeen-year-old Derek Olsson Alison kept hidden in a drawer now sat on her desk, returning her stare with a mute grin.

Propped up next to Olsson's impish face was the picture from the wall behind her: herself at sixteen on the steps of Parliament House. With one hand Alison absently stroked the patchy fur of her childhood favorite, one-armed Ted, perched on her lap. When she looked at the innocent teenager with her future ahead of her, she wondered whether she'd approve of what she had become—knowing what the answer would be. When she looked at Derek, Karla's words—"Murder and violence come with the territory"—weighed on her mind. The more she thought about what Karla had said, the more she believed she was right.

"And tell me, Derek, what happened to your Golden Rule: do no harm?" An unvoiced thought, one she couldn't bring herself to speak aloud, gnawed at her—one she tried to deny even as it came, unasked, into her mind: *Have you hurt others yourself? Or, God forbid, caused someone's death by your own hand?*

If Karla's right, how could you *avoid* it?

We've split. She felt once again her surge of anger as she'd walked out of the Sandview Hideaway Hotel. *It's all over. Why should it make any difference to me what you might have become? Every man I've loved has turned into a chimera, or betrayed me. You worst of all. . . .*

Why can't I let go?

A MONTH AFTER DEREK Olsson had walked unannounced and uninvited back into her life, Alison dialled Ross Traynor's number. She had to dial three times: her fingers kept hitting the wrong buttons. "Will you tell Derek I want to see him, please, Ross?"

She could hear Traynor's surprise through his sharp intake of breath. "Of course, Alison," he said. "The next time I talk to him."

"When will that be, do you know?" She knew she was conveying her impatience, but she couldn't help it.

"Within the week, I'm sure."

"Do you think—" She had to stop to gather her nerve: she knew she was giving away too much, but she had to *know.* "Do you think he'll *want* to see me, after . . . ?"

Traynor paused. When he replied, his tone was somber and definite. "Yes, Alison, he *will.*"

To Alison's ear, Traynor's voice was strangely soothing and reassuring, giving her the feeling she'd experienced in the confession box, when the priest forgave all her sins.

"Thank you, Ross."

Every night that month she'd dreamed—of him. He had opened the Pandora's Box of memories she thought was tightly locked and hidden where it could never be found. Every morning, she woke—wrung out with hurt, excitement, anger, passion, betrayal, or insatiable desire; reliving her every moment, every feeling, every memory of him, now amplified and embellished into untamable dreams and nightmares.

Alison knew that to just start talking with him would be like plunging through a hole in the Arctic ice with no preparation—or protection. She insisted they meet at the *dojo;* Olsson was happy to comply. They danced across the mat on a Saturday a few weeks later and Alison felt some of the old magic return, even though she remained nervous and wary; as they followed each other's movements in flawless harmony. The old sense of connection, of awareness of each other's thoughts and intentions, began to return. The newer students stopped to watch them with awe; even *Sensei* Tozen regarded them both with approval.

"Thank you, Alison," Olsson said as they walked around the corner afterwards. "That was a great idea."

Alison smiled faintly in response, feeling energized and stronger.

It was one of those beautiful Sydney spring days with hardly a cloud in the brilliant blue sky, the sun hot on your skin if you stood outside long enough, cooled by the chilly edge of a gusty breeze that made the leaves of the trees sing. Alison felt like saying, *It's as if God were smiling on us*—and she firmly suppressed her desire to laugh at the incongruity of her sudden thought.

They walked in mutually agreed silence. Olsson grinned as he looked around the familiar coffee shop. With a flourish he held her chair for her; as he took his own seat his soft, hazel-green eyes came to rest on hers. His broad smile and the deep dimple on his cheek spoke of his own pleasure at seeing her. Alison felt herself responding, warming to the way his eyes seemed to glow with admiration and devotion . . . yet, with the sense that the sparkle of his energy came not from within him, but somehow from drawing on *her* strength. And his eyes were now hooded and veiled, as though somewhere behind them shutters had clicked down to hide something from her. Or from everybody. Or even from himself.

Aware his gaze was pulling her towards him, she drew back in surprise at the realization: *He still loves me.*

Really? The voice in her mind was sarcastic and skeptical. *Then where has he been all this time? And why?*

"You still take my breath away—more than ever," Olsson said. His left hand rested on the table near hers; it seemed to tremble as he resisted the urge to reach out and touch her. "And you haven't changed."

"But *you* have."

"I have?" He shook his head, his tousled hair becoming even more unruly as he did.

"Yes. I'm not sure I like it." The way he was sitting, his back to the wall facing the entrance, his eyes now and then scanning the room, suddenly made her think of a scene from an old spy movie. "You're afraid of something."

"Not . . . really. Just . . . cautious. That's all."

"Of what?"

He shrugged. "I guess . . . it's just become a habit."

Why? She had decided not to press him—not yet. Instead, she asked, "Are you and Ross up to something again?"

He grinned. "It's time I came back home. *Way* past time. We're talking business, a partnership—he's a tough negotiator."

No, she thought, feeling a moment of frozen shock. *I don't want you to come back, I don't want you to still love me. I just want a final "Goodbye" so I can get on with my life in peace.*

"What's wrong, Alison?" he said gently.

"Nothing. Just . . . surprised, I guess."

Olsson seemed about to ask a question, but simply said, "I'm . . . sorry. I didn't mean to shock you the other day. But when I saw you in the hotel lobby, I couldn't resist. It was only then I realized I regret every moment of the past seven years. I should never have left."

"But would it be any better today if you'd stayed?"

"*Touché,*" he grinned. "Maybe not. But it would have been *different.*"

"So why didn't you . . . come back?" she asked.

His fingers fidgeted with a napkin; then he said, "I know you want an explanation."

"Yes."

"And you deserve one."

"I do."

Olsson's soulful eyes made Alison think of the stray kitten she'd found when she was three, and how it squirmed when it had done something it *knew* it shouldn't have done.

"I got into a bit of trouble in Hong Kong—"

"What kind of trouble?"

"Oh, nothing serious," he said, attempting an air of lightness that emphasized rather than disguised his imploring tone. "But it was so *embarrassing.* I was young and so terribly naïve. Dumb, even." He laughed. "I would *never* have admitted that to *anybody* then. I'd have denied the very idea. Whenever I *tried* to tell you—started writing a letter—it sounded like a plea for help—"

"I would have helped you," Alison said.

"Thank you," he said softly, almost a whisper, dropping his eyes in embarrassment.

"So . . . why not simply come back?"

"To run back here with my tail between my legs? I couldn't do it."

"I wouldn't have minded, so long as you were back."

"I . . . couldn't have faced you feeling like a dumb loser. It was just a matter of getting back on my feet . . . it would just take a little longer . . . and I knew I could. But then—"

"But then *what?*"

"I . . . got stuck."

"How?"

Olsson's face flushed. "I was so ashamed . . . I still am. Even now."

"Ashamed of what? Breaking your 'Golden Rule'?"

His eyes flashed with a brief energy. "No!" he said. "Never."

"Then . . . what did you do that's so *awful* you couldn't tell me?" Alison demanded. "I would have forgiven you anything . . . then."

"I couldn't forgive myself . . . and still haven't," he said hoarsely.

"Derek," Alison said, her voice cold and commanding. "I don't know what you thought, but there's only *one* reason I wanted to see you. An explanation."

Olsson's face burned red and twisted with pain; his eyes glistened as they looked at her pleadingly, as though without hope; his lips parted as if to speak . . . on words that would choke him. Alison felt the sudden, consuming desire to reach out to him, to cradle his head in her lap and caress and comfort him. She forced her muscles to lock, to hold her body and expression rigid, but she couldn't stop the slight wetness in her eyes as she said, "I'm sorry, Derek. But that's all I want from you. Nothing more; nothing else."

Olsson's head fell. Nodding weakly, he said, "I understand."

The clatter of cups from the coffee shop's counter and the chatter of other patrons were suddenly loud in the silence that followed. Alison waited for Olsson to continue, forcing herself to look at him as coolly, as blankly as she could manage . . . but she couldn't command her mind to follow suit. *"I always feel like I'm leaning on you for your strength,"* he had once said; she wondered where *his* strength that so awed her had gone . . . and what terrible thing he had done that he should end up seeming . . . broken. *". . . you become an irresistible force. Getting in your way then is like standing in front of an express train."* She had the impression he didn't have the energy to get out of the way.

"So you didn't find what you were looking for?" she asked impulsively.

"No," he groaned. "The opposite, if anything." He seemed to be choosing his words carefully, as though he was tip-toeing through his explanation. "I was . . . seduced."

Alison's nostrils flared. "Is this all about another *woman?*" she snapped.

"No, no. I met a man—"

"A *man?*"

"Not like that," Olsson protested weakly. "He bailed me out—"

"Of *jail?*"

"No." He tried to laugh, but the sound he made was more like a sob. "Of my troubles— of my *stupidity*. But, Alison, it was my grandfather all over again—" his voice dropped to barely above a whisper "—but worse. And now I'm trapped. Stuck. Under his thumb."

"You? Trapped?" She shook her head. "I just can't believe that of you, Derek."

He shrugged. "I guess . . . I *have* changed. But I *haven't* given up. I'll *never* give up, Alison." He now looked at her so intently that she had to drop her eyes—and felt certain that, whatever else he was referring to, he was also telling her: *I'll never give you up, Alison.*

"That doesn't explain why you never wrote."

"Shame. And as things got worse for me, shame, disgrace, humiliation all piled on top of each other. In the end, I tried to convince myself that was the best thing—if I just dropped out of your life."

"Why?"

"Because, as I once said, I couldn't go where you were going. Where you *have* gone. And now, against my will but, inexorably, just the same, I'm on an *opposite* road." He shook his head sadly, his gaze, again, becoming intense. "It was the *worst* thing I've ever done."

Keep focused, Alison, she told herself at that thought: *The worst thing for you?— me?—or both of us?* "So you still don't approve of what I'm doing?"

"I still think you're . . . mistaken. But, look at me now" he chuckled sadly. "Who am I to criticize you—or anybody?"

As she did look at him she thought: *There's more to it than what you've told me.* But he appeared so wretched that she didn't have the heart to pry anything more from him.

The moment of silence was broken when he said, "Let me tell you how you're different."

"You said I hadn't changed."

"You haven't, not in any real way—except to become *more* of what you already were. Stronger, more purposeful, more single-minded in going for what you want. And you're obviously flourishing. What's Canberra actually *like?*"

"A bit like a maze," she said with a smile. "Just when you think you've found your way around, suddenly a new dead end appears from nowhere. But it's so exciting. Especially now—"

"—you're moving up the ladder?"

Alison couldn't stop herself from gasping in surprise: all of a sudden, Derek Olsson was transformed into the cheeky and irrepressible, impishly grinning boy who had incessantly challenged and charmed her.

"Of course," she said evenly.

"Now," he said, his eyes shimmering briefly as though a hidden ember had suddenly shot off a spark, "*I've* got a purpose too."

"Which is?"

"You'll see."

"Okay," she said doubtfully, pushing herself to her feet. "And thank you, Derek,—but I have to go."

He followed her out onto the footpath. "I'll walk you home."

"I can find my own way," she said, a little more sharply than she had intended.

"When will I see you again?"

Alison shrugged. "I'll think about it."

Olsson smiled in understanding and she watched Olsson's familiar dimple appear on his cheek. At the same moment she realized he'd moved, she felt his mouth hungrily kissing hers, the sudden touch of his hand, resting gently on her shoulder, inviting but not pressuring. She felt her lips pressing back on his, her body swaying closer to him, and angrily stepped away from him.

"Goodbye, Derek," she said.

"Bye, Alison."

She marched away, all too aware of his insouciant smile, forcing her eyes to stay focused on the footpath ahead. But at the corner she couldn't resist a quick, backward glance. He was standing in the same spot, his arms and stance loose, the grin still on his face.

She hoped she was far enough away from him that he wouldn't be able to see the wetness in her eyes.

*****

SHE VOWED NEVER TO see him again.

But when she visited her parents a few weeks later, a letter was waiting for her. She recognized Olsson's handwriting on the envelope immediately. On the back was a return address—an apartment in the city. The note inside was brief: "I'm back," with his cellphone number and the invitation to call him whenever she was in the mood.

The knowledge that he was now *here* was a powerful acid slowly but relentlessly dissolving her resolution. One Friday night she felt, as she pressed the buzzer of the apartment number etched in her memory, that they were joined by a connection harder than steel, tougher than diamond, yet elastic, stretching and stretching and then snapping them back together again.

"Derek?"

"Alison? I'll be right down."

"No," she replied. "I'll come up."

As she stepped out of the elevator, Olsson stood waiting for her. She fell into his arms, freely admitting her helplessness. "I couldn't wait any longer," she said. Noticing the dark rings under his eyes, she added, "You're tired."

"I was asleep."

"I'll go then."

"Not a chance," he grinned. "I'm wide awake now. If I hadn't been working twenty-eight hour days, I would have come to *you* long ago."

Weeks went by without a word between them, and then he'd suddenly appear on her doorstep or she on his. Now and then they'd spend a weekend in the country, or at a beach. There was nothing furtive about their meetings, but they told no one: what they did together was nobody else's business.

By unspoken agreement, they avoided sensitive topics—but an underlying tension was ever-present, and occasionally erupted.

"And what about *girls?*" she asked one day. "You never said a word about *that.*" Olsson blushed. "I was no monk, if that's what you mean. But I've never met anyone who measured up to you. I don't expect I ever will." He never asked her the same question, but she had to admit, to herself, that she measured every man she ever met against Olsson—and found them wanting.

Now and then she'd grill him about his time in Hong Kong. He'd let slip a few irrelevant non-essentials—that he'd learnt Cantonese and even some Thai—"It just happened," he shrugged. "I must have the ear for it or something"—that this shadowy man, who'd rescued and betrayed him, had studied philosophy . . . about some of the crooked politicians and outright thugs he'd met while in the banking business. But her questions always ended when he clammed up, or said, "It hurts to talk about it, Alison." She took her revenge by staying away. Just when she was about to break, he'd call to tell her, "Hi, Alison, I have to go away for a couple or three weeks. See you when I get back."

Sometimes, not too often, she'd explode in frustration. "I don't know if I can keep going like this. Where's the future for *us,* Derek? Tell me that—if you can."

"I don't know, Alison. But if this is all I can have with you, right now. . . ." He shrugged. "I'll live with it."

"Let's just give everything up, Derek. *Both* of us. Go to a place where no one knows who we are, and live a normal life."

"A 'normal' life, Alison?" he laughed. "What's that? How long could you exist—" he dropped his voice and had looked at her intently "—without your *purpose?*"

"I don't know. But I want to find out."

"Tell you what: I'll come and live with you in Canberra instead. Introduce me to all your friends and associates. But I can't promise to keep my mouth shut, especially in front of that moral vacuum you have for a boss. How long, do you think, before you'd throw me out?"

His renewed drive and energy were evident in the way InterFreight shot a web of routes and terminals across the country, pushing aside its competition like an irresistible river in flood. As before, she thought, when he sets out to do something he does it brilliantly. Despite his success, she was sure the *freight* business was not his calling; whenever she tried to find out the underlying purpose that gave him such drive, he'd merely grin and repeat, "You'll see."

The transport industry viewed him, at first, as an upstart who'd soon flame out. As Derek Olsson streaked into national prominence, they complained about "unfair competition," demanding the government look into what they called his "cutthroat practices." Customers didn't care: they flocked to InterFreight's lower prices and better service. A business magazine wrote admiringly of InterFreight's arrangements with its drivers, which lowered its payroll costs while the drivers took home more cash: the taxman forfeited the difference. A left-wing magazine took the opposite view: that Olsson "wasn't paying his fair share to society," and bitched about InterFreight's refusal to deal with any union. Industry pressure led to a tax audit. The Tax Commissioner reluctantly informed his minister: "These arrangements may be flouting the *spirit* of the tax law. But unquestionably they're well within the *letter.*" There was talk about amending the tax laws; it remained talk as, one by one, the proposal's most vociferous supporters inexplicably changed their minds.

Olsson was voted "Australia's Most Eligible Bachelor" by the readers of a woman's magazine. He was pursued by the gossip columns and the paparazzi—until they gave up: there was nothing for them to write about, never a sensational picture of him with a model or movie starlet—or anyone else. In photos of his rare public appearances, he was always alone. "Have you ever been in love?" a reporter once asked him. "I still am," he smiled, his eyes twinkling—and refused to say more. Business groups and Rotary Clubs invited him to speak, a beauty contest wanted him as a judge; popular TV shows asked him to appear on panels. He turned down every invitation.

One invitation he couldn't refuse was the ceremony for the "Businessman of the Year Award"—presented by a smiling Anthony Royn. From a table in the audience Alison thought she was probably the only person who noticed the flash of distaste that crossed his face as Royn pumped his hand. "I've heard a lot about you, Miss McGuire," he said very properly when they were introduced. He leaned forward and kissed her hand, just a moment longer and a touch harder than was proper; she knew in the glint of his eyes that he was thinking the same as she: of all the other parts of her body that these same lips had kissed, and that he was aware of the tingle that ran up her spine at his touch. "One could hardly *not* hear a lot about you, Mr. Olsson," she had replied, strangely relieved to realize she *wasn't* standing naked in front of hundreds of people. She spoke so coldly that Royn looked at her in puzzlement, assuming she took an instant dislike to Derek Olsson.

He bought a two-storey penthouse apartment in The Rocks. Alison was his first visitor. When she woke she was alone. Pulling on a pair of his pajamas, she padded down the stairs. Olsson was sitting on the balcony watching the orange ball of the sun creep above the horizon. The scattered clouds above were streaked with color, and the sun's strengthening rays sparkled like flashing jewels as they caught and lost the gentle rise and fall of the waves in Sydney's harbor. In the distance, behind the sails of the Opera House below, Alison could just make out North and South Heads, the rocky promontories that framed the harbor's narrow opening to the sea and protected it from the ravages of the ocean, outlined in black shadow as the sun rose behind them. On the harbor, a lone ferry chugged towards Circular Quay, its only companions a scattering of pleasure boats gliding across the water, twinkling in the early morning light.

"It's so beautiful," she breathed as she stepped into the light. Only then did she notice the bottle of champagne and two flutes on the table. "Is it a special occasion?" she asked.

"Being with you is *always* a special occasion," he said solemnly as he stood to welcome her into his arms.

"Oh, Derek."

"But . . . you've forgotten what today is?" he asked with mock surprise.

She searched her memory for what he meant—and looked at him blankly.

"It's our anniversary, Alison. Of the day we met. On the mat."

"Oh," she said, grinning mischievously.

"Want to try it again?" he asked.

She laughed, nestled against him and kissed him, running her hands over his body until her fingers grasped his crotch and gently squeezed.

"You're completely helpless now, aren't you Derek."

"You know I am."

"And you have no defence."

"None," he said as he kissed her back and slid a hand under her pajamas. She gasped at his touch and her nipples hardened as his mouth covered her breast. "Nor do you."

Alison closed her eyes and pulled him closer. "Don't you think we should go inside?" she asked.

He opened his dressing gown and wrapped it around her, binding her body to his at the same time.

"No need," he said as her pajama pants fell to the balcony floor. "This is big enough for both of us."

What turned out to be their last weekend together, in the Sandview Hideaway Hotel, had been idyllic—until she commented, "You know, nobody in Canberra likes your newspapers."

"I'm glad to hear it," Olsson replied. "But I'm surprised that anyone, other than local members, read them."

"It's mainly Karla Preston's column in the Sykes' papers. She's considered a real pain in the neck."

"That would make a great ad." Olsson laughed. "You, or even better, your boss, saying that on TV."

"Oh, be serious, Derek." Alison's voice was scalding.

"I *am* being serious."

"You're impossible," she grinned. "It's one thing to take potshots at politicians—and God knows, some of them deserve it. But this latest series, pushing drug legalization, that's just too much."

"Why, Alison?"

"How can you ignore the terrible damage drugs cause?" Alison stood, her muscles tense, leaning over Olsson, her eyes ablaze. "The lives destroyed. Pushers turning young kids into addicts—who end up as petty criminals and prostitutes just to make money for these murderous, soul-destroying thugs. It's got to be stamped out, not made freely available for anyone to try. Your so-called cure is worse than the disease."

"All these drugs were legal once, and—"

"I've read all your arguments," she snapped.

"Drugs are illegal all around the world. Yet, wherever you go, they're easy to get—despite the decades-long 'War on Drugs.' *Another* government program that's been a screaming success. Why? *Because* drugs are illegal they're *extremely* profitable. That money corrupts the police and the courts which are supposed to *protect* us from criminals, not *co-operate* with them. That's the *real* scourge, Alison."

"You're starting to sound like that Karla Preston woman," she spat.

"Maybe," he said thoughtfully. "She certainly makes a lot of sense. And there's no doubt that I've come to despise government and everything it stands for. Remember my Golden Rule, as you call it? No violence—except in self-defence? The foundation of government—*every* government—is based on breaking that rule every day of the week. It's obvious in places like Thailand and the Philippines. There, government is simply the means for politicians and their cronies to steal money from the people to line their pockets—and everybody knows it."

"Not here."

"Not here? You should know better than that, Alison. What do you think a licence is, for, say, a casino or a TV station, but the monopoly grant of a stream of cash, protected by a government threatening violence to any would-be competitor willing to compete on a free and open market. What are lobbyists except groups trying to get special favors from the government? Which the government can only give by *denying* those same rights to everyone else? What is corruption if it's not an under-the-table, unofficial licence for an exemption from the law that's enforced against everyone else?"

Tears in her eyes, Alison protested, "But government is a force for *good.*"

Olsson shrugged. "Sure, it can do good things. But the Mafia has its own welfare program you know—does that turn them into saints?"

"Don't be ridiculous. How can you compare government with the Mafia?"

"How can you *not?* They both have the same foundation: violence. How many taxes would be paid if they weren't backed up by the threat of being thrown into jail? How many of your 'good works' could the government do if it didn't, first, extort the money at gunpoint to pay for them? At least the criminal is more honest: when he steals your wallet he doesn't try to make you believe he's doing it for your own good."

"So you despise *me,* do you?"

"Oh, no," said Olsson, shocked at the idea. "Quite the opposite."

"You just said my employer and the Mafia are the same. You just said you despise everything I do—how can you *not* despise me as well? What *else* do you expect me to think?"

"That . . . you're mistaken."

"So you just think I'm *dumb?*"

"You know I don't think that."

But Alison was beyond hearing. "So you started your newspapers to fight *me* and everything I stand for."

"No, Alison," he pleaded, "never *you*."

"How can I stand to be with *you*? All this time . . . the man I thought I loved has been my worst enemy . . . and I never knew it."

"No, that's not *true*."

"You've just had a rare attack of honesty," she said coldly. "Don't spoil it."

Five minutes later she walked out of the suite and called for a taxi.

This time, she did not look back.

*****

"ALISON, DINNER'S READY."

"Oh—" Alison flipped Olsson's picture over when she heard her mother's voice and turned her head to see Maggie standing in the doorway "—*what?*" Until that moment, she'd been unaware of the dusk gathering on the other side of the curtains. She was still dressed in the track suit she'd worn to the *dojo;* she hadn't showered since coming home either.

"I guess I completely lost track of the time," she said in surprise.

"Where *were* you?" Maggie smiled; her voice was light, but her eyes were heavy, as if sensing Alison's mental torment. She had seen the way her daughter was staring at Olsson's picture and how she tried to hide it—but Maggie knew that picture, even from the back. "I knocked and knocked and you didn't hear anything."

"Oh—daydreaming, I suppose."

"Like to talk about it?" Maggie asked softly.

"Maybe later." Alison held her smile, but tears welled up in her eyes. "I can't hide anything from you, can I?" she said, smiling despite the tears.

Maggie grinned and came over to cradle Alison's head against her chest as if she were still her baby. "That man," she said, "seems to have caused you nothing but trouble."

"Oh, no, Mama, that's not true." Alison now grinned and reached for a tissue to dab away the tracks of her tears. "Well—not *quite* true."

"If you say so, my dear," Maggie said doubtfully.

"*Later,* Mum. Okay? Just give me five minutes to clean up."

Joe and Maggie smiled with pleasure when Alison joined them at the dining table. "You look a bit tired, my dear," Joe said as she sat down.

"Yes, Daddy, I am," she sighed. "Too many things going on at once."

"What sorts of things?" Joe asked.

"Just . . . stuff, Daddy."

"Well . . . " Joe said, a touch grouchy, "can you at least tell me what Kydd's *real* condition is?"

"Pretty much what's on the news," Alison said. "As far as I know."

"Is he going to make it?" he asked.

"If you mean, 'Will he live?' the answer is, 'Yes'."

"But will he be back?"

Alison grinned. "That's the question everyone's been asking all week."

"What do *you* think?"

"I—" Alison was about to give her stock "we'll have to wait and see" answer. But—perhaps because it was her father who asked the question—her accumulated impressions of Kydd suddenly gave her a different response. "If he *can* come back, even if he has to be carried," she said, speaking in the manner of announcing something that was self-evidently true, like two plus two equals four, "he *will* be back."

"In other words," Joe grinned, "as long as he can breathe."

"Yes, Daddy. I'd say that's about right."

"Pity," Joe said. "I'd like to see you get to where you want to be—even if you *are* working for the wrong side."

"You *would?*" Alison regretted her words the moment she heard them—but she was too surprised to say anything else.

"Of course," Joe said, beaming, unfazed by her reaction. "Whatever our differences, you're still my daughter and I'm proud of what you've done."

Alison suddenly noticed her mother's hand resting gently on Joe's arm. Maggie was smiling at Joe in approval. *You said something to him, didn't you, Mum?* Alison thought as she studied her mother's face. Maggie shifted her gaze as if aware of Alison's look; she smiled at her daughter as if to say, *That's right.*

"You know," Joe continued, "that Karla Preston woman, sometimes—not very often—she makes some sense."

"I'm surprised you read her columns," Alison said.

Joe laughed. "So am I at times. But somehow, I always do—"

"And spitting mad afterwards," Maggie said.

"That's right," said Joe.

"I've met her, you know," Alison said.

"What's she like?" Maggie asked.

"Just like her columns. Abrasive, acerbic, cutting, and sometimes insensitive. But I like her—even though there's a lot about her *not* to like." Seeing how Joe's eye lit up at her description, she asked him, "Why, would you like to meet her?"

"It could be fun," Joe grinned.

"He likes a good fight," said Maggie. Joe nodded vigorously.

"In Karla, you might have met your match, Daddy."

"I'll *have* to meet her now, then," he grinned. "But you've got to admit, she nailed your boss to a 'T' when she said he's 'all show and no substance'. That's what made me think maybe it's better you're working for the bad guys."

"How on *earth—?*" Alison stared at her father, unable to go on.

"It's not as though the Labor Party couldn't *use* you," Joe explained. "But with the Conservatives, at least your common sense can leaven some of their stupidities."

"I . . . see what you mean . . . excuse me . . . " Alison said with a sense of relief as her cellphone chimed. "I'll have to take this call. . . ." It wasn't that she *preferred* her father's usual combative style whenever they talked politics, she reflected. And she glowed, even if awkwardly, from his unusual compliments. She just didn't know how to react to his non-argumentative, conciliatory manner. As she moved away from the dining table for privacy, she smiled at her father and blew him a kiss—and was surprised to see he was as embarrassed as she had been.

"Yes, Jason? What's the matter?"

"I showed the transcript of the interview with Leon Price to the boss, who said it wasn't part of our brief. Nothing to do with the Candyman. More a state than federal matter. A *federal Senator* accused of corruption? *Not* a *federal* matter? What's going on, Alison?"

"From what I hear, it's probably a political deal. I'm sure it's only temporary—"

"This is evidence of a *crime,* Alison. Since when have we let a criminal investigation become *politicized?*" He spat the last word as if it had only four letters.

"I'd guess . . . since the first government set up the first police force." *What am I saying?* she thought, surprised at her own words. *But it's true. . . .*

"Alison, I'm being *serious.*"

"So, unfortunately, am I. Why not pass it to the Sydney police?"

"The *Sydney* police? They're riddled with corruption."

"Surely not *riddled?* Not any more."

"Okay—I'm exaggerating. It's not like the fifties or sixties. It's here and there, especially in the Drug Squad. That's where the money is. But something like this? You've got to be very careful who you give it to."

"Who would you recommend?"

"Your private eyes must know someone."

"I'm sure they do. But I'd rather rely on *your* recommendation."

"Rudi Durant. He's the best there is—straight as an arrow and once he's got his teeth into a case he's tougher to get rid of than AIDS. I've never known him to give up—even when he's been reassigned so some other case."

"That's the kind of policeman we want. You know him?"

"Yes. Not that well, but we know each other."

"Then, how about *you* approach him first? And if he wants to pick it up—"

"He'll want it all right. To put away McKurn? What a feather in his cap *that* would be."

"Thanks, Jason. And I'm sorry—that 'feather' should be yours."

"That's okay, Alison. One of the good things about Rudi is that he doesn't hog all the credit."

"I'd like to meet this guy some day—you make him sound too good to be real."

"He's better."

There was a smile in Jason's voice. Alison laughed. "Thanks again. I owe you one."

"*Another* one, Alison," Jason chuckled. "That makes three."

She turned back to the table to see her father frowning at her.

"Crime? Politicized investigation?" he asked. "Why do *you* need a policeman, Alison?"

"What?" she said, forcing a smile. "Oh . . . I don't. It's . . . an official inquiry that seems to have gone off the rails. Nothing to do with me, *personally.*"

Still frowning, Joe gazed at her and shrugged. "If you say so."

But the skeptical expression on his face, and the way Maggie briefly pursed her lips, told Alison that she had not been convincing.

My God, she sighed. *Now I'm lying to my parents too.*

43 A Matter of Trust

"WHAT DO YOU MAKE of this, Simon?" Rudi Durant asked, gesturing to Monday's newspaper headline: **COPS BUST UP GANG WAR.**
Simon Lee finished reading the internal police report and threw it down angrily on Durant's desk. "We're being used," he snapped.

"By who?"

"One of the other gangs."

The previous night members of the Lebanese gang attacked a drug warehouse in the suburb of Redfern run by the Colombians. Tipped off, the police arrived in force in the middle of a pitched battle and rounded up nearly two dozen members of both gangs, an arsenal of firearms—rifles, shotguns, AK-47s, a variety of pistols—and twenty kilos of cocaine, ecstasy, and heroin.

Durant nodded. "But which one?"

"Several leading candidates. But should we complain too much? We got quite a haul."

"True. But I don't like it." Pointing to the transcript of the interview with Leon Price he'd received over the weekend from Jason Kowalski, Durant asked, "Have you read it?"

Lee nodded. "Fascinating. But," he shrugged, "it's all ancient history now, isn't it?"

"Not to *me.*" Durant's sudden intensity made Lee feel he was about to be scolded for overlooking something obvious. "When I came into the force Price was still in business." Durant's finger stabbed the transcript. "That was the early seventies, around the time all these casinos were finally shut down. I was just a constable then, of course, so I never met Price—he was some bigwig working for the Premier. But I *did* meet a few of the people Price names, and knew of the others. Everyone Price mentions is now dead, or retired—"

"Except for McKurn," said Lee.

"Precisely, Simon. Price accuses McKurn of some pretty serious crimes. If they can be confirmed, he'll go for a row. But McKurn's still around. If you can believe what you read, he's still up to his neck in some racket—or several. He can't be working alone."

"You're wondering who he's working with?"

"Exactly." Durant smiled approvingly. "What should we do with this transcript, then?"

"Take it to Zimmerman, I suppose."

"In theory, yes," said Durant.

"Then—" Lee eyed Durant thoughtfully "—why not?"

Durant rubbed his chin. "Things were very different when I was a constable, Simon. So many policemen were on the take I quickly learnt you could never be sure who you could trust, especially among the police officers who'd been around for a while. If McKurn's as bent as an old rope he's been operating for over thirty years without being discovered. Nor have any of his associates . . . who could be *anybody.*"

"Even you," said Lee.

Durant nodded. *"Everyone* from that era is a suspect. Zimmerman came in about five years before me—"

"You think *Zimmerman* could be bent?"

"Actually, no. But I don't know for *sure.* I knew that Super in Melbourne, you know, the one who was slated to be the next Commissioner down there. I'd never have suspected him."

"Then," said Lee, "how can you be sure of me—or, more to the point, how can *I* be sure of *you?"*

"That's what I'm getting at: how we can be sure of *anybody?"*

"If we're not taking it to Zimmerman, who will we take it to?"

"Nobody," Durant replied. "We'll run a little unofficial moonlighting operation of our own. We could start with a little chat with Mr. Price, don't you think?"

"But," said Lee, "we haven't been *assigned* to this. What if someone like Zimmerman finds out what we're doing?"

Durant growled, "We'd better make sure nobody *does.*"

*****

McKurnWatch.com

"The website that ~~must not~~ can now be named" [Thanks, Frankie!]

Good morning Boys & Girls—and a top o' the morning it is!

Poor Frankie's time has run out: it's 10:29 am, precisely two weeks to the second since the court issued its "temporary" injunction against McKurnWatch.com—and Frankie's lawyers didn't even bother to turn up in court this morning.

McKurnWatch is back in action—not, of course, that we were ever put *out* of business.

With that annoying distraction thankfully behind us, let's continue with the main event.

Frankie's rough and ready ways were one reason (a minor one, mind you) he got a place on the Conservative Party's NSW Senate ticket and was elected some thirty-five years ago: the Conservatives could point to him as evidence that they didn't *all* come from the blue-rinse set.

Today we know that his "origin as a man of the workers" is merely a carefully honed image that's pure tripe.

What's not so well-known is that as he rose in political circles he re-established contacts with his old mates from Cranbrook. Several of these were instrumental in his rise, especially a pollie called Leon Price who (according to the school's records) had been McKurn's classmate at Cranbrook since kindergarten.

Unlike Frankie's dad, Price senior was unaffected by the depression, so young Leon sailed through Cranbrook and Sydney Uni and followed his father's footsteps into politics.

You've probably never heard of Leon Price. He became an MLA (Member of the Legislative Assembly, NSW state's lower house). He never rose to public prominence but became very powerful behind the scenes as a power-broker firmly allied with the then-Premier.

He and Frankie sat at the top of the web of the Premier's money-conduit. They accounted for payoffs up and down the line from all sources—illegal gambling from casinos and SP bookies all the way down to neighbourhood two-up schools, favored abortion clinics, protection rackets, brothels, under-the-table permits and licences, help with "interpreting" the zoning laws and so on—and skimmed off the Premier's (and his cronies') share after, naturally enough, taking a liberal "commission" for their troubles.

Everybody who wanted the Premier's ear and favor had to kowtow to them.

Suffice it to say that it was then extremely difficult (though not totally impossible) to do any illegal business in Sydney without a portion of your profits going through young Frankie's hands.

This is how Frankie—who, until he became a Senator, never received a regular, "above-ground" pay-cheque—managed to accumulate the funds to buy back the mansion in Bellvue Hill that his Dad lost when he went bust—for cash. [Frankie still lives there to this day.]

One reason Frankie has escaped discovery for so long is that his Dad's old house is his only extravagance. Unlike other people of *nouveau* wealth, he appears to have no passion (well . . . no *public* passion) for fast cars, private jets, a flashy lifestyle, dropping the odd million at Monte Carlo, or expensive women.

This lends credence to what I've heard on the grapevine: that to Frankie, power is an aphrodisiac far more potent than money . . . or sex.

— The McKurn Watcher

*****

"There's a Mr. Uqumagani at the gate, sir. He says you're expecting him."

"That's right," said Major McMurray to the sergeant on the phone. "Send him in."

"Good morning, Captain—ah, congratulations are in order I see, *Major* McMurray," Uqu grinned as he was ushered into McMurray's office. "A pleasure to see you again."

"Yes," McMurray smiled. "I received a cryptic email from Miss Preston yesterday suggesting I talk to you."

"I never did get to thank you for rescuing me from the Sandeman soldiers—along with Miss Karla Preston."

"Yes, that was a very nasty business," said McMurray, reaching across to shake Uqu's hand and motioning him into a chair. "You were—"

"Miss Preston's guide."

"Ah . . . yes," McMurray said. "I've always suspected that you had a hand in the . . . ah . . . difficulties Miss Preston caused us."

"That's hardly fair, major," Uqu grinned. "If you know anything about Miss Preston, you know she's perfectly capable of stirring up trouble without any help from me or anyone else."

McMurray nodded. "So I've heard," he said sourly.

"I've come to help *avert* trouble for you, not cause it."

"How can you do that?" McMurray asked skeptically.

"*I* can't. I'm just a messenger for those who can."

"What's your message?"

"We know that a band of terrorists who fled St. Christopher's Island are now on Jazeerat el-Bihar," Uqu said. "They set up shop on el-Bihar selling protection—from themselves, of course—to businesses along the Strip, as it's called."

"Like the Mafia?"

"Exactly. But they were largely unsuccessful."

"The Strip is regularly patrolled by MPs, so that's hardly a surprise."

Uqu chuckled. "Your MPs have no idea what's going on behind the scenes."

"Really? You're telling me our intelligence sucks?"

"It's . . . incomplete," Uqu grinned. "The Strip has its own police force—all members of Islamic Purity."

"Their purpose?"

"Making sure no harm came to any Australian or Sandeman soldier."

"Why should I believe *that?*"

"You now have evidence of their goodwill."

"I do?"

"Who do you think killed that would-be suicide bomber yesterday?"

"You mean—Islamic Purity?"

"That's right," said Uqu.

"Cut it a bit fine, didn't they?"

"As I think your military police will confirm, not a single bullet missed its target."

McMurray nodded. "I take it those terrorists in the hills on el-Bihar are the *'we'* who's sending this message."

"Please, major, don't make the mistake of mislabelling these groups—especially this one."

"That's what Jeremy said," McMurray mumbled to himself.

Uqu understood him nonetheless. "Ah, yes, Lieutenant McGuire."

"You know about that?"

Uqu nodded. "Islamic groups, along with just about everyone else on el-Bihar from village elders on down, would like to see all these *real* terrorists just go away."

"If they knew about this bomber attack, why didn't they just tell us?" McMurray grumbled.

"If they'd left a message, would it have been passed on? If it was, would anyone have believed it? If it had been believed, can you be sure your MPs would have identified the right person? And in time? Perhaps there was a better way, but you must admit that *this* message is loud and clear."

"It is—but why should I trust whoever's sending it?"

Uqu nodded in understanding and passed a sheet of paper across to McMurray.

"These look like coordinates," McMurray said, looking quizzically at Uqu.

"Right. If you point your sky eyes at that location, you'll find a camp of ex-St. Christopher terrorists. Secondly, if you send a few of your MPs along the Strip *with* their Sandeman equivalents and interview the locals, you'll learn that I'm telling you the truth."

"Wait a minute." McMurray picked up the phone and a moment later a sergeant trotted in. "Sarge," he said, reading him the co-ordinates, "tell the . . . ah . . . flyboys—*not* the helicopter jockeys, you understand—to take a look here and tell me what, if anything, they see. ASAP."

"It's okay, Major," Uqu said when the sergeant had gone, "they know all about your Predators."

"They *do?*"

"Of course," Uqu laughed. "The Predator's role in the St. Christopher's operation is all over the Australian press—not to mention being hyped by the manufacturers."

"So what are they suggesting? We drop a bomb on this camp?"

"Yes," said Uqu, "but not yet."

"Why not?"

"You could carpet-bomb the area but you won't kill *every* terrorist. My . . . ah . . . clients would like to ensure that these terrorists are eradicated *completely*. They recommend the camp be attacked at something like three in the morning *after* it's been surrounded—without, of course, giving any warning—so *no one* will escape. And before you do anything, we imagine you'd like to ensure that you're not being used as some pawn in a local squabble."

"Of course not," said McMurray, his cheeks pinkening slightly.

"The leaders of Islamic Purity, with the approval of the village elders, would like to offer themselves as auxiliaries to the Australian-Sandeman forces."

"What can they do?"

"Aside from providing intelligence?" Uqu asked, raising an eyebrow. "They know their way around better than any of your people, to start with."

McMurray nodded, recalling Jeremy's words on the same subject.

"They make this offer with no preconditions, and no preconceptions of who should do what. They suggest a meeting at Inkaya, hosted by the village elder, Tungi-*ga*. They're making just one request—and it's *only* a request: that Lieutenant McGuire be included in your delegation."

"They are—why?"

"They admire him immensely for the risk he took."

"So do I," said McMurray, adding, "excuse me," as his phone rang. McMurray listened silently ending the conversation with a sighed, "Thank you, Sarge." Turning to Uqu he said, "Okay, it looks like there *could* be a camp there. The jungle is very dense so it's hard to see what, if anything, is on the ground. They'll keep an eye on it and wait till dark when the infrared should let them see through the foliage."

"Should you be telling me all this, major?" Uqu asked.

McMurray smiled. "Nothing you can't figure out, I would have thought."

Uqu nodded as if in a salute.

"So how can I get in touch with you—should I need to?"

"My cellphone number," Uqu said, writing it down for McMurray. "Any time, day or night. But—we hope—sooner rather than later."

"That, I'm afraid, is something I can't say. Just between you and me, if everything you've said checks out, I'd like it to be sooner myself."

*****

"You should go for it Tony," Melanie was urging. As she spoke, she leaned forward, her hands on the desk of Royn's Parliament House office, as if to emphasize her words. "Why wait? What *for*? You *know* Kydd's not going to go unless he's forced out."

"You and Dad have told me nothing else—all weekend," Royn sighed, rolling his eyes. Turning to Alison he asked, "What do you think?"

"First, is Kydd going to come back?" Alison asked.

"Yes," said Melanie.

"If he can," said Royn at the same time.

"How is he?" Alison asked.

"A bit better . . . but still weak. He nixed my Royal Commission idea, but," Royn chuckled, "I think he nearly had another heart attack when I mentioned it."

Alison grinned. "Well, that will make Stanley Chow happy."

"I suppose that's something," Royn said. "So, Alison, do you agree with Melanie—that I should go for it?"

"You may have no choice," said Alison.

"How come?"

"I've just been going through the phone taps. McKurn and Cracken may be planning a spill. If they call a meeting while Kydd's still in hospital and he's not there to support you, they figure they'll have an edge."

"*Would* they?" said Melanie. "Tony, you *know* you've got the numbers—"

"*With* Kydd's support," Royn reminded her. "What if we don't have that? What then?"

"Get Bruce to do an assessment. Or *I* will," said Melanie. Bruce Spring was confident that in a straight Royn-Cracken contest, half the members would support Royn while the other half would either support Cracken or were undecided. "But I don't see why the result should be any different if Kydd *isn't* there."

"Has Bruce been asking the right questions?" Alison said.

"Basically, whether members would vote for me or Cracken," said Royn.

"When you're taking a poll," Alison said, "people only answer the questions you *ask*. Sometimes, of course, they tell you what they think you want to hear. It's the questions you *don't* ask that can cause the problems."

"What do you mean by *that?*"

"Well . . . for example, what if it's not just you and Cracken, but a *three-way* contest?"

"Who else would stand?"

Alison shrugged. "I have no idea. And then—will a motion for a spill pass or fail? Shouldn't we have some idea of the answer to *that* question? But the answer could depend on *who's proposing* the spill."

"You mean," said Royn thoughtfully, "if half the members support me, and I *oppose* a spill, they'd vote against it?"

"You can't simply assume you've got fifty percent of the members in your pocket," said Alison. "*Only* on the issue of you versus *Cracken*. And *only* at the time the question was asked."

"I see what you mean," said Royn. "Okay. We better get Bruce in here and get him to organize some more research."

"Does that mean you're going for it?" Melanie asked.

Royn forced a grin. "No, my dear. I'm going to wait and see."

"Just one suggestion, Minister," Alison said. "I think you should advise Kydd what's brewing. Otherwise he might think *you're* behind it."

"An excellent idea. Thank you, Alison. I will."

44 "Get a Dog"

AN AUSTRALIAN ARMY HELICOPTER sat in the Inkaya village square surrounded by excited children. The teachers gave up trying to get their charges back to class and joined them in gawking at the first helicopter they'd ever seen.

In the nearby canteen, the tables had been pulled together into a square. Arang'anat and Uqu sat next to Tungi at the center of one side of the makeshift conference table, the village elders arrayed to his right and left, spilling around the corners.

Facing Tungi sat Colonel Cantrell and his opposite number from the Sandeman army, Colonel Gugamti. Major McMurray, Jeremy McGuire, and the other members of the Australian delegation sat to Cantrell's left; Captain N'gaandi and an equal number of Sandeman officers to Gugamti's right. Two empty chairs remained, one a few seats from Tungi, the other in the center of one connecting side.

A dozen soldiers, half Sandeman and half Australian, formed a loose cordon around the open-air restaurant. All were unarmed, but the rest of Jeremy's and Captain Ranga N'gaandi's platoons were encamped on the beach over the hill.

"Before our remaining participants arrive," Uqu translated for Tungi, "I have been asked to restate the ground rules for this meeting and reaffirm everyone's agreement."

"With due respect," said Cantrell, "we've been over these a dozen times. And we should wait for the representatives of . . . ah . . . Islamic Purity."

"Colonel," Uqu replied, "this meeting has been arranged with such haste that my principals would like to hear your agreement directly from you first. Okay?"

Cantrell shrugged, his eyes flicking to his watch. "Okay."

"It's very straightforward," Uqu smiled. "This meeting is conducted under a flag of truce; all participants affirm they are unarmed, and that no members of this meeting will be in any way harmed by any of the other participants or their agents in the twenty-four hours following this meeting's conclusion. Is that your understanding, Colonel Cantrell?"

Cantrell nodded. "It is."

"And do you concur, Colonel Gugamti?" Uqu asked.

The Sandeman colonel appeared to hesitate before agreeing, his face sour.

"And do you agree to abide by those rules?"

"Of course," said Cantrell.

"And you, sir?"

As the silence, broken only by children's chatter in the background, seemed to grow oppressive some twenty faces turned to watch Gugamti expectantly. With an obvious effort, the Sandeman colonel curtly nodded his head.

Then Tungi spoke. "We abide also . . . " Uqu began his translation when Arang'anat's sudden squeal prompted everyone at the table to look up in surprise: a tall white woman in a native dress, a scarf hiding her hair, deftly slipped between two of the soldiers and strode towards the table.

"Sorry I'm a bit late," Karla Preston said, with a bow to Tungi, as she stepped under the tin roof. "The water—" she waved her hand in the direction of the tip of Papua New Guinea just visible in the distance "—was a bit rough today."

Tungi stood, smiling, and with a gesture directed Karla to the empty chair between the Australian officers and the village elders. *"Matalam,* Tungi-*ga,"* she said with a bow of her head as she took the indicated seat. Uqu translated Tungi's words, "Tungi-*ga* welcomes and would like to introduce Miss Karla Preston to this meeting."

"Karla *Preston?"* Gugamti exploded as the other Sandeman officers eyed her angrily, a few looking as though they were restraining themselves from leaping to their feet. "What is *she—?"*

"Indeed," Cantrell's voice boomed, stopping Gugamti in mid-flow. "What is this, ah, *journalist* doing here?"

"I have a right to be here, Colonel," Karla said, "since Uqu and I were instrumental in making this meeting possible. Isn't that correct, Captain—no, congratulations—*Major* McMurray?"

"That's one way of looking at it, I suppose," McMurray said guardedly.

"You realize, Tungi-*ga,"* Cantrell said coolly, "this is most irregular."

Tungi spoke quietly to Arang'anat, forcing her to turn her eyes away from Karla, and said, "Tungi-*ga,* he say Karla—uh, Miz Presdon—here to witness. She agree, no speak till permission."

Karla nodded. "That's right, gentlemen. I pledge to say nothing and write nothing about this meeting until Tungi-*ga* gives his permission."

"That's totally unacceptable!" Colonel Gugamti exploded. "This woman is not only a fugitive but is obviously here illegally. She should be arrested immediately." He turned and barked an order to the Sandeman soldiers in the cordon who, after a moment's hesitation, strode purposefully towards Karla.

Tungi, glaring at Gugamti, sprang to his feet shouting. *"Stop,"* Arang'anat's voiced boomed in line with Tungi's, her face an expression of surprise at her own audacity, "or meeting over." Tungi spoke again. "You agree rules already," Arang'anat said. "You now break. Not cricket."

Cantrell leaned over and whispered a few words to Gugamti who angrily jerked his head from side to side. Cantrell spoke more urgently, and Gugamti sighed. He barked another order to the Sandeman soldiers who now backed off, but stood behind Karla to block her exit. Cantrell and Gugamti came to their feet. "If you'll excuse us Tungi-*ga,* ladies and gentlemen." Tungi nodded and the two colonels walked away until their words became indistinct, their tone still clearly one of argument. All heads turned at Cantrell's loud but still indistinct words—except Arang'anat's, whose eyes were focused on Karla. Tungi's hand resting on her arm forced her to restrain her impulse to leap from her place at the table.

The two colonels had stopped talking and just stared at each other. Gugamti looked ready to explode. Even the children still thronging around the helicopter lapsed into silence, watching the two men as if they expected a fight to break out any minute.

But with a jerk of his head that was barely discernible, Gugamti nodded and without a word strode back towards his seat. Shaking his head, Cantrell followed.

Glaring at Karla, Gugamti said, "We agree," with as little grace as he could muster.

As if his words were a signal, a short stocky man slipped from the kitchen area behind Tungi moving so quietly that only at the sound of the last empty chair scraping back did everyone become aware of him.

Karla and Jeremy grinned as Mountain Man came into view. Jeremy stood. "Welcome," he said.

Mountain Man grinned back.

"Who is he?" Gugamti growled.

"He's the leader of the Islamic Purity group," Jeremy said as he resumed his seat. "He's the man I trusted with my life—" he turned to look Gugamti in the eye "—and I'd do it again."

"He's the man who killed one of our soldiers," Gugamti stood, leaning towards Mountain Man, one arm pointing at him accusingly.

"I wouldn't be so sure of that, Colonel," Karla said.

"I saw what you wrote," Gugamti said, "and I don't believe a word of it."

"I was there. You weren't."

"*Enough,*" Tungi said sharply to Gugamti. Everyone at the table understood his meaning before it was translated.

"As I understand it," Cantrell said with a nod to Tungi, his voice booming, "we're not here to rake over our past differences, but to explore possible areas of cooperation." Cantrell gripped Gugamti's arm as he spoke, nudging him back to a sitting position. With searching look at the newcomer, he added, "I'm Colonel Cantrell, and you are . . . ?"

"I call him Mountain Man," said Karla, "because he moves like a mountain goat."

Mountain Man grinned at the translation, his eyes laughing.

Cantrell smiled woodenly at Karla. "With your permission, Tungi-*ga,*" he said, "it would seem to me that your status here, Miss Preston, is an *observer,* not a principal. If I am correct, then perhaps it would be *politic* if you kept your counsel for the balance of the meeting."

Tungi nodded his agreement, and Karla leaned back in her chair, her cheeks flushing.

"Perhaps," Cantrell said to Tungi, "the leader of Islamic Purity could be formally introduced."

Tungi nodded. "Amtami-*ga,*" he said.

"We thank you for your information, which we have confirmed," said Cantrell, addressing Amtami, who simply nodded. "Since then, we've monitored comings and goings from their camp. Now, we'd appreciate if you could tell us exactly what it is you have in mind."

"Certainly," said Amtami. "I believe we all have one aim in common: the elimination of this band of refugee terrorists from St. Christopher's Island—*all* of them." Amtami had used the Arabic name, Jazeerat el-Misk; Uqu had also translated the name, much to Tungi's and Amtami's annoyance.

"That's correct," said Cantrell—while Gugamti scowled as if he didn't concur.

"We believe we can help you ensure that aim is achieved—"

"We know where they are," Gugamti said. "What do we need *you* for?"

"With due respect, Colonel," Amtami replied softly, "we know the lay of the land intimately. Our men can guide your men into position in the dark without alerting the enemy."

"They sure can," said Jeremy.

"We can hear your men coming from a kilometer away," Amtami grinned, his glance encompassing both colonels, "and if we can hear them, so will *they*. If the enemy hear you coming, they'll melt away. The jungle around that camp is thick, but not impenetrable. We suggest that the camp be completely surrounded *before* your missiles are used. We can guide your men *silently* into position. Then, any stragglers not killed or injured by the missiles will be caught."

"If we just blanket the area," said Cantrell, "then surely we'll get them all."

Amtami shook his head. "You only have two Predators deployed with two missiles each—"

"How do you know that?"

"Oh, Colonel," Amtami smiled. "It's common knowledge. And the terrorists now know their effects, so they've dug themselves underground shelters for protection."

"How do you know that?" Cantrell snapped.

"We're watching them, twenty-four hours a day.

"You can get that close? Through that jungle? *Without* being detected?"

Amtami nodded.

Cantrell looked at Amtami in wonderment.

"Even if you follow up the Predators by blanketing the area with artillery fire and bring in your helicopters, you won't get every one of them."

Cantrell nodded. "Possibly," he conceded.

"Ridiculous," Gugamti spluttered. "We have thousands of men. We can easily cordon off the whole area so none of those terrorists can escape."

"Colonel, talking doesn't cook rice," Amtami said softly.

"So tell us, colonel," Karla said as Gugamti half-rose from his seat, "how the terrorists we're talking about today managed to escape your thousands of men on the next island?"

Cantrell frowned at Karla, but not fiercely, and turned with barely hidden interest to see how Gugamti would reply. But Gugamti said nothing, merely fell slowly back to his seat while alternately glowering at Karla and Amtami. Cantrell and Gugamti whispered to each other for a few minutes. Then turning to Amtami, Cantrell said, "We propose a joint exercise with your men. If the result is positive, we'll implement your proposal."

Amtami nodded guardedly. "Six of your men," he said, "including M'gire *-ga*."

Cantrell looked at Gugamti who slowly nodded.

"We are agreed, then," said Cantrell. Gugamti slowly nodded. "Captain McGuire and captain N'gaandi will be two of the six men, and we'll determine the next steps based on their reports."

"Agreed," said Amtami.

Amtami was the first to leave when the meeting ended, disappearing as quickly as he'd come. Released from her duties at last, Arang'anat made a bee-line for Karla who grinned widely as Arang'anat threw herself into her arms. "I never think to see you again," she said.

After a word to N'gaandi, Gugamti stomped off to the helicopter while N'gaandi gathered his men and led them towards the pier. "What's going on, Ranga?" Jeremy called, but N'gaandi didn't answer. "Sarge," he said to "Paddy" Byrne, "take a couple of men and see what they're up to."

"So, Miss Preston," Cantrell said as he walked towards Karla, "what do you plan to write about this meeting?"

"I suppose it depends on what happens next," said Karla. "But it wouldn't surprise me if that colonel friend of yours causes some problem."

Now beside her, Arang'anat shuddered. "He . . . bad omen?" she said, looking, questioning, at Karla.

"Bad news, is that what you mean?" Karla smiled.

"Bad *news*. Yes."

Cantrell's face seemed stoic, but Karla had the impression he agreed.

"You could say, colonel," she said, "that my role here is to make sure everyone is honest."

"I hope you'll have wasted your trip," Cantrell replied.

"So do I, Colonel—in that sense at least."

"Colonel?" Jeremy said as he stepped up, "could I have a . . . ah, *private* word, sir?"

He and Cantrell stepped away, Cantrell nodding as Jeremy spoke urgently. In a moment, they returned and Cantrell said, "Miss Preston, I think it's time you left."

"Why is that, Colonel?"

Cantrell nodded at Jeremy who explained, "N'gaandi and his men have arrested the officer on duty at the immigration and customs post. Presumably, for letting you in."

"But . . . he's not at fault," Karla protested, turning towards the pier. "I didn't even come in that way."

"Very honorable of you to go to his rescue, if that's what you have in mind," said Cantrell. "But a very bad idea. I suggest you allow Captain McGuire and his men to escort you to safety before you cause even *more* trouble."

"I—" About to protest, Karla absorbed the serious tone of Cantrell's voice and dipped her head slightly. "Thank you, Colonel," she said softly.

"You stay, just a while?" Arang'anat asked, her eyes wide.

"I'm sorry," Karla said, "but the colonel is right. I have to go. Now."

She hugged Arang'anat saying, "I'll be back, I promise," shook hands with Uqu, and directed Jeremy to where the *banca* that had brought her across the narrow strait was waiting. She waved to Arang'anat who stood watching forlornly until Karla disappeared from view. The last of Karla's words floated back: "Are you related to *Alison* McGuire, by any chance?"

✳✳✳✳✳

ONE HUNDRED AND TWENTY-TWO of the one hundred and twenty-three Conservative Senators and Members of the House filled the Parliament House meeting room assigned to the governing party almost to capacity. Only one member was missing: Randolph Kydd.

At noon, the federal party chair, Helen Arkness, ascended to the small podium and rapped her gavel. "I declare this meeting open," she said, her voice booming into the sudden hush. "There is, at the moment, one item of business before this meeting."

Jack Quigley—who, with the required number of seconders, had called the meeting—caught Helen Arkness' attention.

"Mr. Quigley has the floor," she announced.

"I move," Quigley said, "that the leadership of the Conservative Party be declared vacant."

There was a moment of stunned silence—and the room exploded with sound. "It's a spill!" said one member to another. "Kydd's days are numbered." "I wouldn't be so sure" . . . "What happens now?" a new member asked an older one. "There'll be a call for nominations." "So who do you think will win—Royn or Cracken?" "Who would *you* vote for?"

"*Quigley* of all people is moving the spill motion," Royn whispered to Bruce Spring, next to him. "Very interesting."

"We know Quigley and Cracken did some sort of deal," Spring whispered back, "but I thought it was Cracken and McKurn who were planning a spill."

"That's the word we had," Royn replied. "They must have promised Quigley a big prize for him to agree to take the heat."

"The heat? From who?"

"Kydd," said Royn. "When he hears of it, he'll be after Quigley's blood."

"Order! Order!" Helen Arkness yelled over the tumult, pounding her gavel.

Into the silence a voice came from the now-open door: "Are you sure you don't want to withdraw that motion, Jack?"

Two hundred and forty-four surprised eyes turned as one to see Randolph Kydd, glaring at Quigley, being wheeled into the room by a nurse. Quite a few members had to look twice before they realized it was Kydd: his voice no longer bounced from the walls; his face was sallow, his skin loose folds hanging from his cheeks. He was dressed in one of his trademark suits—which now looked a size too big.

"Helen," Kydd said, "I'm disappointed you started the meeting without me."

"No one told me you were coming, Prime Minister," she replied.

"Point of order!" Quigley shouted. When Helen Arkness nodded in his direction he continued, "There should be no outsiders in the room—" with a wave of one arm Quigley indicated the nurse standing behind Kydd's wheelchair "—unless, of course, the members wish to make an exception for the Prime Minister."

"I so move," said McKurn, grinning at Kydd.

"I second," said Quigley.

"Do you wish to speak to the point of order, Senator?" Arkness asked.

"Just to say," McKurn said as he slowly rose to his feet, "that one look at our Prime Minister shows it would be an unnecessary cruelty to deprive him of obviously much-needed medical support. One hates to think of the reverberations were our Prime Minister to die in this room because help was just out of reach."

Kydd scowled at the scattering of concerned looks and nervous laughter that greeted McKurn's words. Mouthing, *Bugger you,* at McKurn, Kydd said, "That won't be necessary." He motioned the nurse away. "Just wait outside the door." With clear reluctance, the nurse slowly backed out of the room. "It would seem your motion has become moot, *Frankie,*" he said.

"So be it," said McKurn, with a one-shouldered shrug.

"What happened to you?" Kydd asked. "Have an argument with a cement mixer?"

McKurn glanced at his cast and chuckled. "Something like that, you could say. But the cast will come off in a few weeks and I'll be as good as new. Pity you can't say the same."

"Up yours," Kydd hissed. Turning towards Quigley he said, "Well, Jack, now that I'm here, will you withdraw your motion?"

Looking evenly at Kydd, Quigley said, "No, Randolph, I won't."

After a slight pause, Helen Arkness declared, "Mr. Quigley has moved that the leadership be declared vacant—is there a seconder for this motion?" Even before she'd finished speaking, several members jumped to their feet, vying for her attention. Most were Quigley supporters, but one of them was Bruce Spring.

"What are you *doing?*" Anthony Royn hissed, grabbing Spring's arm to pull him back down to his seat.

"What has to be done," Spring replied, resisting Royn's pull.

"You *fool,*" Royn said as he turned to see Kydd glaring at him. *Oh my God,* Royn thought, *he blames me.* Kydd gazed at Royn for what felt like an eternity, his face twisted into a look that Royn knew was reserved for his worst enemies. "You've done it, now," he said to Spring.

As Spring became aware of Kydd's look, he nervously resumed his seat.

"Too late." Royn's head dropped into his hands, facing the reality that the prize of the Prime Minister's office was no longer going to be handed to him on a plate—if, indeed, that was ever Kydd's real intention. "What will we do *now?*" he groaned.

In support of his motion, Quigley did little more than repeat McKurn's words at greater length and add that, "it was past time for a younger man to take the helm."

Kydd replied, invoking the wheelchair-bound American President, Franklin Roosevelt, saying that he was perfectly capable of continuing in office and pointing out that, unlike Roosevelt, "my condition is merely temporary." But his voice, no longer bludgeoning a whispered comment into silence, belied his every word; a murmur that flew from one mouth to another caused members to focus on the way one side of Kydd's face seemed to have less life than the other side. Kydd's anger slowly rose at the doubt he met in most people's eyes.

The debate continued, strong voices taking both sides. Chow, Bergstrom, and several other ministers came out on the side of "stability."

"They just want to keep their jobs," one member commented cynically. "Wouldn't you?" another replied.

"Kydd's been calling in his debts," Royn whispered to Spring, wondering if Alison's suggestion to warn him that a spill could be brewing had backfired.

"Still a few heavyweights sitting on the fence," Spring replied.

"Most prominently Cracken—"

"And you."

"True," Royn nodded. "What's it look like?"

Spring had been keeping a running tab of the likely votes. "The Cracken and Quigley blocs, that's thirty-two. Forty-three with the fellow travellers. Throw in the marginals it's somewhere between forty and sixty-five depending on how marginal you want to go."

"Maybe—but far from certain, then."

"Chow and Bergstrom can deliver a dozen or so votes between them. Kydd?" Spring shrugged. "With his other supporters who've spoken up, somewhere between thirty-five and sixty."

"So it could go either way."

Spring turned to Royn. "But weighted slightly towards a 'no' vote. You can swing the vote the other way—if you want," he said, his face hard, tone challenging.

A young member stood up nervously. "Prime Minister," he began, "we heard that you would be back on your feet in no time. But, with due respect, while I wish it were true I now find that hard to believe. My problem is simple: as you all know, I won my seat in the last election by just four votes—after a recount. We have to face the voters again in ten months. My seat is the most marginal in the party. The slightest swing against us and I'm out. I won't be the *only* one." He looked around the room; over two dozen heads were nodding in agreement. "It's clear to me that if the Prime Minister does *not* fully recover and faces the electorate in anything even halfway like his current condition, I for one will lose my seat. So it is with great reluctance that I have no choice but to support Mr. Quigley's motion for a spill."

"I understand your concern," Kydd said softly, "but I can assure you that I won't need this wheelchair that much longer."

"Maybe," the young member said, a slight tremor in his voice. "But if you were in my position, Prime Minister, would you take the risk?"

Kydd face froze for a fraction of a second; he leaned forward and said, "I guarantee that I will prove you wrong."

"Good for him," Spring whispered. "He really put Kydd on the spot."

"You've primed the marginal members well," Royn said.

With hardly a pause for breath, Kydd turned to Royn. "Perhaps our Deputy Leader, who has been unusually silent and would surely like to keep *his* post, might say a few words on this subject." Kydd's eyes were smouldering black pinpoints fixed on Royn.

"You'd better make *your* position clear," Spring whispered. "You *know* we've got the numbers."

Royn nodded.

"And just *look* at him—" Spring flicked his wrist towards Kydd "—he doesn't have a prayer. And he knows it."

"Maybe," Royn mumbled vaguely; Spring wasn't sure Royn had even heard him.

Royn was thinking: *I could oppose the spill and redeem myself in Kydd's eyes.* Except that he knew, no matter how vociferously he protested that Bruce Spring had acted on his own initiative, Kydd would never trust him again. *And then . . . if the spill succeeds, my position as Deputy Leader will be up for grabs too. Kydd won't back me for Leader or Deputy . . . the opposite if anything. . . .*

"Come on, Tony," Spring urged. "Whatever else you do, you must not *appear* to procrastinate."

"You're right," Royn said, thinking that taking on Cracken or any other member was easy—but now he had to seriously consider opposing *Kydd*. Taking a deep breath as he rose to his feet, he now towered over his . . . former . . . mentor. Looking down, Kydd's appearance seemed to give flesh to the saying "a shadow of his former self"—and Royn suddenly felt lighter.

"I can certainly understand and sympathize with the Prime Minister's wish to continue in the office he has occupied with an unmatched and probably unmatchable record—" Royn began, and recalled Kydd's own advice, *kick 'em while they're down.* For the first time, he returned Kydd's fixed glare evenly. *If I don't put the knife in now,* he thought, *I might as well simply pack it in.* "—but I think it is only fair, so that everyone present has enough information to come to a considered decision, that I should tell you that the Prime Minister's own doctors advise that *months* of complete rest are required if he is to have the chance of a full recovery—"

Kydd exploded. "That's not the case at all."

"Oh, really, Prime Minister?" Royn asked. "*You,* not your doctors, told me that. I am merely repeating your very own words which were, and I quote—" suddenly, Kydd's former voice boomed through the room from Royn's lips "—'the bastards want me to quit.'"

Kydd's eyes blazed at Royn and the color rushed back into his face. McKurn leaned over and said, in a voice that carried to the back of the room, "Careful, Randy. You don't want a *second* heart attack, do you?"

As Kydd spluttered, Quigley jumped to his feet. "I move that the motion be put."

Kydd tried to object but his voice was drowned out by cries of "Yes!" and "Aye!"

Helen Arkness rapped her gavel. "The motion before the floor is: to declare the leadership of the Conservative Party vacant. Those in favor?"

The shouted "Ayes" seemed to outweigh the "Noes."

"I demand a count," said Kydd.

Helen Arkness nodded. Those in favor of the motion moved to one side of the room, those against to the other. The balance was clearly in favor of the "Ayes," but everyone waited until the tellers had made their reckoning. An expected silence fell as Helen Arkness rapped her gavel. "The motion is carried, sixty-three votes to fifty-nine."

"And your vote, Helen?" Kydd asked.

"Would make no difference, Prime Minister." As party chair, she held the casting vote in the event of a tie. "I call for nominations for leader of—"

One of Quigley's supporters interrupted her, yelling, "I nominate Jack Quigley." His voice was followed by several shouts of "Second."

Royn saw Cracken's look of approval as Quigley accepted the nomination. "So *that's* his game," he muttered.

"What?" asked Spring.

"Quigley will draw votes away from me," Royn whispered, "and then, presumably, do his best to switch them to Cracken."

"Unless he wins," Spring said. They both laughed.

In quick succession, both Cracken and Royn were nominated. Then Stanley Chow slowly rose to his feet and waited as the members, one by one, noticed him, and near-silence reigned. "I nominate Randolph Kydd." Two of Kydd's closest supporters rose to second Chow's motion.

"What's he doing?" Spring asked Royn.

Royn shrugged. "He's as unpredictable as ever."

"Do you accept the nomination, Prime Minister?" Helen Arkness asked.

"Of course," said Kydd, with a smile at Chow.

"Any other nominations?" Helen Arkness asked. Silence greeted her question. "In that case," she said, "I declare—" seeing that Kydd had raised a hand she stopped and asked, "Yes, Prime Minister?"

"I nominate Victor Bergstrom." As Kydd spoke, his eyes, glinting with amusement, focused on Royn.

"Is there a seconder?" Arkness asked over the hubbub. When several seconders appeared, she asked, "Do you accept the nomination, Mr. Bergstrom?"

Bergstrom stood sheepishly, looking at Kydd with puzzlement. "Ah . . ." he started to say, in obvious confusion. "If I am called to serve. . . ."

"Is that a 'yes,' Mr. Bergstrom?" Helen Arkness asked.

Bergstrom nodded his head. "Yes," he said softly.

"Are there any other nominations?" Her gaze swivelled twice around the room. "No? Then I declare nominations closed."

Quigley jumped up before anyone else could speak, saying, "I move that we vote *now.*"

He was greeted with shouts of "No!" "It's too soon." "We need time." And from several of his supporters, "I second the motion."

Helen Arkness looked at Quigley. "By the sound of it, your motion will fail. Do you wish to continue with it?"

"Yes, Madam Chair," he answered, "I do."

The tally was: one hundred and three against, nineteen for.

"Today is Wednesday," said Helen Arkness. "I suggest we reconvene either tomorrow or Friday."

Shouts of "Friday" far overshadowed "Thursday."

"Friday it is," Helen Arkness declared. She looked at Quigley but when neither he nor anyone else objected she asked, "Is there any other business? No? In that case, I declare this meeting adjourned until Friday—at nine-thirty AM."

*****

"ALISON!" ANTHONY ROYN YELLED as he strode past Mary without noticing her and disappeared into his office, Bruce Spring close on his heels.

"It must have gone badly," said Melanie as she and Alison watched the two men storm across the outer office.

"Must have," Alison sighed. "Let's go and find out what happened."

"I still don't understand why you had to jump up like that—" Royn stopped in mid flow as Alison and Melanie came into his office; Royn and Spring stood by the open cupboard that contained the bar, each with a brandy in his hand. "Oh . . . hi," he smiled at Melanie. "Medicinal purposes," he said, lifting his brandy snifter and gulping it empty. "Muggins here dropped me in the soup."

"That's hardly fair," Spring complained.

"How else would you describe it?" Royn glared at him.

"Calm down, you two," Melanie ordered. "Sit down and tell us what happened."

"It's a five-way contest," Royn spluttered as he moved towards his desk.

"Oh my God," Alison said. "You, Cracken—and who else?"

"Kydd for heaven's sake," said Spring. "Plus Quigley and Bergstrom—nominated by *Kydd.*"

"Tell us how *that* happened, Tony," Melanie asked as they all took seats around Royn's desk.

Royn quickly summarized the course of the meeting, ". . . and then this numskull jumps up to second Quigley's motion—you should have seen the way Kydd looked at *me.*"

"Tony certainly rose to the occasion," Spring said approvingly.

"You didn't leave me any choice," Royn snapped. Turning to Alison as if for support he began to explain, "There was *no* reason for Bruce—"

"Tony, that's enough." Melanie glared at her husband. "Bruce probably did you a favor—if you'd opposed the motion for a spill, Kydd might still be the leader."

"No 'might' about it," said Spring.

Alison nodded slowly. "You've certainly lost Kydd's support, *permanently.* But that was inevitable the moment you did *anything* Kydd could interpret as opposition to him."

Royn nodded glumly.

"And then . . . ?" Alison prompted.

"The nominations. They went pretty quickly—Quigley, Cracken, me, Kydd, Bergstrom. The only thing of interest, aside from Kydd nominating Bergstrom, was Cracken's look when Quigley accepted the nomination. They're up to something, that's for sure."

Alison nodded. "And McKurn—did he second Cracken?"

"Oh, no," said Royn. "Nothing so obvious. He only spoke to annoy Kydd—*very* successfully."

"Why did Kydd nominate *Bergstrom,* of all people?" Melanie asked.

"Divide and rule," Alison said.

"That's cryptic," Melanie said. "Please explain."

"So many candidates muddy the waters," said Alison. "And Bergstrom . . . a stroke of genius you must admit. The perfect compromise candidate."

"But he'll take away votes from Kydd, won't he?" Melanie asked.

Royn nodded. "Quite possibly."

"But he'll take votes from everyone else, too," Spring said.

"That's right," said Alison, and turned to Royn as she continued, "From what you've said, Minister, Kydd hasn't just withdrawn his support from you; he's out to *deny* you the leadership."

"It certainly looks that way," Royn said, his voice low.

"With Bergstrom in the race," Alison said matter-of-factly, "once he sees which way the wind's blowing, Kydd could drop out and throw his weight behind Bergstrom."

"He'll never do that," Melanie complained bitterly. "He just won't lay down and die."

"That's . . . a bit over the top, my dear," Royn said, looking quizzically at his wife.

"I was . . . speaking metaphorically," she replied, unapologetic. "But now that you mention it . . . a pity."

"He *will* withdraw," said Alison, "but only as a last resort. You said there were fifty-nine votes *against* the spill, Minister?"

"That's right," said Royn.

"So it's a fair assumption that that's the extent of Kydd's support—is that what you're getting at?" Melanie asked.

Alison nodded. "And from what you said about how everyone reacted to his condition—" She shrugged. "That's one of the things we've got to find out. Who's going to support whom. How solid are the numbers for the Minister, and so on."

"I figure that Bergstrom and Quigley will be eliminated first," said Spring. "But then—?" he shrugged. "Who can say?"

"The worst scenario," said Alison thoughtfully, "is that it comes down to you versus Cracken—and Kydd supports Cracken."

"What if it's Tony versus Kydd?" Melanie asked. "Who do you think Cracken would support?"

"Kydd," said Alison without having to think. "If the Minister wins, Cracken might never have another chance at the leadership."

Royn nodded glumly.

"We have to remember," said Spring excitedly, "the polls show that only with Tony as leader are we sure to win. That's our ace-in-the-hole."

"If it were only that simple, Bruce," Alison said coolly, "we'd have nothing to worry about. That poll could now be out of date."

"Why not do another one?" Melanie said excitedly.

"We'd need the results by Friday morning," said Royn. "Is there time, Alison?"

Alison nodded. "Probably. I can find out in ten minutes."

"Do it," said Royn.

*****

ALMOST AS QUICKLY AS news of the leadership spill flashed across the country, a pool was set up in one newsroom after another to bet on the winner: when the result was declared, the money in the pool would be divided amongst those who had bet on the winning candidate.

Most of the money was put on Royn, with Cracken a distant second. In one newsroom, every journalist put his money on Royn—except the editor of the racing pages, who bet on Cracken, Bergstrom, and Kydd. "Why did you do *that?*" someone asked him. "Kydd's dead, Bergstrom doesn't have a hope, and against Royn Cracken doesn't have a frog's chance in a French restaurant."

"What's the point of betting on Royn? Put a dollar on him," the racing editor replied, "and you get a dollar back plus a cent if you're lucky. Sure, I'm taking a long shot. But Kydd isn't dead till he's buried, Bergstrom could win in a deadlock, and if Kydd supports Cracken he'll probably beat Royn. Any one of them wins, I scoop the pool." The editor immediately regretted his comment as the other journalist put some money down on the other candidates, including Quigley for good measure, chopping his potential winnings in half. *I hope,* he thought to himself, *he has the sense to keep his mouth shut . . . unlike me.*

*****

"TONY. DON'T YOU THINK it's time we met?"

A barely tasted drink in his hand, Anthony Royn was one of some six hundred people milling around in Parliament's Great Hall at a cocktail party in honor of the visiting

British Defence Minister. Idly chatting with a somewhat haughty British dowager, he looked around, startled to see the attractive woman who'd addressed him. "Senator . . . ah . . . Strezlecki." He half-bowed as he spoke.

"Vanessa," she said with an amused smile.

"But we *have* met . . . Vanessa." Royn recalled the reception held a couple of months ago to introduce the new Senator to other members of parliament. Like most other members, he had briefly shaken her hand and not thought about her since.

"That hardly counts," Vanessa replied with a beaming smile.

"How are you enjoying being a Senator?" Royn asked, unaware that as they spoke Vanessa was taking tiny steps backwards that drew him away from the people he'd just been talking to.

"It's . . . amusing," she replied, still smiling.

"Is there anything you *don't* find amusing?"

"Not much, now that you mention it."

VANESSA STREZLECKI BECAME THE junior Senator from the island state of Tasmania to complete the term of Senator Reginald "Redge" Thompson who, when hospitalized with cancer, resigned.

When a seat in the House of Representatives becomes vacant, a bye-election is held to elect the new member. But when a Senator dies or resigns from office, the state government appoints the successor who holds office until the next half-Senate election. By an unwritten convention—occasionally honored in the breach—the new Senator is from the same party as the previous one.

Senator Thompson's resignation caused a conundrum for the state Labor government: Thompson, an independent, was affiliated with no party, and had no political organization worth mentioning. Who should be his replacement?

The Labor Premier suggested appointing a Labor man on the basis that "Redge, after all, mostly voted with Labor anyway."

That idea was quickly shot down when a reporter asked Thompson why he didn't cut the controversy short by suggesting a successor himself. Thompson replied, "I'm intrigued to see whether that little shit of a Premier will do the right thing for a change. If he does, it will be the first time since he learnt to wipe his own arse and stopped wearing nappies."

A red-faced Premier invited the public to suggest the best Tasmanian to "pick up and continue Redge's legacy of service to the great state of Tasmania."

One of many names put forward was Vanessa Strezlecki, a widowed, unassuming, personable mother of four, who was active in a number of the environmental and other movements that Redge Thompson favored.

Vanessa was amused by the attention she received. While well known within the state, she was the kind of person who worked tirelessly in the background to support others who—like Thompson—yearned to stand in the limelight. Then a TV station decided to grill some of the suggested candidates. Vanessa was one of those invited.

Vanessa Strezlecki was fifty-nine, not that she ever mentioned her age. At first glance, she didn't look that old at all: a woman of medium height in her forties or, possibly, even late thirties, who moved with a youthful energy, appearing to glide rather than walk. But then you'd notice her silvery hair was silvery-*grey*, the faint hint of crow's feet around her eyes, a strange translucency to her facial skin that made some people think she'd had a facelift, and a poise and grace to her stance that gave the impression of experience rather than youth. So on second glance you'd realize that despite her slim figure, she had to be much older than she looked.

In the makeup room, the suggestion of crow's feet was erased and the slight shininess to her skin masked; when introduced on camera as an about-to-be grandmother, viewers wondered how that could be possible for one so young.

"I'm not a politician," Vanessa said to the interviewer, "and I've never had any desire to be one—God forbid. But if the government asks me I'll say, 'Yes.' Why not? It will be fun—a new experience. And it would only be until the next election, just long enough for me to enjoy it without becoming completely disgusted with all the back-stabbing, back-biting, and two-faced wheeling and dealing that goes on in Canberra all the time."

"So you have no intention of standing for election at the end of your term?" the interviewer asked.

"What a horrible thought," Vanessa replied, her nose wrinkling in disgust. "Canberra's a nice place to visit . . . very occasionally. But I simply can't understand why anyone would actually want to *live* there."

"Have you given any thought to how you might vote in the Senate?"

"Not really. But I'd be very aware that I'd only be Redge's stand-in, his mouthpiece so to speak. Although Redge and I aren't close, our differences are minor and I know him well enough to know how he'd vote on pretty much everything. After all, if I'm ever in doubt I can always phone and ask him. But that doesn't mean I won't speak my own mind as well, of course."

"Does it follow, then, that you agree with Redge's description of the Premier as 'that little shit'?"

Vanessa laughed. "I can assure you that when I express an opinion, I am far more lady-like."

"That doesn't really answer the question."

"Well, let me say that I respect the Premier's talents as a politician—talents I have absolutely no desire to acquire myself."

"A_{ND} _{WHAT} _{ON} _{EARTH} can be so amusing in the Senate?" Royn asked her.

"Well, for one thing," Vanessa said, "the way so many politicians strut around with supreme self-importance they clearly don't deserve."

"Ah . . . yes," said Royn slowly. "And do *I* 'strut around' too?"

"No. You always seem to move very naturally."

"*Seem* to?"

"Yes. . . . I've been watching you, you know."

"Me? Why?"

She laughed. "I'm a people-person, Tony—I watch *everybody*."

"Oh. And what do you see?"

"For example, that you're a chameleon and that Senator McKurn was lying through his teeth about 'the only women I ever loved' on TV the other day."

"He was?"

"Oh, yes."

"How do you know?"

Vanessa's expression became thoughtful, her smile now just a hint from the slight upturn of the corners of her mouth. "It's hard to explain . . . but I could see that while he was genuinely upset—which made his words so convincing—it was like he'd put on a mask. . . . But I suppose you'll just dismiss that as woman's intuition."

"Oh, no," said Royn. "I've no doubt your perceptions are spot on."

"And is my other comment spot on too, then—the one you're avoiding?"

"That I'm a chameleon? I should feel insulted." *Though, strangely, I don't, at all.*

Vanessa shook her head. "It's a compliment, believe it or not. I was in the gallery in the House one day and noticed you sitting on the bench, looking rather self-absorbed, depressed even. Then there was a question for you and you stood up and switched on your charm as if you'd turned on a light. An amazing transformation, just like that." She snapped her fingers.

"You know," Royn said, feeling drawn in by Vanessa's eyes as if they were deep, enticing pools, "I've always wanted to be an actor. That was my passion for as long as I can remember." Royn felt surprise at how those words had just spilled out, wondering how long it had been since he'd spoken them to anyone else . . . or even acknowledged his youthful passion to himself.

Vanessa smiled warmly. "Well, politics is a stage."

"Indeed—but after performing in the theater you don't have to go home and write the script for the next day."

"Why don't you go back to the theater?"

"Start a new career—at my age?" Royn said.

Vanessa laughed at Royn's reaction. Her laughter was infectious. It seemed to infuse her body and somehow reminded Royn of joyous Christmas bells tinkling on clear night. He smiled broadly, then glanced around with a touch of guilt to see if anyone had noticed how much he was enjoying Vanessa's company.

"Why on earth not? You'd be a hit. You're well known and popular. What a novelty for a former high-ranking politician to walk onto a stage. You'd pack the house."

"I would?"

"No doubt whatsoever," Vanessa nodded. "But then . . . maybe you'll be Prime Minister come Friday. In fact," she added, chuckling mischievously, "shouldn't you be canvassing votes right now instead of wasting your time on a lost cause?"

"You're a lost cause?"

"To the Conservative Party, yes."

"And if you *were* a Conservative, who would *you* vote for?"

"I'd probably vote for Victor."

"Why?"

"Because he's the only one who doesn't *want* to be Prime Minister."

I wouldn't be so sure he's the only one, Royn thought.

"Oh, there you are, darling."

Royn turned, his cheeks flushing, as he felt Melanie's hand clutch his arm possessively. "Hi, Mel. This is Senator Strezlecki; my wife, Melanie."

Vanessa smiled warmly at Melanie and held out her hand. "Just Vanessa," she said.

"A pleasure," said Melanie, her eyes coldly looking Vanessa up and down while her lips smiled and she limply shook Vanessa's hand. "Now, if you'll excuse us."

"Of course," said Vanessa, her eyes twinkling. "I wouldn't wish to hinder the next Prime Minister in the pursuit of his destiny."

Melanie's gaze suddenly became intent. "You think he'll win?" she asked.

"I couldn't say," Vanessa said. "But one thing I *can* tell you is that, from what I hear, Labor hopes he *doesn't.*"

"That's very interesting," Melanie said, now smiling. "Thank you, Vanessa."

"Yes, it is," Royn said, not quite sure where to direct his eyes.

45 **Down Payment**

"Morning, Louie."

Louie looked up as Alison walked into his coffee shop. "This is a pleasant surprise."

"Why is that?"

"Because I don't expect to see you on a Friday morning—and you're *much* more attractive, dressed for the office, than on Sundays after your run." Louie froze for an instant in mid-motion, his eyes narrowing. "Want to talk about it?" he asked softly.

"About what?" Alison leant wearily on the counter, forcing a smile.

"About whatever's bothering you."

Is it that obvious? she asked herself. "Thanks, Louie, but no thanks. Just something at the office. It'll sort itself out soon enough."

"Without your help?" Louie grinned. When Alison smiled wanly but said nothing, he asked, "So tell me, who's going to win?"

"Win what?"

"The leadership spill—it's all over the papers you know."

"Oh, that," Alison muttered, puzzled she hadn't immediately realized what he was referring to. *It must be happening now,* she thought, curious that she'd forgotten all about the party meeting which would decide Royn's—and her—fate. For the first time in her fourteen years working for Royn, she'd taken a sickie, promising she'd be in later. Noticing how Louie's eyes narrowed in surprise, she said lightly, "Who do *you* think should win?"

"Your boss."

"Why?"

"Because then you'll get what you want."

Will I? Alison wondered, noticing distantly that she was no longer sure. "Thanks, Louie," she said. "But who do you think would be *best—?*"

"At my age," he grinned, spreading his arms, "what difference would it make?"

"At your age," Alison smiled back, "why are you still working?"

"What? Sit in an old folk's home playing bridge with old battle axes when I could be here and chat with sweet young things like you?"

"Flattery will get you nowhere," Alison chuckled.

"Oh, I wouldn't be so sure."

Alison laughed. "And what, if anything, are your customers saying about it?"

Louie shrugged. "Mainly, that Kydd should do the right thing and give someone else a go." He put a cappuccino on the counter in front of Alison, who realized she hadn't even ordered yet. "On the house today."

"That's very sweet of you, Louie. Thank you."

Louie leaned forward and said in a whisper that no one else would hear, "Would you like a shot of something more . . . stimulating in that?"

"What?" Alison stared at him open-mouthed, and then nodded. "Yes, I think I would," she said quietly.

Louie poured in a generous helping of what looked like water and passed it back to Alison. "Good luck," he said.

Her hand shook slightly as she picked up the cappuccino. "Thank you—again," she said, looking at him gratefully, her eyes watery.

Even though it was a blustery day, clouds scudding between her and the warmth of the sun more often than not, Alison sat at her usual table on the footpath. She spread out the newspaper she'd brought, holding it in place from the wind with an ashtray on one corner and the sugar bowl on another. She spluttered at her first sip of coffee: she'd forgotten about Louie's "additive"; it was certainly strong, whatever it was—and warm, mellowing, and very welcome.

She started reading but the words weren't making sense, as though half of them were from some undiscovered language; she slumped back into her chair and stared blankly into space, oblivious to the gusts of wind that whipped her hair around her face and flapped the folds of her skirt. From time to time, she was vaguely aware of the sounds of footsteps, traffic, and chatter around her until a little voice saying, solemnly, "Don't be silly, Daddy," seized her attention.

A young couple were smiling and laughing and glancing at each other with a look that melted her heart. The husband pushed a pram; his wife held the hands of two toddlers whose non-stop chattering turned the weight of the lump in her stomach into lead. She was frozen in place as the toddlers pulled their parents to a stop, glued to the glittering display of European chocolates wrapped in silver and gold in Louie's window. They requested chocolate and settled for ice cream; the weight in her stomach grew heavier with each tinkle of their voices while, unnoticed, tears formed in the corners of her eyes and rolled slowly, one at a time, down her cheeks.

She thought of Lorraine Adams, her best friend since primary school. *Where did she go?* As the question came to her she knew the answer: *Nowhere.* Lorraine was now married with three children and still lived in Balmain not far from where they'd both grown up—*I'm the one who went somewhere.* It had happened so slowly she'd hardly noticed it: as she spent more time in Canberra, or travelling around the country and the world, they just saw less and less of each other . . . and had less and less in common. *And I'm the godmother of her first child,* she remembered guiltily, failing to recall when she'd last seen her godson. She'd gone to the baptism of Lorraine's second child, but when the third came she was in Rome or somewhere with Royn. If a genie materialized to offer her three wishes, she would, there and then, swap places with Lorraine.

But . . . just as in school, in Canberra Alison was surrounded with friends . . . new friends who had come to replace her old ones. *Everybody here has their own axe to grind; more often than not, like Bruce Spring, their "axe" is their own advancement.* Of all the people she knew in Canberra the image of Louie laughing behind his counter stayed in her mind. *He cares nothing about politics,* she thought of the grandfatherly man she'd known for years, *yet his warmth . . . he would listen.* But Royn? Melanie? Bruce Spring? Jason? The people she hung out with on Wednesday nights talking politics? *Everything goes through a political filter. Politics brought us together and if you take the politics away, there's nothing much left.*

Now licking their ice creams, the toddlers and their parents had moved all of three shop windows away. Alison shook her eyes loose. *I can't bear it . . .* as though she was seeing everything she had given up, the price she had paid. *. . . No . . . that was just a down payment.* She stood, tears blurring her vision; a gust of wind caught the newspaper and she watched the pages flutter across the footpath. *Oh, whatever.* She gulped the rest of her coffee which burned her throat even though it had gone cold, and strode away until the children's happy, piercing voices could no longer jangle her nerves.

Around the corner she slowed . . . and stopped. Across the intersection was a church—no, Manuka *Cathedral.* She walked a few paces, and stopped again. Anywhere in Europe, she thought, it would be nothing more than a large church. Perhaps not even that. Built of light brown-yellow brick, there was nothing prepossessing about it. Nothing . . . awe-inspiring. The church's double doors were open, but nobody was going in, or coming out. She continued walking away; her eyes kept drifting back, her steps slowing every time she looked at the church—she couldn't think of it as a cathedral, despite its name.

At the next corner she stopped. Half-a-dozen wide steps led to the archway of the doors, a dark opening like the mouth of a cave. She took a step to walk on, but the heaviness in her stomach felt like a planet at the farthest reach from its sun, the grip of a far greater gravity preventing it from moving any further away. *A black hole . . . ?* she wondered, standing immobilized.

What am I thinking? She asked herself. *I haven't been near a church since I was. . . . Since before.* Oh—there'd been the weddings of some friends, a baptism. But they didn't count. *And this is a Catholic church. Do I really want to go in there?*

Shrugging, her feet took her back and across the road until she stood in the doorway of the cathedral, wishing there was somewhere else she could go, someone—anyone—she could talk to.

She peered through the doorway. In the dim light inside she could see the pews were nearly empty. Just one or two people praying. People like me, she thought, who need some comfort right now; who have nowhere else to go.

Gathering her courage she took a step into what she once thought was the House of God. *Why didn't I choose another church? Any other church? They wouldn't be the same. But I wouldn't feel scared to go in.*

God lives here, she could remember her younger self thinking, and smiled bitterly at the memory. That was another life . . . *before. . . .*

As she walked through the archway her eyes slowly adjusted to the dim light, straying to the confessional box glowing in the muted rainbow of light filtering through the stained-glass windows. She automatically began to make the sign of the cross. It took conscious effort to still her hand. *Don't be silly.* But she had the uncomfortable feeling she'd just done something wrong, something . . . sacrilegious. She couldn't shake it—remembering something she'd once read, that the child you once were still lives inside you.

Little Alison, she thought. *So carefree, so innocent, so gay, so beautiful. What a wonderful soul she had. What would she think of me now?* Yet it was comforting to think that maybe that five-year-old soul still lived within her . . . somewhere.

That's why I came here. To be five years old again . . . without a care in the world.

But . . . how could that be possible . . . now?

She'd intended to sit right at the back where nobody would notice her. Instead, she found herself walking towards the front, taking a seat on the right-hand side a few rows from the altar. *This is where Alison used to sit,* she remembered, *with Mama on one side and Daddy on the other . . .* and she could almost feel they were there with her now.

She closed her eyes and felt herself drifting back in time. She could imagine the choir singing a hymn and she hummed along. And the rustle of people as they all knelt to pray. She resisted the impulse to kneel too. No words came to her mind, no sound issued from her mouth, but the sense of peace she once experienced flooded back to her, enveloping her. And as had happened when she was five, all her troubles . . . *not that I had any then* . . . seemed to be so far away they just didn't matter any more.

She sat in the pew tasting happy memories, one after another. Memories from *before* . . . she hadn't thought about for years. Her bicycle, and how she sped along the streets, unstoppable. Her dolls—patched and battered but more beautiful and cuddly than anything in a shop window. The little kitten she'd brought home . . . so cute—she never did tell Mama where she found it. And Mama . . . always *fussing*. "Stop fussing, Mama," she heard in her five-year-old voice. And Daddy, poor Daddy, I hurt him so. "I love you, Daddy," she murmured, "I love you. I've *always* loved you. Always."

Strange, she mused, that I can feel these things in this place.

As Father Ryan appeared behind the altar in her imagination and began to preach about the sanctity of life, the heaviness in her stomach which had seemed to have faded away, exploded into her awareness. *No,* she almost shrieked. *I don't want to hear that.* Father Ryan blinked out and she was suddenly back in this church in this time, the seats around her empty.

She sighed with the sense of the irretrievable loss of a time when everything was bright, simple, and clear-cut—while Father Ryan's words continued inexorably in her mind, as though they'd been imprinted on her soul.

She looked up at Jesus' sad, downcast eyes above the altar, her own glistening eyes casting halos all around him. At the blood on his side and on his hands. She could feel his pain in her shoulders, the weight of his body tearing on the nails through her palms.

I'm suffering too. Does that make you feel any better? She studied the face of the . . . idol . . . a painted, wooden image of . . . someone's imagination . . . as if searching for an answer.

What's your purpose in life? She could hear Derek's question in her head as if it was yesterday.

Revenge, she'd answered. Instantly.

The graven image was silent, the deep sorrow in its eyes directed at her, as if it were asking: *And what did you get?*

The weight in her stomach seemed to grow, her breasts distending, her legs swelling, her back aching, and a voice inside whispered, barely audible: *What are you going to do, Alison?*

"No!" she shrieked, her reflexive sound disappearing into the vastness of the cathedral's vaulted ceiling.

That would be a sin.

You mean, another sin.

Alison sighed. *You've got to face it,* she told herself.

For several days she'd been feeling uncomfortable and seemed to tire easily, nothing she could pinpoint. She put it down to stress from overwork until, one morning in the shower, she imagined that her breasts felt a little heavier. She studied herself in the bathroom mirror afterwards and was sure her nipples were slightly darker. Then she looked again. . . . *You're imagining things,* she thought with relief. There was no *reason* to worry—*yet, anyway*—but she bought a pregnancy test kit at a pharmacy. It sat on her dining room table, taunting her for the entire evening until she marshalled the nerve to use it.

The result was positive.

It can't be.

Knowing the test was not foolproof she'd driven across town to the all-night pharmacy and bought three more, each a different brand . . . but they all agreed with one another.

And the first one.

No—God, No! A *baby* growing inside her, moving, kicking, expanding, becoming a part of her, the sense of it pushing, struggling, and the pain of release—and the reward; her breasts growing heavy, the feeling of a baby's mouth sucking . . . to look down and see McKurn on her breast. . . .

This is worse than rape.

And walking along the street holding . . . his or her? . . . hand. *"The sins of the father. . . ."* She shuddered. *How could I curse a child with his rotten genes?*

You'd be taking a life.

Do I believe that any more? She gazed at the suffering Jesus hanging on the cross above the pulpit. *Is that what you want? Every time I looked at my child, I'd remember McKurn. For the rest of my life. I couldn't stand it. . . . It's just a bunch of cells, right now. Hardly begun to divide. Anyway, it's my body—it have the right to do whatever I want to it.*

Would you cut off a finger? Or a toe? In any case, it's not part of you; it's a different biological entity—

Like a wart? She trembled. *Or a tumor or a cancer eating away at my soul?*

It's a life, not a virus. And sacred. A different human being . . . from conception.

When does life begin? When does the soul enter the body?

And if there's no soul?

It has no mind. No brain.

So it's okay then to kill a retarded child . . . ?

Of course not. But I can't—

Give it up for adoption then.

To give up my baby . . . ? She shook her head automatically, violently, her hands cradling her stomach as if she was already aware of its presence even though there was nothing there to feel, yet. . . . Maybe it was already too late. . . .

Never!

Then you have no choice, Alison.

And feel cursed for the rest of my life—either way I turn?

"My child." A concerned male voice. "Can I be of any help to you?"

Alison slowly looked up to see, through a red haze, the priest standing in the aisle looking at her with obvious concern.

"No, I *won't!*" she shrieked, jumping to her feet, unaware of whose question she was answering. "You've done enough damage as it is." She scrambled past the startled man as if he was an obstacle to be avoided and all but ran until she was outside. Blinking at the sudden brightness, she breathed deeply of the cool, fresh, open air.

*****

As Anthony Royn strode towards the party room some fifteen minutes before the meeting was due to start, he was sure of only one thing: that he didn't have the numbers and neither did anyone else.

Worse, aside from Alison calling in sick, the results of the snap poll weren't in yet, despite the premium demanded for a rush job. "They'll be ready any minute"—so they'd been promised, again and again, for the past hour.

The last two days had disappeared in a blur. Phones never stopped ringing, even at night. Supporters needed constant reassurance; waverers, constant persuasion. Rumors and scuttlebutt, often contradictory, about who was going to vote for whom, who'd been seen talking to "guess who?" and what people had overheard, flooded in nonstop. Most damaging was Kydd's comment that Royn "didn't have what it takes" to be party leader, let alone PM, "but he makes a good lapdog." Spring countered it by spreading the news that the only candidate Labor actually *feared* was Anthony Royn.

His office had become his campaign HQ: Royn felt as though Spring and other members of the Push were invaders who'd taken it over. A large whiteboard now dominated the room: Spring continually updated it with his latest guesstimate of the votes for each of the five candidates. "Undecided" had led from the beginning.

To top it off, Kydd had called a cabinet meeting the previous morning to reassert his authority and, Royn was positive, to humiliate him. He called Royn's proposed Royal Commission "the dumbest thing I've heard in my fourteen years as prime minister." With the exception of Royn, who abstained, the Cabinet voted unanimously to kill the idea.

Royn was not alone in thinking that Kydd's strategy may have backfired. Aside from underlining his sudden and clearly personal antagonism to Royn after years of boosting him, Kydd's energy level was clearly low. No longer the forceful presence dominating the room, even when he said nothing, when he cut the Cabinet meeting short it was an admission of weakness. Kydd had not returned to the Prime Minister's Lodge, but was staying in a hospital. "He'll recover—in time," the doctors had assured everyone who asked—but they tried to restrict Kydd's forays to Parliament House . . . without success.

Royn was sure that Kydd's condition would lose him votes. But where those votes would go was still anybody's guess.

Members were strung in small groups along the corridor outside the party room. Royn slowed and chatted briefly as he passed, greeting everyone by name. "I'm glad to hear Betsy's on the road to recovery," he said to a Senator whose wife had just undergone a serious operation; he congratulated a member on a speech he'd made a few days before, and asked another how his son felt about his exams, saying nothing about the real reason they were all there—except when someone asked him, "Ah, Tony, who do you think will win?" He merely smiled and, projecting a confidence he didn't feel, replied, "Hard to say—but it's certainly going to be interesting, don't you think?"

A low buzz of conversation greeted Royn as he turned into the party room. Spring, sitting in one corner with other members of the Push, beckoned to him. Royn nodded back, but wandered in an apparently aimless circle around the room speaking briefly to everyone he passed. About a quarter of the members were already there and more were streaming in. Members were scattered in twos and threes, but identifiable knots gathered in each corner. Quigley sat in one, a few of his supporters grouped around him; the others were working the room in last-minute canvassing. Handfuls of Royn's, Cracken's, and Kydd's supporters occupied the other three corners while the majority were, like Quigley's and Royn himself, gauging the members' mood and chasing waverers—as they had all been doing for the past two days.

Of Bergstrom—the only candidate who had not organized a vigorous campaign—or his supporters, there was no sign.

"Where are those poll results?" Spring whispered as Royn sat down next to him.

"*Still* not ready. Mary will rush them over soon as they arrive."

"Anything preliminary we can use?"

"Kydd comes in third now—but it's just hearsay until we can show the *actual* numbers—the *proof.*"

"Damn," said Spring. As he spoke Kydd, chatting with Bergstrom, wheeled himself into the room a few minutes before the meeting was scheduled to begin; Cracken came in a moment later. "What have *they* been up to, do you think?"

"Nothing good for us," Royn grumbled.

At nine-thirty AM sharp, McKurn and a couple of other stragglers slipped through the door as Helen Arkness rapped her gavel. McKurn grinned at Kydd as he took a nearby seat; Kydd scowled back. "Doesn't look like you're getting any better, Randy," McKurn said.

"Piss off, Frankie."

McKurn laughed.

Helen Arkness frowned at McKurn and rapped her gavel again for silence. "I don't imagine I need to remind anyone why we're here. There are five candidates for the position of party leader. I'll ask each candidate to address us—but keep it brief, please, otherwise we'll be here all day. Then we'll go to the first round of voting, by secret ballot. The candidate with the lowest vote total will drop out, and we'll repeat the process until only the winner remains. Prime Minister, would you like to begin?"

"With your permission, madam chair, I will speak last," said Kydd.

"As is your privilege," said Helen Arkness. "So would—" Quigley's raised hand caught her attention. "Mr. Quigley?"

Familiar with Quigley's rants, few members bothered to listen—at first. But as he spoke he caught their attention and the hum of whispered exchanges died down. Instead of his usual pitch about subsidies, he talked about land and water conservation, suggesting programs so farmers could fight the current severe drought, improve the productivity of their land, and conserve water by, for example, installing drip irrigation to combat the drought "which could be financed by low-cost loans subsidized by a gradual increase in the price of water."

"What's he doing?" Spring whispered. "Increase the price of water? The farmers will go bananas."

"Not if they listen to the whole pitch," said Royn.

"Which most won't. But whatever he's up to, he's not making a *leadership* pitch."

"No—he must be angling for a ministry."

"Maybe that's what Cracken promised."

"Quite likely—how else could Quigley be bought?" said Royn. "It's so unusually rational for him, Paul probably even wrote it."

Victor Bergstrom awkwardly rose to his feet, thanked members "for the honor of being considered for this position," promised to "serve faithfully" if elected, and sat down again to a scattering of applause.

"What are they clapping for?" Spring chuckled. "He didn't say a damn thing."

With a questioning expression, Helen Arkness looked alternately at Royn and Cracken, and there was a moment of expectant silence as members tried to sense who would go next—but both Royn and Cracken sat solidly in place. "Shall I flip a coin?" Helen Arkness asked at length.

"As former Deputy Leader," Royn said, "I would like to exercise the option of speaking before our former Leader."

"So be it," Helen Arkness nodded. "Mr. Cracken."

Cracken's dark, deep-set eyes narrowed into slits as he scowled at Royn. Then he stood and walked slowly to stand in the space in front of the small podium, forcing his shoulders back to compensate for his slight stoop as his eyes travelled slowly from one face to another. "It seems obvious," he began, his gaze stopping with Kydd, "that the current occupant is no longer able to carry the heavy burden of the party leadership and the many trying and *tiring* responsibilities it entails. We must carefully consider what *kind* of leader we need and want now." He dipped his head as if agreeing with those several people who'd nodded theirs. "And here, ladies and gentlemen, you are faced with a fundamental choice between one candidate who has clearly demonstrated his ability to fight and win against all the odds, and another who had everything handed to him on a plate—since the day he was born as the youngest son, the *baby* of one of the country's richest families." Cracken smiled sourly as he turned towards Royn. "Everything, that is, except the ultimate prize he expected to be *given*.

"I would like to remind members that I was *not* born with a silver spoon in my mouth. My parents were poor. I went to a state school until, through my own efforts, I was lucky enough to win a scholarship to Melbourne Grammar. I come from the same side of the tracks as the people who tend to support the opposition party. I believe—and I have certainly demonstrated this in my own electorate, which I have turned from a marginal constituency into a fairly safe seat—that I can connect far more effectively with those voters we need to win away from the opposition than anyone else on the slate. I've done this the hard way, not by grinning on television but by going out and *listening* to people's concerns—and doing something about them. *Only* by bringing more and more Labor supporters into the Conservative fold can we continue to hold firm to the reins of government.

"Another quality I believe is essential for the party leader is his ability as a *manager*. Again, this is a talent I believe I have demonstrated, beyond a shadow of doubt, in successfully running the most difficult ministry of them all: the Treasury. I realize, of course, that the Treasurer is not always the most popular of ministers—often being seen as the one who shoots down everybody else's plans." Cracken shrugged. "It comes with the territory. If you were Treasurer—and wanted to be a *good* one—you'd do the same.

"But our string of budget surpluses—a unique achievement, I should point out, in today's world, for which we can *all* share the credit—have actually provided the soundest possible foundation for the realization of all our goals. Goals that have led to fourteen years of responsible government and can—but *only* with the right leadership—easily lead to fourteen more."

Cracken and Quigley supporters cheered and whistled while others applauded politely. Cracken bowed in appreciation and returned to his seat. As Helen Arkness turned towards Royn he stood in turn.

"I agree with much of what Paul has said," Royn began, and with a grin continued, "but not, of course, *everything*.

"There's no question that Paul is an *excellent* manager, and has done a superb job as Treasurer. He has proved that he's always conversant with and in control of the most minute detail of Treasury's Byzantine operations. Which is why, were you to see fit to elect me party leader, I intend to keep him there.

"Paul claims that he's the better manager—though not in so many words," Royn chuckled. "I agree. I know my limitations and I want to make it clear that I have no intention of micromanaging anything or any*one*. I intend to delegate authority within strict—but *broad*—limits to ministers, and let them get on with it. I'm sure that, in the spirit of Party Unity, I and other ministers will be able to depend on Paul's demonstrated management expertise in these areas whenever necessary.

"But, unlike Paul, I believe that the party leader has a role which is *far* more important. He must inspire others—*especially*, of course, the *voters*—with a vision of where the country should and could be going. And, as you know, my prime objectives are our *security* as a nation and administration at home that is honest and free of corruption at *all* levels of government. A government the people can *trust*.

"*That*, as we're all too aware, is the main issue on the public's mind.

"Finally, I would like to remind all members that various poll results that you have all seen show, time and again, that with Paul as leader we'd have *fewer* seats come the next election; whereas, should you decide to select me, we can all look forward to *increased* majorities. While that, of course, should not be your only consideration, it's clearly a crucial one—not only for those newer members who will be standing for reelection for the first time, but for all of us who wish to remain on the government benches when, after the many years we've been in office, voters could easily be misled into thinking it's time for a change.

"It *isn't*. And I, for one, see no limits on the length of time our great party can continue to occupy the government benches. I hope you will all join me in achieving that goal."

As Royn sank back to his seat the applause was enthusiastic. "You've got the edge—so far," Spring whispered.

"We'll see," said Royn noncommittally.

"Prime Minister?" Helen Arkness said.

"Thank you, Helen," Kydd said gravely. Thrusting with his arms on side of the wheelchair, he levered himself to his feet.

"Let me help you, Randy," McKurn chuckled, making a move to support him. "Your doctors said to take it easy, remember?"

Kydd scowled at McKurn but said nothing. Taking a walking stick from the back of the wheelchair, he puffed and shuffled slowly towards the podium. After a couple of deep, wheezing breaths he smiled. "As you can see, I'm recovering. Slowly, true— but inevitably. Reports of my demise are decidedly premature. I want to thank you all for your many expressions of concern. I appreciate them, but they've been somewhat overdone."

Kydd grinned as he spoke, the color back in his face from his exertion. There was more energy in his voice which now carried easily, though didn't boom, across the room. But the way his jowls sagged loosely, like his clothes, gave him a gaunt appearance. He paused, whether for effect or breathing space his audience couldn't tell.

"As Paul so eloquently put it, you have an important choice. But Paul made a serious error. He spoke as if there were only *two* candidates before you today. I find it puzzling, not to mention disturbing, that our *Treasurer* of all people, is unable to count to three, let alone five.

"Who, I ask you, has led this party to victory for five elections in a row? Who, tell me, has achieved what no other Prime Minister in the history of our federation has achieved: a massive, record-breaking majority in the *fifth* of these elections? Who among us has the most experience in *successfully* wooing the voters? Demoralizing and defeating Labor? *Fourteen* years of managing our complex governmental system—successfully?

"At a time like the present, when we are possibly approaching a crisis of unknowable proportions—" Kydd paused, his glance resting on McKurn for long enough for no further words to be necessary "—to replace the firm hand of experience and demonstrated success with an unproven novice would be of the utmost foolishness, and can, I must warn you, quite easily lead to unmitigated disaster.

"Ladies and gentlemen, the future of our great party rests in your hands. I'm sure I can depend on you to treat this burden of trust with wisdom, not folly."

Kydd gazed solemnly into the silence that followed as if to underline the seriousness of his words. There was a mere scattering of applause and the room erupted into a hubbub of worried conversations. "Disaster? What's he talking about?" "McKurn." "All these revelations." "Who knows what McKurn's really up to?" "Or who else is involved." "Bit enigmatic, don't you think?" "McKurn has to go before he destroys us all." "You're right about that."

Kydd hobbled back to his wheelchair and Helen Arkness rapped her gavel. "Voting will now begin." Three members appointed as tellers placed a ballot box and a pile of voting papers on a small table in the center of the room. Members crowded around to collect their ballot; as each Member or Senator pushed his or her vote through the slot in the top of the ballot box, a name was crossed off the list. A hush descended over the room as, last of all, Helen Arkness stepped down from the podium to put her vote in the box.

One of the three tellers picked up the box and, accompanied by the other two, carried it to a corner of the room where the ballots were laid out on a table. Five other members—a representative of each candidate—stood in a half circle behind the tellers as they separated the votes into five piles. Everyone craned to see if the piles gave a clue to whether there was a dominant candidate—but even close up, the piles looked a fairly similar height. The tellers counted and tabulated the votes, and repeated the process at the request of one of the candidates' representatives. Finally, one teller took the tabulation over to Helen Arkness. As the five representatives turned to face the room, their equally wooden, sour expressions gave no clue to the result.

"Randolph Kydd, thirty-five votes," Helen Arkness read. "Anthony Royn, thirty-two votes. Paul Cracken, twenty-eight. Victor Bergstrom, fifteen, and Jack Quigley, thirteen." She looked at the candidates' representatives. "Any objections?" she asked. When none were forthcoming, she said, "The candidate with the lowest number of votes, Mr. Quigley, is therefore eliminated. Shall we move on to the second round of voting in, say, thirty minutes?"

"Thirty-two votes," said Spring. "We got most of the marginals, I would think. And it looks like a bunch of the undecideds have gone for Victor."

"Still sitting on the fence," Royn replied as Kydd said, "I move that we vote now," several of his supporters shouting "Second!"

"What do you think he's doing?" Royn asked Spring.

"Stampeding Quigley's supporters . . . I think."

"Good idea, even if that's not his motive," said Royn, and raising his voice so it boomed across the room said, "I move that the motion be put." "Second!" Spring yelled immediately.

Kydd gave Royn a puzzled, calculating look, and turned his head away the moment Royn noticed.

The "Ayes" were overwhelming, so the tellers brought out the ballot box again, along with another set of preprinted ballots, crossing off Quigley's name as they handed out each one. The same voting procedure was repeated and about ten minutes later Helen Arkness read out a second tally. Bergstrom, with eighteen votes, was the one to trail this time. But Cracken moved into the lead with thirty-seven votes. Royn picked up just one vote to thirty-three and Kydd's total was unchanged at thirty-five.

"Cracken," Spring hissed. "How can *he* be in front?"

Royn shrugged. "He picked up most of Quigley's votes."

"I thought Quigley could deliver his whole bloc."

"Maybe he did," Royn said, "and a few others switched theirs. We probably got that Quigley supporter in a marginal seat. But Kydd didn't pick a up a *thing*."

"He's got his base—but that's all."

"He should get a few of Victor's votes."

"Probably," Royn said as he sent Mary yet another text. "Now it's down to three, it's time to bring out the big guns—but we don't have any!" As if in response, his phone vibrated. "*Still* not here," he cursed. "No sign of Alison either."

"Not having that poll could kill us," Spring moaned. "What are we going to *do?*"

Royn shrugged weakly and stared blankly at the floor. "I don't know," he said.

Bergstrom caught Helen Arkness' eye and rose uncertainly to his feet, looking everywhere except at Kydd. "Well, I . . . ah . . . must say," he said as though tiptoeing through a minefield, "that I truly appreciate the surprising level of support you chose to give me. I'm most grateful. As you can probably guess, my preference is for the steady hand of experience to remain at the tiller." Kydd smiled at Bergstrom's words. "But should the party . . . I mean, ah, you . . . decide that it's time for a younger man to take the helm—" his gaze flicked towards Cracken and seemed to flick away just as quickly, resting, Royn thought, for an instant longer on him "—then you can be assured of my unwavering support."

Kydd glared at Bergstrom, who looked away in embarrassment.

"Poor Victor," Royn chuckled. "Kydd thought he had a deal, but Victor's having fifty cents each way."

Helen Arkness rapped her gavel. "We'll take a thirty minute break before voting on the third round."

As a good third of the members stood and began heading for the door there were shouts of "No." "Let's vote now." followed by "Don't be ridiculous." "We need a break."

Quigley jumped up and moved that the vote should be taken immediately. Shouts of "Second!" were drowned out by "No way!"

Frowning, Royn leant towards Spring and whispered conspiratorially, "I'm going to lose. I can feel it."

"Why the hell do you think *that?*" Spring growled.

"Where's our ammunition?" Royn asked as he pulled out his mobile phone and sent a message: Paul. A quick word, whispering, "If we vote now, I'm history. Even if we get those poll results in time *and* I'm still in the race after the next round, whoever drops out—Kydd or Cracken—will support the *other*. Not me."

"Yeah," Spring conceded reluctantly. "Between them—"

"—they've got the numbers."

From across the room Cracken studied Royn suspiciously. A moment later, a message appeared on Royn's phone: Why should I talk to YOU?

It's in your interest, I guarantee it.

"Order! Order" Helen Arkness called. "There's a motion before the floor."

One of the members near the door yelled, "Nature calls—so I move the motion be put."

Okay, I'll listen—but that's all I'll promise to do.

Fair enough. Meet me in the men's room—if you help kill the motion.

Across the room, Cracken nodded slowly, and whispered something to his supporters. Royn could see whatever he had said being passed like a wave from one person to another.

"Those in favor of the motion?" Helen Arkness asked.

A clear majority sat sullenly silent as Quigley and his supporters and a handful of others yelled "Aye."

"Those against?"

The volume of the "Noes" was overwhelming.

"The motion fails," Helen Arkness ruled. "Thirty minutes."

*****

"THANK GOD YOU'RE HERE," Mary said as Alison trudged into the office—after a stop in the bathroom to redo her face. But Mary, now peering at her, wasn't fooled. "You don't look at all well—are you sure you should be out of bed?"

"Thanks, Mary, but I'll be okay," Alison smiled sourly. "For a while, anyway."

"The Minister's been throwing a fit about those poll results—they're still not *here*."

"*What?*"

"Doug and I have been calling and calling—but it seems like half the people aren't there today or something."

"I'll call the boss right now." A flood of adrenalin drowned Alison's inner turmoil, giving her the sense she'd just stepped out of a cold shower.

"We haven't been able to find him," Mary wailed.

"I'll get him," Alison said angrily. "I've got all his private numbers."

"If you hadn't turned off your phone," said Mary accusingly, "this wouldn't have happened."

Alison shrugged. "Never mind that now," she said, digging out her cellphone and switching it on. It beeped several times, signalling several text messages and even more missed calls. Alison ignored them. In her office, all but throwing herself into her chair, she punched in a number. "Where are our results? I've got more problems right now than I can shake a stick at so I don't really give a damn about *yours*. I need those results *now*. And I mean *now*, not in five minutes. . . . Then just tell someone to email me the raw data *immediately*, for heaven's sake. Assuming you want to get paid. . . . Damn right I wouldn't pay you. . . . I'm not interested in your excuses. Stop wasting my time."

By the time her computer warmed up, the data was there. She scanned it quickly. She could spend an hour or so getting all the numbers accurate to the last decimal point, but the results were sufficiently obvious. She typed furiously for a few minutes, checked what she'd written, and pressed PRINT. Stepping into the doorway of her office she called to Mary, "It's coming off now. A hundred and twenty-three copies. Can you give them to the Minster?"

"He's still at the meeting," said Mary. "He wants you over there."

"There's something I have to do first," Alison said. "Tell him I'll be there in five minutes."

"Sure." Mary moved to stand by the printer spewing out copies. "It's down to three now. Quigley and Bergstrom dropped out. . . ."

"Later," Alison said vaguely with a sudden listlessness in her voice, and closed her office door.

Slumped in her chair, drained by her unexpected rush of energy, she stared at the phone, Mary's bewildered face was still visible on the other side of the glass wall.

She thought of express trains.

I must have left my locomotive behind at the station.

The churning in her stomach was now no longer masked, and her body trembled slightly in response. She thought of taking something to settle it—but she knew that pills had no cure what she was feeling.

There was only one cure: *revenge.*

. . . and when you have your revenge, Derek's question from long ago rang in her mind, *then what?*

"I don't know, Derek," she said aloud, speaking as if Olsson were sitting on the other side of the desk. "I don't know—but I will *have* it, just the same."

For an instant she felt overwhelmed by his presence, knowing at the same moment she was desperate for his compassion and understanding . . . and the warmth of his arms. *He offered his help,* she remembered, *several times. . . . I could send him an email.*

She turned towards her laptop.

Later, she decided. *Maybe.*

With a sigh she picked up the phone and dialled a number. "Hi, Karla, it's Alison." *Karla would listen,* she thought. "I . . . " *Not now.* "I want to send you a whole bunch of stuff about McKurn—if you're interested . . . ?" *But—should I really blame McKurn? Or myself?*

"Dirt?" Karla asked.

"Right."

"I'm *very* interested."

"I thought you might be," Alison said, her face a twisted grin. "There's just one condition: completely off the record."

"Any way you like!" Karla's voice was exuberant. "Will you be in Sydney again this weekend?"

"I'm not sure. But if I am, I'll call you."

"I'd like that," said Karla.

"So would I," Alison found herself saying.

The wheels are in motion, Alison thought as she put down the phone, *come what may. . . .* "Okay," she said, "let's see what he wants."

On an impulse she walked into Royn's office and stood at the window, warmed by the sun streaming over the prime minister's courtyard below.

As Chief Political Advisor to the *Prime Minister,* she'd have the second-largest office all to herself. No longer cooped up in a cubbyhole, she'd see trees and grass and flowers and be warmed by sunshine on a cold wintry day. *Fourteen years . . . more . . . and I'm nearly there,* she thought. *Maybe just half-an-hour away. . . .*

Or if those poll results are too late, maybe not.

She turned away sadly, aware of only the weight in her stomach. And her indecision.

Trudging along the corridor she crossed paths with Mary. "I gave the printouts to Bruce," she said.

"Not the Minister?" Alison asked.

Mary shook her head. "They were having a break and he'd gone off somewhere with Cracken."

"With *Cracken?* What on earth *for?*"

Mary shrugged. "Ours not to reason why . . . " she smiled.

"Oh, my God." Alison accelerated her pace. She felt the desire to run, but could not find the energy. When she arrived the doors of the meeting room were closing.

Alison waited.

She was not alone.

A handful of other political staff members stood silently in the corridor, trying to hear what was going on behind the closed doors. But the doors were solid and joined together seamlessly. In the corridor, even the occasional yell became an indiscernible whisper, loud applause a distant thunder. They gave up and speculated endlessly about what each sound might mean. All they knew was that five candidates had shrunk to three, that the poll results overwhelmingly favored Royn, and that Royn and Cracken had disappeared together . . . and no one knew why.

Alison listened blankly but said nothing, resting against the wall. As the others gave up trying draw her into their conversation her mind started wandering and she was overcome with the feeling that Royn was going to *lose.* She couldn't shake it, but instead of feeling depressed she felt strangely relieved. *It would be all over. All for nothing. . . . What would I do then?*

She shrugged, surprised not only that she didn't care, but that in a way she looked forward to it.

The crowd by the door had grown: every minute or two another staff member or journalist turned up, waiting for the news. And Melanie. "Any idea what's happening in there?" she asked.

Alison shook her head without moving from the wall. "We'll know very soon," she said listlessly.

Melanie looked at her strangely, but in a moment she knew everything everybody else knew, plus half-a-dozen competing theories about what the result would be.

The sound of sustained applause seeped through the doors and brought a sudden silence in the corridor. A couple of people with their ears to the crack where the two swinging doors joined together shook their heads. "Couldn't make out a thing," one said.

"That must be it, then," somebody said. Slowly, a space appeared in front of the doors as the crowd moved back waiting for the doors to open.

"God. I can hardly breathe," Melanie said, standing tensely, the fingers of one hand nervously fidgeting with the folds of her skirt.

Nothing happened.

"If that was the leader, there's still the deputy to be elected," someone said.

"Not much longer then," Alison said.

"I hope so," Melanie replied, her voice strangely squeaky. "I don't know if I can take this waiting for another minute."

*****

WHEN THE LAST MEMBER had returned from the break and the doors were closed, Helen Arkness rapped her gavel. "Time for the third round of voting." The ballot box and ballot papers were already in place.

Cracken stood and said, "Madam Chair?"

"Yes, Mr. Cracken?"

"I have an announcement to make if I may."

Helen Arkness nodded. "Go ahead."

Cracken turned towards the center of the room. "I withdraw my nomination and urge all my supporters to vote for Anthony Royn. I would like to add that given the results of the poll we have just received, the Prime Minister should do the same and make the result unanimous."

A copy of the poll rested on Kydd's lap. He screwed it into a ball and threw it in Cracken's direction. "That, Paul, is my answer. In any case, what evidence do I have that this so-called poll is objective and believable?"

"In that case," said Helen Arkness, "there'll be just two candidates—"

"Madam Chair, one moment please." Victor Bergstrom had gotten up from his seat and was weaving his way through the other members, zigzagging towards Kydd.

"Yes, Mr. Bergstrom?" she asked.

Bergstrom knelt down by Kydd without answering and began talking in a low whisper. Other conversations in the room died away as everyone tried to make out what Bergstrom was saying. All they could hear was the occasional angry word from Kydd—"No!" "Never." "Don't be ridiculous." "I'll do nothing of the kind!"

Bergstrom whispered more feverishly, and Kydd's face turned from pink to red. Eventually, his teeth grinding, he gave a minimal nod.

Bergstrom stood up. "Madam Chair, the Prime Minister withdraws his candidacy," he announced.

Helen Arkness looked at Kydd. "Is that correct, Prime Minister?"

Kydd looked at Helen Arkness as if she was the cause of all his problems, but after a moment he gave the barest of nods.

"Thank you, Prime Minister," said Helen Arkness. "In that case, I declare Anthony Royn elected to the position of Leader of the Conservative Party. Ladies and gentlemen, shall we make it unanimous?"

Kydd shook his head violently, leaving no one in any doubt to his opinion. Bruce Spring, followed by most of Royn's supporters, jumped up and cheered to the accompaniment of applause thundering around the room. More than one member looked at Kydd with disgust or outright hostility.

Royn sat, grinning happily at Kydd's reaction to his win. "Seems I have the killer instinct after all . . . Randy," he muttered to himself, his voice inaudible against the din of applause. And his father's voice came to him, "Here's your opportunity to show everyone what you're *really* made of." His father and Melanie would be ecstatic at his victory. "And me?" All he could think about was the responsibility that now lay oppressively on his shoulders . . . of the hundreds of thousands of federal employees and party members who now depended on *him* . . . that everyone would pass the buck to *him* . . . there was nowhere else for it to go. . . .

As the clamor died, Helen Arkness called, "The meeting is now open for nominations for the post of Deputy Leader."

Remembering Vanessa's words with wry amusement, Royn "switched on his charm" and rose, majestically, like King Lear in a suit. "I nominate Paul Cracken."

Amid shouts of "Second!" Helen Arkness asked, "Do you accept the nomination?" When Cracken nodded, she continued, "Are there any other nominations?"

Kydd scowled at Royn and Cracken. "I nominate Stanley Chow," he said.

"Mr. Chow," Helen Arkness asked, "do you accept the nomination?"

"I appreciate the Prime Minister's confidence," Chow said with a smile at Kydd, "but I feel that, at this moment, I must sadly decline the nomination and, in the interests of party unity, support Paul Cracken."

"Party unity," Spring chuckled. "That means he knows he'd lose."

"Any other nominations?" Helen Arkness asked. When her question was met with silence she said, "I declare Mr. Cracken elected unopposed."

In their separate corners, well-wishers thronged around Royn and Cracken, shaking hands, slapping them and each other on their backs, and wishing them luck. Slowly, the two groups merged into one as Royn and Cracken moved towards the center of the room, meeting near Kydd's wheelchair which was trapped in the crowd. McKurn stood to his full height, towering over everyone else. "Congratulations, Paul," he said pumping Cracken's hand. "Nice moves, Tony," he added more coolly, dipping his chin in acknowledgement. Turning to Kydd he said, "Well, Randy, don't you think you should congratulate your successor?"

Kydd glowered at McKurn, Royn, Cracken—and everyone else in sight. He spun his wheelchair around and, giving the wheels a shove, pushed his way through the swarm of members, heedless of the toes he ran over or the knees he grazed.

"I guess Randy's not a happy man today," McKurn chuckled.

"So it would seem," said Cracken.

"Quite," Royn nodded. "Well, Paul, we should give a press conference, don't you think? How about on the steps of Parliament House?"

*****

THE DOORS TO THE meeting room opened and Randolph Kydd came barrelling out into the corridor on his wheelchair nearly knocking Melanie over.

Melanie jumped back in surprise. "Prime Minister!"

Kydd's hooded eyes and lips, pressed into an icy frown, exaggerated his shrunken frame, his posture becoming reminiscent of a troll from some nightmarish fairytale. He ignored the many questions from journalists and others alike, and people squeezed back to let him through when he showed no sign of slowing down. A voice carried above the hubbub, "Poor loser."

Alison looked up as she heard the familiar tone to see Robin Cartwright smiling at her. "You get around," she said.

"Well, you know us journalists," he grinned. "Whenever there's a fire, we turn up to fan the flames."

Alison smiled despite herself. "And on a slow news day you light them, I suppose."

Cartwright just laughed.

Members began to leak out of the room into the crowd. One said to Melanie, "Congratulations, Mrs. Prime Minister."

"You mean—?"

"That's right. Your husband is now the party leader."

Melanie shrieked and jumped with excitement, her arms held in a high "V." "That's amazing. That's *fantastic.*"

She was suddenly blinded by the flashlights of half-a-dozen cameras: she'd forgotten about the journalists and sobered immediately. But she could not restrain her wide grin so she turned and tried to make her way into the meeting room against the growing stream of members and Senators coming out. One of them was McKurn who, as always, looked at her appreciatively as he passed.

Alison saw him and smiled. "Good morning, Senator," she said, forcing gaiety into her voice. "Feeling better today, I trust?"

McKurn's look was acid, but then he leered and ogled her openly. "What a pleasant surprise," he said, chuckling.

"Really? I can't imagine why," Alison said sourly.

McKurn leaned towards here and, smirking, said quietly, "Because *now,* when I see you, my dear, I don't have to *imagine* a thing."

Alison flushed and grabbed his good arm hard with one hand, twisting it so McKurn winced. "I'd be careful what you say if I were you."

"And if I were *you*," McKurn snarled, "I wouldn't go out alone at night."

"I'll just have to finish what I started then, won't I," Alison hissed, nudging him so that he stumbled into the person behind him.

McKurn glared at her with undisguised hatred as he turned away. Alison realized she was shaking, as if Mephistopheles had just caressed her soul. *Baiting him was a mistake,* she thought, and thinking of concrete boots, *but thanks for the reminder.*

"What was that all about?"

Alison turned to see Robin Cartwright looking at her with concern—and interest. She had the impression his nose was twitching. *He smells a story.*

"What's going on?" he said. Peering at her, he added, "You look like death warmed up."

She breathed deeply and slowly felt her trembling subside. "Really?" she said, trying to smile as if it was a joke and failing.

Cartwright, she realized, was still studying her intently. "Hell hath no fury—" he began.

"—like a Senator scorned," Alison said.

"I see," said Cartwright; despite his words, his expression was just as puzzled as it had been before.

"Do you?" said Alison, now feeling more in control of herself. "I doubt that very much."

"Why don't you enlighten me, then?" Cartwright asked.

"Aren't you here to cover the spill?"

Cartwright shrugged. "Me—and dozens of others. I'd rather go where no journalist has gone before."

"Try McKurn, then," Alison laughed, surprised to realize that she no longer needed the wall for support. "Good luck." She left him to follow Melanie into the meeting room.

"If you ever change your mind," Cartwright called after her, "you know where to find me."

Alison smiled back at Cartwright as she went through the doors. Her smile faded as she saw Cracken and Royn, his arm around Melanie, walking slowly towards her, still surrounded by a dozen or so members.

"Alison," Royn grinned excitedly as he saw her. "We won!"

"That's great," Alison said, looking at Royn quizzically. "But—*how?*" Then she realized that although he was pleased with himself, he was acting, wearing his political glad-handling, baby-kissing *persona.* She'd worked for him so long she'd learnt to read him . . . no, not like a book, but like the script of a play, complete with stage directions. Melanie was genuinely excited, like a little girl who'd just gotten everything she ever wanted; peering behind Royn's mask, Alison could see he was troubled . . . burdened. *That makes two of us,* she thought, *but why* him?

The other, excited people in the room seemed to disappear as Royn's mask slipped and Alison felt she was looking at a little boy elated with the risk he'd just taken, scared at his own success—and simultaneously aware of her own reaction to his victory. The sense of connection, like a brief handshake, disappeared as quickly as it had come.

"Those results arrived too late, so. . . ." Royn said, his voice trailing off as he remembered that he and Alison were not alone. "Look, Alison, Paul and I have to go and talk to the press." Royn dropped his voice to a whisper. "And I can't tell you here." He turned to Bruce Spring standing behind him. "Bruce, could you bring Alison up to date for me."

"My pleasure," Spring said.

"I'll see you in the office in half an hour or so." With a sigh, he took Cracken by the elbow and said, "Let's go, Paul."

Alison felt doubt gnawing at her stomach. "What's he *done?*" she demanded of Spring.

"Not here," said Spring quietly. "Somewhere private."

"Why? What's wrong with right here and how?"

Spring had started to step away; when Alison stood her ground he came back and whispered, "It's confidential, for heaven's sake Alison. *That's* why."

"Okay," she said guardedly. "But I don't think I'm going to like it."

Spring shrugged. "We won. What else matters? It looked like we were going to *lose* without those poll results—which we'd have had if *you'd* been here, according to Tony," he added with an accusing tone.

"So it's *my* fault, is it?" Alison snapped.

Spring's cheeks flushed. "Well. . . ."

"I can't help it if I'm not feeling well today. In fact, I should still be in bed."

Spring shrugged. "We had to do *something.* We had no choice. Now, if you want to know what happened, follow me."

Alison followed Spring out of the room, the last to leave. The crowd of members, journalists, and onlookers had disappeared. Alison felt relieved when Cartwright was nowhere to be seen. When they reached an empty corridor Spring stopped and said, "He did a deal."

"He did what?"

"He did a deal with Cracken," Spring said, smiling happily. "Tony was sure Cracken would support Kydd against us. But if Kydd won that would merely be delaying the inevitable. Next time, it would be just the two of them, and Tony would beat the pants off him. Cracken knew it.

"And imagine what could happen if we went into an election with Kydd in a wheelchair, still half-paralyzed. We could even lose. Cracken might be tossed out of his own seat—it's better than a marginal, but not *that* much better.

"So he offered Cracken a deal: back Tony against Kydd, and Tony would support him for the Deputy Leadership—and step down two years after the next election. Based on that poll of yours, we'll be reelected with an even *bigger* majority than Kydd's—and Cracken would have a full year as prime minister to consolidate *his* leadership to face the electorate in his own right."

Alison stared at Spring, speechless. *After fourteen years—and McKurn—just two years? That's all I'll have . . . ?* But the words wouldn't come.

"What's the problem?" Spring asked. "Tony said it's only what he and Melanie had already agreed."

"I . . . guess," Alison said. Her eyes fell to the floor and her shoulders slumped. *Except . . . after two years in the Prime Minister's Lodge, Melanie would change her mind. Cracken won't change his.*

"Alison?" Spring said after a moment.

Alison looked up blankly until she remembered Spring was still there. "Sorry. Thanks, Bruce." She turned her back on him and trudged slowly along the corridor back to her office.

Puzzled, and feeling slightly hurt, Spring watched her until she stepped out of sight. He shrugged. "Must be that time of the month," he muttered.

*****

What now? Alison asked herself as she neared the Deputy Prime Minister's office. It would be a busy afternoon, planning the move into Royn's new role—and new offices. There'd be staff decisions to be made—*Who should we keep from Kydd's staff? If anyone?* Then the Cabinet—*Move ministers around—or not?* And hundreds of other things.

By the time Alison opened the door she was already feeling exhausted.

The noise was deafening.

Several bottles of champagne had been opened; Mary and Doug Selkirk were dancing to the music from a golden oldies station, holding glasses brimming with champagne above their heads while trying to keep them from spilling. A circle of people around them cheered them on—and laughed when Doug's glass was the first to spill. He had to drink the rest of his and Mary's glass as well.

"Alison's here." Somebody put a glass of champagne in her hand to thrilled shouts of "We won! We won!"

Alison smiled numbly, their exhilaration making her even more aware of the weight in her stomach. She put the champagne down. "I'm sorry," she said, "but I'm wiped out."

But only Mary seemed to have heard her. "You can take it easy now," she said.

If only that were true, Alison mused as she nodded in acknowledgement.

Get out of here. . . . she thought as she closed the door to her office. She picked up her handbag and laptop and remembered her promise to Karla. *I won't send it, I'll take it to Sydney.*

She gathered her papers, and took Sidney Royn's thick report from the safe. At the prospect of going to Sydney for the weekend, she suddenly felt a little more cheerful. Not because she would see Karla, though that would be nice. Contrary to her thought in the church earlier, she *did* have somewhere to go.

I want to go home.

A sudden "Hip, hip, hooray" broke into her thoughts. She looked up to see Royn and Melanie standing in the doorway, their faces beaming as if in reflection of the staff's appreciation. She saw Royn flash a look of concern at her, and he began to make his way towards her.

"You look like you're leaving," he said as he came into her office, closing the door behind him.

Alison nodded. "I'm sorry, Minister, but I *have* to rest up, maybe for the rest of the weekend."

"But—"

"I know," Alison sighed. "There's so much to do."

"Yes. . . ." Whatever other words were on Royn's lips died as only now, without the distraction of other people, he took in the implications of Alison's pale face. "You're right," he said. "I just hope you're better by Monday."

"So do I Minister," Alison said without conviction. "So do I."

46 Gone Fishing

"G'day, Rog. Nice boat."

The man on the cruiser, a deep-sea fishing tackle fixed behind the cockpit, was getting ready to cast off from the pier at the Brooklyn Marina. In his seventies, he was lean and fit, his skin bronzed and leathery. His hair was white from age—or bleached from too much sun. He looked up startled at the two men in suits standing on the pier.

"Who the hell are you, and what do you want?"

"Surely you haven't forgotten me completely, Rog?" said the heavily built Caucasian who stepped on board across the narrow gangplank.

"Rudi Durant, I do declare." His eyes squinted suspiciously. "I don't remember inviting you *or* your mate on board."

"Shall I get a warrant? I'd be really put out if I had to do that." Durant looked over the cruiser with interest. "I bet this cost a pretty penny, eh Rog? But then, it goes with your house, which cost a helluva lot more."

Rudi Durant and Simon Lee had laboriously interviewed the bed-ridden Leon Price during the week—who confirmed his allegations in their presence and on tape. One of the people he'd named was Roger Kelly, a former police inspector, which brought them to Brooklyn, a small, sleepy, but exclusive village near the mouth of the Hawkesbury River thirty-odd kilometers north of Sydney. Kelly's house sat on a bluff looking over both the ocean and the estuary; Mrs. Kelly told them where to find him—"if he hasn't already gone out to sea."

Roger Kelly dropped the rope he was holding and stared, speechless, at Durant. He sat down heavily on the pilot's seat and said, "I take it you're not interested in going fishing then."

Kelly paled at Durant's smile. "I *am* fishing, Rog."

"Where's your bait?"

"You don't need bait, Rog," Durant chuckled, "when you've got a good, strong hook." He sat on the padded bench at the rear of the cockpit and stretched out languorously while Simon Lee leant against the railing and admired the view. "You know, Rog, I'm curious. You were an inspector when you retired what—getting on for twenty years ago. You and I both know what inspectors' salaries were back then. We both know there's no way you could have bought this boat *or* your house on what an inspector earns."

Kelly shrugged. "I had a good day at the races."

"Just one?" said Durant, raising an eyebrow. "Quite a few, I'd say. In that case, just show me your TAB slips and I'll go away."

"That was *years* ago," Kelly protested. "I've no idea where they are now."

"Not to worry," said Durant. "Easy enough to get the records from the TAB—" Seeing Kelly frown, he stopped. "Or did your winnings came from an SP bookie? In which case you're in deep doo-doo."

"All right," said Kelly. "Tell me what you want to know and—"

"Rog!" Durant raised his hand. "You know I'm not a man who's open to a deal. All I can promise is that if you sing, I'm sure the judge will take that into account."

"Not much of a promise," Kelly growled.

"Better than nothing." Durant said.

"The statute of limitations—"

"Doesn't apply to bent coppers."

Kelly looked at Durant suspiciously. "I'm not sure I want to take legal advice from you," he said.

Durant shrugged. "That's your right."

"In fact, I don't think I'll say another word till I've spoken to my lawyer."

"That's your right, too. Why don't you give him a call now?"

"*Now?* It's Saturday morning."

"So?" Durant leaned forward. "In any case, Rog, I'm not going to arrest you today. In fact, I'm not even going to ask you to come down to the station to answer questions. This is more of a courtesy call on an old colleague just to let you know we'll be investigating your finances, among other things. You have been named as a bagman for the Premier's office back in the sixties and seventies, collecting money from gangsters and other bent coppers and passing it on to Frank McKurn and Leon Price."

"Named? By *who?*" Kelly demanded.

"All in good time, Rog," Durant said soothingly. "Let me put it this way. Since I'm not making an official call right now, anything you tell me will be off the record. In any case, you know the rules—unless it's all taped, videoed, sealed, and made in the presence of your lawyer, it's inadmissible in court."

"Get to the point," Kelly said gruffly.

"It's McKurn and Price we're really after, not you. You're just a sideshow. Just tell me what you know about them—"

"No way," said Kelly, shaking his head. "I couldn't do that."

Kelly's eyes darted from Durant to Lee and back. A faint tremor ran through his body. Durant tensed, sensing Kelly's fear. Gauging from long experience that Kelly was about to run rather than break, he leant back and sighed. "Oh well," he said, looking at Kelly with pity on his face, "you could have been a great help." He stood up, saying, "Let's go Simon," as he took a couple of steps towards the gangplank. "Of course," he said as if in an afterthought, "you could always do a deal with the Attorney-General in return for immunity, and spill the beans. I could help you arrange that if you like."

"Not a chance."

"Pity," said Durant taking another step away, "for you. Oh—just between you and me, how much *did* this boat set you back?"

"None of your business."

"But Rog, it's very much my business. Not to worry. Easy enough to find out . . . as you very well know." Durant smiled. "Have a nice day, Rog—and I trust you don't have any plans to leave town."

WHAT DID YOU MAKE of that?" Durant asked Lee as they got back in their car.

"He's scared shitless."

"That's right."

"But—of *who?* Not *you.*"

"No," said Durant as he swung the car up the hill in the direction of Kelly's house.

"If I didn't know you so well," Lee grinned as he turned to look at Durant, "I'd say you've shown your cards without getting anything in return."

Durant laughed. "What *did* we get in return?"

"Nothing to take to court," Lee said thoughtfully. "But we now *know* Price was telling the truth."

"Exactly," said Durant. "There are lots of other names on the list. And sometimes, it doesn't hurt to set a cat among the pigeons."

"I hope you're right."

"So do I," Durant chuckled as he stopped the car. "Grab the binoculars in the glove box."

"Okay," said Lee. "But *why?*"

"I bet he's going to make a phone call. Jump out here, Simon, and watch what he does for the next twenty minutes or so."

When Durant returned Lee's first words were, "You were right. Two calls, in fact. Doesn't look like he's going fishing now. Pity we don't know who he called."

"We'll be able to find out easily enough," Durant replied, "once this investigation becomes official."

*****

"WHAT THE HELL HAS happened to *you?*"

Alison felt as though her head were being wrenched up by the sharp, rasping sound of Karla's voice; Karla stood, frozen, in the doorway of the coffee shop; her searching eyes locked on Alison's face.

That's the same look Mum gave last night, Alison thought. But Maggie McGuire had silently hugged her daughter—if extra-hard and extra-long—while Karla's words seemed to still linger, echoing, in the air.

Alison smiled wanly as Karla sat down. "I'm just not feeling very well today," she whispered hoarsely. "That's all."

Karla gazed intently at Alison in obvious disbelief, as if she might be able to answer to her question by looking inside her.

Why do I feel like she's trying to trap me? Alison asked herself. Frowning as if to release herself from Karla's gaze, she took two thick ring binders from her shoulder bag and pushed them across the small table, saying, "That's a copy of an investigation carried out while *Sidney* Royn was Attorney-General."

Slowly, with apparent reluctance, Karla turned to look at them. "The one Nash claimed had McKurn as a hidden agenda?" she asked.

"The very same," Alison said, forcing a smile.

"Kydd denied it in question time?"

"Yes," said Alison, "but he lied."

"Why am I not surprised?" Karla laughed. "And you've got more?"

"*Lots* more. . . ." Her voice trailed off as she became aware of other customers' eyes watching them. Mostly male eyes, but she felt their ears were also straining to hear their conversation. "I feel uncomfortable talking about Mc—about this here," she said, her voice low. "It's too . . . public."

Karla glanced around and laughed. "Don't you feel sorry for all those poor pubescent *boys*," she said, her gravelly voice now overwhelming the soft, background music, "who've got nothing better to do than gawp at a couple of pretty girls?"

Alison giggled as she saw several males faces turn red, their eyes suddenly finding the menu or the cars outside of intense interest. "You're incorrigible."

"I couldn't resist," Karla chuckled. "At least I've livened you up a bit. How about coming to my place, then?" she asked. "It's near and *very* private."

Why should I feel so apprehensive? Alison wondered. *But where else can we go?* "Okay."

Karla's apartment was on the fifth floor of a pre-war building near the end of Glebe Point Road. "No lift," Karla commented as they took the stairs. "I've been here since I was a student, when it was all I could afford."

"Very cozy," Alison said, as Karla ushered her inside.

"You mean tiny," Karla chuckled, "as in cramped?"

"Well, true, I suppose. But I like it. Somebody really *lives* here. It's your *home*. And the way you've decorated it, it even *looks* like you."

Colorful posters, pictures, and fabrics covered those walls of the studio apartment that were not lined with books; flowery curtains were drawn across the single, wide window. A vase of flowers stood on top of the computer table. A leafy pot plant sat on the small dining table, with room for just two chairs, which looked like it was mostly used as a desk. A single, large, comfortable armchair took up most of the remaining space. An unmade three-quarter bed was squeezed into a nook. "I wasn't expecting visitors," Karla grinned as she pulled a curtain across the nook, closing off the "bedroom."

"That's neat," Alison said.

"My own idea," Karla smiled. She strode all of two paces to the window and pulled back the curtains. "Look. This is why I loved this place the moment I saw it."

Sunlight streamed through the north-facing window; the ground fell away towards the water. Alison could see the expanse of the harbor beyond the Pyrmont Bridge below. The sweeping view was interrupted only by a tall building under construction. "Wonderful," she said.

"That building wasn't there when I moved in," Karla said sourly. "Rumor has it they're going to redevelop *this* block, too."

"That would be a shame."

"Not if the view gets built out. I feel like a cup of tea," Karla said abruptly, moving to the tiny kitchenette tucked by the front door. "You? There's coffee if you'd rather."

"Tea is fine, thanks," Alison said. Dropping her shoulder bag on the armchair she turned to study the books that lined most of the side wall. In the center, between the books carefully arranged by subject: fiction, history, politics, philosophy—*The sorts of books Derek used to read*—was the green figurine of a fat, Chinese-looking man sitting cross-legged, his arms spread, palms held skywards, laughing. The carving was so intricate that it seemed his entire body, from his eyes to the tiniest folds of his skin, was wobbling in time with his laughter. She reached out to touch it and felt the smooth, cold texture of jade.

"What's this?" she asked. "A *Buddha?*"

Karla looked up and laughed. "That's what I thought. But no, it's a Chinese figure called 'Everybody's Happy.' Not religious at all."

"Where did it come from?"

"It was . . . a present."

Detecting a slight hesitation in Karla's voice, Alison replied firmly, "From Derek, I presume."

Karla nodded.

"Do you miss him?"

Karla's pale cheeks flushed pink. "Of course. Don't *you?*"

About to declaim *"No,"* Alison hesitated as a sudden thought flashed into her mind: *My baby should be* his, *not McKurn's. . . . Where did that come from?* she asked herself, noticing that her hand had come to rest on her now-heavy stomach.

"Sometimes," she said guardedly. "I suppose that makes us rivals."

Shaking her head, Karla laughed.

Alison's fingers slipped from the laughing figurine as she took two quick paces to the counter dividing the kitchenette from the rest of the apartment. *"I* don't see anything to laugh about," she said irritably, her eyes flashing.

Karla finished pouring boiling water into the teapot, covered it with a tea cosy and set it to steep before looking up to face Alison, now leaning over the counter. "You and I can *never* be rivals—not over Derek," she said softly.

"You're talking in riddles, again."

Karla sighed. "Would you want to spend the rest of your life with a man who's in love with someone else?"

"Of course not—you're talking about, Derek, aren't you?"

Karla nodded. "And I don't like illusions—especially *self*-delusions."

Are you telling me he loves you? Alison wondered, her eyes searching Karla's face for the answer. "What's that supposed to mean?" she said.

"If I were some flibbertigibbet who's easily mesmerized by some great, rich, or handsome man, I could easily convince myself that I was in love with Derek and he loved *me*. But it was obvious the first day I met him that he was in love with someone else. We've been hanging around together, but *that* hasn't changed. *That's* what I mean."

"How can you be so sure?"

Karla smiled. "That's easy. The way his voice changes, or his dreamy look when *your* name comes up—which only happens occasionally, I hasten to add. I think Derek is a wonderful man. I admire him, I love the way his mind works—and he really knows how to make a girl feel like a woman. But I'd be deluding myself if I thought he loved me. And there's a part of him that's obscured or buried, never to be seen—" noticing Alison's expression, she added "—you know what I mean, don't you?"

Alison nodded. "Why are you telling me all this?"

"I think I answered that question last time we met."

"When you talked about living with yourself?"

"Right," Karla said. "So I have to be honest with myself—*and* everybody else."

Alison sighed wistfully, aware that as she spoke Karla seemed to exude an aura of internal peace; Alison's sudden longing for that same elusive state only amplified the fluttering in her own stomach.

As if sensing Alison's tension, Karla turned her attention to pouring the tea. Alison gratefully pulled a stool out from under the counter and sank down onto it. For a moment there were only wraiths of steam wafting from the tea as it gurgled and swirled into the cups.

Then Alison chuckled. "You wouldn't last long in Canberra."

"Maybe ten minutes," Karla laughed. "Tell the truth in politics and you only alienate people, create enemies—and lose votes."

"That's pretty cynical."

"Is it?" Karla asked. "Isn't politics the art of deception?—to win the prize, you only have to fool enough of the people enough of the time."

"You're exaggerating."

"Am I? Doesn't that describe McKurn—the Arch Deceiver—who's managed to fool all the people all the time?"

Alison felt the challenge in Karla's words, but her gaze was open and her voice calm, with no hint of mockery. Nevertheless, Alison couldn't stop her eyes from falling away, all too aware that Karla was right. "Until now," she replied softly.

"We're going to lift the veil. You and I—and McKurnWatch, of course."

"That's the idea," Alison said, grinning at the enthusiasm in Karla's voice—and relieved at the change of subject. "I've got stacks of information for you," she said reaching for her shoulder bag and setting the ring binders and her laptop on the counter. "I'll need that report back, but feel free to photocopy anything you need."

"No problem," Karla nodded, opening one of the binders.

"Now, listen to *this.*" About to play one of the geek's earliest phone taps, Alison's finger froze in mid-motion. *"No one else must know,"* she'd told Royn. *I'm going to break that understanding without his consent.* She overrode the tension in her stomach and hit the key.

"Gladys?"

"Yes . . . ah, John. Your usual?"

"Of course."

"That's *McKurn's* voice," Karla gasped, and when the conversation ended she demanded to know, "Who's the woman?"

Alison smiled. "Gladys—which is not her real name. She ran that call-girl agency in Canberra that was shut down for sex slavery. Remember?"

Karla nodded, her eyes narrowing as she asked, "What have you been *up* to?"

Alison grinned. "Research."

"Illegal research, by the sound of it," Karla chucked.

Alison shrugged. "I prefer to describe it as 'unofficial'."

Karla laughed, and leaning forward on the counter said, with growing excitement, "But—it's enough to hang McKurn with. If that recording went public, he'd be thrown out of the Senate on his arse."

"Maybe not, unfortunately,"

"Huh?" Karla looked deflated. "Why on earth not?" she demanded.

"McKurn could simply deny it, and claim someone fabricated it. Just about anyone with a computer could do it."

"I suppose so. But the phone company records—"

"—would show he called the agency, yes. But McKurn's name *doesn't* appear in the agency records, so that's not *proof*—not enough for a court."

"You don't *need* to go to court. Just getting him kicked out of politics, surely. . . ." Karla's voice trailed off as she saw Alison's frown, and the shake of her head. "That's not enough for you. . . ."

"Not *nearly* enough."

"I see," Karla said in a long, drawn-out breath. When she realized Alison was not going to volunteer anything else, she added, "You've got more?"

"Indeed." Alison's eyes glinted as she opened another file.

As Alison played one phone tap after another, Karla scribbled notes fiercely, her eyes glowing excitedly. While Karla listened intently, throwing questions at Alison without looking up, Alison's mind began to wander. *She's hooked,* she thought to herself, *but where will it lead? . . .* She could imagine Royn's approving reaction to whatever Karla would write . . . but *Melanie*—who'd first suggested Alison get in touch with Karla— would make the connection.

I've done it now, she thought glumly. *And if McKurn thinks I'm the one feeding Karla information?* She recalled how he had suspected that she was responsible for McKurnWatch. *He wouldn't bother checking—he'd just act.*

Alison didn't notice when the last recording came to an end until she became aware of a silence that seemed to hang ominously in the air; only then did she look up from her thoughts to see Karla scrutinizing her intensely, as if she was attempting to decipher Alison's every facial movement. Once again she felt the power of Karla's eyes, and the flutters in her stomach suddenly intensified into a swirl, making her feel she was about to be sick.

"You know," Karla said, without relaxing her invasive look, "you're not at ease. Not at all."

"Oh," Alison protested, unable to quell the slight quiver in her voice. "I'm quite comfortable here."

Karla shook her head. "That's not what I meant. You're all tensed up. Something's troubling you—and it's just gotten worse. Would you like something to calm you down?"

"You mean, like a Valium?" Alison said suspiciously.

Karla grinned wryly at Alison. "What," she mused, "made you think of Valium?"

Even though Karla spoke casually, as if she was uttering a throwaway line of no great consequence, Alison felt as though her inner turmoil was exposed to Karla's gaze. She dropped her eyes, and did not reply.

"No, not Valium," Karla said after a moment. "Marijuana. *Much* better. No side-effects."

"I can't."

"You've never tried it?"

"Once, at uni. But after one puff I coughed so much that I gave up, there and then."

"There's another option." Karla pulled a plastic container from the refrigerator behind her, took out a biscuit and placed it on a plate in front of Alison. "Try this then, a chocolate chip *hash* cookie—homemade." Karla carefully broke the cookie in half and then into quarters. "Just a quarter to start with."

Alison jerked back, away from Karla. "What are you trying to do to me?"

"Just offering something to help you relax, that's all," Karla sighed. "Sure, I'm pushy. I know that. But I'm not insensitive. Right now—" Karla paused, as though searching for the right words "—you're radiating enough nervous tension to sink a battleship, if you'll excuse the mixed metaphor."

"Is it that obvious?" Alison asked quietly.

Karla nodded.

"If I eat that, what will happen?"

"You'll relax a bit—and probably get a bit giggly."

"And if I ate the whole thing?"

"You'll get the munchies, and probably go into a dreamy state where you think all sorts of interesting thoughts and have all kinds of interesting insights—some of which, of course, will seem quite ridiculous later. Or—given the way you are right now—you might just go to sleep."

"Where did you get it?"

"You can buy it anywhere, you know," Karla grinned. "But this came from the Sandemans."

"So you're a smuggler yourself—and *you're* upset that *Derek* might be in the drug business?"

"Hey," Karla protested. "I'm just a customer. What I hadn't smoked there was still in my backpack. She shrugged. "It's not a big deal. It's no different from carrying cigarettes or liquor, above the duty-free quota, through customs as far as I'm concerned." She grinned mischievously at Alison and added, "I suppose you've never done *that*."

"Just the same," Alison said sharply, as if to counter the pinkening of her cheeks, "I should call the police."

Karla gestured to the phone sitting on the dining table; as Alison turned her head, Karla said, "But you *won't*."

"Why not?"

"Because you're not going to dob in someone you *like* for a small-time offence which you're ambivalent about."

"Ambivalent?

"I know what you think about drugs—or, at least, what *Royn* thinks—"

"You think I don't agree with him?"

"That's *Royn's* crusade, not *yours*. You don't have his *passion* on the subject—or you would have called the police five minutes ago. You also know that marijuana is not a hard drug, like heroin and cocaine—you've even tried it yourself. So no, you're not going to call the cops."

"What makes you so sure?"

"I have a . . . sense of people," Karla said, "which I trust."

Alison looked away, as if in defeat, and saw her fingers twitching on the countertop. With a sigh, she stilled them. *She's right,* she thought. *I wouldn't call the cops.* But she said nothing.

The sound of Karla's munching broke the brief silence. Alison saw that a quarter of the cookie had disappeared and that Karla was putting the other pieces back into the container. "Never mind," Karla smiled, as she saw Alison look up in surprise. "Maybe we should continue this tomorrow. That's if we have much more ground to cover."

Alison nodded. "We do."

"Get a good night's sleep so you'll feel better in the morning."

"You sound like my mother," Alison grinned.

"I don't think anyone's called me motherly before. Would you rather have a drink instead?"

"No," Alison said impulsively. "I think I'd rather be dreamy than drunk."

"If I can confirm what you've given me—and keep the lawyers happy—we'll blow McKurn away."

"What a picture." Alison shrieked with laughter, tears streaming down her face. She had to force herself to stop to gasp for air. "I've never laughed so much in my life."

Alison sat curled in the armchair, her laptop on her knees. Sprawled beside her on a beanbag, Karla eyed the last of the pictures Alison had just shown her, of McKurn with underworld figures from the sixties and seventies like Perce Galea, Abe "Mr. Sin" Saffron, and "Stan-the-Man" Smith.

"What's so funny," she asked, stabbing her finger at the laptop's screen, "about *that?* He looks like a thug—they *both* do."

"No, no, no. The picture of McKurn being blown up. Blood splattered everywhere—if he has any, the cold-blooded bastard."

Karla chuckled, but her eyes were studying Alison's glee as though a mislaid piece of a jigsaw puzzle had suddenly clicked into place.

Oblivious to Karla's look, Alison reached down for one of the sandwiches they'd made earlier, but her fingers touched an empty plate. "You ate the last one," she said accusingly.

"Sorry," Karla smiled.

"Never mind," Alison said. She placed the laptop on the floor with slow, careful movements, and rose unsteadily to her feet. "I'll see what's left."

"We've eaten everything that doesn't need cooking."

"There are still more of those chocolate chip cookies."

"No, no. You've had enough. Trust me."

"Oh," Alison frowned, slumping back into the armchair. "I *do* feel a bit dizzy," she said, one hand massaging her forehead. "Are you sure there's *nothing?*"

"Well . . . there might be some peanut butter."

"Perfect."

"I'll get it."

As Karla brought back a half-empty jar of peanut butter—and two spoons—she smiled at the way Alison was slouched comfortably in the armchair, her head slightly bowed, her hands clasped loosely over her belly. Thinking Alison might have dozed off, Karla tiptoed carefully, but as she sat down Alison looked up slowly.

"Now I've shown you everything," Alison said. "Except. . . ."

"Except what?" Karla prompted after a moment, dipping her head slightly to hide her curiosity at the way Alison had suddenly jerked upright, her hands clasping her stomach.

Should I? Alison wondered. She looked hard at Karla, pursing her lips thoughtfully, her expression suddenly solemn. She shook her head. "No, I can't show it to you," and then continued, giggling, "but I can *tell* you about it—*if* you promise never to mention it. *Ever.* To *anyone.*"

"I promise," Karla swore between giggles, her hand on her heart.

"Can you say that with a straight face?"

Karla burst out laughing; she shook her head violently. Alison found she had no choice but to join in.

In fits and starts—like someone telling a joke who keeps laughing at the punch line long before reaching it—Alison told Karla about the five Asian sex slaves and what they said about Senator Frank McKurn. At her words "Five-Minute Frankie," Karla whooped so uncontrollably she fell on the floor, flat on her back—yet she continued studying Alison's face with growing intensity, all too aware of the spiteful edge to Alison's voice—and the malicious glitter in her eyes.

Karla slowly pulled herself up, leaning on the edge of the armchair for support. Alison's laughter stopped at the sheer force of Karla's gaze. "And," Karla said, her voice barely above a whisper, "*was* it all over in five minutes?"

"What are you talking about?" Alison shrieked, her feelings of calm and light-headedness suddenly a desperate memory.

"You're pregnant," Karla said, her voice somber.

Numbed, Alison's eyes and mouth opened wide. She had to force out her words. "What on earth made you think *that?*"

"Because," said Karla slowly, "you keep doing *that.*"

Alison's eyes turned to where Karla pointed; she became aware that her fingers had been kneading her stomach—and jerked them away to the arms of the chair. "So? Don't be ridiculous. It must be the marijuana."

"No," Karla smiled sadly, shaking her head slowly. "You've done it all afternoon, every time you tense up."

"I have?" Alison shrugged again. "That's where I feel it."

"Maybe," Karla conceded. "But there are other signs."

"*What* signs?"

"Your body has changed since I first saw you. Just a touch—but a doctor once told me what to look for. When you get pregnant, your breasts start to get heavier, and there's a build-up of fat, especially in your hips, stomach, cheeks and even on the tip of your nose. *That's* what I see in your face—and if you look closely in the mirror, you'll see it too."

Alison gripped the armchair's cushions to hold her body still. "Too many rich dinners this past week," she said curtly.

"Maybe," Karla said. "But you were going to pass me all this stuff about McKurn last Saturday. You didn't. Some deal was done, some compromise reached—and you were okay with that because your motive, then, was *political.* Today, it's a *vendetta.* You're out to cripple McKurn—and to hell with the consequences. When Royn became Prime Minister yesterday, you achieved *your* ambition to be the 'power behind the throne.' But if I print all the stuff you've given me, McKurn is dead. What are the chances of the party that's harbored a murderer and criminal at the very top winning the next election? No longer guaranteed. You're willing to do whatever it takes to get McKurn—and take the risk that, like Samson, you'll bring your own ambitions crashing down around you."

Alison stared at Karla, her lips quivering soundlessly—and doubled over as her self-control disintegrated. Her head fell, her hands and her body trembled as a wordless moan erupted from deep within. With a touch of one arm, Karla gently invited her to rest her head against her chest, and Karla held her until the quaking of her body slowly ceased.

Now breathing deep and fast, her face ashen as though all her blood had drained away, her body limp and her head slumped back in the armchair, Alison slowly dabbed her eyes and forced a wan smile. "It's such a relief to *tell* someone," she said slowly. "Not that I really *did*—"

"Not in so many words," Karla grinned.

"He set out to destroy me."

"Is he succeeding?" Karla asked softly.

"No," Alison said weakly. But . . . she had an eerie sense of being trapped at the center of a spider's web—a tangle of lies. Royn, Melanie, Kydd, and especially the people she was closest to, her mother and father . . . even Derek—she'd told none of them the truth. *Until Karla named it, I was denying the truth to myself.* She touched her stomach, surprised that all her tension had drained away—and suddenly grasped the sheer effort and energy she'd had to expend to face the world through a charade that, at this moment at least, was no longer necessary. She looked softly at Karla and said, "I should resent the way you squeezed the truth from me, but I don't. I feel grateful." But remembering Karla's profession, Alison looked at her with a sudden suspicion. "You're not going to publish any of this—I hope."

"Never," Karla said firmly. "In fact, I won't even use anything you've given me about McKurn if you'd like to change your mind."

"Thank you," Alison said, attempting to push herself to her feet and failing. "Could I ask you for a glass of water," she chuckled. "I don't seem to have any energy."

"Of course," Karla laughed.

Alison gulped the water gratefully and Karla handed her a small packet containing a white, rectangular pill. "Here," she said, "take this. Not now. Think about it first."

"What is it?"

"It's a 'morning after' pill."

"I . . . don't know if I could," Alison said, the fingers holding the pill trembling as she pushed it back into Karla's hand. "Have *you* ever taken one?"

Karla shook her head. "Nope. It's just in case."

"You wouldn't hesitate, would you? You'd have no qualms?"

"None," Karla said softly. "But you obviously do."

"Yes . . . if life doesn't begin at birth or conception, then *when?*"

"Is that your Catholic upbringing talking?"

"Maybe. But even if you don't believe in God, that's still a valid question, *isn't it?*"

"Yes, it is," Karla said quietly. She opened her mouth to say something but, changing her mind, asked instead, "And have thought about what happens to *you* if you *don't* take it?"

"Oh, yes," Alison groaned—and shuddered as, for a fleeting moment, she felt as if she was once again sitting, tormented, in the cathedral under Jesus' sad but watchful eyes.

"Decide later," Karla said with an understanding smile. "I'll put it in your handbag," she added, getting to her feet. "You can always throw it away—but it's meant to be taken the morning after, so it may be too late."

It is, Alison thought numbly as she watched Karla drop the pill in a side pocket of her handbag.

Karla came back with a bottle of brandy and two glasses. "You could probably use some of this."

"You're reading my mind again," Alison said. "But is it a good idea, on top of the marijuana, I mean?"

"It's not a problem," Karla said as she handed Alison a glass, "in moderation. If you're feeling sort of mellow and laid back rather than high, it's starting to wear off."

"That's pretty much how I feel."

"So," Karla grinned, "I've been wondering if you can cast any light on McKurn's supposed 'accident'."

As Karla spoke, the welcome fire of Alison's first sip of brandy was sliding down her throat and met head-on with an irresistible urge to laugh. She shook her head and spluttered, "I think 'cast' is the wrong word."

They both laughed.

"In fact," Alison added, "I really don't want to talk about McKurn any more—not right now anyway."

"Fair enough," Karla smiled. "Shall we go out somewhere and get something to eat?"

"I'm expected home for dinner," Alison said, noticing that the sun was no longer streaming through the window. "At least, thanks to you, I can face my mother now."

"Okay," Karla said. "I'll photocopy that report in the morning, so I could drop it off at your place tomorrow if you like."

Alison laughed, wobbling slightly as she came to her feet.

"What's so funny?" Karla asked.

"My father is keen to meet you—he reads your columns because he likes getting *angry*. He'd just love to have an argument with you."

"Sounds like fun," Karla chuckled. Noticing that Alison seemed a little unsteady, she asked, "Will you be okay? Shall I call a taxi?"

"I'll be fine in a moment," Alison said, giving Karla a hug, "and the walk will do me good."

*****

"You look a lot better. Lighter," Maggie said as Alison came through the front door.

"Yes, Mum, I am." *Even though,* she thought, all-too-aware of the "morning after" pill in her handbag, *nothing's really changed.*

Her mellow state continued all through dinner as she basked in the unconditional acceptance of her parents. Turning to her father she asked him a question that had been slowly forming in the back of her mind. "Daddy, have you ever been faced with a really hard choice . . . whichever path you choose, you'll *hate* the result?"

"Like between the lesser of two evils?" Joe asked, his voice a slow drawl as he gazed thoughtfully at his daughter.

Alison nodded.

Pursing his lips he said, "Why are you asking?"

"Oh, Daddy," Alison protested. "Just wondering . . . because, okay, I have a tough decision to make. That's all."

Alison tensed, thinking her father was going to press her for more details, but then his expression relaxed into a warm smile. "Oh, yes," he said. *"You."*

"Me? What do you mean?"

Maggie nodded, her eyes moist. "I'd had so many miscarriages we were convinced we'd *never* have a child."

Joe clasped Maggie's hand and beamed at Alison. "We'd given up all hope."

"And then, I became pregnant with you—but I was forty. . . ." Maggie bowed her head, unable to continue, dabbing at her eyes with her napkin.

"I'm sorry, Mum," Alison said. She reach out to grip her mother's shoulder and was surprised to feel faint tremors under her touch. *She's afraid,* Alison thought. *She must be remembering. . . .* "I didn't mean to—"

Maggie looked up and smiled, even as tears still trickled from the corners of her eyes. "It's okay, Alison. It turned out for the best, didn't it?"

"We were *both* terrified," Joe said in an eruption of words. He was looking at Alison but not seeing her, his mind trapped somewhere in the past, the pulse on the side of his neck visibly racing. "The doctors said pregnancy would be a sentence of death. For Maggie.—" Joe paused as he focused on Alison "—For *you*. Or *both* of you. They tried to persuade us that Maggie should have an . . . " His mouth froze for an instant until he was able to spit out: *"Abortion."* He made it sound as though the word was coated in castor oil.

"Never," said Maggie.

"I was . . . tempted," Joe admitted shyly.

"So he was," Maggie said, grinning at Joe. "But I soon set him straight."

Joe grinned back. "But if you had died," he said, looking at Maggie as if they were alone, "I would have lost my reason for living."

"But I didn't, did I?" Maggie said softly, her lips stretching into an enormous smile.

Alison gazed in wonder at the sight of her parents behaving like teenagers in love; at the same time she was thinking, *I wish I'd never asked.*

Joe was beaming when he turned back to Alison; his face and neck now loose, his words came easily. "We would have loved to have given you a little brother or sister—but I'm not sure I could have survived *another* nine months of . . . of. . . ." A shudder ran through his body. "Let me put it this way: I *know* I don't want to go to hell because I've already been there."

"That's true," Maggie said. "But it was all worth it, wasn't it, Joe?"

"Oh, yes," he said.

From the radiance of her parents' smiles and the passionate glow in their eyes, Alison had the sense she was staring into the blinding sun and had to look away. She knew the story of her birth—but had never before felt the pain or intensity of her parents' ordeal. She felt her mother's gentle touch on her fingers; gripping her hand tightly she slowly lifted her head. She couldn't bring her mother's face into focus at first until she blinked away the tears in her eyes. "Oh, Mum, I. . . ."

"Not a word," Maggie laughed. "After all, you had no say."

And if I had been asked . . . ? The question came into her mind, incomplete and needing no answer; she imagined she'd felt a faint, almost imperceptible movement in her stomach. Her vision suddenly blurred and she reached for her napkin. "I'm sorry," she said, shaking her head as she smiled through her tears. "It's just too much, to *choose* to face death. . . ."

"We didn't make the choice," said Joe. "We left it in the hands of God."

Or, she thought, hearing Derek's voice, *just let nature run its course.*

"But—what if you'd *known,* for *sure,* that one of us—me or Mum—would die in childbirth?"

"That's what the doctors kept telling us would probably happen," Maggie said.

"So we prayed," said Joe.

"And God must have heard us," said Maggie.

"That's right," said Joe.

I'm proof to them that God exists, Alison thought. "And where was God when I was being raped?" She regretted her words the moment she uttered them.

"I don't know," Maggie said, her voice choking.

Joe gulped, a momentary glint of anger in his eyes. "It's all part of God's Plan. He's made you strong and successful. I don't claim to understand the mind of God but He's obviously been watching over you."

And McKurn is part of "God's Plan" too, Daddy?

"You don't believe any more, do you?" Joe asked.

"Not since—" *There, I've said it now.*

"It doesn't matter," Maggie smiled, cutting Joe off. "God's still looking after you, just the same." She picked up a couple of plates from the table. "Let's clear up, shall we Alison?"

Alison touched the dining table to steady her legs as she walked around it to her father, who sat brooding at his wife's back. "Thank you, Daddy," she said.

"I hope we helped," he said, half-smiling as he stood.

Instead of answering, Alison flung her arms around him and felt him melt against her. "I love you so much, Daddy."

Joe's face lit up and he squeezed her so hard Alison giggled, "Daddy, I can hardly breath."

Joe laughed and kissed her on the cheek.

"Thank you, Daddy, for *everything.*"

Joe nodded, unable to speak. The long moment of communion was not broken until a clatter of dishes came from the kitchen.

AFTER JOE AND MAGGIE had gone to bed Alison half-dozed, sunk into the sofa's deep cushions, without the energy to move. The TV continued to chatter, but lost in the loop of her own thoughts she'd stopped watching it long ago.

If they'd taken the doctors' advice, I wouldn't be here.

To which the ageless voice responded: *But you'd never have known.*

She'd shaken her head. *That doesn't make it right.*

She was gripped by wild optimism when it occurred to her: *Maybe I've inherited Mum's genes and I'll miscarry anyway.* That sudden lift was shattered as she saw the implications: *Maybe I'd never have any children . . . or have to go through Mum's ordeal of choosing between an abortion and probable death.*

All the while she was aware that she'd added one more tangle to her web of deceptions: *I can never tell them what I've been considering.* And if she didn't make *their* choice? *I could never tell them, ever.*

She forced her eyes to focus on the characters flickering across the TV screen as if that would still her thoughts, but with no idea of what was going on she punched hard on the remote to kill the picture.

She started as she noticed her hand was once again caressing her stomach, and wished she'd asked Karla for a chocolate chip cookie for "later." Instead, she pushed herself to her feet and helped herself to a large measure of her father's whisky. *To help me have a dreamless sleep.*

To while away the time until the whisky made an impact she plugged on to the internet, *To make an informed decision,* she told herself—knowing a lack of information was not the issue, that digging for it was just an excuse to procrastinate.

The "morning after" pill, she learnt, inhibited conception or caused the lining of the womb to reject the fertilized egg. Now I'm actually pregnant, she sighed, *there's no point taking it. If only I'd thought of it before. . . .*

But I thought I was safe. She had resumed taking the pill—*Not soon enough.*

Pouring another shot of whisky, she went through several of the phone taps in her inbox, deleting one routine call after another until she heard:

"Frankie. The cops are after me. They seem to know everything."

"Who's this?"

"Rog."

"Oh, right."

"Did you tell them anything?"

"Of course not. But they *know.* Somebody's spilled the beans. And they're going to investigate my *finances.* They're sure to find something funny."

"Calm down, Rog. Who were the cops? Did you know them?"

"Rudi Durant, along with an Asian guy—Chinese maybe."

"Ah, Durant. I'll see what I can do. Just take it easy, okay?"

"Sure, Frankie—easy enough for you to say. And Durant's a hard-boiled egg—"

"There are always ways and means, Rog. Ways and means. Just leave it to me, okay?"

What was that all about? Alison wondered, suddenly alert. *And who's "Rog"?* She played it again, listening to Rog's voice carefully. A memory fragment came into her mind: "I *don't* want to go out to sea one day and end up as shark bait. . . ."

"Shark bait." Was that the voice of Roger Kelly?

"Ways and means," McKurn had said. *Could McKurn put pressure on Durant somehow? Or worse—could Durant be in danger?*

What am I going to do—what can I do? Tell Jason? But then I'd have to tell him how I found out.

She shook her head.

I have to warn Durant—but how? Send him an email. But the police website only listed general inquiry addresses. *I could get Durant's email from Jason . . . or someone else. . . .* She shook her head: *No tracks.* She considered and immediately discarded phone, mail, and fax. *An anonymous note would be best:*

> At 9:07 this (Saturday) morning, a man I'm pretty sure is Roger Kelly called Senator Frank McKurn in a panic. "The cops are after me," he said. "They seem to know everything." He identified you as one of two policemen who visited him.
>
> McKurn told Kelly to "calm down" and that he'd see what he could do, adding, "There are always ways and means, Rog. Ways and means. Just leave it to me, okay?"
>
> From what I know about McKurn, you may be in danger.

She wondered what Durant looked like, trying to imagine how he'd react to her note. *He'd know someone was tapping McKurn's or Kelly's phone.* What had Jason said? "He's as straight as an arrow and tougher to get rid of than AIDS."

He'd probably come after me, too—no, he wouldn't find me, he'd find the geek—I can't put him at risk. She encrypted the note along with the recording and sent it to the geek, asking him to pass them onto Durant somehow "if you're comfortable doing that."

The moment she'd sent the email she felt overcome with exhaustion; she stretched to loosen the tension in her shoulders. She let the last drop of whisky roll around in her mouth before clearing up and heading for bed.

As she reached the door of the spare bedroom she paused. *I faced that. I can face anything.*

Her eyes glued to the doorknob, she could imagine the scene on the other side with only a mild tremor of fear, while thinking: *Maybe that wasn't the worst thing that could ever happen to me.*

*****

It was after midnight when Amtami and his men guided two Australian and two Sandeman platoons towards the guerrillas' hideout. They quietly took station in a loose ring, circling the terrorists' camp.

The moment the Predator missiles struck and the naval artillery barrage began, the Firebird helicopter gunships would lift off from Zulu base to add their firepower.

The soldiers had spent two intensive days training with Amtami's men, learning how to move silently. They first had to discard anything that might rattle, jingle, or clink, and firmly tape down items such as dog tags or spare ammunition that they could not leave behind. They learnt how to observe the different features of the ground and vegetation so they could avoid anything that might make a noise—and then practiced by starlight while communicating only with hand signals. At the end of the two days, Amtami announced, "they'd do"; the Australian and Sandeman troops had come to admire and even befriend the men from Islamic Purity.

As they left Zulu base, N'gaandi took Jeremy aside and whispered. "Can I ask you something?"

"Shoot," said Jeremy.

"If you had received orders you thought were wrong, what would you do?"

"I guess . . . find some way to be unable to carry them out. Do you have an example in mind?" When N'gaandi looked worried, Jeremy added, "A hypothetical example will do, won't it?"

"I guess," N'gaandi doubtfully. Making a decision, he continued, "Say you had orders . . . once the terrorists are all rounded up, to turn our guns on . . . our Islamic Purity guides. To kill as many as you can without warning. What would you do?"

"That's an interesting example," Jeremy said, recalling Gugamti's obvious opposition to coming to *any* arrangement with Amtami. "I'd have to give it some thought."

N'gaandi nodded. "Okay . . . but don't take too long about it."

"I won't," said Jeremy. "Just leave it to me."

"I didn't tell you a thing, Jeremy," N'gaandi said.

"Of course not," Jeremy smiled.

A little while later Jeremy cornered Amtami. "Amtami-*ga*," he whispered, "I'd like to make a suggestion."

Amtami waved over his interpreter.

"I think it would be an excellent idea," Jeremy said, "if you and your men disappeared as quickly as possible—*before* we've finished rounding up all the terrorists."

"Why is that?" Amtami asked, a glimmer of humor in his eye.

"For your own safety."

"No worries," Amtami said, his teeth flashing white in the starlight as he grinned broadly. "You won't see us. *Matalam*, M'gire-*ga*."

When the first Predator missile exploded in a mushroom of flame, Amtami and every one of his men simply disappeared into the jungle. Not that anybody noticed: the soldiers were all too busy staying in position and keeping an eye out for escaping terrorists as they slowly tightened the ring to worry about what the Islamic Purity guerrillas were up to. The only sign of their former presence were the dead bodies of the lookouts, whose throats had been silently cut bare moments before the barrage was scheduled to begin.

By the time the violent down-pouring of fire ceased, and the ring finally closed around the smouldering, pitted terrain of what had once been pristine jungle, two of the guerrillas from St. Christopher's Island had been shot dead while trying to flee, and three had been captured, one them dying of burns before he could be medivaced out. As far as anyone could tell, all that was left of the rest were scattered, mostly unidentifiable chunks of charred meat and the sickening aroma of still-barbecuing pork.

47 Election Fever

A LISON SETTLED BEHIND HER desk, looking forward to an hour by herself before the day began, when Anthony Royn strode into the office at the speed of a marathon walker nearing the finish line; Melanie trailed in moments later, puffing to keep up with him. Spying Alison, Royn changed direction and began asking, even before he reached her office door, "What do you think of calling an early election?"

"Huh?" Alison said, taken aback by Royn's unusual abundance of energy. "I mean, good morning, Minister. What was that you said?"

"A snap election," Royn said. He started to take a chair but changed his mind, as if sitting down was too confining. "Take everyone off guard. Capitalize on the honeymoon period."

An election. Alison nodded distractedly. She'd been involved in countless campaigns . . . for *Royn.* This time around, as the prime minister's right hand, she'd play a central role in creating and directing the campaign for the whole party. *A dream come true. . . . So why don't I feel excited?*

"Catch a tail wind," said Melanie, now standing in the doorway, smiling impishly at Alison.

"Exactly," said Royn, his eyes bright. "Paul and Melanie and I have been talking about nothing else all weekend."

Alison gaped at Royn. "You and *Cracken?* All *weekend?*"

"Well—he's deputy leader now," Royn said as he paced back and forth. "I need to keep him onside. Co-opt him, that's the best policy."

"I suppose so," said Alison, her voice larded with doubt.

"Right," said Royn, taking her words as agreement without registering her tone. "And if the polls we've been doing hold up *after* I'm sworn in as Prime Minister on Wednesday—"

"In just two days," said Melanie.

"Wait a minute, Minister," Alison said, throwing her hands up in the air. "Have you really thought this through? We *must* do another poll first, to *check.* Otherwise we'd be flying blind."

"Of course," Royn said. "Take it Thursday or Friday. We could announce the election on the weekend."

"I'd want to see the poll results first," Alison said, trying to inject a note of caution into the discussion.

"Naturally," Royn said, waving a hand as if there could be no doubt what the poll would show. *"And,* we could put the Royal Commission through Parliament this week— great campaign material, clean government and so on and so forth."

"What about Stanley Chow? He scuttled the idea before."

"He'll agree—if the Royal Commission won't *do* anything until *after* the election."

"And if the opinion poll *doesn't* hold up?" said Alison. "You'd have to postpone the election but be stuck with the Royal Commission."

"Ah, yes, I hadn't thought of that," Royn frowned, coming to a halt.

"Why not take the poll *now?*" Melanie asked. "Why wait till Thursday—Tony's already PM in all but name."

"Great idea," said Royn, immediately full of cheer again.

"Better *after* he's sworn in," said Alison. "All those TV and press pictures will add credibility. And what about McKurn?" she added, suddenly recalling she'd told Karla to go ahead and publish as much as she could.

"The Dump McKurn movement will take care of him."

"It should," Alison said guardedly.

"You don't sound convinced," Royn said, frowning at Alison. "But *surely* we don't have to worry about McKurn any more—not with what we've got on him."

"I'll stop worrying about McKurn when he's dead and buried, and not before."

"Surely—" Royn said.

"Do you think McKurn will go willingly?" Alison demanded.

"Well, I—" Royn began.

"What do you think, Melanie?" Alison asked.

Royn turned to look at Melanie, who slowly shook her head. "No, of course he won't."

"And Cracken's in his pocket," Alison continued. "What's *he* going to do?"

"Paul said he'll protest mildly," Royn said, brightening up again, "but stay on the sidelines."

"I don't trust Cracken any more than I trust McKurn. He'll tell you what you want to hear—but can you guarantee he'll keep his word?" Alison shook her head. "For all we know, he's *already* snitched your plans to McKurn."

"Little Dick," Melanie murmured.

Royn grimaced at Melanie's reminder.

"That's right," said Alison. "You've been rivals since the year dot. Has the vulture suddenly sheathed his claws?"

"I . . . " Royn shrugged, admitting reluctantly, "probably not."

"Don't forget," Alison said, "that even if he's *off* the Senate ticket, McKurn will be hanging over us till the new Senate takes office in June next year."

"Which will be the case *whenever* we hold the election," said Melanie.

"I know," said Alison glumly, looking up to see Melanie peering at her intently.

"You sound like a wet blanket this morning," Melanie said. "That's not like you."

Alison smiled wryly. "You hit me with this idea out of the blue," she said. "It makes a lot of sense—but I get the impression you've already made up your mind. That could be a mistake. And what about the logistics?" She glanced at her list of everything that needed to be done to ensure Royn's smooth transition to Prime Minister: two pages of headings, and far from finished. "The week's agenda is *already* overloaded. Moving into the PM's office, rearranging staff, taking over the party machinery, just to begin with. Parliament's in session too. Preparing for an election *as well* is overwhelming. Don't get me wrong: an early election is a good idea—but there are risks."

"There are risks if we *don't* go for it," said Royn. "If we get a jump in the polls this week, it could be downhill from then on."

Alison nodded. "You're probably right."

Royn glanced at his watch. "Paul will be here in half an hour—we need to talk about who should be the new Minister for Foreign Affairs and other Cabinet changes—"

"Do you plan to involve Cracken in all your major decisions, Minister?" Alison asked. "You're the *Prime* Minister now. Kydd usually made his decision and then persuaded or arm-twisted everyone else to follow along. That, after all, is the Prime Minister's prerogative."

"True," Royn chuckled. "But as someone once said, keep your friends close, but your enemies closer. *That's* my strategy with Paul, but it *doesn't* follow that I haven't already decided on my policy."

"But I'd suggest, Minister, you assume that Cracken, unlike most other people, is totally immune to your charm."

"Unfortunately, Alison, I'm sure you're right."

*****

"Simon! Come and listen to this." Durant played the recording he'd just received of Roger Kelly talking to Frank McKurn.

"Somebody's been tapping somebody's phone,"

"Kelly's?—or McKurn's?" Durant said.

Lee pointed to the covering email:

listen to this! you could be in danger

— a friend from asio

ps. i shouldn't be sending you this. please don't spoil our operation by mentioning it to anyone

"McKurn's, I'd guess."

"More likely. But there could be something wrong with this email. What do you think?"

Lee noticed the return email address for the first time: deep.throat. "Very original" he laughed. "One of those free email services. *Anyone* could have sent it."

"Exactly," said Durant. "Maybe it *is* a friend from ASIO—but that could just be a blind."

"But if Kelly *did* call McKurn, you *have* set the cat among the pigeons—and it looks like we're going to be the pigeons."

Durant's phone shrilled. "Durant speaking. . . . Ah, yes, Boss. . . . Certainly. . . . We're on our way." Durant slammed the phone down. "Zimmerman's on the warpath," he said, looking hard at Lee. "Got your armor on? Looks like the cat has made its first move."

"I've heard you two have been up to a little private snooping," Zimmerman said as Durant and Lee walked into his office. "It's got to stop."

"We have?" Durant asked innocently, sprawling into a chair opposite Zimmerman without waiting for permission. "And which little birdie gave you this intriguing piece of information?"

"Never mind," said Zimmerman sharply. "That's none of your business."

"Oh, but it very much is," Durant replied.

"Really? I don't think so," Zimmerman snapped. Turning on Lee, he asked, "Sergeant Lee, what have you got to say for yourself?"

"We . . . ah . . . followed up a tip," Lee said; still standing, he shifted his weight from one leg to another. "Checked it out."

"And what was the result?"

"Ah. . . ." Lee shrugged. "Too early to say."

"Have you written up your report yet?" Zimmerman demanded, glaring at Durant.

"What makes you think there's something to report, sir?" Durant asked.

"I received—"

"I know. A phone call." Pointing at Monday's *Mercury* on Zimmerman's desk, Durant said, "Been reading the papers, I see. Keeping up to date on the news eh?"

Zimmerman winced as he glanced at the paper's headline, *Queensland's Top Drug Cop Nabbed. "Salted Away Millions" says Anti-Corruption Chief*, and looked quizzically at Durant. "So?"

"Who's next, I wonder?" Durant sounded as if he was musing out loud, but his look was somber. "These days, it can be dangerous to protect friends in high places."

"Are you threatening *me?*"

"Threatening you?" Durant laughed. "Just stating the obvious. That's all."

Zimmerman glowered at Durant. "You're up to something. You know something. It's your *duty* to inform your superior—*Inspector* Durant."

Durant laughed. "I had suspicions—but now they've been confirmed."

"What's *that* supposed to mean?"

Durant studied Zimmerman's face thoughtfully; after a moment he leant forward in his chair and said, "Have you asked yourself *why* this little birdie sang in your ear?"

"I can't—" Now it was Zimmerman's turn to look uncomfortable. "All I can tell you is that it's none of your damn business. Do I make myself clear?"

"Very clear," Durant nodded.

"You have been warned," Zimmerman said.

"Yes, indeed. I appreciate it. You can be assured that I'll take it to heart," Durant said, rising to his feet.

"We haven't finished yet," Zimmerman growled, "so sit back down. It's been a whole week since Jessica Olsson walked off that plane from Bangkok—and there's been zero progress in catching Derek Olsson."

"That's right," said Durant. "Jessica Olsson confirmed she was kidnapped, drugged, and smuggled out of the country, and said she had no idea where she was until she was taken to Bangkok airport. She identified this 'Luk Suk' character from photos provided by the Hong Kong police, but no one else—except that she thought they were all Chinese. We have a report from the Thai police that Olsson is 'believed to be somewhere in Thailand'—so we assume that he traded himself for his sister. Even the false sightings of Olsson have pretty much dried up."

"You haven't told me anything I don't already know," said Zimmerman. "Think I should send you to Thailand, then, to see if you can pick up Olsson's trail?"

"I don't know," Durant shrugged. "Maybe that could help—"

"I was being sarcastic," said Zimmerman, leaning back in his chair. "It seems your taskforce has turned into a bunch of police officers sitting around twiddling their thumbs when they could be doing something useful. For example," he grinned, "there's that grisly double murder yesterday—something right up your street. And it won't leave you any time for wild, off-the-record goose-chases. So I'm assigning you and Sergeant Lee back to your normal duties. Any questions?"

"No . . . *sir*," said Durant. "You've made yourself very clear."

"Good," said Zimmerman. "Dismissed."

*****

I am pregnant!

"Sometimes, that home urine test gives false positives," the smiling doctor, a kindly, middle-aged lady, had told Alison, "*and* false negatives. Although *four* of them agreeing doesn't leave much room for doubt. Still, we'll give you another test, just to be certain."

Alison stood frozen in the doorway to Royn's office, gaping at the text message on her cellphone: *Congratulations, Alison! Your test result is positive.*

On Sunday morning she'd gone to a public clinic which asked only for her first name, and her cellphone number, as a private means of getting in touch with her.

"Alison?" Royn's voice cut into her thoughts.

"What's the matter?" Melanie asked, eyeing Alison's cellphone with obvious interest.

Alison looked up to see Royn, Melanie, Doug Selkirk, Paul Cracken, and two members of his staff all staring at her. She shrugged and tucked her phone back in her handbag. "Just a surprise. That's all."

"I was just saying," said Cracken to Alison as she took a seat, "that I don't think we should elevate any of the junior ministers on your short list."

"I quite agree," said Royn, turning his chair restlessly as he looked from one person to another. "They're all qualified, but it's too early for me to start offending senior ministers—even if one of the juniors *would* do a better job."

"Quite so," said Cracken.

"So . . . Helen Arkness, Victor Bergstrom, or Leonard Underwood for Foreign Affairs," Alison said mechanically, glancing at Cracken, "unless, of course, you want to add anyone else to the list. Yourself, for example."

"A tempting idea," Cracken grinned, "but no thanks."

"The obvious candidates," Royn said, drumming his fingers until Melanie reached over to still his hand with hers.

"If you make Helen Arkness Minister for Foreign Affairs," Alison said, "have you considered how people like Nimabi would react?"

Paul Cracken laughed. "She certainly knows how to put him in his place."

"That's what I mean," said Alison, "given the problems we're having up there."

"Victor is *too* gentlemanly," Cracken said, "and Leonard Underwood—"

"The Undertaker." Leaning forward, Royn chuckled at the nickname for Leonard Underwood, the Trade Minister. "Poor Lenny, he'd bore everyone to death."

"Possibly the better strategy," Alison suggested. She noticed Melanie giving her a strange look, and realized that once again her hand had strayed to her stomach. *How long before Melanie will see it, too?*

"Victor wouldn't care if he was passed over," Cracken said. "But choosing the Undertaker might put Helen's nose out of joint—especially as she wants the job." They all nodded, aware that Helen Arkness, while junior in the hierarchy to Bergstrom was senior to Underwood.

"Let's give it a bit more thought, then," said Royn, smiling at Cracken. "But not too much—we should announce all the Cabinet changes *before* the swearing in on Wednesday."

"Right," said Cracken, "But we shouldn't kowtow to people like Nimabi. Anything else, Tony?"

Melanie and Alison grinned uncomfortably at each other: the Royn-Cracken duumvirate and their new routine of treating each other as the best of mates was going to take some getting used to.

"Yes," Royn said, smiling at Alison as he spoke. "If we're going to announce an election this weekend, we must make sure we're *ready.* Then, while Nash and his people are scrambling to get their act together, we'll have the momentum and the high ground. With any luck we'll keep it till election day."

"Set the election date for as soon as possible," said Cracken. "Keep the campaign short."

"Five weeks is the minimum," Alison said, "assuming it's announced on a Sunday."

"It can't be shorter?" Royn asked.

Alison shook her head. "It's all specified in the Electoral Act."

"Pity," said Cracken.

"*Three* weeks would be better," Royn said impatiently, "but we'll manage." Finally, as if some invisible restraint had suddenly given way, Royn jumped out of his chair. "And the logical person to take charge of the overall campaign—from our side, of course—is Alison," he said, grinning at her.

Alison blanched. Her eyes followed Royn as he paced back and forth behind his desk; she felt suddenly weary, as if her energy was being drained away by Royn's apparently inexhaustible supply. Her eyes dipped towards the floor. With a deep sigh, she forced herself to straighten up, only to see Royn, now standing still and leaning towards her, looking at her expectantly.

"You're *definitely* out of sorts today," Melanie said. "Are you *sure* you've recovered from whatever you had last week?" And leaning closer she whispered, "Are you really up to it?"

Alison shrugged, unable to hold Melanie's gaze. "It's taking a bit longer than expected," she said, forcing a smile. "That's all."

Melanie nodded, but continued to frown at her.

"Is there a problem?" Royn asked.

"Well . . . yes," said Alison, forcing her fingers to remain still on the arms of her chair. "If too many people know we're even *thinking* about an early election, the news will leak. But to be *ready* by this weekend, we need some sort of cover story that's completely believable."

"The press will speculate anyway," Cracken pointed out.

"Can't be helped," Royn grinned. "That's what they do best."

"What *kind* of cover story, Alison?" Melanie asked.

Alison sat blankly, but no idea would come.

Cracken jumped into the silence. "How about calling a meeting of the Party's leaders this weekend to discuss all the options—a sort of mini-Party conference. That gives us a good excuse for anything we want to do. And infuse a sense of urgency into people without giving the game away."

"Excellent idea," said Royn. "Let's do it."

"But," Cracken said forcefully, looking each person in the eye as he spoke, "each of us here knows the *real* reason. So we should all agree to tell *no one else.*"

"Quite so," said Royn, now standing over his desk forcing everyone to look up at him. "No wives, no colleagues, no superiors—and, of course, no journalists. If there *is* a leak—" he paused to make sure he had everyone's complete attention "—I'll know where to look."

One by one, each person present solemnly agreed.

As Cracken and his assistants left, Royn, now leaning against the window, his arms folded, said, "Now Alison, could you—"

"Just a moment, Minister, if you don't mind," Alison protested.

Royn froze for an instant, squinting at Alison. "What's the problem?" he asked softly.

"I'm *already* overloaded. And you want me get us ready for an election this weekend *as well?* It can't be done, Minister."

"Overloaded?" Royn asked.

"That's right! This week we have to move office, reshuffle Cabinet, reorganize staff and settle into our new roles. And you're going to move into the Lodge. That's more than enough to do. To announce an election this weekend, we should have started planning for it the week before *yesterday*. And with you as Prime Minister, it's is going to be a very *different* election campaign: *you're* going to be in charge. So if you want me to focus on that, I don't see how I can do anything else *as well*."

"Fair enough," Royn grinned, resuming his pacing. "How about you hand everything else over to Doug?"

"I'll need Doug's help too," said Alison.

"Actually," said Doug Selkirk slowly, "we now have—" he glanced at Royn "—*you* now have the entire Commonwealth bureaucracy at your disposal—"

"That's right," said Royn thoughtfully. "I guess being Prime Minister is going to take a little getting used to."

"We'll manage," Melanie grinned.

"I'm sure we will," said Royn.

"How about Doug and I, along with whoever else, work out what needs to be done and then put someone *else* in charge," said Alison.

"No worries," said Selkirk. "Mary could handle it once it's all laid out."

"Fine," said Royn. "Do whatever you need to do to clear the decks."

"Thank you, Minister," said Alison, her shoulders slumping against the back of the chair. "Now, have you given any thought to who might replace Kydd?"

"Assuming he resigns his seat," said Melanie sourly. "If he doesn't, you'll have to throw him out. You can't have him sniping at you for the next three years."

"That's true," said Royn.

"There's always Fred," Melanie grinned.

Royn laughed. Fred Ingram had been secretary of the party's main branch in Kydd's constituency for as long as Kydd had been there. Everybody knew he saw himself as Kydd's logical successor in Parliament. "He's a great guy, no question about that. But he'd be mincemeat a week after he got here."

"Well," asked Alison, "what sort of person do you *want?*"

"Someone loyal to me, of course. Someone I could always count on in the party room."

"What other qualities?" Doug Selkirk asked. "A perpetual backbencher? Cabinet material?"

"At the moment, it's *Kydd's* Cabinet," said Royn. "So it would be nice to inject some new ministerial material, loyal to *me*. He'd have to be a *logical* minister. Have the right qualifications. Be popular in the party room too—when you promote a newcomer you're always going to upset *somebody*. But a bit older . . . so he wouldn't have too many expectations of glory." Royn shook his head. "Sounds like too much to hope for. Can't think of anyone like that."

"How about Barry?" said Melanie, smiling.

"My God, yes—Barry." Royn gave her a look of admiration. "He's the obvious one—when you think of it."

"He even lives in the electorate, I think," said Alison.

"He does," said Royn.

Barry Easton was a professor of economics at Macquarie University, in Sydney. He was one of the people Royn had called on to help him learn more about economic issues, and Royn turned to him for informal advice ever since. Easton was a popular lecturer and a skilled debater. Businesses paid for his advice. From that and his investments—"Applied economics," he called them—he'd become independently wealthy. He was also active in the Conservative Party and had served on several government commissions. He'd recently chaired an inquiry into industrial relations, producing a report giving the government almost everything it wanted.

"Can't give you *everything*," Easton had said when Royn asked him about the "almost." "After all, I'm an academic." He laughed. "Can't compromise my independence—be a violation of academic freedom."

"I'll sound him out," Royn said. "But—would he be willing to take on Kydd?"

"It's probably the safest Conservative seat in the country," Doug Selkirk pointed out. "We've held it since the party was founded. Every party hack and his dog will try and grab it. So the main problem will be getting Easton nominated even if Kydd *doesn't* stand."

"That's true," said Royn, now leaning against the window. "We'll have to out-think them then, won't we?"

"We'll have our work cut out whether Kydd stands or not," Melanie grinned. "I'd better get started then, hadn't I?"

Royn reached out to grasp Melanie's shoulder. "Good idea," he grinned. "And while you do that, it's time for my appointment with the Governor-General."

"THESE ARE FOR THE Minister," Mary called as Alison came out of Royn's office. She peered at Alison's face as she gave her a thick package and a thin envelope. "Are you *sure* you're feeling better than you were on Friday?"

Alison laughed. "You asked me that earlier."

"I didn't get a straight answer then," Mary said, "and I suppose you're not going to give me one now, either."

"I'm on the mend," Alison said.

"If you say so." Mary shrugged.

And how long before she sees it too? Alison thought as she headed for her desk. *What would I tell people?* Her step faltered under the sudden extra weight of her stomach. *I couldn't let anyone know McKurn was the father—not even the child . . . I'd be living in a tissue of lies for the rest of my life.*

She sat blankly before taking the envelope and fumbling as she opened it, tearing the letter inside in the process. It was a note from ASIO, advising that the "report you requested on Saudi Arabian activities in Australia and the Sandemans" was now ready and "when would be a convenient time to schedule the briefing?" *Something else to arrange,* she sighed. The package contained three copies of a thick report on Saudi Arabian influence in Australia from the think tank they'd approached several weeks earlier. She grinned weakly: no sign of the requested analysis from Foreign Affairs.

She riffled the pages of the think tank's report. "A hundred and seventy-two." *Is this relevant right now?* she asked herself, thinking of the election. *Probably not—but I have to be able to tell Royn what it says.* She skimmed the summary: the think tank's information about the *extent* of Saudi activities in the country was sketchy, relying on publicly available information. But its conclusion—that Saudi money created anti-democratic, anti-human-rights zealots—and its recommendations were clear:

> Only one thing makes Saudi Arabia powerful and influential: the money that comes from oil. That money funds Wahhabist schools wherever there are Muslims. These schools teach a virulent version of Islam and are the major source of Islamic zealots willing to die for their cause.

Without that money, Saudi Arabia's influence would wither away.

Ultimately, the only way to reduce Saudi Arabia's influence is to remove its source—money—which can only be done by reducing the value of the Saudis' main export, oil, by reducing oil *demand.*

This would require a crash program to replace oil with other sources of energy, which can be sold to the public under a "green" banner.

But Australian demand for oil is a mere 1.05% of world demand, so this objective could only be achieved by a concerted effort led by the United States and Europe.

The simplest way to reduce Saudi influence just within Australia is to ban their activities in the country. But their charitable activities can be claimed as religious in nature, so such a ban could fall foul of the Constitution's guarantee of religious freedom (section 116). If directed solely against Saudi Arabia it would also invite retaliation: for example, banning oil exports to Australia and persuading other Muslim countries to follow suit.

One way to get around section 116 is to simply ban the activities of *all* foreign charities. That would include institutions like the Red Cross and possibly even the Boy Scouts; it would hardly meet with public approval.

A second way is to broaden the definition of "terrorist-related" institutions to include any that propagate "hate-speech" or "unAustralian" ideas, but . . .

. . . the civil libertarians would be up in arms, she thought, her mind wandering to the options the doctor had listed: abortion, adoption, or keep it.

None of the above, she shuddered.

"Some sixty percent of pregnancies," the doctor had said, "fail in the first few weeks for one reason or another. That could still happen. Natural abortion—or God-given, if you prefer."

If that's true, she thought, *God would get a grade of "fail" for his handiwork.* She imagined she heard Derek's mischievous laugh: *"So does He deserve to go to hell along with all the others the churches would send there?"*

She smiled despite herself.

If Nature—or God—pulls the trigger, that's fine. *But if I do? That's the issue.*

"Alison?" Doug Selkirk's voice broke into her thoughts. "Shouldn't we get started?"

Selkirk leant against the door, grinning at her.

"Of course," she said, waving Selkirk to a seat.

"Interesting reading?" Selkirk asked as he sat down.

Nodding, Alison passed him the summary sheets.

"Pretty gruesome," he said, and he reached for the report itself, but Alison pushed it aside.

"Later," she said. "We have more important things to do right now."

Selkirk looked at her. "More *urgent,* perhaps, but more important? I'm not so sure."

48 Hanging Judge

"ON THE COUNT OF murder, *guilty as charged.*"
He shuddered at the words, knowing they were inevitable, and cringed away from the jury spokesman, a dark human shape barely standing out from the fuzzy ovals of the other jurors behind.

"On the counts of accessory to murder," the spokesman continued, "*guilty as charged.*"

"The prisoner will rise."

He struggled to his feet, straining against the overwhelming weight of the judge's looming presence.

The judge sat on high, his white wig distinct; his skin shimmered, the coloring undefined. The glimmering shadow of a face had no expression, but as the words rang out the eyes turned into the black, piercing pinpoints of the last judgement. A dark halo materialized above the wig, drifted slowly down as if time had almost stopped, and morphed into a shapeless cloth of shadow until it touched the wig as a black cap— and the judge and the shadows of the jury slowly closed in on him, their bony, skinless fingers reaching for him as they screamed a ghoulish chorus of "*Guilty, guilty, guilty. . . .*"

He screamed. A long, pulsating wail that jolted him awake.

Derek Olsson jerked himself upright, the voices still echoing from the walls of his mind. *Guilty,* they all seemed to be saying, *of moral bankruptcy.*

Yes, he agreed, *I—whose only moral commandment was* DO NO HARM—*am guilty as charged.*

Yes, Luk Suk had committed countless crimes. Yes, Luk Suk was guilty. Yes, any court where he couldn't bribe the judge would find him guilty if all the evidence was presented. Yes, he'd face execution or a life behind bars. And yes, that's exactly what he deserved.

But now, Olsson's fingers trembled and his throat felt dry as he recalled, once again, feeling Luk Suk's neck under their touch.

I've killed a man. With my own hands. In cold blood. No jury in the world, he knew, would acquit him on the grounds of "pre-emptive self-defence."

He found himself sitting on the edge of the soft, downy, and unfamiliar bed, unable to stop shaking.

He'd slept, but was still tired. As he'd been every morning since his escape from Thailand, waking up feverish, drained from the aftermath of the dreams, visions, and re-lived memories which haunted him ever since . . . Nazarov, Shultz and de Brouw standing over a litter of dead bodies, the death masks of their heads set in a permanent leer that followed him as he moved . . . Luk Suk's body slumping under his touch as its life fled . . . the tortured Thai girl on the tabloid cover . . . and the final judgement.

A doctor in Phnom Penh pumped him full of antibiotics and aspirin, saying, "A severe case of flu," his tone suggesting the doctor didn't believe his own diagnosis. *I know the real reason,* he thought. *I'm exhausted, worn out—and shrouded with gloom.*

Now the fever had gone, but his muscles—and head—still ached.

Forcing his gummy eyes open, he looked around the dark, featureless room.

Where am I?

The only light came from the dancing numbers of the digital clock beside the bed. For a reason he couldn't recall, it was important to know the time. 4:09. AM or PM? He couldn't tell. He fumbled until he found a light switch, shading his eyes from the sudden brilliance. Next to the clock was a room key tagged: AUCKLAND AIRPORT HOTEL. Then he remembered, *I've got a flight . . . haven't I?*

It took a week of soup and water and little else before his fever abated enough for him to get on a plane. Now, he remembered, he was flying the long way around to Brisbane—and Lars. He flew via Auckland using his British passport; for the last leg to Brisbane he would become "Francis Tully," a New Zealander, whose passport had yet to be used.

He stumbled into the bathroom and stared for an indefinite time at his own pale, gaunt image in the mirror. "You look like a ghost," he told himself, "or like you've just seen one." *And they're already stampeding over my grave.*

I put myself in the position where it was all inevitable. I chose a path—dealing in death the inescapable result. Breaking my only moral commandment was impossible to avoid.

As he began the process of transforming himself into the bespectacled Francis Tully, he focused his mind on his goal to mobilize his energy: *Lars . . . and to clear my name.*

"But how," he asked himself, "can I clear my soul?"

*****

"WELL, IT'S NOT THE White House, mate," Collin Renfrew said, gazing around as Anthony Royn greeted him at the front door of the Prime Minister's Lodge.

"Prime Minister to you," Royn grinned.

"Yeah, right," Renfrew chuckled. "Still, congratulations and all that for kicking the Old Goat out of here."

"Old Goat?"

"Christ, Tony. Sometimes I wonder how you made it here. Kydd—goat, got it?"

"I can see inviting you was a mistake," Royn grinned back, giving Renfrew's shoulder a nudge.

As Royn began to greet the next person in line, Renfrew turned to Melanie and kissed her on the cheek. "Hi, Mel," he said. "Bit of a comedown from Toorak, wouldn't you say?"

"Nice to see you, too," Melanie scowled. "But it does come with certain other advantages, you know."

"And the hot seat as well."

"You're holding up the line again," Melanie pointed out.

Renfrew shrugged. "Okay, I know when I'm not wanted—which way is the booze, then?"

"Just follow the scent. I'm sure you'll manage to find it without any help from me—or anyone else," Melanie said, unwrinkling her nose as she turned her attention to the next person who was waiting, politely impatient. "Good evening, Ambassador."

But as she mechanically shook hands with the stream of guests who'd been invited to Royn's inaugural reception, she had to admit Renfrew was right. The Lodge was completed in 1927 as a temporary dwelling until a "monumental" Prime Ministerial residence was built. That never happened: there was no political mileage in putting up a grandiose building at voters' expense in a country where "tall poppies" were regularly knocked over.

The average family would be delighted to move from their three-bedroom house to a two-storey building with forty rooms (including staff quarters), all at the taxpayers' expense. But to Melanie the fact that the Lodge could not, unlike their Toorak house, comfortably accommodate their three children, Royn's and Melanie's parents, and Royn's brother and sister and their families—who'd all come to witness Royn's swearing-in as Prime Minister that morning—meant it was simply too small.

Even a dozen guests for dinner was something of a squeeze, she thought contemptuously. She vowed to find a way to build a residence in keeping with her husband's status as leader of the world's fourteenth-richest state. If she could get her way, she'd model it—in modern style, of course—on the Élysée Palace, home of France's President, with its many *salons* including *La Salle des fêtes* which could host over two hundred people for a sit-down lunch.

To accommodate the Ambassadors, Members, Senators, businessmen, celebrities, journalists, State Premiers and various party officials and hangers-on who received— or wangled—an invitation to the reception, several marquees had been set up on the grounds giving the Lodge, she concluded, all the dignity of a school fête.

Still, there were *definitely* other advantages: she eyed the rich, powerful, and famous all obsequiously flattering, toadying and fawning on the man who now held the reins of power—*her* husband.

Well—almost all of them, she thought as her gaze was drawn to the craggy nose of Senator Frank McKurn. ". . . and don't you think," he was saying to Royn, "that it's time we had a little chat?"

"I'll look forward to it, Senator," Royn responded, his smiling mask almost slipping off his face.

"You look stunning, today," McKurn said as he turned to Melanie. "You grace this old building far more elegantly than your predecessor."

"Thank you, Senator," Melanie said, her hand limp in McKurn's grasp. "I trust your shoulder is healing."

"Tolerably well," McKurn grunted, clearly annoyed to be reminded of it. With a jerk of his head, he strode away.

As Melanie finishing greeting the last person in line Zoë, waving a near-empty flute of champagne, came up to her bubbling, "Isn't this exciting, Mum?"

"Yes, my dear," Melanie grinned, "it is." She hugged her daughter and admired her with warm approval. Zoë had taken Royn's not-so-gentle hint to dye her hair back to its *natural* color with surprisingly good grace; she wore a chic, but conservative, black evening dress, minimal makeup and a single, thin, silver necklace; there was no sign of her usual garish, provocative and rebellious style.

Melanie spied Collin Renfrew coming towards them, his gaze focused on Zoë. "Keep away from *him*," Melanie warned softly.

"Oh, *Mother*," Zoë chided as Renfrew approached. "I can handle him easily. You watch. . . ."

"Young lady," Renfrew said, bowing slightly to kiss Zoë's hand.

"Unca Collin," Zoë replied gaily. Melanie stifled a giggle as Renfrew cringed at Zoë's childish form of address. "Would you be my escort?"

"My pleasure," Renfrew smiled, nodding at Melanie as Zoë linked her arm through his and led him away. A moment later Melanie saw that Renfrew was carrying Zoë's now-empty glass, looking for a refill.

"So, my darling," Royn said, taking Melanie's hand, "shall we mingle? What would you like to drink?"

"Champagne, of course," she said, flashing him a brilliant smile and snuggling up to him. "And you?"

"Later," Royn laughed, pulling slightly away from her. "You're first lady now. You need to behave with a little more decorum, at least in public. And thanks—but *I* don't need a drink at the moment."

Melanie took in his flushed cheeks and glowing eyes. "That's true," she said. "Perhaps just a soda water, then, for appearances."

"Good idea," said Royn. "Where are the boys?"

"They're upstairs somewhere with their cousins. Ricky made some scathing comment about monkey suits."

"Well, he *would,*" Royn, chucked as he looked around. "Have you seen Alison anywhere?"

"She's still not feeling well," said Melanie. "I'm beginning to wonder. . . ." Her voice trailed off as she saw Zoë suddenly stop, say something to Renfrew and turn to Senator McKurn. Royn and Melanie both frowned. Melanie restrained Royn's impulse to head towards his daughter. "Let's just keep an eye on her," she said, "and wander in the same direction."

A small balloon of empty space seemed to encircle McKurn while most of the people crowding the drawing room were congregating expectantly around Royn . . . including the Opposition leader, Ian Nash, who was elbowing his way through the circle of guests.

"Excuse me, Unca Collin," Zoë smiled sweetly, "Senator McKurn looks like he needs cheering up. And I've been *dying* to talk to him."

"Is that wise?" Renfrew asked, still holding Zoë's empty glass. But Zoë had already turned towards McKurn, her long dress a swirl from the slight wiggle of her hips.

"Senator McKurn," Zoë gushed, looking at him the way teenage girls usually reserve for rock stars. "I've heard *so* much about you."

"Is that so?" McKurn said guardedly, his shoulders nevertheless straightening and his eyes glinting as he took in her willowy body. "You have the advantage, madam—I don't think we've met."

"I'm Zoë," she said. "It must be so *intriguing* to be a Senator, especially President of the Senate. What's it like? How did you *rise* to such a position? How—"

"One thing at a time, young lady," McKurn laughed, holding up a hand in mock protest as he inched closer.

"It's just that politics is so *fascinating,* wouldn't you agree, Senator? And you must have some absolutely *riveting* stories to tell." A faint flush swam across Zoë's cheeks as she stood firm under McKurn's intrusive gaze.

McKurn smiled. "I see you are in need of refreshment, madam," he said, offering Zoë his arm. "As am I."

McKurn's breathing quickened as he felt the faint tremble in the touch of Zoë's fingers on his outstretched arm. Absorbed in Zoë's apparently undivided attention, McKurn was unaware that, as he embarked on a highly edited version of his history, she was discreetly guiding him outside, beyond her mother's gaze.

"WELL, TONY," NASH SAID, briefly acknowledging Melanie as he pumped Royn's hand. "How does it feel to be Prime Minister?"

"I only just got here, Ian." Royn grinned in mock protest. "Still finding my way around. But I'm not complaining."

"With any luck," Nash said looking admiringly around the drawing room of the Lodge, "I'll soon be returning the honor with an invitation to *my* first reception."

Royn laughed. "You'll need forty-four gallon drums full of luck is my guess, and lots of them."

"We'll soon see, won't we?" Nash scowled, his unruly red hair spoiling the otherwise elegant effect of his evening dress.

"Soon?" Royn asked, raising an eyebrow. "I've had *so* many *other* things to think about." His shoulders appeared to sag under the enormous weight he was carrying. "But," he added vaguely, as if it had only just occurred to him, "it *will* have to be sometime in the next ten months, won't it?"

"Sure, Tony," Nash laughed. "And I was born yesterday?"

"Not that I've noticed, Ian," Royn laughed, clasping Nash's shoulder. "Don't worry. Whenever a decision is reached, I'll notify you immediately."

"Much appreciated," Nash said sourly.

"With your kind permission, Mr. Nash," the Sandemans' High Commissioner gently interrupted, "if I may have a quiet word, Prime Minister."

"It would be my pleasure," Royn smiled, inclining his head towards Nash, "if you'll excuse me, Ian. Shall we enjoy the fresh air," Royn asked, "and a little more privacy?"

As they moved in the direction Zoë had gone, Melanie looked back to see Nash gazing thoughtfully at their backs, nodding to himself. "Nice performance, darling," Melanie whispered, "but I think he's guessed."

Royn shrugged. "Can't be helped. In his position he should be a good Boy Scout and 'be prepared'."

"Our government congratulates you on becoming Prime Minister," the high commissioner said as they emerged into the cool, wintry air. The sun was low in the cloudless sky, but a mass of tiny colored lights sprinkling the marquees glowed invitingly. "Abdullah Nimabi and our Prime Minister, Aruma Bagambi, send their personal regards and good wishes."

"I truly appreciate that," said Royn with a cordiality he didn't feel: he had a good idea where this conversation was heading.

"They also wish you to know how much they personally, as well as officially, appreciated working with you as foreign minister—a sentiment I, too, share."

"It has indeed been a pleasure," Royn said solemnly, squeezing Melanie's arm as he saw her turn her head away, an impish grin on her lips.

"To that extent—while of course welcoming your ascendance," the high commissioner said, "we also regret it and, naturally, trust our excellent relations will continue."

"That is both our desire and our intent," Royn replied. "And, thankfully, everything *is* going smoothly and successfully—a state of affairs we can all be very proud of. We should make sure it continues that way without substantial change, don't you agree High Commissioner?"

"Quite so, Prime Minister."

"Please convey my heartfelt appreciation to Abdullah and Prime Minister Bagambi. And if you'll excuse me—" Royn waved his hand vaguely at the people milling around them "—this new office comes with a variety of social obligations."

"I am always at your service, Prime Minister." The high commissioner bowed formally, the hint of a sour expression on his face.

Barry Easton stepped into the break of conversation. "Congratulations, Tony."

"Thanks—*again,* Barry." Royn chuckled. "There's something I'd like to talk to you about."

"I'm all ears."

"Stay for a drink after the party winds down, Barry," Royn said, "so we can have a private chat."

"Look, Tony!" Melanie hissed. On the other side of the garden Royn saw his father talking—no, arguing—with McKurn. Vanessa Strezlecki looked as though she was trying to play the role of umpire while Zoë stood calmly watching, wearing Melanie's mischievous grin.

"I don't like the look of that," Royn whispered. "That's *your* expression when you've done something you shouldn't oughta—what do you think Zoë's *doing?*

"My guess is that she's practicing following in your footsteps, my dear."

"Huh?"

"Later, my dear," Melanie said, *when I find out what Zoë did and said.* "Let's go see if she, or Sid, needs rescuing."

Absorbed in his own words and Zoë's doe-like eyes, McKurn barely noticed the other guests until he heard Vanessa Strezlecki's bright, tinkling voice, "Well, if it isn't Senator McKurn."

McKurn stopped in mid flow; Vanessa was smiling at him gaily, while Sidney Royn glanced at his granddaughter with reproof before turning to scowl at McKurn. "I must say," Sidney Royn said, "I'm surprised to see *you* here."

"Why is that, Sid?"

"I thought you might have the decency not to show up tonight," Sidney Royn said, "or didn't you read the papers this morning?"

McKurn winced. "Frankie" McKurn: the Bad Company He Keeps, screamed the page one headline of that morning's *Mercury.* Karla Preston's story was illustrated with pictures of a much younger McKurn in the company of known criminals.

"Ancient history, Sid," McKurn shrugged. "Ancient history."

"And the prison records the papers reproduced," Vanessa asked with apparent innocence, "are *fakes?*"

McKurn shrugged. "So I was a bit rowdy in my youth—"

"A bit rowdy?" Sidney Royn said. "Something of an understatement, don't you think—given the nature of some of the charges?"

"Unsubstantiated BS," McKurn snapped. "Fairy tales!"

"Suspicion of *murder?*" Sidney Royn said. "Reprinted from police records, *unsubstantiated?* Come now, Frankie."

"My name is *Frank,*" McKurn growled. "So I was a wild colonial boy and the cops tried to pin all sorts of stuff on me. And," McKurn grinned widely, "failed."

"Reform school succeeded with you, Senator?" Vanessa asked sweetly, her fingers gently touching McKurn's arm. "Is that what you're saying?"

"Completely, madam," McKurn nodded, moving slightly closer to Vanessa in response to her touch.

"We both know that you know that I know better than that," Sidney Royn responded.

"Whereas I only know what I *see*," Vanessa said before McKurn could react, capturing his eyes with her gaze.

"And what, exactly, do you see, Senator Strezlecki?" McKurn asked.

"I see a strong resemblance to our new Prime Minister."

Sidney Royn, McKurn, and Zoë all looked at her in surprise. "Really?" McKurn said scornfully as, almost simultaneously, Sidney Royn exclaimed disbelievingly, "*What* resemblance?"

Vanessa's laugh tinkled between the two men. "Like Tony," she said, still looking at McKurn, "you're a consummate actor. And politics, after all, is just a stage. Wouldn't you agree, Senator?"

"I see," said McKurn sourly.

"Do you *really* think Daddy's a good actor?" Zoë asked.

"Daddy?" Vanessa asked as her warm eyes studied Zoë's face with interest.

"You're Zoë *Royn?*" McKurn's voice thundered. Zoë took a step back from the implied threat of his clenched fists. "You little minx." Without another word McKurn spun on his heel and stalked away, glowering at Royn and Melanie as he passed them.

Sidney Royn's shoulders loosened as McKurn's back disappeared into the crowd. "My apologies, Vanessa," he said. "I seem to have forgotten my manners. May I introduce my granddaughter, Zoë Royn." He turned to Zoë. "This is Senator Strezlecki."

"Oh," said Zoë, her eyes wide, "you're completing Senator Thompson's term, aren't you?"

"That's right," Vanessa nodded. "And to answer your question, Zoë, yes, your father is a superb actor." Her eyes narrowed with a hint of disapproval. "In fact, I'm wondering if it runs in the family."

"I really don't think so," Sidney Royn said, his tone making it clear that acting was not a profession he held in high regard. "If you'll excuse me," he said abruptly, seeing Royn and Melanie approaching with concerned looks on their faces.

"You should realize, Zoë," Vanessa said when Sidney Royn was out of earshot, "that it's a very dangerous idea to provoke a wild animal even if you're carrying a blunderbuss and know how to use it."

Zoë flushed. "Thank you, Vanessa," she said solemnly. "I'll remember that."

As Sidney Royn neared his son, Doug Selkirk grasped Royn's elbow and pulled him aside. "Prime Minister," he whispered urgently, "you'd better come and take a look at a news item *now.*"

"Later, Doug," Royn said, brushing Selkirk's hand aside.

"Prime Minister! It's important *and urgent.* It won't take long, and *everyone* will know about it in a few minutes. You *must* have a head start."

"That bad?" Royn asked.

"Worse. *Much* worse," Selkirk replied.

Selkirk directed Royn to the upstairs study, closed the door, and flicked the button the TV remote.

"What's this?"

"Just watch," said Selkirk.

"Holy cow," Royn spluttered as the flickering, paused image on the TV leapt into life and the announcer's voice suddenly filled the room. "And I only just got here."

*****

"FINISHED!"

Alison eyed the papers strewn across her dining table, suppressing a yawn. She knew she'd done a good job of outlining recommended election strategies—but was unable to summon any feeling of excitement. She switched on the TV to catch the news.

She thought about the reception she had missed, and shrugged. Her excuse, that she was still not feeling well, wasn't—quite—true. She was behind with her work: for the first time in fourteen years it felt like a chore, not a pleasure. And she lacked the energy, and the desire, to be sociable.

"Top of the news," the news anchor broke into her thoughts, "Melbourne journalist Robin Cartwright has been kidnapped in Toribaya by separatists who are holding him for ransom. In Canberra . . . "

"What?" Alison shrieked, tuning out the rest of the summary. She sank into the sofa waiting impatiently for the ads to come to an end.

". . . and the separatists released this video on the Internet," the anchor was saying. The picture cut to a grainy video of Robin Cartwright and two masked men, each wearing a fez. One held a scimitar-like blade across Cartwright's throat.

"As you can see," Cartwright said in a unsteady voice, "I'm being held captive." Nervously eying the two men, he slowly raised his wrists to the camera: a pair of handcuffs glinted in the lights until one of the men slapped his wrists down. "My captors, members of the separatist group, Islamic Purity, are demanding, as the price of my release, the withdrawal of all Australian and other soldiers from the Sandemans, the release of all political prisoners, and the handing over of control of all oil resources in Jazeerat el-Bihar to its people. A negative response will lead them to sending bits of me—" Cartwright took a deep breath to control his sudden tremble as he eyed the blade "—to various people, starting with Anthony Royn. Congrats, Tony, by the way." He grinned cheekily. "So while I'm waiting I'd really appreciate if someone could send in the Red . . . ah . . . Crescent—I could use a few cases of Scotch."

The camera switched back to the news anchor, Cartwright's frozen face behind him. "In a statement released with the video, the separatists also said—"

Alison's phone shrilled. She tried to listen while she answered it, but Karla's voice, even on the phone, drowned out everything else. "Are you watching the news?" Karla demanded, barely pausing for Alison's response. "There's *no way* Islamic Purity kidnapped Robin. They're not like that."

"How can you be so sure?" Alison asked.

"*They* rescued me from the Sandeman soldiers and—. Have you spoken to your cousin Jeremy lately?"

"Jeremy? No. What's he got to do with it?"

Karla told Alison how, risking his life, Jeremy had gone, *alone,* to Islamic Purity's mountain haven—and about Colonel Gugamti's behavior at the meeting in Inkaya.

"I didn't know that about Jeremy—or about that meeting, for that matter."

"Give Jeremy a call and he'll confirm everything I've said."

"Then . . . " Alison said slowly, "who are the kidnappers?"

"Someone doesn't like Islamic Purity—and it wouldn't surprise me if that Colonel Gugamti had something to do with it."

"An army *officer?* Surely not, Karla."

"An *Australian* army officer, no. But a Sandeman one? Have you already forgotten how we met, and what Robin told Royn?"

"It's just so hard to believe—" Alison began, also recalling Cartwright's exchanges with Rowena Watson on the morning TV program.

"I know," Karla sighed. "Took me a while, too, and I was *there.*"

"I'll pass this information on—if that's okay."

"Absolutely," said Karla. "But I can do more—I can *expose* them."

"How?"

"By interviewing Islamic Purity's *leader*—if I can get ahold of him. Wish me luck."

Alison began to comply, but Karla had already hung up.

She turned the TV off, sat thoughtfully, and called Doug Selkirk. "Doug, have you—?"

"Yes, I've seen it. And so has the Prime Minister," Selkirk replied. Lowering his voice he added, "I think he's in a state of shock."

"I'm not surprised," Alison said. "You'd better revive him."

"A stiff brandy is having its effect," Selkirk said. "But—what's our policy here? Who should be in charge—ASIO? The Federal Police?"

"As far as I know," Alison said, "the government's policy has always been we don't negotiate with terrorists."

"That's been academic—until now."

"True," Alison said. "As to who's in charge, why don't you grab the head of the PM's security and let him sort it out."

"Good idea. You should probably get over here ASAP," Selkirk said. "If you're feeling up to it."

"I'm not dying, Doug," Alison said. *Only inside.* "I have one thing to do first."

She hadn't spoken to Jeremy for quite some time. If she called him *officially* she'd have to "go through channels." God knows how long that would take.

How else could she get in touch with him? *Jeremy's mother—my aunt—will know.*

49 "As Ye Sow . . ."

ALISON PAUSED ON THE threshold of her new office. She closed the door. For the first time in years she felt completely isolated from the rest of the staff.

She was surprised to notice her pleasure at being completely alone.

She stood by the wide windows, leaned against the sill and surveyed the prime minister's private courtyard. The plants were green and welcoming; the sun shone brightly on the opposite wall, leaving her in a well of shadow. She thought of herself at sixteen. . . . *For twenty years, this is where I wanted to be. Here I am—running on empty.*

A police motorcycle roared into the courtyard leading two white limousines. The prime minister's security team leapt from the second car as a scowling Anthony Royn stepped out of the first. Spotting Alison, he beckoned impatiently and marched into the prime ministerial suite, his eyes cast down, looking neither right nor left. Melanie hurried after him. A moment later Barry Easton's mop of thinning, reddish-blond hair appeared from the car. He stood and admired the PM's private space, drinking in the fresh air as if it were tinged with the essence of power. His face lit up when his roving gaze stopped on Alison. Alison grinned faintly. *At least someone's in a good mood today.*

"GOOD MORNING, PRIME MINISTER," Alison said as she trudged along the corridor.

"What's good about it," Royn said sourly as he scurried into his office, Melanie on his heels, "except that Barry's agreed to stand."

"Maybe," said Melanie, looking as grim as Royn.

Easton beamed with delight as he ambled up to Alison. He was dressed, as usual, in a rumpled, tie less white shirt and hound's-tooth blazer with leather patches on the elbows. He was pleasingly pudgy, a perfect candidate for Santa Claus. "You are a glistering rose in what seems to be a mortuary this morning."

"Professor Easton," Alison laughed. "You're not auditioning for Shakespeare." Glancing at Melanie's back she asked, "What's the problem?"

Easton chuckled. "You mean, aside from Cartwright's kidnapping, Karla Preston's report that Islamic Purity had nothing to do with it, or the grenade attack on Zulu base—"

"The *what* attack?"

"Didn't you listen to the radio this morning? Somehow, the terrorists got a hold of a grenade launcher. Three diggers injured."

"Bad to worse."

"But to answer your question," Easton grinned, holding the door to Royn's new office to let Alison go through first, "yes. Several problems it seems."

The fragile Victorian desk had gone; a new sofa suite replaced the one Kydd had worn out; the absence of Kydd's photos made the walls seem naked: they awaited Royn's decision on his preferred paintings, wall-hangings or decoration. The aroma of new leather and the whiff of ammonia in the air—left over from cleaning the remnants of Kydd's smoke from the room—gave it all the stateliness of a furniture showroom.

Royn hardly glanced around as he took his seat. "Somebody's been working Kydd's electorate, a guy called Jake Meldrum," Royn told Alison. "Know anything about him?"

Alison shook her head.

"He's also a lecturer at Macquarie," said Easton. "Sociology. He's been giving talks around the electorate for about a year, signing people up. A few months ago, Meldrum got himself elected Secretary of the Federal Electoral Council for Kydd's electorate."

"How did he manage that?" Alison asked.

"It wasn't hard," Easton grinned. "The previous secretary, an old biddy immobilized with arthritis, was happy to give it up. The party officials there are like Fred Ingram—Kydd cronies and Kydd's vintage. When Meldrum asked if he could nominate for the position, he was welcomed with open arms. I even voted for him, hoping he'd breathe some new life into the local party organization."

"Which is exactly what he's done," Royn said unhappily.

"As FEC secretary, he's in charge of the membership lists," Alison said.

"Exactly," said Melanie.

"But the membership rolls have skyrocketed," Easton said. "There's no doubt he's very efficient—"

"Except when it comes to forwarding lists of new members to Party HQ." Melanie sounded as though she'd just swallowed a large dose of castor oil.

Easton's eyebrows seemed to droop. "So?" he shrugged.

Alison looked at Melanie. "Branch-stacking?"

"That's what I suspect," Melanie said.

"Surely not," Easton protested.

"What's his motive, Barry," Alison asked softly.

Easton shrugged. "He claims he's out to build up the party."

"You're refreshingly naïve, Barry," Melanie laughed.

"I resent your implication, Melanie," Easton said.

"'Everyone in politics is out for himself, until proven otherwise,' according to Kydd." Melanie's tone was that of talking to a wayward child. "He also said he'd never, in fifty years, found an exception to that rule. There are no altruists *or* idealists in politics, Barry. They never get past second base."

All too true, Alison thought. *Which is why scum like McKurn can rise to the top.*

Royn nodded. "*Every* politician's motive is ulterior."

"Including yours, Tony?"

Royn spread his arms to encompass the suite. "Of course," he grinned. "My aim was to get *here,* even when I denied it."

And now that you're here? Revenge was the only word that came to her mind. It took an effort for Alison to recall all the other idealistic goals that had propelled her on this path. *And where will I find the oomph to pursue them?*

"Don't you find the same behavior in your ivory tower?" Melanie asked.

"Sometimes, I suppose," Easton said. His pulled his pipe from his blazer pocket and toyed with it.

"From what I've heard," Royn said, "infighting between professors jockeying for position and status can be as fierce as anything we see here."

"How cynical," Easton said.

"Just realistic, Barry," Alison replied.

"If Meldrum's aim is to be Kydd's successor," Melanie asked Easton, "would he have behaved any differently?"

"I guess not," Easton conceded. "He's certainly been singing Kydd's praises lavishly."

Melanie chuckled. "He's probably just licking arse to ensure Kydd's support."

"Such language," Easton protested. "And from a lady."

"If you think Mel's a lady," Royn laughed, "you've never seen her in action."

"If you're going into politics, Barry," Melanie said, "you'd better get used to it."

"Well," said Easton, "that's the problem isn't it. I'd *love* to stand. But there's no point in me opposing Kydd if he doesn't resign—or Meldrum if he's impossible to beat. Is there another seat I could go for?"

"One West Australian member said he'd resign at the next election," Alison said.

"You'd have to move to Perth, Barry," Royn grinned. "But Stanley Chow's got that electorate sewn up. No point."

"Oh well," Easton shrugged. "It was a nice idea, but if Meldrum's already got the numbers—"

"Think it through carefully, Barry," Royn said. "I love to have you here, but you've already got a good life. Politics could screw it up."

Melanie glared at her husband. "What are you two talking about? We haven't lost yet."

"That's my girl," Royn smiled approvingly.

"Counter-stacking, of course, is out—" Melanie said.

"The six-month rule," Alison interjected. Melanie and Royn both nodded gloomily: a new member of the Conservative Party had to wait six months to be eligible to vote in a preselection contest.

"—but if we can find something fishy about the new members. . . ." Party HQ had to approve every new member's application.

Royn and Alison both nodded sagely; Easton demanded, "Then *what?*"

"If the executive finds any irregularities in the applications, it can reject them," Alison said.

Easton frowned and sucked noisily on his unlit pipe. "I've got a lot to learn." Seeing Melanie's disapproving glance, he added, "I suppose this is a no smoking building," he said.

Melanie nodded.

"Damn smoke Nazis are everywhere," he said, stuffing the pipe back into his pocket.

"Does Meldrum belong to any faction, Barry?" Alison asked. There were, according to the pundits, three main factions in the Conservative Party—the free market radicals on the Right (called the "loonies" by the left), the moderates (otherwise known as the "wishy-washies") and the non-committed (the "Great Unwashed"). Overlaying those groupings was the intricate network of state, local, personal and even family loyalties that cut across the otherwise shifting coalitions.

"I've no idea," Easton said. "What difference does it make?"

"If he's a quiet member of an unpopular faction—" Melanie began.

"Like the loonies," Royn explained.

"—he could lose a lot of support, just like that." Melanie snapped her fingers.

"Wait a minute," Easton protested. "Speaking as an economist, the free market has an enormous amount to offer—"

Royn held up his hand. "Of course it does, Barry," he said soothingly. "But in politics you mustn't be *rigid.*"

"And if you speak like an economist on the hustings," Melanie said, "you'll send everyone to sleep."

"You've seen my talks," Easton said, his eyebrows twitching. "You should know I know that."

"Those people came to *hear* you," Melanie said, "not to *heckle* you."

"I'm a branch president," Easton protested, "so I'm not totally unexposed to political gatherings, Melanie."

"Running tea parties for little old ladies from the blue rinse set hardly counts as preparation for a campaign," Melanie said.

"Indeed," said Royn. "Best to be aware, *now*, of all the pressures you'll face rather than be stumped on the campaign trail."

Easton nodded slowly. "Fair enough, Tony."

"Getting the executive to reject new members may not be enough," Alison said.

"Probably not," Melanie agreed. "But if there's a case for executive intervention into the branch's affairs, Meldrum could even be suspended."

"That's hardly cricket," Easton said.

"We're not playing cricket." Melanie said. "Are you sure you're up to this, Barry?"

"Absolutely," he said, one hand disappearing into his blazer pocket.

"Are there any skeletons in Meldrum's closet?" Melanie continued, "Did he inhale? Sleep with his students?"

"Dirt?" Easton said, a faint flush in his cheeks. "But—that can work two ways," Easton mumbled.

"True," Melanie agreed. "But nominations close ten days after the writs are issued. If our timing's right, Meldrum won't have enough time to respond." She peered intensely at Easton. "*Is* there anything in *your* closet you'd hate to see in tomorrow's paper."

Easton shrugged. "Not that I can think of."

"In politics, Barry," Royn said, "baseless rumors can be just as deadly."

"In that electorate," Alison said, "winning preselection is tantamount to winning the seat. So Meldrum won't be your only opponent. You'll be facing every other Conservative hopeful in the country, all looking for some way—*any* way—to knock out the frontrunners."

Easton gazed into the distance, lost in thought.

"Barry," Melanie said, "when we're finished here, how about I go over the political facts of life."

"Okay," Easton said.

"It's time for the ASIO briefing, Prime Minister," Alison said. Originally scheduled for ASIO to report on its findings about Saudi influence, Robin Cartwright's kidnapping had taken center stage.

"Let's go, then," Royn said, coming to his feet.

*****

Derek Olsson walked up to the front door of a compact, attractive cottage on the outskirts of Noosa, a twenty minute drive from the main beach. *Lars will be surprised,* he thought, twisting the doorknob to see if it was locked. It wasn't. *Don't give him the opportunity to slam the door in my face,* he decided.

"Morning Lars," he said, taking just one step through the front door. "You up?"

Lars Olsson, wearing just a T-shirt and shorts, sprawled on the sofa reading a day-old newspaper. He looked up in surprise, and stiffened. "Who the hell are you?"

Derek Olsson felt he was looking in a slightly distorted mirror. Where Lars was wiry, he was muscly; Lars' shoulders were not quite as broad; he was tanned while Olsson's skin was pale; Lars' hair was a bit darker and tidy in a way Olsson's never naturally was. But, Olsson decided, if you saw Lars Olsson briefly, for the first and only time, as he walked past you in a dim light, when you weren't taking careful notice because he came in with a resident of your building and then, a few days later, you saw *Derek* Olsson in a line-up, it wouldn't be surprising if you thought it was the same person.

"Don't you recognize me, Lars?"

"Should I?" Lars said as he took in Olsson's spectacles, neat black hair, blazer, slacks and briefcase.

Olsson laughed. "Sorry, I forgot." He took off his spectacles. "I've dyed my hair and I don't really wear glasses. But you haven't changed that much, even though it's been eighteen-odd years. . . ."

Lars' gaze scoured Olsson's face. His skin turned pale at his glimmer of recognition. He sprang to his feet, the newspaper's pages scattering on the floor. *"Derek!"*

"That's right, Lars," Olsson sighed.

Lars' brought up his fists into a boxing stance and took two quick steps towards Olsson, bringing one fist back to swing, favoring his now-stronger left arm even though he was right-handed. "Get the hell out of my sight, you louse," he yelled.

"Lars," Olsson laughed without moving, "you should know better than that."

Lars' muscles became rigid, holding him frozen, a still picture of a boxer caught in mid-motion except that his eyes flickered warily between Olsson's hands, hanging loosely by his side. Sluggishly, he let his fists collapse.

"What do you *want?*" he demanded, his angry tone and drooping shoulders an indication that words were the only weapon he had left.

Poor Lars, Olsson thought. The floor of the front room was bare wood, not a rug in sight. The dining table was old and scratched with chairs that didn't match the table—or each other. Only the sofa, armchairs and a large TV set resting on a wooden crate were new. *This must be his proudest possession.* "Nice place you've got here," he commented.

"Yeah, took me a long time to save up for it."

Olsson shook his head sadly. "Not according to my information."

"I don't know what you mean."

"About four weeks before you bought this house, you hardly had enough money to rub two sticks together."

"What have you been doing—looking at my bank statements?"

"Among other things, yes."

"Bullshit," Lars said with a self-satisfied air. "That information is confidential."

"True," Olsson said, "but you can always find someone who'll do something illegal if he's paid enough money. Can't you, Lars?"

"You fucking bastard," Lars shouted as his cheeks flushed. "You've been prying into my private life."

"When my lawyers get a court order to trace the deposit and tell the police who paid you, what will *they* think?"

Lars' jaw dropped and his eyes flicked away from Olsson's face, but he made no sound.

"I see," Olsson sighed, shaking his head with a soft sigh. "Do you really hate me that much?"

Lars held up his weak, right arm. *"This* reminds me a hundred times a day that *you* made me a *cripple."* His scowl turned into a crafty smile as he said, "You're on the run from the cops, aren't you? An escaped convict. I should call the police."

Olsson shrugged. "Go ahead."

Watching Olsson suspiciously, Lars slowly stepped back to pick up the phone on the coffee table, surprised that Olsson made no move. As he put the phone to his ear he frowned and pressed the cradle several times. "It's not working."

"That's right," said Olsson, closing the front door. "The line's been cut."

Lars shrunk away from Olsson, but one hand went to his pocket to pull out his cellphone.

"Not a good idea, Lars," Olsson grinned, shaking his head.

Lars' cellphone hung in mid-air as he cast a wary glance in Olsson's direction. Olsson hadn't moved, hadn't changed his position, was still standing, his arms loose. But as Lars began to punch a number into his phone Olsson uncoiled. Before Lars could hit the CALL key, he twisted Lars' wrist, forced the cellphone from his fingers, scooped it up as it fell towards the floor, and dropped it in his blazer pocket.

Olsson sank into an armchair, dropping his briefcase on the floor within easy reach.

"Goddamn you," Lars said, his shoulders tightening and his fists clenched as he turned in place.

"Sit down Lars, for Chrissake."

Lars stood undecided, let his arms fall, and gracelessly collapsed onto the sofa.

"Lars," Olsson said softly, "I didn't mean to hurt you so much—"

"That's bullshit, and you know it."

Olsson shook his head. "All I wanted to do was to stop you using me as a punching bag. I'm sorry. I really am."

"So am I," said Lars, flexing his weak arm.

"For beating me up?"

"Not for—" Lars shrugged helplessly. "Well . . . I guess. Maybe."

"Why don't you get it fixed?"

"Too expensive."

"Tell me who paid you, and I'll send you to a superb hospital in Bangkok, all expenses paid. Stay there as long as you like. "

"Bangkok, eh?" For just a moment there was a hungry look in Lars' eyes—which disappeared almost as quickly as it had come. "Nah," he said dejectedly, shaking his head. "Why should I trust *you?*"

Olsson reached inside his blazer, pulled out an envelope and dropped it on the coffee table in front of Lars. "Open it."

Lars picked up the envelope gingerly, as if it might burn his fingers. "What's this?" he asked as he studied it, puzzled.

"An airline ticket in your name. To Bangkok. First class."

"First class, eh?" He examined the ticket carefully, as though it might be a forgery, and let it flutter back to the table. "Wouldn't do any good," he said gloomily.

"Why not? I'll do my best to keep your name out if it. If you were in Bangkok when the arrest was made, so much the better."

"Not with my luck."

"In a few weeks, Lars, I won't need your help—and it will be impossible to protect you."

Lars glared at his brother as if Olsson was the cause of everything he'd ever suffered.

"Seven to ten years, Lars. That's the penalty you face as an accessory to murder."

"You'd really like that, wouldn't you?"

Olsson shuddered. "No, Lars, I *wouldn't*. I've spent the last few weeks in prison and it's a God-awful place. I certainly *don't* want to put you there."

"Why should I believe *that?*"

"Because I'm here to give you another option."

"Ha," Lars said, flicking the airline ticket so it fluttered onto the floor. "I've lived my whole life in your shadow. Dad hated me, you were Mum's favorite. Today, everyone I meet goes gooey-eyed and says, 'Oooh, you must be related to that famous *Derek Olsson*—you look just like him.' I just can't escape you, can I?"

So you decided to get even, Olsson thought. "We're adults now," he said. "We can put the past behind us—if we choose to." But as he heard his own words he asked himself, *Can we?*

"Can the sentimental claptrap, Derek."

Olsson nodded slowly. So much for his hope that the passage of eighteen years might have softened Lars' attitude to him.

"What puzzles me, Lars," Olsson said, "is why you're still alive."

"What?" Lars jaw dropped and he stared through wide eyes.

"You accompanied Vincent Leung into his apartment, where he was murdered and evidence was planted to point at me. The doorman saw you come in and picked *me* out of the line-up as the man who'd come in with Leung. They paid you thirty grand for a night's work. You're the only outsider who could identify the murderers. Much simpler to just make you disappear and keep the money."

"You're just making that up." Lars gripped the cushions of the sofa to stop the tremble in his body. "You can't prove a thing."

"But I can, Lars. As soon as my lawyers trace the source of the money I'll know who paid you—and who's the real murderer of Vincent Leung. Then—" he spread his arms and sighed "—there'll be nothing I can do to keep you out of prison."

Lars had slumped into the sofa, but his face was a frozen mask, his mouth clamped firmly shut.

"Assuming you make it to the trial. You're the weak link in the chain. They've killed Leung and God knows how many others. What difference *to them* would one more murder make? You won't even be safe in prison, Lars. But in Bangkok you'll be out of reach."

Lars had difficulty keeping his eyes focused on Olsson, but he still didn't speak.

"And when they see your name in the papers, what will Mum and Jessica think?"

"That's right," Lars snapped. "Make *me* feel guilty."

"Mum's got Alzheimer's—"

Lars hung his head. "I didn't know."

"She *really* misses you. So does Jessica. Mum even goes through your old postcards every day, wondering when the next one will arrive."

Lars shrank into the sofa, his eyes cast to the floor. Other than the sound of Lars' breathing, coming in soft gasps, a long moment of suffocating silence blanketed the room.

"What's it to be, Lars? Prison—if you live to get there? Or Bangkok and your old arm back?"

Lars slowly raised his head, his face still fixed in a scowl, but his eyes glistened redly. "You bastard," he spat.

"I'm sorry, Lars," Olsson said. He leaned over to collect the scattered pages of the airline ticket, picked up his briefcase and rose to his feet.

"You're not leaving *now*."

"You seem to have made your decision, Lars, so I don't see any point in staying."

"I—" Lars moaned, and slowly turned his head away, his shoulders quaking.

Olsson's tread was heavy as he trudged towards the front door without looking back. He gripped the doorknob, about to turn it when he heard Lars' strangled cry:

"Wait!"

Olsson slowly turned around.

Lars gulped. "Okay, I'll tell you."

With a slight nod, Olsson stood still, waiting.

Lars stretched out his hand. "The ticket."

Olsson pulled the ticket from his pocket and moved closer to Lars so he could put it on the coffee table. Lars reached for it hungrily.

"It was that thug in Sydney," Lars said softly, his lips hardly moving, choking on his words. "The one they call the Greek."

"I see," said Olsson softly, sinking slowly back into the armchair.

"I was a waiter in his Bare Bottoms Club for a while—good pay, good tips, good scenery . . . lousy hours." Lars' words now tumbled out as if he'd been relieved of a burden. "He tracked me down, no idea how. Then, you did too."

"Thanks, Lars," Olsson said. "But I need to know exactly what you did."

Lars shrugged. "Not much, really."

"Okay," said Olsson. "Just tell me, blow-by-blow."

"The man—Vincent—was a *poofter*. I befriended him one night in one of those queer hangouts." Lars spat his words, shuddering at the memory. "When we got to his place the Greek was already there with a few of his thugs. They knocked him unconscious and hustled me out the back door. That's all I did. Honest."

"Thanks, Lars," Olsson said. He opened his briefcase and took out his laptop. "Let's look at a few pictures, then."

"Of what?" Lars said suspiciously.

"The Greek's sidekicks." Olsson put the laptop on the coffee table slanted so Lars could see the screen. "Tell me which ones were in the apartment with the Greek."

"How'd you get these pictures?" Lars asked as Olsson flicked through a series of photos of the Greek's henchmen.

Olsson just smiled. "Research."

Lars pointed to one of the pictures. "*He* could have been one of them—the picture's too dark to be certain." Lars looked at Olsson quizzically. "*That* was taken in the Bare Bottoms Club, wasn't it?"

"Looks like it," said Olsson.

"How'd you manage that? The Greek would have had your balls for breakfast if he'd spotted you."

"*I* didn't take them," Olsson replied, "but I assume it was one of those small cameras, easy to hide."

Lars identified two of the three men who'd been with the Greek the night of the murder, "and the other guy was one of those two, though I'm not sure which."

"Thanks, Lars," Olsson said, closing laptop and putting back in the briefcase.

"I—" Lars' body seemed to crumple. "What the fuck have I just done?" he wailed. His eyes looked up helplessly at Olsson. "My life is in your dirty hands—the last person in the world I can trust."

"You're about to find out how wrong you are, Lars." Olsson took a pen from his jacket pocket, leaned over and wrote something on the envelope. "That's an email address if you ever need to contact me. But everything, including the hospital and all expenses, is set with the travel agent. Her name and number's with the ticket." Olsson stood up to leave. "Why don't you visit Mum and Jessica on the way?"

"Maybe."

"I suggest you get going as soon as you can, so you'll be out of the way when the shit hits the fan."

"When will that be?"

Olsson shrugged. "A week or two. Something like that."

"That's not much time. I'd have to quit my job—then who's going to pay the mortgage?"

"I'll cover it for you," Olsson said. "Rates, everything, while you're away."

"If I lose this place—"

Olsson stood transfixed at the quaver in Lars' voice and the slight glistening of his eyes. He wracked his memory, but he could not recall a single example of Lars showing *any* emotion, other than anger. "You won't, Lars," he said, solemnly. "I promise you."

As Olsson turned to the front door, Lars stood up and said, "Hey Derek. What about my cellphone?"

"Sorry, Lars," Olsson grinned. "I forgot." He hesitated and then passed it back to Lars, clasping his hand as he did. About to pull his hand away, Lars smiled tentatively and squeezed Olsson's hand briefly before putting his cellphone back in his pocket.

The Greek, Olsson thought as he reached the car he—or "Francis Tully"—had rented at Brisbane airport the previous evening. When he sat behind the wheel the exhaustion he'd been holding at bay overwhelmed him. *I need more sleep.* First, get some distance from Noosa. He drove south, towards Brisbane, deciding he could take it easy for a few days *Now that I know who I'm looking for.*

*****

"That's the first time I'm glad you won," Cracken told Royn as they walked along the corridors of Parliament House from the ASIO briefing back to Royn's office.

"I'm not sure I like the sound of that," Royn said. "Why?"

"Because you're driving right now, not me."

"If *you* were PM, Paul, what would you do?"

"The same as you've done." Cracken's laugh was almost a cackle. "Delegate the problem to the foreign minister who, if *I* were PM, would be *you*."

"Poor Helen," Royn grinned. Helen Arkness, now Minister for Foreign Affairs, had the unenviable task to—as Cracken had put it—"tell the kidnappers to get stuffed without alienating them."

Cracken shrugged. "She wanted the job."

"Let's just hope she can buy enough time for Sykes' negotiator to come through," Royn said—Cartwright's employer, Henry Sykes, was flying in a top British specialist on negotiating hostage releases—"or for us to find him."

"Ha," Cracken said. "Our spooks have no fucking idea where Cartwright is, who's really holding him, or who lobbed those grenades. What did we learn that we didn't already know last night? Only Alison's confirmation of Karla Preston's report on Islamic

Purity—and they had no idea! Even their recommendations are what we'd already decided to do."

"Let's be fair, Paul. They've got a tough job to do," Royn said. "They *did* confirm that Nimabi's pretty much rolled out the red carpet for the Saudis."

"That's hardly comforting. If the Sandeman Muslims *do* feel they're an oppressed, marginalized minority and wide open to militant Islam, Nimabi must be out of his mind. He's invited the Saudis to come in and light a match in a tinderbox."

"It will take a while, Paul," Royn grinned, "so it probably won't explode until it's your watch."

"Now *that's* something to look forward to," Cracken grumbled. "We'd better find some way to counter Saudi influence *before* it becomes entrenched."

"Agreed," Royn said as they reached the prime minister's suite, "but first things first."

"THE PRELIMINARY POLL RESULTS are positive, Prime Minister," Alison said as she and Doug Selkirk came into Royn's office.

"We should go for it, then," said Melanie.

"I agree," Royn said. "What do you think, Paul?"

"Sure," Cracken nodded.

Prompted by the toneless, noncommittal quality of his voice, Alison wondered what Cracken was really thinking. His hooded eyes and lips of stone gave no hint. *What does he really want?* Shrugging, she turned to Royn, saying, "We won't have final results until later tonight. Shouldn't we wait till tomorrow before making a final judgement?"

"Will final results be any different?" Royn asked.

"In terms of the Conservative Party's increased lead over Labor, a few fractions of a percent."

"Not meaningful," said Melanie. "What else, Alison—if anything?"

"The order of the issues the public thinks are important. At the moment, thanks to all the exposures in the press, corruption is the clear leader. People want it stopped—they're almost unanimous. The Sandemans is second. Opinion—and these questions were asked *before* Cartwright's kidnapping—is almost evenly divided: excluding the 'don't knows,' fifty-two percent are angry and want to send in more troops, while the other forty-eight percent want the troops home yesterday. Everything else—taxes, the economy, schools, pensions, health, jobs, and so on—are way down the list."

"So that won't change materially either," said Melanie.

"Only which issue comes in a distant third," Alison said, placing a thick file on Royn's desk and handing a copy to Cracken. "This is the outline of the election strategy Doug and I recommend."

"Looks comprehensive." Royn riffled through the pages, and grinned. "Why don't you give me the 'Janet and John bit.'"

They all laughed. The "Janet and John bit" was public service idiom for the one- or two-page summary of a 250-page report which, much of the time, was all a minister ever read.

"Except for the two leading issues the polls have identified, we recommend a minimalist campaign. Your popularity means you don't need to make any concrete promises. You could have the unusual situation of winning the election with no actual platform to bind you."

"So the Royal Commission it is," Royn grinned. "That makes our commitment *concrete*. And the commission would, of course, just be the first step in our plan."

"What are the other steps?"

Royn chuckled. "Confidential."

"Meaning, you'll think of something later."

Royn laughed.

"Actually," said Doug Selkirk pointing to the thick file, "we've made several suggestions."

"Thanks," Royn said. "I knew I could count on you and Alison."

"What about Stanley Chow?" Alison asked.

"I told him I'd nominate Justice Herbert Flint to head the Royal Commission," Royn grinned. "He's perfect for the job—Flint by name, flint by nature. He retires from the High Court at the end of next month so he can't start until *after* the election. Stanley thought Flint was an inspired choice."

"If we announce the election on Sunday," Cracken said, "we have to ram the Royal Commission legislation through Parliament today and tomorrow. *And* have a Cabinet meeting first, to approve it."

"The bill's already drafted," Royn grinned. "Not a problem."

"Until it gets to the Senate," Alison pointed out, "where McKurn could try and stall it."

"*He* won't want a Royal Commission into corruption," said Melanie, "*especially* after Karla Preston's revelation today." As she spoke, she began to direct her voice at Alison, but caught herself before the movement of her head became too obvious.

She's guessed, Alison realized.

Karla's article in that morning's *Mercury*, **Company Rips Off NSW and Federal Governments**: *Formerly Associated with Senator Frank McKurn's Wife*, demonstrated that Paper Supplies Pty. Ltd. was clearly overcharging its two customers. By publishing, among other things, the names of the Swiss and Liechtenstein nominee shareholders and the company's supposedly confidential accounts, it was clear that *something* fishy was going on. That the "something fishy" was connected with McKurn was the unstated (and so libel-proof) innuendo.

"True," said Royn, "but Labor and the independents will all support it, so McKurn won't matter. In fact, he'll have to toe the party line and vote for it."

"It has to go through three readings, remember," Alison said. "That's three opportunities to find some procedural or technical delaying tactic."

Royn nodded. "I'll get the whips to take care of it."

"Let's hope they can," Alison said. "How do we handle the Sandemans?"

Royn thought for a moment. Then, standing as if he was facing an audience or the cameras, his face softened and his eyes glistened. When he spoke his voice was slow, deep and comforting, with the hint of a tremor. "I wish with all my heart we could bring all our troops home today." He shook his head. "But to do so when we and our Sandeman compatriots, working hand-in-hand, are on the verge of success would be a grave mistake. And being so close to success—" almost imperceptibly, Royn had straightened his body posture and had half-raised one hand as if he was taking an oath "—I promise you that we will bring our boys home immediately we can."

Melanie clapped her hands together as Doug Selkirk said, "That'll do it—until the pundits pull it apart."

"Fix it so I can make that sound bite on primetime TV," Royn grinned as he sat back down, "and all people will remember is the *impression*. Then the pundits can say what they want and it won't matter."

"Emotion trumps logic," Melanie said.

"Until," Cracken said, "they start sending you bits of Robin Cartwright."

"Always a pleasure to have you around, Paul," Royn scowled. "But—we could use that to our advantage."

"Really?" Cracken drawled, leaning forward as he spoke and looking at Royn with anticipation. "Do tell."

A sudden queasiness in her stomach forced Alison to look anywhere except at Royn or Cracken.

"Arouse people's anger and present the firm hand," Royn said, thumping his fist on his desk. "And send in more troops—we'd have the voters' full support."

Cracken nodded. "And keep it on the boil—at least until the election is over."

"Exactly, Paul."

"Better to get Cartwright out of there," Alison said, "in one piece."

"I quite agree," said Royn, "but you've got to be ready to play the hand you're dealt whether you like it or not."

Alison clenched her fists to still her trembling fingers, thinking, *I can't help but agree.*

"ALISON," MELANIE SAID, "IF you could stay for a bit."

When only Alison, Melanie and Royn remained, Melanie threw the page with Karla's headline, torn from the *Mercury,* on the desk between Royn and Alison.

"What I want to know," Melanie said, looking hard at Alison, "is *where* Karla Preston got her information. She's talking about that company Paper Supplies; the accounts are the *same* ones *you* received from the geek. Those pictures she ran yesterday are the same ones the private eye dug up for us."

"Approaching her was *your* idea," Alison said.

"That was *before* we'd forced McKurn to back off. I'm surprised you didn't discuss it with Tony first."

"She probably should have, Mel—but what's the problem?" Royn leaned back and spread his arms wide. "It's just more fuel for the Dump McKurn movement."

"It will get McKurn's back up. How will he react? Surely, a wrangle in the party *at this moment* won't help us."

"It will," Royn said, "if it gets rid of McKurn. We should do everything we can to push it along, don't you agree?"

"So long as it doesn't rebound on us somehow."

"What could be a greater liability than having McKurn on the ticket?" Royn asked.

"I don't know," Melanie said. "But I *am* sure that if McKurn can think of something, he *will* think of it."

Too right, Alison thought. But she said nothing.

"Maybe, Mel," Royn said, "but what's done is done. And Alison, don't give anyone *anything* unless you check with me first."

"I won't, Prime Minister," Alison said.

*****

AN HOUR FROM NOOSA, Olsson slowed to a crawl, watching for a motel. A newspaper poster grabbed his attention: **McKurn Connection to Company Scam?** He screeched to a halt.

The poster was for *The Queenslander,* the Sykes' Brisbane paper that carried OlssonPress articles. *One of our stories.*

Parking in the first available space, he backtracked to the newsagent. Standing over the stacks of newsprint he ignored the banner headline, **Aussie Journo Kidnapped in Sandemans:** *Held for Ransom,* and focused on Karla's article.

Does Karla understand what she's doing? he asked himself as he quickly skimmed her words. *Second in a series? How many more to come?*

He bought the newspaper and took it to the first coffee shop he passed where he ordered a double espresso. *No sleep for the wicked after all,* he thought. Karla identified a company, he read, that sold pens, pencils, paper and the like to the NSW and Federal governments at inflated prices.

A spokesman for the company insisted the prices were justified. "We don't just sell the supplies, we also handle inventory management and just-in-time delivery," he claimed.

The NSW government contract had been in place for some thirty years.

A source in the NSW Attorney-General's audit department, who spoke off the record, indicated that "the stationery contract did *not* appear to have gone through all requisite bidding procedures before being awarded to Paper Supplies."

The Federal contract was of more recent origin.

"Everything, including the quality of the products, was better before this company got the contract," according to one Commonwealth public servant.

The supporting evidence was compelling: extracts from contracts, company accounts, comparative price lists, shareholder records, and more—with the full text of the documents available online.

And if McKurn *was* behind it. . . .

Olsson reached into his blazer pocket for his cellphone and stopped. *Not here.*

Coming to his feet, he half-stumbled and his vision blurred. Shaking his head seemed to clear it, but he still felt dizzy. *Damn, I don't have the energy.* He carried a second coffee to the car and drove slowly and over-carefully—*Like a "little old lady,"* he chuckled to himself—until he reached the open highway where he pulled off the road.

Now, he sighed, and dialled. "Lynette?"

"Derek?" Lynette McPherson, managing director of the OlssonPress, answered in surprise. "Are you all right? Where are you—where have you *been?"*

"Never mind that now," Olsson said. "Tell Lew to put a twenty-four-hour bodyguard on Karla. *Armed*—whether she likes it or not."

"A bodyguard? Armed? What on earth *for?"*

"Lyn, all the stories and rumors about McKurn are *true.* He'll want Karla's exposé *stopped,* and the obvious way to do it is—"

"I get the picture," Lynette McPherson said, "but it's hard to believe—"

"McKurn lives in a different world, Lyn. Just do it. *Immediately.* And tell Lew to double security at all our offices."

"Derek—"

"Attacking McKurn like this is playing with fire. You don't *play* with fire—you *drown* it. Is that what Karla's series will achieve?"

"Well . . . maybe."

"In other words, maybe not. Spike the rest."

"We can't do that."

"Who do you think was behind the sabotage of our presses, Lyn?"

"You mean—*McKurn?"*

"That's right."

"Can you *prove* it?" Lynette asked excitedly.

"Not yet. Call Lew *now."*

"I will."

He yawned. The seat which gave him a backache yesterday was now seductively comfortable—which clearly had nothing to do with the ergonomics of the cushioning. He forced himself to straighten up, gulped the rest of his coffee and smiled broadly as he pressed the CALL key on his cellphone.

"Kaaaarla," he said softly, drawing out her name.

"Derek!" Karla squealed. "I've been so *worried*—nobody's heard from you for *months. . . .*"

Olsson chuckled. "It's only been six weeks."

"Really? It *feels* like six months. Where *are* you?"

"I'm sitting behind the wheel of a car—"

"*That's* not what I meant," Karla giggled. "You sound like a sleepyhead, so I was picturing you lying in bed—"

"Sorry to disappoint you," Olsson grinned. "That's where I'm heading next."

"What? It's not even noon yet."

"I've been ill—"

"Then you should get lots of rest—"

"Yes, mother," Olsson chuckled.

Karla laughed. "I'm so glad you've come back to life—I've missed your voice."

"Only my voice?"

"Don't be silly."

"I'll be back before long—I just found out who set me up."

"So you can come out of hiding—*at last.*"

"Not yet, unfortunately. I'll have to lie low until I've gathered enough evidence to change Durant's mind."

"Oh," Karla said, her long puff of breath turning into static in Olsson's ear. "That won't take too long, I hope."

"Only a week or two, I expect—but it could be a month."

"Sometimes, I wake up in the middle of the night terrified something so terrible has happened to you that I'll never see you again."

"I'm back Karla, in one piece."

"But you're not *here,* Derek. And back from *where?*"

"I've been . . . keeping on the move."

"Where are you now?"

"Not far away—just a few hundred kilometers."

"That's still too far."

"Yes," Olsson said. "It is."

"And if the police find you—"

"I could walk right past you, Karla, and you wouldn't recognize me, so it's unlikely."

"You think so?"

"I'll prove it to you, one day soon."

"I doubt it. But you're still at risk. I'm not sure I could stand to visit you in prison again."

"I have no intention of ever going anywhere near a prison. But I followed your exploits in the Sandemans—when I could get online," he said, a smile in his voice. "It seems I'm not the only one who's been taking death-defying risks."

"I suppose you're right."

"There must have been times—"

"There were. I was lucky."

"And now, your attacks on *McKurn*—"

"You've seen the paper?"

"Just today's."

"A great scoop, don't you think?"

"Definitely. But now you're probably in *danger.*"

"What danger?"

"Your exposés could bring McKurn down—and you know how McKurn deals with his enemies, don't you?"

Karla was silent.

"Do you want to end up wearing concrete boots?"

"You're serious, aren't you?"

"Very. In fact, I've told Lynette to arrange a twenty-four hour *armed* bodyguard for you—"

"You're overreacting, Derek."

"Am I? I certainly hope so. I just want you safe. That's all."

"Okay," Karla said reluctantly. "I suppose you know more about all this than I do."

It took a moment for Olsson to register the meaning of Karla's tone. "There's something on your mind," he said.

"Yes. We need to talk. But not on the phone."

"It sounds serious."

"I hope not," she breathed, "but it *could* be."

"Okay. I can't come to the surface, so to speak, until I've convinced Durant. But that doesn't mean we can't meet up somewhere."

"I'd like that."

"Give me a couple of days to sort it out."

"I *think* I can wait that long."

"Meanwhile, promise me you'll take care of yourself—"

"Oh, Derek, really."

"—and that you'll keep the bodyguard close to you at all times." When Karla hesitated, he added, "I insist."

"Okay, Derek. I promise."

He pulled onto the highway wondering what Karla's thought *"could* be" so serious. But he found himself thinking, *I can protect her better than any bodyguard.* If he just kept driving he'd reach the airport, where he could take the next plane to Sydney . . . and the Greek. . . .

He jerked upright at the same moment he slammed on the brakes and swerved onto the shoulder, barely missing the car in front. Shaking, he coasted to a halt. *Too damn close. How did that happen?* He realized he'd dozed off at the wheel. *Tomorrow,* he sighed, *after a really long sleep.*

*****

Karla Preston and several other journalists passed through the security guards outside the OlssonPress offices around nine PM; one of the guards, a bulge under his arm, peeled off and trudged behind.

"What's *he* doing?" one of the journalists asked.

"My bodyguard," Karla replied. "Lynette insisted. I argued with her, but she wouldn't take 'no' far an answer."

"What on earth for? What's with all the security anyway?"

"Lynette's in a flap about the McKurn articles. She kept saying, 'What if everything you've heard about McKurn is *true.*'"

"Then he goes for a row."

"Of course," Karla said as they reached the pub across the road. She even pulled my article for tomorrow's paper, saying the lawyers want more fact-checking. Never mind. I need a drink."

The bodyguard sat near enough to catch most of their conversation, his eyes scanning the pub and its customers every few seconds. He perked up when he heard one of the journalists say, "You could give him the slip. Just jump in a taxi—"

Karla shrugged. "Not worth it." She waved her hand as if batting a mosquito. "Lynette would do her block," she said—but she was thinking of her promise to Derek Olsson, and his worried tone of voice. She glanced at the bodyguard at the next table. "He can stand in the corridor or whatever when I get home."

Karla took a front seat on the bus, forcing her minder to sit where she couldn't see him. When she got off he seemed to amble along as though it was pure coincidence he and Karla were going the same way. She made a few purchases in the corner store; he looked as though he couldn't decide which brand or flavor of potato chips to buy.

Karla came out with a shopping bag and marched across the intersection towards her apartment, the bodyguard just behind her. She tried to act as if he wasn't there, but stopped in the middle of the road and was about to turn and say, "Stop stepping on my shadow, for God's sake," when the bodyguard yelled "Look out!" and ran full tilt into Karla to thrust her almost the rest of the way across the street.

The roar of an engine and the screech of tyres all but drowned out his words. A car accelerated along the side street, veering towards where Karla now lay, stunned, on the pavement. The bodyguard had half-regained his balance and was reaching for his gun when the car smashed into him. He rebounded off the bonnet, thumped onto the asphalt and lay still, his body impossibly twisted, blood oozing from his head where it had hit the pavement.

Karla lay on the street, not moving, splotched in red.

The car squealed to a halt in Glebe Point Road. When a couple of people ran from the corner store, the driver stamped on the accelerator and the car disappeared around the next corner.

"Jesus Christ," said the first paramedic to leap out of the ambulance when it arrived. "Do they need us—or a hearse?"

50　Run Like Hell

IN THE FAINT LIGHT of the barely risen sun, Alison McGuire jogged along one side of Telopea Park beneath a curtain of shadow flung by overhanging trees. She forced herself to focus on the pounding of her feet on the pavement and increased her pace to intensify the pleasing ache in her calves and knees. Even so, her stomach weighed too heavily on her mind. She didn't see or return the wave or smile of the occasional jogger and was only vaguely aware of cars whizzing by. So she paid no attention to the man jogging towards her until he suddenly lurched sideways to crash into her. Only then did she see the mask over his eyes, partly hidden by a cap pulled low over his face.

That was when she became aware of a second presence behind her, heard the sound of a vehicle slowing down nearby, and realized from the way the man had gripped her wrist that he, too, was familiar with some marital art.

The thought, *McKurn. Assume they're experts,* flashed into her mind. And disappeared as her awareness filled with the sense of the man's fingers on her wrist and the momentum of his body against hers. She could see herself, as if clairvoyant, falling to the ground, the man's weight pinning her down, her arm being twisted . . . as she had twisted McKurn's.

Unless she could stop him from completing his move.

She struggled, as though she was helpless and ignorant. She sensed the man relax slightly, as if he was thinking: *she's no expert after all.* As she felt herself about to lose her balance and fall, she spun around to *untwist* her arm, reached out with her other hand to grab the man's wrist and leapt into the air. Suddenly she was flying with the man as a counterweight, her body arcing horizontally around him. She heard a grunt as her feet connected with the man coming from behind. As she landed, she twisted her hand to release it from the man's grasp while grabbing his wrist with her other hand. She leapt again to continue her movement. This time, it was her attacker who went flying. Letting him go, she went into a forward roll to regain her balance and ran into the park. Only then did she realize she'd subconsciously made a decision: *If they're both black belts, two-to-one is bad odds. So run like hell.* A quick backward glance told her that the two men were picking themselves up and about to run after her, and that the vehicle was a dark-blue van. Perhaps it was her imagination, but she was sure she'd noticed the same van parked near her apartment building as she'd started her run.

They weren't just going to rough me up.

She shuddered and forced herself to accelerate her pace, Sensei Tozen's voice in her mind matching her rhythm: *Run like hell, run like hell, runlikehell.* She felt she'd gained a second wind—or an adrenalin rush; her aching body faded into the background of her consciousness as her mind filled with her sole objective, *run for your life.*

Alison ran as she'd never run before. Her knees twinged every time her feet pushed back off the ground; her ankles ached; her heart raced and her lungs strained as she gulped breath after breath and kept pushing herself to sprint faster and faster. But every time she looked back she could tell that the two masked pursuers were slowly gaining on her.

Not fast enough.

She angled towards the center of the park and neared the wide, shallow, concrete storm drain that ran down its center. It began across the road from the Manuka swimming pool and drained into the lake. *The pool.* She had to get to somewhere where there were other people—witnesses—and was about to turn towards the pool until she remembered it was closed for the winter. *Damn.* That left the Manuka shopping center, but it was over a kilometer away. Would there be anyone around this early? Was there a police station there? She couldn't remember. They were still gaining on her. They must be as fit as she was—with longer legs. *Manuka is too far.*

She reached the edge of the storm drain without slowing down and leapt, knowing that even a champion long jumper couldn't make it across in one go. A heavy rain turned the drain into a river; now there was just a trickle of muddy, icy water in its center. Her feet slid as she splashed into it, and skidded, sitting in the water, to a painful halt. She pulled herself up to see the two pursuers jump into the drain and close in on her. As she scrambled up the other side one of the men came so close she imagined she could feel his breath on her neck. She looked back to see a wide grin on his face as he stretched his hands forward to grab her. She braced herself against the ground focusing all her energy into one leg and lashed backwards. Her foot slammed into his face with a pleasing crunch. *Right between the eyes.* Pushing off with her other foot she saw the man slowly topple over. *One down.* The second pursuer paused for a second to check his companion, allowing her to increase her lead by ten or so meters. *Not enough.*

At the other side of Telopea Park she ran straight across the road. There was no traffic but as her foot landed on the asphalt an engine screamed and the blue van accelerated around the corner straight at her. She was halfway across—but the van was too close. She'd never make it. She took two longer steps and launched into a forward roll. Just as she thought she was clear she felt something slam into her left foot. She landed on the grass verge and rolled upright, bracing herself for the inevitable pain. But all she could feel in her foot was numbness. *It doesn't hurt,* she thought in surprise. *I got lucky.*

She took off in the direction opposite to the van's, which screeched to a halt and spun around to follow her. Her remaining pursuer was crossing the road in front of her, but she gauged she'd be ahead of him by the time he reached the other side—just. *If* her luck held.

The only other person in sight was an elderly man walking his poodle along the footpath in front of her. He stood gaping at her, the van and the masked pursuer. Alison yelled, "Call the cops, *please,*" as she flashed past him. His eyes followed her and, as though he had just come out of a trance, he reached into his pocket and pulled out a cellphone. Her pursuer stopped, spun around and punched him hard in the stomach. As the old man crumpled over he smashed his fist into the side of the man's head. The little poodle bared its teeth and barked menacingly; the man kicked it aside.

He likes his work.

She ran around the corner; the van screamed past her and braked to a halt. The driver jumped out grinning at her menacingly, holding a truncheon and slapping it lovingly into his other hand. She glanced back: the masked man was coming around the corner behind her.

I'm trapped. She hesitated until the meaning of the truncheon came to her and she speeded up, running straight at the driver. His grin grew even broader and he raised the truncheon ready to strike. Alison seemed to be running straight into his arms, the perfect target. His arm swung the truncheon directly at her head. She reached out with one hand, ducking and pirouetting at the same time. She felt the truncheon skim her hair; her outstretched hand knocked the truncheon and his hand in the direction it was already going; at the same time she pushed herself away from him and sped towards the van. Its engine still running, the driver's door still open, she lunged into the driver's seat and sighed with relief, letting herself relax slightly as she eyed the unfamiliar controls. As if a dam had suddenly burst her body convulsed as an unbearable pain shot upwards from her foot. Gasping for air, she fought her body's desire to collapse. *You're still not clear,* a faint voice reminded her. Gripping the steering wheel with both hands she pushed herself upright, gritting her teeth against the searing jolts of pain that came with every movement.

Through a red haze she registered the van was an automatic. She groped for the gear stick and pushed it into DRIVE—and felt a hand grip her right arm like an iron brace. The masked pursuer was pulling himself through the still-open driver's door—or trying to pull her out. She floored the accelerator and he grabbed at the door with his other hand. While her right arm flailed trying to push him off she spun the steering wheel with her other hand: still accelerating, the van jumped the kerb, bounced, and careened towards a tree. Her attacker held on with one hand on the open door and one foot planted by the driver's seat. He let her arm go, grabbed at the steering wheel, and tried to turn the van away from the tree.

Alison howled at him, a yell of defiance. She took her hand off the wheel and holding her fingers straight stabbed him in the eyes. The man screamed with pain and let go as the van careened into the tree. The driver's door smashed against the tree and slammed shut, the side of the van crumpling against the tree, grinding it to a halt, throwing Alison forward onto the steering wheel.

The sudden silence felt leaden. She wondered vaguely if she'd blacked out and why it hurt to breath. But the pain of breathing was a mild twinge compared to the shrieking of her foot: she remembered planting it against the floor as the van crashed.

She tried to push herself to a sitting position but her muscles had lost their strength. Tears leaked from her eyes as she became aware that something was on her lap. Taking the short, panting breaths that seemed to minimize the pain in the side of her chest, she slowly tilted her head down to see the man's crushed and bloody hand and half his forearm. She had the sense the fingers were still twitching as if they were still groping for a hold.

"Oh my God," she tried to yell—but no sound emerged from her lips.

"'Ullo dearie."

The driver stood by the now-open passenger door grinning at her, his truncheon in his hand.

Without thinking, Alison grabbed the disconnected arm from her lap, wielded it like a club, smashing it again and again into the man's face. "Do you want me to rip your arm off too, you arsehole," she screamed.

The driver cringed away from the bodiless arm, his face stark white. His eyes flicked to Alison's feral grin and he took a few paces back.

Breathing heavily, sobbing, and wincing, Alison slammed the passenger door shut and locked it. She collapsed across the soft passenger seat and closed her eyes: all she wanted to do was escape the continual pain. *Sleep.*

But first, there was something important she had to do, if she could remember. She felt as though she was falling until her hand brushed her pocket and touched the shape of her cellphone. *Phone,* she told herself, fumbling for it.

The screen faded in and out of focus as she tried to find the number. Her fingers had turned into thumbs and she was about to give up when the right number appeared.

"Jason," she breathed weakly. "I've been attacked. Come—armed. Blue van. Near Manuka pool." Jason said something, but she couldn't understand him. "What?"

"Have you called the police?" he asked again.

"Ambulance. I need . . . am . . . bulance. . . ."

The phone slipped from her grasp, Jason's voice still shouted desperately from the speaker but she was now beyond hearing. Her body shook; with the thought *I never took McKurn's threats seriously,* she slipped into blessed unconsciousness.

*****

At nine thirty am, the law firm of Andrews, Zolisky & Smythe filed suit in the NSW Supreme Court against the OlssonPress and Sykes Publications for defamation, libel and slander on behalf of their client, Senator Frank McKurn. They sought damages of a million dollars. The judge set a hearing for the earliest available date, two and half weeks away. Meanwhile, he enjoined the OlssonPress and Sykes Publications from printing any further articles of a similar nature about or related to Senator Frank McKurn.

*****

Absorbed in watching the Senate proceedings on his computer screen, Anthony Royn didn't hear the knock on his door or Mary enter until she said, "Excuse me, Prime Minister. Alison's in hospital."

"What?" Royn said. "Why?"

"She was attacked this morning while out jogging."

"Attacked? *Who* attacked her?"

"I don't know, Prime Minister."

"My God. Is she all right?"

"She'll have to use crutches for a while. Other than that, she'll be okay."

"My God," he mumbled again. Karla Preston left for dead last night. Now Alison. Were they connected? McKurn was the obvious link. His mind wandered to the "little chat" he'd had that morning with McKurn. When he'd obliquely raised the possibility of McKurn announcing his retirement, McKurn merely grinned and shook his head.

"For me to resign *at this time,*" McKurn said, "would be taken as evidence that these scandalous, baseless rumors are *true.* I *must* defend my honor in full—which is *exactly* what I intend to do. I will do *nothing* that might give those accusations any credence."

"Not even for the good of the party?" Royn asked.

"Tony, come now. What is the integrity of the Conservative Party worth if it caves into attacks made by innuendo without evidence by persons too craven to identify themselves? Why should I, or anyone else, have loyalty to such an organization?"

Royn had to call on all the resources he'd mastered in years of dramatic training to keep a straight face. He knew that McKurn was lying, and McKurn knew that he knew. Looking at McKurn's poise, his air of injured innocence, Royn realized he was outclassed by a dissembler whose mastery he could only hope to attain.

"I understand your position, Senator," Royn said. "I hope you understand mine."

"Oh, I do, Tony. I certainly do."

As Mary's voice finally penetrated his awareness, all that remained in his mind was McKurn's mocking grin.

"Prime Minister?" Mary asked again.

"Mary. Sorry. What did you say?"

"Shall I send Alison some flowers, Prime Minister?" Mary asked.

"Good idea," Royn said. His eyes once again glued to the computer screen, he didn't notice Mary's disapproving frown.

All morning he'd kept an eye on the Senate, waiting for Senator Hartman, who represented the Attorney-General in the upper house, to introduce the bill to establish the Royal Commission. But several procedural matters took longer than necessary. When Hartman tried to gain McKurn's attention, McKurn apparently didn't see him and recognized another Senator who launched into a long and tedious speech about . . . Royn couldn't remember, except that it was so boring that other Senators had the same reaction and wandered out of the chamber. Twice, the Senator was interrupted with calls for quorum.

Eventually Hartman took the floor and moved the bill through its first reading. Now McKurn was saying, ". . . it's only a few minutes to noon, Senator, when this morning's half-day session is due to conclude. As you are no doubt aware, most of us have flights to catch or other appointments scheduled. I realize the gravity of this matter, but will it make any difference if this business is not concluded until we resume on Tuesday? Or would you like to ask all your colleagues to rearrange their schedules so we can extend this session into the afternoon?"

Senator Hartman opened his mouth but paused as he slowly looked around the Senate chamber to see several shaking heads.

"In that case," McKurn said before Hartman could speak, "I declare this session of the Senate adjourned until Tuesday."

McKurn must know, Royn thought. *Paul must have told him.*

When an election was called Parliament was prorogued, terminating all pending business. It would not resume, except in exceptional circumstances, until after the election. He'd impressed Senator Hartman with the urgency of getting the Royal Commission bill through the Senate *today*. But to keep a lid on the number of people who knew about the snap election plans, he hadn't told Hartman *why*.

I've finessed myself.

But . . . our intention is clear, Royn thought. The bill will lapse if Parliament is prorogued before Tuesday—but setting up the Royal Commission will be the first act of the new Parliament. In any case, that's about the time Justice Flint will retire, so no time would be lost.

It should make no difference, he decided.

*****

Senator Frank McKurn grinned broadly as he stepped out of the limousine that had ferried him to his apartment. "I'll be leaving for the airport in an hour and a half, John," he said to the driver, "so take a break if you like."

"Th-thank you, Senator," the driver stuttered, unable to hide his surprise: in the years he'd chauffeured McKurn this was first time the Senator had said anything to him that was not an instruction of some kind.

McKurn hummed as he all but ran up the stairs—and stopped cold as he stepped through his front door. Lounging in one of his armchairs was a gaunt man wearing grubby jeans and a tattered T-shirt with a shock of unkempt black hair and equally black stubble on his chin. A bottle of McKurn's favorite beer sat half-drunk on the glass surface of the coffee table. *A bum,* McKurn thought. *How did he get in here?*

"Who the hell are you?" McKurn demanded.

The bum smiled. "Let's just say I'm here to represent your conscience—which you seem to have mislaid somewhere. It's time you and your conscience got reacquainted . . . and had a little chat."

"What the hell is *that* supposed to mean?" McKurn glared. "Get out of here or I'll call the cops."

The intruder grinned. "And how will you do that, Senator," he said languidly, "with two broken arms?"

"What are you talking about?" McKurn said, suddenly apprehensive; even without the heavy cast on his right arm he was no match for the man sitting uninvited in his living room. The visitor might look like a bum, but his biceps rippled when he moved, and he lounged cat-like, commanding the room, making McKurn the intruder in his own home.

With the same half-smile, the bum raised his arm above the coffee table. Thin, clearly expensive leather gloves covered both the bum's hands. *No fingerprints,* McKurn realized.

Holding McKurn's gaze, the intruder's arm flashed down and smashed into the coffee table with a dull thud. Radiating from the point where the edge of his hand hit, a cobweb of thin cracks spread through the thick glass. The beer bottle wobbled but the bum grabbed it up before it toppled over.

"As I said Senator, sit *down.*"

McKurn's fingers trembled as he took a stumbling half-step backwards into the still-open front doorway.

"How far do you think you'd get? Don't even think of it, *Frankie.*" Waving his glove towards the sofa opposite him, the bum added, "Sit."

As if in slow motion, McKurn's lips and the skin on his face began to sag, and his body seemed to shrink a few centimeters in height. Both eyes on the bum, he shambled slowly towards the sofa.

". . . and shut the door behind you."

McKurn glared at him and with a sudden sweep of his left arm he thrust at the door so it slammed with unexpected violence. McKurn glowered as the bum laughed and relaxed even deeper into the armchair, waiting silently as McKurn reluctantly shuffled to the sofa, his eyes darting around the room in a desperate search for something, anything he could use to gain even a tiny advantage.

"What the hell are you after," McKurn spat as he sat down, attempting to recover some of his usual authority.

"It's time, don't you think, to make a down payment on your debt to society?" the bum said as he picked up an envelope and pulled out a few sheets of paper.

"You're talking in riddles. Get to the point."

"Soon enough, Senator. Soon enough." He dropped one sheet of paper in front of McKurn.

"What's this?"

"It's an estimate of Karla Preston's hospital expenses."

"The scribbler? So?"

"You're going to pay it."

McKurn laughed. "Nothing to do with *me.*"

The intruder grinned at McKurn knowingly. "Really, Senator? If you wish to deny any responsibility, why not just consider it the first act of your new role as Good Samaritan."

"Don't make me laugh."

"You should have realized by now, *Frankie,* that this is no laughing matter."

McKurn shrugged, leaning back his lips curled into a faint smile. "If I don't, what will you do? Break my arms and legs as well?"

"That won't be necessary," the bum chuckled, holding out several sheets of paper stapled together.

McKurn eyed them without apparent concern, but his eyes narrowed and his lips trembled slightly, to be quickly replaced by an expression of disinterest.

"Take a careful look, Frankie." The intruder pulled the pages apart and laid them across the coffee table's cracks in front of McKurn. "It the press got hold of this, it would make an interesting story don't you think?"

Despite himself, McKurn's eyes flicked from one page to another, and while his expression didn't change his breaths came more quickly. "Looks like a bank statement," he said.

"You don't recognize the name, the bank—" one gloved finger stabbed at the photocopy of a signature card "—or the signature?"

"A convincing forgery."

"You think so? Take a look at the most recent transaction."

"A withdrawal. Ten thousand francs," McKurn said with deliberate detachment. But then he exploded, "*How did that happen?*"

The bum just smiled. "As you say, Senator, a convincing forgery."

McKurn half stood, glowering over the bum. *"How did you get this?"* he demanded.

"Money talks," the intruder laughed. "Even in Switzerland."

Now standing to his full height, his long arm waving his fist in the direction of the intruder, his face red and twisted in anger, he shouted, "You're stealing my money you bastard."

"Oh, for Chrissakes, Frankie," the bum said calmly, looking up at McKurn with an amused smile, "sit down and shut up. You can't tell me—" he gestured towards the scattered papers "—that there's anything new to you in all this. Except, of course, that you're on the receiving end for a change."

McKurn sat. Picking up the top sheet of the bank statement, he leant slightly towards the intruder with a glint in his eye. "So all I have to do," McKurn said slowly, "is to get the payee's name and I'll know your identity."

The bum laughed, a rumbling, happy laugh. "Actually, no," he said, wiping a glistening drop from one eye. "The payee is a well-known Sydney gangster. If *that* came out you'd just be deeper in the shithole than you already are."

"I see," McKurn said thoughtfully. "And, of course, this is not your only copy."

"Actually," the bum chuckled, "the copy of the statement I have is even better—it's an *original* from your bank in Zurich."

McKurn shook his head sadly. "Who'd have thought that a Swiss bank can't be trusted after all."

"Oh they can be, Senator. But you can always find *someone* who succumbs to Frankie McKurn-style tactics . . . can't you, Senator?"

"I'll take your word for it."

"This is Kar—uh—Miss Preston's account number," the intruder said, placing the last sheet of paper from the envelope on the coffee table. "She's not out of the woods by a long shot, so there'll be further expenses, not to mention her possible loss of earnings and her emotional suffering. A hundred and fifty thousand on top of the hospital's estimate should cover it. Not as much as a court would award, but then, we have no legal fees and so on to worry about."

"You're out of your mind."

"Am I? There's more than enough in just that one account." The intruder leaned forward, his eyes cold, growled intently, "A small price to pay considering the pain you've caused."

"The pain *I've* caused?"

The bum chuckled. "Deny it all you like, Frankie. Fact is, you've got two weeks to put the money in Miss Preston's account or this—" he picked up the bank statement and shoved it in McKurn's face so quickly that McKurn recoiled instinctively "—goes to the press. You know what will happen to you then." He crumpled the paper and tossed it into McKurn's lap. "What's your choice?"

McKurn glared at the bum, but said nothing.

"Offence number one, failing to disclose assets, enough to get you thrown out of the Senate on your arse. Two, failure to declare income—the tax department will put you through the wringer. Think of the fines you'll have to pay. Three, where did the money come from in the first place? The taxman will want the answer and so will the cops who'll put you under a microscope. You'll spend the rest of your life answering questions . . . if you're lucky enough to stay out of jail. Everyone will be *positive* that every single one of those McKurnWatch accusations are *true*."

McKurn sighed. "And if I agree," he said, "I suppose you'll be back later for more."

"You don't have anything I want, Frankie. But now that you mention it, there is one other thing."

"There always is."

"From now on, consider yourself Karla Preston's fairy godmother. Whatever happens to her will happen to you. And you're also to lay off Alison McGuire—on the same basis."

McKurn's eyes narrowed. "What's *your* interest in Karla Preston and Alison McGuire? A knight in shining armor? I don't think so."

"Me? I'm just a messenger—a Greek bearing gifts." The bum's eyes sparkled with interest as McKurn winced at his words. "In fact, Senator," the intruder continued lightly, "perhaps you'd better have someone watch over them both to make sure they don't stub a toe by mistake."

"What?" McKurn protested. "That's ridiculous."

"With *you* involved, Senator, I'm going to assume there are no coincidences. *Do I make myself clear?*"

After a moment, his face tense as he glared at the intruder, McKurn nodded his head imperceptibly.

"Good. Now that we've concluded our business, Senator, we're going for a little drive."

"I don't think so."

In answer, the unwanted visitor simply slapped the center of the cobweb of cracks. The glass surface creaked and groaned; McKurn seemed mesmerized by the way it flexed. After a moment, the bum held out his hand and said, "Your cellphone."

With a show of reluctance, McKurn pulled his cellphone from his jacket pocket and suddenly threw it straight at the bum's face. Without flinching, the bum's hand flashed to pluck the missile out of the air. He let it drop on the glass: finally, the surface of the coffee table shattered sending shards of glass in every direction.

"And now your wallet."

"You're going to rob me too, are you?"

The bum said nothing. The silence was disturbed only by a soft wheeze in McKurn's breathing. Eventually, McKurn took out his wallet and passed it across. Without looking at it the bum flipped it behind him so that it arced up, hitting the ceiling before dropping to the floor. He stood, motioning to McKurn to do the same, and picked up the beer bottle from where it had fallen on the floor. "I'm not dumb enough to leave any trace of my little visit," the bum chuckled as he saw McKurn glance of puzzlement.

As McKurn reached the front door the bum patted his body up and down. He reached into McKurn's other jacket pocket and pulled out a cellphone.

"*Two* cellphones. Now that's very interesting," the bum said, stuffing it in his pocket.

McKurn winced as he felt himself being pulled back into the apartment by a steely grip on his arm. Without letting him go, the bum leaned over for the first cellphone and added it to the other one.

"So you *are* going to rob me after all," said McKurn.

"You have the right to remain silent, Frankie," the bum said, twisting McKurn's arm so he yelped, "so exercise it."

No one was about as they walked down the stairs to the car park. The bum waited while McKurn sat in the passenger seat of the car and threw the beer bottle onto the back seat. "Put on your seatbelt—and don't try anything stupid." When McKurn had awkwardly fastened his seatbelt, the bum ran around to the driver's seat. As he did McKurn opened the passenger door, but before he could undo the seatbelt the bum roughly grabbed McKurn's right wrist sending a shock of pain through his torn shoulder.

"Let go," McKurn yelled.

"I don't think so," the bum said as the car's engine roared into life. "Shut the door."

Still holding McKurn's wrist, he backed out of the parking space and drove one-handed for about ten minutes towards the outskirts of Canberra, and stopped. "You can hop out here and walk back. The exercise will do you good."

"I'll get you for this," McKurn growled as he stepped out of the car.

The bum just laughed.

As the car sped off, McKurn cursed: the car's rear number plate was unreadable, obscured with mud. But he had one lead: the rental car company's sticker on the rear window.

*****

"Look at *you*," Mary said as she carted a pile of paperwork into Alison's apartment. "How long will you be on crutches? Why are you wearing a *boot*—an army boot of all things?" Watching as Alison double-locked the door and shot the bolts home, she added, "And why all the locks?"

"One thing at a time," Alison laughed. Leaning on her crutches, she hobbled over to the dining table while Mary neatly stacked the papers in two piles. "I've got two broken bones in my foot, and they can't put it in a cast. So I have to wear this boot instead, for support. What's really weird is that I *ran* on it *after* it was broken—and didn't feel a thing until I stopped."

"How can that be?"

"The doctor said your body can block pain under stress. He treated a ballet dancer once who cracked a bone in his ankle halfway through a performance and didn't notice anything till the next morning."

"Imagine that. It must hurt."

"It certainly does—if I walk on it," Alison grinned. "I also cracked a rib. *That* hurts if I don't take painkillers."

"It must have been *awful.* Why would anyone attack *you?*" Mary shook her head.

McKurn, of course. She couldn't tell Mary that, so she just shrugged.

"And last night a journalist was in a hit-and-run accident in Sydney—makes you wonder if the streets are safe any more."

"Who?"

Mary shook her head. "I should know her name. A really nice lady—she came to visit the Minister once—"

"Not Karla Preston?"

"*That's* who it was," Mary said.

"*Karla?*" She gaped at Mary. *So it was McKurn,* she thought. *Does he know Karla's information came from me? Or is he simply taking his revenge?*

"That's who I said—what's the matter?"

Alison shrugged. "I know her quite well."

Mary nodded. "Yes, that makes it different, doesn't it." She was admiring the large bouquet on the side table. "Nice flowers."

"Aren't they. I'd better thank Royn for them."

"Ha," Mary scoffed. "He's been totally preoccupied today—barely paid any attention when I told him about your accident. Flowers were *my* idea."

Alison smiled. "They're beautiful, Mary."

"He wants you to call, by the way. I have to get back. Is there anything you need? Shall I make you a coffee first?"

"I can manage," Alison grinned.

Mary went into the kitchen, tidied up and looked in the refrigerator. "Can you go shopping and carry everything up three flights of stairs? I don't think so. I'll look in again after work and bring something—frozen dinners would be best I guess."

"You're right." Alison hobbled back to the front door. At Mary's questioning look she said, "My police friend insisted on the locks, just in case."

Jason had arrived at the scene just in time to scare away the driver who was trying to break into the van. He waited at the hospital until Alison regained consciousness, stayed while the police questioned her and escorted her home. Only when she called a locksmith to turn her apartment into a fortress would he reluctantly consent to leave her alone.

"Is that likely?" Mary asked.

Definitely, Alison thought. "Hopefully," she said, "I was just in the wrong place at the wrong time."

When Mary had gone, Alison leant against the door, suddenly aware of the tightness of the bandages around her chest and foot. Two of her attackers had gotten away, Jason told her, while the man who was "minus half an arm" had nearly bled to death. *Pity he didn't—the bastard.* He'd needlessly pummelled a defenceless old man who was now in hospital with a ruptured spleen, and viciously kicked a poor little dog just for the hell of it. *Whatever he planned to do to me, he was definitely going to enjoy it.* She would make her official statement at the police station in the morning and go through their "rogues' gallery" in the hope she could identify her attackers. She was looking forward to that, but not to taking care of the pile of paperwork Mary had brought—mostly, she assumed, to do with Sunday's meeting.

Just get on with it. First she called Royn who vaguely asked how she was holding up as if his mind was elsewhere. But she got his full attention when she said, "It *has* to be McKurn who hired my attackers—*and Karla Preston's.* This is our chance to get him—and let the *cops* do all the dirty work."

Royn enthusiastically agreed to put pressure on the police to beef up their investigations, so Alison attacked the pile of documents and inevitable emails and phone calls with renewed energy and a smile on her face. She was picking at one of Mary's frozen dinners when she realized all that remained was the pile of phone taps. Her rib, foot and shoulders ached, but she could get them out of the way and still get an early night. She attacked them at random, finding little of interest, until she heard what sounded like a familiar voice: ". . . Senator, sit *down."*

"Derek? It *couldn't* be."

She jumped back until she heard McKurn's voice demanding: "Who the hell are you?"

"Let's just say I'm here to represent your conscience—"

"Derek," she yelped. "What are you *doing?"*

"—which you seem to have mislaid somewhere. . . ."

Alison laughed. "McKurn was born without one, Derek." She listened intently until Olsson's words, ". . . consider yourself Karla Preston's fairy godmother . . . and you're to lay off Alison McGuire on the same basis."

He still cares, she thought, feeling that Olsson had wrapped her in a McKurn-proof security blanket, that she was, at long last, *safe.* Yet a question nagged: . . . *or was I just an afterthought?*

Only when she took off the headphones did she hear the hammering at her front door and a voice, "Alison, it's me!"

Derek?

Grabbing her crutches she hobbled to the door and glued her eye to the peephole. She had a fleeting glance of a thatch of red hair before the man's head disappeared from view.

Not Derek after all. But he disguised himself when they'd met in the . . . in that bar. She began to fumble with the locks and bolts, but hesitated as she remembered her pledge to Jason, "Don't open the door for *anyone."*

But if it was *Derek. . . .*

Before she could make up her mind, there was another knock, and the same voice, "Alison?"

It *sounded* like him.

Through the peephole she saw a pale, gaunt face, topped with unruly red hair. With a sudden inspiration, she ordered, "Smile."

"What?"

"Just smile."

The awkward grin—and the dimple—were unmistakable.

"Derek!"

She swung the door open; Derek Olsson's eyes took in her crutches and the boot and his wide grin disappeared. "What happened to *you?"*

Alison threw her arms around him—her crutches, forgotten, clattering to the floor—and buried her head on his shoulder, pressing her shaking body against his. "I'm so glad you're here," she said between sobs.

She felt Olsson's body stiffen for an instant before, hesitantly, his arms encircled her. "That's not the welcome I anticipated," he said.

She tilted her head to gaze at him; seeing the dark rings under his eyes, she reached up to run the fingers of one hand slowly and softly along his cheek. "You're so pale," she whispered, "and you've lost weight."

"I've been ill."

From along the corridor came the sound of another apartment door opening. "Help me inside."

Olsson half-carried, half-supported her to the sofa. Spying the headphones attached to Alison's laptop he asked, "Been listening to something?"

Alison smiled. "You and McKurn."

"So you bugged his apartment?" Olsson said as he closed and locked the front door.

"*And* his phones," Alison chuckled. "Or your friend the geek did—and what have you been using *him* for?"

"Research." Olsson grinned at Alison as he leant her crutches against the sofa; Alison basked in the warmth of his gaze and, with a gesture of her hand, invited him to sit next to her. Olsson sprawled on the sofa as if he were about to fall asleep. Barely lifting his eyelids, he asked. "What's wrong with your foot?"

"I was attacked this morning."

Olsson jerked to attention, his eyes wide. *"What?"*

Alison's voice faltered under Olsson's silent, searching gaze. One hand unconsciously kneaded her stomach as if that would quell her rising tension; she couldn't understand why it took a conscious effort to keep her eyes from drifting away from Olsson's face.

"McKurn." Air hissed from Olsson's lips as if he'd been holding his breath all the while Alison spoke. "First Karla. Now *you.*"

"But we're both safe now, Derek," Alison said, gently squeezing Olsson's hand, "thanks to you."

"We're dealing with *McKurn*, remember," Olsson groaned, his head slumping to rest on his hands; when he pushed himself up his eyes were red. "Karla was left for dead—and you're lucky to be walking around at all. Why *you*, Alison? Does McKurn know you were the source of Karla's information?"

Alison shook her head. "What makes *you* think I am?"

"The geek, as you call him, sent me the accounts of that Paper Supplies outfit, too. When I saw them in Karla's article—"

"You guessed."

Olsson nodded. "What's going on with McKurn?"

Alison stared at Olsson wordlessly, aware of her fingers digging into her stomach. *You have to tell him,* the ageless voice in her mind prompted her. *Now.* She forced herself to speak, her voice a hoarse whisper. "Blackmail."

"McKurn's been blackmailing *you?* How?"

Alison felt herself falling into the compassion in Olsson's eyes and tried to hold his gaze—but had to turn away in case those same eyes saw too much. Trembling, she crumbled against him. "Just hold me, Derek," she said, resting her head on his shoulder, and slipping one arm behind Olsson's back. Olsson pulled her close. "Not *that* tight. My rib—"

"Sorry," Olsson laughed, relaxing his grip, one hand gently stroking Alison's hair as if that might calm her as he waited for her to continue.

"Remember our weekend in the Sandview Hideaway—"

"Vividly, Alison," he scowled, his fingers stiffening, pressing for an instant into Alison's arm.

Alison felt her cheeks flush, grateful her face was hidden from Olsson's view. "We were recorded—"

"Everything?"

"Every word we said. Everything we did. McKurn threatened to release the . . . pornographic parts on the internet if I didn't . . . cooperate with him."

"Why didn't you *tell* me?"

"I—" Alison's eyes flicked in the direction of her laptop "—I didn't think you could do anything."

"Now you know better."

"And I was really angry with you."

"And now?"

"I'm much angrier with *myself*—" she lifted her foot "—for letting this happen." *For putting myself into the position where something like this could happen.* She resisted the urge to lift her head to look at him. The warmth of his arms and the cadence of his voice was comforting, and it was easier to speak without seeing his reactions.

"You let it happen?"

"Not exactly. . . . In a way. . . ." She squirmed in his arms. "Remember . . . when I first told you I wanted to be in Canberra—"

"—at the center of power?"

"Do you remember what you said?"

"Something like . . . you wanted to be one of *them?*"

"And that's what I'm afraid I'm becoming, Derek." She buried her face in his shirt as if that would hide her tears. "To *survive.*"

Olsson nodded slowly. "Yes," he said, as though he were talking to himself, "you think you can play the game your way . . . but you find that someone else has already set the rules."

"What made you say that? Because that's exactly how I feel."

"Now and then it seems that when I got on that plane to Hong Kong I made a choice . . . and everything that's happened to me since was unavoidable—inevitable."

"You can't believe *that.* Surely not?"

Olsson shook his head. "I don't—yet I can't shake the feeling."

"When I started working for Royn, there seemed to be no limit to what I could achieve."

"And now?"

"I'm surrounded by sharks and vultures who'll tear me apart, given half an opportunity—"

"You mean, they haven't?" Olsson asked softly.

"Not yet."

"Not for want of trying."

Alison squeezed closer to Olsson to quell a sudden shudder. *I was so lucky. If the van had been an inch nearer I'd have lost my foot—and maybe my life.*

"Sharks and vultures?" Olsson chuckled. "What happened to all the good people in Canberra you told me about?"

"Oh, they're there, Derek. But at the top—?" Of all the frontbench MPs and Senators, Royn and Bergstrom stood out in her mind as "good people," plus quite a few of the backbenchers from both sides of the political fence—mostly newbies. Thinking of Bruce Spring, she said, "Most of them have their hearts in the right place, but they'd all sacrifice their principles for political gain. When they *have* principles. Even Royn—"

"Your moral vacuum."

"Exactly. And he's the *best* of them."

"A moral vacuum sitting on top of a moral sewer."

Alison laughed.

"Not so long ago," Olsson said, "you'd have accused me of exaggerating."

"I did, didn't I?" Alison smiled to herself. "But now . . . what pulled me here so long ago seems like an impossible dream—"

"And I was going to congratulate you on getting where you wanted to be."

"I'm no longer sure I'm in the right place," Alison said slowly, pushing herself up, stiffening her body, impelled to, at last, look him in the eye "—and I'm beginning to think you may have been right, all along."

Alison was prepared for Olsson to grin in triumph, or in mockery. She was not ready for his nod of understanding, the sudden tears that came to his eyes, or the tender touch of his fingers gently stroking her cheek. "What's driving you now, then?" he asked.

"McKurn. He's the Great White, completely immoral, the most rotten apple in the whole barrel—and what's scary is that *McKurn* is in his natural element and, it turns out, I'm not." *And is McKurn turning me into a moral vacuum too?*

"And if McKurn wasn't there?"

Alison sighed. "There are others, not so bad, not so cunning, just your everyday, pragmatically *a*moral self-seekers after power."

"So getting rid of McKurn is just pulling up the biggest weed in the garden."

"In Canberra, it would be easier to pull up the grass. There's less of it."

"I never thought I'd hear you say something like that," Olsson chuckled.

Alison laughed. "Nor did I."

"Alison," Olsson said sharply, "don't give up now."

Alison looked at him, struggling against her surprise to find a response. "You, of all people, are *encouraging* me?"

"You've *arrived.* You're at the top. Maybe you can still achieve something—and prove me wrong after all."

"Not while McKurn is around."

"Is he such an obstacle?" Olsson asked. "Or are you still seeking revenge?"

"Both."

"But mainly revenge . . . ?"

Alison nodded. "Will you help me?"

"Of course."

Alison started the sudden vehemence in his voice, surprised to see his eyes watering. "What is it, Derek?"

"I never thought McKurn would move so *fast.*"

"You knew?"

"I suspected when I saw Karla's article. I had no idea he'd go after you, too. I could have *been* there, Alison, I could have saved Karla." Olsson's words brought the color back to his cheeks.

"Maybe, Derek," Alison said softly. "More likely, you'd be in hospital too."

"I know," he groaned. "That's where Karla's bodyguard is—in even worse shape than she is."

"She had a bodyguard?" Alison asked.

"I insisted. You need one too."

"Derek—no," Alison protested.

"After what happened yesterday, how can you refuse? Next time it could be a sniper a hundred meters away. One bullet, that's all it would take. It's too easy, Alison. You need protection, professionals who know what to look for. I'll arrange it. They'll be here tomorrow."

"I have to go to Melbourne tomorrow."

"They'll go with you. They'll go with you *everywhere* until this is over. With Karla, too."

Alison could say "no" to Jason but not, she knew, to Olsson. "Thank you, Derek," she said, sinking back into his arms. "I could have *died* this morning—but it still seems so unreal, as if it happened in some other country, not here."

"McKurn isn't acting alone. You must know that."

"Of course."

Olsson suppressed a yawn. "It's getting late, so tell me *why* McKurn blackmailed you?"

"He threatened to release the video unless I helped him make his stooge, Paul Cracken, Kydd's successor instead of Royn."

"That name, Cracken, rings a bell—should I know who he is?"

Pushed herself upright to look Olsson in the eye, she demanded, "Don't you follow politics at all?"

"Only when I can't avoid it."

"What about voting?"

"By the oddest coincidence, I've always been overseas at election time."

Only when Olsson laughed did Alison realize, "You're having me on . . . aren't you?"

Olsson just grinned. "Seems Cracken and McKurn both failed, doesn't it?"

"You're impossible," she said with a mischievous smile. "I played along with McKurn for a while, but then—" Alison shivered, shrinking away from Olsson.

"But then?" Olsson prompted.

Alison sighed. "I . . . backed out."

"But he hasn't released the video—?"

"We found something to hang over McKurn's head. A Mexican standoff."

"How long will that last?"

"I . . . don't know."

"Maybe these will help." Olsson reached into a side pocket of his trousers and pulled out two cellphones. "These are McKurn's."

Alison reached for them, a sparkle in her eyes. "They're the same model as mine. I have the linking software on my laptop."

"It's late," Olsson said. "Let's do it tomorrow—and I'd like to see everything else you've got on McKurn."

"Leave them with me, then."

Olsson hesitated, then shook his head. "I'd rather not, just in case."

"Just in case *what?*"

"They would link you to McKurn—and the bum who visited him."

"You're being paranoid, Derek."

Olsson grinned. "That's right. That's one reason I'm still in one piece. Tomorrow."

"Then stay with me tonight." As soon as she'd spoken she felt herself pulled down by the leaden weight in her stomach. *I feel dirty, unclean—an Untouchable. . . . Please say no.*

Olsson hugged her tighter but before he could speak she said, "I forgot. Jason's coming early tomorrow to take me to the police station."

"Jason?"

"He's a . . . friend. A policeman. If he knew who you were, he'd arrest you on the spot."

"Probably just as well," Olsson chuckled. "Neither of us would get any rest."

*****

Outside Alison's apartment building everything was quiet. Now and then a car passed by, but not very often: even though it was a Friday night and a few blocks away a few shops and bars were still open, this street had turned in for the night. Only the occasional sound of a car starting in the distance, the scream of a cat-fight or the bark of a dog shattered the silence.

There was no one to notice, except a nondescript man sitting in a nondescript car parked in deep shadow on the road opposite the building—just one parked car of many—a large thermos of coffee at his side. He scanned the building yet again. 11:30. Light coming from just *one* of the apartments.

Hers.

The light snapped out, the entire building was now dark except for the dim bulb in the foyer. A red-haired man now stood beneath it, scanning the parked cars.

Can he see me? The man in the car froze as they appeared to lock eyes. But Red's gaze moved on. He strode towards a car parked opposite.

The man in the car had a photographic memory for faces. He knew he'd never seen Red before, but at the same time he seemed uncannily familiar. He watched Red unlock a car door and get in and was tempted to follow him without knowing why.

He looked up at the dark window. He should sit here all night and follow her wherever she went. *If* she went.

Had Red been visiting *her?* Or did he live in the building, perhaps in an apartment one on the other side, hidden from his view.

As Red's car pulled out he noticed a rental company sticker on the back window. His memory made a connection. *Sydney airport.*

Could it be the same guy? The one he'd trailed from Canberra to Goulburn—and then lost at the airport?

With a final glance at the dark window—she ain't going anywhere right now—he started his engine and slowly pulled out behind Red, staying well back.

He had a score to settle.

51   "Fair Go!"

GREG CANNON GOT LUCKY.

He trailed "Red" to a motel, stayed until the light in Red's room went out and waited half-an-hour before returning to his assignment outside Alison's apartment.

By eight AM, when his partner took over the day watch, Cannon was desperate for sleep. On his way back to Red's motel, he stopped to refill his thermos with coffee and grab some stay-awake pills at a chemist.

Red's car was gone.

I've lost him again, Cannon thought. Loaded with pills and caffeine, his eyelids glued to his eyebrows, he decided to wait. "Red" showed up an hour later and disappeared into his room until around lunchtime. As he threw his suitcase into the back of his car, Cannon managed to snap a few good mugs shots with his cellphone camera.

He followed Red back to Alison's apartment, where a heavily built man now stood in the apartment building's lobby. *A flatfoot,* he thought. *That's interesting.* Cannon drove around the block, stopping in a space from which, while well back, he could keep watch on Red's car and the lobby. He could also see his partner's car parked further along the street.

About ten minutes later, *another* plainclothes flatfoot came out of the building and walked across the road straight to where his partner was sitting. The cop didn't seem very happy as he checked his partner's ID. After what looked like a heated exchange, his partner's car pulled out and disappeared.

Damn, he thought. *Now she'll know she's being watched.* His partner would circle around and resume his watch from a more obscure perch. Just the same, Cannon would have to advise his employer and ask for instructions. But he put his cellphone back in his pocket as he saw Red leave the building.

Red drove to an electronics store and then continued to the airport. Cannon followed, watched him turn in the rental car and check in for a flight to Sydney. He stood close enough to hear the check-in agent say, "Have a good flight, Mr. Brewster."

Now he had the man's *name.*

When the plane pulled away from the gate he took out his phone—and hesitated.

He'd followed "Red" before—then he was "Blackie"—and was still annoyed he'd been given the slip. If he could pin "Red" down, he'd have information his client would definitely want. Until then, he'd have to dip into his own pocket, which wasn't very deep.

And if "Red" *wasn't* "Blackie" . . . ?

What the hell.

Cannon called a colleague in Sydney and arranged to have "Red"—Brewster—tailed from the airport, sending him a mug shot so there'd no identification problem.

Only when the plane was a tiny dot in the sky did he head for bed. Just as he drifted off to sleep, his phone beeped. Good news for a change: the Sydney private eye had picked up "Red's" trail.

*****

ALISON'S HOME NO LONGER felt like her castle.

Olsson's promised bodyguards turned up first thing Saturday morning, swept through her apartment like an invading army—and took up residence. Two men stood guard in the corridor and lobby; the woman's role was as her permanent shadow. Her motherly looks and manners and even her name, Madge, Alison decided, were totally unsuited to her profession. But it was a deceptive cover: underneath she was tough and unyielding and wouldn't even let Alison close the door when she went to the bathroom.

Alison knew it was all for her own safety, but she felt hemmed in, as if *she* were being held hostage. When the time came to catch her mid-afternoon flight to Melbourne she left her apartment feeling a strange sense of relief—with the added irony that, thanks to her crutches, her two male escorts acted as bag-carriers.

Alison grinned when they arrived at Royn's Toorak mansion and the Prime Minister's security detail gave her bodyguards a hard time, the same treatment *they* meted out to her visitors that morning. First Jason, who was annoyed at having his police ID verified before taking her to the police station, where she spent a couple of fruitless hours going through hundreds of pictures, recognizing no one.

Much to the bodyguards' embarrassment, it was Jason who spotted the watcher outside. Then Olsson, masquerading as "Joe Brewster," got the third degree. "I can't take the risk of being identified," he'd explained. So he downloaded the software to read the information on McKurn's phones while Alison copied all McKurn's phone taps onto a couple of discs. When he arrived, the exchange of her discs for Olsson's flash memory took all of a few seconds. As far as her "minders" were concerned, "Joe Brewster" was simply a messenger.

"Who are all those people with you?" Melanie asked as she, Royn, and Alison sat around the Royns' enormous dining table.

When Alison explained her "entourage," Royn said, "Good idea. I should have thought of it."

"Let's talk about Kydd's seat before Doug and the others get here," said Melanie, who'd spent the previous Friday sniffing around Kydd's electorate. "Meldrum is planning to run. I'm sure of it, though none of the fuddy-duddies there agree—they all think the sun shines out of his you-know-what. He's well-known and popular with ordinary members too, as far as I could tell."

"I also have some bad news," Alison said. "Cracken could be backing Meldrum." She read the text message from Cracken that Olsson had found on McKurn's phone: Melanie Royn is in Kydd's electorate. Suspicious. Told Meldrum to watch his back.

"*Another* problem," Royn sighed. "If Meldrum *is* running, with or without Cracken's support, what do you suggest?"

"The Prime Minister," Melanie grinned, underlining Royn's title, "can always intervene and *order* the selection committee to nominate his candidate. But—"

"They'll resent that, and block it if they can," Alison said.

"Exactly."

"Ruffling feathers is a bad idea anyway," Royn said. "That's a last resort. What are our other options?"

"First," said Melanie, "you support Barry. Go and romance everyone up there."

"Will that do it?" Royn said, a smile back on his face.

Melanie shook her head. "It will help. The main work needs to be done behind the scenes. Disallow as many new members as possible, make a case for intervention into branch affairs, see who we can turn on the selection committee and the Federal Electoral Council level where we have another problem—McKurn."

"McKurn?" asked Royn. "How?"

"He's been in the New South Wales party machine for so long it's riddled with his supporters. He might even *control* the preselection machinery."

"If he does," Alison asked, "what then?"

"I'm not sure yet, but I have the feeling I'll be spending next week in Sydney working on it."

"Any other seats up for grabs?" Royn asked.

"Unless some other member decides to retire," Alison said, "only two: that one in Perth Stanley Chow has a lock on, and one in North Queensland—"

"Quigley territory."

"Exactly. In most other seats, candidates have already been preselected," Alison said as the doorbell rang.

"I'll get it," said Melanie. A few moments later, Bruce Spring and a handful of other Royn loyalists, along with Doug Selkirk, took their places around the table. Noticeable by his absence, Alison thought, was Paul Cracken.

"Let's go over our strategy for tomorrow's meeting," Royn said.

*****

ON THE PLANE FROM Canberra, Derek Olsson listened to McKurn's conversations on the MP3 player he'd picked up at an electronics store. He read through the texts on McKurn's phones, and spent the day deep in thought. Late in the afternoon he opened his laptop and began sending emails:

> Demas Chrysanthopoulos, aka "The Greek," murdered Vincent Leung and set me up for the fall, he wrote to his partner Ross Traynor. Can you get the lawyers and private eyes to dig up everything they can about him.

And to the geek:

> Find out everything you can about Demas Chrysanthopoulos: bank accounts, business dealings, wife, kids, what side of the bed he gets out of in the morning— EVERYTHING you can dig up. This is urgent—can you put aside anything else you're doing, double rates?

Finally, he sent a long list of instructions to Nazarov, with pictures of the Greek's four sidekicks Lars identified.

What else can I do?

He'd set things in motion but his plans were still incomplete. He glanced at the bed: sleep beckoned, but it was too early. He sat for a while, his eyes unfocussed, and decided to "walk over" his problems and, no doubt, find something to eat along the way.

An hour or so later he was not surprised when his "aimless" walk turned out to have a destination after all: the "Bare Bottoms Club." He grinned at the doorman who was inviting him inside, but decided against it. *Once was enough.*

*****

WHEN ALISON REACHED HER hotel room, among the usual stack of emails she found an encrypted message from Olsson with a file attached.

Did you listen to this? McKurn must have made this call soon after I saw him.
He'll no doubt get new cellphone numbers. Be nice to find out what they are—any suggestions?

"I could ask him," Alison giggled.

McKurn would hand out his new cellphone numbers to his associates. Have the geek tap one of *their* phones and, when McKurn called. . . . Who? Paul Cracken? *Why not? Listen to what he's saying in private.*

The file Olsson sent was one of McKurn's phone calls, made from his apartment.

"Fritz," came McKurn's voice, "it's Frank. Someone, somehow, has got a copy of the statement of one of my Swiss bank accounts." He reeled off an account number and the name of a bank. "Someone in the bank was paid to supply it. I want you to find out who did it—and take care of the bastard. . . . Exactly. *Permanent* retirement," McKurn chuckled.

Alison suddenly felt so cold she looked up to check if the heating was still on. And shocked: even after her narrow escape, she still couldn't fully believe how McKurn "settled his debts."

She felt very grateful to Olsson for the bodyguards.

She hoped they'd be enough.

The geek's latest missive in her inbox the next morning made her wonder if they would be:

McKurnWatch.com
"The website that ~~must not~~ can now be named" [Thanks, Frankie!]
54,371 McKurnWatchers—and counting.

It's hardly a "good morning" today when Frankie seems to be up to his old tricks again. So if you're going to church this morning, put in a prayer for Karla Preston. She's *still* in a coma—severe concussion, among other things—and needs all the help she can get.

The hit-and-run "accident" that nearly killed her is just too darned convenient, don't you think? Reminds me of the "timely" (for Frankie) death of his first wife in another hit-and-run.

But there's more.

When Frankie was very young, as you may recall, he wriggled out of a charge of manslaughter. The cops interviewed the bystanders, but most gave answers like "I didn't see anything," or "I couldn't really say who started it." One, however, insisted that Frankie threw the first punch and a second swore Frankie kicked the man while he was down. But before the case could get to trial, the two witnesses changed their minds (or *had* them changed . . . ?).

A few years later a young woman was brought screaming to a hospital emergency room, her once-attractive face disfigured by acid. A prostitute, she named her "minder"—none other than our dear Frankie, continuing his ascent of the ladders of the underworld—as the culprit.

Her wounds, while horrific, were not life-threatening. Nevertheless, on her second morning in hospital she woke up dead—from a drug overdose (no one ever figured out "whodunit").

Coincidences? They keep coming.

Twenty-odd years ago, a gangster who was ready to "tell all" about McKurn to a corruption inquiry disappeared before he could spill his beans, never to be seen or heard from again.

And some ten years later, while Frankie was Minister for Mining and Energy, a mid-level bureaucrat from that department, known to be a couch potato whose favorite exercise was walking to and from his car, died on the ski slopes of all places. Even odder: having never skied in his life, he came to grief on an expert-level, double-black-diamond run.

Just *another* fluke that this functionary had blabbed to a journalist about questionable goings-on in Frankie's department? (Did he slide or was he pushed?)

Of course, perhaps this string of convenient "accidents," each one *permanently* removing an obstacle in Frankie's way (with—fingers crossed—the exception of Karla Preston) was nothing more than pure luck.

Sure.

But hey! Wait a minute. I think I just saw a pig zipping past my window, flapping its wings.

— The McKurn Watcher

*****

To the public Anthony Royn, as Prime Minister, sat at the top of the Conservative Party "tree." In reality, the Conservative Party was not a unified, monolithic organization dancing to the prime minister's tune, but a loose confederation of two "wings": the "organizational wing"—autonomous state and territory "divisions," each an independent organization with its own rules and constitution, and the "parliamentary wing," separately constituted State and Federal parliamentary parties. each, in practice if not principle, an independent fiefdom.

All these separately constituted bodies, which sometimes forgot they were all in the same boat and fought like warring tribes, plus associated bodies like the Young Conservative Movement and the Women's Council, came together in the Federal Council—whose decisions, however, were binding on neither the organizational nor parliamentary wings.

The two wings were joined at the hip by mutual dependence: the organizational wing handled membership, raised funds, chose candidates. and provided them with campaign backup—functions all crucial to the main job of the parliamentary parties: winning office and keeping it.

They were also tied together by mutual interest: both wings gained when the party was in government; both wings preferred the trappings of power to the backwater of opposition.

Royn well knew that, excellent poll numbers notwithstanding, election success depended on smooth and friendly cooperation between all these independent bodies. Randolph Kydd, towards the end of his reign, had often announced decisions after talking to just a couple of his cronies—or no one at all. Kydd could depend on the enormous personal authority he'd built within the party; Royn would have to *persuade* where Kydd had *dictated.* No written rule required a Conservative Party prime minister to consult *anyone* in the party before calling an election—or anything else. By inviting the key party members, including those who weren't in his camp—faction leaders like Jack Quigley, loose cannons like Stanley Chow, and even McKurn who, as President of the Senate, could not be ignored—Royn sought to "conscript" them into persuading him to do what he planned to do anyway.

So as not to offend anyone, he also put out the welcome mat for any MP or party official who wanted to come. Some two hundred people said they'd attend; three hundred turned up, including assistants.

The meeting was scheduled to start at noon so attendees could fly in and out the same day. "And keep it short," Doug Selkirk had grinned: from mid-afternoon, everyone would be looking at their watches to be sure they'd get to the airport in time for their flight home. Holding the conference at an airport venue would have been more convenient but, it was explained, "no suitable facilities could be found" at such short notice. They met in a posh hotel in the center of Melbourne.

The noon start allowed Royn and Melanie to go to their neighborhood church—Royn was thankful no one overheard the pastor's quiet welcome, "Haven't seen you here for a while,"—and so be photographed and interviewed as they came out, the more important reason, which was left unstressed.

Inevitably, the reporters' questions centered around the likelihood of a snap poll—the topic of the political pundits' speculations in the weekend papers.

"That issue is bound to come up," Royn grinned. "After all, there *has* to be an election in the next ten months."

"How about telling us something we *don't* know, Prime Minister," one reporter grunted.

"Another time," Royn chuckled, pointing at his watch and striding towards the waiting limousine.

Billed as an informal, getting-to-know-you-better occasion, the meeting was anything but. Royn schmoozed with the State Premiers and opposition leaders, State Presidents, members of federal and state executives, and Members and Senators as they arrived—even greeting Quigley like a long-lost brother and managing to say a few pleasant words to McKurn. Cracken, Spring, and others also "worked the crowd."

When things got under way, well after one, almost everyone was sated from the spread of delicacies—supposedly a "light lunch"; quite a few were also somewhat mellowed by a glass or three of wine. Primed by carefully dropped hints of poll numbers, everyone took their seats in the conference room amid a buzz of excited, anticipatory conversation—and grabbed for the detailed report of the poll results laid out on those seats. For a few minutes the only sound was the shuffling of paper until somebody muttered, "These look pretty conclusive."

A gusty, wintry day outside, the temperature in the room nevertheless rose as three hundred people in a space designed for two hundred taxed the air conditioning. The forty most-senior people squeezed around the long, oval conference table, Royn at its head; the rest packed the walls in concentric circles of status.

Alison perched uncomfortably just behind Royn, with a perfect view of the premiers, presidents, senior MPs and senators—and McKurn, halfway around the table. Her eyes kept coming back to him. He glanced briefly at the poll numbers without apparent interest, observed the proceedings as if he had no stake in the outcome, contributing only his silence to the debate. From time to time his eyes would turn towards Alison, as if he could feel her gaze; she jerked her head away with the taste of bile in her throat.

Royn had intended to kick things off with the question, "*When*, gentlemen, is the best time to call an election?" while Cracken and Spring were set to stage-manage the conversation. But no prompting was needed for an animated discussion of the desirability of an election sooner, rather than later.

After about half an hour in which a few people pleaded they needed more time to prepare, Jim Williams, the NSW President, thumped on the table and announced, in a loud voice, "There are risks in waiting, and risks in *not* waiting. But *these* numbers are unlikely to ever get any better, so I say we should go *now*."

There was a general murmur of assent as Spring asked innocently, as if the idea had only just occurred to him, "Are you implying that we should announce an election *today?*"

"Well," said Williams, "maybe not today, but how about *next* weekend? Give those laggards a little bit more time to get ready."

There was a moment of silent agreement until Stanley Chow interjected, "Whatever we decide is bound to leak. By next weekend, we'll have lost the element of surprise."

"If you've been reading the papers," Helen Arkness chuckled, "people would probably be more surprised if we *didn't* announce a snap poll today."

"It's important that *everyone* be ready," said Williams. "I, for one, am willing to give some resources to those who need a little extra help."

"Thanks, Jim," said one of the laggards. "That will work for us."

"Is the consensus of the meeting that we announce today?" Williams asked. Heads nodded accompanied by a cascade of yeses. Williams turned to Royn. "Prime Minister, what do you think?"

Royn's smiling eyes seemed to caress everyone in the room, even McKurn. He spread his arms as if helpless, saying, "Who am I to oppose the majority?"

"Wait a moment." Helen Arkness' voice was a sudden explosion of sound, slicing across the scent of victory that had settled over the room. "We've been carefully skating around a major problem we *must* face."

"What's that, Helen?" Royn asked. His tone was steady, but there was no mistaking the flash of panic that crossed his face.

At her signal, an aide lifted a heavy stack of newspapers from the floor and dropped them in front of Helen Arkness; the table shook, ice in the water glasses tinkled. Helen Arkness pushed the stack so the newspapers tumbled and slid across the conference table. Every eye in the room—the aides behind craning to see—was uncomfortably glued to the panorama of sleaze and vice strewn across the table: the faces of Senator Haughtry, parliamentarians, top policemen and bureaucrats, every official exposed by the OlssonPress and now facing corruption charges stared back at them.

"Corruption in high places—" Helen Arkness' arm swung in a wide gesture to take in all the pictures "—is the issue that can kill us." She sat in the middle of the long table and glanced at McKurn, sitting opposite, as she spoke.

"We all *know* that, Helen," Stanley Chow grimaced, pointing at the newspapers, "and hardly need to be reminded of it in this overly dramatic fashion. It affects Labor too, you know."

"Quite so," said Royn, evincing an aura of calm in the hope it would prove contagious. "I'm committed to clean government which, unquestionably, should be our stance."

Helen Arkness laughed. "Then we'll be labelled hypocrites, Tony. You'll hand Labor a present Nash will milk to crucify us unless we solve our *real* problem which makes all these—" she indicated the papers again with a sweep of her eyes "—mere background noise."

"What on earth are you talking about, Helen?" Jack Quigley asked, the sly look on his face suggesting he had a good idea of the answer.

Helen Arkness stared at McKurn as she tossed two more papers in the center of the pile, headlining Karla Preston's articles on McKurn, whose face loomed menacingly from both front pages.

Involuntarily, every head turned towards McKurn, whose only reaction was the hint of an amused smile.

"Senator McKurn," Helen Arkness said sternly, "for the good of the party, it's time for you to go."

The atmosphere in the room was now charged, like the second before a thunderstorm shoots its first lightning bolt. Alison found it hard to breathe. Jack Quigley nodded enthusiastically. The Young Conservatives' president said, tentatively, "Hear, hear," but looked around nervously when just a handful of timid voices echoed his—and quickly died away. Jim Williams seemed to shrink, as if that would make him invisible—but his eyes kept flicking to McKurn as if awaiting an eruption. Doug Selkirk muttered, "Straight for the jugular, damn her." Stanley Chow grimaced at Helen Arkness as if *she,* rather than McKurn, was the problem; Chow's preference was well-known: controversial issues should be settled in the backroom, on the quiet. The tendons on the side of Royn's neck stood out like taut ropes; at the other end of the table, Paul Cracken glanced sideways at McKurn and said, "Aren't you being a little hasty, Helen?"

"*Hasty,* Paul?" Helen Arkness demanded, stabbing her finger at a front page so hard that she dented a picture of McKurn's face.

"Then why hasn't the senator been charged? Why are the courts on *his* side—banning any more such stories about him? Where's the *evidence,* Helen?"

"Evidence?" Helen Arkness peered at Cracken, astonished. "I'd assumed, Paul— wrongly it turns out—that someone with *your* political nous would know that an election doesn't happen in a court of law, but in the court of public opinion."

"I'm ashamed of you, Helen."

McKurn's voice was soft, but commanding. His head shook slowly a couple of times, his eyes mournful, those of a puppy hurt for no explicable reason. There was a collective, almost-audible sigh of relief, as though everyone had read that morning's McKurnWatch and was tensed for a violent reaction which hadn't come. But while McKurn's left hand lay, relaxed, on the table, his other hand, held under the table against his belly by the sling, was clenched in a tight fist.

"*You* are ashamed of *me?* I can't believe my ears."

"That's right, Helen. Ashamed that *you,* a senior member of our noble party, would repeat baseless innuendos that should be left in the gutter where they came from. I've been a loyal member of the Conservative Party for my entire career. But now, with my reputation under attack by persons unknown who are spreading vicious rumors which—as Paul so correctly pointed out—have no legal foundation and are backed with no evidence—"

Helen Arkness lifted one of Karla Preston's articles and let the paper thump back on the table. "Baseless? Reform school, time in the nick, associating with criminals—"

"Tony," McKurn asked Royn, lightly, his eyes resting on Alison as he spoke. The crooked bridge of his nose transformed his wry smile into an ominous smirk, making Alison freeze. "Did being photographed with Mao Tse-tung, as our dear Randolph once was, turn him into a communist?"

"That's not the point, as you very well know," Helen Arkness growled, unaware that Royn's mouth hung open, and she'd come to his rescue. "Standing up for 'clean government' with *you* on the Senate ticket will make us a laughing stock."

"What happened to justice? To 'innocent until proven guilty'? To a fair go—which is all I'm asking for?"

McKurn's face reddened when somebody giggled, which spurred a chain reaction of low murmurs and the rustling of chairs. Alison coughed loudly to stifle an automatic laugh.

"What a novel idea," Helen Arkness chuckled. "I can see it now: 'Fair go Frankie'—"

"My name," McKurn snarled, "is Frank."

"'Frank,'" Helen Arkness mused, "means 'forthright, guileless, honest, truthful, candid, blunt.' Aside from the last, you'll be hard pushed to find anyone in the whole country who agrees that you're *frank*, Frankie."

Doug Selkirk leant close to Alison to whisper, "And *she's* our chief diplomat." Alison, her attention fixed on McKurn, seemed deaf to Selkirk's comment. She touched Royn's arm and softly said, "You need to assert your authority, Prime Minister. And Helen's right. He's *got* to go."

Royn leaned his chair back to murmur, "I should support Helen *now?*" He was so close he could feel Alison's hot breath and was surprised at the intense glitter in her eyes.

"Better just to drop a hint," Alison replied.

"Yes . . . a hint. . . ." Royn nodded thoughtfully. He saw McKurn watching him impatiently. He looked at McKurn evenly.

McKurn shrugged and said to Helen Arkness: "Are you implying, Helen, that I'm dishonest, deceitful, a *liar?*"

"I'm not *accusing* you of anything—I'm not even talking about right or wrong, guilt or innocence. I'm talking about what the voters *believe*—"

"Let me make one thing clear, Helen," McKurn declaimed. "I fully intend to protect my reputation from these scurrilous rumors and I will do nothing—*nothing,* you understand—that might give them any credence whatsoever."

"I wish you luck," Helen Arkness grinned. "But you could swear your innocence on a stack of Bibles and no one would believe you were telling the truth. *That's what matters.*"

"Perhaps you could explain that, Helen," Royn said quietly, "with your permission of course, Senator."

Heads swung towards Royn almost in unison, like a military salute. McKurn glared at him, but said nothing. Helen Arkness and Jack Quigley, among others, smiled; Paul Cracken's face was one of many that seemed apprehensive. A background hum of whispered comments was silenced as Helen Arkness' voice boomed:

"Certainly, Tony. People believe these stories about McKurn are true—or *could* be true. If we call an election with *you* as a candidate, Senator, we'll be committing electoral suicide."

"My resignation would be interpreted as an admission of guilt," McKurn said. "It's not an option."

"I'm with Helen," said Quigley. "We'd be fools to go to the electorate with all these charges against our senior member flying around. Maybe Senator McKurn could become ambassador to France—or Paraguay, which might be more appropriate."

"I'm quite happy where I am," McKurn growled.

"You're probably the only one who is, Frankie," said Helen Arkness.

"Goddammit!" McKurn exploded. "Can't we have a little respect around here?"

"Certainly," Helen Arkness replied. "But you have to *earn* respect Frankie. For example, by doing the right thing for a change and handing in your resignation *now.*"

"Not a chance," McKurn glowered. "I've given more years of service to this party than anyone else in this room. If you and the party won't stand behind me when I'm being unfairly and viciously slandered, then why should I stand with *you?*"

"Because politics is about winning," Helen Arkness replied. "Better to make a small sacrifice—you—than risk losing government."

McKurn sighed. "It seems I need to remind you that this gathering is *informal.* It has no official status within the party. *Nothing* decided here is binding on *any* party organ so this whole discussion is irrelevant—"

"I can't say I agree with you, Senator," Royn said. "At the end of the day, after all, it's the *Prime Minister* who decides when to call an election—and what advice he needs to make that decision."

McKurn straightened his posture, using his extra height to look down on Royn, even while seated. It was the imperial movement of a person not used to being interrupted. He studied Royn in silence and spied Alison leaning forward, gazing at him intently. To McKurn's surprise, the tension of her posture, her quick breaths and pink cheeks exuded an air of anticipation, even triumph; his eyes narrowed. Alison grinned at McKurn, whose lips curled into a mocking sneer.

"Even so, *Prime Minister,*" McKurn said, drawing out his words and so Royn's title became an insult, "decisions on *Senate* candidates are reserved to the State divisions. Isn't that so, Jim?"

"Quite so, Senator," Williams said carefully, nodding his head.

"And the New South Wales division has the most to lose—with *you* on the list, Frankie," said Helen Arkness.

Jim Williams nervously cleared his throat. "Ah . . . Senator," he said, "the fact of the matter is . . . as I understand it . . . that within the New South Wales division there's a growing sentiment to . . . ah . . . take your name *off* the Senate list at the next election."

"Let's cross that bridge when we come to it," McKurn growled.

"Since *when* to hold an election is why we're here *today,* we're on that bridge right now," Helen Arkness said.

"You're wrong about that, Helen," McKurn said calmly. "We should all wait for the selection committee's decision."

As he spoke, he watched for Royn's reaction, the hint of a grin on his face. Alison jerked back in her chair, her face suddenly pale, her fingers digging into her stomach. Her movement drew McKurn's eyes; only Alison was aware that, for an instant, those eyes seemed to be caressing her breasts.

She levered herself upright with a crutch, accidentally knocking the table as she moved. The sound drew everyone's attention away from McKurn.

"Sorry," she mumbled.

"Alison—?" Royn asked.

"I'm going to be sick," she muttered.

She hobbled out of the room as quickly as her crutches would allow, squeezing herself between packed chairs, stumbling, and unavoidably knocking a few shoulders and toes. "Too much champagne," somebody said. Deaf to the ripple of laughter, preoccupied in soothing her rebellious stomach, she swung the crutches forward as far as she could, running a one-footed race against her nausea to reach a bathroom in time.

In the corridor, Madge fell in step beside her. "Something wrong, Alison?"

Alison couldn't risk opening her mouth; she nodded curtly, knowing that her mounting disgust at McKurn's silky lies had led her to come to the decision she'd been doing her best to avoid.

Madge followed her into the bathroom where she violently threw up as if the force of her revulsion could expel McKurn's unwanted gift along with everything else in her stomach.

MADGE BECAME ALISON'S NURSEMAID, helping her up to the suite they shared and insisting she rest "to regain your strength." Alison was lying limply on the sofa when Doug Selkirk called. "Royn's holding a press conference now," he told her.

"He's going for it?"

"Yes."

"I don't like it," Alison said.

Selkirk shrugged. "I don't either. The stoush with McKurn will be all over the papers in the morning—if not on the news tonight. It's a gamble."

Alison closed her eyes. "Let's talk about it tomorrow."

"You sound drained. Will you be okay?"

"I'm not sure—but I'll live. Does he need me again today?"

"He said you should take it easy."

"I intend to."

*****

ANTHONY ROYN HAPPILY WATCHED his smiling, photogenic face on the screen announcing a snap election, the lead story on the evening news. Then he scowled as Kydd's drawn and menacing face flashed on the screen.

"Why's *he* being interviewed?" Melanie gasped. "I expected Nash next."

"Nothing good, "Royn shrugged, "that's for sure."

"Mr. Kydd," the reporter asked, "have you made any decision about standing in this election?"

"Of course," Kydd said, wincing at being called "mister" instead of "prime minister." "I owe it to the people of my electorate to continue serving them."

"From the back bench? After being Prime Minister for fourteen years?"

"If necessary," Kydd smiled. "But anyone who thinks I'm ready to lay down and die," he growled, "has got another think coming."

"The bastard," Melanie spat. "He never forgets—and never forgives."

Royn nodded glumly. "He could spoil everything."

"We can't let him." Melanie turned to glare at her husband. "We *won't,* will we, Tony?"

Slowly, reluctantly, almost imperceptibly, Royn shook his head. "But—do you think Barry Easton's got what it takes to trounce *Kydd?*"

"Definitely *not,*" Melanie said. "But Jake Meldrum *does.*"

"But if he's in Cracken's pocket—?"

Melanie shrugged. "Who would you rather have—Kydd sniping from behind your back? Or another Cracken supporter who'll be a nonentity, at least for a while?"

Royn grinned half-heartedly. "That's easy."

"I haven't given up on Barry." Melanie's eyes glittered as they focused into the distance, as if seeing her own thoughts displayed on a wide screen, her lips curled into a half-grin. Royn knew that look: he imagined he could see the cogs of her mind turning as she plotted something devious. Knowing Melanie was now fully involved, he relaxed, and waited patiently until she looked up, smiled at him warmly, and said,

"Maybe we can still get Barry nominated. But we've got to get rid of Kydd—*and* McKurn. Whatever it takes."

52 Blank Cheque

"FIFTEEN MINUTES," ALISON MUTTERED to herself. "That's about all I could take."

Hunched over her laptop, the remains of her half-eaten room-service breakfast scattered across the table, ignoring the flood of emails in her inbox, Alison studied her options.

The abortion pill was actually two pills, taken two days apart, inducing a miscarriage. Which could be painful. An operation was all over in fifteen minutes—under anesthetic, so she'd feel nothing.

Except . . . *another* invasion of her innermost self. Her whole body trembled at the thought.

None of the above is not an option, she told herself.

Madge's voice broke into her thoughts. "Hadn't we better get moving?"

Alison closed her laptop. "I guess so." She pulled the hotel dressing gown tighter and looked up, adding, with a wan smile, "In a hurry to meet the Prime Minister?"

"I can take him or leave him," Madge shrugged. Alison and her minders would all fly to Canberra with Royn on the VIP jet.

"You might be surprised," Alison grinned.

Madge shrugged again. "He's just another man."

Alison studied Madge with renewed interest. *What does she mean by that?* A middle-aged, single woman, perhaps her comment indicated troubled relationships in the past. *Look who's talking.*

"True enough," Alison said as she picked up her cellphone and went into the bedroom. "I have a call to make," she told Madge as she closed the door. "A *private* call." *Before I change my mind.*

Her fingers turned into thumbs as she punched in the number and made the appointment for the coming Saturday afternoon.

"I can always cancel it," she mumbled as she headed for the shower.

*****

"JIM WILLIAMS ASSURES ME McKurn doesn't have the numbers—" Melanie was saying as Alison hobbled into the VIP lounge at the airport.

"I don't believe him," Alison cut in as she took a seat. "McKurn was too sure of himself. It wasn't an act. He must have the selectors in his pocket."

"Since last night," Royn said, "Jim has talked a lot of them all. He's certain the vote will be at least sixty-forty to dump McKurn."

"That's *before* McKurn gets to work," Alison said.

"We've got Jim and Helen Arkness on our side, just for starters," said Melanie. "*We* can bring a lot of pressure to bear."

"Enough pressure to counter McKurn's *threats?*" Alison shook her head. "I don't think so. A 'convenient accident' is a hell of an argument to beat."

"Surely not—"

Alison thumped the floor with her crutch. "Melanie! You can't have any doubts about how McKurn gets his way by now, *surely.*"

"I know, but—"

"And I wouldn't be so sure of Williams' support, either."

"What do you mean by that?" Melanie snapped.

"The way he behaved yesterday. He's *afraid* of McKurn. Wouldn't you agree, Doug?"

Selkirk nodded. "That's right."

Melanie looked at Royn. "What do you say, Tony?"

"I . . . ah . . . don't recall exactly." Royn searched his memory and shook his head. "But if that's what Doug and Alison saw—"

"No question about it," said Alison.

"Maybe," Melanie sighed.

A member of Royn's security detail opened the door. "Your Sydney flight's being called, Mrs. Royn."

"Thanks." Turning to Alison as she stood up, Melanie said, "If you're right, I'm going to have my work cut out for me."

Alison nodded. "We all are."

"It's a lot to handle," Royn said as he hugged her. "Kydd's electorate *and* the Senate selection committee. But if anyone can do it, Mel, *you* can."

"I hope so, Tony," she said. Drawing his head closer she whispered in his ear, "I'm going to miss you."

"Me too," Royn whispered back. "But I'm going to have to come to Sydney to press the flesh, aren't I?"

Melanie grinned. "That's right."

"Good luck, Melanie," Alison said.

"Thanks. This time, I might just need some."

*****

RUDI DURANT WAS ANGRY—not that Superintendent Zimmerman, on the other end of the phone, could tell. "Yes, boss . . . if you insist . . . " Durant was saying, his voice suitably obsequious. But when he slammed the phone down he growled, ". . . and three bags full, sir."

From the other side of Durant's desk Simon Lee watched Durant's changing facial expressions with unabashed interest. "What does Zimmerman want now?"

"No rest for the wicked," Durant said, forcing a ghoulish grin. "That's us, if you haven't guessed—the gospel according to Zimmerman."

"Another case?"

Durant nodded, picking up the phone to make another call. "A hopeless case."

Lee groaned and yawned at the same time. Earlier that morning, they brought in the culprit in the double-murder case—after an all-night vigil. Instead of having time to recuperate, they were to be sent straight out on the streets again. Lee closed his eyes, barely listening as Durant spoke to somebody in a hospital, coming half to attention only when he heard the name, "Karla Preston."

When Durant finished, Lee asked, without opening his eyes, "So, we're being demoted, are we?"

"Huh? What makes you say that?"

"That's not murder, it's a hit-and-run."

Durant nodded. "Karla's Preston's companion died last night, so now it's manslaughter. And Zimmerman *laughed* when he said he was being pressured by the Premier *and* Canberra 'to put his best guy on the case.' Bastard." Durant jerked to his feet and shrugged. "Never mind. Let's go see what they've got at the Glebe police station. Then we'll talk to Karla Preston—if she's awake."

The Glebe station sergeant didn't improve Durant's mood. It was late at night, he told them. No one saw the accident happen. There was a description of the car, reported stolen about the same time as the accident and found abandoned the next day. The only fingerprints were those of its owner and his family. Karla Preston's companion died without regaining consciousness. He was her bodyguard "because of all their exposés," the station sergeant explained, glowering as if he were afraid he might be next. "OlssonPress has security guards from here to breakfast, 'just in case,' so they said."

"Seems like she needed one," said Lee as he drove to the hospital. "But no witnesses. No clues. Sounds like punishment to me."

"As if Zimmerman *wants* us to fail."

"Could have been joyriders."

"Maybe," said Durant. "Except for the lack of fingerprints. Whoever hijacked the car must have worn gloves, which suggests intent. Unlikely to have been a couple of kids out for a lark."

"I don't see how that helps," said Lee, uncomfortably aware that even *with* witnesses, hit-and-run accidents often went unsolved.

"Nor do I, but maybe Karla Preston can tell us something."

At the hospital, the doctor told them Karla was suffering from severe concussion and multiple fractures in her right arm, and had been in a coma until this morning. "A few minutes. That's all, until she's stronger."

Two private security guards stood outside the door of her room in the intensive care ward and refused to let Durant and Lee enter until they'd double-checked their identity.

"Why all the security?" Lee asked.

"Protection. We were told she might still be in danger."

"From who?"

"That," said one of the guards woodenly, "is something we don't know."

Karla Preston lay beneath a confusion of wires and tubes connecting her to monitors and drips. One arm was in a wrist-to-shoulder cast. Her eyelids flickered faintly when Durant, Lee, and the doctor entered.

"We've met before," Durant said as the doctor began to introduce them. "Do you remember that, Miss Preston?"

Karla's lips fluttered and with a visible effort she said, "How k-k-k . . . " And stopped.

"How about I ask you 'yes/no' questions. Blink once for 'yes,' twice for 'no.' Can you do that?"

Karla blinked once.

"Do you have any idea who attacked you?"

One blink. *Yes.*

"Who?"

"Mckur . . . " Karla said, her voice faint.

"McKerr?" said Lee.

Two blinks.

"McKurn?" Durant asked. "Do you mean *Senator* McKurn?"

Yes.

"Are you certain of that?"

Yes.

"Do you have any evidence?"

Two blinks. *No.*

"Makes sense," Lee muttered.

Durant nodded.

Karla's eyes were now fully open, holding Durant's. "Alis. . . ." she started to say, her voice faltering.

"Alice?"

Karla blinked, slowly, once. She opened her eyes and closed them again.

"Miss Preston?" Durant said. Karla's only response was a faint flicker of the muscles around her closed eyelids. "Was that a 'yes' or a 'no'?" he asked Lee, who simply shrugged.

"That's it for today, gentlemen," the doctor said sternly as he ushered them out of Karla's room.

Durant gave him a card. "Please call me the moment she can answer some more questions."

"Do you think McKurn's *really* behind it?" Lee asked as they reached their car.

"Who can say? Absolutely no *evidence*. But it gives us a *valid* excuse to follow up on Leon Price's list." Durant chuckled. "Without knowing it, Zimmerman's given us a blank cheque to snoop on McKurn. God, wouldn't it be nice to reel that bastard in. The look on Zimmerman's face would be something to see."

"Is that what you're you going to write up in your report?"

"Well," Durant grinned, "perhaps I should. But . . . what's to write up? A woman barely out of a coma, no doubt loaded with morphine and God knows what else, makes a couple of incomprehensible sounds which may be no more than vague accusations without evidence—assuming we understood what she was trying to say."

"So you still don't trust Zimmerman?"

"He took us off the taskforce because he gives in to pressure. If the pressure came from *McKurn*—?"

"I see what you mean."

"Let's stop at a bookshop," Durant said.

"What on earth for?"

"Grab one of those books of baby names."

"You can look them up on the internet," said Lee, which he did when they returned to Durant's office, while Durant tracked down Lynette McPherson. He finally reached her on her cellphone.

"I know who you are," she said when Durant introduced himself. "You arrested our boss."

"That's right," said Durant, motioning for Lee to pick up the extension, "and I'm *still* looking for him. But that's not why I need to speak to you. I'm investigating the hit-and-run accident that put Karla Preston into hospital. Her bodyguard died last night."

"Oh my God no," said Lynette.

"Whose idea was it to hire a bodyguard?"

"It came from . . . our security chief."

"Who's that?"

Lynette paused; her voice soft, she said, "Lew Campbell. When . . . he saw Karla's articles about McKurn, he insisted on it. I didn't take it seriously enough."

"I see. So Campbell thought Miss Preston could be in danger from McKurn. Is that right?"

"Yes. Obviously, she was."

"Well," Durant said guardedly, "it's certainly a theory worth following up."

"Is *that* what you think?" Lynette demanded. "Just a *theory?*"

"Until you can print that accusation in your newspapers without getting a libel suit, that's all it is. A *theory.*"

"I guess so, Inspector."

"Thanks," Durant said sourly. "I'm sure I'll be talking to you again."

"I can hardly wait, Inspector."

"Women," Durant said as he slammed down the phone. "Always have to have the last word."

"A tough lady," Lee said. "But I think she was lying about Campbell."

"I agree."

"Why didn't you call her on it?"

"Better, I think, if I talk to Campbell first. Show me what you've got."

Lee passed over the list of names he'd made: Alecia, Aleshanee, Alessa, Alessandro, Alessia, Alice, Alicia, Alison, Alissa, Aliza, Alize, Allie, Allison, Allyson, Alyce, Alysha, Alyshea, Alyson, Alyssa.

"What if it's a *guy?*" Durant asked. He picked up the two brick-thick volumes of the Sydney telephone directory from under his desk and dropped them with a thump in front of Lee. "Maybe it's a *last*, not a first name—" Durant grinned, adding the yellow pages to the pile "—or a business name. When you've got *all* the possibilities, run them all through the police databases, see what you come up with. While you're at it, why not dig up everything on McKurn as well."

Lee groaned. "That will take ages. And McKurn's charges—if that McKurnWatch guy is right—go back to the 1940s. Too old to be online."

"You'll manage."

"And what will *you* do?"

"I'll give this Lew Campbell a call," Durant chuckled. "And then I'm sure I'll think of something."

"She *was* lying," Durant told Lee after he'd spoken to Campbell. *Olsson*, not Campbell, got antsy when he saw Karla's articles, Durant explained. Campbell also said Olsson had been in touch with him a few times, and he reported every contact to the police. "We can double-check that later, but Campbell used to be on the force, so he knows the procedure."

"How come no one on the taskforce ever heard about it?" Lee asked.

"Good question. I'll chew *someone* out. But Olsson keeps changing his number, according to Campbell—or uses the internet, as we know." Durant shrugged. "Maybe we would have gotten lucky and located him from a cellphone trace. And you know what?" Durant grinned.

"I give up," said Lee.

"Olsson will probably call again. So—we have grounds for tapping the OlssonPress phones."

Lee nodded. "Can *we* do it? Shouldn't we hand it over to the taskforce?"

"What's left of it," Durant grumbled. "But dammit, you're right."

"What next? Will you call Lynette McPherson now?"

Durant shook his head—and grinned. "Campbell said he'll talk to her. Then, no doubt, she'll speak to her lawyers. Next time I talk to her, she'll be one thoroughly chastened woman."

Lee showed Durant what he'd mined from the police databases: a petty thief named Alistair with a record going way back when, a woman named Alicia serving time on Long Bay for robbery, a company called Alice Springs Minerals being investigated for accounting irregularities by the tax office, and the report of an attack on one Alison McGuire in Canberra the previous morning.

"No obvious connection to Karla Preston," Durant said, "or McKurn."

"Except, maybe, Alison McGuire. She's Anthony Royn's personal assistant," Lee said. "From what the ACT police say, the attack could have been attempted murder. I also spoke to a Sergeant Jason Kowalski—"

"Kowalski? *He* passed us that Leon Price transcript."

"He's a friend of Alison McGuire and was first at the scene of the accident. He doesn't think Alison was just in the wrong place at the wrong time either. I have her cellphone number if you want to talk to her."

"Politics." Durant rocked back in his chair. "Karla Preston is attacked Thursday night—after accusing McKurn. Alison McGuire the next morning. Coincidence?"

"Could be," said Lee. "But unlikely."

"Gimme that number." All he got was voicemail. After a couple more calls, he got through to Royn's office and left a message. "She's up in the air with the PM," he told Lee. "VIP jet at your disposal—what a life, eh?"

"Yeah," Lee grumbled. "At our expense."

"You're not some kind of revolutionary, are you, Simon?"

"Who, me?" Lee jerked back in his chair but relaxed when he saw Durant's wry grin. "But you've got to admit, with all those perks these pollie bastards get, it's no wonder they can't give us cops decent salaries."

Durant nodded. "You wouldn't be wrong there."

*****

DEREK OLSSON SLOWED HIS step when he saw the discreet sign, FLAT FOR RENT, by the front door of the apartment building where Vincent Leung had been murdered.

He was smiling as he walked into the lobby.

"Could I take a look at that vacant apartment?" Olsson said to the uniformed doorman stationed behind a counter.

"Certainly, sir." The doorman disappeared and came out through a side door. "Just a moment." He shut the lobby door and led Olsson to the lift.

"Security looks pretty good here," said Olsson.

"Yes. It's very important to the residents."

"And there's always someone on duty?"

"Oh, yes, sir. Twenty-four hours a day."

Olsson spent an appropriate amount of time examining the apartment, making the comments expected of a potential renter. "It comes with a car park?" he asked as they went back down.

"That's right, sir," the doorman said. "Like to take a look?"

"Might as well, while I'm here. There's a camera here, I see," Olsson said, pointing to the lens above.

"Yes, sir. We can monitor it in the office."

"Is it recorded?"

The doorman shook his head. "No, sir. But the management committee is considering it."

"I see," Olsson said thoughtfully as they stepped out of the lift into a small, glassed-in lobby.

"I think that would be your car park there, sir."

The car park, Olsson noted, was open to the street. But the door between the lift lobby door and the car park was locked. It could be opened easily from the inside, but access from the car park required a code on a touchpad.

"Fair enough," Olsson said, stepping back into the lift. "I guess when you've seen one car park, you've seen them all."

The doorman laughed.

But Olsson had seen what he was after: the fire stairs by the lift went all the way down to the basement. And no key or code was needed to get *out*.

Once back on the street, he stood surveying the building for a few moments, noting that from the lobby the doorman could *not* see cars entering or leaving the car park. *Yes,* he concluded as he flagged down a passing taxi, *if they had the codes, the Greek and his sidekicks could have entered through the car park, gone up and down the fire stairs and driven out without the doorman seeing a thing.*

"FORGET THE GIRL," GREG Cannon was told by his mysterious client when he reported that Alison McGuire was being "shadowed everywhere she went by flatfeet." So the previous evening he'd flown to Sydney and taken over watching "Red." Now he was waiting once again, sitting on the motor bike he'd borrowed from his Sydney associate, parked half out of sight from the apartment building across the road.

Cannon trailed Red's taxi into the City. He nervously strolled up and down the street while keeping an eye on Red, who just sat in a coffee shop on the ground floor of an office block, reading the paper. Half an hour went by, and Cannon was starting to worry that Red might see him. *Would he recognize me?* he wondered.

He shrugged. Nothing he could do about it now.

Red answered his phone, leapt to his feet, and walked rapidly into the building's lobby. Cannon just managed to catch up and get into the same lift just as the doors were closing. He turned his back as he entered, positive that Red hadn't taken any particular notice of him.

Red stepped out on the fourteenth floor and Cannon followed. He studied the floor directory as if searching for the right office while Red turned down the corridor. In his peripheral vision Cannon saw Red step through a door flanked by two waiting men; he went slowly in the opposite direction, as if looking for the right office. When he turned back he saw that the two men had been joined by a third, and he felt as though all three of them were watching him closely.

He took a slip of paper from his pocket and muttered, loud enough for them to hear, "Wrong floor, dammit all," pressed the UP button on the lift, and stepped inside a moment later.

It wasn't every day, Sir Philip French was thinking, that ASIO invited you to a confidential meeting "on a matter of national security." At least, that was the explanation given by the three men who'd very politely, but insistently, met him as he walked out of the French building on his way to lunch. "Just around the corner," he'd been told. "Fifteen minutes or so, that's all."

He'd been relaxing in the comfortable leather armchair just long enough to start wondering if he'd made a mistake. The three men had showed ASIO badges—but he'd never seen an ASIO ID before. Only one of them had spoken, he now recalled. With a South African accent. The youngest of the three. Somehow, it didn't make sense that this youngster was commanding men almost twice his age. Not in a *government* agency. It didn't feel *right*.

Yet, he—"Alex," he'd said his name was—kept him company while the other two remained in the corridor.

He was about to protest when a red-haired man walked in. "Sorry to keep you waiting, Sir Philip," he said, stretching out his hand. French took it, surprised by the powerful grip, which was soft and gentle at the same time. "Thank you for coming at such short notice. That will be all for now, Alex."

"Very good, sir," Alex said as he closed the door behind him.

"What's this all about? Who are you?" French demanded.

The red-headed man smiled. "I apologize for all this apparent drama, but it's necessary." He showed French another ASIO badge. "We need your help in an investigation. Just a few questions and you'll be on your way."

"This obviously isn't your office," French said.

"It's a rent-an-office," the man said genially. "We won't use it again."

French felt himself drawn to this man even though he still didn't know his name, rank, or anything else about him. He was about to ask again when the man said, "I want you to listen to this."

As he sat down opposite French, he switched on an MP3 player. French gasped as he heard his voice saying:

"Frank, it'll cost you two hundred grand, half up front."

"Where did you get that?" French jerked up to sit on the edge of the seat cushion, one hand unconsciously wiping imagined sweat from his forehead.

"You remember this conversation, do you?"

French hesitated. "Sounds like me," he said guardedly.

"Worth it—if it happens. But where's the guarantee? Twenty-five percent down, no more."

"Sorry, Frank, he says it's a take it or leave it offer."

"Now, who would 'Frank' be?"

French shrugged.

"There's no point in denying that *you* are talking to Frank, Sir Philip. We can prove that with a voiceprint easily enough."

French said nothing.

"We're interested in Frank, not you. *We* know who he is—after all, how do you think we got this recording?" The man chuckled amiably. "We know *you* know who he is. There's no point in denying that, either."

"I don't think I should say anything without a lawyer present."

"Sorry, Sir Philip. We're not the police. In any case, we have no intention of *charging* you with anything. It's Frank we're after."

French swayed back in the armchair, as if pushed by an invisible breeze. His eyes were frozen on the man's face, a face looking at him compassionately. He began to feel he could trust this man—but *should* he?

The man gestured with the MP3 player. "Shall we listen to the rest of your conversation?"

"No. There's no need for that."

"So tell me," the man said with a smile. "Who is Frank?"

French's lips moved soundlessly. He sighed, and bowing his head said, "Frank . . . McKurn."

"And McKurn was willing to pay two hundred thousand dollars to stop the OlssonPress newspapers from coming out."

French nodded. "He was pretty pissed off when it only held up production for a few hours."

The man laughed. "The Sykes papers came out anyway."

"Frank said he could take care of Sykes." He shook his head. "I don't know what went wrong there."

The man laughed again. "We do. We've got that on tape, too."

"You've been tapping his phones?"

"Among other things." The red-haired man stretched lazily back in his armchair. "So you put McKurn in touch with the guy who did the job. Did the money pass through you as well?"

French shook his head. "No. I just passed on the account number. McKurn must have paid direct."

"Can you be sure of that?"

"Absolutely," French nodded. "Otherwise the Greek bastard would have come knocking on *my* door. Which he didn't."

"Did you make a note of the account number?"

"I don't know if I still have it. But it won't do you any good. It was a Swiss bank."

"Do you recall the bank's name?"

"Banque Meridian Lausanne. Something like that."

"And this Greek bastard? Does he have a name?"

"No." French gripped the arms of the chair, his knuckles turning white. "I mean, yes—but there's no way I could tell you."

"You realize, Sir Philip, you've committed a chargeable offence. We can keep your name out of it if you cooperate. But if you don't—" the man shrugged "—our hands are tied."

"Can you pr-pr-protect me?"

"From who? The Greek bastard? McKurn?"

"*Both* of them."

"If you're willing to confess."

"I couldn't do that."

The red-headed man nodded, projecting the sense that he understood French's dilemma.

French sighed helplessly.

The man stood up. "In that case, Sir Philip, thanks for all your help."

"That's it?"

The man nodded.

"But you'll keep my name out of it?"

The man smiled sadly. "If we can—but no guarantees."

"But you said—"

"Not without your full cooperation."

French rose to his feet, stooping as if he was counting the threads in the carpet. Eventually he shook his head and started towards the door.

"One other thing." As French turned his head to look back, the man added softly, so that French had to strain to hear, "Demas Chrysanthopoulos."

French's "No!" was more of a shriek, and though he shook his head violently, the slight involuntary nod that came first gave him away.

"Thank you very much, Sir Philip."

French's eyes widened: the man's amiable manner was gone, replaced with a hard, unforgiving look.

"You can go now."

To French's trembling hand, the door knob felt as though it was cased in slippery ice.

CANNON WAITED IN A discreet corner of the lobby, appearing to read a newspaper—but his eyes tracked every person exiting the lifts. His wait was rewarded when he saw the three men from the fourteenth floor, escorting a fourth, much older man in an obviously expensive, tailored suit. The picture of a successful businessman, he hobbled along like an old age pensioner on his last legs. His three escorts had trouble keeping their pace down to his. Cannon hid his face, but managed to take a couple of snaps with his cellphone, capturing the faces of all four men.

Grainy, but they'd do.

When they reached the street, the old man went one way, the three escorts the other. Cannon walked cautiously to the building entrance. The three men had disappeared; he had no trouble catching up to the old man by window-shopping his way for a few blocks until the old man turned into the French building.

That's who he was: Sir Philip French.

Cannon called his client to tell him he'd tracked down the man he'd lost at Sydney airport. "I'm pretty sure he just met with Sir Philip French."

"You're *sure* of that?"

"He's definitely the same guy. He's dyed his hair red, but he can't change the way he walks. He was with three men, probably flatfeet, who escorted French. I'm sending you a picture now."

After a long pause, the other man moaned, "That's French all right. Do you have a pix of the other guy?"

"Red? Yes, I do."

"Send it to me."

"It's on the way."

"Jesus Christ," the other man said a moment later.

"You know him?" Cannon asked.

"Damn right. I want that bastard."

*****

IT WAS TIME, DEREK Olsson decided as he walked down fourteen flights of stairs and exited through the office building's back entrance, that "Joe Brewster" retired. Permanently.

*****

DURANT, ALISON THOUGHT, STARING at the message Mary had given her when she reached Parliament House. *What could he want?*

A few minutes later, fortified by a strong coffee, she made the call. "Inspector Durant? This is Alison McGuire."

"Ah, Miss McGuire," Durant said. "I'm investigating Karla Preston's accident. Do you know her?"

"Yes, I do."

"I understand *you* were attacked the morning after Miss Preston was."

"That's right."

"Do you have any idea who was behind it?"

"I have . . . suspicions, yes."

"Could be any connection between your attackers and Miss Preston's?"

Alison gasped. "What makes you say that, Inspector?"

"Miss Preston seems to think there might be," Durant said.

"She does? She's regained consciousness?"

"Long enough to answer a few questions, yes."

"How is she?"

"Recovering—slowly."

"I'm glad to hear it."

"Is there a connection?"

Yes, Alison was about to say when she wondered. . . . *Surely not, but*—"How can I be sure you are who you say you are?" she said.

"You're unusually suspicious."

"I have my reasons."

"I understand you know Jason Kowalski."

"And if I do?"

"He could vouch for me."

He already has, she thought. "But he's not here and I don't know your voice. I'll tell you what, Inspector. I'll be in Sydney sometime this week. I'll be happy to talk to you then."

"Okay, then. Perhaps there's one question you would answer now."

"Try me."

"Would you say that the same person was behind the attacks on you and Karla Preston?"

"No doubt about it."

"What do you make of that, Simon?"

"She called the police station," said Lee, "asked for you, and was put through. If she's still suspicious, she must be paranoid."

Durant nodded. "But if it *is* McKurn, she's got a lot to be paranoid about."

*****

Guest houses, Derek Olsson decided, were much cozier than hotels—and were delighted to take "cash and no receipt." Olsson could give any name he liked, no questions asked.

Now back in his room—in Paddington, on the opposite side of the City from Karla's apartment—Olsson rummaged through his fake identities, choosing "Manny Klaus." The rather poor picture on the Australian driver's licence sported a blond crew cut, a moustache, and no glasses.

He remembered having this picture taken, with pads in his cheeks to make him look fatter. A nuisance to wear, but they changed the shape of his face.

Laboriously, he gave himself a haircut, shaved except for his upper lip, and dyed his hair. While waiting for it to dry, he made a quick call to Lew Campbell to learn that Karla was recovering slowly but surely. He shied away from going through his various inboxes, but he recognized one encrypted email as coming from Alison's dummy address:

> I got McKurn's new cellphone number by asking the geek to tap Cracken's phone (remember who he is ☺?). Asked him to copy McKurn's taps to the "Jackal." If you're not getting them, chew him out—Love, "Saith."

Sure enough, there were several emails headed with the new number. But the dye was dry; time to go. *I'll listen to them later.*

To further distance himself from "Joe Brewster," he decided "Manny Klaus" should dress a bit more sharply. The man who emerged from the guest house carried a briefcase instead of a knapsack, and sported a jacket, tie, and well-polished shoes.

WORKING ON HIS OWN, Greg Cannon had three main problems: lack of sleep and *two* entrances to cover on opposite sides of the building. It was also on a quiet, dead-end residential street where someone loitering around stood out like a sore thumb.

His solution was to dress like a local out for exercise and walk past both entrances alternately. That only made him more tired and was no protection from anyone sitting in a front window wondering why the same person kept passing by every ten or fifteen minutes.

On top of that, he didn't know whether Red was back or, worse, *gone.* He itched to go into the guesthouse and find out—which would give the game away.

He took careful note of anyone entering or leaving. He dismissed the somewhat portly, crew cut man carrying a briefcase—until he realized that the man's suitcase looked the same as Red's.

Admittedly, the suitcase was so common there were usually several of them in the baggage claim off any flight. Just the same, he broke into a run, knowing he looked like just another jogger.

He gained on the man and saw his barber had done a pretty poor job—or was that how your hair would look if you cut it yourself?

The same walk. As he flashed by, a sideways glance confirmed it was "Red." A slightly fatter Red, but definitely the same man.

He stopped around the corner. Red—now "Blondie"—stood on the kerb, waiting for a taxi. Cannon took a note of the number and raced back to where he'd parked his motorbike.

*****

ALISON WAS SO RELIEVED to get home she didn't even resent the presence of Madge and her minders. Indeed, since Madge had offered to "make a cuppa," she stretched out on the sofa, put up her feet, and revelled in the sense of being waited on.

It had been a hectic day, except for the half-an-hour in which Royn had visited the Governor-General—a formality that, nonetheless, was necessary to set the electoral machinery in motion. By day's end, the Electoral Office issued the writs and the election date was official: five Saturdays from now.

The rest of the week promised to be worse.

Starting on the plane, it was one meeting after another: pencilling in events for the five-week campaign, deciding themes to emphasize, essential electorates to visit, appearances and speeches that must be made; interspersed with phone calls to make appointments, set up photo ops, interviews, and God-knows-what-else. Alison rubbed her ear, sure it still carried the imprint of the phone. In the fragments of time in between, she and Doug had worked on Royn's campaign speech. He was going to make it on Thursday in Sydney—and they'd barely started.

"Tired?" Madge asked placed a cup of tea on the table.

"Exhausted," said Alison, half-opening her eyes. Madge was beginning to intrigue her. She had giggled—to herself, of course—at Royn's puzzled look as he was introduced to Madge on the plane from Melbourne: Madge was the first woman Alison could recall who seemed totally immune to Royn's charm and sex appeal. *Perhaps she prefers women,* she thought.

Struggling to her feet she said, "This is just Day One—and I haven't finished yet. Just wait till election day, you'll see what exhausted *really* looks like."

"You should rest up."

"I know. Maybe on the weekend." *But maybe not.*

She began by attacking the accumulated phone taps starting, she decided, with McKurn's new number. Half-heartedly . . . until the third call . . .

"I'm pretty sure he just met with Sir Philip French."

"You're *sure* of that?"

She couldn't place the first voice, but the second was McKurn's. She listened to the end; shaking her head, she replayed it.

". . . he's dyed his hair red . . ."

Derek? When he came to her apartment, his hair was red. The other man sent McKurn a picture and she could feel McKurn's fingers creeping up her back when he said,

". . . I want that bastard."

Olsson had been followed from *The Frosty Lady* by someone working for McKurn—was the same guy on his trail now?

French had called McKurn, agitated from being questioned by ASIO about ". . . *you,* Frank."

"That wasn't ASIO," McKurn said.

"It wasn't? They had IDs and everything," said French.

"Nope. They don't operate that way. Whoever that guy is, he's not ASIO. Not a cop either. He's a freelancer up to no good."

"You know who he is?"

"No," said McKurn. "Do *you* have any idea?"

"He never gave his name. . . ."

French paused for so long that McKurn asked, "Phil? Are you still there?"

"I just had a crazy thought," French said. "For some reason, he reminds me of Derek Olsson—"

"Olsson?"

"Maybe. Probably just a vague resemblance—but his mannerisms . . .

"Shit."

I agree.

Has Derek heard these yet? I must warn him.

She tried Olsson's last cellphone number. It was dead; she sent him an email.

For the first time in years, she felt like praying.

*****

IT WAS RUSH HOUR. Red had flagged his taxi on a one-way street. Confident he'd catch up, Cannon pushed his motorbike so it squealed around corners and squeaked through tiny gaps between cars. He slowed at every taxi he passed to check the number—and still hadn't found it by the time he reached the first major intersection.

Did "Blondie" turn right, left, or go straight ahead? Cannon had no idea and no way of knowing.

He pulled his motorcycle onto the pavement to watch each taxi as it reached the lights. After ten minutes he had to admit he'd lost his man.

What to do now? He didn't think his client would be too impressed. Was there another way?

Perhaps his Sydney associate would have some ideas. He called him:

"Listen, mate, I have a problem. Can you meet me somewhere right now? . . . Sure. I'll shout you a beer—a whole fucking barrel—if that's what it takes you get you there immediately."

*****

DESPITE HIS FONDNESS FOR guest houses, Olsson decided a medium-priced hotel better fitted "Manny Klaus's" image. He chose a hotel a short walk from the Greek's headquarters, a citadel to be breached.

Settled in, he put on his headphones and made a call. "Have you looked through the files I sent you?" he asked.

Nazarov's voice came clearly through the headphones. "We have. You want us to pick up those four guys—"

"Correct. Got everything ready?"

"We have the place set up. We're still tracking them to establish their routines. Another day or two."

"Faster is better."

"Not if you want everything to go smoothly."

"I'm impatient," said Olsson.

"In our business, impatience gets you killed."

Olsson sighed. "I know you're right. Let me know when you've got them. I'll need you to warm them up a little before I get there."

"Good cop/bad cop," said Nazarov, "and you're the good cop? Is that it?"

"You could put it that way. Here's what I want you to do—"

LATER, OLSSON GASPED WHEN he reached Alison's message and heard McKurn's words:

". . . I want that bastard."

He had no idea that French had guessed his identity, that someone was tracking him—and that someone was working for McKurn.

I must have lost him, he thought.

Or did I?

53 Lost and Found

Will Kydd "rise back from the dead"? When Randolph Kydd was ousted as PM a couple of weeks back, pretty much everyone "in the know" wrote him off as a dead duck.

Everyone except Kydd himself who, despite hobbling around on crutches when not wheeling a chair, is refusing to "lay down and die."

Word is that Kydd's doctors have told him he needs *months* of complete rest to recuperate from his heart attack. Kydd will have none of that. "I'll be back," he said when Royn announced a snap election.

As CP leader, Kydd never faced opposition come preselection time. Sitting members don't—normally. But with Kydd crippled, Conservative Party hopefuls from around the country are gathering like vultures over a rotting carcass, all lusting after the prize of the safest CP seat in the country. Twenty-seven of them at last count.

Most will fall by the wayside. Two have a sporting chance at beating Kydd to the finish line: Jake Meldrum, a popular local functionary who—until he threw his hat in the ring—cast himself as a loyal Kydd supporter; and Barry Easton, a dark horse backed, so scuttlebutt has it, by Royn himself.

Kydd, according to a "don't-you-dare-use-my-name" insider, is "apoplectic" at the "would-be, mediocre upstarts" who are threatening to "steal his property."

Such comments aren't appreciated by even his most loyal supporters who feel they're being taken for granted. Some are even wondering if Kydd's still got what it takes.

The "big event," when the preselection committee meets, is set for Saturday. Should be plenty more fireworks between now and then.

*****

IN THE EARLY HOURS of the morning, a uniformed police sergeant paid a seemingly routine visit to the headquarters of a taxi company. "A simple question," he said as he showed an ID—not his own—and a taxi number, "to help with our enquiries."

The radio operator found the taxi driver in question in ten minutes. "He dropped the guy off at the Fitzwilliam Hotel."

At the hotel, the sergeant asked for the names of everyone who'd checked in around five PM the previous evening. The duty manager obliged. On the street, the sergeant made a phone call before reporting for duty.

Around ten minutes later, Greg Cannon's phone woke him from a deep sleep.

"I got a cop friend of mine to do a little unofficial investigation," his Sydney associate told him. "It'll cost you—"

"I know that. Just get on with it."

"He traced the taxi to a hotel on William Street. Two men checked in around the time the taxi arrived." He gave Cannon the names of the hotel and the two men—and their room numbers.

"Fantastic."

"You're racking up a big bill, mate. When am I going to get paid?"

"Soon. Soon," Cannon promised.

"Fine. But if you need any more help, you'll have to cough up first."

"Don't worry about it."

"Mate, I'll stop worrying about it when I have cash in hand."

"I've got work to do," Cannon said, hanging up.

He phoned information to get the number of the Fitzwilliam Hotel, called and asked for Jack Chancellor. "I'm sorry sir, Mr. Chancellor just checked out."

Cannon took a deep breath. Fingers crossed, he called again. "Mr. Manny Klaus, please."

"Just a moment, sir."

Cannon breathed again.

"Yes," a sleepy voice answered. "Who is it?"

"Room service, sir. We're worried we made a mistake in your order and wanted to—"

"I didn't order anything."

"My sincere apologies, sir—"

But the phone was dead.

Now, Cannon asked himself, which one was Blackie/Red/Blondie? *Only one way to find out.*

Derek Olsson slammed down the phone and burrowed back under the covers.

Then he jerked up, wide awake. *Was it room service—or . . . ?* He picked up the phone and pressed the room service button. "Did you just call me?" he asked.

"Mr. Klaus? No, sir."

No time.

Dressing quickly, he splashed water over his face, threw his toothbrush, laptop, and a few other essentials into his backpack. At the door he stopped, eyeing his other possessions. *No time.*

He pressed the lift button but had second thoughts and took the stairs. Should he reclaim his spare cash and fake IDs in the hotel safe? *Later,* he decided.

Once on the street he stood looking for a taxi; none were in sight. The rush hour traffic wasn't moving anyway. He began to walk.

Cannon threw on some clothes, ran to his motorcycle, and weaved through the traffic in defiance of every traffic law on the books. He slowed at the hotel, looking for somewhere to park.

A man walked out of the hotel, a cap pulled low on his head. He looked around, and started walking. Cannon pulled down the visor on his helmet, and let the motorcycle coast slowly until he reached the next intersection, stopping at the red light. The man walked up almost beside him before crossing over.

"Blondie." No question.

He turned down the side street and made a call. "I need your help, now, mate."

"Like I said—"

"We'll hit an ATM as soon as we can. That okay with you?"

"All right," his Sydney associate grumbled. "What do you want me to do?"

OLSSON TOOK A BUS to the city, walked from one street to another through a department store, did the same again through a mall, and flagged down a taxi. He kept looking back and around; as far as he could tell, no one was following him. But he couldn't be sure: the stream of people bustling along the streets, heading to their offices, would make it easy for anyone on his tail to stay out of sight.

Sinking into the taxi seat he asked himself: *What now? How to be sure?*

"Where to, mate?" asked the taxi driver.

"Ah—Circular Quay."

"You could have walked it quicker, you know," the driver said as he eased the cab into a gap between two cars.

"Suppose I could have," said Olsson.

At the Quay, he walked slowly along the ferry terminals, stopping to buy a paper and, further along, a coffee and a roll. Surreptitiously, he noted when the different ferries were scheduled to depart. The next one: the Taronga Park Zoo.

Perfect, he thought.

A few minutes before the scheduled departure, he strolled up to the window and bought a ticket. Once seated, he watched a family get on, the two young kids talking excitedly about the animals they would see. They were followed by a middle-aged woman and then, just as the gangplank was about to swing up, a man rushed on board, talking on his cellphone. "Mabel, I just made the ferry. . . . Right, see you at the zoo entrance. I'll wait for you or you wait for me, whoever's there first. . . . Okay, love you too."

*****

KARLA PRESTON WAS NO longer semi-conscious; her first visitors were Rudi Durant and Simon Lee. But Karla merely confirmed what they'd already deduced.

"No progress," Lee said gloomily.

"Nothing new," Durant said. "But tomorrow we'll see Alison McGuire. And let's dig up everything we can find on McKurn in the records—"

"We have to go back to the forties and fifties. The computer database doesn't go back that far."

"You're right." Durant grinned. "You'll have to get them from Archives."

"That will leave a paper trail."

Durant stopped in his tracks. "Okay. We'll to figure out another way to get them. Meanwhile, we'll go through that list of people Leon Price named and decide who to hit first."

*****

OLSSON WANDERED AROUND THE ZOO for an hour or so. Now sure he'd lost whoever was on his trail, he took a taxi to Manly and checked into a hotel on the beach.

He phoned the Fitzwilliam Hotel to tell them he'd been unavoidably called away for a couple of days—"Just leave the room as it is. After all, you've got my credit card details. . . . Yes, it may be irregular, but it's fine by me"—and checked on McKurn's phone conversations, *just to be sure.*

There were quite a few, and he worked back from the latest until, some twenty minutes later, he heard . . .

"We've tailed him to the Taronga Park Zoo—"

"What the hell's he doing there?"

Olsson didn't recognize the first voice, but this was definitely McKurn.

"Trying to lose us, I think. I've got some help but I need more urgently—"

McKurn's reply chilled him.

"Not a problem. Get whatever help you need. I'll send a few people along shortly to take him off your hands. Don't worry—you'll be handsomely rewarded if he *is* the bastard I'm looking for."

Where did I go wrong?

The family who'd got on the ferry after him had disappeared into the zoo ahead of him. The middle-aged lady met a group of other women at the snack shop—to chat. He didn't see them again.

The man who'd just made the ferry waited at the zoo entrance. He saw him a while later, arm-in-arm with a woman—*Mabel, I presume.* He'd seen them several times, but dismissed them as a pair of lovebirds. *That was how they were acting, but. . . .* It could have been all show.

He'd come into the zoo from the ferry entrance; he exited through the main entrance on the other side. *No one,* he was certain, followed him out.

So I'm safe . . . or am I?

Not if someone I didn't see saw me leaving.

And there *was* a motorcycle. A black one. Behind the taxi from the zoo. Just like the one he'd noticed as he'd left the Fitzwilliam Hotel. Coincidence. There must be thousands of black motorcycles on Sydney's streets.

He couldn't take the chance—what if McKurn's thugs were already here and waiting?

Only one thing to do. He called Nazarov. But as he punched in the number the door to his room burst open and several policemen swarmed in.

54   Off the Record

STRIPPED TO HIS UNDERWEAR, Derek Olsson lay, uncovered, on a couch in a small, dark room. Faint light seeped through broken slats of venetian blinds; cold, wintry air through partly opened windows.

His shivered himself awake. Moving to sit up, he winced at a flash of pain from the back of his head.

His head fell back and he grimaced again. Gingerly, he ran his fingers through his hair and groaned as they came to a large, sticky lump.

He peered at his fingertips; they were *all* dark—even the fingertips of the hand which hadn't touched his head.

He remembered policemen bursting into his room and then—

Nothing.

Resting the weight of his head on one hand, he slowly levered himself to a sitting position. The room was narrow and bare, the couch, as far as he could tell in the near-darkness, its only furniture. With the wall as support, he shuffled to the window. Peering through the blinds brought no enlightenment: all he could make out was the wall of a neighboring building. Examining his fingertips in the dim light made him none the wiser.

He shuffled back to the door.

Locked.

Maybe he could break it open—but what lay on the other side?

He yawned, shrugged, and shuffled back to the couch, sure of only one thing: this was not a police cell.

He still shivered, but a more powerful force pulled him back into unconsciousness.

*****

"NICE PERK," SAID RUDI Durant. He and Simon Lee surveyed the panoramic views of Sydney Harbour and the Opera House across the water as they were ushered inside Kirribilli House, the prime minister's official residence in Sydney.

"Fetch millions if they sold it," Lee grumbled. "He could stay in a hotel like he does everywhere else. Be a helluva lot cheaper."

"You're not wrong there," Durant said, eyeing the sweeping, carefully tended lawns that ran down to the harbor's edge.

Scrutinized by the PM's security at the gate, they were again questioned by Alison's bodyguards and finally ushered into a small office where Alison hunched over a desk. Closing her laptop she said, "Inspector Durant, I presume?"

Durant nodded. "This is Sergeant Lee."

"Could I see your IDs please?"

Durant and Lee passed them to Alison who studied them carefully.

"Satisfied now?" Rudi Durant asked as Alison returned them.

"Not quite."

"Made your bodyguards happy," Durant scowled.

"So interview *them*," Alison said as she put her cellphone to her ear. "Yeah, it's me. . . . Do me a quick favor. There's a guy I want you to talk to—can you tell me who he is from his voice? But I want to be *sure*—ask him a question only he could answer."

She passed the phone to Durant.

"Durant, here. Who is this? . . . You playing the same game as Miss McGuire? . . . Okay. You're Jason Kowalski." Durant was silent for a few moments, his lips slowly screwing into a frown, and when he spoke he spat his words, "Leon Price. And it was a Sunday afternoon. Okay now?"

He thrust the phone at Alison.

"I know, Jason. I know," she said. "But I had to be *certain*. Thanks."

"Can we begin now?" Durant asked.

Alison smiled. "Certainly, Inspector. Please take a seat."

Durant looked around the tiny office, his gaze ending at the only other chair in the room.

"We can easily get another one," Alison said.

"No problem, Miss McGuire," said Lee, leaning against the door. "Not enough room anyway."

Alison smiled and Durant took the seat. "If we could begin, Miss McGuire, by asking you to describe exactly what happened on Friday morning."

It was easy for Alison to comply: the attack, and every detail, was engraved on her mind.

"You were very lucky," said Durant when she'd finished.

"Yes. I could have been crippled for life or even killed." *If they'd got their hands on me,* Alison shuddered.

"That too," said Durant. "I meant you were lucky there was a witness."

"What?"

"The old man. Otherwise *they* could have accused *you* of attacking *them*—"

"In self-defence?"

"Your word against theirs. Three-to-one is not good odds."

Alison turned away to dab the wetness from her eyes. "It wasn't very lucky for him."

"No, but he'll recover, so I'm told."

"Thank God for that." *And if he hadn't been there,* she thought, *I wouldn't have escaped.*

"We understand you couldn't identify your attackers."

"No."

"That's because they came from Sydney."

"McKurn's territory."

"Exactly," Durant nodded. "Two of them did—the driver hasn't been identified. The second man was picked up trying to get his face fixed. Looks like you broke his nose—"

"Serves him right."

"The guy who lost half his arm—it was touch and go. But he'll live."

"A pity," said Alison.

"You're a dangerous woman."

Alison waved a crutch. "Was—perhaps."

"How did you fight off *three* of them?"

"Aikido and Karate," said Alison.

"Really?" said Durant, noticing the callused edges of her hands. "So your hands are lethal weapons?"

Alison stared at her hands as if she hadn't seen them before, turning them over, touching the soft tips of her long fingers. She laughed. "Is that what they look like to you?"

"Appearances are often deceptive," said Durant.

"Perhaps," said Alison. "But I have a meeting with the PM coming up, so shouldn't you get on with your questions?"

Durant nodded. "Miss Preston is convinced that Senator McKurn was responsible for her attack. She also believes he's behind yours. Would you agree?"

"Definitely. No doubt whatsoever."

"McKurn's possible motive is clear in the case of Miss Preston: to stop her revelations. But why should he go after *you?*"

"Perhaps he suspects I gave Karla the information she printed in her articles."

"And did you?"

"I'm not sure I should answer that question."

"Leaking official information can be a crime."

Alison grinned. "In that case, I *did* give her some materials, but only *un*official information."

"But do you have any proof, any *evidence* implicating McKurn?"

"None at all, I'm afraid. Just the same, I *know* it was him."

"If everything we're reading about McKurn is true—"

"It certainly is," Alison said. "But it's just the tip of the iceberg."

Durant studied Alison levelly. "That's a pretty bold assertion."

"You've seen Leon Price's statement. Where do you think Jason got it from?"

"*You?*" Durant asked.

"That's right."

"And where did *you* get it?"

"From—" Alison paused, eyeing the notebooks both Durant and Lee held. "Tell me, Inspector, you're writing down everything I say—"

Durant grinned. "To be used in evidence against you?"

Alison laughed. "That's not what I meant. You'll have to write up a report for the police files, is that correct?"

Durant nodded.

"If you put your notebooks away, I'll happily tell you everything I can."

"Will you repeat it on the witness stand?"

"*When* you have an ironclad case against McKurn. Not before."

"Are you saying you're willing to help me get that case?" Durant asked.

"Damn right!"

"No one ever checked my identity as thoroughly as you did. Now, you're willing to tell all. Why the sudden change of heart?"

"Jason gave you a glowing recommendation. I was *always* willing to trust you, Inspector. Once I was sure it was *you.*"

"What did he say?" Lee asked.

"Never mind that, Simon," Durant growled.

Alison grinned at the slight flush on Durant's cheeks. "Among other things, Inspector, that you're tougher to get rid of than AIDS."

Lee chucked. Durant glowered at him and carefully studied his notebook. Only when he snapped it shut did his gaze return to Alison. "It's irregular," he said, "but then so is this whole business."

Alison told Lee and Durant a story of political intrigue; how McKurn threatened to release a video which would damage her and Royn—without specifying the content; their "deal"; of the battle within the Conservative Party over McKurn. And of the information she'd collected; most of it, that is.

She made no mention of the series of events culminating in her breaking McKurn's arm, though she did mention McKurn was a client of the APHRODITE's call-girl service.

"The one that was busted for sex slaves?"

"That's the one."

"Do you have evidence of that?" McKurn asked.

Alison was about to say, "Yes, I do,"—but then she'd have to explain how she came to have a recording of McKurn calling "Gladys." So she said, "No, but I suggest you talk to Jason about getting access to the agency's records."

"I will," Durant said, his eyes narrowing at her slight hesitation. "Thank you, Miss McGuire. You've added a lot to what we know. But as evidence—" Durant shook his head somberly—"not enough to make a case yet."

"*That* is the problem with McKurn," said Alison. "He's covered his tracks too damn well."

"One thing still puzzles me, Miss McGuire," said Durant. "If McKurn thought you were working for *him*, why would he attack you?"

"We had, ah, a disagreement," Alison said.

"So the deal's off?"

Alison nodded.

"Then why hasn't McKurn kept his promise and put that video that so disgusts you on the internet?"

"I have some information that would damage him."

"What information, Miss McGuire?"

"I'm afraid I can't tell you that, at the moment."

"So you haven't told me *everything.*"

"There are certain things I simply *can't* tell you. Yet."

"You said McKurn's blackmailing you, so why not come to us—the police?"

"Would that stop that video coming out?"

"We'd get an injunction—"

"Like McKurn did with McKurnWatch?"

"Ah—I see what you mean."

"It's time for me to go," said Alison, levering herself to her feet.

"If we have more questions—"

"Just call me any time, Inspector."

"There is one other thing, Miss McGuire," Durant said as he also stood. "I was told I was put on Karla Preston's case thanks to pressure from the premier *and* the PM. Inevitably, my superior will learn that McKurn is my focus. Then, he might want to reassign me."

"Why?" asked Alison.

Before Durant could answer, Simon Lee said, "Pretty much because of what Sergeant Kowalski said about him."

Alison's mouth hung open before she said, "You mean—corruption in high places?"

"Not necessarily," Durant said. "In our business, when you tread on powerful toes you can provoke an equal but opposite reaction. My superior gave in to pressure once. He'll quite likely give in again."

"I can't make such promises on behalf of the Prime Minister, you understand," Alison said. "But if you *do* come under pressure let me know. I'll do my *utmost* to persuade Royn." She grinned. "I'm pretty sure he'll help. You see, he's on our side."

DURANT STRODE OUT OF Kirribilli House so fast Lee jogged to keep up. He replayed the conversation with Alison McGuire but couldn't pinpoint what might have energized Durant.

"What's the rush?" he asked.

"Wait," Durant replied.

Only when they were back in their car, doors closed, did Durant speak as if releasing a pent-up breath. "Jason could get McKurn's records for us."

"He *could*," said Lee, "but *will* he?"

"Only one way to find out," Durant said, pulling out his cellphone.

*****

A KEY SCRAPING THE lock brought Olsson half awake.

Resisting the temptation to look, he breathed slowly and deeply, letting himself go into a meditative, trance-like state. His eyes closed, the sense of his body drifting, the throbbing in his head seemed to recede into a distant annoyance and his hearing became more acute.

He listened.

The door creaked as it opened; he counted two, then three pairs of feet coming into the room.

A hand grabbed his arm, lifted it, and let go. His arm flopped down, limp and unmoving.

"Hey, Joseph, he's still out," said a voice, almost over his head.

"You probably gave him too much." Another voice—Joseph?—a little further away, maybe near the window.

Too much of what? Olsson asked himself. He remembered how he'd gone back to sleep despite the cold. *I was drugged.*

"What the hell. He isn't going anywhere." The third speaker, he estimated, was standing just inside the doorway. "Wake the bastard up."

A hand grabbed his shoulder and shook him violently, rocking his head from side to side.

"Aaah!" Olsson screamed as the back of his head hit the couch. He exaggerated the sound into a long, drawn-out release of breath that helped him hold onto his trance-like state. His eyes fluttered, allowing him glimpses of the heavy-set man who shook him. *Legs like tree trunks,* he thought. *All muscle.*

He brought up a hand as if to feel his head—and let it fall back as if the effort was too much.

"You shouldn't have hit him so hard."

"That's the only way I know *how* to hit."

The three men laughed.

Olsson let his eyes come half-open: they were the same men who'd burst into his hotel room. No uniforms. "Where am I?" he said, his voice barely above a whisper. He half-rolled on one shoulder as if about to get up, and collapsed back onto the couch. "Oh, my head."

"Never mind," said the voice in the doorway. "We'll wake him up later."

"Wait," Olsson said. "I gotta pee. And water, please."

"Okay," said the man in the doorway. "Help him up, Ray."

The man standing over Olsson bent down and pulled him to his feet with one hand. "That way," he said, giving Olsson a gentle push.

Olsson swayed, stumbled, and fell back down.

"Haul him up."

"Hey, Tiny, gimme a hand," Ray said to the wiry man. Taking a shoulder each, they half-supported, half-carried Olsson through the door into a long, sparsely furnished room. Olsson stumbled, as though he had difficulty keep upright, but through narrowed eyes he took careful note of the three men's faces—Ray and "Tiny" the two minions; Joseph, the boss—and spotted his laptop sitting on a table, open. Of his clothes and backpack there was no sign.

At one end of the long room a staircase led both up and down; he was taken to the bathroom at the other end.

The three men stood blocking the bathroom door, idly chatting with each other. Olsson stood gratefully at the toilet, propping himself up with one hand on the wall. *A row house,* he was thinking.

As he washed his hands he saw that his fingertips were purple. His thumbs, too. That made no obvious sense. *Think about it later.* His attention was on keeping track of the movements, postures, and relative positions of his three captors.

They stood, relaxed, aware of him but engrossed in their conversation. Ray had biceps that matched his legs; "Tiny" was thin and wiry; they both deferred to the third man who was older with the beginnings of a potbelly—Joseph.

Olsson was sure they were the men who'd "arrested" him. There may have been more, but his memory was fuzzy. If they *are* police, he decided, they're moonlighting. Or, masquerading as cops, they could simply tell the hotel staff they'd arrested a hardened criminal and no one would question them. But sapping him and bringing him to a place like this was *not* normal police procedure.

Gripping the sink with one hand for support, Olsson splashed his face with water and gulped from the tap. He slowly stood and shuffled to the door, leaning against it.

The three men turned to look at him. "Take him back into the room," Joseph ordered. He pulled out his cellphone and made a call. "He can talk now," he said as Ray and Tiny moved to escort Olsson as before.

When they neared him, Olsson's hands flashed out, flat as knives, slashing into the two men's Adams apples. Both men sank to the floor, gasping for air.

Joseph dropped his cellphone, pulled a pistol from his belt and turned towards Olsson. As he brought up the gun Olsson danced two steps to grab Joseph's wrist with one hand while pulling the gun from his grasp with the other. Olsson twirled around Joseph twisting the arm he still held firmly. His other arm swung in a wide circle, which ended with the butt of the gun slamming into the back of Joseph's head.

Tiny lay on the floor, gasping fitfully, but Ray was slowly getting to his feet. He massaged his throat with one hand, gurgling, glaring at Olsson and, one fist clenched, sending an unmistakable message: *I'm going to get you, whatever the cost.*

Olsson twirled towards Ray before he was fully erect. Ray saw the gun butt coming at him and tried to move his head out of the way but he wasn't fast enough and slumped to the floor. One more tap ensured that the wiry man was also out.

Now it was over, Olsson felt overcome by a wave of exhaustion and had to grab at a chair to stop himself collapsing to the floor. He stood, breathing slowly and deeply to quieten his breath. *I'm weaker than I thought.*

He stood, listening: surely, if there was a fourth man, the scuffle of battle would have brought him at a run. But all was silence.

He knelt down, used Joseph's shirt to wipe his fingerprints off the gun, and laid it on the floor near the man's hand. *That will confuse someone no end,* he grinned to himself.

Coming to his feet, he caught sight of his purple fingertips, He recalled the procedure at the police station after his arrest. *I was fingerprinted. Why?*

He shrugged. It didn't matter now.

He stood listening. Hearing nothing, he padded around the room, quietly opening doors until he found his clothes and backpack in a cupboard in one of the other bedrooms. He pulled on his pants, grabbed his shoes and the rest of clothes, stopped to stuff his laptop in the backpack, and tiptoed down the stairs.

He reached the landing. At the bottom of the stairs was the front door—and a man with a double-barrelled shotgun. Olsson threw his backpack at the man, aiming for the shotgun, and ran down the remaining stairs three at a time.

But the man side-stepped.

His shotgun now pointed at Olsson's midriff.

Olsson's backpack thunked against the door with the sound of a door slamming.

The man grinned.

"Where d'ya think you're going, matey?"

*****

ELECTION JOURNAL

Dirty tricks and foul play? Anthony Royn starts "pressing the flesh" here in Sydney today before his official campaign kick-off tomorrow—but the real fun and games is happening over in Randolph Kydd's (former?) seat of Bradfield.

Melanie Royn, the PM's wife, is ferreting around the electorate, digging into membership rolls, questioning how officers gained their posts, scrutinizing votes for the preselection committee and God knows what else.

Mrs. Royn's public face is that of a leading light of Melbourne society—a political lightweight. But inside the Conservative Party she's renowned as one of the canniest, toughest and most formidable backroom operators and numbers "men" in the country.

So what exactly is she up to in Bradfield? The word is she's about to accuse Jake Meldrum of that age-old practice of "branch-stacking"—adding dummy or nominal members to the rolls to gain control of a branch, a stepping-stone to control of electorate committees. She's aiming to have the CP State Executive intervene in the branch's affairs, and commandeer the preselection process to the benefit, no doubt, of Royn's favorite, Barry Easton.

Even for a well-entrenched leader with a fistful of evidence, overturning a branch's jealously guarded independence is a dangerous ploy; for the new boy on the block it could be playing with fire.

MELANIE THREW THE NEWSPAPER onto the table with such force that it skidded to floor. "They're right, damn them," she said. "At the moment, it's a contest between Meldrum and Kydd, and Barry doesn't have a look-in."

"How solid is Kydd's support?" Alison asked.

"That's a good question," Melanie scowled. "The old members are still behind him, though a few can be peeled away. But the membership base has changed dramatically since the last election. If it hadn't, Kydd would have it all locked up."

"Is that Meldrum's doing?" asked Royn.

Melanie nodded. "He's more than doubled the party membership in the electorate over the past year. Kydd's cronies still dominate the machinery, but there are lots of new faces. Meldrum faces."

"On the preselection committee too?"

"See for yourself." Melanie passed a sheet of paper to Royn, Alison, and Doug Selkirk. "A conservative guesstimate."

Bradfield Preselection Committee Makeup						
		Old	*New*	*Probable vote*		
	Total	*members*	*members*	*Kydd*	*Meldrum*	*Unknown*
State Executive	20	19	1	5	1	14
State Councillors	20	20	0	6	0	14
Branch Representatives *(2 from each branch)*	78	37	41	33	27	18
TOTAL	**118**	**76**	**42**	**44**	**28**	**46**
Percent				*37.3%*	*23.7%*	*39.0%*

"Looks like the unknowns have it," Royn grinned.

Melanie shook her head. "Sorry, my dear. That just means I have no idea how they'll vote. Maybe they've already made up their minds."

"What have you got on branch-stacking?" Alison asked.

Melanie frowned. "We could challenge ten to twenty percent of new members."

"Not enough," Alison said.

"Enough to make a weak case—"

"Which is worse than no case."

Melanie nodded. "If I only had more *time*—"

"—and would disallowing even twenty percent of the new members make that much difference anyway?" Selkirk asked.

Melanie shrugged. "Maybe half-a-dozen of the branch reps might change."

"Not enough to make a big deal of difference," Selkirk said. "But enough to piss everyone off."

"You could force the issue." Melanie turned to Royn with a wide grin. "Step in and demand the state executive take over the preselection process."

Royn shifted in his seat as if the soft leather chair had metamorphosed into hardwood. He appeared to be gazing at the blue vista of Sydney Harbour through the wide windows. "With a *strong* case, yes. But with what we've got, it would just look like a power grab. Not a good way to win friends and influence people."

"That leaves kissing babies," Selkirk grinned.

"Right," Melanie nodded. "I've already pushed Barry to get out and talk to people. Especially, of course, the preselectors."

"Is that such a good idea?" Alison asked. "He's a great guy and all that, but he talks too much like an academic. Lecturing people won't win him any votes."

Melanie sighed. "I know. He's a babe in the woods. That's why I've arranged things so Tony can do most of the talking."

"That's my job for today? To schmooze around the electorate?"

"Right," said Melanie, "and *personally* invite every preselector to your opening campaign speech tomorrow."

Royn grinned. "Good idea. We can work on Barry's style while we're at it."

"Good luck," Selkirk chuckled.

"What about the Senate?" Alison asked. "Any better news there?"

Melanie frowned. "You were right," she said to Alison. "Williams is not that confident. Andrew White—a State Councillor and the brains behind the Dump McKurn Movement—is gung ho to get rid of McKurn and is working the phones. McKurn's been doing the same thing. So McKurn might slip from number one, but he'll still be *there*."

"Number three or better?" Alison asked.

Glumly, Melanie nodded. "Maybe."

"So I'll need to schmooze there as well, right?" Royn said.

Melanie nodded and looked at her watch. "In fact, your first appointment will be here in ten minutes, and the rest of your day is packed."

Royn rose to his feet, rubbing his hands together. "Bring 'em on."

*****

"Doesn't look like we're very welcome here," Lee muttered to Durant.

They stood on the steps of a run-down boarding house in Redfern. Two men sitting on the narrow verandah squeezed between the building and the street gave them a brief, contemptuous, glance, and turned back to their conversation and cheap wine as if Lee and Durant didn't exist.

Durant grunted his agreement as he pressed the buzzer for the second time.

"Keep your shirt on," a voice grumbled from the other side of the door. A moment later it opened, and a short, unshaven man stood blinking in the sudden light. "Yeah? Whaddya want?"

"We'd like to see Mr. Brad Folsom," Durant said.

"Yeah?" The man looked Durant and Lee up and down. "Don't think he'll wanna see *you*."

"Why don't you ask *him*?" Durant said.

The man shrugged. "You wait there." Leaving the door open, he shuffled a few paces to the bottom of the stairs and shouted up, "Hey, Brad. Coupla flatfeet to see ya."

"Great introduction," Lee muttered.

"Well, there are plenty more names on the list."

They had decided "to start with a minnow" from Leon Price's testimony. Lee had run several names through the police database; Folsom was chosen simply because he was nearest.

From above came the sound of a voice, its words indistinguishable.

"He says go up," the man said.

"Is *that* what he said?" Lee asked.

"Shut the door behind you," the other man shrugged as he shuffled away.

One feeble bulb cast the corridor at the top of the stairs into semi-darkness. Specks of dust danced in the light seeping from a slightly open door. "Mr. Folsom?" Durant called out. A sound came from the direction of the door; Durant and Lee looked at each other, shrugged, and walked along the corridor.

"Mr. Folsom?" Durant said as he swung the door open.

Brad Folsom looked like a tall man who'd shrunk. The illusion came from the way he sat, hunched over on the edge of an unmade bed. When he raised his head to look at

Durant through reddened eyes, his shoulders did not lift as if his spine was locked in a permanent stoop.

He burped and took a swig from the near-empty bottle of whisky sitting on a small table beside the bed. He held the bottle high to examine the remaining contents. "Shorry," he slurred, "can't offer you gentlemen a drink."

"Thanks," said Durant. "Bit early for us."

"Jusht 's well," said Folsom. His eyes followed the bottle back to the table, his arm jerking erratically; then he shrugged, brought the bottle back to his lips, sucked out the last drop—and burped again.

"Thash better," he said, putting the bottle on the floor where it clanked against others; his head stayed bowed as if mesmerized by the empty bottles.

"Mr. Folsom," Durant said, "do you remember Leon Price?"

Folsom looked up, blinking in surprise, his eyes narrowing in suspicion. It took him a moment to remember he had visitors. "Who's asking?"

"I'm Inspector Rudi Durant. This is Sergeant Lee. We'd appreciate if you could help us in our investigation."

"Investigation of what?"

"Leon Price, among others."

"I heard he was gaga."

"So you do remember him."

"I didn't say that."

"He remembers you well enough."

Folsom shrugged. "So what?"

"You're not exactly famous, Mr. Folsom. So tell me, why would Leon Price remember you?"

"Maybe he saw my name in the papers."

"What did you do to get your name in the papers?"

Folsom's eyes flicked away from Durant. "Don't remember."

"Perhaps I can refresh your memory," said Durant. "You were a clerk in state parliament, working for Leon Price. You were sacked, a pretty good achievement for a public servant."

"I done nothing wrong."

"So what are you doing here?"

"Living. If you'd call it that."

"You had a nice cushy job—"

"Yeah. The bastards took away my pension, too."

"You're lucky that's all they took."

"You reckon?" Folsom's arm swept around the tiny room. "Doesn't look so lucky to me."

"Maybe your luck's about to change," said Durant.

Folsom looked at him incredulously. "Huh? You come to tell me I won the lottery? I don't think so." Folsom lurched to his feet. "I need another drink." He walked unsteadily towards the door, but Durant and Lee didn't move.

"Outta my way."

"Tell you what—"

Folsom straightened up, but his shoulders still remained hunched. "I know my rights."

"I'm sure you do," Durant said. "But I'll make you a deal. You answer my questions, and I'll shout you a bottle."

Folsom squinted suspiciously at Durant. *"You're* going to bribe *me?* That's one for the books."

Durant said nothing, his expression wooden.

"Okay," Folsom said. *"Two* bottles, though."

Durant nodded, took out his wallet and passed a note to Lee.

"Make it Black Label," Folsom said.

"Okay," Durant chuckled. "Get two of those tiny airline bottles of Black Label, Simon," he said, without moving his gaze from at Folsom. "Unless, of course, you'd prefer two of those big ones."

Folsom gave up the effort of keeping his back straight. "Okay," he said, shuffling back to the bed.

"So," said Durant, "you *did* work for Leon Price."

"Yes—" Folsom shook his head. "Let's see what your mate brings back first."

Durant shrugged and they waited in silence until Lee returned. Folsom held out his hand. Lee looked at Durant. "Give him one."

Folsom took two large gulps. "Ah," he said. "Yeah, I did work for Leon Price. So what? So did lots of other people."

"What did you do for Price?"

Folsom shrugged. "Scutwork. Ran messages, filing, answering the phone. That sort of stuff."

"What sort of messages?"

"How should I know? I was at the bottom of the heap—just a kid. Nobody told me a fucking thing. He said take this there, I took it. Pick this up from some guy, I picked it up. I didn't *read* the goddam messages, or open the parcels either."

"So you had no idea what was in any of those parcels?"

Folsom took a deep breath, opened his mouth to speak and then shook his head.

"That's not what Leon Price has testified," Durant said.

"What?"

"There's no point in lying: you'd be guilty of perjury."

"What are you talking about?"

"That's what happens if you lie in court."

"Court? What the fuck do you mean?"

"We're not making a social call. I'll give you a choice. Tell me the truth *now.* Or we'll drag you into court as a witness at the trial and you can tell truth then—or face a charge of perjury."

"I ain't going to no trial."

"You've heard of subpoenas? You'll have no choice."

Folsom said nothing.

Durant sighed. "Simon, take back that bottle. He isn't going to pay for it."

Lee took a step towards Folsom, who pulled the bottle to his chest and hugged it tightly. "No." Folsom's shoulders slumped; in a whisper he added, "I'll tell you whatever you want to know."

"You took a big risk there," Lee said as they drove back towards the station.

"Not really. A drunk doesn't think too straight, and the threat of losing his booze. . . . Well, it worked."

"Sure did," Lee agreed. The whisky had launched Folsom into a diatribe against Leon Price. Initially, Folsom had no idea of what was in the packages he carried. When he learnt it was money, he started skimming a few bills from each package. At first, a few dollars here and there wasn't missed. Price cottoned on when Folsom got too greedy and started taking tens and hundreds. Price's revenge: Folsom was sacked "on a trumped-up charge."

Folsom had drifted into an alcoholic sleep, but not before Lee and Durant managed to squeeze him for the names of the people he'd run messages to and from—mostly names that *weren't* on Price's list.

Price and McKurn clearly hadn't trusted Folsom with any large payoffs: just small fry. Small fry *then,* but now some of those names were in high places. One of them: Zimmerman's boss.

"The 'little birdie' who whispered in his ear, do you think?" Lee asked.

"Most likely."

"Perhaps he's reformed."

"Perhaps he has," said Durant. "But once McKurn's got his claws into someone, do you think he's going to let go?"

"No."

Lee squeezed the car into a parking spot. "We're getting a bit far afield from Karla Preston's attackers." In the sudden silence as the engine died his words seemed to have an ominous overtone.

"That's the problem. In fact, we can only go so much further without making this investigation official."

"By showing everything to Zimmerman—"

Durant shook his head. "I don't know. All we've got is the testimony from someone who's possibly senile and is unlikely to live long enough to testify in person, and off-the-record words of an alcoholic with a score to settle. Not enough *solid* evidence so Zimmerman or *his* boss could just ignore it."

"Think Folsom would repeat his words on video?" They both knew the rules so Lee didn't need to add: *otherwise it's not admissible in court.*

"Not if he had any sense," said Durant. "Anyway, he's hardly a credible witness."

"So what now? Keep plugging away—"

"—until Zimmerman or someone else finds out what we're doing." Durant sighed. "Not a good strategy, but all we've got."

*****

Derek Olsson was back on the couch. Cuffs bit into his wrists and ankles. Wired together, the slightest movement was inordinately painful.

He had a second lump on his head: when the man with the shotgun saw his three comrades lying unconscious he took no further chances with Olsson. One blow with the butt and Olsson joined them on the floor.

Manacled when he was revived—by ice cold water splashed over his head and shoulders—the three men he'd overcome proceeded to take their revenge, mostly with their feet. Then he was dumped on the couch and left alone.

How long had he been lying here? He had no way to judge time—but plenty of time to think.

But couldn't imagine any way out. This time, Nazarov and his "cavalry" would *not* be riding to the rescue.

55 Citizen's Arrest

THE PASSAGE OF LIGHT and darkness seeping through the blinds was the only way Derek Olsson could keep track of time. When he heard the door creak open, the now-fading light meant some twenty-four hours had passed since his failed escape attempt. He looked up expectantly—only to see Senator Frank McKurn striding in. Behind him were Olsson's three captors, all armed with pistols—and covered in bandages.

McKurn's face stretched into a wide grin as Olsson groaned.

"So we meet again—under far more pleasurable circumstances."

"*Again*, Senator?" Olsson replied.

"*Senator?*" said the wiry one known as Tiny. His free hand kept returning to the bandage wrapped round his throat as he spoke. "You're a *Senator?*"

"Meet the infamous Senator Frank McKurn," Olsson said.

"So," Tiny croaked, "everything we've heard about him is *true.*"

"That's right," Olsson said.

McKurn glared at him. "Shut your trap. And *you*—" he took a threatening stop towards Tiny "—mind your manners."

"Or what?" Tiny waved his pistol vaguely in McKurn's direction.

McKurn edged backwards. "To start with, you won't get paid."

"Cool down, Frankie," said Olsson. "What are you worried about? Your face is such a bromide you should feel insulted if you're *not* recognized."

McKurn, his cheeks glowing red, spun towards Olsson and lashed out with a foot that connected with Olsson's knee. "That's enough from *you*," McKurn spat. "There's no point in claiming that you're 'Joe Brewster' or 'Manny Klaus.' Your fingerprints say you're Derek Olsson."

"What possible use is that information to you, Senator?"

"To me?" McKurn laughed. "None at all. But to these fine, public-spirited gentlemen—" he waved his hand to include the three thugs behind him "—two hundred thousand dollars, I believe. The reward the police offered for *you.*"

Joseph, now with a thick bandage around his head, grinned. "That's right. We're making a 'citizen's arrest.'"

"I don't think that's such a good idea, Senator," Olsson said.

"I'm sure you don't." The three men joined in McKurn's laughter.

"For *you*, Senator."

"Oh?" McKurn chuckled. "Do tell."

"Take a seat, Senator," Olsson said.

McKurn looked around—Olsson's couch was the only piece of furniture in the room—and shrugged. "Whatever you've got to say, I'm sure it won't take long."

"As you wish," Olsson said. "Consider, as just one example, a certain Anstalt that recently took a bath in certain mining stock—"

"So?" said McKurn. "What's that got to do with me?"

"You've forgotten the documents I showed you, Senator?" Olsson asked. "Whatever makes you think they're the *only* ones I have?"

McKurn took a step towards Olsson. "You've got—" He stopped. "Could you gentlemen leave us alone for a while," he said to the three men, "and get me a chair."

"Is that wise?" Joseph asked. "He's dangerous." He touched the bandage on his head.

"It's necessary," answered McKurn, stepping closer to Olsson. Experimentally, he tugged the wire linking the hand- and ankle-cuffs.

Olsson groaned.

"Looks like you've got him well and truly tied up."

"Okay. But if it was up to me—"

"It's not," said McKurn.

MCKURN PLACED THE CHAIR by the door. "Remember," he told Olsson, "one tap on the door and my, ah, friends rush in."

Olsson grinned, wincing from pain at the same time. "You don't have anything to worry about—on *that* score."

"You mentioned something about an Anstalt. Tell me more."

"Certainly. From memory, an Anstalt called Meadowfields was formed in Liechtenstein forty-something years ago. Tellingly, its first investment—via an innocuous intermediary, of course—was the purchase of shares in certain Sydney businesses at an astonishingly low price from a lady by the name of Mrs. Frank McKurn."

"Fascinating," said McKurn.

"Isn't it? But not really a surprise when you realize that the beneficial owner of this Anstalt is none other than *you*, Senator."

"Hearsay."

"Oh, no, Senator. I have copies of all the paperwork."

"So?" McKurn shrugged. "Things like that can be fabricated. A Liechtenstein court would *never* verify them."

"True, perhaps, though these days even Switzerland and Liechtenstein are bending over backwards when the source of money is corruption. But we don't need to convince a Liechtenstein court, just the taxman, the Senate ethics committee, and, of course, the public. That will be easy."

"Really?"

"Really. After all, most of this Anstalt's investment profits came from share dealings that can be linked to *you*, Senator."

"Coincidence."

Olsson laughed. "No one's going to believe *that*. Especially when they learn that this same Anstalt owns, through other dummies, a certain Hong Kong company which specializes in the export of stationery supplies to just *one* customer: Paper Supplies Pty. Ltd."

"So what?" McKurn shrugged. With a laugh he added, "It was kind of you to tell me all this, but it hardly matters, does it?"

"What makes you think that, Senator?"

"You're not exactly in a position to release any of that supposed information to anyone. If you simply disappeared from the face of the earth—"

"It wouldn't make any difference."

McKurn grinned, his eyes twinkling, and said nothing.

"Several other people have copies of the files—"

"Including your newspapers?"

"They don't have them. Yet."

"And if you're never seen again—?"

"Then my editors *will* have them. *All* of them."

"There are more?"

"Oh, yes, Senator. I have quite a file on you."

"I'd be interested to see it."

Olsson chucked. "I'll be happy to show you."

"You have them with you?" McKurn asked.

Olsson began to shake his head until a sharp throb reminded him to keep still. "No," he gasped. "They're at the hotel."

"Why should I believe you?"

"That several people have them? Or that they're at the hotel?"

"Either. Both," McKurn said, looking at Olsson with a grin of pleasure. "You could be lying through your teeth, just to buy time."

"You can't afford to take the chance that I'm telling you the truth," said Olsson.

"So you're suggesting we go to your hotel where you'll show me the documents."

"Exactly."

"Good try," McKurn laughed. "But no cigar."

"Whatever," Olsson said. "Making that Swiss bank account of yours public is enough to blow you away."

McKurn laughed hard. "What Swiss bank account? In a few more days it will be gone—and its record at the bank wiped out. So, you see, it never existed."

"Very clever. Just as well I have other information."

McKurn shrugged. "We have your room key. I'll just send one of the boys to get those files."

"Go ahead."

McKurn leaned forward, his eyes searching Olsson's face. "I don't believe you."

"Suit yourself."

"I will," McKurn said rising to his feet. "I'd like to see a demonstration of your good faith. Then I might even agree to your suggestion."

Olsson shifted his head as McKurn came closer.

"The boys tried to look into your laptop and phone. But it seems they need passwords. Just tell me what they are."

"And if I don't?"

McKurn loomed over Olsson, his lips moist—and smiled. He reached out with his good arm, grasped the wire linking Olsson's wrists and ankles, and pulled.

The wires, already tight, cut into Olsson's skin. Droplets of blood oozed from his wrists. His elbows twisted and Olsson dimly wondered whether his forearms were about to come out of their sockets. He began to roll forward, a movement which, if continued, would end with him on the floor. But McKurn let go of the wire and he fell back on the couch. His movement squeezed his wrists and elbows so he was barely aware of the throbbing of his head as it bounced on the cushion. Olsson gasped for air and tried to speak, but all that came out of his mouth was a scream.

McKurn was now breathing heavily, the expression on his face one of admiring his own handiwork, his eyes glowing from his achievement. Letting go of the wire, he said,

"The passwords." But before Olsson could draw breath McKurn's foot slammed towards Olsson's crotch, hitting his thigh instead as Olsson's body rolled back.

Olsson barely felt McKurn's foot: submerged in a river of pain, he was close to blanking out. He shrieked again, a drawn-out wail that seemed to have no end. McKurn's breath came hot and fast as he raised his foot for a second shot.

"What's going on?"

McKurn spun around to see the three men rushing into the room, their pistols pointing at McKurn. "Get outta here," he snapped.

"What the hell are you doing to him?" It was Joseph's voice.

"He's trying." Olsson gasped, "to enlist my willing cooperation."

"Torture, more like it," said Tiny.

"It's none of your damn business," said McKurn.

"You're wrong about that. Get out of the way, Senator," Joseph said, thrusting McKurn aside. He looked carefully at the blood oozing from Olsson's wrists. "He's our paycheck. Two hundred grand. There's no way we can turn in damaged goods—so lay off."

The muscle man, Ray, who'd boasted he only knew one way to hit—hard—turned grey. "I won't be any part of this."

"You haven't got any guts," McKurn sneered.

Ray advanced on McKurn, his pistol steady. "I've killed men for less than that. But I've never *played* with them like *you*. You're a *sicko*."

Taking a deep breath against the pain, Olsson projected his voice. "Do you realize, gentlemen, you just signed your own death warrants?"

The three men looked at him curiously. "Whaddya mean?" Tiny asked.

"Don't listen to him," McKurn shouted angrily.

"Shut up, Senator," said Joseph. "I want to hear what he's got to say." The other two nodded in agreement.

"You know how McKurn operates," Olsson said, gasping between words. "People who oppose him simply disappear."

"That's bullshit," McKurn spat.

"Oh?" said Tiny, waving his hand towards Olsson. "And what did you have in store for *him?*"

McKurn glared. "I was just trying to get some information you *failed* to get."

"What information?" the boss asked.

"The passwords to his computer and phone."

Joseph shrugged. "Why, you want to read his emails or something?"

"Or something."

McKurn now faced away from him, but Olsson could see that McKurn's neck muscles were tense. His left fist, curled behind him, repeatedly clenched and unclenched. *He's not used to being challenged,* Olsson thought, *and he wants to hit someone.*

As the pain slowly receded Olsson wondered, *What did McKurn really want?* He didn't think it was the passwords.

"The cops will ask you a lot of questions before they sign off on that reward," Olsson said.

McKurn turned his head, laughing; the way his face lit up sent shivers up and down Olsson's spine and sparked the image of McKurn's expression as he yanked the wires . . . accompanied by the realization: *McKurn was happy.*

"That won't be a problem," he said, "when I vouch for them."

"More likely," said Olsson, "they'll get locked up along with me."

"Don't be ridiculous," McKurn snapped, his cheeks turning red. His gaze swung back to the three men who were now watching him nervously. "Don't listen to him. He'll say anything. But you can't trust a word he says."

"Two hundred grand," Olsson said. "Cash. No questions asked."

Ray seemed interested. "How do we know you've got the money?"

"You've never heard of him?" Joseph asked. Ray and Tiny both shrugged. "He's one of those rich toffs. He can afford it all right—but whether he's got the *cash* is different question."

"I can also offer you something far more important than money," Olsson said.

"What's that?"

"Protection. Against McKurn."

"How?" Tiny demanded. "Your protection against *us* wasn't much good."

"Gentlemen," McKurn said, his hand now loose against his thigh. "Come outside. I need—I want to make a few things clear."

The three men exchanged glances. Before Ray or Tiny could speak, Joseph shrugged and said, "Sure."

"Now, don't go anywhere," McKurn told Olsson as he left.

The door slammed shut; once again, Olsson was alone.

*****

"Luke, I said no interruptions," Demas Chrysanthopoulos shouted at the man who'd burst into his office.

But when Luke shouted back, as if he hadn't heard a word, "Now Damien's disappeared too." Chrysanthopoulos' face turned from red to grey; he lurched back into his chair, as if he'd been slapped.

"*What?*"

"We can't find him *anywhere*."

"You've looked—?"

"Everywhere. He left his apartment an hour ago according to his girlfriend, but his car's still in the parking lot. The doorman swears he was in the lobby but didn't see him come out. We phoned everyone we could think of. *No one* has seen him. Worse, his cellphone rang when I called it—and then it was turned off."

"Shit." Chrysanthopoulos glared at the floor as if he'd find inspiration there. "That's *three* now—what's going on?"

"I wish I knew, boss," said Luke. "I wish I knew."

The previous day, two other of the Greek's sidekicks—Mitch and "Bruiser"— had disappeared, but hadn't been missed until late evening. As far as they could tell, Mitch hadn't been seen since knocking off in the early hours of the morning. But that supposition was based on a search of his apartment, which suggested that he hadn't gone there from the Club. "He was with some bird," one of his mates said. "He probably ended up at her place. Probably still there. Wouldn't be the first time."

"Bruiser," despite his nickname, was a family man. He'd left home the previous evening at the usual time—but neither he nor his car ever turned up.

"The boys are all worried *they'll* be next," said Luke. "They're all saying we'll never see Mitch, Bruiser, or Damien again."

"They could be right," Chrysanthopoulos nodded. "Any idea what happened to Damien?"

Luke shook his head. "He was supposed to wait till we showed up. He didn't."

"Stupid bastard," said Chrysanthopoulos.

"Let's face it," Luke said. "You didn't hire him for his brains."

"Damn right I didn't."

Luke started to speak, but something on the half-muted TV news program caught Chrysanthopoulos' attention. "Wait a minute, Luke," he said, holding up his hand. Turning up the TV's volume Anthony Royn's voice flooded the room . . .

". . . I promise you a double-barrelled assault on corruption. We'll root out the scourge of addictive drugs, we'll root corruption out at its source, with every means at our disposal. Including a Royal Commission on Corruption with wide-ranging powers.

"Let me assure those offenders who think they're home Scot-free: we will not rest until we find you. We will expose you and punish you to the full extent of the law.

"There's only one way you can alleviate your punishment: confess now. Own up, and we'll go easy on you."

The camera cut to the Opposition Leader, Ian Nash: "Royn pledges his Royal Commission will be Parliament's first act *after* the election. That means two or even three *months* before it gets under way." Nash shook his head. "Plenty of time for the culprits to go into hiding or get on a plane, along with all their ill-gotten gains, to some country which won't extradite them. What's Royn waiting for? That's what I want to know. We need action *right now.*"

Somberly, Nash looked straight into the camera. "Unlike some members of the *Conservative* Party, every Labor member stands united in our determination to get rid of the corruption that is plaguing our country. I challenge Anthony Royn: call a special session of Parliament *today.* Every Labor Party member will be there, ready, willing, and able to vote *for* this Royal Commission. Which is more than can be said for certain members of the Conservative Party."

"So it's war," Chrysanthopoulos mumbled as he flicked off the TV set.

"That's right," Luke said. "Someone has declared war on us."

Chrysanthopoulos blinked as he returned his focus back to Luke. "Yes," he grunted. "So what should we *do?*"

"Okay, Luke. Set up a buddy system. No one goes *anywhere*—not even to have a piss—without his partner. They even sleep together. Understood? And tell everyone to get in touch with their contacts—cops, other gangs, stoolies, whoever—and see if they can get any hint of what gang might be after us. Got it?"

"I'll set it up, just like you say, boss." said Luke, smiling for the first time since he'd come into Chrysanthopoulos' office.

"I'll do the same," said Chrysanthopoulos, reaching for the phone as Luke left.

He gazed at the handset through unseeing eyes for a few moments, and then dialled a number. "Jesse. Three of my men have disappeared, 'poof,' like that. . . . Yeah. Wondering if you've heard anything? Like someone's on the warpath. . . . No? Oh, well. . . . Yes, I saw the news. . . . Doesn't look good, does it? . . . No. . . . So what do you think we could do? Is there *anything* we can do?"

Chrysanthopoulos listened intently for quite a while, adding no more than "Uh-huh," and "I see," to the conversation. Eventually he said, "I like that, Jesse. In fact, I think it's *brilliant.* . . . Yeah, I know. Might *not* work. But worth a shot. Are you free tomorrow night? . . . I'll get most of them here, even if I have to twist a few arms."

*****

"The Greek's gang is spooked," de Brouw told Shultz and Nazarov. "They're going around in twos and threes. Won't be easy to pick up the fourth guy."

"Bit slow on the uptake, aren't they?" Shultz grinned.

"The guy they call 'Bruiser' is ready to talk," Nazarov said.

"Bruiser?" de Brouw laughed. "He can dish it out but can't take it, eh?"

Nazarov nodded, and dialled Olsson's number again. "Jeez," he said. "We've got the bastards primed and ready to spill the beans. One of them anyway. And Olsson's simply disappeared. Where the hell is he?"

*****

OLSSON STRAINED TO MAKE out what McKurn and the three men were saying to each other. The actual words were muffled by the closed door, but a peppering of raised, angry voices suggested an argument.

As darkness descended, Olsson dozed intermittently until sudden blazing light startled him awake.

Joseph stood in the doorway, his hand on the light switch. He took McKurn's chair, kicking the door shut behind him.

"Get anywhere with McKurn?" Olsson asked.

"That's none of your business," Joseph snapped.

"I disagree—" said Olsson.

"It's a free country. So they say. I'm here to listen to what you've got to say. Make me an offer. One I can't refuse."

"You've been negotiating with McKurn—and now you want to talk to *me?* You've burnt your bridges with him—so far as he's concerned you're dead meat. I'm your only chance to live long enough to collect your old age pension."

"So you say."

"There's always one way to find out."

"What's that?"

"The hard way."

Joseph said nothing.

"Okay. There's a price on my head. Two hundred thousand dollars. Maybe the cops will give it you to you. Maybe they won't. They'll know who you are—and locking you up wouldn't hurt the promotion prospects of one of McKurn's paid-for stooges."

Joseph's impassive silence was marred by a slight pursing of his lips.

"You can't argue with that," Olsson said.

"I'm not arguing. I'm just listening."

"Two hundred grand. Is that what you expect? You get me out of here, it's yours."

"It has to be cash."

"I can get ahold of about fifty grand in cash immediately. Might take up to a week to get the rest. Or, it could be in your bank accounts in about twenty-four hours."

"Cash."

"Okay."

"SO WE HAVE A deal?" Olsson said about an hour later.

Joseph nodded.

"Let's shake on it."

Joseph grinned. "Understand," he said, bringing up his pistol, "you won't get another chance like you did yesterday. One move and you'll be dead."

"I'm aware of that."

"Just a moment," Joseph said. "I have some other business to take care of first." He left the room—leaving the door open. Olsson could hear McKurn protesting vociferously. A few minutes later, Joseph came back with Tiny and Ray. A fourth man—the one who'd foiled Olsson's escape—stood in the doorway, his shotgun pointing out. Tiny handed his pistol to Joseph and untied Olsson's hands and feet. Olsson stretched, tried to sit up but fell back on the sofa. "Shake?" he said to Joseph, lifting a hand.

"Keep him covered." Joseph passed the pistol back to Tiny. He stepped towards Olsson and they shook hands, briefly.

"Good," Olsson sight. "But I can't go to the hotel looking like this. Can you get someone to patch me up?"

"Okay," Joseph said.

"And I'm starving."

It was near midnight when Olsson opened the door to his room in the Fitzwilliam Hotel. Everything, he was pleased to see, was as he'd left it.

Joseph, Ray, Tiny, and the fourth man, Mike, crowded in behind him. They'd been his shadows, walking in his every footstep, since they'd left McKurn, alone, lashed to a chair. With one arm in a cast, they figured he'd probably be free in an hour or two.

"I still say we should have killed the bastard," Ray grumbled.

"We've been over that. Again and again," Joseph said.

"I know. I know. Still—" Ray shrugged. "What's done is done."

"Or undone," said Tiny.

Killing a Senator was not something to be done lightly, as Olsson had pointed out. On the other hand, was it better to have McKurn or the police after you? "At least you can see the cops coming," Tiny had said. "When they're in uniform," Ray had responded.

In the end, Joseph decided against it. None of them, Olsson thought, had the stomach for cold-blooded murder.

"The cash," Joseph said.

"First things first," Olsson said as he opened his laptop, fingering the dent in one corner, perilously close to the hard drive.

"What are you doing?" Joseph asked, standing over Olsson's shoulder.

"We can't stay here. This is the first place McKurn will look."

"Okay," Joseph said. "But I don't want to see you doing anything else."

"You won't," Olsson said, pointing at the computer. The screen was blank. "Doesn't work."

He used his phone to access the internet and book another hotel. "Near the airport, where checking in at two in the morning won't raise any eyebrows."

When they left the Fitzwilliam, Joseph's mood was much improved: Olsson had emptied the safe deposit box and Joseph now carried a bag containing fifty thousand dollars in cash in hundred-dollar bills.

Olsson had booked a suite with two bedrooms in the airport hotel. Joseph was happy: he could keep Olsson under guard. Once settled in, Olsson took out his phone.

Joseph's hand gripped his wrist. "What are you going to do—call for help?"

"No," Olsson said. "I've lost two days. I've got other things to attend to."

"Let him use the damn the phone," said Ray. "We've got fifty grand, no worries. Suits me if we just take it and go."

"I want the lot," said Joseph.

"You'll get it," said Olsson.

"I believe him," said Ray.

"In any case," Olsson said, "it's not as if I have a low profile. You can find me any time you like."

"Okay," Joseph agreed reluctantly.

Olsson found a long list of texts and missed calls, most of them from Nazarov. Olsson sent him a text: I got tied up. Be there around lunchtime.

56 What Goes Around . . .

ELECTION JOURNAL

First Round: Royn 1, Nash 1. Royn's campaign kick-off yesterday was hard-hitting, impassioned, and a real tear-jerker: hardly a dry eye in the house when he told of his brother's death from a drug overdose.

Royn looked the part of the winner in a performance which is no doubt drawing A-pluses from his former drama teachers.

His theme: a crack-down on drugs and a no-holds-barred Royal Commission into corruption. *"No one* will be immune," Royn promised. One wonders if that includes a certain prominent Conservative Party politician who's the target of "vicious, unsubstantiated rumors" (as he puts it).

Labor leader Ian Nash punched right back. "What are you waiting for, Tony?" he demanded. "Set up your Royal Commission now. *Today.* We'll back you all the way."

Not a knock-out blow, but it took the wind out of Royn's sails for a first-round draw.

Or—by *supporting* Royn has Nash just left him without a platform? That would put Nash way ahead on points.

Gotta admit, though, Nash's challenge—why wait?—makes a lot of sense.

How about it, Tony?

*****

Anthony Royn felt as though he'd floated rather than walked off the stage after his campaign speech, buoyed by the audience's third standing ovation in thirty minutes. His sense of invincibility, that he'd given a speech that would win the election, lasted until he learned Nash's response just a few hours later.

It was now definitely the morning after—even though he hadn't touched a drop the night before. He, Alison, and Melanie sat silently at one end of the long dining table, the remains of a gloomy breakfast scattered between them.

Finally, Royn looked up and said, "Perhaps we *should* agree to a special session of Parliament."

"Why not just appoint Justice Flint head of the Candyman Inquiry?" said Alison. "Starting when he retires. And give him all the powers of a Royal Commission. Nash would have to agree."

"And you could paint Labor as spendthrifts when there's a much simpler solution," said Melanie.

"That'd work," said Royn.

"But," said Alison, "the central thrust of our campaign was corruption—*anti*-corruption."

"Back to the drawing boards," Melanie grinned. "But get Nash to agree to a *joint* announcement appointing Flint and supporting the Royal Commission—then corruption becomes a non-issue as far as the election is concerned."

"That's brilliant, Mel," Royn said excitedly.

"Will Nash agree?" Alison asked. "He's smart enough to figure that out, too."

"Having made that challenge, he'll look stupid if he *doesn't*," said Melanie.

Royn nodded, and looked at Alison.

"Worth a try," she said.

"I'll do it," said Royn.

"So where do we stand with McKurn?" Alison asked.

"His days are definitely numbered," said Royn. Over the past two days, he'd spoken to every Sydney-based selector, urging them to vote McKurn out "for the good of the party." From their reactions, he was confident McKurn would be dropped.

"I know Jim Williams agrees with you," Melanie said. "But I wonder if the selectors were telling you what they'll *do*—or what you wanted to hear?"

"What about the selectors from *outside* Sydney?" Alison asked. "Most of them won't get in till *tonight*."

"Andy White is sure most will vote to oust McKurn," said Royn. "He's even signed up a few of them for the Dump McKurn Movement."

"If McKurn's lucky, he'll be on the bottom of the ticket," said Melanie. "That's my guess. But in Bradfield, despite your schmoozing, I think we're going to have to write Barry off and get behind Meldrum."

"Pity," Royn nodded. "But at least we've got McKurn on the run."

There was a knock on the door and one of Royn's security guards came in. "Excuse me, Prime Minister. Senator Frank McKurn is here to see you."

*****

OLSSON SLEPT WELL INTO mid-morning. He still ached all over, his eye was puffy, but after soaking in the bath he felt passably human.

"There's only one way you can escape McKurn," Olsson told Joseph and his three henchmen. "You have to disappear for a month or two."

"We can't go home?" said Tiny.

"You can't go *anywhere* you're known if you want to be safe. You mustn't even call your friends."

"Too late," Ray said.

Olsson shrugged. "Can't be helped. To disappear, you'll need new identities—driver's licence, birth certificate, credit card, bank account, the lot.

"And how do we do *that?*" said Tiny.

"I'll give you an address. He can do a rush job in twenty-four hours. It's normally a couple of grand apiece, but with my introduction he'll halve it."

"Then what are we supposed to do?" Joseph said.

"Leave town. If you like, go to Albury. The InterFreight terminal there is always short of people on the night shift."

"That's not my line," said Mike.

"It won't hurt you for a couple of months," Olsson said. "Beats the hell out of concrete boots."

"What about the rest of our money?" Joseph asked.

"I'll transfer it into your new bank accounts . . . is that acceptable?"

Joseph shook his head. "We're not letting you out of our sight until we're paid in full. In cash."

Olsson sighed. "Fair enough, I suppose."

"So when do we get it?" Joseph asked.

Olsson held up a hand. "Wait a minute. I need to think." A few moments later he said. "Okay, not a problem. But I'll need to make a couple of phone calls."

"Who to?"

"Look, Joseph, I can't exactly walk into a bank and withdraw a hundred and fifty grand. I need to call a couple of friends who can do that for me—okay?"

"Come on, Joseph," Ray said. "Give the guy a break."

"Go ahead, then," said Joseph reluctantly, "but I'll be listening."

Olsson called Ross Traynor, who agreed to meet him with the money in a couple of hours.

"Then," Olsson said to Joseph, "we go our separate ways."

*****

"Senator," Royn said, forcing a smile as Frank McKurn walked slowly into the expansive reception room of Kirribilli House. "To what do we owe this pleasure?" Royn noticed McKurn's red-rimmed eyes, and patches of stubble under his jaw as if he'd shaved hurriedly. "You look a little tired, Senator—take a seat."

McKurn glowered at Alison, glared at Melanie, frowned at Royn, and shook his head in response to Royn's offer. "This won't take long."

Alison held herself rigid under McKurn's brief glance, refusing to grant him the pleasure of a response. The winter sun streaming through the windows bathed her in warmth, but she shivered as if caught in a sudden thunderstorm.

McKurn stood near Royn, forcing Royn to crane his neck to look him in the eye. "You know what's going to happen tomorrow," he growled, "when the state preselection committee decides the Senate list, don't you?"

Royn shrugged. "I know what I *hope* will happen," he said with a grin.

"Ha," McKurn snorted. "If you can't count—" he jerked his head to glare at Melanie "—*you* can."

"Damn right I can, Senator," Melanie said, unable to restrain her impish grin. "You don't have the numbers."

"You're off the ticket," Alison said triumphantly.

"*You,*" McKurn said to Royn, "have turned enough people against me to tip the balance."

"We hardly did it by ourselves, Senator," Melanie said. "You gave us lots of support."

"If I'm going down, I'll take you with me."

"Really?" said Alison.

"Damn right." McKurn turned to Royn. "The committee meets tomorrow morning. Use your influence to make sure I'm still on the Senate ticket—or I'll release that video of Alison and her boyfriend fucking like rabbits."

Alison tensed to leap up from her seat—until her complaining foot reminded her she needed the crutch. "You know what will happen then, Senator."

"Why, yes," he smiled. "You'll be out on your pretty little arse. And *you*—" McKurn turned on Royn "—will be a laughing stock. Labor will waltz in. After the election, Cracken will easily kick you out. You'll be *finished.*"

"As will you," Alison said.

"I'm quite aware of that," McKurn snapped. "I don't give a tinker's arse. Why should I? What difference will it make to *me*? But it will make a difference to you." He gazed at their faces. *"All* of you."

Alison's hand kneaded her stomach as she stared blindly at McKurn, frozen with the sense that her world was unravelling. Melanie's response was a sharp, inward breath, and a smile of professional appreciation which she quickly suppressed by turning towards Royn.

To hide his shock, Royn's eyes swept past Alison to finally rest on Melanie. To his surprise she said nothing, but the corners of her lips were curled in the beginnings of a smile, and when they made eye contact she wiggled her nose. It took him a moment to make sense of her impish half-grin, and he slowly turned back to McKurn.

"Well, Senator," he said, assuming his Prime Ministerial voice, "I'd appreciate some time to consider the . . . ah . . . ramifications of your . . . ah . . . proposition. If you wouldn't mind waiting outside—"

McKurn nodded curtly. "I'll give you ten minutes."

*****

MITCH WAS THE FIRST member of the Greek's gang nabbed by Nazarov, Shultz and de Brouw. He left the Bare Bottoms Club with a girl he picked up—so he thought. In reality, *she* had done the picking. She had no trouble letting him grope her in a doorway farther along the street where Nazarov and de Brouw pounced, blindfolding him before he had any idea what was going on. They paid off the girl and bundled him into a van; Shultz hit the accelerator before the doors were closed.

Mitch got the silent treatment. No matter how much he begged, yelled, pleaded, sobbed, or cursed, neither Nazarov, Shultz nor de Brouw said a word. They put him into a room, chained him to the wall, and left him there. Every now and then, one of them, always hooded, brought some food or water—but they never unchained him. He lay there, powerful light bulbs on continuously, in his own piss and excrement for more than forty-eight hours. He had no idea where he was, why, or how long he'd be kept like this—and whether he would ever see daylight again. In that whole time, the only voice he'd heard was his own.

"Bruiser" was next, grabbed some twelve hours after Mitch. He was also handcuffed, gagged, and blindfolded without a word of explanation.

Nazarov had rented a luxurious mansion with half-a-dozen bedrooms on two floors, plus the major attraction: a large basement divided into several storage rooms, easily adapted for use as cells. The building was sited, like a country house, in the middle of a couple of acres. Any noise from the house, no matter how loud, would never be heard by the neighbors. When they arrived with Bruiser, they led him into the room where Mitch was imprisoned and removed the blindfold.

"Bruiser!" Mitch shouted. "Fuck, they've got you too. They're real bastards—look what they've done." He rattled his chains. "Have you any idea what's going on? For Christ's sakes, somebody help me . . . "

Noticing that Bruiser didn't seem to be paying him any attention, Mitch's voice rose in both volume and desperation.

Bruiser stopped breathing. His eyes swivelled between his hooded captors, Mitch, and the heavy chains weighing on Mitch's wrists and ankles. Bruiser tried to back out the door as if to escape the same fate, took a deep breath—and bent over double as his stomach rebelled at the foul stink assaulting his nostrils.

Shultz and de Brouw yanked Bruiser outside.

Mitch wailed.

Before the door slammed shut Bruiser saw tears in Mitch's eyes.

Replacing the blindfold, Shultz and de Brouw had to almost carry Bruiser into another cell where he collapsed, shaking, on the bed.

"When you're ready to tell us everything you know about Vincent Leung," de Brouw said as they immobilized him in exactly the same way as Mitch, "let us know."

Then they left him.

That night, Bruiser barely slept. Worse than being alone in silence was hearing Mitch's unpredictable screams, his raves, his sobs—and his pleas for help which Bruiser, still gagged, was unable to answer.

The following morning, de Brouw and Shultz brought Bruiser his breakfast—a thin, paper bowl of gruel and a bottle of water. While Bruiser greedily ate the meager meal, de Brouw flipped through a handful of pictures. As Bruiser finished eating, de Brouw said, "Now, *that's* a good one. Cute little girl, wouldn't you say?"

He turned the picture so Bruiser could glimpse it. Briefly. It was a picture of his daughter leaving school.

As Bruiser tried to speak, Shultz replaced the gag. Bruiser struggled against his bonds. Shultz and de Brouw closed and locked the door.

Bruiser began to cry.

*****

ALISON EXPLODED THE MOMENT the door closed behind McKurn. "You can't even *consider* this. It's lunacy. It's out of the question."

"Do we have a choice?" Melanie said.

Alison's eyes widened at the calmness in Melanie's voice, as if her very tone were a rebuke. If Melanie was at all shocked, or even surprised at McKurn's "offer," there was no sign of it on her face. "A choice?" Alison said, now standing, leaning on one crutch and waving the other for emphasis. "Of course we have a choice. Just tell him to go to hell. Let McKurn get a hold over you and you're sunk."

"If we turn him down, we lose *everything,*" Melanie said. "You're not thinking rationally."

"You want rational? We neutered the bastard and he comes back from the dead. *Any* deal with McKurn is the kiss of death."

"Alison," Royn cut in, "calm down."

"Calm down? With this in front of us?"

"Yes. If we agree, and news leaks out—"

"Of course it will."

"We have to think this through *calmly,*" Royn said, looking at Alison.

"If we *don't* agree," said Melanie, "we *will* be dead at the polls. Even you should realize *that,* Alison."

"Of course I do—"

Melanie eyed Alison. "What's come over you? You're acting like you don't mind if every sick voyeur in the world salivates over your naked body. You're acting like you don't *care* whether we win the election."

"I—"

Alison froze at the words she'd been about to utter: *I DON'T care.*

They were true.

"Alison!" Royn said sharply. "Sit down. I realize even *thinking* about this is . . . ah . . . unsavory—"

"Unsavory? It *that* how you describe it? It stinks."

"That's *enough*. We *have* to give McKurn an answer whether we like it or not."

"*You* consider it," Alison said as she swung her crutches back to her chair. "I *won't*." As she threw herself down, her cellphone rang. She scrabbled in her handbag, ignoring Royn's annoyed glance. She only vaguely registered Melanie's and Royn's muted discussion as she took the call.

ALISON TURNED ON ROYN and Melanie as she snapped her phone shut. "That was Jason Kowalski," she said, cutting into whatever they were saying. "He told me Durant had asked him to access McKurn's criminal records for him—"

"Why didn't Durant do it himself?" Royn asked.

"—and guess what happened?" Alison said, ignoring Royn's question. "Jason's been kicked off the Candyman Inquiry. 'Reassigned to normal duties,' in police jargon."

"Kicked off? Why?" said Royn.

"For the reason Durant didn't want to access the records himself," said Alison.

"You mean—?"

"Yes. Jason thinks *someone* in the Candyman Inquiry is clogging the works."

"That's a distraction we can't afford right now," Melanie snapped.

"A distraction?" said Alison.

"Yes, Alison," Royn said, suddenly unable to look her in the eye. "Much as we detest it, Melanie and I agree we *have* to give in to McKurn."

Royn felt himself shrinking under Alison's cold, analytical gaze. She spun around on one crutch and swung herself towards the kitchen, followed by Royn's plaintive "Alison!"

If she heard him, she made no sign. There was not the slightest falter in the even *pad-thud, pad-thud* of her foot and crutches on the carpet. For a long moment, Royn watched the kitchen door silently closing behind her.

*****

DAMIEN, THE THIRD OF the Greek's sidekicks Nazarov, Shultz, and de Brouw picked up, was briefly shown Mitch and Bruiser and then imprisoned in the same way.

"Now you know what happened to your mates," Nazarov told him, "so you know what's in store for you. Avoiding that fate is very simple: just tell us everything you know about the murder of Vincent Leung."

Damien shook his head violently, tried to pull the chains from the wall, lashed out with his feet, and shouted curses behind the gag. He couldn't keep it up for long: the gag made it harder to breath. His chest heaving as he gasped for air, Nazarov stepped back to the door laughing, and said,

"You'll sing, just like the others. Sooner. Later," Nazarov shrugged. "Up to you." He slammed the door shut.

NAZAROV SLAMMED HIS PHONE down on the kitchen table. "Where the hell *is* he?"

"That's his problem, isn't it?" Shultz drawled, rocking back in his chair and taking another swig from his beer. "We've done our bit."

"That's right," said de Brouw. "And Bruiser's primed." Each time de Brouw brought Bruiser some food or water, he showed him a few more pictures of his children. By the time Damien was brought in, Bruiser was desperate to talk.

"Olsson wanted us to wait—" Nazarov said.

"Who knows when he's going to show up?" said de Brouw. "But if Bruiser doesn't talk *now,* he might change his mind."

"You're right," said Nazarov. "Let's bring him up here and record what he says. His reward can be a shower, clean sheets, and a decent meal."

*****

"If we agree, Senator," Melanie said, "there's a condition. A price you'll have to pay."

"With due respect, Mrs. Royn, I don't think you are in any position to make *any* demand."

"It's a simple thing Senator: get Jake Meldrum to withdraw from Kydd's old seat and swing his weight behind Barry Easton."

"What makes you think I have any influence on Jake Meldrum?"

"If he's not your boy, he's Cracken's—and Cracken *is* in your pocket," said Royn.

"Is he?" McKurn said. "Paul supports Meldrum, but doesn't *control* him. Paul *may* have some leverage, but you have *none.* Why should Meldrum agree? What could you offer him that's better than the safest Conservative seat in the country?"

"How about ambassador to Paris?" said Melanie.

"That could do it," McKurn grinned. "But why the hell ask *me?*"

"Do you want Kydd back?"

"Why should I give a shit one way or the other?"

"You've been enemies from way back—"

"Randy's political career is *over.* Even if he keeps his seat, he's powerless." McKurn shrugged. "He'll just be a pain in the neck—for *you.*" McKurn's gaze rested on Alison's now-empty seat. "I'd be interested to hear Miss McGuire's opinion."

"She . . . ah . . . had to go to the bathroom," Royn said.

"I see," McKurn said, his grin turning into an unexpected smile. "I tell you what. I'll have a word to Paul about Meldrum. That's the best I can offer. *After* you deliver your side of the deal."

"Okay," Royn said, suddenly tasting the eggs he'd had for breakfast in the back of his throat. "We have an agreement."

After McKurn left, Royn turned to Melanie and asked, "What do you think made McKurn suddenly change his mind?"

"I don't know," Melanie said, continuing to study McKurn's expression in her mind's eye. "But I don't like it. Not one bit."

*****

As he pulled out of the parking space, Ross Traynor looked back at the café where they'd rendezvoused.

"They won't follow us," said Olsson, half-dozing in the passenger seat, his eyes closed. "They'll be too busy counting the money."

"How did you get mixed up with guys like them?" Traynor said. "They don't have anything to do with Luk Suk, do they? You gave me the all clear—"

"No. Luk Suk won't bother us any more, Ross. Those guys worked for Frank McKurn—"

"Senator McKurn?"

"The very same."

"They roughed you up—on *his* say so?"

"McKurn had a go himself."

"Jesus Christ, Derek, what the hell is going on? You've got security guards at all the OlssonPress facilities and—my God. Karla Preston! Her accident—was *that* McKurn's doing too?"

"Afraid so."

"Should I pack up the kids again and go back to South America?"

"I don't think so," Olsson said. "McKurn is pissed off with *me,* and my newspapers. You don't figure there."

"Can you be sure of that?" Traynor shuddered. "I'm not."

Olsson was enjoying an unusual state of lethargy; Traynor's comment jolted him alert. *I've really tweaked McKurn's nose,* Olsson thought, *without considering the implications.* McKurn would upend heaven and earth to find him now—and use any lever he could grab.

"You're right, Ross," he said. "I can't. You should take precautions."

"Like what?"

"Hire some bodyguards."

"Jenny will be furious. You'll be in big trouble next time you see her."

"It won't be for long. In a couple more days, if all goes well, I'll be able to convince Durant he's got the wrong man. *Then* I can do something about McKurn."

"Okay," Traynor said. "Where shall I take you?"

"Just drop me off at the next taxi stand."

*****

ALISON WENT TO HER room, packed a bag, and called for a car. At the bottom of the stairs, Royn stepped into the corridor.

"Alison, what on earth are you doing?"

"I'm going home."

"You can't. Not *now.*"

"I need . . . some time to myself, Prime Minister."

"I understand, Alison. I really do. But—" Royn's shoulders slumped, and he stepped back to let her pass. "Okay," he sighed. "Let's talk again on Monday."

Alison stared at Royn for a long moment, then said, "I'm sorry, Prime Minister, but right now the most honest answer I can give you is maybe."

Royn merely nodded vaguely as she stepped past him.

As she and her three bodyguards got into the car the driver asked, "Where to, Miss?"

Where to? Alison wanted to go *home*—but she couldn't face her parents right now. Fly to Canberra—and do what? A lonely evening in her apartment? No. She wanted company, she wanted a sympathetic, understanding ear . . . *I wish I knew where Derek is.*

She blinked the sudden moisture from her eyes—and thought: *Karla.*

Alison told the driver to take them to the hospital and, later, to Canberra.

"Yes, Miss," he said.

KARLA PRESTON GRINNED IN surprise when Alison poked her head through the door. "Hey, come on in."

"I heard you were on the mend," Alison said.

"Yeah, too damn slowly," Karla said. No longer in the intensive care ward, she was half-sitting in the bed, tubes still connected to her wrists, the remains of her lunch on a tray. "It's great to see you, but it's a bit early on Friday afternoon—"

"I walked out."

"You mean—as in *quit?*"

"I . . . ah . . . don't really know," Alison took a seat. "I just felt overwhelmed. It was too much—more than I could take."

"Tell me all about it," Karla said.

Alison blinked away a tear, and her words came tumbling out. Karla's gaze was warm and penetrating at the same time. When she realized Karla was listening without sitting in judgement, Alison felt her pent-up tension fading away.

"I see," Karla said. "So what now?"

"Well," Alison chuckled, "I could use a few of those cookies of yours."

"You're welcome to them," Karla laughed, "but could you manage five flights of stairs?"

"I guess not."

"At least I can walk," Karla chuckled, "but it's hard to write with one hand. What *are* you going to do?"

Alison shrugged. "I don't know. I'm not sure if I can take it any more. Maybe I'll feel differently tomorrow."

"Think about this: From the polls, it looks like Royn's going to win. Then you'd be sitting at his right hand, so to speak. What happened to the 'power behind the throne' the reporters in the press gallery talk about?"

Alison shrugged, unwilling to acknowledge the phrase that slipped into her mind: *I don't know.*

"If you quit now, how will you feel *then?*"

"Probably . . . a bit of a fool."

"Then why not hang on—it's only a few more weeks, after all."

"You're *encouraging* me? You, of all people?"

"Sounds a bit like that, doesn't it? But no. I'd love to see you walk away from the sewer of politics—with *no regrets.*"

Alison shook her head. "I'd always wonder what I *could* have done—"

"—dealing with scum like McKurn?"

"They're not all as bad as him," Alison protested.

"Aren't they? Name just *one* MP who'd stick to his principles come hell or high water—even if it meant he was going to lose at the polls."

"When you put it that way—" The faces of the politicians Alison knew reasonably well, dozens and dozens of them, flashed through her mind. "—a few backbenchers and an independent or two. But frontbenchers? Not a one, on *either* side of the House."

"I'm not surprised," Karla grinned. "Politics, they say, is the art of compromise. Most compromises are petty, insignificant—hardly on the scale of Royn's so-called 'deal' with McKurn. But *every* political compromise entails a betrayal of one's principles. Of course, that only applies to politicians who *have* principles."

"You're as cynical as Derek."

"Am I? Or just realistic?"

Alison recalled Olsson's description of Royn as "a vote-winning hunk of no fixed ideals—a moral vacuum." *Which he's just proved beyond any doubt.*

And he's the best of them, she'd admitted to Olsson. "Where," she mumbled, "is his spine?"

But Karla caught her words. "*Whose* spine?"

Alison sighed. "Royn's."

"You mean 'spine,' as in 'principles'?"

"I'm . . . afraid so." *I knew that, from the very beginning. I just wouldn't admit it.*

Later, as Alison was about to leave, Karla said, "A thought occurs to me. They say when you've got lemons, make lemonade. But how can you do that if the lemons are all rotten?"

"That's not exactly an uplifting comment," said Alison.

"Perhaps not," Karla replied. "But you've got to admit, it's realistic. Food for thought."

"I'll think about it tomorrow," Alison grinned. *Or the next day.*

*****

IT WAS MID-AFTERNOON when Olsson finally arrived. "We were wondering if you were ever going to show up," Nazarov said as he met Olsson at the front entrance.

"So was I, for a while," Olsson replied.

"We didn't wait for you. *Couldn't.* One of our 'guests' was ready to sing, so we let him."

"What did he say?"

"We videoed it," Nazarov said, leading Olsson into the kitchen where a laptop sat on the table, "so you can see for yourself."

Bruiser told a straightforward, if halting story. Demas Chrysanthopoulos, he said, killed Vincent Leung. "Yes, I was there, I saw him put the knife in. We were already in the apartment. He came in with some poofter guy. Darryl—"

"He's the fourth guy on your list," Nazarov said. "The one we couldn't nab."

"—hustled him out. Me and Mitch held Leung while Demas killed him. Then he did some weird things—wouldn't explain. Like, he had a bag full of stuff. A beer bottle and a glass, for example, which he put on the table. A bunch of empty beer bottles he lined up on a shelf. Of course we wore gloves. We're not that stupid. You want me to tell this to the *cops?* Shit, I wouldn't live long enough. That's not much of a choice. . . . Okay, you guarantee my safety, *and* the safety of my family, and I'll think about it.

"That's what I'm after," said Olsson, "but what the hell have you *done* to the poor guy?"

"Poor guy?" Shultz sneered. "This bastard helped set you up, and you *sympathize* with him? What he and his buddies all deserve is the electric chair."

You, Olsson thought, *are talking about justice?*

"We haven't been following Robert's Rules of Order," Nazarov said. "But hell, you *knew* that."

Yes, Olsson nodded slowly, *I did.*

"Since we grabbed them," Nazarov continued when Olsson didn't speak, "they've all been kept in isolation. They've each seen the others, just once, so they know who else we've got—but we haven't let them say a word to each other. No conversation, no exchange of information."

"Do the others know Bruiser has blabbed?" Olsson asked.

"We've let them all think that the others have all talked. I'd say the other two are ready to sing like Bruiser."

"And the fourth guy, Darryl?"

"We couldn't get to him. The Greek finally cottoned on and they're going around in twos and threes."

"Three should be enough," Olsson said. "Even two—if they're both willing to tell the truth. To the *police.*"

"They will."

Olsson flinched at the undertone in Nazarov's voice.

"But listen carefully," Nazarov said. "If you want to spring this trap, you have to act like one of us. Hold your nose; keep your bleeding-heart feelings to yourself; fix in your mind that these guys are all murderers or accomplices to murder. They're not the smartest bastards on the block, but they're *cunning.* If they sense one hint of weakness in you, they'll take advantage of it till *you* break, not them. Do you get what I'm saying?"

Olsson nodded. *Pretend to be one of you,* he thought. *Like it or not, I am—now.*

"Right," Nazarov said. "To pull this off, we have to play 'good cop, bad cop'. . . ." The good cop's role, he explained, was to give them hope but not *compassion.* Be sympathetic, appear to be their only friend—but let the bad cop keep pushing them so eventually they'll grasp their only way out.

"Confession."

"Right," said Nazarov. "Think you can do that?"

"I'll have to," said Olsson, his breath coming faster.

"Okay. Bring Bruiser up here," he said to Shultz and de Brouw, "and we'll get started. This will work if you can make them believe you're their *savior.*"

"Wait," said Olsson. "I need to clean up first."

About an hour later, Olsson reappeared now looking like himself, his hair back to his normal, tangled brown. "I *want* him to recognize me," he said in response to Nazarov's questioning look.

"Is that wise?" Nazarov asked.

"It's necessary," Olsson grinned. "You'll find out why soon enough."

Nazarov frowned; de Brouw and Shultz left for the basement, pulling on their hoods as they left; Nazarov followed suit and held another one out to Olsson. "I suppose you don't want this, then."

"No, thanks," Olsson said.

As Bruiser was brought into the kitchen he stared at Olsson and came to a sudden halt. *"You."* His eyes remained fixed on Olsson as he sat down at the table.

Olsson said nothing.

"Who?" Nazarov asked.

"Leung's poofter mate—wait a minute." Bruiser looked carefully at Olsson, and began to shake his head. "You sure look like him, but you're not the same."

Olsson stood up.

"He was a bit taller than you—but jeez, you sure look alike."

"Know his name?" Olsson asked, resuming his seat.

"Nah. Demas never said."

"You've told us what happened," said Olsson, "and you've agreed to tell the police."

"If my family is safe."

"We agreed to that," said Nazarov.

"Why should I trust you?"

Nazarov pointed to Bruiser's face on the laptop. "What do you think will happen if we give Chrysanthopoulos a copy of this?"

"You *wouldn't.*"

"That's just one of our options."

"Better if we gave it to the police," said Olsson, "wouldn't you think?"

"Or both," said Nazarov.

"You're not giving me much choice."

"Your only choice is whether you want to live or die," Nazarov snapped.

Bruiser shivered, despite the warmth in the room.

"Let me give you an idea of what will happen," Olsson said.

Reacting to the soft tone of his voice, Bruiser turned to Olsson expectantly.

"The police will ask questions, recording everything. You can have a lawyer there—your own, or a public one. If you agree to be a witness for the prosecution, you'll get a reduced sentence for cooperation—maybe even immunity. The Greek will know nothing—until the cops come to arrest him."

"But—what about my *family?*"

"Would twenty thousand dollars help?" Olsson asked.

"Damn right it would."

"I'll deposit that in your bank account, or your wife's, *after* you've testified."

Before Bruiser could say a word, Nazarov exploded, "Don't be crazy—letting the bastard live is enough reward."

"Hmmm," Olsson said. "You could be right—"

Bruiser sighed, his shoulders slumping in defeat. "No, no! I agree. I agree to *everything.*"

After several hours, Bruiser had his statement down pat. They made another video, and then Olsson said, "Now watch."

Working with Nazarov's laptop, he edited Bruiser's confession, fuzzing Bruiser's face so it was unrecognizable, adding *bleep*s to obscure every name Bruiser mentioned.

"We'll show *this* to the police," said Olsson. "They can't identify you *or* any of your associates. To get your evidence they *have* to make a deal *first.*"

For the first time, a broad grin lit up Bruiser's face. "I like it," he said with a yawn. "So how about a soft bed for a change?"

While Shultz and de Brouw took Bruiser upstairs, Olsson wrote a long email which he sent, along with the edited video, to Ross Traynor. "Now, this show is on the road."

"What about the other two?" Nazarov asked.

"Later. I'm exhausted." Olsson pushed himself upright and turned to leave. "But the *timing*," he muttered. Swinging back to Nazarov he said, "Their resistance should be lowest around one or two AM. *That* might be the best time to confront them."

"Good thinking," said Nazarov. "We'll wake you up then."

"Meanwhile, why don't you dig out all the videos and pictures you took of those two, to see what we have that would give us extra leverage."

"Huh?" said Nazarov. "I sent everything to *you.*"

Olsson grinned. "You sent *copies*—but kept the originals."

After a long moment, Nazarov laughed. "Okay, you got me there."

*****

At around nine pm that evening, when the Bare Bottoms Club in Sydney's Kings Cross began to get busy, no one noticed a handful of customers leaving their tables at discreet intervals for a back room half-hidden beyond the gentlemen's loo. Each was welcomed by the Greek—who scrutinized them carefully, looking for any reaction, any clue that might tell him *which* competing gang was attacking his men.

After helping themselves to a drink from a selection of bottles lined up along one side, each one took a seat at a round conference table. While they waited for the last person to arrive, they sipped their drinks in silence and eyed each other warily.

"Thank you all for coming at such short notice," Demas Chrysanthopoulos said as he took his seat. "We've all agreed that this club is neutral territory for the rest of the evening—" he looked around the table and each of the other seven men nodded "—so feel free to enjoy yourselves afterwards. Drinks on the house."

"Let's get on with it," someone growled.

"Certainly. In case we don't all know each other, this is Ryan O'Malley, Surry Hills Push," said Chrysanthopoulos, going around the table starting with the man on his left, "Carlos Santiago from the Colombians; Aban Haddad, Lebanese; Vuong Lam Tho, Vietnamese; Jesse Rubenstein, Eastern Suburbs; Mr. Smith—"

"Mister *Smith?*" said O'Malley, leaping to his feet and leaning over the table. "He looks like a flatfoot. What's *he* doing here—"

Smith, round-faced and beginning to lose his hair, had the body of a man who'd once been very active, but now spent too much time sitting behind a desk. He sat straight, his hands clasped, his forearms resting on the table. His only reaction was the hint of a smile.

"Ryan," Chrysanthopoulos said, "Mr. Smith is here to represent certain politically connected people in *very* high places who share our interests—"

"And our profits," Rubenstein scowled.

"For services rendered," Chrysanthopoulos said. "I vouch for his reliability."

"Do you?" said O'Malley, turning on the Greek. "I don't really trust *you,* so why should I trust *him*—"

"Wait." Vuong's voice was soft, but it caught O'Malley's attention. "He one. Us six. We listen. Don't like. . . ." Vuong shrugged. "Bye-bye Mr. Smith."

O'Malley stared at Vuong and shrugged. "The chink actually makes sense."

Whatever Vuong thought was hidden by his stone face.

O'Malley sat down and turned to Smith. "*John* Smith, I suppose."

"Jack," said Smith, his lips barely moving.

"Yeah, right."

"Now that we all know each other," Chrysanthopoulos said, glaring at O'Malley as if challenging him to interrupt again, "let's get down to business. We came to talk about two things, the Candyman, and—"

"This Candyman bastard is fucking up our business," O'Malley said. "What the hell could be more important than *that?*"

"Royn made a high-powered Royal Commission into drugs and corruption the central plank of his election campaign. Labor supports it. It doesn't matter who wins, we're going to have to deal with it. *That's* what's more important."

"Who's Royn?" asked Santiago.

"You should keep up with politics," Rubenstein said, rolling his eyes. "Royn's the prime minister."

The Colombian shrugged. "Why don't we just knock him off?"

"We're not in South America, you *schmuck,*" O'Malley said. "That's worse than killing a cop—their gloves would be off and not all the protection money in the world would save you."

"I suppose you don't know what a Royal Commission is, either," Rubenstein said.

"Search me," said Santiago with a shrug.

"It's a government enquiry that can subpoena anyone it likes—cops, politicians, bureaucrats, and *you,* if they feel like it—and dig anywhere it takes a mind to, even 'top secret' documents."

The Colombian shrugged. "So? It sounds just like another bunch of cops—"

"It's bigger. It'll have wide political and public support, lots of money behind it, draw on *all* state and federal police—and its proceedings are *public,*" Rubenstein explained. "There's nothing a corrupt official hates more than publicity."

"You don't want *your* name coming up," said O'Malley. "Especially you wogs and slant-eyes—they won't bother with any legal stuff; they'll just deport you."

"Cheap Irish punk," Santiago sneered.

"Gentlemen." Chrysanthopoulos pounded the table.

"If we can't hit this Royn guy or anyone else, I suppose, what *can* we do?" Haddad shrugged. "Write a letter to the editor?"

"More than you might think," Chrysanthopoulos said, "*I'm* talking to all the cops and officials I know. Warning them, telling they have to watch my back and, if they get the opportunity, do whatever they can to slow this commission down. You might like to do the same."

"If I say anything to my pals, they may just want to scarper," said O'Malley.

"Not a bad idea," said Rubenstein. "Then they can't be called as witnesses—and they can't lead the cops to *you*."

"Then, they can't protect me either."

"That's where the higher-ups Mr. Smith represents come in," said Chrysanthopoulos.

O'Malley looked from the Greek to Smith. "I think I'd rather deal with the bastards I know than the bastards I don't."

"Suit yourself," Smith said indifferently.

"What difference this make?" said Vuong. "Business dying anyway, thanks Candyman. What commission do Candyman can't?"

"Name you publicly, put you in jail, and take away your protection," said Rubenstein. "While the heat's on, your mates down at the cop shop will want to keep their heads down, that's for sure."

Smith nodded curtly. "This Royal Commission threatens *all* our livelihoods—not just yours, but all the people up the line who keep the cops and customs guys off your back—"

"And milk us dry in return," O'Malley grumbled.

Smith merely raised an eyebrow. "If you'd prefer to go to jail, that can be arranged." He paused, but O'Malley glowered back without speaking. "I don't think there's any way we can stop this commission coming into existence. But we *can* slow it down. Maybe even emasculate it."

"How the hell can *we* do *that?*" O'Malley asked.

"That's what I'm here to tell you," said Smith. "We have enough influence to get a bunch of *our* boys onto the Commission's staff. We're already working on it. In fact, the Commission is going to take over from something called the Candyman Inquiry. So far, all they've discovered about this Candyman is how well-concealed he is—"

"Tell us something we don't know," O'Malley grumbled.

Smith squinted at O'Malley. "If you zip your flapping lips," he said evenly, "perhaps I will. If you can't, I'm quite happy to continue without you."

O'Malley glared at Smith, who looked back as if he couldn't give a damn what O'Malley did. After a moment, O'Malley sank back in his chair with a faint nod.

"But the Candyman Inquiry," Smith continued, "keeps going off on tangents, looking for corruption here, there, and everywhere. So far, our boys have managed to stymie these efforts—and keep them focused."

"Didn't this Olsson guy start all this trouble?" said Haddad. "Why don't we knock *him* off?"

"If you can find him," Smith shrugged, "go ahead. He's on the run from a murder charge, so no one will miss him if he never comes back. But what's the point—his papers started spilling the beans *after* he disappeared. It's too late now anyway; the damage is done."

"Royn's Royal Commission will have a wider remit than the Candyman Inquiry," said Rubenstein. "That's how it looks to me—so your tactics won't work so well once it's a going concern."

Smith nodded.

"Feed Candyman to commission," said Vuong. "Maybe one big meal, they shut shop, go home."

For the first time, Smith smiled. "A thinking man, I see."

"A great idea," said Chrysanthopoulos. "But who knows anything about the bastard?"

"I thought you were going to tell us," said Santiago.

"I don't know what gave you *that* idea," the Greek said. "Once, I *thought* I knew who he was—but I was wrong."

"What do you mean?" asked Rubenstein.

The Greek shrugged. "Doesn't matter now, does it?"

"Maybe . . . " said Vuong thoughtfully. "Candyman stole couple guys from me. Pump them, hand over to *my* cops, they look lily white, everybody happy."

"Good thinking," said Rubenstein.

"Yeah," said O'Malley. "Instead of just beating the bastards up."

"But they're just the minnows," said Haddad. "How do we get to the big fish?"

"Pool our resources," said Smith. "Find out everything you can about the Candyman, no matter how trivial. We'll feed it to the commission. But even if they can nail the Candyman, they won't want to stop there. We'll have to serve them up some other fish as well."

"*Whose* fish?" O'Malley demanded. "Not *mine*. That's for sure."

"There'll have to be some sacrifices for the greater good," Smith shrugged. "It's inevitable."

"Fine," said O'Malley. "*You* serve up a couple of your top cops *first*. Then I'll *consider* throwing one of mine to the dogs."

Vuong turned to Smith. "I tell you my cops, Commission take them, you take over my business? Think not, Mr. Smith. Better idea. Use commission. Knock out Candyman, Chinese, Melbourne, other gangs not here, take over *their* business. What you say, Mr. Malley?"

"*O'*Malley."

"Velly solly," Vuong grinned.

O'Malley laughed. "I like the chink better," he said, looking at Smith, and sat back down.

"Not chink," Vuong said calmly. "Vietcong."

"You're not old enough," O'Malley said, studying Vuong's hard face.

"Was ten. Killed first man. American. Look like you."

O'Malley flinched—and began treating Vuong with a lot more respect.

They agreed to feed everything they could find on the Candyman and competing gangs to the commission—but no one trusted Chrysanthopoulos and Smith to pass any tips on without first using the information to their own advantage. Eventually, as the liquor flowed, the meeting broke up when a slanging match developed between O'Malley and Santiago. "If you wanna fight," Chrysanthopoulos shouted, "get the hell outside."

"That might have been a bit of a waste of time," Chrysanthopoulos said to Rubenstein, the only one who remained.

"I'd say it was a good start," said Rubenstein. "That Vuong guy strikes me as pretty astute. Maybe you should cultivate him."

"Why don't you?" asked Chrysanthopoulos.

"Me?" Rubenstein shrugged. "I'm getting a bit long in the tooth—as you can see. This may be the perfect time to check out the south of France and other places I've wanted to see but never have. How long since you've been home for a visit?"

"Greece? A tiny little village tucked away in the middle of nowhere with more chickens and goats than people? Where nothing ever happens? Nah. Too much fun here."

"Suit yourself," Rubenstein grinned. "And that 'Mr. Smith' is an interesting character. You must have good contacts."

Chrysanthopoulos grinned back. "The best."

"Let me guess who Smith represents: McKurn."

Chrysanthopoulos shrugged and spread his arms. "Who knows?"

But Rubenstein had caught the slight widening of the Greek's eyes at the mention of McKurn's name.

"Come to think of it," Rubenstein said, "there's another possibility that makes a lot of sense to me. Who's good at covering his tracks? McKurn. Who else? This Candyman. Perhaps they're one and the same person."

"No," Chrysanthopoulos shook head vigorously. "They *can't* be."

"Really?" Rubenstein shrugged. "Not my problem any more. I guess I'll read about it if it ever hits the French papers. Good luck to you, Demas."

When Rubenstein left, Chrysanthopoulos sat alone for a long while, unable to shake the implications of what it would mean if the Candyman *was* McKurn.

*****

MITCH BURBLED A VAGUE tune to himself, his words barely discernible to a listener, had there been one:

". . . bastards . . . gone bad . . .
fuck 'em all, fuck 'em all
I'll tear . . . make me mad . . .
fuck 'em all, fuck 'em all. . . ."

While he mumbled, he itched and scratched around his crotch in a rhythmic motion mirroring a drumbeat in the background. He could remember a time when he didn't itch, a memory lost in haze along with fragmented images of incidents that *might* have happened when he was four or five years old, but could equally have been dreams. He breathed evenly, distantly aware of some foul smell that, once, had bothered him: he could no longer remember why.

So it was a while before some unusual sounds penetrated his consciousness. When they finally registered, he turned his head to see three forms standing near him; three of the devils which seemed to visit him now and then; he was unaware of his quivering shoulders, his trembling hands, and the spittle dribbling from one corner of his mouth.

No—as his red-rimmed eyes slowly came into semi-focus, he saw just *two* of the black-shrouded aliens. The third figure had a face. He blinked with a sudden sense of relief: a face he recognized. The corners of his lips twitched as if he were trying to smile but couldn't remember how.

"Lars!" Freedom beckoned. But the unused-to effort of raising his voice devolved into a fit of coughing. "Thank God you've come," his voice now croaked. "Let's go! I can't stand this any more. See what these fucking bastards have done to me?"

"Mitch—" The figure he took to be Lars came a step towards him—and stopped, one of the devils restraining it.

"Oh, no! They got you too." Mitch felt tears come to his eyes, not knowing the moisture had drained away long ago.

Then, it seemed there was just the figure of Lars standing before him. He thrust his hands out, his chains clanking, his voice now a rasp, "Take me out of here. Let's go-go-go. . . ." until, it seemed to him, all the air had gone and he had to gulp instead of breathe.

He stared at Olsson, one arm reached out to him clanking the chains. "Lars, Lars!" he screamed, desperation now in his voice. "Say something to me. Say anything!"

"Mitch. I know everything. I know exactly what you did."

"You *couldn't,*" Mitch's voice rose an octave in pitch. "You weren't *there*. Darryl hustled you out before anything happened. Oh, God, the blood. . . . I didn't do it. It wasn't me! Demas. *Him.* I didn't hold the knife . . . I didn't do anything. . . ."

"You and Bruiser held Vincent Leung while the Greek stabbed him."

"It wasn't anything like that. Demas did it. It was all his fault. . . . Oh, Christ, I wasn't even there. . . ."

"I think you need is a long, hot bath. How about it?"

A bath. Somehow, that would be nice . . . but then, he'd stop itching. That was hard to imagine—and, in a strange way he felt comfortable here. Or would, if those devils would go away and never come back.

"And a hamburger or maybe two with fries and a beer. Yes, a beer."

"A beer. . . ." Something cool, cold, trickling down his throat. "A beer. . . ."

"So just tell me what happened, Mitch. From the time Darryl took me out."

"I was . . . I saw. . . ." He saw Demas with the knife. Blood ran down the blade, red drops splattering from the tip. But now with the chains holding him down, Demas leered above him, the knife raised. . . . "No, *no*." He shook his head violently.

Mitch closed his eyes and everything disappeared. In a moment he was burbling again, *"Fuck 'em all . . . fuck 'em all. . . ."*

"HE'S LOST HIS MARBLES," de Brouw muttered as he locked the door to Mitch's cell. Nazarov, one hand on Olsson's shoulder, indicated Damien's door, but Olsson impatiently shook off the touch and strode rapidly towards the stairs. A moment later, Nazarov and de Brouw followed.

Nazarov's briefing left Olsson unprepared for the actual sight of the drooling, babbling, man. He kept a firm lid on his feelings, his pallor—unnoticed by Mitch—the only clue to his inner state. But now he was breathing fast and deep in a vain attempt to clear his mouth and lungs of overpowering odor of stale urine and excrement. At the top of the stairs, the air was clear—but the sense of the taste lingered as he kept swallowing back bile bubbling up in the back of his throat.

Nazarov, Shultz, and de Brouw, sitting around the kitchen table, eyed Olsson with a touch of disdain as he came from the bathroom some ten minutes later. "He needs to be cleaned up," he said as he sat down. "And he's bound to need medical attention."

"Hardly worth the trouble," said de Brouw. "As a witness, he's now useless. Might as well get rid of him."

"Definitely *not*," said Olsson. "I'll not have *another* death on my conscience."

"He's a liability now," Nazarov said. "And he's seen you, though he seems to think you're someone else. Bruiser's seen you too. What's going to happen when they compare notes?"

Olsson shrugged. "I'll cope." *Somehow.* "Clean him up, put him upstairs—and tell him Lars made you do it. In the morning, he might be lucid, and ready to talk."

"We're not nursemaids," Shultz grumbled.

"You don't have to be," Olsson snapped. *Careful,* he thought, *I'm starting to lose it.* "Just let him soak in a hot bath for a while."

Nazarov nodded, though they were all clearly unhappy at the prospect. "What about Damien? I think Mitch's ravings have him totally spooked."

"In the morning. I want to be there."

"As another ghost?"

Olsson shook his head. "He doesn't need to see me—I'll wear that hood."

57 Invasive Procedures

" ... **W**E'VE GOT LEON PRICE'S statement," Simon Lee was saying.

"Who'll be dead by the time we get to court," Rudi Durant said sourly. "*If* we ever do."

"Folsom—"

"The defence will tear him apart."

"What about the other three we interviewed?" Lee protested.

"Small fry. Will any of them testify *willingly?*"

Lee shook his head.

"Even if Price's statement is accepted as the absolute truth, there's no corroboration. Price's word against McKurn's."

"So we have to go after some of the big names he mentioned."

"Which we *can't* do without going to Zimmerman first."

"And he'll just tick us off because for fishing without a licence."

"Exactly," Durant said. "We need a break. Wonder if we'll get one."

The gloomy silence was broken by a knock on the door.

"We meet again," said Durant as Mike Rubin entered his office.

"Under happier circumstances, I trust," Rubin replied, nodding to Simon Lee sitting at one side of Durant's desk.

Durant grimaced. Rubin was Derek Olsson's lawyer; every time Durant had asked a question Rubin advised Olsson, "You don't need to answer that."

"You claim to have some evidence related to the murder of Vincent Leung?" Durant asked.

"That's correct. Mind if I sit down?"

Durant waved his hand impatiently. "Olsson decided to confess?"

Rubin's lips twitched into a smile. "I have something to show you." Pressing a button on his phone, he propped it up on the table so Durant and Lee could see the screen.

"I am making this statement voluntarily. . . ."

"Who is this?" Durant asked. "His face is blurred."

"This man is my client. Please listen to it all. It won't take long." Rubin took Durant's grunt as agreement and restarted the recording.

A couple of times Durant began to object; Rubin raised his hand until the video came to an end.

"He'll confess—if he's granted immunity from prosecution," Rubin said. "But if the rest of his gang knew, his life expectancy will be measured in days, if not hours. So you'd have to protect him, and his family."

"Immunity?" Durant shook his head. "We can't do that."

"The Attorney-General can," said Rubin, "but rarely does."

Durant looked at Rubin skeptically, and turned to Lee: "What do you think, Simon?"

Lee had been lounging back in his chair, watching the interchange like a spectator. He straightened his shoulders and looked quizzically at Durant. *Ah, another of Durant's little tests.*

"Well," Lee said at length, "it's interesting but it's not evidence. As it stands."

"Why not?" Rubin asked.

"Too many gaps," said Lee. "Who is he? Every name he mentions is blanked out."

"And," said Durant, "it could have come from anywhere. Could be completely made up—easy enough to do these days."

"I've questioned him and heard the entire statement, Inspector," Rubin said. "He names names, he identifies the murderer and all the accomplices. He's agreed to make the same statement to you, under oath—"

"Let him do that, then."

"He will," said Rubin, *"if* you accept his offer."

"I don't make deals with criminals," said Durant, "In any case, I'm off the case. You're talking to the wrong person."

"I know that."

"Then why are you here?"

"I'm following instructions," said Rubin, "to approach you before we go to the Director of Public Prosecutions and the Attorney-General. Derek Olsson has insisted all along that he was framed. I'm bringing you, the arresting officer, evidence that clears him of the charge of murdering Vincent Leung."

"Maybe. If he's telling the truth."

"It's enough to clear Olsson and point you in the right direction. For a change."

Durant pursed his lips. "We'll see."

"This man is nervous and could change his mind. So it can be classified under the procedures as an emergency. A ranking officer like *you*, Inspector, must make a direct request to the DPP or AG."

"That's stretching the rules a bit," Durant interjected.

"You're no stranger to doing that," Rubin grinned. "So you're justified in making a phone call right now."

Durant looked at the phone thoughtfully. "I shouldn't, but I want to see this through to the finish."

"Even if you tweak a few noses?" Rubin asked.

"It's happened before," Durant grinned. "But how can I get in touch with either of them on a Saturday morning?"

"I have an appointment with them both in about half an hour."

"Today?" Lee said. *"Together?"*

Rubin smiled. "Not a problem." He rose to his feet. "Shall we go, gentlemen?"

*****

A THICK STEAK, STILL sizzling on a metal plate, topped with two eggs and fried onions, French fries on the side, sat in the center of the kitchen table. Damien ignored the four hooded men sitting on the other side of the table; he couldn't take his eyes off the steak.

Which was just out of his reach.

The moment his chains were attached to the table he grabbed for it—and came up short.

"It's yours," said Olsson behind one of the masks. "When you've told us a few things we'd like to know."

Damien slowly lifted his eyes to look at the hood who'd had spoken.

"What things?"

"The Greek gave you the knife he used to kill Vincent Leung. You broke into an apartment in the Rocks, wrapped it in a shirt you took from a cupboard and stashed it in the boot of a car"

"If you know it all, why are you asking me?"

"You're an accessory to murder. That means you'll spend somewhere between ten and twenty years in prison—"

Damien shrugged. "Prove it."

Olsson gestured to Nazarov who switched on his laptop. A grainy picture showed a dark figure frozen in the act of putting a knapsack on a table; on the other side of the table sat Demas Chrysanthopoulos.

"Recognize anyone?" Olsson asked.

Damien said nothing. If he reacted in any way, it was not reflected on his wooden face.

Nazarov touched a key and the picture sprang to life. The quality was poor, the camera position clearly fixed, but in a moment there was a clear shot of the tall figure: Damien. "Here it is, boss," Damien said. He carefully took out a dozen or so sparkling items from the knapsack, laying them down almost reverentially.

"Aren't they fantastic?" Chrysanthopoulos said, staring at the jewellery winking and glittering in the dim light. He reached out to pick up one of them, but Damien stopped him.

"Your *fingerprints*—"

Chrysanthopoulos laughed. "Not a problem now." Ignoring the gold rings and silver bracelets inset with diamonds or other precious stones, his thick fingers lifted the necklace with surprising delicacy, suspending it in the air from one hand.

It was a thin, almost invisible chain, its full length studded with tiny diamonds. Hanging from the chain was a green, semi-translucent pendant, so cleverly set it was impossible to see what held it suspended in space.

The video came to a halt; the necklace now enlarged and enhanced to fill the laptop's screen.

"This emerald necklace is worth a couple of hundred thousand dollars and rightfully belongs to Lady Thurow," Olsson said. "It was stolen from the safe in her house about four years ago and the cops never figured out who did it."

"So?" Damien said.

"So, don't you think the police would like to see this?"

"I—I—. It's not evidence of anything."

"Isn't it?" Olsson said.

"I wonder," said Nazarov, "if da Greek would agree with you?"

"What?"

"You have a choice," said Olsson. "Confess exactly how and when you planted that knife to the police—"

"You must be out of your mind."

"—in return for immunity from prosecution."

"Trust the cops? Not a chance."

"It's all negotiated in advance, before you tell them a thing."

"The Greek would—. No, not a chance."

"Your other choice," Olsson said, pointing to the necklace still sitting on the laptop's screen, "is that we give *that* to the police."

"Or," Nazarov cut in, "we can take you back downstairs and leave you to rot."

"I'll think about it," Damien said.

At Nazarov's signal, de Brouw and Shultz stood and moved towards Damien. "You'll think better downstairs," Nazarov said, reaching out for the steak and sliding it towards himself. "Since no one else wants it—"

"I do!" Damien exclaimed, twisting in Shultz' grasp. "I'll—I'll tell you everything."

****

ELECTION JOURNAL

Of McKurn, "Skeletons," and "Rabbits." This morning the NSW Conservative Party Senate Selection Committee will gather to decide who gets the top spots on the CP Senate ticket.

For more than twenty years, Frank McKurn has held the number one spot effortlessly. But—unlike House of Reps seats where sitting members are rarely challenged—sitting Senators must pitch themselves to the selectors every six years.

The first two spots are guarantees of election. And unless there's an enormous swing against the Conservatives, so is the third. Whoever gets number four is in the race too, based on current opinion polls.

So the competition to get on the ticket is always fierce—not only is being senator a nice, cushy job for six years minimum, with a handsome pension and lifetime perks, but no door-knocking is required. Would-be senators can leave that kind of stuff up to their "poor" cousins in the lower house.

Ninety-five members of the Selection Committee—two from each state electorate, the rest from the State Executive and State Council—will be screening an almost equal number of wanna-be senators in a long, drawn-out process where each candidate gets his or her say before balloting starts (makes for a very late night). And since the "Dump McKurn Movement" has (unsurprisingly) been particularly strident in New South Wales, many of those candidates are gunning for McKurn. You can be sure the selectors will be reminded of McKurn's every . . . ah . . . indiscretion since the day he was born.

Our "flies on the wall" say sentiment inside the Conservative Party is overwhelmingly in favor of getting McKurn completely off the ticket. But the selectors do not necessarily reflect grass-roots opinion, many of them functionaries from party HQ including, no doubt, quite a few (former?) McKurn loyalists.

Our reading of the tea leaves suggests McKurn has a less-than-even chance of staying on the ticket—and if he does, he'll *definitely* lose that prized Number One position.

The fly in this ointment is that McKurn's walked the corridors of power for close to half a century—so he presumably knows where all the "skeletons" are buried. Don't be surprised if he pulls a rabbit out of the hat at the last minute.

ALISON'S EYES BLURRED AS she read. *Too late,* she thought, letting the paper fall to lap. But her silent tears didn't stop.

"Hey," said Madge, placing a comforting hand on her shoulder. "You've every right to feel nervous. I hate these places myself."

Alison sat in the hospital waiting room with her three "friends." Only Madge knew the real reason she was here—"Men are bastards," she'd said when Alison confided in her. *"All* of them."

Alison tried to smile, but she couldn't control her trembling lips.

Madge leaned over and dabbed the tears from her eyes. "It will all be over soon," she said. *"Gone."*

"Thanks," Alison murmured. She raised her head slowly, spying a patient being wheeled through the doors leading to the operating theaters. She would shortly be asked to go through those doors—but she felt so weighed down she was unsure if she'd be able to stand up. *And if I can,* she thought as she heard the entrance doors swing open, *which direction will I choose to take?*

Her phone beeped—a welcome distraction signalling a new message. *Easton ivory towered nerd. Maybe good academic—should have stayed there. Thumbs down for this selector.* In the old days, reporters gathered outside selection committee venues to glean hints of what was happening during coffee, lunch, and even bathroom breaks. Today, insiders used their phones to post messages instantly on the internet for everyone to see.

Alison thought of Barry Easton facing the selectors with no Royn or Melanie at his elbow telling him what to do. *In over his head.*

A voice called out: "Miss McGuire."

Alison saw a nurse coming towards her.

"This way, please."

Madge and the two other bodyguards rose to their feet, but Alison looked at the nurse, then slowly turned her head towards the door leading to the street outside.

She felt a slight pressure from Madge's hand on her shoulder. "Come on, luv. It won't take long."

"C-can Madge—my friend come in with me?" Alison asked.

"Certainly," said the nurse.

Alison dug into her handbag for a tissue and dabbed her eyes. She felt herself give in to Madge's soft touch as though she no longer had a mind of her own, allowing Madge to lead her in the nurse's footsteps.

Her phone beeped again.

Kydd in top form. Tears Easton apart.

Another beep, this time from the feed collating the comments from the Senate selectors.

Andy White gave McKurn a really hard time. Think McKurn's goose is cooked.

If the bastard's still standing, he's not out.

Too right, Alison thought, unaware that she'd come to a halt.

"You'll have to turn your phone off now, Miss," the nurse said.

The nurse held the double doors open. Beyond them, a wide corridor, the antiseptic hospital smell drifting into her nostrils making it hard to breathe.

*****

AS THE DOOR CLICKED shut Mitch's eyes slowly opened to focus on the figure moving towards him. He recoiled, but then his face was transformed by a tentative smile. "Lars."

"Morning, Mitch," Derek Olsson said, pulling up a chair beside the bed. "I hope you're feeling better. I persuaded those bastards get some medicine for your itch." Olsson handed a tube of ointment to Mitch. "How about a hot shower first?"

Mitch nodded mutely. Olsson unlocked the chain and Mitch allowed himself to be led into the en suite bathroom, his eyes flicking between Olsson and the door. "Wh-what about the b-bastards?"

"We have to hurry," Olsson said. "I've managed to get some time, and if we're quick we can escape."

After his shower, he still needed Olsson's help to negotiate his way back to the bed. While he rubbed in the ointment he looked at Olsson gratefully, his eyes now more alert.

His eyes suddenly widened and the smile disappeared from his face.

"*You're* not Lars."

Mitch cringed back into the pillow, distancing himself from Olsson. "You—you look like him but you're n-not him." His lips trembled as he searched for words. "You're someone else. You're one of *them*—another d-d-devil. You're trying to *tr-trick* me. But I've f-found you out."

Mitch's shoulders shook, his eyes watered. He turned away, burrowing under the bedclothes. In a moment he was humming to himself again, "*Fuck 'em all, fuck 'em all . . .*"

Olsson ineffectually blinked away sudden tears that cast halos around the quivering shell of what had once been a healthy human being. Unbearable tension compounding inside from his pretence of being Mitch's friend and savior suddenly released; all his muscles seemed to fail at the same time and he slumped in the a chair. He sat for a long while shaking uncontrollably, unable to face the answers to his questions . . . *What have I done? What have I become?*

*****

I*T'S NOT TOO LATE*, Alison thought. She leant on her crutches, trembling, at the edge of the operating table, not quite sure how she had gotten this far.

She eyed the still-swinging door to the operating theater anteroom. *I have to get on that table,* but her legs refused to obey her, one way or the other, until Madge's faint nudge propelled her forward.

"Alison," Dr. Angie asked, "are you sure you want to go through with this?"

From the concern in her voice, Alison imagined Angie was smiling at her from behind the mask, and felt impelled to smile in return. But try as she did, all she managed was a faint twitch from the corners of her lips.

"Yes," Alison said, at the same time thinking *No.*

"It wouldn't be the first time someone changed their mind at the last minute, you know."

"I must," Alison said.

"You're not being pressured in any way?"

"No. Nothing like that." *Just the pressure of . . . of consequences.*

She sank slightly into the surface of the padded table, and resisted weakly while Angie put her feet in the stirrups. Angie took her arm and although Alison knew what was coming she flinched nonetheless at the mild jab. "In a few moments," Angie said, attaching the IV drip, "you'll begin to feel drowsy."

Alison became aware she had stopped trembling and was feeling a little more at ease. As the anesthetic flowed through the IV drip in her arm, her eyes blinked and closed, banishing the harsh light; she remained aware of Angie's voice and others', but was losing interest in following whatever they were saying; she felt herself drifting as though she was about to float away until—

A sudden but faint pain jolted her alert, her muscles locking in reaction to a sharp, cold jab. "Wha-a-a-a—?" she gasped, looking accusingly at Angie who had put some instrument into her vagina. *This was worse than—. No, nothing was worse than that.*

She felt mildly annoyed when Angie didn't react, as if she hadn't heard, her eyes closing again at the touch of a comforting touch on her forehead. "Thanks, Madge," she murmured.

The after-image of the lights and the room stayed in her vision, and her body insisted: *I've been here before.*

No reaction from her mind—this is a different table, a different hospital, a different doctor, and a different purpose—had any impact on her body's sense of place . . . and then she heard a voice, her *mother's* voice, at the same instant there was a sudden gush into her loins which felt like . . . *no, don't even think about it.*

She clung to the vague awareness of clinks and rattles in the background, the shuffling of people moving, the sense of Madge's soft fingers holding her hand, of being touched within the numbness even though she couldn't feel a thing, that words were being spoken around her, though in that semi-state between awake and asleep she had neither energy nor interest to make sense of those sounds.

I'm floating away, she realized, wondering how that had happened, wondering why she felt no sense of panic, *high in the sky, floating on the clouds* . . . with an occasional glimpse of the earth miles below through a haze. And above were brilliant stars, "where God lives," said a childish voice from her past, and in the distance was a sound like a vacuum cleaner, something tugging, pulling, sucking, and suddenly bolts of lightning flashed from the sky, and from far below she made out a tiny wail that somehow carried through above the clamor of the thunder all around her.

"Noooooooooo . . . " she screamed. But the muscles around her lips barely moved. The only sound she heard was a gush of air from her mouth.

"Alison, it's all over now." A gentle voice.

Is it? Alison asked herself as she struggled to open her eyes, becoming aware that Angie was standing beside her, watching her with concern written all over her face.

"Alison? How are you feeling?"

Her mind was still woozy, and it took her a moment to find the answer, that she felt lighter: the weight she'd been carrying was gone . . . leaving a sense of emptiness behind. "Drowsy," she answered. "I—I—had a dream." *A nightmare.*

"I think you blanked out," said another voice—Madge.

"I must have."

"We'll wheel you into the recovery room where you can rest for as long as you like," Angie said.

"'kay," Alison said. Before they'd even begun to move her, she drifted into a fitful sleep.

*****

". . . so you'll persuade them to vote *for* McKurn?" Anthony Royn paused his pacing to lean forward, arms outstretched, a posture to emphasize his persuasive empathy—to his audience of one, across the harbor on the other end of the phone.

Jim Williams, his voice on the speakerphone so Melanie could listen in, replied, "I'll do what I can—but I *still* don't understand." Williams' voice was a whisper, drowned out, now and then, by the sounds of water running, toilets flushing, or other voices. The NSW Senate Selection Committee was taking a bathroom break, and Williams was not the only member who had secreted himself in a stall to make a private call.

"I know, Jim. I know," Royn said, his head slightly bowed, his voice now slow and soft. "I appreciate that. You *will*, I promise. Right now, we're running out of time."

"Okay," Williams said with obvious reluctance, "I'll—got to go back in. Bye."

"Bye, Jim."

Royn hung up the phone and sagged, deflating with every out-breath. "Thank the heavens *that's* over." He staggered to the sofa, gratefully collapsed, and wiped the accumulated sweat from his forehead with his handkerchief.

"Darling," Melanie said, her face aglow, "that was a stunning performance." She lowered herself onto his knees, cuddling up to him, leaning her head on his chest, stroking his arm with the bare touch of her fingertips.

"It's the hardest act I've done in my life." Royn sighed, one arm vaguely going around Melanie's waist. "Jim can't understand—he kept feeding me all the arguments I gave *him* for getting rid of McKurn. So did everyone else."

Nestling on Royn's lap rarely failed to provoke a response: this time, to Melanie's annoyance, was an exception. "But he's going to do what you want, isn't he?" she said, unable to completely quell the harsh edge in her voice.

Royn was hardly paying attention. "I guess so."

He was wilting from reactions he'd gotten over the past twenty-four hours—"What's got into you, Tony?" "You made a helluva lot more sense a couple of days ago," and "Has the bastard nobbled you, too?" He switched to calling in favors where he could, and leaning on people, as he had with Williams, when he had to: the change of strategy hadn't made him feel any better. "I'm not sure how much more of this I can take."

"Not much longer, darling," Melanie said. "McKurn was fifth on the first round of balloting. Jim can twist enough arms to get him up to third or fourth."

"Wonderful," said Royn.

"It's like—we've spent all this time climbing Mount Everest and we're nearly at the top."

Royn chuckled. "That's not a very good analogy, Mel." His arms swept the expanse of the reception room of Kirribilli House. "We're already *here*, my love. This *is* the top—"

Melanie purred. It wasn't the response she was expecting, but she had jolted him from his mood. "But not in your own right, darling."

"—and I've spent the last twenty-four hours lying through my teeth—it's a wonder I can stand up straight."

"It's just a temporary expedient. Politically necessary. You know that."

"All the same, if this is what it means to be at the top, I'm not sure I want it. I guess Kydd did this sort of thing all the time, with never a touch of remorse."

"Darling, how *dare* you compare yourself to a calculating monster like Kydd. You're *twice* the man he's ever been."

"You think so?"

"Of course. That's one of the things I love about you, that you have a conscience. More than anyone can say about Kydd."

"That's true."

Melanie touched her lips to his—and grinned to herself as he kissed back.

*****

"That's all my client has to say," said the lawyer when Bruiser had finished his statement.

"Is that correct?" Durant asked.

Bruiser hesitated, glanced sideways at the lawyer, then nodded.

Durant tapped a button on the computer and the DVD of Bruiser's testimony—a copy of the official statement they had taken earlier that afternoon—slid out of the slot.

"Too pat."

"Obviously rehearsed," Lee said.

"*Well*-rehearsed," Durant nodded.

"Want to look at the other one again—Damien?"

Durant shook his head.

"What's bothering you?" Lee asked.

"Aside from Rubin turning up with a *second* gangster willing to confess all? I'll show you." Durant slid the second DVD into the computer; in a moment Damien's face showed on the screen.

"I thought you didn't want to watch that one again."

"I don't." Durant fast-forwarded the DVD. "Here," he said. "We've just gone through the routine of 'you're making this statement voluntarily,' et cetera et cetera. Now, watch his reaction."

Durant hit the PLAY button. Damien stared at Durant, his mouth moving as if he was chewing something over. He turned his head towards the lawyer, paused, and turned back. "Yes." His voice was little more than a loud whisper.

"Was that a 'yes'?" Durant asked.

"Yes," Damien replied, more forcefully.

Durant set the video to play in a short loop so Damien was saying "Yes," over and over again. "Now, Simon, what do you make of *that* expression?"

As Damien said "Yes," his eyes turned away from Durant, flicked towards the lawyer and then stared into the distance. After he'd spoken, his lips closed but the upper lip seemed to vibrate.

"He's frightened of something," Lee said.

"Right. *Two* of them coming forward like this? That's hard to believe. And who brings them in? Olsson's solicitor—"

"—who has every incentive to throw the blame on someone else."

"Actually," said Durant, "I'm pretty sure these two thugs *are* telling the truth."

"You mean, Olsson is innocent?"

"Innocent of murder. Guilty of coercing witnesses."

"But if you prove that, the case against the Greek collapses."

"I know." Durant glared at Damien's face on the computer screen.

"The DPP and AG have gone out on a bit of limb doing a deal with these two gangsters. If you cut them off at the knees, they'll go apeshit."

"I know that too."

"Still, you've got the Greek instead—at last."

"Not until he's locked up." Durant sighed. "Olsson might be a bastard, but the Greek's a worse one. I suppose we shouldn't inspect the teeth in the horse's mouth too closely. Just the same—" Durant straightened his shoulders and his face settled into the look of grim determination Lee knew so well "—I'll get to the bottom of this, if only for my own satisfaction."

Durant reached for the phone.

"Time to get the charges against Olsson withdrawn, get a warrant to arrest the Greek—and go get him."

*****

ONCE HOME, ALISON RETREATED to her bedroom. She wanted to be alone. Now, lying on the bed but wide awake, she yearned for company. But not *any* company.

She was thankful for Madge's comforting presence—but she couldn't share her cheerful, everything-will-be-peachy, "I'm glad you're feeling better now" optimism. Jason would come running at the drop of a hat—for the wrong reasons. Karla would be understanding—but hardly comforting. She wanted to crawl into her mother's embrace . . . *but she must never know.*

Derek. That's who I want now.

To distract herself, she turned on her phone. It beeped endlessly. A blizzard of messages . . .

Kydd's "Baby-Face" moniker for Easton sticks.

McKurn #4 on second round.

The bastard's back in the race.

She shrugged.

SHOCK HORROR Jake Meldrum pulls out. Backs Easton. What's going on here??

Has Jake lost his bananas, or what?

Or what. Smells like a dirty deal somewhere to me. Someone sold us down the river.

Jake, the bastard! Who else?

I suppose it will all come out, more likely sooner than later.

Down to "Baby-Face" and Kydd. Could go either way.

She was surprised she had no feeling about Easton's success—or even McKurn's. She examined her reaction of total indifference with interest—and a question: *Should I be concerned about not being concerned . . . ?*

Several calls from Royn. *He'll call again. . . .* With an impatient flick of her thumb, she turned off the phone.

And come Monday, what will I do?

No answer came to her.

Into the blankness of her mind crept the aches in her foot, her ribs, and the most sensitive part of her body—along with the sense that she had somehow lost more than she had gained.

All McKurn's fault.

No—this time she was *not* a victim of circumstances completely beyond her control. *This* was the result of decisions *she* had made, actions *she* had taken . . . of her own free will. She couldn't escape that realization, no matter how hard she tried.

On her dresser was the photo of her sixteen-year-old self standing, radiant, on the steps of Parliament House.

I'm no longer innocent.

She hobbled from the bed and turned the picture so it was facing the wall, thinking:

"The ends justify the means." Ha. They take you somewhere you never wanted to go. . . .

58 Rue the Day

"**D**AMNATION," SIR PHILIP FRENCH spluttered. His first sip of coffee sprayed across the Sunday newspapers spread out before him.

The angry face of Demas "The Greek" Chrysanthopoulos dominated both front pages, handcuffs plainly in view as he was escorted from the "Bare Bottoms Club" by several hefty policemen, charged with the murder of Sydney gang boss Vincent Leung. One—not *his* Sunday, he was pleased to note—had a small shot of Derek Olsson inset in one corner with the caption: *Olsson innocent.*

"Why didn't the bastards warn me?" he muttered, in the heat of the moment ready to grab a phone and chew out his editor for this sin of omission.

But of course: his editor had no inkling of his interest in the Greek. And rightly so.

A man of regular habits, he was having breakfast on the verandah of his Bellvue Hill home. Oblivious to the sweeping view of the harbor, he glared at the Greek as if *he* were responsible for this interruption of his routine when he heard his butler's voice behind him:

"Excuse me, Sir Philip."

"What the hell is it now?" French said without turning around.

"Senator McKurn is here to see you, Sir Philip."

"Send him in, for heaven's sake."

French looked again at the newspapers: he didn't need to be a mind reader to know the reason for McKurn's visit.

*****

DEREK OLSSON SHOULD HAVE been a happy man.

Instead, he was driving a sedated Mitch to a rendezvous with a psychiatrist Nazarov knew. "He knows his stuff," Nazarov had told Olsson, "but he can't keep away from the horses."

De Brouw laughed. "A psychiatrist with a gambling problem. What next?"

In return for enough money to pay his bookies, who were threatening to send his debts "out for collection," he would commit one "John Doe" to a sanatorium as a private patient for treatment, sight unseen.

Olsson chose one of Sydney's most expensive private hospitals. Acting as the psychiatrist's helper, Olsson accompanied Mitch as he was checked in.

Everything went smoothly. No one questioned the psychiatrist's word and, being a Sunday, questions of continuing payment were deferred to the following day, when Olsson would make the necessary arrangements. Including proper treatment for Mitch.

Nazarov, Shultz and de Brouw argued vociferously that "the problem of Mitch" should "be disposed of."

Olsson firmly overruled them.

"If he recovers and identifies *you?*" Nazarov asked. "What then?"

Olsson shrugged. "That's a risk I *have* to take."

He drove away from the hospital—aimless. *I can go back to being Derek Olsson. But . . . just who is Derek Olsson now?*

He passed a police station. He laughed. *I can't even prove I'm Derek Olsson. I have lots of IDs, none for the real me.*

Idling at a red light, he noticed the tips of tall buildings of the City of Sydney ahead. He'd been on automatic pilot, heading for the Rocks.

Home.

When the light changed he turned off, driving in no particular direction other than *away.*

If only to have a destination, he stopped at a shopping center to wander around, relishing the sense of mingling with ordinary people doing everyday things. Spying the Greek's picture, he bought the Sunday papers. As almost an afterthought, he added a copy of *MoneyWeek,* muttering to himself, "Time to get back to business." He spread out the front pages at a café, gazed at Demas Chrysanthopoulos, asking: *Why did you choose to set up me, of all people?*

A mystery—which had almost worked. Except for. . . . A host of images blurred through his mind, but only one stood out.

Mitch.

Without him, would Bruiser and Damien have confessed?

Probably not.

I've killed a man with my own hands. I've sent another one crazy.

"Guilty as charged. . . ."

"Whatever I can do, Mitch, I will do," he vowed. *Restitution . . . make amends. . . . But, will I ever be able to forgive myself?*

Catching himself staring at a void, he forced his mind to turn to the things he had to do. A new laptop. See Ross—and Jessica. He owed her an explanation, and his mother would be delighted to see him. Karla. He could visit her now—but something held him back. *Not yet.*

Alison.

He reached for his phone. It rang and rang. He was about to give up when Alison answered.

"Derek, you're free at last! Did you get my email?"

"I've been . . . out of touch. What did you say?"

Alison paused. "That I need to see you."

Olsson laughed. "That's why *I* called *you.* Are you in Sydney or Canberra?"

"Canberra."

"I'm in Sydney. Remember the resort we went to once, between Berrima and Moss Vale?"

"Oh, yes."

"That's about halfway. How about meeting there?"

"That sounds lovely."

"I'll make a booking . . . but you must be run off your feet."

"Not . . . exactly."

"It's election time, and you sound like you don't much care," Olsson said. "What's going on?"

"Derek, that's a long story. I'll be happy to tell you . . . in a couple of hours."

"I'll be waiting."

*****

"That bastard Olsson's on the loose again."

McKurn pointed to the Greek's picture. "We've got more important things to worry about. Olsson's a mere pinprick by comparison."

"We? Or you?"

"This time, Phil, it's the same thing."

"Something to do with the Greek?"

"He's only a small part of the problem."

"What problem?"

McKurn sat down. "Your hospitality's slipping, Phil. How about some coffee."

"Sure." French pushed a bell. While the butler brought a fresh pot of coffee and another cup, they eyed each other in silence. French felt himself growing increasingly nervous under McKurn's unforgiving scrutiny.

"The Senate—"

"You're still on the ticket—"

"At number three." McKurn's right fist pounded the table, rattling the cutlery; he winced at the jolt to his shoulder. *"And* I had to pull in every favor and twist every arm in sight."

"I see," French said, his voice suddenly weak. "You're here to twist *my* arm?"

McKurn grinned. "If I have to."

French pointed at the banner across the bottom of Sykes' *Sunday Mercury: Zoning Chief Nabbed At Airport. "There's* the cause of your problem. And you say Olsson's just a pinprick?"

"That's where you come in, Phil. Time to demonstrate the power of the press. Plug me."

"Christ, Frank. You're hardly top of the pops right now. For a newspaper to take the unpopular side of an issue is suicide. Our sales will slump—"

"The *hell* with your sales. And not just your newspapers. Your TV and radio stations as well."

"The goddamn journalists will go on strike."

McKurn shrugged. "Your problem."

French was shaking his head. "You're asking me to pull off the impossible."

"Asking you? Who's *asking?* Have you forgotten who helped you swing all your TV and radio licences—not to mention building permits?"

"Of course not."

"To reawaken your sense of gratitude, there were certain irregularities that, somehow, got papered over. If they ever came to light—" McKurn's grin turned into a leer. "—which, of course, they *won't.* Will they, Phil?"

"They've been paid for long ago, Frank."

"Some things are *never* paid for. Do I make myself clear?"

That's right, French thought, keeping his expression blank. *You're a leech, Frank. Once you've got your hooks in, there's only one way to get rid of you. . . .*

"And then," McKurn continued, "there's this Royal Commission of Royn's."

"Nash's backing makes it a *fait accompli*—Wait. I get it. You're afraid the Royal Commission will turn on *you?"*

"It better hadn't."

"And how the hell am I supposed to help you *there?* Come out for the legalization of drugs?"

"Hell no. That'd kill the business stone dead. The best the Royal Commission can do is cripple it for a while."

"So what's the Greek got to do with all this?"

"He was organizing the underworld to help fight the Commission."

"Fight it? How?"

"In government, Phil, when you can't stop something you can sure as hell slow it down—or misdirect it. Feed the Commission enough palatable meals to keep it happy."

"Serve up your enemies to protect your friends—and consolidate your power."

"You've got it."

"And now the Greek's out of the picture . . . ?"

"He was the only one with enough standing to bring the other gang leaders to the party. Still, we'll manage."

French waved the *Mercury* at McKurn. "They've been running these corruption exposes every day for *weeks.* How can we compete? If we come out too heavily behind you, we could be laughed off the newsstands. We need some ammunition to fight back."

"Like what?" said McKurn.

"Feed us exclusives on some of these 'meals' you're going to serve up."

McKurn smiled. "Good idea. No reason why you can't break a few of them ahead of the cops."

"You need to work on your image. Stand *behind* the Royal Commission. Act like you've got nothing to hide."

McKurn laughed. "And if I have?"

Is the Pope Catholic? French asked himself. "What have you got to lose?"

"You're right, Phil. Go on the offensive."

"Exactly."

French felt his old energy returning. This was not a campaign of his choosing, but it *was* a campaign. *And I'd better protect my backside,* he thought.

The tension of McKurn's presence was ebbing, and he found himself grinning back at his sometime nemesis.

*****

Alison swung her crutches in long strides through the entrance of the Pine Creek Resort. She was vaguely aware of heads turning towards her—the odd sight of a woman on crutches wearing an exquisitely tailored, deep-blue velvety dress with one foot in an army boot. Across the lobby, Derek Olsson's somber face lit up into an insouciant, dimpled smile; from the way he looked at her, she felt they were alone. Alison grinned back—and came to an abrupt halt, the crutches jarring her armpits.

"What happened to you?" she said, staring at the bruise around one of Derek Olsson's eyes, and the faint red marks on a cheek.

Olsson touched his cheek and grinned. "Jessica was pleased to see me."

"Huh?" Alison reached out to touch Olsson's hand. "And your eye?"

"It's a long story."

"How long?"

"It could take all night."

Alison laughed. "Is that an invitation?"

Olsson's cheeks turned a faint pink, and Alison laughed again. "It's been *ages* since I've seen *you* blush." She reached out to touch his waist and tug him closer. Wrapped in the cushion of his arms, she nestled her head on his chest. She sensed the sharp acceleration in the beating of his heart, and held him tighter.

"Many things have changed," Olsson said, a whisper in her ear.

"Yes," she breathed. *"Too* many."

Olsson pulled back slightly, the smile fading from his face. "Alison," he said, the solemn tone of his voice commanding attention, "if I could go back, I would never have gone to Hong Kong."

Alison held his gaze. "And if I could go back," she said, emphasizing her every word, "I would *not* have gone to Canberra."

"That bad?" he said, gently tracing the bandage around her ribs with his fingertips.

"Worse," she said, lost in his soft eyes, welcoming the look that seemed to penetrate to her soul.

Olsson's eyes widened slightly; he whispered, "We have an audience."

Alison laughed. "I'd forgotten." Over Olsson's shoulder, Alison saw two beefy men standing behind him, watching. Behind her, Madge and her two companions—a circle of protection. "Who are those men?" she asked.

"Bodyguards. I decided I shouldn't take any more chances."

"From?"

Olsson touched his bruised eye. "McKurn."

"You too?"

"That's right." Keeping his hand on Alison's waist, Olsson took half a step back. "Perhaps we should continue this in a little more privacy."

Alison grinned. "And I'm famished."

"Your boyfriend?" Madge asked as they all squeezed into the lift.

Alison smiled broadly, her soft eyes turning toward Madge without moving her head nestling on Olsson's shoulder. "That's right."

Madge seemed disappointed, but the expression was so fleeting that Alison decided it was her imagination.

ALISON LAUGHED, ONE HAND holding her ribs where they now ached. "Jessica *slapped* you? Then *hugged* you? *That's* a reaction I can understand. What did you do to the poor girl?"

Startled, Olsson spilled the champagne he was pouring across the remains of their late lunch. Grateful for the interruption, he busied himself pouring two new glasses of champagne. More composed, he carried them to the sofa.

Alison sprawled at one end, gentling him with her eyes as he came towards her. *She looks happy,* Olsson thought—yet, despite her smile, he sensed a new sadness in her eyes.

"Are we celebrating something?" Alison said, sipping her champagne, "or drowning our sorrows?"

Olsson sat down next to her. Close to her warmth. "A bit of both, I'd say."

Outside, grey, roiling clouds were darkening; the pupils of Alison's eyes widened in the dimming light, two dark spots surrounded by misty blue. Olsson wondered if the mist was in her eyes—or his. He admired the peacefulness in her face that he couldn't feel—distracted by a corner of his mind churning over her question about Jessica.

As if sensing his rising nervousness, Alison twined her fingers through his and squeezed his hand softly. "I feel like I'm trapped at the bottom of a dark well, with no way to climb back to the light."

Olsson smiled. "I'm in the well with you—but farther down."

"No," said Alison. "We're together, now."

Olsson nodded. "Yes."

Alison sighed. "I guess it's easier to talk about how to get out of the well than about how we got here."

"You're reading my mind again."

Alison's grin crinkled the skin around her eyes. "I don't need to—you haven't answered my question."

"I—"

Alison stopped him with a slow kiss. "When you're ready," she said. "I suppose it's another long story."

"All part of the same one. It's been a long time."

"Seventeen years since you got on that plane." Alison shrugged. "What's another few days or weeks?"

"I *want* to tell you—but it's hard."

"Because you're not proud of yourself."

"You understand?"

"Oh, yes. Poor Derek—and poor Alison."

The shrill ringing of a phone broke the moment.

"That must be yours," Olsson said. "Shall I get it for you?"

Alison looked across to her handbag on the table and pursed her lips. Then she turned back to Olsson and smiled. "Please. I like it when you wait on me."

Olsson laughed. "You'll have to pay the price, first."

"What price?"

Olsson leaned over and kissed her; they held each other tight long after the phone stopped. Only when Alison released him did he bring her handbag from the table.

"I knew it would be Royn," Alison said. She switched the phone to SILENT mode before slipping it back in her handbag.

Olsson raised his eyebrows. "You're not going to call him back?"

Alison sighed. "He'll want to know whether I'll be back in the office tomorrow. I haven't decided."

"Why *wouldn't* you be there?"

"On Friday, I walked out."

"On Royn? *Why?*"

"He did a deal with McKurn," Alison said, explaining what had happened.

"I see," said Olsson. "Dirty politics."

"To listen to you and Karla, you'd think there's no other kind."

"Is there?"

"Oh yes," said Alison. "But it hardly ever seems to *win*."

"Have you walked away at last? From Royn, Canberra, and everything?"

Alison laughed. "No you don't—it's *your* turn."

"Okay." Taking a deep breath Olsson spoke quickly, "Jessica was kidnapped. I got her free by taking her place."

"Kidnapped?" Alison stared at Olsson, her eyes and mouth frozen wide. Olsson waited for the obvious questions—*Why? Who?*—but Alison only said, "Was she harmed?"

"No. But she was terrified."

"I'll bet. Just one slap? You got off lucky. Is she still living with your mother . . . ?"

Olsson nodded. "My mother—" For a moment, he couldn't breathe. "She's getting worse. Lars visited a couple of weeks ago—the prodigal son returns—and that's all she could talk about. Half the time, she thought *I* was Lars."

"Poor Molly. I wonder if she'll remember me?"

"You made quite an impression, so she might. Did I ever tell you I saw my father? He's now a wino living on the streets." As they talked—about friends, family, memories, and nothing in particular—the sky through the wide windows turned black and rain lashed against the glass. Olsson shivered. "Perhaps I should close the curtains."

"Never mind," said Alison, nuzzling closer. "You stay right here."

When their words subsided, they just leaned against each other, enjoying the comfortable glow of the other's presence, a shield enfolding and protecting them from the storm outside. Whenever a thought of the events that had brought them to this point intruded into Olsson's awareness, he felt his stomach tighten—only to be soothed by the balm of Alison's warmth.

He wanted it to last.

"We could just stay here," he said.

"At the bottom of the well?"

"Yes."

Alison brushed her lips against his ear. "Tempting."

"If only for a few days. . . ." Even as he spoke, Olsson felt the pressure of reality encroaching on the edge of their cocoon of comfort. "I'd just have to call Ross," he muttered, thinking out loud, "and Karla—"

Alison jerked upright, turning to face him. "When you see Karla," Alison said, her voice carrying a hint of warning, "I want to be there."

"You do?"

"She suspects you're involved in the drug trade in some way."

"She does?"

"She told me what she saw in the Sandemans." Alison giggled. "I even tried the hashish she got there—it was really good."

"You did? I'm surprised."

Alison's face clouded. *That's nothing compared to. . . .*

"Are you?" she said.

Olsson stared through the window, feeling the whirl of the storm outside engulfing him through the glass. Slowly, his eyes turned back to Alison, his neck muscles tensing against the impulse to nod. Sensing only compassion and understanding in her expression, he whispered, "Yes."

Alison touched his cheek. "That explains a lot."

Olsson waited, frozen, for questions that never came.

Alison's laugh was an invitation to join her. "No," she said. "I won't ask. I guess it all started in Hong Kong."

"Yes—and no."

"I think I know what you mean," Alison said, remembering her excitement the first time she stepped through the entrance to Parliament House.

She didn't want to think about that. "Derek," she said with sudden inspiration. "We weren't the *only* ones caught by McKurn's cameras. He's been running a blackmail racket." Alison described her visit to Ivan Mettner's office. "There are *hundreds* of other victims, judging by the number of DVDs stacked up there."

"If we could raid it—?"

"Very difficult. You need two sets of codes to get in—and that's just the security I know about. I asked the geek, but I haven't heard back."

"But this *Ivan* has the codes, right? Perhaps we should pay him a visit."

"He's absolutely *terrified* of McKurn," Alison said. "McKurn's got something on him—I've no idea what."

"It's worth a shot." Olsson's voice trailed off. He sank back into the sofa, the pressure of his hand inviting Alison to follow him. "Alison," he said, an unintended hint of pleading in his tone, "I'll miss being at the bottom of the well. With you."

Alison smiled as she cuddled against him. "It's hard to escape the outside world."

"Perhaps we can postpone it—at least, until morning."

"Yes." Alison's response had welled up from somewhere deep inside her, somewhere beyond thought. "But I can't—" *Because of the . . . operation, and other things I can't tell you yet.*

Olsson's hand cradled her rib so gently she barely felt his touch. "How long before this all heals?" he said.

"Another week or so, I think," Alison said. "But the bruises inside—"

Olsson nodded. "They always take much longer."

59 Blowback

ALISON DRIFTED AWAKE, PROMPTED by the slow awareness of her aching ribs. She quelled her instinctive desire to move away from the cause: the pressure of Olsson's arm encircling her, his hand still clasping her breast. She pressed her back closer against his chest, now feeling the faint exhale of his breath on her neck. *This is how I want to wake up every morning.* As she moved, his hand brushed her nipple; she moved her body slightly to slide her breast into the cup of his palm. The sudden thrill from her breast reawakened the longing that had made it so difficult for them to fall asleep the night before. She was poised to roll over, wake him with her hand, and . . .

To hell with doctor's orders.

She sighed as she heard Angie's kindly voice describing the possible complications—and then a very different desire announced itself rather forcefully.

With infinite patience, she moved Olsson's arm, wriggled off the bed, and went to the bathroom. While there, she inspected herself carefully: just a few drops of blood and no pain. That *probably* meant everything was fine.

Donning a hotel dressing gown, she crept—as best she could on crutches—to the door, which creaked as it opened. Olsson stirred, but rolled over without awakening.

The winter sun, low on the horizon, streamed through the windows of the suite's living room. Other than a few scattered clouds, the sky was a clear, brilliant, slowly brightening blue; here and there were white patches of frost glistening in the sunlight. There was no sign of last night's storm. Basking in the warmth of the sun, Alison felt it was an invitation from the outside world for her to return.

But it's so cold outside.

Pivoting away from the windows, she saw the morning papers pushed under the door. She hobbled over, picked them up—and caught herself as she was about to spread them out on the dining table. *It's a habit,* she thought. *A morning ritual . . . and work.*

Instead, she ordered two breakfasts from room service. Sitting down at the dining table to wait, she idly flipped the papers and gasped as she noticed a headline. Automatically, she opened the paper and began to read . . .

ELECTION JOURNAL

"Dump McKurn Movement" fields Senate candidate. Andrew White, a prominent Conservative Party State Councillor, announced he'll be the NSW Senate candidate for the "Dump McKurn Movement."

His campaign slogan: Conservative YES!—McKurn NO!

According to White, "It's disgusting that McKurn is still on the Conservative Party ticket."

The "Dump McKurn" Senate how-to-vote card will be same as the Conservative Party's—with White's name third on the ticket instead of McKurn's. "Conservatives can still vote the party ticket—and express their disgust with McKurn and his back-room shenanigans at the same time."

What made Jake Meldrum run (away)? At the last minute, front-running candidate for ex-PM Kydd's old seat Jake Meldrum pulled out and swung his weight behind Royn's favorite, Barry "Baby Face" Easton. (Even so, Easton only beat Kydd by a nose.)

Meldrum's supporters are livid—"We've been betrayed"—and totally flummoxed—"He was odds-on favorite for the safest seat in the country. He must be insane."

Or, according to whispers going around the electorate, was he bought off?

And what does Meldrum have to say?

Not a squeak.

He's been seen by neither friend nor foe since late Saturday night. Word is he's gone to ground—probably a good idea given that hell hath no fury like a supporter spurned.

It won't be long before they have the full story.

Alison gasped at the page three headline of French's *Mercury: McKurn Backs Royal Commission: "I've Nothing to Hide"*—and laughed as she read the story.

McKurn was up to his old tricks.

In an odd editorial—*Guilty? Till Proven Innocent?*—the Mercury argued that McKurn was being pilloried without trial and without evidence. "Senator McKurn is being unfairly judged in the court of public opinion," the editorial concluded. "If his anonymous accusers have the facts and the guts to make such charges in the proper venue, a court of law, let them come forward. Until that should happen, let us all remember the basic principle of justice, fairness, and decency: the age-old common law principle, innocent until *proven* guilty."

French is supporting McKurn, she concluded, wondering if McKurn had pressured him. *Why does anyone do anything for McKurn?*

The buzz of the doorbell announced the arrival of breakfast. As the waiter finished setting up the table and left, Olsson appeared in a duplicate of her dressing gown, rubbing his eyes. "Ah, good idea." He yawned. "Sleep well?"

"You know better than that."

Standing behind her chair, he leant down and kissed her ear, his hands cupping her breasts. Alison shivered, moving into his embrace. "Derek . . . ." she groaned.

"I know," he said, releasing her and taking the chair beside her. "Is it my fault you're irresistible?"

Alison smiled back. "You're unbearably cheerful this morning."

Olsson laughed. "Why not?" Pointing at the papers he added, "What's happening in the world?"

"Problems."

"For who?"

"Royn, among others."

"Including you?"

Alison sighed. "He needs me."

"But do you need *him?*"

"Gawd!" she said. "Another of your damnable questions. You're back to your normal, infuriating self. I should be pleased . . . I suppose."

"Sorry," Olsson said, the deepness of his dimpled grin signalling that "sorry" was the last thing on his mind.

They ate slowly, prolonging the meal in the mutual awareness that breakfast marked a transition from the night before to the day ahead—a transition neither was quite ready to face. Eventually, it was Alison who broached the subject.

"What are your plans, Derek?"

Olsson shrugged. "I have a new laptop to set up. Some calls to make. Various things to sort out. Here's as good as anywhere. But," he grinned, "I'm in no hurry to start."

"I see." Alison waited for him to return the same question; when he said nothing, she sighed. "I guess I should look after my moral vacuum—at least, until the election is over."

Olsson lifted her hand to his lips, his eyes solemn. "I'll be waiting, Alison."

"Don't make it harder for me, Derek. Be honest. Can *you* just drop everything like that?"

"I—guess not," Olsson conceded.

"Not that I'm asking you to."

Olsson smiled. "Touché."

"Thank you." She pushed herself to her feet. "I need to take a bath," she said. She stood gazing at Olsson, her sapphire eyes now sparkling in the reflected sunlight. "I could use some help," she grinned. "Like to play nursemaid for a while?"

"For as long as you want."

Alison laughed. After all, that certain activities were off-limits didn't mean *everything* was *verboten*.

OLSSON STOOD BY THE hotel entrance watching the car that was taking Alison away. He stood staring at the fork in the road where it disappeared from sight until he could no longer ignore the winter chill penetrating his thin sweater.

It would be simple to get in his car and follow her. *But I, too, have issues to deal with.*

Only when he started to shiver did he trudge slowly back into the warmth of the lobby.

*****

MAJOR PETER MCMURRAY WAS waiting by the gate of the Australian Forces compound in Toribaya with a platoon of military police when a cavalcade of cars and vans pulled up in front. Armed men dressed in a mishmash of uniforms piled out of the two vans and herded half-a-dozen prisoners into the arms of the MPs. Three men stepped out of the center vehicle. McMurray instantly recognized Amtami, the Islamic Purity chieftain, and the short, smiling Uqu who looked, as always, as if he'd just stepped from an air-conditioned office. It took McMurray a few moments to recognize the much taller and older dishevelled Caucasian male awkwardly exiting from the car with Uqu's help: Robin Cartwright.

Cartwright's cheeks were pale and gaunt, his hair unkempt, twelve day's growth of beard obscuring his face, his clothes grubby . . . overall, McMurray thought, he looked more like a wino from the streets of Sydney than the nationally known journalist.

Cartwright had barely stepped two paces when he was suddenly surrounded by the Australian journalists who'd been waiting by the gate.

"How were you treated, Robin?" one asked as cameras flashed and microphones were thrust into his face.

"Tolerably well," Cartwright replied. "But I'm dry as a bone."

The journalists—his regular drinking companions at the hotel bar—all laughed; then the questions tumbled out: "Who kidnapped you?" "How did you escape?" "Did your boss pay the ransom?"

Grinning, Cartwright held up his hands. "Listen, mateys, I've got a hot exclusive and if you think I'm going to share even a tiny piece of it with you, your elevator doesn't run to the penthouse. I'll be happy to talk to you lot in a couple of hours—after I've filed my own story. On one condition: if you want me to talk, I have to be properly lubricated. I've got a lot to catch up on."

"What now then, Robin?"

"A triple scotch, a steak, and a long, hot bath—in that order."

Ignored by the journalists, Amtami and Uqu went up to McMurray. "You realize," he said, glancing at Cartwright, "that you've brought me a bomb that's going to explode both here and in Canberra."

Amtami grinned and nodded his head vigorously like an excited child at Uqu's translation.

"I think, Major," said Uqu, "that's part of his plan."

McMurray laughed. "Please tell him he's a born troublemaker and that I'm very pleased to see him."

Amtami laughed, pumped McMurray's hand—and turned his head away as a photographer snapped a picture.

"Can we offer you and your men some refreshment?" McMurray asked.

Uqu translated Amtami's answer: "He says another time. He won't feel safe until he and his men are well away from Toribaya."

"He'd better get moving, then," said McMurray. "Those journalists will have the story out in fifteen minutes or less, unless—." He turned to the journalists and said, "Listen, guys, like to come in and get your stories out from here? No fighting traffic, and drinks on me."

Most of the journalists trotted towards the gate; a couple held back, looking at McMurray suspiciously. "What's the catch?"

"No catch. And no one listening in, either."

As the last journalist headed for the gate, McMurray whispered to Uqu, "I'll try and get him an hour, but thirty minutes is probably the best I can do."

Amtami held his hand in salute, barked an order to his men, and a few minutes later the convoy accelerated out of sight.

A military ambulance was waiting inside the gate. As a medic took Cartwright's arm he protested, "I'd much rather go to the Officers' Mess than the hospital." But when an attractive nurse came to support him from the other side he put an arm around her shoulder and exaggerated his weakened state.

"Careful, luv," one of the journalists shouted after him, "he's a lecherous old bastard."

"You're just jealous," Cartwright said.

The nurse laughed. "Just wait till Matron gets ahold of him."

*****

Less than five minutes after Alison reached her desk in Parliament House, the door to her office flew open and Anthony Royn strode in. "Thank God you're back. Are you okay, now?"

"Not really, Prime Minister. But I'm here."

"McKurn's slipped, and we got Barry nominated."

Alison was aware that behind the façade of his smile, Royn wanted a sign, from her, of approval. "But," she said, still frowning, "when the story of your deal with McKurn gets out, how will you handle it?"

"You mean it will leak? Surely not."

"The press are already hot on the trail. When Meldrum surfaces, do you think he'll keep his mouth shut?"

"Ah—I guess not. Any suggestions?"

Alison shook her head. "Why don't you put Doug onto it, and give me an hour to catch up with everything?"

"Certainly," said Royn, hesitating before turning back into the corridor.

Alison started sorting through three days' worth of emails and her overflowing in-tray when a new email arrived in her inbox—from Robin Cartwright. "What?" she exclaimed. "He's free?"

Hi Alison: here's advance warning of my column for tomorrow's papers. It should be up on the internet within the hour—Best, Robin.

PS. I'm still after that story! ☺

Alison laughed and quickly replied:

Thanks.

> PS. I'm still after that story! ☺ *Not a chance*

Her smile disappeared when she read his column:

Kidnapped . . . By the Cops!

By Robin Cartwright
Sykes Media exclusive
Monday: **Toribaya, Sandeman Islands**

For the past two weeks, I've been a prisoner of a Muslim terrorist group who threatened to cut off my head if their ransom demands for weren't met.

That's the official story. The reality is very different.

First, these "fanatical Muslims" weren't at all devout. Quite the opposite, spending most of their time drinking beer and whisky and playing penny ante poker—activities that will deny Muslims their 72 virgins, according to the Prophet. Nor did they ever, as far as I could tell, bother about the ritual of praying five times a day, or at any other time.

The farce was revealed when I recognized one of their visitors. I was not, of course, supposed to see him, but my "prison" was a poorly made shack in the slums of Toribaya. It was easy to poke a small hole through the slats so I could see what my kidnappers were up to.

Their visitor was the boss, the master-mind of the operation—a profitable little sideline from his day job as Toribaya's Chief of Police.

That's right, the whole thing was a put-up job.

Why?

It's not always easy to fathom the labyrinthine politics of the Sandemans, but it appears that the "terrorist" group, Islamic Purity, recently helped Australian and Sandeman forces, in a joint operation, to completely destroy a terrorist camp on the westernmost island, Jazeerat el-Bihar.

Off the record, Australian troops involved spoke highly of Islamic Purity. But certain high-ranking Sandeman officers had their noses put out of joint and decided to get even.

So my kidnapping was falsely credited to Islamic Purity.

How can I be so sure?

Simple. *Islamic Purity rescued me*—and served up the kidnappers (minus, unfortunately, the head honcho) to the Australians.

Meanwhile, Sandeman troops have been scouring Jazeerat el-Bihar trying to put Islamic Purity out of business.

A total failure, needless to say, with not a single prisoner (and not much loot, either) to show for their efforts.

"Oh, boy. Talk about *trouble*," she groaned, her mind racing with all the implications. *So much for getting back into things slowly.*

She printed out half-a-dozen copies of Cartwright's article, thumped along the corridor as fast as she could, and burst into Royn's office.

"Cartwright's free," said Melanie.

"I know," said Alison.

"The PM's getting briefed on it now," said Doug Selkirk.

Royn was on the phone; she thrust the article under his nose and passed copies to Melanie and Selkirk.

Royn hung up and said, while skimming Cartwright's article, "Alison, get Paul, Helen, and Victor, on the double."

"Sit down, Alison," Selkirk said. "I'll get Mary onto it."

Alison smiled. "Thanks, Doug."

"Aren't you all overreacting?" Melanie said. "Surely, it's just a rogue cop."

"That's not what Robin implies at all," said Alison.

Royn sighed. "Alison's right. Cartwright is merely confirming what I just heard from Defence. And something Cartwright didn't mention: the Sandeman authorities are hopping mad that they've been left completely out of the loop."

Melanie shrugged. "But it's all happening in the *Sandemans*—"

"What it means," said Alison, "is that we're in bed with a bunch of crooks—and our boys are dying to keep them in power. At least, that's where Nash and the press can take it. If Nash doesn't, the press will."

"Ah," Melanie said, now understanding, "it could be an election issue."

"Exactly," said Royn. "But . . . how can we head it off?"

"Forceful action, darling," Melanie said. "Now is the time to be *seen* to be *decisive.*"

"Worst case," said Selkirk as he returned, "we can bury it."

"How?" said Alison. "Start another war?"

"Alison!" said Royn. "What's come over you?"

Good question, she thought.

*****

KARLA PRESTON WAS RESTLESS. She missed the sedation, now that she was recovered enough to no longer need it: instead of evaporating, time now crawled. If she'd had her druthers, she'd have checked out of the hospital and to hell with the consequences. But the doctors insisted she had to be monitored for a bit longer. "Just a few more days," they said. "It's your *brain* we're talking about, Ms. Preston."

Flicking TV channels for want of something better to do, she suddenly heard a familiar voice: ". . . I'm dry as a bone."

"Robin!" she called in surprise.

As the camera panned back from Cartwright's emaciated face, she saw Uqu talking to Major McMurray and behind them, half-obscured, another very familiar face. . . .

"Mountain Man!" she gasped. "What the hell are *you* doing there?"

What indeed?

Robin had been freed—but by who? How? He hadn't said.

"Your exclusive, eh, Robin? Maybe I can beat you to the punch." Grabbing for her cellphone, she scrolled through her contacts until she reached the number she was looking for.

"Uqu, it's me—Karla. . . ."

Forty-five minutes later, Karla's hospital room was turned into an impromptu recording studio by OlssonPress technicians. When they gave her the thumbs up, she dialled Uqu again. Once he was on the line, the technicians dialled another number, also in the Sandemans, and added a third party to the call.

*****

". . . AND THE TORIBAYA POLICE chief categorically denies Cartwright's accusation," Helen Arkness was saying, her voice coming from a speakerphone.

"Well, *that's* certainly a surprise," said Paul Cracken.

"The prisoners all confirm Cartwright's claim, so I'm told," Victor Bergstrom said from another speakerphone. "But the Sandeman authorities are demanding they be turned over, and we'll have to comply soon: we don't really have any jurisdiction."

"Handed over to whom?" Selkirk asked.

"Well—to the Sandeman police, I guess," Bergstrom said.

Alison wondered: *What would Cartwright—or Karla—say?* She said, "If you do that, they'll never be seen nor heard of again."

"You can't be serious," Royn said.

"There's one way to find out," said Alison. "If I'm right, do you want these five men's death or dismemberment on your conscience?"

"Alison's right," said Cracken. "If that happens, we'll just be giving more meat to the vultures of the press."

"Victor," said Royn, "call the AG and get him—and the military lawyers—to find some legal pretext we can use to keep them out of Sandeman hands." He frowned and shrugged. "I doubt they'll find one. But still—that's what lawyers are for."

"But that won't solve the problem," Melanie said. "How about we. . . ."

Alison, once again, tuned out the conversation. After half-an-hour, the meeting hadn't reached any conclusion, and none seemed to be looming on the horizon. She'd been thinking about something more important. . . . *No sex for two weeks . . . your cervix has been dilated . . . needs time to return to normal . . . danger of complications or an infection.* . . . She decided to visit Dr. Angie early to see if she could negotiate a reprieve from her two week sentence of abstinence. Karla Preston's voice jerked her from her reverie.

Flustered, Mary had come into the room unannounced with a portable radio blaring. "Excuse the interruption, Prime Minister," she said, "but I th-think you really ought to hear this."

Karla's voice, strong despite the tinny sound from the small speaker, flooded the room. ". . . I interviewed Mr. Amtami, the leader of the Islamic Purity group falsely accused of kidnapping Robin Cartwright. He claims that a Sandeman Colonel, Gugamti, was the brains behind Cartwright's kidnapping. The police chief was merely his stooge."

"And you believe this Mr. Amtami was telling the truth?" the interviewer asked, clearly disbelieving that possibility.

"Oh, without a doubt," said Karla. "Amtami is one of the few truly honorable people I met in the Sandemans. Quite the opposite of Colonel Gugamti."

"How can you be so sure?"

Karla briefly described the meeting she'd attended in Inkaya. "Gugamti was ready to kill Amtami there and then. He had to be reminded, forcefully, that he'd given his word of honor to a truce. Even so, Colonel Cantrell—heading the Australian team there—had trouble persuading him to keep his cool."

"What was this Gugamti so upset about?"

"Loss of face, for one thing. The skills of Amtami's soldiers—which even the Australian troops admired—showed up the inferiority of Gugamti's forces. And Amtami's group has wide support within the island of Jazeerat el-Bihar, so it threatens the dominance of the Sandeman authorities."

"But it's a terrorist group, right?"

"So called. But if you talk to the locals, it's the *Sandeman* soldiers who are the terrorists. They regard Islamic Purity as their defenders. Gugamti's attempt to paint Islamic Purity as kidnappers was merely a pretext. While Cartwright was being held captive, Sandeman troops searched the island for Amtami and his men. Who gave the order? Gugamti."

"According to Robin Cartwright, they didn't find anyone or anything."

Karla's deep laugh boomed through the speaker. "Damn right they didn't. Amtami's men are a helluva lot smarter."

"Sounds as if you like this guy. Have you actually met him?"

"Indeed," said Karla. "A month ago, as you may recall, I was captured by Sandeman soldiers. It was Amtami and his men who rescued me and smuggled me out of their clutches."

"From what you've said about the Sandeman soldiers, good for him. Karla, our time's up. If our listeners would like to read the whole interview—"

"—it will be in tomorrow's papers."

"That was Karla Preston on News24/7—all the news, all the time. . . ."

"Thank you, Mary," Royn said handing back the radio. "You were right."

"Thank *you*, Prime Minister," Mary replied, obviously relieved.

"Victor," Royn said. "Is what she said true?"

"I—ah—"

"Find out, *now.*"

"Yes, Prime Minister."

"I've got to run—the press conference, remember?" said Royn, rising to his feet. "Will you keep chewing this over, please. See what you can come up with. I'll be back in an hour."

"What press conference?" Victor asked.

"On the *Sandemans?*" Helen Arkness

"No," Royn said, stopping at the door. "Alison, would you fill them in, please?"

Alison nodded.

"With any luck, the announcement I'm about to make will divert the media's attention," Royn said as he walked out of the office, Selkirk on his heels.

"Don't hold your breath," Alison muttered to herself.

*****

THE LATE AFTERNOON SUN, reflecting from the sheer glass façade, framed in white, of the High Court of Australia, created a pool of warmth in the forecourt against the chill breeze blowing from the lake.

A bevy of reporters congregated on the wide steps, placing lights, TV cameras and other paraphernalia and attaching their microphones to the lectern in front of the building's entrance.

A few minutes before five PM, a limousine pulled up in front and Anthony Royn stepped out. Smiling and chatting with the reporters, Royn strode up the paved ceremonial ramp stretching from the road to the podium, Doug Selkirk in tow.

The entrance doors to the High Court swung open and a thin, grey-haired man blinked as he stepped through into the full force of half-a-dozen powerful arc lights. Drawing his overcoat tighter against the sudden chill, Justice Herbert Flint joined Anthony Royn at the lectern.

Aware of the raw power Flint radiated, the reporters studied Flint's demeanor in breathless silence. Without words, he conveyed the impression of a man entirely comfortable with the authority vested in him to change the course of people's lives—and the nation's—for good or ill. Here, they realized, was a man who, were the death penalty ever reinstated, would don the black cap of justice without a second thought.

"Ladies and gentlemen," Royn said with a sideways glance at his watch—it was five PM, perfect timing for the evening news—"I would like to introduce Justice Herbert Flint, a man with twenty-seven years of outstanding service to our country as a member of the supreme court of our land, the High Court. He will retire at the end of this month—but he's not ready to lay down his gavel and tend to his roses, for which he is also justly famous. On the contrary, he has accepted the burden of far more arduous task: chairmanship of the Special Inquiry into Corruption, colloquially known as the Candyman Inquiry, now in operation under the aegis of the Attorney-General's department. This Inquiry will be transformed into the Royal Commission on Corruption as the first act of the next Parliament. Meanwhile, Justice Flint will have all the wide-ranging powers, the budget, the personnel, *and the independence* of a Royal Commission at his disposal."

Royn turned to Flint. "Justice Flint," he said, "would you like to say a few words?"

Flint stepped up to microphones. "Thank you, Prime Minister. I accept the honor you have bestowed upon me and fully intend to live up to your high expectations. I have spoken with my colleagues on the bench and they all agree that this inquiry *must*, for the good of the country, be completed with the utmost urgency and dispatch. They therefore urged me to take up the appointment *immediately*." Flint turned towards Royn with a happy smile on his face. "I have agreed to do so."

Feeling as if he'd been hit by a physical blow, Royn swayed back from Flint's words; his mouth open in stunned silence as he digested the implications. . . . *Flint will be sitting in judgement while McKurn's on the ticket. . . .*

The flashes of half-a-dozen cameras brought him back to Flint's words.

"By the simple expedient of taking accumulated leave," Flint continued, unaware of Royn's reaction, "I will be able to start my new duties on Thursday of this week."

The picture suddenly cut to Royn's face.

"That's w-wonderful," Royn said, the TV cameras catching his expression in the process of transforming into a grin of delight.

That shot of Royn's face made every evening news program, along with Flint's uncompromising statement, in answer to a reporter's question, "I can assure you, ladies and gentlemen, that I have taken this post on the basis that no one, I repeat, *no one*, is exempt from investigation. Justice will be meted out impartially—and *ruthlessly*."

60   No Sanctuary

DESPITE TEN HOURS OF uninterrupted sleep, Alison had to drag herself out of bed.
"Breakfast?" Madge said cheerfully when Alison finally hobbled into the living room.

"Thanks, Madge. That would be wonderful."

The TV was tuned into *Good Morning Australia*, the volume low. "I hope this didn't disturb you," Madge said.

"Not at all," Alison said, stunned at the face on the screen. "In fact, if you could turn it up."

". . . I was evacuated on a military flight," Robin Cartwright was saying, "for my own safety."

"Along with Mr. Uqumagani," said the host, Rowena Watson. "Would you introduce him to our viewers?"

Cartwright grinned. "Uqu, as he is known, was the liaison between Amtami—the Islamic Purity leader—and the Australians." Turning to Uqu, he added, "How did you describe your work?"

"Helping Australian businessmen negotiate the sliding interface between two incompatible cultures."

"Incompatible cultures?" Rowena repeated. "So could you make sense of Robin's kidnapping for us?"

"Certainly. The Sandeman army came into being only a few years ago. It has even more power than the police—not to mention the opportunities for graft from purchases of expensive military equipment—"

"Graft?" asked Rowena.

"Of course," said Uqu. "In the Sandemans, five percent and usually lots more of *every* dollar spent by the government ends up in someone's pocket."

Rowena appeared to be about to say something, but was stopped by Uqu's matter-of-fact tone of voice. He spoke as if he was stating the incontrovertibly obvious, like, "the sun is shining today."

Uqu continued, "The political families fought tooth and nail to get *their* representatives the plum appointments—say, colonel and up. So the Sandeman army reflects the tribal character of the country: each command is its own little fiefdom. Think of it this way: groups of private militias all wearing the same uniform."

"But isn't the *Australian* army training Sandeman soldiers?"

"The rank and file. The higher ups are all *political* appointments. Whatever military training they have is on-the-job experience—which they try to avoid as their prime interest is not defending the country but protecting their political positions and feathering their own nests."

"It takes an Australian soldier twenty-odd years to work his way up the ranks to colonel or general," Cartwright said. "In the Sandeman army it's who you know."

"And *what* you know is irrelevant," said Uqu.

"Okay," Rowena said, "but Robin says the chief of *police* was behind his kidnapping. How does the army come into the picture?"

"The police chief was just the fall guy," Uqu said. "The brain behind it was the officer Karla Preston mentioned in her column, Colonel Gugamti—"

"A *political* appointment?" Rowena said.

"Right. Gugamti's only military experience was playing with toy soldiers as a kid. He knows it, and he knows his troops know it. They treat the *Australians* as exemplars, not him. The Australians pushed him *against his will* to cooperate with the separatist group, Islamic Purity. Islamic Purity is a competitor for power and loot in his unit's operational area—*his* fiefdom. Remember that in the Sandemans, anyone who's *not* a member of your tribe or your clan is fair game. On top of that, Amtami's men *trained his troops* and Australian soldiers in jungle craft."

"Trained them to do what?" Rowena asked.

"Mainly, to move around the jungle in the dark without making a sound. The Australians loved it, by the way. So now, who do the Sandeman troops admire more: Gugamti or Amtami?"

"Amtami, I imagine."

"Exactly. To get rid of Amtami and his men, Gugamti arranges for Robin to be kidnapped so Islamic Purity can be blamed, giving him a pretext to wipe them out. Except he couldn't find them."

"Then," Cartwright said, "Amtami rescues me, I blow the lid on the story—"

"—and Gugamti must be apoplectic," said Uqu. "The only handy target for his anger was *me.*"

"So you left," said Rowena.

"Exactly. I'm not very popular in Toribaya right now. If I stayed there, I doubt I'd live to see my grandchildren."

After a pregnant pause, Rowena said, "Thank you, gentlemen." The camera zoomed in on her, the background changing to a slow motion replay of Royn's crestfallen expression from his press conference with Flint. "Coming up next, what sent PM Anthony Royn into a state of shock yesterday? Our Canberra correspondents will join us, after the break. . . ."

Simple enough, Alison thought, flicking the TV off, *if you know the full story.*

She turned on her phone to find two missed calls from Doug Selkirk.

"Alison," Selkirk said when she called back, "do you know anything about this McKurn and Meldrum business?"

"What did Royn tell you?" Alison asked.

"Only that he switched from 'dump McKurn' to backing him—not that *he* told me."

So Royn didn't have the guts to tell the truth. She took a deep breath. "I can tell you—on one condition. You know nothing about it."

"Got it."

"Blackmail."

"McKurn? He's blackmailing *Royn?*"

"McKurn's got something that could blow Royn out of the water." *The truth, but not the whole truth.*

"What the hell's he done? What's his *secret?*"

"Doug, that's all I can tell you. McKurn figured he was going be heaved off the Senate ticket so he threatened Royn. Under pressure, Royn agreed to switch. McKurn threw Meldrum to the dogs as part of the deal."

"It sucks, but—" Alison could imagine Selkirk shrugging "—no wonder. I don't know about you, Alison, but this is one of those times I'd rather be selling something wholesome, like junk food or second-hand nappies."

"I know exactly what you mean, Doug."

As she put her phone down it beeped: a message.

Want to join me with Karla this eve?—Love, Derek.

I'll need a pretext to go to Sydney, she thought. *I'll find one,* and answered: Yes.

She chatted with Madge for a few minutes, and then turned to the papers while she picked at her breakfast. . . .

ELECTION JOURNAL

Royn blots his copybook? Last week, Royn and the Conservative Party were so far ahead in the polls that it hardly seemed worth holding an election.

A Conservative walkover doesn't look quite so likely now—and Royn has only himself to blame.

An enthusiastic supporter of the "Dump McKurn" movement, Royn changed his tune at the last minute. Having campaigned hard to persuade selectors to drop McKurn, he turned around and strong-armed them to switch their vote *back to* McKurn. "The hell with him," said more than one selector.

Another rumor: Royn somehow persuaded Jake Meldrum to drop out of the race in the former PM's super-safe seat at the very moment he was about to trump both Kydd and Royn's pet, Barry Easton.

The result: a movement among some CP branch leaders to run Meldrum—or even Kydd—as an independent against Easton.

The party faithful are aghast that McKurn is still on the NSW Senate ticket. Meanwhile, party hacks are grumbling about Royn's high-handed manner, and there's a growing sentiment that Randolph ("Sour Grapes") Kydd is right: Royn doesn't have what it takes.

The CP is still ahead in the polls, but its lead no longer looks impregnable.

Alison sighed. At that moment, travelling the few miles to Parliament House felt as appealing and as difficult as climbing a vertical cliff. She decided to have her rib and foot checked. *And I could see Dr. Angie at the same time.*

*****

GURUNDI STOOD ON THE wide, marble steps of Parliament House, positive every passer-by could hear the sound of his knees knocking.

He waited for the last of the group of schoolchildren to reach the door of the small foyer holding the metal-detector. His nose wrinkled in distaste at the young girls' uncovered knees, arms and faces, their breasts budding through their uniforms, not even segregated from the boys with whom they were flirting shamelessly.

Yet at the same time, he smiled inwardly at what lay ahead.

He looked around, expecting people to be staring at him. Nobody was taking any notice. He remembered the camera hanging around his neck, brought it to his eye and took a couple of snapshots like any other tourist. He swung around as if to take a picture of the broad avenue that pointed to the War Memorial across the lake. He saw the man he knew only as Ahmed, a stone's throw away, turning his back to the camera.

He needn't have bothered, Gurundi chuckled. Ahmed had given him the cheap, throwaway camera and told him it had no film.

Ahmed had met him at Sydney airport and shepherded him everywhere ever since. Just as well. Gurundi got lost in the terminal until a friendly Sandeman traveller guided him through. And with his limited English, Gurundi had trouble picking out the handful of words he thought he knew from the midst of the alien Australian babble.

"Where do the poor people live?" Gurundi asked as Ahmed drove past house after house in an outer Sydney suburb, each with a garden, a TV antenna on the roof, and a car, sometimes two, in the driveway.

"Here," Ahmed answered.

"Impossible," Gurundi muttered. These houses didn't look that much smaller than the ones in the gated village where the Toribaya rich lived. Thinking of the Toribaya shanty he'd just left, he asked, "Where are the shanty towns?"

"There aren't any."

The long drive to Canberra along perfect roads, nary a pothole in sight, was even worse. Scattered trees, cattle and sheep were lost in the almost empty fields that stretched from horizon to horizon. The enormous expanse of the country frightened him; he yearned for the close, pleasing cover of jungle.

And, from what he'd heard, America was ten times bigger.

The world was definitely a hostile place.

Gurundi sensed from the first that "Ahmed" wasn't his guide's—minder's—real name, that he wasn't who he seemed. Clues like his perfect teeth, carefully trimmed hair, and the not-quite-hidden way he viewed Gurundi as a peasant even as he tried to treat him like a colleague, were all confirmed the first time they went through the metal detector at Parliament House: "Ahmed," dressed like Gurundi in cheap jeans and an old sweater against the unfamiliar cold, deposited a gold Rolex watch in the tray.

Gurundi shrugged. "Ahmed" would eventually meet his fate: Allah would see to that. Meanwhile, he was just Allah's tool.

The last schoolgirl disappeared inside, no other visitors behind her.

It was time.

He held himself steady against the desire to fall to his knees, salaam and pray. Instead, he turned towards Mecca and silently thanked Allah for saving him from the soldiers in the jungle and guiding him to the comrades in Toribaya who offered him the chance he was about to take.

Taking a deep breath, he walked towards the entrance for the third and, he knew, last time. At the doorway he paused and looked back. Ahmed grinned at him, lifting one hand in salute.

Once, Ahmed had told him, the imposing entrance doors were always wide open. Now closed, except on special occasions, all visitors had to pass through security in a small ante-room to one side.

He was sure the three policemen manning the metal detector knew why he was there. He hesitated, but they just smiled at him and beckoned him in. Gurundi grinned back, knowing their smiles wouldn't last long.

He took off his watch, and emptied his pockets of some small change and a set of keys—"So you'll look like everyone else," according to Ahmed. Finally, he pulled the old man's crucifix from under his shirt and dropped it and its brand-new metal chain in the tray. Relieved at last of that burden he felt lightheaded, his feet barely touching the floor.

He smiled at the policeman who said something he didn't understand, but he nodded at the wave of the man's hand and walked lightly to the archway of the metal detector.

The alarm beeped.

His heart pounding in his ears, Gurundi stopped in surprise, patting his pockets.

Two of the policemen stood on the other side of the metal detector's conveyor belt. One of them sighed, picked up the hand wand and beckoned to him. "Over here, mate," he said.

Gurundi only understood the word "mate," but nodded and took the two slow, practiced steps to the end of the conveyor belt, barely noticing the tray with his possessions now at his side.

The policeman took a step towards him, his arm pointing to where he wanted Gurundi to stand.

Gurundi ran.

He ran up the steps into the spacious lobby of Parliament House. The schoolchildren were bunched at the bottom of the stairs across the lobby leading to the viewing galleries above.

Gurundi ran towards them.

Klaxons suddenly deafened him.

Behind him he could hear the steps and panting of the policemen chasing him.

From behind a counter to his left, a security guard's head spun between Gurundi and his pursuers; after a split-second's indecision he sprinted around the counter and barrelled towards him.

Someone was yelling "Get down!" Another voice, "Get back! Get out of the way."

The schoolchildren were shrieking in confusion. Some stood looking at him, their mouths gaping; others backed away.

Only a few more meters and Gurundi would be in their midst—but he knew he wouldn't make it.

That didn't matter.

The security guard reached Gurundi and brought him down with a rugby tackle. A moment later one of the policemen landed on top of him.

As Gurundi fell to the floor time stopped, the schoolchildren frozen in front of him. He grinned at them.

"Allahu Akbar!" he shouted and squeezed the button in his pocket.

*****

Anthony Royn, Paul Cracken, Melanie, and Doug Selkirk sat in Royn's office looking at one another in silence. Their faces mirrored the dark sense of gloom they all felt gathering around them.

"I can't see any way to avoid it, Prime Minister," Doug Selkirk said. "The Sandemans is blowing up in our faces again, thanks to Cartwright. And the press are onto the story that you switched a hundred and eighty degrees to backing McKurn. It will be all over the place in the morning—and probably a helluva lot sooner."

"What can I *do?*" Royn said, failing to fully suppress the whine in his tone.

Selkirk shook his head. "You can't deny it, and trying to explain it would only make it look worse."

"If we could only bury it somehow," Cracken said, without hope.

"Maybe we can," Royn said, now pacing back and forth behind his desk, waving his arms with excitement. "Some outfit in the Sandemans is growing marijuana and smuggling it into Australia. If we could—"

Whatever Royn was about to add was lost in the ear-shattering blast of klaxons sounding throughout Parliament House.

Royn froze; Cracken and Selkirk sprang to their feet. "What the hell is that?"

The door burst open and the Prime Minister's security chief burst in, two policemen behind him.

"Ah, Prime Minister. Please stay right here while we secure the area."

"Why, George? What's going on?" Royn demanded.

"An explosion in the lobby.."

"An *explosion?* Was anybody hurt?" Royn asked.

"We don't know yet, sir."

Royn stepped towards the door; George was blocking the doorway and did not move. He held up his hand and said, in a sergeant major's voice, "Prime Minister! Please! My job is to ensure your safety. I can only do that if you all stay right here."

Royn came to a halt. "Yes, of course," he mumbled. "I just want to know what happened."

"As soon as I know anything, I'll tell you. I'll be back shortly."

George turned on his heel and closed the door firmly behind him. He returned a couple of minutes later. "Everything's locked up, and there's no sign of anyone in the courtyard area."

"Any news?" Royn asked.

"The public areas are being cleared and we're cordoning off Parliament House. More police are coming—"

"And ambulances?" said Royn, pacing around the office as if he felt like he was in a cage.

"On the way, sir. When we're sure it's safe, we'll move you out of here."

They waited in an uncomfortable silence broken only by the buzz of George's radio earpiece. He repeated the fragments of information as they came in. "Several schoolchildren are injured . . . two seriously . . . two policemen hurt . . . no, *dead.* . . . it was a suicide bomber!"

"A *what?*"

"Suicide bomber?" Melanie repeated.

Royn was vaguely aware of Melanie's odd tone of voice, but his attention was focused on his security chief. "Just one? Or are there others?"

George listened to his earpiece. "Just one, sir. No one else in sight. As far as we know, Prime Minister."

Royn sat down. "George—one person, acting alone, who's now dead. I'd say I'm perfectly safe here, wouldn't you think?"

"Just the same, Prime Minister—"

"If you're still worried, put some extra guards around this office."

"If you *insist,* sir."

"I do," Royn said—and grinned. "I'll put it in writing, if you insist."

George smiled. "That won't be necessary, sir."

"One other thing. I want to go and see what happened and provide some comfort, if I can. As soon as possible."

"Yes, sir," George said. "I'll go and arrange it."

Melanie waited till George had closed the door. "That's a good idea, darling. I *know,* it's a *tragedy.* It's *terrible.*" Melanie injected compassion into her voice, her attempt convincing nobody. "But don't you see? Now we *can* smother it."

"That's right," Cracken said, his voice cool. "McKurn. The Sandemans. Anything else you like."

Cracken was looking at Melanie in appreciation, Royn noted. *Like they were made for each other.* He suddenly wondered if he really knew the woman he had married. He shook his head, dismissing the thought before it could register.

"My God," said Selkirk, aghast. "This is a *tragedy* and all you can think of is *politics?*"

"We have to do *something*," said Cracken, giving Selkirk a withering glance, "to avert *another* such tragedy—and discover how this one was allowed to happen."

"Like what?" Royn asked, the marijuana fields temporarily forgotten.

"It would appear—without prejudging anything," Cracken said choosing his words with care, "that there's a big hole in our security procedures. Somehow, someone got into Parliament House carrying explosives. That should never have happened. How did he get into the country? If he's not a local, of course. If he *is* a local, how come none of the police or security forces got wind of the plot? You see what I'm getting at?"

"Not really," said Royn. "Review our security—"

"Much more than that, Tony," said Cracken. "*Overhaul* security. We *must* have the laws on the books that give our police the necessary powers to stop such attacks long before they happen. Do we? Let's get the AG and whoever else we need here right now."

"Paul, that's *perfect*," said Melanie, almost squealing with delight.

"Melanie!" Royn's voice was that of a parent scolding an unruly child. Selkirk's face mirrored Royn's look of incomprehension. For an instant, Cracken's lips curled with a hint of contempt.

"We must do whatever is necessary," Cracken said.

"To improve security?" Selkirk asked. "Or to win?"

Cracken shrugged. "What's the difference?"

There was a knock on the door, and George came in. "If you'd like to come now, sir," he said.

Royn rose awkwardly to his feet, surprised he had to support himself with one hand to find the strength.

"And you need to make some kind of appearance on TV tonight," said Melanie.

Royn nodded. "I guess so."

Royn slowly drew himself to his full height, his expression changing as though he was choosing which one to wear. After a moment, he took a deep breath and said, "I'm ready. Let's go, George."

"Break a leg," said Melanie.

Royn smiled and started for the door. "You should come along too, Paul. Good for your image."

As he strode along the corridor, Cracken a couple of paces behind, he reminded himself: *Politics is just a stage.*

If that's true, then who's the real audience?

*****

AROUND THAT TIME, A short item came across newswires:

> SYDNEY, TODAY: The NSW Attorney-General's Department announced it has cancelled the NSW government contract with Paper Supplies Pty. Ltd. for unspecified irregularities and has directed the government to put the contract for stationery supplies up for rebid. Paper Supplies Pty. Ltd. is barred from participating.

In most newsrooms, the deluge of reports on the carnage in Parliament House smothered it.

With a couple of exceptions.

*****

"Derek!" Karla shouted with delight, as Olsson walked into her hospital room, Alison a step behind him. "How wonderful." She stretched her free arm out to him.

"Don't get up," Olsson grinned, leaning in to her embrace and kissing her on the cheek.

"I didn't take your warning seriously enough," Karla said.

"I'm . . . sorry," Olsson said. "I could have *been* there—"

"—and have *you* dead, *too?*" Karla said.

"Probably," Olsson admitted, gently disengaging from Karla's embrace. "I took the liberty of bringing you some things from your apartment." He motioned to the bag on the chair. "Some clothes, *and*—" He pulled a cookie jar from the bag.

"Oh, Derek, you're so thoughtful," Karla said with a laugh. "Better keep those hidden. Wouldn't do for the nurses or the cleaning lady to sample them. Hi, Alison. What happened to your crutches?"

"The doctor gave me this instead." Alison waved the walking stick she had acquired that afternoon.

Noticing that Alison was looking wistfully at the cookie jar, Karla said, "You're welcome to some, if you like."

"Please."

"Who were your visitors?" Olsson asked. Half-a-dozen people were filing out of Karla's room when he and Alison arrived. "They looked like students."

"Most of them are," Karla grinned. "They're a bunch of libertarians who've started a political party. I'm their main advisor." Karla shrugged. "Probably won't amount to much, they're all wet-behind-the-ear idealists. But," she chuckled, "you'll never guess what it's called."

"The party?" Olsson asked. "I give up."

"MYOBB," said Karla.

"My *what?*" Alison asked.

Karla chuckled. "It's short for the Mind Your Own Bloody Business Party."

"What a name," Alison laughed.

"Interesting," said Olsson.

"Right," said Karla. "It doesn't label them, doesn't put them in a convenient box so they can easily be dismissed. We hope."

"You've been giving them ideas, eh?" said Olsson.

"Yes. They even asked me to be a candidate."

Alison laughed. "You turned them down, of course."

"Actually," Karla said, wriggling against some discomfort, "not yet."

"Karla Preston knocking on doors and kissing babies," Alison said between fits of giggling. "What a picture."

"Two excellent reasons to say 'No.' Still," she said wistfully, "it could be fun—so long as I don't win."

"No chance of that," Alison said. "Third parties aren't in the race—so why even consider standing?"

"Because Karla likes arguing with people," Olsson said.

"How true," Alison said. "Nominations close on Thursday, so you've got two days to make up your mind."

"Do you think I should?"

"Speaking as Royn's political advisor, no."

Karla laughed. *"That's* the best argument I've heard for saying *yes."* Karla's eyes swivelled to the TV. "Wait!" she said, turning up the volume.

A somber Anthony Royn sat at a desk, a wall of books behind him.

"That's a studio, not his office," Alison said.

Royn's eyes were steady, fixed, giving each of millions of viewers the sense Royn was looking at and talking directly to each of them—individually.

"Tragedy struck right here in Parliament House this afternoon, when a suicide bomber tricked his way past security. Not for long. But, unfortunately, long enough. Two policemen died valiantly, throwing themselves on the bomber and so averting an even worse tragedy. As it is, two innocent children are in critical condition—" a tear rolled down Royn's check; he paused to wipe his eyes with a handkerchief.

"He's hamming it up for all he's worth," said Karla.

Alison nodded. "True," she said. "But he's a softie. Those tears are real."

"Can you always tell?" Karla asked.

"Most of the time."

"I'm sorry," Royn said, the picture cutting to the Parliament House lobby as Royn continued speaking, "but it's impossible to think of what happened without choking up—and feeling immense anger." The camera panned quickly over the bodies of two policemen lying on top of a third body, lingering barely long enough for the viewer to register that the bodies were not whole, to rest on blood-spattered children crying and shrieking; Royn was assisting a medic to lift one child on to a stretcher.

". . . so we're completely overhauling all our security procedures," Royn concluded, "and I'm calling a special session of Parliament next week to pass a new anti-terrorism bill to give police, immigration, customs, and other officials all necessary powers to ensure that an outrage like the one in our nation's capital today can never happen again, anywhere in our vast land.

"We are rightly known as the 'Lucky Country.' But there are times like these when Lady Luck needs a helping hand. That is exactly what I, and my government, pledge to provide you."

Royn paused, and slowly clasped his hands together.

"I ask you to now join me in a minute of silence, to pray, if you will, for the complete recovery of the injured children, the souls of the valiant policemen—and for the resolve we will all need for the fight ahead."

Royn bowed his head; ten seconds short of a minute, the picture began to slowly dissolve, first losing focus, the colors then fading until the screen went dark.

"Impressive," said Karla. "And he just picked up the God vote, too."

"You're a cynic, Karla," said Olsson.

"He's an actor," Karla said.

The screen slowly faded back to life. "That," the announcer said, her words soft, "was the Prime Minister, Mr. Anthony Royn." There was a touch of reverence in her voice, as if to acknowledge that Royn was, indeed, the leader he wanted to be.

"And in related news," the announcer continued, her pace picking up, "the suicide bomber has been identified—"

Karla gasped as a fuzzy picture, probably from a passport or similar document, came onto the screen.

"—as a Sandeman imam named Gurundi. He arrived in Sydney five days ago. . . ."

"What an arsehole that man is," Karla said.

"You *know* him?"

"Damn right I do. The snake." Snapping the TV off, she briefly summarized her encounter with Gurundi in Inkaya, "and *he's* the one who tipped off the Sandeman army that I was there."

Olsson grinned. "That's a great story. Want to write it up?"

"Sure. Tomorrow." Karla's smile evaporated as she turned to Alison. "This anti-terrorism bill—what's Royn talking about? A police state? Warrantless arrest? Indefinite detention? *Torturing* suspects?"

"I wouldn't be surprised," Alison said. "But I don't really know."

"Shouldn't you be there instead of here?" Karla asked.

"Probably," Alison said. "But I had a doctor's appointment this afternoon. Tonight, as far as they're concerned, I'm visiting my sick mother."

"Who's in perfect health I take it?"

Alison grinned. "I have no reason to doubt it."

"Goofing off, Alison?" Olsson chuckled. "That's not like you."

"You know why."

For a fleeting moment, Karla glimpsed the way Alison and Olsson looked at each other. A tiny tear appeared in the corner of one eye. She turned away. Olsson began to rise; Alison stopped him with a hand and went to sit beside Karla.

"I remember what I told you," Karla said, trying to grin, "but my head doesn't completely rule my heart."

"Not even yours?" Alison asked softly.

"Not even mine."

Silently, Alison passed her a tissue.

"I'll be okay, Derek," Karla said as she dried her eyes. "In time. I've always known that, one day, you and Alison would be together again. But I'm going to miss you, just the same."

"Karla, I—"

"Derek, don't."

"I shouldn't have come," Alison said.

"Sooner is always better than later," Karla said, taking her hand. "I'm glad you're here, but *why?*"

"Because, I said I wanted to be present when—"

"Oh, yes," Karla said.

Now, it was Olsson who felt excluded. "What are you two cooking up?" he asked.

Karla turned to him, her expression now serious. "Uqu was here this morning—"

"Uqu?" Alison asked. "The guy on TV with Cartwright?"

Karla nodded. "My guide in the Sandemans. I asked him a few questions about *you,* Derek. Which he refused to answer. But his body language—he *squirmed.*"

"I see," said Olsson.

"He works for you, Derek—"

"InterFreight," Olsson said.

"*And* InterFreight," Karla said, challenging Olsson to correct her.

"The *Sandemans?*" Alison said to Olsson. "InterFreight has business there?"

Karla quickly responded, "A *little.* But that's not Uqu's main focus, is it, Derek?"

Olsson said nothing.

"Know where the hash for those cookies came from, Alison?" Karla said.

"You told me. The Sandemans."

"Right. From the village of Inkaya. There's a marijuana plantation there, along with a hash factory and everything—"

"I know," Alison said.

"You *do?*" Karla and Olsson both said. Karla's gaze honed in on Olsson's face; Olsson held himself rock steady against her invasive scrutiny.

"Some of our soldiers identified the plants," Alison said. "The information reached Royn."

"How did our 'Drug Czar' react?" Olsson asked.

"He was furious."

"I'll bet," Olsson grinned.

"So, Derek, you know what I'm talking about," Karla said. It was not a question.

"I'm . . . aware of it, yes."

"Just *aware?*" Karla said.

Alison was watching Olsson's discomfort through narrowed eyes.

"You're evading the question, Derek," Alison said.

"What question?"

"Are you involved in the drug trade?"

Olsson hesitated.

"Yes or no?" said Alison.

"I—"

"Anything less than an emphatic *No,*" Karla said, a growing anger in her voice, "is admitting you *are.*"

Olsson shot back, "I thought you were in favor of *legalizing* drugs."

"I am. The problem right now is they're *illegal*—"

"They shouldn't be."

"That's not the point, Derek, and you damn well know it."

"What is, then?"

"Stop playing cat and mouse," Karla said. "I need answers. Honest ones. They're the only kind worth having, you know."

"I know," Olsson sighed.

"Let's talk about Uqu. He works for you, and he knows everything about the marijuana business in Inkaya. He knew everyone there, and everyone knew *him.* The marijuana is shipped out on fishing boats and transferred, in mid-ocean, to another boat—"

"How can you be so sure of all this?" Olsson asked.

"I was smuggled out on a boat, which rendezvoused with another boat in the middle of nowhere. That's not the point. What I want to know is: *are you involved in this?*"

Olsson shrank away from the force of Karla's words but, once again, failed to answer.

Karla shook her head sadly as she said, "I see."

"What do you see?" Alison asked.

"He's answered the question by failing to answer it."

Alison reached out to take Olsson's hand. "Please tell me, Derek," she said, her voice soft, her gaze compassionate, "whether you're involved in this marijuana business?"

Feeling her warmth, sensing that she was not about to sit in judgement upon him, Olsson nodded. "Yes," he said, his voice hoarse.

"The part of you that's hidden," Alison said, gently squeezing his hand.

"Hidden?"

"Yes, Derek." Karla's voice was commanding, penetrating. "Parts of you have been off-limits all the time I've known you—and now we know why."

"Since you came back from Hong Kong," Alison said.

Olsson half turned to Karla, swung back to Alison, and nodded slowly at her words. Karla's voice, now louder and demanding cut into this thoughts.

"What sort of company have you been keeping?"

"What do you mean?" Olsson said.

"You know *exactly* what I mean. Drugs are *illegal.* You're in the drug business dealing with criminals. You can't avoid it. You can't avoid the violence that comes with the territory."

"There are *non*-violent ways," said Olsson.

"Derek, you were spirited out of the prison van taking you to court. A couple of days later you were free—and half-a-dozen gangsters were dead. That's non-violent?"

"No," Olsson groaned. "It was . . . self-defence. I was, ah, captured by members of the Golden Dragon Triad. Vincent Leung, the man I was falsely accused of murdering, was head of the Sydney branch. The supreme boss was convinced, like the police, that I was guilty. He decided to take his own vengeance."

"But you escaped. How?"

"I was rescued."

"Rescued. *Who* rescued you—your *own* gang?" When Olsson said nothing, Karla snapped, "Or was it the Tooth Fairy?"

"No," Olsson sighed, shuddering at the memory.

"What's wrong, Derek?" Alison said, concern in her voice.

"It was terrible. The bodies—"

"It comes with the territory," Karla said. "Violence and death are *inevitable."*

"What happened to your motto, Derek?" Alison said. "Do no harm."

"The law of the jungle," Olsson muttered.

"Have you *ordered* violence?" Karla said. "And people died?"

Olsson slowly nodded.

Karla gazed at him, her eyes wide. "Have you killed someone *yourself?"*

Olsson shied away from Karla's gaze to study the patterns on the floor. "Yes," he whispered, "I did."

"With your own hands?" Karla said.

Olsson nodded.

Alison said suddenly, "So did I!"

"What?" Karla and Olsson said simultaneously.

"I had an abortion."

"You did what?" Olsson asked, now fully focused on Alison.

"That's different," said Karla, nodding approvingly.

"Is it?"

"It's just a bunch of cells—"

"So are *you,* Karla," Alison said. "So are *all* of us."

"It wasn't *conscious.* Wasn't yet a human being."

"It had the *potential*—"

"So does a sperm and an egg."

"That's ridiculous, Karla. What about a brainless cretin who will *never* become a full human being? No potential? Let's put it out of its misery."

Olsson's head twisted from Alison to Karla and back as their words heated up. He was aware of the pressure of Alison's hand gripping his, and that he'd shifted slightly closer to her so their bodies touched, as if to communicate his support.

"That would be—" Karla stopped in mid-sentence.

"Murder," Alison said.

"But—it's your body—"

"Of course it is. I can do what I like with it. But a fetus is *not* part of my body. It's a separate biological entity, the result—in this case—of my own freely chosen decision. Surely you, of all people, believe you should take responsibility for the consequences of your own actions? Nothing you can say, Karla, will absolve me from feeling I *have* committed murder. I've been through all the arguments and it's no good. When does life begin—conception or birth? Somewhere in between? If there's a dividing line, where is it? If there is one, it disappears when a baby can be raised in an artificial womb—from *conception*. A fetus is dependent for its sustenance on others? So is a one-day-old baby. So are most teenagers, for that matter. Only *before* conception is there no life—for *certain*."

"Alison," Karla said, "you're condemning yourself more harshly than anyone else ever could."

"You think I don't know it?"

Olsson stepped into the pause. "Alison," he said, now clasping her hand with both of his.

"Derek, don't ask!" Alison was breathing heavily; she backed away slightly, eying him through the tears streaming unnoticed down her cheeks. Seeing he was shaking his head, reacting to the sense of understanding in his eyes, she felt herself relaxing.

Olsson reached for the box of tissues near Karla's bed. "Tell Karla about your mother," he said softly, as he offered her the tissues.

Alison nodded, gripping his hand again after she had dried her cheeks. "My mother had I don't know how many miscarriages before I was born," she said, turning to Karla, her words now slow and gentle. "When she carried me, the doctors warned her that pregnancy was a sentence of death. They advised abortion. Even Dad thought about it. If they'd followed the doctors' advice, *I wouldn't be here.*"

"I didn't know," Karla whispered.

"Karla, if you could travel back in time to before I was born, what would you advise my mother to do?"

Karla's head fell deep into the pillow, her mouth hanging open in a wide "O." A moment passed before she could say, her voice almost a cry, "M-my God, Alison. What sort of a question is that?"

Alison's hand clenched Olsson's so hard it hurt. He looked at her reassuringly, but she didn't see him. She was staring at Karla, her mouth frozen, as if in shock at her own words. Olsson spoke into the unbearable silence:

"Karla," he said softly, "I killed a gangster. A Hong Kong triad leader. Drugs, prostitution, extortion, smuggling, money laundering, theft, fencing, murder—you name it, he was guilty of it."

"You know this for a fact?"

"Yes."

"*How?*"

"I knew him well," Olsson said, raising his voice a little to pre-empt the words forming on Karla's lips. "I was snatched from the prison van by *his* men. After I escaped he kidnapped my sister, Jessica. He threatened to send my mother bits of her, starting with an ear or a finger—"

"He *what?*"

"That's the kind of animal he was, Karla. Willing to torture a total innocent to get what he wanted: *me.* Could I sit back and let him carve up my sister? Of course not. I traded her freedom for my captivity, knowing full well I'd be lucky to be alive twenty-four hours later."

A look of horror "You *willingly*—" Her voice trailed to a stop.

"Willingly? Hardly. But if anything had happened to Jessica—" Olsson shook his head. *"You*, Karla, taught me there's a big difference between the *illegal* and the *immoral*. Taking the law into my own hands was *illegal*. But was it immoral? I don't think so. Just the same—" Olsson looked at the hand that had squeezed Luk Suk's throat "—I *feel* guilty. Guilty as hell." His body shook as he spoke. "No one, *no one* should have that power of life and death over another human being."

Their attention was distracted by a sharp knock on the door and the entrance of the ward sister.

"Miss Preston," the sister said in reaction to the expression on Karla's face. "Too much stress is bad for you right now. I don't know what you've been discussing—" she delivered a black look in a sideways glance to Alison and Olsson "—but it's late and visiting hours have been over for some time."

Alison began to push herself up, but the strength had fled from her legs. Olsson had to support her as she hobbled over to Karla and embraced her.

"I didn't mean to—" Karla said, tears in her eyes.

"Nor did I."

"I'm going to have to think hard about what you said." As Karla spoke, her gaze widened to include Olsson as well.

"I just wish I could *stop* thinking about it," Alison said.

"So," Olsson said, looking directly at Karla, "do I."

After a moment, Karla turned her head away from him.

"There's one other thing, Karla," Alison said. "Rightly or wrongly, Derek can claim self-defence. I can't."

Karla's eyes were moist. "I—I need some time to myself," she said.

Alison leaned over and kissed her gently on the forehead. "I'll be in touch."

ALISON AND OLSSON TRUDGED in silence, like sleepwalkers, along the deserted hospital corridors. She leaned on Olsson's shoulder while his arm clutched her waist as if they both needed support.

"Alison," Olsson said as they reached the hospital entrance.

"Derek. I can't. Not now. I'm totally drained, exhausted. But by the weekend—"

"Yes. But I don't want to wait any more."

"I don't either. But I *have* to get the first flight back early tomorrow—"

"You don't have to go."

"Derek. I must see this through—for myself."

"To find out how much you can take?"

"If you like. And you?"

"I don't like what I've become. I took the wrong track, and—"

"We both did," Alison said. She pulled his lips towards hers and held him tightly.

Only with great reluctance did Olsson release her.

"Help me into the van, please," she said. As Olsson was about to close the door after her, she said. "Till Saturday."

Olsson nodded. "Till then."

As the van pulled out Olsson thought: *It's long past time that I regained my own self-respect.*

61 Unintended Consequences

Derek: OlssonPress has been subpoenaed by the "Candyman Inquiry." We've been ordered to appear Wednesday next week "with all files, documents, pictures, emails, and persons related to past, current, and future stories on crime and/or corruption, no matter how distant that connection may be."

I've arranged a conference with our lawyers for 11am and really need you to be there—you can appreciate my problem!—Lynette.

Indeed I do, Olsson thought.

He lay back in the chair, meditatively pondering his options for a considerable time. Eventually, a broad smile began to inch across his face.

Coming back to full awareness, he started to reply to Lynette McPherson's email, but decided to call her instead.

"This inquiry's spinning its wheels," Olsson said to Lynette when she answered, "and now it's suddenly come to life. Any idea why?"

"Flint. The subpoena was issued at his order."

"I thought he was due to start tomorrow."

"That's right," Lynette said, "but he wandered into the Inquiry's offices yesterday and started to shake things up."

"I see."

"We *have* to comply with this order, you know—"

"Of course. And we will," said Olsson. "I think I know how to handle it, but I need to make a few phone calls first. I'll see you at eleven."

"Derek, I—"

"Lynette," Olsson said, his voice commanding yet comforting, "I *do* understand your problem. And I think you'll welcome my solution."

Lynette McPherson sighed. "We'll see, won't we?"

Olsson dialled another number. "Inspector Durant. This is Derek Olsson."

"And to what do I owe this dubious pleasure?"

"I understand you're investigating the attack on Karla Preston."

"I am?"

Olsson laughed. "A newspaperman has his sources, Inspector."

"I see. You've talked to Karla Preston, I take it."

"And Alison McGuire. How would you like to arrest the perpetrator?"

"That's a *non sequitur,* Mr. Olsson," said Durant.

"Look, Inspector, I can understand if you feel your nose is a bit out joint—"

"If *that's* what you think, Mr. Olsson, you're dead wrong. We all make mistakes, and I do appreciate being corrected in your case. It was an excellent frame-up. But I still have quite a few unanswered questions—"

"Which I'll answer if I can. But I called you because I have some evidence that will help you arrest the person responsible."

"And who would that be?"

"Frank McKurn."

"You can *prove* McKurn was behind the attack?"

"No—but I've got enough for you to charge him with ten or twenty *other* crimes."

"Why haven't you come forward with this evidence *before?*"

"You've seen our series in the papers—"

"Who hasn't?"

"It's the fruit of a—ah—five-year undercover project. McKurn was to be our *pièce de résistance,*" Olsson said.

"Was?"

"A court has ordered us not to print any allegations regarding McKurn."

"Ah, yes. So you're telling me I could arrest McKurn—but the case I'm assigned to would remain unsolved."

"As things stand, I'm afraid so. Unless," Olsson chucked, "you could persuade McKurn to confess."

"That particular talent seems to be more up your alley than mine, Mr. Olsson."

"You think so?"

"That's one of my unanswered questions."

"Come and look at what I've got—and you can ask me as many questions as you like."

"Will you answer them?"

Olsson laughed. "Well, my lawyer won't be there this time."

"That's not a 'yes'."

"It's not a 'no,' either, Inspector. How about we meet at the InterFreight office—fewer nosey parkers there."

"Why don't you come here, Mr. Olsson?"

"It could be a very long session, Inspector. I'd suggest total privacy."

"I see," said Durant. "Around five, then."

"I'll be there. One other thing: how can I get back my IDs and other stuff that were impounded when I was arrested?"

"How about I bring them with me"

"Thank you, Inspector."

Then he called his partner, Ross Traynor, to advise him he'd be having a meeting that evening at InterFreight. "And, Ross, how would you like to buy out my share of InterFreight?"

"You want to sell? Why?"

"Why don't I come in after lunch and we can talk about it," Olsson said.

"Okay," Traynor said, sounding stunned. "But business is down, you know. I think we'll lose our biggest customer—not that I mind too much."

"Ross, no need to try and knock the price down," Olsson laughed. "I'm happy to sell to *you*—for a dollar."

"A dollar?"

"And Luk Suk's heirs are probably open to a low-ball offer," Olsson said. "You could end up with a hundred percent."

"But, Derek, *why?*"

"Mate, I know it's a bit of a shock. I'll see you this afternoon and all will be explained. Just think about it till then."

Before leaving for the meeting with Lynette and the lawyers, he went through the files Suchart had sent him of mutilated and murdered prostitutes in Thailand, Cambodia, and Laos. He compared the dates against another file. They all checked.

Not stand-up-in court conclusive. . . . There's only one way to find out.

He sent Nazarov an encrypted email:

If you wanted to take a much-deserved vacation, now could be an excellent time.

Appreciate if you could remain "on standby" for a couple of days, just in case. If not, it will be a good ten days before the next assignment.

Will advise within 48 hours.

*****

EMPTY PIZZA BOXES, COFFEE cups, and soft drink cans littered the floor of Derek Olsson's office at InterFreight. The desk was strewn with computer disks and printouts. Simon Lee was munching the last, long-since cold, slice of pizza. Olsson, who'd just finished guiding Durant and Lee through the file gleaming from the computer screen, grinned at Durant. Durant leaned back in his chair and yawned.

"Christ, Derek," Durant said, noticing the time, "it's nearly midnight. Seven hours—"

Over the course of the intense evening, the relationship had changed from "Inspector," "Sergeant Lee," and "Mr. Olsson" to "Rudi," "Simon," and "Derek."

"—and we've hardly begun," said Olsson, indicating the discs which, when stacked, stood over a meter high.

"First things first," Durant said. "The rest can come later." He stood up and stretched.

"Time to go?" Simon Lee asked hopefully.

"Just getting the kinks out," said Durant, sitting back down. "Of course, we can't use *all* that evidence without corroboration or independent investigation. And some of it—" Durant shook his head. "How the hell could we confirm those Swiss bank account records are genuine?"

Olsson shrugged.

"And how the hell did *you* get them?"

Olsson grinned. "I had a visit from my, ah, Fairy Godmother."

"So now you're Cinderella? I don't think so. I'll get to the bottom of it one day, I promise you."

"Maybe, Rudi, I'll tell you—one day."

"I won't hold my breath. Anyway, we don't need them—"

"Maybe the taxman would like to see them," Olsson said.

"I'm sure he would," Durant laughed. "But without them, you've given me enough to sew McKurn up good and proper—once we've tied up a few loose ends."

"Glad to hear it."

Durant's face clouded over. "There's still one bridge to cross," he said, his tone now serious. "I can't just suddenly start an investigation like this on my own. I need to take this to a senior officer—but who can I trust? The same thing applies to all the other men we'll need on the job. In fact, to do this properly, it should be an Australia-wide investigation involving *all* police forces."

"Rudi," said Olsson, "I can only tell you who you probably *can't* trust. There's an index here somewhere. . . ." Olsson scrimmaged through the pile of DVDs and CDs and popped one into his computer. "Who's your immediate superior?"

"Superintendent Zimmerman."

Olsson scrolled down to the Zs. "Not a thing. Who's *his* superior?"

"The Assistant Commissioner."

"He's here all right," said Olsson, pulling up a summary on the screen. "He's up to his eyeballs. Former drug squaddie."

"Like that bastard in Melbourne."

"At least *he's* not in line for Commissioner," Durant sighed. "I'll have to take a chance on Zimmerman, then."

"This evidence on *his* superior should convince him—" Olsson paused, his body suddenly shaking with humor "—*especially* if we plastered his face on our front pages."

Durant's eyes widened. "That'd do it!"

Suddenly wide awake, they discussed the timing—and a few days later Durant had no trouble persuading Zimmerman to assign him to the case of Senator Frank McKurn.

"One other thing, Rudi," Olsson said as he walked with them to the entrance. "I'm going to disappear for a while, just in case McKurn hasn't given up on me." *And,* he thought despondently, *I'm going to have to tell Alison we can't meet this weekend. I hope she'll understand why.*

"Probably a good idea," Durant said. "But—what if I need to get in touch with you?"

Olsson grinned. "Set up one of those free email accounts and send me the address. Then I'll tell you how we can communicate without leaving any tracks."

"Ah," Durant chuckled. "Secrets of the trade."

"Exactly."

Drained, Olsson trudged back to his office. He felt like collapsing—but he had some wheels to set in motion first.

When, finally, Olsson and his two bodyguards reached his Mercedes in the car park, Olsson stopped.

"Something wrong, boss?"

"Yes," Olsson said. "Anywhere we could rent a car?"

The two men looked at him strangely. "It's four o'clock in the morning," said one. "Not a chance."

"Yeah, you're right." Olsson paused, frozen in thought. Passing the keys to one of the men he said, "I'm beat. You drive. To the airport. We'll check in somewhere. Then drop the car back here and return to the hotel in a taxi."

The two men looked at each other as if to say, our client has lost his marbles. "This takes the cake," said one.

"I didn't bring my toothbrush," said the other.

"We can buy stuff in the morning," Olsson said, sinking into the back seat. "Look, I have to disappear for about a week—for the same reason you're here. My safety. You're supposed to check in and advise your HQ where you are at all times, right?"

The bodyguards nodded.

"Check in tomorrow and tell them you *won't* be advising your whereabouts until further notice. I don't want *anyone* to know, okay?"

"You don't trust our security?"

"I don't know the answer to that question—and I don't want to put it to the test," Olsson said. "But once someone *else* knows a secret, it's no longer a secret. Even the three of us is two too many. So no cell phones, no email, no contact of any kind with anyone for about a week." When they reluctantly agreed, Olsson continued, "In the morning, I want one of you to rent a car in your name," Olsson said. "I've got one call to make. Then we're going for a long drive."

THE NEXT MORNING, OLSSON visited Ivan Mettner, the computer nerd who ran McKurn's blackmail operation. It didn't take long. Olsson made his proposition; Mettner was too frozen with fear to answer, even with the single word, "No."

"I suggest you don't say a word to McKurn about my visit. He has a nasty habit of rubbing out evidence. One last word of advice: when the time comes, tell the police everything." Olsson handed him Mike Rubin's card. "But before you say a word, call my lawyer and follow his advice."

Mettner swallowed his fear long enough to stutter, "Wh-what t-time are you t-talking about?"

"When it comes," Olsson said, "you'll *know.*"

*****

THE FIRST RAYS of the sun were beginning to peek over the horizon when an Australian Navy frigate slowly and silently sailed into the bay around the peninsular from the village of Inkaya. Rubber dinghies were lowered quietly over the side and, with muffled oars, landed a platoon of Australian soldiers on the beach, near the site of the abandoned hotel project.

Jeremy McGuire stepped off the first dinghy to hit the shore. When the rest of his platoon landed, they moved slowly and silently along the track leading to the village, exactly as they'd been taught by Amtami and his guerrillas. In addition to their normal weapons, the soldiers carried trench-digging tools and machetes. Accompanying them were five soldiers armed with television cameras and recording equipment.

Once clear of the bay, the Navy frigate—no longer attempting to disguise or muffle its presence—steamed around the peninsula to dock at the Inkaya village jetty. Another platoon of soldiers disembarked and marched into the sleepy village. A third of the platoon cordoned off the village square; the remainder, in pairs, spaced themselves along the track from the village square to the two buildings halfway up the hill. There, the troops joined up with Jeremy's platoon, coming from the other direction.

Within minutes of the square being secured, a sound like distant thunder grew louder as a Chinook helicopter came into view above, swirling dust willies across the village, like miniature tornadoes, as it flew overhead. The chopper hovered over the village, slowly descending and turning to squeeze its bulk diagonally into the center of the square.

People in Inkaya rose early. Even so, when the troops disembarked only a handful of villagers were up and about. When the Chinook landed, the entire village was wide-awake, most of them standing around the square gaping at the strange machine that had fallen from the sky into their midst. The soldiers kept them back.

Tungi was one of the first. He scoured the Australians' faces, recognizing no one. But he could tell, from the man's bearing and the pips on his shoulders, who was in charge. He motioned to one of the young boys standing around and asked him to find Arang'anat, "and run."

Already halfway down the hill, Arang'anat was at Tungi's side just moments later. Tungi pointed to the man standing by the open ramp of the Chinook. They started walking towards him, only to be stopped by a soldier barring their way.

"Captain!" Arang'anat shouted. "What meaning this?"

Her voice was drowned out by the sound of a motor revving up. An army tractor, equipped with shovels and other tools and protuberances the villagers didn't recognize, roared down the ramp and turned towards the track up the hill, to be followed by a second one, plus a group of Army Engineers.

Tungi moved swiftly around the soldiers' cordon to stand in the tractor's path. Arang'anat followed, and a group of villagers assembled behind them, completely blocking the tractor's exit.

The tractor screeched to a halt, its driver shouting, "Get out of the way." The soldiers began to move towards the villagers.

The tractor engine now idling, Arang'anat shouted again to the officer, who was also coming towards them.

"We have a mission to accomplish," the captain said, "and you're in the way."

"Captain, this Tungi-*ga*, head of village council. He says like to welcome Australians to village, like last time."

"Well, we thank you for that," said the captain.

"But this, ah, invasion, cannot."

"Invasion? How dare you."

Flustered, Arang'anat said, "My English not good. Maybe not right word."

Tungi looked around and spoke sharply. Arang'anat translated: "Where Sandeman soldiers?"

"This is an Australian operation."

"What kind operation?"

The captain had had enough. He snapped an order to his troops who began edging forward *en masse* to push the villagers out of the way. When, following Tungi's example, the villagers didn't move, he ordered them to fire a volley over the villagers' heads.

As the soldiers raised their rifles, many of them looking very uneasy, Arang'anat took one step forward, looked the captain in the eye and said, "You shoot me?"

The captain slowly shook his head.

"Let them through," Tungi said, moving aside himself. "We don't want anyone to get hurt."

Slowly, reluctantly, the villagers moved back and the tractors roared up the track.

Tungi leaned down to the nearest boy and with a motion of his hand whispered in his ear. The boy grinned with excitement, nodded and gathered some other boys who all ran off to fulfill their errand.

Following the tractors, Tungi stalked up the hill, Arang'anat at his side. Half-a-dozen of the more adventurous boys skipped ahead of him while villagers trailed behind. A pair of soldiers at the edge of the village held them up. But the boys darted off the track, reappearing twenty-odd meters further up the hill. Others began to follow their example.

"We can't stop them," the captain sighed. "Let them watch."

When he reached the buildings, Tungi saw what the soldiers were doing. The two buildings had been demolished, the equipment in the hashish processing plant exposed for all to see. Soldiers uprooted marijuana plants with machetes and trenching tools, while tractors made short work of the more accessible ones. He saw a familiar face. "M'gire-*ga*," he called.

When Jeremy saw Tungi, his face flushed, his expression turned sheepish.

"You destroy village," Arang'anat said.

"I'm sorry—" Jeremy began.

Tungi turned away and spoke to the villagers behind him—knowing the Australians would not understand a word he said. "Remember how we stopped the hotel on the beach?"

The villagers responded with a chorus of "Yes!"

"We did it once," Tungi said, his voice booming. "We can do it again."

Arang'anat was the first to move. She walked up to Jeremy, sat down in front of a soldier about to dig up a plant, and said, "We stop you."

The operation quickly descended into chaos as the villagers streamed into the soldiers' midst. They hugged the plants. The soldiers had to lift the villagers out of the way, surround the plant while two of them dug it up. The villagers lay down in front of the tractors, to be replaced the moment the soldiers managed to drag them out of the way.

It was slow, frustrating work; unsurprisingly, tempers frayed and more than once Jeremy or one of his noncoms had to remind the men that they'd be on a charge if they used actual violence.

As the hours passed, the number of villagers only increased. "Everyone's here," Sergeant Byrne told him. "The village is deserted and there are *still* more people coming."

"They must be coming in from all over," Jeremy said.

Eventually, the Australians recognized some familiar faces. One came up to Jeremy and said, "M'gire-*ga*."

"Mr. Amtami," Jeremy replied.

"This sad day," Amtami said through his interpreter.

Jeremy nodded. "Unfortunately, I have my orders."

To Jeremy's surprise, Amtami grinned. "And we mission have."

"I understand."

Jeremy saw that with the addition of the guerrillas, progress was all but grinding to a halt. He decided it was time to call in once again. When the radio operator had established a connection to headquarters in Toribaya, he took the mike:

"Hotel, this is Charlie Alpha. Over."

"Charlie Alpha, go ahead."

Jeremy described the situation, concluding, "Either I need a lot more reinforcements to keep the villagers out of the way, or we just can't do this peacefully. No way will I shoot unarmed civilians. Frankly, I think what we're doing is totally wrong. Over."

"Hotel, wait one." The radio was silent. Then: "Charlie Alpha, pull out. For your information, this has caused an awful flap up here and there's even talk of sending Sandeman soldiers to reinforce the villagers. Over."

"Charlie Alpha," Jeremy said, "understood. Out." He sighed with relief, muttering, "A total balls-up."

Later that day, in time for the evening news, the army released video footage of Australian troops clearing "a drug factory and marijuana plantation in the Sandemans that supplied Australia with illegal drugs," also claiming, "we have broken up a big-time smuggling racket."

It was too late. Amateurish, grainy footage, shot from cellphones, of Australian troops threatening unarmed villagers, carting limp, sit-down protestors out of the way, and even Captain Jeremy McGuire on the walkie-talkie clearly saying, "I think what we're doing is totally wrong"—scenes all, unsurprisingly, absent from the official footage—were already freely available on the internet.

In a fiery statement, Sandeman Foreign Minister Abdullah Nimabi called it "an outrage. The Australian army has ruined the livelihood of an entire Sandeman community. Our supposed allies snuck into Inkaya before dawn like thieves in the night to do what? Root out the terrorists known to be hiding on the island? No. They uprooted a *plantation*. An illegal act which cannot and will not go unpunished."

A reporter in Toribaya, relying on "usually reliable sources," claimed, "The order came direct from the Prime Minister, who overruled the protests of Australian diplomats and the army's commanding officers."

And in Inkaya, the villagers trudged dejectedly down the hill. They *had* ground the Australians to a halt; they should feel proud of themselves. They *had* succeeded.

But not before the damage had been done.

*****

A FEW DAYS LATER, solicitors Andrews, Zolisky & Smythe filed suit in the NSW Supreme Court against the Government of Australia on behalf of the Croned Stow Corp., a company incorporated in Dubai. The suit sought millions of dollars in damages "for the illegal and wanton destruction of buildings, equipment, the company's plantation, the return of all equipment stolen from our facilities, plus compensation for the company's ensuing loss of business and income." The "destroyed or stolen" assets specified in the complaint included "731 marijuana plants" and "one hashish processing facility."

The Croned Stow Corp. suit was joined by the Village Council of Inkaya, which sought unspecified damages for "the destruction of our economy."

The Attorney-General appeared in person to oppose the complaint, arguing that "the Government of Australia has sovereign immunity against such proceedings."

After a moment's thought, the judge allowed that argument was, indeed, one the Government could make—*in court*—and set a hearing date two weeks' hence.

A similar suit was filed by the same two entities in the High Court of the Sandeman Islands, in Toribaya, with an added wrinkle: the request to freeze all assets belonging to the Government of Australia within the Sandeman Islands, pending the outcome of the Court's deliberation.

"Tony, we have a problem," Foreign Affairs Minister Helen Arkness told Royn. "From what we can determine, this Dubai outfit has the entire Sandeman High Court in its pocket."

"What do you mean?" said Royn.

"The judges have all been bought. Bribed. Naturally," Helen Arkness laughed, "we can easily outbid them. But then we'd be breaking our own laws."

"Can't we get our friends in the government up there to lean on the court?" Royn asked.

"Tony," said Helen Arkness. "As of right now, we don't have very many friends in Toribaya."

62   Judgement Day

ELECTION JOURNAL

Royn and Conservatives surge ahead. Who'd have thunk it? Royn and the Conservative Party owe a big "thank you" to Gurundi, the so-called imam who blew himself up in Parliament House—and turned out to be election manna "dropped in" from heaven. Faltering in the polls a week ago, Royn's strong-man reaction is supported by most Australians who, according to yesterday's polls, also stand firmly (74-26) behind his proposed anti-terrorist legislation to be introduced in a special session of Parliament today.

Royn's approval rating has also skyrocketed, pipping Kydd's at its highest.

What about the fiasco in the Sandemans? About fifty percent of us applaud Royn's "decisive action." Most of the other half think he did the right thing in the wrong way. And nobody seems to care that much: "After all, it's in the *Sandemans,* for heaven's sake," is a common reaction.

Even better for Royn: Labor's in trouble. The minority left-faction opposes the anti-terror bill as an unwarranted invasion of civil liberties, but Nash has made it clear that any Labor MP or Senator who votes "nay," or even abstains, will face disciplinary action.

With Labor *also* supporting the other bill to come before the House today—to turn the "Candyman Inquiry" into a Royal Commission on Drugs and Corruption—Royn has today's three major issues, terrorism, corruption and drugs, all sewn up.

Labor is flailing to find something—*anything*—that will grab the voters' attention. So far without success.

ALISON SIGHED. A WEEK in politics *is* a long time, she decided. Royn had gone from looking vulnerable, thanks to his weak-kneed, last-minute switch to backing McKurn, to riding the crest of a wave of popularity which swamped everything that would, otherwise, give Royn trouble in the polls.

Just before nominations closed, Nash announced the Labor Party would drop a Senate candidate who was rumored to have connections with the underworld. "When he's cleared," Nash said, "as I'm sure he will be, he'll be reinstated. He agreed to this step to demonstrate that Labor, unlike certain other political parties we shall not name, adhere to the highest standard of ethics."

Labor's sacrifice did not go unnoticed, but was buried in the emotional maelstrom.

Karla Preston's decision to run as a candidate for the MYOBB Party *did* receive a lot of press, sometimes of the humorous variety. Asked by one reporter, "If you win, Miss Preston, what will your first action be?" Karla answered, "Demand a recount!"

"You don't want to win?"

"Of course I want to win. But I have no desire to spend *any* of my precious time in Canberra's—hell, the *country's* biggest cesspit."

As a media personality, she became the public face of MYOBB—"Oh, no. I'm no leader. I don't believe in followers."

"And what does your party stand for?" she was asked.

"Simple," Karla grinned. "You mind your own business, I'll mind mine. You keep your hands out of my pockets and I'll keep my hands out of yours. And that's the proper role of government—to keep *your* hand out of *my* pocket. Government makes too many dumb rules, takes too much money out of our pockets and sends too many busybodies into our lives. We've had enough and are simply saying: *No more.*"

Thanks to Karla—and its name—the "Mind Your Own Bloody Business" Party put all the other third parties in the shade. The two major parties dismissed them as a mere annoyance, brushing them off as flies or mosquitoes. *But flies and mosquitoes,* Alison thought, *keep coming back.*

What caused the greatest stir was the requirement that every MYOBB candidate sign an agreement, to be lodged with a firm of arbitrators, to abide by the party's platform, along with a signed, but undated, resignation letter addressed to the Governor-General. If the arbitrators agreed with *any* voter's complaint that a candidate who won election had broken his or her pledge, the resignation letter would be sent in.

The pledge was clear and simple:

To vote AGAINST—

• ANY increase in any tax, and any new tax, not accompanied by the equivalent reduction in other tax rates, and any spending bill, including the annual budget, in which spending exceeded revenues, and any government invasion of civil liberties;

And to vote FOR—

• The legalization of drugs and all other victimless crimes, the privatization of marriage, and a bill of rights to constitutionally limit the power of government.

"Unconstitutional!" one lawyer said of the resignation agreement. "Won't stand up in court," said another. One commentator asked, "Since pretty much *any* government action can be interpreted as 'an invasion of civil liberties,' the MYOBBs should be more honest and call themselves the Party of No Way." A prominent cartoonist drew a politician at a meeting saying, "I'd be *happy* to sign a pledge to stick to the party platform—" with a voice in audience responding, "If you only knew what it was!"

Most people seemed think it was a good idea. "If you break a promise," said one, "*you* should pay for it, not us."

On TV, radio, and in rallies all over the country, politicians of all parties floundered, embarrassed, when asked why *they* weren't willing to sign a commitment to keep *their* election promises.

Responses ranged from a discourse "in the necessity for flexibility in government" to dismissing the questioners as "libertarian crazies" or "MYOBB plants."

In the minds of the public, the answers were forgotten; the reactions of embarrassment and evasion remained. But the Royn rollercoaster rolled on.

Just the same, Alison had the uncomfortable feeling that the crest of the wave wasn't far away.

She was thinking, for one thing, of the affidavit she'd signed at Olsson's suggestion, identifying one Ivan Mettner, who ran a blackmail operation in the back room of McKurn's lawyers offices—on behalf of Senator Frank McKurn. With it, Durant could get a search warrant and raid McKurn's collection of videos. When *that* came out. . . .

And today, the OlssonPress had to show up at the Candyman Inquiry.

She had no idea what documents and information the OlssonPress journalists and lawyers would present—but given what they'd already printed, she didn't think it would be good news for Royn.

Then there was the "anti-terrorism" bill. A law so hastily drawn up that, as late as yesterday, the drafters were still arguing vociferously over what it should contain. The solution, to have it ready for Parliament today, was simple: create a new "Protection Agency" with broad, almost unlimited powers, and let *it* write the regulations. Pretty much anything it liked.

A blank cheque.

The absence of information—little more than a vague statement from the Attorney-General that it would include "The essential expansion of police powers to allow suspected terrorists to be detained"—was enough for the civil libertarians to thoroughly denounce it. The OlssonPress ran a series showing how successful anti-terrorist operations resulted almost entirely from traditional, foot-slogging police work.

Policemen who spoke up—retired ones openly, others "not for attribution"—by and large agreed.

But most voters, Alison thought, felt the new law would *protect* them, even though they had no more idea than anyone else what it would be or do.

Alison knew that when the critics saw the actual bill, as they would this morning, they'd go bananas—she could imagine Karla's caustic comments and found herself half-agreeing with them. But they'd be dismissed as Pollyannas, at least until after the election when the new agency was up and running. Then, when it was too late, the Pollyannas would turn out to be prophets.

It was unnerving to see the whole political process of emotional reaction and counter-reaction, undented by reason, unravelling in her mind's eye. *I've been here too long.*

There was a knock on the door and Royn walked in. "Have you seen the polls?" he said. "We're riding high."

"Yes, indeed, Prime Minister," Alison said, "but how long will it last?"

Royn shrugged. "It's a bit like a hurricane, I guess—but it's certainly blown everything *else* out of the way."

"True. But hurricanes peter out in a few days, and election day is still three weeks away."

"Alison, you're unusually pessimistic this morning."

"A pessimist, Prime Minister, is merely an optimist with better information."

"Oh, really?" Royn laughed. "And what do you mean by that?"

"That's my job, isn't it?" Alison said, forcing a smile to mask her doubts.

"To be a pessimist?"

"To assume the worst so it won't take us by surprise. But this is hardly the time to spoil your mood with what could easily be nothing more than idle speculation."

"Quite so," said Royn. "Almost nine. Time for me to be in the House," Royn said. "Wish me luck."

"Good luck, Prime Minister," Alison said, wondering how long the spring in Royn's step would last.

A week is a long time. . . .

Three of them to go.

A FEW MINUTES LATER, Alison tuned into the opening of the proceedings of the Candyman Inquiry. Justice Flint looked regal sitting alone on the bench, and then the OlssonPress witness was called.

Witness. *Singular.*

"My God," she breathed as the witness walked in. "What are *you* doing there?"

She shivered as she asked herself: *And what are you going to say?*

*****

AT PRECISELY 9:01 AM, INSPECTOR Rudi Durant, accompanied by a squad of police, assembled at the entrance to the offices of Andrews, Zolisky & Smythe, Solicitors. The receptionist looked up in alarm and picked up the phone. In moments, an elderly, impeccably dressed man strode past the receptionist, came through the glass entrance door—and shut it firmly behind him.

"I'm Andrews," he said, "senior partner. How can I help you?" The tone of his voice conveyed a different message: *abandon all hope, ye who enter here.*

Without a word, Durant handed Andrews a document.

"A *search warrant?*" Andrews exploded. "Unthinkable."

"Then it's time to think the unthinkable," Durant said.

"I must protest," Andrews said.

"Protest all you like," Durant said. "We're coming in."

"But—but—ah—confidential client information—"

"That's not what we're after," Durant said. "*You* should know the law. The warrant specifies the items we're after."

Andrews stood in front of the door as if he could turn his body into a shield that would repel intruders, his stance wilting as he read the warrant.

Durant motioned to a police officer behind him, who came towards the door swinging a sledgehammer.

"As I said, Mr. Andrews, we're coming in. *Which* way we come in is your choice."

Andrews seemed to crumple. "You won't hear the last of this."

"By all means," Durant chuckled, "call your lawyers."

Andrews punched in the access code and the door swung open. Durant and his men charged through, Andrews following behind. They strode past the offices directly to the kitchen area, to startled and apprehensive looks from staff. Durant said, "Open that door, please, Mr. Andrews."

"I—I *can't.*" Beads of sweat had suddenly appeared on Andrews' forehead. "I don't know the code and . . . and that's confidential storage."

"For whom?"

Andrews was silent.

"Do you know what's in there?"

Andrews slowly shook his head.

"Your firm sublets this," Durant said, pointing to the door. "We know what's in there, you don't. But it could involve your firm in a charge of aiding and abetting criminal activity. Do I make myself clear?"

Andrews nodded. He spread his arms, bowed his head, and slowly turned and plodded away like a broken man.

The door was solid; it took fifteen minutes and several policemen, taking turns with the sledgehammer, to break it open. Another hour passed as the police carted disks, computers, servers, and every scrap of paper into the police van in front of the building entrance, seven floors below.

Sergeant Lee was elsewhere: his assignment that morning was to arrest Ivan Mettner.

Remembering Olsson's advice, Mettner said nothing until Mike Rubin arrived at the police station. Then he agreed to confess, "but only if you can guarantee my safety," he wailed.

*****

Two unmarked police vans cruised slowly around Parliament House, dropping off two plain-clothed police officers at each entrance, including the car park exits. A couple of motorcycles took up station where, upon the signal, they could follow any car leaving the building. Additional police in cars and on motorbikes were discreetly parked around the roads leading to and from Parliament House.

To the casual observer, it looked like overkill: barriers cordoned off Parliament House from the public, already manned with enough police to fend off a small invasion.

But this squad of police was on a different mission.

When everyone was on station, Inspector Zack Latham walked up the wide marble steps to the main entrance, and waited. A few minutes later Nathan Shaw, the chief of Parliament House security, came out and said, "Morning, Zack. I don't get it—what's wrong with coming to my office?"

"Well—" Latham stopped, shrugged, and then said, "Mate, you'd better read this." He pulled a thick file from the envelope he was carrying and passed it over.

Shaw's jaw fell as he began reading. He squinted at Latham, started to say something, and went back to the documents. "Corruption . . ." he muttered as he skimmed through it, ". . . misuse of privileged information . . . *four* counts of accessory to *murder?*"

Latham nodded.

"*Nine* counts in total?"

"All open and shut as far as I can tell. More to come, so I'm told."

"Well I'll be darned."

"You're not surprised?"

"At the charges? Not really. But—why are you standing out here?"

"We can't arrest a Senator or Member *in* Parliament while it's in session. We can't even come into the building—we have to wait till he comes out."

Shaw scratched his head. "So what do you want me to do?"

"Keep track of McKurn's movements and let me know the moment he leaves."

Shaw grinned. "And if he doesn't come out?"

Latham laughed. "We'll just have to come in and get him—when Parliament adjourns."

"I swear to tell the truth, the whole truth, and nothing but the truth."

Senator Frank McKurn, hunched over his desk, glowered at the television image of Derek Olsson being sworn in before the Flint Inquiry as the OlssonPress' main witness.

As Olsson lowered his hand the man sitting beside him—his lawyer, no doubt—stood and said, "Your Honor, if I may come to the bench, I have a representation to make."

Justice Herbert Flint perched over the proceedings, a cross between a vulture and a hawk—or maybe, McKurn thought, it was just the camera angle. When the lawyer reached the bench he had to look up, despite his height, to talk to Flint.

The lawyer passed Flint a document, who read it in silence. He dropped the papers, leaned forward, and had a short discussion with the lawyer: whatever they said could not be heard.

Justice Flint rapped his gavel. "Sergeant-at-arms, clear the court. Eject the TV cameras, the press, and all visitors. The testimony of this witness will be given *in camera*. Impound *all* cellphones, laptops, cameras, recorders, and every other device with a wireless or phone connection until the end of today's hearings."

"Bugger it," McKurn swore as the picture faded to an announcer. He flicked the TV off, throwing the remote so it bounced on his desk and shattered—he was now certain whatever Olsson was going to say would not be good.

His private line rang. "Holy shit!" he muttered as he listened to the nervous voice of the senior partner of Andrews, Zolisky & Smythe.

Slamming the phone down without a word of thanks, fury written over his face, he growled, "Alison McGuire! She snitched to the cops—traitorous *bitch!*"

A moment later came another call. It was one of his moles in the ACT Police telling him there was an arrest warrant out for him.

"It must be Olsson's doing!" McKurn's fist smashed on the desk. "I should have broken the bastard's neck when I had the chance. It would have been so easy. . . ." he muttered, lost in the memory of standing over the helpless Olsson, feeling his fingers going around Olsson's neck. . . .

He smiled. "Better late than never." There were, he realized, quite a few things he could do.

He glanced at the clock. The Senate session began at ten, an hour later than the House. By then, the bills should be through their first reading in the House and be ready to be "deliberated upon" by the Senate.

Hah! Rammed through.

He had enough time. If not—

McKurn shrugged. If need be the Senate would have to get along without his presence today. He had more important matters to attend to.

He dialled the first of several phone calls he was to make that morning.

*****

"Your Honor," Derek Olsson said, speaking from the witness table, "in compliance with your order I have brought with me thousands of documents. With your permission, I wish to make a brief statement before submitting them."

"Go ahead, Mr. Olsson," Flint said, "so long as it *is* brief."

"Thank you, Your Honor.

"Five years ago, we began a highly confidential, undercover operation to gather evidence of corruption in our society. You have seen some of the results on the front pages of the OlssonPress and Henry Sykes' newspapers."

"Some?" said Flint.

"What we've published so far, Your Honor, is just the tip of the iceberg. In those files—" Olsson indicated several boxes stacked by his feet "—is evidence that could, with corroboration, convict hundreds of government officials at all levels—federal, state, and local. And break up most of the criminal gangs in the drug trade. That's not all. There are also fragments of information which, if followed up, could indict hundreds, if not thousands more."

"If you've been collecting this information for so long, why wait till *now* to start publishing it?" Flint asked.

Olsson was all too aware he had Flint's full attention. He suppressed a touch of nervousness, sensing there was more to Flint's gaze than simply paying attention would warrant.

"We started at the local level, with cops and councillors who fixed speeding tickets and the like for their mates. Petty stuff. But we quickly found exposing such offenders made absolutely no difference. Arrest a street-corner drug dealer and in days, if not hours, someone else would fill his shoes. Break up a drug ring, and another gang moves into the vacuum. Nothing was changed—"

"Was that your aim? Change?"

"Yes, Your Honor. Our mission became to make a *real* difference."

With over forty years' experience in court, most as a judge, Justice Herbert Flint was confident he could quickly sense when a witness wasn't telling the truth. Which was why Olsson puzzled him. Olsson *was,* he felt, telling the truth as he knew it. Yet, there was something missing, nothing he could put his finger on, nothing that even seemed out of place, something suggesting—*Yes, that's it,* he thought. *He's not telling the whole truth.*

He smiled to himself. *Let's give him enough rope. . . .*

"*Became* your mission?" Flint said. "What does *that* mean?"

"The project started as a way to sell papers. But as one connection led to another, we found it went far deeper—" Olsson paused, groping for words. "To make an analogy, a doctor finds a lesion on a patient's body. He cuts it out. Others appear and he cuts them out too—until he realizes that *cancer* is the underlying cause."

"It doesn't take doctors *that* long to find the cancer."

"*These days,*" Olsson retorted, "doctors know that a lesion of a certain kind is a *symptom* of cancer. A hundred or so years ago, they didn't. Back then, they treated the *symptoms* but never the *cause.*"

"What's this got to do with us, here and now?" Flint demanded.

"This is far from the first inquiry into corruption in our country's history. Over ten years ago, another Royal Commission investigated the drug trade in Dubbo. The result was the breaking up and prosecution of a gang which was a major supplier of marijuana to the Melbourne market, and was also responsible for several murders. Would you rate that Royal Commission as a success, Your Honor?"

"Yes, of course," Flint snapped. "*Obviously.*"

"That's true, Your Honor," Olsson said, "if your measure is the number of bodies locked up. But—is there any shortage of marijuana on Melbourne's street corners? Of course not. Is Dubbo now free of criminal gangs? Don't be ridiculous. That kind of success merely creates a vacuum—and nature abhors a vacuum."

Olsson lifted a box onto the table, spilling out dozens of discs. "The evidence I have brought here today could convict thousands of people. Lock them *all* up, collar *every* cop and bureaucrat on the take, and will our country will suddenly be free of corruption—*forever?* Will the scourge of the drug trade disappear?"

"You are here, Mr. Olsson," Flint growled, "to answer questions, not *ask* them."

"Then I'll answer it. Of course not. If there's demand for heroin and other illegal drugs, it will be supplied. Lock up every crooked cop and customs official, incarcerate every drug dealer in the country, and a few months later it will be business as usual in the drug trade. That's human nature.

"For just sixty-five dollars you can buy a kilo of opium in Afghanistan. Refined into a hundred grams of heroin, that one kilo of opium will retail here for *sixty thousand dollars* at $600 *per gram.* That's a *ninety-two thousand percent markup.* There's no other business in the world with such enormous profit margins—except cocaine and other *illegal* drugs.

"With *that* much money involved, it's child's play to find a mere handful of officials who'll be *eager* to keep their eyes—and mouths—*shut.* With *that* much money on the table, you'll have no trouble recruiting people who are willing to kill other humans beings without the faintest qualm; people who will happily turn your fifteen-year-old granddaughter into a heroin addict who has to prostitute herself to pay for it."

Flint's eyes widened imperceptibly at "granddaughter." He thought: *He's done his research*—Flint's granddaughter had just turned fifteen.

"You can dig up weeds from here to Kingdom Come and they'll just grow back—unless you get rid of what they *feed* on. In the drug business, that's the 'obscene profits.'

"Remove the incentives.

"Corruption in government exists for one reason only: *the law makes illegal activities highly profitable.* The *law,* Your Honor, makes corruption possible. Abolish those laws, and you abolish corruption."

"Are you suggesting, Mr. Olsson, the legalization of *drugs?*"

"Your Honor, nicotine and alcohol are the *only* highly addictive drugs that your fifteen-year-old granddaughter *cannot* buy on the school playground at lunchtime."

"But—" For the first time he could recall, Justice Flint was at a loss for words.

"Yes, your granddaughter goes to an exclusive, very expensive school—about a mile from Kings Cross where pretty much *everything* is for sale. Rich, impressionable kids are the perfect customers for the sharks who ply the trade.

"If she gets drunk, or smokes, you and her parents will probably know. If she's addicted to heroin or worse, you'll never find out—until it's too late. Bring the drug trade into the light of day, Your Honor. Let *honest* companies produce and sell it *openly,* where it can be controlled, regulated—and taxed.

"At one stroke, you'll fulfill your mission.

"What's more, it's the only way you can."

"But *punishment,* Mr. Olsson," Flint interjected. "*That's* a deterrent."

"If it *was,* Your Honor, neither you nor I would be here today."

"Are you implying our criminal justice system is a failure, Mr. Olsson?" Flint said, a touch of anger in his voice. "That is *not* the subject of this inquiry. Please get back on track and make it snappy."

"Certainly, Your Honor," Olsson said. "And I apologize. I have obviously misread your remit. I was not aware of any limits on your discretion in taking this Inquiry wherever it must lead."

Olsson paused, anticipating a response from Flint—who merely glared at him.

"You can only punish the corrupt officials you can *find,*" Olsson continued, "when you can *also* gather enough evidence. What about the cop who 'everybody knows' is on the take—but there's no *proof?* What about the people who are so smart, cunning, or lucky they're never suspected? When this inquiry comes to an end, they'll still be in business. And they'll be very grateful to you for cutting back on their competition."

Olsson scrimmaged through discs scattered across the table and pulled out three. "Consider this man," he said, holding the discs as if offering them to Flint. "He has been firmly ensconced in the highest levels of government for *decades,* has pocketed millions of dollars *illegally,* been responsible for countless murders, perverted the course of justice, and has achieved this and more with hardly a whiff of suspicion, until very recently.

"*Here—*" Olsson strode to the bench and laid the three discs in front of Flint "—is the evidence that will send this man to jail for the rest of his natural life which, given his age, won't be too long."

"*Who?*" Flint demanded.

"Senator Frank McKurn."

"Perhaps we'd better look at this now," Flint said, wondering why Olsson had scanned everybody in the room as he'd spoken.

"I gave that information to the NSW police a week ago," Olsson said. "An arrest warrant is being served on Senator Frank McKurn right now, along with several other officials."

"Mr. Olsson! You are out of order—"

"Your inquiry leaks like a sieve, Your Honor. By the time you can process this evidence, McKurn will have long gone." Olsson suddenly twirled across the room, yanking the arm of one of the court reporters from under the table. In his hand, clear for all to see, was a cellphone. "See what I mean?"

"Sergeant-at-arms," Flint thundered, "arrest that man!"

Olsson wrenched the cellphone from man's grasp. "He's already sent a message. Just one word: 'McKurn.'" Olsson grinned. "Too late."

Olsson handed the cellphone to the sergeant-at-arms as the court reporter was led away.

"Bring in a relief," Flint ordered. When the replacement was seated, Flint said, "Mr. Olsson, please wrap up your statement."

"Perhaps, Your Honor, there will never be another criminal as smart, cunning, and successful as Frank McKurn. *But how do you know?* You simply can't. Just the same, there is one way, and *only* one way, to put the McKurns and his lesser imitators out of business *permanently.*"

Flint stared at Olsson until he realized Olsson had fallen silent. He rapped his gavel. "These proceedings will adjourn for thirty minutes."

Olsson watched Flint stalk out, puzzled about what he might have said to provoke such a reaction. He was wondering what to do with himself for the next half-hour when the issue was decided by the Sergeant-at-arms, who came up and whispered, "Justice Flint would like to see you in his chambers. If you would follow me, sir."

*****

McKurnWatch.com

"The website that ~~must not~~ can now be named" [Thanks, Frankie!]
57,497 McKurnWatchers—and counting.

G'day boys, girls, and those of you who can't make up your minds: it's time to roll out the champagne and pop the corks . . . it's *definitely* party time!

The sun hasn't risen over the yardarm yet, you say? So what! Thanks to one of our more "public-spirited" readers, Frankie's going to go for a row.

At last.

On the McKurnWatch website, you'll find the following documents:

1. several Swiss bank account statements in the name of—you guessed it— "Franklin Julius McKurn" (never knew his middle name before, did you?). One of them even has his Bellvue Hill home address!

Nice stash you've socked away there, Frankie.

2. the incorporation papers of a Liechtenstein Anstalt, including documents showing the beneficial owner is none other than one Franklin Julius McKurn.

(English translations of the original German kindly provided for linguistically-challenged English speaker—let's be honest, that's most of us, right?)

3. a list of the assets owned by this Anstalt as of about a year ago, which make *very* interesting reading.

One item of note is a certain Aussie company that's been in the news recently: Paper Supplies Pty. Ltd., along with a Hong Kong company in the business of . . . exporting stationery supplies to Australia. It's one (that's right, *one, single, only)* customer? None other than our old friend, Paper Supplies.

Also of relevance: brokerage accounts that clearly show our Frankie has profited from inside information.

Tut, tut.

Where did these documents come from?

Our source assures us he (she?) has originals, received direct from the various Swiss and Liechtenstein institutions.

Presumably, "money talks" in Switzerland, too—perhaps louder than anywhere else.

I thought of calling up the Swiss banks in question to check. But aside from the time difference (meaning all good Swiss bankers should be sound asleep), I figured they'd tell me diddley-squat.

So the copies you can see online (and download, if you like) won't, without corroboration, help convict Frankie of anything—in a court. But there are other venues whose rules of evidence aren't quite so strict. For example: the parliamentary committees supervising the ethical or otherwise activities of MPs and Senators.

(Ever wonder *why* the world's legislatures *have* such "ethics" committees? Seems too many of our political "masters" are morally challenged and have great difficulty distinguishing right from wrong.)

Even more potent is the taxman.

Remember! Al Capone wasn't locked up for murder, theft, standover tactics, and Eliot Ness never grabbed him for trafficking alcohol during Prohibition. The Feds got him on *tax evasion!*

The taxman tends to work on the principle: you're guilty unless *you* can prove you're innocent.

Makes it tough to defend yourself—especially if the taxman has frozen all your assets.

I don't see the difference between taxation and theft—except that the burglar, unlike the taxman, at least has the decency *not* to pretend he's stealing your money "for your own good." So the *taxman,* not the tax*payer,* is the one who should be locked up.

But in Frankie's case, I'll make an exception.

Glad I'm not in his shoes right now!

— The McKurnWatcher

PS. I think someone is playing a joke on Frankie. Not that he doesn't deserve it!

I've seen quite a few posts suggesting that our Frankie is that mysterious underworld drug dealer known only as "the Candyman." These posters note that the Croned Stow Corporation—the company that's suing the Australian government for uprooting their cannabis patch in the Sandemans—has hired Andrews, Zolisky & Smythe, the same legal eagles Frankie has been using to try and put McKurnWatch. com out of business (hope they do a better job for the Croned Stow!).

Our Frankie is many things, but Stupid isn't one of them. If it *is* his company, the last thing he'd want to do is call attention to it. While we can't dismiss a "double bluff," my guess is we have a japester in our midst.

And remember: there are lawyers who'll do whatever you ask, so long as there's enough grease on their palms. The firm of Andrews, Zolisky & Smythe, with Frankie as their client, obviously falls into that category.

The clue to the jape is the company's name. The real owner is probably an Australian (but could be anyone familiar with Cockney slang), as in *Crone the stows.* I mean. . . . Well, you know what I mean.

Don't you?

Either way, I doubt it's the sort of name Frankie would choose—and nor does it fit an off-the-shelf company lying around some lawyer's office (even one in Dubai) waiting for a purchaser.

Come to think of it, though, *The Croned Stow* sure would be the perfect name for an Amsterdam-style *ganja* joint, should the "dreaded weed" ever be legalized, don't you reckon?

*****

A FORBIDDING PLACE, DEREK Olsson thought as he stood in the entrance to Justice Flint's office. Dark wooden floor-to-ceiling bookshelves, filled with black leather books, lined the walls. The curtains were drawn, shutting out the sunlight. The only flash of color was a single rose on his desk.

Flint looked up from his papers. "Sit down, Mr. Olsson," he said brusquely, his gaze neither hostile or welcoming, but all business. Without waiting for Olsson to take a seat, he continued, "Your demonstration there was a leaker on the Inquiry's staff was dramatic, but—" Flint shrugged "—one person who should have known better sending a text is hardly *proof* of anything. You've made a serious charge. Can you back it up?"

"Yes, I think I can," Olsson said, taking a moment to get comfortable. "But isn't this a question more appropriate for the courtroom?"

"This is not a court of law, Mr. Olsson," Flint said. "It's an *inquiry*. The procedures might seem similar—but they're not. I have far more discretion than any judge. If what you say is *true*, then I'd rather have the information privately, first. Proceed."

Olsson nodded. "Do you know anything about a Sergeant Jason Kowalski—?"

"He was with the inquiry for a while and then reassigned." Flint shrugged. "So what?"

"Do you know *why* he was 'reassigned'?"

"Is this *relevant*, Mr. Olsson?" Flint said curtly.

"Very. He had evidence against McKurn. He gave it to his superiors—who got rid of Kowalski and buried his evidence somewhere in the files."

"*Bury* evidence? What on earth are you talking about?"

"This Inquiry has been infiltrated by the mob. It—and *you*—are threats to the drug merchants. They and their, ah, 'protectors' in government react to any threat by trying to squash it, emasculate it, obstruct it, or divert its attention."

"They can't do that," Flint growled.

Olsson smiled. "But they *have*. Why do you think this Inquiry has gone nowhere until now? When it was set up someone—most likely McKurn—got enough of his own stooges appointed to 'capture' it. Not totally, but sufficiently to grind it almost to a halt using the arsenal of delaying tactics *every* bureaucracy has at its disposal. They'll also take advantage of you by throwing their competitors to the wolves in the hope you'll be satisfied with a few triumphs and go away."

Flint's steely expression had remained fixed on Olsson since he'd stood in the doorway. But now he had to consciously maintain it to prevent exposing a hint of his rising frustration with this witness, who continually refused to follow *his* script. At the same time, it occurred to him that maybe it was *Olsson* who was trying to divert his attention. If so, from *what?*

"You tell a good story, Mr. Olsson," Flint said. "But, once again, *prove* it."

"*My* evidence is circumstantial. But there's one person who can prove it: *you.* Talk to Sergeant Kowalski, examine his evidence—and find out who spiked it and why."

"What you're suggesting, Mr. Olsson, is far more serious than just a few leaks."

"It is."

"How come you know all this?" The subtext of Flint's words were: if you *do* know it.

"In five years we've built up many contacts in the underworld."

"An expensive business. Where's your return?"

"We were just beginning to get a return when you pre-empted us with your subpoena."

"Are you sure what you're telling me is *true?*"

"Every day for the past few weeks, Your Honor, a high-profile government official has been arrested thanks to *our* evidence. While I haven't focused on the Candyman Inquiry, I've heard the same thing from several sources—"

"Rumors," Flint said, with a dismissive wave of his hand.

"You could call them that, if you like," said Olsson. "But the police would call them information from usually reliable informants—and investigate. What happened to Kowalski is no rumor."

"Maybe not."

"You have a problem, Your Honor: *which* members of your staff can you trust? As things stand, if you hand them the evidence I've brought to them it will *certainly* get into the wrong hands. Your birds will all fly the coop."

"So you say."

"And if I'm right? Can you afford to take that chance?"

Flint scowled at Olsson. "It would be easy to assume that *you,* Mr. Olsson, are the one trying to stymie this inquiry."

"What on earth do you mean?"

"You're implying I should investigate my staff first and put everything on hold in the meantime?"

"A good idea," Olsson said. "But you're overlooking a simple fact, Your Honor. I've put *five years'* worth of investigation at your disposal. There's information there you could *never* dig up. Indeed, I've done most of your work for you."

"Maybe," Flint grunted through tightly pressed lips, the only sign of his growing exasperation. "That will take time."

"Talk to Inspector Rudi Durant of the NSW police, Your Honor."

"What's your connection with him?"

Olsson grinned. "He arrested me for murder. He also issued an arrest warrant for Frank McKurn which should have been served this morning."

"From *your* evidence?"

"That's right," Olsson said. "He's also had a week to examine it. *His* opinion should be worth something—though you already have it: McKurn is just *one* of the people he's arresting today."

"Is this 'Candyman' one of them?" Flint asked.

"Not from *my* information I'm afraid," Olsson said. "He remains an enigma."

"Indeed," said Flint, a raised eyebrow and a slight narrowing of his eyes the only evidence of his sudden intuition that there was a connection here. Olsson, who'd remained annoying relaxed, tensed slightly at his mention of the "Candyman."

"Thank you, Mr. Olsson," Flint said abruptly. "You can go now. But I'll require your presence again in a day or two."

*****

Alison McGuire looked at herself, consumed with ecstasy. Her face, framed by her black hair, spilled in all directions over a downy pillow. Her skin of her face was flushed, her deep blue eyes glowed, her nipples taut as Derek's hand slowly stroked her breast . . . and then the other.

She watched, stunned, unable to move until her body began to shake and the sound of her breathing and her moans of delight from the laptop speakers overwhelmed her.

She slammed the laptop lid shut.

She gazed around her office, blurred through misty eyes. There was no one to see or to hear . . . except for the billions of people with connections to the internet.

Like the friend had alerted her in an email: My Goodness, Alison, what have you been doing?

How many others? she wondered.

By tomorrow—no, tonight—everyone in Parliament House. *This* would go around faster than the news of the police waiting to arrest McKurn.

And tomorrow . . . everyone plugged into cyberspace. *No,* she thought, recalling McKurn's words, ". . . and double-page spreads of the juiciest pictures in the sleazier tabloids."

"If I'm going down, I'll take you with me," McKurn had said. So he made that "one phone call." She held her hand, stiff, over her desk. *It would have been so easy.*

Even now . . . he was still in Parliament House . . . *except I'd be the one going to jail, not him.*

Gingerly, she opened the laptop, killed the video, searched "Alison McGuire Derek Olsson"—and counted the hits. At twenty, she stopped.

She collapsed onto the desk, her head buried in her hands, uncaring about the tears streaming from her face.

What can I do?

Just one possibility kept leaping into her mind. But first, a minor act of revenge.

With a short message from "an avid reader," she emailed *McKurn Watch* the phone tap of McKurn, calling himself "John," phoning "Gladys" of the Aphrodite's call girl agency.

Would it have any effect on McKurn? She shrugged. She *felt* better.

Gathering a few essentials, she walked out into corridor without a word to anyone, including a surprised Mary. Several people gave her strange looks. Was it just her imagination, or . . . ?

She hobbled faster, her trio of protectors puffing to keep up, pretending not to see anyone she knew. Which was everyone bar the rare visitor. Turning a corner she almost barrelled into Royn, who was striding along the corridor as if his feet were wings.

"Alison!" Royn said excitedly. Everything sailed through. No way McKurn could derail it this time. Isn't that wonderful?" He raised his hand to give Alison a "high five."

"Congratulations, Prime Minister," Alison said, her face wooden, making no move to join Royn's ritual by copying his gesture.

"Alison?" Only now did Royn see Alison's pale, drawn face. "What's wrong?"

You'll find out soon enough, she thought. "I'm sorry, Prime Minister. I have to go," she said, hobbling past him before he could react.

Reaching the parking lot, she sat low in the back seat of the van where no one would notice her. "Home," she said to Madge, who was driving.

*****

HE'D RETIRED FROM THE army ten years ago and still missed military *action*. He'd enjoyed it so much he'd refused various offers of promotion which would have taken him out of the field.

He hadn't been pressed too hard: he was *good.*

He knew dozens of other soldiers who'd had trouble adapting to civilian life, and turned to drink or worse to douse their troubles.

He'd been luckier. Or smarter. He'd carved himself a new career.

His services didn't come cheap. But either he succeeded, and got paid, or failed and didn't. Partial success didn't count. Two clients who didn't cough up after he'd done his job didn't live long enough to regret their actions. Since then, he'd never had a collection problem.

Now he sat in the wintry sun looking like an elderly pensioner feeding the pigeons. His grey hair, at least, was real. He hardly noticed the pigeons or the sun: he watched the entrance of the building across the street for his new target, the first of three, to come out.

It had been a bit of a rush getting here—he got the last seat on the flight to Canberra—but he'd made it. He had no idea how long he'd have to wait, but he could hobble down to the lake, wander up and down for a while, yet keep the building entrance in view. Who'd take any notice of an old man who obviously needed a walking stick?

He wasn't planning to do anything rash, like try and make his target *today.* That would be playing with fate.

No. First he'd learn his target's ways; only then could he devise a plan of action—one that wouldn't leave a *signature.*

His enjoyment was in the chase, the stalking. He knew this was his one flaw, his reluctance to let the chase come to an end.

But was *happy:* he was hunting once again.

63   Disappearing Act

MURDER!
CORRUPTION!
BLACKMAIL!

Anthony Royn, Melanie, Doug Selkirk, and Paul Cracken eyed the newspapers strewn across Royn's desk: Frank McKurn's arrest dominated every front page in the country. Even the arrest of a NSW Assistant Police Commissioner only got a brief "see inside" slug on one of the Sydney papers.

Radio and TV were no better.

". . . so now," as one talking head had put it, "the Conservative Party goes to the polls with an alleged murderer, blackmailer, and all-around charlatan on its Senate ticket."

"And that," Cracken said, "is the problem. How will it affect us in the polls?"

"Badly," said Selkirk. "You, Prime Minister, are going to come in for a lot of flak for switching from dumping McKurn to backing him."

"I guess so," Royn sighed.

"There's no way we can get McKurn off the ticket?" Melanie said.

"No," said Selkirk. "I checked. Nominations closed a week ago, and they can't be changed."

"Not even if a candidate dies?" Melanie said.

Selkirk shook his head. "Not even then."

"So we're stuck with McKurn—and he's now in jail," Melanie said.

Her statement was met with a moment of gloomy silence.

"We need Alison," Royn said. "Does anyone know where she is?"

No one answered.

Alison McGuire had disappeared.

She hadn't called in this morning.

Her cellphone was off.

Emails went unanswered.

There was no sign of her at her apartment; her parents and friends had no idea where she might be.

"She's gone into hiding," Melanie said. "*I* would."

"I suppose you're right," Royn said. "I guess she'll be back when it's blown over."

"*If* it blows over," Selkirk said.

"You're a wet blanket this morning, Doug," Melanie said. "At least there's no political fallout from this video."

"Not yet," said Selkirk. "McKurn's arrest has smothered everything else."

"Including everything we did in Parliament yesterday," Cracken said.

"McKurn released it from pure spite," Melanie said.

"What can we *do?*" Royn moaned.

*****

DEREK OLSSON SPENT THE morning at the Sandview Hideaway Hotel with a TV crew. Back in Sydney, he was invited to watch a rough cut of the segment that would air on that evening's TV news.

It began with a clip of Inspector Rudi Durant, standing next to an enormous pile of DVDs; then the scene faded to Derek Olsson walking through the door of a hotel room.

In the center of the room Olsson turned to the camera. "This is where that video was taken," he said.

The crew had urged him to say more than "that video." Olsson refused: the video had gone viral "so everybody knows about it. More's the pity."

The camera swung around the lounge of the Honeymoon Suite. Olsson stood on a corner table and pointed up: the picture zoomed in to a tiny ornament in the corner where two walls and the ceiling met. "It looks perfectly innocent, doesn't it?" said Olsson.

With a hammer and chisel he carefully levered the ornament off the wall: hidden beneath it was a camera. "There are two more cameras hidden, like this, in this room," Olsson said, pointing them out. "And more, of course, in the bedroom."

Olsson walked into the bedroom saying, "As you can see, this is a luxury hotel, cleverly designed to give all guests complete privacy. When a politician, celebrity, or well-known businessman checked in, they were told there was some mistake in their booking—and were upgraded to this suite. The guests were very grateful to be upgraded at no extra charge. But they *did* pay for it—later."

Olsson chipped at another ornament to reveal another camera. "Everything that went on here was recorded. *Everything.*"

The picture cut to Inspector Durant. "We've only just begun analyzing these," he said, his hand on the pile of DVDs, "but these are videos of at least four hundred prominent or wealthy people, all caught in compromising positions—usually with people who aren't their wives or husbands."

The camera switched back to Olsson, now sitting on the bed. "A nice racket. Hundreds of CEOs, prominent politicians, and celebrities, threatened with exposure unless they paid up. Most, I imagine, did.

"Among those caught on camera were myself and Alison McGuire. The recording ended up in the hands of Senator Frank McKurn, who—and I have to add 'allegedly' for legal reasons—used the threat of its release to blackmail Alison for his own political ends. As you can imagine I, for one, am looking forward to his trial."

Olsson watched the program with less than half his attention. He was worried about Alison. He'd called repeatedly; no answer. He'd emailed: no response.

She's hiding, he thought—but the calm voice of reason was overwhelmed by his vivid image of Alison's cold body covered in blood, and his mounting fear for her safety.

Leaving the studio, he called the principal of the agency providing his, Alison's, and Karla's bodyguards.

"I'm sorry, Mr. Olsson," the principal said, "I cannot tell you where she is—assuming I knew. And I have no reason to doubt her safety."

"*I'm* the one who hired you to protect Alison McGuire."

"That's true, Mr. Olsson. But our duty is to Miss McGuire. All I can do is this: *should* she or her bodyguards contact us, I will pass on your message. It's her decision, Mr. Olsson, not ours."

"Your agents are required to keep you informed of their location."

"Indeed. But when our operatives in the field decide to maintain total secrecy, we respect that decision—*as you well know, Mr. Olsson.*"

"I—understand," said Olsson. "She may now be in *greater* danger than ever, so please tell your men to keep their guard up."

"Certainly, Mr. Olsson. "I'll pass that on—if I can."

Olsson was sure he did know where Alison was—*but how can I weasel that information out of him?*

No obvious answer came.

He called Alison's parents. "Oh, Derek," Maggie said. "Can you find her? It's all so *awful.*"

Olsson heard Joe's voice in the background. "Dirty politics!"

"She might be hiding from the world," Olsson said. "Do you have any idea where she could be? Somewhere you took her on holiday, as a child, which is completely isolated."

"No. We never went anywhere like that."

"If you think of something, will you let me know?"

"Of course, Derek. And if—*when* you find her, please tell me immediately."

"I will," Olsson promised.

LATER THAT EVENING, OLSSON received a call from Durant. "Derek, I have some bad news for you. We've heard a rumor from our underworld sources that there's a hit out on you, and possibly others."

"Others? *Who?*"

"I don't know. But assume the worst: Alison McGuire and Karla Preston."

"You mean—*McKurn* is behind it?"

"I have no idea. I interviewed him today in Long Bay—a waste of time. He's vicious, vindictive, and vengeful—a miserable specimen of the human race—and he let slip that he blames *you* for his arrest. If your suspicions are right, he was behind the attacks on Alison McGuire and Karla Preston, so why wouldn't he decide to complete the job?"

"You're making too much sense, Rudi."

"But it gets worse. It's a killer-for-hire called 'the Assassin.' We know nothing about him except that he exists, he's very professional, and his kills are all different so he doesn't leave a *signature.* His reputation in the underworld is unmatched, and his fees are sky high. That's all I can tell you. And in case you were going to ask, I can't offer you police protection. I have no *evidence,* just a rumor."

"But McKurn's behind bars. How could he have set it up?"

"He couldn't be arrested while Parliament was in session, so he had a whole day at his disposal. My guess is releasing that video was just one of the things he did. In any case, prisoners have visitors, can make phone calls—."

"Got it, thanks, Rudi. I'll beef up our security."

From his bodyguards, Olsson got the cellphone number of the principal of the agency. "It's for emergencies only."

"This," said Olsson, "is a *crisis.*"

A sleepy, none-too-happy voice answered.

"Have you heard of a contract killer known as 'the Assassin'?"

"Who's this?"

"Derek Olsson. *Have* you?"

"Can't say that I have."

"He's a hit man for hire. Best in the business according to my police contact, who just told me he's acquired a new assignment. Three, in fact: Alison McGuire, Karla Preston—and me. Beef up your security for Karla, and tell me where Alison is so I can protect her."

"I already told you—"

"I don't believe you. One or more of us may be dead by morning and all you can say is—"

"Mr. Olsson! I'll try and contact our operatives—again. If they respond, you'll hear from me."

The phone in Olsson ear went dead. He stared at it—and emailed the geek.

The next morning, when the computers at the investigative agency were turned on, they all froze and a message popped up on the screens:

YOUR 'SECURITY' SUCKS!

at the request of one of your clients, i have hacked your system

i could have downloaded all your 'protected' information—which is so 'secure' pretty much anyone with hacker 101 skills can read it

have a nice day

The agency's principal was just beginning to recover from the shock when his phone rang. "Mr. Olsson! I'm sorry, I can't talk to you right now. We have a problem—"

"I know. Computer problems."

"*How* do you know? You mean, *you're* responsible for this? I could sue you—"

Olsson laughed. "Sue a client? That would hardly improve your reputation, especially when the *reason* is made public. Now, just tell me where Alison McGuire is and I'll see what I can do about unfreezing your machines."

IT WAS A LONELY house, a mere thirty-odd kilometers from Canberra, tucked away at the end of a narrow dirt track off the Captains Flat Road. This was an area with many such houses, each cut off from the rest of the world by a hectare or two of land, inhabited mostly by people who worked in Canberra but preferred to live in the country.

Their van bounced up the track as Olsson piloted it for speed not, comfort. He skidded to a halt in front the entrance and leapt out. A bodyguard standing on the verandah stiffened and then relaxed as he recognized Olsson and his colleagues. Alison appeared in the doorway. Seeing Olsson, her face reddened.

"Derek, I—"

"Get inside!" Olsson hissed. In two long strides he was at her side, his arms going around her in what Alison expected to be an embrace.

Olsson lifted her up and carried her through the door.

"Put me down," Alison squealed, her arms going around him for support; she felt a strange hardness under his coat. "What are you *wearing?*"

"A bulletproof vest." Olsson let her down gently.

"What?"

"You're in danger. We're *all* in danger."

"Hey, boss," one of the bodyguards called, "we're being tracked."

Olsson stood in the doorway. "How?"

The man was hunched down, looking under the vehicle. "There's a little gadget here. A transmitter."

Olsson froze. "Oh, Christ! I've actually brought the bastard *here.*"

"Shit happens, boss," the bodyguard grinned.

"Are you a Buddhist, by any chance?" Olsson said. "Leave the transmitter in place. Bring everything inside. Act normally, in case we're being watched."

Alison eyed the strange pile of luggage the men carried in. Especially puzzling were the seven long, thin aluminium cases of a type she'd never seen before.

"The vests," Olsson said.

Olsson's bodyguards opened a suitcase and handed out bulletproof vests.

"I'll explain in a minute," Olsson said. "Just put them on first."

"What's going on, Derek?" Alison demanded. "What's in those cases?"

"Rifles," Olsson said.

"Best to do what the man says, Alison," Madge ordered. "I saw a flash of light out the window. Just for a second. I think."

"THE ASSASSIN" FOLLOWED THE van, keeping some ten kilometers behind. Only when the van stopped did he narrow the distance. The first time was on the highway between Sydney and Canberra, at a petrol station. He drove on, parking in a bay further along the road. The van bypassed Canberra and stopped, for the second time, somewhere off a lonely road the other side of Queanbeyan.

Using his GPS, he pinpointed the location on the map.

He parked his car in the bush, out of sight from the road, a couple of kilometers from the van's position. He left his sniper rifle in the boot of the car—if he was seen carrying *that* it would be too obvious. But he was armed with a pistol, a knife, and a stubby AK-47 hidden in his knapsack, just in case.

He hiked cross-country—very slowly. The dead leaves on the ground were dry and he wanted to make no sound. He skirted a couple of houses until he saw the van in the distance.

It was a gentrified countryside, he decided. Manicured lawns around the houses—turning brown from the lack of rain, fields where horses grazed with plenty of scrub in between where he could hide. He selected a spot where trees and undergrowth shielded him from view so he could watch the house and van through his binoculars without being seen. A man he recognized as one of Olsson's two bodyguards carried a suitcase through the front door. A man he did not recognize stood by the door and then went inside.

He put down his binoculars. Now there was nothing to do but wait.

OLSSON OUTLINED THE DANGERS they faced and asked, "If you wanted to attack this house and kill everyone in it, how would you go about it?" Olsson said.

"Fire," Madge said immediately. It's as dry as a bone outside. Canberra has water restrictions and the level of the dam out there is very low."

One of the guards said, "There are seven of us and one of him—"

"As far as we know," said Olsson.

"It's a big house. If he starts a bushfire he can't be sure some of us won't get out the back."

"We have to take him out," said another. "It's the only way."

"He must have a vehicle somewhere. If we could disable it—"

"Or trap him?"

"We have one advantage," Madge said. "He doesn't know we know he's there. How can we use that?"

"Do we need reinforcements?" Olsson said—and thought of calling Nazarov. They were leaving tonight on the vacation he'd suggested. If he called them, they'd come.

"Jason!" Alison suddenly said.

"Your policeman friend?" Madge said. "What could he do?"

"I don't know—arrest him?"

"For what?" said Madge.

"We could ask him," said Alison.

"That's an option." Turning to the bodyguards, Olsson asked, "Any of you ex-military?"

A couple of them nodded.

"Special forces? Anything like that?"

"Sort of," one said. "I had a week's training in jungle craft—"

"Yeah, when you were twenty years younger and twenty kilos lighter."

"If this Assassin is a real pro," Olsson said, "then we don't have the skills to go out there to creep up on him." He thought again of Nazarov. *The kind of skills they have.* But in the end, he shook his head. *Better to let things take their natural course,* he decided. He lost track of what the others were saying and suddenly interrupted:

"Even if we succeed, it won't work. If this Assassin guy fails, there'll just be someone else."

"But McKurn's locked up," Alison protested.

"Yes, he is," Olsson said. "But a prisoner can have visitors, make phone calls, and there are other ways of getting messages in and out. There's a better way."

"What?"

"I need to visit a, ah, friend—in Long Bay."

"McKurn?" Alison said.

Olsson grinned. "No. But it's a thought."

"So we're going back to Sydney?" one of Olsson's bodyguards asked.

"That's right."

"When?"

"Best to go now," Madge said. "Fire, remember."

"Dusk," said Olsson. "It will be harder for him to see what we're doing. We'll take both vans—"

"And split up halfway?" Madge said.

"Right," Olsson said.

"What about the transmitter?"

"Leave it where it is. Then he won't know we're onto him. He'll probably follow it, so Alison and I will go in the *other* van." Remembering Nazarov, he stood up saying, "Excuse me a moment, I have something to attend to." Olsson stepped away to the other side of the room and made a call. "Suchart. It's Derek." Olsson then switched to a language neither Alison nor the others could understand.

"What was that all about?" Alison asked when he put the phone down.

Olsson shrugged. "Just a loose end to be tied up," he said.

"What language were you speaking?" she asked. "Cantonese or Thai?"

Olsson grinned. "You remember. Thai. One last call."

"Also to Thailand?"

Olsson nodded. "General Vanich, *sawadee-krap.* . . ." The conversation continued in Thai, but with a scattering of English words that caught Alison's attention—"Russian," "South African," three names. And an airline.

"I'm dying to know what you're up to," Alison said.

Olsson took a deep breath as he held her gaze, and a smile slowly spread across his face. "No more secrets."

Alison grinned back.

"Sorry to interrupt," Madge said, "but it's time we got going."

64 Mission Accomplished?

Down—but not out? Arrested but still-Senator Frank McKurn hangs over the Conservative Party like a dead albatross.

So it's hardly surprising that the Conservatives have slipped several percent in the latest polls—but, oddly enough, not to Labor's benefit. Nash is no doubt gnashing his teeth at the arrests of a couple of *state* Labor MPs, tarring Labor with the same brush of corruption.

The biggest gainer: "undecided" (including the minor parties and independents), now 14.7% compared to 8.3% a week earlier.

The rise of the "undecideds" is reflected in lower turnouts at CP and Labor rallies. It seems more voters are concluding: "A plague on both your houses."

The Conservatives still lead on a two-party-preferred basis (that's after the projected distribution of preferences)—but if this "plague" of "undecideds" keeps spreading in the two weeks between now and election day, the final result could be anyone's guess.

In case you were wondering: The Conservatives would *love* to get McKurn's name off the ballot—but once nominations have closed, *no* candidate can drop out. Them's the rules. An arrest, even for serious crimes like murder, is no disqualification either. Only a *conviction* putting an MP or Senator in jail for a year or more will get him or her thrown out of Parliament. It will be months, (possibly *years,* given the number of charges) before a judge decides whether McKurn is "innocent" or "guilty."

So the Conservatives are stuck with him till the end of his current term (June next year)—or even longer if he's reelected.

*****

"Pressing the flesh and kissing babies" had energized Anthony Royn since his very first election campaign when he challenged Paul Cracken in high school for the presidency of the Young Conservatives. Weeks without enough sleep never slowed him down.

This campaign was turning into something very different. McKurn's arrest had popped the bubble of popularity he'd enjoyed since the Parliament House explosion. Even worse, Conservative Party loyalists were reminded of his supposed "duplicity"— and blamed *him* for McKurn's continued presence on the Senate ticket.

In the past two days, he'd addressed seven rallies in seven cities and towns. Preceding each rally was a "meet-the-Prime-Minister" reception for Conservative Party members.

He wasn't sure which was worse.

Too many Conservative Party bigwigs skipped the receptions, expressing their feelings by suddenly discovering "a conflicting appointment." Those members who showed up welcomed him, sure enough, but "warm" was not an adjective anyone could use to describe their attitude.

And the "rallies"—well! In previous elections, when the party booked a space for a thousand people, twelve hundred or more showed up and hung on his every word. At *all* seven venues, there'd been empty seats. He even had to raise his voice to compete with the muttering and chattering in the audience. He felt he was trying to wake up the dead—and failing. Each appearance drained his energy until he felt he had none left.

McKurn's arrest made a mockery of *his* anti-corruption, anti-drug, and clean government campaign themes. But, ironically, it hadn't affected *McKurn's* protégé Paul Cracken, who happily turned into a tenacious terrier attacking his former patron, giving no quarter and asking none. "We promised clean government," he said. "We pledged a no-holds-barred, take-no-hostages approach to the menace of corruption—and that's what we've delivered. So Senator McKurn, the senior member of our own party, was the first to be arrested? What's the problem? That just shows we *mean* it, that we're doing exactly what we said we'd do."

When Royn tried the same pitch, it fell flat: even the members who *wanted* to believe him remained skeptical. He wasn't sure he believed it himself.

Doug, Melanie, and the Conservative officials who rallied to him—not necessarily to save *him*, but to save the party—were at a loss for ideas. Without Alison's support, he felt disoriented, and assailed by self-doubts. He'd finally received a message from her: I'm sorry for just disappearing, Prime Minister, but I simply can't face *anyone*. I hope you understand.

He did—which solved nothing.

His enjoyment of politics came from his presence on the stage, his power over the audience—and the limelight. The rest he could do without. Vanessa's suggestion of going back to the theater grew in appeal; he began wondering how soon after the election he could make a graceful exit.

He'd gone to bed feeling exhausted and woke feeling no better. He easily resisted the weak impulse to open his eyes and pulled the blankets over him until he remembered where he was.

Hobart. Arriving late last night for another rally this morning, followed by one in Melbourne this afternoon.

He groaned, wishing he could go back to sleep and wake up on Sunday, when he'd be back home with Melanie and have a day off—as much as that was possible in the middle of an election.

But now, almost against his will, his eyes were wide open. Sluggishly, he crawled out of bed and drew back the curtains. Tasmania's picturesque capital lay spread out before him—but all he could comprehend were the dark, stormy clouds scudding across the sky.

He was still in the shower when Doug Selkirk's frantic phone call reminded him the reception would start in just five minutes.

THE PARTY STALWARTS—THOSE who'd come—were polite enough, but he was aware of the odd strange look, their reserve, and that they found talking with each other of greater interest than talking with him. There were always a few who couldn't resist the attraction of actually meeting *the* Prime Minister, but their curiosity was quickly satisfied. Royn was toying with the idea of going back to his suite "to run through his notes" when he heard a soft, tinkling voice saying.

"Tony. Welcome to Tasmania."

He looked around to see Vanessa Strezlecki smiling at him. "What a pleasant surprise," he grinned. "But—I thought this was members only. How did you get in here?"

Vanessa laughed. "Being a senator helps open doors. Have you had any time to look around our fair city?"

Royn shook his head. "All I've seen of Hobart this time is the view from my suite and the brewing storm."

"It's a grey day, a bit like your mood, perhaps? You should come in autumn. It's so beautiful—my favorite time of year."

"Not summer?" Royn said, aware that he was edging back to draw Vanessa further from the other guests.

"Oh, summer l like. Spring I love too. And curling up by the fire in winter's so *cozy,* don't you think?"

Royn laughed despite himself. "Is there anything you *don't* like?"

"*Every* cloud has a silver lining. All you have to do is look for it."

Royn sighed. "I wish I could believe that."

"On occasion," said Vanessa, "you need to invest some time and energy before you can see it."

"Right now, I don't have either," Royn found himself admitting.

"You *do* look a bit tired."

"Exhausted," Royn nodded, reacting to the compassion in her voice. "It seemed so easy—until I became prime minister. Turns out it's harder than I expected."

"I suppose Kydd used to make all the tough decisions. Now they're all yours."

Royn nodded. *Those decisions* were inescapable—but somehow the weight of them had melted away. At least, for the moment.

"And you could overlook the dark side of politics—all the scheming, backstabbing and under-the-table chicanery?"

"Pretty much," Royn sighed, "but not completely—"

"But not any more?"

"And it won't ignore me," Royn grinned.

"Especially, I suppose, McKurn."

"Do *you* believe those stories?"

"What matters, surely, is that everybody out there—and, by the looks of them, in here—believes them."

"That's true." Royn became aware that he and Vanessa had become the subject of puzzled looks from the party members, who probably wondered why *their* leader was in deep conversation with an independent senator, and a "green" one to boot.

"So—" Vanessa shrugged, as if to defuse the significance of what she was about to say "—what are you going to do about it?"

Royn sighed. "I wish I knew."

"Why don't you try something like, 'Look, sorry everyone, I really messed up.'"

"I *couldn't*—" Then what she'd said struck home and he paused to taste it. "Maybe," he said, searching Vanessa's face, "but I'm not sure I should take advice from the opposition."

"The *loyal* opposition."

Royn laughed. "Loyal to what or whom?"

"Friendship," Vanessa said.

"You're full of surprises, Vanessa. Like being *here*. You're not exactly a Conservative Party voter. Why did you come?"

"This is my hometown. I thought I should welcome you."

Aside from the hotel staff, who most likely acted from professional courtesy, Vanessa was about the only person who'd extended him a genuine welcome. "Thank you," he said with feeling. "But apologize? I'm not sure that would work."

"Has anyone come up with a better idea?"

Royn shook his head. "In fact, they'd probably nix it—"

"Doesn't it seem like the *right* thing to do?" Vanessa asked.

Royn slowly nodded. "I think so."

"Avoiding the issue hasn't worked. Denying it won't. An apology might not—but it will make you more human. And when was the last time a prime minister or president *genuinely* apologized for *anything?*"

"You're tempting me," Royn chuckled. "I should be suspicious of even *considering* any advice from a member of the opposition—even the loyal opposition."

"You think I'm laying a trap?"

"If anyone else had suggested it, I *would*," Royn laughed, glancing at his watch. "Time to start." He paused and then whispered, "Would you have time for a coffee, or even an early lunch afterwards?"

"I'd enjoy that, Tony. Where?"

"Um—perhaps you could make your way up to my suite—?"

"Quietly, you mean?" Vanessa grinned. "I understand. A scandal would not be a good idea right now."

Royn flushed. "That's—"

"What you were thinking. I know. I'll creep up while nobody's looking. Oh, Tony— you might find quite a large crowd today. I suggested my friends all come along—"

"The loyal opposition?"

"Right."

"They'll be here to heckle me."

"Most likely," Vanessa said, her face lighting up with amusement, "but that will be a change from being ignored, don't you think?"

"It should liven things up," Royn said. With new-found energy, he felt ready to take on the world. "Thanks for the warning—and the advice." Dropping his voice, he added, "Will *you* be there?"

Vanessa nodded. "Good luck."

Royn grinned. "See you after."

THE WEATHER IN HOBART that morning was blustery and near-freezing. People cheerfully shed their coats and parkas as they streamed into the hall, happy to come in from the cold. When the influx slowed to a trickle, just a dozen or so empty seats remained.

Good, Royn thought as he peeked through the curtains behind the stage. Assessing the audience's mood, he felt some looked rather bored—probably the party faithful, here from a sense of duty; from others, anticipation. No doubt Vanessa's friends and other opponents polishing their heckles. A hostile audience, perhaps, but an *active* negative reaction was something to look forward to—for a change.

"A lot of faces I don't recognize, Tony," said the emcee, the President of the Tasmanian Conservatives.

"Yes," Royn chuckled. "The hecklers, I'd guess."

"I'll go ahead and introduce you—"

"With this audience, Ron, my sense is it would be better if I just walked out alone."

The President looked slightly miffed. "If you say so," he shrugged.

As Royn strode from the side entrance to the lectern, the noise level dropped; not to zero but to a background of whispers and mutters.

In a departure from his normal practice, he did not look at the audience as he crossed the stage. He dropped the newspaper he was carrying on the lectern and studied his notes. The background voice level rose slightly, accompanied by the creaking of chairs. He sensed a growing restlessness and sure enough, in less than a minute a voice yelled out: "Get on with it, mate. We haven't got all day." The interjection was followed by a small chorus of "Yeah," and "Hear, hear."

Only now did Royn look up. Throwing down his notes, he stepped to one side of the lectern. He saw Vanessa in the back row smiling at him. He smiled back, and let his smile encompass the room.

"I've come in for a quite a lot of criticism lately," Royn began.

"You're not joking!" the same voice yelled.

Royn's head turned towards the heckler. "That's right," he said. "I'm not joking. And I can assure you, it's been a very unpleasant experience."

"Well-deserved!"

"You think so?" Royn grinned at the heckler. "We'll see what you think in a few minutes. Let me start with some background.

"Two months ago, the Special Inquiry into Drugs and Corruption—colloquially known as the 'Candyman Inquiry'—was established by the Attorney-General *at my instigation.*

"The 'Candyman' was just a blind; the primary focus of the Inquiry from its very first day was *Senator Frank McKurn.*

"The Candyman Inquiry became a full Royal Commission because *I pushed it through.*

"Who suggested making Mr. Justice Herbert Flint its head? *I did.*

"When the 'Dump McKurn' movement came into being, who was its most enthusiastic supporter? *Me.*"

"You expect us to believe that?"

"Well, you *should.*" Royn chuckled, looked towards the heckler with a wide grin. "After all, why have I been so severely attacked, condemned and derided? *Because I backed the move to drop McKurn from the Senate ticket—*"

"Until the last moment!"

"That's right," said Royn, his voice turning somber. "Until the very last moment. Then I switched."

"Proving you're just another two-faced Janus."

Royn nodded. "It sure looks that way—"

"You agree!" the heckler shouted triumphantly.

"I agree it *looks that way,*" Royn said. He saw Doug Selkirk alternately nodding and shaking his head, clearly puzzled and concerned. He smiled reassuringly, at the same time wondering how party officials—and the press—would react. *Too late to worry about that now.*

"This all began earlier this year when we stumbled across some, ah, information which, if corroborated, would become evidence against McKurn. Everything came to a head when—" Royn paused, pursing his lips in thought. "McKurn was arrested on

Wednesday on nine different charges. Later that day, a *tenth* charge was added, *blackmail.* When someone is charged with a crime, the legal rule of *sub judice* comes into play. That means we can't talk about anything related to a case until the court reaches a verdict of innocent or guilty."

"McKurn was pressuring *you?*"

The voice from the audience, this time, was Selkirk's. Royn acknowledged him with a faint nod of his head, just enough to give the audience the impression he agreed with Selkirk, while saying, "That, unfortunately, is one of many questions I cannot answer right now. *Sub judice,* remember. What I can say is this: it was imperative that McKurn be kept in the dark about our investigations. McKurn has—*had* enormous clout within the party, even with all the accusations from McKurnWatch and others. To buy enough time for Flint to gather enough evidence to convict McKurn, I felt I had no choice but to, ah, concede, much as I hated to do so. And then—you know the rest.

"I and my colleagues expected it would take *months* for Justice Flint to collect enough evidence against McKurn. No one, least of all me, expected Justice Flint's first witness, Derek Olsson, to turn up with McKurn's head on a plate, so to speak." For emphasis, he waved the newspaper so everyone could see its big, black headline heralding more arrests.

"I wish to acknowledge the enormous debt of gratitude I have—we *all* have—to Derek Olsson. The arrests resulting from his testimony have vindicated everything I've stood for in ways I had never expected."

Royn had moved slowly closer to the audience. Now standing front and center at the edge of the stage, he was composed and commanding, the audience giving him full attention in total silence. His face spread into a wide grin as he added, "And if you haven't heard the latest news, this morning McKurn was denied bail, the judge ruling the risk of him fleeing the country was too high."

The applause started slowly as if his message had taken a while to sink in. It was polite applause, with pockets of enthusiasm and others who clapped a couple of times and then stopped. *Far* from a standing ovation, he thought, but a vast improvement nonetheless.

A movement in the back of the hall caught his eye. Vanessa was edging out of the hall. At the doorway she stopped. With a slight wave of her hand she gave him a thumbs up.

Now feeling ten feet tall, Royn felt as though he could spread himself to encompass every person there.

"Thank you," he said. "If you have questions, fire away."

*****

"*YOU!* WHAT THE FUCK?"

"King Kong" halted in the entrance of Long Bay Jail's visiting room, staring at his surprise visitor.

Derek Olsson grinned back. "I'm pleased to see you too."

"Are you coming or going?" a guard asked the King.

The King shrugged. "Like—my appointment book is full today!" His foot still in plaster, he hobbled across the room towards Olsson.

"No hard feelings?" Olsson asked as the King took a seat on the opposite side of the table.

"Toff, in my business you can't afford 'em. Especially with some guy who can take out me and me four mates like that." He snapped his fingers; then grinned. "But don't hang around in any dark alleys once I'm out."

"Fair enough," Olsson chuckled. "Sorry about the ankle, but I didn't have a lot of choice at the time."

The King shrugged. "I guess we came off better than what we planned for you." His face lit up as he added, "But I tell you what. Them nurses are a sight damn softer on the eyes than them pig uglies round here."

Olsson laughed. "Hear anything from Luk Suk?"

The King shook his head.

"You won't."

"He can't talk any more?" the King said.

Olsson shook his head.

"You have something to do with that?"

Olsson nodded.

"That figures." The King settled back in his chair. "But much as you enjoy my company, don't s'ppose ya come here just to pass the time o' day."

Olsson lowered his voice. "I came to see if you might do me a favor."

"Favors don't come cheap, ya know?"

"So I've heard."

"How about you get me outta here?"

"Sure," Olsson said. "I'll send a limo to pick you up—when you're released."

The King laughed. "What kind of favor?"

"You know Frank McKurn?"

"Yeah," the King sneered. "The 'Solon.' Thinks he's king of the hill, but he don't give no respect so he don't get none. So?"

"Call him 'Frankie,'" Olsson chuckled. "That really gets his back up."

The King laughed. "Good idea. So whaddaya want?"

"I'd appreciate if you could deliver a message for me." Olsson grinned. "I doubt you'll have any trouble, *this time.*"

"With Frankie?" The King laughed. "Except . . . we don't see him much."

"Why is that?"

"He's in the VIP cells. A sort of mini 'Club Fed'."

"I see," said Olsson.

Then the negotiations got serious.

*****

"I hate that place," Alison said as the van sped away from Long Bay Jail. "I couldn't stand it, thinking of you, Derek, when you were in *there*—"

Olsson's arm around her tightened at the trembling of her body against his. "I'm not there now," he said.

"You didn't mind it?" Alison said, looking up in surprise.

"Not too much."

Alison sighed with relief as the jail and its razor-topped fence disappeared from view. Snuggling closer to Olsson she said, "What now, Derek?"

"We have to wait," he said. "A day or two. Three. I don't know."

"Let's wait somewhere far away. From *everything.*"

"Not too far," Olsson said. "Flint wants me back—"

"*No,*" said Alison. "You *can't.* That . . . *killer* might pick up our trail again." Alison jerked around to look through the rear window, something she'd been doing regularly since they'd left her hideout. Again, she asked, "Are you *sure* we've lost him?"

"As sure as we can be," said Madge from the front passenger seat.

"The van's clean," said the bodyguard who was driving. He checked the vehicle thoroughly at every stop, just to make sure.

For the first half of their journey the previous evening from Alison's lonely hideout on the Captain's Flat Road, they'd travelled in convoy with the second van. About halfway to Sydney, they accelerated away from the "wired" van and turned off the freeway, taking back roads the rest of the way. Once in Sydney, they switched vehicles. The two bodyguards in the "wired" van took turns driving non-stop—to Brisbane. They *thought* they'd spotted the tail, but they couldn't say for sure.

"But, Madge," said Alison, "are you one hundred percent *certain?*"

Madge shook her head. "No, Alison," she said softly, "we can't be."

Alison shuddered. "Then we need to get a long way away," she said in a small voice. "Quickly."

Olsson absorbed the pleading look in her eyes. "Head for Bankstown airport," he said. "We'll rent a plane."

THE TWIN-ENGINED CESSNA droned on into the night. Alison dozed fitfully, comforted by the faint vibration and the knowledge that every throb of the propellers carried her further away from the Assassin. For the first time since Olsson had shown up and thrust her into a bulletproof jacket, she felt completely relaxed.

Almost completely. The sense of danger was growing fainter by the second—but would it ever go away? She'd abandoned Royn in the middle of his greatest challenge and was assailed by feelings of guilt. She should go back, said her sense of duty—a small voice overwhelmed by the continuing shock of knowing she could never look anyone in the eye again without wondering: *have you seen me?*

The image of the sixteen-year-old part of herself still stood on the steps of Parliament House—with tears streaming down her face.

Since she'd walked out of the Prime Minister's office, she could hold just one objective in her mind: *escape.* To return to the world that sent her on the run from a killer as if *she* were a fugitive was beyond comprehension.

She nestled closer to Olsson. Since he'd arrived—despite the danger he'd brought—she felt *protected.* She let him make the decisions with nary a murmur or objection, and was pleased to do so. A reversion to childhood when everything was simple, that she knew. A reversal of roles, remembering the time when Olsson said, "I always feel like I'm leaning on you for your *strength.*" Now, *she* was the one without strength, without even the willpower to look beyond the safety of the moment.

Their destination was Dubbo, west of Sydney and the furthest they could fly without running into airport curfews. They touched down with five minutes to spare.

Dubbo was a surprising oasis of green in the parched, drought-stricken land. "Recycled water," said the motel clerk, in response to Olsson's question, as he checked them in. Hiding behind dark glasses and a beret low on her forehead, Alison went unrecognized.

They had dinner by the pool, takeaway from a nearby Chinese restaurant. Alison sat in shadow, shivering when anybody walked by—even on the distant street.

"Fancy a swim?" Olsson asked.

"Not a chance," Alison shuddered. "It's no joking matter."

"I know, Alison," Olsson said softly.

"Let's go inside."

Alison carefully double-locked and chained the door, hobbled to the window and drew the curtains. Awkwardly shrugging off her coat, she surveyed the room in the harsh light of the naked bulb in the center of the ceiling. A double bed, a single, a TV, a bathroom behind. Functional but cheap furniture, a cookie-cutter duplicate of thousands—*millions,* perhaps—of other motel rooms around the world.

"It's not the Ritz," said Olsson.

"No, it's not," Alison said, overcome with the sense that her world had shrunk into four walls like these. Then, looking at Olsson, she began to smile. She let her walking stick fall to the floor and opened her arms invitingly. "But *you're* here."

ALISON LAY, CONTENTED, HER head buried under the covers and on Olsson's chest. Lazily, her lips lay on his skin; her fingers caressed him; his strong arms enfolded her, his hand pressing into the small of her back. She luxuriated in the sense of him, the feeling of spent electricity still tingling along the length of their bodies. Shimmers of light leaked from the outside through the cheap curtains, but as long as she kept her eyes closed she could forget where she was. She was drifting towards welcome sleep when Olsson suddenly said:

"Are you going to let McKurn win?"

"What do you mean?"

"Do I have to explain it?"

"No," Alison groaned, letting her head fall back on the pillow, opening her eyes, the moment broken. "You don't."

"I've got an idea," Olsson said.

Alison looked at him askance: even in the dim light his mischievous grin and deep dimple unmistakably implied he was about to say something she wouldn't like. "Out with it, then," she sighed.

"Let's go on TV. You and me. Together."

"On TV? Me?" Alison said, horrified. She sat up, glaring down on him. "That's the *worst* idea, ever."

"Which is why you should do it."

"Because it's the *worst?*"

"Because it's the *hardest.* Someday, you'll have to face the world. Will waiting make any difference?"

"When I'm old and grey, maybe I won't care any more."

"And what will you do till then?"

"Oh, Derek. I don't know."

65 "... for I Have Sinned ..."

Third Parties Grab for Balance of Power
Hope to up Senate seats, tip election for House
By Robin Cartwright
Sykes Media exclusive
Saturday: **Sydney**

A loose "alliance" of third parties and independents hope to cash in on the dramatic fall of both Labor and Conservative parties in the polls.

The MYOBB Party, along with half-a-dozen independents and a few minor parties, announced they would put each other first on their official How To Vote Cards—and the Labor and Conservative parties *last.*

Karla Preston, the "unofficial" (as she vainly insists) spokesperson for the MYOBB Party, invited all other minor parties and independents to join in. "The only conditions," she said, "are that you put everyone else who's signed up ahead of all other candidates—in any order you like, of course—and the two major parties dead last. That should dramatically increase the chances of an independent winning when no candidate has an absolute majority—especially in the Senate."

Ms. Preston was confident this agreement would result in independents picking up an extra Senate seat in just about every state.

The Labor and Conservative Parties disagreed. "In the end," said Labor leader Ian Nash, "pretty much all preferences end up with us or the Conservatives. All this arrangement will do is make it harder to count the votes."

Federal Conservative President Helen Arkness said, "Minor parties are a vibrant part of Australian democracy. But I think it's a pipe-dream of Ms. Preston's to think that her arrangement will have any significant impact on the final result."

But the major parties' decline in the polls, says Sydney University political science professor Georgina Oldfellow, "could prove Ms. Preston right. Minor parties and independents seem likely to pick up a record number of votes. By streaming preferences to each other, ahead of the major parties, they definitely increase their chances of gaining a few extra Senate seats, though probably not in the House."

The MYOBB Party claims it is the only "party of principle." But *any* minor party is welcome to join, according to Ms. Preston—including the MYOBB's ideological opposites like the Greens and Family Foundation. Ironically, they could be the ones to end up with an extra seat or two—thanks to MYOBB preferences.

"Or it could go the other way," Ms. Preston replied. "Since you have to number all the candidates in order of your preference, starting with number one, your preferences have to go *somewhere* for your vote to be valid. That's how the system works. This is a 'you-scratch-my-back-and-I'll-scratch-yours' deal. It involves no compromise of our principles.

    "In any case, Family Foundation, Greens, Labor, Conservatives—what's to choose? They *all* want to put their hands in your pockets. Their only argument is what they want to take out."

*****

SENATOR FRANK MCKURN HAD never felt so alone.

His "VIP" cell was more comfortable than the ones he remembered from his previous stretches in Long Bay. But back then he was young, had plenty of company—and was only inside for a few weeks or months.

This time, he had a cell all to himself. There was the company of the other politicians, senior policemen and bureaucrats who'd also been arrested on corruption charges. But they universally—and so unfairly—blamed him for their plight. And this time there was no limit to his stay. He'd be very lucky, he knew, if he ever walked out the gates of Long Bay under his own steam.

The four walls of his cell had become his world. A miniature, colorless universe where he was in control of nothing.

He began to suffer from mysterious aches and pains which took him to the prison infirmary. Probably psychosomatic—but at least there was the comforting, sympathetic voice of the prison doctor to look forward to.

Once again, he was sitting in the doctor's waiting room when another prisoner was ushered in, accompanied by two guards. The man was taller than McKurn, broad-shouldered, heavily-muscled, and twice the weight. One leg was in a cast. Grinning, he hobbled on crutches towards McKurn. As he sat in the next chair, one of his crutches landed heavily on McKurn's foot.

McKurn yelped. "Goddammit! Watch where you're putting those bloody things."

"Sorry, Frankie," said the King. "But accidents happen, you know."

"My name," McKurn growled, "is Senator McKurn."

"You might have been a big wheel out there," "King Kong" said without inflection, making his voice more menacing, "but in here Senator don't mean shit, you unnerstand?"

"Really? It means I don't have to mix with the likes of you."

"Then what do you call this?"

"Who the hell are you, anyway?"

"They call me King Kong."

"I can see why."

The King squeezed McKurn's knee. McKurn yelped.

"Just being friendly, Frankie."

"That's friendly?"

"Sorry," the King laughed. "Don't know my own strength."

McKurn shuddered at the imagined sensation of the King's powerful fingers closing around his neck.

"In fact, when you get back to your cell you'll find a little gift. From me."

"What sort of gift?"

"Oh, something I'm sure you'll enjoy. But you'd better enjoy it carefully. It's against prison regulations."

"And how will it get there?"

"Magic," the King laughed, glancing meaningfully at Bob the Swagman.

McKurn caught the King's glance and looked at the prison guard, who just smiled.

The other guard, by the door, simply ignored him. At that moment, McKurn wished he were safely locked inside the four walls of his cell. Except—that was no longer safe, either.

"And the next gift," the King said, "may not be so pleasant."

"You're not supposed to be here at the same time as me."

"True," the King said. "But there are ways and means, Frankie. Ways and means."

McKurn turned to Bob the Swagman. "Officer—"

"Yes, I know, Frankie." He shrugged. "A mix-up. These things happen. Like accidents."

Accidents? McKurn's eyes swivelled between Bob the Swagman and King Kong. The "VIP" section of the prison was off limits to regular prisoners, but prison guards could move around freely. There was obviously something going on between the King and the Swagman. Why not? What could be more natural in a place like this?

McKurn sighed. "So, what are you here for?"

"Murder," said the King. "Several, in fact."

"That's not what I meant."

"You sure?" the King chuckled.

McKurn winced.

"A mate of mine is being threatened by a mate of yours, Frankie. I'd appreciate if you could call him off."

"Why should I?"

The King laid his hand gently on McKurn's good arm. "You got two shoulders," he said softly. "That's one good reason."

McKurn turned towards the Swagman, who just looked on impassively. McKurn inwardly shuddered at the awareness that even the prison guards held him in contempt.

"Whatever you're being paid, I can double it," McKurn said.

The King shrugged. "A million bucks in here is worthless. And when I get out—" the King laughed "—my pension fund is waiting for me. But there is one thing you could do for me."

"What's that?"

"Get me outta here. Now."

McKurn shook his head.

The King shrugged. "Then you got nothing to offer me, Frankie."

McKurn looked at the King blankly. Once upon a time, he was thinking, he could have beaten this "King" to a pulp. I've gotten soft, old—and frail.

"All ya gotta do is tell your mate, the 'Assassin,' to lay off."

"And if don't?"

"Maybe I'll ask the guvnor to gimme a reward for all the money the taxpayers will save when your unfortunate demise means Frankie McKurn won't ever have to stand trial." The King laughed uproariously at his own words. "Look on the bright side, Frankie: you'll never be found guilty."

For a moment, McKurn trembled uncontrollably. As Senator McKurn, he'd been "The King." He'd instilled fear even in tough thugs like this one. He'd been the one who'd threatened—and protected—hundreds of others. Now, he couldn't even protect himself.

He had never felt so helpless in his life.

"Okay," he murmured.

"I gotta friend of mine on the outside who knows the 'Assassin.' You tell me when he's got the message, and my mate will check out he really did. So no backpedalling, no double-dealing—or you know what will happen. We gotta deal?"

McKurn nodded.

"I didn't hear ya."

"Yes," said McKurn, "we gotta deal."

*****

"Do we *have* to keep moving?" Alison sighed as they drove a rented SUV out of Dubbo in the long shadows of the early morning, heading further west.

"The pilots might have recognized you," Madge pointed out. "If so, they're bound to talk."

"And yes, we do," Olsson said. "Until I get a message. Just a day or two now—I hope."

"If the message is 'no'?" Alison said.

Olsson shrugged. "We'll have to think of something else."

"At least," said the driver, "we can be *sure* we're not being followed."

Alison looked behind. The land was flat, the road dead straight, the only vehicle to be seen was moving the opposite direction. "At the moment," she said skeptically.

"Let's see, then," said Madge, who begin noting the number plates of every car they passed. More than once they parked, out of sight, at the top of a hill with clear views of the road for kilometers in each direction. By the time they reached the town of Mildura on the NSW-Victorian border, even Alison was convinced that no one was on their tail. "But," she said, "I still don't feel *safe*."

Alison paced their hotel room, back and forth, driving her walking stick into the floor with extra force on each step to emphasize her growing irritation. "I feel like a prisoner," she said, glaring at Olsson sitting lazily in one of the armchairs as if he hadn't a care in the world. Somehow, that angered her more than the sense of being hemmed in by the claustrophobic walls. She turned on him, demanding:

"Aren't you going to ask me?"

"Ask you what?"

"Who it was?"

"Who what—?" Olsson shook his head. "No."

"Don't you want to know?"

"Do you want to tell me?"

"Dammit, Derek. Why do you always answer my question with another question?"

Olsson grinned. "Why not?"

Alison raised her walking stick, holding it like a club, growling at Olsson in mock attack.

Olsson shrugged. "I figure you'll tell me when you're ready to and not before."

"Does it bother you?"

"Yes." Olsson held up a hand before Alison could react. "Because you're hurting so much it must have been rape, all over again."

"Yes," Alison said, shuddering at the memory, "it was. Except that I *agreed* to it."

Olsson stared at Alison, his mouth hanging open in disbelief. "You agreed to—?"

"Don't say it!" Alison threw herself onto the sofa. "And don't look at me like that. I was under pressure. *Severe* pressure." Her head fell into her hands as her shoulders began to shake.

Olsson leapt up to find a box of tissues; kneeling in front of her, he could hear her mumbled words, ". . . forgive me, Father, for I have sinned . . . " as one hand made the sign of the cross on her chest. Raising her head she looked at Olsson through reddened, tearful eyes. "I come seeking redemption and absolution for my sins. . . ."

Her words were not for him; her eyes glazed, she didn't even see him. He gently dabbed her face with a tissue. "Alison," he said solemnly, "I love you."

A smile trembled on her lips. "But, Derek," she said, "I *have* sinned."

"Against God?"

Alison laughed. "Worse than that. Against myself."

Olsson's head began to nod, as if in agreement, but he was gazing back in time, seeing his life laid out before him in all its grisly details. "As have I, Alison," he said, his voice a hoarse whisper. "But on the scales of judgement, my sins—my *self-betrayal* far exceeds yours."

"That," Alison said, taking his hands, "is not possible. Unless—"

"—abortion is not murder?"

Alison blinked away a sudden tear. "Yes," she whispered.

"I just don't know," Olsson sighed. "As you said, if the dividing line is not conception, where it is?"

"You're such a comfort."

"Okay, then," Olsson grinned. "It was just a bunch of cells."

"This is nothing to joke about." But there was a chuckle in her voice as she spoke.

Olsson's grin faded from his face. "Just the same, Alison—"

"*You're* the greater sinner? Convince me, then. If you can." A tug on his hands directed him to sit beside her. Leaning her head on his chest, she said, "Tell me what happened in Hong Kong. Why you *abandoned* me. *Everything.*"

"It was my grandfather all over again," Olsson said, his arms encircling Alison's body as if to gather strength, "but much worse. His name, his *title*, was Luk Suk. . . ."

In a very few minutes, the sound of Alison's breathing slowed into a purr. Olsson paused, thinking she had fallen asleep. But her voice murmured, "I *am* listening, Derek. Keep going."

Drawing comfort from her warmth and closeness, he continued—surprised at the easy flow of even his most sensitive words, and the deepest secrets he'd never spoken aloud before, even to himself.

". . . *THAT'S* WHEN I SAW you again, in the coffee shop of the Regent Hotel."

"Ross was there?"

"When you stormed out, you walked straight past him."

"I had no idea. I was so *angry.*"

"You had every right to be."

"I did."

"But you're not angry now."

"Not with you, Derek, not with you."

"Even after everything I've told you so far?"

"Derek," Alison smiled, "we're *both* of us at the bottom of the well."

"Nowhere to go but up."

"I hope so," Alison chuckled. "You went into business with Ross to escape Luk Suk?"

"Yes—Luk Suk was *also* a partner. He financed us and was our biggest customer. It went like a dream. No one ever *suspected* a thing."

"*That's* why InterFreight grew so quickly. But drugs—didn't that bother you?"

"I was *free,* out from under Luk Suk's thumb—"

"Except you weren't."

"Not in the end, no. And, yes, the drugs *did* bother me. After all, being illegal, we could not depend on the protection of the law. Karla's right: when you're outside the law, violence comes with the territory. I had to find another way."

"And do no harm?"

"Right. Did you ever wonder why I gathered all that information about crime and corruption? For my little country papers? No. I hit on reverse blackmail. When somebody threatened us, our counter threat was to *expose* them. They backed off peacefully. Always."

"*Who* backed off? You said no one suspected a thing—and then you contradict yourself."

"I, er, branched out."

"Into *what?* Out with it. *Everything,* remember."

Olsson sighed. "*Selling* drugs. The idealist in me: I thought I could transform the trade."

"Derek, you can't be that naïve."

"It seemed to be working, Alison. There are no guarantees of *quality* or *consistency* in the drug business. The buyer can never be sure what's mixed into his drug of choice. Sometimes the additives are fatal. We set out to correct that—"

"We? Ross too?"

"No, Ross never knew."

"*What* drugs?"

"Marijuana, hashish, and heroin."

"Oh, Derek. Heroin's *poison.*"

"Not marijuana?"

"I used to think so. But—just keep going."

"Our products were high quality at a lower price—we even listed the ingredients on the packet—and *branded* them—"

"*Branded* them?" Alison sat up. "Burmese Gold . . . Afghan Number One . . . Colombian High . . . holographic images . . . ?"

"You've . . . *seen* them?"

"You? You're the Candyman?"

Olsson sighed. "Yes."

"You were in competition with Luk Suk?"

"He never knew. *No one* knew. Not another soul—until now."

"Then you were framed—"

"—and everything blew up."

"Violence came to you after all—and you killed a man."

"Yes." *Others died,* Olsson thought. *And Mitch—will he ever recover?*

"But, Derek, *why?*"

"He was convinced, like Durant, that I'd killed Victor Leung. He thought I'd crossed him, and anyone who crossed him died."

"So it *was* self-defence."

"Not right then. He was my prisoner. Alone and defenceless. He was no threat to me *at that moment.* But later he'd hunt me down, just like we're being hunted now."

"Did he deserve it?"

"You name it—he was guilty. But did that give me the right to take the law into my own hands? I didn't think so then, and I don't think so now."

"But—"

"It was him or me. The law of the jungle. If not then, later. I wanted to live. The choice was simple, but to actually *do* it, in cold blood—" Olsson shuddered. "*That* was almost impossible."

"Just like. . . ." Alison said dreamily. "So here we are, everything both of us set out to do a complete shambles, as if—"

"As if it was inevitable?"

"Yes," Alison. "I wish we could start over."

"We *can*," said Olsson. "But first, we have to get back to the starting point."

"Out of the well."

Alison looked around the room. "I don't know *how*, Derek. But I'll go crazy if I stay in a room like this much longer. But I *can't* go out into the world. Not yet, anyway."

"How about a vacation in a place where no one will know who you are?"

"Where in the world would that be? Antarctica?"

Olsson laughed. "I was thinking of the Sandemans."

"Why there?"

"There are some delightful places—secluded beaches, coral reefs, tiny resorts—where no one will have ever heard of Alison McGuire. *Or* Derek Olsson."

*****

VUONG LAM THO WAS a careful man. His many criminal enterprises were structured so he could walk away from them with maximum deniability. His public face was that of a leading businessman in the Vietnamese immigrant community: few people knew that the many legitimate above-ground businesses he owned had been financed by his profits from the underworld.

His favorite was Sydney's foremost—and most expensive—Vietnamese restaurant. *Everything* was authentic Vietnamese, from the décor, the waiters, the table settings, to the meals, prepared with no concessions to the Western palate by the best chefs from Hanoi, Ho Chi Minh City, and wherever else in Vietnam they could be found.

It was Vuong's home away from home—and an instant hit.

This evening he sat, alone in a back room, waiting for his guest. Right on the agreed time, "Mr. Smith" was ushered in by two waiters.

"Kind of you to see me," Smith said.

A faint smile appeared on Vuong's otherwise impassive face. He waved his hand towards the seat opposite. The two men sat in silence while the waiters poured the tea, brought in an enormous array of dishes, and placed a bottle of beer next to Smith. When the waiters departed, without exhibiting any particular interest Vuong said:

"So, Mr. Smith, why you come?"

"You made an enormous impression when we met at the Greek's." Getting no response, he continued, "I came away convinced that you are a man of your word, unlike most of the other gang leaders at that meeting."

"You work for McKurn," Vuong said. It was a statement, not a question.

"I did," Smith said. "Now I have, ah, inherited a nice piece of his organization."

"How about you get to point, Mr. *Smith*."

"Okay, Mr. Vuong. Since the Greek and McKurn were arrested their outfits are falling apart."

"Not only ones. Many arrested last few days."

"That's right," said Smith. "And there'll be more, thanks to this Royal Commission. Many of your competitors will be put out of business. That represents a great opportunity, Mr. Vuong. But to take advantage of it, you need lots more protection. I can help. McKurn had extensive contacts, supporters and plants in both state and federal governments, including the police and many others on his payroll. I know. I am—was—his paymaster, among other things. And you don't want to be one of the targets of the Royal Commission. I have people on the inside and I can tell you that your name hasn't come up so far. If it does, I can help head them off."

Smith grew restless under Vuong's steady, unchanging case. He could divine no clue to Vuong's thoughts. He sighed with relief when Vuong finally said:

"We begin, Mr. Smith, with your real name."

66   End of the Line

When Olsson woke, he found a message on his phone:
The Assassin has gone home.

"Alison! Take a look at this."

Dripping wet, pulling a towel around her, Alison stepped out of the bathroom.

"We can get out of here, at last," Olsson said.

"Who's it from?" Alison said, less than convinced.

"From the King, of course. Who else?"

"I don't know. Even if this 'King' *did* send it, he's a *criminal*. How do you know he's telling the truth? You beat up him *and* his gang of four. How can you be sure that he ever *intended* to keep his word? Or that McKurn didn't outbid you?"

"I trust my sense of him."

"I don't."

"You don't know him," said Olsson.

"I wouldn't trust him even if I did. You may be a good judge of character, Derek, but you aren't *infallible*. Our *lives* are at stake. And Karla's. Can you take the risk? *I* can't."

Olsson stood thoughtfully.

"You know I'm right, Derek. You're just arguing with me for the fun of it."

"Partly," Olsson grinned. "I'll call Inspector Durant. There's a prisoner in Long Bay called 'the Rat' because he knows everything—and *tells* everything. I'll see if Durant can visit him. And no doubt he has other sources of information."

Alison smiled, and kissed the tip of his nose. "I knew you'd see sense."

*****

Honesty is the best policy?

Anthony Royn wondered if that were true—in politics.

The public reaction to his confession was muted, especially in the press where, thanks to *sub judice*, no headline like *McKurn Blackmails Royn* or, worse, *Royn Gives Into McKurn Pressure* could be printed.

The upper echelons of the party were divided between those who, often from personal experience, appreciated the reach of McKurn's power, and those who considered Royn a weakling for bending to it.

Predictably enough in hindsight, Ian Nash twisted Royn's words, thundering, "Is a man who *admits* he's *incapable* of standing up to someone like Frank McKurn a man who has what it takes to lead our country? I say: definitely not."

Melanie was furious, saying, "I told you so," though not in so many words because, of course, she hadn't. Most of his colleagues, even Cracken, were supportive—if piqued at not being consulted in advance.

The only comfort in the party's latest poll was that the slide of the Conservatives' (and Labor's) share of the vote *may* have slowed. Conversely, the MYOBB Party was the main gainer.

Royn spent the previous morning on the phone to his colleagues. By lunchtime it was agreed that "something had to be done." So Paul Cracken, Helen Arkness, Barry Easton, and Doug Selkirk joined Royn and Melanie in Melbourne to sort through the competing ideas.

The plan they evolved by late evening was simple—in theory. A combination of tax cuts, along with hikes in selected welfare and other payments targeted as much as possible at marginal electorates.

The difficult part: to project, convincingly, that the budget surplus would not decline significantly—in the long run.

When journalists and Labor got to tear the proposal apart, the numbers had to stand up. Cracken ordered the Secretary of the Treasury to join them, telling him in no uncertain terms to keep his objections to himself. In another room were several Treasury officials crunching numbers.

In Canberra, another team was researching "little things" Royn could effect immediately, by regulation. Proposals that would cost nothing—well, cost the government nothing, such as allowing employees to take half-a-day off on full pay to take their pets to the vet.

Ideally, every other day until the election, Royn could sign something like that into law on the theory the voters would be grateful—to him.

By early afternoon it looked as though everything would be ready the next day. "So," Royn said, "shall we set up a press conference tomorrow, to announce it?"

When that was agreed, Royn instructed Selkirk to put the wheels in motion. "And give Jack Noble a call. See if he'll come on board for the next two weeks."

Advertising guru Jack Noble had recently retired—again—after selling the third advertising agency he'd created. Retirement obviously hadn't suited him: within two months he'd opened a fourth agency—styled a "marketing boutique" to comply with the non-compete clause in the sale—and in no time had a full house of clients eager for his marketing magic.

He'd worked for the Conservatives before. Indeed, his advertising was considered a key factor in helping Kydd win his first term of office.

When Selkirk told Noble's receptionist, "I'm calling from Mr. Royn's office," he was put straight through.

"G'day, Doug," said Noble before he could utter a word. "Things are looking pretty grim for you guys, eh, mate? That why you're calling?"

Selkirk was taken off guard until he remembered how the efficient receptionist had carefully taken down his name. "You could say that, Mr. Noble."

"Call me Jack."

"Certainly Mr.—ah, Jack. Mr. Royn was wondering if you might be in a position to work some of your advertising magic for him over the next couple of weeks."

"Well. . . ."

The way Noble drew out that single word with a falling tone sounded to Selkirk very much like "No."

". . . I'd say not even Saint Paul could save you guys now."

"Saint *Paul?* What on earth has he got to do with it?"

"The greatest marketing man in history, mate. Took an obscure Jewish sect, repackaged it, sold it to the Greeks and Romans—and now it's the world's biggest religion. Who can top that?"

"Unfortunately, Jack, we don't have two thousand years."

Noble laughed. "Good one, Doug. No, you've only got two weeks. That makes it even tougher—you need a miracle and not even the saintly Paul could help you there. Have you seen the polls? *Of course* you've seen the polls. Between the Greens and Karla Preston—the Mind Your Own Bloody Business Party, a stroke of genius—you *and* Labor are being skewered at both ends. So give Tony my regards. He's a nice enough guy and might even have made a good prime minister. That's history department now. The way things look he could sell his soul to the devil and *that* wouldn't do the trick. You gotta face it, mate, your boss is fucked. Your whole party is fucked, dead in the water."

"Thanks for the encouragement," Selkirk said.

"You're most welcome," Noble chuckled. "Sorry to be the cold shower of reality, mate—but it's usually better to face facts than ignore them."

"No, huh?" Royn said when he saw Selkirk's expression.

"No," Selkirk said.

"What did he say, Doug? Too busy?"

"He sent you his best regards, Prime Minister."

To Royn, Selkirk seemed to be carrying a cloud of gloom that had not been there before. "Out with it Doug. Tell me *exactly* what he said."

Selkirk shook his head. "You don't want to know."

"That bad?"

"Worse."

Royn frowned. "Did he say anything about our plan?"

"I couldn't get that in," Selkirk replied.

"Then," Royn said, brightening up, "let's surprise him."

*****

"That was Rudi," Olsson said as he put down his phone. "He can't go today, but promises he will first thing in the morning."

"Another day to wait," Alison sighed. "What happened?"

"Flint commandeered him for the Royal Commission, so he's handing everything over. But he *did* say he heard a rumor from his underworld informants that the Assassin *has* gone home."

"That's *wonderful*. That means we can—"

"Not so fast," Olsson said. "It's only a rumor. We still need confirmation—unless you've changed your mind."

"No," Alison said, deflating, "I guess I haven't."

"Apparently, Flint also reinstated your friend Jason Kowalski."

"That'll make him happy," Alison said, turning back to the papers she'd been reading for want of something better to do. She had caught up on the state of the parties, the poll results, and absorbed Royn's dilemma. She felt she could project the final election result with surprising clarity, as if she'd acquired clairvoyance. At the same time, she felt as though she were reading about subjects like quantum physics or the biology of plankton, which held neither interest nor relevance, to *her*.

She could see Royn's fate laid out in front of her—and nothing came. No ideas, no policy options, no strategies. No suggestions whatsoever, not even the *glimmer* of one.

"It's weird," she said, flopping back in the chair. "I've been a political junkie all my life, but now I can't find that passion anywhere."

"It's just a passing phase."

"I'm not so sure, Derek. I can see what Royn's up against—and my mind is blank. *Nothing.* I feel empty."

"Do you *care* whether he wins?"

"I'd *like* him to win."

"That's not the same thing."

"No, it's not."

"Does he miss you?"

"Oh, yes," she said, thinking of the flood of unanswered emails and texts from Royn, Doug Selkirk, and even Melanie and Mary. "But I'm fresh out of rabbits."

"Shouldn't you go back, just the same?"

"I *can't,* Derek."

"Because you can't face them?"

"It's not just that. I've been . . . *violated.* By politics—by the *system.* I'm starting to feel I've been living and working in a sewer—could you go back to that?"

"No. Shouldn't you tell him so?"

Alison nodded slowly, sighing, "I'll send him an email."

Taking her hand, Olsson grinned impishly. "Tell me something else, Alison. Did you get your revenge?"

"I suppose so," Alison said, her mood lifting a little when she thought of McKurn locked up in a dark cell—in a *real* prison which made her "confinement" in a luxury hotel suite a vacation by comparison.

"Was it worth the price you paid?"

"No."

Olsson sat beside her. "I can add up two and two, you know."

"What do you mean by that?"

"I know what price you paid."

"You *can't.*"

"You said you'd been 'violated' *by politics,* and you had an abortion. *Another* violation—of your own conscience. I was in McKurn's power for a couple of days. He gets his kicks from controlling and humiliating people."

"That's like the geek's comment," Alison said, "that to McKurn, power is an aphrodisiac far more potent than money or sex."

"The *geek* writes McKurnWatch? Now, *that's* a surprise—though few people can dig up information as well as him."

"Which is what you used him for, your reverse blackmail."

"That's right," Olsson grinned. "Are you trying to change the subject?"

"Yes," Alison whispered. "But—go on. I can take it."

"Who was blackmailing you, Alison? McKurn. You told me that. What's more humiliating than rape? To you, *nothing.*"

But that's not the full price I paid. The image of her sixteen-year-old self flashed into her mind, with McKurn's leering face to one side.

"Oh, Derek, it was terrible—but I broke his arm."

In politics, she now knew, the cream goes sour and the *McKurns* rise to the top. *Where does that leave me?*

*****

Poonchit scanned the customers ogling her and the other girls on the elevated stage—all wearing high heels and nothing else. As she danced she was thinking, *only a few more customers.* Just a week. Maybe less. She'd worked in this bar for nearly two years. She'd saved almost enough money to buy a small house in her village and start the little roadside stall she'd been dreaming of—and return to her village as *somebody.*

She glanced at her reflection in the floor-to-ceiling mirrors. Her breasts were firm, her body slim, her silhouette attractive. Maybe she'd find a man, get married, and have babies. From that package, only children attracted her. Too many of the men in her village were layabouts who'd rather sponge off their girlfriends than get out of bed. And foreigners—well, she surveyed the customers with contempt, making sure it was well-covered by an inviting smile. They were here for just one reason: the only way they could get what they wanted was to pay for it.

One man, she saw, was looking at *her.* She wiggled her hips at him. He was handsome, blond, and reasonably young as customers went. There was something about him she didn't like—and dismissed the thought. The customers she'd *liked* she could count on the fingers of one hand. He was with two older men. She looked at the oldest one but dismissed him. Older men were usually more considerate—and they couldn't keep you up all night. But there was something hard, repellent about him. Maybe the third, secretive one.

Whatever, she mentally shrugged, her feet not missing a beat. What riveted her attention was the money they threw around. Hundred-baht tips to the waitresses who brought their drinks. Stuffing notes—along with their hands—down the girls' panties. Suddenly, the thought of working another week shrank into the possibility of just one more night! The young man was beckoning to her. She gave him her best smile and slipped off the dance floor.

It was hard work. She was just one of many sexy bodies who had spotted the hundred dollar bills bulging from their wallets: the competition for these three was severe. She fended the other girls off by keeping her man on the edge of excitement, titillating him mercilessly without satisfaction to keep his attention from wandering too much.

They kept plying her with drinks which made it harder to keep her focus. But by the time she lost count she knew that if she could earn just *one* of those hundred dollar bills as a tip, she could be on a bus back to her village the very next day.

When she walked into the steamy Bangkok night in a tipsy daze, she felt that the gods had kissed her. Not only was *she* one of the three winners, she'd ended up with the nicest of the three men, the one in the middle. His name was Vlad—or was it? They kept calling each other different names, as if they'd set out to hide their real ones and, as they got drunker, forgot. Vlad spoke English scattered with a few words she recognized as Russian—but then so did the old one. Though his accent was obviously American, he kept calling Vlad *Tovarisch.* The younger one she couldn't place.

A taxi took them to a house in one of the Sois off Sukhumvit. Instead of going up to one of the bedrooms, the three men pulled out bottles of whisky, bourbon, and vodka and seemed to settle into the sofas for the rest of the night. So, she shrugged, they liked to do it together. She'd done kinkier stuff. It wasn't long before they were all naked and everything was proceeding normally, aside from too many whiskies which made her woozy and nauseous.

A piercing scream shattered her mental fog. One of the other girls. The scream sounded endless; too abruptly, it turned into a strange gurgling sound.

She pushed herself up, ignoring the man on top of her, to see the older man holding a knife covered in blood. She was suddenly thrust back onto the sofa by the man's hand gripping her neck. She could barely breathe. She looked into the smile of death and now knew what this man was so secretive about: he was the worst of the three.

He was going to kill her, she knew. Her strength fading, she reached out with both hands, grabbed his balls and squeezed them with every last ounce of energy she could muster.

"Bitch!" the man snarled thought his shriek of agony. He shifted his weight so it bore down on her neck, cutting off her breath completely. His other fist was now raised, about to smash into her face, when his head simply exploded, blood and flesh and bone splattering on her face. His body collapsed on top of her and she desperately gasped for air as the pressure of his hand relaxed.

On the street outside the house Suchart sat, General Vanich at his side, in the back of a nondescript van monitoring the cameras he'd planted in the house the previous day. When he saw the American pull out a knife he said to Vanich, "Now!"

Vanich grinned. He'd already given the signal and was halfway out the van's rear door.

The squad of armed police sprinted towards the house from their hiding places in the seemingly deserted garden. One of them opened the front door with the duplicate keys thoughtfully provided by Suchart. The others didn't bother with such niceties: they simply crashed through the windows. A moment later, two of the *farang* were dead, the third was grovelling on the floor beneath the menace of three guns, held by unforgiving policemen. Blood oozed from wounds in his arm and chest. In a few minutes he lapsed into unconsciousness.

General Vanich came through the front door and began directing the clean-up and the gathering of evidence. Behind him came Suchart, who handed Vanich a couple of DVDs with the words, "The only copies," and removed the planted cameras.

Poonchit could hardly believe her luck as she helped her still-shaking friend out onto the street. The nightmare over, she and her friend each had three hundred dollars in their purses. Thanks to Suchart, who pointed out to Vanich that the girls hadn't been paid. Vanich took a handful of hundred dollar bills from where the police had laid out the men's possessions and divided them between the two girls. When she reached her village—*tomorrow*—she would lay a large offering of thanks at the feet of the Buddha. With a fervent prayer that all three would come back as ants in the next life so she could squash them.

As he walked to the van, Suchart sent a short text in English: Two of the three shot dead while resisting arrest. One, de Brouw, will stand trial.

That story would be splashed across the next day's papers along with the winning smile of the hero of the moment, the man who had put an end to the serial bar-girl murders: General Vanich.

Olsson, Suchart thought, was a man who paid off his debts with style.

67 Inversion

The "Candyman's" Auction of Stolen Goods

By Karla Preston
OlssonPress Syndicate Exclusive

Is your vote for sale?

Anthony Royn thinks it is—and he's out to buy it.

Last night, looking tired and drawn, he came back fighting, reincarnated as the "Candyman" with a slew of goodies up for grabs. All yours—if you vote for him.

Does he think we're all suckers? Unfortunately, to paraphrase P.T. Barnum, "No one ever lost an election by underestimating the intelligence of the Australian public."

Machiavelli anticipated Barnum by several centuries when he noted that "a deceiver will never lack victims for his deceptions."

If politics is the art of deception, then Anthony Royn is the Artful Dodger. If you swallow Royn's promise that his package of tax cuts and welfare handouts "won't significantly impact the budget surplus," then you're a "victim of his deceptions"—one of the suckers.

Make no mistake about it: the "candy" he's throwing at you as a bribe for your vote is *your own money.* Where else do you think he's going to get it?

Sure, maybe you'll be one of the "lucky" ones, the Paul who scoops up the candy stolen from Peter. Except that up to half of Peter's "candy" gets "lost" in Canberra's bureaucratic maze before Paul gets his hands on whatever's left. If you think getting back 50-65 cents on your tax dollar is worth voting for—hey, I've got a great deal for you on the Sydney Harbour Bridge.

The rich, with their legions of accountants, tax advisors, trusts, and offshore companies, won't be footing too much of the bill. Nor will the poor—but you won't find many "Pauls" amongst the poor.

The package of welfare "goodies" is targeted exclusively at the 85+% of voters who comprise the great Australian middle class . . . the same people who'll be sucked dry to pay for it all.

And while we're on the subject, what do you think makes the budget surplus possible in the first place?

Carefully controlled government spending? Economizing bureaucrats?

Ha!

Inflation pushes up wages. When your salary goes up you move into a higher tax bracket. Lots of people pay more tax and—Bingo! Budget surplus!

Without bracket creep, the government would run a permanent deficit.

Royn is following Kydd's well-trodden path of buying your vote with the money the government stole from you last year.

And if you think I'm exaggerating, equating taxation with thievery, just try *keeping* your money instead of coughing it up when the taxman comes knocking. You'll quickly see taxation's true nature when the government sends men with guns to extort it from you—or drag you away.

For your own good, of course.

"KARLA'S IN GREAT FORM," Olsson chuckled, passing the newspaper to Alison.

"I feel sorry for him," Alison said as she skimmed it.

"Royn?"

"Yes. Most of the other reactions are almost as skeptical—"

"—without the dripping sarcasm."

Durant had given the "all clear" the previous afternoon; they were now on a Sandeman Airlines flight to Toribaya which Alison had chosen "since *everyone* on Qantas will have seen . . . it."

"Free at last," Alison said as she said goodbye to Madge and the other bodyguards.

There was just one uncomfortable moment, at passport control at Sydney airport. The immigration officer's eyes widened when he looked at their passports, and said, "Could you remove your sunglasses, Miss, ah, McGuire?"

"You've seen enough already," Olsson growled.

The embarrassed man handed back their documents and waved them on their way.

"How much longer?" Alison asked, twisting in her seat.

"A couple of hours. Are you still feeling cooped up?"

"Not like before, but I *am* looking forward to getting off this plane. And I still regret—"

"Not visiting your parents?"

"We were *there*," Alison sighed. "But I know—better safe than sorry."

"When we get back."

"Yes. And what are we going to *do* in the Sandemans? You still haven't told me."

"We'll stay overnight in Toribaya," Olsson said. "And tomorrow—a surprise."

*****

YET ANOTHER HELICOPTER SAT in the center of the Inkaya village square. This one brought neither a third wave of Australian soldiers nor an overwhelming crowd of gaping villagers. As the rotors slowed to a halt, Abdullah Nimabi, Sandemans Minister for Foreign Affairs and the local MP, stepped out, along with his entourage, to be welcomed by the assembled members of the Inkaya village council.

Over refreshments, Nimabi introduced his passenger: the new imam for the mosque. He was, said Nimabi, a *real,* fully-qualified imam, from Indonesia but trained in Saudi Arabia.

Tungi's reaction was loathing at first sight. He attempted to hide it, only partially succeeding. He sensed from the imam's fleeting expression that the feeling was mutual. The imam, Tungi decided, was here to win the soul of the village. Tungi was his instant enemy. The imam was young, energetic, charismatic. Tungi was old, staid, and led by consensus. That consensus was about to be shattered: this imam was not one to compromise. Tungi's only advantage was that the Indonesian was still learning the villagers' language. From the way the imam had already attacked that deficit, it was clear Tungi's advantage would be fleeting.

Nimabi, totally absorbed in telling the skeptical councillors how the government would help revive Inkaya's economy, was oblivious to the non-verbal interchange between Tungi and the imam. As he half-listened, Tungi watched Nimabi with growing reservations. There was a new power in him, as if he'd grown in stature—and Tungi didn't like it. For one thing, the appointment of a new imam was a matter for the village council. Nimabi had simply ignored that protocol—and seemed to expect to receive gratitude for the omission.

Afterwards, Tungi took Nimabi on a tour of a village filled with people sitting around all day doing nothing, exuding a pall of hopelessness. Two fishing boats lay idle at the dock. Half the shops and stalls were closed and the rest had barely enough customers to keep them afloat.

In a matter of moments, Tungi and the councillors were left behind as Nimabi and his entourage bustled around the village, a tiny bubble of energy in a sea of despair that would soon depart without leaving any impression.

Except, of course, for the imam, now in deep conversation with Nimabi.

Around him, Tungi could hear the low mutterings of his fellow councillors. They, he thought, *have come to similar conclusions—but what can we do?*

At least we stood up to the Australian soldiers, Tungi concluded, *even if we lost. But now, without resources, we are supplicants, dependent on charity—which has just arrived with strings attached. Nimabi had not come humbly, as he had in the past, as their representative, seeking their vote or approval, but as an autocrat dictating what would be done and how.*

Shortly after Nimabi and his helicopter took off, the sound of another engine grew overhead. A strange-looking plane flew over the village and some way out to sea where it turned to land with a splash in the bay. It taxied up like a boat to the wharf. Derek Olsson and Alison McGuire stepped out.

"What are we going to do here?" Alison asked.

"Visit some old friends," Olsson said, "and check on an investment—which looks pretty sick at the moment."

Almost instantly, the dock was crowded with sprinting children and teenagers, come to take in this new and unexpected wonder. Adults followed at a more leisurely pace. Olsson grinned at them and said a few words to the pilot who reluctantly agreed to take groups of them for a short joyride.

They were met at the end of the dock by Tungi and Arang'anat. Seeing the first group climbing into the plane, Arang'anat blurted, "Olsson-*ga*. Our children! Where go?"

"For the thrill of a lifetime," Olsson grinned. Arang'anat didn't understand. When Olsson rephrased his comment, Tungi smiled.

"*Matalam,* Olsson-*ga.*"

Olsson needed no introduction, Alison thought, her mind completing the circle—*Inkaya, Jeremy, marijuana.* His "investment" must be the plantation and factory the Australians had destroyed.

As Olsson introduced Alison, Arang'anat eyes narrowed. "M'gire-*gaat?*" she said, an edge in her voice.

Alison's smile faltered. "What's wrong?"

"M'gire-*ga,* soldier. Thought he friend, but—" Words failing her, she waved her arm to indicate the village.

"My cousin, Jeremy."

To Alison's bewilderment, Arang'anat turned away, fixing her eyes on the path ahead.

"This was such an *active* place," Olsson said as Tungi led them past the village square.

"It looks like a tsunami has hit it," Alison said. "Yet, everyone seems well-fed and well-dressed."

"This *was* the richest place in the Sandemans after Toribaya."

"Was?—oh."

Olsson nodded. "You'll see in a moment. Just up the hill."

For most of the climb, Alison had held Olsson's arm lightly for support. Not that she really needed it: her foot was feeling much better and she could now walk almost normally with hardly a twinge.

Tungi-*ga* showed them the gutted buildings and the deserted remains of the plantation; Arang'anat told them, blow by detailed blow, what had happened. Alison began to feel that only Olsson's arm was keeping her upright. The despair and desolation in Inkaya was centered here, thanks to—

She burst out, "*Our* politics caused *this.*"

"That's right," Olsson nodded.

She had been party to an action which had destroyed prosperity and replaced it with despair. True, she had argued against it—for *political,* not moral reasons. Royn had ordered it over the objections of generals and the diplomats, heads of agencies both far more powerful than she had been. That she could not have stopped Royn didn't make her feel any better.

She might have opposed this action, this *policy,* but she had been an avid supporter of the *system* that made it possible.

Had been? Past tense? Was that right? She wasn't sure.

OVER A MODEST LUNCH in the canteen by the village square, Olsson, Tungi, and Arang'anat discussed what could be done to salvage the plantation. "There are other things you can grow and process," Olsson was saying. "I'll find out."

Alison touched his elbow. "I'll go for a short walk."

"We'll find you," Olsson said.

After wandering around, exchanging smiles and, here and there, a few words of broken English, she stopped thoughtfully in front of a small sewing shop to finger the fabrics. They were light and cool. A simple, white, long-sleeved blouse—more a shirt—caught her eye. She held it against herself and studied her reflection. "How much?" she asked, to be met with blank stares. Smiling, she opened her purse; then they understood and wrote *75t* on a slip of paper. Less than four dollars. Passing over a hundred *tingi* she began to fold the shirt.

The two seamstresses shook their heads. Gently, the blouse was pried from her hands and the two women fussed over her, armed with tape-measures. Moments after she'd chosen the fabric, it was sliced was into pieces, and she watched in awe as the women's fingers flew across the pieces and the garment seemed take shape in no time at all. In less than half-an-hour it was finished. They led her into a back room where she could try it on. After a few alterations—though Alison couldn't see any flaws—it was ready.

She wore it from shop, the two seamstresses standing proudly by the door. She glanced at the idle fishing boats—one of them which must have carried Karla—and asked herself: *why can't they just keep . . . smuggling?*

She laughed at the thought. *The world's turned upside down.*

Fingering her new, *tailor-made* garment, she could imagine many other women would be delighted with one. Men too, for that matter.

Of course, she knew *nothing* about business. Nothing at all. Nor, it occurred to her, did all but a handful of the politicians and public servants who took it upon themselves to dictate and regulate what businessmen could and should do—"for the greater good."

Olsson appeared to be taking his leave when she returned to the canteen. "New clothes, I see," Olsson grinned as he saw her.

Arang'anat's look—at her or, perhaps, the shirt—jogged her memory. "Miss Arang'anat, I have a message for you. From Karla."

Arang'anat's face lit up. "Presdon-*gaat*? You know?"

Alison nodded. "We're friends. Karla invites you to come to Australia, go to university, and learn new ways to teach."

"Australia? Me?"

"Yes," said Olsson. "You. We can arrange all the papers."

"Karla promises to look after you," Alison said.

"Yes, yes, *yes.*" Arang'anat almost jumped onto the table with joy. But as quickly as it had come, her grin transformed into a deep frown. She sank slowly, shrinking as she did, until she was hunched so her body looked like it was about to weep. "I—permission need. My father—"

"What?" Alison said.

"This is a different culture," Olsson said in a low voice. "To do anything, a woman needs the consent of her father—or her husband." He passed an envelope to Arang'anat. "Arang'anat-*gaat*," he said, "here is an official letter of invitation. Show it to your father by all means."

Arang'anat took the letter gingerly. "Thank you, M'gire-*gaat*, Olsson-*ga,*" she said, forcing a smile.

But the tears in her eyes seemed to be expecting: *My father will say no.*

Later that afternoon the plane flew them to a beautiful resort on a small island surrounded by a coral reef where they spent two blissful days.

Mostly blissful days.

Halfway through the second day, Alison became aware that the handful of Australian tourists, and even a few of the male staff, were giving her strange glances.

No escape. Anywhere.

As an experiment, she bought the smallest bikini she could find in the resort's boutique and went sunbathing by the hotel pool. Certain that *everyone* was looking at her, she found she could bear it by keeping her eyes closed. Except she was aware of the murmurs, never hearing precise words, but certain of what they were. Hardly an improvement.

She opened her eyes to see a man on the other side of the pool staring at her. She glared back. The man turned away, embarrassed.

I stared him down.

Alison was absorbed in the realization that the man felt *guilty;* that she could *shame* him. Not everyone would react that way, but she could handle the others—just as she had handled the three boys in the schoolyard after the rape.

She stood up slowly, ignoring everyone around her, took a couple of careful steps to the edge of the pool and lowered herself in. Gingerly at first, she began swimming laps. Breast stroke was easy; the butterfly, she knew without testing it, was out; the Australian crawl was fine so long as she didn't stretch her arms too far and was careful with her foot when she turned. Exercising her muscles after too long as an invalid felt like an uncommon luxury; the renewal of her energy shook off her lassitude.

She swam and swam until her rib began to ache. Deciding enough was enough—for the moment—she came up for air by the side of the pool to see Olsson grinning at her.

"You have quite an audience," he said.

"To hell with them." She stretched out an arm. "Help me up, please."

As she climbed out of the pool she threw her arms around Olsson and kissed him hungrily. Aware of the onlookers, Olsson hesitated, but dismissed them under the pressure of Alison's insistent lips and the closeness of her body.

"Hey," he chuckled, "you're getting my shirt wet."

"So," she whispered, "take it off."

Olsson gazed into eyes that had been dull but now gleamed again like liquid sapphire. "You're back at last," he said. "What happened?"

"I've decided it's time to go."

"Go where?"

Alison grinned. "Back to the real world. I'm ready to start facing it now."

*****

Arang'anat sat on the steps of the empty school, sobbing.

"Poor child," Tungi said, "what on earth can be so terrible?"

"My father won't let me go." Her eyes turned up to Tungi, pleading through her tears. "In Australia, I could learn English properly, go to a real college, learn new better ways to teach."

"Presdon-*gaat* is a good person," Tungi said.

The village was sleepy now, fishing and coconuts once again the main industries. Most of the people who'd worked on the plantation had gone back to their homes where, Tungi thought, they were now sitting around, no job, no money, nothing to do, like the youths in the park.

The village no longer had enough money to finance the school on the same scale. In any case, more than half the students no longer came: they had to help their parents scrape a living off the land.

The world has come to us, Tungi thought, and nothing will ever be the same again. He looked at Arang'anat's tearful eyes. In a few short days, Presdon-*gaat* had given her a new, alien, vision of what a woman could be. He wasn't sure whether he approved or not, but he had to admit there was something about Presdon-*gaat* he admired. What was Allah's will?

Could this new imam really represent that will? he wondered. The words of fire and brimstone, of *jihad* and death to all infidels—the same words Gurundi had preached—were, he said, from the Koran. Was this the same holy book that talked about peace, that demanded the protection of guests regardless of their faith, the source—so he had thought—of everything he held dear?

Tungi didn't know. He understood no Arabic, and the Koran had not been translated into his language—not that he read that well anyway. But he found it hard—nay, impossible to accept that Allah or the Prophet, blessed be His name, had spoken from both sides of His mouth.

Across the square, nearly half the young men of the village streamed into the mosque. While the village school languished, the same could not be said of the imam's new school, a *madrasa*. The transformation of the village was under way. The youths were becoming belligerent; they no longer treated him with their former respect, even casting a few aspersions against "the tired old men" of the village council. They never spoke directly to him, but their words, like everything else that happened in the village, eventually reached him.

His gaze turned back to Arang'anat. She would obey her father, of course. And if she did. . . .

An old woman, bowed under the weight of life and the heavy basket she was carrying from the market, shuffled past him, too tired to notice his presence.

She had given birth to seven children; now her husband had brought a much younger, second wife into the family. While she still held the title of "first wife," her actual status was little more than a servant. Yet, Tungi knew, it was *she* who held the family together, who was the main provider, who somehow managed to keep most of the *tingi* she earned out of the hands of her profligate, ne'er-do-well husband.

He was looking at Arang'anat's lot.

"Go, my child," Tungi said. "There's no future for you here."

"But—"

"*I'll* talk to your father."

Arang'anat smiled through sudden tears of happiness. "Oh, thank you, Tungi-*ga*, thank you!" Without thinking, she threw her arms around Tungi and hugged him.

Tungi carefully pried himself away from Arang'anat's grip.

"Please forgive me," she said, shocked at her own behavior. But she was relieved to see Tungi's understanding look, with no hint of censure in his eyes.

I DID MY BEST, Tungi thought. Then the world invaded us with weapons and money and alien ideas far beyond our ability to resist, and refuses to leave us alone. What will come of it?

Nothing good, he decided. Amtami's band had shrunk to a handful of men, all disheartened by their total inability to protect their people from the Australians.

He looked once again at Arang'anat. *She*, at least, had the chance of a better life. He watched the last of the youths swagger into the mosque. If I was young, I'd probably be one of them. And if they and that *imam* are the future. . . .

He shuddered.

It won't be long, he sighed, his eyes looking towards heaven, and I'll soon be joining you. I won't have to see everything I've helped build finally crumble away.

Tungi shrugged.

Inshallah.

68   Pay the Piper!

F LASH! SANDEMANS NATIONALIZES OZ OIL. SAUDI-ARAMCO TO ADVISE NEW S'MAN OIL CO.

Distracted by the moving ribbon of text flowing across the bottom of the TV screen, Anthony Royn felt the razor bite into his skin. "Darn." The razor clattered to the floor, forgotten, as Royn strode naked into the bedroom.

"Tony!" Melanie said, sitting up in bed in surprise. "What's wrong? You're bleeding."

Reaching the phone by the bed, Royn impatiently waved a hand to shush her, wiped his face with the other—and left red blotches on the white phone. "Doug, did you see the news? . . . Yes. Get Helen to call me ASAP, would you? Thanks."

Melanie reached up with a tissue to dab his face. "What's happened?"

"Nimabi—may he burn in hell—has nationalized oil and invited in the Saudis."

"That sounds bad."

"Bad? It's *awful*. He could at least have waited until *after* the election."

"I guess he's not too happy with us."

"I suppose not," Royn said, and then looked at Melanie sharply. "Your nose is twitching," he grinned. "Are you thinking his timing was *intentional?*"

Melanie nodded slowly. "Why now, instead of in a week or two?"

"Why indeed."

The phone rang and Royn grabbed for it. "Helen? Have you seen the news? No? Nimabi has nationalized oil. Can you believe it? . . . It was on TV—nothing from your department? Get them moving and can you be in my office in, say, thirty minutes?"

Slamming the phone down he leaned down to give Melanie a quick kiss and suddenly hugged her tight.

"You don't have time for that," she said, her tongue slowly licking her upper lip.

"More's the pity. Frankly, I'd much rather stay right here."

Giggling, Melanie brushed her nipples against his chest.

Royn reluctantly pulled himself away, stood uncertainly, and grabbed the phone once more. "Doug? Call Paul and, I guess, Stanley Chow. Meet in the office or we'll get them on speakerphone within the hour."

"Shall I come too?" Melanie asked.

"Please. I'm going to need your support."

Melanie watched Royn until he disappeared into the bathroom, smiling to herself. Since Alison's disappearance, Royn was leaning more and more heavily on *her*. She wondered when—or if—he would notice the change.

ROYN WALKED INTO HIS office, munching on the last of the breakfast Melanie had hastily prepared, to find Doug Selkirk and Helen Arkness already there—looking glum.

Before he could speak, Selkirk handed him a printout. "Prime Minister, "you'd better read this first."

"Sheesh," he said as he saw the headline. "Where's this from?"

"It just went up on the Sykes website. It's not in print yet."

"That's not even a small mercy," Helen Arkness said.

Silent Coup in Toribaya

By Robin Cartwright
Sykes Media exclusive

The surprise nationalization of the Sandemans' only producing oil well, discovered and still part-owned by an Australian company, was announced this morning by Abdullah Nimabi, the Sandemans' *Foreign* Minister.

His announcement won't win any friends in Canberra, a good reason, you'd think, to let some other minister take the blame.

"Why *him?"* was not the first question in anyone's mind, though it turns out to be the most important one.

Six weeks ago, Saudi Arabia rolled out the red carpet for Nimabi—who also happens to be the Sandemans' most high-flying Muslim. Back in Toribaya he announced the Saudis would open an embassy and sponsor the Sandemans for associate membership of OPEC.

Behind the scenes, according to my sources in Toribaya, Nimabi brought back something far more important: Money. Oodles of aid and soft loans that can be paid back on the never-never.

All controlled by Nimabi.

With the Sandemans' finances in a shambles, its credit rating hardly better than junk, this Saudi money has financed a "silent coup" which puts Nimabi in the catbird seat—president in all but name.

Given that the Saudis produce as much oil every hour or two as the Sandemans will in a year—if *every* exploratory drill hole turns into a gusher—what on earth is the Saudis' interest in the place? The coconut trade?

Hardly. They're buying influence and the opportunity to spread their virulent Islamic sect of Wahhabism. Already, they've shipped Saudi-trained imams to four Sandeman mosques, with more on the way. Part of the payback is a slice of Sandeman oil production—I mean, "advisory fees." Hence the nationalization.

Why would a Christian majority nation with a troublesome Muslim minority agree to this deal?

Of course the "Sandemen in the street" weren't asked. Their "glorious leaders" happily signed off on it for a couple of reasons, not counting politicians' usual short-sightedness.

Greed is primary. This new "money gusher" is godsend (Allah-send?) of new graft to help those in power finance their retirement in Monte Carlo or other salubrious and far safer places.

The second factor is more complex. For some time, top officials have been muttering their resentment of the Australians' "high-handed, imperialistic attitude." The Australian army's recent ripping up of a marijuana plantation hasn't helped.

They certainly resent anyone, like me, who states the obvious: that the fruit-salad "generals" of the Sandeman army are political appointees whose grunts wouldn't follow them out of a paper bag, or that the average official's idea of "good governance" is how many backhanders he can collect under the table.

With Saudi money, "we can safely put the Australians in their place," said one Sandeman official.

Money talks—and if there's something Saudi Arabia isn't short of, it's money. But he who pays the piper calls the tune, as the Sandeman people will eventually find out.

Since the successful Australian-Sandeman sweep of St. Christopher's Island, the terrorist threat is seen (except by the Australian army) as pretty much in abeyance. Given a year or two of the new Saudi-financed *madrasas,* that will inevitably change.

If—or when—everything does blow up, it will be the people who'll pay the price: the current powers-that-be will happily watch the chaos from their luxuriously decked-out villas in the far, far away.

If they can get to the airport in time, that is.

Royn threw the printout on his desk. "Holy cow."

"That's a pretty good summary," said Helen Arkness.

Mary put her head through the door. "Prime Minister," she said in surprise. "You're early."

"Coffee all round, please Mary," Royn said, hardly looking at her. "Sandwiches? Anything else?"

Mary felt piqued at Royn's abruptness. Frowning as she took down their orders, she realized: *It must be bad for Royn to be here before me—in such a foul mood.*

Melanie slipped in, taking a seat beside Royn. "Read this," he said passing her Cartwright's article. A moment later a messenger brought Helen Arkness a thick file.

"Foreign Affairs briefing," she said in response to Royn's questioning look. "Give me a moment to skim through it."

"I'll get Stanley Chow and Paul Cracken on the speakerphone," said Selkirk, dialling.

"Here's the gist," Helen Arkness said a few minutes later. "Their options are: Protest note. *Strong* protest note. Carpet the Sandeman High Commissioner. Recall *our* High Commissioner 'for consultations'—or just recall him, period. Withhold or cut off aid. Cut off diplomatic relations. Strong-arm them behind the scenes."

"*Strong-arm* them?" Melanie said. "Did they actually say *that?*"

Helen Arkness laughed. "Not in so many words. 'Use all our available influence, points of leverage, and friends in government,'" she read, "'including, should it become necessary, the possibility of withdrawal of assistance, to persuade the appropriate Sandeman officials to come to a more rational reconsideration of these actions.'"

"Gobbledygook," Selkirk muttered.

"Do we *have* any friends in the government up there?" asked Chow.

"Not *everyone* is happy with Nimabi's power grab," said Helen Arkness.

"What about a counter-coup?" Cracken said. "Did they mention *that* possibility?"

"The CIA have more experience than us with that sort of thing," Chow said. "If we could get *them* to arrange it, we'd have total deniability."

"They won't touch it," said Cracken. "Be too afraid of tweaking the Saudis' noses."

"Except for one thing," said Chow. "I've had the Australian wildcatter on the phone—woke me up, actually—and they're not that badly off. They sold a majority stake to an American oil company."

"So the Americans can be counted on to raise some hell," said Helen Arkness. "I'll get onto the ambassador right away."

"If we pull out," said Cracken, "the Saudis will fill the vacuum. If we can kick the Saudis out, we'd have to go in even more heavily. That's the *real* problem."

"But," said Chow, "if we *do* pull everything out and the Muslim minority becomes radicalized, how long before the Christian *majority* starts hitting back?"

"Civil war on our doorstep?" Royn said, aghast.

"Bosnia? Ethnic cleansing? Is that what you're suggesting?" Selkirk said.

"It *would* be pretty one-sided," Cracken agreed.

"Sometimes," Chow said, "it's better just to let things take their natural course."

"Prime Minister," Selkirk said, his tone suddenly urgent, "we're supposed to be getting on a plane to Brisbane very shortly."

"Gawd, I forgot about that rally. Any way we can postpone it? Cancel it? Send someone else?"

"That would make lots of people very unhappy, Prime Minister," said Selkirk. "Especially everyone who's forked over three hundred bucks a plate to hobnob with you at the fund-raising lunch."

"And tonight I'm supposed to debate with Nash," Royn groaned. "Let's stop talking about what we could *do*, and focus on what in heaven's name I'm going to *say* about all this."

*****

McKurnWatch.com

"The website that ~~must not~~ can now be named" [Thanks, Frankie!]
60,938 McKurnWatchers—and counting.

G'd evening boys and girls, and shed a tear (if you're toked up enough) for Frankie: tomorrow will be his first day in court and the first day of the rest of his life. Which isn't much to look forward to, given his new accommodations in the not-very-stimulating atmosphere of Long Bay Jail.

On second thought, there *is* something worth shedding a tear over: The time has come, as the Walrus might have said,

to no longer talk of cabbages and kings,

or whether Frankie has wings,

but to move along to other more important things,

. . . so our paths must uncross with this, the swansong issue of McKurnWatch.

But . . . shouldn't we spare a thought for Poor Frankie? Don't you *feel* for him, stripped of his power and wealth, locked up in a dungeon along with hundreds of other thugs? Where he'll probably stay until he gets out—in a box?

Oh, you don't? He deserves it? Is that what you're thinking?

Damn right!

When McKurnWatch began, I promised to tell you Frankie's life story—the *real* story that nobody knew about.

Frankie was pretty upset and did his best to shut us down. He failed.

He *more* than failed. He lost. *Everything.* His power and influence—gone. His little and not-so-little scams—all unravelling. His life of luxury—something to look backward to.

In the end, against the odds, I was vindicated.

Now, while I never did finish Frankie's promised "biography," all the gruesome details I haven't covered yet will come out in court, so you won't miss a trick.

And since there's not that much satisfaction in beating a dead horse, I'll let the courts do that for us all.

So the purpose of McKurnWatch has been fulfilled.

A swansong should have some musical accompaniment, don't you think? While not exactly rhythmic, our "swansong" is highly apt, as you'll ~~see~~ hear. Just click on the link to listen to the "soothing" tones of Frankie's sultry voice—"disguised" as "John." But then "Gladys" isn't the name of the woman he's talking to, either.

"Gladys" ran the call girl service in Canberra that was shut down for sex-slavery.

"John," as you'll appreciate, was one of her customers.

Not the wisest choice of pseudonym, Frankie!

— The McKurnWatcher

PS. Two other items of interest before I sign off.

It seems the Royal Commission staff inherited by Mr. Justice Flint is riddled with underworld stooges—most likely McKurn's.

That's hardly a surprise when you think about it: who has the greatest vested interest in delaying, diverting, leaking, and otherwise foiling the Commission's investigations?

The druggies, of course. Given the massive profits in their trade, they've got plenty of moolah to spread around—and when that doesn't work, plenty of whores on tap to trap the most "innocent" bureaucrat.

Flint swooped on NSW Police Inspector Rudi Durant—the man responsible for last week's arrest of McKurn and several other sleazebags.

Durant's first job at the Commission is to clean out this human garbage. Given his record, it probably won't take him very long.

Second, as you probably know, the NSW Attorney-General's office has cancelled the stationery contract Paper Supplies (a company McKurn owns through dummies) had with the NSW government.

That company has a similar contract with the *federal* government—and the *federal* AG is also investigating. One "little" wrinkle that's just been "whispered in my ear": the AG investigators suspect that Paul Cracken may be complicit in awarding that contract to Paper Supplies.

That's right: our Treasurer, Deputy PM, Deputy Leader of the Conservative Party— and, until last week, Frankie McKurn's golden-haired little page-boy.

If that, on Frankie's heels, isn't enough to prove the truth of the statement, Power Corrupts, I don't know what is.

Gottlieb Alten reread the final issue of McKurnWatch with a sigh. It was the first time he'd embarked on a project with no prospect of a financial return. *But it was such fun, and I'll miss it.*

That, he decided, was a strange thought—for him.

With McKurn out of the way, he'd moved back into his Potts Point apartment. He swung his glance around his computer room. All was quiet—*like my business.*

He'd lost his two major customers—"Saith Lord," who'd put him on the track of McKurn, had obviously achieved *his* objective, and "The Jackal," who'd referred "Saith" to him, emailed to tell him "I'm shutting my business down and thanks very much for your help."

Strange that I don't really mind. Must be getting old.

He still had enough customers to pay the rent, but meeting all their requirements would hardly fill his day.

He didn't even need them: he could spend the rest of his life in comfort on the dividends and interest from his investments.

He began to wonder what he should do next.

A career in "public service" had never appealed to him. Before. But McKurnWatch had been such fun, and while it seemed unlikely there'd be another scumbag as clever, nasty, and successful as McKurn, there must be plenty of candidates for second place.

Maybe McKurnWatch—ScumbagWatch?—could continue, he thought.

Maybe.

Something to think about.

69 Black Holes

"**P**AUL, IS THERE any truth in this?" Anthony Royn demanded.

"In what?" said Cracken innocently.

"You mean to tell me you haven't seen the latest McKurnWatch?" Royn kept tight control of his voice to rein in his impulse to shout down the phone.

"Oh, that."

"Yes, *that.* I spoke to the Attorney-General, who says if there's anything in it, it will definitely come out. So you'd best tell me now. Yes, or no."

"I—. Ah. . . ."

"Paul, you have to resign."

"What do you mean? I haven't said anything."

"That's the trouble, mate. At least you didn't lie and say, 'No.'"

Royn pulled the handset away from his ear at the sound of Cracken's long sigh. "And if I don't?"

"I'll reshuffle the Cabinet and you'll be out."

"Not the best time to do that."

"No it isn't. But that's the way it is. So, Paul, do you want to be pushed out in disgrace, or have a chance to redeem yourself?"

Cracken was silent for so long Royn began to wonder if the connection had dropped. "Resign my *seat?*" he said at last, his voice dull.

"No. Treasurer. And Deputy PM."

"How about I, ah, step aside? Temporarily."

"Much better."

"Though it amounts to the same thing."

"Not really," said Royn. "Look. We're not *admitting* anything. You haven't actually *said* anything to me, either. The AG can be counted on to say *nothing,* 'pending the completion of our investigations.' I'll back him up. It's just another rumor—"

"Which is what McKurn said—and look where he is now."

"Unfortunately, true. Giving this too much credence. Another reason for you to get out of the firing line. We'll be seen as doing the right thing—and you've got your seat to think about, too."

"That's a point," Cracken said.

"Where's your energy, Paul? You've been a battler your whole life. Are you going to give up now?"

"Are you on *my* side, all of a sudden?"

"In this, yes. Look, I can leave both posts vacant until we can call a party meeting, which will be impossible until *after* the election."

"Can we *do* that?" Cracken asked.

"I'll have to check." Alison, Royn suddenly thought, would have the answer to that at her fingertips. He sighed. *She's not coming back,* he decided, recalling the long email she'd sent him a couple of days ago. He had followed her suggestion that, "under doctor's orders," she had to rest to recover from nervous exhaustion. No one in his office believed a word of it, but it explained her absence. "Paul, I'll call you right back."

An hour later, Paul Cracken announced he was "stepping aside from all my government and party posts until the Attorney-General cleared the air."

Anthony Royn praised Cracken "for doing the right thing," said "the Assistant Treasurer will fill in for Paul, temporarily, as necessary," and added, "the Attorney-General can say *nothing* until the investigation is completed, but I'm confident these rumors are totally unfounded."

*****

Senator Frank McKurn listened impassively as the long list of charges against him were read out by the prosecution. It took over an hour.

When the judge turned towards him and asked, "How does the defendant plead?" McKurn's barrister, an impressive grey-haired man almost as tall as McKurn, rose slowly to his full height. "Not guilty on all counts, Your Honor."

In another courtroom, attorneys representing The Croned Stow Corporation and the Village of Inkaya completed their reply to the propositions the Attorney-General had argued the previous day. The government claimed, by virtue of its sovereign nature, immunity from such "frivolous" suits. Also: the alleged acts occurred during a time of war in a foreign country—beyond the court's jurisdiction. And since the Commonwealth faced a similar case in Toribaya, the proceedings in this court were a form of double jeopardy and so against the principles of the common law.

After many pointed questions and further discussion, the judges retired for most of the afternoon to consider their ruling.

They decided against the Commonwealth on all but the Attorney-General's third argument, agreeing that any award of costs or damages should not be cumulative between the two jurisdictions.

How that ruling might be decided and enforced, especially if the government of the Sandeman Islands did not agree to it, was left unsaid.

*****

Joe and Maggie McGuire stood on their doorstep, grinning, when Alison and Olsson arrived.

Maggie ran out to the gate and threw her arms around her daughter. "Oh, Alison, I've been so *worried*. Are you still badly injured? Where have you been—what have you been doing—?"

"Mother," Alison laughed, sinking into her mother's warmth. "One thing at a time."

Maggie laughed too, and beamed at Olsson. "Derek, welcome home." Turning back to Alison, she said, "So when's the wedding?"

"Oh, mother," Alison said scornfully. "Really!" But she smiled just the same.

Joe slapped Olsson on the shoulder. "I'm glad it wasn't you, son," he said.

"Not you, too, Dad," Alison said, eyeing her father with puzzled interest.

Joe grinned broadly. "Isn't this what you've always really wanted, Alison?"

Alison blinked at the sudden wetness in her eyes. "Yes," she whispered hoarsely. "Yes, Dad, it *is*."

After a long and pleasant lunch, they visited Olsson's mother and came away depressed. Molly Olsson was delighted to see them both. Although her condition had worsened dramatically, to everyone's surprise she remembered Alison clearly. But she kept talking to Olsson as if he were Lars, to the extent of saying to Alison, mystified, "I thought you were *Derek's* friend. Have you seen him lately? How is he?"

The nurses claimed she would be better off in a home or hospital. A tearful Jessica agreed: half the time, she told them, her mother thought she was just another nurse. "I'm not sure I can stand it much longer, Derek."

When they left, Olsson felt relieved—and guilty for feeling that way. "And there's nothing anyone can *do*," he moaned, "except watch her slowly fall to pieces."

ALISON WAS HUNCHED OVER the dining table, looking at her cellphone.

Alison's mood darkened as they neared the penthouse and Olsson couldn't figure out why. He padded over and sat beside her, one arm loosely around her shoulders. "What's bothering you, Alison?" he asked softly.

Her eyes moist, Alison looked at him as if she'd forgotten he was there.

"Royn," she sighed. "I should call him, *speak* to him. I've been putting it off—"

"Do you know what you want to say to him?"

Alison nodded. "But he'll want to know *why*. And I can't tell him that, can I?"

"Do you want me to go upstairs, leave you in peace?"

Alison shook her head, clutching his hand.

She shifted closer to Olsson as she dialled.

"Prime Minister, it's Alison." She held the phone so Olsson could also hear Royn's voice.

"Alison! At last! What a relief!"

"I just want to apologize for disappearing, and leaving you in the lurch, but—"

"I know," Royn sighed. "The video—"

"I can live with that—now."

"Great! So you can come back. I really need you."

Alison lips parted but no words came out. She looked helplessly at Olsson, squeezing his hand for support.

"Alison! Are you still there?"

"I—I can't, Prime Minister."

"Why not? We've *won*, Alison. McKurn's locked up where he should be, and if the video's no longer a problem—"

"It's more complicated—" She glanced at Olsson, her expression a plea for help. With a deep breath she said, "I just can't, Prime Minister. Can we leave it at that for the moment?"

"I don't understand."

From the tone of his voice, Alison could easily imagine the flush of anger on Royn's cheeks.

"Prime Minister! I just called to apologize—and to wish you luck."

"For fourteen years I've depended on you, Alison. And then you're gone! I have a right—"

Alison sighed. "I know. I owe you an explanation. But . . . for now . . . just let me ask you a question: Now you're Prime Minister, are you happy?"

The sound of Royn's sharp, indrawn breath exploded in Alison's ear. "Huh?"

"If Cracken—or Bruce Spring—were sitting in your chair, they'd be over the moon. *That's* what I mean. They're like Kydd and McKurn—in their natural element. Are you? I don't think so. I used to think I was. But now I've paid the price, I know I'm not. *That's* why I can't come back."

"I—ah . . . " Royn's voice trailed into silence.

"Good luck, Prime Minister."

Royn sighed. "Thank you, Alison—I suppose."

"Maybe I shouldn't have called," Alison said to Olsson, dabbing the tears from her eyes.

"I'd say you didn't tell him anything he doesn't already know."

"I suppose not," Alison said, with a wan attempt at a smile, "but I'm sure he doesn't want to think about it right now."

LATER, THEY SIPPED WINE on the balcony, and watched the city's lights twinkle as the last rays of the setting sun faded into night. "It's a beautiful evening," Olsson said, "and while we have plenty of wine, the cupboard is otherwise bare. How about a walk—a bit of exercise might cheer us both up a bit—followed by dinner?"

"It's Friday night, Derek. There'll be people *everywhere.* I'm not quite up to that yet. Somewhere near—or takeaway."

"Sure," Olsson grinned. "There's a cozy place, just down those steps. A five-minute walk. A quiet table in the back. How about that?"

It had been one of those summery days so characteristic of Sydney in winter. It cooled quickly after the sun went down, but it wasn't really chilly enough to justify the overcoat and scarf, wrapped over her mouth like a muffler, topped off with a beret pulled low over her forehead, that Alison insisted on wearing.

"Welcome back, Derek," the restaurant's owner said as he guided them to a rear booth. Despite his poker face, Alison was aware of the momentary searching of his eyes. *Get used to it,* she told herself.

The light was low, the food excellent, the wine better, and the acoustics superb, dampening the normal restaurant sounds of voices and the clatter of plates and cutlery to a faint, background hum. Alison slowly relaxed into the resultant sense of privacy. About halfway through the meal, the tone of her voice suddenly became serious.

"I've been thinking," she began.

"About what?"

Alison laughed. "The rest of my life. I've been trying to get what I wanted by persuading politicians and bureaucrats to run my projects, my way. When I won—usually after far too many compromises—it was run by other people with different goals. Empire-builders, power-seekers, even those with the best of intentions who just *knew* they knew better. Did I succeed? Sometimes. Sort of. But do you know what my greatest achievement is?"

"The—I don't know—the orphanage program?" said Olsson.

"No," Alison said with a shake of her head. "The Victims' Self-Defence League. And I didn't even start it. I inspired others. They shared my goal—because they shared my experience. *They* built it and made it happen. They're all volunteers—and they still are."

"You're underplaying your role, Alison," Olsson said sternly. "You did more than just inspire them. You set the *example* they followed."

"I suppose so," Alison conceded. "And you know what? *They're* getting the revenge I was after. Defending victims, helping them defend and assert themselves—and bringing justice to the perpetrators. I'm going to get involved again."

"Will that be enough?"

"It's a start, Derek. What about you?"

"Except for my newspapers, I'm selling everything or closing it down."

"Including—?"

"Yes," he said, dropping his voice. "The Candyman has gone out of business. But there's still a lot of tidying up to do. I've a busy week or so ahead of me."

"And then?"

"I'm going on a crusade."

"A what?"

"A crusade. I'm going to—"

Alison grabbed his wrist tightly. "We've been recognized," she hissed. A couple of the other diners stood gazing at them with a look full of curiosity. Alison's mouth tensed. She glared at them. "Let's get out of here."

As they stepped onto the street they were caught in the glare of a camera's flash. A reporter thrust a microphone into Olsson's face. "How do you feel about—"

Olsson's arm flashed out, grabbed the reporter's wrist, and twisted. "Piss off," he growled.

The reporter stumbled back, rubbing his wrist. "That *hurt,* damn you. You can dish it out, but can't take it, eh?"

The owner came up behind them. "Derek, you can slip out the back way."

Alison, he realized, had already gone back through the restaurant door. With a last glare at the reporter, he followed her inside.

THE BRACING NIGHT AIR, the short hike up the steps, and the first sip of brandy when they reached Olsson's apartment revived Alison's spirits.

"It was the shock. Mainly. Being accosted like that." Stretched out on the sofa, Alison shivered in spite of the warmth from Olsson's embrace. "But—all this doesn't seem to bother *you,* Derek."

"I'm angry. Yes. Those bastards are peeping into our most private, personal moments. I wish I'd strangled McKurn when I'd had the chance. But it doesn't affect me in the same way it effects you—who wants to look at *me* in the nude, for heaven's sake?"

"Women don't watch porn? Of course they do. All those poor, lonely, lovesick girls. You're famous; they'll fantasize about having sex with you. They'll *all* want to see your buns."

"Really?" Olsson said.

"Damn you, Derek, that was not a compliment."

"Hey, I've just never thought of myself as a sex object."

"You're not a woman," Alison said.

"But you are, thank God," he said, nibbling her ear.

"Don't do that."

Olsson grinned; his fingers probing the tightness in her shoulders. "I prescribe a massage."

"That would be perfect," Alison said, yawning.

"I had something a little more stimulating in mind."

Alison chuckled. "I've got a headache."

"I've got the aspirin," Olsson said, "upstairs."

"TELL ME ABOUT YOUR 'crusade,'" Alison murmured as Olsson kneaded her shoulders.

"I need to make amends, redeem myself." Olsson slurred his words as if he were drunk from the tingling touch of his hands caressing her skin, and the sight of her naked body stretched out before him.

"You've blown the lid on McKurn and hundreds of others. Isn't that enough?"

Olsson's hands paused as he tasted the thought.

"Hey," Alison said. "Don't stop."

Olsson chuckled. He poured oil over Alison's back and his hands began to move down her spine. "Maybe," he said. "It doesn't *feel* like enough."

"What would?"

"Regaining Karla's respect."

"Karla?" Alison turned her head to glare at him.

"Hold still."

"This is hardly the time or the place to bring up—"

Alison subsided as Olsson pressed a knotted muscle under her shoulder blade, releasing it.

"Aaah," she groaned. "Where did you learn to do that?"

"In Bangkok."

"I see. I imagine that's not the only thing you learned."

Ignoring the sour hint in her voice, Olsson said, "There is this."

His hands slid down to massage the flesh of her behind. His fingers light, they strayed to the top of her legs and between them. Alison began moving in time with his rhythm; moaning, she stretched her arms behind her to reach him. "Wait," he said; with each slow stroke, he increased the pressure.

And then a few minutes later, inexplicably, he stopped.

Alison twisted her head from the pillow so she could look at him. "You should finish what you've started, Derek."

"Exactly," Olsson said, his serious tone undercut by the twinkle in his eyes. "I thought you wanted me to tell you about my crusade."

"Damn you," Alison laughed. "That'll keep."

"If you like," Olsson grinned back. "You claim I'm a sex object. Prove it."

Alison's eyes narrowed. "Okay," she said. "Don't say you didn't ask for it. Roll over!"

Olsson's hand lazily caressed Alison's back. She lay on top of him, her head on his shoulder, their bodies still joined, their skin a slippery mixture of massage oil and sweat.

"You were saying?" Alison murmured sleepily.

"You mean—my crusade? Now?"

"Sure. If you put me to sleep, you'll know it's a bad idea."

Olsson laughed. "Remember back, before Hong Kong—"

"You were searching."

"Yes. And the closest I got was: Do no harm. Live and let live. Neither rule nor be ruled. Good rules, but not enough. Emotional guidelines. On the right track but not *principles.*"

"So what is?"

"The idea of *self-ownership.* That you own your body, your mind, your soul. *And* the products of your labor, of what you create. That ownership is *inviolate.*"

"If I don't own my body, who does?"

"Exactly."

"And that applies to *everyone—?*"

"Yes."

"So," she mused, "rape—"

"Is a violation. Of course. As is murder, theft, extortion—*anything* involving the *initiation* of force."

"Makes sense to me," Alison mused, "except . . . *everyone* includes the government, doesn't it?"

"Of course. A government is just a group of people, after all."

"Hmm. Like the Mafia, as you once told me."

"You remember," Olsson chuckled.

"How could I forget?"

"But you're not going to walk out the door this time?"

"No. That doesn't mean I agree with you."

"Don't you?" Olsson asked. "Isn't that what your Victims' League does? Teaches people that they own their own bodies? That they have the right to defend themselves against aggression? And helps them do just that?"

"In a way, I suppose," Alison conceded. "It's certainly hard to argue with your basic premise. Just the same, it's going to be pretty hard to sell. When, and how, are you going to start?"

"I'm going to use the papers to campaign—"

"They're all in country towns. You won't get much impact."

Olsson chuckled. "I'm going to launch dailies in Sydney and Melbourne. And later, Brisbane."

"Can you afford it?"

"Certainly—if I can squeeze French out."

"French? Oh—*you're* seeking revenge, too?"

Olsson chuckled. "Partly, I suppose."

"Oh, come on, Derek. I'll bet that was a prime motivation."

"It's the icing, Alison."

"That's usually the best part of the cake."

"True enough."

"You'll be very busy," Alison said.

"Yes. Won't you be, too?"

"If I get involved with the League."

"At night," Olsson chuckled, "we can compare notes."

Alison lifted herself so she was looking down on Olsson, her breasts butterflies sliding across his skin. "You mean, like this?" she grinned, squeezing him with her vaginal muscles.

"Oh, my God," Olsson cried. "Can you control that now?"

Alison nodded.

"Then do it again."

She did.

*****

Just one more week, Anthony Royn was thinking, *and it will all be over.*

He rubbed his sleepy eyes. Again. It didn't help. But *next* Sunday *would* be a day of rest.

He could hardly wait.

He picked at his breakfast, scanning one of the two Sunday papers. On the other side of the table, Doug Selkirk was absorbed in the other one, while Melanie sat beside him nursing her coffee and glancing at the headlines over his shoulder. "A penny for your thoughts," she said.

"Sleep," Royn said, trying to sound light. "I'm thinking of sleep."

"Aren't we all?" Doug Selkirk yawned.

"Don't do that, Doug," Royn said, yawning in sympathy.

"Oh-oh," Melanie said as Royn turned a page. "More bad news, by the looks of it."

ELECTION JOURNAL

Labor "falls" ahead. With Paul Cracken joining Anthony Royn under a cloud, the mess in the Sandemans "due to the government's total incompetence," according to Labor leader Ian Nash, and the voters' skeptical reaction to Royn's attempt to "buy himself an election," the psephologists predicted that Labor would pull ahead of the Conservatives.

They were half right.

With one week to go, yesterday's polls show the "undecided"/independent/minor party vote topping twenty percent for the first time as *both* major parties continued to lose popularity. Labor is now in the lead—because the Conservatives dropped more.

Sydney University political science professor Georgina Oldfellow thinks the major parties' vote is "now pretty close to rock-bottom." But as to who's more likely to win? "That's anybody's guess."

"At least Cartwright's kidnappers have been convicted," Royn said.

"Which makes just *one* item of good news," Melanie said.

"Ah—maybe not." Selkirk passed the other Sunday paper across to Royn. "You'd better read this article, Prime Minister."

"Oh, no," Royn moaned as he saw the headline.

Toribaya Chief of Police walks:
Money and Influence
Trump the Law
By Robin Cartwright
Sykes Media exclusive

All charges against the man who masterminded my kidnapping—the Toribaya Chief of Police—were dropped yesterday due to lack of evidence.

At the same time, a warrant was issued for the arrest of the man who *rescued* me from the kidnappers: Amtami and his band of merry men, whose Islamic Purity group has been wrongly tarred with the label "terrorist."

My notarized testimony, identifying the Chief of Police as a member of the gang, was not accepted by the court. I had to appear in person, not something that would increase my life expectancy, or be interrogated by officers of the Sandeman court—in Melbourne. Funds for that not being forthcoming, my employer kindly offered to finance the trip. The offer was turned down as a potential "conflict of interest."

By talking to my contacts in Toribaya—who all, understandably, wish to remain unidentified—I've pieced together the story of what happened.

The man behind it all was Sandeman army colonel Gugamti, whose nose was put of joint when he was "forced by the Australians" (his words) to cooperate with Islamic Purity. The complete success of the resulting mission, which wiped out a terrorist group without a single Australian or Sandeman scratch is, apparently, neither here nor there so far as Gugamti is concerned.

Gugamti persuaded the Chief of Police to set up the kidnapping and blame it on Islamic Purity, thus creating the pretext for Gugamti to send his troops after them.

Although the police chief was freed, the five other men allegedly involved in the kidnapping have been sentenced to life in prison (story and photo on page 7).

I say "allegedly involved" because I was there. I saw every one of the five men who held me hostage—and the faces in the photo are of five *other* men.

Who could they be? Five unfortunates picked up randomly off the street, beaten until they "confessed," and given parts in a show trial worthy of Comrade Stalin at his peak.

My techie colleagues are convinced the photo on page 7 was retouched, presumably to airbrush out bruises and cuts from their faces. The job was poorly done: inspect the picture closely and you'll see the traces for yourself.

All five also "confessed" to being members of Islamic Purity.

A document introduced in court—purportedly discovered in Islamic Purity's abandoned headquarters on Jazeerat el-Bihar by Gugamti's troops—allegedly confirms Islamic Purity's role. As it was withheld from the court-appointed defence lawyer on "national security" grounds, its authenticity cannot be confirmed.

This is a complete parody of justice, the result of pressure on the court and outright bribery. For example, the judge who issued this verdict just ordered himself a nice, new BMW.

"The Sandemans has turned into a black hole," said Selkirk. "Once you're sucked in, there's no known way of escape."

"*That's* exactly how I feel," Royn said gloomily. "*Surrounded* by black holes, all sucking me to pieces."

Melanie took his hand. "It's going to work out, *Prime Minister,*" she grinned. "You'll see."

"Really?" said Royn. "That's how it looked. Just a few *weeks* ago. But now?" He let the question hang.

"You've got church at eleven," Selkirk said with a sideways glance at Melanie. He spoke briskly, his voice matter-of-fact. An attempt to divert Royn's attention.

"Better keep him away from that pastor," Melanie said, mimicking Selkirk's manner. "He made a crack last time, 'haven't seen you for a while.' Don't want any reporters to overhear another one."

"Consider it done," said Selkirk. "Then after that—"

"Doug," Royn sighed. "I know. Another busy electioneering day. Don't worry." Royn straightened his shoulders and put on his winning smile.

"Good. Then—"

Royn held up a hand as he slumped back into his real self. "Doug, I need a break. There's, what, an hour or so before we have to leave? I'm going to do something completely mindless, like watch cartoons."

"How about a good comedy?" Melanie suggested.

"An excellent idea," Royn said, "so long as it's not *Yes, Prime Minister.*"

70 "Chicago Rules"

**On Saturday,
Vote Twice!**
By Karla Preston
OlssonPress Syndicate Exclusive

"Vote early and vote often" was the advice of some long-dead Chicago political machine boss to his supporters.

You can do the same on Saturday.

Australia is the only democracy where we're *forced* to be free: voting is compulsory. If you don't vote on Saturday you get fined.

On the other hand, even though you can (and "must") go to the polls (if only *once),* thanks to our unique preferential voting system you can vote twice, or even three or more times.

Too many of us, unfortunately, don't fully appreciate how it works, so here's a quick guide.

To win a seat in the House of Reps, you have to get fifty percent of the votes, plus one. If there are just two candidates in an electorate, whoever gets more votes wins. When there are three or more candidates it starts to get interesting.

As you know, when you vote you can't just tick the box next to your preferred candidate. You have to number them in the *order* of your preference. So if Bloggs, Jones and Smith are the candidates, and you want *Jones* to win but detest Smith, you might vote like this:

2 Bloggs

1 Jones

3 Smith

When the votes are counted only the *first preferences*—the *1s*—are tallied. Say the count looks like this:

Bloggs	29
Jones	27
Smith	44
TOTAL	100

In countries like the U.S. and Britain with a "first past the post" system, Smith would be the winner—even though a majority of 56% voted *against* him.

But here, since Smith does *not* have fifty percent of the votes plus one, there's a second round: the preferences of the lowest candidate are "distributed." In this case, that's *your* candidate, Jones. All his votes are counted again. But this time the 2s, not the *1s*, are tallied. Those 2s are added to Bloggs' and Smith's 1s to give the final total.

Let's say 5 Jones voters put Smith as their second choice, while the other 22 went for Bloggs. The final result is:

Bloggs	51
Smith	49
TOTAL	100

So even though Jones, your favorite candidate, didn't make it, at least that charlatan Smith didn't get in—because *your* vote was counted *twice.*

(When there are more than three candidates—as always happens in the Senate—the process is the same if a little more complicated. They simply keep distributing preferences until they reach "the last politician standing.")

Why not use this system to your own advantage on Saturday?

Even if you're a dyed-in-the-wool Labor or Conservative supporter, surely there's *something* you're dissatisfied with about your own party? If so, Saturday is your opportunity to tell them, and tell them where it really hurts: at the polling booth.

Simply give your *first* preference to one of the independent candidates in your electorate—for example, one whose stance is closer to your own views on an important issue—and then put your *real* (Conservative or Labor) choice *second.*

The chances of an independent winning a seat in the House are so low it's hardly worth worrying about. When the votes are counted, the independents' preferences will be distributed and your *second* vote will be the one that counts. But you can be sure that the political bosses will see the decline in their first preference vote—and get your message.

That's what I'll be doing on Saturday. I hope you consider doing the same—and remind our "leaders" in Canberra who's the boss.

On Saturday, Vote Twice! was reprinted as a full page ad in every newspaper in the country, every day, for the rest of the week, up to and including election day. It was turned into a video with cartoon-style graphics that became an overnight hit on the internet and was aired on many TV stations. It was all financed by the OlssonPress.

*****

The intercom on Sir Philip French's desk buzzed. "Derek Olsson is here to see you, Sir Philip," his secretary said.

"Olsson? *Here?*"

"Yes, Sir Philip. He's right in front of me. *Wait.* Mr. Olsson—"

Derek Olsson stepped into French's office, shutting the door behind him.

"You don't have an appointment," French growled.

Olsson sat down opposite French. "I do now," he grinned.

"I have no desire to talk to you," French said.

"Just listen, then. I'm here to make you an offer. Five million dollars for the *titles,* only, of your Sydney and Melbourne capital city papers."

"They're worth far more than that!"

"They are," Olsson agreed, "at the moment. But when I'm through with you, they won't be worth a damn thing."

"Are you threatening me?" French demanded.

"That's *your* style, Phil. Not mine."

"What are you talking about?"

"Surely I don't need to remind you of our recent conversation," Olsson said.

"So it *was* you."

"And then you called your mate, Frankie, right?"

French's involuntary flinch was an admission of guilt. He stood up. "The answer is no," he said. "Good day."

Olsson lounged back and grinned. "I thought you might say that. But there's some information you don't have. In just a few weeks, we'll be starting up dailies in competition with yours."

"What?" said French, slowly collapsing into his seat. "The way things are, there's hardly enough business around to support *two.*"

"Very true, Phil. Something will have to give. My guess is it will be you. You're bleeding in Wagga and a couple of other country towns. Peanuts. You can wear it for a while. You've sunk a fortune into the new French building. Until that's finished and you can sell this building, it's a big drain on your finances. You'll have new presses there. The ones you're stuck with now are antiquated. Ours are the latest. State of the art. We're the low-cost providers in the newspaper business. No unions. No featherbedding. No delivery trucks sitting around sixteen hours a day. No one—not you, not Henry—can compete with us there. Your Sydney and Melbourne flagships are weaker than Sykes'. When they're bleeding tens of thousands of dollars a day, your whole empire will be threatened. I don't think your son will be very happy to see his inheritance disintegrate."

French glared at Olsson. "God damn you to hell."

"You're thinking you don't deserve this?" Olsson said, still lounging as if this was an innocuous conversation between two friends. "You've been in bed with McKurn from the year dot. And not just McKurn. You've cultivated connections with the underworld to put pressure on your unions, among other things. Especially with the Greek—"

"Ancient history now," French growled.

"Not if your past came to light, Phil," Olsson said.

"You're going to expose me, *too?*"

"No." Olsson shook his head. "Sure, you've pulled every string in government to get special favors. You've hired thugs to sabotage your competition—oh, yes, I *know*, Phil. You give businessmen a bad name. Now, let's see how you take the heat of honest competition."

French said nothing.

Olsson got to his feet. "A pleasure to chat with you, Phil. For a change. You've got my number. Give me a call if you change your mind. Don't wait too long, though. When our plans reach a certain stage, I'll no longer be interested."

French stared at the door swinging shut behind Olsson until he no longer saw it. He was remembering his heyday, the circulation battles with Sykes and others, the rush to get a hot story on the streets thirty minutes ahead of the competition, the subtle and not-so-subtle tactics they'd used against each other.

Those days were gone. For good.

He began to think about Olsson. He knew too much—where did he get his information? Where, for that matter, did he get his money? The freight business was far more cutthroat than newspapers. Anyone with a truck was your competitor. Today, of course, anyone with an internet connection was *his* competitor.

But, if I could follow Olsson's money to its source. His spirits rose as he began thinking of the mechanics. No, he quickly realized. By the time he could find out anything—*if* there was anything to find—it would be too late.

I'm definitely getting too old.

With a heavy sigh, he picked up the phone to talk with his son.

*****

THE VICTIMS' SELF-DEFENCE League survived on a shoe-string. Its office was in the industrial suburb of Alexandria, a single room on the fourth floor of a rundown building with no elevator, about halfway between the city of Sydney and the airport.

Alison slowly climbed the stairs to the rhythmic *clack* of her walking stick. At the top she paused to rest her now-aching foot. A babble of voices leaked through the door of the League's office.

A few more steps and she was about to knock when the door swung open and Maureen Hendrickson, the League's president, nearly barrelled into her. "Alison! Come with me."

The office was crammed with desks and papers and more people than should logically fit in such a small space. Everyone seemed to be talking earnestly on a phone or on headphones attached to a computer.

"Maureen. What's going on?"

Maureen tugged Alison's arm as she shouted back, "Keep her on the line," to one woman and "Keep trying!" to another. "I'll tell you on the way," she said to Alison.

"Where are we going?"

"To stop a suicide. If we can get there in time."

"Watch out for the cops," Maureen said as she accelerated from the kerb. She bullied her way through the traffic, running red lights, crossing double yellow lines, squealing around corners. A fifteen-year-old girl who was raped last night, she explained as she drove, had called the help line. "She just wants to *die*. She probably *wouldn't* have called if she was *really* going to kill herself. But you never know. Luckily, she lives not too far away."

"Okay," Alison said doubtfully. "But—what can I do that you can't?"

"She'll know who you are, Alison. Everybody knows. You're living proof that you can survive rape and find true love."

"The video—"

"Unfortunately," Maureen said, "yes."

Other than the squealing of tyres and the honking of horns, Alison contemplated that strange thought in silence, until it was shattered by the ringing of her phone.

"Alison McGuire?" said a vaguely familiar voice, "it's Annabelle—Annabelle Myers, remember?"

"Of course. *Sergeant* Annabelle now, I understand. Congratulations."

"Thank you." Annabelle paused, and taking a deep breath said, "We have a DNA match."

"A what?"

"We arrested one of your three rapists. A routine DNA test threw up a match. Do you want to prosecute?"

"I—" Alison stopped. "What about the statute of limitations? Does that apply to rape?"

"Definitely not!" Alison heard Maureen say in one ear as Annabelle said the same thing in the other.

Revenge, Alison thought. She'd been driven, consumed by it. She looked at her hands: they were still. Not long ago, her reaction to Annabelle's news would have been very different. Anger; the immediate stiffening of her hands—and the desire to *kill*.

But now? She could think of her rape dispassionately. *More* dispassionately, she corrected herself.

"Who twisted your soul?" Karla had said the first time they'd met. *They* had, those three men. Or, in my reaction, *did I do it to myself?*

"I don't need to," Alison said.

"You've *forgiven* them?" Annabelle said.

"No way. But I have, if you like, forgiven myself. What about the other two?"

"We've no idea who they might be, but *he* could identify them."

"How about you hang a rape charge over his head, but if he identifies his mates—"

"A great idea," said Annabelle enthusiastically. "This guy's a petty crim, with a long laundry list of minor charges. This time we've got him on robbery and assault. But the other two, what if we have nothing on them?"

"*Then* I'll be happy to testify. Or whatever."

"They found your rapist?" Maureen said the moment Alison put down her phone.

"One of them, yes."

"You've *got* to prosecute the bastard, Alison," Maureen said.

Alison shrugged. "That's how I used to feel, but now. . . ."

"But don't you understand? You can give others *hope*. How long ago was it?"

"Twenty years."

"If *you* can receive justice after twenty years, so can *they*." She slammed on the brakes in front of a small bungalow and leapt out of the car. "We're here."

Knocking gently on the front door she called out, "Rosemarie? It's Maureen. May I come in?"

There was no answer. The door swung open at her touch. She stepped inside. Rosemarie was huddled in an armchair, wearing a nightgown, still talking on the phone. She looked up suspiciously as Maureen entered. But when Alison hobbled in, her eyes goggled.

"*You?* You've come to see *me?*"

Maureen grinned at Alison and mouthed the words: *See, you're famous.*

Within moments, Rosemarie clung to Alison like a lost puppy. Her dependence made Alison feel uncomfortable. But Rosemarie was quick to agree to anything Alison suggested—report her rape to the police, be tested, and prosecute—"so long as you come with me."

The culprit: her mother's boyfriend. "Where was your *mother?*" Maureen asked, incredulous.

"Dead drunk, as usual," Rosemarie replied.

Three hours later, they left the exhausted girl in a League halfway house, staffed by volunteer members.

"But you'll come and visit me?" Rosemarie said, not willing to let Alison go.

"I promise."

"You were magnificent with Rosemarie, you know," Maureen said as they drove away.

"She reminds me of *me*," Alison said.

"Don't they all," Maureen sighed. "We can *really* use your help, Alison. And there's one thing we desperately need. Money."

"But you get grants from the government. Aren't they enough?"

"Almost. But they think that because they fund us, they can tell us what to do and how to do it. We need to be truly independent."

"Is that a hint?" Alison asked, immediately thinking of Olsson, and of everything she'd learnt from the Conservative Party's fund-raising programs.

"It certainly is."

"There might be something I can do," Alison said guardedly.

"Will you have the time?" Maureen asked.

"I could have—" About to tell Maureen she had lots of time on her hands, she switched gears in mid-sentence "—after the election."

"Next week, then."

"Maybe," Alison laughed. "Remember that report you showed me?"

"About the bullies?"

"Yes. I visited a couple of schools and it's not as bad as you think, Maureen," Alison said. "Yes, the bullies *love* the martial arts program. But there's an interesting development in the playgrounds that your researchers overlooked: the *other* students, the non-victims in the program, protect the victims by standing up to the bullies. And since the bullies are in the minority—"

"That's incredible," said Maureen. "Restores my faith in human nature."

ALISON'S TAXI DREW TO a halt at the entrance to Olsson's apartment building. She didn't notice the man standing nearby—until he walked straight up to her and thrust an official-looking envelope into her hand.

"What's this?" she said. "And who are *you?*"

"I'm a process server and this is a subpoena. You're to appear in court on Thursday morning."

"Court? What court?"

"As a prosecution witness at McKurn's trial. It's all there, Miss McGuire."

"*This* Thursday?"

"That's right, Miss McGuire."

"But—I *can't.*"

The process server shrugged. "You'd best take that up with the prosecution, Miss."

With one hand she dialled Royn's number while punching the security code with the other, fumbling both. *Calm down, Alison.*

She called Royn immediately she got upstairs.

"It's the Labor Premier, I'll bet. He's done this on purpose," Royn said.

"That's what I thought, Prime Minister."

The NSW State government was in Labor's hands. Labor, of course, was not going to do the Conservatives any favors. But the Labor Premier had always treated Royn with disdain and contempt, and was taking full advantage of Royn's current troubles.

"But you've got to admit, Prime Minister," Alison said, "that it's a stroke of genius."

All political news and commentary, commercials—*anything* to do with the election— was barred from all TV and radio stations from Thursday morning until the polling booths closed at six PM on Saturday. By definition, court reports did not fall into that category.

"Yes," Royn grudgingly admitted. "But not for *us*. They'll rake you over the coals, Alison, their eyes on the evening news. Right in a middle of the blackout, all our dirty laundry will be hanging out. It will be an enormous political story with no competition— and no way to reply."

"We can in the press—"

"But *not* on the evening news. . . . I'll see what I can do, Alison, and call you back."

Royn phoned the Attorney-General who called his NSW counterpart. "No go, Tony," he reported. "The bastard won't budge."

In desperation, Royn spoke to Ian Nash.

"Ma-a-ate," Nash drawled. "You know I'd help you if I could, but my hands are tied. Right now, we're in the same boat. We *both* need all the help we can get. The New South Wales Premier and his mates must have dreamed this up as a smart move. Which it is, I guess. But they're *really* pissed off with me at the moment. Worried about how Saturday's results are going to affect *them* when they go to the voters in a few months. If I tried to persuade them to help *you,* mate, the bastards will start sharpening their knives to push me out after the election."

Nash sounded friendly enough, but Royn wasn't sure he believed a word he'd said—other than the message that he wouldn't budge, either.

He threw his hands up in the air. "Nothing we can *do.*"

"Anything political is banned, right?" Melanie said.

Royn nodded.

"Could we get Alison's testimony classified as 'political comment'?"

"Maybe," Royn said. "But it would backfire. We'd be accused of censorship."

"Pity."

*****

ALISON SAT AT THE dining table staring at the envelope, arguing with herself.

I can't do this.

I have to. I have no choice.

Royn's return call confirmed what she thought: it was a political stunt. She'd still try to postpone her appearance—knowing she'd be wasting her time. The only other option, Royn said, was to be sick. "But you'd have to *really* be sick. A note from a friendly doctor is too easy to get. They're bound to check."

She didn't hear the key turning in the lock, the door swinging open, or even Olsson's footsteps as he bounded in. Only at the sound of his voice did she slowly look up.

"Alison, I've been invited to speak at the—"

It took Olsson a moment to register the cloud of gloom hanging over Alison's head. His cheery grin disappeared, his bubbling energy seemed to drain away. "What's wrong, Alison?" he said, softly. Seeing the envelope he added, "What's *that?*"

"A present from the Labor Party," Alison sighed. "An *unwelcome* present."

Olsson sat opposite and reached for her hands.

"I'd *love* to testify against McKurn," Alison said after she had explained the situation, "*after* the election."

"Is there anything I can do? I have a few contacts I could call."

"Thanks, Derek. Save them for later. You'd just be wasting your influence. I'll just have to do it. Unless I get food poisoning or something."

"Just eat something that's gone off—"

"No, thanks," Alison shuddered. "I don't *want* to be sick. Certainly not on purpose." She smiled. "Don't worry. I'll live. What were *you* so excited about?"

"I'm going to speak at the Businessmen of the Year Awards on Thursday night. Someone dropped out, so they called me. I've become something of a celebrity, it seems. They'll *hate* what I'm going to say. It's a black tie affair. I was going to ask if you wanted to come?"

"I'd love to. But—*Thursday?* Will Royn be there?"

"Stanley Chow will be doing the honors. And—ah—I'd like Karla to hear what I'm going to say."

"Being seen with you *and Karla?* That's like letting the world know I've parted company with Royn."

"If Karla just happened to be there?"

"Coincidences happen," Alison said with a wan grin.

"Are you still up for dinner with her?"

"Sure," Alison nodded. "That should liven me up a little."

*****

IN A BACK ROOM of the Chinese restaurant, Karla fumbled with the hot teacup. Her right arm in a cast, she was forced to use her left hand for everything, making her life much more difficult. It was one of several things annoying her. Which was, in itself, infuriating. She'd lost the aura of calm and peace with herself, the sense of being in control of her own destiny that she'd taken to be her natural state.

Mostly, she was annoyed with Derek Olsson—or perhaps with herself. Unusually, she couldn't decide which. On one level, she felt she'd been unceremoniously dumped—reacting like a silly schoolgirl whose favorite crush has just announced his engagement to the girl of his dreams. On the other hand, she'd always known it would happen. Which didn't help, either. Derek was the first man who was her equal. She missed the companionship, the union of bodies and like minds she'd never experienced before. Replaced, for the first time in her life, with a feeling of *loneliness.*

Then there was what he had *done.* An unforgiveable sin? That was her immediate reaction. But she'd been doubting her own judgement. Her heart was fighting with her mind, and her mind wasn't winning.

Such confusion was a new and uncomfortable experience.

How, she wondered should she—would she—react when they arrived? Perhaps being here at all was a mistake.

When the door swung open and Alison came in followed by Olsson and a waiter, the teacup wobbled in her fingers as she set it down.

"How *are* you, Karla?" Alison said with a peck on her cheek.

Alison, Karla felt, was tentatively enquiring after her state of mind; Olsson looked uncomfortable, out of place. All three of us, she decided, are on edge.

With an effort, Karla pushed her inner turmoil aside, smiled at Alison, tapped her cast, and said with assumed bravado, "Aside from being one-armed, I'm having a ball."

"Politics *agrees* with you?" Alison said, with disbelief.

"Not at all. Skewering those idiots *does.*"

"We saw you on TV," Olsson said. "You were great."

Karla remained aware of Olsson in her peripheral vision. Whenever she glanced in his direction, her eyes snapped back to Alison, as if pushed away by a repellent force. Now, she forced herself to acknowledge him, to *see* him. The moment she did, her lips began to tremble. She looked away and grabbed the menu. "Let's order!"

They studied the menu in an awkward silence. The dishes came quickly. Karla picked at her food, her inner tension, bubbling below the surface, threatening to boil out.

Raising her eyes to look directly at Olsson for the first time, she said:

"Derek, I'm not myself any more!" Her voice, slow and soft at first, quickly rose in force until Olsson quailed back in shock. "You're the first man I ever *loved.* The first man strong enough for me, who I didn't scare off. Of course there were other men before you. Boys, really. Sexual adventures. Meaningless. Then you're arrested, right under my nose. Disappear to God knows where. Weeks later—weeks of *worry*—you come back in the arms of another woman."

"Karla—" Alison said, reaching a hand towards her.

"It's not your *fault*, Alison." Karla said with a wave of her hand, her gaze locked on Olsson, unaware of the tears trickling from her eyes. "It's not even *your* fault, Derek, though it's easy enough to blame you. I won't, Derek—except for your thoughtlessness. I can see how love turns into hate overnight. It's *hurt*, not hate. I'm hurting inside. You've upset my emotional balance. And goddammit I *miss* you. I miss what we had together."

"Oh, Karla," said Olsson. His eyes fell to the tablecloth. "I—I didn't mean to—"

"There," Karla said, using the napkin to dry her eyes and cheeks. "*That* feels better. I've said what I needed to say—what I've been trying *not* to say." To Olsson's surprise, she smiled at him. "I know you're sorry, that you didn't want to hurt me, that you still care about me. All those things."

"That's all true," Olsson said with a sense of relief. "I just didn't know what to do, what to say to you—"

"It's okay, Derek. Believe me. Sure, you handled it badly." She shrugged. "There's probably no way to handle it well."

Olsson stared at Karla, unable to comprehend her reaction.

Karla laughed. "Derek, you should see yourself."

"I just don't understand you," Olsson said. "All of a sudden you're acting as if nothing has happened."

"Not at all," Karla said. "I had to face reality head on. I'd been avoiding it. Now that I have, I feel like myself again. I'm still raw inside, but I'm over the hump. But there's still something else. I'm not sure I can continue working for you."

"Whyever not?"

"Because of what you've done."

Olsson's chin fell, his shoulders dropped, his presence diminishing. "Luk Suk," he mumbled.

"And the violence."

"Wait!" said Alison, her voice sharp with an edge of excitement. "Something's been bothering me and now I know what it is. Derek, you told me you wanted to leave Luk Suk but he wouldn't let you go. How could he have stopped you?"

"Forcibly, of course," Olsson said. "He wasn't direct about it—but he didn't need to be. I knew that anyone who crossed him died."

"So," Alison continued, "you concocted this complicated plan of going into business with Ross to get away from him?"

"That's right." He shrugged. "Though it didn't work in the end."

"But it could *never* work, Derek. Don't you see?" Alison reached for Olsson's hand, holding him tightly. "You still needed his *permission*. Your sense of freedom was an illusion. He still had you on a leash."

Transfixed, Karla drank in the implications of Alison's words.

"Yes," Olsson muttered. "That's true."

"Luk Suk took away your freedom. If someone took away *yours*, Karla, what would you do? What would you have the *right* to do?"

"Whatever it takes!" Karla said without the slightest hesitation.

"So Derek had the *right* to reclaim his freedom. And to take Luk Suk's life if that was the only way he could do it."

"Of course," Karla tapped the table with her cast in emphasis.

Olsson's eyes glistened, his shoulders straightening as if partially relieved of an intolerable burden. "Thank you," he said, including both Alison and Karla in his gaze. "I feel absolved. Morally justified. But—I took a life. I still *feel* guilty." Olsson shuddered at the memory. "But now I *know* I can redeem myself. And exactly how I'm going to do it."

"Your crusade?" Alison said.

"Exactly."

"Crusade?" Karla said, feeling a pang of envy that Alison knew this about Olsson while she didn't. "What are you talking about?"

"I have a new project. It's right up your alley, Karla." He leapt to his feet, as if sitting was too confining. He began pacing up and down, gesticulating as he talked, his words tumbling out with uncontrollable energy. "I'm going national. I made French an offer for his Sydney and Melbourne papers today. If he doesn't accept it, I'll start dailies in both cities and put him out of business. Plus, we'll be expanding into Brisbane and, later, elsewhere. I want to set up a new department. Working title, *Applied Philosophy*—with *you* in charge."

"Applied philosophy?" said Alison. "What on earth is that?"

"What we've been doing. Exposing corruption, pushing drug legalization, and so on. But on a grander, integrated scale. You convinced me, Karla, that *ideas* move the world. I'm going to use my papers to campaign—to *sell* the concept of self-ownership, and everything it implies."

"Everything?" said Karla, caught up in his enthusiasm—and his concept. "That won't win you any popularity contest. Or circulation battle, for that matter."

"You think so? Depends how it's done," Olsson grinned. "People resist change, no matter how much they grumble about the way things are. *Radical* change is frightening. Pure, logical, theoretical argument won't reach them. You're the master of tying the philosophical to a current issue. *You* get through to people."

"By making them angry with you," Alison grinned. "Like my father."

"At least I've pushed his buttons," Karla chuckled.

"Exactly," said Olsson. "You get a reaction. You make people think. But imagine stories from real life. Ordinary people living in the real world—even if it's an alien one. Written so people can see it. *Live* it. For instance, there are some towns in the States with competing electric companies. Dissatisfied? You can switch in a day. Lower prices, too. An economist might use this as an example of the benefits of competition. But who'd take much notice, except other economists?"

"And not even most of them," Karla said.

Olsson nodded. "So take an average Joe living in one of those towns. He loves it— and feels sorry for his brother in the next town where there's a monopoly supplier of electricity. A human-interest story. A person who *lives* in this real-life place, who treats this supposedly alien situation as *normal*. Written so the reader identifies with him. No comment. No argument. Just straight *reporting*."

"It's tough to make the normal dramatic and exciting," Karla pointed out.

"We'll need excellent writers—"

"—who more or less agree with us," Karla said. "This is going to be much harder than you think."

"But not impossible," Olsson grinned. "Especially with you to choose and educate the writers. We start slow and build up."

"Where will you find *examples?*" Alison asked.

"There's a whole world out there," Olsson said. "Houston has no zoning laws. Does that mean factories next to apartment buildings? No. Why not? In several Asian countries, you don't need a prescription to buy antibiotics and other drugs over the counter. What are the effects? And mine history. For three hundred years, Iceland was peaceful—with no government at all. And Pennsylvania too, when it was a colony, for some thirty years. Until a few hundred years ago, if you moved in together you were married; move out, you're divorced. Simple—and even the Catholic Church recognized them as marriages. Why should the state get involved?

"The world's *full* of different customs. With enough people, we'll be able to find all kinds of examples. Hundreds. Thousands. And push organizations like your Self-Defence League. Anything that's peaceful, anything that's *voluntary*. Open people's minds to possibilities. Change what people talk about. Change the *issues* and eventually the politicians will follow along."

"Keep those corruption exposés going," Karla said, her voice now reflecting her inner excitement. "Continually remind people that the whole *system* is corrupt."

"But surely," Alison said, "they'll pretty much all be locked up soon."

Karla laughed. "Oh no, Alison. As long as the government tries to stop consenting adults doing what they like, the underworld will fill the gap—and need protection from the law. There'll be a new crop of corrupt cops and politicians along in no time at all. You'll see."

"Maybe." Alison turned to Olsson. "This could be something that would interest the geek."

"You're right," Olsson said.

"The geek? Who's the hell is that?" Karla asked.

"The guy behind McKurnWatch. A hacker—"

"Oh," said Karla.

"His specialty," said Olsson.

"So *that's* where you got all that information," Karla said, leaning back in her chair.

"A lot of it, yes," said Olsson.

"Far more than justified by a purely journalistic exercise."

"True enough," Olsson grinned. "We *never* paid a bribe. When a cop, politician, or gangster threatened us, we showed what we had on him and he went away."

"Clever," said Karla. "I'd love to do it, Derek. I can't answer you now. But I will, I promise, consider it very carefully."

"I don't see how I can do it without you, Karla."

"Are you trying to bribe *me?*" Karla asked.

"Incentivize you," Olsson grinned. "It'll be a tough job. You'll have to travel all over the world, see all sorts of new places, talk to all manner of new people—"

"Enough," Karla laughed. "Are you trying to make it hard for me to say no?"

"As hard as I can. I have one request. Before you decide *anything,* come and hear me on Thursday night."

"Saying what?"

Olsson grinned. "I could tell you, but I guarantee you're going to have a lot more fun if you're *there.*"

"Sounds like you're planning something *I* might do," Karla said.

"Indeed," Olsson laughed. "But you're too controversial. They'd never send you an invitation. After Thursday night, they'll never send *me* one, either."

71 Fireworks

"**I** LOVE A MAN in the kitchen," Alison grinned as Olsson brought two plates of bacon and eggs from the kitchen.

"You have a big day coming up," Olsson said as he sat down opposite her.

"Don't remind me." Alison pushed the *Mercury* across to Olsson. "We're in today's gossip column."

"Great."

Tonight's fireworks: Alison McGuire and Derek Olsson, the most elusive celebrities-of-the-moment, are all over the internet. Much to their chagrin, we're sure. But aside from a picture of them leaving a restaurant arm in arm, published on Saturday, neither of them has been seen in public for weeks.

That will change when Derek Olsson addresses the Businessman of the Year Awards dinner tonight.

Today, the organizers must be having second thoughts about inviting him. Olsson's views, it turns out, are somewhat more extreme than Karla Preston's, if you can imagine that.

Yesterday, he published his testimony to the Flint Commission. The title says it all: *Olsson tells Flint: To Kill Corruption, Legalize Drugs Today.* Among other things, he claims that "Nicotine and alcohol are the *only* drugs your fifteen-year-old *CANNOT* buy in school."

Also yesterday, a transcript of a fascinating argument between Alison McGuire and Derek Olsson—which ended with Alison McGuire walking out on her beau—was posted on the internet. It's from the video allegedly used to blackmail Alison McGuire.

The steamy, pornographic excerpts are the number one internet view. But who has watched the *whole* thing, an incredible thirty-six or so hours?

Nobody, we'd thought. Until now.

A few of Mr. Olsson's comments to Miss McGuire:

Drugs "are illegal all around the world. Yet, wherever you go, they're easy to get—despite the decades-long 'War on Drugs.' *Another* government program that's been a screaming success."

Corruption "is an under-the-table, unofficial licence for an exemption from the law that's enforced against everyone else."

Government and the Mafia ". . . both have the same foundation: violence. How many taxes would be paid if they weren't backed up by the threat of being thrown into jail?"

Miss McGuire is Anthony "Drug Czar" Royn's chief political advisor, so it's not hard to imagine why she was upset.

Tonight's function is sure to be packed with people who'll want to hear Olsson's next *bon mots*—and see Alison McGuire "in the flesh," *if* she turns up. We'll be there, with our cameras and recorders rolling, to find out. So watch this space.

"They're expecting fun and games," Olsson grinned. "They got *something* right."

"Does that mean we'll *both* be in the headlines tomorrow?"

"No doubt. Would you like me to come with you?"

"And hold my hand in court?" Alison grinned. "That *would* be a spectacle."

The intercom buzzed. "That should be Mike," Olsson said.

Alison had refused to be prepped by the prosecutor. Instead, she'd spent the previous day rehearsing her testimony with Olsson's lawyer, Mike Rubin—and learning how to counter the tricks prosecution and defence lawyers liked to use to put witnesses off guard. Rubin would accompany her to court and slip her in through a side entrance to avoid reporters.

"Wish me luck, Derek."

"I'll do better than that." Aware of the slight trembling of her body as his arms enfolded her, he kissed her long and hard, his fingers making small circles on her back, moving lower.

"Hey," she laughed. "Not right now."

"I'll be here most of the day, if you need me—"

"I'll call you anyway. Let you know how it goes."

Later, before he got down to work, Olsson phoned the psychiatrist who was treating Mitch.

"How is he, doctor?" Olsson asked.

"He's coming out of it slowly, Mr. Brewster. It's early to be certain, but there's a very good chance of full recovery."

"I'm glad to hear it," said Olsson.

"I'm sure he'd appreciate a visit from an old friend like you, Mr. Brewster."

"I'm not exactly a friend," said Olsson. "But I do owe him a large debt."

"I don't really understand your relationship with him at all."

"It's a complex one that didn't end amicably. So it would be better, as I said, if you didn't mention my name at all."

"As you say," the psychiatrist said doubtfully.

Another debt paid off, Olsson thought. *I hope.*

*****

"Ready for the bad news?" Royn asked.

"No choice," said Doug Selkirk. "We have to know how they play it."

"Fortification," Melanie said, carrying a couple of stiff drinks.

"Not too much," Selkirk warned. "You have another talk tonight."

Royn flicked on the TV, one arm going around Melanie as she snuggled down beside him. As the TV sprang to life, he gazed around the living room of Kirribilli House, and the view of Sydney Harbor beyond, with the ominous sense that this could be the last time he'd see it.

The news reader looked directly into the camera, an unusually grim expression on his face. "Today, police in all states and territories arrested more than a hundred gangsters, politicians from both major parties, public servants—and a couple of businessmen."

As he spoke, a montage of clips rotated behind him—police breaking down doors, handcuffing suspects or leading them away—captioned with city names: Sydney, Melbourne, Adelaide, Townsville, Albury, Canberra, and more.

"The arrests were part of a nation-wide operation coordinated by Inspector Rudi Durant, now with the Flint Royal Commission, seen here detaining Labor Senator Rupert

Taylor in Canberra today. All arrests were based on evidence given to the commission by Derek Olsson."

The screen cut to Royn, saying, "The Flint Commission is doing its job, and doing it superbly. Cleaning house. The scale of the arrests do seem incredible. But they're really just a few rotten eggs—a mere two or three for every *ten thousand* government employees, national, state, and local. Clearing out these few bad apples brings us a step closer to clean government from top to bottom. A government you can unreservedly *trust*."

"Our reporters have been talking to people in the street," said the news reader, "and not everyone agrees with the Prime Minister."

The scene cut to a middle-aged woman with two children in tow. "I'm glad they're all locked up," she said. "But—who's next?"

"It's shocking," said an elderly man. "Just proves you *can't* depend on the government. You can't even trust the police!"

The segment ended with a comment from Inspector Durant: "Today's arrests," he said, "are just the beginning."

The news reader came back on the screen. "Coming up next: Alison McGuire was called as a witness in the trial of Senator Frank McKurn. Her revelations after the break."

"Damn them," Melanie said. "They chose those two clips on purpose. That's biased reporting."

"Based on the questions the PM was asked today," Selkirk said, "maybe they couldn't find anyone who agrees with him."

Royn nodded glumly. Too many of the questions and comments he'd received today were hostile—and from Conservative Party supporters. "I hope you're wrong, Doug."

His cellphone rang. "Yes, Helen? . . . You're not serious. . . . You are? Oh, sheesh. . . . Let me put you on the speakerphone."

"I had a call from Nimabi," Helen Arkness said. "He's confident the Sandeman High Court will rule against us tomorrow."

"Tomorrow?" said Selkirk. "I thought these things took *years* in the Sandemans."

"They do. Normally," Helen Arkness replied. "This case has been on a fast track—"

"For obvious reasons," Royn growled.

"Precisely, Tony," said Helen Arkness. "Nimabi's playing honest broker—not that I believe him for a microsecond. He suggested an out-of-court settlement might be the best way to handle it."

"That's pure blackmail," Royn said. "But a settlement could work. The important thing, Helen, is to string out negotiations so nothing is announced before Sunday."

"Okay," Helen Arkness said, "I'll be with the Attorney-General in a minute. We'll see what we can do and call you back."

Selkirk rose to his feet. "We'd better get going," he said.

Royn sighed. "You're right, I suppose. It's going to be a busy night. And tomorrow, Brisbane and Melbourne."

Squeezing his hand, Melanie grinned. "At least tomorrow night, Tony, we'll be *home*."

*****

Alison held Olsson's arm for support as they entered the hotel ballroom. She was delighted she didn't need the walking stick—which would definitely have clashed with her gown. A sheer, dark blue that matched her sapphire eyes, it hugged her body until flaring from her hips, all supported, so it appeared, only by her breasts. When she moved, the fabric rippled and gleamed to emphasize her curves.

"That," Olsson said as they dressed, "looks like it's about to fall off."

"That's the idea," Alison laughed. "But it won't."

"Really?" Olsson said. He ran his hand down her back. "Ah, you've got something on underneath."

"But not much."

"Your intention is obviously to be *highly* provocative."

"You don't like it?"

"I *love* it. But—"

Alison's eyes sparkled. "Let the bastards feast their senses."

Olsson smiled, but the muscles around his eyes contracted in puzzlement.

"They're all going to look at me," Alison said, scrutinizing her image in the mirror with a critical eye. "They'll be embarrassed when they do." She adjusted the gown to show a little more cleavage. "Now, they'll be *really* embarrassed."

"Are you making some kind of statement?"

"Yes. Isn't that what you're planning to do?"

His broad, dimpled smile was answer enough.

Alison held out a blue cummerbund made from the same material as her gown. "Would you like to wear this?"

"Surely," Olsson said, "that message is far too subtle—"

"For men, yes. The women will get it immediately."

"If you say so." He put it around his waist, and finished tying his white bow tie.

"I thought you said it was black tie."

"I've never been very good at following instructions."

At their entrance, one head after another turned towards them, the background chatter in the ballroom falling as if someone turned the volume control from medium to low. Hugging the darkness of Olsson's black tails, Alison's skin glowed and her gown sparkled all the more. They were talking, grinning, laughing, as if unconcerned or even unaware of anyone outside their own, private universe. The onlookers were expecting . . . something else, *anything* else. Not this. It was like a slap in the face.

Just the same, husbands were transfixed by the way Alison's dress, while perfectly decorous, left nothing to the imagination. Their wives glared at them angrily, while exchanging sharp, muttered comments—"How *could* she?" "Hussy!" "Unforgiveable."

They were greeted by a battery of camera flashes—and the chairman of the Award Committee.

"Ah, Mr. Olsson. Welcome," he said diffidently, his hand limp in Olsson's. "You've become, er, rather controversial. We were rather hoping—"

Olsson laughed. "Don't worry. I won't be talking about drugs or the Mafia or anything like that tonight."

"Ah, good, then. Have you met Stanley Chow, our Minister for—"

"I know who he is," Olsson said.

"The pleasure is mine," said Chow. "Alison." He dipped his head. "We've all missed you recently."

"I've been telecommuting," she said with a smile Chow assumed was for him, but was actually for Karla Preston who she spotted making her way towards them.

"I'm surprised we've never met, Mr. Olsson," Chow said.

"The occasion has not arisen," Olsson said. "Before."

"Now that it has, I'd love to hear your ideas on how we can improve our services to business."

"Do nothing," Olsson said.

"What?"

"I think Stanley is quite shocked, Derek," Alison said. "Every businessman he meets asks him for some favor or other. Isn't that so, Stan?"

"Really?" Olsson said softly, grinning at Alison.

Karla stepped into the small circle, nudging the chairman aside and gripping Chow's arm as if to prevent him from running away. Wearing a plain white dress barely covering her knees, a bright shawl across her shoulders for warmth, and the shoulder-to-wrist cast now covered with signatures, she made—as usual—no concession to proper form.

"I think the concept of a government that does nothing," Karla said, her deep voice suddenly dominant, "is not in Stanley's vocabulary. That's a *fantastic* dress, Alison."

"And very effective." Alison smiled in welcome, partly in reaction to her sense that Karla was a touch nervous.

Karla noticed how Chow's eyes kept returning to the swell of Alison's bosom; her deep laugh echoed through the room.

"It, ah, certainly is unusual," Chow said, frowning at Karla.

"Just so we're clear, Mr. Chow," said Olsson, "I'm using the word 'nothing' in the sense of: stop doing *something.*"

"What? But—but—Mr. Olsson! Our policies are carefully crafted to create jobs and the investment infrastructure necessary for—"

"You want to send investment through the roof? Get rid of the company tax."

"We couldn't do *that,* Mr. Olsson."

"Create jobs? Abolish the GST. Consumers will have more money to spend. Businesses will have to hire left, right, and center."

"But, the *deficit*—

Olsson shrugged. "Cut spending."

"We do our best," Chow sighed, "but it's so *difficult.* Where would *you* start?"

"Everywhere at once, Stanley," Karla Preston cut in. "At the end of every financial year, every government department rushes to spend the last of its money so *next* year's budget won't be cut. Change the incentives. For every dollar they come in *under* budget, pay fifty cents as a bonus to the staff. Hell, pay out the lot. But then, the department's *actual* spending becomes next year's budget. Waste will disappear almost overnight."

"But—but, that could lead to *indiscriminate* cutting. Some essential services could be emasculated."

Karla shrugged. "That all depends how you define 'essential'—doesn't it, Stanley?"

Olsson laughed. "Now, *that* would work."

Chow had moved half a step back, glancing here and there for some reason to escape. Karla grinned at his growing discomfort.

"An interesting proposal," Chow said guardedly. "But I assure you, Mr. Olsson, that I have your best interests at heart."

"How can you, Mr. Chow? You don't even know what my interests are."

"To make money, of course."

"Really? Money is just a fuel, Mr. Chow."

"For what?"

"*That,* Mr. Chow, is the far more important question."

"Indeed. Yes," said Chow, "but you'll have to excuse me. Must talk to—" But he was gone before he finished the sentence.

"I guess he didn't want to hear my ideas after all," Olsson said.

THE DINNER WAS SUPERB but the company was awkward.

Originally, Alison and Olsson were seated at the same table as the chairman, a couple of other committee members, their spouses—and Stanley Chow. But Chow had whispered something in the chairman's ear so they had been re-seated at the next table with prominent businessmen and their wives.

The women were annoyed by the way their husbands eyed Alison; the men all seem to agree that inviting Olsson to speak was a mistake, not that they ever said so directly. Alison, who simply glared back at the men, and Olsson, unaffected by their concerns, made them uncomfortable. Everyone was relieved when coffee was served and the chairman went up to the podium.

"Before we move to this evening's business," he said, "the presentation of the Businessman of the Year Award, I'd like to introduce our guest speaker, a former Award winner and a man who needs no introduction, Mr. Derek Olsson."

Olsson began to stand, but the chairman continued to introduce him anyway, beginning, "I don't need to remind you of his many achievements,"—and then reminded them. The noise level in the ballroom slowly rose until, finally reaching his attention, he concluded, ". . . and with no further ado, Derek Olsson."

As if of one mind, the audience clapped loudly at the chairman's last words, the volume of the applause dropping slowly as Olsson moved closer to the microphone.

He stood silently to make eye contact with the room. Alison smiled at him; Karla, at a table next to Chow, watched him expectantly. The slight frown on Stanley Chow's face gave Olsson the impression that Chow was ready to be angry at whatever he was about to say. Olsson grinned at him, and began:

"Communism tried to change man's nature. Its collapse proved its failure."

Several hundred faces jerked in surprise. Olsson's first words, dispensing with the customary inanities—"Good evening, I'm honored to be here," and so on—signalled this was to be no ordinary speech. Olsson heard a faint groan, and saw the chairman wringing his hands.

"Where Communism failed," Olsson continued, "Christianity and other religions succeeded. Not in *changing* man's nature, but in *controlling* and *suppressing* it.

"How? Guilt.

"You emerged into this world from the womb tainted with original sin. You're guilty.

"You pass an attractive woman on the street and feel a momentary sensation of lust. Even if you'd never *act* on that impulse, Jesus calls you an adulterer.

"Guilty again.

"You have sex with a condom? Or take the pill? You're guilty, says the Pope."

At each "you" Olsson looked directly at a different person, who seemed to squirm back from his accusing gaze.

"It's easier for a camel to pass through the eye of a needle than it is for a rich man to enter heaven. You're all successful businessmen. You've earned a profit. You're going straight to hell because you're guilty."

"Every one of us in this room is *guilty*."

Olsson chuckled. "You doubt me? Everyone—and I mean everyone on the planet— wants two things above all else. To get laid and to get rich. In our culture, thanks to Christianity, *both* are *sins*.

"Even most skeptics, agnostics, and atheists, who'll have no truck with *any* religion, will tell you that greed is a sin, that making money is evil, that your profits are 'excessive' or 'obscene.' 'Tax the rich,' they all chant—after all, what did they do to *deserve* all that money? The atheistic Communists were the worst of all. They made sure that *nobody* could make a profit of any kind. We all know where *that* got them."

Olsson paused and scanned the audience.

"I see I'm making some of you nervous. Am I being sacrilegious? If *that's* how you feel the purveyors of guilt have done a great job. Hardly surprising. They've been at it for over two thousand years.

"Even the world's richest self-made men feel this guilt. They hold their billions, they say, 'in trust for society'—and they're giving it, as they put it, 'back.' It's not really *their* money at all.

"One of them talks about winning the genetic lottery, giving him the unique set of skills which resulted in his massive accumulation of wealth. His fortune is not, it seems, *his* creation at all, but the result of a genetic accident. *He* did nothing to *deserve* it.

"You, like anyone who's succeeded in any field, knows that's total rubbish. The race doesn't go to the smart or the swift. It goes to those who *persevere*. To the single-minded, plodding turtle, not the hare distracted by every temptation.

"In times past, the priest was holy. Never mind that he was buggering little boys, slipping into the nunnery across the street at night to fornicate with the brides of Christ, and lining his pockets with gold from selling phony entrance tickets into heaven.

"That's all shrugged off, even today, with the excuse, 'There are always a few bad apples in every barrel.'

"Today, the priest has been superseded by the *politician*. Unlike the seeker of profit, the politician's motives are not selfish. Oh no, he's an altruist. His is the creed of the 'common good.' Like the clergyman, he worships the poor and hates the rich. After all, there are more poor voters than rich ones.

"When a corrupt politician gets caught—oh, well, 'There are always a few bad apples in every barrel.'

"Politician or clergyman, the hawkers of guilt need a symbol of evil. In times past, the Devil Incarnate and his henchmen—the witches, warlocks, and heretics who were burned at the stake—personified evil.

"Today, it's the *businessman*.

"You're rich and successful?" He leaned forward slightly, pointing accusingly at one table after another. "You must have done *something* underhanded—*that* goes without saying. Your prices are too high? You're price-gouging, victimizing your customers— or both. You undersell the competition? You're trying to put them out of business and establish a monopoly. You charge the *same* price as the competition? You *and* your competitors are *all* guilty—of collusion. You use every legal avenue in the book to reduce your taxes? You're guilty of taking a 'free ride on society'—whatever that means.

"Are there 'good' businessmen? Oh yes, they're the ones who *admit* their guilt, who attempt to atone for their wealth by giving it away. But they're still *businessmen*. No amount of atonement is ever enough.

"Are there businessmen who lie about their products and cheat their customers? Yes. There are, you might say, a few bad apples in every barrel. Except that perception does *not* apply to businessmen. To the public, the occasional 'bad apple' is merely proof that *all* businessmen should be held in contempt.

"The government—any government—is thought morally superior to any business. So is any *non*-profit organization. The only chance *you* have, ladies and gentlemen, of reaching heaven, whether on earth or afterwards, is to *give up the sin of making money.*"

A ripple of laughter, of nervous relief, infected the room.

"What a perversion of morality!

"Are politicians and businessmen completely different species? Of course not. Entering politics doesn't give you a halo, any more than wearing a dog collar does. We're all *homo sapiens*. The same people, with the same drives, the same virtues—and the same faults. Some businessmen are driven by greed. So are some politicians—whose greed is for *power over others,* not money.

"The businessman gives people *what they want.* In the open market, he cannot *force* anyone to buy his products. When he fails, when his customers desert him, he's out of a job and so are all his workers.

"The entrepreneur creates new products people didn't even know they wanted *until* he'd created them. He plants the seeds for giant new industries that create new jobs and new wealth—from *nothing.* The entrepreneur and his associate, the inventor, are the great benefactors of mankind. It is *they*—not the politician, the social worker, the clergyman, or any other self-appointed, self-important 'do-gooding' busybody—who liberated us all from the time when life was hard, brutal, and short.

"And when the entrepreneur fails, *his* investment of time, money, and energy go up in smoke. Nobody else's.

"The entrepreneur and businessman's success depends on one thing and one thing alone: whether enough consumers want the product or service they offer *and* are willing, *voluntarily,* to part with their hard-earned cash to have it.

"The politician, and his henchman the bureaucrat, operate in a different world. They decide what we *should* have. They give it to us whether we want it or not. Then, to make sure we *have* to take it, they establish a monopoly for themselves. Outlawing competition. Outlawing *choice.*

"The politician *produces* nothing that anyone will voluntarily *pay* for. Yet he must finance his activities *somehow.* His solution: just take our money *without* our consent. Call it taxes if you like—it's no different from out and out thievery.

"So who has the greater claim to morality? Who has the greater guilt? The one who deals with others only by mutual, voluntary *consent?* Or the one who resorts to force, giving little or nothing in exchange?

"Who is the more moral? The one you *voluntarily* give your money to again and again and again, because you get so much value in exchange? Or the one you *hide* your money from—because that's the only way you can *keep* it?

"I think the answer is self-evident."

Olsson paused. A number of people started clapping and the applause grew—but quickly began to die away. A few people in the audience got up, thinking Olsson had finished.

So did the chairman. Olsson brusquely gestured that he should sit back down, and continued:

"But there's a problem. It's called competition. Every businessman is in a desperate battle for survival. To keep or win a customer he must produce something that's better, cheaper, or both. If he doesn't, some competitor will. If he's too slow to react, his competitor takes away his customers and he's out on the street.

"Wouldn't it be nice if there was an *easier* way to make a profit? Would you like to learn what it is?"

This time when Olsson paused, there was no shuffling of chairs, no wavering of attention. On the contrary, many heads were nodding. They were keen, it seemed, to learn an easier way to make money from someone who had obviously made so much so fast—willing to put aside, at least temporarily, everything else he'd said.

"So let me ask you: what's the *main* reason you're here tonight? To listen to me? I doubt it. To see who'll be this year's Businessman of the Year? Maybe, if you or one of your mates is in the running.

"The *main* reason you're here tonight is to rub shoulders with Stanley Chow. Oh, yes, I've been watching you, all standing in line to talk to him, like supplicants.

"Mr. Chow has a nice racket going. Nothing illegal, of course. But a racket, a *protection* racket, just the same.

"Having trouble getting a licence or a permit? Want an exemption to some zoning or other law? Need someone to lean on a local council which is gumming up the works? Visit your old mate, Stan. Just coincidentally, send a donation to his slush fund. Or buy a couple of tickets to those thousand-dollar-a-plate 'meet Stan' dinners. Nothing, as I said, illegal about it. But you've all helped make Mr. Chow's position within the Conservative Party unassailable.

"Why? Money. Mr. Chow is the Conservatives' Mr. Moneybags. Their biggest fundraiser. Come election time, Stan gives you and every other businessman in his Rolodex a call. You donate a nice chunk of money to the Conservative Party and a smaller chunk to Mr. Chow's personal campaign funds. This gives him enormous clout within the party. And he, personally, has plenty of spare cash to help out other Conservative candidates—who now owe him big time.

"What do you get from Mr. Chow in return? Protection—from *competition*. I'm sorry. Its proper name is industrial policy."

Stanley Chow stood, his face tense and red from anger, loosening his collar with one hand. "Lies!" he shouted. "Drivel. I'll put you—"

He stopped, bringing his mouth under sudden control.

Olsson's face lit up in a twisted grin, his eyes blazing ominously.

"Do what, Stanley? Put me out of business? Is *that* what you were going to say? A piece of advice, Stan. Be careful what you do and say. Maybe I have a file on you. Maybe I gave it to the Flint Commission. And then again, maybe I didn't."

Chow glared at Olsson, his stance that of a wild animal ready to leap at Olsson's throat. Olsson gazed back, unruffled, his only reaction a broadening of his smile.

A breathless silence lasted until Chow slowly fell back to his seat, muttering under his breath, "I'll get you for this, you bastard!"

But not softly enough. A number of people nearby heard him. One of them, sitting at the next table, was Karla Preston.

Olsson turned slowly back to the audience.

"Tariffs are great. They protect you from foreign competition so you can gouge your customers *legally*. They're an easy sell, too: 'We're protecting Australian jobs from cheap, coolie labor.' Racist, of course. But what the hell—it works.

"Antitrust legislation lets you kill your competitors in court over their supposed 'anti-competitive' practices. No need to dream up a better product to hit them with in the marketplace. And if some upstart threatening you can't afford the legal fees, that's even better—they automatically lose.

"Regulation is good. *More* regulation is better. Why? Compliance costs. All those people you have to employ to fill out all those forms. A nuisance for the large company; a real burden for the small one.

"Patents and licences are best of all. *By law*, you have no competition.

"Why try to be *better* than your competition when you can take the easy road. Lobby—in the name of the 'public good,' of course—for more onerous regulation, more government snooping—I mean supervision. Get Stan's and his mates' support with judicious campaign contributions, junkets, dinners—and the promise of cushy directorships when they retire. Remember to look after the opposition too. They'll be in the saddle some day, and you want to make sure your cozy racket won't be disturbed when they are.

"So you *are* guilty, after all." His voice suddenly became deeper, his stance ominous like an evangelical preacher calling down the demons. "What's more, you deserve that guilt. Not because you make a profit but from the *way* you make it: teaming up with the government to put your competitors out of business. Trading the clean pursuit of profit from voluntary exchange with consenting adults for *security* from honest competition by buying—sorry, I mean lobbying for—the support of the police power of the state to weaken your competitors and screw your customers."

A faint ripple of applause failed to dent the sullen silence that followed Olsson's last words. Scowling at Olsson, the chairman scurried up to the podium. Olsson stood in the silence a moment longer, smiling impishly at everyone, so forcing the chairman to wait impatiently at his side. With a slight dip of his head and a wink in Karla's direction, he stepped down.

He strolled, unhurriedly, over to Alison. Holding a hand towards her, he said quietly, "Let's get out of here. I think I've worn out my welcome. But shall we make a regal exit?"

Alison looped her arm through his and they walked out imperiously. Behind them, the chairman's voice faltered as all eyes followed their progress.

Once the ballroom doors closed behind them Alison began to laugh. "What came over you, Derek?"

"I'm *free,* Alison. No more hiding, no more deception—and I've finally buried my grandfather. Metaphorically speaking."

"And literally. After all, Luk Suk was far worse than your grandfather. Wasn't he?"

"Oh, yes. And now I'm taking your advice, about conquering my *own* defects—remember?"

"That was so long ago."

Olsson grinned. "I guess I'm a slow learner."

They turned at the sound of Karla's voice: "Derek, you were *wonderful.*"

"Thank you," Olsson grinned.

"Stanley Chow was *livid.* You'll never guess what he said after you stared him down. 'I'll get you for this, you bastard!'"

"*Chow's* words?" Alison said.

"He said that out loud?"

"Yep," said Karla, "not that he meant anyone else to hear him. A couple of people next to me confirmed it, so I won't be accused of making anything up."

"Great!" Olsson said.

"And a superb headline, don't you think?" Karla grinned.

"Poor Stanley," Alison giggled. "He has an unfortunate habit of saying the wrong thing in the wrong place at exactly the wrong time."

"Hmm," said Olsson. "We'll *need* the geek."

"Why?" said Alison and Karla together.

"Protection. What's the bet that in few days, every OlssonPress and InterFreight office will be crawling with health inspectors, fire inspectors, safety inspectors, and God knows how many other inspectors? And that I'll be put through the wringer come tax time? When you threaten to take away someone's rice bowl, they become dangerous."

"Not, I trust," Karla shuddered, "as dangerous as McKurn."

"Let's hope not," said Alison.

72 Mandate of Heaven

A cliffhanger coming up? As we head out to vote this morning, predictions of the result are all over the map. Labor leads the Conservatives in the polls with a margin of one or two percent—less than the margin of error.

The two-party-preferred vote predicts a Labor win by one to three seats. "But that's meaningless," says Sydney U pol sci professor Georgina Oldfellow. "The two-party-preferred vote is calculated from an estimate of how preferences will be distributed, based on official how-to-vote cards. But Karla Preston's 'vote twice' article seems to have had a tremendous impact. What people will actually do in the privacy of the polling booth is anybody's guess.

"On top of that, the two major parties have only 65% to 75% of the primary vote, depending on which poll you look at. An unprecedented low. Independents and minor parties representing some 20% of the vote have signed onto Karla Preston's preference-exchange deal. With that mix of uncertainties, it's just plain impossible to have any sense of what the result will be.

"My only guess—and it's nothing more than a guess—is that after this election there'll be more independents in the House of Reps, and *many* more in the Senate."

How many more?

"I doubt even God knows."

An odd footnote: Two of Ms. Oldfellow's former students are high-profile players in this election: Karla Preston and Alison McGuire. How does she feel about that?

"They're both brilliant," Ms. Oldfellow said. "Karla, I think, must have been born a rebel. We never agreed on anything—and we still don't. But, no question, she's sussed the system out superbly. And my heart goes out to Alison. She was doing a wonderful job as Royn's personal assistant. The way she's been pulled over the coals is disgusting. She deserves a much better fate."

*****

"Tony," Melanie yelled as she shook him. "Wake up, for heaven's sake."

Royn rolled over without opening his eyes. "What's the time?" he groaned.

"Seven thirty."

Royn forced himself to sit up. "What happened to the alarm?"

"The alarm wasn't the problem, my dear."

He rubbed his eyes. "I feel like I haven't slept at all."

"Nor did I," Melanie said. "Into the shower with you. The polls open in thirty minutes and the kids are already here!"

They were going to vote as a family, Royn now recalled. He allowed himself to be pushed towards the bathroom.

FOR THE PAST FORTY-EIGHT hours, the papers and the airwaves seemed unable to discuss anything but Durant's wide-ranging arrests, Alison's testimony in court—a.k.a. "hanging out the Conservatives' dirty laundry"—and Stanley Chow's indiscretion. Illustrated, unsurprisingly, by Alison McGuire on Derek Olsson's arm, captioned more than once with a comment along the lines of: *What's Royn's political advisor doing with the man who's bankrolling the MYOBB Party?*

The only "good" news was that Helen Arkness and the Attorney-General managed to string out the Sandemans negotiations so nothing would be announced before election day.

No news was better than more *bad* news.

When Royn joined Melanie, Max, Ricky and Zoë at the breakfast table, he immediately saw from the headlines that this morning's papers were no improvement. Ricky's holey jeans and ragged sweater earned him a frown. Zoë represented the opposite extreme. A smart jacket and skirt, careful makeup a little overdone to his taste, a bright scarf hanging on the chair behind her, all made her seem more an adult than the teenager who would, today, vote for the first time.

"Dad, it's just not fair!" Zoë said. "Durant arrested a Labor Senator. That hardly gets a mention."

"I thought there was supposed to be a blackout," Max said.

"There is," said Royn. "On TV and radio."

"But none of this so-called 'news' is counted as election comment," Melanie said sarcastically.

Max looked up from the paper he was reading. "Dad, it says here—"

"Please don't remind me, Max," Royn said, holding up his hand. "Can we leave politics until later?"

"But, Dad—"

"It's been a tough campaign, Max," Melanie said. "We all need to recharge our batteries."

Two peaceful cups of coffee later, Royn felt he was as ready as he would ever be to face the world. "Nice day for a walk," he said. "Just a couple of kilometers."

"Oh, no," said Zoë. "I just *couldn't*. Not in *these* shoes."

"Why not change them?" Melanie suggested.

"The Princess is worried that someone might take a picture of her *shoes*," Ricky smirked. "Get real, Zoë."

Ah, Royn thought, smiling to himself. She's dressed up for the photographers.

"I'm more worried about being seen with *you*," Zoë said.

"What about Max?" Ricky said, looking offended. "He's dressed the same as me."

"Yeah, but *his* clothes have seen the inside of a washing machine, and he looks like he had a bath sometime this week."

Royn raised his voice. "Let's go!" He opened the front door to see his parents coming up the path.

"Tony," Sidney Royn said, gripping Royn's shoulders with both hands. "I'm proud of you, son."

"You are?" Royn blurted his words, wondering what had come over his father to say such a thing.

"We *both* are," Nancy Royn smiled.

"You made a tough choice, did the right thing—and now McKurn is where he needs to be. *You* did what I couldn't."

"But, Grandpa," said Ricky. "We might *lose* the election."

Sidney Royn grinned. "We might," he said with a shrug. "Sometimes when you do what's *right* instead of what's expedient, you pay a high price. Not many politicians would do what Tony did."

Only Nancy Royn noticed Melanie's disapproving frown at the prospect of losing.

"Thanks, Dad," Royn said giving his father a hug. "We'll be back in an hour or so." He walked with a new spring in his step.

"We'll be waiting for you, son," Sidney Royn said.

As Royn's security detail joined them, Zoë pointed at Ricky and said, "You should arrest him, officer. He looks like a terrorist to me."

"Just a terror," Ricky grinned.

"Oh, shut up you two for heaven's sake," Melanie snapped. "Can we walk the rest of the way in peace?"

*****

"Since I'm in the country for a change," Olsson grinned, "I'd better vote."

"Holy Mother of God," Alison shrieked. "I have to vote, too. Fancy *me* forgetting that. But I'm registered in Canberra."

"Could you get a postal ballot?"

"Maybe. It might be too late. I don't know."

Olsson shrugged. "You could just forget about it and pay the fine for not voting."

Alison's lips curled into an impish grin. "I've got a better idea. Let's go to Canberra."

"Both of us?"

"Of course. Did you have any particular plans?"

"Only to spend time with you," Olsson said.

"That's settled, then. Just for the afternoon."

"Sure," Olsson chuckled. "Why not?"

After Olsson voted, they took a taxi to the airport, ending up in front of Alison's Kingston apartment. "Are we going up?" Olsson asked.

"Later," Alison said.

They took Alison's car. She drove. "That's where I was attacked," she said as they passed Telopea Park. "I used to jog here just about every morning." She stopped in front of Telopea Park High School. "I won't be long."

Voting took her about twenty minutes. Olsson was standing by the park. "Over there," she said as she joined him, pointing to where the two men assaulted her. They wandered through the park. Alison followed the route she'd taken, describing the chase and her escape. They ended up at the tree she'd smashed into. "This tree saved my life." The van had torn a large chunk from one side of the tree. Alison's fingers touched it gently, caressing the wound. "I hope it lives."

"Terrifying."

"It was."

"And now?"

"It's like—" she scanned the grass and trees and the storm channel that ran down the center of the park as if she'd find the right words there "—it happened in a previous life. But I'm not sure I want to go jogging here again."

As they strolled back to the car, Alison said, "I'd like to introduce you to an old friend." A few minutes later she edged into a parking spot in the Manuka shopping center and took Olsson's hand. "Follow me."

"Alison, what a pleasure," Louie said as they walked into his coffee shop. "I've missed you. And this, I presume, is Derek Olsson."

"The very same," said Olsson.

"Derek, meet my old friend Louie," Alison said.

"No need to emphasize the obvious, Alison," Louie grinned.

"That's not what I meant and you know it."

"You two are a hot topic of conversation, you know," Louie said.

"You've seen it?" Alison said, gaping at him.

"I plead guilty," Louie said with a shrug. "But then, so is everyone else in the country. You're a beautiful woman, and I may be old but I'm certainly not dead. You make a stunning couple which, I guess, puts me out of the running. Still, you can do me one last favor."

"What's that?"

"Invite me to the wedding."

Alison and Olsson looked at each other in surprise.

"Oops," Louie grinned. "Did I put my foot in my mouth or something?"

After a moment Alison laughed. "*If* there's a wedding, Louie, the first invitation is yours."

"Cappuccino?" Louie asked.

"Two, please," Alison said.

"I'll bring them out."

While not crowded, there was a constant flow of passers-by along the footpath. But in front of their table, the flow seemed to hesitate.

"I wonder if I'll ever get used to it," Alison sighed.

"I certainly preferred being anonymous."

"On Sunday mornings," Alison said, "I used sit here and read the papers after my morning run."

"Shall I get the papers for you now?" Olsson said.

"I've lost the compulsion to know every little thing that's going on."

Louie came out with three cappuccinos on a tray. "May I join you?"

"Of course, Louie," Alison grinned.

"So what are you going to do now, Alison?" Louie asked.

"What do you mean?" Alison asked innocently.

"Come, now," Louie smiled. "When Parliament's in session, Manuka crawls with political types, journalists, and so on. They talk. I listen. I pick up this and I pick up that. Then I add them together."

"I can't hide anything from you, can I?" Alison laughed. "I'm not really sure, yet."

"You have a great story to tell, I'm sure," Louie said, a strange glint in his eye.

"What are you getting at, Louie?"

"I think," Olsson said, "he's suggesting you write a book."

"He's smarter than he looks," Louie said.

Olsson laughed. "Perceptive, aren't you?"

"A book?" Alison said in surprise. "About what?"

"Your life in politics."

Olsson nodded. "It would be a bestseller, Alison."

"You think so?" she said.

"For sure," said Louie.

"Where to now?" Olsson asked as they walked back to the car.

"I should clear out my office."

As she drove towards Parliament House, Olsson asked, "What did they call you in the press gallery?"

"The power behind the throne."

"There's your title."

Alison laughed. "But I lost it in the end."

"The, ah, 'Hollow Throne' doesn't have quite the same impact. But that could be the moral of your story," Olsson said.

"Maybe."

At the security desk in the Parliament House lobby, Alison signed Olsson in. "Haven't seen you for a while, Miss McGuire," the guard said uncomfortably. "Welcome back."

"Nobody will be here today," Alison said as they passed through security into empty corridors, "except for the guards. And maybe a few reporters."

"There's nothing here to report," Olsson said.

"Their offices are in the press gallery. Would you like the guided tour?"

Olsson had no interest in Parliament House. Alison knew it. So why had she made this offer? He noticed the way her fingers were touching the corridor wall. He was reminded of the way she'd caressed the tree.

"Lead the way," he said.

When they reached the Prime Minister's office some two hours later, Olsson had seen everything that could be seen, with the sole exception of the press gallery. Almost every square foot held a memory for Alison. In the middle of one corridor, no different from any other, she stopped. "I was standing here the first time I saw McKurn. I was sixteen and the way he looked at me *then—*"

They stood inside the chamber of the House of Representatives. "I was up there," she said, pointing to the visitors' gallery, "the first time I saw Royn." She pointed to a chair behind the members' benches. "And I'd often sit there when the House was in session."

Olsson quickly understood she was saying "goodbye." So when she showed him the gym, equipped with every latest exercise gadget, the indoor swimming pool, the air-conditioned squash courts, the plush members' bar, he refrained from making the comments she expected to hear.

The sign on the door of McKurn's office still read:

Senator Frank McKurn

President of the Senate

"He'll be Senator until he's convicted," Alison explained. "His name will stay there until then—though I suppose they'll elect someone else as Senate President in his absence."

Alison unlocked the door to the Prime Minister's suite and took Olsson into her office. "Royn's office used to be up above," she told him. "Having this window on the courtyard was quite a prize."

"I've got an idea," Olsson said, his arms going around her from behind, his hands cupping her breasts.

"I'm not sure I'm going to like it," Alison said, though she let her body press closer to his.

"While we're here, we could make love in the Prime Minister's office."

"Derek Olsson," Alison said sharply. "Don't you have any respect?"

"Do you really want me to answer that?" he chuckled.

Alison sighed. "I guess not." She took his hands, pulling them away from her body. "I'd appreciate a hand somewhere else," she giggled.

Olsson helped her stack files and documents in a corner. "I'll ask Mary to have them sent over to my apartment later."

THEY STOOD ON THE WIDE marble steps of Parliament House, looking at the entrance.

"I've spent nearly half my life here," Alison said. "It was my dream, since I was sixteen."

"And now you're ready to walk away from it. Forever?"

"I—think so, Derek."

"What if we wake up tomorrow and Royn's won. PM in his own right for the next three years. Won't you go back?"

She stared through glass doors, sensing the weight of the building sunk into the top of the hill—and the weight of her memories. *Part of me has died,* she thought. *But at the same time, I feel as if I've been reborn. As if I'm becoming whole.*

"I have to admit, I'd feel tempted. But I *couldn't,* Derek. I've learnt the truth about politics in the hardest possible way. To go back there, now, knowing what I know? I couldn't live with myself."

"That sounds final."

She turned to face him. Even that part of her that had once been afraid of what he might see welcomed his gaze. "It is," she said softly.

"Alison—"

She reacted to the way he'd said her name, lilting, musical, a herald of significance, by leaning closer to him. "Yes?" she said expectantly, puzzled at why he had not continued.

But Olsson's eyes had flicked away for a second, breaking the moment.

"I think, my love," he said, taking her hand, "we should go. Now."

"Why?"

She followed his gaze. They were not alone. There were a few tourists further down the plaza. A couple of them were taking photos of the entrance—or of them?

"Yes, let's go."

When they reached the door of Alison's apartment, Olsson leant down, one arm knocking her knees from behind sending her off-balance, his other arm catching her around her shoulders and scooping her up into the air.

"Derek," Alison shrieked, her arms wrapping around his neck for support. "What are you doing?"

"I'm going to carry you across the threshold."

Alison felt her heart beating faster. She gazed at Olsson through misty eyes, but her lips crinkled with gaiety.

"Are you sure?"

"I've *always* been sure, Alison."

Tightening her hold, Alison buried her head against his neck. "So am I," she said. "Now."

He carried her inside, kicking the door closed behind him.

*****

KARLA PRESTON WAS ACCOSTED by reporters as she exited the polling booth.

"Miss Preston! Who did you vote for?"

Karla laughed. "I didn't vote *for.* I voted against."

"So who did you put first?"

"That," Karla grinned, "is between me and my conscience."

"Who do you think's going to win?"

Karla shrugged. "Does it really matter?"

Tiring of her cryptic answers, the reporters eventually gave up. But as she began to walk away, she was stopped with a last question, "Who's your political favorite—if you have one?"

"Guy Fawkes," Karla said. "He's the only person who ever entered a parliament with honest intentions."

"But he was going to blow it up."

Karla shrugged. "I said *honest* intentions. Not necessarily *intelligent* ones. If he'd succeeded, the politicians would just meet somewhere else."

*****

AT SIX PM, SYDNEY time, the polls closed in the eastern states, the counting of votes began, and the radio and TV blackout was lifted.

There was still thirty minutes to go before the clocks struck six in Adelaide, Darwin, and Alice Springs, in the central time zone. In Western Australia, the country's largest state taking up about a third of the continent, it was only 4:00 PM: the polls there would be open for another two hours. While the airwaves there remained blacked out to any political commentary, anyone with an internet connection could find out what was going on.

That there were no results yet to talk about was no hindrance to the pundits. They recapped the pre-election polls; showed clips of Royn, Nash, and others after they'd voted; analyzed their expressions for a hint to their expectations—and leapt on the exit polls, which did little more than confirm what everyone already knew: the result of this election was going to be totally unpredictable.

By 6:20 PM, less than one percent of the vote was in, enough numbers for some serious prognostications.

"It's unprecedented," said Rowena Watson, host for the evening on Sykes' channel. "The vote so far's divided roughly evenly. Labor, Conservative, and the rest, around a third each."

"Labor's a bit ahead," said Robin Cartwright, one of the two commentators. "The Greens have close to ten percent. If their preferences all go to Labor—as they're supposed to—Labor could win."

"But will they?" Georgina Oldfellow injected a note of skepticism. "The Greens are up nearly double last time. What percentage of those extra votes are Green supporters? And how many are Conservative and Labor voters registering a protest? Nobody knows."

By eight PM, the outlook for some seats was clearer. "Royn, Nash, and Easton—in Kydd's old seat—are all well ahead," Rowena Watson reported. "It looks like Paul Cracken's seat will go to preferences, while Helen Arkness might just squeak in without them."

"Cracken's suffered an enormous drop," said Georgina Oldfellow. "Last election he was shooed in on a clear ten percent majority."

"McKurn's puppet," Cartwright said contemptuously.

When counting for the day stopped at midnight, Labor was ahead with thirty-nine confirmed seats in the House, versus thirty-four for the Conservatives, along with the sole independent in the previous Parliament. With seventy-six seats still undecided, there was still no obvious winner.

"It's amazing," said Rowena Watson. "Half the seats will go to preferences. It will be days, even weeks, before we know the final result."

"A hung parliament wouldn't surprise me," said Georgina Oldfellow.

The swing against the major parties was clearest in the Senate. Each state was a single, multi-member constituency. With half the twelve Senators retiring every three years, there were always six to be elected—more when, as in the case of Tasmania, there was an extra vacancy through death, illness, or resignation.

The early count projected two Labor and two Conservative Senators from each state, "except New South Wales," Georgina Oldfellow pointed out, "where McKurn's still on the Conservative ticket."

"The 'Dump McKurn' alternative isn't making up the difference," Cartwright observed. "Looks like we can say 'bye bye,' Frankie."

"In summary," Rowena Watson said, "neither Labor nor the Conservatives are within striking distance of the seventy-six seats needed to form a government. The Greens and the MYOBB Party seemed set to pick up several seats in the Senate and both have an outside chance of winning a seat in the House."

Robin Cartwright grinned. "Looks like Karla Preston won't have worry about a recount, though."

"It's an impressive result just the same," said Georgina. "She got over ten percent of the primary vote in a safe Labor seat."

Champagne and beer flowed at election parties across the country. Despite the alcohol, Labor and Conservative gatherings were sobering affairs; only at Greens and MYOBB Party get-togethers did the spirits flow in unison.

Interviews with party leaders were broadcast on all channels. Ian Nash, irrepressibly confident, predicted "Labor will form the next government. No question. Yes, our primary vote has fallen, but the Conservatives' vote has collapsed. With the support of the Greens, we only need a small leakage of preferences our way in undecided seats to be the outright winner. So I call on Anthony Royn to recognize the obvious and concede defeat."

"Ian Nash," Royn grinned, heavy makeup masking the worry lines around his tired eyes, "is talking through his hat—once again. His expectation of getting *all* the Greens' preferences is moonshine. Over the next few days he's going to be in for a big, and very disappointing, surprise."

The Greens' Hugo Black called the election "a victory for common sense. It seems clear the Greens will hold the balance of power in the Senate. That means all Australians can look forward to an ecologically sound future, whichever party ends up holding office."

A reporter's question to Karla Preston was drowned by a cheer from the crowd of people behind her. On the small screen, it appeared that hundreds of people were present; in fact, there were only forty or so, squeezed into a room meant for twenty-five.

The question was repeated: "There are claims you and your party have had a major effect on this election. How do you feel about that?"

Karla took a moment to focus. She was more than slightly tipsy, and while elated, Derek Olsson had promised to come—and hadn't. There was no answer at the penthouse; his mobile phone was off; she'd received no message. Nothing. It was disappointing.

"The result is amazing—and gratifying," she said. "But the mandate of heaven is clear. A plague on *both* your houses." She raised her champagne flute. "And I'll drink to *that.*"

*****

"DAMN THAT WOMAN," MELANIE's face flushed in anger as she flicked the TV off, pressing the remote as if she wanted to crush it. "Damn Derek Olsson. Damn Frank McKurn. Damn Flint. I hope they all rot in hell!"

Exhausted, Royn, his eyes barely open, half-dozed on the couch, the remains of his triple scotch resting precariously on the armrest.

He'd registered that Karla Preston was speaking, but had not the faintest idea what she said. It was only an hour since they'd returned from the most dismal election party he'd attended in his entire life—and he immediately collapsed.

The party's only saving grace was the champagne and God knows what else flowing like water. He wasn't the only one who needed its sustenance.

If Melanie's tirade hadn't brought him back to consciousness, he'd have slept where he was for the next twelve hours, if not longer.

Royn stared at her through sleepy eyes, his head nodding in agreement with each of her statements.

"It's all over," Melanie continued, talking to the TV set, unaware that Royn was stirring. "All gone. Everything I've worked for, everything I've ever dreamed about—"

Royn's sullen voice broke into her stream of consciousness. "Everything *you've* ever dreamed about?"

Melanie spun on her heel, mortified to see Royn glaring at her.

"I—Tony—"

Royn's movement disturbed the glass of scotch; he caught it before it could fall into his lap and gulped it down. "What about *my* dreams?" he spluttered. "What do *they* count for? Nothing?" Stumbling to his feet, his hands curled into fists. Melanie took a step backwards.

"At least Dad is proud of me. For something. At last. Not even something I wanted to do— something I was *forced* to do. Something *I* didn't even really do at all. *Other* people deserve the credit for bringing down McKurn. Not *me*. Yet Dad's proud of me. What a *joke* that is."

He took another step towards her; she backed away again. His voice level kept rising as he talked. "I've been attacked, battered, vilified, betrayed by just about everyone in the darned Conservative Party, by Labor, by that blasted Preston woman. The press have hung me out to dry. Even Alison's turned on me. Doug wants to go. Rats leaving a sinking ship. And now you. All *you* care about is being Mrs. Prime Minister. Is that it? What am I? A puppet on a string? Your ticket to glory? Is that all I mean to you—the last person in the world I thought I could count on?"

Even as he spoke, it came to him that the past few weeks of marital bliss were no more that a brief respite from years of discord. Had he *ever* been able to count on her? Resentment exploded from within. Resentment at his father—who saw Anthony Royn as the vehicle for fulfilling his own shattered dreams; at Kydd—who'd treated him as a patsy from the very beginning; at Melanie—the woman he'd unreservedly loved and implicitly trusted who, he was now convinced, had shown him her true nature.

He shambled across to the bar with hardly a pause in his flow of words, grabbed a bottle of scotch and took a long swig. "I've had enough. I'm going to sleep in the guest room tonight. Maybe you'll have come to your senses in the morning."

"Tony. I didn't mean—I'm sorry—" Melanie's voice was a cry of doom. But Royn was halfway up the stairs; if he heard her plea, he ignored it.

Her shoulders shook, her lips trembled, tears leaked from her eyes. What could she do?

Slowly, she followed in his footsteps. She paused at the guest room door and reached for the doorknob.

It was locked.

She leant against the door for a long time, tears streaming down her cheeks, her sense of desolation expanding into a burning ache. Eventually, she stumbled along the corridor and threw herself on the bed, unable to sleep from the confused skein of thoughts whirling through her mind in a haze of alcohol, frustration, anger, and anxiety.

She could make no sense of them. Except the overwhelming feeling of abandonment, of having lost *everything* dear to her.

73   Fun & Games

"R UDI," DEREK OLSSON SAID when he saw Durant's face on the apartment's intercom. "You're not here to arrest me again, are you?"

"Not this time," Durant grinned.

"Come on up, then."

A few minutes later, the lift doors opened and Rudi Durant stepped into the living room.

A voice came from above. "Who's that, Derek?"

Durant looked up to see Alison McGuire at the top of the stairs. *Last time,* Durant thought, *it was Karla Preston. Wonder if that's the same dressing gown?* "Good morning, Miss McGuire," he said.

"Inspector. This *is* a surprise. But—we're not exactly dressed for visitors."

"That's when Rudi prefers to drop in," Olsson said.

"I'll be down in a minute," Alison said.

"Take a seat, Rudi. Coffee? Tea?"

"Whatever you're having," Durant said, crossing to the dining table. Olsson went into the kitchen and came back a moment later with a pot of coffee and three mugs. "You've been a busy man."

"Yes, thanks to your evidence."

"I'm surprised Flint hasn't called me back."

"He probably won't," Durant grinned. "He's got me instead."

"So what brings you here on a sunny Sunday morning?" Alison said as she joined them, now wearing jeans and a sweater. "Won't your family be missing you?"

Durant shook his head. "I was divorced long ago. My wife accused me of bigamy."

"What?"

Durant chuckled. "Said I was married to my job, not her. I guess she was right."

"So this is not a social call?" Alison said.

"Yes—and no," Durant said, turning to Olsson. "I've come across some interesting information. For example, some of that evidence you gave me, Derek, is used."

"Second-hand?" said Olsson. "I don't get it."

"Not second-hand. A few people we arrested were *very* upset when they saw what we had on them. They swore someone had threatened to 'give it to the fuzz' unless they cooperated—but keep it quiet if they did." Durant chuckled. "They cooperated; now they feel betrayed."

"Cooperate? With who?"

"They never really knew. Negotiations were by phone, email, or meetings in dark places with people obviously disguised. But there was a common thread: the activities were all, we think, related to this Candyman."

"Interesting," said Olsson.

"Did you know this Candyman seems to have gone out of business?"

"Really?" Olsson leant forward with sudden interest. "Tell me more."

"Can't be contacted, according to our informants. When the stocks of his products run out, there'll be turmoil in the drug market."

"Thanks for that, Rudi. I'll tell Lynette. Could be a good story there."

Under his mask, Durant was puzzled. *Maybe Flint's suspicions are misplaced,* he thought. He said, "You remember Wong Sui-hung—otherwise known as Luk Suk?"

Alison glanced at Olsson; Durant caught the slight widening of her eyes, quickly suppressed. Under the table, out of Durant's view, Olsson gently squeezed Alison's hand, trying to communicate comfort.

"How could I forget?" Olsson shrugged, unperturbed.

"You used to work for a bank in Hong Kong. Wong was an investor in this bank, through dummies. According to Hong Kong Immigration records, you brought suitcases full of cash from countries like the Philippines and Thailand more than once."

"Perfectly legal back then."

"In Hong Kong. But not the other places."

Olsson shrugged. "I did some crazy things in my younger days, Rudi."

"Wong disappeared in Bangkok recently. The police—in both Bangkok and Hong Kong—are sure he's dead. It appears that his heirs may own forty-nine percent of InterFreight."

"*Somebody* is the beneficial owner," Olsson replied. "But the Swiss owners of record won't say who."

"I find it hard to believe that you don't know who the ultimate owners are."

"We needed their money. It's all paid back now."

"Millions, I believe."

"Expanding as fast as we did was an expensive business."

"Did you know that two Australian residents were recently shot while resisting arrest in Bangkok?"

"I read about it. The hooker homicides, right?"

"Supposedly, yes. One will stand trial—if he recovers from his wounds. It may be a coincidence, but they were in Bangkok at the same time Wong disappeared."

"Think they could have something to do with that?" Olsson asked.

"They *could* have," Durant said. "Interesting trio. A Russian, ex-KGB; an American who was cashiered from the Marines; a South African. All ex-mercenaries. Been in Australia for about five years. All rolling in money with, as far as we can tell, no visible means of support. Very suspicious, don't you think?"

"You think they were gangsters of some kind?"

"Perhaps," Durant shrugged. "They have no record here."

"All very interesting, Rudi," Olsson said, spreading his arms, "but—so what?"

Durant grinned. "That was the time when your sister, Jessica, was kidnapped. Because Luk Suk wanted *you.*"

"Indeed, he did," said Olsson.

"I met Jessica at the airport, so he obviously got you. But now—here *you* are. While he *isn't.* Is that a coincidence? You, Wong, Jessica, and those three thugs were all in Bangkok at the same time. *Another* coincidence?"

Olsson shrugged.

"I don't believe in coincidences, Derek. I talked to some friends in the Hong Kong police. *They* think if Wong just wanted 'justice,' shall we say, you'd have died in the prison van. He wanted something more."

Olsson nodded. "Yes. He wanted me to *pay*."

"But you didn't. You escaped. How?"

"I got lucky," Olsson said.

"Got lucky? Hardly. According to the Thai police, there were dead bodies all over Wong's house in Bangkok."

"Including him?"

"He's never been found, as I said."

"It's all over now, anyway."

"I'm not so sure, Derek. I'll get to the bottom of it one day."

"Well, I wish you luck, Rudi."

Olsson accompanied Durant to the door. As Durant stepped into the lift, he looked back to Alison, still sitting at the dining table. "It might be a good idea, Miss McGuire," he said, "if you and Derek got married."

Alison gaped at him. "Why do you say *that?*"

"In certain circumstances," Durant said, "a wife can*not* be forced to testify against her husband, Miss McGuire."

When the lift doors clanged shut, Alison looked at Olsson in alarm. "He *knows*. And he knows *I* know."

"He *thinks* he knows," said Olsson. "But he can't prove a thing."

"But—"

"Alison, there's no evidence. It all happened in another country, outside his jurisdiction. All you know is what I told you. *Hearsay.* I think Rudi just likes to solve puzzles."

"And those three men—*that's* why you made those calls to Thailand?"

Olsson nodded. "They worked for the Candyman—and they turned out to be merciless killers."

*****

ANTHONY ROYN WOKE LATE and wandered aimlessly around their Toorak home, drank too much coffee, peeked in on Melanie. She was curled under the sheets and didn't move. Should he wake her? Was she asleep—or pretending to be? He looked at her for a long time, but couldn't decide.

Beyond betrayal and misery, he wasn't even sure how he felt.

But—government kept governing even when an election result was up in the air. He was *still* Prime Minister. Somehow, that was a lifebelt to cling to. He made a decision and a bleary-eyed Anthony Royn took the VIP jet to Canberra. Alone.

Parliament House was even worse.

His office suite was empty. Sitting at his desk didn't help him feel like a prime minister at all. A brief stroll through deserted corridors revealed nothing, here, for him.

He called Bruce Spring. He called a few other people. They talked politics—and the hollow of emptiness inside him just kept hardening. But yes, we all need to get together and figure out what to do next. Tomorrow, Tony, they all said. *Tomorrow . . .* there'd be distractions. Things to be done. People to see.

The Lodge, at least, was warm and comfortable. The staff prepared the first decent meal he'd eaten that day.

Being prime minister, he decided, was confining. He couldn't wander along the street, drop into a café, go window-shopping in a mall—he couldn't do *anything* in public without his security guards, reporters in tow, and people staring at him or even accosting him. His world had shrunk.

Melanie called. He watched his cellphone vibrating on the table, unsure of whether he wanted to answer or not. Eventually it stopped. A while later, he called back.

"Tony!" Melanie said. "Where *are* you? I've been worried—?"

"You were?" Royn said in surprise. "In Canberra."

"What are you doing *there?*"

"Nothing. Thinking."

"I could just make the last flight."

He was desperate for company, but. . . . One part of him *wanted* her to come; other parts rebelled; he felt his anger rising.

"Not right now," he said. "I need some time alone."

"I—understand, Tony. I'm sorry. Last night I was upset—"

"What's done is done," Royn said.

"It doesn't need to be. Just—tell me what you want."

"I don't know, Mel. I just don't know."

But he *did.* To rewind his life—to go back to when he and Melanie were *together.* Or was that all an illusion, even then?

He needed someone to talk to. Someone who really *listened.*

Vanessa.

But he had no way of reaching her on a Sunday.

*****

ELECTION JOURNAL

Hung Parliament? With 22 seats in doubt at the close of counting Monday night, the prospect of whether Royn or Nash will form the next government is as muddy as ever.

The Conservatives crawled ahead with 61 confirmed seats to Labor's 60. The chances of either picking up the necessary 17 or 18 seats from the outstanding 22 to reach the needed majority of 76 are, say the pundits, approximately zero.

Yesterday's big news was in the influx of independents and minor parties, *seven* of them to date:

- three independents with no party affiliation;
- one member of Western Australia's Free Mining Party;
- one MYOBB Party member; and,
- two Greens.

Neither Royn nor Nash has mentioned the dreaded "coalition" word—not, at least, in public. But the pollies began descending on Canberra yesterday and are sending out feelers on the quiet to the independents. Scuttlebutt has it that the Greens are open to a deal with Labor, while both major parties are busy framing offers to "buy" enough support to occupy the government benches.

*****

ROYN EYED THE REMNANT of the party's parliamentary leaders at the strategy meeting in the Cabinet room. Bruce Spring, Helen Arkness, Stanley Chow, Victor Bergstrom, a few others including Jack Quigley for heaven's sake. But Quigley's group had survived the rout better than most, making him and his faction even stronger. A couple of newcomers were included. One of them was Barry Easton.

Barry, to Royn's surprise, took to Canberra like a duck to water. In the twenty-four hours since he'd arrived, full of zeal, he'd befriended nearly every MP he met, regardless of party, and was on first-name terms with many of the Parliament House staff as well.

A good but somewhat dry speaker in a controlled setting, he turned out to be one of those people who schmoozed with ease when one on one. He was going to be a great asset to Royn's team.

He was also ambitious, angling for the Treasury. "You'd make a great Treasurer, Barry. But if I appointed a newcomer to the top of the tree, I'd put *everyone's* nose out of joint. I'll push for you as fast as I can. But you'll be here a long time if you choose to be, so give it a couple of years."

"Seniority," said Easton.

Royn shrugged. "That's the way it is."

"I know," Easton grinned. "Got to serve your apprenticeship first."

Oddly, of all the absent faces the one he missed most was Paul Cracken's, whose seat had gone to one of the Greens. Paul, though his nemesis since whenever, was a known quantity. He eyed the rump of the party, distantly aware that internal power relationships were changing and that he should be the one to direct the rearrangement. Someone, he supposed, was already building a base to challenge him down the line. He vaguely wondered who it might be, and refocused his attention to the discussion. Stanley Chow was saying:

". . . I took the liberty of talking to the Free Mining and MYOBB party guys. They're both open to a deal."

"Even the MYOBB guy?" Spring asked.

"Shaun Bernstein. He's a nineteen-year-old student who put his name on the ballot as a lark." Chow laughed. "The last thing he expected was to *win*."

"Then how on earth did he?" Helen Arkness said. "In one of *our* seats, too."

"The Free Mining Party candidate split the Conservative Party vote—"

"What's left of it," someone grumbled.

"Quite so," said Chow with a glance at Royn. "And the local mayor—a popular guy who stood as an independent—split the Labor vote. Bernstein drew a position near the top of the ballot, so he got the Donkey Vote. That Preston woman's preference deal did the rest."

A small but occasionally significant percentage of voters simply filled in their ballots by numbering every candidate in sequence—1, 2, 3, 4, and so on—from top to bottom. This was called the "Donkey Vote," and made a position at the top of the ballot worth an extra couple of percent of the votes.

"So he's a fluke. A one-term member," said Spring.

"Most likely," said Chow, "if he stays with the MYOBBs. *We* can promise him reelection, one reason I think we can wean him away from them."

"What are the others, Stan?" said Royn.

"He's just a kid. Wet behind the ears, doesn't know his arse from his elbow. He was flattered, almost tongue-tied when I called him. If Tony, Helen, Victor, Bruce—all of us invite him to tea, so to speak, he'll be overwhelmed."

"What about that agreement he signed?" Victor Bergstrom said.

"What about it?" Chow said dismissively. "If it's challenged in court and stands up, he'll be out and there'll be a bye-election. We'll get our seat back. If it *doesn't* stand up, he has to stick with us. Either way, we win."

"Okay," said Spring, "I'll put him down as a definite maybe. . . ."

Royn's attention wandered to the memory of Vanessa's tinkling voice. "I'll be there for lunch—if you like," she'd said when he'd tracked her down. At the same time, other thoughts nagged from the back of his mind. Did seeing Vanessa mean he was betraying Melanie? Did that matter any more? He should forgive her—her words came from frustration, exhaustion, and alcohol. No—he was just a piece of furniture in her life, a tool to be used. He'd never felt so small.

Melanie kept phoning, desperation and regret in her voice. He kept putting her off, pleading the immense pressure of events. True. He could have made time for her. He didn't.

Unsurprisingly, the kids were all upset too. Max was stoic, Ricky angry but didn't want to be involved. Withdrawing, Royn thought, like me. Zoë was distraught.

"Mum's crying on my shoulder," she complained. "What did you *do* to her?"

"Me?" said Royn. "I did nothing."

"Then why are you *there* instead of *here?*" she demanded.

Zoë was insistent, persuasive; in the end he escaped by mumbling an excuse and cutting her off.

First, his father, then Melanie, now Zoë. All manipulating him. Paul was right, he thought. I *was* born with a silver spoon in my mouth. I've never had to fight for anything in my life. Now's the time—if only I could be sure what it is I *want* for fight for.

He tried to shut down his mental turmoil by focusing on Bruce Spring's words.

"What about the Free Mining guy, Ralph Nugen?"

"We all know what *he* wants," Chow said. "So we give him some of it."

The Free Mining Party, mostly ex-Conservatives, was a West Australian phenomenon, though it had made some headway in Queensland, the other state where mining was a dominant part of the economy. It rebelled against the controls, restrictions, and taxes on mining and wanted them all gone. Their pitch to the voters, "More investment, more jobs," gained them some traction.

"I think we can sign him up," Spring said. "No way *Labor* will agree to relax a damn thing."

"So," Chow said, "it comes down the question of the minimum price he'll take, right?"

"There are too many controls, anyway," said Spring. "So it's not as though we'd be giving him anything we don't want to give."

"Exactly," said Chow.

Royn's mind drifted away again as the discussion turned to the independents, the undecided seats, and different strategies for hanging onto the Treasury benches. He should, he knew, be more involved. But let Chow and Spring lead the discussion. He'd reassert his authority before the meeting closed—if he could find the energy.

*****

Robin Cartwright grumbled to himself. There was a big story in the air. Labor and Conservative bigwigs were talking to each other—but not to the press. Someone would blab any minute. Cartwright was determined that someone would blab to *him*.

He was on his way to collar a junior minister who'd been in the huddle with Royn, owed him a favor, loved the sound of his own voice—and leaked like a *pissoir*.

He turned a corner to see Vanessa Strezlecki meandering in his direction. As usual, she'd been talking to someone—one of the security guards this time. Universally liked, she was on first name terms with everyone in Parliament House, from janitors to ministers. Probably with God too, he thought. If God had a first name.

"Vanessa!" he said. "What a delightful surprise. But—the Senate's not sitting, so what brings you here?"

Vanessa grinned. "This in a once in a lifetime situation, don't you think? I've come to watch the fun and games."

"Can I quote you on that?"

"Of course you may."

He continued on his way but his pace slowed as a question hit him. Vanessa Strezlecki was an environmentalist who usually voted with Labor, voiced opinions mostly anathema to the government, and though most Conservatives were under the spell of her considerable charms, they held her political views in contempt.

What on earth, he wondered, was she doing in the section of Parliament House where the only offices were those of government *ministers?*

Passing through, perhaps?

Curiosity got the better of him. Turning back, he trailed her until she disappeared into the PM's suite.

Now, he was more puzzled than ever. But his nose was twitching again.

*****

FRANK MCKURN'S EXPENSIVE SUIT now hung loose around him as if he'd shrunk from his two and a half weeks in jail.

The only virtue of being here, McKurn thought as he took his seat for his eighth day in court, was that for the next eight hours he was *not* in Long Bay.

His defending barrister was the best money could buy.

But by the third day of his trial, McKurn knew that the verdict on at least *one* of the now twenty-one charges against him would be *guilty.*

His barrister did his job superbly. He argued, pleaded, objected at every opportunity—but while he never said a word on the subject, McKurn knew the best he could expect was a reduction in the verdict from life to twenty or twenty-five years; or fifteen years to ten.

Maybe.

At his age, it made absolutely no difference.

He sat in the courtroom, his lips compressed, barely listening to the proceedings, holding tight to the one thing that remained of his tattered self-respect: he vowed to never, *ever,* admit a thing to *anyone.*

74   "Et Tu, Mate?"

**Let's Cleanse Our World of Rats, Slugs,
Maggots, Cockroaches and Other Vermin
—While We Can**

By Karla Preston
OlssonPress Syndicate Exclusive

Thanks to Derek Olsson's revelations at the Royal Commission, the police have rounded up hundreds of gangsters—and the bent bureaucrats, cops and politicians who sheltered them from the law.

At the same time as the gangs have been emasculated, the enigmatic drug supplier who dominated the wholesale drug trade, known only as "The Candyman," has disappeared from the market as mysteriously as he came.

The interruption of supply along with the decimation of drug distributors has caused a severe shortage of heroin, cocaine, marijuana and other illegal drugs.

Their prices on the street have skyrocketed.

Anthony Royn and other would-be generals of the "War Against Drugs" see this as a great victory.

They couldn't be more wrong.

Just as nature rushes to fill a vacuum, so underworld entrepreneurs are racing to fill this gaping void in the drug market. Within months if not weeks, addicts will once again be able to satisfy their desires at "normal" prices.

Unfortunately for us, the gap is being filled by elements of the Russian Mafia, Chinese Triads, Colombian drug syndicates, and other scum of the earth. With them comes their culture of violence, the "ethic" of "shoot first—and to *hell* with the questions."

The result is inevitable. Gun battles on our streets. Dead and injured police and bystanders. Assassinations. Even St. Valentine's Day Massacres.

Our home-grown syndicates, now being swept away, are paragons of virtue by comparison.

The police will be powerless to stop it.

The arrest of so many cops has decimated their ranks. Those left are demoralized, wondering which of their buddies they can trust. On top of that, their hands are full with hundreds of prosecutions—which could soon turn into thousands. They won't have the time let alone the energy to go after these new gangsters. They won't even know who they are—until it's too late.

There's a simple way to stop this influx of rats, slugs, maggots, cockroaches and other vermin—and to get rid of most our home-grown ones at the same time:

Legalize drugs. *Today.*

Bring the whole drug trade above ground. Out into the *open.*

Let reputable companies manufacture, distribute and sell your drug of choice to *anyone* over eighteen years old.

Regulate the trade. Tax it.

At one stroke, thousands of gangsters will be out of "work"; there'll be no more massive underworld profits to corrupt cops and other officials—and the government's coffers will be filled.

And since drugs finance the terrorists who are killing our soldiers in Afghanistan, we'll stop underwriting our enemies at the same time.

The "War on Drugs" is a total failure: you can still buy your drug of choice with hardly a hassle anywhere you go.

It's only "successes" are more corruption, more violence, turning addiction into a "sin" that must hidden from view instead of treated—and handing over the supply of addictive substances to amoral thugs who'll turn your daughter into a prostitute without the slightest qualm.

Legalizing drugs *today* is the only moral and rational course of action.

Yes, drugs are harmful. Addiction is dumb. But what you would prefer: to have your son *hide* his addiction from you, finance his habit by thieving or turning his friends into addicts—and end up in jail as a criminal? Or *help* him, as you would if he abused the legal drugs of alcohol and nicotine—the most addictive drug of all?

Your children's futures lie in your hands.

*****

ALISON WAS WALKING OUT the door when Karla rang, her words spilling out in a rush. "Alison! Sorry. Can't meet for lunch today. I have to go to Canberra."

"You? Canberra? *Have* to go? What's come over you, Karla?"

Karla laughed. "It's those bozos, the new MYOBB MPs. Power's gone to their heads."

"What power? There are only two of them—they don't have any."

"Power is like a virus. Just *being* there is infectious. Didn't you ever notice that yourself, Alison?"

"Yes," Alison said, recalling her reaction the first time she had visited Parliament House on a school excursion, "I did."

"They're being courted by Nash and Royn and God knows who else. They think they can make or break the next government. The dream of power and influence has sent them into cloud cuckoo land. I have to set them straight."

"How are you going to do that?"

"I'm going to see the Governor-General."

"The Governor-General? You, Karla? I can't believe this. *Why?*"

"Tell you later. Got to run."

GOVERNMENT HOUSE, THE RESIDENCE and offices of the Governor-General, was set in fifty-three hectares of gardens, lawns, and parklands fronting Lake Burley Griffin. A country estate, Karla thought as her taxi reached the entrance, twenty minutes from the city center.

Technically, the Governor-General of Australia was appointed by the Queen as her representative. In reality, he was chosen by the government who "advised" the Queen to appoint him—which she always did.

Though head of state, the Governor-General's duties were primarily ceremonial. The powers of the office were real, usually exercised as formalities at the Prime Minister's request. The one time a Governor-General had dissolved Parliament and called an election on his own initiative caused a furor.

The current occupant, Alex Herzog, was a kindly, roly-poly man who reminded Karla of Randolph Kydd—without Kydd's inner meanness.

"Miss Preston," he said as Karla was ushered into his office, "one can hardly escape your presence at the moment."

"Do *you* wish to escape?"

Herzog laughed. "No. Not yet, anyway."

"I should tell you up front, that I'm here under false pretences," Karla said.

"You are?"

"My interview request was a pretext. I'll certainly interview you if you wish. My *real* reason is to ask you one simple question."

"Such honesty is refreshing, Miss Preston. I should throw you out—but go ahead."

"If you receive a resignation letter from one of the MYOBB Party members under our rules—"

"I read about that arrangement. Rather quaint, I thought. Do you think it will stand up in court?"

"If it doesn't some very expensive lawyers are going to be very, very sorry they were ever born."

"I see," said Herzog, glad at that moment he wasn't one of those lawyers.

"I want to know what you'll do if you receive one of those letters."

Herzog shrugged. "I really can't say until it happens. *If* it happens."

"Let me put it this way," Karla said. "*If* you do receive one, I imagine you'll study everything carefully—the letter, the agreement, the process, and so on."

"I imagine so."

"And if your conclusions are the same as our legal opinions, you would have to accept it?"

"Speaking hypothetically, that's a reasonable assumption. But it's *only* an assumption. And such acceptance would not immunize it from challenge in court."

"That's understood," Karla grinned. "But who's likely to challenge it—except the member in question? Make him look like a real turncoat, wouldn't it?"

"Quite possibly. You understand, I trust, that it's impossible for me to pre-empt what a future investigation of this issue would determine—assuming, of course, there ever was one."

"In fact, you've really said nothing at all."

"Quite so. I'm curious. *Why* did you want an answer to that question?"

"Two of our candidates were elected, much to everyone's surprise. *Especially* their own. Unfortunately, it seems the moment they walked into Parliament House they checked their rationality and ideals at the door."

Herzog nodded. "I know exactly what you mean. Anything else you wanted to ask me?"

"Since I'm here, yes. It's been a rather interesting election, don't you think? Would you have any comment on that?"

Herzog laughed. "Aside from yes, indeed, it *is* a rather interesting result, nothing at all."

Karla grinned. "I guess my interview idea came to nothing, then."

"A suggestion, Miss Preston, if I may," Herzog said as he accompanied Karla to her waiting taxi. "You're a powerful, even intimidating woman. Don't beat on them too hard, eh?"

*****

PARLIAMENT HOUSE PROVIDED MPs and Senators with state-of-the-art facilities to satisfy their every heart's desire. The one glaring exception: privacy. The building was crammed with people who firmly believed in the inalienable right to know everybody *else's* business—and left no stone unturned in their pursuit of that knowledge.

When they couldn't pin down the truth they put two and two together, not too concerned whether they got three, four, or five.

Robin Cartwright may have been the first, but he wasn't the only one who noticed that Anthony Royn seemed to be spending rather too much time in the company of Vanessa Strezlecki—while Melanie Royn was conspicuous by her absence.

The vague shreds of evidence went into the rumor mill, were hissed from mouth to ear, chewed over, embellished, and with hardly a pause insiders breathlessly called their friends to gloat, "Have you heard the *latest?*"

Inevitably, one of those calls was made to Melanie Royn.

Everything clicked together in Melanie's mind, making so much sense the impulse to cry was overwhelmed by a seething anger. She reached for her phone.

"You're having an affair with that Vanessa woman!" she said when Royn answered.

"I'm *what?*"

"Don't lie to me, Tony. *That's* why you want to be alone. *That's* why you're always too busy for *me.*"

"What rubbish."

"Is it? You're always in her company—you don't even *care* about me enough to keep it quiet."

"Always? I've talked to her a few times—"

"A *few* times? Just talked? That's not what *I* hear. Why, Tony? *Why?*"

"Because she *listens.*"

"Meaning I don't? I'm listening to you now—but you're not *talking.* Tell me what do you *really* want, Tony—a divorce?"

"A what?" He glanced at the clock. "Mel—I'm running late for a meeting—"

"With *her?*"

"Don't be silly. A party meeting. I *have* to be there."

"Aren't you going to answer my question?"

"Later, Mel. I'll call you later—"

"That's what you *always* say," Melanie said, cutting off the call.

DIVORCE? VANESSA? WHAT'S COME over her?

By the time he reached the party room, Royn had reduced his whirling thoughts to a faint point of tension in the back of his mind. He paused at the door, going through a routine he'd learnt years ago to counter stage fright. Satisfied he had assumed the character of Prime Minister, he went in.

Not everyone's here yet, was his reaction to the empty spaces in the party room.

But when Helen Arkness saw him come in, she rapped her gavel to open the meeting and he chuckled at his own absentmindedness. There were, of course, now *fewer* Conservative MPs.

"The first item of business," Helen Arkness announced, "is to elect a new Deputy Leader. So I now call for nominations."

Stanley Chow rose to his feet. "Point of order, madam chair. With one leadership position vacant, shouldn't the other be vacant too?"

"You are correct, Mr. Chow, for all cases *except* the situation we face now where the deputy leader lost his seat."

"In that case, madam chair, I move for a spill."

Amidst the uproar, there were several shouts of "Second!"

So, thought Royn, it's *Stan* who's making the grab.

"I wasn't prepared for *this*," Bruce Spring said.

"I expected this would happen sometime—" Royn's voice more observer than participant "—but not so *soon*."

"Stanley? You should have warned me."

"I had no idea *who*. And I figured it wouldn't happen for months. Never mind that. Let's start counting the numbers."

"There's a motion on the floor," said Helen Arkness. "Will you speak to it, Stanley?"

"Most assuredly." Chow strode to the center of the floor, glanced at Royn, and began.

"Tony had his chance—and bumbled it. Elected leader when *all* the polls projected he'd *beat* Kydd's all-time record, in less than two months Tony achieved the remarkable feat of engineering the biggest decline of any political party in Australian history. Anthony Royn: you're a *loser*. It's time for you to *go*.

"But we can salvage victory from the jaws of Tony's debacle. We all know that the next government will be a coalition. And *we* are the only ones who can put it together.

"Look at the numbers. Four seats remain undecided. We should get two and Labor the others. We'd have seventy-one seats to Labor's sixty-nine. Labor's done a deal with the Greens who—and here we can thank Tony again—have *three* seats instead of *none*. That takes them to seventy-two. We've lined up Ralph Nugen of the Free Mining Party. We're neck and neck with Labor at seventy-two each.

"That leaves the four independents and the two MYOBB Party members. Labor's signed up one of the independents. Another's leaning their way. We've got the other two *almost* in the bag. It's now just a question of price. We'll meet it—after we try to knock them down.

"Seventy-four each. *Both* parties are within two seats of a majority. There's only one place to get those seats—the MYOBB Party. *Without* those two seats, *neither* party can form a government.

"But *we* have the advantage. Labor *cannot* invite the MYOBBs into their coalition. The Greens would go berserk. Labor's left faction would revolt. They'd be lucky to hold them together for three minutes.

"But *we* can live with the MYOBBs' absurd conditions."

Several groans greeted his remark.

"I know, I know. But balancing the budget and limiting government spending are right out of our own playbook. And if something has to be cut—" Chow paused, spread his arms and grinned "—*everyone* will know who to blame."

A few members frowned, but most leaned forward in their seats, their heads nodding with rising enthusiasm as they once again breathed in the scent of power they felt they'd irretrievably lost.

"Everyone thinks because the MYOBBs signed that pledge, they're inflexible. They're not. But, like everyone else they have a price. They will join *our* coalition if we agree to legalize drugs."

Suddenly, the breathless silence dissolved into chatter, murmurings, shouts of "No way." and "No! No! No!"

Royn relaxed. "He's just lost it," he whispered to Spring.

"He has?"

"The majority won't agree to legalize drugs. Not a chance."

"Are you sure, Tony? If it's the only way to stay in power—"

"You're tempted, eh?" Royn grinned. "But it's *not* the only way."

"Ladies and gentlemen!" Chow's voice boomed to cut through the clamor—but now, not everyone was listening. "Think of the tax revenue from legalized drugs. We can—we'd have to, of course—cut other taxes. How popular is that going to be? Silly question. *Immensely* popular. And who's going to take the credit? *Us,* of course."

Royn's eyes narrowed when he saw Easton's head nodding sagely.

"As a leader," Chow's voice now one of growing desperation, "Tony's washed up. We *can* hold onto to the Treasury benches—but only without him."

Polite but hardly enthusiastic applause accompanied Chow as he returned to his place.

"Now watch," Royn whispered to Spring. "This will be my best performance yet."

Chuckling at the doubt written on Spring's face, Royn ambled up to the front wearing an amused smile, as if he didn't have a care in the world. Spring's eyes widened in amazement as Royn's lassitude disappeared, transformed into a sense of carefree energy. Even the tired, worn look on his face had gone.

"Well, Stanley," Royn said, "it would certainly be a new experience for all of us to have a leader with foot-in-mouth disease."

Uneasy laughter, accompanied by a few of Chow's more inappropriate comments, rippled from one member to the next.

Half-rising from his seat before thinking better of it, Chow glared at Royn's unflappable grin, his hands closing into fists.

"Oh, yes," Royn said when he spotted a few puzzled expressions. "That's what Stanley's *really* angling for. Just as well that's not going to happen, isn't it?

"Why not? Simple. Ninety percent of Australians *oppose* the legalization of drugs. Follow Stanley and you're handing the reins of government to Labor. Not three years from now but at the next bye-election.

"But—" Royn paused, his amusement gone. He leaned slightly into his audience with a gaze of solemn intensity "—there are a few minor items that Stanley has naïvely overlooked. Just *whisper* 'drug legalization' to *one* of those independents Stan's so confident are 'almost in the bag' and he'll *sprint* across to Labor's side. Stan's so-called majority will disappear just like that.

"*My* stance on drugs is well-known. I don't need to repeat it. It's unshakeable—and has been ever since my brother died from a heroin overdose. It's so firm that should you, Stan, or anyone else in this room bring a bill onto the floor of the House to legalize drugs, I'll cross the floor to vote *against* it."

There were scattered murmurings of "Hear, hear."

"And I won't be the only one!"

Shouts of "Damn right!" and "That's for sure," greeted Royn's pledge. As he'd known all along, he was not the only member in the room who'd risk expulsion from the party to vote "Nay" on legalizing drugs.

Royn's voice roared above the commotion, "I move the motion be put!"

"Second!" shouted Spring, a split second before a chorus of other voices echoed him, followed by an explosion of sound, "Aye!"

Rapping her gavel, Helen Arkness announced, "The motion before us is that there be a spill for the party leadership. Those in favor—"

The sound of "Aye!" rang out from those who wanted Royn to go.

One of those shouting "Aye!" at the top of his voice was Barry Easton.

Easton's voice fell silent when he saw Royn studying him—and turned his head away.

Brutus, Royn thought.

Helen Arkness "Those against—"

Led by Royn and Spring, the volume of "Nays" was clearly louder.

"The nays have it," Helen Arkness announced. "The motion fails."

"I demand a division," Chow said, his cheeks reddening.

Royn grinned. "Is there any point, Stanley?"

Chow glanced at the faces around him. "I guess not," he said after a moment, glaring at Royn. Appearing resigned and shrunken in defeat, he sank back into his chair muttering to himself, "The fools."

It only took a few minutes to wrap up the rest of the meeting's business: Royn's nominated candidate, Victor Bergstrom, was elected deputy leader. Unopposed.

After the meeting, Barry Easton sucked nervously on his unlit pipe until Royn and Spring were deep in conversation before edging past them.

But Spring saw him. "Et tu, mate?" he said, just loud enough for Easton to hear.

"Barry!" Royn said, his voice cold.

Easton's reaction was that of a rabbit Royn once caught in a spotlight, desperate to escape but frozen with terror. Royn suppressed his chuckle at the memory. He sprang up, took Easton by one arm and began walking him into the corridor. Spring followed so Easton, his head bowed, was sandwiched between them.

"What did Stan promise you, Barry?"

"The, ah, Treasury."

Through the nervousness in Easton's voice, Royn detected an undertone of pride. He laughed. "Would Stan have *kept* his promise?"

Easton's head jerked up in surprise. "What do you mean?"

"Barry, you're playing in the big leagues now, where rules *and* promises are made to be broken. If you break a promise and *win,* nobody minds too much. But losers are held in contempt. Let's go, Bruce."

Royn strode away without waiting for Spring.

Easton stood frozen, staring into the distance, chewing on his unlit pipe.

I WHEELED AND DEALED, Royn mused to himself, moved mountains, put noses out of joint to give Barry the best seat in the country—and the moment he gets here he turns his back on me. I never really believed Kydd's two rules of politics—but how right he was.

"Trust your enemies—*but not your friends,*" was Kydd's first rule. Always followed by a chuckle when he added, The second rule, Tony, is *far* more important: *"Always Remember Rule Number One."*

Your enemies, Kydd had explained more than once, can be trusted. You *know* what they want. They're *predictable.* You don't know *how* they're going to scupper you. But you know they will if they can. Keep your guard up and your eyes open and you'll see them coming.

Your friends are another story. Friends are people you tend to trust. You let your hair down. You confide in them. But friends in *politics?* One day they'll see an opportunity— and pounce. Suddenly, they're your *enemy,* using your confidences against you.

In politics, Tony, you *never* have any *real* friends. Only allies. Alliances are always temporary. *Always.* Every ally is an enemy in waiting. Everyone in this building is out for himself at all times. All else is appearances.

You don't really believe me, do you Tony? I just hope for your sake, Kydd sighed, you don't learn the truth the hard way.

Now, as he replayed his memory of Kydd's words, Royn nodded in agreement, to the extent of sighing in unison with Kydd at his own folly.

*****

"KARLA PRESTON! WHAT A pleasure. An honor!" Shaun Bernstein gazed Karla in admiration as he welcomed her to his office. "Your article this morning—brilliant as usual!"

"Thank you, Shaun, but my head's starting to swell," Karla laughed.

"I'm glad you're here," Kurt Jenkins said. The second MYOBB MP shook her hand with a firm, strong grip. "I think we're a bit out of our depth."

They were, Karla decided, a contrast of opposites. Bernstein wore his new suit as if he'd rather be in jeans and T-shirt. Jenkins, probably twice Bernstein's age, had the authority of self-possession but looked at everything with a touch of awe and uncertainty, as if he'd been suddenly pitched into a strange and unfamiliar land.

"*I* think we've been doing pretty well," said Bernstein, offering her a seat. "We've got a lot to tell you—everybody's been knocking on our door."

"Yes," said Jenkins, "they have."

"Nash, Royn, Chow—all of them! It's amazing!" Bernstein said, his eyes aglow. "*We* hold the balance of power. Isn't that something?"

Jenkins grinned at Karla, shaking his head at the same time, as if to say: he's just a kid.

"And they wanted—"

"Government," said Jenkins. "With our help."

"I trust you turned them down," Karla said.

"Well, ah, not exactly," Bernstein said sheepishly.

Nervously, in fits and starts, they explained the "tentative arrangement" they'd come to with Stanley Chow.

"Demanding drug legalization on top of everything else," Karla said, deciding to follow Herzog's advice and be gentle with them, "was a stroke of genius."

"Thank you," Bernstein grinned, his posture straightening.

"But," Karla said, "Royn will never agree. Chow doesn't have enough influence to push it through. In any case, if you join a coalition, you're stuffed."

"Surely not," said Bernstein.

"You become *part of the government*. You're supposed to support it even when you don't agree with it. You lose your independence."

"They promised to respect our voting conditions."

"And you *believed* them? Politicians make promises all the time! How often do they *keep* them?"

"They've been treating us like we're babes in the wood," said Jenkins. "And they're right."

"Remember the agreement you signed? Before coming here, I saw the Governor-General. If he receives your resignation letter, and agrees with our lawyers' advice, he'll accept it."

"But—but they, Chow said—"

"—the agreement wouldn't stand up in court?"

Bernstein nodded.

"Shaun. Would you take legal advice from a used car salesman?"

"Of course not."

"Politicians are just used car salesmen in fancy dress. They're trying to seduce you. But they're just setting you up the for the kill. If you and Kurt *do* hold the balance of power, there are only two ways *any* law can get through the House. Either Labor and Conservatives *both* vote for it, or you vote with one or the other. Join a coalition and you give that up. If it's influence you want, you've got it right now."

Bernstein's phone beeped. Relieved at the distraction, he grabbed for it. "They've rejected it."

"That's a relief," said Jenkins. At Karla's puzzled look, he added, "I thought it was a good idea but, somehow, it didn't *feel* right."

"Now you've got a different problem. The press will be after you."

"Reporters," Jenkins said. "I don't really know how to handle them."

Karla grinned. "How about I coach you?"

*****

ANTHONY ROYN. PRIME MINISTER. By default.

His eyes roved vacantly around his office, *still* not properly furnished.

How appropriate.

He'd continue to occupy it until he or Nash could form a government.

Until then, he was a caretaker, an interloper.

He'd beaten back Stanley Chow today—but had probably used up what was left of his authority in the party room. The *next* leadership spill would *not* be a Stanley Chow, spur-of-the-moment special. It would be carefully planned. He'd lose for sure.

Alison had formally resigned. Doug Selkirk was going to leave—reluctantly agreeing to wait another month to help Royn "save face." And Melanie—

Sighing, he shook his head. *Politics,* he thought, *is easier to deal with than women.*

What should he do?

He could just resign. Walk away. Admit total defeat.

Hardly a graceful exit.

But Vanessa's words kept running through his head.

"What does Melanie object to? Acting, the theater—what?"

"She hates the idea of me kissing other girls."

"That's easy." Vanessa's voice tinkled with laughter. "Just refuse those parts. Anyway, unless you're going to play the lead in *Lolita,* there aren't that many plays where older guys kiss bright young things."

She was right.

"If you *know* what you want to do and be when you grow up, drop everything else and *do* it. What are you waiting for—the next life?"

And Alison's: "Now you're Prime Minister, are you happy?"

No. The answer he couldn't—wouldn't—admit to himself before.

Just quit, and go on the stage? Fulfill his real ambition?

Yes, he told himself.

Just not yet.

*****

WHEN A FAMILY MEMBER was in residence at the Prime Minister's home in Toorak, a policeman was stationed outside twenty-four hours a day. The advantage, Melanie thought as she went to answer the doorbell, was that unwanted visitors—door-to-door salesman and the like—could never make it past first base. So she froze in shock when she saw Vanessa Strezlecki, of *all* people, standing in front of her.

"What do you think *you're* doing here?" Melanie snapped, glaring at her.

"May I come in?" Vanessa said, mildly.

"I think not." But when Melanie began to slam the front door shut, Vanessa thrust a foot in the way.

"I have something important to tell you to do with your husband," Vanessa said, "that you need to hear."

"What? You're going to run away with him?"

Vanessa laughed, a gay sound of wry amusement that, Melanie realized, did not offend her. It was a laugh directed not at her, but at the absurdity of her statement.

"On the contrary, Mrs. Royn," Vanessa said, "he is deeply in love with you."

"Why doesn't *he* tell me that?"

"I imagine he has. Did you hear him?"

"I—" Their recent conversations flashed through Melanie's mind—all dominated by *her* anger. "So what *have* you been doing with *my* husband?"

"He needs someone to talk to. I'm a good listener."

Studying Vanessa's face, Melanie was surprised to find that she believed her. Hesitantly, she let the door swing open. "Would you care for a cup of tea?"

"That would be delightful," Vanessa said. Over Melanie's objections, Vanessa insisted on accompanying her to the kitchen and helped prepare the tea. Somehow, that simple domestic task helped break the ice between them, and they began to talk.

By the time they were halfway through their second pot of tea, years had melted from Melanie's face. The lines of sour, obsessive jealously faded, the anger that filled her boiled away, and her eyes glowed.

"So I've been a fool," Melanie said. *Again,* she thought, thinking of Alison.

"No," Vanessa said softly, "you're in love and *afraid* at the same time. You've seen, time and again, that Tony excites other women. There's something about him, a sexual charisma, that all women respond to. Didn't someone say once that just shaking hands with him was a sexual experience?"

"Exactly," Melanie said.

"It scares you, doesn't it?"

"And it always makes me angry. I can't help it."

"What you haven't seen—or haven't believed—is that other women don't excite him. Not the way you do."

"But for Tony to go on the stage—"

"—he'll be brilliant. But he'll always come home to you."

"All those young actresses. . . ." Melanie sighed. "I wish I could believe that."

"Melanie, he talks about you—all the time. Sitting on a verandah growing old—with you. Isn't that what *you* want?"

"Oh, *yes.*"

"And about some special place where something wonderful happened—"

"He told you about *that?*"

"Not a thing. He'd start to say something, and then drift off into a dream—or a memory, I suppose."

"That's what I *want* to believe."

"Then pretend you believe it for a while. What have you got to lose?"

Melanie let herself absorb that thought. "Not much, I suppose," she murmured.

"And think of what you've got to gain."

"Yes," Melanie said dreamily, her attention distracted by the abrupt image in her mind of a gazebo on Virginity Hill.

"Why don't you call him now?" Vanessa said.

Melanie stared at the phone, began to stand—and fell back into the chair. "No," she said, grinning impishly, "not the phone. I've got a *much* better idea."

Melanie waited for a reaction, but Vanessa simply gazed at her with curiosity.

"I'm going to the airport."

"May I come with you?" Vanessa asked.

"To *Canberra?*" Melanie said, suddenly suspicious.

Vanessa's smile never faltered. "No," she said. "Just to the airport. I'm on my way home. To Hobart."

75   "Why Not?"

A RANG'ANAT'S BIGGEST-EVER ADVENTURE had been leaving her family and Jazeerat el-Bihar to attend teachers' college in Toribaya. There, she lived with a distant aunt. Aside from the relative freedom of attending classes, the only change was to replace the authority of her father with that of her uncle—who was far stricter. More than once he'd stressed the "enormous responsibility" of guarding his niece's virtue.

But today, she was squeezed into the middle seat on a plane.

Alone.

A rather fat and sweaty Australian man in the aisle flirted with her despite getting no response. At the window, an ascetic-looking Sandeman woman's every glance shouted disapproval as if *she* were responsible for the Australian man's advances.

She sat frozen with apprehension until, about halfway through the flight, she could no longer contain her need to go the bathroom. By the time she figured out why people were lining up in the back of the plane, she was near bursting.

Throughout the flight, the woman at the window read a thick, black book filled with small print, mumbling quietly as she read—except for occasional censorious glances in her direction. Soon after take-off she pulled the window blind shut. Arang'anat was delighted when, as they began to land, the hostess made her raise it. Now, she could look through the window at the tops of the clouds and the strange city of Sydney as it appeared, spread out before her.

Never had she thought a place could be so big.

The plane touched down with a bounce; Arang'anat's stomach fell; she gripped the arms of her seat as if that would save her life. That feeling was forgotten as they taxied past planes like mammoths that, surely, could never fly, strange-looking vehicles—so much incomprehensible activity. Her excitement mounted as she stepped off the plane. She was actually in Sydney. In another country. With no one to order her around. Except Karla, she supposed—but Karla was not her father, not even a figure of authority like Tungi-*ga*.

The prospect of freedom for the first time in her life was more than a little frightening.

She dawdled in the same direction as the other passengers, drinking in every new sight. There seemed to be as many women wearing uniforms as men. The long-legged Australian women strode past her, jostling for position on equal terms. She passed a couple who were barely moving. The reason for their lack of haste was obvious when she looked back: they were kissing each other in public, passionately, like something in a forbidden movie.

She gazed at the girl's blissful face, wondering if any man would ever kiss her like that. Wondering if she would ever meet a man who would make her *want* to be kissed like that.

Then she had no alternative but to walk through a store of some kind where hundreds of bottles of liquor were on display. She stopped to admire leather handbags and fancy scarves, fingering her own scarf, still carefully tied around her head. No one else in sight was wearing one. *If I took mine off,* she thought, *no one would mind.*

Except me. To uncover her hair in public—*I'd feel naked.*

She stood quietly in line at immigration when the woman in front of her started arguing with the uniformed official behind the counter. Her accent was strange—of course, she couldn't be Australian; they were both in the "Other Passports" line—and the words came too fast for her to understand. But Arang'anat didn't need to catch a single word to know exactly what was happening: a woman was arguing with a man, refusing to do whatever she was told. Not just any man: an *official.*

Arang'anat couldn't stop shaking. Right in front of her was the undoable—the *unthinkable.*

A second man in uniform had joined the first, and now the woman argued with *both* of them. Arang'anat was rescued by the officer at the next counter who waved her across.

"Going to school, eh?" the man said as he examined her papers.

"Y-y-yes, sir," Arang'anat said, still trembling. "I English learn."

The man grinned at her—a kindly grin, though it took more than a moment for that to register. "Good on yer, luv," he said as he banged a stamp in her passport and handed it back to her along with her papers.

Arang'anat stood there, dazed, wondering what kind of English she had just heard, until the man said, "That way to get your baggage."

She'd barely taken two steps when the woman who'd been in front of her stormed past. Triumphant.

Unable to even think, she slowly followed. Later, she could never remember exactly how she found her suitcases and wheeled them through the exit, as though she'd been sleep-walking until the sight of Karla's grinning face woke her up.

Beside Karla was another familiar face. Uqu! She began to bow her head in deference, but Karla's hand cupping her chin prevented her movement. "None of that here, girl," Karla said with a smile.

Uqu extended his hand; awkwardly, she shook it. "Welcome to Australia," he said in her own language, and then in English, "It's cold outside. You'll need this." Folded over one arm was a long coat, which he passed to her.

"It, it yours?" she stammered.

"I didn't think one of mine would fit you," Karla said.

Her fingers delighted in the soft, almost-silky fabric; it was the most beautiful garment she had ever seen. How she must stand out, she thought, dressed so shabbily, so cheaply, compared to the richness of everyone around her.

Taking her arm, Karla said, "Perhaps the first thing we should do is take you shopping." And with a vague wave of her other arm, "Uqu, would you do the honors?"

With an elaborate flourish of his hand, Uqu bowed deeply to Karla. "At your service, Your Ladyship," and he took the trolley from Arang'anat before she knew what he was doing.

"Got to keep men in their proper place," Karla said.

Arang'anat looked at Uqu, at Karla, and back, until it dawned on her that they were grinning at each other. She began to laugh. This was all just too absurd.

Her arm linked with Karla's, one hand sensuously stroking the glorious coat, she turned her head to see Uqu behind, pushing her luggage. Automatically she slowed her step so Uqu could pass to his rightful place. But Karla's tight grip tugged her forward, overwhelming the resistance of her sense of wrongness from walking in front of a man.

Hesitantly, Arang'anat stepped into the bright sunlight on the other side of the exit doors—and into the great unknown.

BEHIND THEM, UNNOTICED, A man off a different flight wheeled his trolley out the door. Blinking, he had to shade his eyes from the harsh Australian sun. Aside from his pasty face, he was just another nondescript traveller in the crowd.

In less than a year, that would change. He would become famous—when he joined the nation's Most Wanted list.

His name: Andrei Mikhailovich Kuznetsov. *Not* the name on his British passport.

His previous residence: a prison in Siberia. His previous position: Moscow drug lord. Neither of which, needless to say, he declared on the immigration card.

Russia was too hot. He bribed his way out of prison. But he had too many enemies. The ones in government would send him back to Siberia if they ever caught him. The others were worse: they'd just shoot, knife, or strangle him.

He decided to move to greener fields. Right now, in his profession, Australia was unique in the world.

Virgin territory.

*****

DEREK OLSSON WHISTLED TUNELESSLY as he left the pandemonium of the OlssonPress offices. Stepping onto the street, he paused. The air was bracing, invigorating; he breathed it deeply.

He was running a race against time. In just one week the first issue of the French papers under his management would hit the streets. They were still hiring reporters, renting new office space, testing dummy layouts, dry runs, logistics, and a hundred and one other things. But the geek was on board, intending to revive *McKurnWatch* as *ScumbagWatch,* and Karla's team of investigators was taking shape. It was hectic. Still on schedule, but very tight.

The fresh air brushed all that from his mind. Tucking the wad of papers under his arm, with long, effortless strides he flew past weary pedestrians on their way home as if they were standing still, quickly reaching the penthouse where Alison would be—writing. An imaginary but nevertheless real DO NOT DISTURB sign pasted to her forehead. In an idle moment, toying with Louie's suggestion, she'd made a few notes—and ever since, when she wasn't working with Maureen at the Victims' Self-Defence League, she was glued to her laptop.

He thought *he* was busy; Alison was even busier.

Tonight, he grinned, would be different. Not that she knew that yet.

Alison was hunched over her laptop, her black hair swinging forward, partially covering her face. Olsson paused in the doorway. Alison frowned at the screen, then smiled. Her lips moved soundlessly, testing words as she typed. She brushed a stray lock of hair back over her ear; almost immediately it fell forward again and she didn't notice.

"Hi, Alison," he said, letting the door close with a thunk.

"Hi," she grunted, nary a falter in her fingertips' dance over the keyboard.

He dropped the papers he'd been carrying on the table. "Did you see this?"

Her eyes flicked to the headline and back to the screen. "Uh huh."

"This" was a proof copy of Karla's profile of Alison, scheduled to run in a couple of days. She *couldn't* have seen it. Grinning with suppressed laughter, Olsson shook his head, shrugged, and went into the kitchen.

Half an hour later he was back with a bottle of champagne and two flutes. Alison looked up at the sound of the cork popping. "No, thanks, Derek, I'm busy."

"It's our anniversary."

"It is?"

Finally, he had her attention. "You've forgotten?"

As she searched her memory, he handed her a glass; she took it automatically. Then her expression of puzzlement turned into a frown. "Anniversary of what?" she said, glaring at the dimple on Olsson's cheek. "You're just trying to distract me."

"Among other things." He glanced at the laptop. "Am I in it?"

"Wait and see."

He moved behind her to look over her shoulder. "I want to know what you've said about me. Maybe I'll object."

Alison slammed the lid of her laptop shut, twisting her head to glare at him. "When I'm ready to show it to someone, you'll be the first. Maybe."

"Thanks to Louie," he said, sliding his hands over her breasts to her waist. "I hardly ever see you." He leant down to kiss her upturned lips.

"You're seeing me now," Alison growled; but her annoyance dissolved in the touch of his lips. Turning her body within his arms, she rose in slow motion, pressing herself to him and melting into his embrace.

When their lips parted, the glow of his touch lingered. Smiling, she said, "Tell me, Derek. What's the occasion—if there *is* one?"

"Two years ago today, you walked out of the Sandview Hideaway Hotel."

She pulled back against his arms. "You want to commemorate *that?*"

"It's behind us now," Olsson grinned. "*That's* worth celebrating."

Alison slowly nodded. "Only two years ago? It feels like forever." Lifting her glass, she reached for his and they came together in a silent salute.

Olsson led her out on the balcony. They leant over the railing. The stars and moon were veiled behind clouds, the dark mass of the harbor glimmered, reflecting the dense sprinkling of lights spreading to the horizon in every direction.

"Remember sitting on the verandah at the Traynor's place, watching the lights of the city?"

"Oh, yes," Alison said, her voice soft; then she laughed. "Except we weren't giving them much attention." She sniffed the air, now recognizing the aroma coming from the kitchen. "So *that's* what you're cooking. Spaghetti."

"The very same."

Olsson gestured, his arm encompassing the breadth of the city beyond. "Millions of people out there. Do you think we'll reach them? Persuade them? You'd think it would be easy—don't they all want to be left alone to pursue their own lives in peace?"

"Yes," said Alison. "But they *also* want to be looked after."

Olsson nodded. "Security versus freedom. The age-old conflict. Funny, but sometimes I miss my grandfather."

"You *do?*"

"Oh, not him. The *idea* of him."

"You're not making sense."

"We're born into the world completely helpless. Totally dependent. Our parents walk the earth like gods and we tremble at their approach. As teenagers, we reject them in the name of independence—and rush into the arms of a substitute—"

"Just as you did. You walked out on your grandfather—and searched desperately for *another* guru."

"I did, didn't I?"

"Ending up with Luk Suk."

"Yes. I thought I was grown up and free—but all I did was choose someone else's chains." He looked out to the city. "So did they. I want to wake them all up."

"I think I beat you to it," Alison chuckled.

"You did? How?"

"The League. When someone comes for help, we hope to transform them so they're able *and willing* to fight back. Without victims," she grinned, "tormentors are helpless."

"Like my father," Olsson said, "when I finally stood up to him."

"Leaders are the same. No followers—they're out of a job."

Olsson stared across the city, the discrete lights sparkling in his unfocussed gaze. "A world of independent people," he murmured, a voice from a dream. "No one who wants to rule; no one who's willing to *be* ruled. Wouldn't *that* be wonderful."

"Yes. But can you change the world?" Alison said. "That's what I thought I could do. Once."

Olsson turned towards her, holding her eyes with his. "Who knows?" he grinned. "I'm pulling out all the stops. But even if I fail to influence a single person I'll still succeed, Alison, if I live that life *fully*—myself."

"Yes," she breathed—and with a sudden shiver stepped into his warmth. "It's getting chilly. Shall we go inside?"

Alison turned in his arms—and stopped.

"Look!" she said, leaning towards one side of the balcony, pointing at a tiny, green shoot peeking between two bricks. "You'd think nothing could grow there."

"How on earth did a seed land *there*, let alone take root? Amazing. Like ideas. Spread them, and you never know where they'll germinate."

"Or *when*."

Her sudden shift of tone startled him. Her eyes, caught in the rhythmic blinks of a neon sign, sparkled and flashed hypnotically; her mischievous grin made him curious—and wary.

"A long time ago, you made me a promise."

"I did?"

"Yes. And you've still to keep it. So you owe me—with interest."

"I do? What?"

"Christmas. In London *and* New York."

He looked at Alison in surprise, his expression changing into a slow grin.

Derek Olsson laughed.

"Why not?"

Acknowledgements

I owe an enormous debt to Jo Ann Skousen. Her comments on a much earlier draft (v2.0 in computer speak; the book you are holding is v8.99+many-somethings) saved this novel from oblivion by forcing me to rethink (and rewrite) everything I had done to that point. The characters' names survived, and not much else.

Raquel Narca diligently read (and reread) every page as it came off the computer; her comments and reactions added enormously to the quality of this story—especially when it comes to understanding the female of the species (I'm still learning).

Marby Villaceran reviewed the manuscript and made many suggestions which improved it, and Michael Morrison, an eagle-eyed editor, picked up errors I'd never even heard of!

Senior Sergeant Gerard O'Connor of the NSW Police gave me for invaluable advice (and corrections!) regarding police methodology and practice; from Roger Martindale, I received a seasoned and detailed review of scenes involving parliament house security and police procedure; and Mick Shaw also gave me the benefit of his many years as a detective ; and the staff at the Surry Hills police station kindly showed me the arrest and interview procedures. None of them (unfortunately?) gave away anything of a confidential nature.

Damian Balkin, General Manager of Border Mail Printing, generously showed me over the printing plant of the *Border Mail* which serves the "twin cities" of Albury and Wodonga—and became the inspiration for the OlssonPress.

For advice on legal matters I turned to Mark Hodges, George Forrai, and Gerard Pike; while Celia Tier carefully corrected my naïve assumptions on various medical procedures, and my father, Don Tier (Brigadier, ret.) critiqued everything military.

Staff members of the Australian Electoral Commission and the Department of Immigration and Citizenship patiently answered my questions about some of the finer points of Australian election procedure and immigration law, as did the people I spoke to at the Liberal Party HQ, who similarly helped with some of my arcane inquiries about preselection and other matters.

And I owe much to everyone who read all or part of the manuscript while it was in preparation. Some gave me serious (and, occasionally, scathing) criticisms which helped improve it while others, who patiently waited for the next installment with bated breath, inspired me to continue. So my thanks go to Larry Abrams, Gregory Barton, Tanya Birman, Bay Butler, Ivy Choy, Ginnie Faustino-Galgana, Nick Horden, Neville Kennard, Chris Lonsdale, Benjamin Marks, Ron Manners, Debbie McInnes, Ahmed Meandahawi, Jon Motley, Andrea Rich, Dan Rosenthal, Desiree Samson, Tim Staermose, Elaine Thompson, Bruce Tier, Natasha Tier, Tamsin Tier, Patrick Walters, Kris Wadia, Ellen Young, Duncan Yuille, and John Zube— and the unknown co-passenger on a flight whose appearance inspired the character of Vanessa Strezlecki. Thank you!

And finally, Google and the internet make it possible to do an enormous amount of research anywhere in the world—without leaving home. An enormous saving in time, not to mention the travel expense that would otherwise be required.

Trust Your Enemies is as authentic as I can make it. Any mistakes that remain are, of course, completely my responsibility.

Cast of Characters and
Glossary of Terms

ABC. Australian Broadcasting Commission. Australian equivalent of the BBC.

Abdullah Nimabi. Foreign Minister of the **Sandeman Islands**.

ACT. Abbreviation for Australian Capital Territory. Formerly a part of **NSW**, it is now the site of Canberra, the Australian Capital.

Alex Herzog. Governor-General of Australia.

Alison McGuire. Chief Political Advisor to Anthony Royn.

ALP. Abbreviation for the Australian Labor Party.

Annabelle Myers. Constable, **NSW** Police.

Anstalt. A Liechtenstein entity which is a hybrid of a company and a foundation. Has a "founder" (not shareholders) whose identity can be hidden.

Anthony Royn. Deputy Prime Minister and Minister of Foreign Affairs. Deputy Leader of the **Conservative Party**. Married to **Melanie Royn**.

Arang'anat. Teacher in the **Sandeman** village of Inkaya.

Arthur Riddell. General; Chief of the Australian Defence Forces.

Aruma Bagambi. Prime Minister of the **Sandeman Islands**.

ASIC. Australian Securities and Investments Commission. Regulatory body equivalent to the American SEC.

Australian Army Ranks follow the British system. For example, Brigadier-General was retitled Brigadier in 1922. Otherwise, officer ranks are the same as in the US Army, except that the insignia are different so terms like "2-star general" do not apply. The structure of other ranks in the British system is, again, different from the American. See http://en.wikipedia.org/wiki/Australian_Defence_Force_ranks_and_insignia for more.

ASIO. Australian Security and Intelligence Organization. Equivalent to the CIA and MI5.

Barry Easton. Economics professor who becomes a CP candidate for parliament.

Bruce Spring. Minister for Justice and Customs; leading member of **Anthony Royn**'s "**push**."

Candyman, the. Nickname for the mysterious underworld drug lord who is taking over Australia's supply of heroin and marijuana.

Cantrell. Australian Army colonel.

Chuasiriporn. General, Royal Thai Police.

Collin Renfrew. Anthony Royn's lawyer.

Conservative Party. Australia's two major political parties are the Labor Party, and a coalition of the Liberal and National (formerly Country) Parties. The Conservative Party of *Trust Your Enemies* does not exist: for all practical purposes it can be considered an amalgamation of the Liberal and National Parties, its structure and procedures based on those of the Liberal Party.

CP. Abbreviation for the **Conservative Party**.

Demas Chrysanthopoulos, aka "The Greek." Major figure in Sydney's underworld.

Derek Olsson. Owner of the **OlssonPress**; partner with his high school chum **Ross Traynor** in **InterFreight**.

distribution of preferences. See **preferences, distribution of.**

Doug Selkirk. Anthony Royn's press secretary.

Edward Tozen. *Aikido* Sensei.

Feliks Ilyich Nazarov. Ex-KGB *Spetsnaz* assassin; former mercenary; leader of a gang consisting of him, **Nick Schulz**, and **Mats de Brouw**.

Frank McKurn. Federal Senator from the state of New South Wales; President of the Senate.

French Publishing. Media group owned by **Sir Philip French**.

go for a row. Get caught and probably punished.

Golden Dragon Triad. Hong Kong based triad.

Gottlieb Alten. Computer hacker.

Greg Cannon. Private investigator.

Gugamti. Sandeman Army colonel.

Gurundi. Khatib in the **Sandeman** village of Inkaya.

Hanson McLeod. Former policeman, now a private detective. Married to **Orawan McLeod**.

Helen Arkness. Immigration Minister; chair of the parliamentary **Conservative Party**.

Henry Sykes. Owner of media group **Sykes Media**.

Herbert Flint. Justice of the High Court.

High Commissioner. Title for ambassadors between members of the British Commonwealth.

Ian Nash. Leader of the Federal Australian Labor Party and so also Leader of the Opposition.

InterFreight. Road transport company 51% owned by **Derek Olsson** and **Ross Traynor**.

Jack Dent. Derek Olsson's grandfather.

Jack Quigley. Conservative Party MP.

Jake Meldrum. CP candidate for parliament.

Jason Kowalski. Sergeant, Federal Police.

Jazeerat el-Bihar. Arabic for "Spice Island," the westernmost island of the **Sandemans**. Population almost 100% Muslim.

Jazeerat el-Misk. The name (Arabic for "Fragrant Island") preferred by **Sandeman**'s Muslims for the island officially called **St. Christopher's Island**.

Jennifer Dent. Derek Olsson's grandmother.

Jeremy McGuire. Lieutenant in the Australian Army; cousin of **Alison McGuire**.

Jessica Olsson. Derek Olsson's "kid sister."

Jim Williams. Chair of the **NSW** division of the **Conservative Party.**

Joe McGuire. Alison McGuire's father.

Karla Preston. Columnist for the **OlssonPress. Derek Olsson**'s current girlfriend.

Khatib. Delivers the sermon at Friday prayers in the mosque; senior Muslim figure in the absence of an imam.

Kurt Jenkins. Member of the **MYOBB Party.**

Lars Olsson. Derek Olsson's older brother.

Leon Price. MLA, retired.

Lester Edleton. Western Australian mining stock promoter.

Lew Campbell. OlssonPress security chief.

Luk Suk. Title of the chieftain of the **Golden Dragon Triad.**

Lynette McPherson. Managing Director of the **OlssonPress.**

Maggie McGuire. Alison McGuire's mother.

Mats de Brouw. South African; former mercenary; member of **Nazarov**'s gang.

Maureen Hendrickson. President of the Victims' Self-Defence League.

Max Royn. Son of **Anthony** and **Melanie Royn.**

Melanie Royn. Married to **Anthony Royn.**

Mike Rubin. OlssonPress lawyer.

MLA. Member of the Legislative Assembly, the lower house of the **NSW** state parliament.

Molly Olsson. Derek Olsson's mother.

MP. Abbreviation for Member of Parliament; refers to members of the lower house of Australia's federal parliament.

MYOBB Party. Read on . . . ☺.

Nancy Royn. Anthony Royn's mother.

Nick Schulz. American; ex-Marine (cashiered); former mercenary; member of **Nazarov**'s gang.

NSW. Abbreviation for the Australian state of New South Wales, capital Sydney.

OlssonPress. Small newspaper publishing company started and owned by **Derek Olsson.**

Orawan McLeod. Former policewoman; now assists her husband **Hanson McLeod.**

"Paddy" Byrne. Sergeant in the Australian Army.

Paul Cracken. Treasurer.

Peter McMurray. Captain in the Australian Army.

Philip French, Sir. Owner of media group **French Publishing.**

Poonchit. Bangkok bar girl.

porridge. Jail time.

preferences, distribution of. When no candidate has 50% of the vote plus one, the candidate with the lowest number of votes (first preferences) is eliminated. That candidates second preferences (2's) are then counted, being added to the first preferences (1's) of the other candidates. This process is continued until one candidate is the winner. (See **preferential voting.**)

preferential voting. Also termed "The Australian Ballot," all candidates must be numbered in order of preference (1, 2, 3, 4, and so on) for the vote to be valid.

push. Australian slang for a gang.

Pty. Ltd. Abbreviation for "Proprietary Limited," signifying a privately-held company.

QLD. Abbreviation for the Australian state of Queensland, capital Brisbane.

Randolph Kydd. Prime Minister of Australia; Leader of the **Conservative Party.**

Ranga N'gaandi. Captain in the **Sandeman** Army.

Richard ("Ricky") Royn. Son of **Anthony** and **Melanie Royn.**

Robin Cartwright. Journalist for the *Melbourne Examiner.*

Ross Traynor. Partner with his high school chum **Derek Olsson** in **InterFreight.**

Rowena Watson. TV anchor.

Rudi Durant. Detective-Inspector in the **NSW** Police.

Sam Royn. Anthony Royn's older brother.

St. Christopher's Island. Immediately east of **Jazeerat el-Bihar**; population approximately half Muslim (to the west) and half Catholic. The Muslims demand it should be called by its original Arabic name: **Jazeerat el-Misk.**

Sandeman Islands. A fictitious country located in the Coral Sea northeast of Australia, with the Solomon Islands to its north, Papua New Guinea to the west, and Vanuatu and New Caledonia to the southeast. (Note: there are, in fact, no islands there at all as the ocean in that area is some 11,000 feet deep.)

scarper. Flee, disappear, beat it—but with more haste.

Sean Reynolds. Inspector, Federal Police.

Shaun Bernstein. Member of the **MYOBB Party.**

Sidney Royn. Anthony Royn's father.

Simon Lee. Detective-Sergeant in the **NSW** Police; assistant to **Rudi Durant.**

SP Bookie. Abbreviation for Starting Price Bookmaker. Usually means an illegal, off-course bookmaker.

spill. The term used when the parliamentary members of a political party vote to oust the current party leader.

standover. Extortion. *Standover tactics:* using power or the threat of force to obtain property, money, etc. *Standover merchant:* someone who uses standover tactics. Usually (though not exclusively) applied to gangsters.

Stanley Chow. Minister for Trade.

Suchart. Thai associate of **Derek Olsson.**

Sven Olsson. Derek Olsson's father.

Sykes Media. Media group owned by **Henry Sykes.**

TAB. Totalisator Agency Board. State government betting monopoly.

Thierry. Brigadier. Commander of Australian forces in the **Sandeman Islands.**

Toff. Rich, well-dressed, upper-class person, usually male. Can be used as a term of respect, or as an insult (e.g., "rich bastard").

Toribaya. Capital of the **Sandeman Islands.**

two-party-preferred vote. Projection of the winning party after the estimated distribution of preferences (See also: **preferential voting, preferences, distribution of.**)

Tungi. Chief Elder in the **Sandeman** village of Inkaya.

Uqumagani, aka Uqu. InterFreight employee in the **Sandeman Islands.**

Vanessa Strezlecki. Independent Senator from the state of Tasmania.

Vanich. General, Royal Thai Police.

VIC. Abbreviation for the Australian state of Victoria, capital Melbourne.

Victor Bergstrom. Minister for Defence.

Vincent Leung. Chief of the Sydney wing of the **Golden Dragon Triad.**

Vuong Lam Tho. Head of Sydney's Vietnamese gang.

Zimmerman. Superintendent in the **NSW** Police and **Rudi Durant**'s immediate superior.

Zoë Royn. Daughter of **Anthony** and **Melanie Royn.**

About the Author

Mark Tier is an Australian writer and businessman based in Hong Kong "partly because paying taxes is against my religion."

Founder of the investment newsletter *World Money Analyst,* which he published and edited until 1991, he is also the author of *Understanding Inflation,* which became a bestseller in Australia in 1974, and *The Nature of Market Cycles.*

In 1984 he wrote *How To Get A Second Passport* which sold like hotcakes around the world— and was shamelessly plagiarized in Greece, the Philippines, the UK and Canada.

He was Hong Kong correspondent for the New York *Journal of Commerce* in the late '70s, a columnist for *The Australian Stock Exchange*

Journal and *Business Traveller,* and his articles on investing and other themes have appeared in *Reason* magazine, *Time, The Australian, Quadrant, Liberty, The South China Morning Post,* and elsewhere, and has been a featured speaker at seminars in the USA, London, Canada, Australia, Hong Kong, Johannesburg and Singapore. He is also co-editor (with Martin H. Greenberg) of two collections of science fiction stories: *Give Me Liberty* and *Visions of Liberty.* Both were later reissued by the publisher, Baen Books, in one volume titled *Freedom!*

Since 1991, in addition to helping start five new (and highly successful) investment publications, he has been a marketing consultant and acted as a coach and counsellor. A graduate in economics from the Australian National University, he began a PhD program in economics at UCLA. He is also a Master Practitioner of Neuro-Linguistic Programming.

His book, *The Winning Investment Habits of Warren Buffett & George Soros* (first published in 2004) became an international bestseller with three editions in English (Hong Kong, New York and London), and twelve (so far) in other languages. Adopting those "winning investment habits" himself, he sold all his business interests and now lives solely from the returns on his investments—which enables him to do what he really loves to do: write.

His latest books are *When God Speaks for Himself: The Words of God You'll <u>Never</u> Hear in Church or Sunday School,* written with George Forrai, and *Trust Your Enemies,* a political thriller which is "up there with *The Girl With the Dragon Tattoo,*" according to the first review on Amazon.com.

He is currently writing another financial book—and planning his next novel.

FOR MORE, VISIT MARK TIER'S WEBSITE: www.marktier.com

www.ingramcontent.com/pod-product-compliance
Lightning Source LLC
Chambersburg PA
CBHW080652010826
48976CB00026B/2658